CAPTIVATED BY YOU

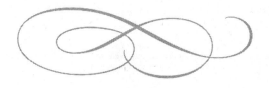

Sylvia Day

BERKLEY
New York

BERKLEY
An imprint of Penguin Random House LLC
penguinrandomhouse.com

Copyright © 2014 by Sylvia Day

BERKLEY and the BERKLEY & B colophon are registered trademarks of Penguin Random House LLC.

Library of Congress Cataloging-in-Publication Data

Day, Sylvia.
Captivated by you / Sylvia Day. — Berkley Trade paperback edition.
p. cm. — (A crossfire novel ; 4)
ISBN 978-0-425-27386-9 (pbk.)
I. Title.
PS3604.A9875C37 2014
813'.6—dc23
2014035820

First edition: November 2014

Printed in the United States of America
6th Printing

*This one is for all the readers who
waited patiently for this next chapter in
Gideon and Eva's story.
I hope you love it as much as I do!*

ACKNOWLEDGMENTS

There are innumerable people behind me who make it possible for me to write, keep up with my commitments, and stay sane.

Thanks to Hilary Sares, who keeps me on track by editing each book as I go. I rely on you more than you know.

Thanks to Kimberly Whalen, agent extraordinaire, for all that you do, but especially for all of your support. I'm grateful for you every day.

Thanks to Samara Day, for all the stress you take off my shoulders. I can't imagine how far behind I'd be without you.

Thanks to my children, who tolerate being without me for long stretches while I work (and all the inconveniences associated with that). I couldn't do what I do without your support. I love you.

Thanks to all the amazing teams at Penguin Random House: Cindy Hwang, Leslie Gelbman, Alex Clarke, Tom Weldon, Rick Pascocello, Craig Burke, Erin Galloway, Francesca Russell, Kimberley Atkins . . . and that's just scratching the surface of the US and UK. There are teams hard at work in Australia, Ireland, Canada, New Zealand, India, and South Africa. I'm grateful to you all for the time and effort you put into publishing my books.

Thanks to Liz Pearsons and the team at Brilliance Audio for making audio editions readers rave about!

And thanks to all of my international publishers, who work tirelessly in their territories. I wish I could thank you all personally here. Please know that I feel blessed to work with you.

1

Icy needles of water bombarded my overheated skin, the sting chasing away the clinging shadows of a nightmare I couldn't fully remember.

Closing my eyes, I stepped deeper into the spray, willing the lingering fear and nausea to circle the drain at my feet. A shiver racked me, and my thoughts shifted to my wife. My angel who slept peacefully in the apartment next door. I wanted her urgently, wanted to lose myself in her, and hated that I couldn't. Couldn't hold her close. Couldn't pull her lush body under mine and sink into it, letting her touch chase the memories away.

"Fuck." I placed my palms flat against the cool tile and absorbed the chill of the punishing deluge into my bones. I was a selfish asshole.

If I'd been a better man, I would've walked away from Eva Cross the moment I saw her.

Instead, I'd made her my wife. And I wanted the news of our

marriage broadcast via every medium known to man, rather than hidden away as a secret between less than a handful of people. Worse, since I had no intention of letting her go, I would have to find a way to make up for the fact that I was such a fucking mess we couldn't even sleep in the same room together.

I lathered, quickly washing away the sticky sweat I'd woken up in. Within minutes I was heading out to the bedroom, where I pulled on a pair of sweats before heading to my home office. It was just barely seven in the morning.

I'd left the apartment Eva shared with her best friend, Cary Taylor, only a couple of hours earlier, wanting to give her time to catch a few hours of sleep before she headed into work. We had been at each other all night, both of us too needy and greedy. But there'd been something else, too. An urgency on Eva's part that gnawed at me and left me uneasy.

Something was bothering my wife.

My gaze drifted to the window and its view of Manhattan beyond it, then settled on the empty wall where photos of her and us hung in the same space in my penthouse office in our home on Fifth Avenue. I could imagine the collage clearly, having spent countless hours studying it over the last few months. Looking out at the city had once been the way I encapsulated my world. Now, I accomplished that by looking at Eva.

I sat at my desk and woke my computer with a shake of the mouse, taking a deep slow breath as my wife's face filled my monitor. She wore no makeup in the photo that was my desktop wallpaper, and a smattering of light freckles on her nose made her appear younger than her twenty-four years. My gaze slid over her features—the curve of her brows, the brightness of her gray eyes, the fullness of her lips. In the moments when I let myself think of it, I could almost feel those lips against my skin. Her kisses were benedictions, promises from my angel that made my life worth living.

With a determined exhalation, I picked up the phone and speed-dialed Raúl Huerta. Despite the earliness of the hour, he answered swiftly and alertly.

"Mrs. Cross and Cary Taylor are heading to San Diego today," I said, my hand curling into a fist at the thought. I didn't have to say more.

"Got it."

"I want a recent photo of Anne Lucas and a detailed rundown of where she was last night on my desk by noon."

"At the latest," he affirmed.

I hung up and stared at Eva's captivatingly beautiful face. I'd caught her in a happy, unguarded moment, a state of being I was determined to keep her in for the rest of her life. But last night she'd been distressed by a possible run-in with a woman I'd once used. It had been a while since I'd crossed paths with Anne, but if she was responsible for aggravating my wife, she'd be seeing me again. Soon.

Opening my inbox, I started sifting through my e-mails, drafting quick answers when required and working my way toward the subject line that had caught my eye the moment my e-mail opened.

I felt Eva before I saw her.

I lifted my head and my keystrokes slowed. A sudden rush of desire soothed the agitation I felt whenever I wasn't with her.

I leaned back to better appreciate the view. "You're up early, angel."

Eva stood in the doorway with her keys in hand, her blond hair in a sexy tangle around her shoulders, her cheeks and lips flushed from sleep, her curvy body clad in a tank top and shorts. She was braless, her lush tits swelling softly beneath the ribbed cotton. Petite and built to take a man to his knees, she often pointed out how different she was from the women I'd been photographed with before her.

"I woke up missing you," she replied, with the throaty voice that never failed to make me hard. "How long have you been up?"

"Not long." I pushed the keyboard drawer in to make room for her on my desk.

She padded over on bare feet, effortlessly seducing me. The moment I first saw her I'd known she would wreck me. The promise was there in her eyes and the way she moved. Everywhere she went, men stared at her. Coveted her. Just like I did.

I caught her by the waist when she came close enough, choosing to pull her onto my lap instead. Bending my head, I caught her nipple in my mouth, drawing on her with long, deep sucks. I heard her gasp, felt her body jolt at the sensation, and smiled inwardly. I could do whatever I wanted to her. She'd given me that right. It was the greatest gift I had ever been given.

"Gideon." Her hands went to my hair, sifting through it.

I felt infinitely better already.

Lifting my head, I kissed her, tasting the cinnamon of her toothpaste and the underlying flavor that was uniquely her. "Hmm?"

She touched my face, her gaze searching. "Did you have another nightmare?"

I exhaled in a rush. She'd always been able to see right through me. I wasn't sure I would ever get used to it.

I stroked the pad of my thumb over the damp cotton clinging to her nipple. "I'd rather talk about the wet dreams you're inspiring right now."

"What was it about?"

My lips thinned at her persistence. "I don't remember."

"Gideon—"

"Drop it, angel."

Eva stiffened. "I just want to help you."

"You know how to do that."

She snorted. "Sex fiend."

I cuddled her closer. I couldn't find the words to tell her how she felt in my arms, so I nuzzled her neck, breathing in the well-loved scent of her skin.

"Ace."

Something in the tone of her voice set me on edge. I pulled back slowly, my gaze gliding over her face. "Talk to me."

"About San Diego . . ." Her eyes dropped and she caught her lower lip between her teeth.

I stilled, waiting to see where the conversation would go.

"Six-Ninths is going to be there," she said finally.

She hadn't tried to hide what I'd already known, which was a relief. But a different kind of tension flooded me instead.

"You're telling me that's a problem." My voice remained steady, but I was anything but calm.

"No, it's not a problem," she said softly. But her fingers were tangling restlessly in my hair.

"Don't lie to me."

"I'm not." She took a deep breath and then held my gaze. "Something's not right. I'm confused."

"About what, exactly?"

"Don't be like that," she said quietly. "Don't get all icy and freeze me out."

"You'll have to forgive me. Listening to *my wife* tell me she's confused over another man doesn't put me in a good mood."

She squirmed out of my lap and I let her, so I could watch her—gauge her—with some distance between us. "I don't know how to explain it."

I deliberately ignored the cold knot in my gut. "Try."

"It's just—" Looking down, she chewed on her lower lip. "There's something . . . not finished."

My chest grew tight and hot. "Does he turn you on, Eva?"

She stiffened. "It's not like that."

"Is it the voice? The tattoos? His magic dick?"

"Stop it. It's not easy talking about this. Don't make it harder."

"It's damned hard for me, too," I snapped, pushing to my feet.

I raked her from head to toe, wanting to fuck her and punish her at the same time. I wanted to tie her up, lock her up, safe from anyone who could threaten my grip on her. "He treated you like shit, Eva. Did seeing the 'Golden' video make you forget that? Is there something you need that I'm not giving you?"

"Don't be an ass." Her arms crossed, a defensive pose that angered me further.

I needed her open and soft. I needed her completely. And there were times when I was maddened by how much she meant to me. She was the one thing I couldn't imagine losing. And she was saying the one thing I couldn't bear hearing.

"Please don't be ugly about this," she whispered.

"I'm being remarkably civilized, considering how violent I feel at the moment."

"Gideon." Guilt darkened her gray eyes, and then tears glistened.

I looked away. "Don't!"

But she saw into me the way she always did.

"I didn't mean to hurt you." The diamond on her ring finger—my claim to her—caught the light and shot sparks of multihued fire against the wall. "I hate that you're upset and pissed off at me. It hurts me, too, Gideon. I don't want him. I swear I don't."

Restless, I went to the window, trying to find the calm I needed to deal with the danger Brett Kline presented. I'd done everything I could. I had said the vows, slid the ring on her finger. Bound her to me in every way. Yet it still wasn't enough.

The city spread out before me, the view obstructed by taller buildings. From the penthouse, I could see for miles. But from the Upper West Side apartment I'd taken next door to Eva's, the vista was limited. I couldn't see the endless ribbons of streets clogged with yellow taxis or sunlight glinting off the many skyscraper windows.

I could give Eva New York. I could give her the world. I couldn't love her more than I did; it consumed me. And still, an asshole from her past was making strides on edging me out.

I remembered her in Kline's arms, kissing him with a desperation she should feel only for me. The possibility that lust for him might still affect her made me want to tear something apart.

My knuckles popped as my hands fisted. "Do we need to take a break already? Take some time for Kline to clear up your confusion? Maybe I should do the same and help Corinne deal with hers."

She sucked in a shaky breath at the mention of my former fiancée. "Are you *serious*?"

There was a terrible stretch of silence.

Then, "Congratulations, dickhead. You just hurt me worse than he ever did."

I turned in time to see her stalking out of the room, her back rigid and tense. The keys she'd used to let herself in were left on my desk, and the sight of them abandoned triggered something desperate. "*Stop.*"

I caught her and she struggled, the dynamic between us so familiar—Eva running, me chasing.

"Let me go!"

My eyes closed and I pressed my face against her. "I won't let him have you."

"I'm so mad at you right now, I could hit you."

I wanted her to. Wanted the pain. "Do it."

She clawed at my forearms. "Put me down, Gideon."

I turned her around and pinned her to the hallway wall. "What am I supposed to do when you tell me you're *confused* about Brett Kline? I feel like I'm hanging on the edge of a cliff and my grip is slipping."

"So you're going to tear at me to hold on? Why don't you get that I'm not going anywhere?"

I stared down at her, scrambling for something to say that would make things right between us. Her lower lip began to quiver and I . . . I unraveled.

"Tell me how to handle this," I said hoarsely, circling her wrists and exerting gentle pressure. "Tell me what to do."

"Handle *me*, you mean?" Her shoulders went back. "Because I'm what's wrong here. I knew Brett during a time in my life when I hated myself but wanted other people to love me. And now he's acting the way I wanted him to back then and it's giving me a head trip."

"Christ, Eva." I pressed harder, flattening my body against her. "How am I not supposed to feel threatened by that?"

"You're supposed to trust me. I told you because I didn't want you to get weird vibes and jump to conclusions. I wanted to be honest about it so you *wouldn't* feel threatened. I know I've got some stuff to work out in my head. I'm going to see Dr. Travis this weekend and—"

"Shrinks aren't a cure-all!"

"Don't yell at me."

I fought the urge to slam my fist into the plaster behind her. My wife's blind faith in the healing properties of therapy frustrated the hell out of me. "We're not running to a damned doctor every time we've got a problem. It's you and me in this marriage. Not the god-damned psychiatric community!"

Her chin lifted, her jaw taking on the determined slant that drove me crazy. She never gave me an inch unless my cock was inside her. Then she gave me everything.

"You may think you don't need help, ace, but I know I do."

"What I need is you." I cupped her head in my hands. "I need my wife. And I need her thinking about me and not some other guy!"

"You're making me wish I hadn't said anything."

My lip curled in a sneer. "I knew how you felt. I've seen it."

"God. You jealous, crazy . . ." She moaned softly. "Why don't you understand how much I love you? Brett's got nothing on you. *Nothing*. But honestly, I don't want to be around you right now."

I felt her resistance, the pushback of her trying to get away. I clutched her like a lifeline. "Can't you see what you're doing to me?"

Eva softened in my arms. "I don't get you, Gideon. How can you just flip a switch and turn your feelings off? Knowing how I feel about Corinne, how could you throw her in my face like that?"

"You're the reason I breathe, I can't turn it off." I slid my mouth across her cheek. "I think of nothing but you. All day. Every day. Everything I do, I do with you in mind. There's no room for anyone else. It kills me that you have room for him."

"You're not listening."

"Just stay the hell away from him."

"That's avoidance, not a solution." Her fingers dug into my waist. "I'm broken, Gideon, you know that. I'm piecing myself back together."

I loved her just the way she was. Why wasn't that enough?

"Thanks to you I'm stronger than I've ever been," she went on, "but there are still cracks, and when I find them, I have to figure out what made them and how to seal them up. Permanently."

"What the fuck does that mean?" My hands pushed beneath her top, seeking her bare skin.

She stiffened and pushed at me, rejecting me. "Gideon, no . . ."

I sealed my mouth over hers. Lifting her off her feet, I took her to the floor. She struggled and I growled, "Don't fight me."

"You can't just screw our problems away."

"I just want to screw you." My thumbs hooked into the waistband of her shorts and shoved them down. I was frantic to be in her, possessing her, feeling her surrender. Anything to drown out the voice in my head telling me I'd fucked up. *Again*. And this time, I wouldn't be forgiven.

"Let me go." She rolled onto her stomach.

My arms banded around her hips when she tried to crawl away. She could throw me off as she'd been trained to and she could cut me off with a word. Her safe word . . .

"Crossfire."

Eva froze at the sound of my voice and the one word meant to convey the riot of emotions she shattered me with.

It was in that eye of the storm that something snapped. A fierce and familiar quiet exploded within me, silencing the panic shaking my confidence. I stilled, absorbing the sudden absence of turmoil. It had been a long time since I'd last felt the dizzying switch between chaos and control. Only Eva could rock me so deeply, sending me hurtling back to a time when I'd been at the mercy of everything and everyone.

"You're going to stop fighting me," I told her calmly. "And I'm going to apologize."

She went lax in my arms. Her submission was total and swift. I had the upper hand again.

I pulled her up and back, so that she was sitting on my thighs. Eva needed me in control. When I was reeling, she scattered, which only shook me more. It was a vicious cycle and I had to get a better grip on it.

"I'm sorry." Sorry for hurting her. Sorry for losing my command of the situation. I'd been edgy after the nightmare—something she'd intuited—and getting hit with Kline immediately after hadn't given me time to get my shit together.

I would deal with him. I'd keep a tight grasp on her. Period. There were no other options.

"I need your support, Gideon."

"I need you to tell him you're married."

She leaned her temple against my cheek. "I'm going to."

I shifted her to sit across my lap and leaned back against the wall, cradling her close. Her arms wrapped around my neck and my world righted itself again.

Her hand slid down my chest. "Ace . . ."

The coaxing note in her voice was one I knew well. I was hard in an instant, my blood hot and thick. Submitting to me turned Eva on, and that reaction from her fired me up like nothing else.

I pushed my hand into her hair and fisted the soft gold strands, watching the way her eyes grew heavy-lidded at the feel of the gentle tug. She was restrained and at my mercy, and she loved it. Needed it, just as much as I did.

I took her mouth.

Then I took her.

WHILE Angus drove Eva and me to work, I scrolled through my appointment calendar and thought of my wife's eight-thirty flight.

I glanced at her. "You'll take one of the jets to California."

She had been looking out the window of the Bentley, city-scoping with her usual eager interest. She turned her gaze to me.

I was born in New York. I'd grown up in and near the city and eventually began to make it my own. At some point, I'd stopped noticing it. But Eva's fascination and delight with my hometown had reintroduced it to me. I didn't study the city with the intensity she did, but I saw it with fresh eyes all the same.

"Will I?" she challenged, her eyes betraying her countering attraction to me.

Her fuck-me look kept me redlined constantly.

"Yes." I closed my tablet case. "It's faster, more comfortable, and safer."

Her mouth curved. "All right."

That hint of teasing amusement captivated me, made me want to do everything wicked and raw to her until only complete surrender remained.

"You get to tell Cary," she went on, switching the cross of her legs and revealing the lacy edge of her stockings and a peek of her garter.

She was wearing a red sleeveless shirt and a white skirt with strappy heels. A perfectly acceptable businesslike outfit that was elevated by the body inside it to understated sexiness. Electricity arced between us, the instinctive recognition that we had been made to fit together perfectly.

"Ask me to come with you," I said, hating the thought of her being away from me for an entire weekend.

Her smile faded. "I can't. If I'm going to start telling people we're married, I have to start with Cary, and I can't do that with you around. I don't want him to feel like he's on the outside of a life I'm creating with you."

"I don't want to be on the outside, either."

She linked her fingers with mine. "Spending private time with friends doesn't make us any less of a couple."

"I prefer to spend time with you. You're the most interesting person I know."

Her eyes widened and she stared at me. Then she exploded into movement, hitching up her skirt and straddling me before I realized what she was doing. Cupping my face in her hands, she pressed her gloss-slick lips to mine and kissed me senseless.

"Umm," I moaned, as she pulled away breathlessly. My fingers flexed into the generous curve of her gorgeous ass. "Do that again."

"I'm so hot for you right now," she breathed, rubbing my lips clean with her thumb.

"I'm good with that."

Her husky laugh slid all around me. "I feel so awesome right now."

"Better than you did in the hallway?" Her joy was infectious. If I could've stopped time, I would have at that moment.

"That's a different kind of awesome." Her fingertips tap-danced on my shoulders. She was . . . *radiant* when she was happy, and her plea-sure brightened everything around her. Even me. "That was the best compliment, ace. Especially coming from *the* Gideon Cross. You meet fascinating people every day."

"And wish they'd go away so I can get back to you."

Her eyes glistened. "God, I love you so much it hurts."

My hands shook and I dug them into the backs of her thighs to hide it from her. My gaze wandered, trying to latch on to something that would anchor me.

If she only knew what she did to me with those three little words.

She hugged me. "I want you to do something for me," she murmured.

"Anything. Everything."

"Let's have a party."

Seizing the opportunity to move on to other topics . . . "Great. I'll set up the swing."

Pulling back, Eva shoved at my shoulder. "Not *that* kind of party, fiend."

I sighed. "Bummer."

She gave me a wicked smile. "How about I promise the swing in return for the party?"

"Ah, now we're talking." I settled back, enjoying her immensely. "Tell me what you have in mind."

"Booze and friends, yours and mine."

"All right." I considered the possibilities. "I'll see you your booze and friends, and raise you a quickie in a dark corner somewhere during."

Her throat worked on a quick swallow and I smiled inwardly. I knew my angel well. Indulging her closet exhibitionism was a complete 360 turnaround for me, and though it still amazed me when I thought about it, I didn't mind in the least. There was nothing I wouldn't do for those moments when the only thing that mattered to her was being filled with my cock.

"You drive a hard bargain," she said.

"Exactly my intention."

"Okay, then." She licked her lips. "I'll see you your quickie and raise you a hand job under the table."

My brows rose. "Clothed," I countered.

Something that sounded like a purr rumbled in the air between us. "I think you need to revisit and revise, Mr. Cross."

"I think you'll need to work harder to convince me, Mrs. Cross."

She was, as always, the most invigorating negotiation of my day.

WE separated on the twentieth floor, where she exited the elevator into the Waters Field & Leaman foyer. I was determined to get her on my team and working for me. It was an objective I strategized every day.

When I reached my office, my assistant was already at his desk.

"Good morning," Scott greeted me, standing as I approached. "PR called a few minutes ago. They're fielding an unusual amount of inquiries about a rumored engagement between you and Miss Tramell. They'd like to know how to respond."

"They should confirm." I passed him and went to the coatrack in the corner behind my desk.

He followed. "Congratulations."

"Thank you." I shrugged out of my jacket and slung it on a hook. When I glanced at him again, he was grinning.

Scott Reid handled myriad tasks for me with quiet care, which led others to often underestimate him and allow him to go unnoticed. On more than one occasion, his detailed observations of individuals had proven extremely insightful, and so I overpaid him for his position to keep him from going anywhere else.

"Miss Tramell and I will marry before the end of the year," I told him. "All interview and photo requests for either of us should be routed through Cross Industries. And tell security downstairs the same. No one should get to her without going through me first."

"I'll let them know. Also, Mr. Madani wanted to be notified when you got in. He'd like a few minutes with you before the meeting this morning."

"I'm ready when he is."

"Great," Arash Madani said, walking in. "There used to be days when you were here before seven. You're slacking off, Cross."

I shot the lawyer a warning look that carried no heat. Arash lived to work and was damned good at it, which is why I hired him away from his former employer. He'd been the toughest counsel I had ever run across, and in the years since, that hadn't changed.

Gesturing at one of the two chairs in front of my desk, I took my seat and watched him take his. His dark blue suit was simple but bespoke, his wavy black hair tamed by a precision cut. Sharp intelligence marked his dark brown eyes, extending to a smile that was more warning than greeting. He was a friend as well as an employee, and I valued his lack of bullshit.

"We've received a respectable bid on the property on Thirty-sixth," he said.

"Oh?" A tangle of emotions held my reply for a moment. The hotel Eva hated remained a problem as long as I owned it. "That's good."

"That's curious," he shot back, setting one ankle on the opposite knee, "considering how slowly the market's recovering. I had to dig through several layers, but the bidder is a subsidiary of LanCorp."

"Interesting."

"Cocky. Landon knows the next highest bid is a ways off—about ten million ways. I recommend we pull the property off the market and revisit in a year or two."

"No." Sitting back, I waved away the suggestion. "Let him have it."

Arash blinked. "Are you shitting me? Why are you in such a hurry to get rid of that hotel?"

Because I can't keep it in my holdings without hurting my wife. "I have my reasons."

"That's what you said when I advised you to sell it a few years ago and you chose to sink millions in renovations into it instead. An expense that you're just finally breaking even on, and *now* you want to offload it in a still-shaky market to a guy who wants your head?"

"It's never a bad time to sell real estate in Manhattan." And certainly, never a bad time to dump something Eva called my "fuck pad."

"There are better times, and you know it. Landon knows it. You sell to him, you'll only be encouraging him."

"Good. Maybe he'll up his game."

Ryan Landon had an ax to grind; I didn't hold it against him. My father had decimated the Landon fortune and Ryan wanted a Cross to pay for that. He wasn't the first or last businessman to come after me because of my father, but he was the most tenacious. And he was young enough to have plenty of time to dedicate to the task.

I looked at the photo of Eva on my desk. All other considerations were secondary.

"Hey," Arash said, lifting his hands in mock surrender, "it's your business. I just need to know if the rules have changed."

"Nothing's changed."

"If you believe that, Cross, you're further out of the game than I thought. While Landon's plotting your ruin, you're off at the beach."

"Stop kicking my ass for taking a weekend off, Arash." I'd do it again in an instant. Those days I'd spent with Eva in the Outer Banks had been every fucking dream I'd never allowed myself to have.

I stood and walked to the window. LanCorp's offices were in the high-rise two blocks over, and Ryan Landon's office had a prime view of the Crossfire Building. I suspected he spent more than a few moments every day staring at my office and planning his next move. Occasionally, I stared back and dared him to bring it harder.

My father was a criminal who'd destroyed countless lives. He was also the man who'd taught me how to ride a bike and to sign my name with pride. I couldn't save Geoffrey Cross's reputation, but I could damn sure protect what I'd built out of his ashes.

Arash joined me at the window. "I'm not going to say I wouldn't hole up with a babe like Eva Tramell if I could. But I'd have my goddamn cell phone with me. Especially in the middle of a high-stakes negotiation."

Remembering how melted chocolate tasted on Eva's skin, I thought a hurricane could've been ripping shingles off the roof and I wouldn't have given it a second's attention. "You're making me pity you."

"LanCorp's acquisition of that software set you back years in research and development. And it's made him cocky."

That was what really got Arash's blood up, Landon's pleasure in his own success. "That software's next to worthless without PosIT's hardware."

He glanced at me. "So?"

"Agenda item number three."

He faced me. "It said *To Be Determined* on my copy."

"Well, it says *PosIT* on my mine. That game enough for you?"

"Damn."

My desk phone beeped, followed by Scott's voice projecting from the speaker. "A couple things, Mr. Cross. Miss Tramell is on line one."

"Thank you, Scott." I headed for the receiver with the thrill of the hunt coursing through my blood. If we acquired PosIT, Landon would be back to square one. "When I'm clear, I need Victor Reyes on the line."

"Will do. Also, Mrs. Vidal is at reception," he went on, stopping me in my tracks. "Would you like me to postpone the morning meeting?"

I looked out the glass partition that divided my office from the rest of the floor, even though I couldn't see my mother from that distance. My hands clenched at my sides. According to the clock on my phone, I had ten minutes to spare and my wife on the line. The urge was there to make my mother wait until I could fit her in my schedule, not hers, but I shoved it down.

"Buy me twenty minutes," I told him. "I'll take the calls with Miss Tramell and Reyes, then you can bring Mrs. Vidal back."

"Got it."

I waited a beat. Then I picked up the phone and hit the rapidly blinking button.

2

"ANGEL."

The impact of Gideon's voice on my senses was as hard-hitting as it had been the first time I'd heard it. Cultured yet smoky with sensuality, it knocked me for a loop both in the darkness of my bedroom and over the phone, where I couldn't be distracted by that incomparably gorgeous face of his.

"Hi." I slid my swivel chair a little closer to my desk. "Is it a bad time?"

"If you need me, I'm here."

Something in his voice didn't hit me right. "I can call back later."

"Eva." The authoritative bite when he said my name had my toes flexing in my nude sling-back Louboutins. "Say what you need."

You, I almost said, which was more than a little insane considering he'd just fucked my brains out only a couple hours before. After he'd fucked my brains out damn near all night long.

Instead, I told him, "I need a favor."

"I'll enjoy the payback."

Some of the tension left my shoulders. He'd hurt me by mentioning Corinne the way he had, and the argument that followed was still fresh in my mind. But I had to push it aside, let it go. "Does security have the home addresses of everyone who works in the Crossfire?"

"They have copies of IDs. Tell me why you're asking."

"The receptionist here at work is a friend of mine and she's been out sick all week. I'm worried about her."

"If you're hoping to head over to her place and check up on her, you should get the address from her."

"I would if she'd return my calls." I ran my fingertip around the lip of my coffee mug and stared at the collage of pictures of Gideon and me that decorated my desk.

"Are you not on speaking terms at the moment?"

"No, we're not fighting or anything. It's just not like her to not get in touch with me, especially when she's calling in sick to work every day. She's a chatty girl, you know?"

"No," he drawled. "I have no idea."

If it had been any other guy who'd said that, I would think he was being sarcastic. But not Gideon. I didn't think he'd ever really talked with women in any meaningful way. He was too often clueless when interacting with me, as if his social development hadn't quite been well rounded when it came to dealing with the opposite sex.

"Then you'll have to take my word for it, ace. I just . . . I want to make sure she's all right."

"My lawyer's standing right here, but I don't have to ask him about the legality of giving you the information you're asking for via the means you've suggested. Call Raúl. He'll find her."

"Really?" An image of the dark-haired, dark-eyed security specialist ran through my mind. "Is he going to be okay with that?"

"Angel, he's paid to be okay with everything."

"Oh." I fiddled with my pen. I knew I shouldn't feel uncomfortable using Gideon's resources, but it made me feel as if our relationship were unbalanced in his favor. While I didn't believe he would ever hold that over me, I didn't think he'd see me as equal to him, either, and that was really important to me.

He had already taken care of issues on his own that I should've been a part of. Like Sam Yimara's horrid sex tape of Brett and me. And Nathan.

Still, I asked, "How do I reach him?"

"I'll text you his number."

"Okay. Thanks."

"I want either myself, Angus, or Raúl with you when you go see her."

"And that wouldn't be awkward at all." I glanced at Mark's office to make sure my boss didn't need me for anything. I tried not to make personal calls at work, but Megumi had been out for four days straight without a single returned call or text the whole time.

"Don't throw me that 'chicks before dicks' line, Eva. You need to give me something here."

I got the subtext. He was worried about me going to San Diego and was letting that issue slide. I had to bend a little somewhere else in return. "Okay, okay. If she's not back in the office on Monday, we'll figure out how to handle it."

"Good. Anything else?"

"No. That's it." My gaze returned to a photo of him and my heart hurt just a little, the way it always did when I looked at him. "Thank you. I hope you have an amazing day. I love you madly, you know. And no, I don't expect you to say it back while your lawyer's hanging around."

"Eva." There was an aching note in his voice that moved me more than words ever could. "Come see me when you get off work."

"Sure. Don't forget to call Cary about taking your jet."

"Consider it done."

I hung up and sat back in my chair.

"Good morning, Eva."

I swiveled to face Christine Field, the executive chairman. "Good morning."

"I wanted to congratulate you again on your engagement." Her gaze went past my shoulder to the framed photos behind me. "I'm sorry, I hadn't realized you and Gideon Cross were dating."

"That's okay. I try not to talk about my personal life at work."

I made the statement casually, because I didn't want to antagonize one of the partners. Still, I hoped she got the hint. Gideon was the center of my life, but I needed some parts of it to belong only to me.

She laughed. "That's good! But just goes to show that I'm not keeping my ear close enough to the ground."

"I doubt you're missing anything important."

"Are you the reason Cross approached us with the Kingsman campaign?"

I winced inwardly. Of course she'd think I would recommend my employer to my boyfriend, because she'd assume Gideon and I had been dating at least long enough to make an engagement plausible. Telling her I had been with Waters Field & Leaman longer than I'd been with Gideon, when I had been employed there only a couple of months, would open up speculation I didn't want floating around.

Worse, I was pretty certain Gideon *had* used the vodka campaign as an excuse to draw me into his world on his terms. That didn't mean Mark hadn't done a phenomenal job on the request for proposal. I didn't want my relationship with Gideon to shift any of the focus away from my boss and his accomplishments.

"Mr. Cross approached the agency on his own," I replied, sticking to the truth. "Which was a great decision. Mark rocked that RFP."

Christine nodded. "He did. All right. I'll let you get back to work. Mark's been singing your praises, too, by the way. We're glad to have you on our team."

I managed a smile, but my day was off to a rocky start. First, Gideon knocked me sideways with his Corinne bullshit. Then, finding Megumi still out sick. Now, I'd rolled into being treated differently at work because my name was connected to Gideon's in a significant way.

Opening my inbox, I started going through the morning's e-mail. I understood that Gideon wanted to make me feel what he was feeling, so he'd leveraged Corinne against me. I'd known talking about Brett was going to be a problem, which was why I'd put it off, but I hadn't had an ulterior motive in bringing it up or when I'd kissed Brett, either. I had hurt Gideon, yes, but could sincerely say I hadn't consciously intended to do so.

On the flip side, Gideon had deliberately set out to hurt me. I hadn't realized he was capable of that or willing to do it. Something important had shifted between us that morning. I felt as if a core column of trust had been shaken.

Did he know that? Did he understand how big a problem that was?

My desk phone rang and I answered with my usual greeting.

"How long were you going to wait to tell me about your engagement?"

A sigh escaped me before I could hold it back. My Friday really was shaping up to be a trial. "Hi, Mom. I was going to call you during my lunch."

"You knew last night!" she accused. "Did he ask you on the way to dinner? Because you didn't say anything about a proposal when we talked about him asking your father and Richard for permission. I saw the ring at Cipriani's and was pretty sure, but when you didn't say anything, I didn't push because you've been so touchy lately. And—"

"And you've been violating the law lately," I shot back.

"—Gideon was wearing a ring, too, so I thought maybe it was some kind of promise thing or something—"

"It is."

"—and then I read about your engagement online! I mean, really, Eva. No mother should find out on the Internet that her daughter is getting married!"

I stared at my monitor blankly, my heart rate kicking up. "What? Where on the Internet?"

"Take your pick! Page Six, HuffPost . . . And let me tell you again, there is *no way* I can pull together a proper wedding before the end of the year!"

My daily Google alert hadn't hit my inbox yet, so I did a quick search, typing so quickly I spelled my own name wrong. It didn't matter.

Socialite Eva Tramell has nabbed the brass ring. Not literally, of course. Multibillionaire entrepreneur Gideon Cross, whose name is synonymous with excess and luxury, wouldn't slide anything less than platinum onto the finger of the woman who'll bear his name. (see photo at left) A source at Cross Industries confirmed the significance of the giant rock on Tramell's left hand. No comment was made regarding the ring Cross has been seen wearing. (see photo at right) A wedding is planned before year's end. We have to wonder what the rush is. Operation Gideva Baby Bump Watch has commenced.

"Oh my God," I breathed, horrified. "I have to go. I have to call Dad."

"Eva! You need to come over after work. We have to talk about the wedding."

Thankfully my dad was on the West Coast, which bought me at least three hours, depending on his work schedule. "I can't. I'm going to San Diego this weekend with Cary."

"I think you need to put off any travel for a while. You need to—"

"Start without me, Mom," I said desperately, glancing at the clock. "I don't have anything specific in mind."

"You can't be seri—"

"Gotta go. Have to work." I hung up, then pulled open the desk drawer that held my smartphone.

"Hey." Mark Garrity leaned over the top of my cubicle and offered me one of his charming crooked smiles. "Ready to roll?"

"Uh . . ." My finger hovered over the home button on my phone. I was torn between doing what I was paid to do—work—and making sure my dad heard about the engagement from me. Usually, it wouldn't be a dilemma at all to choose. I loved my job too much to risk it by slacking off. But my dad had been in a funk since he'd messed around with my mom and I was worried about him. He wasn't the kind of guy to take sleeping with a married woman lightly, even one he was in love with.

I put the phone back in the drawer. "Absolutely," I replied, pushing back from my desk and grabbing my tablet.

When I settled into my usual seat in front of Mark's desk, I sent my dad a quick text from my tablet saying I had something important to share with him and that I'd call at noon.

It was the best I could do. I could only hope it was enough.

3

"MAN, YOU ARE smooth."

I looked up at Arash after setting the receiver back in its cradle. "Are you still here?"

The attorney laughed and settled back in his seat on my office sofa. The view wasn't nearly as pleasant as the one my wife had given me not too long ago.

"Schmoozing the father-in-law," he said. "I'm impressed. I expect Eva will be impressed, too. Bet you're counting on that heading into the weekend."

Damn right. I would need all the points I could earn when I met up with Eva in San Diego. "She's about to go out of town. And you have to head into the conference room before they get too restless in there. I'll join you as soon as I can."

He stood. "Yes, I heard. Your mother's here. Let the wedding insanity begin. Since you're free this weekend, how about we round up some of the usual suspects at my place tonight? It's been a while, and your bachelor days are numbered. Well, technically they're over, but no one else knows that."

And he was bound by attorney-client privilege.

It took me a beat to decide. "All right. What time?"

"Eight-ish."

I nodded, then caught Scott's eye. He got the message and rounded his desk to head up to reception.

"Great." Arash grinned. "See you at the meeting."

During the two minutes I had alone, I texted Angus about getting to California. I still had unfinished business there, and taking care of it while Eva was visiting her dad gave me a legitimate excuse to be where she was. Not that I absolutely needed one.

"Gideon."

As my mother entered, my fingers curled into my palms.

Scott followed and asked, "Are you sure I can't get you something, Mrs. Vidal? Coffee, maybe? Or water?"

She shook her head. "No, thank you. I'm fine."

"All right." He smiled and left, pulling the door closed behind him.

I hit the remote on my desk that controlled the opacity of the glass wall, blocking the view from everyone on the main floor. My mother approached, looking slim and elegant in dark blue slacks and white blouse. She'd pulled her hair back into a sleek ebony bun, showing off the flawless face that my father had adored. Once, I'd adored it, too. Now, I had trouble looking at her.

And since we looked so much alike, I sometimes had trouble looking at myself.

"Hello, Mother. What brings you into the city?"

She set her purse on the edge of my desk. "Why is Eva wearing my ring?"

The small pleasure I'd felt at seeing her dissipated instantly. "It's *my* ring. And the answer to your question is obvious: She's wearing the ring because I gave it to her when I proposed."

"Gideon." She pulled her shoulders back. "You don't know what you're getting into with her."

I forced myself to remain facing her. I hated when she looked at me with hurt in her eyes. Blue eyes that were so like mine. "I don't have time for this. I've put an important meeting on hold to see you."

"I wouldn't have to come to your office if you'd answer my calls or come home once in a while!" Her pretty pink mouth tightened with disapproval.

"That is *not* my home."

"She's using you, Gideon."

I retrieved my coat. "We've had this discussion."

She folded her arms across her chest like a shield. I knew my mother; she was just getting started. "She's involved with that singer, Brett Kline. Did you know that? And she's got an ugly side you've never seen. She was downright vicious to me last night."

"I'll speak with her." Straightening my coat with a brisk tug on the lapels, I headed toward the door. "She shouldn't be wasting her time."

My mother's breath caught. "I'm trying to help you."

"It's a little too late for that, don't you think?"

She took a shaky step back from the look I gave her. "I know Geoffrey's death was hard on you. It was a difficult time for all of us. I tried to give you—"

"I'm not doing this here!" I snapped, furious that she would bring up something as personal as my father's suicide while I was working. That she would bring it up at all. "You've hijacked my morning and pissed me off. Let me make it clear to you. There is no scenario pitting you against Eva where you come out on top."

"You're not listening to me!"

"There's nothing you could say that would affect anything. If she wanted my money, I'd give her every cent. If she wanted another man, I'd make her forget him."

She lifted an unsteady hand to her hair, smoothing it although not a single glossy strand was out of place. "I only want the best for you, and she's stirring up crap that has been put away a long time. It can't be a healthy relationship for you. She's creating a rift with your family that—"

"We've been estranged, Mother. Eva has nothing to do with that."

"I don't want it to be like this!" Stepping closer, she held out her hand. A strand of black pearls peeked out from between the lapels of her blouse, and a sapphire-faced Patek Philippe adorned her wrist. She hadn't rebooted her life after my father's death; she'd done a complete wipe and restart. And never looked back. "I miss you. I love you."

"Not enough."

"That's not fair, Gideon. You won't give me a chance."

"If you need a ride, Angus is at your service." I caught the handle of the door and paused. "Don't come here again, Mother. I don't like arguing with you. It would be best for both of us if you just stay away."

I left the door open behind me and headed toward the conference room.

"You took this shot today?"

I looked up at Raúl, who stood in front of my desk. Dressed in a plain black suit, he had the steady, watchful gaze of a man who made his living by seeing and hearing everything.

"Yes," he answered. "Not more than an hour ago."

I returned my attention to the photo in front of me. It was difficult looking at Anne Lucas. The sight of her foxlike face, with its sharp chin and sharper eyes, brought back memories I wished I could erase from my mind. Not just of her, but of her brother, who'd been similar in ways that made my skin crawl.

"Eva said the woman had long hair," I murmured, noting that Anne still had cropped hair. I remembered the plastic feel of it, the sharp-gelled spikes scratching my thighs as she deep-throated my cock, working desperately to get me hard enough to fuck her.

I handed the tablet back to Raúl. "Find out who it was."

"Will do."

"Did Eva call you?"

He frowned. "No." But he pulled out his smartphone and checked it. "No," he said again.

"She may wait until you fly out to San Diego. She wants you to find a friend of hers."

"No problem. I'll take care of it."

"Take care of *her*," I said, holding his gaze.

"Doesn't need to be said."

"I know. Thank you."

As he left my office, I sat back in my chair. There were a number of women in my past who might cause problems for me with my wife. The women I'd slept with were aggressive by nature, ones who put me in the position of needing to take the upper hand. Eva was the only woman who'd ever grabbed the lead and made me want more.

It was getting harder to let her be away from me, not easier.

"The team from Envoy is here," Scott said through the speaker.

"Send them in."

I powered through my day, wrapping up the week's agenda and laying the groundwork for more to come. There was a lot I needed to get off my plate before I could take time off with Eva. Our daylong honeymoon had been perfect, but far too short. I wanted at least two weeks away with her, preferably a month. Someplace far away from work and other commitments, where I could have her all to myself with no interruptions.

My smartphone vibrated on my desktop and I looked at it, surprised to see my sister's face on the screen. I'd texted Ireland earlier to let her know about the engagement. Her reply had been a short and simple, Yay! Stoked. Congrats, bro!

I'd barely answered the call with a quick hello when she cut me off.

"I'm so fucking excited!" she yelled, forcing me to pull the phone away from my ear.

"Watch the mouth."

"Are you kidding? I'm seventeen, not seven. This is so awesome. I've wanted a sister forever, but figured I'd be old and gray before you and Christopher stopped bouncing around and settled down."

I sat back in my chair. "I live to serve."

"Ha. Yeah, right. You done good, you know. Eva's a keeper."

"Yes, I know."

"Thanks to her, I get to harass you now. Always a highlight of my day."

My chest tightened, forcing me to take a minute before I could reply in an easy tone of voice. "Oddly enough, it's a highlight of mine as well."

"Well, yeah. It should be." Her voice lowered. "I heard Mom losing her shit over it earlier. She told Dad she went to your work and you guys got in a fight or something. I think she's kinda jealous. She'll get over it."

"Don't worry about it. Everything's fine."

"I know. It just sucks that she couldn't keep it together today of all days. Anyway, I'm thrilled and wanted you to know that."

"Thank you."

"But I'm not going to be the flower girl. I'm too old for that. I'm up for being a bridesmaid, though. Even a groomswoman or whatever. Just sayin'."

"All right." My mouth curved. "I'll pass that along to Eva."

I'd just hung up when Scott buzzed through my office line.

"Miss Tramell is here," he announced, making me realize how late in the day it was. "And, as a reminder, your videoconference with the development team in California is in five minutes."

Pushing back from the desk, I saw Eva round the corner and come into view. I could watch her walk for hours. She had a sway to her hips that made me ache to fuck her and a determined tilt to her chin that challenged every dominant instinct I had.

I wanted to fist her ponytail in my hand, take her mouth, and grind against her. Just the way I'd wanted to the first time I saw her. And every time since.

"Send along the proposal deck to the team," I told Scott. "Tell them to review and I'll join in shortly."

"Yes, sir."

Eva swept through the door.

"Eva." I stood. "How was your day?"

She rounded the desk, then grabbed me by the tie.

I was instantly hard and totally focused on her.

"I fucking love you," she said, before yanking my mouth down to meet hers.

I hooked one arm around her waist and felt around for the opacity controls with my other hand, all the while letting her kiss me as if she owned me. Which she did. Absolutely.

The feel of her lips against mine and the unmistakable possessive-ness of her actions were exactly what I needed after the day I'd had. Holding her close, I turned and half-sat on the edge of the desk, pull-ing her in between my thighs. I could say it was a more secure way to hold her, but honestly, my knees were weak.

Her kisses did that to me. Did what three hours of sparring with my trainer couldn't do.

Inhaling through the rising lust, I breathed her in, allowing the delicate fragrance of her perfume and the provocative scent that was hers alone to intoxicate me. Her lips were soft and damp against mine, demanding in the subtlest of ways. Her tongue licked delicately, savoring, teasing and arousing me effortlessly.

Eva kissed me as if I were the most delicious thing she'd ever tasted, a flavor she craved and was helplessly addicted to. The feeling was heady and had become necessary. I lived for her kisses.

When she kissed me, I knew I belonged right where I was.

Tilting her head, she moaned into my mouth, a soft sound of pleasure and surrender. Her fingers were in my hair, sliding through it, tugging it. That sensation of being caught—*claimed*—challenged me on the deepest level. I drew her closer, until the firmness of her belly pressed against the hardness of my erection.

My dick was throbbing, aching.

"You'll make me come," I murmured. All the effort I'd once had to expend to become aroused enough to orgasm was unnecessary with my wife. The fact that she existed stirred my blood. The strength of her desire was enough to set me off.

She leaned back slightly, breathless like me. "I don't mind."

"I wouldn't, either, if I didn't have a meeting waiting."

"I don't want to hold you up. I just want to thank you for what you said to my dad."

Smiling, I gave her ass a two-handed squeeze. "My lawyer said I'd score major points for that."

"Work was so busy, and I didn't have a chance to call him until lunch. I was so worried he'd hear about our engagement before I could tell him." She shoved at my shoulder. "You could've given me a heads-up that you were announcing it to the world!"

I shrugged. "It wasn't planned, but I wasn't going to deny it when asked."

Her lips twisted wryly. "Of course not. Did you see that ridiculous post about a baby bump?"

"A frightening thought at this point," I said, trying to keep my tone light despite the sudden rush of alarm I felt. "I'm planning on keeping you all to myself for a while."

"I know, right?" She shook her head. "I was freaked out that my dad would think I was engaged *and* pregnant, and just couldn't be bothered to let him know. It was such a relief to call him and find out you'd explained everything and smoothed the way."

"My pleasure." I would set the world on fire to clear a path for her, if that's what it took.

Her hands went to work unbuttoning my vest. My brows arched in silent query, but I wasn't going to stop her.

"I haven't even left yet, and I'm missing you already," she said quietly, straightening my tie.

"Don't go."

"If I were just going to hole up with Cary for a bit, I'd do it here at home and not in San Diego." She lifted her gaze to my face. "But he's a head case over Tatiana being pregnant. Plus, I need to spend time with my dad. Especially now."

"Is there something you should be telling me?"

"No. He sounded good when I talked to him, but I think he was hoping we'd have more time together before I got married. To him, it seems like you and I just met."

I knew I should keep my mouth shut, but I couldn't. "And we can't forget Kline."

Her jaw hardened. She dropped her attention back to where her fingers were buttoning my vest. "I'm leaving soon. I don't want to fight again."

I caught her hands. "Eva. Look at me."

Staring into her stormy eyes, I felt the tug in my chest: a slow wrenching that could turn me upside down. She hadn't stopped being angry with me, and I couldn't stand it. "You still don't understand what you do to me. How crazy you make me."

"Don't give me that. You shouldn't have brought up Corinne the way you did."

"Maybe not. But be honest, you brought up Kline this morning because you're worried about seeing him."

"I'm not worried!"

"Angel." I gave her a patient look. "You're worried. I don't think you'd sleep with him, but I do think you're anxious about crossing a line you shouldn't. You needed a strong reaction from me, so you were blunt and you got it. You needed to see what it would do to me. How just the thought of you with him makes me insane."

"Gideon." She gripped my biceps. "*Nothing* is going to happen."

"I'm not making excuses." I brushed my fingertips across her cheek. "I hurt you and I'm sorry."

"I'm sorry, too. I wanted to avoid causing any problems and they happened anyway."

I knew she regretted our fight. I could see it in her eyes. "We're learning as we go. We'll fuck up now and again. You just have to trust me, angel."

"I have, Gideon. It's why we've gotten so far. But the fact that you'd hurt me at all—*on purpose* . . ." She shook her head and I could see how what I'd said was eating at her. "You were always supposed to be the one I could count on to never hurt me deliberately."

Hearing her doubt her trust in me was a hard blow. I took the hit, then explained myself the way I'd only ever done with her. I would explain anything, talk for hours, write the promise in blood . . . if that was what it took to make her believe in me.

"There's a difference between deliberation and malicious intent, wouldn't you agree?" I cupped her face in my hands. "I promise I'll never cause you pain just to hurt you. Don't you see that I'm just as vulnerable? You have the same power to hurt me."

Her face softened, became even more stunning. "I wouldn't."

"But I did. You'll have to forgive me."

She stepped back. "I hate when you use that tone of voice."

Inclined toward self-preservation, I didn't allow the smile I felt to show. "But it makes you wet."

Tossing a glare at me over her shoulder, Eva moved to the window and stood in the same spot I'd occupied that morning. Her ponytail showed off her beauty—and left her no way to conceal her emotions. Hot color rose in her cheeks.

Did she know how often I thought about tying her up when she was riled like this? Not to cage her or leash her, but to hold that vibrant energy of hers, that lust for life I'd never learned to have. She gave that to me, surrendered it fully.

"Don't try to control me with sex, Gideon," she said with her back to me.

"I don't want to control you at all."

"You manipulate me. You do things . . . say things . . . just to get a particular response out of me."

My arms crossed as I remembered her kissing Kline. "As do you, which we just discussed."

She faced me. "I'm allowed to, I'm a woman."

"Ah." I smiled then. "I knew that."

"You're such an enigma to me." She sighed and I could see her letting the lingering resentment go. "But you've got me pegged. You know all my buttons and just how to push them."

"If you think I don't spend a good percentage of every day trying to figure you out, you're not paying attention. Think about that while I handle this meeting, and then we'll say good-bye properly."

As I sat in my chair, her gaze followed me. I adjusted the fit of my headset and paused when I realized she was staring. She liked looking at me. And hers was the only avid hunger that had ever made me feel good about myself. I'd never had the knee-jerk defensive reaction to her sexual interest that others provoked. She made me feel loved and wanted in a way that wasn't the least threatening.

"Watching you get into business mode makes me hot," she explained, her voice just husky enough to prevent me from fully focusing on work. "Sexy as hell."

My lips twisted wryly. "Angel, behave for fifteen minutes."

"What would be the fun in that? Besides, you like me bad."

Damn straight.

"Fifteen minutes," I reiterated. Considering I'd planned for the meeting to take close to an hour, that was a major concession.

"Do what you have to do." Eva stopped by my chair and bent over like a pinup girl to breathe in my ear. "I'll find something to occupy myself with while you're on the phone playing with your millions."

My cock was abruptly, painfully hard. She had said something similar to me when we'd first started dating, and I had dreamed of it in the weeks since.

I would have told her to wait, but I knew she wouldn't. She had a determined look in her eye and a taunting swing to her hips as she circled my desk. I'd fucked up and she wanted to get a piece of her own back. Some couples punished each other with pain or deprivation. Eva and I, we punished each other with pleasure.

The moment she stepped out of view, I logged into the meeting without activating my camera and I muted my microphone. All half-dozen participants were actively discussing the materials Scott had provided. I gave them a moment to register that I'd logged in . . .

. . . and used the time to stand and open my fly.

Eva kicked off her heels. "Good. It'll go easier on you if you cooperate."

"You don't actually believe having your mouth wrapped around my dick while I'm on a videoconference is going to be easy at any level." Even then, the team in California was chiming in with greetings through my headset. I ignored them for the moment, thinking only of what was about to happen right there in my office.

Only weeks ago the possibility that I'd play while working would've been nonexistent. If Eva had been wired any differently, I would've made her wait until I had the time and attention to devote fully to her.

But my angel was a dangerous lover, one who got off on the thrill of being *this close* to discovery. I would never have known I enjoyed that edge if not for her. There were times I wanted to fuck her for the entire world to see, so it would be known definitively how completely I possessed her.

Her grin was pure wickedness. "If you liked things easy, you wouldn't have married me."

And I was going to marry her again, as soon as possible. It wouldn't be the last time. We'd be renewing our vows often, reminding each other that we made a promise to be together forever, no matter what life threw at us.

Lowering gracefully to her knees on the far side of my desk, Eva set her hands on the floor and prowled toward me like a lioness on the hunt. Through the smoked-glass surface of my desktop, I watched her move into place, her tongue darting out to wet her lips.

Anticipation coursed through me, the rush of the challenge and erotic expectation. Everything about my wife gave me pleasure, but her mouth was in a class by itself. She sucked me off as if she were starved for my cum, as if the taste were something she was hooked on. Eva gave me head because she loved it. Watching me unravel while she did it was just a bonus.

I adjusted the spread of my fly and pushed down the waistband of my boxer briefs, studying her face as I revealed how she'd affected me. Her lips parted as her breath quickened, her body shifting back until she was sitting on her heels like a supplicant.

Settling into my chair, I absorbed the unaccustomed feeling of restraint around my thighs and the pull of elastic beneath my balls. My reaction was swift and unpleasant, the sensation of being bound dredging up memories I kept ruthlessly buried.

Reconsidering, I started to roll back in my desk chair, my heart rate rising . . .

Eva swallowed me.

"Fuck," I hissed, my fingers digging into the armrests as her fingers dug into my hips.

The rush of wet heat over the sensitive crown of my cock was shockingly intense. Hard suction tightened around me and a satin-soft tongue massaged the perfect spot. Through the pounding of my heart, I heard the team questioning whether my webcam and headset were working properly . . .

Straightening my spine, I slid forward and activated my feeds. "Excuse the delay," I said briskly as Eva took more of me. "Now that you've had the chance to review the deck, let's discuss the steps you'll be taking to implement the recommended adjustments."

Eva hummed her approval and the vibration reverberated through me. I was hard enough to drive nails and her slender fingers were teasing me, stroking with just enough pressure to make me want more.

Tim Henderson, the project manager and team leader, spoke first. I could barely focus, seeing him more from memory than the monitor in front of me. A tall, painfully thin man with pale skin and a wild mane of dark curls, he liked to talk, which was a blessing considering how dry my mouth had become.

"I'd like more time to review this," he began, "but off the cuff, I'm thinking this is a seriously accelerated schedule. Some of this is great and I'm excited about seeing what we can do with it, but phasing into consumer beta testing is at least a year away, not six months."

"That's what you told me six months ago," I reminded him, my fist clenching as Eva took my cock to the back of her throat. Sweat bloomed on the back of my neck when she pulled off, her mouth a hot velvet suction.

"We lost our top designer to LanCorp—"

"And I offered a replacement, which you declined."

Henderson's jaw tightened. He was a coding genius with a brilliant creative mind, but he didn't play well with others and was resistant to outside intervention. That would be his prerogative . . . if he weren't eating my time and money.

"A creative team is a delicate balance," he argued. "You can't just plug a random person into the void. We've got the right man on the job now—"

"Thank you," Jeff Simmons interjected, his angular face breaking into a grin at the praise.

"—and we're making progress," Tim went on. "We—"

"—keep blowing through your self-imposed deadlines." My tone was gruffer than I intended due to my wife's wickedly agile tongue. Soft, playful licks from root to tip were driving me half out of my mind. My thighs ached with strain, the muscles hardened by the force it took to keep me in my chair. She was following the line of every sensitive vein, stroking over the throbbing ridges with the flat of her tongue.

"While creating an exceptional and groundbreaking user experience," he shot back. "We're getting the job done and we're doing it right."

I wanted to bend Eva over my desk and fuck her. Hard.

To do that, I needed to get through the damn meeting.

"Excellent. Now, you just need to do it faster. I'm sending out a team to help you achieve the objectives on time. They'll—"

"Now, wait a minute, Cross," Henderson snapped, leaning closer to the webcam. "You send some corporate bean counters over to breathe down our necks and you're only going to slow us down! You need to leave the development to us. If we need your help, we'll ask for it."

"If you thought I'd give you my money and be a silent partner, you didn't do your homework."

"Uh-oh," Eva murmured, her eyes bright with laughter beneath the glass.

I reached beneath the desk and cupped her nape, squeezing. "The app space is highly competitive. That's why you approached me. You presented me with a unique and intriguing gaming concept, and a one-year development-to-rollout timeline, which was judged by my team to be reasonable and achievable."

I paused on a breath, tormented by the feel of warm lips gliding up and down my raging dick. Eva was working with purpose now, driving me on with hard pumps of her fist. There was no more buildup, no teasing. She wanted me to come. Now.

"You're looking at this from the wrong perspective, Mr. Cross," Ken Harada said, running his hand over a blue goatee. "Technical timelines don't make allowances for an organic creative process. You don't understand how—"

"Don't make me the villain here." The urge to thrust, to fuck, was clawing. Aggression built in me like a tidal wave, forcing me to fight for any semblance of civility. "You guaranteed on-time delivery of all elements on a schedule you created and you're not holding up your end. I'm now forced to help you keep the promises you made."

The artist slumped back in his seat, muttering under his breath.

Tightening my grip on Eva's neck, I tried to slow her down. Then I gave up and started moving her, urging her roughly to suck faster. Harder. To drain me. "This is how this is going to play out. You'll work with the team I'm sending. If you miss another deadline, I'm pulling Tim off oversight."

"Bullshit!" he shouted. "This is my fucking app! You can't take it from me."

I needed finesse but had none, my brain hazed with the animal need to mate. "You should've read the contract more carefully. Do that tonight and we'll revisit tomorrow after the team arrives."

After I come . . .

Tingles raced along my spine. My balls drew up. I was a minute away, and Eva knew it. Her cheeks were hollowing with the force of her suction, her tongue fluttering over the sensitive underside of my cockhead. My heart was pounding, my palms damp with perspiration.

Staring into a half-dozen angry faces with a riot of protests exploding from my earpiece, I felt the orgasm hit me like a freight train. I fumbled for the mute button and let the groan tear from my throat as I spurted powerfully into Eva's greedily working mouth. She moaned and milked my dick with both hands, pulling and squeezing as I kept coming in a flood I couldn't stop.

I felt the heat race up into my face. Staring stonily into my monitor, I fought the urge to close my eyes and throw my head back, to free myself to absorb the singular pleasure of coming for my wife. Coming *because* of her.

As the pressure eased, I released her hair and touched her cheek with my fingertips.

I unmuted my microphone.

"My admin will call you in a few minutes," I cut in, my voice hoarse, "to arrange tomorrow's meeting. I hope we can come to an amicable agreement. Until then."

I shut down my browser and yanked off my headset. "Come here, angel."

My chair was shoved back and I'd hauled her out before she had the chance to come out on her own.

"You're a machine!" she gasped, her voice as rough as mine, her lips red and swollen. "I can't believe you didn't even twitch! How can you— Oh!"

The tiny scrap of lace she wore as underwear dropped to the floor in pieces.

"I liked those panties," she said breathlessly.

Lifting her, I set her bare ass on the cool glass, aligning her perfectly to take my cock. "You'll like this more."

"Angel."

Like a sleepy kitten, Eva blinked at me as I stepped out of my office washroom. "Hmm?"

I grinned at finding her still slumped in my desk chair. "I assume you're okay."

"Never better." She reached up and ran a hand over her hair. "Missing the brain you just fucked out of me, but otherwise, I'm feeling excellent, thank you very much."

"You're welcome." I headed toward her with a warm damp washcloth.

"Are you trying to set a new record for most orgasms in a single day?"

"An intriguing proposition. I'm willing to give it a shot."

She held out her hand as if to ward me off. "No more, maniac. You screw me again and I'll be a drooling, babbling idiot."

"Let me know if you change your mind." I kneeled in front of her and urged her legs open. Waxed smooth and pretty pink, her cunt was lovely. Perfect.

She watched me as I cleaned her, her fingers reaching out to comb through my hair. "Don't work too hard this weekend, okay?"

"As if there's something else worth doing without you around," I murmured.

"Sleep in. Read a book. Plan a party."

My mouth quirked. "I haven't forgotten. I'm asking the guys tonight."

"Oh?" The laziness left her eyes. I pulled back before her legs closed. "What guys?"

"The ones you want to meet."

"You're calling them?

I stood. "We're getting together."

"To do what?"

"Drink. Hang out." Returning to the bathroom, I tossed the washcloth in the hamper and washed my hands.

Eva followed me. "At a club?"

"Maybe. Probably not."

She lounged against the doorjamb and crossed her arms. "Are any of them married?"

"Yes." I slung the hand towel back on the rack. "Me."

"That's it? Is Arnoldo going to be there?"

"Maybe. Likely."

"What's up with the short answers?"

"What's up with the interrogation?" I asked the question, but I knew. My wife was a jealous, possessive woman. Lucky for both of us, I liked it. A lot.

She shrugged, but it was a defensive gesture. "I just want to know what you're doing, that's all."

"I'll stay home if you will."

"I'm not asking you to do that."

There was a smudge of dark makeup beneath her eyes. I loved mussing her up and giving her that just-fucked look. No woman wore it better. "Get to the point, then."

She made a frustrated noise. "Why won't you tell me what you guys have planned?"

"I don't know, Eva. Usually we meet at one of our places and drink. Play cards. Sometimes we go out."

"Trolling. A group of hot guys who've got a buzz and want a good time."

"That's not a crime. And who said they're attractive?"

She shot me a look. "They're trolling with you. That means they're either hot enough not to completely pale in your shadow or too confident to worry about it."

I held up my left hand. The bloodred rubies in my wedding band caught the light. I never took the ring off and never would. "Remember this?"

"I'm not worried about you," she muttered, her arms dropping to her sides. "If I'm not fucking you enough, you need help."

"Says the wife who couldn't wait fifteen minutes."

She stuck her tongue out at me.

"That's what got you fucked right there."

"Arnoldo doesn't trust me, Gideon. He doesn't really want you with me."

"It's not his decision to make. And some of your friends aren't going to like me, either. I know Cary's on the fence."

"What if Arnoldo tells the others how he feels about me?"

"Angel." I went to her and caught her by the hips. "Talking about feelings is predominantly female territory."

"Don't be sexist."

"You know I'm right. Besides, Arnoldo knows how it is. He's been in love before."

She looked up at me with those uniquely beautiful eyes. "Are you in love, Mr. Cross?"

"Irrevocably."

MANUEL Alcoa slapped me on the back as he rounded me. "You just cost me a thousand dollars, Cross."

I leaned against the kitchen island and shoved my hand into the pocket of my jeans, wrapping it around my smartphone. Eva was mid-flight and I was alert for any word from her or Raúl. I'd never feared flying, never worried over someone's safety while traveling. Until now.

"How so?" I asked, before taking a swig of my beer.

"You are the last man I figured would tie the knot and you turn out to be the first." Manuel shook his head. "Kills me."

I lowered the bottle. "You bet against me?"

"Yeah. Although I suspect someone had the inside scoop." The portfolio manager narrowed his eyes across the island at Arnoldo Ricci, who lifted one shoulder in a shrug.

"If it's any consolation," I said, "I'd have bet against me, too."

Manuel grinned. "Latinas rule, my friend. Sexy, curvy. More than a handful in bed and out. Hot tempered. Passionate." He hummed. "Good choice."

"Manuel!" Arash yelled from the living room. "Bring those limes over here."

I watched Manuel leave the kitchen with the bowl of lime slices. Arash's condo was modern and spacious with a panoramic view of the East River. There was a notable lack of walls except for those hiding the bathrooms.

Circling the granite-topped island, I approached Arnoldo. "How are you?"

"Good." His gaze dropped to the amber liquid he swirled in a tumbler. "I'd ask you the same, but you look well. I'm glad."

I didn't waste time with small talk. "Eva worries that you've got a problem with her."

He glanced at me. "I've never been disrespectful to your woman."

"She never said you were."

Arnoldo drank, taking a moment to savor the fine liquor before swallowing it. "I understand that you are—what's the word?—held captive by this woman."

"Captivated," I provided, wondering why he didn't just speak in Italian.

"Ah, yes." He gave me a slight smile. "I have been there, my friend, as you know. I don't judge you."

I knew Arnoldo understood. I'd found him in Florence, recovering from the loss of a woman by drowning in liquor and cooking like a madman, producing so much five-star cuisine he was giving it away. I had been fascinated by the totality of his despair and unable to relate.

I'd been so certain I would never know anything like it. Like the opacity and soundproofing of the glass wall in my office, my view of life had been dulled. I knew I'd never be able to explain to Eva how she'd appeared to me the first time I saw her, so vibrant and warm. A colorful explosion in a black-and-white landscape.

"*Voglio che sia felice.*" It was a simple statement, but the crux of the issue. *I want her to be happy.*

"If her happiness depends on what I think," he answered in Italian, "you ask too much. I will never say anything against her. I'll always treat her with the respect I feel for you as long as you are together. But what I believe is my choice and my right, Gideon."

I looked over at Arash, who was lining up shot glasses on the bar in the living room. As my lead attorney, he knew about both my marriage and Eva's sex tape, and he didn't have a problem with either one.

"Our relationship is . . . complex," I explained quietly. "I've hurt her as much as she's ever hurt me—likely more."

"I'm not surprised to hear that, but I am sorry." Arnoldo studied me. "You couldn't choose one of the other women who've loved you and would give you no trouble? A comfortable ornament who would settle into your life without a ripple?"

"As Eva says, what would be the fun in that?" My smile faded. "She challenges me, Arnoldo. Makes me see things . . . think about things, in ways I didn't before. And she loves me. Not like the others." I reached for my phone again.

"You didn't allow the others to love you."

"I couldn't. I was waiting for her." A thoughtful expression crossed his face and I said, "I can't imagine your Bianca was hassle-free."

He laughed. "No. But my life is simple. I can use complications."

"My life was ordered. Now, it's an adventure."

Arnoldo sobered, his dark eyes growing serious. "But that wildness in her that you love is what worries me most."

"Stop worrying."

"I will mention this only once, then never again. You may be angry with me for what I say, but understand that my heart is in the right place."

My jaw tightened. "Get it off your chest."

"I sat with Eva and Brett Kline at dinner. I observed them together. There is chemistry there, not unlike what I saw between Bianca and the man she left me for. I wish I believed Eva would ignore it, but she's already proven that she can't."

I held his gaze. "She had her reasons. Reasons I gave her."

Arnoldo took another drink. "Then I'll pray that you don't give her more reasons."

"Hey," Arash shouted. "Cut it out with the Italian and get your asses in here."

Arnoldo touched his glass to my bottle before passing me.

I finished my beer alone, taking a moment to consider what Arnoldo had said.

Then I joined the party.

4

"WHAT'S GOT YOU frowning, baby girl?" Cary asked, his voice
low and sleepy from the Dramamine he'd downed at takeoff.

Staring at the choices in the dropdown menu my cursor hovered
over, I debated which to pick. *Engaged* or *It's complicated*? Since *Married* also applied, I thought *All of the above* should've been an option.

Wouldn't that be fun to explain?

Glancing across the luxurious cabin of Gideon's private jet, I found
my best friend sprawled along the white leather sofa with his hands
tucked behind his head. Long and lean, he was a pretty picture with
his shirt riding high and his cargo pants riding low, exposing the
amazing abs that were helping Grey Isles to sell jeans, underwear, and
other men's clothing.

Cary had no problem whatsoever accustoming himself to the
luxurious conveniences of Gideon's immense wealth. He'd settled
immediately and comfortably into the elegant appointments of the

ultra-modern cabin. And somehow, even casually dressed, he looked perfectly at home amid the brushed steel and gray oak.

"I'm trying to set up some social media accounts," I answered.

"Whoa." He sat up with effortless grace, his posture surprisingly and instantly alert. "Big step."

"Yeah." Nathan had kept me hiding, afraid to put myself out there and risk making it easy for him to find me. "But it's time. I feel like . . . Never mind. It's just time."

"All right." He set his elbows on his knees and tapped his fingertips together. "Then why is your face all scrunched up like that?"

"Well, there's a lot to consider. I mean, how much do I share out there? I don't have to worry about Nathan anymore, but Gideon is under constant scrutiny."

With my thoughts on Gideon, I ran a search for his profile. It popped up with the little blue check mark that told me it was verified as belonging to him. The sight of his picture, a shot of him in a black three-piece suit and the blue tie I loved, sent a pang of longing through me. He'd been photographed on a rooftop with the skyline of Manhattan fuzzily out of focus behind him, while he was sharply and vividly captured by the camera's lens.

He was even sharper and more vibrant in reality. I stared into Gideon's eyes, getting lost in that impossible blue. His black hair framed that perfect fallen-angel face in strands of glossy, inky silk.

Poetic? Yes. But then his looks could inspire sonnets. To say nothing of spur-of-the-moment marriage.

When had the photo been taken? Before we'd met? He had the implacable, remote look that made him seem like such an impossible dream.

"I'm married," I blurted out, tearing my gaze away from the most gorgeous man I'd ever seen. "To Gideon, of course. Who else would I be married to?"

Cary froze while I rambled. "Come again?"

I rubbed my palms on my yoga pants. It was a cop-out telling him the news while motion sickness drugs lulled his brain, but I'd take any advantage I could get. "When we went away last weekend. We eloped."

He was quiet for a long, weighted minute. Then he exploded to his feet. "Are you shitting me?"

Raúl's head turned in our direction. The movement was casual and unhurried, but his gaze was vigilant and watchful. He sat in the far corner, being eerily unobtrusive for such a hard-to-miss guy.

"What's the damned rush?" Cary snapped.

"It just . . . happened." I couldn't explain it. I'd thought it was too soon. Still did. But Gideon was the only man I would ever love so completely. When I considered that, I knew Gideon had been right; we'd only be postponing the inevitable. And Gideon needed my promise that I was his forever. My amazing husband who found it so hard to believe he could be loved. "I'm not sorry."

"Not yet." Cary shoved both hands into his hair. "Jesus, Eva. You don't up and marry the first guy you have a serious relationship with."

"It's not like that," I protested, awkwardly avoiding looking at Raúl. "You know how we feel about each other."

"Sure. You two are whack jobs separately. Together, you're a god-damn nut house."

I flipped him the bird. "We'll work on it. Wearing a ring doesn't mean we stop figuring things out."

He dropped into the chair across from me. "What incentive has he got to fix anything? He's bagged and tagged the prize. You're stuck with his psychotic dreams and Grand Canyon–sized mood swings."

"Wait a minute," I said tightly, feeling the sting of truth in his words. "You didn't get upset when I told you we were engaged."

"Because I figured it'd be a year, at the very least, before Monica got the wedding worked out. Maybe a year and a half. At least some time for you two to try living together."

I let him rant. Better that he did it at thirty thousand feet than in some public venue where the whole world could hear.

He leaned closer, his green eyes fierce. "I'm having a baby and I'm not getting married. You know why? Because I'm too fucked up and I know it. I've got no business hitching a passenger on this wild ride. If he loved you, he'd be thinking about *you* and what's best for *you*."

"I'm so glad you're happy for me, Cary. That means a lot."

The words dripped with sarcasm, but they were honest in their own way. There were girlfriends I could call who would tell me what an amazingly lucky bitch I was. Cary was my closest friend because he always gave it to me straight, even when I desperately wanted sugar-coating.

But Cary was thinking only about the darkness. He didn't understand the light Gideon brought into my life. The acceptance and the love. The safety. Gideon had given me my freedom back, a life without terror. Giving him vows in return was too simple a repayment for that.

I turned my attention back to Gideon's profile, scrolling down to see that the most recent post was a link to an article about our engagement. I doubted he'd posted it himself; he was too busy to bother with something like that. But I figured he'd approved it. If not, he had somehow already made it clear that I was important enough to become the one bit of personal news that was okay to be shared on an otherwise business-focused profile.

Gideon was proud of me. Proud to be marrying me, a hot mess with a history of bad choices. Whatever anyone else thought, I knew *I* was the one who'd bagged and tagged the prize.

"Fuck." Cary slouched into the chair. "Make me feel like an ass."

"If the shoe fits . . ." I muttered, clicking on the link to view other photos of Gideon.

It was a mistake.

All the pictures posted by his social media admin were business-related, but the unofficial pictures he'd been tagged in weren't. There, in living color, were images of him with beautiful women. And they hit me hard. Jealousy clawed and twisted my stomach.

God, he looked amazing in a tuxedo. Dark and dangerous. His face savagely beautiful, his cheekbones and mouth chiseled perfection, his posture confident and more than a little arrogant. An alpha male in his prime.

I knew the photos weren't recent. I knew the women in them didn't have firsthand knowledge of his insanely mad skills in bed; he had a rule about that. Neither of which stopped the images from making me twitchy.

"Am I the last to know?" Cary asked.

"You're the only one." I glanced at Raúl. "At least on my side. Gideon wants to tell the world, but we're going to keep it under wraps."

He studied me. "For how long?"

"Forever. The next wedding we have will be our first as far as anyone else is concerned."

"You having second thoughts?"

It killed me that Cary didn't care that we had an audience. I was hyperaware that every move I made, every word I said was being witnessed.

Not that Raúl's presence had any effect on my answer. "No. I'm glad we're married. I love him, Cary."

I was glad Gideon was mine. And I missed him. Worse after seeing those pictures.

"I know you do," Cary said with a sigh.

Unable to help myself, I opened the messaging app on my laptop and sent Gideon a text. I miss you.

He texted back almost instantly. Turn the plane around.

That made me smile. It was so like him. And so unlike me. Wasting the pilots' time, the fuel . . . it seemed so frivolous to me. More than that, though, would be the proof of how dependent on Gideon I'd become. That would be the kiss of death in our relationship. He could have anything, any woman, at any time. If I ever became too easy for him, we'd both lose respect for me. Losing his love wouldn't be far behind.

I returned to my new profile and uploaded a selfie I'd taken with Gideon that I synced from my smartphone. I made it the masthead image. Then I tagged him and gave it a description: *The love of my life.*

After all, if his photos were going to include him with women, I wanted at least one of them to be me. And the one I'd chosen was undeniably intimate. We lay on our backs, our temples touching, my face bare of makeup and his relaxed with a smile in his eyes. I dared anyone to look at it and not see that I had a private bond with him the world would never know.

I suddenly wanted to call him. So badly that I could almost hear that amazingly sexy voice, as intoxicating as top-shelf liquor, smooth with just a hint of bite. I wanted to be with him, my hand in his, my lips against his throat where the smell of his skin called to something hungry and primitive inside me.

It scared me sometimes, how much I needed him. To the exclusion of everything else. There was no one I wanted to be with more, including my best friend, who was at that moment needing me almost as fiercely.

"It's all good, Cary," I assured him. "Don't worry."

"I'd be more worried if I thought you actually believed that." He shoved the bangs off his forehead with an impatient hand. "It's too soon, Eva."

I nodded. "But it'll work out."

It had to. I couldn't imagine my life without Gideon in it.

Cary's head dropped back and his eyes closed. I might have thought he was succumbing to the motion sickness pills, except his knuckles were white from gripping the armrests too tightly. He was taking the news hard. I didn't know what I could say to reassure him.

You're still heading in the wrong direction, Gideon texted.

I almost asked him how he knew that, but caught myself. Are you having a good time with the guys?

I'd have more fun with you.

I grinned. I would hope so. My fingers paused, then: I told Cary.

The answer wasn't instantaneous. Still friends?

He hasn't disowned me yet.

He didn't say anything to that, and I told myself not to read too much into his silence. He was out with his guys. It had been asking a lot to even hear from him at all.

Still, I was super happy to get a text from him ten minutes later.

Don't stop missing me.

I looked over at Cary and found him watching me. Was Gideon facing similar disapproval from his friends?

Don't stop loving me, I texted back.

His answer was simple and very much Gideon. Deal.

"SoCal, baby, I missed you." Cary descended the steps from the plane to the tarmac, tilting his head back to look up at the night sky. "God, it's good to leave that East Coast humidity behind."

I scrambled down after him, eager to get to the tall, dark figure waiting by a shiny black Suburban. Victor Reyes was the kind of male who commanded attention. Part of that was due to his being a cop. The rest was all him.

"Dad!" I ran full bore toward him and he unfolded from where he'd been leaning against the SUV and opened his arms to me.

He absorbed the crash of my body into his and lifted me off my feet, squeezing me so tightly I couldn't breathe. "It's good to see you, baby," he said gruffly.

Cary sauntered up to us. My dad put me down.

"Cary." My dad clasped Cary's hand, then pulled him in for a quick hug and a hearty slap on the back. "Looking good, kid."

"I try."

"Got everything?" my dad asked. He eyed Raúl, who'd exited the plane first and now stood silently near a black Benz that had been parked and waiting close by.

Gideon had told me to forget that Raúl was there. That wasn't easy for me to do.

"Yep," Cary answered, adjusting the weight of his duffel strap on his shoulder. He carried my bag, which was lighter than his, in his hand. Even with all my makeup and three pairs of shoes, Cary had packed more than me.

I loved that about him.

"You two hungry?" My dad opened the passenger door for me.

It was just past nine in California, but after midnight in New York. Too late for me to eat usually, but we hadn't grabbed dinner.

Cary answered before climbing into the backseat. "Starved."

I laughed. "You're always hungry."

"So are you, sweet cheeks," he shot back, sliding into the center seat so he could lean forward and be in the mix. "I've just got no guilt about it."

We pulled away from the jet and I watched it grow smaller as we cruised down the tarmac toward the exit. I glanced at my dad's profile, looking for any hint of his thoughts about the lifestyle I'd be living as Gideon's wife. The private jets. The full-time bodyguards. I knew how he felt about Stanton's wealth, but that was my stepdad. I was hoping a husband would be cut some slack.

Still, I knew the change in routine was glaring. Previously, we would've flown into San Diego's harbor. We would have headed to the Gaslamp and grabbed a table at Dick's Last Resort, spending an hour or more laughing at the silliness and enjoying a beer with dinner.

There was tension now that hadn't been there before. Nathan. Gideon. My mom. They were all hovering between us.

It sucked. Massively.

"What about that place in Oceanside with the slushy beer and peanut shells on the floor?" Cary suggested.

"Yeah." I twisted in my seat to give him a grateful smile. "That'd be fun."

Laid-back and familiar. Perfect.

I could tell my dad thought so, too, when I looked at him and his mouth quirked. "You got it."

We left the airport behind. I dug out my phone and turned it on, wanting to sync it to the Suburban's sound system so we could listen to music that would take us back to less complicated times.

Texts popped up so fast, they filled my screen then scrolled off.

The most recent one was from Brett. Call me when you get into town.

And right on cue, "Golden" started playing on the radio.

I was climbing the steps of my dad's tiny porch the next day when my phone started vibrating. I pulled it out of my shorts pocket and felt a tingle of happiness at the sight of Gideon's picture on the screen.

"Good morning," I answered, settling into one of the two cushioned wrought-iron chairs near the front door. "Did you sleep well?"

"Well enough." The beloved soft rasp of his voice slid sweetly through me. "Raúl says Victor's coffee could wake a hibernating bear."

I glanced at the Benz parked across the narrow street. The tinted windows were so dark I couldn't see the man inside. It was a bit freaky that Raúl had somehow managed to talk to Gideon about the coffee I'd just barely taken over to him before I even made it back to the house. "Are you trying to intimidate me with how closely you're watching me?"

"If intimidation were my goal, I wouldn't be subtle about it."

I picked up the mug I'd dropped off on the small patio table prior to making my java delivery to Raúl. "You do know that tone of voice makes me want to irritate you back, don't you?"

"Because you like the way I rise to the challenge," he purred, sending little goose bumps across my skin despite the warmth of the summer day.

My mouth curved. "So, what exactly did you guys end up doing last night?"

"The usual. Drink. Give each other a hard time."

"Did you go out?"

"For a couple of hours."

My grip tightened on the phone as I pictured a pack of hot guys out on the prowl. "I hope you had fun."

"It wasn't bad. Tell me your plans for the day."

I picked up the same note of tightness in his words that I'd just had. Unfortunately, marriage wasn't a cure for jealousy. "When Cary wakes up and rolls his ass off the couch, we'll grab a quick lunch with my dad. Then we're going down to San Diego to see Dr. Travis."

"And tonight?"

I took a sip of my coffee, steeling myself for an argument. I knew he was thinking about Brett. "The band's manager sent me an e-mail about where to claim VIP tickets, but I've decided not to see the show. I figure Cary can take a friend, if he wants. What I have to say won't take very long, so either I'll see Brett tomorrow before I leave or we can chat on the phone."

He exhaled softly. "I expect you have an idea of what you're going to tell him."

"I'm gonna keep it simple. With 'Golden' and my engagement, I don't think it's appropriate for us to see each other socially. I hope we'll be friends and keep in touch, but e-mail and texts are better, unless you're with me."

He was silent long enough that I thought maybe the call had dropped. "Gideon?"

"I need to know if you're afraid to see him."

Uneasy, I took another drink. The coffee had cooled, but I barely tasted it anyway. "I don't want to fight about Brett."

"So your solution is to avoid him."

"You and I have enough shit to fight about without throwing him into the mix. He's not worth it."

Gideon was quiet again. This time, I waited him out.

When his voice came again, it was confident and decisive. "I can live with that, Eva."

My shoulders relaxed and something inside me eased. And then, paradoxically, my chest tightened. I remembered what he'd said to me once, that he'd live with me loving another man just so long as he had me.

He loved me so much more than he loved himself. It broke my heart that he'd sell himself short like that. It made it impossible to hold myself back.

"You're everything to me," I breathed. "I think about you all the time."

"It's no different for me."

"Really?" I lowered my voice further, trying to keep it down. "Because I have it so bad for you. I get—well, hot. Like I'm overcome with this desperate *need* to be touching you. My brain scatters and I have to take a minute to ride it out, but it's so hard to deal. So many times I've almost dropped whatever I'm doing to get to you."

"Eva—"

"I have fantasies about barging into one of your meetings and just running right into you. Have I told you that? When the craving is really bad, I can almost *feel* you pulling at me."

I rushed on when I heard him growl softly. "I lose my breath every time I see you. If I close my eyes, I can hear your voice. I woke up this morning and I panicked a little because you're so far away. I would've given *anything* to be able to get to you. I wanted to cry because I couldn't."

"Christ. Eva, please—"

"If you're going to worry about anything, Gideon, it should be *me*. Because I can't be rational when it comes to you. I'm crazy about you. Literally. I can't think about a future without you—it freaks me out."

"Goddamn it. You'll *never* be without me. We're going to grow old together. Die together. I'm not going to live a single day without you."

A tear slid from the corner of my eye. I scrubbed it away. "I need you to understand that you'll never have to settle for pieces of me. You shouldn't be settling at all. You deserve so much better. You could have anyone—"

"That's enough!"

I jumped at the lash of his voice.

"You will not ever say anything like that to me again," he snapped. "Or I swear to God, angel, I will punish you."

Shocked silence filled the space between us. The words I'd spoken circled restlessly in my mind, taunting me with how pathetic I could be. I never wanted to be dependent on him, but I already was.

"I have to go," I said hoarsely.

"Don't hang up. For God's sake, Eva, we're *married*. We're in love. There's no shame in that. So what if it's crazy? It's *us*. It's who we are. You need to come to grips with that."

The screen door squeaked as my dad stepped onto the porch. I looked at him and said, "My dad's here, Gideon. I'll have to talk to you later."

"You make me happy," he said, in the deep firm tone he used when making an unswayable decision. "I'd forgotten what that feels like. Don't devalue what you mean to me."

God.

"I love you, too." I ended the call and set the phone down on the table with a shaky hand.

My dad settled into the other chair with his coffee. He wore long shorts and a dark olive T-shirt, but his feet were bare. He'd shaved and his hair was still damp, the ends curling slightly as they dried.

He was my father, but that didn't stop me from appreciating the fact that he was ridiculously attractive. He kept himself in great shape and had a naturally confident bearing. I could see why my mother hadn't been able to resist him when they'd met. And apparently still couldn't.

"I heard you talking," he said without looking at me.

"Oh." My stomach dropped. It was bad enough spilling my guts to Gideon. Knowing that my dad had heard me do it only made it worse.

"I was going to talk to you about whether you knew what you were doing, getting engaged so soon and so young."

I pulled my legs up and crossed them under me. "I figured you would."

"But now I think I understand what you're feeling." He looked at me, his gray eyes soft and searching. "You express it far better than I ever could, back in the day. The most I could ever get out was 'I love you,' and it's just not enough."

I could see he was thinking about my mom. I knew it must be hard not to when I looked so much like her. "Gideon doesn't think those words are enough, either."

I looked down at my rings. The one Gideon had given me to express his need to hold on to me, and the other both a symbol of his commitment and a tribute to a time in his past when he'd last felt loved. "He shows me, though. All the time."

"I've talked to him a few times now." My dad paused. "I have to remind myself that he's in his twenties."

That made me smile. "He's very self-possessed."

"He's also very hard to read."

My smile widened. "He's a poker player. But he means what he says."

I believed Gideon implicitly. He always told me the truth. The problem was, there was a lot he didn't tell me.

"And he wants to marry my daughter."

I shot him a look. "You gave him your blessing."

"He said he would always take care of you. He promised to keep you safe and make you happy." He stared across the street at the Benz. "I still don't know why I believe him, even with him staking out my place for you. Doesn't help that he lied about waiting to ask you."

"He couldn't wait, Dad. Don't hold it against him. He loves me too much."

He looked at me again. "You didn't sound happy when you were just talking to him."

"No. I sounded desperate and insecure." I sighed. "I love him like mad, but I hate when I get needy with it. We should be balanced in our relationship. Equals."

"Good goal. Don't lose sight of it. Does he want that, too?"

"He wants us to be together. In everything. But he's built a reputation and an empire, and I want to build my own. Not necessarily the empire, but the reputation for sure."

"Have you talked to him about this?"

"Oh yeah." My mouth quirked. "But he believes Mrs. Cross should naturally play on Team Cross. And I can see his point."

"It's good to hear that you've been thinking this through."

I heard the pause. "But?"

"But that could be a serious issue, couldn't it?"

I loved the way my dad urged me to explore without trying to sway me or judge. He'd always been that way. "Yes. I don't think it would become a deal breaker for us, but it could cause problems. He isn't used to not getting what he wants."

"Then you're good for him."

"He thinks so." I shrugged. "Gideon isn't the problem. It's me. He's been through a lot in his life and he's had to deal with it on his own. I don't want him to feel like he's got to handle everything himself anymore. I want him to feel like we're a unit and that I'm here to support

CAPTIVATED BY YOU · 63

him. That's a hard message to send when I want my own independence, too."

"You're a lot like me," he said with a soft smile, looking so handsome that my heart swelled with pride.

"I know you'll get along with him. He's a good man, with a beautiful heart. He'd do anything for me, Dad." *Even kill for me.*

The thought made me queasy. The possibility that Gideon would have to answer for Nathan's death in some way was all too real. I couldn't let anything happen to him.

"Would he let me pay for the wedding?" My dad snorted out a laugh. "I guess I should ask how much of a fight you think your mother would give me."

"Dad . . ." My chest tightened again. After the discussions we'd had about paying for my college tuition, I knew better than to say he didn't have to stretch his finances to the breaking point for me. It was a point of pride and my father was a very proud man. "I don't know what to say except thank you."

He gave me a relieved smile and I realized that he'd been expecting me to be resistant, too. "I've got about fifty large. I know it's not much—"

I reached for his hand. "It's perfect."

I could already hear my mom's freakout in my head. I'd cope with that when the time came.

It would be worth it for the look on my father's face at that moment.

"It hasn't changed." Cary paused on the sidewalk outside the former recreation center and pulled the sunglasses off his face. His gaze slid over the gym's entrance. "I've missed this place."

I reached for his hand and linked our fingers. "Me, too."

We headed up the walk and nodded at the couple standing by the door smoking. Then we went inside and were greeted by the sights and sounds of a hoops match in progress. Two teams of three played a half-court game, taunting each other and laughing. I knew from experience that sometimes Dr. Travis's unusual offices were the only place one felt free and safe enough to laugh.

We waved at the players, who paused just long enough to register us, and then we made a beeline for the door that still had *Coach* emblazoned on the glass inset. It was ajar and a beloved figure lounged in a worn desk chair with his feet propped on the desk. He tossed a tennis ball against the wall and caught it deftly, over and over, while a fellow patient I knew from before vaped on an electronic cigarette and talked.

"Oh my God." Kyle stood in a rush, her pretty red mouth falling open and a cloud of vapor billowing out. "I didn't know you two were back!"

She launched herself at Cary, barely giving me time to let his hand go.

Dr. Travis folded his legs and then stood, his kind face splitting with a welcoming grin. He was dressed in his usual khakis and dress shirt, with the leather sandals on his feet and the earrings in his ears giving him away as a tad unconventional. His sandy brown hair was shaggy and messy, and his wire-rimmed glasses were slightly skewed on the bridge of his nose.

"I wasn't expecting you two until sometime after three," he said.

"It's after three in New York," Cary rejoined, disentangling himself from Kyle.

I had my suspicions that Cary had slept with the pretty blonde at some point, and that she hadn't brushed it off as easily as he had.

Dr. Travis caught me up in a quick hug, then did the same to Cary. I watched my best friend's eyes close and his cheek rest for a moment on Dr. Travis's shoulder. My eyes stung as they always did whenever I saw Cary happy. Dr. Travis was the closest thing to a father that he had and I knew how much Cary loved him.

"You two still watching each other's backs in the Big Apple?"

"Of course," I replied.

Cary jerked his thumb at me. "She's getting married. I'm having a baby."

Kyle gasped.

I elbowed Cary in the ribs.

"Oww," he complained, rubbing his side.

Dr. Travis blinked. "Congratulations. Quick work, both of you."

"I'll say," Kyle muttered. "What's it been? A month?"

"Kyle." Dr. Travis tucked his chair into his desk. "Would you give us a minute?"

She snorted and sauntered toward the door. "You're good, Doc, but I think you're going to need more time than that."

"ENGAGED, huh?" Kyle took another drag off her e-cigarette, her eyes on Cary as he leaped above Dr. Travis's head and made a slam dunk. We sat on the worn bleachers about three rows from the top, enough distance away that we couldn't overhear the therapy session taking place on the court.

Cary got restless when he opened up. Dr. Travis had quickly learned to keep Cary physically active if he wanted to keep him talking.

Kyle looked at me. "I always kinda figured you and Cary would end up together."

I laughed and shook my head. "It's not like that with us. Never has been."

She shrugged. Her eyes were the color of the San Diego sky and heavily rimmed with electric blue liner. "You known this guy you're marrying long?"

"Long enough."

Dr. Travis nailed a bank shot and then ruffled Cary's hair affectionately. I saw him glance at me and knew it was my turn.

I stood and stretched. "Catch you later," I said to Kyle.

"Good luck."

My mouth twisted wryly and I made my way down the stairs until I reached Dr. Travis.

He was about Gideon's height, so I stopped before I hit the bottom stair so that we were briefly at eye level. "You ever consider moving to New York, Doc?"

He smiled his crooked smile. "As if California taxes aren't bad enough."

I sighed dramatically. "I had to try."

His arm slung around my shoulders when I joined him courtside. "So did Cary. I'm flattered."

We went to his office. I shut the door while he nabbed a dinged metal chair and spun it around to sit facing backward with his arms draped along the backrest. It was one of his quirks. He sat in the desk chair when he was just hanging out; he straddled the relic when he got down to business.

"Tell me about your fiancé," he said, when I took my usual spot on the green vinyl sofa that was held together with duct tape and decorated with signatures of former and existing patients.

"Come on," I chided. "We both know Cary filled you in."

Cary always started his sessions with talk about my life and me. That eventually dovetailed into talk about him.

"And I know who Gideon Cross is." Dr. Travis tapped his feet in that way he had that somehow never seemed restless or impatient. "But I want to hear about the man you're going to marry."

I thought for a minute and he sat quietly while I did, not waiting, just observing. "Gideon is . . . God, he's so many things. He's complicated. We have some issues to work out, but we'll get there. My more immediate problem is the feelings I'm having for this singer I used to . . . see."

"Brett Kline?"

"You remember his name."

"Cary reminded me, but I remember our discussions about him."

"Yeah, well." I looked at my stunning wedding ring, twisting it around my finger. "I'm so in love with Gideon. He's changed my life in so many ways. He makes me feel beautiful and precious. I know it seems too fast, but he's the one for me."

Dr. Travis smiled. "It was love at first sight for me and my wife. We were in high school when we met, but I knew she was the girl I was going to marry."

My gaze drifted to the pictures of his wife on his desk. There was one when she was younger, and another more recent. The office itself was a mess of papers, sports equipment, books, and ancient posters of bygone sports personalities, but the frames and glass protecting the photos were spotless.

"I don't understand why Brett has any effect on me at all. It's not that I want him. I can't imagine being with anyone else but Gideon. Sexually or otherwise. But I'm not indifferent to Brett."

"Why should you be?" he asked simply. "He was a part of your life at a pivotal time, and the end of your relationship caused a bit of an epiphany for you."

"My . . . interest—that's not the right word—doesn't feel like nostalgia."

"No, I'm sure it doesn't. I would guess you're feeling some regret. Thinking about what-ifs. It was a highly sexual relationship for you, so there may be some lingering attraction, even if you know you'd never go there again."

I was almost sure he was right about that.

His fingertips drummed on the back of the chair. "You said your fiancé is a complicated man and you're working on some issues. Brett was very simple. You knew what you were getting with him. In the last few months, you've had a big move, you're closer to your mother, and you're engaged. You may, occasionally, wish things were simpler."

I stared at him as that sank in. "How do you make sense like that?"

"Practice."

Fear made me say, "I don't want to screw things up with Gideon."

"Do you have someone you're talking with in New York?"

"We're in couples therapy."

He nodded. "Practical. That's good. He wants it to work, too. Does he know?"

About Nathan? "Yes."

"I'm proud of you, kiddo."

"I'm going to avoid Brett, but I wonder if that means I'm not dealing with the root of the problem. Like an alcoholic who doesn't drink is still an alcoholic. The problem is still there, they're just staying away from it."

"Not quite true, but interesting that you'd use an addiction analogy. You're prone to self-destructive behavior with men. A lot of individuals with your history are, so it's not unexpected and we've addressed that before."

"I know." That was why I was so afraid of getting lost in Gideon.

"There are a few things you have to consider," he continued. "You're engaged to a man who, on the surface, is very much the sort of man your mother would want for you. Considering how you feel about your mother's dependence on men, there might be some resistance you're feeling."

My nose wrinkled.

He wagged his finger at me. "Ah, a possibility? The other is that you might not feel you deserve what you've found with him."

A rock settled in my gut. "And I deserve Brett?"

"Eva." He gave me a kind smile. "The fact you're even asking that question . . . that's your problem right there."

5

"I DIDN'T EVEN recognize you without the suit and tie," Sam Yimara said, as I settled into the seat across from him. He was a compact man, well shy of six feet in height but muscled. His head was shaved and tattooed, his earlobes pierced so that I could see right through them.

Pete's 69th Street Bar wasn't located on Sixty-ninth Street, so I had no idea where the name originated. I did understand that Six-Ninths had derived their name from it, after playing on its stage for a number of years. I also understood that the restrooms in the back had provided a place for Brett Kline to screw my wife.

I wanted to lay my fists into him for that. She deserved palaces and private islands, not seedy bar bathroom stalls.

Pete's wasn't quite a dive, but it was classless. A beach bar that looked best under cover of darkness and known mostly as a place for

SDSU students to hook up and drink 'til they couldn't remember what they did or whom they fucked.

After I tore the place to the ground, they wouldn't remember the bar, either.

The choice in venue was deliberate and quite brilliant on Yimara's part. It put me on edge and drove home what was at stake. If my decision to show up alone and dressed in jeans and T-shirt threw him off in return, I'd consider the challenge well met.

I leaned back in my seat, watching him carefully. The bar had a few patrons, most of whom were seated on the patio. Only a handful of us occupied the beach-themed interior. "Have you decided to accept my offer?"

"I've considered it." He crossed his legs and angled so that he could lay his arm along his seat back. Overconfident and not smart enough to exercise caution. "But hey, considering what you're valued at, I'm surprised Eva's privacy isn't worth more than a million dollars to you."

I smiled inwardly. "Eva's peace of mind is priceless to me. But if you think I'll up my offer, you aren't thinking clearly. The injunction against you *will* go through. And then there's the pesky little detail regarding the legality of filming Eva without her consent, a very different scenario from a mutually agreed-upon private sex tape gone public."

His jaw tightened. "I thought you wanted to keep this quiet, not make it part of public record. Eva would be on her own with any lawsuit, you know. I've already talked to Brett and we've worked things out."

Tension tightened my shoulders. "He's seen the footage?"

"He has it." Sam reached into his pocket and pulled out a flash drive. "Here's a copy for Eva. I figured you should see what you're paying for."

The thought of Kline viewing sexual images of Eva sent rage surging through me. His memories were bad enough. A recording was unacceptable.

My hand fisted around the flash drive. "It's going to come out that the footage exists; I can't stop it. You contacted too many reporters with your offer to sell it. What I can do is destroy you. Personally, that would be my preference. I want to watch you burn, you piece of shit."

Sam shifted in his seat.

I leaned forward. "You got more than Eva and Kline with your cameras. There are dozens of other victims who didn't sign releases. I own this bar. Hell, I own the band. It didn't take much effort to find the regulars and Six-Ninths followers who were here when you were illegally filming in the bathrooms."

The last bit of avarice in his gaze dimmed, then blinked out completely.

"If you were smarter," I went on, "you would've leveraged for long-term gain instead of an immediate payout. Instead, you're going to sign the contract I'm about to put in front of you and walk away with a check for a quarter million."

He straightened. "Fuck that! You said one million. That was the deal."

"Which you didn't accept." I stood. "It's no longer on the table. And if you take any longer to decide, the new offer won't be, either. I'll just run you into the ground and straight into a jail cell. It's enough that I can tell Eva I tried."

As I walked away, I shoved the flash drive into my pocket, where it promptly burned a hole I couldn't ignore. My gaze met Arash's as I passed where he sat at the bar waiting for his cue to step in.

He hopped off his bar stool. "Always a pleasure watching you scare the hell out of someone," he said, before heading toward the seat I'd just vacated, the necessary contract and check in hand.

I stepped outside the dim bar into the bright San Diego sunshine.

Eva didn't want me to view the footage; she'd made me promise I wouldn't.

But she was feeling something for Kline. He remained a very real threat. Seeing them together, intimately, might give me the information I needed to fight him off.

Had she been as sexually raw with him as she was with me? Had she been as desperate and greedy for him? Could he make her come like I could?

I squeezed my eyes shut against the images in my head, but they wouldn't go away.

Remembering my promise, I crossed the parking lot to my rental car.

Is it silly that I'm nearly as excited to be your "friend" as I am to be your wife?

I laughed inwardly as I read Eva's text and replied. I'm as excited to be your lover as I am to be your husband.

OMG . . . fiend.

That had me laughing aloud.

"What was that sound?" Arash looked at me over the edge of his tablet, having made himself at home on the couch in my hotel suite. "Was that a laugh, Cross? Were you seriously just laughing? Or were you having a stroke?"

I flipped him off.

"Seriously?" he shot back. "The finger?"

"Eva says it's a classic."

"Eva's hot enough to get away with it. You're not."

I opened a new window on my laptop and logged into my social media profile, linking it to Eva's with the *Engaged to* designation now that we were "friends." As I waited for her to accept the relationship link, I clicked on her profile and smiled again at the cover image she'd selected. She was exposing herself to the world for the first time, and she was doing so as the woman who was mine.

I texted her back when she approved our joined status. Now you're both.

☺ I'm keeping my half of our deal.

My gaze moved from the message window to the photo of us on her profile. I brushed over her face with my fingertips, resisting the urge to go to her. It was too soon. She needed what space I could bear to give her.

So am I, angel mine.

THE theater in the casino wasn't a huge venue, but it wasn't small, either, and it was easier to fill. It was better for Six-Ninths to boast sold-out concerts than to risk embarrassingly empty seats, even in their hometown. Christopher would've thought of that.

My brother was good at what he did. I'd learned not to tell him so, though. It only made him more of an asshole.

As the rows of seats slowly emptied, I made my way toward backstage. Not my turf, despite the all-access pass I carried as primary shareholder of Vidal Records. Kline definitely had the advantage.

But I hadn't been able to stay away until morning, even though I knew it was the wiser move. Then, he'd be exhausted. Possibly hungover. *I* would have the upper hand then.

I couldn't wait that long. He had the footage. He would've watched it at least once. Maybe more than that. I couldn't stomach the thought of him watching it again. Getting it away from him was the most important thing on my agenda.

And I wanted him to know I was close by before he met with Eva. I was marking my territory, so to speak, and I chose to do so in the jeans and T-shirt I'd worn when I met Yimara. Anything to do with Eva was a personal matter, not business, and I wanted that to be clear the moment Kline saw me.

I entered stage left and walked straight into chaos. Scantily clad women fucked up on their drug or booze of choice lined the scuffed, narrow corridor. Dozens of tattooed and pierced men broke down and packed up equipment with efficient, practiced skill and speed. Hard-grinding music piped out of hidden speakers, clashing with the tunes spilling out of individual rooms. I weaved through the pandemonium, searching for a distinctive head of frosted spikes.

An achingly familiar blonde stumbled out of an open doorway several feet away, her hair falling around her shoulders and drawing attention to the lush curves of a great ass.

My footsteps slowed. My heartbeat quickened. Kline followed her out, a beer in one hand and the other reaching for her. She caught it and pulled him out into the wing.

I knew how that delicate hand felt, how smooth the skin was. How firm the grip. I knew how those nails felt digging into my back. How those fingers tugged at my hair as she came against my mouth. The electric sizzle of her touch. The primal awareness.

I stood frozen, my gut knotting. She stood close, too close, to Kline. Her shoulder leaned against the wall. Her hip was cocked provocatively, her fingertips brushing suggestively over Kline's stomach. He gave her a cocky, flirtatious smile, his hand rubbing her upper arm in a far too intimate way.

No one who saw them together could mistake that they were lovers.

Rage fired my blood. A sick darkness radiated through me.

Pain. Searing and soul deep. It took my breath and every ounce of control.

A woman's arm draped over my shoulder. Her hand slid beneath the neck of my T-shirt to touch my chest, while her other wrapped around my hip to stroke my dick. Cloying perfume assaulted my nose,

CAPTIVATED BY YOU · 75

spurring me to shrug her off violently even as a model-thin brunette with heavily made-up blue eyes tried to sandwich me from the front.

"Back off!" I growled, glaring at both in a way that had them stumbling back and calling me an asshole.

In another time, I would've fucked them both, turning the feel of being hunted into one of complete control.

I'd learned how to handle sexual predators after Hugh. How to put them in their place.

I surged forward, pushing through the crowd, remembering the feel of Kline's jaw against my fist. The unforgiving hardness of his torso. The grunt of air leaving his body when I hit him with everything I had.

I wanted him laid out and battered. Bloody. Broken.

Kline bent over her, speaking close to her ear. My hands clenched. She threw her head back and laughed, and I stumbled to a halt. Startled and confused. Despite the volume of noise, the sound struck me as wrong.

It wasn't Eva's laugh.

It was too high. My wife's laugh was low and throaty. Sexy. As unique as the woman it belonged to.

The blonde turned her head and I saw her in profile. She wasn't Eva. The body and hair were similar. Not the face.

What the fuck?

My mind caught up with reality. The girl was the one from the "Golden" music video. The Eva stand-in.

Roadies and groupies filtered around me, but I remained fixed in place as Kline caressed and seduced a pale imitation of my incomparable wife.

My phone vibrated in my pocket, startling me. I cursed and pulled it out, reading the text from Raúl: She just arrived at the casino.

So, she'd changed her mind about seeing Kline. Working the situation to my benefit, I typed back: Get her to the left wing now.

Got it.

I backed up against the wall, sidestepping into an alcove half hidden by steel equipment cases stacked on hand trucks. The minutes ticked by slowly.

I sensed her before I saw her, felt the frisson of recognition. Turning my head, I found her easily. Unlike her imitator, who wore a small tight dress, Eva was dressed in jeans that hugged every curve and a simple gray tank top. She wore heeled sandals and hoop earrings, casual and relaxed.

Hunger hit me with brutal force. She was the most beautiful woman I'd ever seen and easily the sexiest woman alive. Other women turned their heads to follow her when she walked by, envying her effortless beauty and sexuality. Men eyed her with heated interest, but she didn't seem to notice, her attention on Kline.

Her gaze narrowed as she took in the same scene I had moments earlier. I watched her assess the situation and knew when she reached the same conclusion I had. A myriad of emotions crossed her face. It had to be odd for her, seeing a former lover so desperate to recapture what he'd once had with her.

It was inconceivable to me. If I couldn't have Eva, I would have no one.

Her shoulders went back. Her chin lifted. Then a smile curved her mouth. I could see the acceptance settle over her, a new kind of peace. Whatever she'd needed, she had found it.

Eva passed by without spotting me, but Raúl joined me.

"Awkward," he said, his attention on Kline as the singer looked up and spotted my wife, his body visibly stiffening.

"Perfect," I replied, as my wife greeted Kline by extending her left hand to him. My ring on her finger sparkled brilliantly, impossible to miss. "Keep me posted."

I left.

As my muscles burned through my eightieth push-up, my gaze was on the flash drive lying on the carpet in front of me. The way I'd dealt with Yimara and Kline had been effective but unsatisfying. I was still tense and aggravated, spoiling for a fight.

My eyes stung as rivulets of sweat ran down my forehead. My chest heaved with exertion. Knowing Eva was out clubbing with Cary and some of their SoCal friends only sharpened the edge I hovered on. I knew how primed she got when out drinking and dancing. I loved nailing her when her body was damp and steamy with perspiration, her cunt slick and greedy.

Jesus. My dick throbbed and hardened further. My arms trembled as I neared the point of muscle fatigue. Veins stood out in harsh relief along my forearms and hands. I needed a cold shower, but I wouldn't get myself off. I always saved it for Eva. Every thick, creamy drop.

The message app on my laptop pinged and I slowed the vicious pace, hitting one hundred before I pushed to my feet. I grabbed the flash drive and dropped it on the desk, then retrieved the towel I'd hung over the back of the chair. Wiping my face before opening the window on my laptop, I expected to read the latest update on Eva's evening. What I saw was a text from her.

What room are you in?

I stared at the screen for a moment, processing the question. Another ping announced a text from Raúl: She's heading toward your hotel.

Anticipation shifted my focus from working out to my delectable, clever wife. I typed a reply to her: 4269.

I reached for the phone on the desk and called room service. "A bottle of Cristal," I ordered. "Two flutes, strawberries, and whipped cream. Have it here in ten. Thanks."

Returning the receiver to its base, I slung the towel around the back of my neck. A quick glance at the clock told me it was half past two in the morning.

By the time the doorbell chimed, I'd turned on all the lights in both the living room and bedroom and opened the curtains that had been blocking the view of the moonlit ocean.

I went to the door and opened it, finding both Eva and room service waiting. Dressed as I'd seen her earlier, Eva looked like a bad girl, renewing my hard-on in an instant. Her hair was limp and her face shiny, her mascara running slightly. She smelled like clean sweat and alcohol.

If the server hadn't been standing behind her, I would've had her on her back on the foyer tile before she knew what hit her.

"Holy fuck," she breathed, eyeing me from head to toe.

I glanced down. I was still overheated, my skin shiny with sweat. The waistband of my sweats was wet with it, drawing attention to the erection I didn't even try to will away. "Sorry, you caught me mid-workout."

"What are you doing in San Diego?" she demanded from the hallway.

Stepping back, I gestured for her to come in.

She didn't move. "I'm not getting sucked into your sex-god vortex until you answer me."

"I'm here on business."

"Bullshit." Her arms crossed.

Reaching out, I caught her by the elbow and tugged her in. "I can prove it."

Room service rolled the cart in after her.

"You're way too optimistic," she muttered, looking at the order as I signed the receipt.

I handed the bill and stylus back, waited for the server to leave, then walked over to the phone by the sofa. I dialed Arash's room.

"Are you serious?" he answered, sounding groggy. "Some of us sleep, Cross."

"My wife wants to talk to you."

"What?" Sheets rustled. "Where are you?"

"In my room." I held the receiver out to Eva. "My attorney."

"Are you nuts?" she asked. "It's five in the morning in New York! On a Sunday!"

"He's in the room next door. Take it. Ask him if I've been working today."

She marched over and snatched the phone out of my hand. "You should get a new job," she told him. "Your boss is insane."

He replied and she sighed. "Before." She glanced at me. "Thank God he's hot. Still, I might get my head checked. Sorry he woke you up. Go back to sleep."

Eva held the phone out to me.

I took it and put it to my ear. "As she said, go back to sleep."

"I like her. She gives you shit."

My gaze slid over her. "I like her, too. Good night."

I hung up and reached for her.

She backed up, avoiding my grasp. "Why didn't you tell me you were here?"

"Didn't want to cramp your style."

"Don't you trust me?"

My brows rose. "Asks the wife who tracked my phone to my hotel."

"I was just curious if you were staying in the penthouse or not!"

She pouted when I only continued to eye her. "And . . . I missed you."

"I'm right here, angel." I opened my arms to her. "Come and get me."

Her nose wrinkled. "I have to shower. I stink."

"We're both sweaty." I went to her. This time, she didn't pull away. "And I love the way you smell. You know that."

I put my hands on her waist, sliding them up until I hugged her delicate rib cage just beneath the full swell of her tits. I cupped them through her top, gently hefting their weight, squeezing softly.

I'd never had a fetish for particular parts of the female body, until Eva. I worshipped every inch of her, cherished all of her generous curves.

The pads of my thumbs circled her nipples, feeling them harden. "I love the way you feel."

Lowering my head, I found the crook of her neck and nuzzled her, rubbing my damp hair against her.

She moaned. "No fair. You're all ripped and shiny and mostly naked, and I have no willpower."

"You don't need any." I pushed my hands beneath her tank and freed the clasp of her bra. "Let me have you, Eva."

I sucked in a slow, deep breath as she reached under the elastic of my waistband and gripped my cock.

"Yum," she whispered. "Look what I found."

"Angel." I cupped her ass. "Tell me you want it exactly the way I want to give it to you."

She looked up at me with heavy-lidded eyes. "And how would that be?"

"Here. On the floor. Your jeans caught around one ankle, your shirt pushed up, your underwear shoved to the side. I want my cock inside you, my cum filling you." I slid my tongue along the racing pulse in her neck. "I'll take care of you once I get you to bed, but right now . . . I just want to use you."

She trembled. "Gideon."

Banding one arm behind her thighs, I pulled her feet out from under her and lowered her carefully to the carpet. My mouth found hers soft and hot and wet, her tongue licking mine. Her arms wrapped around my neck, trying to hold me. I let her, my knees straddling her hips, my fingers opening her jeans.

Her belly was flat and silky smooth, concaving with a giggle when my knuckles brushed her sides. Her ticklishness made me smile into our kiss, joy filling my chest until it felt too small to contain it.

"You'll stay with me," I told her. "Wake up with me."

"Yes." Her hips lifted to help me yank her pants down.

I freed one leg and left the other trapped, my hands pushing her thighs open so I could see her. Her panties were skewed from pulling off her jeans, giving her just the look I wanted.

She was my wife. My most valuable possession; I treasured her. But I loved her slutty and dirty, too. A sexual object for my pleasure. The one woman who could silence the memories in my head and set me free.

"Angel." I slid down, lying prone, my mouth watering for the taste of her.

"No," she protested, her hands covering herself.

I pinned her wrists at her sides and glared. "I want you like this."

"Gideon—"

I licked her through the silk and she arched with a whimper, her heels digging into the carpet and lifting her cunt to my mouth. I pulled her panties aside with my teeth and uncovered the impossibly soft skin. A rough sound left me, my dick hardening to the point of pain.

Wrapping my lips around her clit, I sucked her, licked her. Felt her tense up. I released her hands, knowing she was mine now, helpless to fight me.

"Oh God," she breathed, writhing. "Your mouth . . ."

Spreading her wide with my shoulders, I tongued her, driving her to come. Her fingers pulled at my hair, tugging painfully at the roots, spurring me on until she climaxed with a startled cry. I licked inside her, fucking her, feeling her quiver around my tongue. She grew slicker, hotter.

I rubbed against her clit and slid two fingers inside her, grinding my hips into the floor at the feel of her tight plushness. My cock ached to sink into that snug heat, knowing how amazing it felt, craving the constriction.

"Please," Eva begged, grinding into the thrust of my fingers, needing the slide of my dick to fill her.

I wanted to fuck. To come. Not because I needed sex, but because I needed *her*.

Her body twisted and tensed with another orgasm, her neck arching as she cried out.

Wiping my wet mouth on her inner thigh, I rose to my knees and shoved my sweats down. I placed one hand on the floor and used the other to aim my cock, levering over her and notching the throbbing head against her. I thrust hard, putting the weight of my body behind it, surging through the tight clasp with a groan.

"Gideon."

"Christ." I rubbed my sweat-slick forehead against her cheek, wanting her to smell like me. Her nails were in my back, digging in. I wanted them to mark me, scar me.

Cupping her ass, I lifted her, angled her, digging my feet into the carpet for the leverage I needed to push all the way in. Eva gasped and churned her hips, working to fit me.

"Take me," I hissed through clenched teeth, fighting the need to come before she took all of my cock. "Let me in."

Her cunt rippled, sucking at me. I pinned her shoulder to hold her still and thrust harder. She gave, letting me have her.

The feel of her clutching the entire length of my dick was all I needed. Wrapping myself around her, I held her against me, kissing her roughly, coming with a violence that left me trembling in her arms.

STEAM curled around us as I cradled Eva in the suite's massive sunken tub. Her wet hair clung to my chest, her arms draped over mine where they hugged her waist.

"Ace."

"Hmm?" I pressed my lips to her temple.

"If we couldn't be together—not that it would ever happen, just hypothetically—would you sleep with someone who looked like me? I mean, I know I'm not your usual type, but would you want to pretend with someone who reminded you of me?"

"I'm not going to speculate on situations that will never occur."

"Gideon." She leaned to the side, tilting her head back to look at me. "I get it. I tried to think if I would find any comfort in being with someone similar to you. Like maybe if it was dark and his hair was your length—"

My hold tightened. "Eva. Don't tell me about fantasies of other men."

"God. As usual, you're not listening."

"What the fuck is this about?" I knew, of course. But there were no avenues in the topic I wanted to explore.

"Brett's sleeping with that girl from the 'Golden' video. The one who looks like me."

"No one looks like you."

She rolled her eyes.

"She may have your curves," I conceded, "but she doesn't sound like you. She doesn't have your sense of humor, your wit. She doesn't have your heart."

"Oh, Gideon."

I brushed wet fingertips over her brow. "Turning off the lights wouldn't help me at all. A random, stacked blonde wouldn't smell like you. She wouldn't move the way you do. She wouldn't touch me the same way, need me the same way."

Her face softened and she pressed her cheek against my shoulder. "That's what I thought, too. I couldn't do it. And the moment I saw Brett with that girl, I knew that you wouldn't do it, either."

"Not with anyone. Ever." I kissed the tip of her nose. "You've changed what sex means to me, Eva. I couldn't go back. I wouldn't even try."

She shifted around to straddle me, sending water sloshing up and over the rim of the tub. I looked at her, taking in the slicked-back hair the color of wheat, the smudges left by her makeup, the sheen of water on her golden skin.

Her fingers massaged the nape of my neck. "My dad wants to pay for the wedding."

"Does he now?"

She nodded. "I need you to be okay with that."

I was okay with anything when I had my naked, wet, and frisky wife wrapped around me. "I've had the wedding I wanted. You can do whatever you like this time around."

Her brilliant smile and enthusiastic kiss were all the reward I needed. "I love you."

I pulled her closer.

She bit her lower lip, then said, "My mom is going to have a fit. She can blow through fifty thousand dollars in just flowers and invitations."

"So tell your parents your dad is paying for the wedding and your mom can pitch in for the reception. Problem solved."

"Ooh. I like that. You're handy to have around, Mr. Cross."

I lifted her and licked across her nipple. "Let me prove it."

THE bedroom was lightening with the coming dawn when Eva's breathing settled into the deep, even rhythm of sleep. I extricated my-self from both her arms and the sheets as carefully as possible, stand-ing beside the bed to watch her. Her hair was tumbled around her shoulders, her lips and cheeks flushed from sex. I rubbed my chest, pained by how tight it had become.

Leaving her like this was always hard and became more difficult by the day. My skin hurt from being parted from hers.

I closed the curtains in the bedroom, then moved into the living room and did the same there, plunging the room into darkness.

Then I settled on the sofa and fell asleep.

A sudden flash of light woke me. Blinking, I scrubbed at my gritty eyes and saw that the curtains had been parted to send sunlight shafting across my face. Eva walked toward me, the light haloing around her naked body.

"Hey," she whispered, sinking to her knees beside me. "You said I'd wake up with you."

"What time is it?" I looked at my watch, saw I'd only been asleep an hour and a half. "You were supposed to sleep longer."

She pressed her lips to my abs. "I don't sleep well without you."

Regret pierced me. My wife needed things I couldn't give her. She woke me with light instead of a touch because she feared my reaction. She was right to be cautious. In the grip of a nightmare, the stroke of a hand might have me waking up with fists flying.

I brushed her hair back from her face. "I'm sorry." *For everything. For all you're giving up to be with me.*

"Shh." She lifted the elastic waistband of my sweats and pushed it down past my cock. I was hard for her. How could I help it when she came to me naked and sleepy-eyed?

Her mouth wrapped around the head of my dick.

I squeezed my eyes shut and groaned, surrendering.

KNOCKING at the door woke me the next time. Eva stirred in my arms, cuddled against me on the narrow stretch of the sofa.

"Goddamn it," I muttered, pulling her tighter against me.

"Ignore it."

The knocking continued.

I leaned my head back and yelled, "Go away."

"I come bearing coffee and croissants," Arash shouted back. "Open up, Cross, it's after noon and I want to meet your lady."

"Christ."

Eva blinked up at me. "Your lawyer?"

"He was." I sat up and shoved my hands through my hair. "We're going away, you and me. Soon. Far away."

She kissed the small of my back. "Sounds good."

I shoved my feet into the legs of my sweats, then stood to pull them up. Eva took the opportunity to smack me on the bare ass.

"I heard that!" Arash yelled. "Cut it out and open up."

"You're fired," I told him, striding toward the door. I glanced back to tell Eva to cover herself, but she was already running into the bedroom.

I found Arash waiting outside my suite with a room service cart. "What the fuck is the matter with you?"

I had to back out of the way before he rolled right through me.

"Quit your bitching." He grinned, pushing the cart off to the side and raking me with a glance. "Save the marathon sex for your honeymoon."

"Don't listen to him!" Eva shouted through the bedroom door.

"I won't." I turned away from him. "He doesn't work for me anymore."

"You can't hold it against me," Arash said, following me into the living room. "Wow. Your back looks like you got into a brawl with a mountain lion. No wonder you're tired."

"Shut up." I snatched my shirt off the floor.

"You didn't tell me Eva was in San Diego, too."

"It was none of your business."

He held up both hands in surrender. "Truce."

"Don't say a word about Yimara," I told him quietly. "I won't have her worrying about that."

Arash sobered. "It's done. I won't mention it again."

"Good." I went to the cart and poured two cups of coffee, preparing Eva's the way she liked it.

CAPTIVATED BY YOU · 87

"I'll take a cup," he said.

"Serve yourself."

His lips curved wryly as he joined me. "Is she coming out?"

I shrugged.

"She's not mad, is she?"

"I doubt it." I took both mugs to the coffee table, then went to the wall where the controls for the drapes were. "It takes some work to piss her off."

"You're good at it." He smiled and settled into one of the armchairs. "I recall that viral video of you two scrapping in Bryant Park."

I shot him a look as sunlight began pouring into the room. "You must really hate your job."

"Tell me you wouldn't be curious if I eloped with a chick I knew only a couple of months."

"I'd send her my condolences."

He laughed.

The bedroom door opened and Eva stepped out dressed in her clothes from the night before. Her face was freshly washed, but the dark circles under her eyes and her swollen mouth made her look both well fucked and extremely fuckable. With her bare feet and barely tamed hair, she was stunning.

Pride swelled my chest. Uncovered by the lack of makeup, the dusting of freckles on her nose made her adorable. Her body told you she was a dream to fuck, the confidence in her posture told you she'd take no shit from anyone, and the mischievous amusement in her eyes told you there would never be a dull moment.

She was every promise, every hope, every fantasy a man could have. And she was mine.

I stared. Arash stared, too.

Eva shifted her stance and smiled shyly. "Hi."

The sound of her voice snapped him out of it. He pushed to his feet so quickly he spilled his coffee. "Shit. Sorry. Hi."

He set his mug down and brushed the stray droplets off his pants. He went to her and held out his hand. "I'm Arash."

She shook it. "Nice to meet you, Arash. I'm Eva."

I joined them, pushing Arash back with my forearm. "Stop drooling."

He glanced at me. "Funny, Cross, you ass."

Eva laughed and leaned into me when I slid my arm around her shoulders.

"It's good to see he works with people who aren't afraid of him," she said.

Arash winked, blatantly flirting. "I know how he operates."

"Really? I'd love to hear all about it."

"I think not," I drawled.

"Don't be a spoilsport, ace."

"Yeah, ace," Arash taunted. "What have you got to hide?"

I smiled. "Your corpse."

He looked at my wife and sighed. "See what I have to deal with?"

6

A LATE-AFTERNOON OUTDOOR lunch, in beautiful San Diego, with the three most important men in my life definitely ranked at the top of my best-moments-ever list. I sat between Gideon and my dad, while Cary lounged in the seat directly across the table from me.

If you had asked me a few months ago, I would have said I was apathetic about palm trees. I had a new appreciation for them now that I hadn't seen one in a while. I watched them sway gently in the warm ocean breeze and felt the kind of peace I chased but rarely caught. Seagulls competed with pigeons for the scraps under tables, while the not-too-distant crash of waves against the beach underpinned the bustle of the packed restaurant.

My best friend's mirrored shades hid his eyes, but his smile came often and easy. My dad wore shorts and a T-shirt and had started out the meal unusually quiet. He'd loosened up after a beer and now looked as comfortable as Cary. My husband wore tan cargo pants and a white T-shirt, the first time I'd ever seen him in light-colored clothing. He looked cool and relaxed in aviators, his fingers linked with mine on the arm of my chair.

"An early-evening wedding," I thought aloud. "Around sunset. Just family and close friends." I looked at Cary. "You'll be the man of honor, of course."

His mouth curled up on one side in a lazy smile. "I better be."

I glanced at Gideon. "Do you know who you'll ask to stand with you?"

The tightening of his lips was nearly imperceptible, but I caught it. "I haven't decided yet."

My happy mood dimmed a little. Was he debating whether Arnoldo would be suitable, considering the chef's feelings toward me? It made me sad to think I might strain that relationship.

Gideon was such a private person. Although I didn't know for sure, I suspected he was tight with his friends but that there weren't many of them.

I squeezed his hand. "I'm going to ask Ireland to be a bridesmaid."

"She'll like that."

"What do we do about Christopher?"

"Nothing. With luck, he won't come."

My dad frowned. "Who are we talking about?"

"Gideon's brother and sister," I answered.

"You don't get along with your brother, Gideon?"

I explained, not wanting my dad to hold anything against my husband. "Christopher's not a nice guy."

Gideon's head turned toward me. He didn't say it aloud, but I got the message: He didn't want me speaking for him.

"He's a total douche, you mean," Cary interjected. "No offense, Gideon."

"None taken." He shrugged and then elaborated for my father.

"Christopher views me as a competitor. I'd have it differently, but it's not my choice."

My dad nodded slowly. "That's too bad."

"While we're discussing the wedding," Gideon segued smoothly, "it would be my pleasure to provide transportation. It would give me a chance to contribute, which I'd appreciate."

I took a deep breath, understanding—as I knew my father would—that my husband's directness and tact made him hard to refuse.

"That's very generous of you, Gideon."

"It's a standing offer. With an hour's notice, we can have you in the air and on your way. It'll make it easier for you and Eva to work around your schedules and maximize your time together."

My dad didn't answer right away. "Thank you. It might take me a while to get used to the idea. It's a bit extravagant, and I don't want to be a burden."

Gideon pulled his shades off, baring his eyes. "That's what money's for. All I want is to make your daughter happy. Make that easy on me, Mr. Reyes. We all want to see Eva smiling as much as possible."

It sank in then why my dad was so opposed to Stanton paying for anything. My stepdad didn't do it for me; he did it for my mom. Gideon would only ever consider *me* when making decisions. I knew my dad could live with that.

I caught Gideon's gaze and mouthed, *I love you.*

His grip on my hand tightened until it hurt. I didn't mind.

My dad smiled. "Making Eva happy. How can I argue with that?"

THE smell of freshly brewed coffee brought my well-trained senses to life the following morning. I blinked up at the bedroom ceiling of my Upper West Side apartment and gave a sleepy smile when I discovered Gideon standing beside my bed, stripping out of his shirt. The sight of his leanly muscular torso and washboard abs almost made up for the fact that I'd obviously spent the night alone after falling asleep in his arms.

"Good morning," I murmured, rolling onto my side as he pushed his pajama bottoms down and kicked them off.

Whoever said Mondays sucked had obviously never woken up to a naked Gideon Cross.

"It will be," he said, lifting the covers and sliding between the sheets with me.

I shivered as his cool skin touched mine. "Yikes!"

His arms slipped around me, and his lips touched my neck. "Warm me up, angel."

By the time I was done with him he was sweating and the coffee he'd brought me was cold.

I didn't mind in the least.

I was in an excellent mood when I got to work. Morning sex contributed to that, of course. Also the sight of Gideon getting dressed for the day, watching him transform from the private man I knew and loved into the dark and dangerous global magnate. The day only got better when I exited on the twentieth floor and saw Megumi sitting at her desk.

I waved at her through the glass security doors, but my smile faded the moment I got a good look at her. She was pale and had dark circles under her eyes. Her usually sassy asymmetrical haircut looked limp and overlong, and she was wearing a long-sleeved blouse and dark slacks that were out of place with the August mugginess.

"Hey," I greeted her when she buzzed me through. "How are you? I've been worried about you."

She gave me a weak smile. "I'm sorry I didn't call you back."

"Don't worry about it. I'm totally antisocial when I get sick. I just want to curl up in bed and be left alone."

Her lower lip quivered and her eyes grew shiny with tears.

"Are you okay?" I glanced around, worried about her privacy as other employees passed through the reception area. "Did you see a doctor?"

She started crying.

Horrified, I stood frozen for a minute. "Megumi. What's *wrong*?"

She pulled off her headset and stood, tears spilling down her face. She shook her head violently. "I can't talk about it now."

"When is your break?"

But she was already hurrying to the bathroom, leaving me staring after her.

I headed to my cubicle and dropped off my bag, then went down the hall to Will Granger's desk. He wasn't there, but I found him in the break room when I stopped to grab some coffee.

"Hey, you." His eyes behind his square-framed glasses looked as worried as I felt. "Did you see Megumi?"

"Yeah. She looks wiped out. And she started crying when I asked how she's doing."

He slid the carton of half-and-half over to me. "Not good, whatever it is."

"I'm bad with not knowing. My imagination runs wild. I'm bouncing between cancer, pregnancy, and everything in between."

Will shrugged helplessly. With his neatly trimmed sideburns and subtly quirky-patterned shirts, he was the sort of affable and easy-natured guy who was hard to dislike.

"Eva." Mark stuck his head in the door. "I've got news."

My boss's bright eyes told me he was excited about something. "I'm all ears. Coffee?"

"Sure. Thanks. See you in my office." He ducked back out again.

Will grabbed his mug off the counter. "Have a good one."

He left. I hurried to get the coffee ready, then went to Mark's office. He'd taken his jacket off and was studying something on his monitor. He looked up, smiling when he saw me.

"We've got a new RFP request." His smile widened. "And they asked for me specifically."

I tensed. Setting his coffee down, I asked warily, "Is it another Cross Industries product?"

As much as I loved Gideon and admired all that he'd accomplished, I didn't want to be totally overshadowed by his world. Part of who we were as a couple was two people who had separate working lives. I enjoyed riding to work with my husband, but I needed to say good-bye to him, too. I needed those few hours when he didn't consume me.

"No, it's bigger."

My brows rose. I couldn't think of anything or anyone bigger than Cross Industries.

Mark slid a picture of a silver-and-red box across the desk to me. "It's the new PhazeOne gaming system from LanCorp."

I settled into the seat in front of his desk with an inner sigh of relief. "Sweet. Sounds fun."

IT was a little after eleven when Megumi called to see if I was free for lunch.

"Of course," I told her.

"Someplace quiet."

I considered our options. "I've got an idea. Leave it to me."

"Great. Thanks."

I sat at my desk. "How's your morning been?"

"Busy. I have to get caught up."

"Let me know if I can help with anything."

"Thank you, Eva." She took a deep, shaky breath, her composure slipping. "I appreciate you."

We hung up. I called Gideon's office, and his secretary answered.

"Hey, Scott. It's Eva. How are you?"

"I'm good." I could hear the smile in his voice. "What can I do for you?"

My feet tapped restlessly. I couldn't help but be worried about my friend. "Could you ask Gideon to give me a call when he has a free minute?"

"I'll put you through now."

"Oh. Okay, great. Thanks."

"Hang on."

A moment later I heard the voice I loved. "What do you need, Eva?"

I was startled for a minute by his brusqueness. "Are you busy?"

"I'm in a meeting."

Fuck. "My bad. Bye."

"Eva—"

I hung up, and then called Scott again to discuss how we should handle calls in the future so I didn't come out looking like an ass. Before he answered, the secondary line flashed with an incoming call. I switched over. "Mark Garrity's office—"

"Don't ever hang up on me," Gideon snapped.

I bristled at his tone. "Are you in a meeting or not?"

"I was. Now I'm dealing with you."

Hell if anyone was going to "deal" with me. I could be as pissy as him any day of the week. "You know, I asked Scott to give you a message when you had time for it and he patched me through. He shouldn't have done that, if you were busy with—"

"He has standing orders to always connect your calls. If you want to leave me a message, send a text or an e-mail."

"Well, excuse me for not knowing the etiquette for getting in touch with you!"

"Never mind that now. Say what you need."

"Nothing. Forget it."

He exhaled roughly. "Don't play games with me, angel."

I was reminded of the last time I'd called him at work and how off he'd sounded then, too. If something was bugging him, he sure wasn't sharing it.

I hunched over my desk and lowered my voice. "Gideon, your attitude pisses me off. I don't want to *deal with you* when you're aggravated. If you're too busy to talk to me, you shouldn't have standing orders that interrupt you."

"I'm never going to be unreachable."

"Really? 'Cause you seem that way right now."

"For fuck's sake."

Hearing his exasperation gave me a surge of satisfaction. "I didn't text you because I didn't want to bother you in a meeting. I didn't send an e-mail, because it's a time-sensitive favor and I don't know how often you get to your inbox. I figured a message with Scott would get the job done best."

"And now you have my complete attention. Tell me what you want."

"I want to get off the phone, and I want you to get back to your meeting."

"What you're going to get," he said, with dangerous evenness, "is me at your desk if you don't cut the shit and explain why you called."

I glared at his photo. "You make me want to find a job in New Jersey."

"You make me crazy." He growled softly. "I can't function when we're fighting, you know that. Just say what you need, Eva, and forgive me for now. We can argue and have makeup sex later."

The tension left me. How could I stay mad at him after he admitted how vulnerable I could make him?

"Damn you," I muttered. "I hate when you get reasonable after irritating me."

He made a low sound of reluctant amusement. I instantly felt better.

"Angel mine." His voice took on the sexy, raspy warmth I needed to hear. "Definitely not a quiet, comfortable ornament."

"What are you talking about?"

"Don't worry about it. You're perfect. Tell me why you called."

I knew that tone. I'd turned him on somehow. "You're a maniac. Seriously."

Lucky me.

"Anyway, ace, I wanted to see if I could borrow one of your conference rooms for lunch with Megumi. She's back, but she's a mess and I think she wants to talk about it but there's really not a good place to go nearby that's private and quiet."

"Use my office. I'll have something ordered in and you'll have the space to yourself while I'm out."

"For real?"

"Of course. However, I have to remind you that when you work for Cross Industries you'll have your own office to lunch in."

My head fell back. "Shut up."

THE research involved in prepping for the PhazeOne RFP kept me hopping, but I was antsy for information from Megumi, so the hour seemed to drag anyway.

I met up with her at the reception desk at noon. "If it's not too weird," I said, as she pulled her purse out of a drawer, "we're going to use Gideon's office for lunch. He's out and it's private."

"Oh man." She shot me an apologetic look. "I'm sorry, Eva. I should've congratulated you. Will told me about your engagement, but I spaced."

"It's totally okay. Don't worry about it."

She reached out and squeezed my hand. "I'm really happy for you."

"Thank you."

My concern deepened. Megumi always followed the latest gossip. The friend I knew would've heard about the engagement almost before I did.

We took an elevator to the top floor. The Cross Industries vestibule was as striking as Gideon himself. It was much bigger than others in the building and decorated with lilies and ferns in hanging baskets. Cross Industries was etched into the smoked-glass security doors in a masculine but elegant font.

"Impressive," Megumi murmured, as we waited for the receptionist to buzz us through.

The redhead I was used to seeing at the reception desk must have been out to lunch, because a guy with dark hair let us in.

He stood when we approached. "Good afternoon, Miss Tramell. Scott said you should just go right in."

"Has Mr. Cross left?"

"I'm not sure. I just took over here."

"All right. Thank you." I led Megumi back. We rounded the corner to reach Gideon's office just in time to see him stepping out.

Fierce pride and possession moved me. Pleasure, too, when his stride faltered just a bit when he saw me. We met each other halfway.

"Hi," I greeted him.

He gave me a nod in return and held his hand out to Megumi. "I don't think we've been officially introduced. Gideon Cross."

"Megumi Kaba." She gave him a firm shake. "Congratulations to you and Eva."

A ghost of a smile touched his sexy mouth. "I'm a lucky man. Make yourselves comfortable. If you need anything, just call up to reception and Ron will see to it."

"We'll be fine," I told him. "You won't even know we had a raging party in there while you're gone."

He smiled outright. "Good. I have a meeting later. Shot glasses and streamers would be interesting to explain."

I expected him to head out. Instead, he cupped my face, tilted my head to the angle he wanted, and pressed his lips to mine in an unhurried, chaste kiss that left me with little stars in my eyes.

Then he whispered in my ear, "Looking forward to making up later."

My toes curled.

Pulling back, he slid easily into the reserved persona he showed the rest of the world. "Enjoy your lunch, ladies."

He walked away with the confident, innately sexual stride that turned heads.

"And you're still standing upright," Megumi murmured, shaking her head. "Kills me."

I couldn't explain how weak Gideon made me. How shaken and needy I could so easily become. "Come on," I said breathlessly. "Let's eat."

She followed me into Gideon's office. "I don't think I can."

While she took in the sprawling space with its panoramic views and monochromatic color scheme, I went to the bar, where lunch awaited us. I remembered how I'd felt the first time I walked into the room. Despite the multiple seating areas that might have invited guests to sit and stay awhile, the progressively contemporary, cutting-edge design kept visitors from getting too comfortable.

There were so many sides to the man I'd married. His office reflected only one. The classically European style of his penthouse reflected another.

"Have you ever experimented with BDSM?" Megumi asked, seizing my attention.

Surprise made me drop the napkin-rolled utensils I'd been holding. I spun to face her and found her staring out the window at the city. "That acronym covers a lot of ground."

She rubbed her wrist. "Being tied up and gagged. Helpless."

"I've been helpless, yes."

Her head turned. Her eyes were twin shadows in her pale face. "Did you like it? Did it turn you on?"

"No." I walked over to the nearest couch and sat. "But I wasn't with the right person."

"Were you scared?"

"Terrified."

"Did he know that?"

The formerly appetizing smell of lunch started to turn my stomach. "Why are you asking me these questions, Megumi?"

She answered by rolling up her sleeve, exposing a wrist so bruised it was nearly black.

7

I T WAS AFTER eight when I let myself into Eva's apartment and found her sitting with Cary on the living room's white sectional sofa, holding a glass of red wine in both hands.

My wife gravitated toward modern traditional furnishings, but I could see touches of her mother and roommate in the décor. I didn't resent those pieces of Monica and Cary, but I looked forward to the day when I shared a home with Eva that reflected *us*, undiluted.

Still, the apartment would always be a special place to me. I would never forget the way Eva had looked the first time I'd come over. Naked beneath a thigh-length silk robe, her face made up for the night ahead, a diamond anklet winking at me. Teasing me.

I had lost all rational thought. I'd put my mouth on her, my hands all over her, and my fingers and tongue inside her. I hadn't even thought about getting her to the "fuck pad." I wouldn't have been able to wait, even if I had. She wasn't like any woman who'd come before her. Not just because of who she was, but also because of who *I* was when I was with her.

It was unlikely I would ever allow the property management to lease the space out again. It held too many memories, both good and bad.

I tipped my chin at Cary in greeting and sat beside Eva. My wife's best friend was dressed to go out, while Eva wore a Cross Industries T-shirt and had her hair twisted up in a clip. They both glanced at me, and I knew something was wrong.

There were things to discuss, but whatever was troubling Eva was the pressing priority.

Cary stood. "I'm heading out. Call me if you need me."

She nodded. "Have fun."

"My middle name, baby girl."

The front door shut behind him as Eva's head fell gently against my shoulder. Sliding my arm around her, I settled deeper into the sofa and tucked her closer. "Talk to me, angel."

"It's Megumi." She sighed. "There's this guy she was into and things weren't working out—he was hot-and-cold and couldn't commit—so she broke it off. But afterward, he stepped it up and she let him come over. They started messing around with a little bondage, but things got out of hand in a bad way."

The mention of bondage put me on alert. I ran my hand down her back and tucked her tighter against me. I was nothing if not patient in aligning my desires with her fears. Setbacks were expected and accommodated, but I didn't want someone else's misadventures to create new hurdles for Eva and me to face.

"Sounds like bad judgment all around," I said. "One of them should've known what they were doing."

"That's the thing." She pulled away and faced me. "I went over it with Megumi. She said no—*a lot*—until he gagged her. He got off on her pain, Gideon. And now he's terrorizing her with texts and photos he took of her that night. She's asked him to stop, but he won't. He's sick. Something's wrong with him."

I weighed how best to respond. I went with blunt. "Eva. She broke it off, and then took him back. He might not realize she's serious this time."

She recoiled, then slid off the couch in a rush of curvy, golden legs. "Don't make excuses for him! She's bruised everywhere. It's been a week and the bruises are still dark. She couldn't sit down for days!"

"I'm not excusing him." I stood with her. "I would never justify an abuser—you know that. I don't have the whole story, but I know *your* story. Her situation isn't like yours. Nathan was an aberration."

"I'm not projecting here, Gideon. I saw the pictures. I saw her wrists, her neck. I saw his texts. He's crossed a line. He's dangerous."

"Even more reason for you to stay out of it."

Her hands went to her hips. "Oh my God. You did not just say that! She's my friend."

"And you're my wife. I know that look on your face. There are some battles that aren't yours to fight. You will not confront this man the way you did my mother and Corinne. You will not put yourself in the middle of this."

"Did I say I was going to do that? No, I didn't. I'm not an idiot. I asked Clancy to find him and talk to him."

I went still inside. Benjamin Clancy was her stepfather's man, not mine. Totally outside my control. "You shouldn't have done that."

"What was I supposed to do instead? Nothing?"

"Preferably. At most, you should've asked Raúl."

She threw up her hands. "Why would I do that? I don't know Raúl enough to ask him for a personal favor."

I checked my exasperation. "We discussed this. He works for you. You don't have to ask him for favors, you just need to tell him what you need done."

"Raúl works for *you*. Besides, I'm not some godfather sending out hired thugs to teach people lessons. I asked someone I trust, as a friend, to help another friend of mine."

"However you rationalize it, the result is the same. You forget, Ben Clancy is employed to protect your stepfather's interests. He looks after you only because it gives him more control in securing Stanton's safety and reputation."

She bristled. "How would you know what his motives are?"

"Angel, let's simplify. Focus on the fact that your mother and Stanton have been invading your privacy for some time. You're keeping that door open by using their resources."

"Oh." Eva caught her lower lip in her teeth. "I hadn't thought of it that way."

"You sent a trained professional to 'talk' to this guy. But you didn't fully assess the possibility of blowback. If you'd tapped Raúl to help you, he would've known to be extra vigilant." My jaw clenched. "Damn it, Eva. Don't make it hard for me to keep you safe!"

"Hey." She reached for me. "Don't worry, okay? I told you what was happening as soon as you walked in the door. And Clancy was with me until an hour ago, when he dropped me off after my Krav Maga class. Nothing's happened yet that would put me in danger."

I pulled her into me and held on, wishing I could be certain she was right. "I want Raúl to escort you wherever you go," I said gruffly. "To your classes, the gym, shopping . . . whatever. You need to let me look after you."

"You do, baby," she said soothingly, her temper cooled. "But you can be obsessive about it."

I would always be obsessive when it came to her. I'd come to accept that. Eventually, she would, too. "There are things I can't give you. Don't fight me on the things I can."

"Gideon." Her face softened. "You give me everything I need."

I brushed my fingers across her jaw. She was so soft. Delicate. I had never anticipated my sanity hinging on something so fragile. "You come home to another guy. You make your living by working for some-one else. I'm not as necessary to you as I'd like to be."

Her eyes brightened with humor. "While I'm about as dependent on you as I can stand to be."

"It's mutual." Running my hands down her arms, I caught her by the wrists and squeezed with just enough pressure to capture her focus. I watched her pupils dilate and her lips part, her body instinctively responding to the restraint. "Promise you'll come to me first from now on."

"Okay," she breathed.

The undercurrents of arousal and surrender in her voice sent my blood humming. She swayed into me, her body softening. "I'd like to come now, actually."

"I am, as always, at your service."

GIDEON.

The shock of hearing panic in Eva's voice reverberated through me. My body jolted, jerking me out of the deepest sleep. Rolling to my side with a low moan, I struggled awake, shoving my hair out of my face to find her kneeling on the edge of the bed.

A heavy, inescapable sense of dread had my heart racing and cold sweat coating my skin.

I pushed up onto one elbow. "What's wrong?"

Moonlight slanted through the room and haloed her. She'd come to me in our bedroom in the apartment next door to hers. Something had woken her, and I was afraid. Fear chilled me to the bone.

"Gideon." She slid into me in a rush of silken skin and shining hair. Curled against me, she reached up and touched my face. "What were you dreaming about?"

The stroke of her fingertips left a trail of wet across my skin. Star-tled, horrified, I scrubbed at my eyes and smeared more tears across my cheek. In a corner of my mind, I sensed the lingering shadow of a dream.

The brush of memory had me shivering, spiraling further downward.

I rolled into her and pulled her tight against me, hearing her gasp as I squeezed too hard. Her skin was cool to the touch, but her flesh was warm beneath and I absorbed her heat, breathed in her scent, felt the terrible lingering grief inside me ease with her nearness.

I couldn't grasp the dream I'd had, but it refused to let go of me.

"Shh," she crooned, her fingers pushing through the sweat-damp roots of my hair, her hand stroking up and down my back. "It's okay. I'm here."

I couldn't breathe. I fought for air and a horrible sound ripped from my burning lungs.

A sob. Christ. Then another. I couldn't stop the violent contractions.

"Baby." She hugged me harder, her legs tangling with mine. She rocked us gently, whispering words I couldn't hear over the pounding of my heartbeat and the outcry of my phantom pain.

I wrapped myself around her, holding on to the love that could save me.

"GIDEON!"

Eva's back arched as I thrust hard, my knees spreading her thighs wide, my cock tunneling deep. Her wrists were pinned by my hands, her head thrashing as I fucked her hard.

Some days I woke her with tenderness. Today wasn't one of those mornings.

I'd woken to a throbbing erection, the head of my dick wet with pre-cum against the curve of Eva's ass. I aroused her hungrily, impatiently, sucking her nipples to hard points, slickening her cunt with the demanding drive of my fingers. She'd ignited to my touch, gave herself over to me, gave herself *to* me.

God. I loved her so much.

The need to come was like a vise around my balls, the pressure exquisite. She was tight, so amazingly snug, and so wet. I couldn't get enough. Couldn't get deep enough, even when I felt the end of her clasping at the head of my cock.

She thrashed beneath my pounding drives, her heels sliding across the sheets, her tits rocking with the force of my thrusts. She was so small, so soft, and I was fucking her lush body with everything I had in me.

Take me. Take all of me. The good and the bad. Everything. Take it all.

The headboard banged into the shared wall between our two apartments in a hard-driving rhythm that screamed *crazed sex* to anyone listening. As did the growls spilling from my throat, the animalistic sounds of my pleasure I didn't try to hold back. I loved fucking my wife. Craved it. Needed it. And I didn't care who knew what she did to me.

Eva arched up, sinking her teeth into my biceps, her bite sliding over my sweat-slick skin. The mark of possession drove me wild, had me thrusting so hard I shoved her up the bed.

She cried out. I hissed as she tightened around me like a greedy fist.

"Come," I bit out, my jaw clenched against the urge to do the same, to let go and pump every drop I had into her.

Rolling my hips, I ground against her clit, pleasure sizzling up my spine when she moaned my name and climaxed around me in pulsing ripples.

I kissed her roughly, drinking in her taste, spilling into her with a shuddering groan.

EVA stumbled a little as I helped her out of the back of the Bentley in front of the Crossfire.

A hot flush spread across her face and she shot me a look. "You suck."

My brows rose questioningly.

"I'm shaky and you're not, sex machine."

I smiled innocently. "I'm sorry."

"No, you're not." Her wry smile faded as she glanced down the street. "Paparazzi," she said grimly.

I followed her gaze and spotted the photographer aiming a camera out of the open passenger window of his car. Gripping her by the elbow, I led her into the building.

"If I have to start actually styling my hair every day," she muttered, "you're dealing with morning wood on your own."

"Angel," I tugged her into my side and whispered, "I'd hire a full-time hairdresser for you before I gave up your cunt every morning."

She elbowed me in the ribs. "God, you're crude, you know that? Some women take offense to that word."

She went ahead of me through the security turnstiles and joined the mass of bodies waiting for the next elevator car.

I stood close behind her. "You're not one of them. However, I might be willing to revise. I recall *orifice* being a favorite of yours."

"Oh God. Shut up," she said, laughing.

We separated when she exited on the twentieth floor and I went up to Cross Industries without her. I wouldn't be doing so for long. Someday, Eva would be working with me, helping to build our future as a team.

I was debating the myriad avenues to achieving that goal when I rounded the corner on approach to my office. My stride slowed when I saw the willowy brunette waiting by Scott's desk.

I steeled myself to deal with my mother again.

Then her head turned and I saw it was Corinne.

"Gideon." She rose gracefully to her feet, her eyes brightening with a look I'd come to recognize, having seen it on Eva's face.

It gave me no pleasure to see that warmth in Corinne's eyes. Unease slid down my spine, stiffening my back. The last time I had seen her had been shortly after she'd tried to kill herself.

"Good morning, Corinne. How are you feeling?"

"Better." She came toward me and I took a step back, causing her to slow and her smile to waver. "Do you have a moment?"

I gestured to my office.

With a deep breath, she turned and preceded me. I glanced at Scott. "Give us ten."

He nodded, his gaze sympathetic.

Corinne walked to my desk and I joined her, hitting the button that closed the door behind us. I kept the glass clear and didn't remove my jacket, sending her every signal that she shouldn't settle in for long.

"I'm sorry for your loss, Corinne." Saying the words wasn't enough, but they were all I could give her. The memories of that night in the hospital would be with me for a while.

Her lips whitened. "I still can't believe it. All these years of trying . . . I thought I couldn't get pregnant." She picked up the photo of Eva on my desk. "Jean-François told me you called a couple times asking about me. I wish you'd called me. Or returned my calls."

"I don't think that's appropriate, under the circumstances."

She looked at me. Her eyes weren't the same shade of blue as my mother's, but they were close, and their sense of style was similar. Corinne's elegant blouse and trousers were notably like something I'd once seen my mother wear.

"You're getting married," Corinne said.

It wasn't a question, but I answered anyway. "Yes."

Her eyes closed. "I'd hoped Eva was lying."

"I'm very protective when it comes to her. Tread lightly."

Opening her eyes, she set the picture down hard. "Do you love her?"

"That's none of your business."

"That's not an answer."

"I don't owe you one, but if you need to hear it, she's everything to me."

The tightness of her mouth softened with a quiver. "Would it make a difference if I told you I'm getting divorced?"

"No." I exhaled roughly. "You and I will never be together again, Corinne. I don't know how many times or in how many ways I can say it. I could never be what you want me to be. You dodged a bullet when you broke our engagement."

She flinched, her hair sliding over her shoulder to flow down to her waist. "Is that what's keeping us apart? You can't forgive me for that?"

"Forgive you? I'm thankful." My voice softened when tears filled her eyes. "I don't mean to be cruel. I can guess how painful this might be. But I didn't want you to have hope when there isn't any."

"What would you do if Eva said these things to you?" she challenged. "Would you just give up and walk away?"

"It's not the same." I raked a hand through my hair, struggling to find the words. "You don't understand what I have with Eva. She needs me as much as I need her. For both our sakes, I wouldn't ever give up trying."

"*I* need you, Gideon."

Frustration made me curt. "You don't know me. I played a role for you. I let you see only what I wanted you to see, what I thought you could accept." And in return, I saw only what I wanted to see in her, the girl she'd once been. I had stopped paying real attention long ago, and so I'd failed to see how she had changed. She'd been a blind spot for me, but no longer.

She stared at me in shocked silence for a moment. "Elizabeth warned me that Eva was rewriting your past. I didn't believe her. I've never known you to be swayed by anyone, but I guess there's a first time for everything."

"My mother believes what she wants and you're welcome to join her." They were similar in that way, too. Good at believing what they wanted and ignoring any proof to the contrary.

It was a revelation to realize I had been comfortable with Corinne because I'd known she wouldn't pry. I'd been able to fake normalcy with her and she never dug deeper. Eva had changed that for me. I wasn't normal and I didn't need to be. Eva accepted me the way I was.

I wasn't going to reveal my past to everyone, but my days of playing along with the lies were over.

Corinne reached a hand out to me. "I love you, Gideon. You used to love me, too."

"I was grateful to you," I corrected. "And I will always be. I was attracted to you, had fun with you, for a time I even needed you, but it would never have worked out between us."

She dropped her hand back to her side.

"I would have found Eva eventually. And I would've wanted her, given up everything to have her. I would have left you to be with her. The end was inevitable."

Corinne turned away. "Well . . . at least we'll always be friends."

It was an effort to strip any apology out of my tone. I wouldn't encourage her. "That won't be possible. This is the last time you and I will speak to each other."

Her shoulders shook with a ragged indrawn breath, and I turned my head, fighting with discomfort and regret. She'd been important to me once. I would miss her, but not in the way she wanted me to.

"What do I have to live for if I don't have you?"

I turned at her question and barely caught her when she ran into me, holding her at bay with a grip on her upper arms.

The devastation on her beautiful face got to me before I could process what she'd said. Then it registered. Horrified, I shoved her away. She stumbled back as her heels caught in the carpet.

"Don't put that on me," I warned, my voice low and hard. "I'm not responsible for your happiness. I'm not responsible for you at all."

"What's *wrong* with you?" she cried. "This isn't you."

"You wouldn't know." I went to the door and yanked it open. "Go home to your husband, Corinne. Take care of yourself."

"Fuck you," she hissed. "You're going to regret this, and I might be too hurt to forgive you."

"Good-bye, Corinne."

She stared at me for a long minute and then stormed out of my office.

"Damn it." I pivoted, not knowing where to go or what to do, but I had to do *something*. Anything. I paced.

I'd pulled out my smartphone and called Eva before I consciously made the decision to do so.

"Mark Garrity's office," she began.

"Angel." The one word betrayed my relief at hearing her voice. She was what I needed. Something in me had known that.

"Gideon." She read me immediately, as she so often did. "Is everything all right?"

I glanced out at my staff in the distant cubicles getting into the groove of the day. I hit the controls to frost the glass, carving out a moment alone with my wife.

I lightened my tone, not wanting to cause her stress. "I miss you already."

She waited a beat before replying, adjusting to my mood. "Liar," she shot back. "You're too busy."

"Never. Now, tell me how much you're missing me."

She laughed. "You're terrible. What am I going to do with you?"

"Everything."

"Damn straight. So what's up? It's going to be a busy day and I have to get going."

I went to my desk and studied her photo. My shoulders relaxed. "Just wanted you to know I'm thinking about you."

"Good. Don't stop. And FYI, it's nice to hear you not grumpy at work."

It was nice to hear her, period. I'd given up trying to figure out why she affected me the way she did. I just appreciated that she could reset my day. "Tell me you love me."

"Madly. You rock my world, Mr. Cross."

I stared into her laughing eyes, my fingertip brushing lightly over the glass. "You're the center of mine."

THE rest of the morning passed swiftly and uneventfully. I was wrapping up a meeting regarding a possible investment in a proposed resort chain when yet another personal interruption showed up. So much for workflow.

"You've got to fuck up everything, don't you?" my brother accused, barging into my office with Scott on his heels.

With a look, I gave Scott the okay to back out. He shut the door behind him.

"Good afternoon to you, too, Christopher."

We shared blood but could not have been less alike. Like his father's, his hair was wavy and fell somewhere between brown and red. His eyes were a gray mixed with green, while I was most definitely our mother's son.

"Did you forget that Vidal Records is Ireland's legacy, too?" he snapped, his eyes hard.

"I never forget that."

"Then you just don't give a shit. Your vendetta against Brett Kline is costing us money, damn you. You're hurting all of us, not just him."

Moving to my desk, I leaned against it and crossed my arms. I should've seen it coming, considering how irate Christopher had become at the Times Square launch of the "Golden" video. He wanted Kline and Eva together. More than that, he wanted Eva and me apart.

It was the sad truth that I brought out the worst in my brother. The only times he ever acted cruelly or rashly was when he was trying to hurt me. I'd seen him give brilliant speeches, charm people with his natural charisma, and impress board members with his industry savvy, but he never displayed those traits toward me.

Frustrated by his unprovoked animosity, I baited him. "I'm assuming you're going to get to the point soon."

"Don't play innocent, Gideon. You knew exactly what you were doing when you systematically destroyed every media opportunity Vidal secured for Six-Ninths."

"If those opportunities were centered on Eva, they had no business being pursued to begin with."

"That's not your decision to make." His mouth twisted in a scornful smile. "Do you even comprehend the damage you've done? *Behind the Music* has delayed their special because Sam Yimara no longer owns the rights to the footage he compiled of the band's early years. *Diners, Drive-Ins and Dives* can't include Pete's 69th Street Bar in their San Diego episode, because it's being demolished before they can film their segment. And *Rolling Stone* isn't interested in pursuing their proposed piece on 'Golden' since your engagement was announced. The song loses its interest without the happy ending."

"I can get you the footage VH1 wants. Put them in touch with Arash and he'll take care of it."

"After you remove all traces of Eva? What's the point?"

My brows lifted. "The point is supposed to be Six-Ninths, not my wife."

"She's not your wife yet," he shot back, "and that's your problem. You're afraid she's going to go back to Brett. You're not really her type and we all know it. You can eat her pussy at parties, but what she really likes is blowing rock stars in public—"

I was on him before he blinked. My fist hit his jaw; his head jerked back. I caught him with a follow-up left and he stumbled, crashing into the glass wall.

Through it, I glimpsed Scott shoving to his feet, and then I braced for the impact of Christopher's body hurtling into mine. We went down. I rolled, punching his ribs until he groaned. He slammed his head into my temple.

The room spun.

Dazed, I rolled away and clambered to my feet.

Christopher pulled himself up by the coffee table, blood running from the side of his lips and onto the carpet. His jaw was swelling and he gasped for air, dragging in harsh breaths. My fists ached and I flexed my hands, tensing with the need to hit him again. If he'd been anyone else, I would have.

"Do it," he taunted, wiping his mouth on his sleeve. "You've wanted me dead since the day I was born. Why stop now?"

"You're insane."

Two security guards rounded the corner at a run, but I held up a hand to stop them.

"I'm fucking onto you, asshole," my brother growled, pushing heavily to his feet. "I've talked to members of the board. Explained what you're doing. You want to take me down, I'm fighting you all the way."

"You've lost it, you fucking idiot. Take your crazy somewhere else. And leave Eva alone. You want to make an enemy out of me, screwing around with her is the way to do it."

He stared at me for a long minute, then laughed harshly. "Does she know what you're doing to Brett?"

I winced through a deep breath, a dull ache in my side from a forming bruise. "I'm not doing anything to Kline. I'm protecting Eva."

"And the band is just collateral damage?"

"Better him than her."

"Fuck that," he snarled.

"Fuck you."

Christopher stalked toward the door.

I should've let him go but found myself speaking instead. "For Christ's sake, Christopher, they're talented. They don't need a gimmick to be successful. If you weren't so damned eager to make me pay for something you've imagined I've done, you'd be concentrating on better angles than making them into a one-hit wonder."

He rounded on me with clenched fists. "Don't tell me how to do my job. And don't get in my way or I'll shove you out."

I watched him leave, escorted by security. Then I went to my desk and checked my message log. Scott had noted that two of Vidal Records' board members had called over the course of the day.

I opened the line between Scott and me. "Get me Arash Madani."

If Christopher wanted a war, I'd give him one.

I arrived at Dr. Lyle Petersen's office on time at six o'clock. The psychologist greeted me with a welcoming smile, his dark blue eyes warm and friendly.

After the day I'd had, spending an hour with a shrink was the last thing I wanted to do. Spending an hour alone with Eva was what I needed more.

Our session began as they always did, with Dr. Petersen asking how my week had been and me answering as succinctly as possible. Then he said, "Let's talk about the nightmares."

I leaned back, laying my arm on the sofa's armrest. I'd been up front about my sleep problems from the beginning in order to get the prescription medication that made me marginally safer for Eva to be near at night, but dissecting the dreams had never been one of the topics on discussion.

That meant someone else had brought them up. "You talked to Eva."

It wasn't a question, since the answer was evident.

"She sent me an e-mail earlier," he confirmed, folding his hands atop his tablet screen.

My fingers drummed silently.

His gaze followed the movement. "Does it bother you that she contacted me?"

I weighed my response before giving it. "She worries. If talking to you alleviates that, I won't complain. You're also *her* therapist, so she has a right to discuss it with you."

"But you don't like it. You'd prefer to choose which issues you share with me."

"I'd prefer Eva to feel safe."

Dr. Petersen nodded. "That's why you're here. For her."

"Of course."

"What does she hope the outcome of our sessions will be?"

"Don't you know?"

He smiled. "I'd like to hear your answer to that question."

After a moment, I gave it to him. "Eva previously made bad decisions. She learned to rely on the advice of therapists. It worked well for her and it's what she knows."

"How do you feel about that?"

"Do I have to feel anything?" I countered. "She asked me to try it out and I agreed. Relationships are about compromise, aren't they?"

"Yes." Picking up his stylus, he tapped at the screen of his tablet. "Tell me about your previous experience with therapy."

I took a breath. Let it out. "I was a child. I don't remember."

He glanced at me over the rim of his glasses. "How did you feel about seeing someone? Angry, frightened, sad?"

Glancing down at my wedding ring, I replied, "A little of all that."

"I imagine you felt similarly about your father's suicide."

I stilled. Studying him, my gaze narrowed. "Your point?"

"We're just talking, Gideon." He leaned back. "I often feel like you're wondering what the angle is. I don't have an angle. I just want to help you."

I forced my posture to relax.

I wanted the nightmares to stop. I wanted to share the same bed as my wife. I needed Dr. Petersen to help me do that.

However, I didn't want to talk about things that couldn't be changed to get there.

8

"Hey, girl. What are your thoughts on karaoke?" Shawna Ellison asked the second I answered the phone.

I dropped my pencil onto the notepad I'd been scribbling in, then sat back on the couch and curled my legs onto the cushion. It was rolling past nine o'clock and I hadn't heard from Gideon yet. I didn't know if that was a good or bad sign, considering he'd had an appointment with Dr. Petersen earlier.

The sun had set nearly an hour before, and I'd been trying not to think of my husband every five seconds since. Chatting with Shawna was a welcome distraction.

"Well," I hedged, "since I'm tone deaf, my thoughts on singing in public are pretty much nonexistent. Why?"

In my head, I pictured the vibrant redhead who was quickly becoming a friend. In a lot of ways, she was like her brother Steven, who happened to be engaged to my boss. They were both fun and easygoing, quick to tease and yet rock solid, too. I liked the Ellison siblings a lot.

"Because I was thinking we could go to this new karaoke bar I heard about today at work," she explained. "Instead of those cheesy background tracks, this place has a live band. You don't have to sing if you don't want to. A lot people go just to watch."

I reached for the tablet lying on the coffee table. "What's the name of this place?"

"The Starlight Lounge. I thought it might be fun for Friday."

My brows went up. Friday was our bringing-the-crew-together night. I tried to imagine Arnoldo or Arash singing karaoke and just the thought made me smile. Why the hell not? At the very least, it'd break the ice.

"I'll mention it to Gideon." I ran a search for the bar and pulled up its website. "Looks nice."

The name had conjured thoughts of old-school crooner hangouts, but the images on the site were of a contemporary club decorated in shades of blue with chrome accents. It looked upscale and swank.

"Right? I thought so, too. And it'll be entertaining."

"Yeah. Wait 'til you see Cary with a mic. He's shameless."

She laughed and I grinned at the sound, which was as bubbly as champagne. "So is Steven. Let me know what you decide. Can't wait to see you."

We hung up, and I tossed my phone onto the cushion beside me. I was leaning forward to get back to my project when I heard the ping of a text message.

It was from Brett. We need to talk. Call me.

I stared at his picture on the screen for a long minute. He'd been calling all day but hanging up when he got my voice mail. I would be lying if I said I wasn't conflicted about him still reaching out, but it was a dead end. Maybe we'd be friends someday, but not now. I wasn't up for it or the stress it caused Gideon.

I used to think facing issues that made me uncomfortable showed strength and responsibility. Now, I realized that sometimes resolution wasn't the purpose. Sometimes, you just had to take the opportunity to examine yourself better.

I'll give you a ring when I can, I typed back. Then I set the phone aside again. I'd call him when Gideon was with me. No secrets and nothing to hide.

"Hey." Cary strolled into the living room from the hallway dressed in pajama bottoms and a threadbare T-shirt. His dark brown hair was still damp from the shower he must have taken after Tatiana left an hour earlier.

I was glad she hadn't spent the night. I wanted to like the woman who said she was carrying my best friend's baby, but the leggy model didn't make it easy for me. I felt like she deliberately baited me whenever she could. I got the strong impression that she would like nothing more than to keep Cary all to herself and I was viewed as a big roadblock to that end.

My best friend sprawled facedown on the other section of the sofa, his head near my thigh and his long legs stretched out. "Whatcha working on?"

"Making lists. I want to get started on something for abuse survivors."

"Yeah? What are you thinking?"

One of my shoulders lifted in a helpless shrug. "I don't really know. I keep thinking about Megumi and how she didn't tell anyone. I didn't tell anyone, either. Neither did you, until way later."

"Because who's going to give a shit?" he said gruffly, propping his chin on his hands.

"And it's scary to talk about it. There are a lot of hotlines and shelters for victims. I want to find something else that makes a difference, but I don't have any groundbreaking ideas."

"So talk to idea people."

My mouth curved. "You make it sound so easy."

"Hell, why reinvent the wheel? Find someone who's doing it right and help 'em out." He rolled onto his back and scrubbed at his face with both hands.

I knew that gesture and what it signified. Something was eating at him.

"Tell me about your day," I said. I'd ended up spending more one-on-one time with Gideon in San Diego than I had with Cary, and I felt bad about that. Cary said he'd had a good time hanging with his old crowd, but that hadn't been the purpose of our trip. I felt like I'd let him down, even though he didn't accuse me of doing so.

He dropped his hands to his sides. "I had a shoot this morning, and then I saw Trey for a late lunch."

"Did you say anything to him about the baby?"

He shook his head. "I thought about it, but I couldn't do it. I'm such a dick."

"Don't be hard on yourself. It's a rough spot you're in."

Cary's eyes closed, shuttering the vivid green of his irises. "I was thinking the other day how much easier it'd be if Trey swung both ways. Then we could both be banging Tat and each other, and I could have it all. Then I realized I didn't want to share Trey with Tat. Don't mind sharing her. But not him. Tell me that doesn't make me a total douche."

Reaching out, I ruffled my fingers through his dark hair. "It makes you human."

I'd been in a similar situation with Gideon, thinking I could work out a way to be friends with Brett, even while I was aggravated that Gideon was friends with Corinne. "In a perfect world, none of us would be selfish, but that's not the way it goes. We just do our best."

"You're always making excuses for me," he muttered.

I thought about that for a second. "No," I corrected gently, bending over to press a kiss to his forehead. "I just forgive you. Someone has to, since you won't forgive yourself."

WEDNESDAY morning came and went in a flurry. Lunch was on me before I knew it.

"We were celebrating our engagement two weeks ago," Steven Ellison said, as I settled into the chair he held out for me. "Now we get to celebrate yours."

I smiled; I couldn't help it. There was something infectiously joyful about my boss's fiancé, which you couldn't help but pick up on. "Must be something in the water."

"Must be." He glanced at his partner, then back at me. "Mark's not losing you, is he?"

"Steven," Mark admonished, shaking his head. "Don't."

"I'm not going anywhere," I answered, which earned me a surprised and pleased grin from my boss. His goatee-framed smile was as contagious as Steven's gregariousness. Really, our scheduled lunches were worth the price of admission.

"Well, I'm happy to hear that," Mark said.

"Me, too." Steven opened his menu with a decisive snap, as if something important had been decided. "We want you to stick around, kid."

"I'm sticking," I assured them.

The server set a basket of olive oil–drizzled garlic bread on the table between us, then rattled off the day's specials. The restaurant the guys had selected had two menus: Italian and Greek.

Like most Manhattan eateries, the location was small and the tables packed tightly together, close enough that one party flowed into the next and you had to watch your elbows. The scents flowing out of the kitchen and wafting from the trays of passing servers had my stomach growling audibly. Thankfully the noise from the lunch crowd frenzy was loud enough to cover me.

Steven ran a hand through the bright red hair many women would kill for. "I'm having the moussaka."

"Me, too." I closed my menu.

"Pepperoni pizza for me," Mark said.

Steven and I teased him about being adventurous.

"Hell," he shot back, "marrying Steven is adventure enough."

Grinning, Steven set his elbow on the table and his chin on his fist. "So, Eva . . . how'd Cross propose? I'm guessing he didn't blurt it out in the middle of the street."

Mark, who was sitting on the bench seat next to his partner, gave him an exasperated look.

"No," I agreed. "He broke the news to me on a private beach. I can't say he asked, because he pretty much just told me that we're getting married."

Mark's mouth twisted in thought, but Steven was blunt as always. "Romance, Gideon Cross style."

I laughed. "Absolutely. He'll be the first to tell you he's not romantic, but he's wrong about that."

"Let me see the ring."

I held my hand out to Steven and the Asscher cut diamond shot sparks of multihued fire. It was a beautiful ring, which held beautiful memories for Gideon. Elizabeth Vidal's thoughts on the subject couldn't touch that.

"Whoa. Mark, darlin', you have got to get me one of those."

The picture in my head of the flame-haired, burly contractor wearing a ring like mine was comical.

Mark shot him a look. "So you can shatter it on a job site? Let me get right on that."

"Diamonds are tough little beauties, but I'll take good care of it."

"You'll have to wait until I run an agency of my own," my boss retorted with a snort.

"I can do that." Steven winked at me. "You register anywhere yet?"

I shook my head. "You?"

"Hell, yeah." He twisted to open the messenger bag next to him and pulled out his wedding binder. "Tell me what you think about these patterns."

Mark raised his gaze heavenward with a long-suffering sigh. I grabbed a piece of garlic bread and leaned forward with a happy hum.

I worked on the LanCorp RFP the remainder of the afternoon.

When my day ended, I headed to my Krav Maga class with Raúl. On the way, I reread Clancy's reply to my text saying I wouldn't need a ride from him. He had typed back that it was no problem, but I felt the need to explain further.

Gideon wants to have his ppl with me moving forward, so you're free from now on. ☺ TY for all your help.

It didn't take him long to answer. Anytime. Holler when you need me. BTW, your friend shouldn't have any more trouble.

The "thank you" I sent back didn't seem like enough. I made a note to send him something that would better express my gratitude.

Raúl parked outside the brick-faced converted warehouse that was Parker Smith's Krav Maga studio and then escorted me inside, taking a seat on the bleachers. His presence threw me off a little bit. Clancy had always waited outside. Having Raúl watching made me a little self-conscious.

The massive open space still managed to look crowded, thanks to all the clients on the mats and in one-on-ones with instructors. The noise was nearly deafening, a cacophony of bodies hitting padding, flesh colliding with flesh, and the various shouts as participants psyched themselves up while psyching each other out. Giant metal delivery-bay doors added to both the industrial feel of the studio and the heat, which even the air-conditioning and multiple standing fans couldn't quite alleviate.

I was stretching in preparation for the grueling drills ahead when a pair of lanky legs came into my line of sight. I straightened and faced NYPD detective Shelley Graves.

She wore her curly brown hair in a bun as severe as her face, and her blue eyes assessed me with sharp impassiveness. I was afraid of her and what she could do to Gideon, but I admired her a lot, too. She was fierce and confident in a way I could only aspire to.

"Eva," she greeted me.

"Detective Graves." She was dressed for work in dark slacks and a red jersey top. She wore a black blazer that didn't hide either her badge or her firearm. Her boots were scuffed and no-nonsense, much like her attitude.

"Spotted you on my way out. Heard about your engagement. Congratulations."

My stomach flipped a little. Part of Gideon's alibi—if one could call it that—was that we'd been broken up when Nathan was killed. Why would a powerful, upstanding public figure kill a guy over an ex he'd left behind without looking back?

Getting engaged so quickly had to look suspicious. Graves had told me she and her partner had moved on to other cases, but I understood what kind of cop she was. Shelley Graves believed in justice. She believed Nathan had gotten his, but I knew something inside her questioned whether Gideon had something to pay for, too.

"Thank you," I replied, pulling my shoulders back. In this, Gideon and I were a team. "I'm a lucky girl."

She glanced at the bleachers. At Raúl. "Where's Ben Clancy?"

I frowned. "I don't know. Why?"

"Just curious. You know, one of the feds I talked to about Yedemsky also has the last name Clancy." Her gaze bored into me. "You think they're any relation?"

The blood drained out of my head at the mention of the Russian mobster whose corpse had been sporting Nathan's bracelet. I swayed a little with a sudden rush of dizziness. "What?"

She nodded, as if she'd expected as much. "Probably not. Anyway, I'll see you later."

I watched her walk away, her attention on Raúl. Then, she paused and faced me again. "You inviting me to the wedding?"

I fought through the buzzing in my head to say, "The reception. We're keeping the wedding small, just family."

"Really? Didn't expect that." Something like a smile transformed her thin face. "He's full of surprises, isn't he?"

I couldn't even begin to decipher what that meant. I was too busy trying to process everything else she'd said. I didn't even realize I'd chased after her until I had her elbow in my hand.

She stopped, her body taut in a way that told me to let go. Which I did. Immediately.

I stared at her for a beat, trying to pull my thoughts together. Clancy. Gideon. Nathan. What the hell did it mean? Where was she going with it?

Most of all, why did I feel as if she were helping me? Looking out for me. For Gideon.

What I ended up saying startled me. "I'm looking to support an organization that does good work for abuse survivors."

Her brows rose. "Why are you telling me?"

"I don't know where to start."

She shot me a look. "Try Crossroads," she said dryly. "I've heard good things about that one."

I was sitting cross-legged on the floor of my bedroom's sitting room when Gideon came home. He walked in wearing loose-legged jeans and a V-neck white T-shirt, the keys to my place spinning around his finger.

I stared. I couldn't help it. Would he always stop my heart? I hoped so.

The room was small and girly, decorated by my mother with antiques, such as the silly escritoire I was supposed to use as a desk. Gideon infused a drugging dose of testosterone into the space, making me feel soft and feminine and eager to be ravished.

"Hi, ace." The love and longing he inspired were exposed in those two words.

The keys were caught in his hand abruptly and he came to a stop, looking down at me much as he had that first day in the Crossfire lobby. His eyes took on the brooding fierceness I found wildly exciting.

For some reason I would probably never understand, he felt the same about me.

"Angel mine." He dropped gracefully into a crouch, his hair sliding briefly along his cheekbones in a loving caress. "What are you working on?"

His fingers rifled through the papers scattered on the floor around me. Before my research into his Crossroads Foundation distracted him, I caught his hand and squeezed it.

I blurted out what I knew, as abruptly as the info had been sprung on me. "It was Clancy, Gideon. Clancy and his brother in the FBI planted Nathan's bracelet on that mobster."

He nodded. "I figured."

"You did? How?" I smacked him on the shoulder. "Why didn't you say something? I've been worried sick."

Gideon settled on the floor in front of me, crossing his long legs in a pose mirroring mine. "I don't have all the answers yet. Angus and I have been narrowing it down. Whoever was responsible was either watching Nathan or me and following our movements, so we started there."

"Or watching both of you."

"Precisely. Who would do that? Who had a stake in it? In you?"

CAPTIVATED BY YOU · 129

"Jesus." I searched his face. "Detective Graves knows. The FBI. Clancy—"

"Graves?"

"She brought it up at Parker's studio tonight. Tossed it at me in passing just to see how I'd take the news."

His gaze narrowed. "Either she's fucking with you or she wants you to stop worrying. My bet is on the latter."

I almost asked why, but then I realized I'd come to the same conclusion. The detective was tough as nails, but she had a heart. I had caught glimpses of it during the few times we'd interacted with one another. And she was good at her job, obviously.

"We have to trust her, then?" I asked, crawling over the brochures and paperwork to curl into his lap.

He pulled me into him, fitting me into the hard planes of his body as if I were meant to be there always. I felt that way when he held me. Safe. Treasured. Adored.

His lips touched my forehead. "I'm going to talk to Clancy just to be sure, but he's no fool. He wouldn't leave anything to chance."

My hand tightened around a fistful of his T-shirt, hanging on to him with everything I had. "Don't keep things like this from me, Gideon. Stop trying to protect me."

"I can't." His grip on me tightened, too. "Maybe I should have said something, but we have only a few hours alone every day and I want them to be perfect."

"Gideon. You've got to let me in."

His chest expanded beneath my cheek, his heart beating strong and sure. "I'm working on it, Eva."

That was all I could ask for.

THE next morning I padded into the kitchen on bare feet to find Gideon pouring coffee. I could say the smell of java is what added a spring to my step, but it was the sight of my husband, freshly shaved and dressed with his vest hanging open, that did it. I loved seeing him a little undone.

He looked me over as I went to him, my heels rapping on the marble, his face impassive and his eyes warm. Did he get the same kick when he caught sight of me ready to tackle my day? I doubted it. I was convinced men just saw hot . . . or not.

Wrapping my fingers around his wrist, I led his hand around me and up the back of my skirt to cup the undercurve of my buttock.

A smile teased the corners of his lips. "Hello to you, too, Mrs. Cross."

He snapped the back of my garter against my thigh. I jumped at the sting and gasped as warmth spread outward from the spot.

"Hmm . . . you like that." He smirked.

My lower lip stuck out in a pout. "It hurt."

Gideon shifted to lean back against the counter and pulled me between his spread legs, both of his hands lightly gripping the back of my thighs. He nuzzled his nose against my temple and massaged the place that burned. "I'm sorry, angel."

Then he snapped my garter on the other side.

I arched in surprise, my body aligning with his. He was hard. Again. A low moan escaped me. "Stop it."

"It's turning you on," he murmured in my ear.

"It hurts!" I complained, even as I rubbed against him. He'd woken me with soft kisses and provocative hands. I had thanked him in the shower with my mouth. Still, he could go again. I could, too. We were addicted to each other.

"Want me to kiss it and make it better?" His fingers slid between my thighs and found me warm and ready. He groaned. "Christ. What you do to me, Eva. I've got so much to do . . ."

God, he felt good. Smelled even better. My arms wrapped around his neck. "We have to go to work."

He yanked me up to my toes, grinding me against his erection. "We're playing with these garters later."

I kissed him. I put my open mouth over his and devoured him, my tongue touching his. Stroking it greedily. Sucking.

Gideon's hand fisted in my ponytail, holding me in place as he took over the kiss, fucking my mouth, drinking me in. In an instant, I was hot, my skin humid with perspiration.

His lips were firm yet soft against my own, his grip angling me just the way he wanted, his teeth scraping gently across my lower lip. The taste of him, flavored delectably with a hint of rich black coffee, intoxicated me. Drunk on him, I clutched his hair in my hands, holding on, my toes flexing to push me closer. Always closer. But never close enough.

"Whoa." Cary's voice broke me out of the sensual spell Gideon had cast. "Don't forget we eat in here."

I started to pull away from my husband, but he held me tight, allowing me only to break the kiss. My gaze met his. His eyes were sharply alert beneath heavy lids, his lips softened and damp.

"Good morning, Cary," he said, his attention shifting to my best friend as Cary joined us by the coffeemaker.

"For you two, maybe." Cary opened the cupboard that held the mugs and pulled one out. "Sadly, I'm too tired to get turned on by the show. Not making me feel too optimistic about the rest of the day."

He was dressed in skinny jeans and a navy T-shirt, his hair skillfully arranged in a trendy pompadour. I pitied the single Manhattanites who'd see him out and about that day. He was such a striking man, both physically and in the false confidence he exuded.

"Do you have a shoot today?" I asked.

"No. Tat does, and she wants me there. She's got morning sickness and shit, so I'm going to be around to help her out if she's not feeling well."

I reached out and rubbed his biceps in sympathy. "That's awesome, Cary. You're the best."

His lips twisted wryly as he lifted his steaming cup to his mouth. "What else can I do? I can't get sick for her, and she's got to work as long as she can."

"You'll let me know if there's anything I can do?"

He shrugged. "Sure."

Gideon's hand stroked up and down my back, offering wordless support. "If you've got the time, Cary, I'd like you to be there for the appointment with the designer who's renovating our place on Fifth Avenue."

"Yeah, I've been thinking about that." Cary cocked his hip into the counter. "I haven't totally worked things out with Tat, but I figure we'll be shacking up together at some point. You guys aren't going to want a screaming baby next door. When you're ready for that, you'll have your own, not put up with mine."

"Cary . . ." My best friend rarely looked beyond the next fifteen minutes of his life. To hear him stepping up to the plate so solidly made me love him all the more.

"Both sections of the penthouse are fully soundproofed," Gideon said, his voice holding the firm note of command that reassured everyone who heard it. "We can make anything work, Cary. You just tell me what concerns you have and we'll address them."

Cary looked into his mug, his beautiful face suddenly looking worn and tired. "Thanks. I'll talk to Tat about it. It's hard, you know? She doesn't want to think about what's next and I can't stop thinking about it. There's going to be this person who's totally dependent on us, and we need to be prepared for that. Somehow."

I stepped back and Gideon let me go. It was hard to watch Cary struggling. It was scary, too. He didn't handle challenges well and I was so afraid he'd slip back into familiar, self-destructive coping mechanisms. It was a threat we both faced on a daily basis. I had a group of people who kept me anchored. Cary had only me.

"That's what families are for, Cary." I offered a smile. "To drive each other crazy and straight into therapy."

He snorted, then hid his face behind his mug. The lack of a glib reply made me even more anxious. A heavy silence descended.

Gideon and I both gave him a minute, taking the time to grab our own cups of java and caffeinate ourselves. We didn't speak or even look at each other, not wanting to create a unit that left Cary out, but I felt how in sync we were. It meant so much to me. I'd never had someone in my life who was a true partner, a lover who was there for more than just a good time.

Gideon was a miracle in so many ways.

It struck me then that I had to make some adjustments, compromise a little more on the issue of working with Gideon. I had to stop thinking of Team Cross as being his alone. I had to own it, too, so I could share in it with him.

"I've got time next week," Cary said finally, looking at me, then Gideon.

Gideon nodded. "Let's plan on Wednesday, then. Give us some room to recover from the weekend."

Cary's mouth twitched. "So it's that kind of party."

I smiled back. "Is there any other kind?"

"How are you?" I asked Megumi when we sat down for lunch on Thursday afternoon.

She looked better than she had on Monday, but she was still overdressed for the heat of the summer. Because of that, I'd ordered salads for delivery and we settled in the break room instead of braving the steamy day outside.

She managed a wan smile. "Better."

"Does Lacey know what happened?" I wasn't sure how close Megumi was to her roommate, but I hadn't forgotten that Lacey had dated Michael first.

"Not all of it." Megumi pushed at her salad with a plastic fork. "I feel so stupid."

"We're always quick to blame ourselves, but no means no. It's not your fault."

"I know that, but still . . ."

I knew just how she felt. "Have you thought about talking to someone?"

She glanced at me, tucking her hair behind her ear. "Like a counselor or something?"

"Yes."

"Not really. How do you even start looking for someone like that?"

"We've got mental health benefits. Call the number on the back of your insurance card. They'll give you a list of providers to choose from."

"And I just . . . pick one?"

"I'll help you." And if I got my act together, I'd find a way to help more women like her and me. Something good had to come of our experiences. I had the motivation and the means. I just had to find the way.

Her eyes glistened. "You're a good friend, Eva. Thanks for being here."

I leaned over and hugged her.

"He hasn't texted me lately," she said when I pulled back. "I keep dreading that he's going to, but every hour that goes by that he doesn't, I feel better."

Settling back in my seat, I sent a silent thank-you to Clancy. "Good."

⌒

CAPTIVATED BY YOU · 135

five o'clock, I left work and took the elevator up to Cross Industries, hoping to catch some time with Gideon before our appointment with Dr. Petersen.

I'd been thinking about him all day, about the future I wanted *us* to have together. I wanted him to respect my individuality and my personal boundaries, but I also wanted him to open up some of his own. I wanted more moments like this morning with Cary, when Gideon and I stood together, facing a situation as one. I couldn't really push for that if I wasn't willing to make the same effort.

The redheaded receptionist at Cross Industries buzzed me in. She greeted me with a hard smile that didn't reach her eyes. "Can I help you?"

"No, I'm good, thanks," I replied, breezing past her. It would be nice if all of Gideon's employees could be as easy-natured as Scott, but the receptionist had an issue with me and I'd just come to accept it.

I headed back to Gideon's office and found Scott's desk empty. Through the glass, I saw my husband at work, presiding over a meeting with casual authority. He stood in front of his desk, leaning back against it with one ankle crossed over the other. He wore his jacket and faced an audience composed of two suit-clad gentlemen and one woman wearing a great pair of Louboutins. Scott sat off to the side, taking notes on a tablet.

Settling into one of the chairs by Scott's desk, I watched Gideon as raptly as the others in the room with him. It never ceased to amaze me how self-assured he was for a man who was only twenty-eight. The men he was meeting with looked to be twice his age, and yet their body language and focused attention told me they respected my husband and what he was saying.

Yes, money talked—loudly—and Gideon had tons of it. But he conveyed command and control with subtle actions. I recognized that after living with Nathan's father, my mom's first husband, who'd wielded power like a blunt instrument.

Gideon knew how to own a room without thumping his chest. I doubted the setting made any difference; he would be a formidable presence in anyone's office.

His head turned and his gaze met mine. There was no surprise in those brilliantly blue eyes of his. He'd known I was there, had sensed me just as I often sensed his approach without looking. We were connected somehow, on a level I couldn't explain. There were times when he wasn't with me and I just wished he was, but I still felt him nearby.

I smiled, then dug in my bag for my phone. I didn't want Gideon to feel like I was just sitting around waiting, not that doing so would pressure him at all.

There were dozens of e-mail messages from my mother with photo attachments of dresses and flowers and wedding venues, reminding me that I needed to talk with her about Dad paying for the ceremony. I'd been putting off that conversation all week, trying to steel myself for her reaction. There was also another text from Brett, telling me that we needed to talk . . . urgently.

Standing, I looked around for a quiet corner where I could make that call. What I saw was Christopher Vidal Sr. rounding the corner.

Gideon's stepfather was dressed in the khakis and loafers I'd come to expect, with a pale blue dress shirt open at the collar and rolled up at the sleeves. The dark copper waves he'd passed on to Christopher Jr. were neatly cut around his neck and ears, and his slate green eyes were capped with a frown behind old-school brass-framed glasses.

"Eva." Chris slowed as he neared me. "How are you?"

"Good. You?"

He nodded, looking over my shoulder at Gideon's office. "Can't complain. Do you have a minute? I'd like to talk to you about something."

"Sure." The door opened behind me and I turned to see Scott stepping out.

"Mr. Vidal," he said, coming toward us. "Miss Tramell. Mr. Cross will be another fifteen minutes or so. Can I get either of you something to drink while you wait?"

Chris shook his head. "Nothing for me, thank you. But if you have a private room we could use, that would be great."

"Of course." Scott looked at me.

"I'm good, thanks," I answered.

Leaving his tablet on his desk, Scott led us to a conference room with a sweeping view of the city. A long, polished wood table gleamed beneath the recessed lighting, with a matching cabinet covering one wall and a large monitor lining the other.

"If you need anything," he began, "just dial one and we'll take care of it. There's coffee in the cabinet there, and water."

Chris nodded. "Thank you, Scott. Appreciate it."

Scott left. Chris gestured for me to sit, then took the chair to the right of mine, spinning it to face me.

"First, let me congratulate you on your engagement." He smiled. "Ireland speaks very highly of you, and I know you've been instrumental in bringing her and Gideon closer together. I can't thank you enough for that."

"I didn't do much, but I appreciate the thought."

He reached for my left hand, which was resting on the table. His thumb rubbed gently over my engagement ring and his mouth curved ruefully.

Was he thinking about the fact that Geoffrey Cross had selected the ring for Elizabeth?

"It's a beautiful ring," he said finally. "I'm sure it meant a great deal to Gideon to give it to you."

I didn't know what to say to that. It meant a lot to my husband because it was a symbol of the love between his parents.

Chris released my hand. "Elizabeth is taking this very hard. I'm sure there are a lot of complicated emotions a mother must feel when her first child decides to get married, especially with a son. My mother used to say that a son is a son until he gets married—then he's a husband—but a daughter is a daughter for life."

The conciliatory explanation rubbed me the wrong way. He was trying to be kind, but I was tired of all the excuses, especially when it came to Elizabeth Vidal. The pretending had to end or Gideon would never stop hurting.

I needed the pain to stop. Every time he woke up crying, it shattered me a little more. I could only imagine the damage it was doing to him.

Still, I debated letting it go for now. I could argue and push forever, but Gideon needed to be the one to demand the answers and hear them given.

Put it away. When the time is right, it'll happen.

But I found myself leaning forward instead, unable to hold the silence Gideon had kept for too long.

"Let's be honest," I insisted quietly. "Your wife didn't have this reaction when Gideon became engaged to Corinne." I didn't know that for sure, but having seen Elizabeth with Corinne's parents at the hospital, it seemed likely.

His sheepish smile proved me right. "I think that was different because Gideon had been with Corinne awhile and we knew her. You and Gideon haven't been together long, so there's still some adjusting to do. I don't want you to take it personally, Eva."

The smile chafed, but it was the words that were too much for me. Resentment welled and flowed over the wall I tried to contain it behind.

Chris wasn't blameless, either. Taking a grieving, troubled boy into his home had to have been hard—especially when he'd been building his own family with Christopher Jr. and Ireland on the way. But he'd accepted the role of stepfather when he married Elizabeth. He shared responsibility for pursuing justice for a wounded and exploited child. Hell, a *stranger* would have an obligation to report the crime.

Leaning forward, I let him see how angry I was. "It's *very* personal, Mr. Vidal. Elizabeth is feeling threatened because I'm not going to put up with this bullshit anymore. You both owe Gideon an apology and she needs to admit to the abuse. I'm going to keep pressuring her to make things right. You can count on that."

His posture stiffened visibly. "What are you talking about?"

I snorted with disgust. "Seriously?"

"Elizabeth would never abuse her children," he said tightly when I didn't reply. "She's a wonderful, devoted mother."

I blinked, then stared at him. Was he as delusional as Elizabeth? How could they both act like they didn't know?

"I think you'd better explain yourself, Eva. Fast."

I sagged back into the chair, stunned. If he was acting, he deserved a goddamned Academy Award.

He surged forward without getting up, bristling and aggressive. "Start talking. *Now.*"

My voice came quiet. Small. "He was raped. By the therapist he was seeing."

Chris froze. For a long minute, he didn't even breathe.

"He told Elizabeth, but she didn't believe him. She knows he was telling the truth, but she's denied it for whatever screwed-up reason she's come up with."

He straightened, shaking his head vehemently. "No."

The one-word rebuff pushed me to my feet. "Are you going to deny it, too? Who would lie about something like that? Do you have any idea how hard it was for him to admit to what was happening? How confused he must have been that a man he trusted would do those things to him?"

Chris looked up at me. "Elizabeth would never ignore . . . something like that. There's a misunderstanding. You're confused."

I took in his dilated pupils and white-rimmed lips but refused to feel bad for him. "She went through the motions. That's all. When push came to shove, she chose to side with everyone but her own child."

"You don't know what you're saying."

I grabbed the handle of my bag and slung it over my shoulder. I bent into him, meeting him at eye level. "Gideon was raped. One of these days, you and your wife are going to look him in the eye like I'm looking at you and you're going to admit it. And you're going to apologize for all the years he's lived with that alone."

"*Eva.*"

Gideon's voice cracked through the air, making me jump. Straightening in a rush, I stumbled as I faced him.

He stood in the open doorway, his hand gripping the handle with such force it should've broken off. His face was hard, his body stiff, his gaze searing me with a different kind of heat.

Fury. I'd never seen him so angry.

Chris pushed heavily to his feet. "Gideon. What's going on? What is she saying?"

Gideon's arm shot out and grabbed me. He yanked me into the hallway with such force I yelped in alarm. I felt the bite of his fingers even after he released me.

With his hand at the small of my back, he propelled me forward, his stride so long and quick I had to scramble to keep pace.

"Gideon, wait," I said breathlessly, my heart pounding. "We—"

"Not a fucking word," he snapped, pushing me roughly through the etched glass security doors into the elevator vestibule.

I heard Chris calling Gideon's name. I caught sight of him rushing toward us just before the elevator doors shut him out.

9

As I led Eva out of the Crossfire, Angus took one look at my face and his smile disappeared. He opened the rear door to the Bentley and stepped aside, watching me urge my wife into the backseat.

Our gazes met over her head as she slid into the back. I read the message in his faded blue eyes. *Be gentle with her.*

He didn't know how hard it was for me to show as much restraint as I was managing. I could feel the vein pulsating in my temple, echoing the driving pulse beat that had my cock throbbing.

I'd nearly stopped the elevator halfway down to fuck Eva against the wall like an animal. The only things that deterred me were the security cameras and watchful guard eyes monitoring the feed.

I wanted to leash her. Sink my teeth into her shoulder as I nailed her. Dominate her. She was a tigress, clawing and hissing at everyone she felt had done me wrong, and I needed to pin her down. Make her submit.

"Goddamn it," I bit out, rounding the back of the car to get in on the other side. Eva was a wild card. I couldn't control her.

I folded into the seat and slammed the door shut, staring out the window because I was afraid of what I'd do if I looked at her. She was the air I breathed and at the moment, I couldn't catch my breath.

She set her hand on my thigh. "Gideon . . ."

Grabbing that slender hand wearing my ring, I shoved it between my legs and thrust my aching dick into her palm. "Open your mouth again and that's what I'm putting in it."

She gasped.

Angus slid behind the wheel and started the car. I felt Eva's gaze on the side of my face. Her hand pulled away and I nearly groaned at the loss of her touch. Then she shifted, curling into my side. Her other hand slid back between my legs, cupping my cock possessively. Her lips pressed a kiss against my jaw.

My arm went around her back. I took a deep breath, inhaling her scent.

The Bentley pulled away from the curb and we melded into midtown traffic.

IT wasn't until we pulled over in front of the office building where Dr. Petersen kept his office that I remembered our appointment. I'd been counting the minutes until we got home and I could take Eva the way I needed to . . . fast . . . hard . . . furious.

She started sitting up when Angus got out of the car. I tightened my arm around her. "Not today," I said tightly.

"Okay," she whispered, kissing my jaw again.

Angus opened the door. She pulled away, then got out of the car anyway. She spun through the revolving doors and left me staring after her.

"Jesus."

Ducking down, Angus peered in at me. "Couples therapy means the both of you."

I glared at him. "Stop enjoying this."

The smile in his eyes curved his lips into a broad grin. "She loves you, lad, whether you like it or naw."

"Of course I like it," I muttered, glancing over my shoulder to check the traffic before opening my door and stepping out. I rounded the trunk. "That doesn't mean she's not a loose cannon."

Angus shut the door. A rare summer breeze ruffled the graying red hair that peeked out from beneath his chauffeur's hat. "Sometimes you'll lead, sometimes you'll follow. Expect you'll grumble about the following part for a while yet."

I growled, exasperated. "She talked to Chris."

His brows rose with surprise even as he nodded. "I saw him go in."

"Why won't she leave it the hell alone?" I stepped onto the sidewalk, tugging my vest into place and wishing I could straighten my thoughts as easily. "She can't change the past."

"It's not the past she's thinking of." He set his hand briefly on my shoulder. "It's the future."

I found Eva pacing in Dr. Petersen's office, her hands waving as she spoke. The good doctor sat in his customary chair, his attention on his tablet as he took notes.

"The whole situation makes me so mad," she seethed. Then she caught sight of me standing in the doorway and paused midstride.

"Gideon." A brilliant smile lit up her beautiful face.

There wasn't anything I wouldn't do to put that happy look on her. The fact that she smiled like that just because she saw me . . .

"Eva. Doctor." I took a seat on the sofa. How much had she told him?

Dr. Petersen followed me with his gaze. "Hello, Gideon. I'm glad you could join us after all."

I patted the cushion next to me and waited for Eva to sit.

"We're making plans to move back into the penthouse on Fifth with Cary," I said smoothly once she'd settled beside me, deflecting the conversation into territory I was more comfortable addressing. "I expect it will be a rocky transition for all of us."

Eva gaped.

Dr. Petersen set his stylus down. "Eva was just telling me about a visit with your stepfather. I would like to hear more about that before we move on."

I linked my fingers with Eva's. "It's not open for discussion."

She stared at me. I turned my head to meet her gaze and my breath left me in a pained rush.

The new look on her face made me ache for a different reason altogether.

The session had barely started and already it couldn't end soon enough for me.

I told Angus to take us home—to the penthouse.

It was obvious Eva was lost in her own thoughts by the surprise she displayed when the valet opened the door for her. We were in the sub-terranean garage beneath the building.

She glanced at me.

"I'll explain," I told her, as I took her elbow and led her to the elevator.

We rode up in silence. When the car doors opened into our private foyer, I felt her tense beneath my hand. We hadn't been to the penthouse together in nearly a month. The last time we'd been in the foyer had been the night she confronted me about Nathan's death.

I'd been afraid then, too. Terrified I had done something she couldn't forgive me for.

We'd had many explosive moments here. The penthouse hadn't

CAPTIVATED BY YOU · 145

seen as much joy and love between us as the secret apartment on the Upper West Side. But we would change that. One day, we would look back and this place would remind us of all the steps in our journey together, good and bad. I refused to envision anything else.

I opened the door, gesturing her in before me. She dropped her purse into an armchair and kicked off her shoes. I shrugged out of my jacket, hung it on the back of one of the bar stools in the kitchen, and then pulled a shiraz off the wine rack.

"You're disappointed in me," I called out, uncorking the wine.

Eva padded to the open archway and leaned against the tumbled stone. "No, not in you."

Retrieving a decanter and two glasses, I considered my reply. It was difficult bargaining with my wife. In every other deal, I went in with the knowledge that I could take it or leave it. There was no agreement anywhere I couldn't walk away from.

Except those that endangered my hold on Eva.

As I poured the wine from its bottle into the decanter, she joined me at the island.

Her hand came to rest on my shoulder. "We haven't been together long, Gideon, and you've come so far already. I'm not going to push you to go farther so soon. These things take time."

I let the decanted wine sit and turned to face her, pulling her close. She'd felt so far away the last hour or so and the distance had been killing me.

"Kiss me," I murmured.

Tilting her head back, Eva lifted her mouth to me. I pressed my lips to hers but otherwise did nothing else, wanting her to be the one to reach out. Needing her to be.

The stroke of her tongue over the seam of my lips made me groan. The feel of her fingers sliding into the hair at my nape soothed me. There was an apology in the softness of her lips gliding across mine and love in her quiet moan of surrender.

I caught her up, lifting her feet from the floor, so relieved she still wanted me that I felt dizzy with it. "Eva . . . I'm sorry."

"Shh, baby, it's okay." She pulled back and touched my face, cupping it in both hands. "You don't have to apologize to me."

The back of my throat burned. I lifted her onto the counter, stepping between her spread legs. Her skirt rose up, baring the ends of her garters. I wanted her. In every way.

My forehead touched hers. "You're upset that I didn't want to talk about Chris."

"I wasn't expecting you to avoid it so completely, that's all." She kissed my brow, her fingers brushing the hair from my face. "I should've considered the possibility, considering how angry you were when we left the Crossfire."

"Not with you."

"At Chris?"

"At the situation." I exhaled roughly. "You're expecting people to change and that doesn't happen. In the meantime, you're stirring up trouble at a time when we've got enough on our plates. I just want to have some peace with you, Eva. Days when we're alone and happy and free of any bullshit."

"And nights where you go to sleep in another bed? In another room?"

My eyes squeezed shut. "Is that what this is all about?"

"Not completely, but some of it, yeah. Gideon, I want to be with you. Waking and sleeping."

"I understand, but—"

"That peace you're looking for? You're pretending you have it during the day and suffering without it at night. It's tearing you up from the inside, and it's shredding me watching it happen to you. I don't want you to live like this forever. I don't want *us* to live forever like this."

I looked at her, my soul bared to those amazing steel-colored eyes that didn't let me hide anything. There was so much love in the look she gave me. Love and worry, disappointment and hope. The pendant lamps over the island backlit her blond hair, reminding me of how precious she was. A gift I'd never expected.

"Eva . . . I am talking to Dr. Petersen about the nightmares."

"But not about what's causing them."

"You're assuming Hugh is the problem," I said evenly, feeling the burn of hatred and humiliation in my gut. "We've been talking about my father instead."

She pulled back. "Ace . . . I don't know exactly what's in your dreams, but I've seen you wake up in two different ways: ready to beat up someone or crying like your heart is breaking. When you come out swinging, the things you say make me damn near certain you're fighting off Hugh."

I sucked in a quick, deep breath. It infuriated me that my former therapist—and molester—could reach out from the grave and touch Eva through me.

"Listen." She wrapped her legs around my hips. "I said I wasn't going to push you and I meant it. If we were two years into our relationship, I'd put up a fuss, maybe. But it's only been a few months, Gideon. The fact that you're seeing someone and talking about your dad is enough for now."

"Is it?"

"Yes. But there are things we can never discuss that are haunting you, too. Dr. Petersen is already working with a handicap because of that. The more you keep from him, the less he can help."

Nathan. She didn't have to say the name.

"I'm making an effort, Eva."

"I know." Her hands smoothed over my shoulders, then reached for the buttons of my vest. "Just tell me that you're not hoping to avoid talking about it forever. Tell me you're just working up to it."

My heart rate sped up. I reached for her wrists, holding them firmly, anchoring myself to her. I felt cornered, trapped between her needs and my own, which seemed terribly divergent at that moment.

Her lips parted at the pressure of my grip, her breasts lifting with a quickened breath. A restraining touch, a heated look, the tone of my voice . . . Eva reacted to my unspoken demands as if she'd been trained to.

"I'm doing my best," I told her.

"That's not an answer."

"It's all I've got right now, Eva."

She swallowed, her thoughts scattering as her body stirred. "You're playing with me," she said quietly. "You're manipulating me."

"I'm not. I'm giving you the truth, even though it's not what you want to hear. You told me you wouldn't push. Did you mean it?"

Wetting her lower lip with a brush of her tongue, she stared up at me. Then nodded. "Yes."

"Good. Let's have some wine and dinner. Afterward, if you'd really like to play, let me know."

"Play? How?"

"I have some silk cord I bought for you."

Her eyes widened. "Silk cord?"

"Crimson, of course." I released her and stepped back, giving her some space to think while I reached for the decanter to pour her a glass. "I'd like to tie you down when you're ready for that. If not tonight, then someday. I won't push you, either."

We were both steering each other in directions that were uncomfortable. She chose to believe an educated observer was part of the answer we were looking for. I believed we could find a lot of the answers on our own, just the two of us connecting in the most intimate ways possible.

Sexual healing. What could be more perfect for two people who had the history Eva and I shared?

CAPTIVATED BY YOU · 149

Eva accepted the wine I handed her. "When did you buy that?"

"A week ago. Maybe two. I had no expectation of using it soon, but you made me want to today." I took a sip, letting the shiraz roll around my tongue. "That said, I'm perfectly happy with just fucking you hard."

The wine sloshed a little in her glass as she lifted it to her mouth. She gulped it down, leaving a few drops in the bottom. "Because you're mad at me for talking to Chris."

"I told you I wasn't."

"You were furious when we left."

"Furiously turned on." I smiled wryly. "I can't explain why, because I don't understand it myself."

"Try."

I reached up and brushed the pad of my thumb over her lips. "I see you angry, passionate, ready to fight, and I want all that violence trapped beneath me. You make me want to hold you down, clawing and screaming, your cunt milking my cock as I pound it into you. Mine. All mine."

"Gideon." She set her glass aside and grabbed me, claiming my mouth with a wild hunger I hoped would never abate.

"How come you never told Chris about what happened with Hugh?"

That unwelcome question came out of the fucking blue. I paused midchew, suddenly finding the bite of pizza in my mouth unappetizing. Dropping what was left of my slice onto the plate in front of me, I grabbed a napkin and wiped my mouth. "Why are we discussing this again?"

Eva frowned at me from where she sat beside me on the floor in between the coffee table and the couch in the living room. "We didn't talk about it."

"Didn't we? In any case, it doesn't matter. My mother told him."

Her frown deepened. She reached for the TV remote and lowered the volume, muting the voices of the NYPD detectives on the screen. "I don't think so."

I pushed to my feet and grabbed my plate. "She did, Eva."

"Do you know that for sure?" She followed me into the kitchen.

"Yes."

"How?"

"They discussed it at the dinner table one night, something I don't want to do."

"He acted like he didn't know." She braced her hands against the counter as I dropped my leftovers into the trash. "He seemed genuinely confused and horrified."

"Then he's as conveniently obtuse as my mother. You shouldn't be surprised."

"What if he didn't know?"

"So what?" I set the plate in the sink, the lingering smell of food making my stomach roil. "What the fuck does it matter now? It's done, Eva. Done and over with. Let it go."

"Why are you so mad?"

"Because I was settled in for the night with my wife. Dinner, wine, a little TV, a couple hours making love . . . after a long, rough day." I left the kitchen. "Forget it. I'll see you in the morning."

"Gideon, wait." She grabbed my arm. "Don't go to bed pissed. Please. I'm sorry."

I paused and removed her hand from my arm. "So am I."

"START out slow," he whispers, his lips near my ear.

I can feel him becoming excited. He reaches around my hip to where I'm stroking my penis. His hand covers mine. His breath is quick and shallow. His erection brushes against my buttocks.

My stomach feels sick. I'm sweating. I can't stay hard, even as my oiled fist slides up and down, guided by his.

"You're thinking too much," he tells me. "Concentrate on how good it feels. Look at that woman in front of you. She wants you to fuck her. Imagine how it'd feel to push your cock into her. Soft. Hot. Wet. And tight." His grip closes harder over mine. "So tight."

I look at the centerfold spread over the top of my toilet's water tank. She's got dark hair and blue eyes, and her legs are long. They always look like that, the women in the pictures Hugh brings.

He pants in my ear, and the sickness is back. Wrong. There's something wrong with me. This feels wrong. His eagerness makes me feel dirty. Bad. I'm a bad boy, even Mom says so. She yells it at me when she's crying, when she's angry with me about Dad.

A low moan cuts through the sound of his heavy breaths. It's me making that noise. It feels good, even though I don't want it to.

It's hard to breathe, to think, to fight . . .

"That's it," he coaxes. His other hand pushes between my buttocks.

I try to pull away, but he's got me trapped. He's bigger than me, stronger. No matter how I struggle, I can't push him off.

"Don't," I tell him, squirming.

"You like it," he grunts. His hand pumps me harder. "You shoot off like a geyser every time. It's okay. It's supposed to feel good. You'll be better once you've come. You won't fight with your mother so much . . ."

"No. Don't! Oh, God . . ."

He pushes two slick fingers inside me. I cry out, writhing away, but he won't quit. He's rubbing and thrusting into me, hitting the spot that makes me want to come more than anything. The pleasure grows despite the tears burning my eyes.

My head falls forward. My chin touches my heaving chest. It's coming. I can't stop it . . .

Abruptly, I look down from a higher vantage. My hand is suddenly bigger, my forearm thicker and coursing with veins. Dark hair dusts my arms and chest, my abdomen ripples with muscle as I fight the orgasm I don't want.

I am not a child anymore. He can't hurt me anymore.

There's a knife atop the centerfold, gleaming in the light from the vanity beside me. I grab it and jerk free of the fingers fucking me. I turn and the blade sinks into his chest.

"Don't touch me!" I roar, grabbing his shoulder and yanking him into the knife, all the way to the hilt.

Hugh's eyes widen with horror. His mouth falls open in a silent scream.

His face morphs into Nathan's. My childhood bathroom shimmers and transforms. We're in an eerily familiar hotel room.

My heart pounds harder. I can't be here. They can't find me here. Can't find any trace of me. I have to leave.

I stumble back. The knife withdraws in a smooth, blood-soaked glide. Nathan's eyes turn milky with death. They're gray. Gray eyes. Beautiful, beloved dove gray irises. Eva's eyes. Clouding over . . .

Eva is bleeding in front of me. Dying *in front of me. I've killed her. My God . . .*

Angel!

Can't move. Can't reach her. She crumples and pools onto the floor, those stormy eyes dull and sightless—

I jerked awake with a gasp, sitting up in a rush that sent an air-conditioned breeze across my sweat-soaked skin. I couldn't breathe through the panic and fear choking me. Shoving off the sheet tangled around my legs, I stumbled out of bed, blind with terror. My stomach heaved in protest and I lurched into the bathroom, barely reaching the toilet before I vomited.

I showered, washing away the sticky sweat covering me.

The grief and despair weren't so easy to get away from. As I scrubbed a dry towel over my skin, they weighed heavily, suffocating me. The memory of Eva's pale face etched with betrayal and death haunted me. I couldn't get it out of my head.

I stripped the bed with rough, jerky movements, then yanked a clean fitted sheet over the mattress.

"Gideon."

I straightened and turned at the sound of Eva's voice. She stood in the doorway to my bedroom, her hands twisting in the hem of the T-shirt she wore. Regret hit me hard. She'd gone to sleep alone in the room I'd had redesigned to look like her bedroom on the Upper West Side.

"Hey," she said softly, tentatively, shifting on her feet in a way that told me how uncomfortable she felt. How wary. "Are you okay?"

The light from the bathroom lit her face, revealing dark circles and reddened eyes. She'd fallen asleep crying.

I'd done this to her. I had made her feel unwelcome, unwanted, her thoughts and feelings less of a concern to me than my own. I'd let my past drive a wedge between us.

No, that wasn't true. I had let my fear push her away.

"No, angel, I'm not."

She took a single step closer, then stopped herself.

Opening my arms, I said hoarsely, "I'm sorry, Eva."

She came to me in a rush, her body lush and warm. I held her too tightly, but she didn't complain. Pressing my cheek to the top of her head, I breathed in her scent. I could face anything—I *would* face anything—as long as she stayed with me.

"I'm afraid." My voice was scarcely a whisper, but she heard it.

Her fingers dug into the muscles of my back as she pulled me closer. "Don't be. I'm here."

"I'll try harder," I promised. "Don't give up on me."

"Gideon." She sighed, her breath soft against my chest. "I love you so much. I just want you to be happy. I'm sorry for pushing you after I said I wouldn't."

"It's my fault. I fucked up. I'm sorry, Eva. So sorry."

"Shh. You don't have to apologize."

I picked her up and carried her to the bed, laying her down carefully. I crawled into her arms, wrapping myself around her and resting my face against her belly. She ran her fingers through my hair, massaging my scalp, then my nape, then my back. Accepting me, despite all my flaws.

The cotton of her T-shirt grew wet with my tears and I curled in tighter, ashamed.

"I love you," she murmured. "I'll never stop."

GIDEON.

I stirred at the sound of Eva's voice, then at the feel of her hand sliding down my chest. Opening my tired, burning eyes, I saw her leaning over me, the room softly lit by the coming dawn, her hair aglow in the meager light.

"Angel?"

She shifted, sliding a leg over me. Rising, she straddled me. "Let's make today our best ever."

I swallowed hard. "I'm on board with that plan."

Her smile rocked my world. She reached for something she'd left on her pillow and a moment later, haunting strains of music piped softly out of the speakers in the ceiling.

It took me a moment to recognize it. "Ave Maria."

She touched my face, her fingertips gliding over my brow. "Okay?"

I wanted to answer her, but my throat was too tight. I could only nod. How could I tell her it felt like a dream, a breathtaking heaven I didn't deserve?

She reached behind her to push the sheet below my hips and out of the way. Her arms crossed her torso to pull her shirt up and over her head. She threw it aside.

Awed, I struggled for my voice. "God, you're beautiful," I said hoarsely.

CAPTIVATED BY YOU · 155

My hands lifted, gliding over the plush curves and valleys of her voluptuous body. I sat up and dug my heels into the bed, pushing us backward until I was leaning against the headboard. My hands went into her hair and down her throat. I could touch her for days and not get my fill.

"I love you," she said, tilting her head to take my mouth in a hot, demanding kiss.

I let her have me, opening to her. Eva licked deep, stroking me with her tongue, her lips soft and wet against mine.

"Tell me what you need," I murmured, lost to the gently muted music. Lost to her.

"You. Just you."

"Take me, then," I told her. "I'm yours."

"I hate to be the one to break it to you, Cross," Arash said, his fingers drumming on the armrest of the chair in front of my desk, "but you've lost your killer instinct. Eva's tamed you."

I glanced up from my monitor. After spending two hours of my morning making love with my wife, I could concede that I wasn't feeling particularly aggressive. Slaked and relaxed was more apt. Still . . . "Just because I don't think LanCorp's PhazeOne gaming system is a threat to the GenTen doesn't mean I'm not paying attention."

"You're aware," he corrected, "which isn't the same as paying attention, and I guarantee Ryan Landon has noticed. You used to do something every week or two to poke at him, which—for better or worse—gave him something to do."

"Wasn't it just last week that we closed the PosIT deal?"

"That's reactive, Cross. You need to make a move he didn't prompt."

My office phone started ringing on the line synced to my smartphone. Ireland's name popped up on the screen and I reached for the receiver. "I have to take this."

"Of course you do," he muttered.

I narrowed my eyes at him as I answered. "Ireland, how are you?"

It wasn't like my sister to call. We usually texted back and forth, a form of communication we were both comfortable with. No awkward silences, no need to fake cheeriness or ease.

"Hey, sorry to call you in the middle of the day." Her voice was off.

I frowned, concerned. "What's wrong?"

Ireland paused. "Maybe now's not a good time."

I cursed inwardly. Eva had similar reactions when I was too brusque. The women in my life needed to cut me some slack. I had a big learning curve when it came to social interactions. "You sound upset."

"So do you," she shot back.

"You can call Eva and complain about it to her. She'll sympathize. Now, tell me what's wrong."

She sighed. "Mom and Dad were fighting all night. I don't know what about, but Dad was yelling. He never yells, you know that. He's the most laid-back guy ever. Nothing gets to him. And Mom hates fighting. She's a conflict avoider."

Her astuteness both startled and impressed me. "I'm sorry you had to hear that."

"Dad took off early this morning and Mom's been crying ever since. Do you know what's going on? Is it about Eva and you getting married?"

A strange but recognizable quiet settled over me. I didn't know what to say to her, and I refused to jump to conclusions. "That probably has something to do with it."

The only thing I knew for certain was that I didn't want Ireland listening to her parents fighting. I remembered what it had felt like when my parents fought in the days after my dad's financial fraud had been exposed. I could still feel echoes of the panic and fear. "Is there a friend you can stay with over the weekend?"

"You."

The suggestion was unnerving. "You want to stay with me?"

"Why not? I've never seen your place."

I stared at Arash, who was watching me. He leaned forward, setting his elbows on his knees.

I didn't know how to refuse, but I couldn't agree. The only person who'd ever spent the night with me was Eva, and obviously, that hadn't turned out well.

"Never mind," she said. "Forget it."

"No, wait." Damn it. "Eva and I have plans with friends tonight, that's all. I'll need some time to change them."

"Oh, gotcha." Her voice softened. "I don't want to fuck up your plans. I've got some friends I can call. Don't worry about it."

"I'm worried about *you*. Eva and I can make some adjustments; it's not a problem."

"I'm not a kid, Gideon," she said, clearly exasperated. "I don't want to hang around your place knowing you and Eva were supposed to be out having fun. That would totally suck, so no thanks. I'd rather chill with my own friends."

Relief relaxed my spine. "How about dinner on Saturday instead?"

"Yeah? I'm down. Can I stay the night then?"

I had no idea how I was going to manage it. I had to trust that Eva would know what to do. "That can be arranged. Will you be okay until then?"

"Jeez, listen to you." She laughed. "You sound like a big brother. I'll be fine. It was just weird, you know, hearing them going at it. It freaked me out. Most people are probably used to their parents fighting, but I'm not."

"They'll be fine. All couples fight eventually." I said the words, but I was both uneasy and curious.

Eva couldn't have been right about Chris not knowing. I found that impossible to believe.

∽

I'D just finished rolling up the sleeves of my black dress shirt when Eva stepped into the reflection of the mirror. I froze, my gaze raking over her.

She had chosen short shorts, a sheer sleeveless blouse, and high-heeled sandals. She'd pulled her hair up in its usual ponytail, but she had done something to it to make it look wild and bedhead messy. Her eye makeup was dark, her lips pale. Big gold hoops hung from her ears, and bangles decorated her wrists.

I'd woken up to an angel. I would be going to bed with a different woman entirely.

I whistled in appreciation, turning my back to the mirror to take in the real deal. "You look like a bad, bad girl."

She wiggled her ass and gave a cocky toss of her head. "I am."

"Come here."

She eyed me. "I don't think so. You've got the fuck-me look and we have to go."

"We can be a little late. What would it take to talk you into wearing those shorts just for me?"

I wanted others to want her and know she was mine. I also wanted to keep her all to myself.

Her eyes took on a calculating gleam. "We could renegotiate the hand job."

Remembering the deal we'd struck—a quickie for a clothed hand job—I realized the shorts were going to make the former a bit more difficult than it could be. As for the latter, I could work something out.

Tilting my head in agreement, I told her, "Put on a skirt, angel, and let's get this party started."

"WAS this your idea?" Arash asked, when we met him outside the ground-floor entrance to the Starlight Lounge.

Through the lobby glass, I watched a bouncer oversee the number of patrons entering the elevator that would take them to the rooftop. Two more bouncers stood guard at the exterior door, holding back the surging crowd hoping to get in based on their looks, their clothes, and/ or their charm.

"It's as much of a surprise to me as it is to you."

"I meant to tell you." Eva was literally hopping with excitement. "Shawna's heard good things about this place and I thought it'd be fun."

"Great reviews online," Shawna said, "and some of my regulars were raving about it."

Manuel checked out the eager crowd behind the ropes, while Megumi Kaba stood cautiously between Cary and Eva. Mark Garrity, Steven Ellison, and Arnoldo all stood back, keeping the way clear for those whose names were on the VIP List.

Cary slung his arm around Megumi. "Stick with me, kid." He gave her a wide smile. "We'll show 'em how it's done."

Eva grabbed my arm. "Your surprise is here."

I followed her gaze, spotting a couple approaching us. My brows rose when I recognized Magdalene Perez. Her hand was linked with that of the man next to her and her dark eyes were brighter than I'd seen in a long time.

"Maggie," I greeted her, clasping her extended hand and leaning down to kiss her cheek. "I'm glad you came."

Gladder still that Eva had asked her. The two women had gotten off to a rocky start, which was entirely Maggie's fault. The rift between them had strained my relationship with Maggie in the weeks since, and I'd been prepared to accept that as an indefinite state of affairs. It was nice, however, that I didn't have to.

Maggie grinned. "Gideon. Eva. This is my boyfriend, Gage Flynn."

I took the man's hand after he shook Eva's, noting the strength of his grip and the steady way he met my perusal. He gave me a once-over, too, but mine would be more thorough. Before the week was out, I would know everything worth knowing about the man. Maggie had been through enough with Christopher. I didn't want to see her hurt again.

"And here's Will and Natalie," Eva said, as the last of our group arrived.

Will Granger had a retro beatnik look that worked for him. His arm was snug around the small blue-haired woman next to him, who dressed in the same fifties style and sported twin sleeves of tattoos.

While Eva made the introductions, I nodded at the bouncer to signal the arrival of the final members of our party. He held the line and cleared the doorway for us.

My wife shot me a suspicious glance. "Don't tell me you own this place."

"Okay, I won't."

"You mean you do?"

My hand slid down her back and rested lightly on the curve of her hip. She'd ditched the shorts in favor of a fitted skirt with a split up the back. I almost wished she hadn't changed. The shorts had shown off her legs; the skirt showed off her amazing ass.

"You need to decide if you want me to answer the question or not," I said, as we made our way into the club. The music was loud, the amateur singer on the stage louder. Strategic lighting illuminated walkways and tables while still allowing the Manhattan nightscape to dazzle patrons. Air-conditioning pumped out of the walls and floors, cooling the open air to a comfortable temperature.

"Is there anything you *don't* own in New York?"

Arash laughed. "He doesn't own the D'Argos Regal on Thirty-sixth anymore."

Eva stopped walking, causing Arash to bump into her from behind and send her stumbling. I shot him a glare.

Grabbing my arm, Eva yelled over the volume of the crowded club. "You got rid of the hotel?"

I looked down at her. The wonder and hope on her face more than made up for the financial hit I'd taken. I nodded.

She threw herself at me, her arms twining around my neck. She peppered my jaw with quick, fierce kisses and I smiled, my gaze meeting Arash's.

"And suddenly," he said, "it all makes sense."

10

"GOD, THOSE TWO are so sweet," Shawna said, watching Will and Natalie sing "I Got You, Babe" on the stage.

"They're giving me diabetes." Manuel stood with his drink. "Excuse me, everyone. I see something interesting."

Gideon's voice near my ear was laced with amusement. "Say goodbye, angel. We won't be seeing him again."

I followed his line of sight and saw a pretty brunette giving Manuel a blatant once-over.

"Bye, Manuel!" I yelled after him, waving. Then I leaned into Gideon, who was semisprawled on the expensive leather upholstery. "How come all the guys you work with are hot?"

"Are they?" he drawled, nuzzling my neck and along the curve of my ear. "Maybe they won't be working with me much longer."

"Oh God." I looked up at the starry sky. "Whatever, caveman."

His arm tightened around my hips, tugging me closer so that I was pressed fully against him from knee to shoulder. Joy spread through me. After all the crap we'd been through the day before, it was so awesome to just enjoy each other.

Megumi leaned over the low coffee table that filled the center of the rectangular seating area we occupied. Bordered by two sectionals, the VIP section held our entire party comfortably. "When are *you* getting up there to make fools of yourselves?" she asked.

"Um . . . never."

It had taken a few drinks and Cary's undivided attention to make Megumi comfortable enough to enjoy herself. My best friend had kicked things off with a rousing rendition of "Only the Good Die Young," and then he'd dragged Megumi up there to sing "(I've Had) The Time of My Life." She'd come back to the table glowing.

I owed Cary big-time for taking care of her. Even better, he seemed to have no intention of ditching us to cruise the place for conquests like Manuel had. I was really proud of him.

"Come on, Eva," Steven coaxed. "You picked this place. You have to sing."

"Your sister picked this place," I shot back, looking to her. Shawna just shrugged innocently.

"She's sung twice!" he countered.

I deflected. "Mark hasn't sung anything."

My boss shook his head. "I'm doing you all a favor, trust me."

"You're telling me. Squealing tires sound more lyrical than I do!"

Arnoldo pushed the tablet with the song choices my way. It was the first time all night he'd made any overture toward me, aside from saying hello at the entrance. He'd spent most of the evening focused on Magdalene and Gage, which I tried not to take as a personal snub.

"No fair," I complained. "You're all ganging up on me! Gideon hasn't sung yet, either."

I glanced at my husband. He shrugged. "I'll go up if you will."

Astonishment widened my eyes. I'd never heard Gideon sing, had never even imagined it. Singers exposed and expressed emotion with their voices. Gideon's still waters ran very deep.

"Hell, you gotta do it now," Cary said, reaching over to tap the menu open at a random page.

My stomach twisted a little. I looked helplessly at the songs in front of me. One jumped out and I stared at it.

Taking a deep breath, I stood. "Okay. Just remember, you all asked for this. I don't want to hear any shit about how bad I suck."

Gideon, who'd risen to his feet when I had, pulled me close and murmured in my ear, "I think you suck excellently, angel."

I elbowed him in the ribs. His low laughter followed me as I made my way to the stage. I loved hearing that sound, loved spending time with him when we forgot our troubles and had fun with people who loved us. We were married, but we still had so much dating to catch up on, so many nights with friends yet to experience. Tonight was just the first of many, I hoped.

I regretted threatening the fragile peace with my song choice. But not enough to change my mind.

I high-fived Will as he and Natalie passed me on the way back to our group. I could have input my song choice into the tablet at the table, the same way we placed our food and drink orders, but I didn't want Gideon seeing the title.

Plus, I'd noticed that every other party in the place had to wait for their turn in the queue, but our selections were fast-tracked. I was hoping that adding my name to the list in person would buy me some time to build up the courage I needed.

I should've known better. When I gave the hostess my selection, she typed it into the system and said, "Okay, stay right here. You're next."

"You're kidding." I glanced back at our table. Gideon winked at me. Ooh, he was going to pay for that later.

The chick on the stage singing "Diamonds" wrapped it up, and the place exploded into applause. She'd been decent, but really, the live band made up for a lot of faults. They were really good. I had my fingers crossed that they'd be good enough for me, too.

I was shaking when I climbed the short steps to the stage. When the loud whistles and cheers erupted from our table, I couldn't help but laugh despite my nervousness. I gripped the mic in its stand and the beat kicked in immediately. The familiar song, one I loved, gave me the boost I needed to start.

Looking at Gideon, I warbled my way through the opening lyrics, telling him he was amazing. Even over the music, I could hear the laughter at my horrible voice. My own table erupted with it, but I had expected that.

I'd chosen "Brave." I had to be it to sing it—that, or crazy.

I stayed focused on my husband, who wasn't laughing or smiling. He just stared intently at my face as I told him via Sara Bareilles's lyrics that I wanted to see him speak up and be brave.

The catchy composition plus the skill of the band backing me began to win over the crowd, who started singing along, more or less. My heart strengthened my voice, giving power to the message meant only for Gideon.

He needed to stop holding his silence. He needed to tell his family the truth. Not for me or for them, but for him.

When the song ended, my friends surged to their feet in applause and I grinned, energized. I gave a lavish bow and laughed when the strangers at the tables in front of the stage joined in the unearned praise. I knew my strengths. My singing voice certainly wasn't one of them.

"That was fuckin' awesome!" Shawna shouted when I got back to the table, grabbing me in a fierce hug. "You owned that, girl."

"Remind me to pay you later," I said dryly, feeling my face heat as the rest of our party kicked in with praise. "You guys are full of it."

"Ah, baby girl," Cary drawled, his green eyes bright with laughter, "you can't be good at everything. It's a relief to know you're flawed like the rest of us."

I stuck my tongue out at him and picked up the fresh vodka cranberry sitting in front of my spot.

"Your turn, lover boy," Arash goaded, grinning at Gideon.

My husband nodded, then looked at me. His face held no hint to his thoughts, and I began to worry. There was no softness on his lips or in his eyes, nothing to give me a clue.

And then some idiot started singing "Golden."

Gideon stiffened, his jaw visibly tightening. Reaching for his hand, I gave it a squeeze and felt a bit of relief when he squeezed back.

He kissed my cheek and headed to the stage, cutting through the crowd with easy command. I watched him go, seeing other women's heads turn to follow him. I was biased, of course, but knew for a certainty that he was the most striking man in the room.

Seriously, it should be criminal for a man to be that sexy.

I looked at Arash and Arnoldo. "Have either of you heard him sing?"

Arnoldo shook his head.

Arash laughed. "Hell, no. With any luck, he'll sound like you. Like Cary says, he can't be good at everything or we'd all have to hate him."

The guy onstage wrapped it up. A moment later, Gideon walked on. For some reason, my heart started pounding as badly as it had when I was up there. My palms grew clammy and I wiped them on my skirt.

I was afraid of what it would be like to watch Gideon up there. Much as I hated to think it, Brett was a hard act to follow and hearing "Golden," even sung by someone who shouldn't ever have access to a microphone, brought those two worlds too close together.

Gideon grabbed the mic and pulled it off the stand as if he'd done the move a thousand times before. The women in the audience went crazy, yelling about how hot he was and making suggestive remarks I chose to ignore. The man was delicious physically, but his command-ing, confident presence was the real kicker.

He looked like a man who knew how to fuck a woman senseless. And God, did he ever.

"This one," he said, "is for my wife."

With a pointed glance, Gideon signaled the band to start. An in-stantly recognizable bass beat ratcheted up my pulse.

"Lifehouse!" Shawna crowed, clapping her hands. "I love them!"

"He's calling you his wife already!" Megumi yelled, leaning toward me. "How freakin' lucky are you?"

I didn't glance at her. I couldn't. My attention was riveted on Gideon as he looked directly at me and sang, telling me in a lusciously raspy voice that he was desperate for change and starving for truth.

He was answering my song.

My eyes burned even as my heart began to beat with a different rhythm. Had I thought he'd be unemotional? My God, he was killing me, baring his soul in the rough timbre of his voice.

"Holy fuck," Cary said, his eyes on the stage. "The man can sing."

I was hanging by a moment, too, hanging on to every word, hear-ing his message about chasing after me and falling more in love. I shifted in my seat, turned on beyond bearing.

Gideon dominated the attention of everyone in the bar. Of all the voices we'd heard that night, his was truly professional grade. He stood in the single spotlight, feet set a foot apart, dressed elegantly while singing a rock song, and he made it work so well I couldn't imagine it sung any other way. There was no comparison to Brett, not in Gideon's delivery or my reaction to it.

I was on my feet before I knew it, making my way through the crowd to get to him. Gideon finished the song and the bar went bal-listic, cutting off my route to him. I became lost in the crush, too short to see beyond the shoulders around me.

He found me, pushing his way through to catch me up in his arms. His mouth claimed mine, kissing me roughly, inciting a new round of catcalls and cheers. In the periphery, I heard the band begin a new song. I practically climbed up Gideon, panting in his ear, "Now!"

I didn't have to explain. Setting me down, he grabbed my hand and led me across the bar and back through the kitchen to the service elevator. I plastered myself against him before the doors closed behind us, but he was pulling out his phone and lifting it to his ear, tilting his head back as my mouth slid feverishly over his throat.

"Bring the limo around," he ordered gruffly, and then the phone was back in his pocket and he was kissing me back with all the passion he'd once kept locked inside.

Ravenous, I devoured him, catching his lower lip between my teeth and tasting it with swift lashes of my tongue. He groaned when I pushed him against the elevator's padded wall, my hands running down his chest to cup the heft of his erection in my palms.

"Eva . . . Christ."

We stopped descending and he exploded into movement, grabbing me by the elbow and pushing me ahead of him out the doors with brisk, impatient strides. We exited from a service hallway into the lobby, once again maneuvering through a crowd until we stepped out into the summer night heat. The limo idled in the street.

Angus jumped out, quickly pulling the rear door open.

I scrambled in with Gideon crowding in behind me.

"Don't go far," he told Angus.

We settled onto the bench seat with a foot of distance between us, both of us looking anywhere but at each other as the privacy partition slowly rose and the limo began to move.

The moment the divider locked into place, I fell back against the seat and yanked my skirt up, brazenly tearing off my own clothes in my eagerness to be fucked.

As Gideon dropped to his knees on the floorboard, his hands went to his waistband, opening his slacks.

I shimmied out of my underwear, kicking them off along with my sandals.

"Angel." His growl had me moaning with anticipation.

"I'm wet. I'm wet," I chanted, not wanting him to play with me or wait.

Still, he tested me, cupping my sex in his hand. His fingers parted me, stroking over my clit, pushing inside me.

"Jesus, Eva. You're soaked."

"Let me ride you," I begged, pushing away from the seat back. I wanted to set the pace, the depth, the rhythm . . .

Gideon pushed his pants and boxer briefs down to his knees, then sat on the bench, yanking his shirttails out of the way. His cock rose up thick and long between his thighs, as savagely beautiful as the rest of him.

I slid down to kneel between his legs, stroking his penis with my hands. He was hot and silky soft. My mouth was on him before I formulated the thought. His breath hissed out between his teeth, one hand grasping my ponytail as his head fell back.

His eyes squeezed shut. *"Yes."*

I swirled my tongue around the broad head, tasting him, feeling the thick veins throbbing against my palms. Tightening my lips, I pulled off, then sucked him back in.

He groaned and arched upward, pushing into my mouth. "Take it deep."

I squirmed as I obeyed him, ragingly turned on by his pleasure. Gideon's eyes opened, his chin lowering so he could take in the sight of me.

"Come here." The low command sent a shiver of desire through me.

I crawled up his magnificent body, straddling his hips and draping my arms over his shoulders. "You are so fucking hot."

"Me? You're burning up, angel."

I moved my hips to position him. "Wait 'til you feel me from the inside."

He reached around me and gripped his cock, holding himself steady as I began to sink down. My legs shook as the thick crest of his penis pushed inside me, stretching me.

"Gideon." The feeling of being taken, possessed, was one I never got over.

Gripping my hips, he supported me. I took him deeper, my eyes on his as they grew heavy. A rumbling sound filled the space between us and I grew slicker, hotter.

It didn't matter how many times I had him, I always wanted more. More of the way he responded to me, as if nothing had ever felt the same, as if I gave him something he could get nowhere else.

I clung to the back of the seat and rolled my hips, taking a little more. I could feel him pressing against the deepest part of me, but I couldn't fit all of him. I wanted to. I wanted everything he had.

"Our first time," he said hoarsely, watching me. "You rode me right here, drove me out of my mind. You blew the top of my fucking head off."

"It was so good," I breathed, dangerously close to coming. He was so thick, so hard. "Ah, God. It's better now."

His fingers dug into my hips. "I want you more now."

Gasping, I pressed my temple to his. "Help me."

"Hold on." Yanking my hips down, he thrust upward, shoving into me. "Take it, Eva. Take it all."

I cried out and ground into him, moving on instinct, taking the last of him.

"Yes . . . yes . . ." I gasped, slamming my hips into his, pumping my sex up and down the rigid length of his erection.

Gideon's face was harsh with lust, brutally etched with his need. "I'm going to come so hard for you," he promised darkly. "You'll feel me in you all night."

The sound of his voice . . . the way he'd looked onstage . . . I'd never been so excited. He wasn't the only one who'd be coming hard.

His head fell back against the seat, his chest heaving, harsh sounds of pleasure scraping from his throat. His hands released me, clenching into fists against the seat. He let me fuck him the way I needed to, let me use him.

Arching back, I climaxed with a cry, my entire body shaking, my sex grasping, rippling along his cock. My rhythm faltered, my vision blackened. An endless moan poured out of me, the relief dizzying.

The world shifted and I was on my back, Gideon rising over me, his arm hooking beneath my left leg to lift it to his shoulder. He dug his feet into the floorboard, thrusting again and again, sinking deep. So deep.

I writhed, the feel of him so good it hurt.

He kept me pinned, opened and defenseless, using me as I'd used him, his control shattered by the need to orgasm. The power of his body as he pounded into me, the force with which he drove his cock into my tender sex, had me quivering on the verge again.

"I love you," I moaned, my hands stroking down his flexing thighs.

He growled my name and started coming, his teeth clenching, his hips pressed tight to my own, screwing deep. It set me off, the feel of him coming inside me.

"So good," he groaned, rocking into the spasms of my sex.

We strained together, grasping at each other.

He buried his face in my throat. "Love you."

Tears stung my eyes. He said the words so rarely.

"Tell me again," I begged, holding on to him.

His mouth found mine. "I love you . . ."

"More," I demanded, licking my lips.

Gideon glanced over his shoulder at me. Bacon sizzled in the pan in front of him and my mouth watered for another slice. "And here I'd thought two packs of bacon would last us all weekend."

"Grease is a must after a night of drinking," I told him, wiping some off my plate with my fingertip and lifting it to my mouth. "When you're not hung over, that is."

"Which I am," Cary muttered, walking into the kitchen in just his jeans, which he hadn't bothered buttoning all the way. "Got any beer?"

Gideon pointed at the fridge with his tongs. "Bottom drawer."

I shook my head at my best friend. "Hair of the dog this morning?"

"Hell, yeah. My head feels like it's splitting in two." Cary pulled a beer out and joined me at the island. He popped the cap off and tipped the bottle back, gulping down half the contents at once.

"How'd you sleep?" I asked, mentally crossing my fingers.

He'd stayed the night in the attached single-bedroom apartment, and I hoped he loved it. It had all the beautiful prewar details of Gideon's penthouse and was furnished similarly. I knew Cary's style was more contemporary, but he couldn't fault the view of Central Park. All the rest could be changed, if he just said the word.

He lowered the bottle from his mouth. "Like the dead."

"Do you like the apartment?"

"Of course. Who wouldn't?"

"Do you want to live there?" I persisted.

Cary gave me a lopsided smile. "Yeah, baby girl. It's a dream. Thank you for the pity fuck, Gideon."

My husband turned away from the stove with a plate of bacon in his hand. "There is neither pity nor fucking included in the offer," he said dryly. "Otherwise, you're welcome."

I clapped my hands. "Yay! I'm stoked."

Gideon snagged a piece of bacon and stuck it in his mouth. Leaning forward, I parted my lips. He bent toward me, letting me bite off the end.

"Come on," Cary groaned. "I'm fighting nausea as it is."

I shoved him gently. "Shut up."

He grinned and finished his beer. "Gotta give you guys a hard time. Who else is going to stop you two from singing 'I Got You, Babe' in a few years?"

Thinking of Will and Natalie made me smile. I'd discovered even more to like about Will and found that I got along well with his girl, too. "Aren't they adorable? They've been together since high school."

"Exactly my point," he drawled. "Spend enough years with someone and either you start bickering or you fall down the lovey-dovey hole, never to be seen again."

"Mark and Steven have been together for years, too," I argued. "They don't fight or moon at each other."

He shot me a look. "They're gay, Eva. No estrogen in the mix to cause drama."

"Oh my God. You sexist pig! You did not just say that."

Cary glanced at Gideon. "You know I'm right."

"And with that," Gideon declared, grabbing three strips of bacon, "I'm out."

"Hey!" I complained after him, as he exited to the living room.

My best friend laughed. "Don't worry. He hitched himself to your brand of female."

I glared at him as I munched another piece of bacon. "I'm giving you a pass, because I owe you for last night."

"It was fun. Megumi's good people." His humor fled, his face darkening. "I'm sorry she's going through what she is."

"Yeah, me, too."

"You make any decisions about how you're going to help others like her?"

I set my elbows on the island. "I'm going to talk to Gideon about working with his Crossroads Foundation."

"Hell. Why didn't you think of that before?"

"Because . . . I'm stubborn, I guess." I glanced over my shoulder at the living room, then lowered my voice. "One of the things Gideon likes about me is that I don't always do everything he wants just because he wants it. He's not like Stanton."

"And you don't want to be like your mom. Does this mean you're keeping your maiden name?"

"No way. It means a lot to Gideon for me to become Eva Cross. Besides, it sounds kick-ass."

"It does." He tapped the end of my nose with his finger. "I'm here for you when you need me."

Sliding off the stool, I hugged him. "Same goes."

"I'm taking you up on that, obviously." His chest heaved with a deep sigh. "Big changes happening, baby girl. You ever get scared?"

I looked up at him, feeling the affinity that had gotten us both through some hard times. "More than I let myself think about."

"I have to run to the office," Gideon interjected, stepping back into the kitchen wearing a Yankees ball cap. He'd kept the same gray T-shirt on but had swapped out his pajama bottoms for sweats. A ring of keys twirled around his finger. "I won't be long."

"Is everything all right?" I asked, backing away from Cary. My husband was wearing his game face, the one that told me his mind was already on whatever he was going to deal with.

"Everything's fine." He came to me and gave me a quick kiss. "I'll be back in a couple of hours. Ireland won't be here 'til six."

He left. I stared after him.

What was important enough to drag him away from me on a weekend? Gideon was possessive about a lot of things when it came to me, but our time together topped the list. And the key-twirling thing was kind of weird. Gideon wasn't a man given to wasted movement. The only times I'd seen him fidget were when he was completely relaxed or the opposite—ready to throw down.

I couldn't shake the feeling that he was hiding something from me. As usual.

"I'm gonna take a shower," Cary said, grabbing a bottled water out of the fridge. "You want to watch a movie when I get out?"

"Sure," I said absently. "Sounds like a plan."

I waited until he'd gone back into the attached apartment, then went to find my phone.

11

"WHERE'S EVA?"

    I rounded the front of the Benz and stepped onto the curb in front of Brett Kline. My fingers twitched, the habit of extending my hand in greeting ruthlessly suppressed. The singer's hands had touched my wife intimately in the past . . . and recently. I didn't want to shake them. I wanted to break them.

"At our home," I answered, gesturing at the entrance to the Crossfire Building. "Let's go up to my office."

Kline smiled coldly. "You can't keep me from her."

"You did that all by yourself." I noted the worn Pete's T-shirt he was wearing with black jeans and leather boots. Without a doubt, his choice of attire wasn't a coincidence. He wanted to remind Eva of their history together. Maybe even remind me, too. Had Yimara given him the idea? I wouldn't be surprised.

It was the wrong move for both men to have made.

He walked through the revolving doors ahead of me. Security took his information and printed out a temporary ID, then we headed through the turnstiles to the elevators.

"You can't intimidate me with your money," he said tightly.

I entered the car and hit the button for the top floor. "There are eyes and ears all over the city. At least in my office, I know we won't be putting on a show."

His lip curled in disgust. "Is that all you care about? Public perception?"

"An ironic question, considering who you are and what you want."

"Don't act like you know me," he growled. "You know shit."

In the confined space of the elevator car, Kline's aggression and frustration permeated the space between us. His hands gripped the handrail behind him, his stance hostile and expectant. From the platinum tips of his spiked hair to the black-and-gray tattoos covering his arms, the front man of Six-Ninths couldn't be more different from me in appearance. I used to feel threatened by that and his history with Eva, but no longer.

Not after San Diego. And certainly not after last night.

I could still feel the marks of Eva's nails in my back and ass. She'd pushed me to my limits all night and into the early hours of the morning. The insatiable hunger she felt for me left no room for anyone else. And the catch in her voice when she told me she loved me, the sheen of tears in her eyes when I yielded to what she did to me . . .

I leaned back against the opposite wall and tucked my hands into the pockets of my sweats, knowing my nonchalance would goad him.

"Does she know we're meeting like this?" he asked harshly.

"I figured I'd leave it up to you to decide whether to mention it."

"Oh, I'm mentioning it all right."

"I hope you do."

We exited into the Cross Industries foyer and I led him through the security doors and back to my office. There were a few people at their desks and I took note of them. Those who worked on their days off weren't always better employees than those who didn't, but I respected ambition and rewarded it.

When we got to my office, I shut the doors behind us and frosted the glass. A folder sat on my desk, as I'd instructed before leaving the penthouse. I set my hand atop it and gestured for Kline to take a seat.

He remained standing. "What the fuck is this about? I come into town to see Eva and your goon brings me here instead."

The "goon" was security provided by Vidal Records, but he wasn't wrong in thinking the man worked for me. "I'm prepared to offer you a great deal of money—along with other incentives—for the exclusive rights to the Yimara footage of you and Eva."

He gave me a hard smile. "Sam told me you were going to try this. That tape is none of your business. It's between me and Eva."

"And the entire world if it leaks, and that would destroy her. Does that matter to you at all, how she feels about it?"

"It's not going to leak, and of course I give a shit about how she feels. It's one of the reasons we need to talk."

I nodded. "You want to ask her what you can use. You think you can talk her into letting you exploit some of it."

He rocked back on his feet, a restless move that signaled a direct hit.

"You're not going to get the answer you hope for," I told him. "The very existence of that tape horrifies her. You're an idiot if you think otherwise."

"It's not all sex. There's some good stuff of us hanging out. Her and I, we had something. She wasn't just a lay to me."

Piece of shit. I had to control the impulse to deck him.

He smirked. "Not that you'd understand. You had no problem banging away at that brunette until I came back into the picture, then you changed up your game. Eva's a toy you got bored with. Until someone else wanted her."

His mention of Corinne hit a harsh chord. The charade of dating my ex had nearly cost me Eva, a close call that still haunted me.

That didn't prevent me from noticing how good he was at shifting the blame. "Eva knows what she means to me."

He stepped closer to my desk. "She's too blinded by your billions to realize there's something really wrong with you hiding that bogus wedding in a foreign country. Is it even legal?"

It was a question I'd anticipated. "Absolutely legal."

Opening the folder, I pulled out the photo inside. It was taken on the day of my wedding, at the very moment I first kissed Eva as her husband. The beach and the pastor who had officiated at the ceremony were behind us. I cupped her face, our lips touching softly. Her hands held my wrists, my ring sparkling on her finger.

I turned the picture around so that it faced him. I slid a copy of the marriage license into place beside it. I used my left hand, proudly displaying my ruby-encrusted wedding band.

I wasn't sharing such personal things to prove a point. I intended to provoke Kline, which I'd been deliberately doing from the moment he arrived in New York. When he reached out to my wife again, I wanted him off-balance and at a disadvantage.

"So you and Eva are done," I said evenly. "If you doubted it, now you know it for sure. In any case, I don't think you want my wife as much as you want the memory of her for the band's use."

Kline laughed. "Yeah, paint me as the sleaze. You can't handle the thought of her seeing that tape. You've never made her get that wild and you never will."

My forearms twitched with the need to pound the smugness out of his face. "Believe what you like. Here are your options: You can take the two million I'm offering, give me the footage, and walk away—"

"I don't want your damn money!" Setting his hands on the edge of my desk, he leaned toward me. "You don't get to own my memories. You may have her—for now—but I have those. Fuck if I'm selling them to you."

The thought of Kline watching the footage . . . watching himself fuck my wife . . . set my blood on a slow boil. The thought of him suggesting that Eva sit through a viewing of it, knowing how that would shatter her, pushed me to the raw edge of violence.

Keeping my tone even was a struggle. "You can reject the money and keep the existence of the footage to yourself until you die. Make it a secret gift to Eva she never has to know about."

"What the fuck are you talking about?"

"Or you can be a selfish asshole," I continued, "and hit her up with it, shocking her with the goal of destroying her marriage and making yourself more famous."

I stared him down. Kline stood his ground, but his gaze dropped for a fraction of a second. A small victory, for what it was worth.

With a swipe of my hand, I withdrew the contract Arash had drawn up. "If you care about her at all, you'll make a different decision than the one that brought you to New York."

He grabbed the documents off my desk and ripped them in half, throwing the pieces back onto the glass. "I'm not leaving until I see her."

Kline strode out of my office, bristling with anger.

I watched him go. Then I placed a call via a secure line. "Did I give you enough time?"

"Yes. We took care of the laptop and tablet in his luggage as soon as you took him upstairs. We're handling his e-mail and backup provider servers as we speak, and the backups to those servers. We searched his residence over the weekend, but he hasn't been there in weeks. We cleaned everything on both Yimara and Kline's equipment, as well as the accounts and equipment of those who received teasers of the full-length footage. One of the execs at Vidal had a full copy on his hard drive, but we wiped it. We found no evidence that he forwarded it anywhere."

Ice slid through my veins. "Which executive?"

"Your brother."

Fuck. I gripped the edge of my desk so hard my knuckles cracked with the strain. I remembered the video of Christopher with Magdalene, knew how perverse his hatred toward me was. Thinking about him seeing Eva so intimately . . . so vulnerable . . . took me to a place I hadn't been since I'd first heard about Nathan.

I had to believe that the private military security firm I'd hired had dealt with the situation thoroughly. Their tech teams were trained to handle far more sensitive information.

I shoved the mess on my desk into the folder. "I need that footage to cease to exist anywhere."

"Understood. We're on it. Still, it's possible there's a hard copy floating around, although we've searched Kline and Yimara's transaction records for security deposit boxes and the like. We'll continue to monitor the situation until you say otherwise."

I never would. I'd search for a lifetime, if that was what it took, for any hint that the footage survived somewhere outside of my control. "Thank you."

Hanging up, I left my office and headed home to Eva.

"You're really good with those," Ireland said, eyeing Eva as she lifted a chopstickful of kung pao chicken from its white box to her mouth. "I never got the hang of 'em."

"Here, try holding them like this."

I watched my wife adjust my sister's grip on the slender sticks, her blond head a bright contrast against Ireland's black hair. Sitting on the floor at my feet, they both wore shorts and tank tops, their tanned legs stretched out beneath the coffee table, one long and lean, the other petite and voluptuous.

I was more of an observer than a participant, sitting on the couch behind them and envying their easy rapport even while I was grateful for it.

It was all so surreal. I hadn't ever imagined a night like that, a quiet evening at home with . . . family. I didn't know how to contribute or even if I could. What could I say? How should I feel?

Besides awed. And thankful. So very thankful for my amazing wife, who brought so much to my life.

Not long ago, on a similar Saturday night, I would have been at a highly publicized social function or event, focusing on business unless or until a woman's keen interest spurred a need to fuck. Whether I returned to the penthouse by myself or ended up at the hotel with a one-night stand, I'd be alone. And since I hardly remembered what it felt like to belong anywhere, to anyone, I didn't know what I was missing.

"Ha! Look at that," Ireland crowed, holding up a tiny bit of orange chicken, which she promptly ate. "Made it to my mouth."

I swallowed the wine in my glass in a single gulp, wanting to say *something*. My mind raced with options, all of which sounded insincere and contrived. In the end what came out was, "The chopsticks have a large target. Ups your chances."

Ireland turned her head toward me, revealing the same blue eyes I saw in the mirror every day. They were much less guarded, far more innocent, and bright with laughter and adoration. "Did you just call me a big mouth?"

Unable to resist, I ran my hand over the crown of her head, touching the silky soft strands of her hair. Those, too, were like mine and yet not. "Not my words," I said.

"Not *in so many* words," she corrected, leaning briefly into my touch before turning back to Eva.

Eva glanced up at me, offering an encouraging smile. She knew I drew strength from her, and she gave it unconditionally.

My throat tight, I rose from the couch and grabbed Eva's empty wineglass. Ireland's glass of soda was still half full, so I left it and headed to the kitchen, trying to regain enough equanimity to make it through the rest of the evening.

"Channing Tatum is so hot," Ireland said, her voice traveling from the living room. "Don't you think?"

I frowned. My baby sister's idle question triggered uncomfortable thoughts of her dating. She had to have started a few years ago—she was seventeen. I knew it was unrealistic to want her to stay away from boys. I knew it was my fault that I'd missed so much of her childhood. But the thought of her having to deal with younger versions of men like me and Manuel and Cary roused an unfamiliar defensive reaction.

"He's very good-looking," Eva agreed.

Possessiveness rose to join the mix. My gaze narrowed on the two glasses in front of me as I refilled them.

"He's this year's Sexiest Man Alive," Ireland said. "Look at those biceps."

"Ah, now on that, I have to totally disagree. Gideon is way sexier." My mouth curved.

"You're such a goner," my sister teased. "Your pupils turn into little hearts when you think about Gideon. It's so cute."

"Shut up."

Ireland's musical laugh floated through the air. "Don't worry. He's goofy over you, too. And he's been on every Sexiest Man Alive list for ages. I never hear the end of it from my friends."

"Gah. Don't tell me stuff like that. I'm jealous by nature."

Laughing inwardly, I dropped the empty bottle into the recycling bin.

"So is Gideon. He's going to flip out when you start hitting the

Hottest Women Alive lists. No way to avoid it now that everyone's heard of you."

"Whatever," Eva scoffed. "They'd have to Photoshop fifteen pounds off my ass and thighs to sell that."

"Um, have you seen Kim Kardashian? Or Jennifer Lopez?"

I paused on the threshold of the living room, taking in the picture Ireland and Eva made over the rim of my glass. An ache bloomed in my chest. I wanted to freeze the moment, protect it, keep it safe forever.

Ireland looked up and spotted me, then rolled her eyes. "What did I tell you?" she said. "Goofy."

SITTING back in my chair, I sipped coffee and studied the spreadsheet on my monitor. I rolled my shoulders back, trying to loosen the kink in my neck.

"Dude. What the hell? It's three in the morning."

I looked up to find Ireland standing in the doorway to my home office. "Your point?"

"Why are you working so late?"

"Why are you Skyping so late?" I countered, having heard her laughter and occasionally raised voice over the last hour or so since I'd left Eva sleeping.

"Whatev," she muttered, coming in and dropping into one of the chairs in front of my desk. She slouched, her shoulders even with the chair back and her legs sprawled out in front of her. "Can't sleep?"

"No." She didn't know how literally true that was. With Ireland sleeping in Eva's bed and Eva sleeping in mine, I couldn't risk going to sleep myself. There was only so much I could expect Eva to take, only so many times I could frighten her before it destroyed the love she felt for me.

"Christopher texted me a bit ago," she said. "Guess Dad's staying at a hotel."

My brows rose.

She nodded, her face forlorn. "It's bad, Gideon. They haven't spent a night apart ever. At least that I can remember."

I didn't know what to say. Our mother had been calling me all day, leaving messages on my voice mail and ringing the penthouse so often I'd been forced to disconnect the main receiver so that none of the phones would ring. I hated that my mother was struggling, but I had to protect my time with Ireland and Eva.

It felt heartless to focus on myself, but I'd already lost my family twice before—once when my father died and again after Hugh. I couldn't afford to lose any more. I didn't think I could survive it a third time, not with Eva in my life.

"I just wish I knew what caused the fight," she said. "I mean as long as they didn't cheat on each other, they should be able to get through it, right?"

Exhaling roughly, I straightened. "I'm not the person to ask about relationships. I have no idea how they work. I'm just stumbling my way through, praying not to fuck things up, and grateful that Eva is so forgiving."

"You really love her."

I followed her gaze to the collage of photos on the wall. It hurt sometimes, looking at those pictures of my wife. I wanted to recapture and relive every moment. I wanted to hoard every second I'd ever had with her. I hated that time slipped away so quickly and I couldn't bank it for the uncertain future.

"Yes," I murmured. I'd forgive Eva anything. There was nothing she could do or say that would break us apart, because I couldn't live without her.

"I'm happy for you, Gideon." Ireland smiled when I looked at her.

"Thank you." The worry in her eyes lingered and sparked restlessness. I wanted to fix the problems troubling her, but I didn't know how.

"Could you talk to Mom?" she suggested. "Not now, of course. But tomorrow? Maybe you can find out what's going on?"

I hesitated a moment, knowing a conversation with our mother was certain to be unproductive. "I'll try."

Ireland studied her nails. "You don't like Mom very much, do you?"

Weighing my answer carefully, I said, "We have a fundamental difference of opinion."

"Yeah. I get it. It's like she's got this weird form of OCD that applies to her family. Everyone has to be a particular way or at least pretend to be. She's so worried about what people think. I saw an old movie the other day that reminded me of her. *Ordinary People*. Ever seen it?"

"No, can't say I have."

"You should watch it. It has Kiefer Sutherland's dad in it and some other people. It's sad, but it's a good story."

"I'll look it up." Feeling the need to explain our mother, I tried my best. "What she dealt with after my father died . . . It was brutal. She's insulated herself since then, I think."

"My friend's mother says Mom used to be different before. You know, when she was married to your dad."

I set my cooled coffee aside. "I do remember her differently."

"Better?"

"That's subjective. She was more . . . spontaneous. Carefree."

Ireland rubbed at her mouth with her fingertips. "Do you think it broke her? Losing your dad?"

My chest tightened. "It changed her," I said quietly. "I'm not sure how much."

"Ugh." She sat up, visibly shaking off her melancholy. "You going to be awake awhile?"

"Probably all night."

"Wanna watch that movie with me?"

The suggestion surprised me. And pleased me. "Depends. You can't tell me what happens. No spoilers."

She shot me a look. "I already told you it's sad. If you want happily ever after, she's sleeping down the hall."

That made me smile. Standing, I rounded my desk. "You find the movie, I'll grab the soda."

"A beer would be good."

"Not on my watch."

She pushed to her feet with a grin. "Okay, fine. Wine, then."

"Ask me again in a few years."

"You'll have kids by then. It won't be as fun."

I paused, hit by anxiety sharp enough to mist my skin with sweat. The thought of having a baby with Eva both thrilled and terrified me. It wasn't safe for my wife to live with me. How could it ever be safe for a child?

Ireland laughed. "Holy fuck, you should see your face! A classic case of playboy panic. Didn't they tell you? First comes love, then comes marriage, then comes the baby in the baby carriage."

"If you don't shut up, I'm sending you to bed."

She laughed harder and linked her arm with mine. "You're a riot. Seriously. I'm just messing with you. Don't flip out on me. I've got enough family members doing that."

I willed my heart to stop pounding so damn hard.

"Maybe *you* should have a drink," she suggested.

"I think I will," I muttered.

"I'm going to give major props to Eva for getting a ring out of you. Did you have a panic attack when you proposed, too?"

"Stop talking, Ireland."

Leaning her head against my shoulder, she giggled and led me out of my office.

THE sun had been up for over two hours by the time I returned to bed. I stripped silently, my gaze roaming over the delectable bump under the covers that was my wife.

Eva was curled in a ball, mostly hidden except for the bright strands of hair splayed over the pillow. My mind filled in the blanks, knowing she was naked between the sheets.

Mine. All mine.

It killed me to sleep away from her. I knew it hurt her, too.

Lifting the edge of the blankets, I slid in beside her. She gave a soft little moan and rolled toward me, her lush warm body wriggling into place against me.

I was instantly hard. Desire simmered in my blood; awareness tingled along my skin. It was combustible sexual chemistry but also something more. Something deeper. A strange, wonderful, frightening recognition.

She filled an emptiness in me I hadn't known was there.

Eva buried her face in my throat and hummed softly, her legs tangling with mine, her hands gliding over my back. "Hard and yummy all over," she purred.

"All over," I agreed, cupping her ass and pulling her tighter against my hard-on.

Her shoulders shook with a silent laugh. "We have to be quiet."

"I'll cover your mouth."

"Me?" She nipped at my throat. "You're the noisy one."

She wasn't wrong. As rough and impatient as I could get when aroused, I'd never been loud . . . until her. It was a struggle to be discreet when situations called for it. She felt too good, made me feel too much.

"So we'll take it slow," I murmured, my hands roaming greedily over her silky skin. "Ireland will be sleeping for hours; there's no rush."

"Hours, huh?" Laughing, she pulled back and rolled away from me, reaching for the nightstand drawer. "Overachiever."

Tension stretched across my shoulders as she dug out the breath mints she kept handy. I was reminded of similar situations, when women had reached into the nightstand drawer for condoms.

Eva and I had used condoms only twice. Before her, I'd never fucked a woman without one. Avoiding pregnancy was something I'd religiously adhered to.

Yet since those first two times with Eva, we'd gone bare, relying on her birth control to prevent conception.

It was a risk. I knew that. And considering how often I had her—at least two, sometimes three or four times a day—the risk was not inconsiderable.

I thought of it sometimes. I questioned my control, my selfishness in putting my own pleasure above the consequences. But the reason for my recklessness wasn't as simple as pleasure. If it were, I could deal. Be responsible.

No, it was much more complicated.

The need to come inside her was primitive. It was a conquest and surrender in one.

I had wanted to fuck her raw before I'd even had her the first time, before I knew definitively how explosive it would be between us. I'd gone so far as to warn her prior to our first date that I needed it, needed her to give me that, something I'd never wanted with anyone else.

"Don't move," I said roughly, sliding over her while she was still stretched out on her stomach. My hand pushed between her hip and the bed, reaching between her legs to cup her cunt in my palm. She was moist and warm. My stroking fingers made her slick and hot.

She muffled a moan.

"I want you just like this," I told her, brushing my lips across her cheek.

Reaching for my pillow with my free hand, I yanked it over and then shoved it under her, lifting her hips to an angle that would let me sink balls-deep.

"Gideon . . ." The way she said my name was a plea, as if I wouldn't get down on my knees and beg for the privilege of having her.

I shifted, urging her legs apart and pinning her wrists beside her head. Holding her down, I thrust into her. She was ready for me, plush and tight and wet. My teeth gritted together to restrain the growl that surged from my throat, a tremor racking my body from head to toe. My chest heaved against her back, my violent exhalations ruffling her hair lying across the pillow.

Just like that, just by taking me, she had me right on the edge.

"God." My hips churned without volition, screwing my cock into her, pushing me deeper until I was in her to the hilt. I could feel her all around me, from root to tip, clenching in ripples that milked me like a greedy little mouth. "Angel—"

The pressure at the base of my dick was insistent, but I was capable of staving it off. It wasn't a question of control, but of will.

I *wanted* to come inside her. Wanted it enough to consider the risk—as terrifying as it was—acceptable.

Closing my eyes, I dropped my forehead to her cheek. I inhaled the scent of her and let go, coming hard, my ass flexing as I filled her up in thick, hot spurts.

Eva whimpered, writhing under me. Her cunt tightened, then trembled around my cock. She climaxed with a soft, sweet moan.

I growled her name, searingly aroused by her orgasm. She came because I did, because my pleasure turned her on as much as my touch. I would reward her for that, show her the depth of my gratitude. She would get hers, over and over again, as many times as she could take it.

"Eva." I rubbed my damp cheek against hers. "Crossfire."

Her fingers tightened their grip on mine. Her head turned, her lips seeking.

"Ace," she breathed into the kiss. "I love you, too."

It was shortly after five in the evening when I drove the Bentley through the gates of the Vidal estate in Dutchess County and into the circular drive out front.

"Aw, you drove too fast," Ireland complained from the backseat. "We're here already."

I put the SUV in park and left it idling. One look at the house, and a knot tightened in my gut. Eva reached over, taking my hand and giving it a squeeze. I focused on her steely gray eyes instead of the Tudor-style mansion at her back.

She didn't say a word, but she didn't have to. I felt her love and support and saw the glimmer of anger in her eyes. Just knowing she understood gave me strength. She knew every dark and dirty secret I had, and yet she believed and loved me anyway.

"I want to stay over again sometime," Ireland said, poking her head between the two front seats. "It was fun, right?"

I looked at her. "We'll do it again."

"Soon?"

"All right."

Her smile more than made the promise worth what it would cost me in sleep and anxiety. I'd stayed away from her for many reasons, but the main one was that I didn't know what I could offer her of any value. I'd channeled everything into keeping Vidal Records afloat for her well into the future, taking care of her the only way I knew I wouldn't screw up.

"You'll have to help me out," I told her honestly. "I don't know how to be a brother. You will probably have to forgive me. Frequently."

The smile left Ireland's face, transforming her from a teenager to a young woman. "Well, it's like being a friend," she said somberly. "Except you *have* to remember birthdays and holidays, you have to forgive me for everything, and you should introduce me to all your hot, rich guy friends."

My brow lifted. "Where's the part about me picking on you and giving you a hard time?"

"You missed those years," she shot back. "No do-overs."

She meant to tease, but the words struck home. I *had* missed years and I couldn't get them back.

"You get to pick on her boyfriends instead," Eva said, "and give *them* a hard time."

Our eyes met and I knew she understood exactly what I was thinking. My thumb stroked over her knuckles.

Behind her, the front door opened and my mother stepped out. She stood on the wide top step dressed in a white tunic and matching pants. Her long, dark hair hung loosely around her shoulders. From a distance, she looked so much like Ireland, more of a sister than a parent.

My grip on Eva's hand tightened.

Ireland sighed and opened her door. "I wish you guys didn't have to work tomorrow. I mean, what's the point of being a gazillionaire if you can't play hooky when you want?"

"If Eva worked with me," I said, looking at my wife, "we could."

She stuck her tongue out. "Don't start."

I lifted her hand to my mouth and kissed the back. "I haven't stopped."

Opening my door, I stepped out of the car and hit the hatch release. I rounded the back of the car to retrieve Ireland's bag and found my arms full of her instead. She hugged me tightly, her slender arms wrapped around my waist. It took me a moment to unfreeze from my surprise, and then I hugged her back, my cheek coming to rest on the crown of her head.

"I love you," she mumbled into my chest. "Thanks for having me over."

My throat closed tight, preventing me from saying anything. She was gone as quickly as she'd come at me, her duffel in hand as she met Eva on the passenger side and hugged her, too.

CAPTIVATED BY YOU · 193

Feeling as winded as if I'd been punched, I closed the hatch and watched as my mother met Ireland halfway across the blue-gray gravel drive. I was about to return to the wheel and leave, when she signaled at me to wait.

I glanced at Eva. "Get in the car, angel."

She looked as if she might argue, and then she nodded and slid back into the front passenger seat and closed the door.

I waited until my mother came to me.

"Gideon." She caught me by the biceps and lifted onto her tiptoes to press a kiss to my mouth. "Won't you and Eva come in? You drove all this way."

I took a step backward, breaking her hold. "And we have to drive back."

Her gaze reflected her disappointment. "Just for a few minutes. Please. I'd like to apologize to both of you. I haven't handled the news of your engagement well and I'm sorry about that. This should be a happy time for our family, and I'm afraid I've been too worried about losing my son to appreciate it."

"Mom." I caught her arm when she moved toward the passenger side. "Not now."

"I didn't mean all those things I said about Eva the other day. It was just a shock, seeing the ring your father gave me on another woman's hand. You didn't give the ring to Corinne, so I was surprised. You can understand that, can't you?"

"You antagonized Eva."

"Is that what she told you?" She paused. "I never meant to, but— Never mind. Your father was very protective, too. You're so like him."

I looked away, gazing absently at the trees beyond the drive. I never knew how to take comparisons to Geoffrey Cross. Were they meant as praise or a backhanded compliment? There was no telling with my mother.

"Gideon . . . please, I'm trying. I said some things to Eva I shouldn't have, and she responded as any woman would under the circumstances. I just want to smooth things over." She set her hand over my heart. "I'm happy for you, Gideon. And I'm so glad to see you and Ireland spending time together. I know it means so much to her."

I pulled her hand away gently. "It means a lot to me, too. And Eva made it possible in ways I won't explain. Which is just one of the reasons I won't have her upset. Not now. She has to work in the morning."

"Let's make plans for lunch this week, then. Or dinner."

"Will Chris be there?" Eva asked through the window before pushing the door open again and stepping out. She stood there, so small and bright against the dark hulking SUV, formidable in the way her shoulders were set.

My wife would fight the world for me. It was miraculous to know that. When no one else had fought for me, I'd somehow found the one soul who would.

My mother's lips curved. "Of course. Chris and I are a team."

I noted the brittleness of her smile and doubted her, as I so often did. Still, I conceded. "We'll make plans. Call Scott tomorrow and we'll work something out."

My mother's face brightened. "I'm so glad. Thank you."

She hugged me and I braced myself, my body stiff with the need to push her away. When she approached Eva with her arms outstretched, Eva thrust out her hand between them to shake instead. The interaction was awkward, with both women so obviously on the defensive.

My mother didn't want to mend fences; she wanted an agreement to pretend the fences were sound.

We said good-bye, and then I slid into the driver's seat. Eva and I took off, leaving the estate behind us. We hadn't gone far when she said, "When did your mother talk to you?"

Damn it. I knew what that bite in her tone signified.

Reaching over, I set my hand on her knee. "I don't want you worrying about my mother."

"You don't want me worrying about anything! That's not the way this is gonna work. You don't get to deal with all the crap alone."

"What my mother says or does isn't important, Eva. I don't give a shit and neither should you."

She twisted in the seat to face me. "You need to start sharing stuff. Especially things that have to do with me, like your mother saying things behind my back!"

"I won't have you getting pissed off over an irrelevant opinion." The road curved. I accelerated out of the turn.

"That would be better than me getting pissed off at *you*!" she snapped. "Pull over."

"What?" I glanced at her.

"Pull the damn car over!"

Cursing inwardly, I removed my hand from her leg and gripped the wheel. "Tell me why."

"Because I'm mad at you, and you're sitting there looking all hot and sexy driving and you need to stop."

Amusement warred with exasperation. "Stop what? Looking hot and sexy? Or driving?"

"Gideon . . . don't push me right now."

Resigned, I eased off the gas and pulled to a stop on the narrow shoulder. "Better?"

She got out of the car and went around the hood. I stepped out, giving her a questioning glance.

"*I'm* driving," she announced when she was standing in front of me. "At least until we get to the city."

"If that's what you want."

I knew next to nothing about relationships, but it was a no-brainer to make concessions when your woman was mad at you. Especially when you entertained hopes of getting laid in a few hours, which I most definitely was. After spending the weekend with friends and Ireland, I was feeling a renewed need to show my wife just how much I appreciated her.

"Don't look at me like that," she muttered.

"Like what?" I raked her with a glance, admiring how pretty she looked in a strappy white sundress. The evening was hot and muggy, but she looked airy and fresh. I wanted to strip off my clothes and press up against her, cool off a little before heating things up.

"Like I'm a ticking time bomb ready to go off!" Her arms crossed. "I am *not* being irrational."

"Angel, that's not the look I'm giving you."

"And don't try to distract me with sex," she bit out, her jaw clenched. "Or you won't get any for a week!"

My arms crossed, too. "We've already talked about issuing ultimatums like that. You can bitch at me all you like, Eva, but I'll have you when I want you. Period."

"Never mind whether I want you?"

"Asks the wife who gets wet watching me drive a damn car," I drawled.

Her gaze narrowed. "I may just leave you here on the side of the road."

Clearly, I wasn't navigating the situation well. So I switched tactics, taking the offensive position.

"You don't tell me everything," I countered. "What about Kline? Has he completely stopped communicating with you since San Diego?"

I'd been holding back the question all weekend, wondering how Kline was going to handle Eva.

I was torn about how I wanted him to proceed. If he approached her about the tape he no longer possessed, it would hurt her but also drive her closer to me. If he walked away for her sake, it would betray deeper feelings for her than I was comfortable with. I hated that he wanted her, but I feared he might actually love her.

She gasped. "Oh my God. Have you been looking at my phone again?"

"No." My reply was swift and decisive. "I know how you feel about that."

I followed her every move, knew where she was and who she was with at every moment of the day, but she'd set a hard limit with her cell phone and I honored it, even though it drove me crazy.

Eva studied me a minute but must have seen the truth on my face. "Yes, Brett has sent me a few texts. I was going to talk to you about it, so don't even try to say it's the same thing. I totally intended to tell you. You had absolutely no intention of telling me."

A car rushed by on the road, turning my concern toward her safety. "Get in and drive. We'll talk in the car."

I waited until she climbed into the seat, and then I shut the door behind her. By the time I settled in the passenger side, she'd adjusted the mirrors and seat to suit her and put the car in gear.

The minute she was fully merged in the lane, she started in on me again. I was vaguely aware of her speaking, my attention more focused on the way she handled the Bentley. She drove fast and with confidence, her grip light and easy on the wheel. She kept her gaze on the road, but I couldn't take my eyes off her. My California girl. On an open road, she was fully in her element.

I found myself pleasantly aroused by watching Eva handle the powerful SUV. Or maybe it was that she was chastising me, challenging me.

"Are you listening to me?" she demanded.

"Not really, angel. And before you get more riled, it's entirely your fault. You're sitting there looking hot and sexy, and I'm distracted."

Her hand whipped out and smacked my thigh. "Seriously? Stop cracking jokes!"

"I'm not kidding. Eva . . . you want me to share, so you can support me. I get it. I'm working on it."

"Not hard enough apparently."

"I'm not going to share things that aggravate you unnecessarily. There's no point."

"We have to be straight with each other, Gideon. Not just occasionally, but all the time."

"Really? I don't expect the same from you. For example, feel free to keep all the unflattering comments your father and Cary make about me to yourself."

Her lips pursed. She chewed on that for a bit, then, "Using that logic, wouldn't it be okay for me to not say anything about Brett?"

"No. Kline impacts our relationship. My mother does not."

She snorted.

"I'm right about this," I said evenly.

"Are you telling me that your mom talking crap about me doesn't bother you?"

"I don't like it. That said, it doesn't change how I feel about you or her. And telling you won't change your feelings about her, either. Since the result is the same either way, I choose the path of least disruption."

"You're thinking like a guy."

"I should hope so." I reached over and brushed the hair off her shoulder. "Don't let her cause trouble between us, angel. She's not worth it."

Eva glanced at me. "You're pretending that what your mom says and does has no effect on you, but I know that's not true."

I debated denying it, just to shut down the topic, but my wife saw everything I'd rather hide. "I don't let it affect me."

"But it does. It hurts and you push it into that place where you push everything you don't want to deal with."

"Don't analyze me," I said tightly.

Her hand touched my thigh. "I love you. I want to stop the pain."

"You already have." I gripped her hand. "You've given me everything she took away. Don't let her take any more."

With her eyes on the winding road, Eva lifted our joined hands and kissed my wedding band. "Point taken."

She gave me a quick smile that told me she was done—for now—and drove us home.

12

I DARED ANYONE to come up with a more awe-inspiring sight than Gideon Cross taking a shower.

It amazed me that he could be so matter-of-fact about running his hands over all that taut, tanned skin and those perfectly defined slabs of muscle. Through the misted glass of my bathroom shower, I watched the rivulets of soapy water run down the hard ridges of his abdomen and the length of his strong legs. His body was a work of art, a machine he kept in prime shape. I loved it. Loved looking at it, touching it, tasting it.

Reaching out, he swiped a hand through the condensation, revealing that breathtaking face. One darkly winged brow arched in silent query.

"Just enjoying the show," I explained. The scent of his soap teased senses that had become trained to recognize the fragrance as belonging to my mate. The man who stirred and pleasured my body to delirium.

I licked my lips when he casually stroked the heavy length of his cock. He'd once told me he used to masturbate every time he took a shower, a release he had considered as routine as brushing his teeth. I could see why, knowing how powerful his sexual appetite was. I would never forget the way he'd looked when he had jacked off in the shower for me, so virile and potent and hungry for orgasm.

Since he'd met me, he didn't pleasure himself anymore. Not because he couldn't still satisfy me if he did, and not because I took care of him enough to make the effort redundant. For both of us, being ready for sex with each other was never a problem, because the hunger we felt was deeper than physical.

Gideon teased me by saying he saved himself to satisfy my insatiability, but I saw the self-restraint for what it was—he gave me the right to his pleasure. It was mine and mine alone. He had none without me, which was a tremendous gift. Especially in light of his past, when sexual release had been used as a weapon against him.

"It's an interactive exhibition," he said, his eyes warm with amusement. "Join me."

"You're an animal." My thighs were wet with his semen beneath my robe, since I was the lucky girl who woke up to his desire.

"Only for you."

"Ooh, right answer."

He smirked. His cock lengthened. "You should reward me."

I moved away from the threshold and stepped closer. "How would you suggest I do that?"

"Any way you like."

That was a gift, too. Gideon rarely relinquished control, and then only to me.

"I don't have enough time to do you justice, ace. I'd hate to cut things short when they're just getting interesting." I set my hand on the glass. "How about we revisit after my workout tonight? You, me, and whatever I want to do to you?"

He shifted and faced me head on, his hand lifting to press against mine through the glass. His gaze slid over my face in a heated caress that was damn near tangible. His face was impassive, a strikingly handsome mask that revealed nothing. But his eyes . . . those stunning blue depths . . . they exposed tenderness and love and vulnerability.

"I'm all yours, angel," he said, his words so quiet I saw them more than heard them.

I pressed a kiss to the cool glass. "Yes," I agreed. "You are."

NEW week. Same ultrafocused Gideon. He started working as soon as the Bentley pulled away from the curb, his fingers flying across the keyboard built into a dropdown tray table. I watched him, finding his intense concentration and confidence extremely sexy. I was married to a powerful, driven man, and watching him flex that ambition was a major turn-on.

I was so into watching him that I jumped when my smartphone vibrated in my purse against my hip.

"Jeez," I muttered, digging it out.

Brett's name and photo appeared on the lock screen. Knowing I needed to deal with him at some point if I expected him to stop calling, I answered.

"Hey," I answered cautiously.

"Eva." The timbre of Brett's now-famous voice hit me as forcefully as it always had, but not in the same way. I loved the way he sang, but that love wasn't intimate anymore. It wasn't personal. I admired him the way I did a dozen other singers. "Damn it, I've been trying to reach you for a week!"

"I know. I'm sorry, I've been busy. How are you?"

"I've been better. I need to see you."

My brows rose. "When are you coming to town?"

He laughed harshly, a humorless sound that rubbed me the wrong way. "Incredible. Listen, I don't want to get into it on the phone. Can we get together today? We need to talk."

"You're in New York? I thought you were on tour . . . ?"

Gideon's rapid-fire typing didn't slow and he didn't look at me, but I could feel his energy shift. He was paying attention, and he knew who was on the line.

"I'll tell you what's going on when I see you," Brett said.

I frowned out the window as we idled at a light, my gaze on the flood of pedestrians crossing the street. New York was teeming with life and frenetic energy, gearing up to do world-changing business. "I'm on my way to work. What's going on, Brett?"

"I can meet you for lunch. Or after you get off for the day."

I debated saying no, but the determination in his tone gave me pause. "Okay."

Reaching over, I set my hand on Gideon's thigh. The toned muscle was hard beneath my palm, even though he was at rest. The tailored suits polished his form into civility, but I knew the truth about the vigorously fit body that was only hinted at underneath. "I can see you at lunch, if we stick close to the Crossfire Building."

"All right. What time should I be there?"

"A little before noon would be best. I'll meet you in the lobby."

We hung up and I dropped the phone back into my purse. Gideon's hand captured mine. I glanced at him, but he was reading a lengthy e-mail, his head bent slightly so that the ends of his hair brushed his sculpted jaw.

The warmth of his touch soaked into me. I looked down at the band he wore on his finger, the one that told the world he belonged to me.

Did his business associates pay attention to his hands? They weren't those of a man who pushed paper and tapped on keyboards all day.

They were the hands of a fighter, a warrior who practiced mixed martial arts and pounded out his aggression with both boxing bags and sparring partners.

Kicking off my shoes, I curled my legs under me and leaned into Gideon's side, setting my other hand on top of his. I ran my splayed fingers between his knuckles and fingers, forward and back, carefully resting my head against his shoulder so that I didn't mess up his pristine black jacket with my makeup.

I breathed him in, feeling the effect of him—his nearness, his support—permeate my being. The smell of his soap was muted now, the naturally seductive scent of his skin altering the fragrance into something richer and more delicious.

When I was restless, he settled me.

"There's nothing for him," I whispered, needing him to know that. "I'm too filled with you."

His chest expanded abruptly, his sharp inhalation audible. He pushed the tray table up and away, then patted his lap in invitation. "Come here."

I crawled into his lap, sighing happily when he shifted me into a spot that felt made for me. Every peaceful moment we had with each other was treasured. Gideon deserved the respite, and I longed to be that for him.

His lips touched my forehead. "You okay, angel mine?"

"I'm in your arms. Life doesn't get better than this."

I spotted three paparazzi outside the Crossfire when we arrived.

With a hand at the small of my back, Gideon ushered me through the entrance ahead of him, escorting me quickly but unhurriedly into the cool lobby.

"Vultures," I muttered.

"Can't be helped that we're such a photogenic couple."

"You're such a humble man, Gideon Cross."

"You make me look good, Mrs. Cross."

We stepped into the elevator with a few other people and he took the rear corner, hooking me to him with an arm around my waist, his hand pressed flat against my belly, his chest warm and hard against my back.

I savored those few minutes with him, refusing to think about work or Brett until we parted on the twentieth floor.

Megumi was already at her desk when I approached the glass security doors, and the sight of her made me smile. She'd trimmed her hair since I'd seen her Friday night and polished her nails a bright red. It was good to see the small signs that she was reclaiming her spirit.

"Hey, you," she greeted me after buzzing me in, pushing to her feet.

"You look great."

Her smile widened. "Thanks. How'd it go with Gideon's sister?"

"Awesome. She's a lot of fun. It makes me melt seeing Gideon with her."

"He makes me melt, period. You lucky bitch. Anyway, I put a call through to your line earlier. They wanted to leave a message."

I shifted on my feet, thinking of Brett. "Was it a guy?"

"No, a woman."

"Hmm, I'll go check it out, thanks."

I headed back to my desk and got settled in, my gaze coming to rest on the collage of photos of Gideon and me. I still needed to talk to him about Crossroads. There hadn't been a good time over the weekend. We'd had enough on our plates having Ireland over.

He hadn't slept Saturday night. I'd hoped he would but hadn't really expected him to. It was hard for me, thinking of his inner struggle, his worry and fear. He carried shame, too, and an inherent belief that he was broken. Damaged goods.

He didn't see in himself what I saw—a generous soul who wanted so much to belong to something greater than himself. He didn't recognize what a miracle he was. When he didn't know what to do in a given situation, he let instinct and his heart take over. Despite all he'd been through, he had such an amazing capacity to feel and to love.

He'd saved me, in so many ways. I was going to do whatever needed to be done to save him, too.

I listened to my messages. When Mark came in, I stood, and met him with a grin and bouncing anticipation.

His brows rose. "What's got you so excited?"

"A gal from LanCorp called this morning. They want to meet with us sometime this week to talk a bit more about what they're hoping to achieve with the launch of the PhazeOne system."

His dark eyes took on a familiar sparkle. He'd become a happier man overall since he and Steven had become engaged, but there was a whole different energy to him when he was eager about a new account. "You and me, kid, we're going places."

I hopped a little on my feet. "Yeah. You've got this. Once they meet with you in person, you'll have them eating out of your hand."

Mark laughed. "You're good for my confidence."

I winked at him. "I'm good for you, period."

We spent the morning working on the PhazeOne RFP, putting together comps to better grasp how we might position the new gaming system against its competition. I had a momentary pause when I realized how much buzz surrounded the upcoming release of the next-generation GenTen console—which happened to be a product of Cross Industries, making it PhazeOne's primary rival in the marketplace.

Pointing the situation out to Mark, I asked, "Is it going to be a problem? I mean, could LanCorp possibly see a conflict of interest with me working for you on this?"

He straightened in his chair, leaning back. He'd shucked his coat earlier but remained smartly attired in a white dress shirt, bright yellow tie, and navy slacks. "It shouldn't be an issue, no. If our proposed positioning wins out over the other RFPs they're collecting, the fact that you're engaged to Gideon Cross isn't going to make a damn bit of difference. They're going to make their decision based on our ability to deliver their vision."

I wanted to feel relieved, but I didn't. If we were awarded the PhazeOne campaign, I'd be helping one of Gideon's competitors steal some of his market share. That really bothered me. Gideon worked so hard and had overcome so much to lift the Cross name up from infamy to a level where it inspired awe, respect, and a healthy amount of fear. I never wanted to set him back, in anything.

I'd thought I would have a little more time before I was forced to make a choice. And I couldn't help feeling like the choice to be made was between my independence and my love for my husband.

The dilemma niggled at me all morning, chipping away at the excitement I felt over the RFP. Then the hours crept toward noon and Brett took over my thoughts.

It was time to take responsibility for the mess I'd made. I had opened the door to Brett, and then I'd kept it open because I couldn't get my head on straight. It was my job now to fix the problem before it impacted my marriage any more than it already had.

I headed down to the lobby at five minutes to noon, having asked permission from Mark to leave a little early. Brett was already waiting for me, standing near the entrance with his hands shoved into his jeans pockets. He wore a plain white T-shirt and sandals, with sunglasses propped atop his head.

My stride faltered a little. Not just because he was hot, which was undeniable, but because he looked so out of place in the Crossfire. When he'd met me here before the video launch in Times Square, we had rendezvoused outside. Now, he was in the building, occupying a spot too near to where I'd first run into Gideon.

The differences between the two men were stark and didn't have anything to do with clothing or money.

Brett's mouth curved when he saw me, his body straightening, shifting in that way men moved when their sexual interest was piqued. Other men, but not Gideon. When I'd first met my husband, his body, his voice, gave nothing away. Only his eyes had betrayed his attraction, and only for an instant.

It was later I realized what had happened in that moment.

Gideon had claimed me . . . and given himself to me in return. With a single look. He'd recognized me the moment he saw me. It took me longer to understand what we were to each other. What we were meant to be.

I couldn't help but contrast the possessive, tender way Gideon looked at me against the earthier, lustful way Brett raked me from head to toe.

It seemed so obvious suddenly, that Brett had never really thought of me as *his*. Not the way Gideon did. Brett had wanted me, still did, but even when he'd had me, he hadn't asserted any ownership and he certainly hadn't ever given anything *real* of himself to me.

Gideon. My head tilted back, my gaze searching for and finding one of the many black domes in the ceiling that hid the security cameras. My hand went to my heart, pressing over it. I knew he probably wasn't looking. I knew he'd have to deliberately access the feed in order to see me and that he was far too busy with work to think of it, but still . . .

"Eva."

My hand dropped to my side. I looked at Brett as he approached me with the easy prowl of a man who knew his appeal and was confident of his chances.

The lobby was swarming with people flowing around us in steady streams, as one would expect in a midtown skyscraper. When his arms lifted as if to embrace me, I stepped back and held out my left hand instead, just as I had done when we last met in San Diego. I would never again cause Gideon to feel the pain I'd inflicted when he saw me kissing Brett.

Brett's brows lifted and the heat in his eyes cooled. "Really? Is this where we're at now?"

"I'm married," I reminded him. "Hugging each other isn't appropriate."

"What about the women he's tapped all over the tabloids? That's okay?"

"Come on," I chided. "You know you can't always believe what the press feeds you."

His lips pursed. He shoved his hands back in his pockets. "You can believe what they say about how I feel about you."

My stomach fluttered. "I think *you* believe it."

Which made me a little sad. He didn't know what Gideon and I had, because he'd never had it. I hoped he would someday. Brett wasn't a bad guy. He just wasn't meant to be *my* guy.

Cursing under his breath, Brett turned and gestured toward the exit. "Let's get out of here."

I was torn. I wanted privacy, too, but I also wanted to stay where there were witnesses who could reassure Gideon. In any case, we couldn't exactly have a picnic in the Crossfire lobby.

Reluctantly, I fell into step beside him. "I had some sandwiches delivered a little bit ago. Figured that would give us more time to talk."

Brett nodded grimly and held out his hand for the bag I was carrying.

I took him to Bryant Park, weaving beside him through the frenetic lunchtime crowds on the sidewalks. Taxis and private cars honked insistently at the streams of pedestrians too time-strapped to obey the signals. Heat shimmered off the asphalt, the sun high enough in the sky to spear down between the towering skyscrapers. An NYPD squad car hit its siren, the piercing robotic chirps and rumbles doing little to expedite the cruiser's movement through the clogged street.

It was Manhattan on an average day and I loved it, but I could tell Brett was frustrated by the intricate dance required to get through the city. The shifting of shoulders and hips to let people pass, the quick inhales to squeeze by too-big bags or too-slow pedestrians, the swift-footedness needed to avoid the abrupt appearance of new bodies filing out of the many doorways that lined the sidewalks. Life as usual in NYC, but I remembered how overwhelming it felt when you weren't used to so many people occupying relatively little space.

Entering the park just behind the library, we found an unoccupied bistro table and chairs in the shade near the carousel and settled in. Brett pulled out the sandwiches, chips, and bottled water I'd ordered, but neither of us started eating. I scouted our surroundings instead, aware that we could be photographed.

I'd considered that when I chose the location, but the alternative was a noisy, crowded restaurant. I was hyperconscious of my body language, trying to ensure that nothing could be misconstrued. The world at large could think we were friends. My husband would know, in every way I could show him, that Brett and I had actually said good-bye.

"You got the wrong impression in San Diego," Brett said abruptly, his eyes shielded behind his shades. "Brittany isn't a serious thing."

"It's none of my business, Brett."

"I miss you. Sometimes, she reminds me of you."

I winced, finding the comment anything but flattering. I lifted one hand and gestured helplessly. "I couldn't go back to you, Brett. Not after Gideon."

"You say that now."

"He makes me feel like he can't breathe without me. I couldn't settle for less." I didn't need to say that Brett had never made me feel like that. He knew.

He stared at his steepled fingertips, then straightened abruptly and dug his wallet out of his back pocket. He pulled a folded photograph out and set it on the table in front of me.

"Look at that," he said tightly, "and tell me we didn't have something real."

I picked up the photo and spread it open, frowning at the image. It was a candid shot of Brett and me, laughing together over something lost to memory. I recognized the interior of Pete's in the background. There was a crowd of blurred faces around us.

"Where did you get this?" I asked. There'd been a time when I would've given anything to have an unposed photo with Brett, believing that such an insubstantial thing would give me some kind of proof that I was more than a piece of ass.

"Sam took that after one of our sets."

I stiffened at the mention of Sam Yimara, abruptly reminded of the sex tape. I looked at Brett, my hands shaking so hard I had to put the photo down. "Do you know about . . . ?"

I couldn't even finish the sentence. Turned out, it wasn't necessary for me to.

Brett's jaw tensed, his forehead and upper lip beaded with sweat from the summer heat. He nodded. "I've seen it."

"Oh my God." I recoiled from the table, my mind filled with all the possibilities of what was captured on video. I had been desperate to win Brett's attention, with a complete lack of self-respect that shamed me now.

"Eva." He reached for me. "It's not what you think. Whatever Cross told you about the video, I promise it isn't bad. A little raw sometimes, but that's the way it was between us."

No . . . Raw was what I had with Gideon. What I'd had with Brett was something much darker and unhealthy.

I clasped my trembling hands together. "How many people have seen it? Have you shown it to— Has the band watched it?"

He didn't have to answer; I saw it on his face.

"Jesus." I felt sick. "What do you want from me, Brett?"

"I want—" Shoving up his sunglasses, he rubbed at his eyes. "Hell. I want you. I want us to be together. I don't think we're over yet."

"We never got started."

"I know that's my fault. I want you to give me a chance to fix it."

I gaped. "I'm married!"

"He's no good, Eva. You don't know him like you think you do."

My legs quivered with the urge to get up and leave. "I know he'd never show footage of us to anyone! He respects me too much."

"The whole point was to document the rise of the band, Eva. We had to sort through it all."

"You could've watched it alone first," I said tightly, horribly aware of the people sitting not too far away. "You could've cut us out before the others saw it."

"We're not the only ones Sam got on video. The other guys had stuff, too."

"Oh God." I watched as he shifted restlessly. Suspicion bloomed. "And there were other girls with you," I guessed, my nausea worsening. "What did it matter when I was just one of many."

"It mattered." He leaned forward. "It was different with you, Eva. *I* was different with you. I was just too young and full of myself to appreciate it at the time. You need to see, Eva. Then you'll understand."

I shook my head violently. "I don't want to see it. Ever. Are you crazy?"

That was a lie. What was in the video? How bad was it?

"Goddamn it." He yanked off his shades, throwing them on the table. "I didn't want to talk about the fucking video."

But there was a defensiveness to his posture that made me doubt him. His shoulders were high and tight, his mouth a hard line.

Whatever Cross told you . . .

He knew Gideon was aware of the tape. He had to know Gideon was fighting to keep it buried. Sam would've told him.

"What do you want?" I asked again. "What was so damned urgent you had to come out to New York?"

I waited for him to answer, my heart pounding. It was hot as hell and humid, but my skin felt chilled and clammy. He couldn't tell me he loved me, not after I'd caught him with Brittany. He couldn't warn me away from Gideon; I was already married. Brett was in Manhattan midtour, something the band had to agree with. And Vidal. Why would they do that? What would they get out of interrupting their schedule?

When Brett just sat there, his jaw working, I stood and turned blindly away, hurrying across the grass toward the nearest gate in the wrought-iron fence.

He called after me, but I kept my head down, achingly aware of the number of people in the park whose heads turned in my direction. I was making a scene, but I couldn't stop. I left my bag behind and didn't care.

Get away. Get somewhere safe. *Get to Gideon.*

"Angel."

The sound of my husband's voice made me stumble. I turned my head. He rose from a chair near the piano by Bryant Park Grill. Cool and elegant, seemingly impervious to the sultry heat.

"Gideon."

The concern in his eyes, the gentle way he enfolded me in a hug, gave me strength. He'd known this meeting with Brett wouldn't go well. That I would be upset and needy. That I would need *him.*

And he was there. I didn't know how, and I didn't care.

My fingers dug into his back, practically clawing at him.

"Shh." His lips brushed against my ear. "I've got you."

Raúl appeared beside us with my bag in hand, his stance conveying a protectiveness that added to the shield Gideon's body gave me. The riotous panic inside me began to ease. I wasn't freefalling anymore. Gideon was my net, always prepared to catch me.

He led me down the steps to where the Bentley waited, with Angus standing ready to open the back door. I slid inside and Gideon joined me, his arm wrapping around me when I curled into him.

We were right back to where we'd started that morning. But in a matter of hours, everything had changed.

"I've got this," he murmured. "Trust me."

I lifted my nose to his throat. "They want to use the footage, don't they?"

"They won't. No one will." There was a razor-sharp edge to his words.

I believed him. And I loved him more than I ever thought possible.

WHAT an afternoon. I avoided thinking about Brett by working hard on game console comps, including GenTen; my mind was firmly on Gideon when five o'clock rolled around.

It wasn't just PhazeOne that worried me anymore. It was also me, the girl I'd once been. The sex tape could do more damage to the Cross name than anything a rival company could do.

I texted Gideon. I hoped for a quick answer but didn't expect one. Are you in your office?

He replied almost instantly. Yes.

Heading home, I typed back. Want to say bye first.

Come up.

I released the breath I hadn't realized I'd been holding. See you in ten.

Megumi was already gone when I passed reception, so I reached Gideon faster than I'd planned on. His receptionist was still at her station, her long red hair hanging sleekly around her shoulders. She gave me a curt nod and I gave her a smile, unfazed.

Scott wasn't at his desk when I got back there, but Gideon was standing at his, his hands on the desktop as he perused documents spread out in front of him. Arash was seated in one of the chairs, his posture relaxed and easy as he spoke. Neither of them wore a coat, and both of them looked mighty fine.

Arash glanced at me as I came closer, and Gideon's head came up. My husband's eyes were so blue, the hue struck me even across the distance between us. His face remained austerely handsome, so classically Gideon, and yet his gaze softened at the sight of me. My mouth curved when he beckoned me with a crook of his finger.

I entered his office and held out my hand to Arash when he stood. "Hey," I greeted him. "You keeping him out of trouble?"

"When he lets me," the lawyer replied, catching my hand and pulling me in for an air kiss on my cheek.

"Back off," Gideon said dryly, his arm sliding around my waist.

Arash laughed. "This new jealous streak of yours is vastly entertaining."

"Your sense of humor is not," Gideon shot back.

I leaned into my husband, loving the feel of his hard body against mine. There was no give to him, no yielding. Except when he looked at me.

"I've got a meeting in thirty," Arash said, "so I'll head out. Thanks for Friday night, Eva. I'd love to do it again sometime."

"We will," I told him. "For sure."

As he left the office, I turned to Gideon. "Can I hug you?"

"You never have to ask."

My heart felt squeezed by the warm indulgence in his eyes. "The glass is clear."

"Let them see," he murmured, wrapping his arms around me. He exhaled long and slow when I clung to him. "Talk to me, angel."

"I don't want to talk." Didn't want to think about the mess I'd made of my life, which was now impacting the man I loved. "I want to hear your voice. Say anything, I don't care."

"Kline won't hurt you. I promise you that."

My eyes squeezed shut. "Not about him. Tell me about work."

"Eva . . ."

I felt the tension in his body, the strain of concern and worry, so I explained. "I just want to close my eyes for a minute and feel you. Smell you. Hear you. I need to just soak you in for a minute, and then I'll be okay."

His hands rubbed up and down my back, his chin resting on the top of my head. "We're going away. Soon. For at least a week, although I'd prefer two. I was thinking we might go back to Crosswinds. Spend the time naked and lazy—"

"You're never lazy. Especially when you're naked."

"Especially when *you're* naked," he corrected, nuzzling me. "But I've never had you that way for an entire week. You could wear me out."

"I doubt that's possible, fiend. But I'm willing to try my best."

"It won't be our honeymoon, per se. I want a month for that."

"A month!" I pulled back and looked at him, my mood lifting. "The entire economy of New York could collapse if you're out of the game that long."

He cupped the side of my face, his thumb brushing over my brow. "I think my highly capable team can manage a few weeks without me."

I caught his wrist and let a little of my anxiety out. "I couldn't manage it. I need you too much."

"Eva." He lowered his head and pressed his lips to mine, his tongue teasing them open.

Gripping his nape in my hand, I held him still while I deepened the kiss. Fell into it. He pulled me closer, lifting me onto my tiptoes.

His head tilted, tightening the seal until every breath was shared, every moan and whimper.

I gasped when we broke for air. "When will you be home?"

"When you want me there."

"That would be when your day is done. You've lost enough time over me today." I smoothed his perfectly placed tie. "You weren't just spying on me this afternoon. You knew my lunch with Brett was going to go south."

"It was a possibility."

"The spying? Or the heading south?"

He shot me a look. "You're not going to give me a hard time about being there for you. You would've done the same had the situation been reversed."

"How did you know what he wanted?" Was the video's existence eating at him, too? What I'd done and who I'd been before?

"I know he's getting pressure from Christopher, who's also putting pressure on the rest of the band."

"Why? To get to you?"

"In part. You're not just some random hot blonde. You're Eva Tramell and you're news."

"Maybe I should dye my hair. Get rid of the 'Golden.' How about red?" I couldn't go brunette, not with Gideon's history of dark-haired women. It would kill me to look in the mirror every day.

His face shuttered, closed up like a steel trap even though nothing else about him gave away any tension. I got a tingle at the back of my neck, a prickling warning that something had shifted.

"Don't like the idea?" I prodded, abruptly reminded of a redhead from his past—Dr. Anne Lucas.

"I like you just the way you are. That said, if you want a change, I won't object. It's your body, your right. But don't do it just because of them."

"Would you still want me?"

The tightness around his mouth eased, the inflexibility on his face fading away nearly as swiftly as it had appeared. "Would you still want me if I had red hair?"

"Hmm." I tapped my chin with my finger, pretending to contemplate the change. "Maybe we should stick with what we've got."

Gideon kissed my forehead. "That's what I signed up for."

"You also signed up for letting me have my way with you tonight."

"Name the time and place."

"Eight o'clock? Your apartment on the Upper West Side?"

"*Our* apartment." He kissed me softly. "I'll be there."

13

"BY THE WAY, congratulations on your engagement."

My gaze shifted from the project engineer's face on my monitor to the photo of Eva blowing kisses. "Thank you."

I would much rather look at my wife. For an instant, I pictured Eva as she'd been the night before, those plush lips wrapped around my cock. I had given her carte blanche with my body and all she'd wanted was to suck me off. Again and again. And again. *Christ.* I had been thinking about the night we'd had all day long.

"I'll keep you posted on the impact of the storm," he said, bringing my attention back to work. "I appreciate you calling personally to check on us. The weather conditions may set us back a week or two, depending, but we'll open on time."

"We have a cushion. Take care of yourself and your crew first."

"Will do. Thanks."

I closed the chat window and checked my schedule, needing to know exactly how much time I had to prepare for my next meeting with the lead R and D team at PosIT.

Scott's voice projected from my phone's speaker. "Christopher Vidal Sr. is on line one. It's his third call today. I've already told him you'll get back to him when you can, but he's insistent. How do you want me to handle?"

Calls from my stepfather never boded well, which meant delaying them ate into the time I had to fix whatever problem he needed to impose on me. "I'll take it."

I hit the speaker button. "Chris, what can I do for you?"

"Gideon. Listen, I'm sorry to disturb you, but you and I need to talk. Would it be possible for us to meet today?"

Prodded by the urgency in his voice, I picked up the receiver and took him off speaker. "My office or yours?"

"No, your penthouse."

I sat back, surprised. "I won't be home until close to nine."

"That's fine."

"Is everyone all right?"

"Yes, everyone's fine. Don't worry about that."

"It's Vidal, then. We'll take care of it."

"God." He laughed harshly. "You're a good man, Gideon. One of the best I know. I should've told you that more often."

My gaze narrowed at the edge in his tone. "I've got a few minutes now. Just lay it out."

"No, not now. I'll see you at nine."

He hung up. I sat for a long minute with the receiver in my hand. There was a knot in my gut, one that was cold and sharp.

I returned the receiver to its cradle and my attention to work, pulling up schematics and reviewing the packet Scott had placed on my desk earlier. Still, my mind raced.

I couldn't control what happened with my family, had never had any power there. I could only clean up the messes Christopher made and try to keep Vidal from going under. I drew the line, however, at using the footage of Eva. Nothing Chris could say would change that.

Time was racing toward the PosIT meeting when the message app popped up on my monitor and Eva's avatar appeared.

I can still taste you. Yummy. ☺

A dry laugh escaped me. The knot I'd been ignoring eased, then disappeared. She was my clean slate. My fresh start.

Soothed, I replied. The pleasure was mine.

"I'VE got a lead."

My head turned to find Raúl entering my office.

He came to my desk with brisk strides. "I'm still running through the guest list for that event you attended a couple weeks ago. I've also been running twice-daily searches for photos. Got an alert on this one today. I secured a copy and made some zoom views."

I glanced at the photos he slid across my desk. Picking them up, I examined them more closely, one by one. There was a redhead in the background. In each successive picture, she was brought closer to the fore. "Emerald green dress, long red hair. This is the woman Eva saw."

It was also Anne Lucas. Something about the way she was standing, with her face averted, spurred a familiar sickness in my gut.

I looked up at Raúl. "She wasn't on the guest list?"

"Not officially, but she was on the red carpet, so I'm thinking she had to have been someone's plus-one. I don't know who her escort was yet, but I'm on it."

Restless, I stood, shoving my chair back. "She went after Eva. You need to keep her away from my wife."

"Angus and I are developing new protocols for event security."

Turning, I retrieved my jacket from its hook. "You'll tell me if you need more men."

"I'll let you know." He scooped up the photos and started toward

222 · SYLVIA DAY

me. "She's at her office today," he said, accurately gauging my intention. "Was still there when I headed up to see you."

"Good. Let's go."

"Excuse me." The petite brunette behind the desk stood in a rush as I walked by. "You can't go in there. Dr. Lucas is with a patient now."

I grabbed the knob and opened the door, walking into Anne's office without breaking stride.

Her head snapped up, her green eyes widening the instant before her red mouth curved in a satisfied smile. The woman on the couch across from her blinked at me in confusion, swallowing whatever she'd been about to say.

"I'm so sorry, Dr. Lucas," the brunette said breathlessly. "I tried to stop him."

Anne slithered to her feet, her eyes on me. "An impossible task, Michelle. Don't worry, you can go."

The receptionist backed out. Anne glanced at her patient. "We'll have to cut today's appointment short. I apologize for this incredibly rude interruption"—she glared at me—"and of course I won't charge you. Please talk to Michelle about rescheduling."

I waited in the open door as the flustered woman gathered her stuff, and then I moved aside as she stepped out.

"I could've called security," Anne said, leaning back against the front of her desk and crossing her arms.

"After going to all the trouble of luring me here? You wouldn't."

"I don't know what you're talking about. Regardless, it's good to see you." She dropped her arms and gripped the edge of her desk in a deliberately provocative pose, exposing her bare thigh as the slit in her blue wrap dress slid open.

"I can't say the same."

Her smile tightened. "Break your toys, then throw them away. Does Eva know her days are numbered?"

"Do you?"

Unease dimmed her bright eyes and shook her smile. "Is that a threat, Gideon?"

"You'd like for it to be." I stepped closer, watched her pupils dilate. She was becoming aroused and that revolted me as much as the smell of her perfume. "Might make your game more interesting."

She straightened and came toward me, her hips swaying, her red-soled black stilettos sinking into the plush carpet.

"You like to play, too, lover," she purred. "Tell me, have you tied up your pretty fiancée? Flogged her into a frenzy? Shoved one of your extensive array of dildos into her ass, so that it fucked her while you pounded her pussy for hours? Does she know you, Gideon, the way I do?"

"Hundreds of women know me the way you do, Anne. Do you think you were special? The only thing memorable about you is your husband and how it eats at him that I've had you."

Her hand swung up to slap me and I didn't stop her, taking the hit unflinchingly.

I wish what I'd said were true, but I had been particularly depraved with her, seeing ghosts of her brother in the curve of her smile, her mannerisms—

I caught her wrist when she made a grab for my cock. "Leave Eva alone. I won't tell you twice."

"She's the chink in your armor, you heartless piece of shit. You've got ice in your veins, but she bleeds."

"Is that a threat, Anne?" I asked, calmly tossing her words back to her.

"Absolutely." She yanked free of my grip. "It's time to pay, and your billions won't cover the debt."

"Raising the stakes with a declaration of war? Are you that stupid? Or don't you care what this will cost you? Your career . . . your marriage . . . everything."

I moved toward the door, my stride leisurely even as fury burned through me. I'd brought this down on Eva. I had to clean it up.

"Just watch me, Gideon," she called after me. "See what happens."

"Have it your way." I paused with my hand on the doorknob. "You've started this, but make no mistake, the final move will be mine."

"HAVE you had any nightmares since we last saw each other?" Dr. Petersen asked, his demeanor laid back and quietly interested, the requisite tablet in his lap.

"No."

"How often would you say you have them?"

I sat as comfortably as the easygoing doctor but was irritably restless inside. I had too much to deal with to waste an hour of my time. "Lately, once a week. Sometimes a little longer in between."

"What do you mean by *lately*?"

"Since I met Eva."

He jotted something down with his stylus. "You're facing unfamiliar pressures as you work on your relationship with Eva, but the frequency of your nightmares is lessening—at least for now. Do you have any thoughts as to why?"

"I thought you were supposed to be explaining that to me."

Dr. Petersen smiled. "I can't wave a magic wand and give you all the answers, Gideon. I can only help you sort through it."

I was tempted to wait for him to say more, make him do most of the talking. But the thought of Eva and her hopes that therapy was going to make some sort of difference goaded me to speak. I'd promised to try, so I would. To a degree. "Things are smoothing out for us. We're in sync more than we're not."

"Do you feel that you're communicating better?"

"I think we're better at gauging the motives behind each other's actions. We understand each other more."

"Your relationship has moved very quickly. You're not an impulsive man, but many would say marrying a woman you've known such a short time—and one you admit you're still getting to know—is extremely impulsive."

"Is there a question there?"

"An observation." He waited a moment, but when I didn't say anything, he went on. "It can be difficult for spouses of individuals with Eva's history. Her commitment to therapy has helped both of you; however, it's likely she'll continue to change in ways you may not expect. It will be stressful for you."

"I'm no picnic myself," I said dryly.

"You're a survivor of a different sort. Have you ever felt that your nightmares were aggravated by stress?"

The question irritated me. "What does it matter? They happen."

"You don't feel there are changes that can be made to lessen their impact?"

"I just got married. That's a major life change, wouldn't you say, Doctor? I think that's enough for now."

"Why must there be a limit? You're a young man, Gideon. You have a variety of options available to you. Change doesn't have to be something avoided. What's the harm in trying something new? If it doesn't work out, you always have the option to go back to what you were doing before."

I found that wryly amusing. "Sometimes, you can't go back."

"Let's try a simple change now," Dr. Petersen said, setting his tablet aside. "Let's go for a walk."

I found myself standing when he did, not wanting to be seated while he towered above me. We stood face-to-face with the coffee table between us. "Why?"

"Why not?" He gestured toward the door. "My office may not be the best place for us to talk. You're a man used to being in charge. In here, I am. So we'll level the playing field and hit the hallway for a bit. It's a public space, but most of the individuals who work in this building have gone home."

I exited his office before him, watching as he locked both his inner and outer office doors before joining me.

"Ah, well. This is certainly different," he said, his mouth curving wryly. "Knocks me off my stride a bit."

I shrugged and started walking.

"What are your plans for the rest of the evening?" he asked, falling into step beside me.

"An hour with my trainer." And then I said more. "My stepfather is coming over later."

"To spend time with you and Eva? Are you close to him?"

"No, to both." I stared straight ahead. "Something's wrong. That's the only reason he ever calls me."

I sensed his gaze on my profile. "Do you wish that were different?"

"No."

"You don't like him?"

"I don't dislike him." I was going to leave it at that, but again I thought of Eva. "We just don't know each other very well."

"You could change that."

I huffed out a laugh. "You're really pushing that angle tonight."

"I told you, I don't have an angle." He stopped, forcing me to stop, too.

Tipping his chin up, he eyed the ceiling, clearly thinking. "When you're considering an acquisition or exploring a new avenue of doing business, you bring in people to advise you, right? Experts in their respective fields?" He looked at me again, smiling. "You could think of me the same way, as an expert consultant."

"On what?"

"Your past." He resumed walking. "I help you with that, you can figure out the rest of your life yourself."

"GET your head in the game, Cross."

My gaze narrowed. Across the mat, James Cho hopped on his bare feet, taunting me. He grinned evilly, knowing the unspoken challenge would spur me on. Half a foot shorter than me and lighter by at least thirty pounds, the former MMA champion was lethally quick and had the belt to prove it.

Rolling my shoulders back, I adjusted my stance. My fists came up, closing the opening that had allowed his last punch to connect with my torso.

"Make it worth my while, Cho," I fired back, irritated that he was right. My brain was still back in Dr. Petersen's office. A switch had been thrown tonight and I couldn't get a handle on what it was or what it meant.

James and I circled, feinting and striking out, neither of us scoring a hit. As always, it was just the two of us in the dojo. The driving beat of taiko drums rumbled in the background from speakers cleverly hidden in the floor-to-ceiling bamboo paneling.

"You're still holding back," he said. "Falling in love turn you into a pussy?"

"You wish. Only way you'd beat me."

James laughed, then came at me with a roundhouse kick. I dropped low and swept him, taking him down. He scissored his legs with lightning speed, taking me down with him.

We hopped back up. Squared off again.

"You're wasting my time," he snapped, his fist lashing out.

I ducked to the side. My left fist shot out, grazing his side. His fist hit my ribs straight on.

"No one piss you off today?" He came at me in a rush, giving me no option to do anything but defend myself.

I growled. Rage was simmering in the back of my mind, tucked away until I had the time and attention to deal with it.

"Yeah. I see that fire in your eyes, Cross. Let it out, man. Bring it on."

She's the chink in your armor . . .

I lashed out with a left/right combo, driving James back a step.

"That all you got?" he jeered.

I feigned a kick and then threw out a punch, snapping his head back.

"Fuck yeah," he gasped, flexing his arms, getting pumped. "There you are."

She bleeds . . .

Snarling, I lunged forward.

REFRESHED from a shower, I had barely finished dressing by pulling a T-shirt over my head when my smartphone started ringing. I picked it up off the bed where I'd left it and answered.

"A couple things," Raúl said after greeting me, the background noise of a crowd and music quickly fading, then disappearing completely. "I've noticed that Benjamin Clancy is still keeping an eye on Mrs. Cross. Not constantly, but consistently."

"Is that so," I said quietly.

"Are you good with that? Or should I talk to him?"

"I'll deal with him." Clancy and I were due for a chat. It had been on my list, but I would move it up.

"Also—and you may know this already—Mrs. Cross had lunch with Ryan Landon and some of his executives today."

I felt that terrible quiet settle over me. Landon. Fuck.

He'd slid in somewhere I hadn't been watching.

"Thank you, Raúl. I'll need a private number for Eva's boss, Mark Garrity."

"I'll text it to you when I have it."

Ending the call, I shoved the phone in my pocket, barely resisting the urge to throw it at the wall instead.

Arash had warned me about Landon and I'd brushed his concerns off. I'd been focused on my life, my wife, and while Landon had a wife of his own, his primary focus had always been me.

The ringing of the penthouse phone jolted me. I went to the receiver on the nightstand and answered with an impatient, "Cross."

"Mr. Cross. It's Edwin at the front desk. Mr. Vidal is here to see you."

Jesus. My grip tightened on the receiver. "Send him up."

"Yes, sir. Will do."

Grabbing my socks and shoes, I carried them out to the living room and pulled them on. As soon as Chris left, I was heading home to Eva. I wanted to open a bottle of wine, find one of the older movies she knew by heart, and just listen to her recite the corny lines of dialogue. No one could make me laugh like she did.

I heard the elevator car arrive and pushed to my feet, running a hand through my damp hair. I was tense and despised the weakness.

"Gideon." Chris paused on the threshold of the foyer, looking grim and worn, which he so rarely did and only then because of my brother. "Is Eva here?"

"She's at her place. I'm heading over there when you leave."

He gave a jerky nod, his jaw working but nothing coming out of his mouth.

"Come in," I said, gesturing at the wingback chair by the coffee table. "Can I get you something to drink?"

God knew I needed one myself after the day I'd had so far.

He stepped wearily into my living room. "Anything strong would be great."

"Sounds good to me." I went to the kitchen and poured us both a glass of Armagnac. As I was setting the decanter down, my phone vibrated in my pocket. Pulling it out, I saw a message from Eva.

It was a selfie of her bare leg glistening with water and draped over the rim of her bathtub with candles in the background. Join me?

I swiftly revised my plans for the evening. She'd been sending me provocative texts all day. I was more than happy to both satisfy and reward her.

I saved the photo and typed back. Wish I could. Promise to make you wet again when I get there.

Tucking my phone away, I turned and found Chris joining me at the island. I slid a tumbler over to him and took a sip from mine. "What's going on, Chris?"

He sighed, both of his hands wrapping around the crystal. "We're going to reshoot the 'Golden' video."

"Oh?" That was an unnecessary expense, something Chris wisely avoided as a rule.

"I overheard Kline and Christopher arguing in the offices yesterday," he said gruffly, "and got the story. Kline wants a redo and I agreed."

"Christopher doesn't, I'm sure." I leaned back against the counter, my jaw set. Apparently, Brett Kline had some serious feelings for Eva after all. I wasn't okay with that. Not even close.

"Your brother will get over it."

I doubted that, but it would do no good to say so.

But Chris read what I didn't say and gave a nod. "I know the video has caused stress for you and Eva. I should've been paying more attention."

"I appreciate you being flexible about it."

He stared into his glass and then took a long drink, nearly downing the contents in a single swallow. "I've left your mother."

I took a quick, deep breath, grasping that the reason for his visit had nothing to do with work. "Ireland told me you two had a fight."

"Yeah. I hate that Ireland had to hear it." He looked at me, and I saw the knowledge in his eyes. The horror. "I didn't know, Gideon. I swear to God, I didn't know."

My heart jerked in my chest, then began to pound. My mouth went dry.

"I, uh, went to see Terrence Lucas." Chris's voice grew hoarse. "Barged into his office. He denied it, the lying son of a bitch, but I could see it on his face."

The brandy sloshed in my glass. I set it down carefully, feeling the floor shift under my feet. Eva had confronted Lucas, but Chris . . . ?

"I decked him, knocked him out cold, but God . . . I wanted to take one of those awards on his shelves and bash his head in."

"Stop." The word broke from my throat like slivers of glass.

"And the asshole who did . . . That asshole is dead. I can't get to him. Goddamn it." Chris dropped the tumbler onto the granite with a thud, but it was the sob that tore out of him that nearly shattered me. "Hell, Gideon. It was my job to protect you. And I failed."

"Stop!" I pushed off the counter, my hands clenching. "Don't fucking look at me like that!"

He trembled visibly, but didn't back down. "I had to tell you—"

His wrinkled dress shirt was in my fists, his feet dangling above the floor. "Stop talking. Now!"

Tears slipped down his face. "I love you like my own. Always have."

I shoved him away. Turned my back to him when he stumbled and hit the wall. I left, crossing the living room without seeing it.

"I'm not expecting your forgiveness," he called after me, tears clogging his words. "I don't deserve it. But you need to hear that I would've ripped him apart with my bare hands if I'd known."

I rounded on him, feeling the sickness clawing up from my gut and burning my throat. *"What the fuck do you want?"*

Chris pulled his shoulders back. He faced me with reddened eyes and wet cheeks, shaking but too stupid to run. "I want you to know that you're not alone."

Alone. Yes. Far away from the pity and guilt and pain staring out at me through his tears. "Get out."

Nodding, he headed toward the foyer. I stood immobile, my chest heaving, my eyes burning. Words backed up in my throat; violence pounded in the painful clench of my fists.

He stopped before he left the room, facing me. "I'm glad you told Eva."

"Don't talk about her." I couldn't bear to even think of her. Not now, when I was so close to losing it.

He left.

The weight of the day crashed onto my shoulders, dropping me to my knees.

I broke.

14

I WAS DREAMING of a private beach and naked Gideon when I was jerked awake by the sound of my phone ringing. Rolling to my side, I thrust my arm out and smacked around on the top of my nightstand, trying to find my smartphone in the dark. My fingers brushed against the familiar shape and I grabbed it, sitting up.

Ireland's face lit up my screen. I frowned and glanced at the space beside me in the bed. Gideon wasn't home. Of course, he could've found me sleeping and gone next door to go to bed . . .

"Hello?" I answered, noting that the time on the cable box said it was after eleven o'clock.

"Eva. It's Chris Vidal. I'm sorry to call so late, but I'm worried about Gideon. Is he all right?"

My stomach dropped. "What do you mean? What's wrong with Gideon?"

There was a pause. "You haven't talked to him tonight?"

I slid out of bed and turned on the lamp. "No. I fell asleep. What's going on?"

He cursed with an intensity that made the hairs rise on my arms. "I met with him earlier about . . . the things you told me. He didn't take it well."

"Oh my God." I spun around blindly. Something to wear. I needed something to put on over the racy teddy I'd planned to seduce Gideon with.

"You have to find him, Eva," he said urgently. "He needs you now."

"I'm going." I tossed the phone on my bed and yanked a wool trench coat out of my closet before racing out of my room. I grabbed the keys to the next-door apartment from my purse and ran down the hall. Fumbling with the deadbolt, I took too long to open the door.

The place was as shadowy and silent as a tomb, the rooms empty.

"Where are you?" I cried into the darkness, feeling the scratch of panicked tears in my throat.

I ended up back in my apartment, my fingers trembling as I opened the app on my smartphone that would track his.

He didn't take it well.

God. Of course, he didn't. He hadn't taken it well when I'd told Chris initially. Gideon had been furious. Aggressive. He'd had a horrible nightmare.

The blinking red dot on the map was right where I was hoping it would be. "The penthouse."

I shoved my feet into flip-flops and hurried back out to my purse.

"What the hell are you wearing?" Cary asked from the kitchen, jolting me.

"Jesus, you just scared the shit out of me!"

He sauntered up to the breakfast bar in just his Grey Isles boxer briefs, his chest and neck glistening with sweat. Since the air-conditioning was working fine and Trey was spending the night, I knew exactly how and why Cary was overheated.

"It's a good thing I did—you can't go out like that," he drawled.

"Watch me." I slung my bag over my shoulder and headed toward the door.

"You're a freak, baby girl," he shouted after me. "A woman after my own heart!"

GIDEON's doorman didn't bat an eye when I climbed out of the back of the taxi in front of his building. Of course, the man had seen me in worse shape before. So had the concierge, who smiled and greeted me by name as if I didn't look like a crazy homeless person. Albeit one in a Burberry coat.

I walked as fast as I could in flip-flops to the private penthouse elevator, waited for it to descend to me, then keyed in the code. It was a straight shot up, but the ride felt endless. I wished I could pace the confines of the small, elegantly appointed car. My worried face stared back at me from the spotless mirrors.

Gideon hadn't called. Hadn't sent me a text after the flirtatious one promising me a steamy night. Hadn't come to me, even if only to sleep next door. Gideon didn't like being away from me.

Except when he was hurting. And ashamed.

The elevator doors slid open and pounding, screaming heavy metal music poured in. I cringed and covered my ears, the volume of the ceiling-mounted speakers so loud it hurt to hear them.

Pain. Fury. The raging violence of the music crashed over me. I ached deep in my chest. I knew. I understood. The song was an audible manifestation of what Gideon felt inside himself and couldn't let out.

He was too controlled. Contained. His emotions so tightly leashed, along with his memories.

I dug into my purse for my phone and ended up dropping the whole bag, spilling the contents onto the elevator car floor and across the checkerboard foyer. I left it all where it fell except for my smartphone, which I picked up and swiped through to get to the app that controlled the surround sound. I synced it to softer music, lowered the volume, and hit enter.

The penthouse fell silent for an endless moment, and then the gentle chords of "Collide" by Howie Day began to play.

I felt Gideon approaching before I saw him, the air crackling with the violent energy of an impending summer storm. He rounded the corner from the hallway leading to the bedrooms. I lost my breath.

He was shirtless and barefooted, his hair a silky tousled mane that brushed his shoulders. Black sweats clung to the lowest point of his hips, underlining the tight lacing of his abs. He was bruised on his ribs and up by his shoulder, the signs of battle only strengthening the impression of rage and ferocity tightly leashed.

My choice of music clashed with the emotion seething from him. My beautiful, savagely elegant warrior. The love of my life. So tormented that the sight of him brought hot, stinging tears to my eyes.

He jerked to a halt when he saw me, his hands clenching and releasing at his sides, his eyes wild and nostrils flaring.

My phone slid out of my hand and hit the floor. "Gideon."

He sucked in a breath at the sound of my voice. It changed him. I watched the shift come over him, like a door slamming shut. One moment, he was bristling with emotion. The next, he was cool as ice, his surface as smooth as glass.

"What are you doing here?" he asked, his voice dangerously even.

"Finding you." Because he was lost.

"I'm not fit company now."

"I can deal with it."

He was too still, as if he were afraid to move. "You should go. It's not safe for you here."

My pulse leaped. Awareness sizzled across my senses. I felt the heat of him from across the room. His need. The demand. I was suddenly melting in my jacket. "I'm safer with you than anywhere else on earth." I took a deep breath for courage. "Does Chris believe you?"

His head went back. "How do you know?"

"He called. He's worried about you. I'm worried about you."

"I'll be fine," he snapped. Which told me he wasn't fine now.

I made my way to him, feeling the burn of his gaze as it tracked me. "Of course, you will be. You're married to me."

"You need to go, Eva."

I shook my head. "It almost hurts worse, doesn't it, when they believe you? You wonder why you waited to tell them. Maybe you could've stopped it sooner, if you'd just told the right person?"

"Shut up."

"There's always that little voice inside us that thinks we're to blame for what happened."

His eyes squeezed as tightly closed as his fists. "Don't."

I closed the distance between us. "Don't what?"

"Don't be what I need. Not now."

"Why not?"

Those fiercely blue eyes snapped open, pinning me so thoroughly that I paused midstep. "I'm hanging on by a thread, Eva."

"You don't have to hang on," I told him, holding my hands out to him. "Let go. I'll catch you."

"No." He shook his head. "I can't . . . I can't be gentle."

"You want to touch me."

His jaw worked. "I want to *fuck* you. Hard."

I felt the heat sweep up to my cheeks. It was a testament to how much he wanted me that he could still find me desirable despite my ridiculous clothes. "I'm totally up for that. Always."

My fingers went to the lapels of my coat. I'd partially buttoned up on the cab ride over, not wanting to flash anyone by accident. Now the trench was sweltering, my skin damp with perspiration.

Gideon lunged and caught my wrists, squeezing them too hard. "Don't."

"You don't think I can handle you? After all we've done together? All we've talked about and plan on doing?"

God. His entire body was straining, tense, every muscle thick and hard. And his eyes, so bright against his tanned skin, so agonized. My Dark and Dangerous.

He gripped my elbow and started walking.

"What—?" I stumbled.

He dragged me toward the elevator. "You have to go."

"No!" I struggled, kicking off my flip-flops and digging my feet in.

"Damn it." He rounded on me and yanked me up, facing me nose to nose. "I can't promise to stop. If I take you too far and you safe word, I might not stop and this—*us*—will all go to hell!"

"Gideon! For chrissakes, don't be afraid to want me too much!"

"I want to punish you," he snarled, gripping my face in both hands. "You did this! You brought this on. Pushing people . . . pushing me. Look what you've done!"

I smelled the liquor on him then, the rich vapor of some expensive spirit. I'd never seen him truly drunk—he valued his control too much to completely dull his senses—but he was drunk now.

The first hint of wariness rippled through me.

"Yes," I said shakily, "this is my fault. I love you too much. Will you punish me for that?"

"God." He closed his eyes. His hot, damp forehead touched mine, nuzzling hard. His sweat coated my skin, imprinting me with the lushly masculine scent that was his alone.

I felt him soften, relaxing infinitesimally. I turned my head and pressed my lips to his feverish cheek.

He stiffened. "No."

Gideon pulled me toward the elevator, yanking me into the foyer and kicking the scattered contents of my purse out of the way.

"Stop it!" I yelled, trying to tug my arm free.

But he wouldn't listen. His finger stabbed at the call button. The car doors opened instantly, the private elevator always waiting to take him down. He threw me in and I stumbled into the rear wall.

Desperate, I yanked at the belt of my coat, my urgency giving me strength. I tore at the buttons, sending them rolling in every direction. The doors were closing when I spun to face him, holding the lapels of my coat wide open so he could see what I was wearing beneath.

His arm shot out, blocking the door from closing. He shoved it open. The teddy I'd worn was bloodred—our color—and had scarcely any material to it at all. Sheer mesh exposed my breasts and sex, while bandagelike cutouts caged my waist.

"Bitch," he hissed, stalking into the confined space, shrinking it too small. "You can't stop pushing."

"I'm *your* bitch," I shot back, feeling the tears well and fall. It was painful to have him so angry with me, even though I understood. He needed an outlet and I'd positioned myself as the target. He'd warned me . . . tried to protect me . . . "I can take you, Gideon Cross. I can take whatever you've got."

He tackled me back into the wall so hard the impact knocked the breath from me. His mouth covered mine, his tongue plunging deep. His hands squeezed my breasts roughly, his knee pressing hard between my legs.

I arched into him, fighting to shrug off my coat. I was too hot, sweat sliding down my back and belly. Gideon wrenched the trench off, tossing it aside, his mouth sealed to mine. A moan of gratitude escaped me, my arms wrapping around his neck, my heart swelling with the relief of holding him. My fingers pushed into his hair, my grip tightening to give me leverage to crawl up him.

Gideon tore his mouth away, then my hands. "Don't touch me."

"Fuck you," I snapped, too hurt to hold the words back. Just to spite him, I broke free of his grip and let my hands roam over his rock-hard shoulders and biceps.

He pushed me back, holding me to the wall with a single hand against the middle of my chest. No matter how I shoved or scratched at his steely arm, I couldn't budge him. I could only watch as he yanked the drawstring free of his sweats.

Desire and apprehension twisted together inside me. "Gideon . . . ?"

His gaze met mine, so dark and haunted. "Can you keep your hands off me?"

"No. I don't want to."

With a nod, he released me, only to spin me around to face the rear of the car. Caged by his body, I had little room to maneuver.

"Don't fight me," he ordered, his lips to my ear.

Then he tied my wrists to the handrail.

I froze, startled that he was actually restraining me. So surprised and disbelieving that I barely struggled. It was only after I watched him knot the thin cord that I realized he was serious.

Gripping my hips, he nuzzled my hair aside and sank his teeth into my shoulder. "I say when."

I gasped, tugging at my hands. "What are you doing?"

He didn't answer me.

He just left.

Twisting around as much as I was able, I caught him walking into the living room just as the doors slid shut.

"Oh my God," I breathed. "You wouldn't."

I couldn't believe he'd send me away like this . . . tied up in the elevator in only lingerie. He was presently screwed up in the head, yes, but I couldn't believe my wildly jealous husband would expose me that way, to whoever might be in the lobby, just to get rid of me.

"*Gideon!* Goddamn it. Don't you dare leave me in here like this! Do you *hear* me?! Get your ass back in here!"

I wrenched at the cord binding my wrists, but it was knotted tight.

Seconds passed, then minutes. The car didn't move and after screaming myself hoarse, I realized it wouldn't. It waited for the push of a
button, standing by for Gideon's command.

Just like I was.

I was going to kick his fucking ass when I got loose. I'd never been
so pissed. *"Gideon!"*

Bending over, I walked backward, then lifted and stretched one leg
to reach the button that opened the doors. I pushed it with my big toe.
As they slid open, I sucked in a deep breath to scream . . .

. . . then promptly lost it in a startled rush.

Gideon strode through the living room toward the foyer . . .
completely naked. And drenched from head to toe. His cock was so hard
it curved up to his navel. His head was tipped back as he guzzled bottled water, his stride loose and easy, yet entirely predatory.

I straightened as he drew closer, panting from both the riot of my
emotions and the depth of my hunger. Asshole or not, I wanted him
with a ferocity I couldn't fight. He was complicated and sexy, damaged
and perfect.

"Here." He brought a crystal tumbler to my lips that I hadn't noticed because I'd been too busy ogling his magnificent body. The glass
was nearly full, the reddish-gold liquid sloshing against my lips as he
tipped it.

My mouth opened by instinct and he poured the liquor in, the potent proof burning my tongue and throat. I coughed and he waited,
his gaze heavy-lidded. He smelled clean and cool, refreshed from a
shower.

"Finish it."

"It's too strong!" I protested.

He simply poured another large swallow past my parted lips.

I kicked at him, cursing when I hurt my foot—and didn't do any
damage to him at all. "Stop it!"

He dropped the empty water bottle and cupped my face in his

hand. His thumb brushed away the drops of liquor on my chin. "You need to let me settle, and you need to mellow out. We go at it like this, we'll tear each other apart."

A stupid tear slipped out of the corner of my eye.

Gideon groaned and bent toward me, his tongue licking the trail of the droplet off my cheek. "I'm shattered and you're beating at me with your fists. I can't take it, Eva."

"I can't take you shutting me out," I whispered, tugging at the damned cord. The liquor was spreading fire through my veins. I could feel the tendrils of intoxication curling around my senses already.

He put his hand over mine, stilling my restless movements. "Stop that. You'll hurt yourself."

"Cut me loose."

"You touch me and I can't keep it together. I'm hanging by a thread," he said again, sounding desperate. "I can't snap. Not with you."

"With someone else?" My voice became shrill. "You need someone else?"

I couldn't keep it together, either. Gideon was the rock in our relationship, the anchor. I thought I could be the same for him. I wanted to shelter him, be his haven. But Gideon didn't need shelter from the storm; he *was* the storm. And I wasn't strong enough to bear up under the weight of his crashing mood.

"No. Christ." He kissed me. Hard. "You need me in control. *I* need to be in control when I'm with you."

I felt the panic building. He knew. He knew I wasn't enough. "You were different with the others. You didn't hold back—"

"*Fuck!*" Gideon spun away, slamming his fist into the control panel. The doors opened to the sound of Sarah McLachlan singing about possession and he threw the tumbler, shattering it against the foyer wall. "Yes, I was different! *You* made me different."

"And you hate me for that." I started crying, my body sagging into the car wall.

"No." He wrapped himself around me, his water-chilled body curving over my back. He rubbed his face against me, his embrace so tight I could barely breathe. "I love you. You're my *wife*. My goddamn life. You're everything."

"I just want to help you," I cried. "I want to be here for you, but you won't let me!"

"God. Eva." His hands began to move, to pet and glide. To stroke. To soothe. "I can't stop you. I need you too much."

I gripped the handrail with both hands, my cheek pressed to the cool mirror. The liquor began to work its magic. A heated languor slid through me, drowning my anger and what fight I had left until they drifted away, leaving me sad and afraid and so desperately, terrifyingly in love.

His hand pushed between my legs, rubbing, searching. With a forceful tug, he opened the snaps that held the front and back of the teddy together. I moaned at the sudden release of pressure. My sex was wet and swollen from the skilled movements of his hands and the image in my mind of the way he'd looked walking toward me.

My head fell back against his shoulder and I saw his reflection. His eyes were closed, his lips parted. The vulnerability etched on his gorgeous face undid me. He was hurting so badly. I couldn't bear it.

"Tell me what I can do," I whispered. "Tell me how to help."

"Shh." His tongue rimmed the shell of my ear. "Let me settle."

The featherlight stroke of his thumb over the mesh covering my nipple was driving me mad. The slide of his fingers between the slick folds of my cleft had me quivering. He knew where to touch me, how much pressure.

I cried out when he pushed two fingers inside me, my feet flexing, lifting me onto my toes. My knees weakened, my legs quivering with the strain. The air in the elevator felt thick and steamy, heavy with the need that pumped off him in waves.

"Ah, Christ." He groaned when my sex tightened around him, his hips rolling against me to grind his erection into my buttocks. "I'm going to bruise this sweet cunt, Eva. I can't stop it."

His arm banded around my waist and lifted me, pulling me back so that my arms were straight and I was bent over. He kneed my legs apart, his fingers sliding wetly from my cleft. I felt his hand graze my hip, and then he was dragging the wide crest of his penis through the seam of my buttocks and notching it between the lips of my sex.

I held my breath, squirming against that plush pressure. I'd wanted him all day, craving the feel of his big cock inside me, needing him to make me come.

"Wait," he groaned, reaching for both my waist and my shoulder, his fingers flexing impatiently. "Let me—"

My sex clenched, tightening around the thick head.

Gideon cursed and thrust, one hard stroke that shoved him deep. I cried out in pleasured pain, arching away from the rigid fullness, feeling the burn of stretching inner muscles and tender tissues.

"Yes," he hissed, yanking me back into him until the lips of my sex hugged the thick root of his penis. His hips circled, his balls lying heavily against my engorged clitoris. "Fucking tight . . ."

I moaned and tried to hold on to the handrail; my body rocked as he began to fuck. The sensation was devastating, being filled so completely, then emptied abruptly. My knees gave out, my core spasming in delight as he reamed me hard and thoroughly. All the emotion he'd pent up inside him was hammered into me, the relentless drives of his cock massaging every sensitive nerve.

I was coming before I knew the orgasm was on me, gasping his name as pleasure racked my body in violent trembles.

My head dropped between my arms, my muscles weak and useless. Gideon held me up with his hands, with his erection. Using my body. Taking it. Grunting primitively every time he hit the end of me.

"So deep," he growled. "So good."

In the periphery, I caught movement, my dazed eyes focusing on our reflection. With a low, pained cry I started coming again, if I'd ever stopped. Gideon was the most searingly erotic thing I'd ever seen—his biceps thick and hard as he supported my weight, his thighs straining with exertion, his ass flexing as he pistoned, his abs rippling with power as he rolled his hips with every stroke.

He'd been built to fuck, but he had mastered the skill, using every inch of his amazing body to enslave a woman to pleasure. It was innate to him, instinctive. Even drunk and near feral with anguish, his rhythm was tight and precise, his focus absolute.

Every thrust took him deep inside me, hitting the sweetest spots again and again, driving the ecstasy into me until I couldn't resist the onslaught. Another climax churned through me like a tidal wave.

"That's it," he groaned. "Milk my dick, angel. God . . . You're making me come."

I felt his cock thickening, lengthening. Tingles raced across my skin; my lungs heaved for air.

Gideon threw back his head and roared like an animal, spurting hotly. Gripping my hips, he pumped me onto his ejaculating cock, coming hard and forever, filling me until semen slicked my sex and inner thighs.

He slowed the thrust of his hips, gasping, bending over to press his cheek to my shoulder.

I started sinking to my knees. "Gideon . . ."

He pulled me up. "I'm not done," he said roughly, still thick and stiff inside me.

Then he started again.

I woke to the feel of his hair brushing over my shoulder and the press of warm, firm lips. Exhausted, I tried to roll away, but an arm around my waist pulled me back.

"Eva," he rasped. His hand cupped my breast, clever fingers rolling my nipple.

It was dark and we were in bed, although I barely remembered him carrying me there. He'd undressed me, washed me with a damp cloth, and rained kisses over my face and wrists. They were bandaged now, slicked with ointment and wrapped with care.

It had turned me on to feel his tender caresses over the chafing, the mix of pleasure and pain. He'd noticed.

With eyes hot with lust, he'd spread my legs and eaten me with an insistent demand that robbed me of the ability to think or move. He'd licked and sucked my cleft endlessly, until I lost count of how many times he made me come around his wicked tongue.

"Gideon . . ." Turning my head, I looked at him over my shoulder. He was propped on one arm, his eyes glittering in the faint light of the moon. "Did you stay with me?"

Maybe it was reckless to hope he'd stayed with me while I slept, but sharing a bed with him was something I loved. And craved.

He nodded. "I couldn't leave you."

"I'm glad."

He rolled me over and into him, taking my mouth, kissing me softly. The coaxing licks of his tongue stirred me again, made me moan.

"I can't stop touching you," he breathed, gripping my nape to hold me still as he deepened the kiss, his teeth tugging gently on my lower lip. "When I touch you, I don't think about anything else."

Tenderness blended with the love. "Can I touch you, too?"

Closing his eyes, he begged. "Please."

I surged into him, my hands sliding into his hair to hold him as he held me. I brushed my tongue against his, our mouths hot and wet. Our legs tangled, my body arching to press against the hardness of his.

He hummed softly and slowed me down, rolling to pin me to the bed. Pulling back, he broke the seal of our mouths, nibbling, sucking. Tracing the curves of my lips with the tip of his tongue.

I whimpered in protest, wanting deeper, harder. Instead, he licked leisurely, stroking the roof of my mouth, the lining of my cheeks. I tightened my legs, dragging him closer. He rocked his hips, pressing his erection into my thigh.

Gideon kissed me until my lips were hot and puffy and the sun was rising in the sky. He kissed me until he came in a hot rush against my skin. Not once but twice.

The feel of him coming, the sound of his low pained moans of pleasure, knowing I could bring him to orgasm with just my kiss . . . I slicked his thigh with my need and ground against him until I climaxed.

As the new day began, he closed the distance he'd put between us in the elevator. He made love to me without sex. He pledged his devotion by making me the center of his world. There was nothing beyond the edges of our bed. Only us and a love that stripped us bare even as it made us whole.

WHEN I woke again, I found him sleeping beside me, his lips as kiss-swollen as mine. Gideon's face was soft in repose, but the faint frown between his brows told me he wasn't resting as deeply as I would wish. He lay on his side, his body stretched long and lean across the mattress, the sheet tangled around his legs.

It was late, nearly nine, but I didn't have the heart to either wake him or leave him. I hadn't been at my job long enough to miss a day, but I decided to do it anyway.

I'd been putting my needs first when it came to my career, giving it the power to someday put a wedge between us. I knew my desire to be independent wasn't wrong, but at that moment, it didn't feel right, either.

Pulling on a T-shirt and boyshorts, I slipped out of the bedroom and down the hall to Gideon's home office, where his smartphone was bitching that he was ignoring the alarm to wake him up. I turned it off and went to the kitchen.

Mentally checking off the things I needed to do, I called and left a message for Mark about missing work due to a family emergency. Then I called Scott's desk and left a message telling him that Gideon wasn't going to make it in by nine and might not be there at all. I told him to call me and we could talk about it.

I hoped to keep Gideon home all day, although I doubted he would agree to that. We needed time together, alone. Time to heal.

I retrieved my smartphone from the foyer and called Angus. He answered on the first ring.

"Hello, Mrs. Cross. Are you and Mr. Cross ready to go?"

"No, Angus, right now we're staying put. I'm not sure we'll be leaving the penthouse today. I was wondering, do you know where Gideon gets those bottles of hangover cure?"

"Yes, of course. Do you need one?"

"Gideon might when he wakes up. Just in case, I'd like to have one waiting for him."

There was a pause. "If you don't mind me asking," he asked, his Scottish burr more pronounced, "does this have something to do with Mr. Vidal's visit last night?"

I rubbed at my forehead, feeling the warning signs of an impending headache. "It has everything to do with it."

"Does Chris believe?" he asked quietly.

"Yes."

He sighed. "Ach, that's why, then. The lad wouldna been prepared for that. Denial is what he knows and can handle."

"He took it hard."

"Aye, I'm certain he did. It's good he has you, Eva. You're doing the right thing for him, though it may take him time to appreciate it. I'll get that bottle for you."

"Thank you."

With that accomplished, I turned my attention to cleaning the place up. I washed the empty decanter and tumbler I found on the kitchen island first, then took the broom and dustpan into the foyer to clean up the shattered glass. I talked to Scott when he called while I was picking up all the crap that had fallen out of my purse, and when we hung up, I turned my attention to scrubbing the foyer wall and floor to remove the dried traces of brandy.

Gideon had said he felt shattered the night before. I didn't want him to wake up and find his place that way.

Our place, I corrected myself. Our home. I needed to start thinking of it that way. And so did Gideon. We were going to have a conversation about him trying to kick me out. If I was going to make a better effort at entwining our lives, then he had to as well.

I wished there were someone I could talk to about it all, a friend to listen and give sage advice. Cary or Shawna. Even Steven, who had a way about him that made him so easy to talk to. We had Dr. Petersen, but that wasn't the same thing.

For now, Gideon and I had secrets we could share only with each other, and that kept us isolated and codependent. It wasn't only innocence our abusers had taken away from us; they'd also taken our freedom. Even after the abuse was long over, we were still caged by the false fronts we lived behind. Still caged by lies, but in a different way.

I had just finished polishing all the smudges off the mirror in the elevator when it began descending with me inside. In only a T-shirt and underwear.

"Seriously?" I muttered, yanking off my rubber gloves to try to put order to my hair. After rolling around with Gideon all night, I looked like an epic mess.

The doors slid open and Angus started to step in, his footstep halting midair when he spotted me. I shifted position, trying to hide the cord still tied to the handrail behind me. Gideon had cut me loose with scissors, freeing my wrists but leaving the evidence.

"Uh, hi," I said, squirming with embarrassment. There was no good way to explain how I happened to be in the elevator, scarcely dressed and holding yellow rubber gloves, when Angus had called it down to pick him up. To make things worse, my lips were so red and swollen from kissing Gideon for hours that there was no way to hide what I'd been up to all night.

Angus's pale blue eyes lit with amusement. "Good morning, Mrs. Cross."

"Good morning, Angus," I replied, with as much dignity as I could manage.

He held out a bottle of the hangover "cure," which I was pretty sure was just a shot of alcohol mixed with liquid vitamins. "Here you go."

"Thank you." The words were heartfelt and carried additional gratitude for his lack of questions.

"Call me if you need anything. I'll be nearby."

"You're the best, Angus." I rode back up to the penthouse. When the doors opened, I heard the penthouse phone ringing.

I made a run for it, sliding into the kitchen on my bare feet to snatch the receiver off its base, hoping the noise hadn't woken Gideon.

"Hello?"

"Eva, it's Arash. Is Cross with you?"

"Yes. He's still sleeping, I think. I'll check." I headed down the hall.

"He's not sick, is he? He's never sick."

"There's a first time for everything." Peeking into the bedroom, I found my husband sprawled magnificently in sleep, his arms wrapped around my pillow with his face buried in it. I tiptoed over to put the hangover bottle on his nightstand, and then I tiptoed back out, pulling the door closed behind me.

"He's still crashed," I whispered.

"Wow. Okay, change of plan. There are some documents you both have to sign before four this afternoon. I'll have them messengered over. Give me a call when you're done with them, and I'll send someone to pick them up."

"*I* have to sign something? What is it?"

"He didn't tell you?" He laughed. "Well, I won't ruin the surprise. You'll see when you get them. Call me if you have any questions."

I growled softly. "Okay. Thanks."

We hung up and I stared down the hall toward the bedroom with narrowed eyes. What was Gideon up to? It drove me crazy that he set things in motion and handled issues without talking to me about them.

My smartphone started ringing in the kitchen. I ran back across the living room and took a look at the screen. The number was an unfamiliar one but clearly based in New York.

"Good grief," I muttered, feeling like I'd already put in a full day of work and it was just past ten thirty in the morning. How the hell did Gideon manage being pulled in so many directions at once? "Hello?"

"Eva, it's Chris again. I hope you don't mind that Ireland gave me your number."

"No, it's fine. I'm sorry I didn't call you back sooner. I didn't mean to make you worry."

"Is he okay, then?"

I went to one of the bar stools and sat. "No. It was a rough night."

252 · SYLVIA DAY

"I called his office. They told me he was out this morning."

"We're home. He's still sleeping."

"It's bad, then," he said.

He knew my man. Gideon was a creature of habit, his life rigidly ordered and compartmentalized. Any deviation from his established patterns was so rare it was cause for concern.

"He'll be all right," I assured him. "I'll make sure of it. He just needs some time."

"Is there anything I can do?"

"If I think of anything, I'll let you know."

"Thank you." He sounded tired and worried. "Thank you for saying something to me and being there for him. I wish I had been when it was happening. I'll have to live with the fact that I wasn't."

"We all have to live with it. It's not your fault, Chris. Doesn't make it easier, I know, but you need to keep it in mind or you'll beat yourself up. That won't help Gideon."

"You're wise beyond your years, Eva. I'm so glad he has you."

"I got lucky with him," I said quietly. "Big-time."

I ended the call and couldn't help but think of my mother. Seeing what Gideon was going through made me appreciate her all the more. She had been there for me; she'd fought for me. She had the guilt, too, which made her overprotective to the point of craziness, but there was a part of me that hadn't gotten quite so damaged as Gideon because of her love.

I called her and she answered on the first ring.

"Eva. You've been deliberately avoiding me. How am I supposed to plan your wedding without your input? There are so many decisions to make and if I make the wrong one, you'll—"

"Hi, Mom," I interrupted. "How are you?"

"Stressed," she said, her naturally breathy voice conveying more than a little accusation. "How could I be anything else? I'm planning one of the most important days of your life all by myself and—"

"I was thinking we could get together on Saturday and hash it all out, if that fits into your schedule."

"Really?" The hopeful pleasure in her voice made me feel guilty.

"Yes, really." I had been thinking of the second wedding as being more for my mother than anyone else, but that was wrong. The wedding was important to Gideon and me, too, another opportunity for us to affirm our unbreakable bond. Not for the world to see, but for the two of us.

He had to stop pushing me away to protect me, and I had to stop worrying that I would disappear when I became Mrs. Gideon Cross.

"That would be wonderful, Eva! We could have brunch here with the wedding planner. Spend the afternoon going over all our options."

"I want something small, Mom. Intimate." Before she argued, I pressed forward with Gideon's solution. "We can go as crazy as you want with the reception, but I want our wedding to be private."

"Eva, people will be insulted if they're invited to the reception and not the ceremony!"

"I really don't care. I'm not getting married for them. I'm getting married because I'm in love with the man of my dreams and we're going to spend the rest of our lives together. I don't want the focus to ever shift from that."

"Honey . . ." She sighed, as if I were clueless. "We can talk more about this on Saturday."

"Okay. But I'm not changing my mind." I felt a tingle race down my back and turned.

Gideon stood just beyond the threshold to the kitchen, watching me. He'd pulled on the sweatpants from the night before and his hair was still mussed from sleep, his eyes heavy-lidded.

"I've got to go," I told my mom. "I'll see you this weekend. Love you."

"I love you, too, Eva. That's why I only want the best for you."

I killed the call and set my phone down on the island. Sliding off the seat, I faced him. "Good morning."

"You're not at work," he said, his voice raspier, sexier, than usual.

"Neither are you."

"Are you going in late?"

"Nope. And you're not, either." I went to him, wrapping my arms around his waist. He was still warm from the bed. My sleepy, sensual dream come true. "We're going to hole up today, ace. Just you and me hanging out in our pajamas and relaxing."

His arm cinched around my hips, his other hand lifting to brush the hair back from my face. "You're not mad."

"Why would I be?" Lifting onto my tiptoes, I kissed his jaw. "Are you mad at me?"

"No." He cupped my nape, pressing my cheek to his. "I'm glad you're here."

"I'll always be here. Until death do us part."

"You're planning the wedding."

"You heard that, huh? If you've got requests, tell me now or forever hold your peace."

He was quiet for a long time, long enough that I figured he didn't have anything to add.

Turning my head, I caught his lips and gave him a quick, sweet kiss. "Did you see what I left you by the bed?"

"Yes, thank you." A ghost of a smile touched his mouth.

He looked like a man who'd been well fucked, which filled me with feminine pride. "I got you off the hook at work, too, but Arash said he had some papers to send over to us. He wouldn't tell me what they were."

"Guess you'll have to wait and find out."

I brushed my fingertips over his brow. "How are you doing?"

His shoulder lifted in a shrug. "I don't know. Right now, I just feel like shit."

"Let's revisit that bath you missed last night."

"Umm, I'm feeling better already."

Linking our fingers together, I started leading him back toward the bedroom.

"I want to be the man of your dreams, angel," he said, surprising me. "I want that more than anything."

I looked back at him. "You've got that in the bag already."

I stared down at the contract in front of me, my heart racing with a dizzying combination of love and delight. I looked up from the coffee table as Gideon entered the room, his hair still damp from our bath, his long legs encased in black silk pajama bottoms.

"You're buying the Outer Banks house?" I asked, needing his confirmation despite having the proof in front of me.

His sexy mouth curved. "*We're* buying the house. We agreed we would."

"We talked about it." The agreed-upon price was a bit staggering, telling me the owners hadn't been easy to persuade. And he'd asked them to convey the copy of *Naked in Death* with the property, along with the furnishings in the master bedroom. He always thought of everything.

Gideon settled on the couch beside me. "Now, we're doing something about it."

"The Hamptons would be closer. Or Connecticut."

"It's a quick hop down by jet." He tipped my chin up with his finger and pressed his lips to mine. "Don't worry about the logistics," he murmured. "We were happy there on the beach. I can still picture you walking along the shore. I remember kissing you on the deck . . . spreading you across that big white bed. You looked like an angel and that place, for me, was like heaven."

"Gideon." I rested my forehead against his. I loved him so much. "Where do we sign?"

He pulled back and slid the contract over, finding the first yellow *sign here* flag. His gaze roved over the coffee table and he frowned. "Where's my pen?"

I stood. "I've got one in my purse."

Catching my wrist in his hand, he tugged me back down. "No. I need my pen. Where's the envelope this came in?"

I spotted it lying on the floor between the couch and table, where I'd dropped it when I realized what Arash had sent over. Picking it up, I realized it was still weighted and upended it over the table to let the rest of the items inside spill out. A fountain pen clattered onto the glass and a small photo floated out.

"There we go," he said, taking the pen and slashing his signature on the dotted line. As he went through the rest of the pages, I picked up the picture and felt my chest tighten.

It was the photo of him and his dad on the beach, the one he'd told me about in North Carolina. He was young, maybe four or five, his small face screwed up in concentration as he helped his dad build a sand castle. Geoffrey Cross sat across from his son, his dark hair blowing in the ocean breeze, his face movie-star handsome. He wore only swimming trunks, showing off a body very much like the one Gideon boasted today.

"Wow," I breathed, knowing I was going to make copies of the image and frame one for each of the places we lived in. "I love this."

"Here." He pushed the contract, with the pen lying atop it, over to me.

I set the photo down and picked up the pen, turning it over to see the *GC* engraved on the barrel. "You superstitious or something?"

"It was my father's."

"Oh." I looked at him.

"He signed everything with it. He never went anywhere without it tucked in his pocket." He raked his hair back from his face. "He destroyed our name with that pen."

I set my hand on his thigh. "And you're building it back up with the same pen. I get it."

His fingertips touched my cheek, his gaze soft and shining. "I knew you would."

15

"HIS-AND-HERS MASTER SUITE—a classic." Blaire Ash smiled as his pen flew across the large notepad clipped to a board.

His gaze lifted to roam the entirety of Eva's bedroom in the penthouse, the one I'd had him design specifically to look exactly like the room my wife had in her Upper West Side apartment.

"How big a change are you looking for?" the designer asked. "Do you want to start with a blank slate, or are you just looking for the easiest structural change that will combine the two rooms?"

I left it to Eva to answer. It was difficult for me to participate, knowing this change was one neither of us really wanted. Our home would soon reflect how fucked up I was and how badly our marriage was affected because of it. The whole exercise was like a knife in the gut.

She glanced at me, then asked, "What would the easy way look like?"

Ash smiled, revealing slightly crooked teeth. He was attractive—or so Ireland assured me—and sported his usual attire of ripped jeans and a T-shirt under a tailored blazer. I couldn't care less about his looks. What mattered was his talent, which I'd admired enough to hire him to decorate both my office and my home. What I didn't like was the way he was looking at my wife.

"We could simply adjust the layout of the master bath and knock out an arched entry through this wall, effectively joining the two rooms via the bathroom."

"That's just what we need," Eva said.

"Right. It's quick and efficient, and the actual construction wouldn't be all that disruptive to your lives. Or"—he went on—"I could show you some alternatives."

"Like what?"

He moved to her side, so close that his shoulder pressed against hers. Ash was nearly as blond as Eva, the image of them striking as he bent his head to hers.

"If we work with the square footage of all three bedrooms and master bathroom," he replied, speaking only to her as if I weren't there, "I could give you a master suite that's balanced on both sides. Both bedrooms would be the same size, with his-and-hers adjoining home offices—or sitting room, if you prefer."

"Oh." She nipped absently at her lower lip for a second. "I can't believe you sketched that up so quickly."

He winked at her. "Fast and thorough is my motto. And getting the job done so well that you think of me when you want to do it again."

I lounged against the wall, my arms crossing as I watched them. Eva seemed oblivious to the designer's double entendre. I was anything but.

The house phone rang and her head came up. She looked at me. "I bet Cary's here."

"Why don't you get that, angel?" I drawled. "Maybe you should bring him up yourself, share your excitement."

"Yes!" She ran her hand over my arm as she hurried from the room, a fleeting touch that reverberated through me.

I straightened, focusing on Ash. "You're flirting with my wife."

He stiffened abruptly, the smile leaving his face. "I'm sorry. I didn't mean anything by it. I just want Miss Tramell to feel comfortable."

"I'll worry about her. You worry about me." I didn't doubt that he questioned the arrangement we'd consulted him to implement. Everyone who saw it would. What red-blooded man in his right mind would have a wife like Eva, yet sleep not just in a different bed but a different room altogether?

The knife dug in a little deeper and twisted.

His dark eyes went flat and hard. "Of course, Mr. Cross."

"Now, let's see what you've sketched so far."

"WHAT do you think?" Eva asked, between bites of pepperoni and basil pizza. She leaned over the island, with one leg kicked up behind her, having chosen to stand on the opposite side from where Cary and I sat.

I debated my reply.

"I mean the idea of a master suite with two mirroring sides is lovely," she went on, wiping at her mouth with a paper napkin, "but if we go the easy route, it'll be faster. Plus we could close up the wall again one day, if we want to use the room for something else."

"Like a nursery," Cary said, shaking crushed red pepper onto his slice.

My appetite died and I dropped the slice I'd been eating onto my paper plate. Lately, eating pizza at home hadn't been working out for me.

"Or a guest room," Eva corrected. "I liked what you talked to Blaire about for your apartment."

Cary shot her a look. "Quick dodge."

"Hey, you may have babies on your mind, but the rest of us have other things to check off our lists first."

She was saying exactly what I wanted her to say, but . . .

Did Eva have the same fears I did? Maybe she'd taken me as a husband because she couldn't help herself, but drew the line at taking me as a father to her children.

I carried my plate to the trash and tossed it in. "I have some calls to make. Stay," I said to Cary. "Spend time with Eva."

He gave me a nod. "Thanks."

Leaving the kitchen, I crossed the living room.

"So," Cary began, before I stepped out of earshot, "hot-designer-dude's got a thing for your man, baby girl."

"He does not!" Eva laughed. "You're crazy."

"No argument there, but that Ash guy barely glanced at you all night and kept his eyes glued on Cross."

I snorted. Ash had gotten the message, which reaffirmed my belief in his intelligence. Cary was free to read that however he liked.

"Well, if you're right," she said, "I have to admire his taste."

I headed down the hallway and entered my home office, my gaze landing on the collage of Eva's photos on the wall.

She was the one thing I couldn't tuck neatly away in my mind. She was always at the forefront, driving everything I did.

Settling down at my desk, I got to work, hoping to catch up on what I could so that the rest of the week wouldn't be thrown completely off. It took me a bit to get my head in the game, but once I did, I felt relief. It was a reprieve to focus on problems with concrete solutions.

I was making headway when I heard a yell from the living room that sounded like it had come from Eva. I paused, listening. It was quiet a moment, and then I heard it again, followed by Cary's raised voice. I went to the door and opened it.

"You could talk to me, Cary!" my wife said angrily. "You could tell me what's going on."

"You know what the fuck is going on," he retorted, the edge in his tone drawing me out of my office.

"I didn't know you were cutting again!"

I moved down the hall. Eva and Cary squared off in the living room, the two friends glaring at each other across the span of several feet.

"It's none of your business," he said, his shoulders high and chin canted defensively. He glanced at me. "Not yours, either."

"I don't disagree," I replied, although that wasn't quite true. How Cary self-destructed wasn't my concern; how it affected Eva was.

"Bullshit. That's total fucking bullshit." Eva's gaze shot to me as she turned to bring me into their conversation. Then she looked back at Cary. "I thought you were talking to Dr. Travis."

"When do I have time for that?" he scoffed, raking his hair back off his forehead. "Between my work and Tat's, plus trying to keep Trey, I don't have time to sleep!"

Eva shook her head. "That's a cop-out."

"Don't lecture me, baby girl," he warned. "I don't need your shit right now."

"Oh my God." She tipped her head back and looked at the ceiling. "Why the fuck do the men in my life insist on shutting me out when they need me most?"

"Can't speak for Cross, but you're not around for me anymore. I'm getting by the best I can."

Her head snapped down. "That's not fair! You have to tell me when you need me. I'm not a damn mind reader!"

Turning on my heel, I left them to it. I had problems of my own to work out. When Eva was ready, she'd come to me and I would listen, being careful not to offer too much of my opinion.

I knew she didn't want to hear that I thought she would be better off without Cary.

THE early-morning light slanted across the bed and caught the ends of Eva's hair as she slept. The soft blond strands glowed like burnished gold, as if they were lit from within. Her hand curled gently on the pillow beside her beautiful face, the other tucked safely between her breasts. The white sheet was draped over her from hip to thigh, her tanned legs exposed by the tangle we'd made before falling asleep.

I wasn't a man given to whimsy, but at that moment my wife looked like the angel I believed she was. I focused the camera on the sight she made, wanting to preserve that image of her for all time.

The shutter snapped and she stirred, her lips parting. I took another shot, grateful I'd bought a camera that just might do justice to her.

Her eyelids fluttered open. "What are you doing, ace?" she asked, in a voice as smoky as her irises.

I set the camera on the dresser and joined her in the bed. "Admiring you."

Her lips curved. "How are you feeling today?"

"Better."

"Better is good." Rolling, she reached for her breath mints. She turned back to me smelling of cinnamon. Her gaze slid over my face. "You're ready to tackle the world today, aren't you?"

"I'd much rather stay home with you."

Her eyes narrowed. "You're just saying that. You're itching to get back to global domination."

Bending down, I kissed the tip of her nose. "You know me so well."

It still amazed me how well she could read me. I was feeling restless, a bit shaky. Distracting myself with work—seeing concrete progress made on any of the projects I was personally overseeing—would ease that. Still, I pointed out, "I could work the morning at home, and then spend the afternoon with you."

She shook her head. "If you want to talk, I'll stay home. Otherwise, I've got a job to get back to."

"If you worked with me, you could cybercommute, too."

"You'd rather push me on that, huh? That's the tack you wanna take?"

I rolled onto my back and slung my forearm over my eyes. She hadn't pushed me the day before and I knew she wouldn't push me today. Or tomorrow. Like Dr. Petersen, she'd wait patiently for me to open up. But knowing she was waiting was pressure enough.

"There's nothing to say," I muttered. "It happened. Now Chris knows. Talking about it after the fact won't change anything."

I felt her turn toward me. "It's not talking about the events themselves that matters, it's how you feel about them."

"I don't feel anything. It . . . surprised me. I don't like surprises. Now, I'm over it."

"Bullshit." She slid out of bed faster than I could catch her. "If you're just going to lie, keep your mouth shut."

Sitting up, I watched her round the foot of the bed, the tight set of her shoulders doing nothing to detract from how stunning she was. My need for her was a constant thrumming in my blood, so easily provoked by her fiery Latin temper into a restlessly impatient craving.

I'd heard some say my wife was as breathtaking as her mother, but I disagreed. Monica Stanton was a cool beauty, one who gave off the air of being slightly out of reach. Eva was all heat and sensuality—you could reach her, but her passion would scorch you.

I jumped out of bed and waylaid her before she reached the bathroom, gripping her by the upper arms. "I can't fight with you right now," I told her honestly, staring down into the roiling depths of her turbulent gaze. "If we're out of sync, I won't make it through the day."

"Then don't tell me you're over it when you're struggling to keep it together!"

I growled, frustrated. "I don't know what to do with this. I don't see how Chris knowing changes anything."

Her chin tilted up. "He's worried about you. Are you going to call him?"

My head turned away. When I thought of seeing my stepfather

again, my stomach churned. "I'll talk to him at some point. We do manage a business together."

"You'd rather avoid him. Tell me why."

I pushed back from her. "We're not suddenly going to be the best of friends, Eva. We rarely saw each other before, and I see no reason for that to change."

"Are you angry with him?"

"Jesus. Why the fuck is it my job to make him feel better?" I headed for the shower.

She followed. "Nothing is going to make him feel better, and I don't think he expects that of you. He just wants to know that you're back on your stride."

I reached into the stall and turned the taps on.

Her hand touched my back. "Gideon . . . you can't just shove your feelings into a box. Not unless you want an explosion like the other night. Or another nightmare."

It was the mention of my recurrent nightmares that had me rounding on her. "We managed the last two nights just fine!"

Eva didn't back down in the face of my fury the way others did, which only aggravated me further. And seeing the myriad reflections of her naked body in the mirrors didn't help.

"You didn't sleep on Tuesday night," she challenged. "And last night you were so exhausted, I doubt you even dreamed at all."

She didn't know I'd slept part of the night in the other bedroom, and I didn't see any reason to mention it. "What do you want me to say?"

"This isn't about me! It helps to talk things over, Gideon. Laying it all out helps us gain perspective."

"Perspective? I've got that just fine. There was no mistaking the pity on Chris's face last night. Or yours! I don't need anyone feeling sorry for me, damn it. I don't need their fucking guilt."

Her brows shot up. "I can't speak for Chris, but that wasn't pity you saw on me, Gideon. Sympathy, maybe, because I know what you're feeling. And pain, certainly, because my heart is connected to yours. When you're hurting, I'm hurting, too. You'll have to learn to deal with that, because I love you and I'm not going to stop."

Her words ripped into me. Reaching out, I gripped the edge of the shower's floating glass.

Relenting, she came to me, wrapped herself around me. My head bowed as I soaked her in. The smell of her, the feel. My free arm slid around her hips, my hand cupping the full curve of her ass. I wasn't the same man I'd been when we met. I was stronger in some ways and weaker in others. It was the weakness I struggled with. I used to feel nothing. And now—

"He doesn't see you as weak," she murmured, reading me the way she always could. Her cheek lay over my heart. "No one could. After what you've been through . . . to be the man you are today. *That's* strength, baby. And I'm impressed."

My fingers flexed into her supple flesh. "You're biased," I muttered. "You're in love with me."

"Of course I am. How could I be anything else? You're amazing and perfect—"

I grunted.

"Perfect for *me*," she corrected. "And since you belong to me, that's a good thing."

I tugged her back and into the shower, leading her under the pounding jets of warm water. "I feel like this changed things," I admitted, "but I don't know how."

"We figure it out together." Her hands ran over my shoulders and down my arms. "Just don't push me away. You have to stop trying to protect me, especially from yourself!"

"I can't hurt you, angel. Can't take any risks."

"Whatever. I can take you down, ace, if you get out of hand."

If that were true, it might have been a comfort.

I switched gears, hoping to avoid a fight that would send ripples through the rest of my day. "I've been thinking about the penthouse renovations."

"You're changing the subject."

"We exhausted the subject. It's not closed," I qualified, "just tabled until there are additional variables to address."

She eyed me. "Why does it turn me on when you go all alpha mogul on me like that?"

"Don't tell me there are times when I don't turn you on."

"God, I wish. I'd be a more productive human being."

I brushed the wet hair back from her forehead. "Have you thought about what you want?"

"Whatever ends with your cock inside me."

"Good to know. I was talking about the penthouse."

She shrugged, her eyes lit with mischievous amusement. "Same goes either way."

IT was the sort of local eatery that tourists never spared a glance. Small and lacking in aesthetics, it boasted a vinyl marquee that did nothing to brand it as unique or welcoming. It specialized in soup, with sandwich options for those with heartier appetites. A cooler by the door offered a limited selection of beverages, while an ancient register was only capable of taking cash.

No, travelers would never come to this place run by immigrants who'd decided to take a bite out of the Big Apple. They'd head to the spots made famous by movies or television shows, or those that dotted the garish spectacle of Times Square. The locals, however, knew the gem in their neighborhood and lined up outside the door.

I slid through that line to reach the back, where a tiny room held a handful of chipped enamel-topped tables. A lone man sat at one of them, reading the day's paper while steam curled out of his cup of soup.

Pulling out the chair opposite him, I sat.

Benjamin Clancy didn't look up when he spoke. "What can I do for you, Mr. Cross?"

"I believe I owe you thanks."

He folded the paper leisurely and then set it aside, his gaze meeting mine. The man was solidly built, thick with muscle. His hair was dark blond, cut short in a military style. "Do you? Well, then, I accept. Although I didn't do it for you."

"I didn't think you did." I studied him. "You're still keeping watch."

Clancy nodded. "She's been through enough. I'm going to see she doesn't go through any more."

"You don't trust me to do that?"

"I don't know you enough to trust you. In my opinion, neither does she. So I'll keep an eye on things for a while."

"I love her. I think I've proven how far I'll go to protect her."

His gaze hardened. "Some men need to be put down like rabid dogs. Some men need to be the ones to do it. I didn't peg you as one of those guys either way. That makes you rogue in my book."

"I take care of what's mine."

"Oh, you took care of it all right." His smile didn't quite reach his eyes. "And I took care of the rest. As long as Eva is happy with you, we'll leave it at that. You decide someday she's not what you want, you cut her off clean and with respect. If you hurt her in any way at all, then you've got a problem, whether I'm still breathing or in the grave. You got me?"

"You don't have to threaten me to be good to her, but I heard you." Eva was a strong woman. Strong enough to survive her past and to pledge her future to me. But she was vulnerable, too, in ways most people didn't see. That was why I would do anything to shield her, and it seemed Benjamin Clancy felt the same.

I leaned forward. "Eva doesn't like being spied on. If you become a problem for her, we'll sit down like this again."

"You planning on making it a problem?"

"No. If she catches you at it, it won't be because I tipped her off. Just keep in mind that she's spent her life looking over her shoulder and being suffocated by her mother. She's breathing easy for the first time. I won't let you take that away from her."

Clancy narrowed his eyes. "I guess we understand each other."

I pushed back from the table and stood, extending my hand. "I'd say we do."

As my day ended and I cleared off my desk, I felt solid and settled.

There in my office, at the helm of Cross Industries, I had a handle on every detail. I doubted nothing, least of all myself.

The ground had leveled beneath my feet. I'd smoothed the feathers ruffled by my Wednesday cancellations, while staying on track with my Thursday. Despite missing a full day, I was no longer behind.

Scott walked in. "I've confirmed your agenda for tomorrow. Mrs. Vidal will meet you and Miss Tramell at The Modern at noon."

Shit. I'd forgotten about lunch with my mother.

I glanced at him. "Thank you, Scott. Have a good night."

"You, too, Mr. Cross. See you tomorrow."

Rolling my shoulders back, I walked over to the window and looked out at the city. Things had been easier before Eva. Simpler. During the day, while consumed with work, I'd taken a moment to miss that simplicity.

Now, with the evening upon me and time to think, the prospect of major alterations to the home I'd come to see as a refuge bothered me more than I would admit to my wife. On top of the other personal pressures we faced, I felt almost crushed by the scale of the adjustments I was making.

Waking up to Eva as she'd been that morning was worth it all, but that didn't mean I wasn't struggling with the aftermath of her entry into my life.

"Mr. Cross."

I turned at the sound of Scott's voice and found him standing in the doorway to my office. "You're still here."

He smiled. "I was on my way out to the elevators when Cheryl caught me at reception. There's a Deanna Johnson in the lobby asking for you. I wanted to confirm that I should tell her you're no longer available today."

I was tempted to turn her away. I had little patience for reporters and even less for former lovers. "They can send her up."

"Do you need me to stay?"

"No, you can go. Thank you."

I watched him leave, then watched Deanna arrive. She strode toward my office on long legs and high heels, her thin gray skirt skimming the tops of her knees. Long dark hair swayed around her shoulders, framing the zipper that gave her otherwise traditional blouse an edge.

She tossed me a megawatt smile and held out her hand. "Gideon. Thanks for seeing me on such short notice."

I shook her hand briefly and briskly. "I expect you wouldn't go to the trouble of coming here directly unless it was important."

The statement was both fact and a warning. We had come to an understanding, but it wouldn't last if she thought she could exploit our connection beyond what I'd already conceded.

"Worth it for the view," she said, her eyes on me for just a second too long before shifting sideways to the window.

"I'm sorry, but I've got an appointment, so we'll have to make this quick."

"I'm in a hurry, too." Tossing her hair over her shoulder, she moved to the nearest chair and sat, crossing her legs in a way that showed more of her toned thigh than I wanted to see. She started digging into her large bag.

I pulled my smartphone out of my pocket, checked the time, and called Angus. "We'll be ready in ten," I told him when he answered.

"I'll bring the car around."

Ending the call, I glanced at Deanna, impatient for her to get to the point.

"How's Eva?" she asked.

"She'll be here in a few moments. You can ask her yourself."

"Oh." She looked up at me, one eye hidden behind the fall of her hair. "I should probably be gone before she gets here. I think our . . . history makes her uncomfortable."

"She knows how I was," I said evenly, "and she knows I'm not that way now."

Deanna nodded. "Of course she does, and of course you're not, but no woman likes when her man's past gets rubbed in her face."

"Then you'll have to make sure you don't do that."

Another warning.

She withdrew a thin folder from her bag. Standing, she walked toward me. "I wouldn't. I accepted your apology and appreciate it."

"Good."

"It's Corinne Giroux you might want to worry about."

What patience I'd had disappeared. "Corinne is her husband's concern, not mine."

Deanna held the folder out to me. I took it and opened it, finding a press release inside.

As I read, my grip tightened until I crumpled the edges.

"She's sold a tell-all book about your relationship," she said redundantly. "The release officially hits the wire Monday morning at nine."

16

"OTHER COUPLES MEET, hit things off, their friends nitpick a little but are mostly supportive, and they coast for a while in that couple stage just enjoying each other." I sighed and glanced at Gideon, who sat beside me on the couch. "We, on the other hand, can't seem to catch a break."

"What kind of breaks are you referring to?" Dr. Petersen asked, eyeing us with fond interest.

That fondness gave me hope. As soon as Gideon and I had arrived, I'd noticed the change in the dynamic between him and Dr. Petersen. There was something looser between them, a new ease. Less wariness.

"The only people who really want us to be together are my mother—who thinks us loving each other is a bonus to his billions—and his stepfather and sister."

"I don't think that's a fair assessment of your mother," Dr. Petersen said, sitting back and holding my gaze. "She wants you to be happy."

"Yeah, well, a lot of being happy for my mom is being financially secure, which I just don't understand. It's not like she's ever struggled for money, so why is she so afraid of not having any? Anywayyyy . . ." I shrugged. "I'm just irritated with everyone right now. Gideon and I get along great when it's just the two of us. I mean we fight sometimes, but we always get through it. And I feel like we're always stronger once we do."

"What do you fight about?"

I glanced at Gideon again. He sat beside me totally at ease, looking gorgeous and successful in his beautifully tailored suit. It was on my to-do list to go with him the next time he updated his wardrobe. I wanted to watch them measure that stunning body of his, see them select the materials and style.

I found him sexy as sin in jeans and a T-shirt, and mind-blowing in a tuxedo. But I'd always have a special fondness for the three-piece suits he favored. They reminded me of how he'd been when I first met him, so beautiful and seemingly unattainable, a man I'd wanted so desperately that the need overrode even my sense of self-preservation.

I looked back at Dr. Petersen. "We still argue about the things he doesn't tell me. And we argue when he tries to shut me out."

He turned his gaze to Gideon. "Do you feel the need to maintain a certain distance from Eva?"

My husband's mouth curved wryly. "There is no distance between us, Doctor. She wants me to dump everything on her that's an irritant to me and I won't do that. Ever. It's bad enough if one of us has to bother with it."

I narrowed my eyes at him. "I think that's crap. Part of a relationship is sharing the load with someone else. Maybe sometimes I can't do anything about the problem, but I can be a sounding board. I think you don't tell me things just because you'd rather shove them into a corner where you can ignore them."

"People process information in different ways, Eva."

I wasn't buying Gideon's dismissive reply. "You're not processing, you're ignoring. And I'm never going to be okay with you pushing me away when you're hurting."

"How does he push you away?" Dr. Petersen asked.

I looked at him. "Gideon . . . separates himself. He goes somewhere else where he can be alone. He won't let me help him."

"'Goes somewhere else' how? Do you emotionally withdraw, Gideon? Or physically?"

"Both," I said. "He shuts down emotionally and goes away physically."

Gideon reached over and took my hand in his. "I can't shut down with you. That's the problem."

"That's not a problem!"

I shook my head. "He doesn't need space," I said to Dr. Petersen, "he needs me, but he cuts me off because he's afraid he'll hurt me if he doesn't."

"How would you hurt her, Gideon?"

"It's . . ." He exhaled harshly. "Eva has triggers. I keep them in mind, all the time. I'm careful. But sometimes, when I'm not thinking clearly, it's possible I could cross the line."

Dr. Petersen studied us. "What lines are you worried about crossing?"

Gideon's grip tightened on my hand, the only outward sign he gave of any uneasiness. "There are times when I need her too much. I can be rough . . . demanding. Sometimes, I don't have the control I need."

"You're talking about your sexual relationship?" He returned Gideon's nod. "We've touched on that briefly before. You said you have sex multiple times a day, every day. Is that still the case?"

I felt my face heat.

Gideon's thumb stroked over the back of my hand. "Yes."

Dr. Petersen set his tablet aside. "You're right to be concerned.

Gideon, you may be using sex to keep Eva at an emotional distance. When you're making love, she's not talking, you're not answering. There's a point when you're not even thinking, your body is in charge and your brain is just along for the endorphin ride. Conversely, sexual abuse survivors like Eva often use sex as a way to establish an emotional connection. Can you see the problem there? You may be trying to achieve distance through sex, while Eva is trying to get closer."

"I've already told you there's no distance." Gideon leaned forward, pulling my hand into his lap. "Not with Eva."

"So tell me, when you're struggling emotionally and you initiate sex with Eva, what is it you're looking for?"

I twisted a little to look at Gideon, totally invested in his answer. I'd never questioned *why* he needed to be inside me, only *how*. For me, it was as simple as him needing and me giving.

His gaze met mine. The shield over his eyes, that mask of his, slipped away. I saw the longing there, the love.

"The connection," he answered. "There's this moment. She opens and I . . . I open, and we're there. Together. I need that."

"You need it rough?"

Gideon looked at him. "Sometimes. There are times when she holds back. But I can get her there. She wants me to get her there, needs it like I do. I have to push. Carefully. With control. When I don't have the control, I need to back off."

"How do you push?" Dr. Petersen asked quietly.

"I have my ways."

Dr. Petersen turned his attention to me. "Has Gideon ever gone too far?"

I shook my head.

"Do you ever worry that he might?"

"No."

His gaze was soft and capped with a frown. "You should, Eva. You both should."

∾

I was stirring vegetables and cubed chicken into a curry mix on the stove when I heard the front door opening. Curious, I waited to see who came into view, hoping Cary had come home alone.

"Smells good," he said, walking up to the breakfast bar to watch me. He looked cool and casual in an oversized white V-neck T-shirt and khaki shorts. Sunglasses hung off his collar and wide brown leather cuffs hugged each forearm, hiding the threadlike cuts I'd spotted the night before.

"Got enough for me?" he asked.

"Just you?"

He smiled his cocky smile, but I saw the tightness around his mouth. "Yep."

"Then I've got enough, *if* you pour the wine."

"You got yourself a deal."

Joining me in the kitchen, he looked over my shoulder and into the pot. "White or red?"

"It's chicken."

"White it is, then. Where's Cross?"

I watched him head to the wine fridge. "With his trainer, working out. How was your day?"

He shrugged. "Same shit as always."

"Cary." I lowered the heat and turned to him. "Just a few weeks ago, you were so happy to be here in New York and getting jobs. Now . . . you're so unhappy."

Pulling a bottle out, he shrugged again. "That's what I get for fucking around."

"I'm sorry I haven't been here for you."

He glanced at me as he dug out the bottle opener. "But . . . ?"

I shook my head. "No buts. I'm sorry. I will say that you've had company most nights I'm home, so I figured that's why we weren't talking as much, but that doesn't excuse me from not reaching out when I know you're going through a difficult time."

Cary sighed, his head bowing. "It wasn't fair to dump everything on you last night. I know Cross has got his own shit to wade through and you're dealing with that."

"That doesn't mean I'm not here for you." I put my hand on his shoulder. "Anytime you need me, just let me know and I'll be there."

Turning abruptly, he caught me up in a powerful hug, squeezing the air out of me. Sympathy did the rest of the work, squeezing my heart.

I hugged him in return, one hand stroking the back of his head. His dark brown hair was as soft as silk, his shoulders as hard as granite. I guessed they'd have to be to hold up the weight of the stress he was carrying. Guilt made me hold him even tighter.

"God," he muttered. "I've fucked this all up to hell and back."

"What's going on?"

He set me down, then turned back to the bottle to open it. "I don't know if it's hormones or what, but Tat is a raging fucking bitch right now. Nothing is good enough. Nothing makes her happy, especially being pregnant. What shot has the poor kid got with me as a father and a self-centered diva who hates him as his mother?"

"Maybe it's a girl," I said, handing over the wineglasses I'd pulled out of the cupboard.

"Jesus. Don't say that. I'm panicked enough as it is." He poured two hefty glasses, slid one over to me, and drank deep from his own. "And I feel like an asshole talking about the mother of my baby that way, but it's the truth. God help us, it's the damned truth."

"I'm sure it's just the hormones. It'll all settle in, and then she'll get that glow and be happy." I took a sip, hoping like hell everything I was saying would come true. "Have you told Trey yet?"

Cary shook his head. "He's the one sane thing I've got going on right now. I lose him, I'll lose my mind."

"He's stayed with you so far."

"And I have to work for it, Eva. Every day. I've never worked so hard. And I'm not talking about fucking."

"I didn't think you were." I pulled two clean bowls out of the dishwasher, along with spoons. "What I think is that you're an amazing guy and anyone would be lucky to have you. I'm pretty sure Trey feels the same way."

"Don't. Please." His gaze met mine. "I'm trying to be real here. I don't need you to blow smoke at me."

"I'm not. Maybe what I said wasn't deep, but it's true." I paused in front of the rice cooker. "Gideon doesn't tell me what's going on with him a lot of the time. He says he's trying to protect me, but what he's really doing is protecting himself."

And it took saying the words aloud to really make them sink in for me.

"He's afraid that the more he tells me, the more reason he gives me to walk away. But it's just the opposite, Cary. The more he doesn't say, the more I don't feel like he trusts me, and that's hurting us. You and Trey have been together as long as Gideon and I have." I reached out and touched his arm. "You have to tell him. If he finds out about the baby some other way—and he will—he might not forgive you."

Cary sagged against the island, suddenly looking so much older and so tired. "I feel like if I just had more time to get a handle on things, I could deal with Trey."

"Waiting isn't helping," I said gently, scooping rice into the bowls. "You're backsliding."

"What else have I got?" His voice came hard with anger. "I don't fuck around anymore. A monk gets off more than I do."

I winced, knowing Cary was a man who exemplified what Dr. Petersen had talked about. When Cary had sex, he could turn his brain off and let his body make him feel good, if only for a little while. He didn't have to think or feel beyond the sensory. It was a coping mechanism he'd had to perfect back when he was the one being fucked, long before he was old enough to even want to.

"You've got me," I countered.

"Baby girl, I love you, but you're not always what I need to get by."

"Cutting yourself and banging everyone who'll let you isn't getting you by, either. They certainly don't help you feel good about yourself."

"Something has to."

I poured curry over the rice and passed the bowl over along with a spoon. "Taking care of yourself will do it. Trusting the people you love will help, too. Being honest with yourself and with them. Sounds simple, but we both know it's not. Still, it's the only way, Cary."

He flashed me a quick, sad smile and took the food I handed him. "I'm scared."

"There," I said softly, returning his smile. "That was honest. Would it help if I'm with you when you talk to Trey?"

"Yeah. I'll feel like a pussy for not doing it alone, but yeah, it'd help."

"Then I'll be there."

Cary caught me in a hug from behind, his cheek resting against my shoulder. "You really are always there for me. I love you for that."

Reaching back, I ran my fingers through his hair. "I love you, too."

THE comforter lifted away from my skin, waking me, and then the mattress shifted under the weight of the man sliding into my bed.

"Gideon."

Eyes closed, I turned to him. Breathing deep, I inhaled the scent of his skin. My hands found the cool strength of his body, slid over him, pulled him close to warm him.

He took my mouth in a deep, urgent kiss. The shock of his hunger woke me the rest of the way; the greed in his touch sent my heart racing. He slid over me, then down, his mouth searing my nipples, then my belly, then my sex.

I gasped and arched. He tongued my clit with demanding focus, driving me higher, his hands pinning my hips as I writhed under the lash of his tongue.

I came hard, crying out. He wiped his lips on my inner thigh and rose, a seductive looming shadow in the dark of night. He mounted me, thrust hard inside me.

Over my moan, I heard him growl my name as if the pleasure of taking me were too great to bear. I gripped his waist; he gripped the sheets. His hips surged and rolled, stroking that magnificent penis deep and tirelessly inside me.

When I woke again the sun was up, and the place beside me in the bed was cold and empty.

17

I WAS FIXING a cup of coffee for Eva the next morning when my smartphone started ringing. Leaving the half-and-half on the counter, I crossed to the bar stool where I'd hung my coat and pulled my phone out of the pocket.

Steeling myself, I answered, "Good morning, Mother."

"Gideon. I'm sorry to cancel on such short notice"—she took a shaky breath—"but I won't be able to make lunch this afternoon."

I returned to my coffee, knowing I'd need it for the long day ahead. "That's fine."

"I'm sure you're relieved," she said bitterly.

I took a drink, wishing it were something stronger though it was barely past eight. "Don't. If I didn't want to have lunch with you, *I* would've canceled."

She was quiet a minute, then asked, "Have you seen Chris lately?"

282 · SYLVIA DAY

I took another sip, my gaze on the hallway as I waited for Eva. "I saw him Tuesday."

"That long ago?" There was a note of fear in her voice. It gave me no pleasure to hear it.

Eva rushed into the living room in bare feet, her body encased in a pale beige sheath dress that managed to be professional while still hugging all her curves. I'd picked it out for her knowing the color would showcase the color of her skin and the paleness of her hair.

Pleasure at the sight of her slid through my veins like the liquor I'd wished were in my coffee. She could do that to me, intoxicate and captivate me.

"I have to go," I said. "I'll call you later."

"You never do."

I set my mug down to pick up Eva's. "I wouldn't say it if I didn't mean it."

Ending the call, I shoved the phone in my pocket and handed the coffee to my wife. "You look stunning," I murmured, bending to press a kiss to her cheek.

"For a man who claims not to know a damn thing about women, you sure know how to dress one," she said, eyeing me over the lip of her mug as she took a sip.

A low moan of pleasure escaped her as she swallowed, a sound very similar to the one she made when I slid my cock inside her. Coffee, I'd learned, was one of Eva's addictions.

"I've made mistakes, but I'm learning." I leaned back against the counter and pulled her between my spread legs. Had she noticed one less Vera Wang dress in the closet? I'd removed it from her wardrobe after realizing just how much of her luscious tits it exposed.

She held the mug up. "Thank you for this."

"My pleasure." I brushed my fingertips across her cheek. "I have to talk to you about something."

"Oh? What's up, ace?"

"Do you still have a Google alert on me?"

She looked into her mug. "Is this when I should plead the Fifth?"

"That won't be necessary." I waited until she looked up at me again. "Corinne has sold a book about our time together."

"What?" Her eyes darkened from pale gray to slate.

I cupped her nape and stroked over her racing pulse with my thumb. "From what I read in the press release, she kept a diary during that time. She's also sharing personal photos."

"Why? Why would she sell that stuff for people to paw through?"

The hand holding her mug trembled, so I took it from her and set it back on the counter. "I don't think she knows why."

"Can you stop it?"

"No. However, if she lies outright and I can prove it, I can go after her for that."

"But only after it's released." Her hands came to rest on my chest. "She knows you'll have to read it. You'll have to see all the photos and read about how much she loves you. You'll read about things you did that you don't even remember now."

"And it won't matter." I pressed my lips to her forehead. "I never loved her, not the way I do you. Looking back on that time isn't going to make me suddenly wish I were with her and not you."

"She didn't push you," she whispered. "Not like I do."

I spoke against her skin, wishing I could press the words into her mind in a way that she would never doubt them. "She also didn't make me burn. Didn't make me hunger, and hope, and dream like you do. There's no comparison, angel, and no going back. I would never want to."

Her beautiful eyes closed. She leaned into me. "The hits just keep on coming, don't they?"

I looked over her head and out the window beyond, at the world that waited for us once we stepped outside. "Let 'em come."

She exhaled roughly. "Yeah, let 'em come."

∝

I entered Tableau One and spotted Arnoldo immediately. Dressed in his pristinely white chef's jacket paired with black slacks, he stood by a small table for two in the back, talking to the woman I'd come to see.

Her head turned toward me as I approached, her long dark hair sliding across her shoulder. Her blue eyes lit brightly for a moment when she spotted me, and then that light was quickly banked. Her smile when she greeted me was cool and more than a little smug.

"Corinne." I greeted her with a nod before shaking hands with Arnoldo. The restaurant he ran and I backed was crowded with lunch guests, the buzz of numerous conversations loud enough to drown out the instrumental Italian-themed music piping through recessed speakers.

Arnoldo excused himself to see to the kitchen, lifting Corinne's hand to his lips in farewell. Before he walked away, he shot me a look that I understood to mean we'd talk later.

I took the seat across from Corinne. "I appreciate your taking the time to see me."

"Your invitation was a pleasant surprise."

"I don't believe it was unexpected." I leaned back, absorbing the soft lilt of Corinne's speech. While Eva's throaty voice stirred a deep craving, Corinne's had always soothed me.

Her smile widened as she brushed at an invisible speck on the plunging neckline of her red dress. "No, I suppose not."

Irritated by the game she was playing, I spoke curtly. "What are you doing? You value your privacy as much as I do mine."

Corinne's lips flattened into a firm line. "I thought the exact same thing when I first saw that video of you and Eva arguing in the park. You say I don't know you, but I do, and having your private life splashed all over the tabloids isn't something you would ever allow under normal circumstances."

"What's normal?" I shot back, unable to deny that I was a different man with Eva. I'd never indulged women who tested me expecting some grand gesture. If they pursued me aggressively enough, I let them catch me for a night. With Eva, I'd always been the one chasing.

"That's exactly my point—you don't remember. Because you're wrapped up in a passionate affair and you can't see beyond it."

"There is nothing beyond it, Corinne. I will be with her until I die."

She sighed. "You think so now, but stormy relationships don't last, Gideon. They burn themselves out. You like order and calm, and you won't have that with her. Ever. Somewhere inside you, you know that."

Her words struck home. She had unwittingly echoed my own thoughts on the subject.

A server came by our table. Corinne ordered a salad; I ordered a drink—a double.

"So you've sold a tell-all to do . . . what?" I asked, when the server walked away. "Get back at me? Hurt Eva?"

"No. I want you to remember."

"This isn't the way."

"What is the way?"

I held her gaze. "It's over, Corinne. Exposing your memories of us isn't going to change that."

"Maybe not," she conceded, sounding so sad it sent a pang of regret through me. "But you said you never loved me. At the very least, I'll prove that wrong. I gave you comfort. Contentment. You were happy with me. I don't see that same sort of tranquillity when you're with her. You can't tell me you feel it."

"Everything you're saying tells me you don't care if I end up with you. But if you're leaving Giroux, maybe you care about the money. How much did they pay you to prostitute your 'love' for me?"

Her chin lifted. "That's not why I'm writing the book."

"You just want to be sure I don't end up with Eva."

"I just want you to be happy, Gideon. And since you've met her, I've seen you be anything but."

How would Eva take the book when she read it? No better, I imagined, than I was taking "Golden."

Corinne's gaze dropped to my left hand, which rested on the table-top. "You gave Eva your mother's engagement ring."

"It hasn't been hers for a long time."

She took a sip of the wine she'd had on the table when I joined her. "Did you have it when you and I were together?"

"Yes."

She flinched.

"You can tell yourself that Eva and I are incompatible," I said tightly, "that we're either fighting or fucking with nothing of substance in between. But the truth is that she's the other half of me and what you're doing is going to hurt her, which will hurt me. I'll buy you out of the publishing contract if you'll withdraw the book."

She stared at me for a long minute. "I . . . I can't, Gideon."

"Tell me why."

"You're asking me to let you go. This is a way for me to do that."

I leaned forward. "I'm asking you, Corinne, if you feel anything for me at all, to please drop this."

"Gideon . . ."

"If you don't, you're going to turn what were good memories for me into something I hate."

Her turquoise eyes shone with tears. "I'm sorry."

I pushed back from the table and stood. "You will be."

Turning away, I walked out of the restaurant to the waiting Bentley. Angus opened the door, his gaze shifting to look beyond me into Tableau One's massive front window.

"Damn it." I slid into the back. "God fucking damn it!"

People who felt I'd wronged them in some way were crawling out of the shadows like spiders, lured by the presence of Eva in my life.

She was my biggest vulnerability, one I wasn't hiding well. And that was becoming a problem I had to get a handle on. Christopher, Anne, Landon, Corinne . . . they were only the beginning. There were others who had grievances against me. Still more who held grudges toward my father.

I'd long dared them all to come at me, enjoying the challenge. Now, the bastards were coming at me through my wife. All at once. And I was being stretched thin because of it. If I didn't have my guard up completely, my focus absolute, I would leave Eva open and unprotected.

Whatever I had to do, I had to prevent that.

"I still want to see you tonight," Eva said, her seductive voice drifting through the phone receiver like smoke.

"That's not in question," I told her, leaning back in my desk chair. Outside the windows, the sun hung lower in the sky. The workday was over. Somewhere in the madness of the week, August had given way to September. "You deal with Cary, I'll sit down with Arnoldo, and you and I will start the weekend when we're done."

"God, this week just flew by. I need to work out. I skipped too many days."

"Spar with me tomorrow."

She laughed. "Yeah, right."

"I'm not joking." I thought of Eva in her sports bra and body-hugging pants, and my dick stirred with interest.

"I can't fight you!" she protested.

"Of course you can."

"You know too much. You're too good."

"Let's put those self-defense skills of yours to the test, angel." The idea I'd thrown out on a whim suddenly seemed like the best one I'd had all day. "I want to know you can take care of yourself in the unlikely case that you have to."

She never would, but it would give me peace of mind to know that she could get away from a threat.

"I've got wedding stuff tomorrow, but I'll think about it," she said. "Hang on."

I heard the car door open and Eva greet her doorman. She said hi to her concierge, and then I heard the ding of an arriving elevator in her lobby.

"You know"—she sighed—"I'm putting on a brave face for Cary, but I'm worried about what's going to happen with Trey. If he walks out, I think Cary just might totally self-destruct."

"He's asking a lot," I warned her, hearing another ding from the elevator. "Cary's basically telling this guy that he's got a pregnant sidepiece that he intends to hang on to. No, scratch that. He's saying that Trey is going to be the sidepiece. I can't see that going over well with anyone."

"I know."

"I'll have my phone on me all night. Call me if you need me."

"I always need you. I'm home, so I have to go. See you later. I love you."

Would those words always hit me hard enough to steal my breath?

We hung up just as a familiar figure rounded the corner leading to my office. I stood as Mark Garrity reached my open doorway, and I met him halfway with my hand extended.

"Mark, thank you for making time for me."

He smiled and shook my hand in a strong grip. "I'm the one feeling thankful, Mr. Cross. There are a large number of people in this city—in the world, actually—who'd kill to be where I am right now."

"Call me Gideon, please." I gestured toward the seating area. "How's Steven?"

"He's doing great, thank you. I'm beginning to think he missed a calling as a wedding planner."

I smiled. "Eva's about to dig into that this weekend."

Unbuttoning his suit jacket, Mark tugged up the legs of his slacks and sat on the sofa. His gray suit contrasted well with his dark skin and striped tie, pulling together the appearance of an urban professional on the rise.

"If she has half as much fun with it as Steven," he said, "she'll have the time of her life."

"Let's hope she doesn't have too much fun," I drawled, remaining on my feet. "I'd like to get past the planning and into the actual wedding."

Mark laughed.

"Can I get you something to drink?" I asked.

"I'm good, thanks."

"Okay. I'll make this quick." I took a seat. "I asked you to meet me after work, because it wouldn't be appropriate for me to offer you a position with Cross Industries while you're on Waters Field and Leaman's time."

His brows shot up.

I let that sink in for a second or two. "Cross Industries has a number of diverse international holdings, with a concentration on real estate, entertainment, and premium brands—or assets we believe we can elevate to that status."

"Like Kingsman Vodka."

"Precisely. For the most part, advertising and marketing campaigns are managed on the ground level, but brand overhauls or adjustments to messaging are approved here. Due to the diversity I mentioned, we're always reviewing new strategies for rebranding or strengthening an established brand. We could use you."

"Wow." Mark rubbed his palms over his knees. "I'm not sure what I was expecting, but this has caught me off guard."

"I'll pay you twice what you're making, to start."

"That's a hell of an offer."

"I'm not a man who likes the word *no*."

His grin flashed. "I doubt you hear it very often. I guess this means Eva is leaving Waters Field and Leaman?"

"She hasn't made that decision yet."

"No?" His brows shot up again. "If I leave, she'll lose her job."

"And gain another one here, of course." I kept my replies as brief and unrevealing as possible. I wanted his cooperation, not questions he might not like the answers to.

"Is she waiting for me to agree before she takes any steps?"

"Your decision will be a catalyst."

Mark ran a hand over his tie. "I'm both flattered and excited, but—"

"I understand it's not a move you were planning on making," I interjected smoothly. "You're happy where you're at, and feel a measure of job security. So I'm prepared to guarantee you the position—and reasonable bonuses and annual raises—for the next three years, barring any misconduct on your part."

Leaning forward, I set my fingers on the folder that Scott had left atop the table. I pushed it toward Mark. "All the information is laid out in detail in this. Take it home with you, discuss it with Steven, and let me know your decision on Monday."

"Monday?"

I stood. "I expect you'll want to give Waters Field and Leaman ample notice and I don't have a problem with that, but I'll need to have your commitment as soon as possible."

He picked up the folder and rose to his feet. "What if I have questions?"

"Call me. My card is in the folder." I glanced at the watch on my wrist. "I'm sorry. I have another appointment."

"Oh, yes, of course." Mark accepted my extended hand. "I'm sorry. This happened so fast I feel like I haven't quite processed it all yet. I understand you've offered me a fantastic opportunity, though, and I appreciate that."

"You're good at what you do," I told him honestly. "I wouldn't make the offer if you weren't worth it. Think about it, then say yes."

He laughed. "I'll give it some serious thought and you'll hear from me on Monday."

As he left, my head turned toward the building that housed Lan-Corp's headquarters. Landon wouldn't find me with my back turned again.

"She started crying the minute you walked out."

I looked at Arnoldo over the rim of my tumbler, which held two fingers of scotch. I swallowed, then asked, "Do you want me to feel guilty about that?"

"No. I wouldn't feel sorry for her, either. But I thought you should know that Corinne isn't completely heartless."

"I never thought she was. I just thought she'd given that heart to her husband."

Arnoldo lifted one shoulder in a shrug. Dressed in well-worn jeans and a tucked-in white dress shirt that was open at the collar and rolled up at the cuffs, he was drawing a lot of female attention.

The bar was packed, but our section of the VIP balcony was guarded well, keeping the rest of the patrons at bay. Arnoldo sat on the crescent-shaped sofa where Cary had sat the first night I'd met with Eva outside the Crossfire. The place would always hold strong memories because of her. It was that night when I realized she was changing everything.

"You look tired," Arnoldo said.

"It's been one of those weeks." I caught his look. "No, it's not Eva."

"Do you want to talk about it?"

"Nothing to say, really. I should've been smarter. I let the world see how much she means to me."

"Passionate kisses on the street, even more passionate fights in the park." He smiled ruefully. "What is it they say? Wearing your heart on your sleeve?"

"I opened the door, now everyone wants to walk through it. She's the most direct way to fuck with my head, and everyone knows it."

"Including Brett Kline?"

"He's not an issue any longer."

Arnoldo studied me and must have seen whatever he needed to. He nodded. "I'm glad, my friend."

"So am I." I took another drink. "What's new with you?"

He waved off the question with a careless sweep of his hand, his gaze sliding around us to take in the women nearby who were swaying to the music of Lana Del Rey. "The restaurant is doing well, as you know."

"Yes, I'm very pleased. Exceeded profit projections in every way."

"We just filmed some promotional teasers for the new season earlier this week. Once the Food Network starts airing them and the new episodes, we should see a nice boost in business."

"I can always say I knew you when."

He laughed and clinked his glass to mine when I held it up in a toast.

We were back on track, which settled some of the unrest I'd been feeling. I didn't lean on Arnoldo the way Eva leaned on her friends or Cary leaned on her, but Arnoldo was important to me all the same. I didn't have many people in my life who were close to me. Finding the rhythm he and I had lost was at least one major victory in a week that had seemed like a losing battle.

18

"OH MY GOD," I moaned around a bite of chocolate toffee cupcake, "this is divine."

Kristin, the wedding planner, beamed. "It's one of my favorites, too. Hold on, though. The butter vanilla is even better."

"Vanilla over chocolate?" My gaze slid over the yummies on the coffee table. "No way."

"I would usually agree," Kristin said, making a note, "but this bakery made me a convert. The lemon is also very good."

The early-afternoon light poured in through the massive windows that made up one side of my mother's private sitting room, illuminating her pale gold curls and porcelain skin. She'd redecorated recently, opting for soft gray-blue walls that lent a new energy to the space—and complemented her well.

It was one of her talents, showcasing herself in the best light. It was

294 · SYLVIA DAY

also one of her major flaws, in my opinion. She cared so damn much about appearances.

I didn't understand how my mom could not get bored with decorating to the latest trends, even if it did seem to take over a year to cycle through every room and hallway in Stanton's six-thousand-plus-square-foot penthouse.

My one meeting with Blaire Ash had been enough to tell me that the decorating gene had skipped my generation. I'd been interested in his ideas but couldn't get worked up over the details.

While I popped another mini cupcake into my mouth with my fingers, my mother daintily speared one of the coin-sized cakes with a fork.

"What are your floral arrangement preferences?" Kristin asked, uncrossing and recrossing long, coffee-hued legs. Her Jimmy Choo heels were elegant but still sexy; her Diane von Furstenberg wrap dress was vintage and classic. She wore her shoulder-length dark hair in tight curls that framed and flattered her narrow face, and pale pink gloss highlighted full, wide lips.

She looked fierce and fabulous, and I'd liked her the moment we met.

"Red," I said, wiping frosting from the corner of my mouth. "Anything red."

"Red?" My mother gave an emphatic shake of her head. "How garish, Eva. It's your first wedding. Go with white, cream, and gold."

I stared at her. "How many weddings do you expect me to have?"

"That's not what I meant. You're a first-time bride."

"I'm not talking about wearing a red dress," I argued. "I'm just saying the primary accent color should be red."

"I don't see how that will work, honey. And I've put together enough weddings to know."

I remembered my mother going through the wedding planning

process before, each successive nuptial more elaborate and memorable than the last. Never overdone and always tasteful. Beautiful weddings for a youthful, beautiful bride. I hoped I aged with half as much grace, because Gideon was only going to get hotter as time went on. He was just that kind of man.

"Let me show you what red can look like, Monica," Kristin said, pulling a leather portfolio out of her bag. "Red can be amazing, especially with evening weddings. The important thing is that the ceremony and reception represent both the bride and groom. To have a truly memorable day, it's important that we visually convey their style, history, and hopes for the future."

My mother accepted the extended portfolio and glanced at the collage of photos on the page. "Eva . . . you can't be serious."

I shot a look of appreciation at Kristin for having my back, especially when she'd come on board expecting my mother to be footing the bill. Of course, the fact that I was marrying Gideon Cross probably helped sway her to my side. Using him as a future reference would certainly help her draw new clientele.

"I'm sure there's a compromise, Mom." At least I hoped so. I hadn't dropped the biggest bomb on her yet.

"Do we have an idea of the budget?" Kristin asked.

And there it was . . .

I saw my mom's mouth open in slow motion and my heart lurched into a semipanicked beat. "Fifty thousand for the ceremony itself," I blurted out. "Minus the cost of the dress."

Both women turned wide eyes toward me.

My mom gave an incredulous laugh, her hand lifting to touch the Cartier trinity necklace that hung between her breasts. "My God, Eva. What a time to make jokes!"

"Dad's paying for the wedding, Mom," I told her, my voice strengthening now that the moment I'd dreaded had passed.

She blinked at me, her blue eyes revealing—just for an instant—a sweet softening. Then her jaw tightened. "Your dress alone will cost more than that. The flowers, the venue . . ."

"We're getting married on the beach," I said, the idea just coming to me. "North Carolina. The Outer Banks. At the house Gideon and I just bought. We'll only need enough flowers for the members of the wedding party."

"You don't understand." My mom glanced at Kristin for support. "There's no way that would work. You'd have no control."

Meaning *she* wouldn't.

"Unpredictable weather," she went on, "sand everywhere . . . Plus, asking everyone to travel that far out of the city will make it likely some won't be able to attend. And where would everyone stay?"

"Who's everyone? I told you, the ceremony is going to be small, for friends and family only. Gideon's taking care of travel. I'm sure he'd be happy to take care of lodging arrangements, too."

"I can help with that," Kristin said.

"Don't encourage her!" my mother snapped.

"Don't be rude!" I shot back. "I think you're forgetting that it's *my* wedding. Not a publicity op."

My mom took a deep, steadying breath. "Eva, I think it's very sweet that you want to accommodate your father this way, but he doesn't understand what a burden he's placing on you by asking this. Even if I matched him dollar for dollar, it wouldn't be enough—"

"It's plenty." My hands linked tightly together in my lap, pressing the rings on my fingers uncomfortably against the bone. "And it's not a burden."

"You're going to offend people. You have to understand that a man in Gideon's position needs to take every opportunity to solidify his network. He's going to want—"

"—to elope," I bit out, frustrated by the too-familiar clash of our viewpoints. "If he had his way, we'd run off somewhere and get married on a remote beach with a couple of witnesses and a great view."

"He may say that—"

"No, Mother. Trust me. That's *exactly* what he would do."

"Um, if I may." Kristin leaned forward. "We can make this work, Monica. Many celebrity weddings are private affairs. A limited budget will keep us focused on the details. And, if Gideon and Eva are open to it, we can arrange to have select photographs sold to the celebrity lifestyle magazines, with the profits going to charity."

"Oh, I like that!" I said, even as I wondered how that could work with the forty-eight-hour exclusive deal Gideon had offered Deanna Johnson.

My mom looked distraught. "I've dreamed of your wedding since the day you were born," she said quietly. "I always wanted you to have something fit for a princess."

"Mom." I reached over and took her hand in mine. "You can go wild with the reception, okay? Do whatever you want. Skip the red, invite the world, whatever. As for the wedding, isn't it enough that I found my prince?"

Her hand tightened on mine and she looked at me with tears in her blue eyes. "I guess it'll have to be."

I'D just slid into the back of the Benz when my smartphone started ringing. Pulling it out of my purse, I looked at the screen and saw it was Trey. My stomach twisted a little.

I couldn't get the shattered look on his face last night out of my mind. I'd stayed tucked away in the kitchen while Cary sat with Trey in the living room and told him about Tatiana and the baby. I had put a pot roast in the oven and sat at the breakfast bar with my tablet, reading a book while staying in Cary's line of sight. Even in profile, I could see how hard Trey had taken the news.

Still, he'd stayed for dinner and then overnight, so I hoped things would work out in the end. At least he hadn't just walked out.

"Hi, Trey," I answered. "How are you?"

"Hey, Eva." He sighed heavily. "I have no idea how I am. How are you doing?"

"Well, I'm just leaving my mother's place after spending hours talking about the wedding. It didn't go as badly as it could have, but it could've been smoother. But that's pretty usual when dealing with my mom."

"Ah . . . well, you've got a lot on your plate. I'm sorry to bother you."

"Trey. It's fine. I'm glad you called. If you want to talk, I'm here."

"Could we get together, maybe? Whenever it's convenient for you?"

"How's now?"

"Really? I'm at a street fair on the west side. My sister dragged me out and I was miserable company. She ditched me a few minutes ago and now I'm wondering what the hell I'm doing here."

"I can meet you."

"I'm between Eighty-second and Eighty-third, close to Amsterdam. It's packed here, just FYI."

"Okay, hang tight. I'll see you in a few."

"Thanks, Eva."

We hung up and I caught Raúl's gaze in the rearview mirror. "Amsterdam and Eighty-second. Close as you can get."

He nodded.

"Thanks." I looked out the window as we turned a corner, taking in the city on a sunny Saturday afternoon.

The pace of Manhattan was slower on the weekends, the clothes more casual, and the street vendors more plentiful. Women in sandals and light summer dresses window-shopped leisurely, while men in shorts and T-shirts traveled in groups, taking in the women and discussing whatever it was men discussed. Dogs of all sizes pranced on the ends of leashes, while children in strollers kicked up their heels or napped. An elderly couple shuffled along hand in hand, still lost in the wonder of each other after years of familiarity.

I was speed-dialing Gideon before I realized I'd thought of it.

"Angel," he answered. "Are you on your way home?"

"Not quite. I'm done at my mom's, but I'm going to meet Trey."

"How long will that take?"

"I'm not sure. Not more than an hour, I think. God, I hope he doesn't tell me he's done with Cary."

"How did it go with your mother?"

"I told her we were getting married on the beach by the Outer Banks house." I paused. "I'm sorry. I should've asked you first."

"I think that's an excellent idea." His raspy voice took on the special timbre that told me he was moved.

"She asked me how we're planning on lodging everyone. I kinda dropped that on you and the wedding planner."

"That's fine. We'll work something out."

Love for him spread through me in a warm rush. "Thank you."

"So the big hurdle's behind you," he said, understanding as he so often did.

"Well, I don't know about that. She got all teary about it. You know, she had big dreams that aren't coming true. I hope she lets them go and gets on board."

"What about her family? We haven't talked about making arrangements for them to come."

I shrugged, then remembered he couldn't see me. "They're not invited. The only things I know about them are what I found with a Google search. They disowned my mom when she got pregnant with me, so they've never been a part of my life."

"All right, then," he said smoothly. "I've got a surprise for you when you get home."

"Oh?" My mood instantly brightened. "Will you give me a hint?"

"Of course not. You'll have to hurry home if you're curious."

I pouted. "Tease."

"Teases don't deliver. I do."

My toes curled at the rough velvet of his voice. "I'll be home as soon as I can."

"I'll be waiting," he purred.

THE traffic near the fair was impossible. Raúl left the Benz in the garage beneath my apartment building, then walked me over to the street fair.

When we were half a block away, I started smelling the food and my mouth watered. Music drifted in the air and when we reached Amsterdam Avenue, I saw that it came from a woman singing on a small stage for a packed audience.

Vendors lined either side of the overflowing street, their wares and heads shielded from the sun by white tent tops. From scarves and hats, to jewelry and art, to fresh produce and multinational eats, there was nothing one could want that couldn't be found.

It took me a few minutes to spot Trey in the crowd. I found him sitting on steps not too far from the corner we'd agreed upon. He was dressed in loose jeans and an olive-hued T-shirt, with sunglasses perched on the crooked bridge of his once-broken nose. His blond hair was as unruly as ever, his attractive mouth tightened into a firm line.

He stood when he saw me, holding out his hand for me to shake. I pulled him into a hug instead, holding him until I felt him relax and hug me back. Life flowed by around us—New Yorkers were comfortable with all sorts of public displays. Raúl moved a discreet distance away.

"I'm a fucking mess," Trey muttered against my shoulder.

"You're normal." I pulled back and gestured toward the steps where I'd found him. "Anyone would be reeling right now."

He sat down on the middle step. I perched next to him.

"I don't think I can do this, Eva. I don't think I should. I want someone in my life full-time, someone who's there to support me while I get through school, then try to build my practice. Cary's going to be supporting that model instead and fitting me in when he can. How am I not going to resent that?"

"That's a valid question," I said, stretching out my legs in front of me. "You know Cary won't be sure the baby is his until a paternity test is done."

Trey shook his head. "I don't think it'll matter. He seems invested."

"I think it'll matter. Maybe he won't just walk away, maybe he'll play uncle or something. I don't know. For now, we have to go with the assumption that he's the dad, but maybe he's not. It's a possibility."

"So you're telling me to hang in there for another six months?"

"No. If you want me to give you answers, I don't have any. All I can tell you for sure is that Cary loves you, more than I've ever seen him love anyone. If he loses you, it's going to break him. I'm not trying to guilt you into staying with him. I just think you should know that if you leave, you're not the only one who'll be hurting."

"How is that helpful?"

"Maybe it's not." I set my hand on his knee. "Maybe I'm just small enough to find that comforting. If Gideon and I didn't work out, I'd want to know he was as miserable as I was."

Trey's mouth curved in a sad smile. "Yeah, I see your point. Would you stay with him if you found out he'd knocked someone else up? Someone he was sleeping with while dating you?"

"I thought about that. It's hard for me to imagine not being with Gideon. If we weren't exclusive at the time and the woman was in his past, if he was with me and not her, maybe I could handle it."

I watched a woman hang yet another bag of purchases onto the overburdened handle of her kid's stroller. "But if he was mostly with her and seeing me on the side . . . I think I'd walk."

It was tough being honest when the truth was the opposite of what Cary would want me to say, but I felt like it was the right thing to do.

"Thanks, Eva."

"For what it's worth, I wouldn't think less of you if you toughed it out with Cary. It's not weak to stand by the person you love when they're trying to fix a big mistake, and it's not weak to decide to put yourself first. Whatever decision you make, I'll still think you're a helluva guy."

Leaning into me, he rested his head on my shoulder. "Thanks, Eva."

I linked my fingers with his. "You're welcome."

"I'LL go get the car and pull it around," Raúl said, as we entered the lobby of my apartment building.

"Okay. I'm just going to check the mail." I waved at the concierge as we passed the desk. I turned into the mailroom, while Raúl headed to the elevator.

Sliding my key into the lock, I pulled the brass door open and bent low to peer inside. There were a few postcard advertisements and nothing else, which saved me a trip upstairs. I slid them out, tossed them in the nearby trash can, then shut and locked the mailbox.

I headed back into the lobby just in time to catch a woman exiting the building. Her spiky red hair caught my attention and held it. I stared hard, waiting for her to turn onto the street, hoping I'd catch a glimpse of her profile.

My breath caught. The hair was familiar from a Google image search. The face I remembered from the shelter fund-raiser Gideon and I had attended a few weeks back.

Then she was gone.

I ran after her, but when I reached the sidewalk she was already sliding into the back of a black town car.

"Hey!" I shouted.

The car sped off, leaving me staring after it.

"Everything all right?"

I turned to face Louie, the weekend doorman. "Do you know who that was?"

He shook his head. "She doesn't live here."

Going back inside, I asked the concierge the same question.

"A redhead?" she asked, looking perplexed. "We haven't had any visitors who came in without a tenant today, so I haven't really paid attention."

"Hmm. Okay, thank you."

"Your car's here, Eva," Louie said from the doorway.

I thanked the concierge and headed out to Raúl. I spent the ride between my place and Gideon's thinking about Anne Lucas. By the time I stepped out of the private elevator into the foyer of the penthouse, my spinning thoughts had me distracted.

Gideon was waiting for me. Dressed in worn jeans and a Columbia T-shirt, he looked so young and handsome. Then he flashed me a smile and I almost forgot the world altogether.

"Angel," he purred, crossing the black-and-white checkerboard flooring on bare feet. He had that look in his eye I knew well. "Come here."

I walked right into his open arms, cuddling up tightly to his hard body. I breathed him in. "You're going to think I'm crazy," I mumbled against his chest, "but I could swear I just saw Anne Lucas in the lobby of my building."

He stiffened. I knew the shrink wasn't his favorite person.

"When?" he asked tightly.

"Twenty minutes ago, maybe. Right before I came over here."

Releasing me, he reached into his back pocket and pulled out his smartphone. His other hand caught mine and pulled me into the living room.

"Mrs. Cross just saw Anne Lucas in her apartment building," he said to whoever answered.

"I *think* I did," I corrected, frowning at his hard tone.

But he wasn't listening to me. "Find out," he ordered, before hanging up.

"Gideon. What's going on?"

He led us to the couch and sat. I settled next to him, putting my purse down on the coffee table.

"I saw Anne the other day," he explained, holding on to my hand. "Raúl confirmed that the woman who spoke to you at the fund-raiser was her. She admitted it, and I warned her to stay away from you, but she won't. She wants to hurt me and she knows she can do that if she hurts you."

"Okay." I processed that.

"You need to tell Raúl the moment you see her anywhere. Even if you just *think* it's her."

"Hold on a minute, ace. You went to see her the other day and didn't tell me?"

"I'm telling you now."

"Why didn't you tell me then?"

He exhaled roughly. "It was the day Chris came over."

"Oh."

"Yeah."

I gnawed on my lower lip a minute. "How would she hurt me?"

"I don't know. It's enough for me that she wants to."

"Like would she break my leg? My nose?"

"I doubt she'd resort to violence," he said dryly. "It would be more fun for her to play mind games. Showing up where you are. Letting you catch glimpses of her."

Which was more insidious. "So that you'll go to her. That's what she really wants," I muttered. "She wants to see you."

"I won't be obliging her. I said what I needed to."

Looking down at our joined hands, I played with his wedding band. "Anne, Corinne, Deanna . . . It's a bit crazy, Gideon. I mean, I don't think this is normal for most men. How many more women are going to lose their minds over you?"

He shot me a look that was patently not amused. "I don't know what's gotten into Corinne. None of what she's done since she returned to New York is like her. I don't know if it's the medication she was on, the miscarriage, her divorce . . ."

"She's getting divorced?"

"Don't take that tone, Eva. It doesn't make a damn bit of difference to me if she's married or single. *I'm* married. That's never going to change, and I'm not a man who cheats. I have more respect for you—and me—than to be that kind of husband."

I leaned forward, offering my mouth, and he took it in a soft, sweet kiss. He had said exactly what I needed to hear.

Gideon pulled back, nuzzling his nose against mine. "As for the other two . . . You have to understand that Deanna was collateral damage. Fuck. My entire life has been a war zone and some people have gotten caught in the line of fire."

I cupped his jaw, trying to stroke the tension away with soothing brushes of my thumb. I knew just what he meant.

He swallowed hard. "If I hadn't used Deanna to send a message to Anne that the door was closed between us, she would've been just a one-night stand. Over and done with."

"But she's okay now?"

"I think so." His fingertips brushed my cheek, the touch reflecting the one I'd given him. "Since I'm sharing, I'll say that I don't think she'd turn me down if I tried to hook up—which I won't—but I don't think she falls in the woman-scorned category any longer."

"Yeah, I knew she'd hit the sheets with you again if she could. Not that I blame her. Do you have to be so damn good in bed? Isn't it enough that you're hot, and have an amazing body and a huge cock?"

He shook his head, clearly exasperated. "It's not *huge*."

"Whatever. You're hung. And you know how to use it. And women don't get awesome sex very often, so when we do, we can go a little nuts over it. I guess that answers my question about Anne, since she had you repeatedly."

"She never had me." Gideon sat back, slouching. Scowling. "At some point you're going to get sick of hearing what an asshole I am."

I curled into his side, resting my head on his shoulder. "You're not the first insanely hot guy on the planet to use women. And you won't be the last."

"It was different with Anne," he grumbled. "It wasn't just about her husband."

I stilled, then forced myself to relax so that I didn't make him any more nervous than he already was.

He sucked in a quick, deep breath. "She reminds me of Hugh sometimes," he said in a rush. "The way she moves, some of the things she says . . . There's a familial resemblance. And more. I can't explain it."

"Then don't."

"Sometimes the line between them blurred in my mind. It was like I was punishing Hugh through Anne. I did things to her I've never done with anyone else. Things that made me feel sick when I thought about them later."

"Gideon." I slid my arm around his waist.

He hadn't told me this. He'd said before that it was Dr. Terrence Lucas he was punishing, and I was sure that was part of it. But now I knew it wasn't all of it.

Gideon sat back. "It was twisted between Anne and me. I twisted her. If I could go back and do things differently—"

"We'll deal with it. I'm glad you told me."

"Had to. Listen, angel, you need to tell Raúl the moment you see her anywhere. Even if you're not sure. And don't go anywhere alone.

I'll figure out how to deal with her. In the meantime, I need to know that you're safe."

"Okay." I wasn't sure how that plan would work over the long haul. We lived in the same city with the woman and her husband, and Lucas himself had approached me before. They were a problem and we needed a solution.

But we weren't going to come up with it today. Saturday. One of the two days of the week I most looked forward to because I got to spend so much private time with my husband.

"So," I began, sliding my hand up beneath Gideon's shirt to touch his warm skin. "Where's my surprise?"

"Well . . ." The sexy rasp in his voice deepened. "Let's wait a bit before that. How about we start with some wine?"

Tilting my head back, I looked up at him. "Are you trying to seduce me, ace?"

He kissed my nose. "Always."

"Umm . . . Go right ahead."

I knew something was up when Gideon didn't join me in the shower. The only time he missed an opportunity to put his hands on me while drenched and dripping was in the mornings, after he'd already had his way with me.

When I came back out to the living room dressed in shorts and tank top sans bra, he was waiting for me with a glass of red wine. We settled on the couch with *3 Days to Kill*, which only proved to me that my husband knew me well. It was just the sort of movie I enjoyed—a bit funny, a lot over-the-top. And it had Kevin Costner, who was always a win for me.

Still, as much fun as I had just being lazy with Gideon, the anticipation started to make me twitchy as the hours passed. And Gideon, the devious man, knew it. He built on it. He kept my wineglass full and his hands on me—tangled in my hair, brushing over my shoulder, running along my thigh.

By nine o'clock, I was crawling all over him. I slid into his lap and pressed my lips to his throat, my tongue darting out to stroke over his pulse. I felt it leap, then accelerate, but he made no move in response. He sat as if absorbed in the rerun we'd channel-surfed to after the movie ended.

"Gideon?" I whispered in my fuck-me voice, my hand sliding between his legs to find him as hard and ready as always.

"Hmm?"

I caught the lobe of his ear in my teeth, tugging gently. "Would you mind if I fucked myself on your big cock while you're watching TV?"

His hand rubbed absently down my back. "I might not be able to see around you," he replied, sounding distracted. "Maybe you better get on your knees and suck it instead."

Pulling back, I gaped at him. His eyes laughed at me.

I shoved at his shoulder. "You're terrible!"

"My poor angel," he crooned. "Are you horny?"

"What do you think?" I gestured at my chest. My nipples were hard and tight, straining against the thin cotton in a silent demand for his attention.

Cupping my shoulders, he pulled me closer and caught the tip of my breast in his teeth, his tongue stroking softly. I moaned.

He released me, his eyes now so dark they were like sapphires. "Are you wet?"

I was getting there, fast. Whenever Gideon looked at me like that, my body softened for him, grew moist and eager. "Why don't you find out?" I teased.

"Show me."

The authoritative bite in his command made me hotter. I slid off him carefully, feeling inexplicably shy. He pushed the coffee table back with one foot, giving me more room to stand in front of him. His gaze slid over me, his face expressionless. The lack of encouragement made me even more anxious, which I guessed was his intention.

He was pushing in that way he had.

Rolling my shoulders back, I caught his gaze with my own and ran my tongue along my bottom lip. His eyes became heavy-lidded. I slid my thumbs beneath the elastic waistband of my athletic shorts and pushed them down, wriggling my hips a little to make it look more like a striptease and less like I was feeling awkward.

"No panties," he murmured, his gaze on my sex. "You're a bad girl, angel."

I pouted. "I'm trying to be good."

"Open yourself for me," he murmured. "Let me see you."

"Gideon . . ."

He waited patiently and I knew that patience would hold. Whether it took me five minutes or five hours, he would wait for me. And that was why I trusted him. Because it was never a question of whether I would submit, but *when* I was ready to, and that was a decision he most often left to me.

I widened my stance and tried to slow the quickness of my breathing. Reaching down with both hands, I touched the lips of my sex and spread them, exposing my clit to the man it ached for.

Gideon straightened slowly. "You have such a pretty cunt, Eva."

As he leaned closer, I held my breath. His hands lifted from his thighs, reaching for mine to hold me steady. "Don't move," he ordered.

Then he licked me in a leisurely glide.

"Oh God," I moaned, my legs shaking.

"Sit down," he said hoarsely, sliding to his knees on the floor as I obeyed.

The glass was cool against my bare buttocks, a sharp contrast to the heat of my skin. My arms stretched back, gripping the far edge of the table for balance as he pressed my thighs wide with his palms, splaying me open.

His breath was hot against my damp flesh, his focus fully on my sex. "You could be wetter."

I watched, panting, as he lowered his head and wrapped his lips around my clit. The heat was searing, the lash of his tongue devastating. I cried out, wanting to writhe but held fast by his grip. My head fell back, my ears ringing with the rush of blood and the sound of Gideon's groan. His tongue fluttered over the tight bundle of nerves, driving me relentlessly toward orgasm. My stomach tightened as the pleasure built, the soft silk of his hair brushing along my sensitive inner thighs.

A low moan escaped me. "I'm going to come," I gasped. "Gideon . . . God . . . I'm going to come."

He drove his tongue inside me. My elbows weakened, dropping me lower. His tongue fucked into the clutching opening of my sex, stroking through the sensitive tissues, teasing me with a promise of the penetration I truly craved.

"Fuck me," I begged.

Gideon pulled back, licking his lips. "Not here."

I made a sound of protest as he stood, so close to orgasm I could taste it. He held his hand out to me, helped me straighten and then stand. When I wobbled, he caught me up, tossing me over his shoulder.

"Gideon!"

But then his hand was between my legs, massaging my wet, swollen sex, and I didn't care how he carried me, as long as he got me someplace where he'd take me.

We reached the hallway and turned, then stopped too quickly to have reached his bedroom. I heard the doorknob turn and then the light flicked on.

We were in the bedroom that was mine. He set me down on my feet, facing him.

"Why here?" I asked. Maybe some men would head to the nearest bed, but Gideon had more control than that. If he wanted me in the second bedroom, he had a reason for it.

"Turn around," he said quietly.

Something about his voice . . . the way he looked at me . . .

I looked over my shoulder.

And saw the swing.

IT wasn't what I expected.

I'd looked up sex swings on the Internet when Gideon had first mentioned one. What I'd found were rickety things you hung from door frames, not-so-rickety things that hung from four-legged frames, and ones that hung from an eyebolt in the ceiling. All of them consisted of some combination of chains and/or straps that acted as slings for various body parts. Pictures of women actually harnessed in the damn things looked uncomfortable.

Honestly, I couldn't see how anyone could get past the awkwardness and fear of collapse, let alone manage an orgasm.

I should've known Gideon would have something else in mind.

Turning, I faced the swing head-on. Gideon had cleared out the bedroom at some point. The bed and furnishings were gone. The only object in the room was the swing itself, suspended from a sturdy cage-like structure. A wide, solid metal platform anchored steel sides and roof, which supported the weight of a padded metal chair and chains. Red leather cuffs for wrists and ankles hung in the appropriate places.

His arms wrapped around me from behind, one hand sliding up beneath my shirt to cup my breast, while the other slid between my legs to push two fingers inside me.

Nuzzling my hair out of the way, he kissed my throat. "How do you feel, looking at that?"

I thought about it. "Intrigued. A little apprehensive."

His lips curved against my skin. "Let's see how you feel once you're in it."

A shiver of expectation and apprehension moved through me. I could see from the position of the cuffs that I would be helpless, unable to move or pull away. Unable to exert any control whatsoever over what might happen to me.

"I want to do this right, Eva. Not like that night in the elevator. I want you to feel it when I'm in control and we're in it together."

My head fell back against him. Somehow, it was harder giving the consent he wanted. There was less . . . responsibility when he just took charge.

But that was a cop-out.

"What's your safe word, angel?" he murmured, his teeth scoring gently across my throat. His hands were magic, his fingers gliding shallowly inside me.

"Crossfire."

"You say the word and everything stops. Say it again."

"Crossfire."

His dexterous fingers tugged at my nipple, milking it expertly. "There's nothing to be afraid of. You just have to sit back and take my cock. I'm going to make you come without you having to do a thing."

I took a deep breath. "I feel like that's always how it is between us."

"Try it this way," he coaxed, his hands moving to pull my shirt off. "If you don't like it, we'll hit the bed instead."

For a moment, I wanted to delay, take more time to let it all settle in. I'd promised the swing, but he wasn't holding that over me . . .

"Crossfire," he breathed, hugging me from behind.

I didn't know if he was reminding me of my safe word or telling me he loved me so much there were no words for how he felt. Either way, the effect on me was the same. I felt safe.

I also felt his excitement. His breathing had quickened the moment I'd spotted the swing. His erection was like steel against my buttocks and his skin was hot against mine. His desire spurred my own, made me want to do whatever it took to give him as much pleasure as he could stand.

If he needed something, I wanted to be the woman who gave it to him. He gave so much to me. Everything.

"Okay," I said softly. "Okay."

He kissed my shoulder, then stepped beside me, taking my hand in his.

I followed him to the swing, studying it intently. The narrow seat hung at waist level for Gideon, which meant he had to turn me to face him, then lift me up into the chair. His mouth touched mine as my bare ass touched the cool leather, his tongue teasing the seam of my lips. I shivered. Whether that was from the chill, his kiss, or anxiety, I didn't know.

Gideon pulled away, his gaze heavy-lidded and hot. He eased me into position, holding the chains steady as I leaned into the seat back, which was angled away from him, making me want to stretch my legs out for balance.

"You settled?" he asked, watching me intently.

I knew the question was about more than my physical comfort. I nodded.

He stepped back, his gaze never leaving my face. "I'm going to secure your ankles. You tell me if anything doesn't feel right."

"All right." My voice was breathy, my pulse racing.

His hand slid down my leg, the stroke warm and provocative. I couldn't look away as he wrapped the crimson leather around my ankle and cinched the metal buckle. The cuff was fit securely but not too tightly.

Gideon moved quickly and confidently. A moment later, my other leg was suspended as well.

He looked at me. "Okay so far?"

"You've done this before." I pouted. His actions seemed too practiced to be those of a beginner.

He didn't answer. Instead he began to strip as slowly and methodically as he'd restrained me.

Mesmerized, I greedily drank in every inch of skin he revealed. My husband had such an amazing body. He was so hard and tight, so virile. It was impossible not to become aroused seeing him naked.

His tongue slid along the bottom curve of his mouth in a leisurely, erotic caress. "Still good, angel?"

Gideon knew exactly what the sight of him did to me, and it turned me on even more that he was arrogant enough to use that weakness against me. God knew I did the same to him when I could.

"You are so fucking hot," I told him, licking my own lips.

He smiled and came toward me, his thick, long cock curving upward to his navel. "I think you'll really enjoy this."

I didn't have to ask why he said so, because it was evident as he reached me and took my hands in his. My vantage of him from the swing seat was completely unhindered. From the thighs upward, he was totally exposed between the spread of my legs.

He bent and kissed me again. Softly. Sweetly. I moaned at the unexpected tenderness and the lushness of his flavor.

Releasing one of my hands, he reached between us, gripping his cock and angling it downward to stroke between the lips of my sex. The wide head slid through the slickness of my desire, then nudged against my exposed clit. Pleasure rippled through me and I discovered just how vulnerable I was. I couldn't arch my hips. I couldn't tighten my inner muscles to chase the sensation.

A low whimper escaped me. I needed more, but could only wait for him to give it to me.

"You trust me," he whispered against my mouth.

It wasn't a question, but I answered anyway. "Yes."

Gideon nodded. "Grab the chains."

There were wrist restraints above my head. I wondered why he didn't use them, but I trusted him to know best. If he didn't think I was ready, it was because he knew me so well. In some ways, he knew me better than I knew myself.

The love I felt for him unfurled in my chest until it filled me, pushing aside the vestiges of fear that hovered in the dark corners of my mind. I'd never felt so close to him, never known it was possible to believe in someone so completely.

I did as Gideon ordered and gripped the chains. He stepped close again, his abs glistening with the first mist of perspiration. I could see his pulse throbbing in his neck, his arms, his penis. His heart was racing like mine. The head of his cock was as wet with excitement as my sex. The hunger between us was a living thing in the room, sliding sinuously around us, narrowing the world to just the two of us.

"Don't let go," he ordered, waiting until I nodded my agreement before he proceeded.

He gripped a chain where it met with the seat. His other hand guided his cock to my cleft. The thick crown pressed teasingly against me, taunting me with the promise of pleasure. I was panting as I waited for him to take the step forward that would slide him into me, my core aching with the need to be filled.

Instead, he gripped the seat of the chair in both hands and pulled me onto his cock.

The sound that ripped from my throat was inhuman, the savagely erotic feeling of being so deeply penetrated driving me wild. He sank deep in that one easy glide, my body unable to offer any resistance.

Gideon snarled, a tremor running through his powerful body. "Fuck," he hissed. "Your cunt is so good."

I started to reach for him, but he pushed the swing back, gliding me off his rock-hard erection. The feeling of being emptied made me moan in distress.

"Please," I begged softly.

"I told you not to let go," he said, with a wicked gleam in his eyes.

"I won't," I promised, gripping the chains so hard it hurt.

His arms flexed as he pulled me back, sliding me onto his cock. My toes curled. The feeling of weightlessness, of total surrender, was indescribable.

"Talk to me," he bit out. "Tell me you like this."

"Damn it," I gasped, feeling sweat slide down my nape. "Don't stop."

One moment I was held stationary, the next I was swinging fluidly, my sex sliding on and off Gideon's rigid cock with breathtaking speed. His body worked like a well-oiled machine, his arms, chest, abs, and thighs straining with the exertion of masterfully handling the swing. The sight of his powerful movements, the intensity of his focus on pleasuring us both, the feel of him pumping so deep and fast into me . . .

I orgasmed with a scream, unable to contain the rush that surged through me. He fucked me through it, growling roughly, his face flushed and etched with lust. I'd never come so hard, so fast. I couldn't see or breathe for an endless moment, my body wracked by a pleasure more ferocious than any I'd ever felt before.

The swing slowed, then stopped. Gideon took an extra step toward me that kept him buried inside me. He smelled decadent, primal. Pure sin and sex.

His hands cupped my face. His fingers brushed tendrils of hair off my damp cheeks. My sex spasmed around him, all too aware of how hard and thick he still was.

"You didn't come," I accused, feeling far too vulnerable after the insanity of my orgasm.

Gideon took my mouth in a harsh, demanding kiss. "I'm going to restrain your wrists. Then I'm going to come in you."

My nipples tightened into painful points. "Oh God."

"You trust me," he said again, his gaze searching my face.

I touched him while I still could, my hands sliding over his sweat-slick chest, feeling the desperate beat of his heart. "More than anything."

19

"**G**OOD MORNING, ACE."

I looked over my shoulder at the sound of Eva's voice, smiling as I watched her circle the island on her way to the coffeemaker. Her hair was a wild tangle, her legs sexy beneath the hem of the T-shirt she wore.

Returning my attention to the stove and the French toast I was browning in the pan, I asked, "How are you feeling?"

"Umm . . ."

I looked at her again and found her blushing.

"I'm sore," she said, inserting a coffee pod into the machine. "Deep inside."

I grinned. The swing had positioned her perfectly, allowing for optimal penetration. I'd never been as deep in her before. I had been thinking about it all morning and decided that I would be speaking to

Ash about his plans for the renovations. One of the bedrooms would need to have two closets—one for clothes, the other for the swing.

"Jeez," she muttered, "Look at that cocky smirk. Men are pigs."

"And here I am, slaving over a hot stove for you."

"Yeah, yeah." She swatted my ass as she passed me with a steaming cup of coffee in hand.

I caught her by the waist before she got too far, giving her a quick hard kiss on the cheek. "You were amazing last night."

I'd felt something click into place between us so strongly that the change had been as tangible as the rings I wore on my fingers, and I cherished it as dearly.

She flashed me a dazzling smile, then opened the fridge to pull out the carton of half-and-half. While she took care of that, I plated the finished French toast.

"I've been wanting to talk to you about something," she said, joining me at the island and wriggling onto a bar stool.

My brows lifted. "Okay."

"I'd like to become involved with the Crossroads Foundation—financially and administratively."

"That could encompass a lot of things, angel. Tell me what you have in mind."

Shrugging, she picked up her fork. "I've been thinking about the settlement money I got from Nathan's dad. It's just sitting in the bank, and after what Megumi has been through . . . I've realized that I need to put that money to work and I don't want to wait. I'd like to help fund the programs offered by Crossroads and help brainstorm ways to expand them."

I smiled inwardly, pleased to see her moving in the right direction. "All right. We'll work something out."

"Yeah?" She brightened like the sun, the shining light in my world.

"Of course. I'd like to commit more time to it, too."

"We can work together!" She bounced up and down. "I'm excited about this, Gideon."

I let the smile show. "I can tell."

"It just feels like a natural progression for us. An extension of *us*, really." She cut into her food and forked a bite to her mouth. She hummed her appreciation. "Yummy," she mumbled.

"I'm glad you like it."

"You're hot *and* you can cook. I'm a lucky girl."

I decided not to tell her I'd just downloaded the recipe that morning. Instead, I considered what she'd said.

Had I made a tactical error by moving too quickly with Mark? It was possible that if I'd left it alone just a little longer, Eva might have come around to working at Cross Industries on her own.

But did I have the luxury of giving her more time with Landon closing in? Even now, I didn't think so.

Seeking to mitigate any possible fallout, I debated the merits of broaching the topic of Mark's move to Cross Industries now versus later. Eva had opened the door by talking about us working together. If I didn't walk through it, I ran the risk of her finding out another way.

I had taken that chance on Saturday, knowing Eva and Mark were friends who talked outside work. He could've called her at any time, but I'd banked on him thinking it over first, discussing it with his partner, and coming to peace with leaving Waters Field & Leaman.

"I have to talk to you about something, too, angel."

"I'm all ears."

Shooting for nonchalance, I grabbed the maple syrup and poured some onto my plate. "I offered Mark Garrity a job."

There was a moment of stunned silence, and then, "You did what?"

The tone of her voice confirmed that I'd been right to be up front sooner rather than later. I looked at her. She was staring at me.

"I've asked Mark to work for Cross Industries," I repeated.

Her face paled. "When?"

"Friday."

"Friday," she parroted. "It's Sunday. You're just bringing this up now?"

Since the question was rhetorical, I didn't reply, choosing to wait for a clearer assessment of the situation before possibly making things worse.

"Why, Gideon?"

I took the same tack I'd used with Mark—I told the parts of the truth most likely to be accepted. "He's a solid employee. He'll bring a lot to the team."

"Bullshit." The color came back into her face in an angry rush. "Don't patronize me. You're putting me out of a job and you didn't think that was something you should discuss with me first?"

I switched tactics. "LanCorp asked for Mark directly, didn't they?"

She was silent a minute. "That's what this is about? The PhazeOne system? Are you fucking serious?"

I'd wondered what product Ryan Landon would use as an excuse to approach Eva. I was surprised he'd gone with a product so vital to his bottom line, then chastised myself for not expecting it. "You didn't answer my question, Eva."

"What the hell does it matter?" she snapped. "Yeah, they asked for Mark. So what? You don't want your competitors using him? Are you trying to say this was a business decision?"

"No, this was personal." I set my utensils down. "Eric Landon, Ryan Landon's father, invested heavily with my dad and lost everything. Ryan Landon has been gunning for me ever since."

A frown marred the space between her brows. "So you didn't want us working on any campaigns for him? Is that what you're saying?"

"I'm saying that Ryan Landon asked for Mark as a way to get to you."

"What? Why?" Irritation mixed with anger on her face. "He's

married, for chrissakes. He brought his wife to lunch with us the other day. You've got no reason to be jealous."

"He wouldn't be interested in you that way," I agreed. "It's more of a triumph to have you working for him. He wants the satisfaction of knowing he can give an order and you'll have to jump to get it done."

"That's ridiculous."

"You don't know the whole of it, Eva. How many years he's spent trying to undercut me in every way possible. Every business decision he makes is driven by the need to rewrite the connection between the Landon and Cross names. Every success he's had has been accompanied by a mention of his father's failure to see my dad as a fraud and what that cost the Landons."

"Of course I don't know," she said coldly. "Because you didn't see fit to tell me."

"I'm telling you now."

"When it doesn't matter anymore!" She slid off the bar stool and stalked out of the kitchen.

I went after her, as I always did. "Eva."

I caught her by the elbow, but she yanked free, spinning to face me. "Don't touch me!"

"Don't walk away from me," I growled. "If we're going to fight, let's get it over with."

"That's what you were counting on, right? You figured you'd do whatever you wanted, then sweet-talk or fuck your way through it later. But you can't fix this, Gideon. You can't say a few words or screw me brainless and get away with it this time."

"Fix what? I saw someone maneuvering to take advantage of you and I took care of it."

"Is that how you see it?" Her hands went to her hips. "I don't see it that way at all. Landon is taking the risk. What if Mark and I do a crappy job? He's got a lot riding on PhazeOne."

"Exactly. He has in-house advertising, marketing, and promotion, just like I do. Why take something he's sunk a fortune into—even by my standards—and set himself up for leaks or a massive fail?"

She threw her hands up with a snort.

"Right," I bit out. "You can't answer that because there is no good answer. It's an unnecessary gamble. The only people handling the launch of the next-generation GenTen are people whose souls I own."

"What are you saying?"

"That Landon's waited a long time for his pound of Cross flesh. Maybe he doesn't care that you married into the name. I don't know what he has in mind. At the very least, he's forcing us into a place where we're unable to share information with each other."

Her brow arched. "How is that any different from how our relationship usually works?"

"Don't." I clenched my hands at my sides, frustrated by her stubbornness. "Don't make this about us when it's about him. I'll be damned if Landon drags you through hell because of me."

"I'm not saying you're wrong! If you'd told me about this, I would've made the right decision on my own. Instead, you forced me out of a job I love!"

"Back up. What decision would that have been?"

"I don't know." She gave me a cold, hard smile that chilled my blood. "And now we'll never find out."

She turned her back to me again.

"Stop."

"No," she tossed over her shoulder. "I'm getting dressed. Then I'm leaving."

"Like hell." I followed her into the bedroom.

"I can't be around you right now, Gideon. I don't even want to look at you."

My mind raced, searching for something to say that would calm her down. "Mark hasn't taken the job."

She shook her head and yanked open a drawer to pull out a pair of shorts. "He will. I'm sure you made him an offer he can't refuse."

"I'll withdraw it." God. I was backpedaling and it rankled, but she was so angry I couldn't reach her. She was as distant as I'd ever seen her. Remote and untouchable. After the wildly erotic night we'd had, when we had been as close as ever, her attitude was unbearable.

"Don't bother, Gideon. The damage is done. But you'll get a solid employee who'll bring a lot to your team." She tugged the shorts on and went into the closet.

I was right behind her, blocking the doorway while she shoved her feet into flip-flops. "Listen to me, damn it. They're coming after you. Everyone. They want to get at me through you. I'm doing the best I can, Eva. I'm trying to protect us the only way I know how."

She paused, facing me. "That's a problem. Because this way doesn't work for me. It will *never* work for me."

"Goddamn it, I'm *trying!*"

"All you had to do was talk to me, Gideon. I was halfway there on my own. Working with you on Crossroads was just the first step. I was going to make the decision to work with you, and you took that away from me. You took it away from both of us. And we'll never get it back."

The icy finality in her tone made me crazed. I could deal when discussions went sideways. I could spin and switch strategy on the fly. What I couldn't handle was when my grip on Eva slipped. When we'd said our vows, I had made the irrevocable decision to let everything go—my ambition, my pride, my heart—to hang on to her. If I couldn't do that, I had nothing.

"Don't throw that at me now, angel," I warned. "Every time I've brought up working together you shut me down."

"So you just bulldoze right through me?"

"I was willing to give you time! I had a plan. I was going to seduce you with the possibilities, let you decide that the best way to develop your potential was alongside me."

"You should've stuck with the plan. Get out of my way."

I held my ground. "How could I stick with any plan the last few weeks? While you're feeling righteous, think about what I've dealt with. Brett, the damned tape of you with him, Chris, my brother, therapy, Ireland, my mother, Anne, Corinne, fucking Landon—"

Eva crossed her arms. "Gotta handle it all yourself, don't you? Am I really your wife, Gideon? I'm not even your friend. I bet Angus and Raúl know more about your life than I do. Arash, too. I'm just the pretty cunt you fuck."

"Shut up."

"You need to get out of my way before this gets any uglier."

"I can't let you leave. You know I can't. Not like this."

Her jaw tightened. "You're asking me to give you something I don't have right now. I'm hollowed out, Gideon."

"Angel . . ." I reached for her, my chest so tight I found it hard to breathe. The devastation on her face was killing me. I'd destroy anyone who put that look on her face, but this time, I had done it. "What does it matter if you would've made the same decision anyway?"

"You need to stop talking," she said hoarsely. "Because every word coming out of your mouth makes me think we're so far apart on this that we've got no business being married."

If she'd stabbed me in the chest, it couldn't have hurt worse. The air in the closet became hot and stale, drying my throat and making my eyes burn. The floor seemed to tilt beneath my feet, the foundation of my life shifting as Eva slipped further and further away.

"Tell me what to do," I whispered.

Her eyes glistened. "Let me go for now. Give me some space to think. A few days—"

"No. *No!*" Panic swelled until I was forced to grip the door frame to stay upright.

"Maybe a few weeks. I need to find a new job, after all."

"I can't," I gasped, panting for air. A black ring encroached on my vision, until Eva was the lone pinpoint of light. "For God's sake, something else, Eva!"

"I have to figure out what to do now." She rubbed at her forehead with rough fingers. "And I can't think when you're looking at me like that. I can't think . . ."

She moved to pass me and I grabbed her by the arms, kissing her, groaning when I felt her soften for an instant. I tasted her, tasted her tears. Or maybe they were mine.

Her hands went to my hair, fisting it, pulling it hard. She turned her head, breaking the seal of my mouth.

"Crossfire," she sobbed, the word cracking like a gunshot.

I released her abruptly, stumbling back, even as my mind screamed at me to hang on.

I let her go, and she left me.

THE *sea breeze blows through my hair and I close my eyes, absorbing the feel as it buffets me. The rhythmic push and pull of the waves against the beach and the raucous cries of seagulls anchor me in the moment, in this place.*

It's home in a way I haven't known for a long time, although I've spent less than a handful of days here. It is a place I've shared only with Eva, so all of my memories of here are as drenched with her as the sand is with rays of the sun. Like the sand, I've been crushed down into fine, tiny bits by the forces around me. And like the sun, Eva has brought joy and warmth to my existence.

She joins me on the deck, standing behind me at the railing. I feel her hand on my shoulder, then the press of her cheek against my bare back.

"Angel," I murmur, and place my hand over hers.

This is what we needed, to come back to this place. It's our retreat when the world closes in on us, trying to separate us. We heal each other here.

Relief washes through me. She's back. We're together. She understands now why I did what I did. She was so angry, so hurt. For a moment, I had felt crippling fear that I'd destroyed the most precious part of my life.

"Gideon," she breathes, in that husky siren's voice. One arm slides around my waist to hold me from behind.

I tilt my head back and let the power of her love pour through me. Her fingers glide over my hip, and then she's holding my cock in her hand. Stroking it from root to tip. I harden and thicken, ready for her. I live to serve her, to please her. How could she have doubted it?

A moan rumbles up from the very depths of my soul, the desire I always feel for her climbing through me. Pre-cum leaks from the swollen head of my dick, my balls growing heavy and full.

Her hand on my shoulder glides down my back, pressing lightly, urging me to bend forward.

I obey because I want her to see how she owns me. I want her to understand that I would do anything, give anything, to make her safe and happy.

Her hand traces my spine, kneading lightly. I grip the wooden handrail that circles the deck and spread my legs at her urging.

Now, both of her hands are between my thighs, her breath hot and panting against my back. She's pumping my cock with a firm, practiced grip. Harder than I'm used to from her. Demanding. Her other hand is massaging my sac, driving the urgency into me.

Her grip slickens as the pre-cum streams steadily from the slit at the tip of my dick. The salty air washes over me, cooling the sweat misting my skin.

"Eva . . ." I gasp her name, so hard for her, so desperately in love.

Her fingers, now creamy and always cleverly agile, slide back and tease the dark rosette of my anus. It feels good, even though I don't want it to. The stroking of my penis is making it hard to breathe, to think, to fight . . .

"That's it," she coaxes.

I try to arch away, but she's got me trapped with my dick in her hand.

"Don't," I tell her, squirming.

"You like it," she purrs, working my cock, her touch something I crave and can't resist. "Show me how much you want me."

She pushes two slick fingers inside my ass. I cry out, writhing away, but she's rubbing and thrusting into me, hitting the spot that makes me want to come more than anything. The pleasure grows despite the tears burning my eyes.

My head falls forward. My chin touches my heaving chest. It's coming. I'm coming. I can't stop it. Not with her . . .

The fingers inside me thicken, lengthen. The thrusting becomes frenzied, the slap of flesh against flesh drowning out the sounds of the ocean. I hear a rough, lusty growl but it's not mine. A cock is in me, fucking me. It hurts and yet the pain is tinged with a sick, unwanted pleasure.

"Keep stroking it," he pants. "You're almost there."

Agony explodes in my chest. Eva isn't here. She's gone. She's left me.

Vomit rises into my throat. I throw him off violently, hearing him crash through the sliding door behind us, the glass shattering. Hugh laughs hysterically and I round on him, finding him sprawled amid the glistening slivers, his hair as red as his blood, his eyes lit with that vile lustful avarice.

"You think she'd want you?" he taunts, clambering to his feet. "You told her everything. Who'd want you after that?"

"Fuck you!" I lunge and tackle him back down. My fist pounds into his face again and again.

The shards of glass pierce me, cut into me, but the pain is nothing next to what I feel inside.

Eva is gone. I'd known she would leave, that I couldn't keep her. I'd known it, but I had hoped. I couldn't fight the hope.

Hugh won't stop laughing. I feel his nose shatter. His cheekbone, his jaw. His laughter turns to gurgles, but it's still laughter.

My arm pulls back to hit him again—

Anne is lying beneath me, her face battered nearly beyond recognition.

Horrified at what I've done, I jerk away, scrambling to my feet. The glass digs deep into the soles of my feet.

Anne laughs as bubbling blood pours from her nose and mouth, spreading through the home that was once a sanctuary. Staining everything, the taint washing away the sun until only a blood moon remains . . .

I woke up with a scream in my throat. Sweat drenched my hair and skin. Darkness suffocated me.

Scrubbing at my eyes, I rolled onto my hands and knees, sobbing. I crawled toward the only light I could see, the weak silver glow that was my only guide.

The bedroom. God. I collapsed on the floor, racked by tears. I'd fallen asleep in the closet, unable to move after Eva left me, afraid to take one literal step in any direction toward a life without her in it.

The face of the clock glowed brightly in the darkened room.

It was one A.M.

A new day. And Eva was still gone.

"YOU'RE here early."

Scott's cheery voice lured my gaze from the photo of Eva on my desk.

"Good morning," I greeted him, feeling as if I were still in a nightmare.

I'd come to work shortly after three A.M., unable to sleep anymore and unable to go to Eva. I wanted to, would have—nothing could keep me away from her—but when I tracked her phone I found her at Stanton's penthouse, a place I couldn't reach. The anguish of that, knowing she was deliberately keeping herself from me, ate at me from the inside out like acid.

I couldn't stay home and go through the morning routine of preparing for work without Eva. It had been easier to revert to the schedule I'd often kept before her, coming into work while the moon was high, finding peace in the place where I exercised complete control.

But today there was no peace. Only the torment of knowing that she was in the same building I was by now, so damn close and yet farther away than she'd ever been.

"Mark Garrity was waiting by reception when I came in," Scott continued. "He said you'd discussed having him come in today . . . ?"

My gut knotted. "I'll see him."

I pushed back from my desk and stood. I'd thought of nothing but Eva and the offer I had made to Mark, trying to reason out how I could have done anything differently. I knew Eva too well. Telling her about Ryan Landon wouldn't have made her leave Waters Field & Leaman any more than telling her about Anne would cause her to be more cautious.

Eva would face them head-on instead, growling like a lioness to defend me and failing to see the danger to herself. It was her way and I loved her for it, but I would also protect her when the situation called for it.

"Mark." I extended my hand as he entered, knowing immediately that he was going to say yes. Energy radiated off him and his dark eyes were lit with anticipation.

We agreed that he would begin in October, giving Waters Field & Leaman nearly a month's notice. He wanted to bring Eva along with him and I encouraged him to make the offer, even as I doubted that she would accept it. He countered some of my terms and I negotiated by instinct, keeping him in check without my heart being in it.

In the end, he left happy and pleased with his changed situation. I was left with the deepening fear that Eva would not forgive me.

MONDAY blurred into Tuesday. There were only three times a day when I felt any life at all—at nine when I knew Eva arrived for work, at lunch, and again at five when she finished for the day. I waited with endless hope for her to reach out to me. To call or communicate in any way. Another horrible fight would be better than the aching silence.

She didn't. I could only watch her on the security monitors, devouring the sight of her coming and going like a man dying of hunger, scared to approach her and risk widening the chasm between us.

I stayed in the office overnight, afraid to go home. Afraid of what I would do if I entered any of the residences I shared with her. Even my office was a torment, the couch where I had fucked her an inescapable reminder of what I'd had only days before. I showered in my office's washroom and changed into one of the many suits I kept at work.

I'd never thought it strange to live for work before. Now, I was overwhelmed by emotion I couldn't express, comprehending just how much of my life Eva had come to fill.

She stayed at Stanton's again. It didn't escape my notice that she preferred to spend time with her mother than to risk having to deal with me.

I texted her constantly. Pleas for her to call me. *I just need to hear your voice.* Notes about nothing. *Cooler today, isn't it?* Comments about work. *Never realized Scott always wears blue.* And most of all, *I love you.* For some reason, it was easier to type those three words than to say them. I typed them a lot. Over and over again. I didn't want her to forget that. Whatever my faults and fuck-ups, everything I did or thought or felt was love for her.

Sometimes I got mad, hating what she was doing to me. To us. *Goddamn you! Call me. Stop doing this to me!*

"You look like shit," Arash said, eyeing me as I reviewed the contracts he'd placed on my desk. "You getting sick again?"

"I'm fine."

"My man, you are anything but fine."

I glared at him, shutting him up.

⟨~⟩

IT was nearly six and I was on my way to Dr. Petersen's office when Eva finally reached out to me.

I love you, too.

The words wavered as my eyes stung. I typed back with shaking fingers, nearly dizzy with relief. I miss you so much. Can't we talk, please? I need to see you.

She didn't reply before I reached Dr. Petersen's, which blackened my mood to the point of violence. She was punishing me in the worst possible way. I was as jittery as a junkie, desperate for a hit of her to function. To think.

"Gideon." Dr. Petersen greeted me at the door to his office with a smile that quickly faded when he saw me. Concern drew his brows down. "You don't look well."

"I'm not," I snapped.

He calmly gestured for me to take a seat. I remained standing, roiling inside, debating leaving and searching for my wife. I couldn't stand around and wait anymore. It was too much to ask of me.

"Maybe we should walk again," he said. "I could stand to stretch my legs."

"Call Eva," I ordered. "Tell her to come here. She'll listen to you."

He blinked at me. "You're having trouble with Eva."

Shrugging out of my suit jacket, I threw it on the couch. "She's being irrational! She won't see me . . . won't talk to me. How the fuck are we supposed to work things out if we're not even talking?"

"That's a reasonable question."

"Damn right! I'm a reasonable man. She, however, is out of her damn mind. She can't keep doing this. You have to get her here. You have to make her talk to me."

"All right. But first I need to understand what's happened." He sat in his chair. "I'm not going to be much use to you if I don't know what's going on."

I pointed a finger at him. "Don't play your head games with me, Doc. Not today."

"I think I'm being as reasonable as you are," he said smoothly. "I want you to work things out with Eva, too. I think you know that."

Exhaling in a rush, I sank onto the edge of the sofa, then dropped my head into my hands. It was throbbing viciously, pounding front and back.

"You're fighting with Eva," he said.

"Yes."

"When's the last time you spoke with her?"

I swallowed hard. "Sunday."

"What happened on Sunday?"

I told him. It came out in a rush that had him scribbling frantically on his tablet. The words spewed out in an angry purge, leaving me feeling wiped out and exhausted.

He continued to write for a few moments after I finished, and then his gaze lifted to my face. I saw compassion and it tightened my throat.

"You cost Eva her job," he pointed out, "a job she's told us both that she enjoys very much. You can see why she'd be upset with you, can't you?"

"Yeah, I get it. But I had valid reasons. Reasons she understands. That's what I don't get. She understands and she's still cutting me off."

"I'm not sure *I* understand why you didn't discuss this with Eva beforehand. Can you explain that to me?"

I rubbed at the back of my neck, where the tension felt like steel cables. "She would've stewed over it," I muttered. "It would've taken her time to come around. In the meantime, I'm trying to manage a ton of other shit. We're getting hit from all sides."

"I saw the news about Corinne Giroux's book about you."

"Oh, yeah." My mouth curved grimly. "She probably got the idea from Six-Ninth's 'Golden' video. Landon got to Eva through a hole in my guard. I couldn't risk giving him another opening while I was distracted with everything else Eva and I are dealing with right now."

Dr. Petersen nodded. "You're facing a lot of pressure. Don't you trust Eva to help you reach the decisions you're making? You have to know that her conflicts with her mother often stem from not being consulted before actions are taken."

"I know that." I tried to articulate my chaotic thoughts. "But I need to take care of her. After what she's lived through . . ."

My eyes squeezed shut. Knowing what she'd suffered was almost too much for me to think about sometimes. "I have to be strong for her. Make the tough calls."

"Gideon, you're one of the strongest men I know," he said quietly.

I opened my eyes and looked at him. "You haven't seen me the way she has."

Crying like a child. Brutalized by memories. Masturbating while unconscious. Violent in my sleep. Weak, so weak. Helpless.

"Do you think she doubts you because you've let her see you vulnerable? That doesn't sound like Eva to me."

My eyes stung. "You don't know everything. You just . . . You don't know."

"But Eva does. And she married you anyway. She loves you—very much—anyway." He offered a kind smile that somehow slashed like a blade, cutting me open. "You asked me once if relationships were about compromise. Do you remember that?"

I jerked a nod.

"That compromise means you don't always have to be the strong one, Gideon. You can do the heavy lifting on occasion, and you can let Eva do it sometimes. Marriage isn't about whether you're strong enough as an individual. It's about how strong you are together and the luxury of taking turns carrying the load."

"I . . ." My head bowed again. Eva had said the same thing. "I'm trying. I swear to God, I'm trying."

"I know you are."

"She has to take me back. She has to come back. I need her. She's killing me right now. She's ripping me apart." I stared at my hands, at the rings she'd given me that made me hers. "What do I do? Tell me what to do."

"Eva is going to want to know that you're willing to change. She'll want to see you taking steps to demonstrate that. You won't face these big decisions too often, so she may adopt a wait-and-see attitude. That will be hard for you, I think. Very hard."

I nodded slowly, but I couldn't wait anymore. If Eva needed proof that I'd do anything to keep her, I would give it to her.

My hands clenched into fists. My gaze stayed on the carpet between my feet. "I was—" I cleared my throat. "The therapist. The one I had when I was a child."

"Yes?"

"He . . . he molested me. For nearly a year. He . . . raped me."

20

I miss you so much. Can't we talk, please? I need to see you.

"Still staring at that text?" Cary asked, rolling onto his back on the bed beside me and pressing his temple to mine.

"I can't sleep." It was torture to stay away from Gideon. I spent every minute—waking and sleeping—feeling like someone had hacked out my heart and left a gaping hole in my chest.

I looked up at the canopy above my mom's guest bed. Like her sitting room, the bedroom she'd put me in was newly redecorated. With its palette of cream and moss green, the room was soothing and tastefully elegant. The guest bedroom Cary occupied was done in a more masculine style with grays and navy, with walnut furnishings on the opposite end of the spectrum from the white gilded pieces in my room.

"When are you going to talk to him, baby girl?"

"Soon. I just . . ." I lowered the phone to my chest and pressed it against my heart. "I think we both need a little time."

It was so hard to think when Gideon and I were fighting. I hated it.

And it was worse because he was the one who'd fucked up, and like everything he did, he had done so spectacularly. I couldn't imagine how I could forgive him and live with myself. On the other hand, I couldn't imagine how I could go forward without him and live, period. I felt dead inside. The only thing keeping me going was the belief that somehow we'd work things out and be together. How could we not? How could I give so much of myself to someone and then let that person go?

I thought about the advice I'd given to Trey and how we were both facing the same decision—did we choose love or did we choose ourselves? I was so pissed off at Gideon for being the one who forced my hand. I'd recognized that certain situations were pushing me into that spot, but I had never thought my husband would.

And why the hell did the two choices have to be mutually exclusive? It wasn't fair.

"You're running him through the wringer," Cary pointed out, unnecessarily.

"*He's* done it, not me." Gideon had taken something precious from me, but worse, he had taken something precious away from *us*—my free will and the trust I'd given him to respect it. After that last night we'd had . . . as much as I had trusted him and opened myself to him . . . And he'd already talked to Mark. The feeling of betrayal was heartrending. "Thanks for sticking with me."

He shrugged. "I like Stanton. It's no hardship hanging at his place a few days. We *are* eventually going home, right?"

"I can't hide forever."

"So you've always said," he muttered. "Personally, I like hiding. Just taking a fucking break and forgetting about all the crap."

"But the crap's always out there waiting for you." And knowing that, I always preferred to face it head-on. Get it out of the way and behind me.

"Let it wait," he said, reaching up to ruffle my hair.

Turning my head, I pressed a kiss to his cheek. I'd cried gallons on him the last three days and curled up against him at night. At times, it felt like his arms were the only things holding me together.

God. I hurt all over. I was a fucking mess, a zombie in the vibrantly lively city of New York.

Where was Gideon now? Was the pain of our separation starting to ease? Or was he still as devastated by it as I was?

"Mark asked me to move to Cross Industries with him," I said, just to force my mind onto something else.

"Well, you saw that coming."

"I guess, but it was still surreal when he brought it up." I sighed. "He's so excited, Cary. He's getting a hefty raise, and that will change a lot of things for him and Steven. They'll be able to afford a really fancy wedding plus a long honeymoon, and they're looking for a condominium now. It's hard to hold on to my resentment when this is such a good thing for him."

"Are you going to work for Gideon?"

"I don't know. I wasn't kidding when I told him I was halfway toward making that decision on my own. But now . . . I kinda want to apply elsewhere just to spite him."

Cary lifted his fists and shadowboxed. "Show him he's not the boss of you."

"Yeah." I threw a few punches, too, just to give myself a little lift. "But that's stupid. I'd never know if I got hired for me or for his name, whether that turned out to be a good or a bad thing. Anyway, I've got a month before Mark moves on. I've got time to think about it."

"Maybe Waters Field and Leaman will keep you. Have you considered that?"

"It's a possibility. I'm not sure how I would respond. It would save

CAPTIVATED BY YOU · 339

me a job search, but I wouldn't have Mark, and he's the reason I love my job. Would I still want to be there without him?"

"You'd still have Megumi and Will."

"There's that," I agreed.

We lay there in companionable silence for a while.

Then he said, "So it looks like you and me are just floating around in the hell-if-I-know boat."

"Trey *is* going to call," I assured him, even though I still had no idea what Trey would say when he did.

"Sure. He's a nice guy. He won't leave me hanging." Cary sounded so weary. "It's *what* he's going to say, not *when*, that's the kicker."

"I know. Love should be easier than this," I complained.

"If this were a romantic comedy, it'd be called *Love Actually Sucks*."

"Maybe we should've stuck with *Sex and the City*."

"Tried that. Ended up *Knocked Up*. I should've gone for being a *40-Year-Old Virgin*, but I had way too much of a head start."

"We can write a manual on How to Lose a Guy in 10 Weeks."

Cary looked at me. "Fucking perfect."

WEDNESDAY morning hit me like a hangover.

Getting ready for work at my mom's place helped me to not miss Gideon so much, but it sure as hell didn't separate me from my mother, who was driving me nuts talking about the wedding nonstop. Even Stanton, with his endless capacity for indulging my mom's neurosis, gave me sympathetic looks when he was around.

I couldn't think about the wedding now. I couldn't think beyond each and every hour of the day. That was how I was getting by—one hour at a time.

When I stepped out of the lobby onto the street, I found Angus waiting for me with the Bentley rather than Raúl with the Benz.

I managed a smile, genuinely pleased to see him, but I was wary, too.

"Good morning, Angus." I jerked my chin toward the car and whispered, "Is he in there?"

He shook his head, then touched the brim of his vintage chauffeur's hat. "Good morning, Mrs. Cross."

I squeezed his shoulder briefly before sliding past the door he opened and into the backseat. In short order we were easing into the snarl of morning traffic and heading toward midtown.

Leaning forward, I asked, "How is he?"

"Worse than you, I expect." He glanced at me briefly before returning his attention to traffic. "He's suffering, lass. Last night was the hardest."

"God." I sank back into the seat, at a loss for what to do.

I didn't want Gideon to hurt. He'd been hurt too much already.

Pulling out my smartphone, I texted him. I love you.

His reply was almost immediate. Calling. Pls answer.

A moment later the phone vibrated in my hand and his picture appeared on my screen. It was like a quick stab to the heart to see his face after spending the last few days avoiding any image of him. I was equally afraid to hear his voice. I didn't know if I could be strong. And I didn't have the answers he needed from me.

My voice mail kicked in and the phone quieted. It started vibrating again right away.

I answered, lifting the phone to my ear without speaking.

There was silence on the line for a long, breathless moment. "Eva?"

My eyes watered at the sound of Gideon's voice, the rasp in it so deep, as if his throat were rough. What was worse was the hope I heard in the way he said my name, the desperate longing.

"It's okay if you don't talk," he said gruffly. "I just . . ." He gave a shaky exhale. "I'm sorry, Eva. I want you to know I'm sorry and that I'll do whatever you need me to. I just want to fix this."

"Gideon . . ." I heard him suck in a sharp inhalation when I said his name. "I believe that you're sorry we're not together now. But I also believe that you would do something like this again. I'm trying to figure out if I can live with that."

Silence hung on the line between us.

"What does that mean?" he asked finally. "What would be the alternative?"

I sighed, suddenly feeling so tired. "I don't have any answers. That's why I've stayed away. I want to give you everything, Gideon. I never want to say no to you, it's so hard for me. But right now, I'm afraid that if I make this compromise, if I stay with you knowing how you are and that you're not going to change, I'm just going to resent you and, eventually, fall out of love with you."

"Eva . . . Christ. Don't say that!" His breath snagged. "I told Dr. Petersen. About Hugh."

"What?" My head snapped up. "When?"

"Last night. I told him everything. About Hugh. Anne. He's going to help me, Eva. He said some things . . ." He paused. "They made sense to me. About me and the way I am with you."

"Oh, Gideon." I could imagine how difficult that must have been for him. I'd lived through that confession myself. "I'm very proud of you. I know it wasn't easy."

"You have to stick with me. You promised. I told you I was going to fuck this up. I'll fuck up again. I don't know what the hell I'm doing, but God . . . *I love you.* I love you so fucking much. I can't do this without you. I can't live without you. You're breaking me, Eva. I can't . . ." He made a low, pained noise. "I need you."

"Ah God, Gideon." Tears poured down my face and splattered onto my chest, sliding down beneath the neckline of my dress. "I don't know what to do, either."

"Can't we figure it out together? Aren't we better—*stronger*—together?"

I wiped at my face, knowing my makeup was ruined and not caring. "I want us to be. I want that more than anything. I just don't know if we can get there. There hasn't been a single time when you've let me figure things out with you. Not once."

"If I did . . . if I do—and I *will*—you'll come back to me?"

"I haven't left you, Gideon. I don't know how." I looked out the window, spotted a young couple kissing each other good-bye in front of a revolving door before the man ran off. "But yes, if we could really be a team, nothing could keep me away."

"HEARD you guys landed the PhazeOne campaign."

I turned my attention from the coffee I was sweetening to raise my brows at Will. "I haven't heard that."

He grinned, his eyes sparkling behind his glasses. He was such a happy guy, anchored solidly in a relationship that worked. I was so envious of that serenity. I had felt it only a few times since I'd been with Gideon, and every time it was . . . bliss. How amazing would it be if we could get there and *stay* there?

"That's the buzz I've been hearing," he said.

"Man." I gave an exaggerated sigh. "I am always the last to know."

I'd been putting on an Oscar-worthy performance all week. Between Mark's excitement, the imminent adjustment in my work situation, starting my period, and dealing with the mess in my private life, I was focusing every ounce of energy I had left on acting calm. As a result, I'd avoided the office gossip cliques to limit my contact with people. There was only so much happiness/joy/contentment I could fake.

"Mark's going to kill me for telling you." Will looked completely unapologetic. "I wanted to be the first to congratulate you."

"Okay. Thank you. Maybe."

"I'm dying to get my hands on that system, you know. The tech blogs are wild with rumors about PhazeOne's features." He leaned against the counter next to me and gave me a hopeful look.

I wagged my finger at him. "You won't be hearing any leaks from me."

"Damn it. A guy's gotta hope." He shrugged. "They're probably going to lock you in solitary somewhere until the release just to keep a lid on it."

"Makes you wonder why LanCorp would take it to an outside agency, doesn't it?"

He frowned. "Yeah. I guess. Hadn't thought about it."

Neither had I. But Gideon had.

I looked back down at my mug, stirring absently. "There's a new GenTen coming out soon."

"I heard. That's a no-brainer, though. Everyone's going to buy it."

Flexing my fingers, I studied my wedding ring and thought about the vows I'd made when I accepted it.

"You got plans for lunch?" he asked.

I picked up my mug and faced him. "Yes, I'm going out with Mark and his partner."

"Oh, right." He moved toward the coffeemaker when I got out of the way. "Maybe we could grab drinks after work sometime this week. Drag our significant others with us. If Gideon's up for it. I know he's a busy guy."

I opened my mouth. Closed it again. Will had given me the perfect opening to excuse Gideon. I could take it, but I wanted to share the social parts of my life with my husband. I wanted him with me. If I started excluding him from my life, wasn't that the beginning of the end?

"Sounds like fun," I lied, imagining a tension-fraught evening. "I'll talk to him about it. See what we can work out."

Will nodded. "Cool. Lemme know."

344 · SYLVIA DAY

⤶

"I've got a problem."

"Oh?" I looked across the table at Mark. The Cuban restaurant Steven had chosen was both large and popular. Sunlight streamed in through a massive skylight, while colorful murals decorated the space with parrots and palm fronds. Festive music made me feel like I'd gone on vacation to somewhere exotic, while the rich smell of spices made my tummy perk up for the first time in days.

I rubbed my hands together. "Let's fix it."

Steven nodded. "Eva's right. Lay it on us."

Mark pushed the menu aside and set his elbows on the table. "So Mr. Waters told me this morning to start working on the LanCorp brief."

"Yay!" I applauded.

"Not so fast. In light of that, I had to give him my notice. I'd been hoping to wait until Friday, but they need someone who can stick with the client all the way through, not just the first month."

"You've got a point," I conceded, my smile fading. "What a bummer, though."

"It sucked, but . . ." He shrugged. "It is what it is. Then he called in the other partners. They told me that the LanCorp brass was insistent that I head the campaign when they first approached the agency, enough so that the partners are worried they'll lose the account if I'm not managing it."

Steven grinned and slapped him on the shoulder. "That's what we like to hear!"

Mark gave a sheepish smile. "Yeah, it was a boost, for sure. So anyway, they offered me a promotion and a raise if I'll stay."

"Whoa." I sat back. "That's a *serious* boost."

"They can't offer what Cross did. Not even half, but let's be honest, he's overpaying me."

"Says you," Steven scoffed. "You're worth every penny."

I nodded, even though I had only a vague idea of what Gideon had put on the table. "I agree with that."

"But I feel like I owe Waters Field and Leaman some loyalty." Mark rubbed at his jaw. "They've been good to me and they want to keep me, even knowing I can be poached by someone else."

"You've given them good work for years," Steven countered. "They got a lot out of you. You don't owe them any favors."

"I know that. And I was fine with leaving an empty office behind, because they could fill that quick enough. But I'm having a hard time with possibly costing them the LanCorp campaign when I go."

"But that decision isn't yours to make," I pointed out. "If LanCorp doesn't retain the agency, that's up to them."

"I've tried spinning it that way, too. But it's still not something I want to see happen."

The server came by to take our order. I looked at Steven. "Can you do the honors?"

"Sure." He looked at Mark, who gave a quick nod to signal the same request. Steven ordered for all of us.

I waited until we were alone again to speak, unsure of how to say what needed to be said. In the end, I went with blunt. "I can't work on the PhazeOne campaign."

Mark and Steven stared at me.

"Look, the Landons and the Crosses go way back," I explained, "and there's bad blood between them. Gideon's got some concerns, and I see his point. It's strong enough for me to be cautious."

Mark frowned. "Landon knows who you are. He doesn't have a problem with it."

"I know. But the PhazeOne system is a pretty big deal. There's risk involved with having access to it, and I don't need to contribute to that in any way." It was hard admitting that Gideon was right, because I knew I was right, too. Which left us at an impasse I didn't know how to get around.

Steven leaned closer and studied me. "You're serious."

"Afraid so. Not that your decision is in any way affected by me, Mark, but I thought I should put that out there."

"I'm not sure I understand," Mark said.

"She's telling you that if you stay with your job, you'll be losing both the money and your assistant," Steven clarified. "Or you can move to Cross Industries as you've already agreed to do, get the money, and keep Eva."

"Well . . ." God. This was harder than I'd thought it would be. I had heard it but now I was living it: Any woman who loses or gives up a job she loves because of a man will resent it . . . What had ever made me think I would be somehow exempt? "I can't say yet that I'll be making the move with you."

Mark fell back against the burgundy vinyl booth. "This just keeps getting worse."

"I'm not saying definitively that I won't." I tried to shrug it off as no big deal. "I'm just not sure that Gideon and I should be working together. I mean I'm not sure he should be my boss . . . or whatever. You know what I mean."

"I hate to say it," Steven said, "but she's got a point."

"This is not helping my problem," Mark muttered.

"I'm sorry." I couldn't tell them how sorry I really was. I didn't even feel like I could offer advice. How could I be nonbiased about Mark's options?

"On the bright side," I offered instead, "you're definitely a hot commodity."

Steven elbowed Mark with a grin. "I knew that already."

⌀

"So"—Cary slung his arm around me when I curled into his side— "here we are again."

Another night at my mom's. She'd finally gotten suspicious, considering it was our fourth night in a row at her place. I confessed to arguing with Gideon, but not why. I didn't think she would understand. I'm sure she would think it was perfectly normal for a man in Gideon's position to handle all the pesky little details. And as for me possibly losing my job? Why would I want to work when I had no financial reason to?

She didn't understand. Some daughters wanted to grow up to be just like their mothers; I wanted the opposite. And my need to be the anti-Monica was the main reason I struggled so much with what Gideon had done. Any advice from her would only make things worse. I almost resented her as much as I did him.

"We'll go home tomorrow," I said.

After all, I'd be seeing Gideon at Dr. Petersen's office at the very least. I was desperately curious about how that would go. I couldn't help but hope that Gideon had turned a major corner with therapy. If so, maybe there were other corners we could turn. Together.

I crossed my fingers.

And really, I had to give Gideon credit for doing his best to give me the space I'd asked for. He could've caught me in an elevator or the lobby of the Crossfire. He could have told Raúl to drive me to him instead of wherever I directed. Gideon *was* trying.

"Have you heard from Trey?" I asked.

It was kind of miraculous how often Cary and I ended up in the same place at the same time. Or maybe it was a shared curse.

"He sent me a text saying he was thinking about me but wasn't ready to talk yet."

"Well, that's something."

His hand ran up and down my back. "Is it?"

"Yes," I said. "I'm in the same place with Gideon. I think about him all the time, but I don't have anything to say to him right now."

"So what's next? Where do you go from here? When do you decide you've got something more to say?"

I thought about that a minute, absently watching Harrison Ford hunt for answers in *The Fugitive*, which we had on mute. "When something changes, I guess."

"When *he* changes, you mean. What if he doesn't?"

I didn't have that answer yet, and when I tried to think about it, I went a little crazy.

So I asked Cary a question instead. "I know you want to put the baby first and that's the right thing to do. But Tatiana's not happy. And you're not, either. Trey's definitely not. This isn't working out for any of you. Have you thought about being with Trey and the two of you helping Tatiana with the baby?"

He snorted. "She's not gonna go for that. If she's miserable, everyone else has to be, too."

"I don't think that should be her choice to make. She's as responsible for getting pregnant as you are. You don't have to do some sort of penance, Cary." I put my hand over the arm he had lying in his lap, my thumb brushing carefully over the fresh scars on his inner forearm. "Be happy with Trey. Make him happy. And if Tatiana can't be happy with having two hot guys looking after her, then she's . . . not doing something right."

Cary laughed softly and pressed his lips to the crown of my head. "Solve your own problem that easily."

"I wish I could." I wished for that more than anything. But I knew it wouldn't be easy.

And I feared it might be impossible.

THE vibration of my smartphone woke me.

When I realized what the buzzing was, I began searching blindly for my phone, my hands sliding around the bed until I found it. By then, I'd missed the call.

Squinting at the glaringly bright screen, I saw it was just past three A.M. and Gideon had called. My heart skipped as worry chased away sleep. Once again I'd gone to bed cradling my phone, unable to stop reading the many texts he had sent me.

I called him back.

"Angel," he answered on the first ring, his voice hoarse.

"Is everything okay?"

"Yes. No." He blew out his breath. "I had a nightmare."

"Oh." I blinked up at the canopy that I couldn't see in the dark. My mother was a fan of blackout drapes, saying they were necessary in a city that was never truly dark. "I'm sorry."

It was a lame reply, but what else could I say? It would be pointless to ask if he wanted to talk about it. He never did.

"I'm having them a lot lately," he said wearily. "Every time I fall asleep."

My heart hurt a little more. It seemed impossible that it could take so much pain, but there was always more. I'd learned that long ago.

"You're stressed, Gideon. I'm not sleeping well, either." And then, because it had to be said, "I miss you."

"Eva . . ."

"Sorry." I scrubbed at my eyes. "Maybe I shouldn't say that."

Maybe it was a mixed signal that would only make things worse for him. I felt guilty for staying away, even though I knew I had good reason to.

"No, I need to hear it. I'm scared, Eva. I've never felt fear like this. I'm afraid you won't come back . . . that you won't give me another chance."

"Gideon—"

"I dreamed about my father at first. We were walking on the beach and he was holding my hand. I've been dreaming about the beach a lot lately."

I swallowed hard, my chest aching. "Maybe that means something."

"Maybe. I was little in the dream. I had to look up a long way to see my dad's face. He was smiling, but then I always remember him smiling. Even though I heard him fighting with my mom a lot toward the end, I can't remember any other expression on his face but a smile."

"I'm sure you made him happy. And proud. He probably always smiled when he looked at you."

He was quiet for a minute, and I thought maybe that was it. Then he went on. "I saw you up ahead on the beach, walking away from us."

I rolled onto my side, listening intently.

"Your hair was blowing in the breeze and the sun lit it up. I thought it was beautiful. I pointed you out to my dad. I wanted you to turn your head so we could see your face. I knew you were gorgeous. I wanted him to see you."

Tears welled in my eyes and slid down to wet my pillow.

"I tried to run after you. I was pulling at his hand and he was holding me back, laughing about chasing pretty girls at my age."

I could picture the scene so clearly in my mind. I could almost feel the brisk breeze whipping through my hair and hear the seagulls calling. I could see the young Gideon in the picture he'd given me and the handsome, charismatic Geoffrey Cross.

I wanted a future like that. With Gideon walking down the beach with our son who looked just like him, my husband laughing because our troubles were behind us and a bright, happy future lay ahead of us.

But he'd called it a nightmare, so I knew that future I envisioned wasn't one he saw.

"I was tugging so hard on his hand," he continued, "digging my bare feet into the sand for traction. But he was so much stronger than me. You were walking farther and farther away. He laughed again. Only this time, it wasn't his laugh. It was Hugh's. And when I looked up again, it wasn't my father anymore."

"Oh, Gideon." I sobbed his name, unable to hold back the sympathy and grief. And the relief that he was talking to me at last.

"He told me you didn't want me, that you were going away because you knew everything and it made you sick. That you couldn't get away fast enough."

"That's not true!" I sat up in bed. "You know that's not true. I love you. It's because I love you so much that I'm thinking so hard about this. *Us.*"

"I'm trying to give you space. But I feel like it would be so easy for us to drift apart. A day goes by, then another. You'll find a new routine without me in it . . . Christ, Eva, I don't want you to get over me."

I spoke in a rush, my thoughts tumbling out of my mouth. "There's a way to get through this, Gideon, I know there is. But when I'm with you I lose myself in you. I just want to be with you and to be happy, so I let things ride and put them off. We make love and I think we'll be okay, because we have that and it's perfect."

"It *is* perfect. It's everything."

"When you're inside me, looking at me, I feel like we can conquer anything. But we've really got to work on this! We can't be afraid to deal with our baggage because we don't want to lose each other."

He growled softly. "I just want us to spend time together not dealing with all this other shit!"

"I know." I rubbed at the pain in my chest. "But we have to earn it, I think. We can't manufacture it by running away for a weekend or a week."

"How do we earn it?"

I swiped at the tears drying on my cheeks. "Tonight was good. You calling me, telling me about your dream. It's a good step, Gideon."

"We'll keep making steps, then. We have to keep moving together or we're going to end up moving apart. Don't let that happen! I'm fighting here, with everything I've got. Fight for me, too."

My eyes stung with fresh tears. I sat for a while, crying, knowing he could hear me and that it was hurting him.

Finally, I swallowed the pain down and made a snap decision. "I'm going to that all-night café on Broadway and Eighty-fifth for coffee and a croissant."

He was silent for a long minute. "What? *Now?*"

"Right now." I tossed back the covers on the bed and slid to the floor.

Then he got it. "Okay."

Killing the call, I dropped the phone on the bed and fumbled for the light. I ran to my duffel bag, digging out the butter yellow maxi dress I'd shoved in there because it was easy to pack and comfortable to wear.

Now that I was decided on seeing Gideon, I was anxious to get to him, but I had my vanity, too. I took the time to brush out my hair and put a little makeup on. I didn't want him to see me after four days and wonder why he was so gone over me.

My phone buzzed a notification of a text and I hurried over to it, seeing a note from Raúl: I'm out front with the car.

A little zing went through me. Gideon was anxious to see me, too. Still, he never missed a trick.

I shoved my phone into my purse, my feet into sandals, and hurried out to the elevator.

GIDEON was waiting on the street when Raúl pulled up to the curb. Many of the storefronts on Broadway were shuttered and dark, although the street itself remained well lit. My husband stood within the light cast by the café's awning, his hands shoved into the pockets of his dark jeans and a Yankees ball cap tugged low over his brow.

He could've been any young man out late at night. Clearly attractive by the way his hard body filled his clothes and the confidence in the way he carried himself. I would've given him a second and third look. He wasn't as intimidating outside the three-piece suits he wore so well, but he was still dark and dangerous enough to hold me back from the lighthearted flirting most devastatingly handsome men inspired.

In jeans or Fioravanti, Gideon Cross was not a man to be taken lightly.

He was at the car almost before Raúl pulled to a complete stop, yanking the door open and then freezing in place, staring at me with such scorching hunger and possessiveness that I found it hard to breathe.

I swallowed past the lump in my throat, my equally ravenous gaze sliding all over him. He was unbelievably more beautiful, the expertly sculpted planes of his face honed further by his torment. How had I lived the past few days without seeing that face?

He held his hand out to me and I reached for it, my own trembling in anticipation of his touch. The brush of his skin against mine sent tingles of awareness racing through me, my bruised heart surging with life at being in contact with him again.

He helped me out, then pushed the door closed, rapping twice on the roof to send Raúl away. As the Benz left us, we stood barely a foot apart, the air crackling with tension between us. A taxi raced by, honking its horn as another car turned onto Broadway without looking. The harsh sound jolted Gideon and me both.

He took a step toward me, his eyes dark and hot beneath the brim of his hat. "I'm going to kiss you," he said roughly.

Then he cupped my jaw and tilted his head, fitting his mouth over mine. His lips, so soft and firm and dry, pressed mine open. His tongue slid deep and rubbed, withdrew, slid deep again. He groaned as if he were in the greatest pain. Or pleasure. For me, it was both. The hot stroke of his tongue into my mouth was like a sweet, slow fucking. Smoothly rhythmic, skilled, with just the perfect tease of leashed passion.

I moaned as euphoria sparkled through me like champagne, the ground shifting beneath my feet so that I clung to him for balance, my hands wrapping around his wrists.

I whimpered in protest when he pulled away, my lips feeling achy and swollen, my sex wet with desire.

"You'll make me come," he murmured, unable to resist brushing his lips over mine one last time. "I'm right there."

"I don't care."

His mouth curved and chased the shadows away. "The next time I come will be inside you."

I sucked in a shaky breath at the thought. I wanted that, and yet I knew it would be too soon now. That we'd fall too easily back into the unhealthy pattern we had established. "Gideon . . ."

His smile turned rueful. "Guess we'll settle for coffee and a croissant for now."

I loved him so much in that moment. Impulsively, I pulled off his hat and gave him a great big smacking kiss on the mouth.

"God," he breathed, his gaze so tender it made me feel like crying again. "I've missed you so damn much."

I slid the hat back on his head and grabbed his hand, leading him around the little metal fences cordoning off an outside seating area from the pedestrian traffic. We entered the café and settled at a table by the window, Gideon on one side and me on the other. But we didn't stop holding hands, our fingers stroking and rubbing, each of us touching the other's wedding bands.

We ordered when the server walked over with the menus, then turned our attention back to each other.

"I'm not even hungry," I told him.

"Not for food, anyway," he rejoined.

I shot him a mock glare that made him smile. Then I told him about the retention offer Waters Field & Leaman had made Mark.

It seemed wrong to talk about something so practical, so mundane, when my heart was giddy with love and relief, but we had to keep talking. Reconnecting wasn't enough; I wanted a full and total reconciliation. I wanted to move into the renovated penthouse with him, start our life together. To do that, we had to keep communicating about the things we'd spent our relationship avoiding.

Gideon nodded grimly when I finished. "I'm not surprised. An account like that should be handled by one of the partners. Mark's good, but he's a junior manager. LanCorp would've had to push to get him. And you. The request is unusual enough to give the partners cause for concern."

I thought about Kingsman Vodka. "You did the same thing."

"I did, yes."

"I don't know what he's going to do." I looked at our joined hands. "But I told him I couldn't work on the PhazeOne campaign even if he stayed to manage it."

Gideon's grip tightened on mine.

"You have good reasons for doing the things you do," I said quietly, "even if I don't like them."

He took a slow, deep breath. "Will you come with him to Cross Industries if he moves?"

"I'm not sure yet. I'm feeling pretty resentful right now. Unless that changes, it wouldn't be a healthy working relationship for either of us."

He nodded. "Fair enough."

The server came back with our order. Gideon and I released each other by necessity to give her room to put the plates on our settings. When she walked away, a heavy silence descended between us. There was so much to say, but so much that had to be figured out first.

He cleared his throat. "Tonight—after Dr. Petersen—could I take you out to dinner?"

"Yes." I accepted eagerly, grateful to move past the awkwardness into action. "I'd like that."

I could see similar relief soften the hard line of his shoulders and wanted to do my share to build it. "Will asked if we'd be up for grabbing a drink with him and Natalie this week."

A hint of a smile touched Gideon's mouth. "I think that'd be great."

Small steps. We would start with those and see where they took us.

I pushed back from the table and stood. Gideon pushed to his feet quickly, eyeing me warily. I rounded the table and took the seat next to him, waiting until he sat again so that I could lean into him.

His arm came around me and he settled me into the crook of his neck. A soft sound escaped him when I snuggled in.

"I'm still mad at you," I told him.

"I know."

"And I'm still in love with you."

"Thank God." His cheek rested against the top of my head. "We'll figure out the rest. We'll get back on track."

We sat together and watched the city rouse from sleep. The sky lightened. The pace of life quickened.

It was a new day, bringing with it a new chance to try again.

ENTWINED WITH YOU

Sylvia Day

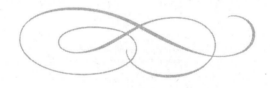

BERKLEY
New York

BERKLEY
An imprint of Penguin Random House LLC
penguinrandomhouse.com

Library of Congress Cataloging-in-Publication Data

Day, Sylvia.
Entwined with you / Sylvia Day. — Berkley trade paperback edition.
pages cm
ISBN 978-0-425-26392-1
1. Secrecy—Fiction. I. Title.
PS3604.A9875E58 2013b
813'.6—dc23
2013004326

First Edition: June 2013

PRINTED IN THE UNITED STATES OF AMERICA
16th Printing

ACKNOWLEDGMENTS

My gratitude to editor Hilary Sares for all her hard work on *Entwined with You* and the previous two books in the Crossfire series. Without her, there would be some rambling, many Latinate words, brief lapses into historical jargon, and other offenses that would distract readers from the beauty of Gideon's love for Eva. Thank you so much, Hilary!

Huge thanks to my agent, Kimberly Whalen, and my editor, Cindy Hwang, for helping me recapture the magic of Gideon and Eva when writing this story. When I needed help, they were there for me. Thank you, Kim and Cindy!

Thank you to my publicist, Gregg Sullivan, for keeping me organized and being a big help in managing my schedule.

Thanks to my agent, Jon Cassir at CAA, for all his hard work and patience in answering my questions.

I'm grateful to all of my international publishers, who've been so tremendously supportive and enthusiastic about the Crossfire series.

And to my readers, I cannot thank you enough for your patience and support. I'm grateful to be sharing Gideon and Eva's continuing journey with you.

1

NEW YORK CABBIES were a unique breed. Fearless to a fault, they sped and swerved through crowded streets with unnatural calm. To save my sanity, I'd learned to focus on the screen of my smartphone instead of the cars rushing by only inches away. Whenever I made the mistake of paying attention, I'd find my right foot pushing hard into the floorboard, my body instinctively trying to hit the brakes.

But for once, I didn't need any distractions. I was sticky with sweat from an intense Krav Maga class, and my mind was spinning with thoughts of what the man I loved had done.

Gideon Cross. Just thinking of his name sent a heated flare of long-ing through my tightly strung body. From the moment I first saw him—saw through his stunning and impossibly gorgeous exterior to the dark and dangerous man inside—I'd felt the pull that came from finding the other half of myself. I needed him like I needed my heart to beat, and he'd put himself in great jeopardy, risking *everything*—for me.

The blare of a horn snapped me back to the present.

Through the windshield, I saw my roommate's million-dollar smile flashing at me from the billboard on the side of a bus. Cary Taylor's lips had a come-hither curve and his long, lean frame was blocking the intersection. The taxi driver was hitting his horn repeatedly, as if that would clear the way.

Not a chance. Cary wasn't moving and neither was I. He lounged on his side, bare-chested and barefooted, his jeans unbuttoned to show both the waistband of his underwear and the sleek lines of his ripped abs. His dark brown hair was sexily mussed and his emerald eyes were bright with mischief.

I was suddenly struck with the knowledge that I would have to keep a dreadful secret from my best friend.

Cary was my touchstone, my voice of reason, my favorite shoulder to lean on—and a brother to me in every way that mattered. I hated the thought of having to hold back what Gideon had done for me.

I wanted desperately to talk about it, to get help working it out in my head, but I'd never be able to tell anyone. Even our therapist could be ethically and legally bound to break our confidence.

A burly, neon-vested traffic cop appeared and urged the bus into its lane with an authoritative white-gloved hand and a holler that meant business. He waved us through the intersection just before the light changed. I sat back, my arms around my waist, rocking.

The ride from Gideon's Fifth Avenue penthouse to my apartment on the Upper West Side was a short one, but somehow it felt like an eternity. The information that NYPD detective Shelley Graves had shared with me just a few hours earlier had changed my life.

It had also forced me to abandon the one person I *needed* to be with.

I'd left Gideon alone because I couldn't trust Graves's motives. I couldn't take the chance that she'd told me her suspicions just to see if I'd run to him and prove that his breakup with me was a well-crafted lie.

God. The riot of emotions I felt had my heart racing. Gideon needed me now—as much as, if not more than, I needed him—yet I'd walked away.

The desolation in his eyes as the doors to his private elevator separated us had ripped me open inside.

Gideon.

The cab turned the corner and pulled up in front of my apartment building. The night doorman opened the car door before I could tell the driver to turn around and take me back, and the sticky August air rushed in to chase the air-conditioning away.

"Good evening, Miss Tramell." The doorman accompanied the greeting with a tap of his fingers to the brim of his hat and waited patiently while I swiped my debit card. When I'd finished paying, I accepted his help out of the back of the cab and felt his gaze slide discreetly over my tearstained face.

Smiling as if everything were okay in my world, I rushed into the lobby and headed straight for the elevator, with a brief wave at the front desk staff.

"Eva!"

Turning my head, I discovered a svelte brunette in a stylish skirt-and-blouse ensemble rising to her feet in the lobby seating area. Her dark hair fell in thick waves around her shoulders, and her smile graced full lips that were a glossy pink. I frowned, not recognizing her.

"Yes?" I replied, suddenly wary. There was an avid gleam in her dark eyes that got my back up. Despite how battered I felt and probably looked, I squared my shoulders and faced her directly.

"Deanna Johnson," she said, thrusting out a well-manicured hand. "Freelance reporter."

I arched a brow. "Hello."

She laughed. "You don't have to be so suspicious. I'd just like to chat with you a few minutes. I've got a story I'm working on, and I could use your help."

"No offense, but I can't think of anything I want to talk to a reporter about."

"Not even Gideon Cross?"

The hairs on my nape prickled. "Especially not him."

As one of the twenty-five richest men in the world, with a New York real estate portfolio so extensive it boggled the mind, Gideon was always news. But it was also news that he'd dumped me and gotten back together with his ex-fiancée.

Deanna crossed her arms, a move that accentuated her cleavage, something I took note of only because I was eyeing her again with more care.

"Come on," she coaxed. "I can keep your name out of it, Eva. I won't use anything that identifies you. This is your chance to get a bit of your own back."

A rock settled in the bottom of my stomach. She was so exactly Gideon's type—tall, slender, dark-haired, and golden-skinned. So very unlike me.

"Are you sure you want to go down this road?" I asked quietly, intuitively certain she'd fucked my man at some point in the past. "He isn't someone I'd want to cross."

"Are you afraid of him?" she shot back. "I'm not. His money doesn't give him the right to do whatever the hell he wants."

I took a slow, deep breath and remembered when Dr. Terrence Lucas—someone else who was at odds with Gideon—had said something similar to me. Now that I knew what Gideon was capable of, how far he would go to protect me, I could *still* answer honestly and without reservation, "No, I'm not afraid. But I've learned to pick my battles. Moving on is the best revenge."

Her chin lifted. "Not all of us have rock stars waiting in the wings."

"Whatever." I sighed inwardly at her mention of my ex, Brett Kline, who was front man for a band on the rise and one of the sexiest men I'd ever met. Like Gideon, he radiated sex appeal like a heat wave. Unlike

Gideon, he wasn't the love of my life. I was never going to wade in that pool again.

"Listen"—Deanna pulled a business card out of a pocket of her skirt—"pretty soon you're going to figure out that Gideon Cross was using you to get Corinne Giroux jealous enough to come back to him. When you smell the coffee, call me. I'll be waiting."

I accepted the card. "Why do you think I know anything worth sharing?"

Her lush mouth thinned. "Because whatever Cross's motivation was for hooking up with you, you got to him. The iceman thawed a bit for you."

"Maybe he did, but it's over."

"That doesn't mean you don't know something, Eva. I can help you figure out what's newsworthy."

"What's your angle?" I'd be damned if I would sit back while someone took aim at Gideon. If she was determined to be a threat to him, I was determined to head her off at the pass.

"That man has a dark side."

"Don't we all?" What had she seen of Gideon? What had he revealed in the course of their . . . association? *If* they'd had one.

I wasn't sure I'd ever get to the point where thinking of Gideon being intimate with another woman didn't trigger ferocious jealousy.

"Why don't we go somewhere and talk?" she cajoled.

I shot a glance at the staffer at the front desk, who made a good show of politely ignoring us. I was too emotionally raw to deal with Deanna, and was still reeling from the conversation with Detective Graves.

"Maybe some other time," I said, leaving the option open because I intended to keep tabs on her.

As if he sensed my uneasiness, Chad, one of the night crew at the front desk, approached.

"Ms. Johnson was just leaving," I told him, consciously relaxing. If

Detective Graves hadn't been able to pin anything on Gideon, a nosy freelance reporter wasn't going to do better.

Too bad I knew what kind of information could be leaked from the police, and how easily and often it was done. My father, Victor Reyes, was a cop, and I'd heard plenty on that subject.

I turned toward the elevators. "Good night, Deanna."

"I'll be around," she called after me.

I stepped into the elevator and hit the button for my floor. As the doors slid shut, I sagged into the handrail. I needed to warn Gideon, but there was no way for me to contact him that couldn't be traced.

The ache in my chest intensified. Our relationship was so fucked up. We couldn't even talk to each other.

I exited on my floor and let myself into my apartment, crossing the spacious living room to dump my purse on one of the kitchen bar stools. The view of Manhattan showcased through my living room's floor-to-ceiling windows failed to stir me. I was too agitated to care where I was. The only thing that mattered was that I wasn't with Gideon.

As I headed down the hallway toward my bedroom, the sound of muted music floated outward from Cary's. Did he have company over? If so, who was it? My best friend had decided to try juggling two relationships—one with a woman who accepted him the way he was and one with a man who hated that Cary was involved with someone else.

I shed my clothes across the bathroom floor en route to the shower. While I lathered, it was impossible not to think of the times I'd showered with Gideon, occasions when our lust for one another had fueled starkly erotic encounters. I missed him so much. I needed his touch, his desire, his love. My craving for those things was a gnawing hunger, making me restless and edgy. I had no idea how I was supposed to fall asleep when I didn't know when I'd get a chance to talk to Gideon again. There was so much that had to be said.

Wrapping a towel around me, I left the bathroom—

Gideon stood just inside my closed bedroom door. The sight of him spurred a reaction so abrupt it was like a physical blow. My breath caught and my heart lurched into an excited rhythm, my entire being responding to the sight of him with a potent rush of yearning. It felt like years since I'd last been with him, instead of a mere hour.

I'd given him a key, but he owned the building. Getting to me without leaving a trail that could be followed was possible with that advantage . . . just as he'd been able to get to Nathan.

"It's dangerous for you to be here," I pointed out. That didn't stop me from being thrilled that he was. My gaze drank him in, roaming avidly over his lean, broad-shouldered frame.

He wore black sweats and a well-loved Columbia sweatshirt, a combination that made him look like the twenty-eight-year-old man he was and not the billionaire mogul the rest of the world knew. A Yankees ball cap was pulled low over his brow, but the shadow cast by its brim did nothing to diminish the striking blue of his eyes. They stared at me fiercely, his sensual lips drawn into a grim line. "I couldn't stay away."

Gideon Cross was an impossibly gorgeous man, so beautiful that people stopped and stared when he walked by. I'd once thought of him as a sex god, and his frequent—and enthusiastic—displays of prowess constantly proved me right, but I also knew he was all too human. Like me, he'd been broken.

The odds were against our making it.

My chest expanded on a deep breath, my body responding to the proximity of his. Even though he stood several feet away, I could feel the heady attraction, the magnetic pull of being near the other half of my soul. It'd been that way with us from the very first meeting, both of us inexorably drawn together. We'd mistaken our ferocious mutual captivation for lust until we realized we couldn't breathe without each other.

I fought the urge to run into his arms, the place where I so desperately wanted to be. But he was too still, too tightly reined. I waited in exquisite anticipation for his cue.

God, I loved him so much.

His hands fisted at his sides. "I need you."

My core tightened in response to the roughness of his voice, the rasp of it warm and luxurious.

"You don't have to sound so happy about it," I teased breathlessly, trying to lighten his mood before he got me beneath him.

I loved him wild, and I loved him tender. I'd take him any way I could get him, but it'd been so long . . . My skin was already tingling and tightening expectantly, craving the greedy reverence of his touch. I feared what would happen if he came at me full force when I was so starved for his body. We might tear each other apart.

"It's killing me," he said gruffly. "Being without you. Missing you. I feel like my fucking sanity depends on you, Eva, and you want me to be *happy* about that?"

My tongue darted out to wet my dry lips and he growled, sending a shiver through me. "Well . . . *I'm* happy about it."

The tension in his posture visibly eased. He must've been so worried about how I would react to what he'd done for me. To be honest, *I'd* been worried. Did my gratitude mean I was more twisted than I realized?

Then I remembered my stepbrother's hands all over me . . . his weight pressing me into the mattress . . . the tearing pain between my legs as he rammed into me over and over . . .

I trembled with renewed fury. If being glad the fucker was dead made me twisted, so be it.

Gideon took a deep breath. His hand reached up to his chest and rubbed at the area over his heart as if it hurt him.

"I love you," I told him, my eyes stinging with fresh tears. "I love you so much."

"Angel." He reached me with quick strides, dropping his keys on the floor and shoving both hands into my damp hair. He was shaking, and I cried, overwhelmed by the knowledge of how much he needed me.

Tilting my head to the angle he wanted, Gideon took my mouth with searing possession, tasting me with slow, deep licks. His passion and hunger exploded across my senses, and I whimpered, my hands tangling in his sweatshirt. His answering groan vibrated through me, tightening my nipples and sending goose bumps racing across my skin.

I melted into him, my hands pushing the cap from his head so that my fingers could sink into the silky black mane of his hair. I fell into the kiss, swept away by the lush carnality of it. A sob escaped me.

"Don't," he breathed, pulling back to cradle my jaw. He looked into my eyes. "It shreds me when you cry."

"It's too much." I trembled.

His beautiful eyes looked as weary as mine. He nodded grimly. "What I did—"

"Not that. How I feel about you."

He rubbed the tip of his nose against me, his hands sliding reverently along my bare arms—hands with proverbial blood on them, which only made me love his touch all the more.

"Thank you," I whispered.

His eyes closed. "God, when you left tonight . . . I didn't know if you'd come back . . . if I'd lost you—"

"I need you, too, Gideon."

"I won't apologize. I'd do it again." His grip tightened on me. "The options were restraining orders, increased security, vigilance . . . for the rest of your life. There was no guarantee you'd be safe unless Nathan was dead."

"You cut me off. Shut me out. You and me—"

"Forever." His fingertips pressed against my parted lips. "It's over, Eva. Don't argue about something that's too late to change."

I brushed his hand away. "*Is* it over? Can we be together now, or are we still hiding our relationship from the police? Are we even *in* a relationship?"

Gideon held my gaze, hiding nothing, letting me see his pain and fear. "That's what I'm here to ask you."

"If it's up to me, I'll never let you go," I said vehemently. "Never."

Gideon's hands slid down my throat to my shoulders, blazing a hot trail across my skin. "I need that to be true," he said softly. "I was afraid you'd run . . . that you'd be afraid. Of *me*."

"Gideon, no—"

"I would never hurt you."

I caught the waistband of his sweats and tugged, even though I couldn't budge him. "I *know* that."

And physically, I had no doubts; he'd always been careful with me, always cautious. But emotionally, my love had been used against me with meticulous precision. I was struggling with reconciling the absolute trust I had in Gideon's awareness of my needs and the wariness that came from a shattered heart still healing.

"Do you?" He searched my face, as attuned as always to what wasn't said. "Letting you go would kill me, but I wouldn't hurt you to keep you."

"I don't want to go anywhere."

He exhaled audibly. "My lawyers will be talking to the police tomorrow, to get a feel for where things stand."

Tilting my head back, I pressed my lips gently to his. We were colluding to hide a crime, and I'd be lying if I said that didn't seriously bother me—I was the daughter of a police officer, after all—but the alternative was too awful to consider.

"I have to know that you can live with what I've done," he said softly, wrapping my hair around his finger.

"I think so. Can you?"

His mouth found mine again. "I can survive anything if I have you."

I reached under his sweatshirt, seeking and finding his warm, golden skin. His muscles were hard and ridged beneath my palms, his body a seductive and virile work of art. I licked his lips, my teeth catching the full curve along the bottom and biting gently. Gideon groaned. The sound of his pleasure slid over me like a caress.

"Touch me." The words were an order, but his tone was a plea.

"I am."

Reaching behind him, he grabbed my wrist and pulled my hand around. He thrust his cock shamelessly into my palm, grinding. My fingers curled around the thick, heavy length, my pulse quickening at the realization that he was commando beneath his sweats.

"God," I breathed. "You make me so hot."

His blue eyes were fierce on my face; his cheeks flushed and his sculpted lips parted. He never tried to hide the effect I had on him, never pretended that he had any more control over his response to me than I had to him. It made his dominance in the bedroom all the more exciting, knowing that he was similarly as helpless to the attraction between us.

My chest tightened. I still couldn't believe that he was mine, that I got to see him this way, so open and hungry and sexy as hell . . .

Gideon tugged my towel open. He inhaled sharply when it hit the floor and I stood before him completely naked. "Ah, Eva."

His voice throbbed with emotion, making my eyes sting. He yanked his shirt up and over his head, tossing it aside. Then he reached for me, stepping carefully into me, prolonging the moment when our bare skin would touch.

He gripped my hips, his fingers flexing restlessly, his breathing quick and harsh. The tips of my breasts touched him first, sending a sudden rush of sensation through my body. I gasped. He crushed me to him with a growl, lifting my feet from the floor and carrying me backward toward the bed.

2

M Y THIGHS HIT the mattress and I landed on my butt, falling to my
   back with Gideon leaning over me. He hitched me up with an
arm banded around my back, centering me on the bed before he settled
atop me. His mouth was on my breast before I knew it, his lips soft and
warm, the suction fast and greedy. He plumped the heavy weight in his
hand, kneading possessively.

"Christ, I've missed you," he groaned. His skin was hot against my
cool flesh, his weight so welcome after the long nights without him.

I hooked my legs around his calves and shoved my hands beneath
his waistband to grip his taut, hard ass. I tugged him into me, arching
my hips to feel his cock through the cotton that separated us. Wanting
him inside me, so that I'd know for certain he was mine again.

"Say it," I coaxed, needing the words he swore were inadequate.

He pushed up and looked down at me, gently brushing my hair back
from my forehead. He swallowed hard.

Rearing, I caught his beautifully etched mouth in a kiss. "I'll say it first: I love you."

He closed his eyes and quivered. Wrapping his arms around me, Gideon squeezed so tight I almost couldn't breathe.

"I love you," he whispered. "Too much."

His fervent declaration reverberated through me. I buried my face in his shoulder and cried.

"Angel." His fist clenched in my hair.

Lifting my head, I took his mouth, our kiss flavored with the salt of my tears. My lips moved desperately over his, as if he'd be gone at any second and I had no time to get my fill of him.

"Eva. Let me . . ." He cupped my face, licking deep into my mouth. "Let me love you."

"Please," I whispered, my fingers linking behind his neck to capture him. His erection lay hot and heavy against the lips of my sex, the weight of him the perfect pressure on my throbbing clit. "Don't stop."

"Never. I can't."

His hand cupped my buttock, lifting me into a deft roll of his hips. I gasped as the pleasure radiated through me, my nipples beading hard and tight against his chest. The light dusting of crisp hair was an unbearable stimulation. My core ached, begging for the hard-driving thrust of his cock.

My nails raked his back from shoulder to hips. He arched into the rough caress with a low growl, his head thrown back in deliciously erotic abandon.

"Again," he ordered gruffly, his face flushed and lips parted.

Surging upward, I sank my teeth into his pectoral, just over his heart. Gideon hissed, quivering, and took it.

I couldn't contain the ferocious swell of emotion that needed release—the love and need, the anger and fear. And the pain. God, the pain. I still felt it keenly. I wanted to tear into him. To punish as well as pleasure. To make him experience some small measure of what I had when he'd pushed me away.

My tongue stroked over the slight indentations left by my teeth and his hips rocked into me, his cock sliding through the parted lips of my sex.

"My turn," he whispered darkly. Leaning on one arm, the biceps thick and beautifully defined, he squeezed my breast in his other hand. His head lowered and his lips surrounded the taut point of my nipple. His mouth was scorching hot, his tongue a rough velvet lash against my tender flesh. When his teeth bit into the furled tip, I cried out, my body jerking as sharp need arrowed to my core.

I clutched at his hair, too impassioned to be gentle. My legs wrapped around him, tightening, echoing my need to claim him. Possess him. Make him mine again.

"Gideon," I moaned. My temples were wet from the trails of my tears, my throat tight and hurting.

"I'm here, angel," he breathed, nibbling across my cleavage to my other breast. His diabolical fingers tugged at the wet nipple he'd left behind, pinching it gently until I pushed up and into his hand. "Don't fight me. Let me love you."

I realized then that I was pulling at his hair, trying to urge him away even as I fought to get closer. Gideon had me under siege, seducing me with his stunning male perfection and intimate expertise with my body. And I was surrendering. My breasts were heavy, my sex wet and swollen. My hands roamed restlessly as my legs caged him.

Still, he slipped farther away from me, his mouth whispering temptation across my stomach. *Missed you so much . . . need you . . . have to have you . . .* I felt a hot wetness slide over my skin and looked down to see that he was crying, too, his gorgeous face ravaged by the same surfeit of emotion flooding me.

With shaking fingers, I touched his cheek, trying to smooth away the wetness that only returned the instant it was wiped away. He nuzzled into my touch with a soft, plaintive moan, and I couldn't bear it. His pain was harder for me to deal with than my own.

"I love you," I told him.

"Eva." He slid back onto his knees and rose, his thighs spread between mine, his cock thick and hard and bobbing under its weight.

Everything in me tightened with ravenous greed. His big body was carved with rock-hard slabs of tautly defined muscle, his tanned skin sheened with perspiration. He was so powerfully elegant, except for his penis, which was bluntly primal with its thick coursing veins and wide root. His sac, too, hung large and heavy. He would make a statue as beautiful as Michelangelo's *David*, but with a flagrantly erotic edge.

Honestly, Gideon Cross had been designed to fuck a woman right out of her mind.

"Mine," I said harshly, pushing up and scrambling gracelessly into him, pressing my torso tightly into his. "You're mine."

"Angel." He took my mouth in a rough, lust-fueled kiss. Lifting me, he moved, turning us so that his back was to the headboard and I was spread over him. Our flesh slid against each other, slickened by sweat.

His hands were everywhere, his muscled body straining upward as mine had done. I cupped his face, licking fast into his mouth, trying to satisfy my thirst for him.

He reached between my legs, his fingers delving reverently into my cleft. The roughened pads stroked over my clit and skirted the trembling opening to my sex. With my lips pressed to his, I moaned, my hips circling. He fingered me leisurely, building my need, his kiss gentling into a slow, deep fucking of my mouth.

I couldn't breathe for the pleasure, my entire body quivering as he cupped me in his hand and his long middle finger slid lazily into me. His palm rubbed against my clit, his fingertip stroking over delicate tissues. His other hand gripped my hip, holding me in place, restraining me.

Gideon's control seemed absolute, his seduction wickedly precise, but he was trembling harder than I was and his chest was heaving more forcefully. The sounds spilling from him were tinged with remorse and entreaty.

Pulling back, I reached for his cock with both hands, gripping him firmly. I knew his body well, too, knew what he needed and desired. I pumped him from root to tip, drawing a thick bead of pre-ejaculate to the wide crest. He pushed back against the headboard with a groan, his finger curving inside me. I watched, riveted, as the thick drop rolled to one side of his glans, then slid down the length of him to pool at the top of my fist.

"Don't," he panted. "Too close."

I stroked him again, my mouth watering as a gush of pre-cum streamed out of him. I was wildly aroused by his pleasure and the knowledge that I had such a profound effect on such a blatantly sexual creature.

As he cursed, his fingers left me. He grabbed my hips, dislodging my grip on him. He yanked me forward, then down, his hips bucking upward, his raging cock driving into me.

I cried out and gripped his shoulders, my sex clenching against the thick penetration.

"*Eva.*" His jaw and neck taut with strain, he started coming, spurting hot and hard inside me.

The gush of lubrication opened me, my sex sliding down his pulsing erection until he filled me too full. My nails dug into his unyielding muscles, my mouth opened to draw in desperate breaths of air.

"Take it," he bit out, angling my descent to gain that last little part of me that let him to sink in to the root. "Take me."

I moaned, welcoming the familiar soreness of having him so deep. The orgasm took me by surprise, my back bowing as the heated pleasure tore through me.

Instinct took over, my hips moving of their own volition, my thighs clenching and releasing as I focused only on the moment, the reclaiming of my man. My heart.

Gideon yielded to my demands.

"That's it, angel," he encouraged hoarsely, his erection still as hard as if he hadn't just had a teeth-grinding climax.

His arms fell to his sides. His hands fisted in the comforter. His biceps clenched and flexed with his movements. His abs tightened every time I took him to the hilt, the rigid lacing of muscles glistening with sweat. His body was a well-oiled machine and I was taking it to its limits.

He let me. Gave himself to me.

Undulating my hips, I took my pleasure, moaning his name. My core clenched rhythmically, another orgasm rushing up too quickly. I faltered, my senses overwhelmed.

"Please," I gasped. "Gideon, please."

He caught me by the nape and waist, and slid down until we were flat on the bed. Pinning me tightly, he held me immobile, thrusting upward . . . over and over . . . shafting my sex with fast, powerful lunges. The friction of his thick penis rubbing and surging was too much. I jolted violently and came again, my fingers clawing into his sides.

Shuddering, Gideon followed me over, his arms tightening until I could barely breathe. His harsh exhalations were the air that filled my burning lungs. I was utterly possessed, completely defenseless.

"God, Eva." He buried his face in my throat. "Need you. I need you so much."

"Baby." I held him close. Still afraid to let go.

BLINKING up at the ceiling, I realized I'd fallen asleep. Then the panic hit, the horrible inevitability of waking from a blissful dream into a nightmare reality. I surged up, gulping air into a chest that was too tight.

Gideon.

I nearly sobbed when I found him sprawled next to me, his lips barely parted with his deep, even breathing. The lover my heart had broken for, returned to me.

God . . .

Sinking back against the headboard, I forced myself to relax, to savor the rare pleasure of watching him sleep. His face was transformed when he was unguarded, reminding me of how young he really was. That was easy to forget when he was awake and radiating the powerful force of will that had literally knocked me on my ass when I'd first met him.

With reverent fingers, I brushed the inky strands of hair away from his cheek, noting the new lines around his eyes and mouth. I'd also noted that he'd grown leaner. Our separation had taken a toll on him, but he'd hidden it so well. Or maybe I viewed him as flawless and inviolate.

I hadn't been able to hide my devastation at all. I'd believed we were over and it showed to everyone who'd looked at me, which Gideon had counted on all along. *Plausible deniability,* he'd called it. I called it hell, and until we could stop pretending we'd broken up, I'd still be living in it.

Shifting carefully, I propped my head on my hand and studied the decadent man who graced my bed. His arms were wrapped around his pillow, showing off chiseled biceps and a muscular back adorned with scratches and crescent marks from my nails. I'd gripped his ass, too, insanely turned on by the feel of it clenching and releasing as he fucked me tirelessly, stroking his long, thick cock deep inside me.

Again and again . . .

My legs shifted restlessly, my body stirring with renewed hunger. For all his polished urbanity, Gideon was an untamed animal behind closed doors, a lover who bared me to the soul every time he made love to me. I had no defenses against him when he was touching me, help-less to resist the drugging pleasure of spreading my thighs for such a virile, passionate male—

His eyes opened, stunning me with those vivid blue irises. He gave me a lazily seductive once-over that made my heart skip a beat. "Hmm . . . You're wearing the fuck-me look," he drawled.

"And that would be because you're so extremely fuckable," I shot back. "Waking up to you is like . . . presents on Christmas morning."

His mouth curved. "For your convenience, I'm already unwrapped. Batteries not required."

My chest tightened with terrible yearning. I loved him too much. I was constantly worried that I wouldn't be able to hold on to him. He was lightning in a bottle, a dream I tried to hold in my hands.

I let out a shaky breath. "You're a delicious extravagance for a woman, you know. A luscious, mouthwatering—"

"Shut up." He rolled over and dragged me under him before I knew his intent. "I'm filthy rich, but you just want me for my body."

I looked up at him, admiring the way his dark hair framed that extraordinary face. "I want the heart inside the body."

"You have it." His arms tucked against my sides and his legs tangled with mine, the coarse hair on his calves stimulating my hypersensitive skin.

I was restrained. Possessed. His warm, hard body felt so good against mine. I sighed, feeling some of the fearful hesitation easing.

"I shouldn't have fallen asleep," he said quietly.

I stroked his hair, knowing he was right, that his nightmares and atypical sexual parasomnia made sleeping with him dangerous. He sometimes lashed out in his sleep, and if I was too close, I took the brunt of the simmering rage inside him. "I'm glad you did, though."

He caught my wrist and pulled my fingers to his mouth for a kiss. "We need time together when we aren't looking over our shoulders."

"Oh, God. I almost forgot. Deanna Johnson was here tonight." The moment the words left my mouth I regretted the wall they put up between us.

Gideon blinked, and in that split second, the warmth in his eyes was gone. "Stay away from her. She's a reporter."

My arms slid around him. "She's going for blood."

"She'll have to get in line."

"Why is she so interested? She's a freelancer. No one assigned her to you."

"Drop it, Eva."

His dismissal of the subject irked me. "I know you fucked her."

"No, you don't. And what you should be focused on is the fact that I'm about to fuck *you*."

Certainty settled in my gut. I released him, pulling away. "You lied."

He reared back as if I'd slapped him. "I have never lied to you."

"You told me you've had more sex since you met me than you've had in the last two years combined, but you told Dr. Petersen you've been getting laid twice a week. Which is it?"

Rolling to his back, he scowled at the ceiling. "Do we have to do this now? Tonight?"

His body language was so tight and defensive that my irritation with his evasiveness left me in a rush. I didn't want to fight with him, especially over the past. What mattered was now and the future. I had to trust that he'd be faithful.

"No, we don't," I said softly, turning onto my side and reaching over to place my hand on his chest. Once the sun came up, we'd be right back to pretending we weren't together. I had no idea how long we'd have to keep up the charade or when I'd get to be with him again. "I just wanted to warn you that she's digging. Watch out for her."

"Dr. Petersen asked about sexual encounters, Eva," he said flatly, "which isn't necessarily fucking, as far as I'm concerned. I didn't think that distinction would be appreciated when answering the question. So

ENTWINED WITH YOU · 21

let me be clear: I took women to the hotel, but I didn't always nail them. It was the exception when I did."

I thought of his fuck pad, a stocked-with-sexual-paraphernalia suite reserved in one of his many hospitality properties. He'd given it up, thank God, but I'd never forget it. "Maybe it's better I don't hear any more."

"You opened this door," he snapped. "We're walking through it."

I sighed. "Fair enough."

"There were times when I couldn't stand to be alone with myself, but I didn't want to talk. I didn't want to even *think*, let alone feel anything. I needed the distraction of focusing on someone else, and using my dick was too much involvement. Can you understand that?"

Sadly, I could, recalling times when I'd dropped to my knees for a guy just to shut off my brain for a while. Encounters like those had never been about foreplay or sex.

"So is she one of the girls you screwed or not?" I hated asking the question, but we had to get it out of the way.

He turned his head to look at me. "Once."

"Must've been some lay for her to be so bent out of shape over it."

"I couldn't say," he muttered. "I don't remember."

"Were you drunk?"

"No. Jesus." He scrubbed at his face. "What the hell did she tell you?"

"Nothing personal. She did mention you having a 'dark side.' I'm assuming that's a sexual reference, but I didn't ask her for details. She was playing it like we had an affinity because we'd both been thrown over by you. The 'Dumped by Gideon Sisterhood.'"

He glanced at me with cold eyes. "Don't be catty. It doesn't suit you."

"Hey." I frowned. "I'm sorry. I wasn't trying to be a total bitch. Just a little one. I think I'm entitled, all things considered."

"What the hell was I supposed to do, Eva? I didn't know you existed." Gideon's voice deepened, roughened. "If I'd known you were out there, I would've hunted you down. I wouldn't have waited a second to find you. But I didn't know, and I settled for less. So did you. We both wasted ourselves on the wrong people."

"Yeah, we did. Dumbasses."

There was a pause. "Are you pissed?"

"No, I'm good."

He stared.

I laughed. "You were getting ready to fight, weren't you? We can play it that way if you want. Personally, I was hoping to get laid again."

Gideon slid over me. The look on his face, the melding of relief and gratitude, caused a sharp pain in my chest. I was reminded of how important it was for him to be trusted to share the truth.

"You're different," he said, touching my face.

Of course I was. The man I loved had killed for me. A lot of things became inconsequential after a sacrifice like that.

3

"ANGEL."

I smelled the coffee before I opened my eyes. "Gideon?"

"Hmm?"

"If it's not at least seven o'clock, I'm going to kick your ass."

His soft laugh made my toes curl. "It's early, but we need to talk."

"Yeah?" I opened one eye, then the other, so I could fully admire his three-piece suit. He looked so edible, I wanted to take it off him—with my teeth.

He settled on the edge of my bed, the embodiment of temptation. "I want to make sure we're solid before I leave."

I sat up and leaned against the headboard, making no effort to cover my breasts because we were going to end up talking about his ex-fiancée. I played dirty when warranted. "I'll need that coffee for this conversation."

Gideon handed me the mug, then stroked the pad of his thumb over my nipple. "So beautiful," he murmured. "Every inch of you."

"Are you trying to distract me?"

"You're distracting me. Very effectively."

Could he possibly be as infatuated with my looks and body as I was with his? The thought made me smile.

"I missed your smile, angel."

"I know the feeling." Every time I'd seen him and he hadn't gifted me with his smile had been another cut to my heart until I'd been bleeding nonstop. I couldn't even think of those occasions without feeling echoes of the pain. "Where did you hide the suit, ace? I know it wasn't in your pocket."

With a change of clothes, he'd transformed himself into a powerful, successful businessman. The suit was bespoke, and his shirt and tie were immaculately matched. Even his cuff links gleamed with understated elegance. Still, the fall of dark hair that skimmed his collar warned others he was far from tamed.

"That's one of the things we need to talk about." He straightened, but the warmth in his gaze remained. "I took over the apartment next door. We'll have to make our reconciliation seem suitably gradual, so I'll keep up the appearance of using my penthouse for the most part, but I'll be spending as much time as possible as your new neighbor."

"Is it safe?"

"I'm not a suspect, Eva. I'm not even a person of interest. My alibi is airtight, and I have no known motive. We're just showing the detectives some respect by not insulting their intelligence. We're making it easy for them to justify their conclusion that they're at a dead end."

I took a sip of coffee, giving me time to contemplate what he'd said. The danger might not be immediate, but it was inherent in his guilt. I felt the pressure of it, no matter how he tried to reassure me.

But we were working our way back to each other, and I sensed his need for reassurance that we were going to recover from the strain and separation of the last few weeks.

I deliberately took a light tone when I replied, "So my former boyfriend will be on Fifth Avenue, but I've got a hunky new neighbor to play with? This could be interesting."

One of his brows arched. "You want to role-play, angel?"

"I want to keep you satisfied," I admitted with brutal honesty. "I want to be everything you ever found in the other women you've been with." Women he'd taken to a fuck pad with toys.

His irises were cool blue fire, but his voice came smooth and even. "I can't keep my hands off you. That should be enough to tell you I don't need more."

I watched him stand. He took my mug and set it on the nightstand, then caught the edge of the sheet and threw it deftly aside, exposing me completely.

"Scoot down," he ordered. "Spread your legs."

My pulse quickened as I obeyed him, sliding to my back and allowing my thighs to fall open. There was an instinctive urge to cover myself—the feeling of vulnerability under that piercing gaze was so intense—but I resisted it. I'd be dishonest if I didn't admit that it was wildly exciting to be totally naked while he was irresistibly clothed in one of his sexy-as-hell suits. It created an instantaneous power advantage for him that was a serious turn-on.

He stroked a finger through the lips of my sex, gliding teasingly over my clit. "This beautiful cunt is mine."

My belly quivered at the rasp in his voice.

Cupping me in his palm, he met my gaze. "I'm a very possessive man, Eva, as I'm sure you've noticed by now."

I shivered as the tip of his finger circled the clenching opening. "Yes."

"Role-play, restraints, modes of transportation, and varied locations . . . I look forward to exploring all of that with you." Eyes glittering, he slid a finger oh-so-slowly inside me. He made a low purring noise and caught his lower lip between his teeth, a purely erotic look that told me he felt his semen inside me.

Being penetrated and so gently pleasured left me unable to speak for a moment.

"You like that," he said softly.

"Umm."

His finger went deeper. "I'll be damned if plastic, glass, metal, or leather will make you come. B.O.B. and his friends will have to find other amusements."

Heat swept over my skin like fever. He understood.

Bending over me, Gideon placed one hand on the mattress and lowered his mouth to mine. His thumb pressed against my clit and rubbed expertly, massaging me inside and out. The pleasure of his touch spread, tightening my stomach and hardening my nipples. I clutched my bare breasts in my hands, squeezing as they swelled. His touch and desire were magic. How had I ever lived without him?

"I ache for you," he said hoarsely. "Crave you constantly. Snap your fingers and I'm hard." He traced my lower lip with his tongue, inhaling my panting breaths. "When I come, I come for you. Because of you and your mouth, hands, and insatiable little cunt. And it'll be that way for you in reverse. My tongue, my fingers, my cum inside you. Just you and me, Eva. Intimate and raw."

I had no doubt I was the focal point of his world when he was touching me, the only thing he saw or thought of. But we couldn't have that physical connection all the time. Somehow, I had to learn to believe in what I *couldn't* see between us.

Shameless, my body writhed as I rode his plunging finger. He added another and I dug in my heels, arching up to meet his thrusts. "Please."

"When your eyes turn soft and dreamy, *I'll* be the one who put that look on you, not a toy." He nibbled my jaw, then moved to my chest, nudging my hands aside with his lips. He claimed my nipple in a gentle bite, his mouth surrounding the tender peak and sucking softly. The ache he created was needle-sharp, my hunger spurred by the sense that there was a lingering gulf between us, something that hadn't yet been recognized and resolved.

"More," I gasped, needing his pleasure as much as my own.

"Always," he murmured, his mouth curving in a wicked smile against my skin.

I groaned in frustration. "I want your cock inside me."

"As you should." His tongue curled around my other nipple, flickering teasingly over it until it ached for suction. "Your craving should be for *me*, angel, not an orgasm. For *my* body, *my* hands. Eventually, you won't be able to come without my skin touching yours."

I nodded frantically, my mouth too dry to speak. Need was coiled like a spring in my core, tightening with every circle of Gideon's thumb on my clit and every thrust of his fingers. I thought of B.O.B., my trusty Battery-Operated Boyfriend, and knew that if Gideon were to stop touching me now, nothing would get me off. My passion *was* for him, my desire inflamed by his desire for me.

My thighs quivered. "I'm g-going to come."

His mouth covered mine, his beautiful lips soft and coaxing. It was the love in his kiss that pushed me over. I cried out and shuddered through a quick, hard orgasm. My moan was long and broken, my body quivering violently. I pushed my hands under his jacket to grip his back, holding him close, my mouth claiming his until the wracking pleasure eased.

Licking the taste of me from his fingers, he murmured, "Tell me what you're thinking."

I consciously tried to slow my racing heart. "I'm not thinking. I just want to look at you."

"You don't always. Sometimes you close your eyes."

"That's because you're a talker in bed and your voice is so sexy." I swallowed hard with remembered pain. "I love to hear you, Gideon. I need to know that I'm making you feel as good as you make me feel."

"Suck me off now," he whispered. "Make me come for you."

I slid from the bed in a breathless rush, my hands reaching eagerly for his fly. He was hard and thick, his erection straining. Lifting his shirttail and pushing down his boxer briefs, I freed him. He fell heavily into my hands, the thick length already glistening at the tip. I licked the evidence of his excitement away, loving his control, the way he reined in his own hungers to satisfy mine.

My eyes were on him as my open mouth slid over the plush head. I watched his lips part on a sharply indrawn breath and his eyelids grow heavy, as if the pleasure were intoxicating.

"Eva." His hooded gaze was hot on my face. "Ah . . . Yes. Like that. Christ, I love your mouth."

His praise spurred me on. I took him as deep as I could. I loved doing this to him, loved the uniquely masculine taste and smell of him. I ran my lips down the length of him, suckling gently. Worshipfully. And I didn't feel wrong for adoring his virility—I deserved it.

"You love this," he said gruffly, pushing his fingers into my hair to cup my head. "As much as I do."

"More. I want to do this for hours. Make you come over and over again."

A growl rumbled in his chest. "I would. I can't get enough."

The tip of my tongue traced a pulsing vein up to the head, and then I took him in my mouth again, my neck arching back as I lowered to sit on my heels, my hands on my knees, offering myself to him.

Gideon looked down with eyes that glittered with lust and tenderness.

"Don't stop." He widened his stance. He slid his cock to the back of my throat, then pulled back out, coating my tongue with a trail of creamy pre-ejaculate. I swallowed, savoring the rich flavor of him.

He groaned, his hands cupping my jaw. "Don't stop, angel. Suck me dry."

My cheeks hollowed as we found a rhythm, *our* rhythm, the syncing of our hearts and breaths and drive to pleasure. We had no problem overthinking our way into trouble, but our bodies never got it wrong. When we had our hands on each other, we both knew we were in the one place we needed to be, with the one person we needed to be with.

"So fucking good." His teeth ground audibly. "Ah, God, you're making me come."

His cock swelled in my mouth. His hand fisted in my hair, pulling, his body shuddering as he came hard.

Gideon cursed as I swallowed. He emptied himself in thick, hot bursts, flooding my mouth as if he hadn't come all night. By the time he finished, I was gasping and trembling. He pulled me to my feet and stumbled to the bed, settling heavily with me tucked into his side. His lungs labored, his hands rough as he pulled me closer.

"This wasn't what I had in mind when I brought you coffee." He pressed a quick, rough kiss to my forehead. "Not that I have any complaints."

I curled into him, beyond grateful to have him in my arms again. "Let's play hooky and make up for lost time."

His laugh was husky from his orgasm. He held me for a while, his fingers sifting through my hair and gliding gently down my arm.

"It ripped me apart," he said quietly. "Seeing how hurt and angry you were. Knowing I was causing you pain and that you were pulling away from me . . . It was hell for us both, but I couldn't take the risk that you might become a suspect."

I stiffened. I hadn't thought of that possibility. It could be argued that I was Gideon's motive to kill. And it could be assumed that I was aware of the crime as well. My complete and utter ignorance hadn't been my only protection; he'd made sure I had an alibi, too. Always protecting me—whatever the cost.

He pulled back. "I put a burner phone in your purse. It's pre-programmed with a number that will put you in touch with Angus. If you need me for anything, you can reach me that way."

My hands clenched into fists—I had to reach my boyfriend through his chauffeur. "I hate this."

"So do I. Clearing my way back to you is my number one priority."

"Isn't it dangerous for Angus to be put in the middle?"

"He's former MI6. Clandestine phone calls are child's play for him." He paused, then said, "Full disclosure, Eva: I can track you through the phone and I will."

"What?" I slid out of bed and stood. My thoughts bounced back and forth between MI6—British secret service!—to geotracking my cell, unsure of what to latch on to first. "No way."

He stood, too. "If I can't be with you or talk to you, I at least need to know where you are."

"Don't be this way, Gideon."

His face was composed. "I didn't have to tell you."

"Seriously?" I stalked to the closet to grab a robe. "And you said warning someone about ridiculous behavior isn't an excuse for it."

"Cut me some slack."

Glaring at him, I shoved my hands into the sleeves of a red silk dressing gown and yanked the belt into a knot. "No. I think you're a control freak who likes having me followed."

He crossed his arms. "I like keeping you alive."

I froze. After a moment, my brain rewound to look at the events of the last few weeks again—with the addition of Nathan in the picture. Abruptly, everything made sense: the way Gideon had freaked out when I'd tried to walk to work one morning, why Angus had shadowed me around the city every day, Gideon's fury when he commandeered the elevator I was riding . . .

All those times I'd almost hated him for being an asshole, he'd been thinking about keeping me safe from Nathan.

My knees weakened, and I sank inelegantly to the floor.

"Eva."

"Give me a minute." I'd figured out a lot of it already during the time we'd been apart. I'd realized Gideon would never allow Nathan to simply stroll into his office with photos of me being abused and violated, then just stroll back out again. Brett Kline had only *kissed* me and Gideon had beaten him up. Nathan had *raped* me repeatedly for years and documented it with pictures and video. Gideon's reaction to meeting Nathan the first time had to have been violent.

Nathan must have visited the Crossfire Building the day I'd found Gideon freshly showered with a crimson stain on the cuff of his shirt. What I'd originally suspected was lipstick was Nathan's blood. The sofa and sofa pillows in Gideon's office had been skewed from a fight, not from a lunch quickie with Corinne.

Scowling fiercely, he crouched in front of me. "Damn it. Do you think I *want* to micromanage you? There have been extenuating circumstances. Give me credit for trying to balance your independence with keeping you safe."

Wow. Hindsight didn't just make things crystal clear; it smacked me upside the head and knocked some sense into me. "I get it."

"I don't think you do. This"—he gestured impatiently at himself—"is just a fucking shell. *You're* what drives me, Eva. Can you understand that? You're my heart and soul. If something ever happened to you, it would kill me, too. Keeping you safe is goddamned self-preservation! Tolerate it for me, if you won't do it for yourself."

I surged into him, knocking him off-balance and onto his back. I kissed him hard, my heart pounding and blood roaring in my ears.

"I hate to freak you out," I muttered between desperate kisses, "but you've got it real bad for me."

Groaning, he squeezed me tightly. "So we're okay?"

I wrinkled my nose. "Maybe not about the burner phone. The cell stalking is nuts. Seriously. Not cool at all."

"It's temporary."

"I know, but—"

He put a hand over my mouth. "I put directions on how to track *my* phone in your purse."

That news left me speechless.

Gideon smirked. "Not such a bad idea on the flip side."

"Shut up." I slid off him and smacked his shoulder. "We are totally dysfunctional."

"I prefer 'selectively deviant.' But we'll keep that to ourselves."

The warmth I'd felt bled away, replaced by a flare of panic at the reminder that we were hiding our relationship. How long would it be before I saw him again? Days? I couldn't repeat the last few weeks of my life. Even thinking about going without him for any length of time made me feel sick.

I had to swallow past a painful lump to ask, "When can we be together again?"

"Tonight. *Eva.*" His beautiful eyes were haunted. "I can't bear that look on your face."

"Just be with me," I whispered, my eyes stinging all over again. "I need you."

Gideon's fingertips glided softly down my cheek. "You were with me. The whole time. There wasn't a second that passed when you weren't on my mind. You own me, Eva. Wherever I am, whatever I'm doing, I belong to you."

I leaned into his touch, letting it soak into me and chase the chill away. "No more Corinne. I can't stand it."

"No more," he agreed, startling me. "I've told her already. I'd hoped we could be friends, but she wants what she and I used to have, and I want you."

"The night that Nathan died . . . she was your alibi." I couldn't say more. It hurt to think of how he might have filled the hours with her.

"No, the kitchen fire was my alibi. It took most of the night dealing with the FDNY, the insurance company, and making emergency arrangements for food service. Corinne stuck around for some of that, and when she left, I had plenty of staff on hand to vouch for my whereabouts."

The surge of relief I felt must have shown on my face, because Gideon's gaze softened and filled with the regret I'd seen so many times now.

He stood and held his hand out to help me up. "Your new neighbor would like to invite you over for a late dinner. Let's say eight o'clock. You'll find the key—and the key to the penthouse—on your keychain."

I accepted his hand up and tried to lighten the mood with a teasing reply. "He's seriously hot. I wonder if he puts out on the first date?"

His returning smile was so wicked it revved me up a notch. "I think your odds of getting laid are pretty good."

I gave a dramatic sigh. "How romantic!"

"I'll give you romance." Pulling me into him, Gideon dipped me with consummate ease.

Pressed against him from hip to ankle and bowed backward in a yielding curve, I felt my robe slide apart, exposing my breast. He deepened my arch, until my tender sex hugged his hard thigh and I couldn't help but be hyperaware of the power of his body as he supported my weight and his.

That quickly, he seduced me. Despite hours of pleasure and a very recent orgasm, I was primed for him in that moment, aroused by his skill and strength and self-assurance, his command of himself and of me.

I rode his leg with a slow slide, licking my lips. He growled and surrounded my nipple with the wet heat of his mouth, his tongue worrying the hardened point. Effortlessly he held me, aroused me, possessed me.

I closed my eyes and moaned my surrender.

≈

BECAUSE of the heat and humidity, I chose a lightweight linen sheath dress and pulled my blond hair back in a ponytail. I accessorized with a small pair of gold hoop earrings and kept my makeup light.

Everything had changed. Gideon and I were back together. I was now living in a world without Nathan Barker in it. I was never going to turn a corner and run into him. He was never going to appear on my doorstep out of the blue. I no longer had to worry that Gideon would learn things about my past that would drive a wedge between us. He knew it all and wanted me anyway.

But the budding peace that came with that new reality was accompanied by fear for Gideon—I needed to know that he was safe from prosecution. How could he definitively be proven innocent of a crime he actually *did* commit? Were we going to have to live with the perpetual fear that his actions would come back to haunt us? And how had this changed *us*? Because there was no way we could be what we'd been before. Not after something so profound.

Leaving my room, I headed out for work, looking forward to the hours of distraction I'd find at my job with Waters Field & Leaman, one of the leading advertising firms in the country. When I went to grab my purse off the breakfast bar, I found Cary in the kitchen. He'd clearly been as Busy with a capital *B* as I had.

He was leaning back into the counter, his hands gripping the edge as his boyfriend, Trey, cupped his face and kissed him passionately. Trey was fully dressed in jeans and a T-shirt, while Cary wore only gray sweats that hung low and sexy on his lean hips. They both had their eyes closed and were too lost in each other to realize they were no longer alone.

It was rude to look, but I couldn't help it. For one, I'd always found it fascinating to watch two hot men make out. And two, I found Cary's pose very telling. While his handsome face was markedly vulnerable, the fact that he was holding on to the counter instead of the man he loved betrayed his lingering distance.

I picked up my purse and backed out as quietly as I could, tiptoeing from the apartment.

Because I didn't want to be totally melted by the time I got to work, I hailed a cab instead of walking. From the backseat, I watched Gideon's Crossfire Building come into view. The gleaming and distinctive sapphire spire was home to both Cross Industries and Waters Field & Leaman.

My job as assistant to junior account manager Mark Garrity was a dream come true. While some—namely my stepfather, megafinancier Richard Stanton—couldn't understand why I'd take an entry-level position considering my connections and assets, I was really proud to be working my way up. Mark was a great boss, both hands-on and hands-off, which meant I was learning a lot both by instruction and from doing it myself.

The cab turned a corner and pulled up behind a black Bentley SUV I knew all too well. My heart skipped a beat at the sight of it, knowing that Gideon was nearby.

I paid the cabdriver and climbed out of the cool interior into the steamy early-morning air. My eyes were riveted to the Bentley in the hope that I might catch a glimpse of Gideon. It was crazy how excited I was by the idea, especially after a night spent rolling around with him in all his naked glory.

Smiling wryly, I spun through the Crossfire's copper-framed revolving doors and entered the vast lobby. If a building could embody a man, the Crossfire did for Gideon. The marble floors and walls conveyed an aura of power and affluence, while the cobalt glass exterior was as striking as one of Gideon's suits. Altogether, the Crossfire was sleek and sexy, dark and dangerous—just like the man who'd created it. I loved working there.

I passed through the security turnstiles and took the elevator up to the twentieth floor. When I exited the car, I spotted Megumi—the receptionist—at her desk. She buzzed me through the glass security doors and stood as I approached.

"Hey," she greeted me, looking chic in black slacks and a gold silk shell. Her dark sloe eyes sparkled with excitement, and her pretty mouth was stained a daring crimson. "I wanted to ask you what you're doing on Saturday night."

"Oh . . ." I wanted to spend the time with Gideon, but there was no guarantee that would happen. "I don't know. I don't have plans yet. Why?"

"One of Michael's friends is getting married and they're having a bachelor party on Saturday. If I stay home, I'll go nuts."

"Michael's the blind date?" I asked, knowing she'd been seeing a guy her roommate had set her up with.

"Yeah." Megumi's face lit up for a second, then fell. "I really like him and I think he likes me, too, but . . ."

"Go on," I prompted.

She lifted one shoulder in an awkward shrug and her gaze skittered away. "He's a commitment-phobe. I know he's into me, but he keeps saying it's not serious and we're just having fun. But we spend a lot of time together," she argued. "He's definitely rearranged his life to be with me more often. And not just physically."

My mouth twisted ruefully, knowing the type. Those kinds of relationships were tough to quit. The mixed signals kept the drama and adrenaline high, and the possibility of awesomeness if the guy would just accept the risk was hard to let go of. What girl didn't want to attain the unattainable?

"I'm game for Saturday," I said, wanting to be there for her. "What did you have in mind?"

"Drinking, dancing, getting wild." Megumi's grin came back. "Maybe we'll find you a hot rebound guy."

"Uh . . ." Yikes. Awkward. "I'm doing pretty good, actually."

She arched a brow at me. "You look tired."

I spent the entire night getting nailed to my bed by Gideon Cross . . . "I had a tough Krav Maga class yesterday."

"What? Never mind. In any case, it won't hurt to check out the scenery, right?"

I shifted the straps of my bag on my shoulder. "No rebound guys," I insisted.

"Hey." She set her hands on her trim hips. "I'm just suggesting you be open to the possibility of meeting someone. I know Gideon Cross has got to be a hard act to follow, but trust me, moving on is the best revenge."

That made me smile. "I'll keep an open mind," I compromised.

The phone on her desk rang and I waved good-bye as I headed down the hallway to my cubicle. I needed a little time to think about the logistics of playing the role of a single woman when I was very much taken. If I owned Gideon, he possessed me. I couldn't imagine belonging to anyone else.

I was just starting to play with how to bring up Saturday night to Gideon when Megumi called after me. I turned back around.

"I've got a call on hold to send your way," she said. "And I hope it's personal, because holy hell is his voice smokin' hot. He sounds like S-E-X rolled in chocolate and covered in whipped cream."

Nervous excitement raised the hairs on my nape. "Did he give his name?"

"Yep. Brett Kline."

4

I REACHED MY desk and dropped into my chair. My palms were damp just thinking about talking to Brett, and I was steeling myself for the little charge I'd get from hearing his voice and the guilt that would follow it. It wasn't that I wanted him back or wanted to be with him. It was just that we had history and a sexual attraction that was purely hormonal. I couldn't shut it off, but I had absolutely no desire to act on it.

I dropped my purse and the bag holding my walking shoes into a desk drawer, my eyes caressing the framed collage of photos of Gideon and me together. He'd given it to me so he would always be on my mind—as if he ever left it. I even dreamed of him.

My phone rang. The rerouted call from reception. Brett hadn't given up. Determined to keep it businesslike to remind him that I was at work and not available for inappropriately personal conversations, I answered, "Mark Garrity's office, Eva Tramell speaking."

"Eva. There you are. It's Brett."

My eyes closed as I absorbed that S-E-X-rolled-in-chocolate voice. It sounded even more decadently sexual than when he was singing, which had helped to propel his band, Six-Ninths, to the brink of stardom. He was signed with Vidal Records now, the music company run by Gideon's stepfather, Christopher Vidal Sr.—a company Gideon inexplicably had majority control over.

Talk about a small world.

"Hi," I greeted him. "How's the tour coming along?"

"It's unreal. I'm still trying to get a grip on it all."

"You've wanted this a long time and you deserve it. Enjoy it."

"Thanks." He fell silent for a minute, and in that space of time, I pictured him in my mind. He'd looked amazing when I saw him last, his hair spiked and tipped with platinum, his emerald eyes dark and hot from wanting me. He was tall and muscular without being too bulky, his body ripped from constant activity and the demands of being a rock star. His golden skin was sleeved in tattoos, and he had piercings in his nipples that I'd learned to suck on when I wanted to feel his cock harden inside me . . .

But he couldn't hold a candle to Gideon. I could admire Brett just like any other red-blooded woman, but Gideon was in a class by himself.

"Listen," Brett said, "I know you're working, so I don't want to hold you up. I'm coming back to New York and I'd like to see you."

I crossed my ankles under my desk. "I'm thinking that's not a good idea."

"We're going to debut the music video for 'Golden' in Times Square," he went on. "I want you there with me."

"There with— Wow." I massaged my forehead. Momentarily thrown by his request, I chose to think about how my mom would bitch at me for rubbing at my face, which she swore caused wrinkles. "I'm really flattered you asked, but I have to know—are you cool with just being friends?"

"Hell, no." He laughed. "You're single, golden girl. Cross's loss is my gain."

Oh, crap. It'd been almost three weeks since the first pictures of Gideon and Corinne's staged reunion had hit the gossip blogs. Apparently, everyone had decided it was time for me to move on with another guy. "It's not that simple. I'm not ready for another relationship, Brett."

"I asked you out on a date, not for a lifetime commitment."

"Brett, really—"

"You have to be there, Eva." His voice lowered to the seductive timbre that had always made me drop my panties for him. "It's your song. I'm not taking no for an answer."

"You have to."

"You'll hurt me bad if you don't go," he said quietly. "And that's not bullshit. We'll go as friends, if that's what it takes, but I need you there."

I sighed heavily, my head bowing over my desk. "I don't want to lead you on." *Or piss Gideon off . . .*

"I promise to consider it a favor from one friend to another."

As fucking *if.* I didn't answer.

He didn't give up. He might never give up. "Okay?" he prodded.

A cup of coffee appeared at my elbow and I looked up to see Mark standing behind me. "Okay," I agreed, mostly so I could get to work.

"Yesss." There was a note of triumph in his voice that sounded like it was accompanied by a fist pump. "Could be either Thursday or Friday night; I'm not sure yet. Give me your cell number, so I can text you when I know for sure."

I rattled the number off in a hurry. "Got it? I've got to run."

"Have a great day at work," he said, making me feel bad for being rushed and unfriendly. He'd always been a nice guy, and could have been a great friend, but I blew that chance when I kissed him.

"Thanks. Brett . . . I'm really happy for you. Bye." I returned the handset to its cradle and smiled at Mark. "Good morning."

"Everything all right?" he asked, his brown eyes capped with a slight frown. He was dressed in a navy suit with a deep purple tie that did great things for his dark skin.

"Yes. Thank you for the coffee."

"You're welcome. Ready to get to work?"

I grinned. "Always."

It didn't take long for me to realize something wasn't right with Mark. He was distracted and moody, which was very unlike him. We were working on a campaign for foreign-language-learning software, but he wasn't into it at all. I suggested we talk a bit about the whole-foods locavore campaign, but that didn't help.

"Is everything okay?" I asked finally, sliding uncomfortably into friend territory, where we both made an effort not to go during work.

We put work aside every other week when he invited me along to lunch with his partner, Steven, but we were careful about maintaining our roles as boss and subordinate. I appreciated that a lot, considering Mark knew my stepfather was rich. I didn't want people giving me considerations I hadn't earned.

"What?" He glanced up at me, then ran a hand over his close-cut hair. "Sorry."

I laid my tablet flat in my lap. "Seems like you've got something weighing on your mind."

He shrugged, swiveling away and back again in his Aeron chair. "Sunday is my seventh anniversary with Steven."

"That's awesome." I smiled. Out of all the couples I'd seen over the course of my life, Mark and Steven were the most stable and loving. "Congratulations."

"Thanks." He managed a weak smile.

"Are you going out? Do you have reservations or do you want me to handle that?"

He shook his head. "Haven't decided. I don't know what would be best."

"Let's brainstorm. I haven't had many anniversaries myself, I'm sad to say, but my mom is spectacular with them. I've picked up a thing or two."

After playing hostess to three wealthy husbands, Monica Tramell Barker Mitchell Stanton could've been a professional event planner if she ever had to work for a living.

"Do you want something private," I suggested, "with just the two of you? Or a party with friends and family? Do you exchange gifts?"

"I want to get married!" he snapped.

"Oh. Okay." I sat back in my chair. "As far as romance goes, I can't top that."

Mark barked out a humorless laugh and followed it with a miserable look at me. "It should be romantic. God knows when Steven asked me a few years ago, it was hearts and flowers to the max. You know drama is his middle name. He went all out."

Startled, I blinked at him. "You said no?"

"I said not yet. I was just starting to get my legs under me here at the agency, he was starting to get some really lucrative referrals, and we were picking up the pieces after a painful breakup. It seemed like the wrong time and I wasn't sure he wanted to marry for the right reasons."

"No one ever knows that for sure," I said softly, as much to myself as to him.

"But I didn't want him to think I had doubts about us," Mark went on, as if I hadn't spoken, "so I blamed my refusal on the institution of marriage, like a total ass."

I suppressed a smile. "You're not an ass."

"Over the last couple years, he's made more than a few comments about how right I was to say no."

"But you didn't say no. You said not yet, right?"

"I don't know. Jesus, I don't know what I said." He leaned forward, resting his elbows on the desktop and dropping his face into his hands. His voice came low and muffled. "I panicked. I was twenty-four. Maybe some people are up for that kind of commitment then, but I . . . I wasn't."

"And now you're twenty-eight and ready?" The same age as Gideon. And thinking of that made me quiver, in part because I was the same age Mark had been when he'd said not yet and I could relate.

"Yes." Lifting his head, Mark met my gaze. "I'm beyond ready. It's like some timer is counting down the minutes, and I'm getting more impatient by the hour. But I'm afraid he's going to say no. Maybe his time was four years ago and now he's over it."

"I hate to sound trite, but you won't know unless you ask." I offered him a reassuring smile. "He loves you. A lot. I think your odds of hearing yes are pretty darn good."

He smiled, revealing charmingly crooked teeth. "Thank you."

"Let me know about those reservations."

"I appreciate that." His expression sobered. "I'm sorry to bring this up when you're going through a tough breakup."

"Don't worry about me. I'm fine."

Mark studied me a minute, then nodded.

"You up for lunch?"

I glanced up into Will Granger's earnest face. Will was the newest assistant at Waters Field & Leaman and I'd been helping him settle in. He wore sideburns and square-framed black glasses that gave him a slightly retro beatnik look, which worked for him. He was super laid-back and I liked him. "Sure. Whatcha feelin' like?"

"Pasta and bread. And cake. Maybe a baked potato."

My brows rose. "All right. But if I end up passed out and drooling on my desk from a carbohydrate coma, you'd better get me out of trouble with Mark."

"You're a saint, Eva. Natalie's on some low-carb kick and I can't go another day without starch and sugar. I'm wasting away. Look at me."

Will and his high school sweetheart, Natalie, seemed to have it together, from the stories he told. I never doubted he'd walk on hot coals for her, and she seemed to look after him as well, although he grumbled good-naturedly about her fussing.

"You got it," I said, suddenly feeling wistful. Being separated from Gideon was torture. Especially when surrounded by friends who were invested in relationships of their own.

Noon rolled around and while I waited for Will, I sent a quick text to Shawna—Mark's almost-sister-in-law—asking if she was available for a girls' night out on Saturday. I'd just hit the send button when my desk phone rang.

I answered briskly, "Mark Garrity's office—"

"*Eva.*"

My toes flexed at the sound of Gideon's low, raspy voice. "Hi, ace."

"Tell me we're okay."

I bit my lower lip, my heart twisting in my chest. He had to be feeling the same unsettling rift between us that was troubling me. "We are. Don't you think so? Is something wrong?"

"No." He paused. "I just had to hear it again."

"I didn't make it clear last night?" *When I was clawing at your back . . .* "Or this morning?" *When I was on my knees . . .*

"I needed to hear you say it when you're not looking at me." Gideon's voice caressed my senses. I turned hot with embarrassment.

"I'm sorry," I whispered, feeling awkward. "I know you get annoyed with women objectifying you. You shouldn't have to put up with it from me."

"I would never complain about being what you want, Eva. Christ." His voice turned gruff. "I'm damned glad you like what you see, because God knows I fucking love looking at you."

I closed my eyes against a surge of longing. To know what I did now—how important he thought I was to him—made it so much harder to stay away. "I miss you so much. And it's weird because everyone thinks we're broken up and I need to move on—"

"No!" The one word exploded across the line between us, sharp enough to make me jump. "Goddamn it. Wait for me, Eva. I waited my whole life for you."

I swallowed hard, opening my eyes in time to see Will walking toward me. I lowered my voice. "I'd wait forever for you, as long as you're mine."

"It won't be forever. I'm doing everything I can. Trust me."

"I do."

In the background, another phone beeped for his attention. "I'll see you at eight sharp," Gideon said briskly.

"Yes."

The line clicked off in my ear, and I instantly felt lonely.

"Ready to chow down?" Will asked, rubbing his hands together with anticipation. Megumi was having lunch with her commitment-phobe, so she'd taken a rain check. It was Will, me, and all the pasta he could eat within an hour.

Thinking a carbohydrate-induced stupor might be just what I needed, I stood and said, "Hell yeah."

I picked up a zero-carb energy drink at a Duane Reade drugstore on the way back from lunch. By the time five o'clock rolled around, I knew I was hitting a treadmill after work.

I had a membership at Equinox, but I really wanted to go to a Cross-Trainer gym. I was feeling the gulf between Gideon and me keenly. Spending time in a place where we had good memories would help lessen it. Plus, I felt a sense of loyalty. Gideon was my man. I was going to do everything I could to spend the rest of my life with him. To me that meant supporting him in everything he did.

I walked back to my place, no longer caring if I wilted since I was going to get messy at the gym anyway. When the elevator in my apartment building let me out on my floor, I found my gaze drifting to the door next to mine. My fingers toyed with the key Gideon had given me. The idea of letting myself in to check out his apartment was intriguing. Would it be similar to his Fifth Avenue place? Or totally different?

Gideon's penthouse was stunning, with prewar architecture and old-world charm. It was a space that exuded affluence, while still remaining warm and inviting. I could as easily picture children in the space as I could foreign dignitaries.

What would his temporary digs be like? Scarce furniture, nonexistent art, and a bare kitchen? How settled in was he?

Pausing outside my apartment, I stared at his door and debated with myself. In the end, I resisted the temptation. I wanted him to walk me inside.

I stepped into my living room to the sound of female laughter. I wasn't surprised to find a long-legged blonde curled up next to Cary on my white couch, her hand in his lap, stroking him through his sweats. He was still shirtless, his arm tossed around Tatiana Cherlin's shoulders, his fingers idly stroking her biceps.

"Hey, baby girl," he greeted me with a grin. "How was work?"

"Same old. Hi, Tatiana."

Her reply was a chin jerk. She was striking, which was to be expected since she was a model. Looks aside, I hadn't really liked her all that much the first few times I met her, and I still didn't. But looking at Cary, I had to admit she might be good for him for now.

His bruises were gone, but he was still recovering from a brutal beating, an ambush by Nathan that had set in motion the events separating me from Gideon now.

"I'm going to change and head out to the gym," I said, moving toward the hallway.

Behind me, I heard Cary tell Tatiana, "Hang on a sec, I've got to talk to my girl."

I entered my room and tossed my purse on my bed. I was digging in my dresser when Cary came to lounge in my doorway. "How are you feeling?" I asked him.

"Better." His green eyes glittered wickedly. "How 'bout you?"

"Better."

He crossed his arms over his bare chest. "Is that thanks to whoever was knocking boots with you last night?"

Closing the drawer with my hip, I shot back, "Seriously? I can't hear you in your room. How come you can hear me in mine?"

He tapped his temple. "Sex radar. I has it."

"What does that mean? That I don't have sex radar?"

"More like Cross blew your circuits during one of his sexathons. Still can't get over that man's stamina. Wish he'd swing my way and wear *me* out."

I threw my sports bra at him.

He caught it deftly, laughing. "So? Who was it?"

I bit my lip, not wanting to lie to the one person who always gave it to me straight, even when it hurt. But I had to. "A guy who works in the Crossfire."

His smile fading, Cary stepped into the room and shut the door behind him. "And you just up and decided to bring him home and fuck his brains out all night? I thought you went to your Krav Maga class."

"I did. He lives near here and I ran into him after class. One thing led to another . . ."

"Should I be worried?" he asked quietly, studying my face as he handed my sports bra back to me. "You haven't had a random screw in a long time."

"It's not like that." I forced myself to hold Cary's gaze, knowing that if I didn't, he'd never believe me. "I'm . . . seeing him. We're having dinner tonight."

"Am I going to meet him?"

"Sure. Not today, though. I'm going to his place."

His lips pursed. "You're not telling me something. Spit it out."

I sidestepped the question. "I saw you kissing Trey in the kitchen this morning."

"Okay."

"Things going good with you two?"

"Can't complain."

Yikes. When Cary was on to something, he wouldn't let it go. I sidestepped again.

"I talked to Brett today," I said as casually as possible, trying not to make a big deal out of it. "He called me at work. And no, he wasn't the guy from last night."

His brows rose. "What'd he want?"

Kicking off my shoes, I headed to the bathroom to wash off what was left of my makeup. "He's coming back to New York for the debut of a music video for 'Golden.' He asked me to go with him."

"Eva—" he began, in that low warning tone parents save for bratty children.

"I want you to come with."

That set him back a bit. "As a chaperone? Don't you trust yourself?"

I looked at his reflection in the mirror. "I'm not getting back together with him, Cary. Not that we were ever really together to begin with, so stop worrying about that. I want you there because I think you'll have fun and I don't want to lead Brett on. He agreed we'd go as friends, but I think the concept needs to be drummed into him, just to be safe. And fair."

"You should've said no."

"I tried."

"No is no, baby girl. Not that difficult."

"Shut up!" I scrubbed at one eye with a makeup remover towelette.

"It's bad enough I got guilted into going! You thought it'd be funny for me to attend that concert without knowing who I'd see there. I don't need shit from you."

Because I was sure to get enough of that from Gideon . . .

Cary scowled. "What the hell do you have to feel guilty for?"

"Brett got his ass kicked because of me!"

"Nooo, he got an ass-kicking because he kissed a beautiful girl without thinking about the consequences. He should've expected you to be taken. And what burrowed up your anal cavity and rotted?"

"I don't need a lecture about Brett, okay?" What I needed was Cary's take on my relationship with Gideon and the concerns I had, but I couldn't reach out to my best friend. That made everything going wrong in my life even more unsettling. I felt totally alone and adrift. "I've told you, I'm not taking that road again."

"Glad to hear it."

I told him what I could of the truth, because I knew he wouldn't judge. "I'm still in love with Gideon."

"Of course you are," he agreed simply. "For what it's worth, I'm sure your breakup is eating at him, too."

I hugged him. "Thank you."

"For what?"

"Being you."

He snorted. "I'm not saying you should wait for him. Whatever Cross's deal is doesn't matter—he snoozes, he loses. But I don't think you're ready to jump into some other dude's bed. You can't do casual sex, Eva. It means something to you; that's why you get so fucked up when you just give it away."

"It never works," I agreed, stepping away to finish cleaning my face. "Will you go with me to the video premiere?"

"Yeah, I'll go."

"Want to bring Trey or Tatiana?"

Shaking his head, he turned to the mirror and arranged his hair with practiced sweeps of his hands. "Then it'd be like a double date. Better if I'm the third wheel. More impact."

I watched his reflection, my mouth curving in a soft smile. "I love you."

He blew me a kiss. "Then take care of yourself, baby girl. That's all I need."

My favorite housewarming gift was Waterford martini glasses. To me, it was just the right blend of luxury, fun, and usefulness. I'd given a set to a college friend who had no idea what Waterford crystal was but loved appletinis, and I'd given a set to my mother, who didn't drink martinis but loved Waterford. It was a gift I'd even feel comfortable giving to Gideon Cross, a man who had more money than was comprehensible.

But stemware wasn't what I clutched in my hands as I knocked on his door.

Nervous, I shifted on my feet and ran a hand down my hip to smooth my dress. I'd dolled myself up after getting back from the gym, taking the time to really work my New Eva hairstyle and smoky eye shadow. My pale pink lipstick was smudgeproof and I wore a little black dress that was a halter with a low draping neckline and an even lower back.

The short dress showed a lot of leg, which I accentuated with peep-toe Jimmy Choos. I wore the diamond hoops I'd chosen for our first date and the ring he'd given me, a striking piece that had interlacing gold ropes hugged by diamond Xs—the Xs representing Gideon holding on to the various threads of me.

The door opened and I swayed a little on my feet, struck by the gorgeous, sexy-as-sin man who greeted me. Gideon must have been feeling sentimental, too. He had on the same black sweater he'd worn to the nightclub where we'd first really hung out together. It looked amazing on him—the perfect blend of casual and elegant sexiness. Paired with graphite gray dress slacks and bare feet, the effect on me was pure, white-hot desire.

"Christ," he growled. "You look amazing. Next time warn me before I open the door."

I smiled. "Hello, Dark and Dangerous."

5

GIDEON'S MOUTH CURVED in a devastating grin as he held his hand
out to me. When my fingers touched his palm, he caught me and
drew me inside, pulling me close to place his lips softly over mine. The
door shut behind me and he reached past me to lock it, shutting the
world out.

My hand clenched around a fistful of his sweater. "You're wearing
my favorite sweater."

"I know." Abruptly, he sank into a graceful crouch, taking my hand
that he held and placing it on his shoulder. "Let's make you comfortable,
angel. You won't need these heels until you're ready for me to fuck you."

My core clenched with anticipation. "What if I'm ready now?"

"You're not. You'll know when the time comes."

As Gideon removed my shoes, I shifted my weight from one foot to
the other. "Will I? How?"

He glanced up at me with those intensely blue eyes. He was nearly on his knees, taking my shoes off, yet he was undeniably in command of himself and of me. "I'll be pushing my cock inside you."

I shifted on my feet for a different reason. *Yes, please . . .*

Straightening, he once again loomed over me. His fingertips drifted across my cheek. "What's in the bag?"

"Oh." I mentally shook off the sexual spell he had me under. "Housewarming gift."

I looked around. The space was a mirror image of my own. The apartment was lovely and comfortably inviting. I'd partly expected a semi-lived-in space, mostly bare with only the essentials. Instead, it was very much a home. One that was lit only by candlelight, which cast a warm golden glow on furniture I recognized because it was Gideon's *and* mine.

Stunned, I barely noticed when he took the gift bag and my purse from my fingers. Barefoot, I skirted him, seeing my coffee and end tables placed around his sofa and side chairs; my entertainment center holding his knickknacks and framed photos of the two of us together; my drapes with his unlit floor and table lamps.

On the wall, where my flat-screen TV would be hanging, was a massive photo of me blowing him a kiss, a much larger version of the photo I'd given him that he kept on his desk in his Crossfire office.

I turned slowly, trying to take it all in. He'd shocked me like this once before, when he'd re-created my bedroom in his penthouse, giving me a familiar place to run when things got too intense.

"When did you move in here?" I loved it. The mix of my modern traditional with his old-world elegance was oddly perfect. He'd blended just the right pieces to create a space that was . . . *us.*

"The week Cary was in the hospital."

I glanced at him. "Are you serious?"

That was when Gideon had begun pulling away from me, cutting me off. He'd started hanging out with Corinne again and become difficult to reach.

Getting this place set up must have kept him busy, too.

"I needed to be near you," he said absently, looking into the bag. "I had to be sure I could get to you quickly. Before Nathan could."

Shock rippled through me. At a time when I'd felt Gideon drifting further and further away from me, he'd been physically close. Watching over me. "When I called you from the hospital"—I swallowed past a dry lump—"you had someone with you . . ."

"Raúl. He was coordinating the move-in. I had to get it done before you and Cary came home." He looked up at me. "Towels, angel?" he asked, with more than a hint of amusement.

He pulled the white hand towels embroidered with CROSSTRAINER out of the bag. I'd picked them up at the gym. At the time, I'd been envisioning him having a bare bones bachelor pad. Now, they were ridiculous.

"I'm sorry," I said, still reeling from his disclosure about the apartment. "I had a different idea of what this place looked like."

He pulled the towels away when I reached for them. "Your gifts are always thoughtful. Tell me what you were thinking about when you bought these."

"I was thinking about making you think about me."

"Every minute of every day," he murmured.

"Let me clarify: Me—all hot and sweaty and desperate for you."

"Umm . . . a fantasy I indulge in often."

Abruptly, the memory of Gideon pleasuring himself in my shower punched into my mind. There really were no words for how fucking amazing that sight was. "Do you think about me when you get yourself off?"

"I don't masturbate."

"What? Come on. Every guy does."

Gideon caught my hand and laced our fingers, then drew me toward the kitchen from which the most heavenly smell was emanating. "Let's talk over wine."

"Are you trying to ply me with alcohol?"

"No." He released me and set the bag of towels on the counter. "I know the way to your heart is with food."

I slid onto a bar stool just like the ones in my apartment, touched by his unique way of making me feel at home. "The way to my heart? Or into my pants?"

He smiled as he poured a glass of red wine from a bottle he'd previously opened to let breathe. "You're not wearing pants."

"Not wearing any panties, either."

"Careful, Eva." Gideon shot me a stern look. "Or you'll derail my attempt to seduce you properly before I ride you on every flat surface in this apartment."

My mouth went dry. The look in his eyes when he brought my glass over made me feel flushed and light-headed.

"Before you," he murmured, with his lips to the edge of his glass, "I stroked off every time I took a shower. It was as much a part of my ritual as washing my hair."

That I believed. Gideon was a very sexual man. When we were together, he'd fuck me before bed, first thing in the morning, and sometimes fit in a quickie during the course of the day.

"Since you, only once," he continued. "You were there with me."

I paused with my glass halfway to my mouth. "Really?"

"Really."

I took a drink, gathering my thoughts. "Why did you stop? The last few weeks . . . We went a long time without."

A ghost of a smile curved his lips. "I don't have a drop to waste if I'm going to keep up with you."

I set the wineglass down and pushed at his shoulder. "You're always making me sound like a nymphomaniac!"

"You like sex, angel," he purred. "Nothing wrong with that. You're greedy and insatiable, and I love it. I love knowing that once I get inside you, you're going to suck me dry. Then you'll want to do it again."

I felt my face heat. "For your information, I didn't get off even once while we were apart. Never even got the urge because we weren't together."

He leaned into the counter, resting one elbow on the cool black granite. "Hmm."

"I like fucking you because you're *you*, not because I'm a cock-hungry slut. If you don't like it, grow a gut or stop showering or *something*." I slid off the stool. "Or just say no, Gideon."

I marched into the living room, trying to get away from the unsettled feeling I'd had all day.

Gideon's arms came around me from behind, halting me midstep. "Stop," he said, with the familiar authoritative bite that always turned me on.

I tried to squirm free.

"Now, Eva."

I gave up, my hands falling to my sides to clench my dress.

"Explain what the fuck just happened," he said calmly.

My head bowed and I didn't say anything, because I didn't know what to say. A moment of silence later, he moved, swinging me up into the cradle of his arms and carrying me to the couch. He sat and arranged me on his lap. I snuggled into him.

His chin came to rest on the crown of my head. "You want to pick a fight, angel?"

"No," I mumbled.

"Good. Me neither." His hands stroked up and down my back. "So let's talk instead."

I pressed my nose into his throat. "I love you."

"I know." He tilted his head back, giving me room to nestle.

"I'm not a sex addict."

"I don't see why it'd be a problem if you were. God knows making love with you is my favorite thing to do. In fact, if you ever wanted me to take care of you more often, I'd go so far as to schedule sex with you into my day."

"Oh my God!" I nipped him with my teeth, and he laughed softly.

Gideon wrapped my hair around his fist and tugged my head back. His gaze on my face was soft and serious. "You're not upset about our incredible sex life. It's something else."

Sighing, I admitted, "I don't know what it is. I'm just . . . *off*."

Adjusting me in his lap, Gideon snuggled me closer, pulling me into his warmth. We fit so perfectly together, my curves aligning with his sculpted lines. "Do you like the apartment?"

"I love it."

"Good." His voice was laced with satisfaction. "Obviously, it's an example—taken to the extreme."

My heart rate jumped a little. "Of what our place could look like?"

"We'll start fresh, of course. Everything new."

I was moved by his pronouncement. Still, I had to say, "It was so risky doing this. Moving in here, getting in and out of the building. It makes me nervous just thinking about it."

"On paper, someone lives here. So of course, he'd move furniture in, and come and go. He enters through the garage, just like all the other tenants with cars. When I'm being him, I dress a little differently, take the stairs, and check the security feeds so I know if I'm going to run into anyone before it happens."

The amount of planning involved was mindboggling to me, but then he'd had practice getting to Nathan without a trace. "All this trouble and expense. For me. I can't— I don't know what to say."

"Say you'll plan on moving in with me."

I savored the surge of pleasure his words brought me. "Do you have a time frame in mind for this fresh start?"

"As soon as we can get away with it." His hand on my thigh squeezed gently.

I set my hand over his. There was so much standing in the way of us living together: the lingering trauma of our pasts; my dad, who disliked rich guys and thought Gideon was a cheater; and me, because I liked my apartment and believed that striking out in a new city meant doing as much as I could on my own.

I jumped to the biggest issue for me, though. "What about Cary?"

"The penthouse has an attached guest apartment."

Pulling back quickly, I stared at him. "You'd do that for Cary?"

"No, I'd do it for you."

"Gideon, I ... ." My words trailed off because there were no words. I was awed. Something inside me shifted a little.

"So you're not upset about the apartment," he said. "Something else is on your mind."

I decided to save Brett for last. "I've got a girls' night out on Saturday."

He stilled. Maybe someone who didn't know him as well as I did wouldn't catch that subtle, sharp alertness, but I caught it. "Girls' night doing what, exactly?"

"Dancing. Drinking. The usual."

"Is it a manhunt?"

"No." I licked my dry lips, mesmerized by the change in him. He'd gone from intimately playful to intensely focused. "We're all attached. At least I think we all are. I'm not sure about Megumi's roommate, but Megumi's got a man and you know Shawna's got her chef."

He was suddenly all business when he said, "I'll make the arrangements—car, driver, and security. If you stick with a circuit of my clubs, your security will stay in the car. You want to branch out, he's going in with you."

Blinking in surprise, I said, "Okay."

From the kitchen, the oven timer began beeping.

Gideon went from sitting to standing, with me in his arms, in one powerfully graceful surge. My eyes widened. My blood hummed through my veins. I wrapped my arms around his neck and let him carry me to the kitchen. "I love how strong you are."

"You're easy to impress." Settling me on a bar stool, he gave me a lingering kiss before heading to the oven.

"You cooked?" I wasn't sure why the thought surprised me, but it did.

"No. Arnoldo had ready-to-cook lasagna and a salad delivered."

"Sounds awesome." I knew from having eaten in celebrity chef Arnoldo Ricci's restaurant that the food would be killer.

Grabbing my glass, I wasted the wonderful wine by gulping it down for courage, thinking it was time to tell him what he wouldn't want to hear. I took the plunge and said, "Brett called me at work today."

For a minute or two, I didn't think Gideon heard me. He slid on a pot holder, opened the oven, and pulled out the lasagna without looking my way. It wasn't until he set the pan on the stovetop and glanced at me that I knew for certain he hadn't missed a word.

He tossed the glove onto the counter, grabbed the wine bottle, and came directly to me. Calmly, he took my wineglass and refilled it before he spoke. "I expect he wants to see you when he's in New York next week."

It took me the space of a breath to respond. "You knew he was coming back!" I accused.

"Of course I knew."

Whether that was because Brett's band was signed to Vidal Records or because Gideon was keeping an eye on him, I didn't know. Both reasons were entirely plausible.

"Did you agree to meet up?" His voice was smooth and soft. Dangerously so.

Ignoring the fluttering of nerves in my belly, I held his gaze. "Yes, for the reveal of the new Six-Ninths music video. Cary's going with me."

Gideon nodded, leaving me anxious and clueless about his feelings.

I slid off the stool and went to him. Wrapping me up in his arms, he rested his cheek against the top of my head.

"I'll back out," I offered quickly. "I don't really want to go anyway."

"It's okay." Swaying from side to side, rocking me, he whispered, "I broke your heart."

"That's not why I agreed to go!"

His hands came up and pushed through my hair, combing it back from my forehead and cheeks with a gentleness that brought tears to my eyes. "We can't just forget the last few weeks, Eva. I cut you deep and you're still bleeding."

It struck me then that I hadn't been ready to pick up the pieces of our relationship as if nothing had gone wrong. A part of me was holding a grudge, and Gideon had picked up on it.

I struggled out of his hold. "What are you saying?"

"That I have no right to leave you and hurt you—for whatever reason—then expect you to forget how that felt and forgive me overnight."

"You killed a man for me!"

"You don't owe me anything," he snapped. "My love for you is not an obligation."

It still tore through me like a bullet every time he said he loved me, despite how often he proved it with his actions.

My voice was softer when I said, "I don't want to hurt you, Gideon."

"Then don't." He kissed me with heartrending tenderness. "Let's eat, before the food gets cold."

I changed into a Cross Industries T-shirt and a pair of Gideon's pajama bottoms that I rolled up at the ankles. We took candles over to the coffee table and ate cross-legged on the floor. Gideon kept my favorite sweater on but swapped his slacks for a pair of black lounging pants.

Licking a dab of tomato sauce off my lip, I told him about the rest of my day. "Mark's gathering the nerve to ask his partner to marry him."

"If I'm remembering correctly, they've been together awhile."

"Since college."

Gideon's mouth curved. "I suppose it's still a tough question to ask, even if the answer is a sure thing."

I looked down at my plate. "Was Corinne nervous when she asked you?"

"Eva." He waited until the lengthy silence brought my head up. "We're not going to talk about that."

"Why not?"

"Because it doesn't matter."

I searched his face. "How would you feel if you knew there was someone out there I'd said yes to? Theoretically."

He shot me an irritated look. "That would be different because you wouldn't say yes unless the guy really meant something to you. What I felt was . . . panic. The feeling didn't go away until she broke the engagement."

"Did you buy her a ring?" The thought of him shopping for a ring for another woman hurt me. I looked down at my hand, at the ring he'd bought for me.

"Nothing like that one," he said quietly.

My hand fisted, guarding it.

Reaching over, Gideon set his right hand over mine. "I bought Corinne's ring in the first store I went to. I had nothing in mind, so I picked one that looked like her mother's. Very different circumstances, don't you agree?"

"Yes." I hadn't designed the ring Gideon wore, but I'd searched six shops before I found the right one. It was platinum studded with black diamonds, and it reminded me of my lover, with its cool masculine elegance and bold, dominant style.

"I'm sorry," I said, wincing. "I'm an ass."

He lifted my hand to his lips and kissed my knuckles. "So am I, on occasion."

That made me grin. "I think Mark and Steven are perfect for each other, but Mark has this theory that men get the urge to marry, and then it goes away if it isn't acted on quickly enough."

"I would think it'd be more about the right partner than the right time."

"I've got my fingers crossed for it to work out for them." I picked up my wine. "Want to watch TV?"

Gideon leaned his back against the front of the sofa. "I just want to be with you, angel. I don't care what we're doing."

WE cleaned up the mess from dinner together. As I reached for the rinsed dish Gideon held out for me to put in the dishwasher, he faked me out. He grabbed my hand instead and deftly set the plate on the counter. Catching me around the waist, he spun us into a dance. From the living room, I caught the strains of something beautiful laced with a woman's pure, haunting voice.

"Who is this?" I asked, already breathless from the feel of Gideon's powerful body flexing against mine. The desire that always smoldered between us flared, making me feel vibrant and alive. Every nerve ending sensitized, preparing for his touch. Hunger coiled tight with heated anticipation.

"No clue." He swept me around the island and into the living room.

I surrendered to his masterful lead, loving that dancing was a passion we shared and awed by the obvious joy he felt in just being with me. That same pleasure effervesced within me, lightening my steps until it felt like we were gliding. As we approached the sound system, the music rose in volume. I heard the words *dark and dangerous* in the lyrics and stumbled in surprise.

"Too much wine, angel?" Gideon teased, pulling me closer.

But my attention was riveted to the music. The singer's pain. A tormented relationship she likened to loving a ghost. The words reminded me of the days when I believed I'd lost Gideon forever, and my heart ached.

I looked up into his face. He was watching me with dark, glittering eyes.

"You looked so happy when you were dancing with your dad," he said, and I knew he wanted treasured memories like that between us.

"I'm happy now," I assured him, even as my eyes stung at the sight of his yearning, a longing I knew intimately. If souls could be mated with wishes, ours would be inextricably entwined.

Cupping his nape, I pulled his mouth down to mine. As our lips touched, his rhythm faltered. He stopped, hugging me so tightly my feet left the floor.

Unlike the heartbroken singer, I wasn't in love with a ghost. I was in love with a flesh-and-blood man, one who made mistakes but learned from them, a man who was trying hard to better himself for me, a man who wanted *us* to work as desperately as I did.

"I'm never happier than when I'm with you," I told him.

"Ah, Eva."

He took my breath away with his kiss.

"It was the kid," I said.

Gideon's fingertips drew circles around my navel. "That's twisted."

We were sprawled lengthwise on the couch, watching my favorite police procedural television show. He was spooned behind me, his chin on my shoulder and his legs tangled with mine.

"That's the way these things work," I told him. "Shock value and all that."

"I think it was the grandmother."

"Oh my God." I tilted my head to look back at him. "And you don't think *that's* twisted?"

He grinned and smacked a kiss on my cheek. "Wanna bet on who's right?"

"I don't gamble."

"Aw, come on." His hand splayed against my belly, anchoring me as he rose up on his elbow to look down at me.

"Nope." I felt him against the curve of my buttocks, a solid, weighty length. He wasn't erect, but that didn't stop him from gaining my attention. Curious, I reached between us and cupped him in my hand.

He hardened instantly. One black brow arched. "You copping a feel, angel?"

I squeezed him gently. "Now I'm hot and bothered, and wondering why my new neighbor isn't putting the moves on me."

"Maybe he doesn't want to push you too far, too fast and scare you off." Gideon's eyes glittered in the light of the television.

"Is that so?"

He nuzzled his nose against my temple. "If he has half a brain, he'd know not to let you get away."

Oh . . . "Maybe I should make the first move," I whispered, wrapping my fingers around his wrist. "But what if he thinks I'm too easy?"

"He'll be too busy thinking he's damned lucky."

"Well, then . . ." I wriggled around to face him. "Howdy, neighbor."

He traced my eyebrow with the tip of his finger. "Hi. I really like the view around here."

"The hospitality isn't bad, either."

"Oh? Plenty of towels?"

I pushed at his shoulder. "Do you want to suck face or not?"

"Suck face?" His head fell back and he laughed, his chest vibrating against me. It was a lusty, full-bodied sound and my toes curled at hearing it. Gideon laughed so rarely.

My hands slid under his sweater and glided over warm skin. My lips moved over his jaw. "Is that a no?"

"Angel, I'll suck on any part of your body I can get my mouth on."

"Start here." I offered him my lips and he took them, sealing his mouth softly over mine. His tongue traced the seam, then dipped inside me, licking and teasing.

I burrowed into his body, moaning when he shifted to lie half over me. My hands slid up and down his back, my leg lifting to hook over his hip. I caught his lower lip between my teeth and stroked the curve with the tip of my tongue.

His groan was so erotic it made me wet.

My back arched as his hand crept beneath the hem of my T-shirt and captured my bare breast, rolling my nipple between his thumb and forefinger.

"You're so soft," he murmured. He kissed his way to my temple, and then buried his face in my hair. "I love touching you."

"You're perfect." I pushed beneath his waistband to grip his bare buttocks. The scent and heat of his skin intoxicated me, made me feel drunk with lust and longing. "A dream."

"You're *my* dream. Christ, you're so beautiful." His mouth covered mine and I fisted a hand in his hair, clutching him to me with my arms and legs wrapped around him.

My world narrowed to just him. The feel of him. The sounds he made.

"I love how much you want me," he said hoarsely. "I couldn't stand being in this alone."

"I'm with you, baby," I promised, my mouth moving feverishly beneath his. "I am *so* with you."

Gideon possessed me with one hand at my nape and the other at my waist. Settling over me, he aligned his hardness to my softness, his cock to my sex, and rolled his hips. I gasped, my nails digging into the rockhard cheeks of his ass.

"Yes," I moaned shamelessly. "You feel so good."

"It'd feel better inside you," he purred.

I bit his earlobe. "Are you trying to talk me into going all the way?"

"We don't have to go anywhere, angel." He sucked gently on my throat, making my sex clench hungrily. "I can put it in right here. I promise I'll make you feel good."

"I don't know. I've changed my ways. I'm not that kind of girl anymore."

His hand at my waist pushed my pants down. I gave a token wiggle and made a soft sound of protest. My skin tingled where he'd touched me, my body awakening to his demands.

"Shh." Brushing his mouth over mine, he whispered, "If you don't like it once it's in you, I promise I'll pull out."

"Has that line ever worked for anyone?"

"I'm not feeding you lines. I mean every word."

I gripped the steely curves of his butt and rocked up against him, knowing damn well he didn't need any lines. A crook of his finger was all it would take for him to get laid by anyone he wanted.

Thankfully, he only wanted me.

Reveling in his playfulness, I teased, "I bet you say that to all the girls."

"What other girls?"

"You've got a rep, you know."

"But you're the one wearing my ring." As he lifted his head, his fingertips brushed the hair from my temple. "Day One of my life was the day I met you."

The words hit me like a blow. I swallowed hard and whispered, "Okay, that's a winner. You can put it in."

The shadows left his face, chased away by his smile. "God, I'm crazy about you."

I smiled back. "I know."

6

I WOKE IN a cold sweat, my heart pounding violently. I lay in the master bed, panting, my mind clawing up from the depths of sleep.

"Get off me!"

Gideon. My God.

"Don't fucking touch me!"

Throwing off the covers, I scrambled out of bed and ran down the hallway to the guest room. I searched frantically for the switch on the wall, hitting it with the flat of my palm. Light exploded in the room, exposing Gideon writhing on the bed, his legs twisted in the bedding.

"Don't. Ah, Christ . . ." His back arched up from the bed, his hands fisting in the fitted sheet. "It *hurts*!"

"Gideon!"

He jerked violently. I raced to the bedside, my heart twisting to see him flushed and drenched with sweat. I placed my hand on his chest.

"Don't fucking touch me!" he hissed, seizing my wrist and

squeezing it so hard I cried out in pain. His eyes were open, but unfocused, still trapped in his nightmare.

"Gideon!" I struggled to get away.

He jackknifed upward, his lungs heaving and his eyes wild. "Eva."

Releasing me as if I had burned him, he shoved his damp hair out of his face and lunged out of bed. "Jesus. Eva . . . did I hurt you?"

I held my wrist with my other hand and shook my head.

"I want to see," he said hoarsely, reaching for me with trembling hands.

I dropped my arms and stepped into him, hugging him as tightly as I could, my cheek pressed to his sweat-slick chest.

"Angel." He clung to me, shaking. "I'm sorry."

"Shh, baby. It's okay."

"Let me hold you," he whispered, sinking to the floor with me. "Don't let go."

"Never," I promised, my lips whispering over his skin. "Never."

I ran a bath and climbed into the triangular corner tub with him. Sitting behind him on the highest step, I washed his hair and ran soapy hands over his chest and back, washing the icy sweat of the nightmare away. The heat of the water stopped his quivering, but nothing so simple could remove the dark desolation in his eyes.

"Have you ever talked to anyone about your nightmares?" I asked, squeezing warm water out of the sponge onto his shoulder.

He shook his head.

"It's time," I said softly. "And I'm your girl."

He took a long time to speak. "Eva, when you have nightmares . . . are they more like re-creations of actual events? Or does your mind switch them around? Change them?"

"They're mostly memories. True to life. Are yours not?"

"Sometimes. Sometimes they're different. Make-believe."

I absorbed that a minute, wishing I had the training and knowledge to be truly helpful. Instead, I could only love him and listen. I hoped that was enough, because his nightmares were ripping me apart as surely as they were him. "Are they changed in a good way? Or bad?"

"I fight back," he said softly.

"And he still hurts you?"

"Yes, he still wins, but at least I hold him off as long as I can."

I dipped the sponge again, squeezing water over him, trying to maintain a soothing rhythm. "You shouldn't judge yourself. You were only a child."

"So were you."

My eyes closed tightly against the knowledge that Gideon had seen the photos and videos Nathan had taken of me. "Nathan was a sadist. It's natural to struggle against physical pain, so I did. That's not bravery."

"I wish it had hurt me more," he bit out. "I hate that he made me enjoy it."

"You didn't enjoy it. You felt pleasure and that's not the same thing. Gideon, our bodies react to things by instinct, even when we don't con-sciously want them to." I hugged him from behind, resting my chin on the top of his head. "He was your therapist's assistant, someone you're supposed to be able to trust. He had the training to fuck with your head."

"You don't understand."

"Then make me understand."

"He . . . seduced me. And I let him. He couldn't make me want it, but he made sure I didn't resist."

Moving, I pressed my cheek to his temple. "Are you worried you're bisexual? It won't freak me out if you are."

"No." He turned his head and brushed his mouth across mine, his hands lifting out of the water to link our fingers together. "I've never been attracted to men. But the fact that you'd accept me if I were . . . Right now I love you so much it hurts."

"Baby." I kissed him sweetly, our lips parting and clinging. "I just want you to be happy. Preferably with me. And I really want you to stop hurting yourself over what was done to you. You were raped. You were a victim and now you're a survivor. There's no shame in that."

He turned and pulled me deeper into the water.

I settled beside him, my hand on his thigh. "Can we talk about something? Sexual?"

"Always."

"You told me once that you don't do anal play." I felt him tense. "But you've . . . we've . . ."

"I've had my fingers and tongue inside you," he finished, studying me. He'd altered with the change of subject, his hesitation replaced by calm authority. "You enjoy it."

"Do you?" I asked, before I lost the courage.

He breathed heavily, his cheekbones burnished by the heated water, his face exposed by his slicked-back hair.

After long moments, I feared he wasn't going to answer me. "I'd like to give you that, Gideon, if you want it."

His eyes closed. "Angel."

I reached a hand between his legs, cupping his heavy sac. My middle finger extended beneath him, brushing lightly over the puckered opening. He jerked violently, his legs slamming shut, sending water sloshing to the lip of the tub. His cock hardened like stone against my forearm.

I pulled my trapped hand free and gripped his erection in my fist, stroking, my mouth taking his when he groaned. "I'll do anything for you. There are no limits in our bed. No memories. Just us. You and me. And love. I love you so much."

His tongue thrust into my mouth, a greedy and slightly angry foray. His hand at my waist tightened, his other hand covering mine and urging me to tighten my grip.

Gentle waves lapped against the sides of the bathtub as I pumped his erection. His moan tightened my nipples.

"*I* own your pleasure," I whispered into his mouth. "I'll take it if you won't give it to me."

He growled, his head falling back. "Make me come."

"Any way you want," I vowed.

"WEAR the blue tie. The one that matches your eyes." I had a direct view into the walk-in closet, where Gideon was picking out the suit he'd wear to wrap up the week.

He glanced over to where I sat on the edge of the bed in the master bedroom, a cup of coffee in my hands. His mouth curved in an indulgent smile.

"I love your eyes," I told him with an easy shrug. "They're gorgeous."

He unhooked the tie from the rack and stepped back into the bedroom with a graphite gray suit draped over his forearm. He wore only black boxer briefs, affording me the joy of admiring his leanly ripped body and taut golden skin.

"It's uncanny how often we think alike," he said. "I picked out this suit because the color reminds me of *your* eyes."

That made me smile. I swung my legs, too full of love and happiness to sit still.

Laying his clothes on the bed, Gideon came to me. I tilted my head back to look up at him, my heart beating strong and sure.

He cupped the sides of my head, his thumbs brushing over my eyebrows. "Such a beautiful stormy gray. And so very expressive."

"A totally unfair advantage for you. You read me like a book, while you've got the best poker face I've ever seen."

Bending over, he kissed my forehead. "And yet I can never get away with anything with you."

"So you say." I watched him start to dress. "Listen, I want you to do something for me."

"Anything."

"If you need a date and it can't be me, take Ireland."

He paused in the act of buttoning up his shirt. "She's seventeen, Eva."

"So? Your sister is a beautiful, classy young woman who adores you. She'd do you proud."

Sighing, he grabbed his slacks. "I can't imagine her being anything but bored at the few events appropriate for her to attend."

"You said she'd be bored having dinner at my place and you were wrong about that."

"*You* were there," he argued, yanking up his pants. "She had fun with *you*."

I took a drink of my coffee. "You said anything," I reminded.

"I don't have a problem going dateless, Eva. And I told you I won't be seeing Corinne anymore."

I stared at him over the rim of my mug and didn't say anything.

Gideon shoved his shirttails into his slacks with obvious frustration. "Fine."

"Thank you."

"You could refrain from grinning like the Cheshire cat," he muttered.

"I could."

He stilled, his narrowed eyes sliding down my body to where my robe had fallen away from my bare legs.

"Don't get any ideas, ace. I already put out this morning."

"Do you have a passport?" he asked.

I frowned. "Yes. Why?"

Nodding briskly, he reached for the tie I loved. "You'll need it."

Excitement tingled through me. "For what?"

"For travel."

"Duh." I slid off the bed onto my feet. "Travel to where?"

His eyes held a wicked gleam as he swiftly and expertly knotted his tie. "Somewhere."

"Are you shipping me off to parts unknown?"

"Wouldn't I love to," he murmured. "You and me on a deserted tropical island where you'd be perpetually naked and I could slide into you at any moment."

I set one hand on my hip and shot him a look. "Sunburned *and* bow-legged. Sexy."

He laughed and my toes flexed into the carpet.

"I want to see you tonight," he said, as he shrugged into his vest.

"You just want to put it in me again."

"Well, you did tell me not to stop. Repeatedly."

Snorting, I put my coffee down on the nightstand and shrugged out of my robe. Naked, I crossed the room, skirting him when he made a grab for me. I was opening a drawer to choose one of the lovely Carine Gilson bra and panty sets he kept stocked for me, when he came up behind me, slid his arms beneath mine, and cupped my breasts in both hands.

"I can remind you," he purred.

"Don't you have a job to get to? Because I do."

Gideon pressed against my back. "Come work with me."

"And pour your coffee while waiting for you to fuck me?"

"I'm serious."

"So am I." I spun so quickly to face him that I knocked my purse onto the floor. "I have a job and I like it a lot. You know that."

"And you're good at it." He gripped my shoulders. "Be good at it for me."

"I can't, for the same reason I didn't accept help from my stepfather. I want to make it on my own!"

"I know that. I respect that about you." His hands caressed my arms. "I clawed my way up, too, with the Cross name trying to drag me down. I'd never take the effort away from you. You wouldn't get anything you didn't earn."

I suppressed the twinge of sympathy I felt for Gideon's suffering over his father, a Ponzi scheme swindler who'd taken his own life rather than face jail time. "Do you really think anyone is going to believe I got the job for any reason other than I'm the chick you're sticking it to now?"

"Shut up." He shook me. "You're pissed off and that's fine, but don't talk about us that way."

I pushed at him. "Everyone else will."

Growling, he released me. "You signed up for a CrossTrainer membership even though you've got Equinox and Krav Maga. Explain why."

I pivoted to yank a pair of panties on so I wasn't arguing while buck naked. "That's different."

"It's not."

I faced him again, stepping on stuff that had fallen out of my purse, which only made me madder. "Waters Field and Leaman isn't in competition with Cross Industries! You use the agency's services yourself."

"Do you think you'll never work on a campaign for one of my competitors?"

Standing there in his unbuttoned vest and impeccable tie, he was making it hard for me to think properly. He was beautiful and passionate and everything I'd ever wanted, which made it nearly impossible for me to deny him anything.

"That's not the point. I won't be happy, Gideon," I said with quiet honesty.

"Come here." He held his arms open for me and hugged me when I walked into them. He spoke with his lips against my temple. "One day, the 'Cross' in Cross Industries won't refer to just me."

My anger and frustration simmered. "Can we not talk about this now?"

"One last thing: You can apply for a position just like anyone else,

ENTWINED WITH YOU · 75

if that's the way you need to do it. I won't interfere. If you get the job, you'd be working on a different floor of the Crossfire and climbing the career ladder all on your own. Whether you advance won't be up to me."

"It's important to you." It wasn't a question.

"Of course it is. We're working hard to build a future together. This is a natural step in that direction."

I nodded reluctantly. "I have to be independent."

His hand cupped my nape, holding me close. "Don't forget what matters most. If you work hard and show skill and talent, that's what people will base their judgments on."

"I have to get ready for work."

Gideon searched my face, then kissed me softly.

He released me and I bent down to pick up my purse. Then I noticed that I'd stepped on my mirrored compact and shattered its case. I wasn't heartbroken over it, because I could always pick up another at Sephora on the way home. What froze my blood was the electrical wire sticking out of the cracked plastic.

Gideon crouched down to help me. I looked at him. "What is this?"

He took the compact from me and broke off more of the shell to expose a microchip with a small antenna. "A bug, maybe. Or a tracking device."

I looked at him with horror. My lips moved silently. *The police?*

"I've got jammers in the apartment," he answered, shocking me further. "And no. There's no way any judge would've authorized a tap on you. There's nothing to justify it."

"Jesus." I fell back on my ass, feeling sick.

"I'll have my guys look at it." He lowered to his knees and brushed the hair back from my face. "Could it be your mother?"

I stared at him helplessly.

"Eva—"

"My God, Gideon." I held him off with an uplifted hand and

grabbed my phone with the other. I dialed Clancy, my stepfather's bodyguard, and the moment he answered, I said, "Is the bug in my compact one of yours?"

There was a pause, then, "Tracking device, not a bug. Yes."

"For fuck's sake, Clancy!"

"It's my job."

"Your job sucks," I shot back, picturing him in my head. Clancy was solid muscle. He wore his dirty-blond hair in a military crew cut and radiated a vibe that was deadly dangerous. But I wasn't afraid of him. "This is bullshit and you know it."

"Keeping you safe became a bigger concern when Nathan Barker showed up again. He was slippery, so I had to cover both of you. The minute his death was confirmed, I turned off the receiver."

I squeezed my eyes shut. "This isn't about the damn tracker! I don't have a problem with that. It's the keeping-me-in-the-dark part that's wrong on so many levels. I feel violated, Clancy."

"I don't blame you, but Mrs. Stanton didn't want you to worry."

"I'm an adult! I get to decide if I worry or not." I shot a look at Gideon when I said that, because what I was saying was totally applicable to him, too.

His arch look told me he got the message.

"You won't hear me arguing," Clancy said gruffly.

"You owe me," I told him, knowing just how I was going to collect. "Big-time."

"You know where to find me."

I killed the call, then sent a text to my mom: We need to talk.

My shoulders sagged with disappointment and frustration.

"Angel."

I shot Gideon a look that warned him not to push me. "Don't you dare make excuses—for yourself or for her."

His eyes were soft and shadowed, but the set of his jaw was resolute.

"I was there when you were told Nathan was in New York. I saw your face. There's no one who loves you who wouldn't do whatever they could to shield you from that."

And that was really hard for me to deal with, because I couldn't deny that I was glad I hadn't known about Nathan until after he was dead. But I also didn't want to be insulated from bad things. They were part of living.

Reaching for his hand, I gripped it tightly. "I feel the same way about you."

"I've taken care of my demons."

"And mine." But we were still sleeping apart from each other. "I want you to go back to Dr. Petersen," I said quietly.

"I went on Tuesday."

"You did?" I couldn't hide my surprise at learning he'd kept his regular schedule.

"Yeah, I did. I only missed the one appointment."

When he'd killed Nathan . . .

His thumb brushed over the back of my hand. "It's just you and me now," he said, as if he'd read my mind.

I wanted to believe that.

I was dragging when I got to work, which wasn't a good omen for the rest of the day. At least it was Friday and I could be a slug over the weekend, which would probably be a necessity Sunday morning if I partied too hard Saturday night. I hadn't had a girls' night out in ages and I felt the need for a good stiff drink or two.

In the previous forty-eight hours, I'd learned that my boyfriend had killed my rapist, one of my exes was hoping to spread me across his sheets, one of my boyfriend's exes was hoping to smear him in the press, and my mother had microchipped me like a damned dog.

Really, how much was a girl supposed to take?

"You ready for tomorrow?" Megumi queried, after she buzzed me through the glass doors.

"Hell, yeah. My friend Shawna texted me this morning and she's in." I mustered a genuine smile. "I arranged for a club limo for us. You know . . . one of those that take you to all the VIP spots, cover included."

"What?" She couldn't hide her excitement, but still had to ask, "How much is that?"

"Nada. It's a favor from a friend."

"Some favor." Her grin made me happy, too. "This is going to be *awesome*! You'll have to tell me the deets over lunch."

"You're on. I expect you to dish about your lunch yesterday, too."

"Talk about mixed signals, right?" she complained. "'We're just having fun,' but he shows his face at my work? I would never pop into a guy's office for an impromptu lunch if we were just messing around."

"Men," I huffed sympathetically, even as I acknowledged that I was grateful for the one who was *mine*.

I went to my desk and got ready to start my workday. When I saw the framed photos of Gideon and me in my drawer, I was struck by the need to reach out to him. Ten minutes later, I'd asked Angus to place an order for black magic roses to be sent to Gideon's office with the note:

> You've got me under your spell.
> I'm still thinking about you.

Mark came to my cubicle just as I was closing the window on my browser. One look at his face and I could tell he wasn't doing so hot. "Coffee?" I asked.

He nodded and I stood. We headed to the break room together.

"Shawna was over last night," he began. "She said you're going out tomorrow night."

"Yes. Is that still okay with you?"

"Is what still okay?"

"If your sister-in-law and I hang out," I prodded.

"Oh . . . yeah. Sure. Go for it." He ran a restless hand over his short, dark curls. "I think it's cool."

"Great." I knew there was more on his mind, but I didn't want to push. "Should be fun. I'm looking forward to it."

"So is she." He reached for two single-serving coffee pods, while I took mugs from the shelf. "She's also looking forward to Doug getting back. And popping the question."

"Wow. Now *that's* cool! Two weddings in your family in a year. Unless you're planning a long engagement . . . ?"

He handed the first cup of coffee to me and I went to the fridge for half-and-half.

"It's not going to happen, Eva."

Mark's tone was weighted with dejection, and when I turned to face him, his head was down.

I patted his shoulder. "Did you propose?"

"No. There's no point. He was asking Shawna if she and Doug were planning on having kids right away, since she's still in school part-time, and when she said they weren't, he went into this lecture about how marriage is for couples ready for a family. Otherwise, it's better to keep things simple. It's the same crap I once shoveled to him."

I rounded him and lightened my coffee. "Mark, you won't know Steven's answer until you ask him."

"I'm scared," he admitted, looking into his steaming mug. "I want more than we've got, but I don't want to ruin what we have. If his answer is no and he thinks we want different things out of our relationship . . ."

"Cart before the horse, boss."

"What if I can't live with no?"

Ah . . . I could understand that. "Can you live with not knowing for sure either way?"

He shook his head.

"Then you have to tell him everything you've told me," I said sternly.

His mouth quirked. "Sorry to keep dumping this on you. But you're always great at giving me perspective."

"You know what to do. You just want a kick in the ass to do it. I'm always up for ass-kicking."

He smiled full on. "Let's not work on the divorce attorney's campaign today."

"How about the airline instead?" I suggested. "I have some ideas."

"All right, then. Let's hit it."

WE hard-charged through the morning, and I was energized by our progress. I wanted to keep Mark too occupied to worry. Work was a cure-all for me, and it quickly became clear that it was for him as well.

We'd just wrapped up for lunch and I had stopped by my desk to drop off my tablet when I saw the interoffice envelope on my desk. My pulse leaped with excitement and my hands shook slightly as I unwound the thin twine and let the note card inside slide out.

YOU'RE THE MAGIC.

YOU MAKE DREAMS COME TRUE.

X

I held the card to my chest, wishing it were the writer I was holding instead. I was thinking about sprinkling rose petals on our bed when my desk phone rang. I wasn't all that surprised when I heard my mother's breathy bombshell voice on the other end.

"Eva. Clancy talked to me. Please don't be upset! You have to understand—"

"I get it." I opened my drawer and tucked Gideon's precious note into my purse. "Here's the thing: You don't have Nathan as an excuse anymore. If you've got any more bugs or trackers or whatever in my stuff, you better fess up now. Because I promise you, if I find something else moving forward, our relationship will be irrevocably damaged."

She sighed. "Can we talk in person, please? I'm taking Cary out to lunch and I'll just stay over until you get home."

"All right." The irritation that had started prickling at me dissipated just as quickly as it had come up. I loved that my mother treated Cary like the brother he was to me. She gave him the maternal love he'd never had. And they were both so appearance- and fashion-conscious that they always had a blast together.

"I love you, Eva. More than anything."

I sighed. "I know, Mom. I love you, too."

My other line flashed a call from reception, so I said good-bye and answered it.

"Hey." Megumi's voice was low and hushed. "The chick who came by for you once before, the one you wouldn't see, she's here again asking for you."

I frowned, my brain taking a second to latch on to what she was talking about. "Magdalene Perez?"

"Yep. That's the one. What should I do?"

"Nothing." I pushed to my feet. Unlike the last time Gideon's friend-who-wished-she-were-more had come around, I was prepared to deal with her myself. "On my way."

"Can I watch?"

"Ha! I'll be there in a minute. This won't take long, then we'll head out to lunch."

Vanity had me smearing on some lip gloss before I slung my purse over my shoulder and headed out front. Thinking of Gideon's note put the smile on my face that greeted Magdalene when I found her in the waiting area. She stood when I came into view, looking so amazing I couldn't help but admire her.

When I'd first met her, her dark hair had been long and sleek, like Corinne Giroux's. Now, it was cut in a classic bob that showed off the exotic beauty of her face. She wore cream slacks and a black sleeveless shell that had a big bow tied at the hip. Pearls at her ears and throat completed the elegant look.

"Magdalene." I gestured for her to return to her seat and took the armchair on the opposite side of the small conversation table. "What brings you here?"

"I'm sorry to barge in on you at work like this, Eva, but I was visiting Gideon and thought I'd stop here, too. I have something to ask you."

"Oh?" I set my purse down beside me and crossed my legs, smoothing my burgundy skirt. I resented her for being able to spend time with my boyfriend openly when I couldn't. There was no way around it.

"A reporter stopped by my office today, asking personal questions about Gideon."

My fingertips curled into the cushion of the armrest. "Deanna Johnson? You didn't answer her, did you?"

"Of course not." Magdalene leaned forward, setting her elbows on her knees. Her dark eyes were somber. "She's already talked to you."

"She tried."

"She's his type," she pointed out, studying me.

"I noticed," I said.

"The type he doesn't stick with long." Her full red lips twisted ruefully. "He's told Corinne that it's best if they remain long-distance friends, rather than social ones. But I suspect you know that."

I felt a ripple of pleasure over that news. "How would I know?"

"Oh, I'm sure you have ways." Magdalene's eyes sparkled with knowing amusement.

Oddly, I found myself at ease with her. Maybe because she seemed so at ease with herself, which hadn't been the case the previous times we'd crossed paths. "Seems like you're doing good."

"I'm getting there. I had someone in my life who I thought was a friend but was really just toxic. Without him around, I can think again." She straightened. "I've just started seeing someone."

"Good for you." In that respect, I wished her only the best. She'd been horribly used by Gideon's brother, Christopher. She didn't know I knew. "I hope it works out."

"Me, too. Gage is different from Gideon in a lot of ways. He's one of those brooding artist types."

"Deep souls."

"Yes. Very deep, I think. I hope I get to find out for sure." She stood. "Anyway, I don't mean to keep you. I was worried about the reporter and wanted to discuss her with you."

I corrected her as I rose. "You were worried about me discussing Gideon with the reporter."

She didn't deny it. "Bye, Eva."

"Bye." I watched her exit through the glass doors.

"That didn't look too bad," Megumi said, joining me. "No scratching or hissing."

"We'll see how long it lasts."

"Ready for lunch?"

"I'm starved. Let's go."

WHEN I walked in my front door five and a half hours later, Cary, my mom, and a dazzling silver Nina Ricci formal gown laid out on the sofa greeted me.

"Isn't it fantastic?" my mother gushed, looking fantastic herself in a fifties-style fitted dress with cap sleeves and a pattern of tiny cherries. Her blond hair framed her beautiful face in thick, glossy curls. I had to hand it to her; she could make any era look glamorous.

I'd been told my whole life that I looked just like her, but I had my father's gray eyes instead of her cornflower blue, and my abundant curves were from the Reyes side. I had a butt no amount of exercise would rid me of and breasts that prevented me from wearing anything without a lot of support. It still amazed me that Gideon found my body so irresistible when he'd previously been drawn only to tall, slender brunettes.

Dropping my bag and purse on a bar stool, I asked, "What's the occasion?"

"A shelter fund-raiser, a week from Thursday."

I looked at Cary for confirmation that he'd be escorting me. His nod allowed me to shrug and say, "Okay."

My mother beamed, looking radiant. In my honor, she supported charities benefiting abused women and children. When the fundraisers were formal, she always purchased seats for Cary and me.

"Wine?" Cary asked, clearly picking up on my restless mood.

I shot him a grateful look. "Please."

As he headed off to the kitchen, my mom glided over to me on sexy red-soled slingbacks and pulled me in for a hug. "How was your day?"

"Weird." I hugged her back. "Glad it's over."

"Do you have plans this weekend?" She pulled away, her gaze sliding warily over my face.

That got my back up. "Some."

"Cary tells me you're seeing someone new. Who is he? What does he do?"

"Mom." I got to the point. "Are we good? Clean slate and all that? Or is there something you want to tell me?"

She started to fidget, almost wringing her hands. "Eva. You won't be able to understand what it's like until you have children of your own. It's terrifying. And knowing for certain that they're in danger—"

"Mom."

"And there are additional dangers that come just from being a beautiful woman," she rushed on. "You're connected to powerful men. That doesn't always make you safer—"

"Where are they, Mom?"

She huffed. "You don't have to take that tone with me. I was only trying—"

"Maybe you should go," I cut in coldly, the chill I felt on the inside leaching out through my voice.

"Your Rolex," she snapped, and it was like a slap to my face.

I staggered back a step, my right hand instinctively covering the watch on my left wrist, a treasured graduation gift from Stanton and my mother. I'd had the silly sentimental idea of passing it on to my daughter, should I be lucky enough to have one.

"Are you shitting me?" My fingers clawed at the clasp and the watch fell to the carpet with a muffled thud. It hadn't been a gift at all. It'd been a shackle on my wrist. "You've seriously crossed the line!"

She flushed. "Eva, you're overreacting. It's not—"

"Overreacting? Ha! My God, that's laughable. Really." I shoved two pinched-together fingers in her face. "I'm this close to calling the police. And I've half a mind to sue you for invasion of privacy."

"I'm your mother!" Her voice trailed off, took on a note of pleading. "It's my job to look after you."

"I'm a twenty-four-year-old adult," I said coldly. "By law, I can look after myself."

"Eva Lauren—"

"Don't." I lifted my hands, then dropped them. "Just don't. I'm going to leave now, because I'm so pissed off I can't even look at you. And I don't want to hear from you, unless it's with a sincere apology. Until you admit you're wrong, I can't trust you not to do it again."

I walked to the kitchen and grabbed my purse, my gaze meeting Cary's just as he was coming out with a tray of half-filled wineglasses. "I'll be back later."

"You can't just walk out like this!" my mother cried, clearly on the verge of one of her emotional fits. I couldn't deal with it. Not then.

"Watch me," I muttered under my breath.

My goddamned Rolex. Just thinking of it hurt like hell, because the gift had meant so much to me. Now, it meant nothing at all.

"Let her go, Monica," Cary said, his voice low and soothing. He knew how to deal with hysteria better than anyone. It was crappy sticking him with my mom, but I had to go. If I went to my room, she would just cry and plead at my door until I felt sick. I hated seeing her like that, hated causing her to feel that way.

Exiting my apartment, I went to Gideon's next door, rushing to get inside before the tears overwhelmed me or my mother came after me. There was nowhere else for me to go. I couldn't go out in public shell-shocked and crying. My mother wasn't the only one who had me under surveillance. There was also the possibility of the police, Deanna Johnson, and maybe even some paparazzi.

I got as far as Gideon's couch, sprawling across the cushions and allowing the tears to flow.

"ANGEL."
Gideon's voice and the feel of his hands on me pulled me from sleep. I mumbled a protest as he shifted me onto my side, and then the heat of his body was warming my back. One of his muscular arms wrapped around my waist, tucking me close.

Spooned with him, the biceps of his other arm hard beneath my cheek, I slid back into unconsciousness.

WHEN I woke again, it felt like days later. I lay on the couch with my eyes closed for long minutes, soaking in the warmth of Gideon's powerful body and breathing air that smelled of him. After a while, I decided that sleeping longer would only throw off my body clock even more. We'd had a lot of late nights and early mornings since we had gotten back together, and they were taking their toll.

"You've been crying," he murmured, burying his face in my hair. "Tell me what's wrong."

I wrapped my arms over his, snuggling into him. I told him about the watch. "Maybe I overreacted," I finished. "I was tired, which makes me irritable. But God . . . it hurt like hell. It totally ruined a gift that meant a lot to me, you know?"

"I can imagine." His fingers drew gentle circles across my stomach, caressing me through the silk of my shirt. "I'm sorry."

I looked toward the windows and saw that night had fallen. "What time is it?"

"A little after eight."

"What time did you get in?"

"Half past six."

I wriggled around to face him. "Early for you."

"Once I knew you were here, I couldn't stay away. I've wanted to be with you since your flowers arrived."

"You liked them?"

He smiled. "I have to say, reading your words in Angus's handwriting was . . . interesting."

"I'm trying to be safe."

He kissed the tip of my nose. "While still spoiling me."

"I want to. I want to ruin you for other women."

The pad of his thumb brushed over my bottom lip. "You did that the moment I saw you."

"Sweet talker." My depression lifted just from being with Gideon and knowing I was his sole focus at that moment. "You trying to get in my pants again?"

"You're not wearing pants."

"Is that a no?"

"That's a yes, I want under your skirt." His eyes darkened when I nipped his thumb with my teeth. "And inside your hot, wet, tight little cunt. I've wanted that all day. I want it every day. I want it now, but we'll wait until you're feeling better."

"You could kiss it and make it better."

"Kiss what, exactly?"

"Everything. Everywhere."

I knew I could get used to having him all to myself like this. Knew I wanted to. Which was impossible, of course.

Thousands of little pieces of him were committed to thousands of people and projects and commitments. If I'd learned anything from my mother's multiple marriages to successful businessmen, it was that wives were often mistresses, almost invariably taking second place because their husbands were also married to their work. There was a reason why a man became a captain in his chosen field—he gave it his all. The woman in his life got what was left.

Gideon tucked my hair behind my ear. "I want this. Coming home to you."

It always startled me when it seemed like he'd read my thoughts. "Would it have been better if you'd found me barefoot in the kitchen?"

"I wouldn't be opposed, but naked in bed would work best for me."

"I'm a decent cook, but you just want me for my body."

He smiled. "It's the very delicious package holding everything else I want."

"I'll show you mine, if you show me yours."

"Love to." His fingertips slid gently down my cheek. "But first, I want to make sure you're in the right frame of mind after the situation with your mother."

"I'll get over it."

"Eva." His tone warned me that he wouldn't be put off.

I sighed. "I'll forgive her, I always do. I don't have a choice, really, because I love her and I know she means well, even if she is seriously misguided. But this thing with the watch . . ."

"Go on."

I rubbed at the ache in my chest. "It broke something in our relationship. And no matter how we move forward, there's always going to be that crack there that didn't exist before. *That's* what hurts."

Gideon was quiet for a long time. One of his hands slid into my hair, while the other curled possessively over my hip. I waited for him to say what was on his mind.

"I broke something in our relationship, too," he said finally, his voice somber. "I'm afraid it's always going to be between us."

The sadness in his eyes twisted into me, hurting me. "Let me up."

He did, reluctantly, watching me warily as I stood. I hesitated before I unzipped my skirt. "Now I know what it feels like to lose you, Gideon. How badly it hurts. If you shut me out, it's probably going to make me panic a little. You'll just have to be careful of that, and I'll just have to trust that your love is going to stick."

He nodded his understanding and acceptance, but I could see it was eating at him.

"Magdalene came by today," I said, to take his mind off the lingering rift between us.

He tensed. "I told her not to."

"It's okay. She was probably concerned about me nursing a grudge, but I think she realized I love you too much to hurt you."

He sat up as I let my skirt drop. It pooled on the floor, revealing my garters and stockings, which earned me a slow hiss through his clenched teeth. I climbed back onto the couch and straddled his thighs, draping my arms around his neck. His breath was hot through the silk of my shirt, stirring my blood.

"Hey." I ran both hands through his hair, nuzzling my cheek against him. "Stop worrying about us. I think we need to be worrying about Deanna Johnson. What's the worst she could possibly dig up on you?"

His head fell back, his gaze narrowing. "She's my problem. I'll deal with her."

"I think she's after something really juicy. Calling you out as a heartless playboy isn't going to be enough."

"Stop worrying. The only reason I would care is because I don't want my past shoved in your face."

"You're too confident." My fingers went to his vest and began freeing the buttons. I exposed his shirt and removed his tie, draping it carefully over the back of the sofa. "Are you going to talk to her?"

"I'm going to ignore her."

"Is that the right way to handle this?" I went to work on his shirt.

"She wants my attention; she's not going to get it."

"She'll find another way, then."

He settled deeper into the seat back, his neck tilting to look up to me. "The only way for a woman to get my attention is to be you."

"Ace." I kissed him, tugging at his shirttails. He shifted to make it easier for me to pull them out of his pants. "I need you to explain Deanna," I murmured. "What set her off like this?"

He sighed. "She was a mistake in every sense. She made herself available once, and I make it a rule to avoid overly eager women a second time."

"And that doesn't make you sound like an asshole at all."

"I can't change what happened," he said coldly.

I could tell he was embarrassed. He could be as much of a dick as any guy, but he was never proud of it.

"Deanna happened to be covering an event where Anne Lucas was making me uncomfortable," he continued. "I used Deanna to keep Anne from approaching me. I didn't feel good about it afterward and I didn't handle it well."

"I get the picture." I pushed his shirt apart, exposing his warm, firm skin.

Remembering how he reacted after the first time we'd had sex, I could imagine how he'd handled Deanna. With me, he'd immediately shut down and shut me out, leaving me feeling used and worthless.

He'd fought to win me back after that, but the reporter hadn't been so lucky.

"You don't want to lead her on with any contact," I summed up. "She's probably still digging on you."

"I doubt that. I don't think I said more than a dozen words to her altogether."

"You were an ass to me, too. I fell in love with you anyway."

My hands slid lovingly across his hard chest, caressing the light dusting of dark hair before coasting down the thin, silky trail that led below his waistband. His abs quivered beneath my touch, the tempo of his breathing changing.

Sinking to sit on his lap, I adored his body. My thumbs circled the tiny points of his nipples and I watched his reaction, waiting for him to succumb to the subtle pleasure of my touch. I lowered my head and pressed a kiss to his throat, feeling his pulse leap beneath my lips and inhaling the virile scent of his skin. Enjoying him was something I didn't get to do enough of, because he always turned it back around on me.

Gideon groaned, his hand coming up to grip my hair. "Eva."

"I love the way you respond to me," I whispered, seduced by having such an unabashedly sexual male completely at my mercy. "Like you can't help yourself."

"I can't." He let the sleep-tousled strands sift through his fingers. "You touch me like you worship me."

"I do."

"I feel it in your hands . . . your mouth. The way you look at me." His throat worked on a swallow and I followed the movement with my eyes.

"I've never wanted anything more." I caressed his torso, tracing muscled pecs, then the line of every rib. Like a connoisseur admiring the perfection of a priceless work of art. "Let's play a game."

His tongue did a slow sweep along the curve of his lip, making my sex clench with jealousy. He knew it, too. I saw it in the way his eyes glittered dangerously. "Depends on the rules."

"Tonight, you're mine, ace."

"I'm always yours."

I unbuttoned my blouse and shrugged out of it, exposing my white lace demi-bra and matching thong.

"Angel," he breathed, his gaze so hot I felt it slide over my bared flesh. His hands moved to touch and I caught his wrists, staying him.

"Rule number one: I'm going to suck you, stroke you, and tease you all night long. You're going to come until you can't see straight." I cupped him through his slacks, massaging his rigid length with my palm. "Rule number two: You're just going to lie back and enjoy it."

"No returning the favor?"

"No."

"Not happening," he said decisively.

I pouted. "Pretty please."

"Angel, getting you off is ninety-nine percent of the fun for me."

"But then I'm so busy coming I don't get to enjoy you!" I complained. "Just for once—one night—I want you to be selfish. I want you to let go, be an animal, come just because it feels good and you're ready."

His lips thinned. "I can't do that with you. I need you with me."

"I knew you'd say that." Because I'd once told him that feeling used by a man for his pleasure was a trigger for me. I needed to feel loved and wanted, too. Not as an interchangeable female body to ejaculate into, but as Eva, an individual woman who needed genuine affection with sex. "But this is my game and it's played by my rules."

"I haven't agreed to play."

"Hear me out."

Gideon exhaled slowly. "I can't do it, Eva."

"You could do it with other women," I argued.

"I wasn't in love with them!"

I melted. I couldn't help it. "Baby . . . I want this," I whispered. "Real bad."

He made an exasperated noise. "Help me understand."

"I can't hear your heart racing when I'm gasping for breath. I can't feel you shaking when I'm shaking, too. I can't taste you when my mouth is dry from begging you to finish me off."

His beautiful face softened. "I lose my mind every time I come inside you. Let that be enough."

I shook my head. "You've said I'm like your favorite wet dream made real. Those dreams couldn't have all been about getting the girl off. What about the blowjobs? The hand jobs? You love my tits. Don't you want to fuck them until you come all over me?"

"Jesus, Eva." His cock thickened in my grip.

Brushing my parted lips across his, I deftly opened his slacks. "I want to be your dirtiest fantasy," I whispered. "I want to be filthy for you."

"You're already what I want you to be," he said darkly.

"Am I?" I ran my nails lightly down his sides, biting my lower lip when he hissed. "Then do it for me. I love those moments after you've seen to me and you're chasing your own orgasm. When your rhythm and focus changes, and you get ferocious. I know you're just thinking about how good it feels and how hot you are and how hard you're going to come. It makes me feel so good to get you that worked up. I want a whole night of feeling like that."

His hands squeezed my thighs. "With one stipulation."

"What is it?"

"You get tonight. Next weekend, the game's on me."

My mouth fell open. "I get a night, you get a whole weekend?"

"Umm . . . a whole weekend of seeing to you."

"Man," I muttered, "you drive a hard bargain."

His smile was razor sharp. "That's the plan."

$\backsim$

"OUR mom says that our dad is a real sex machine."

Gideon glanced at me, grinning, from where he sat beside me on the floor. "You've got a weird catalog of movie lines in that gorgeous head of yours, angel."

I took a swig from my bottled water and swallowed just in time to recite the next line from *Kindergarten Cop*. "My dad's a gynecologist and he looks at vaginas all day long."

His laughter made me so happy I felt as if I could float away. He was bright-eyed and more relaxed than I'd seen him since forever. Some of that had to do with the straight-to-the-point blowjob I'd given him on the couch, followed by a long, slow, slippery hand job in the shower. But a lot of it came from me, I knew.

When I was in a good mood, he was, too. It amazed me that I had a profound influence on such a man. Gideon was a force of nature, his magnetic self-possession so powerful it put everyone around him in his shadow. I saw flashes of it every day and was awed by it, but not nearly as much as I was by the charming, wryly amusing lover I had entirely to myself in our private moments together.

"Hey," I said, "you won't be laughing when your kids tell their teachers the same things about you."

"Since they'd have to hear it from you, I'd know who it was that really needed the spanking."

He turned his head to resume watching the movie, as if he hadn't just knocked the wind out of me. Gideon was a man who'd lived an entirely solitary life, and yet he'd accepted me into it so completely that he could envision a future I was afraid to imagine. I was so scared I'd only be setting myself up for a heartbreak I couldn't survive.

Noting my silence, he set his hand on my bare knee and glanced at me again. "Still hungry?"

My gaze remained trained on the open Chinese take-out boxes on the coffee table in front of us, and the black magic roses, which Gideon had brought home from work so we could enjoy them over the weekend.

Not wanting to make more of his statement than he'd intended, I said, "Only for you."

I put my hand in his lap, feeling the soft heft of his cock within the black boxer briefs I'd allowed him to wear for dinner.

"You are a dangerous woman," he murmured, leaning closer.

Moving quickly, I caught his mouth with my own, sucking on his lower lip. "Have to be," I murmured, "to keep up with you, Dark and Dangerous."

He smiled.

"I need to check in with Cary again," I said with a sigh. "See if Mom's left yet."

"You okay?"

"Yeah." I leaned my head on his shoulder. "There's nothing like a little Gideon therapy to make things look up."

"Did I mention I make house calls? Twenty-four-seven."

I sank my teeth into his biceps. "Let me take care of this, then I'll make you come again."

"I'm good, thanks," he shot back, clearly amused.

"But we haven't played with the girls yet."

He bent down and buried his face in my cleavage. "Hello, girls."

Laughing, I shoved at his shoulders and he pushed me backward until I sprawled on the floor between the sofa and coffee table. He hovered above me, his arms tight and hard from supporting his weight. His gaze roamed, caressing my bra, then my bare tummy, then my thong and garters. The ensemble I wore post-shower was fire-engine red, chosen to keep Gideon revved.

"You're my lucky charm," he said.

I squeezed his biceps. "Really?"

"Yep." He licked the upper swell of my breast. "You're magically delicious."

"Oh my God!" I laughed. "Cheesy."

His eyes smiled at me. "I did warn you about me and romance."

"You lied. You're the most romantic guy I've ever dated. I can't believe you hung those CrossTrainer towels in your bathroom."

"How could I not? And I wasn't kidding about you being lucky." He kissed me. "I've been working on offloading my share of a casino in Milan. Those black magic roses arrived just as a bidder threw in a small winery in Bordeaux that I've had my eye on. Guess what it's called . . . La Rose Noir."

"A winery for a casino, huh? So you remain the god of sex, vice, and recreation."

"Endeavors that help me satisfy you, my goddess of desire, pleasure, and corny one-liners."

I ran my hands down his sides and slid my fingers beneath his waistband. "When do I get to try the wine?"

"When you're helping me brainstorm the advertising campaign for it."

With a sigh, I said, "You don't give up, do you?"

"Not when I want something, no." He rose to his knees and then helped me sit up. "And I want you. Very, very much."

"You have me," I said, using his words.

"I have your heart and your insanely sexy body. Now, I want your brain. I want everything."

"I need to save something for me."

"No. Take me instead." Gideon's hands reached around to cup the bare cheeks of my ass. "Not an even trade in quality, I'm sorry to say."

"You're bargaining like mad today."

"Giroux was happy with his deal. You will be, too, I promise."

"Giroux?" My heart thudded. "No relation to Corinne?"

"Her husband. Although they're estranged and facing divorce, as you know."

"No way. You do business with *her husband*?"

His mouth twisted ruefully. "First time. And likely the last, although I did tell him that I'm involved with a special woman—and she's not his wife."

"The problem is that she's in love with you."

"She doesn't know me." He cupped the back of my head and rubbed our noses together. "Hurry up and call Cary. I'll clean up dinner. Then we'll suck face."

"Fiend."

"Sexpot."

I scrambled up to head to my purse for my phone. Gideon grabbed a garter and snapped it, sending a shock wave of sensation across my skin. Surprisingly aroused by the nip of pain, I slapped his hand away and hurried out of reach.

Cary answered on the second ring. "Hey, baby girl. You still doing okay?"

"Yes. And you're still the best friend ever. Is Mom still hanging around?"

"She bailed a little over an hour ago. You stayin' over at loverman's?"

"Yeah, unless you need me."

"Nah, I'm good. Trey's on his way over now."

That news made me feel a lot better about spending a second night away. "Say hi to him for me."

"Sure. I'll kiss him for you, too."

"Well, if it's from me, don't make it too hot and wet."

"Spoilsport. Hey, remember how you asked me to do some digging on the Good Doctor Lucas? So far, I've come up with a whole lotta nada. He doesn't seem to do much else besides work. No kids. Wife is a doctor, too. A shrink."

I glanced at Gideon, cautiously ensuring that he didn't overhear. "Seriously?"

"Why? Is that important?"

"No, I guess not. I just . . . I guess I expect psychologists to be astute judges of character."

"Do you know her?"

"No."

"What's going on, Eva? You're all cloak-and-dagger lately, and it's starting to piss me off."

Climbing onto a bar stool, I explained as much as I could. "I met Dr. Lucas at a charity dinner one night, then again when you were in the hospital. Both times he said some nasty things about Gideon and I'm just trying to figure out what his deal is."

"Come on, Eva. What else could it be besides Cross banged his wife?"

Unable to reveal a past that wasn't mine to share, I didn't answer. "I'll be home tomorrow afternoon. I've got that girls' night out. You sure you don't want to come?"

"Go ahead, change the subject," Cary bitched. "Yes, I'm sure I don't want to come. I'm not ready to hit the scene. Just thinking about it gives me hives."

Nathan had jumped Cary outside a club, and Cary was still recovering physically from that. Somehow, I'd forgotten that it was the mind that took longer to heal. He played it so cool, but I should've known better. "The weekend after next, you want to fly out to San Diego? See my dad, our friends . . . maybe even Dr. Travis, if we're up for it?"

"Subtle, Eva," he said dryly. "But yeah, sounds good. I may need you to front me some money, since I'm not working right now."

"No problem. I'll make the arrangements and we can square up later."

"Oh, before you hang up. One of your friends called earlier—

Deanna. I forgot to tell you when we talked before. She has news and she wants you to call her back."

I shot a look at Gideon. He caught my eye and something on my face must have given me away, because his eyes took on that familiar hard gleam. He headed toward me with that long, agile stride, the remnants of dinner carted neatly in the original delivery bag.

"Did you tell her anything?" I asked Cary in a low voice.

"*Tell* her anything? Like what?"

"Like something you wouldn't want to tell a reporter, because that's what she is."

Gideon's face took on a stony cast. He passed me to drop the trash in the compactor, then came back to my side.

"You're friends with a reporter?" Cary asked. "Are you nuts?"

"No, I'm not friends with her. I have no idea how she got my home number, unless she called up from the front desk."

"What the hell does she want?"

"An exposé on Gideon. She's starting to get on my bad side. She's all over him like a rash."

"I'll blow her off if she calls back."

"No, don't." I held Gideon's gaze. "Just don't give her any information about anything. Where did you tell her I was?"

"Out."

"Perfect. Thanks, Cary. Call if you need me."

"Have a banging good time."

"Jesus, Cary." Shaking my head, I killed the call.

"Deanna Johnson called you?" Gideon asked, his arms crossing his chest.

"Yep. And I'm about to call her back."

"No, you're not."

"Shut up, caveman. I'm not into that 'me Cross, you Cross little woman' bullshit," I snapped. "In case you've forgotten already, we made a trade. You got me, and I got you. I protect what's mine."

"Eva, don't fight my battles for me. I can take care of myself."

"I know that. You've been doing it your whole life. Now, you've got me. I can handle this one."

Something shifted over his features, so swiftly I couldn't identify whether he was getting pissed. "I don't want you to have to deal with my past."

"You dealt with mine."

"That was different."

"A threat is a threat, ace. We're in this together. She's reaching out to me, which makes me your best shot at figuring out what she's up to."

He threw up one hand in frustration, then raked it through his hair. I had to force myself not to get distracted by the way his entire torso flexed with his agitation—his abs clenching, his biceps hardening. "I don't give a shit what she's up to. You know the truth, and you're the only one who matters."

"If you think I'm going to sit around while she crucifies you in the press, you need to revisit and revise!"

"She can't hurt me unless she hurts you, and it's possible that's what she's really after."

"We won't know unless I talk to her." I pulled Deanna's card out of my purse and dialed, blocking my number from showing on her Caller ID.

"Eva, damn it!"

I put the phone on speaker and set it on the counter.

"Deanna Johnson," she answered briskly.

"Deanna, it's Eva Tramell."

"Eva, hi." The tone of her voice changed, assuming a friendliness we hadn't yet established. "How are you?"

"I'm good. You?" Studying Gideon, I tried to see if hearing her voice had any effect whatsoever. He glared back, looking deliciously pissed off. I'd become resigned to the fact that whatever his mood, I always found him irresistible.

"Things are churning. In my line of work that's always good."

"So is getting your facts straight."

"Which is one of the reasons I called you. I have a source who claims Gideon walked in on a ménage composed of you, your roommate, and another guy, and flew into a rage. The guy ended up in the hospital and is now pressing assault charges. Is that true?"

I froze, my hearing drowned by my roaring blood. The night I'd met Corinne, I'd come home to find Cary in a four-body sexual tangle that included a guy named Ian. When Ian had lewdly—and nakedly—propositioned me to join them, Gideon had refused the offer with his fist.

I looked at Gideon and my stomach cramped. *It was true.* He was being sued. I could see the proof of it in his face, which was devoid of all emotion, his thoughts hidden behind a flawless mask. "No, it's not true," I answered.

"Which part?"

"I have nothing further to say to you."

"I also have a firsthand account of an altercation between Gideon and Brett Kline, allegedly over you being caught in a hot clinch with Kline. Is that true?"

My knuckles whitened as I gripped the edge of the counter.

"Your roommate was recently assaulted," she went on. "Did Gideon have anything to do with that?"

Oh my God . . . "You're out of your mind," I said coldly.

"The footage of you and Gideon arguing in Bryant Park shows him being very aggressive and physically rough with you. Are you in an abusive relationship with Gideon Cross? Is he violent with an uncontrollable temper? Are you afraid of him, Eva?"

Gideon spun on his heel and walked away, striding down the hallway and turning into his home office.

"Fuck you, Deanna," I bit out. "You're going to rip an innocent man's reputation apart because you can't deal with casual sex? Way to represent the sophisticated modern woman."

"He answered the phone," she hissed, "before he was done. He answered the fucking phone and started talking about an inspection at one of his properties. Midconversation he looked at me lying there waiting for him and he said, 'You can go.' Just like that. He treated me like a whore, only I didn't get paid. He didn't even offer me a drink."

I closed my eyes. *Jesus.* "I'm sorry, Deanna. I mean that sincerely. I've met my share of assholes and it sounds like he was one to you. But what you're doing is wrong."

"It's not wrong if it's true."

"But it's not."

She sighed. "I'm sorry you're in the middle of this, Eva."

"No, you're not." I hit the end button and stood with my head bent, holding on to the counter while the room spun around me.

8

I FOUND GIDEON pacing like a caged panther behind his desk. He had an earpiece in his ear and he was either listening or on hold, since he wasn't talking. He caught my eye, his face hard and unyielding. Even dressed in boxer briefs, he seemed invulnerable. No one would be fool enough to take him for anything else. Physically, his power was evident in every slab of muscle. Beyond that, he radiated a ruthless menace that sent a chill down my spine.

The indolent, well-pleasured male I'd eaten dinner with was gone, replaced by an urban predator who dominated his competition.

I left him to it.

Gideon's tablet was what I wanted, and I found it in his briefcase. It was password protected and I stared at the screen for a long while, startled to realize I was shaking. Everything I'd feared was happening.

"Angel."

Looking up, I caught his eye as he appeared from the hallway.

"The password," he explained. "It's *angel*."

Oh. All the rampant energy inside me vanished, leaving me feeling drained and tired. "You should've told me about the lawsuit, Gideon."

"At this point in time there isn't a lawsuit, only the threat of one," he said without inflection. "Ian Hager wants money, I want nondisclosure. We'll settle privately and be done with it."

I sagged back into the couch, dropping the tablet onto my thighs. I watched as he walked toward me, drinking him in. It was so easy to become dazzled by his looks, enough that one could fail to see how alone he was at heart. But it was past time he learned to include me when he faced difficulties.

"I don't care if it's a nonstarter," I argued. "You should've told me."

His arms crossed his chest. "I meant to."

"You meant to?" I shoved to my feet. "I tell you I'm broken up over my mother not telling me something and you don't say a word about your own secrets?"

For a moment, he remained hard-faced and immovable. Then he cursed under his breath and unfolded. "I came home early, planning to tell you, but then you told me about your mom and I thought that was enough shit for you to deal with in one day."

Deflating, I sank back onto the couch. "That's not the way a relationship works, ace."

"I'm just getting you back, Eva. I don't want all the time we spend together to be about what's wrong and fucked up in our lives!"

I patted the cushion beside me. "Come here."

He took a seat on the coffee table in front of me instead, his spread legs bracketing mine. He caught my hands in both of his, lifting them to his lips to kiss my knuckles. "I'm sorry."

"I don't blame you. But if there's anything else you have to tell me, now would be the time."

He pressed forward, urging me to stretch out on the couch. Coming over me, he whispered, "I'm in love with you."

With everything going wrong, that was the one thing that was totally right.

It was enough.

WE fell asleep on the couch, wrapped up in each other. I drifted in and out of consciousness, plagued by anxiety and thrown off my schedule by our earlier long nap. I was awake enough to sense the change in Gideon, hear his fast breathing, followed by the tightening of his grip on me. His body jerked powerfully, shaking me. His whimper pierced my heart.

"Gideon." I wriggled around to face him, my agitated movements waking him. We'd drifted off with the lights on and I was grateful that he woke to the brightness.

His heart was pounding beneath my palm, a fine mist of sweat blooming on his skin. "What?" he gasped. "What's wrong?"

"You were slipping into a nightmare, I think." I pressed soft kisses over his hot face, wishing my love could be enough to banish the memories.

He tried to sit up and I clung tighter to hold him down.

"Are you okay?" He ran a hand over me, searching. "Did I hurt you?"

"I'm fine."

"God." He fell back and covered his eyes with his forearm. "I can't keep falling asleep with you. And I forgot to take my prescription. Goddamn it, I can't be this careless."

"Hey." I propped myself up on my elbow and ran my other hand down his chest. "No harm done."

"Don't make light of this, Eva." He turned his head and looked at me, his gaze fierce. "Not this."

"I would never." God, he looked so weary, with dark smudges under his eyes and deep grooves framing that wickedly sensual mouth.

"I killed a man," he said grimly. "It's never been safe for you to be with me when I'm sleeping, and that's even truer now."

"Gideon . . ." I suddenly understood why he'd been having his nightmares more frequently. He could rationalize what he'd done, but that didn't alleviate the weight on his conscience.

I brushed the thick strands of hair off his forehead. "If you're struggling, you need to talk to me."

"I just want you safe," he muttered.

"I never feel safer than when I'm with you. I need you to stop beating yourself up for everything."

"It's my fault."

"Wasn't your life perfectly uncomplicated before I came along?" I challenged.

He shot me a wry look. "I seem to have a taste for complicated."

"Then stop bitching about it. And don't move, I'll be right back."

I went to the master bedroom and swapped my garters, stockings, and bra for an oversized Cross Industries T-shirt. Pulling the velour throw off the foot of the bed, I went to Gideon's room and grabbed his medicine.

His gaze followed me as I dropped off the throw and prescription before heading to the kitchen for a bottle of water. In short order, I had him settled in, the both of us huddled together beneath the blanket and the majority of the lights turned off.

I snuggled closer, hooking my leg over his. The medication prescribed for Gideon's parasomnia was no cure, but he was religious about taking it. I loved him all the more for that dedication, because he did it for me. "Do you know what you were dreaming about?" I asked.

"No. Whatever it was, I wish it were you instead."

"Me, too." I laid my head on his chest, listening to his heartbeat slow. "If it had been a dream about me, what would it be like?"

I felt him relax, sinking into the sofa and into me.

"It would be a cloudless day on a Caribbean beach," he murmured.

"A private beach, with a cabana on the white sand, enclosed on three sides with the view in front of us. I'd have you spread out on a chaise longue. Naked."

"Of course."

"You'd be sun-warmed and lazy, your hair blowing in the breeze. You'd be wearing that smile you give me after I've made you come. We would have nowhere to go, no one waiting. Just the two of us, with all the time in the world."

"Sounds like paradise," I murmured, feeling his body growing heavier by the moment. "I hope we swim naked."

"Umm . . ." He yawned. "I need to go to bed."

"I want a bucket of iced beer, too," I said, hoping to detain him long enough that he'd fall asleep in my arms. "With lemons. I'd squeeze the juice over your eight-pack and lick it off."

"God, I love your mouth."

"You should dream about that, then. And all the naughty things it can do to you."

"Give me some examples."

I gave him plenty, talking in a low soothing voice, my hands stroking over his skin. He slipped away from me with a deep exhalation.

I held him close until long after the sun rose.

GIDEON slept until eleven. I'd been strategizing for hours by then and he found me in his office, his desk littered with my notes and drawings.

"Hey," I greeted him, lifting my lips for his kiss as he rounded the desk. He looked sleep-mussed and sexy in his boxer briefs. "Good morning."

He looked over my work. "What are you doing?"

"I want you caffeinated before I explain." I rubbed my hands together, excited. "Want to grab a quick shower while I make you a cup of coffee? Then we'll dig in."

His gaze slid over my face and he gave me a bemused smile. "All right. However, I suggest I grab *you* in the shower. Then we'll have coffee and dig in."

"Save that thought—and your libido—for tonight."

"Oh?"

"I'm going out, remember?" I prodded. "And I'm going to drink too much, which makes me horny. Don't forget to take your vitamins, ace."

His lips twitched. "Well, then."

"Oh, yeah. You'll be lucky if you can crawl out of bed tomorrow," I warned.

"I'll make sure to stay hydrated, then."

"Good idea." I returned my attention to his tablet, but had to look when he walked his very fine ass out of the room.

When I saw him again, he was damp-haired and wearing black sweats that hung low enough on his hips that I knew he was commando underneath. Forcing myself to focus on my plans, I gave him the desk chair and stood next to him.

"Okay," I began, "following the adage that the best defense is a good offense, I've been taking a look at your public image."

He took a sip of his coffee.

"Don't look at me like that," I admonished. "I didn't pay any attention to your personal life, since *I'm* your personal life."

"Good girl." He gave me an approving pat on my behind.

I stuck my tongue out at him. "I'm mostly thinking of how to combat a smear campaign focused on your temper."

"It helps that I haven't previously been known as having one," he said dryly.

Until you met me . . . "I'm a terrible influence on you."

"You're the best thing that ever happened to me."

That earned him a quick, smacking kiss to the temple. "It took me a ridiculous amount of time to find out about the Crossroads Foundation."

"You didn't know where to look."

"Your search optimization really blows," I countered, pulling up the website. "And there's only this splash page, which is pretty, but ridiculously bare. Where are the links and info about the charities that have benefited? Where's the About page on the foundation and what you hope to accomplish?"

"A packet detailing all of that information is sent out to charities, hospitals, and universities twice a year."

"Great. Now, let me introduce you to the Internet. Why isn't the foundation tied to you?"

"Crossroads isn't about me, Eva."

"The hell it isn't." I met his raised brows with my own and shoved a to-do list in front of him. "We're defusing the Deanna bomb before it blows. This website needs to be overhauled by Monday morning, with the addition of these pages and the information I've outlined."

Gideon took a cursory glance at the paper, then picked up his mug and leaned back in his chair. I studiously focused on the mug and not his amazing torso.

"The Cross Industries site should cross-link with the foundation from your Bio page," I continued. "Which also needs an overhaul and updating."

I slid another paper in front of him.

He picked it up and began reading the biography I'd drafted. "This was clearly written by someone in love with me."

"You can't be shy, Gideon. Sometimes you just have to be blunt and say, 'I rock.' There's so much more to you than a gorgeous face, hot body, and insane sex drive. But let's focus on the stuff I don't mind sharing with the world."

Flashing a grin, Gideon asked, "How much coffee have you had this morning?"

"Enough to take you to the mat, so watch out." I bumped my hip into his arm. "I also think you should consider a press release announcing the acquisition of La Rose Noir, so that your name and Giroux's are linked. Remind people that Corinne—who you've been seen around with so much lately—has a husband, so Deanna can't paint you as a total bad guy for cutting Corinne off. *If* she decides to go that route."

He caught me unawares and pulled me into his lap. "Angel, you're killing me. I'll do whatever you want, but you need to understand that Deanna has nothing. Ian Hager isn't going to risk a nice settlement to publicize his story. He'll sign the necessary releases, take the money, and go away."

"But what about—"

"Six-Ninths isn't going to want their 'Golden' girl linked with another guy. Ruins the love story of the song. I'll be speaking to Kline and we'll get on the same page."

"You're talking to Brett?"

"We're in business together," he pointed out, with a twist to his lips, "so yes. And Deanna's using Cary's attack as a bluff. You and I both know there's nothing there."

I considered all that. "You think she's yanking my chain? Why?"

"Because I'm yours, and if she had a press pass to any event we attended together, she knows it." He leaned his forehead against mine. "I can't hide how I feel around you, which is what's made you a target."

"You hid it well enough from me."

"Your insecurity made you blind."

I couldn't argue with that. "So she freaks me out with the threat of the story. What does she achieve?"

He leaned back. "Think about it. The lid is about to blow on a scandal involving you and me. What's the swiftest way to defuse it?"

"Stay away from me. That's what you'd be advised to do. Distancing yourself from the source of a scandal is Crisis Management 101."

"Or do the opposite and marry you," he said softly.

I froze. "Is that—? Are you—?" Swallowing hard, I whispered, "Not now. Not like this."

"No, not like this," Gideon agreed, rubbing his lips back and forth over mine. "When I propose, angel, trust me, you'll know it."

My throat was tight. I could only nod.

"Breathe," he ordered gently. "One more time. Now, reassure me that's not panic."

"Not really. No."

"Talk to me, Eva."

"I just . . ." I blurted it out in a rush. "I want you to ask me when I can say yes."

Tension gripped his body. He leaned back, his eyes wounded beneath his frown. "You couldn't say yes now?"

I shook my head.

His mouth thinned into a determined line. "Lay out what you need from me to make that happen."

I wrapped my arms around his shoulders, so that he'd feel the connection between us. "There's so much I don't know. And it's not that I need to know more in order to make up my mind, because nothing could make me stop loving you. Nothing. I just feel like your hesitance to share things with me means that *you're* not ready."

"I think I followed that," he muttered.

"I can't take the risk that you won't want forever with me. I won't survive you, either, Gideon."

"What do you want to know?"

"Everything."

He made a frustrated noise. "Be specific. Start with something."

The first thing that came to mind was what came out of my mouth, because I'd been buried in his business all morning. "Vidal Records. Why are you in control of your stepfather's company?"

"Because it was going under." His jaw hardened. "My mother had already suffered through one financial meltdown; I wasn't going to let it happen to her again."

"What did you do?"

"I was able to convince her to talk them—Chris and Christopher—into taking the company public, then she sold Ireland's shares to me. In addition to what I acquired, I had the majority."

"Wow." I squeezed his hand. I'd met both Christopher Vidal Sr.—Chris—and Christopher Vidal Jr. As alike as father and son were in appearance, with their dark copper waves and grayish-green eyes, I suspected they were very different men. Certainly I knew Christopher was a douche. I didn't think his father was. At least I hoped he wasn't. "How did that go over?"

Gideon's arch look was all the answer I needed. "Chris would ask for my advice, but Christopher always refused to take it and my stepdad wouldn't choose sides."

"So you did what had to be done." I kissed his jaw. "Thank you for telling me."

"That's it?"

I smiled. "No."

I was about to ask him more when I heard my phone ringing with my mother's ring tone. I was surprised it had taken her so long to call; I'd taken my smartphone off mute around ten o'clock. Groaning, I said, "I have to get that."

He let me up, his hand stroking over my butt as I walked away. When I turned at the doorway to look back, he was poring over my notes and suggestions. I smiled.

By the time I reached my phone on the breakfast bar, it had stopped ringing, but it immediately started up again. "Mom," I answered, jumping in before she started flipping out. "I'm going to come over today, okay? And we'll talk."

"Eva. You have no idea how worried I've been! You can't do this to me!"

"I'll be over in an hour," I interjected. "I just need to get dressed."

"I couldn't sleep last night, I was so upset."

"Yeah, well, I didn't sleep much, either," I retorted. "It's not just about you all the time, Mom. I'm the one who had her privacy violated. You're just the one who got caught doing it."

Silence.

It was rare for me to be assertive with my mother because she always seemed so fragile, but it was time to redefine our relationship or we'd end up not having one. I looked to my wrist for the time, remembered I didn't have a watch anymore, and glanced at the cable box by the television instead. "I'll be over around one."

"I'll send a car for you," she said quietly.

"Thank you. See you soon." I hung up.

I was about to drop my phone back into my purse when it beeped with a text from Shawna: What r u wearing 2nite?

A number of ideas ran through my mind, from casual to outrageous. Even though I was inclined toward outrageous, I was checked by thoughts of Deanna. I had to think about what I'd look like in the tabloids. LBD, I replied, thinking the little black dress was a classic for a reason. Wild heels. Too much jewelry.

☺ Got it! See u at 7, she texted back.

On the way to the bedroom, I paused by Gideon's office and lounged against the doorjamb to watch him. I could watch him for hours; he was such a joy to look at. And I found him very sexy when he was focused.

He glanced up at me with a soft curve to his lips, and I knew he'd been aware of my staring. "This is all very good," he praised, gesturing at his desktop. "Especially considering you pulled this together in a matter of hours."

I preened a little, thrilled to have impressed a businessman whose acumen had made him one of the most successful individuals in the world.

"I want you at Cross Industries, Eva."

My body reacted to the unwavering determination in his voice, which reminded me of when he'd said, *I want to fuck you, Eva*, when he'd first come on to me.

"I want you there, too," I said. "On your desk."

His eyes gleamed. "We can celebrate that way."

"I like my job. I like my co-workers. I like knowing I've earned every milestone I reach."

"I can give you that and more." His fingers tapped against the side of his coffee mug. "I'm guessing you went with advertising because you like the spin. Why not public relations?"

"Too much like propaganda. At least with advertising, you know the bias right away."

"You mentioned crisis management this morning. And clearly"—he gestured at his desk—"you have an aptitude for it. Let me exploit it."

I crossed my arms. "Crisis management is PR and you know it."

"You're a problem solver. I can make you a fixer. Give you real, time-sensitive problems to solve. Keep you challenged and active."

"Seriously." I tapped my foot. "How many crises do you have in a given week?"

"Several," he said cheerfully. "Come on, you're intrigued. I can see it on your face."

Straightening, I pointed out, "You have people to handle that kind of stuff already."

Gideon leaned back in his chair and smiled. "I want more. So do you. Let's have it together."

"You're like the devil himself, you know that? And you're stubborn as hell. I'm telling you, working together would be a bad idea."

"We're working together just fine now."

I shook my head. "Because you agreed with my assessment and suggestions, plus you had me sitting in your lap and you copped a feel of my ass. It's not going to be the same when we're not on the same page and arguing about it in your office in front of other people. Then we'll have to bring that irritation home and deal with it here, too."

"We can agree to leave work at the door." His eyes slid over me, lingering on my legs, which were mostly bared by my silk robe. "I won't have any problem thinking of more enjoyable things."

Rolling my eyes, I backed out of the room. "Sex maniac."

"I love making love with you."

"That's not fair," I complained, having no defense against that. No defense against *him*.

Gideon grinned. "I never said I play fair."

WHEN I entered my apartment fifteen minutes later, it felt weird. The floor plan was identical to Gideon's next door, but reversed. The blending of his furniture and mine had helped to make his space feel like *ours* but had the side effect of making me feel like my home was . . . alien.

"Hey, Eva."

I looked around and saw Trey in the kitchen, pouring milk into two glasses. "Hey," I greeted him back. "How are you?"

"Better."

He looked it. His blond hair, which was usually unruly, had been nicely styled—one of Cary's talents. Trey's hazel eyes were bright, his smile charming beneath his once-broken nose.

"It's good to see you around more," I told him.

"I rearranged my schedule a bit." He held up the milk and I shook my head, so he put it away. "How are you?"

"Dodging reporters, hoping my boss gets engaged, planning on setting one parent straight, fitting in a phone call to the other parent, and looking forward to hitting the town with the girls tonight."

"You're awesome."

"What can I say?" I smiled. "How's school? And work?"

I knew Trey was studying to be a veterinarian and juggling jobs to pay for it. One of those gigs was as a photographer's assistant, which was how he'd met Cary.

He winced. "Both brutal, but it'll pay off someday."

"We should have another movie-and-pizza night when you get a chance." I couldn't help rooting for Trey in the tug-of-war between him and Tatiana. It could just be me, but she'd always seemed very adversarial toward me. And I didn't like the way she'd put herself forward when she met Gideon.

"Sure. I'll see what Cary's schedule is like."

I regretted bringing it up to Trey first instead of Cary, because some of the light left his eyes. I knew he was thinking about Cary having to fit him in between time with Tatiana. "Well, if he's not up for it, we can always go out without him."

His mouth tilted up on one side. "Sounds like a plan."

At ten minutes to one, I exited the lobby to find Clancy already waiting for me. He waved aside the doorman and opened the town car door for me, but no one looking at him would believe he was just a driver. He carried himself like the weapon he was, and in all the years I'd known him, I couldn't recall ever seeing him smile.

Once he'd resumed his seat behind the wheel, he turned off the police scanner he routinely listened to and pulled his sunglasses down enough to catch my eye in the rearview mirror. "How are you?"

"Better than my mom, I'm guessing."

He was too professional to give anything away in his expression. Instead, he slid his shades back into place and synced my phone to the car's Bluetooth to start my playlist. Then he pulled away from the curb.

Reminded of his thoughtfulness, I said, "Hey. I'm sorry I took it out on you. You were doing a job and you didn't deserve to get bitched at for it."

118 · SYLVIA DAY

"You're not just a job, Miss Tramell."

I was silent for a bit, absorbing that. Clancy and I had a distant, polite association. We saw each other quite a bit because he was responsible for getting me to and from my Krav Maga classes in Brooklyn. But I'd never really thought about him having any sort of personal stake in my safety, although it made sense. Clancy was a guy who took pride in his work.

"It wasn't just that one thing, though," I clarified. "A lot of stuff happened before you and Stanton ever came into the picture."

"Apology accepted."

The brusque reply was so like him that it made me smile.

Settling more comfortably into the seat, I looked out the window at the city I'd adopted and loved passionately. On the sidewalk beside me, strangers stood shoulder to shoulder over a tiny counter, eating individual slices of pizza. As close as they were, they were distant, each displaying a New Yorker's ability to be an island in a crashing tide of people. Pedestrians flowed past them in both directions, avoiding a man pushing religious flyers and the tiny dog at his feet.

The vitality of the city had a frenetic pulse that made time seem to move faster here than anywhere else. It was such a contrast to the lazy sensuality of Southern California, where my dad lived and I'd gone to school. New York was a dominatrix on the prowl, cracking a mean whip and tantalizing with every vice.

My purse vibrated against my hip and I reached into it for my phone. A quick glance at the screen told me it was my dad. Saturdays were our weekly catch-up days and I always looked forward to our chats, but I was almost inclined to let the call go to voice mail until I was in a better frame of mind. I was too aggravated with my mom, and my dad had already been overly concerned about me since he'd left New York after his last visit.

He'd been with me when the detectives had come to my apartment to tell me Nathan was in New York. They'd dropped that bomb before they revealed that Nathan had been murdered, and I hadn't been able to hide my fear at the thought of him being so close. My dad had been after me about my violent reaction ever since.

"Hey," I answered, mostly because I didn't want to be at odds with both my parents at the same time. "How are you?"

"Missing you," he replied in the deep, confident voice I loved. My dad was the most perfect man I knew—darkly handsome, self-assured, smart, and rock solid. "How 'bout you?"

"I can't complain too much."

"Okay, complain just a little. I'm all ears."

I laughed softly. "Mom's just driving me a little batty."

"What'd she do now?" he asked, with a note of warm indulgence in his voice.

"She's been sticking her nose in my business."

"Ah. Sometimes we parents do that when we're worried about our babies."

"*You've* never done that," I pointed out.

"I haven't done it *yet*," he qualified. "That doesn't mean I won't, if I'm worried enough. I just hope I could convince you to forgive me."

"Well, I'm on my way to Mom's now. Let's see how convincing she can be. It would help if she'd admit she's wrong."

"Good luck with that."

"Ha! Right?" I sighed. "Can I call you tomorrow?"

"Sure. Is everything all right, sweetheart?"

I closed my eyes. Cop instincts plus daddy instincts meant I rarely got anything by Victor Reyes. "Yep. It's just that I'm almost to Mom's now. I'll let you know how it goes. Oh, and my boss might be getting engaged. Anyway, I have stuff to tell you."

"I may have to stop by the station in the morning, but you can reach me on my cell no matter what. I love you."

I felt a sudden surge of homesickness. As much as I loved New York and my new life, I missed my dad a lot. "I love you, too, Daddy. Talk to you tomorrow."

Killing the call, I looked for my wristwatch, and its absence reminded me of the confrontation ahead. I was upset with my mother about the past, but was most concerned with the future. She'd hovered over me for so long because of Nathan, I wasn't sure she knew any other way to behave.

"Hey." I leaned forward, needing to clarify something that was bothering me. "That day when me, Mom, and Megumi were walking back to the Crossfire and Mom freaked out . . . Did you guys see Nathan?"

"Yes."

"He'd been there before and got his ass beat by Gideon Cross. Why would he go back?"

He glanced at me through the mirror. "My guess? To be seen. Once he made himself known, he kept the pressure up. Likely, he expected to frighten you and managed to scare Mrs. Stanton instead. Effective in either case."

"And no one told me," I said quietly. "I can't get over that."

"He wanted you frightened. No one wanted to give him that satisfaction."

Oh. I hadn't thought of it that way.

"My big regret," he went on, "is not keeping an eye on Cary. I miscalculated, and he paid the price."

Gideon hadn't seen Nathan's attack on Cary coming, either. And God knew I felt guilty about it, too—my friendship was what had put Cary in danger to begin with.

But I was really touched that Clancy cared. I could hear it in his gruff voice. He was right; I wasn't just a job to him. He was a good man who gave his all to everything he did. Which made me wonder: How much did he have left over for the other things in his life?

"Do you have a girlfriend, Clancy?"

"I'm married."

I felt like an ass for not knowing that. What was she like, the woman married to such a hard, somber man? A man who wore a jacket year-round to hide the sidearm he was never without. Did he soften for her and show her tenderness? Was he fierce about protecting her? Would he kill for her?

"How far would you go to keep her safe?" I asked him.

We slowed at a light and he turned his head to look at me. "How far wouldn't I go?"

9

"WHAT WAS WRONG with that one?" Megumi asked, watching the guy in question walk away. "He had dimples."

I rolled my eyes and polished off my vodka and cranberry. Primal, the fourth stop on our club-hopping list, was pumping. The line to get in wrapped around the block and the guitar-heavy tracks suited the club's name, the music pounding through the darkened space with a primitive, seductive beat. The décor was an eclectic mix of brushed metals and dark woods, with the multihued lighting creating animal-print silhouettes.

It should've been too much, but like everything Gideon, it skirted the edge of decadent excess without falling over it. The atmosphere was one of hedonistic abandon and it did crazy things to my alcohol-fueled libido. I couldn't sit still, my feet tapping restlessly on the rungs of my chair.

Megumi's roommate, Lacey, groaned at the ceiling, her dark blond hair arranged in a disheveled updo I admired. "Why don't *you* flirt with him?"

"I might," Megumi said, looking flushed, bright-eyed, and very hot in a slinky gold halter dress. "Maybe *he'll* commit."

"What do you want out of commitment?" Shawna asked, nursing a drink as fiery red as her hair. "Monogamy?"

"Monogamy is overrated." Lacey slid off her bar stool at our tallboy table and wriggled her butt, the rhinestones on her jeans glittering in the semidarkness of the club.

"No, it's not." Megumi pouted. "I happen to like monogamy."

"Is Michael sleeping with other women?" I asked, leaning forward so I didn't have to shout.

I had to lean back right away to make room for the waitress, who brought another round and cleared the previous one away. The club's uniform of black stiletto boots and hot pink strapless minidresses stood out in the crowd, making it easy to know who to flag. It was also really sexy—as was the staff wearing them. Had Gideon had any hand in picking the outfit? And if so, had anyone modeled it for him?

"I don't know." Megumi picked up her new drink and sucked at her straw with a sad face. "I'm afraid to ask."

Grabbing one of the four shot glasses in the center of the table and a lime wedge, I shouted, "Let's do shots and dance!"

"Fuck yeah!" Shawna tossed back her shot of Patrón without waiting for the rest of us, then shoved a lime in her mouth. Dropping the juiceless wedge into her empty glass, she shot us all a look. "Hurry up, laggers."

I went next, shuddering as the tequila washed away the tang of cranberry. Lacey and Megumi went together, toasting each other with a loud *"Kanpai!"* before downing theirs.

We hit the dance floor en masse, Shawna leading the way in her electric blue dress that was damn near as bright under the black lights as the club uniform. We were swallowed into the mass of writhing dancers, quickly finding ourselves pressed between steamy male bodies.

I let go, giving myself over to the grinding beat of the music and the sultry atmosphere of the rocking club. Lifting my hands in the air, I swayed, releasing the lingering tension from the long, pointless afternoon with my mother. At some point, I'd lost my trust in her. As much as she promised that things would be different without Nathan, I found I couldn't believe her. She'd crossed the line too many times.

"You're beautiful," someone yelled by my ear.

I looked over my shoulder at the dark-haired guy curved against my back. "Thanks!"

It was a lie, of course. My hair clung to my sweat-damp temples and neck in a sticky tangle. I didn't care. The music raged on, songs sliding into each other.

I reveled in the utter sensuality of the venue and the shameless drive for casual sex that everyone seemed to exude. I was pressed between a couple—the girlfriend at my back and her boyfriend at my front—when I spotted someone I knew. He must have seen me first, because he was already working his way toward me.

"Martin!" I yelled, breaking out of my bump-and-grind sandwich. In the past, I'd only crossed paths with Stanton's nephew during the holidays. We'd met up once since I moved to New York, but I hoped we would eventually see each other more.

"Eva, hi!" He caught me up in a hug, then pulled back to check me out. "You look fantastic. How are you?"

"Let's get a drink!" I shouted, feeling too parched to hold a conversation at the decibel level required in the crowd.

Grabbing my hand, he led me out of the crush and I pointed to my table. The moment we sat down, the waitress was there with another vodka and cranberry.

It'd been that way all night, although I'd noted that my drinks were getting darker as the hours progressed, a sure sign that the vodka-to-cranberry ratio was slowly becoming more cranberry than not. I knew that was deliberate and was suitably impressed by Gideon's ability to carry his instructions from club to club. Since no one was stopping me from supplementing with shots, I didn't mind too much.

"So," I began, taking a welcome sip before rolling the icy-cold tumbler across my forehead. "How have you been?"

"Great." He grinned, looking quite handsome in a camel-hued V-neck T-shirt and black jeans. His dark hair wasn't nearly the length of Gideon's, but it fell attractively across his forehead, framing eyes that I knew were green although no one would be able to tell in the club's lighting. "How's the ad biz treating you?"

"I love my job!"

He laughed at my enthusiasm. "If only we could all say that."

"I thought you liked working with Stanton."

"I do. Like the money, too. Can't say I love the job, though."

The waitress brought his scotch on the rocks, and we clinked glasses.

"Who are you here with?" I asked him.

"A couple friends"—he looked around—"who are lost in the jungle. You?"

"Same." I caught Lacey's eye on the dance floor and she gave me two thumbs up. "Are you seeing anyone, Martin?"

His smile widened. "No."

"You like blondes?"

"Are you hitting on me?"

"Not quite." I raised my brows at Lacey and jerked my head toward Martin. She looked surprised for a minute, then grinned and rushed over.

I introduced them and felt pretty good about the way they hit it off. Martin was always fun and charming, and Lacey was vivacious and attractive in a unique way—more charismatic than beautiful.

Megumi made her way back over and we did another round of shots before Martin asked Lacey to dance.

"You got any other hot guys in your pocket?" Megumi asked, as the couple melted away.

I was wishing I had my smartphone in my pocket. "You're miserable, girl."

She looked at me for a long minute. Then her lips twisted. "I'm drunk."

"That, too. Want another shot?"

"Why not?"

We did a shot each, polishing them off just as Shawna came back with Lacey, Martin, and his two friends, Kurt and Andre. Kurt was gorgeous, with sandy brown hair, square jaw, and cocky smile. Andre was cute, too, with a mischievous twinkle in his dark eyes and shoulder-length dreadlocks. He focused on Megumi, which cheered her right up.

Our expanded group was roaring with laughter in no time.

"And when Kurt came back from the bathroom," Martin finished his story, "he sacked the whole restaurant."

Andre and Martin started howling. Kurt threw limes at them.

"What does that mean?" I asked, smiling even though I didn't get the punch line.

"It's when you leave your sac hanging out of your fly," Andre explained. "At first people can't figure out what it is they're seeing, then they try to figure out if you just somehow don't know your nads are swinging in the breeze. No one says a word."

"No shit?" Shawna nearly fell off her chair.

We got so rowdy, our waitress asked us to tone it down—with a smile. I caught her by the elbow before she walked away. "Is there a phone I can use?"

"Just ask one of the bartenders," she said. "Tell them Dennis—he's the manager—okayed it and they'll hook you up."

"Thanks." I slid off my seat as she moved on to another table. I had no idea who Dennis was, but I'd just been going with the flow all night, knowing Gideon would've set up everything flawlessly. "Anyone up for water?" I asked the group.

I got booed and pelted with wadded-up napkins. Laughing, I went

to the bar and waited for an opening to ask for Pellegrino and the phone.
I dialed Gideon's cell number, since it was the one I had memorized. I
figured it was safe since I was calling from a public place he owned.

"Cross," he answered briskly.

"Hi, ace." I leaned into the bar and covered my other ear with my
hand. "I'm drunk-dialing you."

"I can tell." His voice changed for me, slowed and grew warm. It
captivated me even over the music. "Are you having a good time?"

"Yes, but I miss you. Did you take your vitamins?"

He had a smile in his voice when he asked, "Are you horny, angel?"

"It's your fault! This club is like Viagra. I'm hot and sweaty and dripping in pheromones. And I've been a bad girl, you know. Dancing like
I'm single."

"Bad girls get punished."

"Maybe I should be really bad, then. Make the punishment worth
it."

He growled. "Come home and be bad with me."

The thought of him at home, ready for me, made me even more
eager for him. "I'm stuck here 'til the girls are done, which looks to be
a while."

"I can come to you. Within twenty minutes, you could have my cock
inside you. Do you want that?"

I glanced around the club, my entire body vibrating with the hard-
driving music. Imagining him here, fucking me in this no-holds-barred
place, made me squirm with anticipation. "Yes. I want that."

"Do you see the skywalk?"

Turning around, I looked up and saw the suspended walkway hugging the walls. Dancers dry-fucked to the music from twenty feet above
the dance floor. "Yes."

"There's a section where it wraps around a mirrored corner. I'll meet
you there. Be ready, Eva," he ordered. "I want your cunt naked and wet
when I find you."

I shivered at the familiar command, knowing it meant he'd be rough and impatient. *Just what I wanted.* "I'm wearing a—"

"Angel, a crowd of millions couldn't hide you from me. I found you once. I'll always find you."

Longing seared my veins. "Hurry."

Reaching over to replace the receiver on the business side of the bar, I grabbed my mineral water and drank until the bottle was empty. Then I headed to the bathroom, where I waited in line forever in order to get ready for Gideon. I was giddy with booze and excitement, so thrilled that my boyfriend—arguably one of the busiest men in the world—would drop everything to . . . service me.

I licked my lips, shifting on my feet.

I hurried through the ladies' room to a stall, ditching my panties before hitting the sink and mirror to freshen up with a damp napkin. Most of my makeup had melted off, leaving me with smudged eyes and cheeks reddened by heat and exertion. My hair was a mess, both wildly mussed and wet around my face.

Oddly, I didn't look half bad. I looked sexual and ready.

Lacey was in line and I stopped by her as I inched my way through the crowded bathroom threshold.

"Having fun?" I asked her.

"Yeah!" She grinned. "Thanks for introducing me to your cousin."

I didn't bother to correct her. "You're welcome. Can I ask you something? About Michael?"

Shrugging, she said, "Go for it."

"You went out with him first. What didn't you like about him?"

"No chemistry. Good-looking guy. Successful. Sadly, I didn't want to fuck him."

"Toss him back," the girl next in line interjected.

"I did."

"Okay." I could totally respect not progressing with a relationship lacking sexual heat, but I was still bothered by the situation. I didn't like seeing Megumi so bummed. "I'm going to go grind against some hot guy."

"Hit it, girl," Lacey said with a nod.

I took off in search of the stairs to the skywalk. I found them guarded by a bouncer policing the number of bodies allowed to venture up. There was a line and I eyed it with dismay.

As I debated how much of a delay I was facing, the bouncer unfolded his powerful arms from across his chest and pressed his earpiece deeper into his ear with one hand, clearly focusing on whatever was being relayed through his receiver. He could have been Samoan or Maori, with dark caramel skin, a shaved head, and massive barrel chest and biceps. He had a baby face and was downright adorable when his fierce scowl was replaced by a wide grin.

His hand dropped away from his ear and he crooked a finger at me. "You Eva?"

I nodded.

He reached behind him and unhooked the velvet rope blocking the stairway. "Head on up."

A roar of protests came from those who were waiting. I offered an apologetic smile, then raced up the metal stairs as fast as my heels would allow. When I reached the top, a female bouncer let me through and pointed to my left. I saw the corner Gideon had mentioned, where two mirrored walls connected and the skywalk wrapped around it in an L shape.

I weaved my way through writhing bodies, my pulse rate increasing with every step. The music was less loud up here and the air more humid. Sweat glistened on exposed skin and the elevation lent a sense of danger, even though the glass railing surrounding the skywalk was shoulder-high. I was almost to the mirrored section when I was caught around the waist and pulled back into a man's rolling hips.

Looking over my shoulder, I saw the guy I'd danced with before, the one who'd called me beautiful. I smiled and started dancing, closing my eyes to lose myself in the music. When his hands started to slide over my waist, I caught them, pinning them to my hips with my own. He laughed and dipped his knees, aligning his body with mine.

We were three songs out before I felt the ripple of awareness that told me Gideon was nearby. The electrical charge swept over my skin, heightening every sensation. Abruptly the music was louder, the temperature hotter, the sensuality of the club more arousing.

I smiled and opened my eyes, spotting him arrowing toward me. I was instantly hot for him, my mouth watering as I ate up the sight of him in a dark T-shirt and jeans, his hair pulled back from that breathtaking face. No one seeing him would put him together with Gideon Cross, the international mogul. This guy appeared younger and rougher, distinctive only for his incredible smokin' hotness. I licked my lips with anticipation, leaning into the guy behind me and rubbing my ass voluptuously into the next roll of his hips.

Gideon's hands fisted at his sides, his posture aggressive and predatory. He didn't slow as he neared me, his body on a collision course with mine. Turning, I met him the last step, surging into him. Our bodies crashed together, my arms encircling his shoulders and my hands pulling his head down so I could take his mouth in a wet, hungry kiss.

With a growl, Gideon cupped my ass and yanked me up hard against him, my feet leaving the floor. He bruised my lips with the ferocity of his passion, his tongue filling my mouth with hard, deep plunges that warned me of the violent shades of his lust.

The guy I'd been dancing with came up behind me, his hands in my hair and his lips at my shoulder blade.

Gideon pulled back, his face a gorgeous mask of fury. "Get lost."

I looked at the guy and gave a shrug. "Thanks for the dance."

"Anytime, beautiful." He caught the hips of a girl walking by and moved away.

"Angel." With a growl, Gideon pressed me into the mirror, his hard thigh thrust between my legs. "You're a bad girl."

Shameless and eager, I rode him, gasping at the feel of denim against my tender sex. "Only for you."

He gripped my bare buttocks beneath my dress, spurring me on. His teeth caught the shell of my ear, my silver chandelier earrings brushing my neck. He was breathing hard, low rumbles vibrating in his chest. He smelled so good and my body responded, trained to associate his scent with the wildest, hottest of pleasures.

We danced, straining together, our bodies moving as if there were no clothes between us. The music pounded around us, through us, and he moved his amazing body to it, captivating me. We'd danced before, ballroom style, but never like this. This sweaty, dirty grinding. I was surprised, turned on, fell even deeper in love.

Gideon watched me with a hooded gaze, seducing me with his need and his uninhibited moves. I was lost in him, wrapped around him, clawing to get closer.

He kneaded my breast through the thin black jersey of my spaghetti-strapped dress. The built-in shelf bra was no barrier. His fingers stroked, then tugged the hardened point of my nipple.

As I moaned, my head fell back against the mirror. Dozens of people surrounded us and I didn't care. I just needed his hands on me, his body against mine, his breath on my skin.

"You want me," he said harshly, "right here."

I quivered at the thought. "Would you?"

"You want them to watch. You want them to see me fuck my cock into your greedy little cunt until you're dripping in cum. You want me to prove you're mine." His teeth sank into the top of my shoulder. "Make you feel it."

"I want to prove that *you're* mine," I shot back, shoving my hands into the pockets of his jeans to feel his hard ass flex. "I want everyone to know it."

Gideon hitched one arm beneath my rear and lifted me, his other hand slapping flat against a pad on the wall by the mirror. I heard a faint beeping, and then a door opened in the mirror at my back and we stepped into almost total darkness. The concealed entrance closed behind us, muting the music. We were in an office, with a desk, a seating area, and a 180-degree view of the club through two-way mirrors.

He put me down and spun me, pinning my front to the transparent side of the glass. The club was spread out before me, the dancers on the skywalk only inches away. His hands were up my skirt and in the bodice of my dress, fingers sliding into my cleft and rolling my nipple.

I was snared. His big body covered mine, his arms around me, torso to hips, his teeth in my shoulder holding me in place. He owned me.

"Tell me if it's too much," he murmured, his lips drifting up my throat. "Safeword before I scare you."

Emotion flooded me, gratitude for this man who always—*always*— thought of me first. "I provoked you. I want to be taken. I want you wild."

"You're so hot for it," he purred, pumping two fingers quick and hard into me. "You were made for fucking."

"Made for you," I gasped, my breath fogging the glass. I was on fire for him, my desire pouring out from the inside, from the well of love I couldn't contain.

"Did you forget that tonight?" His hand left my sex to reach between us and yank open his fly. "When other men were touching you, rubbing against you? Did you forget you're mine?"

"Never. I never forget." My eyes closed as his erection, so stiff and warm, rested heavily against the bare cheek of my ass. He was hot for it, too. Hot for me. "I called you. Wanted you."

His lips moved over my skin, forging a scorching trail to my mouth. "Take me, then, angel," he coaxed, his tongue touching mine with teasing licks. "Put me inside you."

Arching my back, I reached between my legs, my hand circling his thickness. He bent his knees, lining himself up for me.

I paused, turning my head to press my cheek to his. I loved that I could have this with him . . . be this way with him. Circling my hips, I stroked my clit with the wide crest of his cock, making him slick with my arousal.

Gideon squeezed my swollen breasts, plumping them. "Lean into me, Eva. Push away from the glass."

With my palm to the two-way mirror, I pushed back, my head pillowed on his shoulder. He wrapped my throat with his hand, gripped my hip, and thrust so hard into me that my feet left the floor. He held me there, suspended in his arms, filled with his cock, his groan cascading over my senses.

On the other side of the glass, the club raged on. I abandoned myself to the wickedly intense pleasure of seemingly exhibitionist sex, an illicit fantasy that always drove us wild.

I writhed, unable to bear the decadent pressure. My hand between my legs reached lower, cradled his sac. He was tight and full, so ready. And inside me . . . "Oh God. You're so hard."

"I was made to fuck you," he whispered, sending shivers of delight through me.

"Do it." I set both hands on the glass, beyond needy. "Do it now."

Gideon lowered me to my feet, his hands steadying me as I bent at the waist, opening myself to him so he could slide deep. A low, keening cry escaped as he seized my hips and angled me, knowing just how to position me to make me fit him. He was too big for me, too long and thick. The stretching was intense. Delicious.

My core trembled, clenching desperately around him. He made a rough sound of pleasure, pulling out just a little before sliding back slowly. Again, then again. The wide crest of his cock massaging the bundle of nerves deep inside me that only he'd ever reached.

Fingers clawing restlessly, leaving steamy trails on the glass, I moaned. I was achingly aware of the distant throb of the music and the mass of people I saw as clearly as if they were in the room with us.

"That's it, angel," he said urgently. "Let me hear how much you like it."

"Gideon." My legs shook violently on a particularly skillful stroke, my weight supported only by the glass and his secure hold.

I was unbearably excited, greedy, feeling both the submission of my pose and the dominance of being serviced. I could do nothing but take what Gideon gave me, the rhythmic slide and retreat, the sounds of his hunger. The scrape of his jeans against my thighs told me he'd pushed them down only far enough to free his cock, a sign of impatience that thrilled me.

One of his hands left my hip, then returned to rest atop my ass. I felt the pad of his thumb, wet from his mouth, rubbing over the tight pucker of my rear.

"No," I begged, afraid I'd lose my mind. But it wasn't my safe-word—*Crossfire*—and I flowered open for him, giving way under the questing pressure.

He growled as he claimed that dark place. He came over me, his other hand moving to finger my sex, to spread me and rub my pulsing clit. "Mine," he said gruffly. "You're mine."

It was too much. I came with a scream, shaking violently, my hands squeaking on the glass as my sweaty palms slipped. He began pounding the ecstasy into me, his thumb in my rear an irresistible torment, his clever fingers on my clit driving me insane. One orgasm rolled into another, my sex rippling along his plunging cock.

He made a rough sound of desire and swelled inside me, chasing his climax. I gasped, "Don't come! Not yet."

Gideon's tempo slowed, his breathing harsh in the darkness. "How do you want me?"

"I want to watch you." I moaned as my core tightened again. "Want to see your face."

He withdrew and pulled me upright. Turned and lifted me. Pressed me to the glass and thrust hard into me. In that moment of possession, he gave me what I needed. The glazed look of helpless pleasure, the instant of vulnerability before the lust seized his control.

"You want to watch me lose it," he said hoarsely.

"Yes." I pulled the straps from my shoulders and exposed my breasts, lifting and squeezing them, toying with my nipples. The glass was vibrating with the beat against my back; Gideon was vibrating against my front, his body barely reined.

I pressed my lips to his, absorbing his panting breaths. "Let go," I whispered.

Holding me effortlessly, he withdrew, dragging the thick, heavy crown across the hypersensitive tissues inside me. Then he powered into me, taking me to my limits.

"Ah, God." I writhed in his grip. "You're so deep."

"Eva."

He fucked me hard, thrusting like a man possessed. I held on, trembling, spread wide for the relentless drives of his rigid penis. He was lost to instinct, the insistent desire to mate. Raw moans spilled from him, making me so hot and slick that my body offered no resistance, welcoming his desperate need.

It was rough and messy and sexy as hell. His neck arched and he gasped my name.

"Come for me," I demanded, tightening around him, squeezing.

His whole body jerked hard, then shuddered. His mouth twisted in a grimace of agonized bliss, his eyes losing their focus as the climax built.

Gideon came with an animal roar, spurting so hard I felt it. Over and over, heating me from the inside with thick washes of semen.

My lips were all over him, my arms and legs holding tight.

He collapsed against me, his lungs heaving for breath.

Still coming.

10

THE FIRST THING I saw when I woke up Sunday morning was an amber bottle labeled HANGOVER CURE in an old-fashioned font. A raffia bow adorned the neck and a cork stopper kept the stomach-turning contents safe. The "cure" worked, as I'd learned the last time Gideon had given me the stuff, but the sight of it reminded me of how much alcohol I'd consumed the night before.

Squeezing my eyes shut, I groaned and buried my head in the pillow, willing myself back to sleep.

The bed shifted. Warm, firm lips drifted down my bare spine. "Good morning, angel mine."

"You sound ridiculously pleased with yourself," I muttered.

"Pleased with you, actually."

"Fiend."

"I was referring to your crisis management suggestions, but of course the sex was phenomenal, as always." His hand slid beneath the sheet that was pooled around my waist and he squeezed my ass.

I lifted my head and found him propped against the headboard beside me with his laptop on his thighs. He looked mouthwatering, as usual, completely relaxed in drawstring lounging pants. I was certain I was looking far less attractive. I'd taken the limo home with the girls, then met up with Gideon at his apartment. It was nearly dawn before I'd finished with him and I'd been so tired, I crashed with hair still wet from a hasty shower.

A tingle of pleasure moved through me at finding him next to me. He'd slept in the guest room, and he had an office to work in. The fact that he chose to work in the bed I slept in meant he'd just wanted to be near me, even while I was unconscious.

I turned my head to look at the bedside clock, but my gaze snagged on my wrist instead.

"Gideon . . ." The watch that had been placed on my arm while I slept enchanted me. The Art Deco–inspired timepiece sparkled with hundreds of tiny diamonds. The band was a creamy satin and the mother-of-pearl face was branded with both Patek Philippe and Tiffany & Co. "It's *gorgeous.*"

"There are only twenty-five of those in the world, which isn't nearly as unique as you are, but then, what is?" He smiled down at me.

"I love it." I pushed up onto my knees. "I love you."

He shoved his laptop aside in time for me to straddle him and hug him tightly.

"Thank you," I murmured, touched by his thoughtfulness. He would've gone out for it while I was at my mother's or maybe just after I left with the girls.

"Umm. Tell me how to earn one of these naked hugs every day."

"Just be you, ace." I rubbed my cheek against his. "You're all I need."

I slid out of bed and padded over to the bathroom with the small amber bottle in my hand. I guzzled the contents down with a shudder, brushed my teeth and hair, and then washed my face. I pulled on a robe and returned to the bedroom, finding Gideon gone and his laptop lying open in the middle of the bed.

I passed him in his office, seeing him standing with his feet planted wide and his arms crossed, facing the window. The city stretched out in front of him. Not the skyline view he had in his Crossfire office or his penthouse, but a closer vantage. More grounded and immediate. The connection with the city more intimate.

"I don't share your concern," he said briskly into his earpiece mic. "I'm aware of the risk . . . Stop talking. The subject isn't open to debate. Draw up the agreement as specified."

Recognizing that all-business note of steel in his voice, I kept walking. I still wasn't sure exactly what was in the bottle, but I suspected it was vitamins and liquor of some sort. Hair of the dog. It was warming my belly and making me feel lethargic, so I went to the kitchen and made a cup of coffee.

Supplied with caffeine, I plopped down on the couch and checked my smartphone for messages. I frowned when I saw that I'd missed three calls from my dad, all before eight in the morning in California. I also noted a dozen missed calls from my mom, but I figured Monday was soon enough to deal with her again. And there was a text from Cary that shouted, CALL ME!

I called my dad back first, trying to swallow a quick drink of coffee before he answered.

"Eva."

The anxious way my dad said my name told me something was wrong. I sat up straighter. "Dad . . . Is everything all right?"

"Why didn't you tell me about Nathan Barker?" His voice was hoarse and filled with pain. Goose bumps swept across my skin.

Oh, fuck. He *knew*. My hand shook so badly, I spilled hot coffee on my hand and thigh. I didn't even feel it; I was so panicked by my father's anguish. "Dad, I—"

"I can't believe you didn't tell me. Or Monica. My God . . . She should've said something. Should've told me." He sucked in a shaky breath. "I had the right to know!"

Sorrow spread through my chest like acid. My dad—a man whose self-control rivaled Gideon's—sounded like he was crying.

I set my mug on the coffee table, my breathing fast and shallow. Nathan's sealed juvenile records had broken open upon his death, exposing the horror of my past to anyone who had the knowledge and means to find it. As a cop, my dad had those means.

"There's nothing you could've done," I told him, stunned, but trying to hold it together for his sake. My smartphone beeped with an incoming call, but I ignored it. "Before or after."

"I could've been there for you. I could've taken care of you."

"Daddy, you did. Putting me together with Dr. Travis changed my life. I didn't really start dealing with anything until then. I can't tell you how much that helped."

He groaned, and it was a low sound of torment. "I should've fought your mother for you. You should've been with me."

"Oh, God." My stomach cramped. "You can't blame Mom. She didn't know what was happening for a long time. And when she did find out, she did everything—"

"She didn't *tell me!*" he shouted, making me jump. "She should've fucking told me. And how could she not know? There must've been signs . . . How could she not see them? Jesus. *I* saw them when you came to California."

I sobbed, unable to contain my anguish. "I begged her not to tell you. I made her promise."

"That wasn't your decision to make, Eva. You were a child. She knew better."

"I'm sorry!" I cried. The insistent, relentless beeping of an incoming call pushed me over the edge. "I'm so sorry. I just didn't want Nathan to hurt anyone else I loved."

"I'm coming to see you," he said, with a sudden burst of calm. "I'm getting the next flight out. I'll call you when I land."

"Dad—"

"I love you, sweetheart. You're everything."

He hung up. Shattered, I sat there in a daze. I knew the knowledge of what had been done to me would eat my father alive, but I didn't know how to combat that darkness.

My phone started vibrating in my hand and I just stared down at the screen, seeing my mother's name and unable to think of what to do.

Standing on unsteady feet, I dropped my cell on the low table as if it had burned me. I couldn't talk to her then. I didn't want to talk to anyone. I just wanted Gideon.

I stumbled down the hallway, my shoulder sliding along the wall. I heard Gideon's voice as I neared his office and my tears came faster, my steps quickening.

"I appreciate that you thought of me, but no," he said in a low, firm voice that was different from the one I'd heard him using before. It was gentler, more intimate. "Of course we're friends. You know why . . . I can't give you what you want from me."

I rounded the corner into his office and saw him at his desk, his head down as he listened.

"Stop," he said icily. "This isn't the tack you want to take with me, Corinne."

"Gideon," I whispered, my hand gripping the doorjamb with white-knuckled force.

He glanced up, then straightened abruptly, surging to his feet. The scowl on his face fled.

"I have to go," he said, pulling the earpiece from his ear and dropping it on the desk as he rounded it. "What's wrong? Are you sick?"

He caught me as I rushed into him, needing him. Relief flooded me as he pulled me close and held me tight.

"My dad found out." I pressed my face to his chest, my mind filled with echoes of my father's pain. "He knows."

Gideon swung me up in his arms, cradling me. His phone started ringing. Cursing under his breath, he walked out of the room.

In the hallway, I could hear my phone rattling on the coffee table. The irritating sound of two phones going off simultaneously ratcheted up my anxiety.

"Let me know if you need to get that," he said.

"It's my mom. I'm sure my dad's called her already, and he's so angry. God . . . Gideon. He's devastated."

"I understand how he feels."

He carried me into the guest bedroom and kicked the door closed behind him. Laying me on the bed, he grabbed the remote off the nightstand and turned on the television, lowering the volume to a level that drowned out all other sound but my hiccupping sobs. Then he lay down beside me and hugged me, his hands rubbing up and down my back. I cried until my eyes felt raw and I had nothing left.

"Tell me what to do," he said when I quieted.

"He's coming here. To New York." My stomach knotted at the thought. "He's trying to fly out today, I think."

"When you find out, I'll go with you to pick him up."

"You can't."

"The hell I can't," he said without heat.

I offered my mouth and sighed when he kissed me. "I should really go alone. He's hurt. He won't want anyone else to see him that way."

Gideon nodded. "Take my car."

"Which one?"

"Your new neighbor's DB9."

"Huh?"

He shrugged. "You'll know it when you see it."

I didn't doubt that. Whatever it was, the car would be sleek, fast, and dangerous—just like its owner.

"I'm scared," I murmured, my legs tangling even tighter with his. He was so strong and solid. I wanted to hang on to him and never let go.

His fingers sifted through my hair. "Of what?"

"Things are already fucked up between my mom and me. If my parents have a falling-out, I don't want to get stuck in the middle. I know they wouldn't handle it well—especially my mom. They're crazy in love with each other."

"I hadn't realized that."

"You didn't see them together. Major sizzle," I explained, remembering that Gideon and I had been separated when I learned the sexual chemistry between my parents was still white-hot. "And my dad confessed to still being in love with her. Makes me sad to think about it."

"Because they're not together?"

"Yes, but not because I want one big happy family," I qualified. "I just hate the thought of going through life without the person you're in love with. When I lost you—"

"You've *never* lost me."

"It was like part of me died. Going through a whole lifetime like that . . ."

"Would be hell." Gideon ran his fingertips across my cheek and I saw the bleakness in his eyes, the lingering specter of Nathan haunting him. "Let me handle Monica."

I blinked at him. "How?"

His lips curled on one side. "I'll call her and ask how you're dealing with everything and how you're doing. Start the process of publicly working my way back to you."

"She knows I told you everything. She might break down on you."

"Better me than you."

That was almost enough to make me smile. "Thank you."

"I'll distract her and get her thinking about something else." He reached for my hand and touched my ring.

Wedding bells. He didn't say it, but I got the message. And of course that was what my mother would think. A man in Gideon's position didn't come back to a woman through her mother—especially one like Monica Stanton—unless his "intentions" were serious.

That was an issue we'd tackle another day.

For the next hour, Gideon pretended like he wasn't hovering. He stayed close, following me from room to room on some pretext or another. When my stomach growled, he tugged me immediately into the kitchen, pulling together a plate of sandwiches, potato chips, and prepared macaroni salad.

We ate at the island, and I let the comfort of his attentiveness soothe my nerves. As rough as things were, he was there for me to lean on. It made a lot of the troubles we were facing seem surmountable.

What *couldn't* we accomplish, as long as we stayed together?

"What did Corinne want?" I asked. "Besides you."

His features hardened. "I don't want to talk about Corinne."

There was an edge to his voice that niggled at me. "Is everything all right?"

"What did I just say?"

"Something lame that I'm choosing to ignore."

He made an exasperated noise, but relented. "She's upset."

"Screaming upset? Or crying upset?"

"Does it matter?"

"Yes. There's a difference between being mad at a guy and being a teary mess over him. For example: Deanna is mad and can plot your destruction; I was a teary mess and could barely crawl out of bed every day."

"God. Eva." He reached over and set his hand over mine. "I'm sorry."

"Cut it out with the apologies, already! You'll make it up to me having to deal with my mother. So is Corinne mad or teary?"

"She was crying." Gideon winced. "Christ. She lost it."

"I'm sorry you're dealing with that. Don't let her guilt-trip you, though."

"I used her," he said quietly, "to protect you."

I set my sandwich down and narrowed my gaze at him. "Did you or did you not tell her that all you could offer was friendship?"

"You know I did. But I also deliberately fostered the impression that we might be more, for the sake of the press and the police. I sent her mixed signals. *That's* what I feel guilty about."

"Well, stop. That bitch tried to make me think you'd banged her"—I wiggled two fingers—"*twice*. And the first time she did, it hurt so bad I'm still getting over it. Plus she's married, for fuck's sake. She's got no business making moves on my man when she's got her own."

"Back up to the part about banging her. What are you talking about?"

I explained the incidents—the lipstick-on-the-cuff disaster at the Crossfire and my impromptu visit to Corinne's apartment, when she'd tried to play it like she'd just got done screwing him.

"Well, that changes things considerably," he said. "There's nothing more she and I need to say to each other."

"Thank you."

He reached over to tuck my hair behind my ear. "We'll eventually be on the other side of all this."

"Whatever will we do with ourselves then?" I muttered.

"Oh, I'm sure I can think of something."

"Sex, right?" I shook my head. "I've created a monster."

"Don't forget work—together."

"Oh my God. You don't quit."

He crunched on a chip and swallowed. "I want you to see the revamped Crossroads and Cross Industries websites when we're done with lunch."

I wiped my mouth with a napkin. "Really? That was fast. I'm impressed."

"Let's have you look at them first before you decide that."

GIDEON knew me well. Work was my escape and he put me to it. He set me up with his laptop in the living room, made my phone stop ringing, then went into his office to call my mother.

For the first few minutes after he'd left me alone, I listened to the low murmur of his voice and tried to focus on the websites he'd pulled up for me, but it was no use. I was too scattered to pay attention. I ended up calling Cary instead.

"Where the fuck are you?" he barked by way of greeting.

"I know it's been crazy," I said quickly, having no doubt my mother and father would've been calling the apartment Cary and I shared when I didn't answer my smartphone. "I'm sorry."

The background noise on Cary's end told me he was somewhere out on the streets.

"Mind telling me what's going on? Everyone's calling me—your parents, Stanton, Clancy. They're all looking for you and you're not answering your cell. I've been freaking out wondering what happened to you!"

Crap. I closed my eyes. "My dad found out about Nathan."

He was silent, the sounds of distant traffic and honking the only indication he was still on the line. Then, "Holy shit. Oh, baby girl. That's bad."

The compassion in his voice made my throat too tight to speak. I didn't want to cry any more.

The background noise suddenly muted, as if he'd stepped into someplace quiet. "How is he?" Cary asked.

"He's torn up. God, Cary, it was *awful*. I think he was crying. And he's furious with Mom. That's probably why she's calling so much."

"What's he going to do?"

"He's flying out to New York. I don't know when, but he said he'd be calling when he landed."

"He's flying out *now*? Like today?"

"I think so," I said miserably. "I'm not sure how he's managing to get time off work again so soon."

"I'll fix up the guest room when I get home, if you haven't done it already."

"I'll take care of it. Where are you?"

"Catching lunch and a matinee with Tatiana. I had to get out for a while."

"I'm so sorry you've been fielding my calls."

"Not a big deal," he dismissed, in his usual Cary way. "I was more worried than anything. You haven't been around much lately. I don't know what you're doing or *who* you're doing. You're not acting like yourself."

The note of accusation in his tone deepened my remorse, but there was nothing I could share. "I'm sorry."

He waited, as if for an explanation, then said something under his breath. "I'll be home in a couple hours."

"All right. See you then."

I hung up, then called my stepfather.

"Eva."

"Hi, Richard." I dug right in. "Did my dad call Mom?"

"Just a moment." There was silence on the phone for a minute or two, then I heard a door shut. "He did call, yes. It was . . . unpleasant for your mother. This weekend has been very hard on her. She's not well, and I'm concerned."

"This is hard on all of us," I said. "I wanted to let you know that my dad is coming back to New York and I'll need to spend some quiet time with him."

"You need to talk to Victor about being a little more understanding of what your mother went through. She was on her own, with a traumatized child."

"You need to understand that we've got to give him time to come to grips with this," I shot back. My tone was harsher than I intended, but reflective of my feelings. I was not going to be forced to take sides between my parents. "And I need you to deal with Mom and get her to stop calling me and Cary nonstop. Talk to Dr. Petersen if you have to," I suggested, referring to my mother's therapist.

"Monica's on the phone now. I'll discuss it with her when she's free."

"Don't just discuss it. Do something about it. Hide the phones somewhere if that's what it takes."

"That's extreme. And unnecessary."

"Not if she doesn't quit!" My fingers drummed on the coffee table. "You and me, we're both guilty of tiptoeing around Mom—*Oh no, don't upset Monica!*—because we'd rather just give in than deal with her meltdowns. But that's emotional extortion, Richard, and I'm done paying out."

He was silent, then, "You're under a lot of strain right now. And—"

"You think?" In my head I was screaming. "Tell Mom I love her and I'll call when I can. Which won't be today."

"Clancy and I are available if you need anything," he said stiffly.

"Thank you, Richard. I appreciate that."

I hung up and fought the urge to throw the phone at the wall.

I'D managed to calm down enough to go over the Crossroads website before Gideon reappeared from his office. He looked wiped and a bit dazed, which was to be expected, considering. Dealing with my mom when she was upset was a challenge for anyone, and Gideon didn't have much experience to fall back on.

"I warned you," I said.

He lifted his arms over his head and stretched. "She'll be all right. I think she's tougher than she lets on."

"She was stoked to hear from you, wasn't she?"

He smirked.

I rolled my eyes. "She thinks I need a rich man to take care of me and keep me safe."

"You've got one."

"I'm going to assume you meant that in a noncaveman way." I stood. "I have to head out and get ready for my dad's visit. I'll need to be home at night for however long he's here, and it's probably not wise for you to sneak into my apartment. If he mistakes you for a burglar, it won't be pretty."

"It's also disrespectful. I'll use the time to be seen at the penthouse."

"So we've got a plan." I stood and scrubbed at my face before admiring my new watch. "At least I've got a lovely way to count the minutes until we're together again."

He came to me, catching me by the nape. His thumb drew tantalizing circles on the back of my neck. "I need to know you're okay."

I nodded. "I'm tired of Nathan running my life. I'm working toward that fresh start."

I imagined a future in which my mom wasn't a stalker, my dad was back on solid footing, Cary was happy, Corinne was in another country far away, and Gideon and I weren't ruled by our pasts.

And I was finally ready to fight for it.

11

MONDAY MORNING. TIME to go to work. I hadn't heard from my dad, so I got ready to head in. I was digging in my closet when a knock came on my bedroom door.

"Come in," I yelled.

A minute later, I heard Cary shout back, "Where the hell are you?"

"In here."

His shadow darkened the doorway. "Any word from your dad?"

I glanced at him. "Not yet. I sent him a text and didn't get a reply."

"So he's still on the plane."

"Or he missed a connection. Who knows?" I scowled at my clothes.

"Here." He came in and stepped around me, pulling a pair of gray linen palazzo pants off the bottom rack and a black lace cap-sleeved shirt.

"Thank you." And because he was close, I hugged him.

His returning hug was so tight it squeezed the air out of me. Startled by his exuberance, I held him for a long while, my cheek over his heart. For the first time in a few days, he was dressed in jeans and a T-shirt, and as usual, he managed to look striking and expensive.

"Everything okay?" I asked him.

"I miss you, baby girl," he murmured into my hair.

"Just trying to make sure you don't get sick of me." I tried to sound like I was teasing, but his tone niggled at me. It lacked all the vivacity I was so used to hearing in it. "I'm taking a cab to work, so I've got some time. Why don't we have a cup of coffee?"

"Yeah." He pulled back and smiled at me, looking boyishly beautiful.

Taking my hand, he led me out of the closet. I tossed my clothes on an armchair before we headed out to the kitchen.

"Are you going out?" I asked.

"I've got a shoot today."

"Well, that's good news!" I headed to the coffeemaker while he went to pull half-and-half out of the fridge. "Sounds like another occasion to dig into the case of Cristal."

"No way," he scoffed. "Not with everything that's going on with your dad."

"What else are we going to do? Sit around staring at each other? There's nothing more that can be done. Nathan is dead and even if he weren't, what he did to me is long over." I pushed a steaming mug over to him and filled another. "I'm ready to shove his memory in a cold, dark hole and forget about him."

"Over for you." He lightened my coffee and slid it back. "It's still news to your dad. He'll want to talk about it."

"I am *not* talking about it with my dad. I'm not talking about it *ever*."

"He might not go along with that."

I turned and faced him, leaning back into the counter with my mug cradled between my hands. "All he needs is to see me doing okay. This isn't about him. It's about me, and I'm surviving. Pretty well, I think."

He stirred his coffee, a thoughtful look on his face.

"Yeah, you are," he said after a few seconds. "Are you going to tell him about your mystery man?"

"He's not a mystery. I just can't talk about him, and that has nothing to do with our friendship. I trust you and love you and rely on you like always."

His green eyes challenged me over the rim of his mug. "Doesn't seem like it."

"You're my best friend. When I'm old and gray, you'll still be my best friend. Not talking about the guy I'm seeing isn't going to change that."

"How am I not supposed to feel like you don't trust me? What's the big deal with this guy that you can't even give me a name or anything?"

I sighed and told him a partial truth. "I don't know his name."

Cary stilled, staring. "You're shitting me."

"I never asked him what it is." As evasive answers went, it begged to be challenged. Cary gave me a long look.

"And I'm not supposed to be worried?"

"Nope. I'm comfortable with the whole thing. We're both getting what we need and he cares about me."

He studied me. "What do you call him when you're coming? You've got to be shouting something if he's any good at it. Which I assume he is, since you obviously aren't getting to know each other by talking."

"Uh . . ." That tripped me up. "I think I just say, 'Oh, God!'"

Throwing his head back, he laughed.

"How are you holding up with juggling two relationships?" I asked.

"I'm good." He shoved one hand in his pocket and rocked back on his heels. "I think Tat and Trey are as close to monogamy as I've ever been. It's working out for me so far."

I found the whole arrangement fascinating. "Ever worry about shouting out the wrong name when you're coming?"

His green eyes sparkled. "Nope. I just call 'em all *baby*."

152 · SYLVIA DAY

"Cary." I shook my head. He was incorrigible. "Are you going to introduce Tatiana to Trey?"

He shrugged. "I don't think that's the best idea."

"No?"

"Tatiana's a bitch on a good day, and Trey's just a nice guy. Not a great combo, in my book."

"You once told me you didn't like Tatiana very much. Has that changed?"

"She is who she is," he said dismissively. "I can live with it."

I stared at him.

"She needs me, Eva," he said quietly. "Trey wants me, and I think he loves me, but he doesn't need me."

That I understood. It was nice to be needed sometimes. "Gotcha."

"Who says there's only one person in the world who can give us everything?" He snorted. "I'm not sure I'm buying that. Look at you and your no-name guy."

"Maybe a mix-and-match situation can work for people who don't get jealous. It wouldn't work for me."

"Yeah." He held out his mug and I tapped it with my own.

"So Cristal and . . . ?"

"Hmm . . ." His lips pursed. "Tapas?"

I blinked. "You want to take my dad out?"

"Bad idea?"

"It's a great idea, if we can get him to go along with it." I smiled. "You rock, Cary."

He winked at me and I felt a little more settled.

Everything in my life seemed to be shaken up, most especially my relationships with the people I loved most. That was hard for me to deal with, because I relied on them to keep me on an even keel. But maybe when everything settled down, I'd be a bit stronger. Able to stand a bit straighter on my own.

It would be worth all the turmoil and pain if so.

"Want me to fix your hair?" Cary asked.

I nodded. "Please."

WHEN I got to work, I was disappointed to find a very unhappy Megumi. She gave me a lethargic wave as she buzzed me in, then dropped back into her chair.

"Girl, you need to kick Michael to the curb," I said. "This is *not* working out for you."

"I know." She brushed back the long bangs of her asymmetrical bob. "I'm going to break it off the next time I see him. I haven't heard from him since Friday, and I'm driving myself crazy wondering if he picked up anyone while doing his bachelor barhopping thing."

"Eww."

"I know, right? It's just not cool worrying about if the guy you're sleeping with is shagging someone else."

I couldn't help but be reminded of my earlier conversation with Cary. "Me and Ben and Jerry's are only a phone call away. Holler if you need us."

"Is that your secret?" She gave a short laugh. "What flavor got you over Gideon Cross?"

"I'm not over him," I admitted.

She nodded sagely. "I knew that. But you had fun on Saturday, right? And he's an idiot, by the way. One day, he's going to figure that out and come crawling back."

"He called my mom over the weekend," I said, leaning over the desk and lowering my voice. "Asking about me."

"Whoa." Megumi leaned forward, too. "What did he say?"

"I don't know the details."

"Would you get back together with him?"

I shrugged. "I can't say. Depends on how well he grovels."

"Totally." She high-fived me. "Your hair looks great, by the way."

I thanked her and headed to my cubicle, mentally preparing my request to take off from work if my dad called. I'd barely turned the corner at the end of the hall when Mark bounded out of his office with a huge grin.

"Oh my God." I stopped midstep. "You look insanely happy. Let me guess. You're engaged!"

"I am!"

"Yay!" I dropped my purse and bag on the floor and clapped. "I'm so excited for you! Congratulations."

Bending down, he picked up my stuff. "Come into my office."

He gestured me in ahead of him, then closed the glass door behind us.

"Was it tough?" I asked him, taking a seat in front of his desk.

"Toughest thing I've ever done." Mark handed me my bags. Sinking into his chair, he rocked back and forth. "And Steven let me stew over it. Can you believe that? He knew all along I was going to propose. Said he could tell by how I freaked out I was."

I grinned. "He knows you well."

"And he waited a minute or two before he answered me. And let me tell you, it seemed like hours."

"I bet. So was all of his anti-marriage talk a front?"

He nodded, still grinning. "His pride took a hit when I put him off before, so he wanted a little payback. Said he'd always known I'd come around eventually. Wanted to make me work for it when I finally did."

It sounded like Steven, who was playful and gregarious. "So where did you pop the question?"

He laughed. "I couldn't do it somewhere with atmosphere, right? Like the candlelit restaurant or the nice dark bar after the show. No, I had to wait until the limo dropped us off at home at the end of the night and we were standing outside our brownstone and I knew I was going to lose my chance. So I just blurted it out right there on the street."

"I think that's really romantic."

"I think *you're* a romantic," he shot back.

"Who cares about wine and roses? Anyone can do that. Showing somebody you can't live without them? *That's* romance."

"As usual, you make a good point."

I blew on my nails and buffed them on my shirt. "What can I say?"

"I'll let Steven give you all the details at lunch on Wednesday. He's told the story so many times already, he's got the delivery down pat."

"I can't wait to see him." As excited as Mark was, I was sure Steven was bouncing off the walls. The big, muscled contractor had a personality as vibrant as his bright red hair. "I'm so thrilled for you both."

"He's going to rope you into helping Shawna with the planning, you know that, right?" He sat up and set his elbows on the table. "Besides his sister, he's recruiting every woman we know. I'm sure the whole thing will be over-the-top craziness all the way."

"Sounds fun!"

"You say that now," he warned, his dark eyes laughing. "Let's grab some coffee and get this week started, shall we?"

I stood. "Um, I hate to ask this, but my dad is making an emergency trip into the city this week. I'm not sure when he'll be coming in. It could be today. I'll need to pick him up and get him settled when he arrives."

"Do you need to take some time off?"

"Just to get him situated in my apartment. A few hours at most."

Mark nodded. "You said 'emergency trip.' Is everything all right?"

"It will be."

"Okay. I don't have a problem with you taking time when you need it."

"Thank you."

As I dropped my stuff off at my desk, I thought—for the millionth time—how much I loved my job and my boss. I understood how much Gideon wanted to keep me close and I appreciated the vision of us building something together, but my work nurtured me as an individual. I didn't want to give that up, and I didn't want to end up resenting him if he kept pushing me to do so. I'd have to come up with an argument Gideon would accept.

I started working on it as Mark and I headed to the break room.

ALTHOUGH Megumi hadn't yet kissed Michael good-bye, I took her out to lunch at a nearby deli with delicious wraps and a decent selection of Ben & Jerry cups. I chose Chunky Monkey, she went with Cherry Garcia, and we both enjoyed the cool treat in the middle of the hot day.

We sat at a small metal table in the back, the remnants of our lunch on a tray between us. The deli wasn't as crazed during the noon hour as some of the other restaurants and full-service eateries in the area were, which suited us both fine. We could hold a conversation without raising our voices.

"Mark's floating," she said, licking her spoon. She wore a lime green dress that went really well with her dark hair and pale skin. Megumi always dressed in bold colors and styles. I envied her ability to pull them off so well.

"I know." I smiled. "It's so cool to see someone that happy."

"Guilt-free happiness. Unlike this ice cream."

"What's a little guilt every now and then?"

"A fat ass?"

I groaned. "Thanks for the reminder that I have to hit the gym today. I haven't worked out in days."

Unless one counted mattress gymnastics . . .

"How do you stay motivated?" she asked me. "I know I should go, but I can always find an excuse not to."

"And you keep that amazing figure anyway?" I shook my head. "You make me sick."

Her lips quirked. "Where do you work out?"

"I alternate between a regular gym and a Krav Maga studio in Brooklyn."

"Do you go after work or before?"

"After. I am *not* a morning person," I said. "Sleep is my friend."

"Would you mind if I tag along sometime? I don't know about that Krav what-a, but the gym. Where do you go?"

I swallowed a bit of chocolate and was about to reply when I heard a phone ringing.

"Are you going to get that?" Megumi asked, which alerted me to the fact that the phone was mine.

The burner phone, which was why I didn't recognize it.

I dug it out quickly and answered with a breathless "Hello?"

"Angel."

For a second, I savored the rasp of Gideon's voice. "Hey. What's up?"

"My attorneys just notified me that the police might have a suspect."

"What?" My heart stopped. My stomach began to revolt against lunch. "Oh my God."

"It's not me."

I don't remember getting back to the office. When Megumi asked me for the name of my gym, she had to ask twice. The fear I felt was like nothing I'd ever suffered before. It was so much worse when you felt it on behalf of someone you loved.

How could the police possibly suspect someone else?

I had the horrible feeling they were just trying to shake Gideon up. Shake me up.

If that was the goal, it was working. At least on me. Gideon had sounded calm and collected during our brief conversation. He'd told me not to get upset, that he just wanted to warn me that the police might come by with more questions. Or they might not.

Jesus. I walked slowly back to my desk, my nerves shot. I felt like I'd gulped down an entire pot of coffee. My hands were trembling and my heart was beating too fast.

I sat down at my desk and tried to get back to work, but I couldn't concentrate. I stared at my monitor and didn't see anything.

What if the police did have a suspect who wasn't Gideon? What would we do? We couldn't let an innocent person go to prison.

And yet there was a tiny voice in my head whispering that Gideon would be safe from prosecution if someone else were convicted of the crime.

The moment the thought entered my mind, I felt sick over it. My gaze went to the photo of my dad. He was in his uniform, looking dashingly handsome standing next to his patrol car.

I was so confused, so frightened.

When my smartphone started vibrating on my desk, I jumped. Dad's name and number flashed on the screen. I answered quickly. "Hey! Where are you?"

"Cincinnati. I'm switching planes."

"Hang on, let me write down your flight info." I snagged a pen and jotted down the details he gave me. "I'll be waiting for you when you land. I can't wait to see you."

"Yeah . . . Eva. Sweetheart." He sighed heavily. "I'll see you soon."

He hung up, and the subsequent silence was deafening. I knew then that the strongest emotion he was feeling was guilt. It colored his voice and made my chest ache.

Standing, I made my way over to Mark's office. "I just heard from my dad. His flight lands at LaGuardia in a couple hours."

He looked at me, then frowned, his gaze searching. "So go home, get ready, and pick him up."

"Thanks." That one word would have to do. Mark seemed to understand that I didn't want to stick around and talk.

I used the burner phone to send a text while I took a cab ride home: Heading to the apt. Leaving in 1 hour to get dad. Can u talk?

I needed to know what Gideon was thinking . . . how he was feeling. I was a wreck and I didn't know what to do about it.

When I got home, I changed into a simple, lightweight summer dress and sandals. I answered a text from Martin, agreeing that it was great we'd hung out Saturday night and that we should do it again. I double-checked the kitchen, making sure all of my dad's favorite foods that I'd stocked up on were exactly where I'd put them. I checked the guest room again, even though I'd gone over it the day before. I got online and checked my dad's flight.

Done. I had enough time left over to drive myself crazy.

I did a search for "Corinne Giroux and husband" on Google, looking specifically at images.

What I discovered was that Jean-François Giroux was a really good-looking guy. Hot, actually. Not as hot as Gideon, but then who was? Gideon was in a league by himself, but Jean-François was a head-turner in his own right, with dark wavy hair and eyes the color of pale jade. He was tan and had a goatee, which *really* worked for him. He and Corinne made a stunning couple.

My burner phone rang and I lunged to my feet in a rush, stumbling around the coffee table to get to it. I snatched it out of my purse and answered, "Hello?"

"I'm next door," Gideon said. "I don't have a lot of time."

"I'm coming."

I grabbed my purse and left my place. One of my neighbors was just unlocking her door, so I offered a polite, distant smile and pretended to wait for the elevator. The moment I heard her go inside her apartment, I darted over to Gideon's door. It opened before I could use my key.

The Gideon who greeted me was in jeans and T-shirt, with a ball cap on his head. He caught my hand and pulled me inside, tugging the hat off before lowering his mouth to mine. His kiss was surprisingly sweet, his firm lips soft and warm.

I dropped my purse and wrapped my arms around him, snuggling into him. The feel of his strength eased my anxiety enough to allow me to take a deep breath.

"Hi," he murmured.

"You didn't have to come home." I could only imagine how doing so had disrupted his day. Changing clothes, making the trip back and forth . . .

"Yes, I did. You need me." His hands slid up my back, and then he pulled away just enough to look down into my face. "Don't worry about this, Eva. I'll take care of it."

"How?"

His blue eyes were cool, his expression one of confidence. "Right now, I'm waiting on more information. Who are they looking at? Why are they looking at him? Chances are very good that it won't pan out. You know that."

I search his face. "What if they do?"

"Will I let someone else pay for my crime?" His jaw tightened. "Is that what you're asking?"

"No." I smoothed his brow with my fingertips. "I know you won't let that happen. I'm just wondering how you'll prevent it."

His scowl deepened. "You're asking me to predict the future, Eva. I can't do that. You just have to trust me."

"I do," I promised fervently. "But I'm still scared. I can't help being freaked out."

"I know. I'm worried, too." His thumb brushed over my bottom lip. "Detective Graves is a very intelligent woman."

His observation clicked with me. "You're right. That makes me feel better."

I didn't know Shelley Graves, not really. But in the few interactions I'd had with her, she'd struck me as being intelligent *and* street-smart. I hadn't factored her into the equation, and I should have. It was odd to be in a position where I both feared who she was and appreciated it.

"You set up for your dad?"

The reminder brought some of the jitters back. "Everything's ready. Except me."

His eyes softened. "Any idea how you're going to handle him?"

"Cary went back to work today, so we'll celebrate with champagne and then head out to dinner."

"You think he's going to be up for that?"

"I don't know if *I'm* up for it," I admitted. "It's screwy to be making plans to drink Cristal and kick up my heels in the middle of everything going on. But what else can I do? If my dad doesn't see I'm okay, he's not going to get over finding out about Nathan. I have to show him all of that ugliness is in the past."

"And you need to let me handle the rest," he admonished. "I *will* take care of you, of *us*. Focus on your family for a while."

Stepping back, I grabbed his hand and led him toward the couch. It was weird being home so early after going in to work. Seeing the brightness of the afternoon sun beating down on the city outside the windows had me feeling out of step, reinforcing the notion that we'd stolen time to be together.

I sat, curled my legs, and faced him, watching as he settled beside me. We were so alike in many ways, including our pasts. Did Gideon need to get everything out in the open with his family, too? Is that what he'd need to fully heal?

"I know you have to get back to work," I said, "but I'm glad you came home for me. You're right—I needed to see you."

He lifted my hand to his lips. "Do you know when your father's heading back to California?"

"No."

"My appointment with Dr. Petersen would've made tomorrow a late night for us anyway." Gideon looked at me with a slight smile. "We'll find a way to be together."

Having him near . . . touching him . . . seeing him smile . . . hearing those words. I could get through anything as long as I had him next to me after a long day.

"Can I have five minutes?" I asked.

"You can have whatever you want, angel," he said softly.

"Just this." I slid closer and curved into his side.

Gideon's arm came around my shoulders. Our hands linked together in our laps. We formed a perfect circle. Not as glittering as the rings we wore on our fingers, but priceless all the same.

After a moment, I felt him lean into me. He sighed. "I needed this, too."

I hugged him tighter. "It's okay to need me, ace."

"I wish I needed you a little less. Just enough to make it bearable."

"What would be the fun in that?"

His soft laugh made me fall even harder for him.

GIDEON had been right about the DB9. As I watched the parking attendant pull the sleek metallic gray Aston Martin to a stop in front of me, I thought it was pretty much Gideon on wheels. It was sex with a gas pedal; so much brute elegance it damn near made my toes curl.

I was scared as hell to get behind the wheel.

Driving in New York was *nothing* like driving in Southern California. I hesitated before accepting the keys from the bow-tied attendant, debating the wisdom of just calling for a town car.

The burner phone started ringing and I fumbled for it quickly. "Hello?"

"Just do it," Gideon purred. "Stop worrying and drive it."

I spun around, my gaze searching for security cameras. Awareness shivered down my spine. I could *feel* Gideon's gaze on me. "What are you doing?"

"Wishing I were with you. I'd love to spread you across the hood and fuck you real slow. Push my cock deep inside you. Give those shocks a workout. Umm. God, I'm hard."

And he was making me wet. I could listen to him endlessly; I loved his voice so much. "I'm scared I'm going to screw up your pretty car."

"I don't give a shit about the car, only about your safety. So scratch it up all you want, just don't get hurt."

"If that was supposed to calm me down, it didn't work."

"We could have phone sex until you come, that should do it."

I narrowed my gaze at the parking attendants, who were pretending not to watch me. "Should I be worried about what got you so horny in the short time since I was with you?"

"Thinking about you driving the DB9 turns me on."

"Does it now?" I fought to hold back a smile. "Remind me, which one of us has the transportation fetish?"

"Slide behind the wheel," he coaxed. "Imagine I'm in the passenger seat. My hand between your legs. My fingers fucking your soft, slick cunt."

Stepping closer to the car on shaky legs, I muttered, "You must have a death wish."

"I'd take my cock out and stroke it with my fist while I fingered you, get us both good and hot."

"Your lack of respect for this vehicle's upholstery is appalling." I settled into the driver's seat and spent a minute figuring out how to move it forward.

His voice rasped through the car's sound system. "How does it feel?"

It totally figured that he'd synced my burner phone to the car's Bluetooth. Gideon always thought of everything.

"Expensive," I answered. "You're crazy for letting me drive this."

"I'm crazy about *you*," he replied, sending delight skipping through me. "LaGuardia is programmed in the GPS."

It made me feel good to know that coming home to see me had lightened his mood so much. I knew just how he felt. It meant a lot to know he felt the same way.

I pulled up the GPS, then hit the button to put the transmission into drive. "You know what, ace? I want to blow you while you're driving this thing. Throw a pillow across this center console here and suck your cock for *miles*."

"I'm going to take you up on that. Tell me how she feels."

"Smooth. Powerful." I waved at the attendants as I eased out of the subterranean parking garage. "Very responsive."

"Just like you," he murmured. "Of course, you're my favorite ride."

"Aw, that's sweet, baby. And you're my favorite joystick." I merged carefully into traffic.

He laughed. "I better be your only joystick."

"But I'm not your only ride," I pointed out, loving him so much in that moment because I knew he was looking out for me, making sure I was comfortable. Back in California, driving had been like breathing to me, but I hadn't been behind the wheel of a car since I moved to New York.

"You're the only one I enjoy naked," he said.

"That's real lucky for you, because I'm very possessive."

"I know." His voice was filled with masculine satisfaction.

"Where are you?"

"At work."

"Multitasking, I'm sure." I stepped on the gas and prayed as I cut across lanes. "What's a little calming distraction for your girlfriend in the midst of world entertainment domination?"

"I'd stop the world from spinning for you."

That silly line oddly touched me. "I love you."

"Liked that one, did you?"

I grinned, startled and pleased by his ridiculous sense of humor.

I was hyperaware of my surroundings. There were signs in every direction prohibiting everything. Driving in Manhattan was a fast trip to nowhere. "Hey, I can't turn left or right. I think I'm heading for the Midtown Tunnel. I could lose you."

"You'll never lose me, angel," he vowed. "Wherever you go, however far, I'll be right here with you."

WHEN I spotted my dad outside the baggage claim area, I lost all the confidence Gideon had instilled in me since I'd left work. Dad looked drawn and haggard, his eyes reddened and his jaw shadowed by stubble.

I felt the sting of tears as I walked toward him, but I blinked them back, determined to reassure him. Holding my arms open, I watched him drop his carry-on and then all the air left my lungs as he hugged me tightly.

"Hi, Daddy," I said, with a tremor in my voice I hoped he missed.

"Eva." His lips pressed hard to my temple.

"You look tired. When's the last time you slept?"

"On the leg out of San Diego." He pulled back and looked at me with gray eyes that were the same as mine. He searched my face.

"Do you have more luggage?"

He shook his head, still studying me.

"Are you hungry?" I asked.

"I grabbed something in Cincinnati." Finally, he backed up and retrieved his bag. "But if you're hungry . . . ?"

"Nope. I'm good. But I was thinking we could take Cary out for dinner later, if you're up for it. He went back to work today."

"Sure." He paused with his bag in his hand, looking a bit lost and unsure.

"Dad, I'm okay."

"*I'm* not. I want to hurt something and there's nothing for me to hit."

That gave me an idea.

Grabbing his hand, I started leading him out of the airport. "Hold that thought."

12

"HE'S REALLY MAKING Derek work for it," Parker noted, wiping the light sheen of sweat off his shaved head with a hand towel.

I turned to watch, seeing my father wrestling with the instructor who was twice his size, and my dad wasn't a small guy. Standing over six feet tall and weighing in at two hundred pounds of solid, rippling muscle, Victor Reyes was a formidable opponent. Plus, he'd told me he was going to check out Krav Maga himself after I'd shared my interest in it, and it seemed he had—he had some of the moves down pat. "Thanks for letting him jump in."

Parker looked at me, his dark eyes steady and calm in that way he had. He'd been teaching me more than just how to defend myself. He had also taught me to focus on the steps to be taken, not the fear.

"Usually I'd say class isn't the place to bring your anger," he said, "but Derek needed the challenge."

Although he didn't ask it, I could feel the unspoken question in the air. I decided it was best to answer it, since Parker was doing me a favor by letting my dad monopolize his co-instructor. "He just found out that someone hurt me a long time ago. Now it's too late to do anything about it and he's having a hard time with that."

He reached down and grabbed the bottle of water sitting just off the side of the training mat. After a minute, he said, "I have a daughter. I can imagine how that feels."

When he looked at me before taking a drink, I saw the understanding in his thickly lashed dark eyes and I was reassured that I'd brought my dad to the right place.

Parker was easygoing and had a great smile, and was genuine in a way that I'd rarely come across. But he had an air about him that warned people to tread carefully. One knew right away that it would be stupid to try to pull anything over on him. His street smarts were as obvious as his tribal tattoos.

"So you bring him here," he said, "let him work it out and let him see you taking care of your own protection. Good idea."

"I don't know what else to do," I confessed. Parker's studio was located in a revitalizing area of Brooklyn. It was a converted warehouse, and the exposed brick and giant sliding loading-bay doors added to the atmosphere of tough chic. It was a place where I felt confident and take-charge.

"I've got some ideas." He grinned and jerked his chin toward the mat. "Let's show him what you can do."

I dropped my towel over my water bottle and nodded. "Let's."

I didn't see any of the uniformed parking attendants as we pulled into the underground garage of my apartment building. Since I wanted to do the honors myself anyway, that worked for me. I slid the DB9 into an empty slot and cut the engine. "Fabulous. Right by the elevator."

"So I see," my dad said. "Is this your car?"

I'd been waiting for that question. "No. A neighbor's."

"Friendly neighbor," he said dryly.

"A cup of sugar. An Aston Martin. It's all the same, right?" I glanced at him with a smile.

He looked so tired and worn, and not from the workout. The weariness came from the inside, and it was killing me.

Turning the car off, I released my seat belt and turned to look at him. "Dad. I . . . It's shredding me to see you torn up over this. I can't stand it."

Heaving out his breath, he said, "I just need some time."

"I never wanted you to find out." I reached out and gripped his hand. "But I'll be glad you did, if we can put Nathan behind us for good."

"I read the reports—"

"God. Daddy . . ." I swallowed back a rush of bile. "I don't want that stuff in your head."

"I knew there was something wrong." He stared at me with such sorrow and pain in his eyes it hurt to look into them. "The way Cary went to sit beside you when Detective Graves said Nathan Barker's name . . . I knew you weren't telling me something. I kept hoping you would."

"I've tried very hard to put Nathan in my past. You were one of the few things in my life he hadn't infected. I wanted to keep it that way."

His grip on my hand tightened. "Tell me the truth. Are you okay?"

"Dad. I'm the same daughter you came to see a couple weeks ago. The same daughter who hung out with you in San Diego. I'm *okay*."

"You were pregnant—" His voice broke and a tear slid down his cheek.

I brushed it away, ignoring my own. "And I will be again someday. Maybe more than once. Maybe you'll be crawling with grandkids."

"Come here."

Leaning across the console, he hugged me. We sat in the car for a long time, crying. Getting it out.

Was Gideon watching the security feeds, sending me silent support? It gave me comfort to think he might be.

DINNER out that night wasn't quite as boisterous a meal as usual for Cary, my dad, and me, but it wasn't as grim as I'd feared it might be. The food was great, the wine better, and Cary was snarking out.

"She was worse than Tatiana," he said, talking about the model he'd shared the shoot with that day. "She kept going on about her 'good side,' which I personally thought was her ass as it walked out the door."

"You've done shoots with Tatiana?" I asked, then explained to my dad, "She's a girl Cary's seeing."

"Oh, yeah." Cary licked red wine off his lower lip. "We work together a lot, actually. I'm the Tatiana Tamer. She starts one of her fits and I calm her down."

"How do— Never mind," I said quickly. "I don't want to know how."

"You already know." He winked.

I looked at my dad and rolled my eyes.

"How about you, Victor?" Cary asked around a bite of sautéed mushroom. "You seeing anyone?"

My dad shrugged. "Nothing serious."

That was by his choice. I'd seen how women acted around him—they fell all over themselves trying to get his attention. My dad was hot, with an amazing body, gorgeous face, and Latin sensuality. He had his pick of women and I knew he wasn't a saint, but he never seemed to meet anyone who really got to him. I'd recently realized that was because my mother had gotten there first.

"You think you'll ever have more kids?" Cary asked him, surprising me with the question.

I'd long ago become resigned to being an only child.

My dad shook his head. "Not that I'm opposed to the idea, but Eva is more than I ever thought I'd have in my life." He looked at me with so much love it made my throat tight. "And she's perfect. Everything I could ever hope for. I'm not sure there's room in my heart for anyone else."

"Aw, Daddy." I leaned my head into his shoulder, so glad he was with me, even if it was for the worst possible reason.

When we got back to the apartment, we decided to watch a movie before calling it a night. I went to my room to change and was stoked to find a gorgeous bouquet of white roses on my dresser. The card, written in Gideon's distinctive bold penmanship, made me almost giddy.

I'M THINKING OF YOU, AS ALWAYS.
AND I'M HERE.
YOURS, G.

I sat on the bed, hugging the card, certain he was thinking of me that very moment. It was also starting to sink in that he'd been thinking of me every moment of the weeks we'd been apart, too.

That night, I fell asleep on the couch after watching *Dredd*. I woke briefly to the feeling of being lifted and carried to my room, smiling sleepily as my dad tucked me into bed like a child and kissed my forehead.

"Love you, Daddy," I murmured.

"Love you, too, sweetheart."

I woke up before my alarm the next morning and felt better than I had in a long while. I left a note on the breakfast bar telling my dad to call me if he wanted to get together for lunch. I wasn't sure if he had anything planned for the day. I knew Cary had a shoot in the afternoon.

During the cab ride to work, I answered a text from Shawna squeeing over her brother's engagement to Mark. So happy for all of u, I texted back.

I'm drafting u! she shot back.

I smiled down at my phone. What's that? Signal's breaking up . . . Can't read u . . .

As the cab stopped in front of the Crossfire, the sight of the Bentley at the curb gave me the usual thrill. When I hopped out, I peeked into the front seat and waved when I saw Angus sitting inside.

He stepped out, setting his chauffeur hat on his head. Like Clancy, you couldn't tell he was carrying a sidearm by looking at him; he wore it so comfortably.

"Good morning, Miss Tramell," he greeted me. Although he wasn't a young man and his red hair was liberally threaded with silver, I'd never had any doubts about Angus's ability to protect Gideon.

"Hi, Angus. It's good to see you."

"You're looking lovely today."

I glanced down at my pale yellow dress. I'd chosen it because it was bright and cheery, which was the impression I wanted my dad to have of me. "Thank you. I hope your day rocks." I backed up toward the revolving door. "See you later!"

His pale blue eyes were kind as he tipped his hat to me.

When I got upstairs, I found Megumi looking more like her usual self. Her smile was wide and real, and her eyes had the sparkle I enjoyed seeing every morning.

I stopped by her desk. "How are you?"

"Good. Michael's meeting me for lunch and I'm ending it. Nice and civilized."

"That's a killer outfit you've got on," I told her, admiring the emerald green dress she wore. It was fitted and had leather piping that gave it just the right amount of edge.

She stood and showed off her knee-high boots.

"Very Kalinda Sharma," I said. "He's going to be scrambling to hold on to you."

"As if," she scoffed. "These boots were made for walking. He didn't call me back until last night, which made it nearly four days without contact. Not totally unreasonable, but I'm ready to find a guy who's crazy about me. A guy who thinks about me as much as I'm thinking about him and hates it when we can't be together."

I nodded, thinking about Gideon. "It's worth it to hold out for one. Do you want me to give you a bailout phone call during your lunch?"

She grinned. "Nah. But thank you."

"All right. Let me know if you change your mind."

I headed back to my desk and dug right in to work, determined to get ahead to make up for leaving early the day before. Mark was fired up, too, segueing from work only long enough to tell me that Steven had a binder full of wedding ideas he'd been collecting for years.

"Why am I not surprised?" I said.

"I shouldn't be." Mark's mouth curved with affection. "He's kept it in his office all this time so I wouldn't know about it."

"Did you get a look at it?"

"He went through the whole thing with me. It took *hours*."

"You're going to have the wedding of the century," I teased.

"Yeah." The word held more than a little exasperation, but his expression remained so happy I couldn't stop smiling.

My dad called just before eleven.

"Hey, sweetheart," he said, in reply to my usual work greeting. "How's your day going?"

"Great." I leaned back in my chair and looked at the picture of him. "How'd you sleep?"

"Hard. I'm still trying to wake up."

"Why? Go back to bed and be lazy."

"I wanted to let you know that I'm going to take a rain check on lunch. We'll get together tomorrow. Today, I need to talk to your mom."

"Oh." I knew that tone. It was the same one he used when he pulled people over, that perfect mixture of authority and disapproval. "Listen. I'm not going to step in the middle of this with you two. You're both adults and I'm not picking sides. But I have to say that Mom wanted to tell you."

"She should have."

"She was alone," I pressed on, my feet tapping restlessly on the carpet, "going through a divorce and the trial against Nathan, and dealing with my recovery. I'm sure she desperately wanted a shoulder to lean on—you know how she is. But she was drowning in guilt. I could've gotten her to agree to anything then, and I did."

He was quiet on the other end of the line.

"I just want you to keep that in mind when you talk to her," I finished.

"All right. When will you be home?"

"A little after five. Want to go to the gym? Or back to Parker's studio?"

"Let me see how I'm feeling when you get in," he said.

"Okay." I forced myself to ignore how anxious I was over the upcoming conversation between my parents. "Call me if you need anything."

We hung up and I got back to work, grateful for the distraction.

When lunch rolled around, I decided to grab something quick and bring it back to my desk to work through the hour. I braved the midday sauna outside to hit the local Duane Reade for a bag of beef jerky and a bottled health drink. I'd skipped my workouts pretty frequently since Gideon and I had gotten back together, and I figured it was time to pay a penalty for that.

I was debating the wisdom of sending Gideon an "I'm thinking of you" note when I twirled through the revolving front door of the Crossfire. Just a little something to say thanks for the flowers, which had made a tough day more bearable.

Then I saw the woman I'd prefer never to see again—Corinne Giroux. And she was talking to my man, with her palm resting intimately against his chest.

They stood off to the side, sheltered by a column outside the stream of traffic heading in and out of the security turnstiles. Corinne's long black hair fell nearly to her waist, a glossy curtain that stood out even against her classic black dress. Both she and Gideon were in profile so I couldn't see her eyes, but I knew they were a gorgeous aquamarine hue. She was a beautiful woman and together, they made a stunning couple. Especially right then, with both of them dressed in black, the only spot of color being Gideon's blue tie. My favorite one.

Abruptly, Gideon's head turned and found me, as if he'd felt me watching him. The instant our gazes met, I felt that soul-deep recognition pierce through me, that primitive awareness I'd only ever felt with him. Elementally, something inside me knew he was *mine*. Had known it from the moment I first laid eyes on him.

And some other woman had her hands on him.

My brows rose in a silent *WTF?* At that moment, Corinne followed his gaze. She didn't look happy to see me paused in the middle of the massive lobby, staring at them.

She was lucky I didn't go up to her and yank her away from him by her hair.

Then she cupped his jaw, urged his attention back to her, and lifted onto her tiptoes to press a kiss against his hard mouth, and I really considered doing it. Even took a step toward them.

Gideon's head jerked back just before she accomplished her goal, his hands catching her by the arms and thrusting her away.

Reining in my temper, I exhaled my irritation and left him to it. I can't say I didn't feel jealous, because of course I did—Corinne could be with him publicly and I couldn't. But I didn't have the sick fear in my gut I'd felt before, the horrible insecurity that told me I was going to lose the man I loved more than anything.

It was weird not to feel that panic. There was still a little voice in my head cautioning me against being too confident, telling me it'd be better to be afraid, to guard myself from getting hurt. But for once, I was able to ignore it. After all Gideon and I had been through, all that we were still going through, all he'd done for me . . . it was harder to disbelieve than to believe.

Despite everything, we were stronger than we'd ever been.

I hopped on an elevator and headed up to work, my thoughts drifting to my parents. I was choosing to take it as a good sign that neither my mother nor Stanton had called to bitch about my dad. I crossed my fingers and hoped that when I got home we could all put Nathan behind us for good. I was so ready for that. Beyond ready to move on to the next phase of my life, whatever that might be.

The elevator car slowed to a stop on the tenth floor and the doors opened to the high-pitched whirring sound of power tools and the rhythmic banging of hammers. Directly ahead of the elevator, plastic sheeting hung from the ceiling. I hadn't realized any part of the Crossfire was under construction, and I peered around the people in front of me, trying to get a look.

"Anyone getting out?" the guy nearest the door asked, looking over his shoulder.

I straightened and shook my head, even though he hadn't been talking to me personally. No one else moved. We waited for the doors to close and shut out the construction noise.

But they didn't move, either.

When the guy began hitting the elevator buttons to no avail, I realized what was going on.

Gideon.

Smiling to myself, I said, "Excuse me, please."

The occupants of the car shifted to let me out and another guy stepped out with me. The doors closed behind us and the car continued on.

"What the hell?" the guy said, scowling as he turned and surveyed the other three elevators. He was a little taller than me, but not much, and wore dress slacks with a short-sleeved shirt and tie.

The ding announcing the arrival of another car was nearly drowned out by the construction noise. When the doors to that elevator opened, Gideon stepped out, looking suave and dashing and irritated.

I wanted to jump him, he looked so hot. Plus, I'll admit it totally turned me on when he went all alpha male on me.

I'd stop the world from spinning for you. Sometimes, it felt like he did.

Grumbling under his breath, the short-sleeved guy walked into Gideon's vacated elevator and left us.

Gideon's hand went to his hips, his jacket parting to reveal the sleekness of his suit. All three pieces were black with a subtle sheen that was unmistakably costly. His dress shirt was black and his cuff links were a familiar gold and onyx.

He was dressed as he'd been that very first day I'd met him. At the time, I'd wanted to climb up his scrumptious body and screw him senseless.

All these weeks later, that hadn't changed.

"Eva," he began in that toe-curlingly sexy voice of his. "It's not what you think. Corinne came by because I'm not taking her calls—"

I held up my hand to cut him off and glanced at his gift, my beautiful watch, on my other wrist. "I've got thirty minutes. I'd rather fuck you than talk about your ex, if you don't mind."

He stood silent and unmoving for a long minute, staring at me, trying to gauge my mood. I watched his brain and body switch gears, adjusting from aggravation to awareness. His gaze narrowed, his eyes darkened. A flush came to his cheekbones and his lips parted on a sharp breath. His weight shifted as his blood heated and his cock thickened, his sexuality stirring like a panther stretching after a lazy nap.

I could almost feel the sexual current crackle between us, sparking to life. I responded to it as I'd been trained to do, softening and quickening, my core clenching gently. Begging for him. The commotion around us only made me hornier, adding urgency to the beat of my heart.

Gideon reached into an inner pocket of his jacket and withdrew his phone. He speed-dialed, then lifted the phone to his ear, his eyes locked with mine. "I'm running thirty minutes late. If that won't work for Anderson, reschedule."

He hung up, casually dropping his phone back in his pocket.

"I'm so hot for you right now," I told him, my voice husky with want.

Reaching down, he adjusted himself, then approached me, his eyes smoldering. "Come on."

He set his hand at the small of my back in that way I loved so much, the pressure and warmth hitting a spot that sent tingles of anticipation through me. I looked up at him over my shoulder and saw the slight smile on his mouth, proof that he knew what that innocent touch was doing to me.

We pushed through plastic sheeting, leaving the bank of elevators behind us. In front of us was sunlight and cement and hanging sheeting everywhere I looked. Through the plastic I could see the watery, foggy shadows of workers. I heard music that was nearly drowned out by the din, and men shouting to each other.

Gideon led me through the plastic, knowing his way. His silence was spurring me on, the weight of expectation growing with every step we took. We reached a door and he opened it, urging me into a room that would be someone's corner office.

The city was spread out before me, the view of the modern urban jungle dotted with buildings that wore their history proudly. Steam billowed into the cloudless blue sky at irregular intervals, and the cars seemed to flow along the streets like tributaries.

I heard the door lock behind me and I turned to face Gideon, catching him shrugging out of his jacket. There was furniture in the room. A desk and chairs, and a seating area positioned in the corner. All of it was draped in tarps, the space still unfinished.

With methodical deliberation, he removed his vest, tie, and shirt. I watched him, obsessed with the masculine perfection of him. "We could be interrupted," he said. "Or overheard."

"Would that bother you?"

"Only if it bothers you." He approached me with his fly open and the waistband of his boxer briefs clearly visible in the gap.

"You're provoking me. You'd never risk us being interrupted."

"Not that I'd stop. I can't think of anything capable of stopping me once I'm inside you." He took my purse from my hand and dropped it into one of the chairs. "You've got too many clothes on."

Wrapping his arms around me, Gideon lowered the zipper at my back with practiced ease, his lips whispering across mine. "I'll try not to get you too messy."

"I like messy." I stepped out of my dress and was about to unhook my bra when he tossed me over his shoulder.

I squealed in surprise, smacking his taut ass with both of my hands. He spanked me hard enough to sting, then threw my dress aside so perfectly it landed directly across his jacket. He was walking across the room when his hand reached up and tugged my panties down below the curve of my butt.

He caught the edge of the tarp draped over the couch and threw it back, then sat me down, crouching in front of me. As he pulled my underwear past my strappy heels, he asked, "Everything okay, angel?"

"Yeah." I smiled and touched his cheek, knowing that question encompassed everything from my parents to my job. He always checked to see where my head was at before he took over my body. "Everything's good."

Gideon pulled my hips to the very edge of the sofa with my legs on either side of him, exposing my cleft to his gaze. "So tell me what's got this pretty cunt so greedy today."

"You."

"Excellent answer."

I pushed at his shoulder. "You're wearing the suit you wore when I met you. I wanted to fuck you so bad then, but I couldn't do anything about it. Now I can."

He pressed my thighs wide with gentle hands, his thumb stroking over my clit. My sex quivered as pleasure pulsed through me.

"And now *I* can," he murmured, his dark head lowering.

I grasped desperately at the cushion beneath me, my stomach tightening as his tongue licked leisurely through my slit. He rimmed the trembling opening to my sex, teasing me before his tongue sank into me. I arched violently, my back bowing while he tormented the tender flesh.

"Let me tell you how I imagined you that day," he purred, circling my clit with the tip of his tongue, his hands holding me down when I would've bucked into the caress. "Spread beneath me on black satin sheets, your hair fanned all around you, your eyes wild and hot from the feel of my cock pounding into your tight, silky cunt."

"God. Gideon," I moaned, seduced by the sight of him savoring me so intimately. It was a fantasy come true—the dark and dangerous sex god in the breathtaking suit, servicing me with that sculpted mouth made for driving women wild.

"I imagined your wrists pinned down by my hands," he went on roughly, "me forcing you to take it over and over. Your hard little nipples swollen from my mouth. Your lips red and wet from sucking my cock. The room filled with those sexy sounds you make . . . those helpless whimpers when you can't stop coming."

I whimpered then, biting my lip as he fluttered over my clit with the wicked lash of his tongue. I hooked one leg over his bare shoulder, the heat of his skin scorching the sensitive flesh at the back of my knee. "I want what you want."

His grin flashed. "I know."

He sucked me, drawing on the tight bundle of nerves. I climaxed with a breathless cry, my legs shaking with the rush of release.

I was still quivering with pleasure when he urged me back lengthwise on the couch, his big body looming over me, his cock thrusting upward from where he'd shoved his briefs down just enough to free it. I reached for him, wanting to feel him in my hands, but he caught my wrists and pinned my arms.

"I like you like this," he said darkly. "Held prisoner for my lust."

Gideon's eyes were intent on my face, his lips glistening from my climax, his chest heaving. I was mesmerized by the difference between the virile male about to take me like an animal and the civilized businessman who'd inspired my searing lust to begin with.

"I love you," I told him, panting as the broad head of his cock slid heavily through my swollen cleft. He pushed against me, parting the slick opening.

"Angel." With a groan, he buried his face in my throat and surged inside me, the thick length of his rigid penis tunneling deep. Gasping my name, he ground his hips against me, trying to get deeper, shoving and circling, screwing. "Christ, I need you."

The desperation in his voice took me by surprise. I wanted to touch him, but he held me down, his hips working restlessly. The feel of him inside me, so hot, the wide crest rubbing and massaging, was driving me out of my mind. I screwed him back, unable to stop, the two of us straining together.

His lips brushed against my temple. "When I saw you standing in the lobby just now, in your pretty yellow dress, you looked so bright and beautiful. So perfect."

My throat tightened. "Gideon."

"The sun was shining behind you, and I thought you couldn't possibly be real."

I struggled to get my hands free. "Let me touch you."

"I came after you because I couldn't stay away and when I found you, you wanted me." He held both my wrists in one hand and cupped my butt in the other, lifting me as he pulled out, then thrust deep.

I moaned, rippling around him, my sex sucking ravenously at his thickness. "Oh God, it's so good. You feel so good . . ."

"I want to come all over you, come inside you. I want you on your knees and on your back. And *you want me this way.*"

"I need you this way."

"I push inside you and I can't take it." His mouth lowered to mine, sucking erotically. "I need you so much."

"Gideon. Let me touch you."

"I've captured an angel." His kiss was wild and wet, passionate. His lips slanted over mine, his tongue fucking deep and fast. "And I put my greedy hands all over you. I defile you. And you love it."

"I love *you.*"

He stroked into me and I writhed, my thighs grasping his pumping hips. "Fuck me. Oh, Gideon. Fuck me hard."

Digging his knees in, he gave me what I begged for, powering into me. His cock plunged into me over and over, his groans and fevered words of lust gusting against my ear.

My core tightened, my clit throbbing with every impact of his pelvis against mine. His heavy sac smacked against the curve of my buttocks and the couch thumped against the bare concrete, inching forward as Gideon pounded into me, every muscle in his body flexing on his downstrokes.

The obscene sounds of furious sex drowned out the awareness of the workers only yards away. The race to climax drove us both, our bodies the outlet for the violence of our emotions.

"I'm going to come in your mouth," he growled, sweat sliding down his temple.

Just the thought of him finishing that way set me off. My sex spasmed in climax, clutching and grabbing at his driving cock, the endless pulses of orgasm radiating outward to my fingers and toes. And still he didn't stop, his hips circling and lunging, expertly pleasuring me until I sagged limp beneath him.

"Eva. *Now*." He reared back and I followed, scrambling to my knees and sliding my mouth down his glistening erection.

At the first hint of suction, he was coming, spilling over my tongue in powerful bursts. I swallowed repeatedly, drinking him down, relishing the gruff sounds of satisfaction that rumbled from his chest.

His hands were in my hair, his head bowed over me, sweat glistening on his abs. My mouth slid up and down his cock, my cheeks hollowing on drawing pulls.

"Stop," he gasped, pulling me off. "You'll make me hard again."

He was still hard, but I didn't point that out.

Gideon cupped my face in his hands and kissed me, our flavors mingling. "Thank you."

"What are you thanking me for? You did all the work."

"There's no work involved in fucking you, angel." His slow smile was pure satiated male. "I'm grateful for the privilege."

I sank back onto my heels. "You're killing me. You can't be that gorgeous and sexy and say stuff like that. It's overload. It fries my brain. Sends me into a meltdown."

His smile widened and he kissed me again. "I know the feeling."

13

MAYBE IT WAS because I'd just gotten laid myself that I saw the signs on Megumi. Or maybe my sex radar, as Cary called it, wasn't on the fritz anymore. Whatever the reason, I knew my friend had slept with the guy she'd been planning on breaking up with and I could tell she wasn't happy about it.

"Is it on or off?" I asked leaning on the reception counter.

"Oh, I broke it off," she said glumly. "After I hit it with him again first. I figured it'd be liberating. Plus who knows how long my next dry spell will last."

"Are you second-guessing your decision to end it?"

"Not really. He just acted all hurt about it, like I'd used him for sex. Which I guess I did, but he's a no-strings-attached guy. I figured he wouldn't have a problem with a no-strings-attached nooner."

"So now your head's all fucked up." I gave her a sympathetic smile.

"Remember, this is the guy who hadn't called you since Friday. He got lunch with a beautiful girl and an orgasm, not a bad deal."

Her head canted to the side. "Yeah."

"Yeah."

Her mood visibly lifted. "Are you working out tonight, Eva?"

"I should, but my dad's in town and I'm playing it on his schedule. If we go, you're welcome to tag along, but I won't know until after work."

"I don't want to intrude."

"Is that an excuse I hear?"

Her grin was sheepish. "Maybe a little one."

"If you want, you can come home with me after work and meet him. If he wants to work out, you can borrow something of mine to wear. If not, we can come up with something else to do."

"I'd like that."

"Okay, then we're set." It would be good for both of us. It would give my dad another look at the normalcy in my life and it would keep Megumi from torturing herself over Michael. "We'll head out at five."

"You live here?" Megumi tipped her head back to look at my apartment building. "Nice."

Like the others on the tree-lined street, it had history and showed it off with the kinds of architectural detailing contemporary builders didn't use anymore. The building had been updated and now sheltered residents with a modern glass overhang above the entrance. The addition meshed surprisingly well with the façade.

"Come on," I said to her, smiling at Paul as he opened the door for us.

When we exited the elevator on my floor, I forced myself not to glance at Gideon's door. What would it be like to take a friend home to a place I shared with Gideon?

I wanted that. Wanted to build that with him.

I unlocked my apartment and took Megumi's purse when we stepped inside. "Make yourself at home. I'm just going to let my dad know we're here."

She stared wide-eyed at the open floor plan of the living room and kitchen. "This place is huge."

"We don't need all this room, really."

She grinned. "But who's going to complain?"

"Right."

I was turning toward the hallway leading to the guest room when my mom emerged from the hall leading to my bedroom and Cary's, which was on the opposite side of the living area. I came to a halt, startled to see her wearing my skirt and blouse. "Mom? What are you doing here?"

Her reddened eyes locked on a point somewhere around my waist, her skin pale enough to make her makeup look overdone. That was when I realized she was wearing my cosmetics, too. Although we'd been mistaken for sisters on occasion, my gray eyes and soft olive skin tone came from my dad and necessitated a different color palette than the pastels my mom used.

Queasiness spread through my stomach. "Mom?"

"I have to go." She wouldn't meet my gaze. "I hadn't realized it was so late."

"Why are you wearing my clothes?" I asked, even though I *knew*.

"I spilled something on my dress. I'll get these back to you." She rushed past me, coming to another abrupt stop when she saw Megumi.

I couldn't move; my feet felt rooted to the carpet. My hands fisted at my sides. I knew the walk of shame when I saw it. My chest tightened with anger and disappointment.

"Hi, Monica." Megumi came forward to give her a hug. "How are you?"

"Megumi. Hi." My mom clearly scrambled for more to say. "It's great to see you. I wish I could stay and hang out with you girls, but I really have to run."

"Is Clancy here?" I asked, not having paid attention to the other vehicles on the street when I'd arrived.

"No, I'll grab a cab." She still didn't look directly at me, even when she turned her head in my direction.

"Megumi, would you mind sharing a cab with my mom? I'm sorry to flake on you, but I'm suddenly not feeling well."

"Oh, sure." She searched my face and I could see her picking up on my change of mood. "No problem."

My mom looked at me then and I couldn't think of a thing to say to her. I was almost as disgusted by the look of guilt on her face as I was by the thought of her cheating on Stanton. If she was going to do it, she could at least own it.

My dad chose that moment to join us. He walked into the room dressed in jeans and a T-shirt, with bare feet and hair still damp from a shower.

As always, my luck was impeccably bad.

"Dad, this is my friend Megumi. Megumi, this is my dad, Victor Reyes."

As my dad walked to Megumi and shook her hand, my parents gave each other a wide berth. The precaution did nothing to stop the electricity arcing between them.

"I'd thought maybe we could hang out," I told him to fill the sudden awkward silence, "but now I'm not feeling up to it."

"I have to go," my mom said again, grabbing her purse. "Megumi, did you want to ride with me?"

"Yes, please." My friend hugged me good-bye. "I'll call you later and see how you're feeling."

"Thanks." I caught her hand and squeezed it before she pulled away.

The moment the door shut behind them, I headed to my room.

My dad came after me. "Eva, wait."

"I don't want to talk to you right now."

"Don't be childish about this."

"Excuse me?" I rounded on him. "My stepdad pays for this apartment. He wanted me to have a place with great security so I'd be safe from Nathan. Were you thinking about that when you were fucking his wife?"

"Watch your mouth. You're still my daughter."

"You're right. And you know what?" I backed up toward the hallway. "I've never been ashamed about that until now."

I lay on my bed and stared up the ceiling, wishing I could be with Gideon, but knowing he was in therapy with Dr. Petersen.

I texted Cary instead: I need u. Come home ASAP.

It was close to seven when the knock came on my bedroom door. "Baby girl? It's me. Let me in."

I rushed to open it and surged into him, hugging him tight. He picked me up so that my feet left the floor and carried me into the room, kicking the door shut behind him.

He dropped me on the bed and took a seat beside me, his arm around my shoulders. He smelled good, his cologne familiar. I leaned into him, grateful for his unconditional friendship.

After a few minutes, I told him. "My parents slept with each other."

"Yeah, I know."

I tilted my head back to look up at him.

He grimaced. "I heard 'em when I was heading out to the shoot this afternoon."

"Eww." My stomach churned.

"Yeah, doesn't work for me, either," he muttered. His fingers sifted through my hair. "Your dad's on the couch looking beat. Did you say something to him?"

"Unfortunately. I was mean, and now I'm feeling awful about it. I need to talk to him but it's weird, because the person I'm feeling most loyal to is Stanton. I don't even like the guy half the time."

"He's been good to you, and to your mom. And getting cheated on is never cool."

I groaned. "I'd be less freaked about it if they'd gone somewhere else. I mean, it'd still be wrong, but these are Stanton's digs. That makes it worse."

"It does," he agreed.

"How would you feel about moving?"

His brows rose. "Because your parents shagged here?"

"No." I stood and started pacing. "Security was the reason we got this place. It made sense to let Stanton help out when Nathan was a threat and safety was a priority, but now . . ." I looked at him. "It's all different now. It doesn't seem right anymore."

"Move where? Someplace else in New York we can afford on our own? Or out of New York altogether?"

"I don't want to leave New York," I assured him. "Your work is here. Mine, too."

And Gideon.

Cary shrugged. "Sure. Whatever. I'm game."

Walking over to where he still sat on my bed, I hugged him. "Would you mind ordering something in for dinner while I talk to my dad?"

"Got anything particular in mind?"

"Nope. Surprise me."

I joined my dad on the couch. He'd been surfing through my tablet but put it aside when I sat.

"I'm sorry about what I said earlier," I began. "I didn't mean it."

"Yeah, you did." He scrubbed wearily at the back of his neck. "And I don't blame you. I'm not proud of myself right now. And I have no excuse. I knew better. She knew better."

190 · SYLVIA DAY

Pulling my legs up, I sat facing him with my shoulder resting against the back of the sofa. "You guys have a lot of chemistry. I know what that's like."

He shot me an examining glance, his gray eyes stormy and serious. "You have that with Cross. I saw it when he came over for dinner. Are you going to try to work things out with him?"

"I'd like to. Would you have a problem with that?"

"Does he love you?"

"Yes." My mouth curved. "But more than that, I'm . . . necessary to him. There's nothing he wouldn't do for me."

"So why aren't you together?"

"Well . . . it's complicated."

"Isn't it always?" he said ruefully. "Listen. You should know . . . I've loved your mother since the moment I saw her. What happened today shouldn't have happened, but it meant something to me."

"I get it." I reached for his hand. "So what happens now?"

"I head home tomorrow. Try to get my head on straight."

"Cary and I were talking about coming out to San Diego the weekend after next. We thought we'd drop in and just hang out. See you and Dr. Travis."

"Did you talk to Travis about what happened to you?"

"Yes. You saved my life hooking me up with him," I said honestly. "I can't thank you enough for that. Mom had been sending me to all these stuffy shrinks and I just couldn't connect with any of them. I felt like a case study. Dr. Travis made me feel like I was normal. Plus I met Cary."

"Are you two done talking about me?" As if on cue, Cary walked into the room waving a take-out menu. "I know I'm fascinating, but you might want to save your jaws for the Thai food we've got coming. I ordered a ton of it."

꧁

ENTWINED WITH YOU · 191

My dad caught an eleven o'clock flight out of New York, so I had to leave it to Cary to see him off. We said our good-byes before I left for work, promising to make plans for the trip to San Diego the next time we talked.

I was in the back of a cab on the way to work when Brett called. For just a moment, I debated letting the call go to voice mail, and then I got over it and answered. "Hi, you."

"Hello, gorgeous." His voice rolled over my senses like warm chocolate. "Ready for tomorrow?"

"I will be. What time is the video launch? When do we need to be in Times Square?"

"We're supposed to arrive at six."

"Okay. I don't know what to wear."

"You'll look amazing no matter what you've got on."

"Let's hope. How's the tour going?"

"I'm having the time of my life." He laughed, and the husky, sexy sound brought back memories. "It's a helluva long way from Pete's."

"Ah, Pete's." I'd never forget that bar, although some of the nights I'd spent there were a bit hazy. "Are you excited about tomorrow?"

"Yeah, I get to see you. I can't wait."

"That's not what I meant, and you know it."

"I'm excited about the video launch, too." He laughed again. "I wish I could see you tonight, but I'm taking a red-eye into JFK. Plan on dinner tomorrow, though."

"Can Cary come? I invited him to the video launch already. You two know each other, so I figured you wouldn't mind. Too much, anyway."

He snorted. "You don't need a cockblocker, Eva. I can restrain myself."

The cab pulled over in front of the Crossfire and the driver stopped the meter. I pushed cash through the Plexiglas slot and slid out, leaving the door open for the guy rushing over to hop in. "I thought you liked Cary."

"I do, but not as much as I like having you to myself. How about we compromise and agree that Cary comes to the launch and you come to dinner alone?"

"All right." I figured it wouldn't hurt to make the situation easier for Gideon to deal with by picking a restaurant he owned. "How about I make the reservation?"

"Awesome."

"I've got to run. I'm just getting to work."

"Text me your address, so I know where to pick you up."

"Will do." I spun through the revolving door and headed toward the turnstiles. "We'll talk tomorrow."

"I'm looking forward to it. See you around five."

Tucking my phone away, I entered the nearest open elevator. When I got upstairs and was buzzed through the glass security doors, I was greeted by Megumi's phone thrust in my face.

"Can you believe this?" she asked.

I pulled back enough to bring the screen into focus. "Three missed calls from Michael."

"I *hate* guys like him," she complained. "Hot and cold and all over the place. They want you until they have you, then they want something else."

"So tell him that."

"Really?"

"Straight up. You could just avoid his calls, but that'll drive you crazy. Don't agree to meet with him, though. Having sex with him again would be bad."

"Right." Megumi nodded. "Sex is bad, even when it's really good."

Laughing, I headed back to my cubicle. I had other things to do besides referee someone else's love life. Mark was juggling several accounts at once, with three campaigns rolling into the final stages. Creatives were at work and mock-ups were slowly making their way across his desk. That was my favorite part—seeing all the strategizing come together.

By ten o'clock, Mark and I were deep into debating the various approaches to a divorce attorney's ad campaign. We were trying to find the right mix of sympathy for a difficult time in a person's life and the most prized qualities of a lawyer—the ability to be cunning and ruthless.

"I'm never going to need one of these," he said, somewhat out of the blue.

"No," I replied, once my brain caught up to the fact that he was talking about divorce attorneys. "You never will. I'm dying to congratulate Steven at lunch. I'm really so thrilled for you two."

Mark's grin exposed his slightly crooked teeth, which I thought were cute. "I've never been happier."

It was nearing eleven and we'd switched to a guitar manufacturer's campaign when my desk phone rang. I ran out to my cubicle to grab it and had my usual greeting cut off by a squeal.

"Oh my God, Eva! I just found out we're both going to be at that Six-Ninths thing tomorrow!"

"Ireland?"

"Who else?" Gideon's sister was so excited, she sounded younger than her seventeen years. "I *love* Six-Ninths. Brett Kline is so freakin' hot. So is Darrin Rumsfeld. He's the drummer. He's fine as hell."

I laughed. "Do you happen to like their music, too?"

"Pfft. That's a given. Listen"—her voice turned serious—"I think you should try talking to Gideon tomorrow. You know, just kinda walk by and say hi. If you open the door, he'll totally barge through it, I swear. He misses you like crazy."

Leaning back in my chair, I played along. "You think so?"

"It's so obvious."

"Really? How?"

"I don't know. Like how his voice changes when he talks about you. I can't explain it, but I'm telling you, he's dying to get you back. You're the one who told him to bring me along tomorrow, didn't you?"

"Not precisely—"

"Ha! I knew it. He always does what you tell him." She laughed. "Thanks, by the way."

"Thank him. I'm just looking forward to seeing you again."

Ireland was the one person in Gideon's family for whom he felt untarnished affection, although he tried hard not to show it. I thought maybe he was afraid to be disappointed or afraid he might ruin it somehow. I wasn't sure what the deal was, but Ireland hero-worshipped her brother and he'd kept his distance, even though he needed love terribly.

"Promise me you'll try to talk to him," she pressed. "You still love him, right?"

"More than ever," I said fervently.

She was quiet for a minute, then said, "He's changed since he met you."

"I think so. I've changed, too." I straightened when Mark stepped out of his office. "I have to get back to work, but we'll catch up tomorrow. And make plans for that girls' day we talked about."

"Sweet. Catch you later!"

I hung up, pleased that Gideon had followed through and made plans with Ireland. We were making progress, both together and on our own.

"Baby steps," I whispered. Then I got back to work.

AT noon, Mark and I headed out to meet Steven at a French bistro. Once we entered the restaurant, it was easy to spot Mark's partner, even with the size of the place and the number of diners.

Steven Ellison was a big guy—tall, broad shouldered, and heavily muscled. He owned his own construction business and preferred to be working the job sites with his crew. But it was his gloriously red hair that really drew the eye. His sister Shawna had the same hair—and the same fun-loving nature.

"Hey, you!" I greeted him with a kiss on the cheek, able to be more familiar with him than I was with my boss. "Congratulations."

"Thank you, darlin'. Mark is finally going to make an honest man out of me."

"It'd take more than marriage to do that," Mark shot back, pulling out my chair for me.

"When haven't I been honest with you?" Steven protested.

"Um, let's see." Mark got me settled in my seat, then took the one beside me. "How about when you swore marriage wasn't for you."

"Ah, I never said it wasn't for *me*." Steven winked at me, his blue eyes full of mischief. "Just that it wasn't for most people."

"He was really twisted up over asking you," I told him. "I felt bad for the guy."

"Yeah." Mark flipped through the menu. "She's my witness to your cruel and unusual punishment."

"Feel bad for me," Steven retorted. "I wooed him with wine, roses, and violin players. I spent days practicing my proposal. I still got shot down."

He rolled his eyes, but I could tell there was a wound there that hadn't quite healed. When Mark placed his hand over his partner's and squeezed, I knew I was right.

"So how'd he do it?" I asked, even though Mark had told me.

The waitress, asking if we wanted water, interrupted us. We held her back a minute and ordered our food, too, and then Steven started relaying their anniversary night out.

"He was sweating like mad," he went on. "Wiping at his face every other minute."

"It's summer," Mark muttered.

"And restaurants and theaters are climate controlled," Steven shot back. "We went through the whole night with him like that and finally headed home. I got to thinking he wasn't going to do it. That the night was gonna end and he still wasn't going to get the damn words out. And there I am wondering if I'll have to ask him again, just to get it over with. And if he says no again—"

196 · SYLVIA DAY

"I didn't say no the first time," Mark interjected.

"—I'm going to deck him. Just knock his ass out, toss him on a plane, and head to Vegas, because I'm not getting any younger here."

"Definitely not mellowing with age, either," Mark grumbled.

Steven gave him a look. "So we're climbing out of the limo, and I'm trying to remember that fan-fucking-tastic proposal I came up with before, and he grabs my elbow and blurts out, 'Steve, damn it. You *have* to marry me.'"

I laughed, leaning back as the waitress put my side salad in front of me. "Just like that."

"Just like that," Steven said, with an emphatic nod.

"Very heartfelt." I gave Mark a thumbs-up. "You rocked it."

"See?" Mark said. "I got it done."

"Are you writing your own vows?" I asked. "Because that'll be really interesting."

Steven guffawed, snagging the attention of everyone nearby.

I swallowed the cherry tomato I was munching on and said, "You know I'm dying to see your wedding binder, right?"

"Well, it just so happens . . ."

"You didn't." Mark shook his head as Steven reached down and pulled a bulging binder out of a messenger bag on the floor by his chair.

It was so packed that papers were sticking out of the top, bottom, and side.

"Wait 'til you see this cake I found." Steven pushed the breadbasket aside to make room to open the binder.

I bit back a grin when I saw the dividers and table of contents.

"We are *not* having a wedding cake in the shape of a skyscraper with cranes and billboards," Mark said firmly.

"Really?" I asked, intrigued. "Let me see."

WHEN I got home that night, I dropped my purse and bag off in their usual place, kicked off my shoes, and went straight to the couch. I sprawled across it, staring up the ceiling. Megumi was going to meet me at CrossTrainer at six thirty, so I didn't have a lot of time, but I felt like I just needed a breather. Starting my period the afternoon before had me riding the edge of irritation and grumpiness, with a dash of exhaustion tossed in for shits and giggles.

I sighed, knowing I was going to have to deal with my mom at some point. We had a ton of crap to work through, and putting it off was starting to bug me. I wished it were as easy to work things out with her as it was with my dad, but that wasn't an excuse to avoid addressing our issues. She was my mother and I loved her. It was hard on me when we weren't getting along.

Then my thoughts drifted to Corinne. I guess I should have figured that a woman who would leave her husband and move from Paris to New York for a man wasn't going to give up on him easily, but still. She had to know Gideon well enough to realize hounding him wasn't going to work.

And Brett . . . what was I going to do about him?

The intercom buzzed. Frowning, I pushed to my feet and headed over to it. Had Megumi misunderstood and thought we were meeting here? Not that I minded, but . . .

"Yes?"

"Hi, Eva," the guy at the front desk said cheerfully. "NYPD detectives Michna and Graves are here."

Crap. Everything else lost significance in that moment. Fear spread through me with crawling fingers of ice.

I wanted a lawyer with me. Too much was on the line.

But I didn't want to seem like I had anything to hide.

I had to swallow twice before I could answer. "Thanks. Can you send them up, please?"

14

My heart was pounding as I hurried to my purse and silenced the burner phone, tucking it into a zippered pocket. I turned around, looking for anything that might be out of place, anything I should hide. There were the flowers in my bedroom and the card.

Unless the detectives had a warrant, though, they could only take note of what was in plain sight.

I ran to shut my door, then went ahead and shut Cary's, too. I was breathing hard when the doorbell rang. I had to force myself to slow down and walk calmly to the living room. When I reached the front door, I took a deep, calming breath before opening it.

"Hello, detectives."

Graves, a rail-thin woman with a severe face and foxlike blue eyes, was in the lead. Her partner, Michna, was the quieter of the two, an older man with receding gray hair and a paunch. They had a rhythm between the two of them—Graves was the heavy who kept the subjects occupied and off-balance. Michna was obviously good at fading into the background while his cop's eyes cataloged everything and missed nothing. Their success rate had to be pretty high.

"Can we come in, Miss Tramell?" Graves asked in a tone that made the question a demand. She'd tied her curly brown hair back and wore a jacket to cover her holstered gun. There was a satchel in her hand.

"Sure." I pulled the door open wider. "Can I get you anything? Coffee? Water?"

"Water would be great," Michna said.

I led them to the kitchen and pulled bottled water out of the fridge. The detectives waited at the breakfast bar—Graves with her eyes pinned to me while Michna scoped out his surroundings.

"You just get home from work?" he asked.

I figured they knew the answer, but replied anyway. "A few minutes ago. Would you like to sit in the living room?"

"Here's good," Graves said in her no-nonsense way, putting the worn leather satchel on the counter. "We'd just like to ask you a few questions, if you don't mind. And show you some photos."

I stilled. Could I bear to see any of the photos Nathan had taken of me? For a wild moment, I thought they might be pictures taken at the death scene or even autopsy shots. But I knew that was highly unlikely. "What's this about?"

"Some new information has come to light that could be related to Nathan Barker's death," Michna said. "We're pursuing all leads, and you may be able to help."

I took a deep, shaky breath. "I'm happy to try, of course. But I don't see how I can."

"Are you familiar with Andrei Yedemsky?" Graves asked.

I frowned at her. "No. Who's that?"

She dug in her bag and pulled out a sheaf of eight-by-ten photos, setting them down in front of me. "This man. Have you seen him before?"

Reaching out with shaking fingers, I pulled the top photo toward me. It was of a man in a trench coat, talking to another man about to climb into the back of a waiting town car. He was attractive, with extremely blond hair and tanned skin. "No. He's not someone you'd forget meeting, either." I looked up at her. "Should I know him?"

"He had pictures of you in his home. Candid shots of you on the street, coming and going. Barker had the same photos."

"I don't understand. How did he get them?"

"Presumably from Barker," Michna said.

"Is that what this Yedemsky guy said? Why would Nathan give him pictures of me?"

"Yedemsky didn't say anything," Graves said. "He's dead. Murdered."

I felt a headache coming on. "I don't understand. I don't know anything about this man, and I have no idea why he'd know anything about me."

"Andrei Yedemsky is a known member of the Russian mob," Michna explained. "In addition to smuggling alcohol and assault weapons, they've also been suspected of trafficking women. It's possible Barker was making arrangements to sell or trade you for that purpose."

I backed away from the counter, shaking my head, unable to process what they were saying. Nathan stalking me was something I could believe. He'd hated me on sight, hated that his father had remarried instead of mourning his mother forever. He'd hated me for getting him locked up in psychiatric treatment, and my being awarded the five-million-dollar settlement he thought of as his inheritance. But the Russian mob? Sex trafficking? I couldn't comprehend that at all.

Graves flipped through the photos until she came to one of a platinum sapphire bracelet. An L-square ruler framed it—unmistakably a forensics shot. "Do you recognize this?"

"Yes. That belonged to Nathan's mother. He had it altered to fit him. He never went anywhere without it."

"Yedemsky was wearing it when he died," she said without inflection. "Possibly as a souvenir."

"Of what?"

"Of Barker's murder."

I stared at Graves, who knew better. "You're suggesting Yedemsky could be responsible for Nathan's death? Then who killed Yedemsky?"

She held my gaze, understanding the motivation behind my question. "He was taken out by his own people."

"You're sure about that?" I needed to know that *they* knew Gideon wasn't involved. Yes, he'd killed for me—to protect me—but he'd never kill just to avoid going to jail.

Michna frowned at my query. It was Graves who replied. "There's no doubt. We have the hit on surveillance footage. One of his associates didn't take too kindly to Yedemsky sleeping with his underage daughter."

Hope surged, followed by chilling fear. "So what happens now? What does this mean?"

"Do you know anyone who has connections to the Russian mob?" Michna asked.

"God, no," I said vehemently. "That's . . . another world. I'm having trouble believing Nathan had any connections. But then it's been years since I knew him . . ."

I rubbed at the tightness in my chest and looked at Graves. "I want to put this behind me. I want him to stop ruining my life. Is that ever going to happen? Is he going to haunt me even after he's dead?"

She quickly and efficiently collected the photos, her face impassive. "We've done all we can. Where you go from here is up to you."

I showed up at CrossTrainer at quarter after six. I went because I'd told Megumi I would and I'd already flaked on her once. I also felt a tremendous restlessness, an urge to move that I had to exhaust before it drove me insane. I'd sent a text to Gideon as soon as the detectives left, telling him I needed to see him later, but I hadn't heard back by the time I'd put my purse in a locker.

Like all things Gideon, CrossTrainer was impressive in both size and amenities. The three-story club—one of hundreds around the country—had everything a fitness enthusiast could want, as well as spa services and a smoothie bar.

Megumi was slightly overwhelmed and needed help with some of the high-tech machinery, so she was taking advantage of the trainer-supervised workout for new members and guests. I got on a treadmill. I started out at a brisk walk, warming up, and then eventually progressed to a run. Once I hit my stride, I let my thoughts run, too.

Was it possible that Gideon and I were free to pick up the pieces of our lives and move on? How? Why? My mind raced with questions that I needed to ask Gideon—with the hope that he was as clueless as I was. He couldn't be involved in Yedemsky's death. I wouldn't believe he was.

I ran until my thighs and calves burned, until sweat ran down my body in steady streams and my lungs ached with the effort of breathing.

It was Megumi who finally got me to stop, waving her hand in my line of sight as she moved in front of my treadmill. "I am so totally impressed right now. You're a machine."

I slowed my pace to a jog, then a walk, before stopping altogether. Grabbing my towel and water bottle, I stepped off, feeling the effects of pushing myself too long and hard.

"I hate running," I confessed, still panting. "How'd your workout go?"

Megumi looked chic even in gym clothes. Her chartreuse racerback tank had bright blue threading that matched her spandex leggings. The ensemble was summer-bright and stylish.

She bumped shoulders with me. "You make me feel like an underachiever. I just did a circuit and checked out the hot guys. The trainer I worked with was good, but I wish I'd gotten *that* guy instead."

I followed the point of her finger. "That's Daniel. Want to meet him?"

"Yes!"

I walked with her toward the mats in the center of the open space, waving at Daniel when he lifted his gaze and caught sight of us. Megumi quickly yanked out the rubber band holding her hair back, but I thought she'd looked great with it on, too. She had beautiful skin and I envied her mouth.

"Eva, great seeing you." Daniel extended his hand to me for a shake. "Who's this you have with you?"

"My friend Megumi. She just joined today."

"I saw you working with Tara." He flashed Megumi his megawatt smile. "I'm Daniel. If you ever need help with anything, just let me know."

"I'm going to take you up on that," she warned, as she shook his hand.

"Please do. Do you have any particular fitness goals?"

As they started talking more in-depth, my gaze wandered. I checked out the equipment, looking for something easy I could do while I waited for them to wrap it up. Instead I found a familiar sight.

Tossing my towel over my shoulder, I noticed my not-so-favorite reporter on the floor. I took a deep breath and walked over, watching her do curls with a ten-pound hand weight. Her dark brown hair was in a fishtail braid, her long legs on display in skintight shorts, and her stomach tight and flat. She looked great. "Hi, Deanna."

"I'd ask if you come here often," she replied, setting the weight back on the rack and standing, "but that's too clichéd. How are you, Eva?"

"I'm good. You?"

Her smile had the edge that never failed to get my back up. "Doesn't it bother you that Gideon Cross buries his sins under all his money?"

So Gideon had been right about Ian Hager disappearing once he'd gotten paid. "If I really thought you were after the truth, I'd give it to you."

"It's all true, Eva. I've talked to Corinne Giroux."

"Oh? How's her husband?"

Deanna laughed. "Gideon should hire you to manage his public image."

That struck uncomfortably close to home. "Why don't you just go to his office and chew him out? Let him have it. Throw a drink in his face or slap him."

"He wouldn't care. It wouldn't make a damn bit of difference to him."

I wiped at the sweat still sliding down my temples and admitted that might be true. I knew damn well Gideon could be a coldhearted ass. "Either way, you'd probably feel a whole lot better."

Deanna snatched her towel off the bench. "I know exactly what'll make me feel better. Enjoy the rest of your workout, Eva. I'm sure we'll be talking again soon."

She sauntered off and I couldn't shake the feeling that she was on to something. It made me twitchy not knowing what it was.

"Okay, I'm done," Megumi said, joining me. "Who was that?"

"No one important." My stomach chose that moment to growl, loudly announcing that I'd burned off the boeuf bourguignon I'd had for lunch.

"Working out always makes me hungry, too. You want to grab dinner?"

"Sure." We set off toward the showers, skirting equipment and other members. "I'll call Cary and see if he wants to join us."

"Oh, yes." She licked her lips. "Have I told you I think he's delicious?"

"More than once." I waved bye to Daniel before we left the floor.

We reached the locker room and Megumi tossed her towel in the discard bin just inside the entrance. I paused before dropping mine, my thumb rubbing over the embroidered CrossTrainer logo. I thought of the towels hanging in Gideon's bathroom.

Maybe next time I'd be calling him, too, asking him to join friends and me for dinner.

Maybe the worst was over.

WE found an Indian restaurant near the gym and Cary showed up for dinner with Trey, the two of them walking in with their hands linked together. Our table was right in front of the street-level window by the entrance, which lent the pulse of the city to our dining experience.

We sat on cushions on the floor, drank a little too much wine, and let Cary run commentary on the people passing by. I could almost see little hearts in Trey's eyes when he looked at my best friend, and I was happy to see Cary being openly affectionate in return. When Cary was really into someone, he held himself back from touching him or her. I deliberately chose to see his frequent, casual touching with Trey as a sign of the two men growing closer, rather than Cary losing interest.

Megumi got another call from Michael while we were eating, which she ignored. When Cary asked if she was playing hard to get, she told him the story.

"If he calls again, let me answer it," he said.

"Oh, God, no," I groaned.

"What?" Cary blinked innocently. "I can say she's too tied up to get to the phone and Trey can bark out sex commands in the background."

"Diabolical!" Megumi rubbed her hands together. "Michael's not the right guy for that, but I'm sure I'll take you up on that offer someday, knowing my luck with men."

Shaking my head, I dug stealthily into my purse for the burner phone and was bummed to see there was still no reply from Gideon.

Cary made a show of peering over the table. "You hoping for a booty call from loverman?"

"What?" Megumi's mouth fell open. "You're seeing someone and didn't tell me?"

I shot a narrow-eyed look at Cary. "It's complicated."

"It's the total opposite of complicated," Cary drawled, rocking back on his pillow. "It's straight-up lust."

"What about Cross?" she asked.

"Who?" Cary shot back.

Megumi persisted. "He wants her back."

It was Cary's turn to glare at me. "When did you talk to him?"

I shook my head. "He called Mom. And he didn't say he wanted me back."

Cary's smile was sly. "Would you ditch your new loverman for a repeat with Cross, the marathon man?"

Megumi poked me in the leg. "Gideon Cross is a marathon man in bed? Holy shit . . . And he looks like that. Jesus." She fanned herself with her hand.

"Can we *please* stop talking about my sex life?" I muttered, looking to Trey for a little support.

He jumped in. "Cary tells me you two are going to a video premiere tomorrow. I didn't realize music videos were a big thing anymore."

I grasped at the lifeline gratefully. "I know, right? Surprises me, too."

"And then there's good ol' Brett," Cary said, leaning across the table toward Megumi like he was about to impart a secret. "We'll call him backstage man. Or backseat man."

I stuck my fingers in my glass and flicked water at him.

"Why, Eva. You're making me wet."

"Keep it up," I warned," and you'll be soaked."

I still hadn't heard from Gideon by the time we got home at quarter to ten. Megumi had taken the subway back to her place, while Cary, Trey, and I shared a cab back to the apartment. The guys headed straight to

Cary's room, but I lingered in the kitchen, debating whether I should run next door and see if Gideon was there.

I was about to pull my keys out of my purse when Cary came into the kitchen, shirtless and barefoot.

He grabbed whipped cream out of the fridge but paused before he headed back out. "You okay?"

"Yep, I'm good."

"You talk to your mom yet?"

"No, but I'm planning on it."

He leaned his hip against the counter. "Anything else on your mind?"

I shooed him off. "Go have fun. I'm all right. We can talk tomorrow."

"About that. What time should I be ready?"

"Brett wants to pick us up at five, so can you meet me at the Crossfire?"

"No problem." He leaned over and pressed a kiss to the top of my head. "Sweet dreams, baby girl."

I waited until I heard Cary's door shut, then grabbed my keys and went next door. The moment I entered the dark and quiet apartment, I knew Gideon wasn't there, but I searched the rooms anyway. I couldn't shake the feeling that something was . . . off.

Where was he?

Deciding to call Angus, I walked back to my apartment, grabbed the burner phone, and took it into my bedroom.

And found Gideon gripped in a nightmare.

Startled, I shoved my door shut and locked it. He thrashed on my bed, his back arching with a hiss of pain. He was still dressed in jeans and a T-shirt, his big body stretched atop the comforter as if he'd fallen asleep waiting for me. His laptop had been knocked to the floor, still open, and papers were crackling under the violence of his movements.

I rushed to him, trying to figure out a way to wake him that wouldn't put me in danger, knowing he'd hate himself if he hurt me by accident.

He growled, a low feral sound of aggression. "Never," he bit out. "You'll *never* touch her again."

I froze.

His body jerked violently, and then he moaned and curled to his side, shuddering.

The sound of his pain galvanized me. I climbed onto the bed, my hand touching his shoulder. The next moment I was on my back, pinned as he loomed over me, his eyes fixed and sightless. Fear paralyzed me.

"You're going to know what it feels like," he whispered darkly, his hips ramming against mine in a sick imitation of the love we shared.

I turned my head and bit his biceps, my teeth barely denting the rigid muscle.

"Fuck!" He yanked away from me and I dislodged him as Parker had taught me to do, throwing him to the side and freeing myself to leap from the bed and run.

"Eva!"

Spinning, I faced him, my body poised to fight.

He slid from the bed, nearly landing on his knees before he found his balance and straightened. "I'm sorry. I fell asleep . . . Christ, I'm sorry."

"I'm fine," I said, with forced calm. "Relax."

He raked a hand through his hair, his chest heaving. His face was sheened with sweat, his eyes reddened. "God."

I stepped closer, fighting the lingering fear. This was part of our lives. We both had to face it. "Do you remember the dream?"

Gideon swallowed hard and shook his head.

"I don't believe you."

"Damn it. You have to—"

"You were dreaming about Nathan. How often do you do that?" I reached him and took his hand.

"I don't know."

"Don't lie to me."

"I'm not!" he snapped, bristling. "I rarely remember my dreams."

I pulled him toward the bathroom, deliberately keeping him moving forward both physically and mentally. "The detectives came to see me today."

"I know."

The hoarseness of his voice concerned me. How long had he been asleep and dreaming? The thought of him tormented by his own mind, alone and in pain, wounded me. "Did they visit you, too?"

"No. But they've been making inquiries."

I flicked the lights on and he stopped, his grip tightening to make me stop, too. "Eva."

"Hop in the shower, ace. We'll talk when you're done."

He cupped my face in his hands, his thumbs brushing over my cheekbone. "You're moving too fast. Slow down."

"I don't want to get hung up every time you have a nightmare."

"Take a minute," he murmured, lowering his forehead to rest against mine. "I frightened you. *I'm* frightened. Let's just take a minute and deal with that."

I softened, my hand coming up to rest over his racing heart.

He buried his nose in my hair. "Let me smell you, angel. Feel you. Say I'm sorry."

"I'm okay."

"It's not okay," he argued, his voice still low and coaxing. "I should've waited for you at our place."

I rested my cheek against his chest, loving the idea of "our" place. "I've been checking my phone all night, waiting for a text or message."

"I worked late." His hands slid under my shirt, brushing over the

bare skin of my back. "Then I came here. I wanted to surprise you . . .
make love to you . . ."

"I think we might be free," I whispered, clutching at his shirt. "The
detectives . . . I think we're going to be okay."

"Explain."

"Nathan had this bracelet he always wore—"

"Sapphires. Very feminine."

I looked up at him. "Yes."

"Go on."

"They found it on the arm of a dead mob guy. Russian Mafia.
They're running with the theory that it was a criminal association gone
bad."

Gideon stood very still, his gaze narrowed. "That's interesting."

"It's *weird*. They were talking about photos of me and sex trafficking, which just doesn't mesh with—"

His fingers pressed against my lips, quieting me. "It's interesting
because Nathan was wearing that bracelet when I left him."

I watched Gideon take a shower while I brushed my teeth. His soapy
hands slid over his body with economical indifference, his movements
brisk and rough. There was none of the intimate worship I caressed him
with, none of the awe or love. He was done in minutes, stepping out of
the shower in all his nude glory before grabbing a towel and scrubbing
away the water on his skin.

He came up behind me when he was done, gripping my hips and
pressing a kiss to my nape. "I don't have any underworld ties," he murmured.

I finished rinsing my mouth and looked at him through the mirror.
"Does it bother you to have to say that to me?"

"I'd rather say it than have you ask."

"Someone went to a lot of trouble to protect you." Turning, I faced him. "Could it be Angus?"

"No. Tell me how the mob guy died."

My fingertips drifted over the ridges of his abdomen, loving the way the muscles flexed and clenched in response to my touch. "One of his own took him out. Retaliation. He was under surveillance, so Graves said they've got proof of that."

"So it's someone connected, then. To either the mob or the authorities, or both. Whoever's responsible, they chose a fall guy who could take the blame and not pay for it."

"I don't care who arranged it, just so long as you're safe."

He kissed my forehead. "We need to care," he said softly. "To protect me, they have to know what I did."

15

Shortly after five in the morning, I went from unconscious to wide awake in a heartbeat. The remnants of a dream clung to me, one in which I'd still believed Gideon and I had broken up. Loneliness and grief weighed me down, pinning me to the bed for several minutes. I wished Gideon were beside me. I wished I could just roll over and press my body to his.

Partly due to my period, we hadn't had sex the night before. Instead, we had enjoyed the simple comfort of just being together. We'd curled up on my bed and watched television until the exhaustion of my over-kill run on the treadmill pulled me under.

I loved those quiet moments when we just held each other. When the sexual attraction simmered just beneath the surface. I loved the feel of his breath on my skin and the way my curves fit into his hard planes as if we'd been designed for each other.

Sighing, I knew what had me on edge. It was Thursday and Brett was coming to New York, if he wasn't in the city already.

Gideon and I were just starting to find a new rhythm again, which made it the worst possible time for Brett to come back into my life. I was anxious about something going wrong, some gesture or look that would be misconstrued and cause fresh problems for Gideon and me to work through.

It'd be the first time Gideon and I would be out together in public since our "breakup." That was going to be torture. Standing next to Brett while my heart was with Gideon.

Sliding from bed, I went to the bathroom and cleaned up, and then pulled on a pair of shorts and a tank top. I needed to be with Gideon. We needed to spend some time together before the day started with a vengeance.

I moved quietly from my apartment to his, feeling slightly naughty as I ran down the corridor to his—*our*—front door.

Once I'd gone inside, I tossed my keys on the breakfast bar and headed down the hallway to the guest room. He wasn't there and my heart sank, but I kept searching, because I could *feel* him. There was a tingling awareness I experienced only when he was nearby.

I found him in the master bedroom, his arms wrapped around my pillow as he slept partially on his stomach. The sheet clung to his hips, leaving his powerful back and sculpted arms bare, and revealing just a hint of the topmost curve of his amazing ass.

He looked like an erotic fantasy come to life. And he was *mine*.

I loved him so much.

And I wanted him to wake up to me, at least once, with pleasure instead of fear, sadness, and regret.

I undressed quietly in the early light of dawn, my thoughts spinning with ways I could pleasure my man. I wanted to run my hands and mouth all over him, make him breathless and hot, feel his body quiver. I wanted to reaffirm our connection to each other, my whole and irrevocable commitment to him, before the harsh realities we faced came between us.

As my knee sank into the mattress, he stirred. I crawled to him, pressing my lips to the small of his back and working my way up slowly.

"Umm. Eva," he said in a husky voice, lightly stretching beneath me.

"You better hope it's me, ace." I nipped his shoulder blade. "This would turn out bad for you, if not."

I lowered onto him, laying my body over his. His warmth was divine and I took a moment to savor it.

"It's early for you," he murmured, resting easily, just as content as I was to be touching each other.

"Way," I agreed. "You're hugging my pillow."

"Smells like you. Helps me sleep."

I brushed his hair aside and pressed my lips to his throat. "That's a beautiful thing to say. I wish I could lie around like this with you for the entire day."

"You remember I want to take you away this weekend."

"Yes." I ran my hand over his biceps, my fingers gliding over the hard muscle. "I can't wait."

"We'll leave as soon as you get off work on Friday and fly back just in time for work Monday. You won't need anything but your passport."

"And you." I kissed his shoulder, then spoke in a nervous rush. "I want you and came prepared to have you, but it could be messy. I mean, it's the tail end, so maybe not, but if period sex isn't your thing—which I'd totally get, because it has *never* been my thing—"

"*You're* my thing, angel. I'll take you any way I can get you."

He flexed, warning me he was going to turn around. I slid to the side, watching his body roll with a fluid rippling of muscle.

"Sit up for me," I told him, thinking he was even more amazing than I'd given him credit for. Or more horny, which I would never hold against him. "With your back against the headboard."

He arranged himself to my liking, looking sleepy-eyed and sexy, his jaw shadowed with stubble. I climbed into his lap, straddling him. I took a long moment to savor the attraction between us, the delicious and provocative edge of danger he exuded even while at rest. Because Gideon wasn't tamed and never would be. Just like a panther still had its claws, even when they were sheathed.

That was one of my joys. He gentled for me but remained true to himself. He was still the man I'd fallen in love with—hard with rough edges—yet he'd changed, too. He was all things to me, everything I wanted and needed in one imperfect man.

Smoothing his hair back from his face, I traced the curve of his lower lip with the tip of my tongue. His hands, so warm and strong, gripped my hips. His mouth opened, his tongue touching mine.

"I love you," I whispered.

"Eva." Tilting his head, he took over the kiss, deepening it. His lips, so firm yet soft, pressed against mine. His tongue stroked deep, licking and tasting. The soft rasp of it against the tender flesh inside my mouth caused goose bumps to spread in a wave over my skin. His cock began to thicken and lengthen between us, the silky flesh hot against my lower belly.

My nipples tightened, aching, and I shimmied, rubbing them against his chest.

One of his hands cupped my nape, capturing me, holding me steady as he kissed me passionately. His mouth slanted across mine, seeking and ravenous, sucking on my lips and tongue. Moaning, I arched into him, my fingers clutching at his black hair.

"Christ, you turn me on," he growled, pulling his knees up. He urged me back, his body forming a cradle that supported me. His hands cupped my breasts, his thumbs circling the hard points of my nipples. "Look at you. You're so fucking gorgeous."

Warmth spread through me. "Gideon . . ."

"Sometimes you're this icy, hands-off blonde." His jaw tightened and he slipped one hand between my legs, his fingers gliding gently through my cleft. "And then you're like this. So hot and needy. Wanting my hands all over you, my cock inside you."

"I'm like this *for you*. This is what you do to me. What you've been doing to me from the moment I met you."

Gideon's gaze slid over me, followed by his hand. As his fingertips caressed the outside curve of my breast and stroked over my clit at the same time, I shivered.

"I want you," he said gruffly.

"And here I am—naked."

His mouth curved in a slow, sexy smile. "I couldn't miss that."

The tip of his finger circled my opening. I lifted a little to give him better access, my hands sliding over his shoulders.

"But I wasn't talking about sex," he murmured. "Although I want that, too."

"With me."

"Only you," he agreed. His thumb brushed feather light over my nipple. "Forever and always."

I moaned and reached for his cock, gripping him in my hands, stroking him from root to tip.

"I look at you, angel, and I want you so badly. I want to be with you, listen to you, talk to you. I want to hear you laugh and hold you when you cry. I want to sit next to you, breathe the same air, share the same life. I want to wake up to you like this every day forever. I *want* you."

"Gideon." I leaned forward and kissed him softly. "I want you, too."

He teased the tip of my breast, tugging and rolling the hardened peak between his fingers. He rubbed my clit and a soft sound escaped me. Gideon hardened in my hands, his body responding to my growing desire.

The room was lightening as the sun rose higher, but the world outside seemed a lifetime away. The intimacy of the moment was both searing and sweet, filling me with joy.

My hands caressed his erection with tender reverence, my only goal to please him and show him how much I loved him. He touched me the same way, his eyes windows to a wounded soul that needed me as much as I needed him.

"I'm happy with you, Eva. You make me happy."

"I'll make you happy the rest of your life," I promised him. My hips churned, desire sliding hot and thick through my veins. "There's nothing I want more."

Leaning forward, Gideon flicked the tip of his tongue over my nipple, a quick swipe that sent a sharp ache through my breast. "I love your tits. Did you know that?"

"Ah, so that's what did you in—the rack."

"Keep teasing me, angel. Give me an excuse to spank you. I love your ass, too."

He pressed a hand to my back, arching me toward his mouth. Hot wetness surrounded the sensitive peak of my breast. His cheeks hollowed on a deep suck and my sex echoed his mouth, hungry for his cock.

I felt him everywhere, all around me and inside me. His heat and warmth. His passion. In my hands, his cock was hard and throbbing, the plush head slick with pre-cum.

"Tell me you love me," I pleaded.

Gideon's eyes met mine. "You know I do."

"Imagine if I never said the words to you. If you never heard them from me."

His chest expanded on a deep breath. "Crossfire."

My hands stilled on him.

He swallowed, his throat working. "It's your word for when things get to be too much, when it's too intense. It's my word, too, because that's how you make me feel. All the time."

"Gideon, I . . ." He'd made me speechless.

"When you say it, it means stop." His fingertips left my breast and slid down my cheek. "When I say it, it means never stop. Whatever you're doing to me, I need you to keep doing it."

Lifting, I hovered above him. "Let me."

"Yes." His fingers left my cleft, and a heartbeat later his cock was filling me, the flared crown stretching sensitive tissues.

"Slow," he ordered softly, his gaze hooded as he licked his fingers with long, sensuous laps of his tongue. He looked so wicked, so shamelessly decadent.

"Help me." It was always more difficult for me to take him this way, using only gravity and the weight of my body. As desperate as he'd made me, he was still a tight fit.

He caught my hips, sliding me up and down leisurely, working me onto his thick erection. "Feel every inch, angel," he crooned. "Feel how hard you make me."

My thighs trembled as he rubbed over a tender spot inside me. I gripped his wrists, my sex rippling.

"Don't come," he warned, with that authoritative bite that practically ensured I would. "Not until you've taken all of me."

"Gideon." The slow, steady friction of his careful penetration was driving me insane.

"Think of how good it feels when I'm in you, angel. When your greedy little cunt has something to tighten down on when you're coming."

I tightened down on him then, seduced by the coaxing rasp in his voice. "Hurry."

"You're the one who has to let me in." His eyes gleamed with humor. He urged me to lean back, changing the angle of my descent.

I slid onto him, taking him to the root in one smooth, slick glide. "Oh!"

"Fuck." His head fell back, his breathing quick and rough. "You feel amazing. You're squeezing me like a fist."

"Baby." I couldn't hide the plea in my voice. He was so hard and thick inside me, so deep I could barely catch my breath . . .

He shot me a look that scorched. "I want *this*. You and me, nothing between us."

"Nothing," I said fervently, panting. Wriggling. Losing my mind. I needed to come so badly.

"Shh. I've got you." Lifting his thumb to his mouth, Gideon licked the pad, then reached between us, rubbing my clit with expertly applied pressure. Heat bloomed across my skin in a mist of sweat, the flush spreading until I felt feverish.

I climaxed in a searing rush of pleasure, my sex spasming in hard, desperate clutches. His growl was a sound of pure animal sexuality, his cock swelling in response to the covetous milking of my body.

But he didn't come, which made my orgasm all the more intimate. I was open, vulnerable, wrenched by desire. And he watched me fall apart with those haunting blue eyes, his control absolute. The fact that he didn't move, just held himself deep, enhanced the feeling of connection between us.

A tear slid down my cheek, the orgasm pushing my emotions over the edge.

"Come here," he said hoarsely, his hands sliding up my back and pulling me into him. He licked the tear away, then nudged me sweetly with the tip of his nose. My breasts pressed against his chest, my arms went around his waist, slipping into the space between him and the headboard. I held him close, my body quivering with aftershocks.

"You're so beautiful," he murmured. "So soft and sweet. Kiss me, angel."

Tilting my head, I offered him my mouth. The melding was hot and wet, an erotic mixture of his unsated lust and my overwhelming love.

I pushed my fingers into his hair, cupping the back of his head to hold him still. He did the same to me, the two of us communicating without words. His lips sealed over mine, his tongue fucking my mouth even as his cock remained unmoving inside me.

I felt the undercurrent of strain in his kiss and his touch, and I knew he worried about the day's events, too. I arched my back, curving into him, wishing I could make us inseparable. His teeth caught my lower lip, sinking gently into the swollen curve. I whimpered and he murmured, soothing me with rhythmic strokes of his tongue.

"Don't move," he said hoarsely, restraining me with his grip at my nape. "I want to come just feeling you around me."

"Please," I breathed. "Come in me. Let me feel you."

We were completely entwined, grasping and pulling at each other, his cock rigid inside me, our hands in each other's hair, our lips and tongues mating frantically.

Gideon was mine, completely. Yet still some part of my mind was stunned that I had him like this, that he was naked in a bed we shared, in an apartment we shared, that he was inside me, a part of me, taking every bit of my love and passion and giving me back so much more.

"I love you," I moaned, tightening my core and squeezing him. "I love you so much."

"Eva. God." He shuddered, coming. He groaned into my mouth, his hands flexing against my scalp, his breath gusting hard across my lips.

I felt him spurting inside me, filling me, and I trembled with another orgasm, the pleasure pulsing gently through me.

His hands roamed restlessly, rubbing up and down my back, his kiss that perfect blend of love and desire. I felt his gratitude and need, recognized it because I felt the same way.

It was a miracle that I'd found him, that he could make me feel this way, that I could love a man so deeply and completely and sexually with all the baggage I carried. And that I could offer the same refuge to him in return.

Laying my cheek against his chest, I listened to his heart pounding, his perspiration mingling with mine.

"Eva." He exhaled harshly. "Those answers you want from me . . . I need you to ask the questions."

I held him for a long minute, waiting for our bodies to recover and my own panic to subside. He was still inside me. We were as close as we could be, but it wasn't enough for him. He had to have more, on every front. He wasn't going to quit until he possessed every part of me and infiltrated every aspect of my life.

Pulling back, I looked at him. "I'm not going anywhere, Gideon. You don't have to push yourself if you're not ready."

"I am ready." His gaze held mine, blazing with power and determination. "I need *you* to be ready. Because it won't be long before I'm going to ask you a question, Eva. And I'm going to need you to give me the right answer."

"It's too soon," I whispered, my throat tight. I lifted slightly, trying to gain some distance, but he pulled me back and held me down. "I don't know if I can."

"But you're not going anywhere," he reminded, his jaw set. "And neither am I. Why put off the inevitable?"

"That's not the way you need to look at it. We've got too many triggers. If we're not careful, one or both of us will shut down, cut the other one—"

"Ask me, Eva," he commanded.

"Gideon—"

"Now."

Frustrated by his obstinacy, I stewed for a minute, then decided that whatever the reason, there *were* questions that needed answers no matter what. "Dr. Lucas. Do you know why he lied to your mother?"

His jaw worked as he clenched his teeth, his eyes turning hard and cold. "He was protecting his brother-in-law."

"What?" I sat back, my thoughts spinning. "Anne's brother? The woman you were sleeping with?"

"Fucking," he corrected harshly. "Everyone in Anne's family is in the mental health field. The whole fucked-up lot of them. She's a shrink. Did any of your Google searches dig *that* up?"

I nodded absently, more concerned with the vehemence with which he said the word *shrink*, practically spitting it out. Was that why he hadn't gotten help before? And how much did he love me to make the effort to see Dr. Petersen despite his loathing?

"I didn't know it right away," he went on. "I couldn't figure out why Lucas lied. He's a pediatrician, for chrissakes. He's supposed to care about kids."

"Screw that. He's supposed to be human!" Rage filled me, a white-hot desire to find Lucas and hurt him. "I can't believe he could look me in the eye like he did and say all that shit he said."

Blaming Gideon for everything . . . trying to drive a wedge between us . . .

"It wasn't until I met you that I finally started to get it," he said, his hands tightening around my waist. "He loves Anne. Maybe as much as I love you. Enough to overlook her cheating and cover up for her brother to spare her the truth. Or embarrassment."

"He shouldn't be practicing medicine."

"I don't disagree."

"So why is his office in one of your buildings?"

"I bought the building because his practice is in it. Helps me keep an eye on him and how well he's doing . . . or not."

Something about the way he said "or not" led me to wonder: Did he have anything to do with Lucas's less profitable times? I remembered when Cary had been taken to the hospital and how special arrangements had been made for him and for me, because Gideon was such a generous benefactor. How much could he influence?

If there were ways to put Lucas at a disadvantage, I was certain Gideon knew them all.

"And the brother-in-law?" I asked. "What happened to him?"

Gideon's chin lifted and his gaze narrowed. "The statute of limitations ran out for me, but I confronted him, told him if he ever went into practice or laid a hand on another child I'd set up an unlimited fund dedicated to prosecuting him civilly and criminally on behalf of his victims. Shortly after that, he killed himself."

The last was said without inflection, which made the hairs on my nape stand on end. I shivered with a sudden chill that came from inside me.

He rubbed his hands up and down my arms, trying to warm me, but he didn't pull me into him. "Hugh was married. Had a child. A boy. Just a few years old."

"Gideon." I hugged him, understanding. He'd lost a father to suicide, too. "What Hugh chose to do isn't your fault. You're not responsible for the decisions he made."

"Aren't I?" he asked, with that ice in his voice.

"No, you're not." I held him as tight as I could, willing my love into his tense, rigid body. "And the boy . . . His father's death might have prevented him from experiencing what you did. Have you thought of that?"

His chest lifted and fell roughly. "Yes, I've thought of it. But he doesn't know what his father was. He only knows that his dad is gone, by choice, and he's left behind. He'll believe his father didn't care enough about him to stay."

"Baby." I pulled his head toward me, urging him to rest against me. I didn't know what to say. I couldn't make excuses for Geoffrey Cross and I knew Gideon was thinking of him, as well as the boy he himself had once been. "You didn't do anything wrong."

"I need you to stay, Eva," he whispered, his arms finally coming around me. "And you're holding back. It's driving me crazy."

I rocked gently, cradling him. "I'm being cautious because you're so important to me."

"I know it's not fair to ask you to be with me"—his head tilted back—"when we can't even sleep in the same bed, but I'll love you better than anyone else could. I'll take care of you and make you happy. I know I can."

"You do." I brushed his hair back from his temples and wanted to cry when I saw the longing on his face. "I want you to believe I'll stay with you."

"You're afraid."

"Not of you." I sighed, trying to pull the words together in a way that made sense. "I can't . . . I can't just be an extension of you."

"Eva." His features softened. "I can't change who I am, and I don't want to change who you are. I just want us to be who we are—together."

I kissed him. I didn't know what to say. I wanted us to live the same life, too, to be together in every way we could be. But I also believed that neither of us was ready.

"Gideon." I kissed him again, my lips clinging to his. "You and me, we're barely strong enough on our own. We're getting better all the time, but we're not there yet. It's not just about the nightmares."

"Tell me what it's about, then."

"Everything. I don't know . . . It's not right for me to live in a place Stanton pays for anymore now that Nathan isn't a threat. And especially not now that my parents hooked up."

His brows shot up. "Excuse me?"

"Yeah," I confirmed. "Total mess."

"Move in with me," he said, rubbing my back to comfort me.

"So . . . I skip right over making it on my own? Am I always going to live off someone else?"

"For fuck's sake." He made a frustrated noise. "Would you feel better if we shared the rent?"

"Ha! Like I could afford your penthouse, even paying just a third of it. And there's no way Cary could."

"So we'll move in here or next door, if you want, and take over the lease. I don't care where, Eva."

I stared at him, wanting what he was offering but afraid I'd miss a big pitfall that would hurt us.

"You came to me as soon as you got up this morning," he pointed out. "You don't like being away from me, either. Why torture ourselves? Sharing the same space should be the least of our problems."

"I don't want to screw this up," I told him, my fingers brushing over his chest. "I *need* us to work, Gideon."

He caught my hand and pressed it over his heart. "I need us to work, too, angel. And I want mornings like this and nights like last night while we do it."

"No one even knows we're seeing each other. How do we go from being broken up to living together?"

"We start today. You're taking Cary with you to the video launch. I'll come up to the both of you with Ireland, say hi—"

"She called me," I interrupted, "and told me to go up to you. She wants us to get back together."

"She's a smart girl." He smiled and I felt a little thrill at the thought that he might be opening up to her. "So one of us will approach the other, make small talk, and I'll say hi to Cary. You and I won't have to fake the attraction between us. Tomorrow, I'll take you out to lunch. Bryant Park Grill would be ideal. We'll make a show of it."

It all sounded wonderful and easy, but . . . "Is it safe?"

"Finding Nathan's bracelet on a criminal's corpse opens the door to reasonable doubt. That's all we need."

We looked at each other, sharing the feeling of hope, the sense of excitement and expectation in a future that had seemed so much more uncertain just yesterday.

He touched my cheek. "You made a reservation at Tableau One for tonight."

I nodded. "Yeah, I had to use your name to get on the list, but Brett asked me out to dinner and I wanted us to go to a place connected with you."

"Ireland and I have a reservation at the same time. We'll join you."

I shifted awkwardly, nervous at the thought, and Gideon thickened inside me. "Uh . . ."

"Don't worry," he murmured, his focus clearly shifting to more heated thoughts. "It'll be fun."

"Yeah, right."

Banding his arms around my hips and shoulder blades, Gideon scooped me up and moved, rolling and putting me beneath him. "Trust me."

I was going to reply, but he kissed me quiet and fucked me senseless.

I showered and dressed at Gideon's, then hurried back down the hallway to my apartment for my purse and bag, trying not to look like I was sneaking around. It was easy to get ready at Gideon's apartment, since he'd stocked the bathroom with all my usual toiletries and cosmetics, and had purchased enough clothes and underwear for me to never have to wear anything from my own closet.

It was too much, but that was the way he was.

I was rinsing off the mug I'd used for a quick cup of coffee when Trey came into the kitchen.

He smiled sheepishly. Dressed in a pair of Cary's sweats and his own shirt from last night, he looked right at home. "Good morning."

"Back atcha." I put the mug in the dishwasher and faced him. "I'm glad you came to dinner."

"Me, too. I had fun."

"Coffee?" I asked him.

"Please. I have to get ready for work, but I'm dragging."

"I've had those days." I fixed him a cup and slid it over.

He took the mug and lifted it in a salute of thanks. "Can I ask you something?"

"Shoot."

"Do you like Tatiana, too? Is it weird for you, having us both around?"

I shrugged. "I don't really know Tatiana, to be honest. She doesn't hang with Cary and me the way you do."

"Oh."

I started heading out and squeezed his shoulder before I passed him. "Have a good one."

"You, too."

I checked my phone while taking a cab to work. I almost wished I'd walked, since the cabbie kept the front windows down and was apparently averse to wearing deodorant. The only saving grace was that it was faster than walking.

There was a text from Brett sent around six in the morning: On the ground. Can't wait to c u 2nite!

I sent him back a smiley face.

Megumi looked good when I met up with her at work, which made me happy, but Will was looking glum. As I was putting my purse in a drawer, he stopped by my cubicle and rested his crossed arms along the low wall.

"What's the matter?" I asked him, looking up at him from my chair.

"Help. Need carbs."

Laughing, I shook my head. "I think it's sweet that you're suffering through this diet for your girl."

"I shouldn't complain," he said. "She's lost like five pounds—that I didn't think she had to lose, mind you—and she looks amazing and has all this energy. But God . . . I feel like a slug. My body's not built for this."

"Are you asking me out to lunch?"

"Please." He clasped his hands together like he was praying. "You're one of the few women I know who actually enjoys eating."

"I've got the butt to show for it, too," I said ruefully. "But sure. I'm game."

"You're the best, Eva." He backed up and bumped into Mark. "Oops. Sorry."

Mark grinned. "No problem."

Will headed back to his cubicle and Mark turned his smile to me.

"We've got the Drysdel team coming in at nine thirty," I reminded him.

"Right. And I've got an idea I'd like to run past strategy before they get here."

I grabbed my tablet and stood, thinking we'd be running down to the wire. "You're living on the edge, boss."

"Only way to do it. Come on."

The day flew by and I rushed full-bore all through it, filled with restless energy. Getting up so early, then eating a plate of pierogi for lunch, didn't slow me down.

I wrapped up exactly at five and did a quick change in the bathroom, switching from my skirt and blouse into a more casual jersey dress in pale blue. I slipped on a pair of wedge sandals, swapped out my diamond studs for silver hoops, and turned my ponytail into a messy bun. Then I headed down to the lobby.

As I moved toward the revolving entrance door, I saw Cary standing outside on the sidewalk talking to Brett. I slowed, giving myself a minute to absorb the sight of my old flame.

Brett's short-cropped hair was naturally dark blond, but he'd had the tips dyed platinum and the look was a good one for him, with his tanned skin and irises of a beautiful emerald green. On stage he was usually shirtless, but today he was dressed in black cargo pants and bloodred T-shirt, his arms covered in sleeves of tattoos that writhed over his muscles.

He turned his head then, looking inside the lobby, and I started walking again, my stomach fluttering a little when he caught sight of me, and his ruggedly handsome face was softened by a smile that revealed a killer dimple.

Jesus, he was sexy as hell.

Feeling a little too exposed, I pulled out my sunglasses and slipped them on. Then I took a deep breath as I spun through the revolving doors, my gaze shifting to the Bentley parked just behind Brett's limo.

Brett whistled. "Damn, Eva. You're more gorgeous every time I see you."

I shot a strained smile at Cary, my pulse racing madly. "Hey."

"You look great, baby girl," he said, reaching for my hand.

Out of the corner of my eye, I saw Angus step out of the Bentley. In that moment of distraction, I totally missed Brett reaching for me. A split second after I registered his hands at my waist, I realized he was going to kiss me and barely turned my head in time. His lips touched the corner of my mouth, feeling warm and familiar. I stumbled back, tripping over Cary, who caught me by the shoulders.

Flushed with embarrassment and disoriented, I looked anywhere but at Brett.

And found myself looking into the icy blue eyes of Gideon.

16

STANDING FROZEN JUST outside the revolving doors of the Crossfire, Gideon stared at me with such intensity I squirmed.

Sorry, I mouthed, feeling awful, knowing how I would've felt if Corinne had gotten her lips on him the other day.

"Hi," Brett greeted me, too focused on me to pay attention to the dark figure standing with his fists and jaw clenched just a few feet away.

"Hey." I could feel Gideon watching me, and it was painful not to go to him. "Ready?"

Without waiting for the guys, I yanked the limo door open and crawled in. I'd barely gotten my ass on the seat when I pulled the burner phone out of my purse and sent a quick text to Gideon: I love you.

Brett settled on the bench seat beside me, and then Cary slid in.

"I've been seeing your pretty mug everywhere, man," Brett said, talking to Cary.

"Yeah." Cary shot me a crooked smile. He looked great in distressed jeans and designer T-shirt, with leather cuffs on his wrists that matched his boots.

"Did the rest of the band fly in with you?" I asked.

"Yep, they're all here." Brett flashed that dimple at me again. "Darrin crashed the minute we got to the hotel."

"I don't know how he drums for hours. It's exhausting just watching."

"When you're high off the rush of being on stage, energy isn't a problem."

"How's Erik?" Cary asked with more than casual interest, making me wonder—not for the first time—if he and the band's bassist had ever hooked up. As far as I knew, Erik was straight, but there had been little signs here and there that made me think he might have experimented a little with my best friend.

"Erik's dealing with some issues that have come up on the tour," Brett replied. "And Lance hooked up with a girl he met when we were in New York the last time. You'll be seeing them all in a few minutes."

"The life of a rock star," I teased.

Brett shrugged and smiled.

I looked away, regretting my decision to bring Cary along. Because having him there meant I couldn't say what I needed to say to Brett— that I was in love with someone else and there was no hope for us.

A relationship with Brett would be entirely different from what I had with Gideon. I'd have had a lot of time on my own while he was on tour. I could do all the things I thought I should do before settling down—living by my own means and spending time unattached with friends and by myself. Kind of the best of both worlds: having a boyfriend but enjoying plenty of individuality.

But although I was worried about jumping from college into a lifetime commitment, I had no doubts that Gideon was the man I wanted. We were just out of sync with our timing—I thought there was no reason to rush, while he thought there was no reason to wait.

"We're here," Brett said, looking out the window at the crowd.

Despite the muggy heat of the day, Times Square was packed as usual. The ruby-red glass stairs in Duffy Square were full of people taking pictures of each other, and pedestrian traffic clogged the overflowing sidewalks. Police officers dotted the corners, keeping a sharp eye out for trouble. Street performers outshouted each other, and the smells emanating from food carts competed with the much less savory smell of the street itself.

Massive electronic billboards plastered on the sides of buildings fought for attention, including one of Cary with a female model wrapped around him from behind. Cameramen and boom operators loitered around a mobile video screen, which was attached to a traveling platform and positioned in front of the bleacherlike stair seating.

Brett climbed out of the limo first and was immediately bombarded by the excited screams of avid fans—most were female. He flashed that killer smile and waved, then reached in a hand to help me out. My reception was much less warm, especially after Brett put his arm around my waist. Cary's appearance, however, started a hum of murmurs. When he slipped on a pair of shades, he elicited his own swell of excited yells and catcalls.

I was overwhelmed by the sensory input but quickly focused when I spotted Christopher Vidal Jr. talking with the host of an entertainment gossip show. Gideon's brother was dressed for business in shirt, tie, and navy slacks. His dark auburn hair caught the eye even in the early evening shade cast by the towering buildings surrounding us. He waved when he caught sight of me, which turned the host's gaze to me as well. I waved back.

The rest of Six-Ninths stood in front of the bleachers signing autographs, clearly enjoying the attention. I looked at Brett. "Go do your thing."

"Yeah?" He studied me, trying to make sure I was okay with him abandoning me.

"Yeah." I waved him off. "This is for you. Enjoy it. I'll be here when it's time for the show."

"Okay." He smiled. "Don't go anywhere."

He bounded off. Cary and I walked over to the tent bearing the Vidal Records logo. Protected from the crowds by private security, it was a tiny oasis in the madness of Times Square.

"Well, baby girl, you've got your hands full with him. I forgot how it was with you two."

"*Was* being the operative word," I pointed out.

"He's different from before," he went on. "More . . . settled."

"That's great for him. Especially with all that's going on in his life right now."

He scoped me out. "Aren't you even the slightest bit interested in seeing if he can still bang you brainless?"

I shot him a look. "Chemistry is chemistry. And I'm sure he's had plenty of chances to bone up on his already fabulous skills."

"Bone up, ha! That's punny." He waggled his brows at me. "You seem solid."

"Ah, now that would be an illusion."

"Well, look who's here," he murmured, turning my attention to Gideon, who was approaching with Ireland at his side. "And heading straight toward us. If there's a brawl over you, I'm watching from the bleachers."

I shoved at him. "Thanks."

It amazed me that Gideon could look so cool in his suit when it was still so hot. Ireland looked fantastic in a low-rise flared skirt and tummy-baring fitted tank top.

"Eva!" she shouted, running over and leaving her brother behind. She met me with a hug, then pulled back to check me out. "Awesome! He's got to be kicking himself."

I looked around her at Gideon, searching his face for any signs that he was pissed about Brett. Ireland turned and hugged Cary, too,

234 · SYLVIA DAY

surprising him. In the meantime, Gideon walked straight up to me, grabbed me gently by the upper arms, and kissed both of my cheeks French style.

"Hello, Eva." His voice was flavored with a soft rasp that had my toes curling. "It's good to see you."

I blinked up at him, not having to fake my astonishment at all. "Uh, hi. Gideon."

"Doesn't she look delish?" Ireland asked, making no attempt at subtlety.

Gideon's eyes never left my face. "She always does. I need a minute of your time, Eva."

"Sure." I shot a what-the-fuck look at Cary and let Gideon lead me to a corner of the tent. We'd taken a few steps when I said, "Are you mad? Please don't be."

"Of course I am," he said evenly. "But not at you or him."

"O-kay." I had no idea what that meant.

He stopped and faced me, raking a hand through his gorgeous hair. "This situation is intolerable. I could stand it when there was no other choice, but now . . ." His gaze was fierce on my face. "You're mine. I need the world to know that."

"I've told Brett that I'm in love with you. Cary, too. My dad. Megumi. I've never lied about how I feel about you."

"Eva!" Christopher came up to me and pulled me into him for a kiss on the cheek. "I'm so glad Brett brought you. You know, I had no idea you two used to be an item."

I managed a smile, hyperaware of Gideon's gaze. "It was a long time ago."

"Not that long." He grinned. "You're here, aren't you?"

"Christopher," Gideon said, by way of greeting.

"Gideon." Christopher's smile didn't waver, but he noticeably cooled. "You didn't have to come. I've got this covered."

They were half brothers but had so little in common physically.

Gideon was taller, bigger, and undeniably dark in both coloring and demeanor. Christopher was a handsome man with a sexy smile, but he had none of Gideon's sizzling magnetism.

"I'm here for Eva," Gideon said smoothly, "not the show."

"Really?" Christopher looked at me. "I thought you and Brett were working things out."

"Brett's a friend," I replied.

"Eva's personal life is none of your business," Gideon said.

"It shouldn't be yours, either." Christopher looked at him with such hostility it made me uncomfortable. "The fact that 'Golden' is a true story, and that Brett and Eva are here together, is a great marketing angle for Vidal and the band."

"The song is the end of that story."

Christopher frowned and reached into his pocket, pulling out his smartphone. He read the screen, then scowled at his brother. "Call Corinne, will you? She's going nuts trying to reach you."

"I talked to her an hour ago," Gideon said.

"Stop giving her mixed signals," Christopher snapped. "If you didn't want to talk to her, you shouldn't have gone over to her place last night."

I tensed, my pulse leaping. I looked at Gideon, saw his jaw tighten, and remembered how I'd waited for a reply text from him. He'd been at my place when I got home, but he'd never explained why he hadn't texted me back. He certainly hadn't said anything about going to Corinne's apartment.

And hadn't he said he wasn't taking her calls?

I backed away with my stomach in knots. I'd felt off all day, and facing the simmering dislike between Gideon and Christopher was too much on top of it. "Excuse me."

"Eva," Gideon said sharply.

"It was good seeing you both," I murmured, playing my scripted part before turning away and heading the few feet over to Cary.

Gideon caught up with me after only two steps, gripping me by the elbow and whispering in my ear. "She's calling my phone and work all the time. I had to talk with her."

"You should've told me."

"We had more important things to talk about."

Brett glanced over at us. He was too far away for me to see his expression, but his posture looked tight. People, all of them pushing to get closer, surrounded him and he was focused on me instead.

Damn it. He'd seen me with Gideon and it was spoiling what should be a wonderful experience for him. As I'd feared, the whole outing was a mess.

"Gideon," Christopher said tightly from behind us. "I wasn't finished talking to you."

Gideon glanced at him. "I'll get to you in a minute."

"You'll talk to me now."

"Walk away, Christopher." Gideon stared at his brother so coldly I shivered despite the heat. "Before you make a scene that takes all the attention away from Six-Ninths."

Christopher seethed for a long minute, then seemed to realize his brother wasn't kidding. He cursed under his breath and turned, only to be confronted by Ireland.

"Leave them alone," she said, with her hands on her hips. "I want them to get back together."

"You stay out of this."

"Whatever." She wrinkled her nose at him. "Come show me around."

He paused, his gaze narrowed. Then he sighed and took her by the elbow, leading her away. I realized they were close.

It made me sad that Gideon didn't have that kind of bond with them.

Gideon brought my attention back to him with a brush of fingertips to my cheek, a soft caress that conveyed so much love . . . and possession. No one looking at us could mistake the claim. "Tell me you know nothing happened with Corinne."

I sighed. "I know you didn't do anything with her."

"Good. She's not acting like herself. I've never seen her so . . . Damn it. I don't know. Needy. Irrational."

"Devastated?"

"Maybe. Yes." His face softened. "She wasn't like this when she broke our engagement."

I felt bad for both of them. Ugly good-byes weren't fun for anyone. "She walked away that time. This time, it's you. It's always harder being the one left behind."

"I'm trying to settle her down, but I need you to promise me that she's not going to get in between us."

"I won't let her. And you're not going to worry about Brett."

It took him a few seconds, but he finally said, "I'll worry, but I'll handle it."

I could tell it wasn't an easy concession for him to make.

His lips thinned. "I have to go deal with Christopher. Are we okay?"

Nodding, I said, "I'm good. You?"

"As long as Kline doesn't kiss you." The warning was clear in his voice.

"Same goes."

"If he kisses me, he's getting decked."

I laughed. "You know what I meant."

He caught my hand and rubbed his thumb over my ring. "Crossfire."

My heart hurt in the best way. "Love you, too, ace."

BRETT disengaged from his fans and headed over to the tent, looking grim.

"Having fun yet?" I asked him, hoping to keep him feeling positive.

"He wants you back," he said bluntly.

I didn't hesitate. "Yes."

"If you're going to give him a second chance, I should get one, too."

"Brett—"

"I know it's tough with me being on the road—"

"And based in San Diego," I pointed out.

"—but I can make it out here often enough and you can always meet up with me, see some new places. Plus, the tour ends in November. I can come stay out here for the holidays." He looked at me with those green eyes of his, and the attraction hummed between us. "Your dad's still in SoCal, so you've got more than one reason to come out."

"You'd be reason enough. But, Brett . . . I don't know what to say. I'm in love with him."

He crossed his arms and looked exactly like the wickedly delicious bad boy he was. "I don't care. It's not going to work out for you with him, and I'll be around, Eva."

Staring at him, I realized nothing would convince him but time.

Brett stepped closer, then reached out to run his hand down my arm. He stood over me, his body curved into mine. I remembered other times we'd stood like this, the moments right before he pressed me back against something and fucked me hard.

"It's only going to take once," he murmured in my ear, his voice sinful as always. "One time inside you and you'll remember how it is between us."

I swallowed past a dry throat. "That's not going to happen, Brett."

His mouth curved in a slow smile, revealing that decadent dimple. "We'll see about that."

"I can't believe they're so much hotter in person," Ireland said, looking over at where the guys were doing their prelaunch interview with the TV show host. "You, too, Cary."

He smiled, his teeth dazzlingly white. "Well, thank you, darlin'."

"So . . ." She looked at me with those blue eyes that were so like Gideon's. "You used to date Brett Kline?"

"Not really. Honestly, we just used to mess around."

"Did you love him?"

I thought about that for a minute. "I think I was close, maybe. I could have fallen in love with him under different circumstances. He's a great guy."

Her lips pursed.

"What about you?" I asked. "Are you seeing anyone?"

"Yes." Her lips twisted ruefully. "I really like him—a lot—but it's weird, because he can't let his parents know he's dating me."

"Why not?"

"His grandparents lost most of their money to that scheme Gideon's dad ran."

My gaze went to Cary, whose brows were lifted above the line of his shades.

"That's not your fault," I said, angry on her behalf.

"Rick says his parents think it's 'convenient' that Gideon is so rich now," she muttered.

"Convenient? They think it's *convenient*?"

"Angel."

I turned around at the sound of Gideon's voice, not having realized he'd come up behind me. "What?"

He just stared at me. I was irritated enough that it took me a minute to note the hint of a smile on his face.

"Don't start," I told him, narrowing my gaze in warning. I turned back to Ireland. "Tell Rick's parents to look up the Crossroads Foundation."

"If you're done being offended for my sake," Gideon said, coming up so close behind me that he brushed up against me, "they're about five minutes from starting the video."

My gaze searched out Brett, who'd rejoined the crowd, and found him waving me over.

I looked at Cary.

"Go on," he said with a jerk of his chin. "I'll hang here with Ireland and Cross."

I headed over to the band, smiling when I saw how excited they were. "Big moment, guys," I said to them.

"Ah, well." Darrin grinned. "This whole event was set up just to get us on this TV show and Internet simulcast. It was the only way Vidal could get them to give us any coverage. Let's hope it pays off, because fuckin' A, it's hot as hell out here."

The host announced the exclusive premiere of the video, and then the screen switched from showing the logo of the show to the start of the video and the first chords of the song began.

The black screen suddenly lit up, revealing Brett sitting on a stool in front of a mic in a puddle of light, just as he'd been at the concert. He began to sing, his voice deep and rough. Crazy sexy. The effect his voice had on me was powerful and immediate, just as it'd always been.

The camera slowly backed away from Brett, revealing a dance floor in front of the stage where he sang. There was a crowd dancing, but they were cast in black and white while a lone blonde was strikingly colored.

I stilled as shock spread through me. The camera was careful to film only her backside and profile, but the girl was undeniably meant to be me. She was my height, with the same hair color and style as mine before I'd recently cut it. She had my curvy butt and hips, and her profile was similar enough to mine to understand immediately who she was meant to be.

The next three minutes of my life passed in a horrified daze. "Golden" was a sexually charged song and the actress did all the things Brett sang about—dropping to her knees for a Brett lookalike, making out with him in a bar restroom, and straddling his lap in the back of a classic '67 Mustang just like the one Brett owned. Those intimate memories were intercut with shots of the real Brett still singing onstage with the rest of the guys in the band.

The fact that actors were playing us helped me deal with it a little better, but one glance at Gideon's stony face told me it didn't matter to him. He was seeing one of the wildest times in my life relived before his eyes and it was very real to him.

The video ended with a shot of Brett looking soulful and tormented, a single tear sliding down his cheek.

I pulled away and faced him.

His smile slowly faded when he got a good look at my expression.

I couldn't believe how personal the video was. I was freaking out that millions of people were going to see it.

"Wow," the host said, leaning into the band with mic in hand. "Brett, you really put yourself out there with this. Was it the song that brought you and Eva back together?"

"In a roundabout way, yeah."

"And Eva, did you play yourself in the video?"

I blinked, realizing he was outing me as *the* Eva on national television. "No, that's not me."

"How do you feel about 'Golden'?"

I licked my dry lips. "It's an amazing song by an amazing band."

"About an amazing love story." The host smiled into the camera and rambled on, but I tuned him out, my gaze searching for Gideon. I couldn't spot him anywhere.

The host talked to the band a bit more and I wandered away, searching. Cary came up to me with Ireland in tow.

"Some video," he drawled.

I looked at him miserably before my gaze slid over to Ireland. "Do you know where your brother is?"

"Christopher's schmoozing. Gideon left." She winced apologetically. "He asked Christopher to take me home with him."

"Damn it." I dug in my purse for the burner phone and typed out a quick text: I love you. Tell me you'll c me 2nite.

I waited for a reply. When it didn't come after a few minutes, I just held the phone in my hand, willing it to vibrate.

Brett ambled up to me. "We're done here. Wanna bail?"

"Sure." I turned to Ireland. "I'm out of town the next two weekends, but let's get together after that."

"I'll keep my schedule open," she said, hugging me hard.

Turning to Cary, I caught his hand and squeezed it. "Thanks for coming."

"Are you kidding? I haven't been this entertained in a long time." He and Brett did some complicated handshake. "Good job, man. I'm stoked for you."

"Thanks for coming. We'll catch you later."

Brett set his hand at the small of my back and we took off.

17

G IDEON DIDN'T SHOW up at Tableau One.
    In a way, I was grateful, because I didn't want Brett thinking
I'd planned the interruption. Outside his long-term hopes for our relationship, Brett was someone who'd been important to me in the past
and I wanted to be friends with him, if possible.

But I was preoccupied with imagining what Gideon was thinking
and feeling.

I picked at my dinner, too unsettled to eat. When Arnoldo Ricci
stopped by to say hello, looking very dashing and handsome in his
white chef coat, I felt bad that so much of his fine food was still on my
plate.

The celebrity chef was a friend of Gideon's. Gideon was a silent
partner in Tableau One, which was the reason I'd chosen the restaurant. If he had any doubts about how the dinner with Brett would go,
he'd have people to ask that he trusted.

Of course, I hoped Gideon would trust me enough to believe *me*, but I knew our relationship had its issues and our mutual possessiveness was just one of them.

"It's good to see you, Eva," Arnoldo said with his lovely Italian accent. He pressed a kiss to my cheek, then pulled out one of the empty chairs at our table and sat.

Arnoldo extended his hand to Brett. "Welcome to Tableau One."

"Arnoldo's a Six-Ninths fan," I explained. "He came to the concert with Gideon and me."

Brett's lips twisted ruefully as the two men shook hands. "Nice to meet you. Did you see both shows?"

He was referring to the brawl he'd had with Gideon. Arnoldo understood. "I did. Eva is very important to Gideon."

"She's important to me, too," Brett said, grabbing his frosty mug of Nastro Azzurro beer.

"Well, then." Arnoldo smiled. "*Che vinca il migliore.* May the best man win."

"Ugh." I sat back in my chair. "I'm not a prize. Or I should say: I'm no prize."

Arnoldo shot me a look. Obviously he didn't wholly disagree with me. I didn't blame him; he knew I'd kissed Brett and had seen the effect it'd had on Gideon.

"Is there a problem with your meal, Eva?" Arnoldo asked. "If you liked it, your plate would be empty."

"You serve big helpings," Brett pointed out.

"And Eva is a big eater."

Brett looked at me. "You are?"

I shrugged. Was he catching on to how little we really knew about each other? "One of my many flaws."

"Not to me," Arnoldo said. "How did the video show go?"

"I think it went well." Brett searched my face as he answered.

I nodded, not wanting to spoil what was supposed to be a celebratory time for the band. What was done, was done. I couldn't fault Brett's intentions, only his execution. "They are well on the road to megastardom."

"And I can say I knew you when." Arnoldo smiled at Brett. "I bought your first single on iTunes when it was still your only single."

"Appreciate the support, man," Brett said. "We wouldn't have made it without our fans."

"You wouldn't have made it if you weren't so good." Arnoldo looked at me. "You will have dessert, won't you? And more wine."

As Arnoldo settled back in his chair, I realized he intended to fill the role of chaperone. When I glanced at Brett, I could tell from his wry smile that he caught that, too.

"So," Arnoldo began, "tell me how Shawna is doing, Eva."

I sighed inwardly. At least Arnoldo was a babysitter who was fun to look at.

BRETT's hired driver dropped me off at my apartment a little after ten. I invited Brett up, because I couldn't see any way to avoid it that wasn't rude. He took in the exterior of the building with some surprise, as well as the night doorman and the front desk.

"You must have a smokin' job," he said as we walked toward the elevators.

The clicking of heels on marble chased after me. "Eva!"

I cringed at the sound of Deanna's voice. "Reporter alert," I whispered, before turning around.

"That's a bad thing?" he asked, turning with me.

"Hi, Deanna." I greeted her with a strained smile.

"Hello." Her dark eyes raked Brett from head to toe, and then she thrust her hand at him. "Brett Kline, right? Deanna Johnson."

"A pleasure, Deanna," he said, turning on the charm.

"What can I do for you?" I asked her as they shook hands.

"Sorry for interrupting you on your date. I didn't realize you two were back together until I saw you at the Vidal event earlier." She smiled at Brett. "I take it there's no harm done from your altercation with Gideon Cross?"

Brett's brows rose. "You lost me."

"I'd heard you and Cross exchanged a few blows in an argument."

"Someone's got a big imagination."

Had Gideon talked to him? Or had media training taught Brett the pitfalls to avoid?

I hated that Deanna had been nearby earlier, watching me. Or, more accurately, watching Gideon. He was the one she was fixated on. I was just easier to access.

Her answering smile was brittle. "Bad source, I guess."

"It happens," he said easily.

She turned her attention back to me. "I saw Gideon with you today, Eva. My photographer got some great shots of you two. I stopped by to ask you for a statement, but now that I see who you're with, would you comment on the status of your relationship with Brett?"

She directed the question at me, but Brett stepped in, grinning and flashing that dazzling dimple. "I think 'Golden' says it all. We've got history and friendship."

"That's a great quote, thanks." Deanna eyed me. I eyed her right back. "Okay. I don't want to hold you up. I appreciate your time."

"Sure." I caught Brett's hand and tugged it. "Good night."

I hurried him to the elevators and didn't relax until the doors closed.

"Can I ask why a reporter's so interested in who you're dating?"

I glanced at him. He was lounging against the handrail, his hands gripping the brass on either side of his hips. The pose was hot and he was undeniably sexy, but my thoughts were with Gideon. I was anxious to be with him and talk to him.

"She's an ex of Gideon's with a grudge."

"And that doesn't send up any flags for you?"

I shook my head. "Not like you're probably thinking."

The elevator arrived on my floor and I led the way to my apartment, hating that I had to walk by Gideon's to get there. Had he felt like this when he'd spent time with Corinne? Weighted with guilt and worry?

I opened the door and was sorry that Cary wasn't hanging out on the couch. It didn't even seem like my roommate was home. The lights were off, which was a strong indicator that he was out. He always left lights on in his wake when he was around.

Hitting the switch, I turned in time to see Brett's face when the recessed ceiling fixtures lit up the place. I always felt weird when people first realized I had money.

He looked at me with a frown. "I'm rethinking my career choice."

"My job doesn't pay for this. My stepdad does. For now, anyway." I went to the kitchen and dropped my purse and bag off on a bar stool.

"You and Cross hang in the same circles?"

"Sometimes."

"Am I too different for you?"

The question unsettled me, even though it was perfectly valid. "I don't judge people by their money, Brett. Do you want something to drink?"

"Nah, I'm good."

I gestured toward the couch and we settled there.

"So, you didn't like the video," he said, laying his arm over the back of the sofa.

"I didn't say that!"

"Didn't have to. I saw your face."

"It's just really . . . personal."

His green eyes were hot enough to make me flush. "I haven't forgotten one thing about you, Eva. The video proves that."

"That's because there wasn't a whole lot for you to remember," I pointed out.

"You think I don't know you, but I bet I've seen sides of you Cross never has and never will."

"That's true in reverse."

"Maybe," he conceded, his fingers tapping silently into the cushion. "I'm supposed to fly out at the butt-crack of dawn tomorrow, but I'll catch a later flight. Come with me. We've got shows in Seattle and San Francisco over the weekend. You can head back Sunday night."

"I can't. I have plans."

"The weekend after that we're in San Diego. Come there." His fingers slid down my arm. "It'll be like old times, with twenty thousand extra people."

I blinked. What were the chances that we'd be home at the same time? "I've got plans to be in SoCal then. Just me and Cary."

"So we'll hook up next weekend."

"Meet up," I corrected, standing when he did. "Are you leaving?"

He stepped closer. "Are you asking me to stay?"

"Brett . . ."

"Right." He gave me a rueful smile and my heart raced a little. "We'll see each other next weekend."

We walked together to the door.

"Thank you for inviting me along today," I told him, feeling oddly sorry that he was going so soon.

"I'm sorry you didn't like the video."

"I do like it." I caught his hand. "I do. You did a great job with it. It's just weird seeing myself from the outside, you know?"

"Yeah, I get it." He cupped my cheek with his other hand and bent in for a kiss.

I turned my head and he nuzzled me instead, the tip of his nose rubbing up and down my cheek. The light scent of his cologne, mingled with the scent of his skin, teased my senses and brought back heated memories. The feel of his body standing so close to mine was achingly familiar.

I'd once had a mad crush on him. I had wanted him to feel the same way about me in return and now that he did, it was bittersweet.

Brett gripped my upper arms and groaned softly, the sound vibrating through me. "I remember how you feel," he whispered, his voice deep and husky. "On the inside. I can't wait to feel it again."

I was breathing too fast. "Thank you for dinner."

His lips curved against my cheek. "Call me. I'll call you no matter what, but it'd be nice for you to call me sometime. Okay?"

I nodded and had to swallow before speaking. "Okay."

He was gone a moment later and I was running to my purse for the burner phone. There was no message from Gideon. No missed call or text.

Grabbing my keys, I left my apartment and hurried to his, but it was dark and lifeless. I knew the moment I entered that he wasn't there without having to check the artfully colored glass bowl he emptied his pockets into.

Feeling like something was very off, I headed back to my place. I dropped my keys on the counter and went to my room, heading straight for the bathroom and a shower.

The unsettled feeling in my stomach wouldn't go away, even as I washed the stickiness and grime of the hot afternoon down the drain. I scrubbed shampoo into my scalp and thought over the day, growing angrier by the moment because Gideon was off somewhere doing whatever, instead of being home with me working things out.

And then I sensed him.

Rinsing soap out of my eyes, I turned and found him yanking off his tie as he stepped into the room. He looked tired and worn, which troubled me more than anger would have.

"Hey," I greeted him.

He watched me as he stripped with quick, methodical movements. Magnificently naked, he joined me in the shower, walking right into me and pulling me into a tight embrace.

"Hey," I said again, hugging him back. "What's the matter? Are you upset about the video?"

"I hate the video," he said bluntly. "I should've screened the damn thing when I realized the song was about you."

"I'm sorry."

He pulled back and looked down at me. The mist from the shower was slowly dampening his hair. He was infinitely sexier than Brett. And the way he felt about me—and I felt about him in return—was infinitely deeper. "Corinne called right before the video finished. She was . . . hysterical. Out of control. It concerned me and I went to see her."

I took a deep breath, fighting off a flare of jealousy. I had no right to feel that way, especially after the time I'd spent with Brett. "How did that go?"

He urged my head back with gentle fingers. "Close your eyes."

"Talk to me, Gideon."

"I will." As he rinsed the suds from my hair, he said, "I think I figured out what the problem is. She's been taking antidepressants and they're not the right prescription for her."

"Oh, wow."

"She was supposed to let the doctor know how they were working out, but she didn't even realize she's been acting so bizarre. It took hours of talking to her to get her to see it, and then pinpoint why."

I straightened and wiped my eyes, trying to stem my growing irritation over another woman monopolizing my man's attention. I couldn't discount her making up a problem just to keep Gideon spending time with her.

He swapped places with me, sidestepping under the shower spray. Water coursed down his amazing body, running lovingly over the hard ridges and slabs of muscle.

"So what now?" I asked.

He shrugged grimly. "She'll see her doctor tomorrow to discuss getting off the pills or switching to something else."

"Are you supposed to walk her through that?" I complained.

"She's not my responsibility." His gaze held mine, telling me without words that he understood my fear and worry and anger. Just as he'd always understood me. "I told her as much. Then I called Giroux and told him, too. He needs to come take care of his wife."

He reached for his shampoo, which rested on a glass shelf with the rest of his personal shower items. He'd moved his stuff into my place pretty much the minute I agreed to date him, just as he had stocked his place with duplicates of my everyday items.

"She was provoked, though, Eva. Deanna visited her earlier tonight with pictures she took of you and me at the video launch."

"Fabulous," I muttered. "That explains why Deanna was here waiting to ambush me."

"Was she really?" he purred dangerously, making me pity Deanna— for about half a second. She was digging herself a nice grave.

"She probably got shots of you showing up at Corinne's place and wanted to rile me." I crossed my arms. "She's stalking you."

Gideon tipped his head back into the water to rinse, his biceps flexing as he ran his fingers through his hair.

He was so flagrantly, sexually, beautifully male.

I licked my lips, aroused by the sight of him despite my irritation with his exes. I closed the distance between us and squeezed some of his body wash into my palm. Then I ran my hands over his chest.

Groaning, he looked down at me. "I love your hands on me."

"That's good, since I can't keep my hands off you."

He touched my cheek, his eyes soft. He searched my face, maybe gauging whether I was wearing the fuck-me look or not. I didn't think I was. I wanted him, that never stopped, but I also wanted to enjoy just being with him. That was hard when he was blowing my mind.

"I needed this," he said. "Being with you."

"It seems like so much is coming at us, doesn't it? We can't catch a break. If it's not one thing, it's another." My fingertips traced the hard ridges of his abdomen. Desire hummed between us, and that wonderful sense of being near someone who was precious and necessary. "But we're doing okay, aren't we?"

His lips touched my forehead. "We're hanging in pretty good, I'd say. But I can't wait to take you away tomorrow. Get out of here for a while, away from everyone, and just have you all to myself."

I smiled, delighted by the thought. "I can't wait, either."

I woke when Gideon slipped out of my bed.

Blinking, I noted that the television was still on, though muted. I'd fallen asleep curled up with him, enjoying our time alone together after all the hours and days we'd been forced to spend apart.

"Where are you going?" I whispered.

"To bed." He touched my cheek. "I'm crashing hard."

"Don't go."

"Don't ask me to stay."

I sighed, understanding his fear. "I love you."

Bending over me, Gideon pressed his lips to mine. "Don't forget to put your passport in your purse."

"I won't forget. Are you sure I shouldn't pack something?"

"Nothing." He kissed me again, his lips clinging to mine.

Then he was gone.

I wore a light jersey wrap dress to work on Friday, something that could go from work to a long flight easily. I had no idea how far Gideon was taking me, but knew I'd be comfortable no matter what.

When I got to work, I found Megumi on the phone, so we waved at each other and I headed straight to my cubicle. Ms. Field stopped by just as I settled into my chair.

The executive chairman of Waters Field & Leaman looked powerful and confident in a soft gray pantsuit.

"Good morning, Eva," she said. "Have Mark stop by my office when he gets in."

I nodded, admiring her triple-strand black pearl necklace. "Will do."

When I passed along the request to Mark five minutes later, he shook his head. "Betcha we didn't get the Adrianna Vineyards account."

"You think?"

"I hate those damned cattle-call RFPs. They're not looking for quality and experience. They just want someone who's hungry enough to give their services away."

We'd dropped everything to meet the deadline for the request for proposal, which had been given to Mark to spearhead because he'd done such an amazing job with the Kingsman Vodka account.

"Their loss," I told him.

"I know, but still . . . I want to win 'em all. Wish me luck that I'm wrong."

I gave him a thumbs-up and he headed to Christine Field's office. My desk phone rang as I was pushing to my feet to grab a cup of coffee from the break room.

"Mark Garrity's office," I answered, "Eva Tramell speaking."

"Eva, honey."

I exhaled at the sound of my mother's watery voice. "Hi, Mom. How are you?"

"Will you see me? Maybe we could have lunch?"

"Sure. Today?"

"If you could." She took a breath that sounded like a sob. "I really need to see you."

"Okay." My stomach knotted with concern. I hated hearing my mother so upset. "Do you want me to meet you somewhere?"

"Clancy and I will come get you. You take lunch at noon, right?"

"Yes. I'll meet you at the curb."

"Good." She paused. "I love you."

"I know, Mom. I love you, too."

We hung up and I stared down at the phone.

How was our family going to move forward from here?

I sent a quick text to Gideon, letting him know I'd have to take a rain check on lunch. I needed to get my relationship with my mom back on track.

Knowing I needed more coffee to tackle the day ahead, I set off to fill up.

I left my desk exactly at noon and headed down to the lobby. As the hours passed, I grew more and more excited about getting away with Gideon. Away from Corinne, and Deanna, and Brett.

I'd just passed through the security turnstiles when I saw him.

Jean-François Giroux stood at the security desk, looking distinctly European and very attractive. His wavy dark hair was longer than it had been in the pictures I'd seen of him, his face less tan and his mouth harder, framed by a goatee. The pale green of his eyes was even more striking in person, even though they were red with weariness. From the small carry-on at his feet, I suspected he'd come straight to the Crossfire from the airport.

"*Mon Dieu*. How slow are the elevators in this building?" he asked the security guard in a clipped French accent. "It's impossible that it should take twenty minutes to come down from the top."

"Mr. Cross is on his way," the guard replied staunchly, remaining in his chair.

As if he sensed my gaze, Giroux's head swiveled toward me and his gaze narrowed. He pushed away from the counter, striding toward me.

The cut of his suit was tighter than Gideon's, narrower at the waist and calves. The impression I got of him was too neat and rigid, a man who assumed power by enforcing rules.

"Eva Tramell?" he asked, startling me with his recognition.

"Mr. Giroux." I offered my hand.

He took it, then surprised me by leaning in and kissing both of my cheeks. Perfunctory, absentminded kisses, but that wasn't the point. Even for a Frenchman, it was a familiar gesture from someone who was a total stranger to me.

When he stepped back, I looked at him with raised brows.

"Would you have time to speak with me?" he asked, still holding my hand.

"I'm afraid not today." I tugged away gently. Anonymity was created just by being in a massive space crowded with people rushing to and fro, but with Deanna lurking around, I couldn't be too careful about who I was seen with. "I have a lunch date and then I'm leaving directly after work."

"Tomorrow, perhaps?"

"I'll be out of town this weekend. Monday would be the earliest."

"Out of town. With Cross?"

My head canted to the side as I examined him, trying to read him. "That's really none of your business, but yes."

I told the truth so he'd know that Gideon had a woman in his life who wasn't Corinne.

"Does it not bother you," he said, his tone noticeably cooling, "that he used my wife to make you jealous and bring you back to him?"

"Gideon wants to be friends with Corinne. Friends spend time together."

"You're blond, but surely you can't be so naïve as to believe that."

"You're stressed," I countered, "but surely you know you're being an ass."

I registered Gideon's presence before I felt his hand on my arm.

"You'll apologize, Giroux," he interjected with dangerous softness. "And do so sincerely."

Giroux shot him a look so filled with anger and loathing, it made me shift restlessly on my feet. "Making me wait is classless, Cross, even for you."

"If the insult were intentional, you'd know it." Gideon's mouth thinned into a line as sharp as a blade. "The apology, Giroux. I've never been anything but polite and respectful to Corinne. You will show Eva the same courtesy."

To the casual observer, his pose was loose and relaxed, but I felt the fury in him. I sensed it in both men—one hot and one icy cool, the tension building by the moment. The space around us felt like it was closing in, which was insane considering how wide and deep the lobby was, and how high the ceiling soared.

Afraid they'd come to blows right there, regardless of being in such a populated space, I reached over and caught Gideon's hand in mine, giving it a light squeeze.

Giroux's gaze dropped to our linked hands, then rose to meet my eyes. "*Pardonnez-moi*," he said, inclining his head slightly to me. "You are not at fault here."

"Don't let us hold you up," Gideon murmured to me, his thumb brushing over my knuckles.

But I lingered, hating to walk away. "You should be with your wife," I said to Giroux.

"She should be with me," he corrected.

I reminded myself that he hadn't come after her when she'd left him. He'd been too busy blaming Gideon instead of fixing his marriage.

"Eva," my mom called, having come inside to find me. She approached on nude Louboutins, her slender body draped in a soft silk halter dress in a matching hue. In the dark marble-lined lobby, she was a bright spot.

"Let's get you on your way, angel," Gideon said. "Give me a minute, Giroux."

I hesitated before walking away. "Good-bye, Monsieur Giroux."

"Miss Tramell," he said, tearing his gaze away from Gideon. "Until next time."

I left because I didn't have a choice, but I didn't like it. Gideon walked me over to intercept my mom, and I looked at him, letting him see the worry on my face.

His eyes reassured me. I saw the same latent power and uncompromising control that I'd recognized when we first met. He could handle Giroux. He could handle anything.

"Enjoy your lunch," Gideon said, kissing my mom's cheek before facing me and giving me a quick, hard kiss on the mouth.

I watched him walk away and was unnerved by the intensity with which Giroux's eyes followed his return.

My mom's arm linking with mine brought my attention to her.

"Hi," I said, trying to push my unease away. I waited for her to ask if the guys were going to join us, since she loved nothing more than spending time with rich handsome men, but she didn't.

"Are you and Gideon trying to work things out?" she asked instead.

"Yes."

I glanced at her before I preceded her through the revolving door. She looked more fragile than ever, her skin pale and her eyes lacking their usual sparkle. I waited until she joined me outside, my senses struggling to adjust to the change wrought by stepping out of the cool, cavernous lobby into the sweltering heat and explosion of noise and activity on the street.

I smiled at Clancy as he opened the back door to the town car. "Hey, Clancy."

As my mom slid gracefully into the back of the car, he smiled back. At least I think it was a smile. His mouth twitched a little.

"How are you?" I asked him.

He gave me a brisk nod in reply. "And you?"

"Hanging in there."

"You'll be all right," he said, just as I slid into the car beside my mom. He sounded a lot more confident about that than I felt.

THE first few minutes of lunch were filled with an awkward silence. Sunlight flooded the New American bistro my mom had selected, which only made the unease between us more obvious.

I waited for my mom to start things off, since she was the one who wanted to talk. I had plenty to say, but first I needed to know what the priority was for her. Was it the trust she'd broken by putting a tracking device in my Rolex? Was it her cheating on Stanton with my dad?

"That's a beautiful watch," she said, looking at my new one.

"Thank you." My hand covered it, protecting it. The timepiece was priceless to me, and deeply personal. "Gideon bought it for me."

She looked horrified. "You didn't tell him about the tracker, did you?"

"I tell him everything, Mom. We don't have any secrets."

"Maybe *you* don't. What about him?"

"We're solid," I said confidently. "And getting stronger every day."

"Oh." She nodded, her short curls swaying gently. "That's . . . wonderful, Eva. He can take good care of you."

"He already does, in the way I need him to, which has nothing to do with his money."

My mother's lips tightened at my bitter tone. She didn't actually frown, something she studiously avoided to protect the flawlessness of her skin. "Don't be so quick to dismiss money, Eva. You never know when or why you'll need it."

Irritation simmered through me. She'd put money first my whole life, no matter who she hurt—like my father—in the process.

"I don't," I argued. "I just won't let it rule my life. And before you blurt out something like, oh it's easy for me to say that, I can guarantee if Gideon lost every cent he had, I'd still be with him."

"He's too smart to lose it all," she said tightly. "And if you're lucky, you'll never have anything happen that will drain you financially."

I sighed, exasperated with the topic. "We're never going to see eye to eye on this, you know."

Her beautifully manicured fingers stroked over the handle of her silverware. "You're so angry at me."

"Do you realize Dad's in love with you? He's so in love with you, he can't move on. I don't think he'll ever get married. He'll never have a steady woman in his life who'll take care of him."

She swallowed hard and a tear slid down her cheek.

"Don't you dare cry," I ordered, leaning forward. "This isn't about you. You're not the victim here."

"I'm not allowed to feel pain?" she retorted, her voice harder than I'd ever heard it. "I'm not allowed to cry over a broken heart? I love your father, too. I would give anything for him to be happy."

"You don't love him enough."

"Everything I've done is for love. *Everything.*" She laughed humorlessly. "My God . . . I wonder how you can stand to be with me when you hold such a low opinion."

"You're my mother and you've always been on my side. You're always trying to protect me, even if you go about it the wrong way. I love you and Dad both. He's a good man who deserves to be happy."

She took a shaky sip of water. "If it weren't for you, I'd wish we had never met. We both would've been happier that way. There's nothing I can do about it now."

"You could be with him. Make him happy. You seem to be the only woman who can."

"That's impossible," she whispered.

"Why? Because he's not rich?"

"Yes." Her hand went to her throat. "Because he's not rich."

Brutal honesty. My heart sank. There was a bleak look in her blue eyes I'd never seen before. What drove her to need money so desperately? Would I ever know or understand? "But *you're* rich. Isn't that enough?"

Over the course of three divorces, she'd amassed millions in personal wealth.

"No."

I stared at her, incredulous.

She looked away, her three-carat diamond studs catching the light and glittering with a rainbow of colors. "You don't understand."

"So explain it to me, Mom. Please."

Her gaze returned to me. "Maybe someday. When you're not so upset with me."

Sitting back in my chair, I felt a headache building. "Fine. I'm upset because I don't understand, and you won't explain because I'm upset. We're getting nowhere fast."

"I'm sorry, honey." Her expression was pleading. "What happened between your father and me—"

"Victor. Why don't you ever say his name?"

She flinched. "How long will you punish me?" she asked quietly.

"I'm not trying to punish you. I just don't get it."

It was crazy that we were sitting in a bright, busy space filled with people and dealing with painful personal crap. I wished she'd had me over to her place instead, the home she shared with Stanton. But I guessed she had wanted the buffer of an audience to keep me from totally losing it.

"Listen," I said, feeling tired. "Cary and I are going to move out of the apartment, get something on our own."

My mom's shoulders straightened. "What? Why? Don't be reckless, Eva! There's no need—"

"There is, though. Nathan's gone. And Gideon and I want to spend more time together—"

"What does that have to do with you moving away?" Her eyes flooded with tears. "I'm *sorry*, Eva. What more can I say?"

"This isn't about you, Mom." I tucked my hair behind my ear, fidgeting because her crying always got to me. "Okay, honestly, it does feel weird living in a place Stanton pays for after what happened between you and Dad, but more than that, Gideon and I want to live together. It just makes sense to start fresh someplace."

"Live together?" My mother's tears dried up. "Before marriage? Eva, no. That would be a horrible mistake. What about Cary? You brought him out to New York with you."

"And he'll stay with me." I didn't feel like telling her I hadn't brought up the Gideon-as-a-roommate idea to Cary yet, but I was confident he'd be okay with it. I would be around more and the rent would be easier to bear when split in thirds. "It'll be the three of us."

"You don't live with a man like Gideon Cross if you're not married to him." She leaned forward. "You have to trust me on this. Wait for the ring."

"I'm not in a rush to get married," I said, even as my thumb rubbed over the back of my ring.

"Oh my God." My mother shook her head. "What are you saying? You love him."

"It's too soon. I'm too young."

"You're twenty-four. That's the perfect age." Determination straightened my mother's spine. For once, that didn't bother me, because it restored some of her spirit. "I'm not going to let you ruin this, Eva."

"Mom—"

"No." Her eyes took on a calculating gleam. "Trust me and slow down. I'll handle this."

Crap. That wasn't at all reassuring when she was on Gideon's side of the marriage argument and not mine.

18

I WAS STILL thinking about my mom when I left the Crossfire at five o'clock. The Bentley waited at the curb and as I walked up to it, Angus climbed out and smiled at me.

"Good evening, Eva."

"Hi." I smiled back. "How are you, Angus?"

"Excellent." He rounded the rear of the car and opened the back door for me.

I searched his face. How much did he know about Nathan and Gideon? Did he know as much as Clancy? Or even more than that?

Slipping into the cool backseat, I pulled out my smartphone and called Cary. It went to voice mail, so I left a message. "Hey, just reminding you that I'll be gone this weekend. Would you do me a favor and think about moving into a place we share with Gideon, and we can talk about it when I get back? Someplace new, that we can all afford. Not that he has to worry about that," I added, imagining Cary's expression. "Okay. If you need me and you can't reach me on my cell, send me an e-mail. Love you."

I'd just hit the end button when the door opened and Gideon joined me. "Hi, ace."

He caught me by the back of the neck and kissed me, his mouth sealing over mine. His tongue licked into my mouth, tasting me, making my thoughts grind to a halt. I was breathless when he let me go.

"Hi, angel," he said roughly.

"Wow."

His mouth curved. "How was lunch with your mom?"

I groaned.

"That good, huh?" He caught my hand. "Tell me about it."

"I don't know. It was weird."

Angus got in the driver's seat and pulled into traffic.

"Weird?" Gideon prompted. "Or uncomfortable?"

"Both." I looked out the tinted window as we slowed due to traffic. The sidewalks were clogged with people, but they were moving briskly. It was the cars that were stuck. "She's so focused on money. That's nothing new, but I'm used to her acting like it's just common sense to want financial security. Today, she seemed . . . sad. Resigned."

His thumb stroked soothingly over my knuckles. "Maybe she's feeling guilty for cheating."

"She should! But I don't think that's it. I think it's something else, but I don't have a clue."

"Do you want me to look into it?"

I turned my head to meet his gaze. I didn't answer right away, thinking it over. "I do, yes. But I feel icky about it, too. I researched you, Dr. Lucas, Corinne . . . I keep digging for people's secrets instead of just asking about them outright."

"So ask her," he said, in that matter-of-fact male way.

"I did. She said she'd talk about it when I wasn't upset."

"Women," he scoffed, with warm amusement in his eyes.

"What did Giroux want? Did you know he was coming by?"

He shook his head. "He wants someone to blame for his marriage troubles. I'm convenient."

"Why doesn't he stop blaming and start fixing? They need to go into counseling."

"Or get a divorce."

I stiffened. "Is that what you want?"

"What I want is you," he purred, releasing my hand to grab me instead and pull me onto his lap.

"Fiend."

"You have no idea. I have diabolical plans for you this weekend."

The heated look he raked me with had my thoughts shifting in a much naughtier direction. I was pulling his head down for a kiss when the Bentley turned, and it was suddenly dark. Looking around, I realized we'd pulled into a parking garage. We drove around two levels, pulled into a spot, then immediately pulled out again.

Along with four other black Bentley SUVs.

"What's going on?" I asked, as we headed back toward the exit with two Bentleys in front of us and two behind us.

"Shell game," he said, nuzzling my throat.

We pulled back out into traffic, heading in different directions.

"Are we being followed?" I asked.

"Just being cautious." His teeth sank gently into my flesh, making my nipples hard. Supporting my back with one arm, he brushed the side of my breast with his thumb. "This weekend is ours."

He'd taken my mouth in a lush, deep kiss when we pulled into another parking garage. We slid into a spot and the door was yanked open. I was trying to figure out what was going on, when Gideon swung his legs to the side and slipped out of the Bentley with me held firmly in his arms, only to immediately step into the back of another car.

We were on the road again in less than a minute, with the Bentley pulling out into traffic in front of us and heading in the opposite direction.

"This is insane," I said. "I thought we were leaving the country."

"We are. Trust me."

"I do."

His eyes were soft on my face. "I know you do."

We didn't have any more stops on the way to the airport. We pulled right onto the tarmac after a brief security check, and I preceded Gideon up the short flight of steps into one of his private jets. The cabin was luxurious yet understated in its elegance, with sofa seating on the right and table and chairs on the left. The flight attendant was a handsome young guy with black dress slacks and vest embroidered with the Cross Industries logo and his name, Eric.

"Good evening, Mr. Cross. Miss Tramell," Eric greeted us with a smile. "Would you like something to drink as we prepare for takeoff?"

"Cranberry and Kingsman for me," I said.

"The same," Gideon replied, shrugging out of his jacket and handing it over to Eric, who waited while Gideon stripped off his vest and tie, too.

I watched appreciatively, throwing in a whistle for good measure. "I'm liking this trip already."

"Angel." He shook his head, his eyes laughing.

A gentleman in a navy suit entered the plane. He greeted Gideon warmly, shook my hand when introduced, then requested our passports. He was gone as quickly as he'd come, and the cabin door was closed. Gideon and I were buckled in at the table with our drinks when the plane started taxiing down the runway.

"Are you going to tell me where we're headed?" I asked, lifting my drink in a toast.

He clinked his crystal tumbler against mine. "Don't you want it to be a surprise?"

"Depends on how long it takes to get there. I might go crazy with curiosity before we land."

"I expect you'll be too busy to think about it." His mouth curved. "This is a mode of transportation, after all."

"Oh." I glanced back, seeing the little hallway of doors at the back of the plane. One would be a lavatory, one an office, and the other a bedroom. Expectation coursed through me. "How much time have we got to kill?"

"Hours," he purred.

My toes curled. "Oh, ace. The things I'm going to do to you."

He shook his head. "You're forgetting this is my weekend to have you any way I want. That was the deal."

"On our trip? That doesn't seem fair."

"You said that before."

"It was true then, too."

His smile widened and he took a drink. "As soon as the captain gives the go-ahead to get up, I want you to head into the bedroom and get naked. Then lie on the bed and wait for me."

One of my brows arched. "You love the idea of having me rolling around naked waiting for you to fuck me."

"I do, yes. I recall the reverse being a fantasy of yours."

"Hmm." I took a drink, relishing the way the vodka went down icy and smooth, then heated in my stomach.

The plane leveled out and the captain made a brief announcement freeing us to move about the cabin.

Gideon shot me a look that said, *Well? Run along now.*

Narrowing my gaze at him, I got up, taking my drink with me. I took my time, provoking him. And making myself more excited. I loved being at his mercy. As much as I loved making him lose his mind over me, I couldn't deny that his control was a major turn-on. I knew how absolute that control could be, which made it possible for me to trust him completely. I didn't think there was anything I wouldn't allow him to do to me.

Which was a conviction that would be tested sooner rather than later, I realized when I entered the sleeping cabin and saw the red silk-and-suede restraints lying so prettily on the white comforter.

Turning my head, I looked at Gideon only to find him gone. His empty glass sat on the table, the square cubes of ice glittering like diamonds.

My heart thudded. I stepped into the room, tossing back the rest of my drink. I couldn't bear to be restrained during sex, unless it was by Gideon. By his hands or the weight of his muscled body. We'd never gone beyond that. I wasn't sure I could.

I set my empty tumbler on the nightstand, my hand shaking slightly. I didn't know if that was due to fear or excitement.

I knew Gideon would never hurt me. He worked so hard to make sure I was never afraid. But what if I disappointed him? What if I couldn't give him what he needed? He'd mentioned bondage before and I knew one of his fantasies was to have me completely restrained and open to him, my body spread and helpless for him to use. I understood that desire, the need to feel total and utter possession. I felt that way toward him.

I undressed. My movements were slow and careful, because my pulse was already thrumming too quickly. I was practically panting, the anticipation painfully acute. I hung my clothes on a hanger in the small closet, then climbed gingerly onto the raised bed. I was holding the restraints in my hands, doubting and second-guessing myself, when Gideon walked in.

"You're not lying down," he said gently, closing and locking the door behind him.

I held up the restraints.

"Custom made, just for you." He approached, his nimble fingers already freeing the buttons of his shirt. "Crimson is your color."

Gideon undressed as slowly as I had, affording me the opportunity to appreciate every inch of skin he exposed. He knew the rippling of his muscles beneath the rough silk of his tanned flesh would be an aphrodisiac to me.

"Am I ready for this?" I asked softly.

His gaze stayed on my face as he removed his pants. When he stood in just his black boxer briefs, his cock a thick bulge in the front, he answered, "Never more than you can take, angel. I promise you that."

Taking a deep breath, I lay back, setting the cuffs on my belly. He came to me, his face tight with lust. He settled on the bed beside me and lifted my hand to his mouth, kissing my wrist. "Your pulse is racing."

I nodded, not knowing what to say.

He picked up the cuffs, deftly unhooking the strip of crimson silk that held the two suede wrist pieces together. "Being bound helps you surrender, but it doesn't have to be literal. It just has to be enough to get you in the right headspace."

My stomach quivered as he laid the strap across it. He set one cuff on his thigh and held up the other.

"Give me your wrist, angel."

I extended my hand to him, my breathing quickening as he fastened the suede snugly. The feel of the primitive material against my fluttering pulse was surprisingly arousing.

"That's not too tight, is it?" he asked.

"No."

"You should feel the constriction enough to be constantly aware of it, but it shouldn't hurt you."

I swallowed. "It doesn't hurt."

"Good." He bound my other wrist similarly, then straightened to admire his handwork. "Beautiful," he murmured. "Reminds me of the red dress you wore the first time I had you. That was it for me, you know. You devastated me. There was no coming back from that."

"Gideon." My apprehension left me, chased away by the warmth of his love and desire. I was precious to him. He would never push me further than I could go.

"Reach up and grip the sides of the pillow," he ordered.

I did, and the tightening of my wrists made me even more aware of the cuffs. I felt bound. Captured.

"Feel it?" he asked, and I understood.

I loved him so much in that moment it hurt. "Yes."

"I'm going to tell you to close your eyes," he went on, standing and taking off the final bit of clothing he wore. He was heavily aroused, his thick cock bobbing under its own weight, the wide crown shiny with pre-cum. My mouth flooded, hunger pulsing through me. He was so hot for me, so hungry, and yet you'd never know it from his voice or the calm he radiated.

His perfect restraint made me wet. Gideon was the best of everything for me, a man who wanted me ferociously—which I so urgently needed to feel secure—but with enough self-possession to keep from overwhelming me.

"I want you to keep your eyes closed if you can," he continued, his voice low and soothing, "but if it gets to be too much, open them. But say your safeword first."

"Okay."

He picked up the satin strap and ran it lightly over my skin. The cool metal of the fastener at one end caught on my nipple, making it pucker. "Let's be very clear about this, Eva. Your safeword isn't for me. It's for *you*. All you have to say to me is *no* or *stop*, but just like wearing the cuffs makes you feel bound, saying your safeword will put your mind in the right place. Do you understand?"

I nodded, growing more comfortable and eager by the moment.

"Close your eyes."

I followed the command. Almost instantly, I became sharply aware of the pressure at my wrists. The vibration and dull hum of the plane's engines became more pronounced. My lips parted. My breathing sped up.

The strap glided over my cleavage to my other breast. "You're so beautiful, angel. Perfect. You have no idea what it does to me seeing you like this."

"Gideon," I whispered, desperately in love with him. "Tell me."

His splayed fingertips touched my throat, and then began a slow slide down my torso. "My heart's beating as fast as yours."

I arched and shivered beneath his slightly ticklish touch. "Good."

"I'm so hard it hurts."

"I'm wet."

"Show me," he said roughly. "Spread your legs." His fingers slid through my cleft. "Yes. You're slick and hot, angel."

My sex clenched hungrily, my entire body responding to his touch.

"Ah, Eva. You've got the greediest cunt. I'm going to spend the rest of my life keeping it satisfied."

"You should start now."

He laughed softly. "Actually, we're starting with your mouth. I need you to suck me off so I can fuck you straight through until we land."

"Oh my God," I moaned. "Please tell me it's not a ten-hour flight."

"I might have to spank you for that," he purred.

"But I'm a good girl!"

The mattress dipped as he climbed onto it. I felt him work his way toward me until he knelt beside my shoulder. "Be a good girl now, Eva. Turn toward me and open your mouth."

Eager, I obeyed. The silky soft crest of his cock brushed over my lips and I opened wider, absorbing the shock of pleasure I felt at the sound of his tormented groan. His fingers pushed into my hair, his palm cupping the back of my neck. Holding me where he wanted me.

"God," he gasped. "Your mouth is just as greedy."

The position I was in, on my back with my hands gripping the pillow, prevented me from taking more than the thick head. I mouthed

him, my tongue flickering over the sensitive hole at the tip, thrilled by
the joy of focusing on Gideon. Going down on him wasn't selfless for
me. In fact, it was mostly for me that I loved it so much.

"That's it," he encouraged, rocking his hips to fuck my mouth. "Suck
my cock just like that . . . so good, angel. You make me come so hard."

I breathed him in, feeling my body respond to his scent, instinctively reacting to its mate. With all of my senses saturated with Gideon,
I gave myself over to our mutual pleasure.

I dreamed I was falling, and it jerked me awake.

My heart raced from the surprise, and then I realized the plane had
dropped suddenly. Turbulence. I was fine. And so was Gideon, who'd
fallen asleep beside me. That made me smile. I'd almost passed out
when he'd finally given me an orgasm after fucking me so thoroughly
I was nearly incoherent with the need to come. It was only fair that he'd
be a little wiped out, too.

A quick glance at my watch told me we'd been in the air almost
three hours. I guessed we'd napped about twenty minutes, maybe even
less than that. I was pretty sure he'd been at me for close to two hours.
I could still feel the echo of his thick cock sliding in and out of me,
stroking and rubbing all of my sensitive spots.

I slid carefully out of bed, not wanting to wake him, and was super
quiet when closing the pocket door that concealed the en suite lavatory.

Outfitted with dark wood and chrome fixtures, the lavatory was
both masculine and elegant. The toilet had armrests, which made it
look like a throne, and a frosted window allowed sunlight into the
space. A walk-in shower had a hand wand showerhead that looked very
tempting, but I was still wearing the crimson cuffs. So I took care of
business, washed my hands, then spotted hand lotion in one of the
drawers.

The fragrance was subtle but wonderful. As I rubbed it on, a wicked idea entered my mind. Grabbing the tube, I took it back to the bedroom with me.

The sight that greeted me when I reentered made my breath catch.

Gideon sprawled across the queen-size bed, dwarfing it with his beautiful golden body. One arm was tossed over his head, the other draped across his pecs. He had one leg bent and fallen off to the side, while the other stretched out until his foot hung off the end of the mattress. His cock lay heavily across his lower abs, the crown nearly reaching his navel.

God, he was so virile. Stunningly so. And powerful, his entire body a study in physical strength and grace.

And yet I could bring him to his knees. That humbled me.

He woke when I climbed onto the bed, blinking up at me.

"Hey," he said gruffly. "Come here."

"I love you," I told him, lowering into his outstretched arms. His skin felt like warm silk and I snuggled into him.

"Eva." He took my mouth in a sweet, hungry kiss. "I'm not nearly done with you."

Taking a deep breath of courage, I set the tube of lotion on his stomach. "I want to be inside you, ace."

He glanced down, frowning, then stilled. I was close enough to feel his breathing change. "That isn't our deal," he said carefully.

"I think we need to revisit and revise. Besides, it's still Friday, so it's not quite the weekend yet."

"Eva—"

"It turns me on just thinking about it," I whispered, wrapping my legs around his thigh and rubbing against him, letting him feel that I was wet. The coarse hair sliding against my sensitive sex made me moan, as did the sense of being shameless and naughty. "You say stop and I will. Just let me try."

His teeth ground audibly.

I kissed him. Pressed my body against him. When Gideon was

walking me through something new, he talked me through it. But with him, sometimes talking wasn't the answer. Sometimes it was best to help him turn his mind off.

"Angel—"

I slid over him, straddling him, setting the lotion aside so he wasn't thinking about it so much. If I took him someplace new, I didn't want either of us to overthink it. And if it didn't feel natural, I wouldn't do it. What we had together was too precious to spoil.

Running my hands down his chest, I gentled him, let him feel my love for him. How I worshipped him. There was nothing I wouldn't do for him, except give up.

His arms came around me, one hand pushing into my hair, the other settling at the small of my back, urging me closer. His mouth was open to me, his tongue licking and tasting. I sank into the kiss, angling my head to get at him.

His cock hardened between us, thickening against my belly. He arched his hips upward, increasing the pressure between us, and moaned into my mouth.

I moved across his cheek to his throat, licking the salt from his skin before latching on. I sucked rhythmically, scoring him with my teeth, marking him. With his hand at my nape, he held me close, rough sounds of pleasure vibrating against my lips.

Pulling back, I looked at the bright red hickey I'd left him with. "Mine," I whispered.

"Yours," he vowed roughly, his eyes hooded and hot.

"Every inch of you." I moved lower, finding and teasing the flat disks of his nipples. I licked over the tiny points, then around them, my touch feather light until I suckled him.

Gideon hissed as my cheeks hollowed on a drawing pull, his hands falling away to grip the comforter on either side of his hips.

"Inside and out," I said softly, as I turned to his other nipple and lavished similar attention on it.

274 · SYLVIA DAY

As I made my way down his straining body, I felt his tension grow. When my tongue rimmed his navel, he jerked violently.

"Shh," I soothed him, rubbing my cheek against his throbbing cock.

He'd washed up after our earlier round, leaving him smelling clean and delectable. His sac hung heavily between his legs, the satiny flesh bared by his meticulous grooming. I loved that he was as smooth as I was. When he was inside me, the connection was complete in every way, the sensations emphasized by touching skin to skin.

With my hands on his inner thighs, I urged him to spread open wider, giving me room to settle comfortably. Then I licked along the seam of his taut sac.

Gideon growled. The untamed, animalistic sound sent a ripple of apprehension through me. Still, I didn't stop. I couldn't. I wanted him too much.

Using only my mouth, I worshipped him, sucking softly and caressing him with my tongue. Then I suspended his testicles on the pads of my thumbs, lifting them to access the sensitive skin beneath. His balls drew up, the skin tightening and pulling close to his body. My tongue reached a little lower, an exploratory foray toward my ultimate goal.

"Eva. Stop." He panted. "I can't. Don't."

My mind raced as I continued to touch him, my hand gripping his cock and stroking it. He was still too much inside his own head, too focused on what was to come instead of what was happening now.

But I knew how to get him to focus on something else.

"Why don't we do this together, ace?" Shifting, I turned around, straddling him backward.

His hands grabbed my hips before I was fully balanced, yanking my sex down to his waiting mouth. I cried out in surprise as he latched onto my clit, sucking hungrily. Swollen and sensitive from earlier, I could hardly bear the sudden rush of pleasure. He was wild and ravenous, his passion driven by his frustration and fear.

Wrapping my lips around his cock, I gave him back what he was giving to me.

As I sucked hard on the head of his erection, his groan vibrated against my clit and nearly made me come. He held me to him, his fingers digging into my hips with bruising force.

I loved it. He was unraveling, and while he was afraid of what that meant, it thrilled me. He didn't trust himself with me, but I trusted him. It was a level of trust we'd worked hard for, shed tears and blood for, and I valued it more than anything else in my life.

Fisting his cock, I pumped him, lapping up the surges of pre-cum that spilled from him. I'd just realized he was trembling when he wrenched us to our sides, placing us side by side instead of one on top of the other.

He ate me hard and fast, his tongue pushing into my sex and driving me mad with furious thrusts. I touched the pucker of his anus with the tip of my finger, my mouth sliding feverishly up and down his thickness. He shuddered and the low sound that escaped him sent goose bumps racing across my sweat-misted skin.

My hips were working without volition, grinding my slick sex against his working mouth. I was moaning uncontrollably, my core trembling with tiny shivers of delight. He was fucking me so good with his tongue . . . driving me insane.

And then his fingertip was mimicking mine, rubbing against my rear entrance. My free hand searched blindly for the lotion.

Gideon pushed the tube into my grip, a much-needed sign of consent.

I'd barely flipped the cap open when his finger pushed inside me. As I arched my back, his cock slipped out of my mouth and I gasped his name, my body absorbing the shock of his unexpected entry. He'd lubed his fingers before passing the tube.

For a moment, I was overwhelmed by him. He was everywhere— around me, inside me, plastered against me. And he wasn't gentle. His finger in my rear plunged and retreated, fucking me, his forcefulness still tinged with that hint of anger. I was pushing him where he didn't want to go and he was punishing me with pleasure that came too quick to manage.

I was gentler with him. Opening my mouth, I sucked his cock. I let the lotion warm on my fingers before I rubbed it against him. And I waited for him to push out for me, to flower open, before I pushed inside with a single finger.

The sound that rattled from him then was like nothing I'd ever heard. It was the cry of a wounded animal, but filled with soul-deep pain. He froze against me, breathing hard against my sex, his finger buried deep, his hard body quivering.

I pulled my mouth off him and crooned, "I'm in you now, baby. You're doing so good. I'm going to make you feel so good."

He gasped when I slid a little deeper, my fingertip gliding over his prostate. *"Eva!"*

His cock swelled even further, turning red, the thick veins standing out along its length, pre-ejaculate spurting onto his lower belly. He was hard as stone, curving up to a point just past his navel. I'd never seen him so aroused and it made me so hot.

"I've got you." I stroked gently inside him, my tongue licking along his raging hard-on. "I love you so much, Gideon. I love touching you like this . . . seeing you this way."

"Ah, Christ." He shook violently. "Fuck me, angel. Now," he bit out, as I rubbed him again. *"Hard."*

I swallowed his erection and gave him what he demanded, massaging the spot inside him that made him curse and writhe, his body fighting the bombardment of sensation. His hands left me, his big frame arching away, but I held on with my lips and hands, driving him onward.

"Ah, God," he sobbed, ripping the comforter in his fists, the tearing sound reverberating through the enclosed space. "Stop. Eva. No more. Damn it!"

I pressed inside the same moment I sucked hard outside and he came with such force, I choked on the heated flood. He spurted across my lips as I pulled away, over his stomach and my breasts, releasing in a gushing torrent that made it hard to believe he'd already come twice in as many hours. I could feel the contractions against my fingertip, the wrenching pulses that propelled the semen from his cock.

It wasn't until his body stilled that I pulled away, turning around shakily to pull him into my arms. We were a sweaty, sticky mess and I loved that it didn't matter.

Gideon buried his damp face between my breasts and cried.

19

G IDEON'S CHOSEN LOCATION was paradise. His pilot took us over the Windward Islands, flying low over the impossibly beautiful blue waters of the tranquil Caribbean into a private airport not far from our ultimate destination, the Crosswinds resort.

We were both still pretty shell-shocked when the plane landed. Gideon had had the orgasm of his life, after all. We had our passports stamped with our hair still wet, our hands linked tightly together. We hardly spoke, either to each other or to anyone else. I think we were both too raw.

We slid into a waiting limousine and Gideon poured himself a stiff drink. His face gave nothing away, his guard up and impenetrable. I shook my head when he held up the crystal decanter in silent query.

He settled on the seat beside me and put his arm around my shoulders.

I snuggled into him, draping my legs over his lap. "Are we okay?"

He pressed a hard kiss to my forehead. "Yes."

"I love you."

"I know." He tossed back his drink and set the empty tumbler in a cup holder.

We didn't say anything else on the long drive from the airport to the resort. It was dark by the time we arrived, but the open-air lobby was brightly lit. Framed by lush potted plants and decorated in dark woods and colorful ceramic tiles, the front desk welcomed guests with a carefree yet elegant style.

The hotel manager was waiting on the circular front drive as we rolled to a stop. His appearance was immaculate, his smile wide. He was clearly excited to have Gideon in residence and doubly so that Gideon knew his name—Claude.

Claude spoke animatedly, as we followed along behind him with our hands linked firmly together. No one could tell from looking at Gideon how intimate and exposed to each other we'd been only an hour or so before. While my hair had dried in a messy mop, his looked as gorgeous and sexy as ever. His suit was perfectly pressed and beautifully worn, while my dress looked a little limp after the long day. My makeup had washed off in the shower, leaving me pale with the remnants of raccoon eyes.

Yet Gideon's possessiveness toward me was clear in the way he gripped me, and how he steered me into our suite in front of him with his hand at the small of my back. He made me feel safe and accepted, even though he was in his work persona and I wasn't at my best, which reflected on him.

I loved him for that.

I just wished he weren't so quiet. It made me worry. And it totally made me doubt my decision to push him after he'd told me to stop more than once. What the hell did I know about what he needed to get better?

As the manager continued to talk to Gideon, I moved slowly through the massive living area, with its wide-open terrace and white couches spread across bamboo floors. The master bedroom was equally impressive, with a large bed framed by mosquito netting and another open terrace that led directly to a private swimming pool with an infinity edge that made it look like part of the shimmering ocean just beyond it.

A warm breeze blew in, kissing my face and sifting through my hair. The rising moon cast a trail over the ocean, and the distant sounds of laughter and reggae made me feel isolated in a way that wasn't quite pleasant.

Nothing was right when Gideon was off.

"Do you like it?" he asked quietly.

I turned to face him and heard the front door shut in the other room. "It's fantastic."

He gave a curt nod. "I ordered dinner in. Tilapia and rice, some fresh fruit and cheese."

"Awesome. I'm starving."

"There are clothes for you in the closet and drawers. You'll find bikinis, too, but the pool and beach are private, so you don't need them unless you want them. If there's anything missing, just let me know and we'll get it brought in."

I stared at him, noting the several feet between us. His eyes glittered in the soft light cast by the dimmed cam lighting and bedside table lamps. He was edgy and distant, and I felt tears building in the back of my throat.

"Gideon . . ." I held my hand out to him. "Did I make a mistake? Did I break something between us?"

"Angel." He sighed. He came close enough to catch my hand and lift it to his lips. Up close I could see how his gaze darted away, as if he had a hard time looking at me. A sick feeling settled in my gut. "Crossfire."

The one word came out so low, I almost thought I'd imagined it. Then he pulled me into his arms and kissed me sweetly.

"Ace." Pushing onto my tiptoes, I cupped the back of his neck and kissed him back with everything I had.

He pulled away too quickly. "Let's change for dinner before it gets here. I could stand being in less clothes."

I stepped back reluctantly, acknowledging that he had to be hot in his suit, but still sensing that something wasn't right. That feeling worsened when Gideon left the room to change and I realized we wouldn't be sharing the same bedroom.

I kicked off my shoes in the walk-in closet that was filled with way too many clothes for a weekend trip. Most were white. Gideon liked me in white. I suspected it was because he thought of me as his angel.

Did he still think of me that way now? Or was I the devil? A selfish bitch who made him face demons he'd rather forget?

I changed into a simple cotton slip dress in black, which matched my funereal mood. I felt like something had died between us.

Gideon and I had stumbled many times before, but I'd never felt this level of withdrawal from him. This discomfort and unease.

I'd felt it with other guys, when they were getting ready to tell me they didn't want to see me anymore.

Dinner arrived and was neatly laid out on the terrace table overlooking the secluded beach. I saw a white tent cabana on the sand and remembered Gideon's dream of us rolling around on a chaise for two by the water, making love.

My heart hurt.

I gulped two glasses of crisp, fruity white wine and went through the motions of eating, even though I'd lost my appetite. Gideon sat across from me in loose white linen drawstring pants and nothing else, which just made everything worse. He was so handsome, so goddamned sexy it was impossible not to stare at him. But he was miles away from me. A silent, forceful presence that made me *want* with every fiber of my soul.

The emotional gulf between us was growing. I couldn't reach across it.

I pushed my plate away once I'd cleared it and realized Gideon had hardly eaten at all. He'd just forked his food around and helped me drain the bottle of wine.

Taking a deep breath, I told him, "I'm sorry. I should've . . . I didn't . . ." I swallowed hard. "I'm sorry, baby," I whispered.

Shoving back from the table with a loud screech of the chair legs across the tile, I hurried away from the patio.

"Eva! Wait."

My feet hit the warm sand and I ran toward the ocean, pulling my dress off and colliding with water that felt as hot as a bath. It was shallow for several feet, then dropped off suddenly, plunging me in below my head. I bent my knees and sank, grateful to be submerged and hidden as I cried.

The weightlessness soothed my heavy heart. My hair billowed around me and I felt the soft brush of fish as they darted past the invader in their silent, peaceful world.

Being yanked back into reality had me sputtering and flailing.

"Angel." Gideon growled and took my mouth, kissing me hard and furious as he stalked out of the water and up the beach. He took me to the cabana and dropped me onto the chaise, covering me with his body before I fully caught my breath.

I was still dizzy when he groaned and said, "Marry me."

But that wasn't why I said, "Yes."

GIDEON had gone into the water after me with his pants on. The soaked linen clung to my bare legs as he sprawled over me and kissed me as if he were dying of a thirst only I could quench. His hands were in my hair, holding me still. His mouth was frantic, his lips swollen like mine, his tongue greedy and possessive.

I lay beneath him unmoving. Shocked. My startled brain quickly caught up.

He'd been agonizing over popping the question, not because he was leaving me.

"Tomorrow," he bit out, rubbing his cheek against mine. The first tingle of stubble roughened his jaw, the sensation jolting me into a deeper awareness of where we were and what he wanted.

"I—" My mind stuttered to a halt again.

"The word is *yes*, Eva." He pushed up and stared down at me fiercely. "Real simple—yes."

I swallowed hard. "We can't get married tomorrow."

"We can," he said emphatically, "and we will. I need it, Eva. I need the vows, the legality . . . I'm going crazy without them."

I felt the world spinning, like I was on one of those fun-house barrel rides that revolve so fast you're stuck to the wall with centrifugal force when the floor drops away from your feet. "It's too soon," I protested.

"You can say that to me after the flight over?" he snapped. "You fucking *own* me, Eva. I'll be damned if I don't own you back."

"I can't breathe," I gasped, inexplicably panicked.

Gideon rolled, pulling me on top of him, his arms banding around me. Possessing me. "You want this," he insisted. "You love me."

"I do, yes." I dropped my forehead to his chest. "But you're rushing into—"

"You think I'd ask you this on the fly? For God's sake, Eva, you know me better than that. I've been planning this for weeks. It's all I've thought about."

"Gideon . . . we can't just run off and elope."

"The hell we can't."

"What about our families? Or friends?"

"We'll get married again for them. I want that, too." He brushed the wet hair off my cheek. "I want pictures of us in the newspapers, magazines . . . everywhere. But that will take months. I can't wait that long. This is for us. We don't have to tell anyone, if you don't want. We can call it an engagement. It can be our secret."

I stared at him, not knowing what to say. His urgency was both romantic and terrifying.

"I asked your dad," he went on, shocking me all over again. "He didn't have any—"

"What? When?"

"When he was in town. I had an opportunity and I took it."

For some reason, that hurt. "He didn't tell me."

"I told him not to. Told him it wasn't going to happen right away. That I was still working on getting you back. I recorded it, so you can listen to the conversation if you don't believe me."

I blinked down at him. "You recorded it?" I repeated.

"I wasn't leaving anything to chance," he said unapologetically.

"You told him it wouldn't be right away. You lied to him."

His smile was razor sharp. "I didn't lie. It's been a few days."

"Oh my God. You're crazy."

"Possibly. If so, you've made me this way." He pressed a hard kiss to my cheek. "I can't live without you, Eva. I can't even imagine trying. Just the thought makes me insane."

"*This* is insane."

"Why?" He frowned. "You know there's no one else for either of us. What are you waiting for?"

Arguments rushed through my mind. Every reason we should wait, every possible pitfall seemed crystal clear. But nothing came out of my mouth.

"I'm not giving you any options here," he said decisively, twisting up and standing with me cradled in his arms. "We're doing this, Eva. Enjoy your last remaining hours as a single woman."

"GIDEON," I gasped, my head thrashing as the orgasm poured through me.

His sweat dripped onto my chest, his hips tireless as he stroked his magnificent penis into me over and over, rolling and thrusting, shallow then deep.

"That's it," he praised hoarsely, "squeeze my dick just like that. You feel so good, angel. You're going to make me come again."

I panted for breath, boneless and tired from his unrelenting demands. He'd woken me twice before, taking me with skilled precision, imprinting onto my brain and my body that I belonged to him. That I was his and he could do whatever he wanted to me.

It made me so hot.

"Umm . . ." He purred, sliding his cock deep. "You're so creamy with my cum. I love the way you feel when I've been at you all night. A lifetime of this, Eva. I'll never stop."

I draped my leg over his hip, holding him in me. "Kiss me."

His wickedly curved mouth brushed over mine.

"Love me," I demanded, my nails digging into his hips as he flexed inside me.

"I do, angel," he whispered, his smile widening. "I do."

WHEN I woke, he was gone.

I stretched in a tangle of sheets that smelled of sex and Gideon and breathed in the salt-tinged breeze drifting through the open patio doors.

I lay there for a while, thinking over the night and the day before. Then the weeks before, and the few months since I'd met Gideon. Then beyond that. Back to Brett and others I had dated. Back to a time when

I'd been so certain I would never find a man who loved me for who I was, with all my emotional scars and baggage and neediness.

What else could I say besides yes, now that by some miracle I'd found him?

Rolling out of bed, I felt a flutter of excitement at the thought of finding Gideon and agreeing to marry him without reservation. I loved the idea of eloping with him, of our first vows spoken in private, with no one watching who harbored doubts or dislike or bad wishes. After all we'd both been through, it made perfect sense for our new beginning to be filled with nothing but love and hope and happiness.

I should've known he'd plan it all perfectly, from the privacy to the exclusive locale. Of course we'd get married on a beach. Beaches held fond memories for both of us, not the least of which was our last time away at the Outer Banks.

When I saw the breakfast tray on the coffee table in the bedroom's seating area, I smiled. There was a white silk robe draped over the back of the chair, too.

Gideon never missed a trick.

I pulled the robe on and reached to pour myself a cup of coffee, wanting a caffeine boost before I searched for him in the suite and gave him my answer. That was when I saw the prenuptial agreement tucked beneath the covered breakfast plate.

My hand froze halfway to the carafe. The agreement was tastefully arranged beneath the single red rose in a slender white vase, with the silverware gleaming from an artfully folded cloth napkin.

I don't know why I was so surprised and . . . crushed. Of course, Gideon would've planned everything down to the last detail—starting with the prenup. After all, hadn't he tried to start our relationship with an agreement?

All of my giddy happiness left me in a rush. Deflated, I turned away from the tray and headed into the shower instead. I took my time washing up, moving in slow motion. I decided I'd rather say no than read a legal document that put a price on my love. A love that was precious and priceless to me.

Still, I feared it was too late, that the damage was already done. Just knowing he'd had a prenup drafted changed everything and I couldn't blame him for that. For God's sake, he was Gideon Cross. One of the twenty-five richest men in the world. It was inconceivable that he *wouldn't* demand a prenuptial agreement. And I wasn't naïve. I knew better than to dream of Prince Charming and castles in the sky.

Showered and clothed in a light sundress, I pulled my hair back in a wet ponytail and went for the coffee. I poured a cup, added cream and sweetener, then slid the prenup free and stepped out to the patio.

Down on the beach, preparations were under way for the wedding. A flower-covered arch had been placed by the shoreline and braided white ribbon had been draped across the sand to mark an impromptu aisle.

I chose to sit with my back to the view, because it hurt to look at it.

I took a sip of coffee, let it soak into me, then took another. I was halfway done with my cup when I gathered enough courage to read the damn legalese. The opening few pages detailed the assets we owned separately prior to marriage. Gideon's holdings were staggering. *When did he find time to sleep?* I thought the dollar amount attributed to me was wrong, until I considered how long the principal had been sitting in investments.

Stanton had taken my five million and doubled it.

It struck me then how stupid I was for just sitting on it, instead of investing it where it could help those who needed it. I'd been acting like that blood money didn't exist when I should've been putting it to work. I made a mental note to tackle that project as soon as I got back to New York.

After that, the reading got interesting.

Gideon's first stipulation was that I take the Cross name as my own.

I could keep Tramell as an additional middle name, but with no hyphenation as a surname. *Eva Cross*—it was nonnegotiable. And so very like him. My domineering lover made no apologies for his caveman tendencies.

His second stipulation was that I accept ten million from him upon the wedding, doubling my personal estate just for saying *I do*. Every year thereafter, he gave me more. I would receive bonuses for each child we had together, be paid for going to couples therapy with him. I agreed to counseling and mediation in the event of a divorce. I agreed to share a residence with him, bimonthly vacations, date nights . . .

The more I read, the more I understood. The prenup didn't protect Gideon's assets at all. He gave them freely, going so far as to stipulate up front that fifty percent of everything he acquired from our marriage onward was irrefutably mine. Unless he cheated. If that happened, it cost him severely.

The prenup was designed to protect his heart, to bind me and bribe me to stay with him no matter what. He was giving everything he had.

He joined me on the terrace when I flipped to the last page, strolling out in a pair of partially buttoned jeans and nothing else. I knew his perfectly timed arrival wasn't coincidental. He'd been watching me from somewhere, gauging my reaction.

I brushed the tears from my cheeks with studied nonchalance. "Good morning, ace."

"Morning, angel." He bent and pressed a kiss to my cheek before taking the chair at the end of the table to my left.

A member of the staff came out with breakfast and coffee, arranging the place settings quickly and efficiently before disappearing as swiftly as he'd appeared.

I looked at Gideon, at the way the tropical breeze adored him and played with that sexy mane of hair. Sitting there as he was, so virile and casual, he wasn't at all the cut-and-dried presentation of dollar signs I'd seen in the prenup.

Allowing the pages to flip back to the first page, I set my hand on top of it and said, "Nothing in this document can keep me married to you."

He took a quick, deep breath. "Then we'll revisit and revise. Name your terms."

"I don't want your money. I want this," I gestured at him. "Especially this." I leaned forward and placed my hand over his heart. "You're the only thing that can hold me, Gideon."

"I don't know how to do this, Eva." He caught my hand and held it pressed flat to his chest. "I'm going to fuck up. And you'll want to run."

"Not anymore," I argued. "Haven't you noticed?"

"I noticed you running into the ocean last night and sinking like a damn stone!" Leaning forward, he held my gaze. "Don't argue the prenup on principle. If there are no deal breakers for you in it, live with it. For me."

I sat back. "You and I have a long way to go," I said softly. "A document can't force us to believe in each other. I'm talking about trust, Gideon."

"Yeah, well—" He hesitated. "I don't trust myself not to fuck this up, and you don't trust that you've got what I need. We trust each other just fine. We can work on the rest together."

"Okay." I watched his eyes light up and knew I was making the right decision, even if I was still partially convinced that it was a decision we were making too soon. "I do have one revision."

"Name it."

"You just did. The name issue."

"Nonnegotiable," he said flatly, with an empathic swipe of his hand for good measure.

I arched a brow. "Don't be a fucking Neanderthal. I want to take my dad's name, too. He's wanted that and it's bothered him my whole life. This is my chance to fix it."

"So, Eva Lauren Reyes Cross?"

"Eva Lauren Tramell Reyes Cross."

"That's a mouthful, angel," he drawled, "but do what makes you happy. That's all I want."

"All I want is you," I told him, leaning forward to offer him my mouth for a kiss.

His lips touched mine. "Let's make it official."

I married Gideon Geoffrey Cross barefoot on a Caribbean beach with the hotel manager and Angus McLeod as witnesses. I hadn't realized Angus was there, but I was pleased that he was.

It was a quick, beautifully simple ceremony. I could tell from the beaming smiles of the reverend and Claude that they were honored to officiate over Gideon's nuptials.

I wore the prettiest dress I'd found in the closet. Strapless and ruched from breasts to hips, with petals of organza floating down to my feet, it was a sweet yet sexy romantic gown. My hair was up in an elegantly messy knot with a red rose tucked into it. The hotel provided a bouquet of white-ribboned jasmine.

Gideon wore graphite gray slacks and an untucked white dress shirt. He went barefoot, too. I cried when he repeated his vows, his voice strong and sure, even while his eyes betrayed a heated yearning.

He loved me so much.

The entire ceremony was intimate and deeply personal. Perfect.

I missed my mom and dad and Cary. I missed Ireland and Stanton and Clancy. But when Gideon bent to seal our marriage with a kiss, he whispered, "We'll do this again. As many times as you want."

I loved him so much.

Angus stepped up to kiss me on both cheeks. "It does me good to see you both so happy."

"Thank you, Angus. You've taken good care of him for a long time."

He smiled, his eyes glistening as he turned to Gideon. He said something so heavily accented by his Scottish heritage, I couldn't be sure it was any form of English at all. Whatever it was, it made Gideon's eyes shine, too. How much of a surrogate father had Angus been to Gideon over the years? I would always be grateful to him for giving Gideon support and affection when he desperately needed it.

We cut a small cake and toasted with champagne on the terrace of our suite. We signed the register the reverend offered and were given our certificate of marriage to sign as well. Gideon's fingers brushed over it reverently.

"Is this what you needed?" I teased him. "This piece of paper?"

"I need you, Mrs. Cross." He pulled me close. "I wanted this."

Angus took both the certificate and prenup with him when he made himself scarce. Both had been duly notarized by the hotel manager and would end up wherever Gideon kept such things.

As for Gideon and me, we ended up in the cabana, tangled naked with each other. We sipped chilled champagne, touched each other playfully and greedily, and kissed lazily as the day crawled by.

That was perfect, too.

"So, how are we handling this when we get back?" I asked him, as we ate a candlelit dinner in the dining room of our suite. "The whole we-ran-off-and-got-hitched explanation."

Gideon shrugged and licked melted butter off his thumb. "However you want."

I pulled the meat out of a crab leg and considered the options. "I want to tell Cary for sure. And I think my dad will be okay with it. I kind of talked around it when I called him earlier and he told me you'd asked him, so he's prepared. I don't think Stanton will care much either way, no offense."

"None taken."

"I'm worried about my mom, though. Things are already rough

between us. She'll be totally stoked that we're married"—I paused a minute, absorbing that for the millionth time—"but I don't want her to think that I left her out because I'm mad at her."

"Let's just tell her and everyone else we're engaged."

I dunked the crabmeat into drawn butter, thinking I wanted to get *very* used to seeing Gideon shirtless and sated and relaxed. "She'll have a conniption if we live together before the wedding."

"Well, then she'll have to plan fast," he said dryly. "You're my wife, Eva. I don't care if anyone else knows it or not, *I* know it. And I want to come home to you, have coffee in the morning with you, zip up the back of your dresses, and unzip them at night."

Watching him snap a crab leg with his hands, I asked, "Will you wear a wedding band?"

"I'm looking forward to it."

That made me smile. He paused and stared at me.

"What?" I prompted, when he didn't say anything. "Do I have butter splashed on my face?"

He sat back with a deep exhalation. "You're beautiful. I love looking at you."

I felt my face heat. "You're not so bad yourself."

"It's starting to go away," he murmured.

My smile faded. "What? What's going away?"

"The . . . worry. It feels safe, doesn't it?" He sipped his wine. "Settled. It's a good feeling. I like it. A lot."

I hadn't had as much time to get used to the idea of being married, but as I sat back and really thought about it, I had to agree. He was mine. No one could doubt it now. "I like it, too."

He lifted my hand to his lips. The ring he'd given me caught the candlelight and glimmered with multihued fire. It was a tastefully large Asscher-cut diamond in a vintage setting. I loved the timeless sophistication of it, but more so because it was the ring his father had married his mother with.

Even though Gideon was deeply wounded by his parents' betrayals, their time together as a family of three was the last true happiness he remembered before meeting me.

And he swore he wasn't romantic.

He caught me admiring the ring. "You like it."

"I do." I looked at him. "It's one of a kind. I was thinking we could do something unusual with our home, too."

"Oh?" He squeezed my hand and resumed eating.

"I understand the need to sleep apart, but I don't like having doors and walls between us."

"I don't, either, but your safety comes first."

"How about a master suite with two bedrooms connected by a bathroom with no doors. Just archways or passageways. So technically, we're still in the same open space."

He considered that a minute, then nodded. "Draw it up and we'll bring in a designer to make it happen. We'll continue staying on the Upper West Side for now while we have the penthouse refinished. Cary can take a look at the adjoining one-bedroom apartment and make any changes he wants at the same time."

I rubbed my bare foot along the back of his calf as a thank-you. The sounds of music drifted in on the evening wind, reminding me that we weren't alone on a deserted island.

Was Angus having a good time somewhere? Or was he stuck standing outside the door to our suite?

"Where's Angus?" I asked.

"Around."

"Is Raúl here, too?"

"No. He's in New York working out how Nathan's bracelet ended up where it did."

"Oh." I suddenly lost my appetite. Picking up my napkin, I wiped my fingers. "Should I be worried?"

It was a rhetorical question, since I'd never stopped worrying. The mystery of who was responsible for sending the police in another direction was always there, niggling at the back of my mind.

"Someone handed me a get-out-of-jail-free card," he said evenly, licking his lower lip. "I expected that was going to cost me something, but no one's approached me yet. So, I'll approach them."

"Once you find them."

"Oh, I'll find them," he murmured darkly. "Then we'll know why."

Beneath the table, I wrapped my legs around his and held on.

WE danced on the beach by the light of the moon. The lush humidity was sensuous at night, and we reveled in it. Gideon shared my bed that night, even though I could tell how difficult it was for him to take the risk. I couldn't imagine sleeping alone on my wedding night and trusted that his prescription combined with the previous night's lack of sleep would help him sleep deeply. It did.

Sunday, he gave me the choice of going to a fabulous waterfall or taking the resort's catamaran out to sea or rafting down a jungle river. I smiled and told him next time, and then I had my wicked way with him.

We lazed around all day, skinny-dipping in the private pool and napping when the mood struck us. It was after midnight when we left, and I was sorry to go. The weekend had been far too short.

"We've got a lifetime of weekends," he murmured as we drove back to the airport, reading my mind.

"I'm selfish with you. I want you all to myself."

When we boarded the jet, the clothes we'd had at our disposal at the resort came with us. It made me smile, thinking of how little we'd worn over the two days.

I took the cosmetic case into the bedroom so I could brush my teeth before sleeping the duration of the flight home. That was when I saw the patent leather and brass luggage tag attached to it, engraved with *Eva Cross.*

Gideon slipped into the lavatory behind me and kissed my shoulder. "Let's crash, angel. We need some sleep before work."

Pointing at the luggage tag, I said, "Was my saying yes really that much of a foregone conclusion?"

"I was prepared to hold you hostage until you did."

I didn't doubt him. "I'm flattered."

"You're married." He smacked me on the ass. "Now hurry up, Mrs. Cross."

I hurried and slipped into the bed beside him. He immediately spooned behind me, tucking me close.

"Sweet dreams, baby," I whispered, wrapping my arms over his around my middle.

His mouth curved against my neck. "My dreams already came true."

20

I T WAS WEIRD going to work on Monday morning and having no one realize my life was profoundly different. Who knew how much saying a few words and slipping on a ring of metal could change a person's perception of themselves?

I wasn't just Eva, the New York newbie trying to make it on her own in the big city with her best friend. I was a mogul's wife. I had a whole new set of responsibilities and expectations. Just thinking about it intimidated me.

Megumi stood as she buzzed me through the security doors at Waters Field & Leaman. She was dressed with unusual sedateness in a black sleeveless dress with an asymmetrical hemline and bright fuchsia heels. "Wow. You've got an amazing tan! I'm so jealous."

"Thanks. How'd your weekend go?"

"Same old, same old. Michael stopped calling." Her nose wrinkled. "I miss the harassment. Made me feel wanted."

I shook my head at her. "You're nuts."

"I know. So tell me where you went. And did you go with the rock star or Cross?"

"My lips are sealed." Although I was tempted to reveal everything. The only thing that held me back was that I hadn't told Cary yet and he needed to come first.

"No way!" Her dark eyes narrowed. "Are you seriously not going to tell me?"

"Of course I will." I winked. "Just not right now."

"I know where you work, you know," she called after me as I headed down the hallway to my cubicle.

When I reached my desk, I got ready to type a quick text to Cary and discovered that he'd sent me a few over the weekend that hadn't come through until later. They certainly hadn't been there when I'd placed my usual Saturday call to my dad.

Wanna have lunch? I texted.

When I didn't get a reply right away, I silenced my phone and set it in my top drawer.

"Where did you spend the weekend?" Mark asked me as he came in to work. "You've got a great tan."

"Thanks. I lazed it up in the Caribbean."

"Really? I've been scoping out the islands for possible honeymoon spots. Would you recommend it for that, wherever you stayed?"

I laughed, happier than I'd been in long time. Maybe in forever. "Absolutely."

"Get me the deets. I'll add the spot to the list of possibilities."

"You have honeymoon scouting duty?" I stood so we could grab coffee together before we started the day.

"Yep." Mark's mouth quirked on one side. "I'll leave the wedding

298 · SYLVIA DAY

stuff to Steven, since he's been planning for so long. But the honey-moon is mine."

He sounded so happy, and I knew just how he felt. His good mood made the start of my day even better.

THE smooth sailing ended when Cary called my desk phone shortly after ten o'clock.

"Mark Garrity's office," I answered. "Eva Tramell—"

"—needs an ass-kicking," Cary finished. "I can't remember the last time I was this mad at you."

I frowned, my stomach tightening. "Cary, what's wrong?"

"I'm not going to talk about important shit on the phone, Eva, un-like some people I know. I'll meet you for lunch. And just so you're aware, I turned down a go-see this afternoon to set you straight, be-cause that's what friends do," he said angrily. "They make time in their schedule to talk about things that matter. They don't leave cutesy voice-mail messages and think that handles it!"

The line went dead. I sat there, shocked and a bit scared.

Everything in my life ground to a screeching halt. Cary was my an-chor. When things weren't right with us, I scattered real quick. And I knew it was the same for him. When we were out of touch, he started fucking up.

I dug out my cell phone and called him back.

"What?" he snapped. But it was a good sign that he'd answered.

"If I screwed up," I said quickly, "I'm sorry and I'll fix it. Okay?"

He made a rough sound. "You fucking piss me off, Eva."

"Yeah, well, I'm good at pissing people off, if you haven't noticed, but I hate when I do it to you." I sighed. "It's going to drive me nuts, Cary, until we can work it out. I need us solid, you know that."

"You haven't acted like it matters lately," he said gruffly. "I'm an afterthought and that fucking hurts."

"I'm always thinking about you. If I haven't shown it, that's my bad."

He didn't say anything.

"I love you, Cary. Even when I'm messing up."

He exhaled into the receiver. "Get back to work and don't stress about this. We'll deal with it at lunch."

"I'm sorry. Really."

"See you at noon."

I hung up and tried to concentrate, but it was hard. It was one thing having Cary angry with me; it was totally another to know I'd hurt him. I was one of the very few people in his life he trusted not to let him down.

AT eleven thirty, I received a small pile of interoffice envelopes. I was thrilled when one of them revealed a note from Gideon.

> MY GORGEOUS, SEXY WIFE,
> I NEVER STOP THINKING ABOUT YOU.
> YOURS,
> X

My feet tapped out a little happy dance beneath my desk. My skewed day righted itself a little.

I wrote him back.

> *Dark and Dangerous,*
> *I'm madly in love with you.*
> *Your ball and chain,*
> *Mrs. X*

I tucked it in an envelope and dropped it in my out-box.

I was drafting a reply to the artist working on a gift card campaign when my desk phone rang. I answered with my usual greeting and heard a reply in a familiar French accent.

"Eva, it's Jean-François Giroux."

Sitting back in my chair, I said, "*Bonjour*, Monsieur Giroux."

"What time is best for us to meet today?"

What the hell did he want from me? I supposed if I wanted to know, I'd have to follow through. "Five o'clock? There's a wine bar not too far from the Crossfire."

"That would be fine."

I gave him directions and he hung up, leaving me feeling somewhat whiplashed by the call. I swiveled in my chair, thinking. Gideon and I were trying to move forward with our lives, but people and issues from our pasts were still trying to hold us back. Would the announcement of our marriage, or even an engagement, change that?

God, I hoped so. But was anything ever that easy?

Glancing at the clock, I refocused on work and returned to writing my e-mail.

I was down in the lobby by five after noon, but Cary hadn't arrived yet. As I waited for him, my nerves started getting to me. I'd gone over my brief conversation with Cary again and again and knew he was right. I had convinced myself he'd be okay with having Gideon join our living arrangements because I couldn't imagine facing the alternative— having to choose between my best friend and my boyfriend.

And now there was no choice. I was married. Ecstatically so.

Still, I found myself grateful that I'd tucked my wedding ring into the zippered pocket of my purse. If Cary felt a growing distance between us, finding out I'd gotten hitched over the weekend wouldn't help.

My stomach twisted. The secrets between us were mounting. I couldn't stand it.

"Eva."

I jerked out of my thoughts at the sound of my best friend's voice. He was striding toward me wearing loose-fitting cargo shorts and a V-neck T-shirt. He kept his shades on, and with his hands shoved in his pockets, he seemed distant and cool. Heads turned as he walked by and he didn't notice, his attention on me.

My feet moved. I was hurrying toward him before I thought of it, then ran straight into him so hard, his breath left him with a grunt. I hugged him, my cheek pressed to his chest.

"I missed you," I said, meaning it with all my heart, even though he wouldn't know exactly why.

He muttered something under his breath and hugged me. "Pain in the ass sometimes, baby girl."

Pulling back, I looked up at him. "I'm sorry."

He linked his fingers with mine and led me out of the Crossfire. We went to the place with the great tacos that we'd gone to the last time he had met me for lunch. They also had great slushy virgin margaritas, which were perfect on a steamy summer day.

After waiting in line about ten minutes, I ordered only two tacos, since I hadn't hit the gym in way too long. Cary ordered six. We snagged a table just as its former occupants cleared away, and Cary inhaled a taco before I'd barely taken the wrapper off my straw.

"I'm sorry about the voice mail," I said.

"You don't get it." He swiped a napkin across lips that turned sane women into giggling girls when he smiled. "It's the whole situation, Eva. You leave me a message telling me to think about sharing a place with Cross, *after* you tell your mom that it's a done deal and *before* you fall off the face of the earth for the weekend. I guess however I feel about it means jack shit to you."

"That's not true!"

"Why would you want a roommate when you're living with a boyfriend anyway?" he asked, clearly getting warmed up. "And why would you think I'd want to be a third wheel?"

"Cary—"

"I don't need any fucking handouts, Eva." His emerald eyes narrowed. "I've got places I can crash, other people I can room with. Don't do me any favors."

My chest tightened. I wasn't ready to let Cary go yet. Someday in the future, we'd be heading our separate ways, maybe only seeing each other on special occasions. But that time wasn't now. It couldn't be. Just thinking about it screwed with my head.

"Who says I'm doing it for you?" I shot back. "Maybe I just can't bear the thought of not having you nearby."

He snorted and ripped a bite out of his taco. Chewing angrily, he swallowed his food down with a long draw on his straw. "What am I, your three-year chip marking your recovery? Your celebratory token for Eva Anonymous?"

"Excuse me." I leaned forward. "You're mad, I get it. I've said I'm sorry. I love you and I love having you in my life, but I'm not going to sit here and get kicked because I fucked up."

I pushed away from the table and stood. "I'll catch you later."

"You and Cross getting married?"

Pausing, I looked down at him. "He asked. I said yes."

Cary nodded, as if that were no surprise, and took another bite. I grabbed my purse from where it hung on the back of my chair.

"Are you afraid of living alone with him?" he asked around his chewing.

Of course he'd think that. "No. He'll be sleeping in his own bedroom."

"Has he been sleeping in a separate room the last few weekends you've been shacking up with him?"

I stared. Did he know for a fact that Gideon was the "loverman" I'd been spending time with? Or was he just fishing? I decided I didn't care. I was tired of lying to him. "Mostly, yes."

He set his taco down. "Finally, some truth out of you. I was beginning to think you'd forgotten how to be honest."

"Fuck you."

Grinning, he gestured at my vacant chair. "Sit your ass back down, baby girl. We're not done talking."

"You're being a jerk."

His smile faded and his gaze hardened. "Being lied to for weeks makes me cranky. Sit down."

I sat and glared at him. "There? Happy?"

"Eat. I've got shit to say."

Exhaling my frustration, I slung my purse over the chair again and faced him with my brows raised.

"If you think," he began, "that being sober and working steadily broke my bullshit meter, now you know better. I knew you were nailing Cross again from the moment you started back up."

Biting into my taco, I shot him a skeptical look.

"Eva honey, don't you think that if there were another man in New York who could bang it out all night like Cross, I would've found him by now?"

I coughed and nearly spit out my food.

"No one's lucky enough to find two guys like that in a row," he drawled. "Not even you. You should've had a dry spell or at least a couple of really bad lays first."

I threw my wadded-up straw wrapper at him, which he dodged with a laugh.

Then he sobered. "Did you think I would judge you for getting back together with him after he jacked up?"

"It's more complicated than that, Cary. Things were . . . a mess. There was a lot of pressure. Still is, with that reporter stalking Gideon—"

"Stalking him?"

"Totally. I just didn't want . . ." *You exposed. Vulnerable. Open to accusation as an accomplice after the fact.* "I just had to let it play out," I finished lamely.

He let that sink in, then nodded. "And now you're going to marry him."

"Yes." I took a drink, needing to loosen the lump in my throat. "But you're the only one who knows that besides us."

"Finally, a secret you let me in on." His lips pursed for a few seconds. "And you still want me to live with you."

I leaned forward again, holding out my hand for his. "I know you can do something else, go somewhere else. But I'd rather you didn't. I'm not ready to be without you yet, married or not."

He gripped my hand so tightly, my bones pressed together. "Eva—"

"Wait," I said quickly. He was far too serious all of a sudden. I didn't want him to cut me off before I put everything out there. "Gideon's penthouse has an adjacent one-bedroom apartment he doesn't use."

"A one-bedroom apartment. On Fifth Avenue."

"Yeah. Great, right? All yours. Your own space and entrance and view of Central Park. But still connected to me. The best of both worlds." I rushed on, hoping to say something he'd latch on to. "We'll stay on the Upper West Side for a bit, while I make changes to the penthouse. Gideon says we can have whatever changes you want made to your apartment done at the same time."

"My apartment." He stared at me, which made me even more nervous. A man and a woman tried to squeeze between our table and the back of an occupied chair that was pushed too far out into the walkway, but I ignored them.

"I'm not talking about a handout," I assured him. "I've been thinking that I'd like to put that money I've been sitting on to work. Create a foundation or something to decide how to use it in support of causes and charities we believe in. I need your help. And I'll pay you for it. Not just for your input, but for your face. I want you to be the foundation's first spokesperson."

Cary's grip on my hand slackened.

Alarmed, I tightened mine. "Cary?"

His shoulders sagged. "Tatiana's pregnant."

"What?" I felt the blood drain from my face. The little restaurant was hopping, and the shouting of orders behind the counter and the clatter of trays and utensils made it hard to hear, but I'd caught the two words that fell out of Cary's mouth as if he'd shouted them at me. "Are you kidding?"

"I wish." He pulled his hand away and scooped back the bangs that draped over one eye. "Not that I don't want a kid. That part's cool. But . . . fuck. Not now, you know? And not with her."

"How the hell did she get pregnant?" Cary was religious about protecting himself, knowing damn well he lived a high-risk lifestyle.

"Well, I shoved my dick in her and pushed it around—"

"Shut up," I bit out. "You're *careful*."

"Yeah, well, putting a sock on it isn't guaranteed protection," he said wearily, "and Tat doesn't take the pill because she says it makes her break out and eat too much."

"Jesus." My eyes stung. "Are you sure it's yours?"

He snorted. "No, but that doesn't mean it's not. She's six weeks along, so it's possible."

I had to ask. "Is she going to keep it?"

"I don't know. She's thinking it over."

"Cary . . ." I couldn't hold back the tear that slid down my cheek. My heart was aching for him. "What are you going to do?"

"What can I do?" He slumped back in his chair. "It's her decision."

His powerlessness had to be killing him. After his mother had given birth to him, unwanted, she'd used abortion as birth control. I knew that haunted him. He'd told me so. "And if she decides to go through with the pregnancy? You'll have a paternity test done, right?"

"God, Eva." He looked at me with reddened eyes. "I haven't thought that far ahead yet. What the hell am I supposed to say to Trey? Things are just starting to smooth out between us and I've got to hit him with this? He's going to dump me. It's over."

Sucking in a deep breath, I straightened in my chair. I couldn't let Cary and Trey fall apart. Now that Gideon and I were good, it was time to fix all the other areas of my life I'd been neglecting. "We'll take it a step at a time. Figure things out as we go. We'll get through this."

He swallowed hard. "I need you."

"I need you, too. We'll stick together and work it out." I managed a smile. "I'm not going anywhere and neither are you. Except to San Diego this weekend," I amended hastily, reminding myself to talk to Gideon about that.

"Thank God." Cary sat forward again. "What I wouldn't give to shoot hoops at Dr. Travis's right now."

"Yeah." I didn't play basketball, but I knew I could use a one-on-one with Dr. Travis myself.

What would he say when he learned how far off the rails we'd slid in the few months we'd been in New York? We had spun some big dreams the last time we'd all sat down together. Cary had wanted to star in a Super Bowl ad and I'd wanted to be the one behind the scenes of that ad. Now he was facing the possibility of a baby and I was married to the most complicated man I had ever met.

"Dr. Trav's gonna flip," Cary muttered, reading my mind.

For some reason, that made us both laugh 'til we cried.

WHEN I got back to my desk, I found another small pile of interoffice envelopes. Catching my lower lip between my teeth, I searched each one until I found the one I was hoping for.

I CAN THINK OF MANY USES FOR THAT CHAIN,

MRS. X.

YOU WILL ENJOY THEM ALL IMMENSELY.

YOURS,

X

Some of the dark clouds from lunch floated away.

AFTER Cary's mind-blowing revelation, meeting Giroux after work barely registered on my what-else-could-possibly-go-wrong-next scale.

He was already at the wine bar when I arrived. Dressed in perfectly pressed khakis and white dress shirt rolled up at the sleeves and open at the throat, he looked good. Casual. But that didn't make him seem more relaxed. The man was strung tight as a bow, vibrating with tension and whatever else was eating at him.

"Eva," he greeted me. With that overt friendliness I hadn't liked the first time, he kissed me on both cheeks again. *"Enchanté."*

"Not too blond for you today, I take it?"

"Ah." He gave me a smile that didn't reach his eyes. "I deserved that."

I joined him at his table by the window and we were served shortly after.

The place had the look of an establishment that had been around a long time. Tin tiles covered the ceiling, while the aged hardwood floors and intricately carved bar suggested the place had been a pub at some point in its history. It had been modernized with chrome fixtures and a wine rack behind the bar that could have been an abstract sculpture.

Giroux openly studied me as the server poured our wine. I had no idea what he was looking for, but he was definitely searching for something.

As I took a sip of a lovely shiraz, he settled comfortably in his chair and swirled his wine around in his glass. "You've met my wife."

"I have, yes. She's very beautiful."

"Yes, she is." His gaze dropped to his wine. "What else did you think of her?"

"Why does it matter what I think?"

He looked at me again. "Do you see her as a rival? Or a threat?"

"Neither." I took another drink and noticed a black Bentley SUV easing into a tight spot at the curb just outside the window I sat beside. Angus was behind the wheel and apparently uncaring of the No Park-ing sign he was camping out in front of.

"You are that certain of Cross?"

My attention returned to Giroux. "Yes. But that doesn't mean I don't wish you would pack up your wife and take her back to France with you."

His mouth quirked on one side in a grim smile. "You are in love with Cross, yes?"

"Yes."

"Why?"

That made me smile. "If you think you can figure out what Corinne sees in him by what *I* see in him, forget it. He and I, we're . . . different with each other than we are with other people."

"I saw that. With him." Giroux took a drink, savoring it before swallowing.

"Forgive me, but I don't know why we're sitting here. What do you want from me?"

"Are you always so direct?"

"Yes." I shrugged. "I get impatient with being confused."

"Then I will be direct as well." He reached out and caught my left hand. "You have a tan line from a ring. A sizable one, it appears. An engagement ring, perhaps?"

I looked at my hand and saw he was right. There was a square-sized spot on my ring finger that was a few shades lighter than the rest of my skin. Unlike my mother, who was pale, I'd inherited my father's warm skin tone and I tanned easily.

"You're very perceptive. But I would appreciate you keeping your speculations to yourself."

He smiled and for the first time, it was genuine. "Perhaps I will get my wife back after all."

"I think you could, if you tried." I sat up, deciding it was time to leave. "You know what your wife told me once? She said you're indifferent. Instead of waiting for her to come back, you should just take her back. I think that's what she wants."

He stood when I did, standing over me. "She has chased Cross. I do not think a woman who chases will find a man chasing her attractive."

"I don't know about that." I pulled a twenty out of my pocket and set it on the table, despite his scowl at the sight of it. "She said yes when you asked her to marry you, didn't she? Whatever you did before, do it again. Good-bye, Jean-François."

He opened his mouth to speak, but I was already halfway out the door.

ANGUS was waiting beside the Bentley when I exited the wine bar.

"Would you like to go home, Mrs. Cross?" he asked, as I slipped into the back.

His greeting made me grin. Combined with my recent conversation with Giroux, it sparked an idea. "Actually, I'd like to make a stop, if you don't mind."

"Not at all."

I gave him directions, then sat back and relished the building anticipation.

IT was half past six when I was ready to call it a day, but when I asked Angus where Gideon was, I learned he was still in his office.

"Will you take me to him?" I asked.

"Of course."

Returning to the Crossfire after hours was weird. Although there were still people moving through the lobby, it had a different feel from the daytime. When I reached the top floor, I found the glass security doors to Cross Industries propped open and a cleaning crew at work emptying trash cans, wiping down the glass, and vacuuming.

I headed directly to Gideon's office, noting the number of empty desks, which included that of Scott, his assistant. Gideon stood behind his, an earpiece in his ear, and his jacket hung on the coat rack in the corner. His hands were on his hips and he was talking, his lips moving rapidly and his face a mask of concentration.

The wall across from him was covered in flat screens streaming news from around the world. To the right of that was a bar with jeweled decanters on lighted glass shelves that were the only spot of color in the office's cool palette of black, white, and gray. Three distinct seating areas offered comfortable spaces for less formal meetings, while Gideon's black desk was a miracle of modern technology, serving as the conduit for all the electronics in the room.

Surrounded by his expensive toys, my husband looked nothing short of edible. The beautifully tailored lines of his vest and pants showed off the perfection of his body, and the sight of him at his command center, wielding the power that had built his empire, did crazy things to my heart. The floor-to-ceiling windows that surrounded him on two sides allowed the view of the city to make an imposing backdrop, yet the vista didn't diminish him in any way.

Gideon was master of all he surveyed, and it showed.

Reaching into my purse, I unzipped the small pocket and drew out the rings inside it, slipping mine on. Then I stepped closer to the glass wall and double doors that separated him from everyone else.

His head swiveled toward me and his gaze heated at the sight of me. He hit a button on his desk, and the double doors swung open automatically. A moment later, the glass turned opaque, ensuring that no one lingering in the office would be able to see us.

I went in.

"I agree," he said, to whomever he was talking to. "Get it done and report back to me."

As he pulled off his earpiece and dropped it on his desk, his gaze never left me. "You're a welcome surprise, angel. Tell me about your meeting with Giroux."

I shrugged. "How did you know?"

His mouth tilted up on one side and he shot me a look that said, *Really? You're going to ask?*

"Are you here for a while?" I queried.

"I have a conference call with the Japanese division in half an hour, then I'm done. We'll go to dinner afterward."

"Let's get something to take home and eat with Cary. He's having a baby."

Gideon's brows shot up. "Come again?"

"Well, he might be having a baby." I sighed. "He's messed up over it and I want to be there for him. Plus, he should get used to having you around again."

He raked me with an assessing glance. "You're messed up over it, too. Come here." He rounded the desk and opened his arms. "Let me hold you."

I dropped my purse on the floor, kicked off my heels, and walked right into him. His arms came around me, and his lips, so firm and warm, pressed against my forehead.

"We'll figure it out," he murmured. "Don't worry."

"I love you, Gideon."

His embrace tightened.

Leaning back, I looked up into his gorgeous face. His eyes were so blue, seemingly even more so with the touch of sun he'd gotten during our trip away. "I have something for you."

"Oh?"

I backed up, catching his left hand before it dropped away from me. Holding it, I slid the ring I'd just bought him onto his finger, twisting it to fit over his last knuckle. He was still the entire time. When I released his hand so he could get a better look, it didn't move at all from where it'd been when I was holding it, as if he'd frozen in place.

Canting my head, I admired the ring on him, thinking it had just the effect I was looking for. But when a moment passed without a word from him, I looked up and saw him staring at his hand as if he'd never seen it before.

My heart sank. "You don't like it."

His nostrils flared on a deep breath and he turned over his hand to look at the backside, which was the same. The design I'd chosen wrapped continuously around.

The platinum wedding band was very much like the ring he wore on his right hand. It had the same beveled grooves cut into the precious metal, which gave it a similar industrial, masculine look. But the wedding band was garnished with rubies, making it impossible to miss. The bloodred hue stood out against his tanned skin and dark suits, a conspicuous sign of my possession.

"It's too much," I said quietly.

"It's always too much," he said hoarsely. And then he was on me, his hands cupping my head and his lips on mine, kissing me fiercely.

I grabbed his wrists, but he moved too quickly, lifting me up by the waist so my feet left the floor, and then carrying me to the same couch where he'd first laid his body over mine so many weeks ago.

"You don't have time for this," I gasped.

He sat me down with my butt on the edge of the sofa. "This won't take long."

He wasn't kidding. Reaching beneath my skirt, he slid my panties down my legs, then spread them wide and lowered his head.

There in his office, where I'd just admired his power and commanding presence, Gideon Cross knelt between my thighs and ate me with ruthless skill. His tongue fluttered over my clit until I writhed with the need to come, but it was the sight of him—in his suit, in his office, servicing me so thoroughly—that brought me to climax with a cry of his name.

I was shivering with pleasure while he licked inside me, the sensitive tissues trembling around the shallow plunges of his wickedly knowledgeable tongue. When he opened his fly and freed his erection, I was desperate for him, my body arching toward him in a shameless silent plea.

Gideon took the heavy length of his cock in hand and stroked the thick crest through my cleft, coating himself in the slickness of my orgasm. The fact that we were both still dressed except for what we needed to get out of the way made it all the hotter.

"I want you to submit," he said darkly. "Bend over and spread wide. I'm going to fuck you deep."

A whimper escaped me at the thought and I scrambled to obey. Aware of how tall he was, I moved to the side of the couch and folded over the armrest, reaching behind me to pull up my skirt.

He didn't hesitate. With a powerful thrust of his hips, he was inside me, stretching me. *"Eva."*

Gasping, I clawed at the sofa cushions. He was thick and hard and so, so deep. With my stomach pressed over the curve of the couch arm, I swore I could feel him pressing outward from the inside.

Folding over me, he wrapped his arms around me and sank his teeth into the side of my neck. The primitive claiming made my sex clench around him, caressing him.

He growled and ran his lips over me, lightly abrading me with the hint of evening stubble on his jaw. "You feel so good," he said hoarsely. "I love fucking you."

"Gideon."

"Give me your hands."

Unsure of what he wanted, I slid my arms closer to my body and he circled my wrists with his fingers, pulling my hands gently around to the small of my back.

Then he was fucking me. Pounding into my sex with relentless drives, using my arms to pull me back to meet the thrusts of his hips. His heavy sac smacked against my clitoris, the rhythmic slaps spurring me toward another orgasm. He grunted on every plunge, mirroring my cries.

His race to orgasm was wildly exciting, as was his complete control of my body. I could only lie there and take it, take his lust and hunger, servicing him as he had me. The friction of his thrusts was delicious, a steady rubbing and pulling that made me crazed with desire.

I wished I could see him; see his eyes when they lost their focus and pleasure took him, his face a grimace of agonized ecstasy. I loved that I could affect him so fiercely, that my body felt so good to him, that sex with me shattered his defenses.

He shuddered and cursed. His cock lengthened, thickening as his balls tightened and drew up. "Eva . . . Christ. I love you."

I felt the lash of his semen inside me, pumping hot and thick. I bit my lip to stem my cry. I was so hot for him, so close.

Releasing my wrists, he wrapped me up, the fingers of one hand sliding into my cleft and rubbing my swollen clit. I came while he was still pumping, my sex milking his spurting cock as he emptied himself inside me. His lips were on my cheek, his breath gusting hot and moist across my skin, low rumbles spilling from his chest as he came hard and long.

We were both panting as our orgasms eased, leaning heavily on each other.

Swallowing hard, I spoke breathlessly. "I guess you like the ring."

His rough laugh filled me with joy.

FIVE minutes later, I lay wilted and sated on the couch, unable to move. Gideon sat at his desk looking pristine and perfect, radiating the health and vitality of a well-fucked male.

He went through the teleconference without a hitch in his stride, speaking mostly English, but opening and closing with conversational Japanese, his voice deep and smooth. His gaze slid over me now and again, his mouth curving in a ghost of a smile laced with undeniable masculine triumph.

I supposed he was entitled to it, considering I had so many post-orgasmic endorphins floating through my system I felt almost drunk.

Gideon finished his call and stood, shrugging out of his jacket again. The gleam in his eyes told me why.

Mustering the energy to raise my brows, I asked, "We're not leaving?"

"Of course we are. But not yet."

"Maybe you should cut back on those vitamins, ace."

His lips twitched as he freed the buttons of his vest. "I've spent too many days fantasizing about fucking you on that couch. We haven't covered even half of those fantasies yet."

I stretched, deliberately enticing him. "Can we still be naughty now that we're married?"

From the spark that lit his amazing eyes, I could guess his views on that.

By the time we left the Crossfire at nearly nine o'clock, Gideon had answered the question definitively.

21

GIDEON AND I were sitting on the floor of my living room eating pizza in our sweats when Cary came in a little after ten o'clock. Tatiana was with him. I reached across Gideon for a packet of Parmesan cheese and whispered, "Baby mama."

He winced. "She's trouble. Poor guy."

That was my thought exactly as the tall blonde walked in and wrinkled her nose rudely at our pizza. Then she caught sight of Gideon and flashed a come-hither smile.

I took a deep breath and told myself to let it go.

"Hey, Cary," Gideon greeted my best friend before tossing his arm over my shoulder and burying his face in my neck.

"Hey," Cary said. "What are you guys watching?"

"*End of Watch*," I answered. "It's really good. You two want to join us?"

"Sure." Cary caught Tatiana's hand and led her toward the couch.

She didn't have the grace to hide her disapproval of the idea.

They sat on the couch and settled into a comfortable tangle that was obviously familiar for them. Gideon pushed the pizza box their way. "Help yourselves, if you're hungry."

Cary snagged a slice, while Tatiana complained about him jostling her. I was bummed that she couldn't be more comfortable hanging out. If she was going to have Cary's baby, she was going to be in my life, and I hated the thought of that relationship being awkward.

In the end, they didn't stay in the living room long. She insisted that the handheld camera shots in the movie made her queasy, and Cary took her back to his room. A short while later, I thought I heard her laughing, making me think her biggest problem was the need to keep Cary all to herself. I could understand that insecurity. I was intimately familiar with it myself.

"Relax," Gideon murmured, urging me to lean into his chest. "We'll work it out with them. Give it some time."

I caught his left hand hanging over my shoulder and toyed with his ring.

He pressed his lips to my temple and we finished watching the movie.

ALTHOUGH Gideon slept in his apartment next door, he came over early enough to zip me into a sheath dress and fix me some coffee. I'd just finished putting on some pearl earrings and was stepping into the hallway when Tatiana appeared heading from the direction of the kitchen with two water bottles in her hands.

She was buck naked.

My temper almost boiled over, but I kept my tone calm. The pregnancy certainly didn't show, but knowing about it was reason enough to skip the shouting match. "Excuse me. You need to have clothes on if you're going to walk around my apartment."

"It's not just your apartment," she shot back, tossing her tawny mane over her shoulder as she moved to pass me.

I thrust my arm across the hallway, blocking her way. "You don't want to play games with me, Tatiana."

"Or what?"

"You'll lose."

She stared at me for a long minute. "He'll pick me."

"If it came to that, he'd resent you and you'd lose anyway." I dropped my arm. "Think about that."

Cary's door opened behind me. "What the fuck are you doing, Tat?"

Turning my head, I saw my best friend filling his doorway wearing only his boxers. "Giving you a good excuse to buy her a nice robe, Cary."

His jaw tightened and he waved me off, opening his door wider in a silent order for Tatiana to get her bare ass back in there.

I resumed my trek to the kitchen, my teeth grinding together. My mood worsened when I found Gideon in the kitchen, leaning back into the counter and leisurely drinking his coffee. He wore a black suit and pale gray tie and looked unbearably handsome.

"Enjoy the show?" I asked tightly. I hated that he'd seen another woman naked. And not just any woman, but a model with the lean, willowy body type he'd been known to prefer.

He lifted one shoulder in a careless shrug. "Not especially."

"You like 'em tall and skinny." I reached for the cup of coffee waiting for me on the counter beside him.

Gideon set his left hand over mine. The rubies on his wedding band sparkled in the bright kitchen lights. "Last I checked, the wife I can't resist was petite and voluptuous. Spectacularly so."

I closed my eyes, trying to push past my jealousy. "Do you know why I chose your ring?"

"Red is our color," he said quietly. "Red dresses in limos. Red fuck-me heels at garden parties. A red rose in your hair when you married me."

That he understood soothed me. I turned into him, pressing my body to his.

"Umm," he purred, hugging me close. "You're a soft, delicious little handful, angel."

I shook my head, my anger melting into exasperation.

He nuzzled his nose against my cheek. "I love you."

"Gideon." Tilting my head back, I offered my mouth and let him kiss my bad mood away.

The feel of his lips on mine never stopped making my toes curl. I was slightly dazed when he pulled back and murmured, "I have my appointment with Dr. Petersen tonight. I'll call you when I'm finished and we'll see what we want to do about dinner."

"Okay."

He smiled at my blissfully nonchalant reply. "I can set up an appointment for us to see him Thursday."

"Make it for next Thursday, please," I said, sobering. "I hate to miss any more therapy, but Mom wants me and Cary to go to a charity gala this Thursday. She bought me a dress and everything. I'm afraid if I don't go, she'll take it the wrong way."

"We'll go together."

"Yeah?" Gideon in a tuxedo was an aphrodisiac to me. Of course, Gideon in anything or nothing turned me on, too. But in a tux . . . Dear God, he was sizzling.

"Yes. It's as good a time as any to be seen out together again. And to announce our engagement."

I licked my lips. "Can I take advantage of you in the limo?"

His eyes laughed at me. "By all means, angel mine."

WHEN I got to work, Megumi wasn't at her desk so I didn't get to see how she was faring. It kind of gave me an excuse to call Martin, though, and see if things with him and Lacey had panned out after our wild night at Primal.

I pulled out my smartphone to program a reminder and saw that my mom had left a voice mail the night before. I listened to it on the way to my desk. She wanted to see if I wanted hair and makeup done before the dinner on Thursday, suggesting that she come over with a beauty crew and we could get dolled up together.

When I reached my desk, I texted her back, letting her know I loved the idea, but time would be tight, since I wouldn't be getting off work until five.

I was settling in for the day when Will stopped by.

"Got plans for lunch?" he asked, looking cute in a plaid shirt only he could pull off so well and a solid navy tie.

"Not another carb feast, please. My butt can't take it."

"No." He grinned. "Natalie's past the brutal phase of her diet, so it's getting better. I was thinking a soup and salad bar."

I smiled. "I'm game for that. Want to see if Megumi wants to come?"

"She's not here today."

"Oh? Is she sick?"

"Don't know. I only heard about it because I was the one who had to call the temp agency for someone to cover for her."

I sat back with a frown. "I'll give her a call on my break and see how she's feeling."

"Tell her I said hi." He drummed a beat on the top of my cubicle wall and headed off.

THE rest of the day passed in a blur. I left a message for Megumi on my break, then tried to reach her again after work as Clancy drove me to

Brooklyn for my Krav Maga class. "Have Lacey call me back if you're feeling too sick," I said in my voice mail message. "I just want to know you're okay."

I killed the call, then sat back and appreciated the grandeur of the Brooklyn Bridge. Going through the massive stone arches soaring over the East River always felt like traveling to a different world. Below, the waterway was dotted with commuter ferries and a lone sailboat heading out into the busy New York harbor.

We reached the long off-ramp in less than a minute and I turned my attention back to my phone.

I called Martin.

"Eva," he answered cheerfully, clearly recognizing my number from his contact list. "I'm glad to hear from you."

"How are you?"

"I'm good. You?"

"Hanging in there. We should get together sometime." I smiled at a cop who was artfully directing traffic at the hugely complicated inter-section on the Brooklyn side. She kept things moving with a whistle between her teeth and fluid hand gestures that had serious sass to them. "We could grab a drink after work or double-date for dinner."

"I'd like that. Are you seeing someone in particular?"

"Gideon and I are working things out."

"Gideon Cross? Well, if anyone can hook him, it'd be you."

I laughed and wished I had my ring on. I didn't wear it around dur-ing the day the way Gideon wore his. He didn't care who knew he was taken or by whom, but I still had everyone in my life to tell. "Thanks for the vote of confidence. What about you? You seeing anyone?"

"Lacey and I are dabbling. I like her. She's a lot of fun."

"That's great. I'm glad to hear it. Listen, if you talk to her today, can you ask her to let me know how Megumi's doing? She's out sick and I just want to make sure she's all right and doesn't need anything."

"Sure thing." The receiver filled with a sudden rush of noise, the unmistakable sound of him stepping outside. "Lacey's out of town, but she's supposed to give me a call tonight."

"Thank you. I appreciate it. You're on the move, so I'll let you go. Let's plan on getting together next week and we'll work out the details in the next couple of days."

"Sounds good. I'm glad you called."

I smiled. "Me, too."

We hung up and because I felt like reaching out, I sent a text to Shawna and another to Brett. Just quick hellos with smiley faces.

When I looked up, I caught Clancy looking at me in the rearview mirror.

"How's Mom?" I asked.

"She'll be fine," he said, in his usual no-nonsense way.

I nodded and looked out the window, catching sight of a gleaming steel bus stop shelter displaying Cary's billboard. "Family is so hard sometimes, you know."

"I know."

"You have any brothers or sisters, Clancy?"

"One of each."

What were they like? Were they tough as nails and deadly like Clancy? Or was he the black sheep? "Are you close, if you don't mind my asking?"

"We're tight. My sister lives out of state, so I don't see her much, but we talk on the phone once a week at least. My brother's in New York, so we catch up more often."

"Cool." I tried to picture a relaxed Clancy tossing back beers with someone who resembled him, but couldn't pull it off. "Does he work security, too?"

"Not yet." His mouth did that little lip twitch, almost-smile thing. "He's with the FBI for now."

"Is your sister in law enforcement?"

"She's in the Marines."

"Whoa. Awesome."

"Yes, she is."

I studied him and his military crew cut. "You were in the service, too, weren't you?"

"I was." He didn't volunteer any more than that.

When I opened my mouth to pry further, we turned a corner and I realized we'd reached the former warehouse where Parker had his studio.

I grabbed my gym bag and got out before Clancy could open the door for me. "See you in an hour!"

"Knock 'em out, Eva," he said, watching me until I got inside.

The door had barely closed behind me when I saw a familiar brunette I would've rather not seen again. Ever. She stood to the side, just off the training mats, with her arms crossed. She was dressed in black workout pants with a bright blue stripe down the sides that matched her fitted long-sleeve shirt. Her brown curly hair was scraped back into an unforgiving ponytail.

She turned. Cool blue eyes raked me from head to toe.

Facing the inevitable, I took a deep breath and approached her. "Detective Graves."

"Eva." She gave me a curt nod. "Great tan."

"Thanks."

"Cross take you away for the weekend?"

Not exactly a casual question. My back went up. "I had some time off."

Her thin mouth quirked on one side. "Still cautious. Good. What does your dad think of Cross?"

"I believe my dad trusts my judgment."

Graves nodded. "I'd keep thinking about Nathan Barker's bracelet if I were you. But then, loose ends make me twitchy."

A shiver of unease ran down my back. The whole thing made me twitchy, but who could I talk to about it? No one but Gideon, and I knew him too well to doubt that he was doing everything in his considerable power to solve that mystery.

"I need a sparring partner," the detective said suddenly. "You're up."

"Uh, what?" I blinked at her. "Is that . . . ? Can we . . . ?"

"The case has gone cold, Eva." She stalked onto the mat and began to stretch. "Hurry up. I don't have all night."

GRAVES kicked my ass. For such a rail-thin, wiry woman, she packed some strength. She was focused, precise, and ruthless. I actually learned a lot from her over the hour and a half we sparred, most especially never to let down my guard. She was lightning quick and swift to exploit any advantage.

When I stumbled into my apartment a little after eight, I headed straight to the bathtub. I soaked in vanilla-scented water, surrounded by candles, and hoped Gideon would show up before I pruned.

He ended up coming in just as I was wrapping a towel around me, his damp hair and jeans telling me he'd showered after a visit with his trainer.

"Hi, ace."

"Hi, wife." He came up to me, tugged open my towel, and lowered his head to my breast.

My breath left me when he sucked a nipple into his mouth, drawing rhythmically until it hardened.

Straightening, he admired his handiwork. "God, you're sexy."

I lifted onto my tiptoes and kissed his chin. "How'd things go tonight?"

He looked at me with a wry curve to his lips. "Dr. Petersen congratulated us, then went on about how important couples therapy would be."

"He thinks we got married too soon."

Gideon laughed. "He didn't even want us having sex, Eva."

Wrinkling my nose, I resecured my towel and grabbed a comb for my wet hair.

"Let me," he said, taking the comb and leading me to the wide lip of the tub. He urged me to sit.

As he combed my hair, I told him about seeing Detective Graves at my Krav Maga class.

"My lawyers tell me the case has been shelved," Gideon said.

"How do you feel about that?"

"You're safe. That's all that matters."

There was no inflection in his voice, which told me it mattered to him more than he'd tell me. I knew that somewhere, deep down inside him, Nathan's murder was haunting him. Because *I* was haunted by what Gideon had done for me and we were two halves of the same soul.

That was why Gideon had wanted us to get married so badly. I was his safe place. I was the one person who knew every dark, tormented secret he had, and I loved him desperately anyway. And he needed love more than anyone I'd ever met.

There was a vibration against my shoulder and I teased, "Is that a new toy in your pocket, ace?"

"Should've turned the damn thing off," he muttered, digging his phone out. He looked at the screen, then answered with a clipped, "Cross."

I heard a woman's agitated voice coming through the receiver, but I couldn't make out the words.

"When?" After hearing the answer, he asked, "Where? Yes. I'm on my way."

He hung up and raked a hand through his hair.

I stood. "What's wrong?"

"Corinne's in the hospital. My mother says it's bad."

"I'll get dressed. What happened?"

Gideon looked at me. Goose bumps swept across my skin. I'd never seen him look so . . . shattered.

"Pills," he said hoarsely. "She swallowed a bottle of pills."

WE took the DB9. While we waited for the attendant to bring the car to us, Gideon called Raúl, telling him to meet us at the hospital to take over the Aston Martin when we arrived.

When Gideon slid behind the wheel, he drove with tight focus; every turn of the wheel and press of the accelerator was skilled and precise. Enclosed in the small space with him, I knew he'd shut down. Emotionally, he was unreachable. When I placed my hand on his knee to offer comfort and support, he didn't even twitch. I wasn't sure he even felt it.

Raúl was waiting for us when we pulled up to the emergency room. He opened the door for me, then rounded the hood and took the driver's seat after Gideon got out. The gleaming car was moved out of the drop-off driveway before we walked through the automatic doors.

I took Gideon's hand, but I wasn't sure he felt that, either. His attention was riveted on his mother, who stood when we entered the private waiting area we'd been directed to. Elizabeth Vidal barely glanced at me, going straight to her son and hugging him.

He didn't hug her back. But he also didn't pull away. His grip on my hand tightened.

Mrs. Vidal didn't even acknowledge me. Instead, she turned her back to me and gestured at the couple seated together nearby. They were clearly Corinne's parents. They'd been talking to Elizabeth when Gideon and I came in, which seemed odd to me since Jean-François Giroux was standing alone by the window, looking as much like an outsider as Elizabeth was making me feel.

Gideon's hold on my hand slackened as his mother pulled him toward Corinne's family. Feeling awkward standing in the doorway alone, I went to Jean-François.

I greeted him softly. "I'm very sorry."

He looked at me with dead eyes, his face seeming to have aged a decade since we'd met at the wine bar the day before. "What are you doing here?"

"Mrs. Vidal called Gideon."

"Of course she did." He looked over to the seating area. "One would think he was her husband and not I."

I followed his gaze. Gideon was crouched in front of Corinne's parents, holding her mother's hand. A sick feeling of dread spread through me, making me cold.

"She would rather be dead than live without him," he said tonelessly.

I looked back at him. Suddenly, I understood. "You told her, didn't you? About our engagement."

"And look how well she took the news."

Jesus. I took a shaky step toward the wall, needing the support. How could she not know what a suicide attempt would do to Gideon? She couldn't be that blind. Or had his reaction, his guilt, been her aim all along? It made me sick to think of anyone being that manipulative, but there was no denying the result. Gideon was back at her side. At least for now.

A doctor entered the room, a kind-looking woman with cropped silvery blond hair and faded blue eyes. "Mr. Giroux?"

"*Oui.*" Jean-François stepped forward.

"I'm Dr. Steinberg. I'm treating your wife. Could we speak privately for a moment?"

Corinne's father stood. "We're her family."

Dr. Steinberg smiled gently. "I understand. However, it's Corinne's husband I need to speak with. I can tell you that Corinne will be fine after a few days' rest."

She and Giroux stepped out of the room, which effectively cut off the sound of their voices, but they were still visible through a glass wall. Giroux towered over the much shorter doctor, but whatever she said to him had him crumbling visibly. The tension in the waiting room ratcheted up to an unbearable degree. Gideon stood beside his mother, his attention snared by the heartrending scene unfolding before us.

Dr. Steinberg reached out and placed a hand on Jean-François's arm, still speaking. After a moment, she stopped and left him. He just stood there, staring at the floor, his shoulders slumped as if a great weight pressed down on them.

I was about to go to him, when Gideon moved first. The moment he stepped outside the waiting room, Giroux lunged at him.

The thud as the two men collided was teeth-rattling in its violence. The room shook as Gideon slammed into the thick glass wall.

Someone shouted in surprise, then yelled for security.

Gideon threw Giroux off and blocked a punch. Then he ducked, avoiding a blow to the face. Jean-François bellowed something, his face contorted with fury and pain.

Corinne's father rushed out at the same moment security arrived with stun guns drawn and aimed. Gideon shoved Jean-François off again, defending himself without once throwing a punch of his own. His face was stony, his eyes cold and nearly as lifeless as Giroux's.

Giroux shouted at Gideon. With the door left open by Corinne's father, I caught part of what was said. The word *enfant* needed no translation. Everything inside me went deathly still, all sound lost to the buzzing in my ears.

Everyone rushed out of the room as both Gideon and Giroux were flex-cuffed and hustled toward a service elevator by the guards. I blinked when Angus appeared in the doorway, certain I was imagining him.

"Mrs. Cross," he said softly, approaching me carefully with his cap in his hands.

I could only imagine how I looked. I was stuck on the word *baby* and what that could possibly mean. After all, Corinne had been in New York as long as I'd known Gideon . . . but her husband hadn't been.

"I've come to take you home."

I frowned. "Where's Gideon?"

"He texted me and asked me to come get you."

My confusion turned into a sharp pain. "But he needs me."

Angus took a deep breath, his eyes filled with something that looked like pity. "Come with me, Eva. It's late."

"He doesn't want me here," I said flatly, latching on to the one thing I was beginning to comprehend.

"He wants you home and comfortable."

My feet felt rooted to the floor. "Is that what the text said?"

"That's what he's thinking."

"You're being kind." I started to walk, running on autopilot.

I passed one of the orderlies picking up the mess made when Giroux had been shoved into a cart of supplies. The way he avoided looking at me seemed to confirm the harsh reality.

I'd been set aside.

22

GIDEON DIDN'T COME home that night. When I checked his apartment on my way out to work, I found the beds neatly made.

Wherever he'd spent the night, it hadn't been near me. After the revelation of Corinne's pregnancy, I was stunned that I'd been left on my own with no explanation. I felt like this huge bomb had exploded in front of me and I was left standing in the rumble, alone and confused.

Angus and the Bentley were waiting for me downstairs when I stepped outside. Irritation simmered. Every time Gideon pulled away from me, he sent Angus in as a surrogate.

"I should've married *you*, Angus," I muttered, as I slid into the backseat. "You're always there for me."

"Gideon makes sure of it," he said, before shutting the door.

Always loyal, I thought bitterly.

When I got to work and learned that Megumi was still out sick, I was equally concerned about her and relieved for me. It wasn't like her to miss work—she was always at her desk early—so the repeated absences told me something was really wrong with her. But not having her there meant she couldn't catch my mood and ask questions I didn't want to answer. Couldn't answer, actually. I had no idea where my husband was, what he was doing or feeling.

And I was angry and hurt about it. The one thing I *wasn't* was scared. Gideon was right about marriage fostering a settled feeling. I had a grip on him he'd have to work to break. He couldn't just disappear or ignore me forever. No matter what, he would have to deal with me at some point. The only question was: When?

Focusing on work, I willed the hours to rush by. When I got off at five, I still hadn't heard from Gideon and I hadn't reached out to him, either. As far as I was concerned, *he* needed to bridge the gap he'd created between us.

I headed to my Krav Maga class after work, where Parker worked one-on-one with me for an hour.

"You're on fire tonight," he said, when I threw him to the mat for the sixth or seventh time.

I didn't tell him I was imagining Gideon in his place.

When I got home, I found Cary and Trey hanging out in the living room. They were eating torpedo sandwiches and watching a comedy show.

"We've got plenty," Trey said, pushing half of his sandwich toward me. "There's beer in the fridge, too."

He was a great guy, with an awesome personality to match. And he loved my best friend. I looked at Cary and for a second, he let me see his confusion and pain. Then he hid it behind his bright, gorgeous smile. He patted the cushion next to him. "Come sit, baby girl."

"Sure," I agreed, partly because I couldn't bear the thought of being alone in my room with my thoughts driving me crazy. "Just let me take a shower first."

332 · SYLVIA DAY

Once I was freshly scrubbed and cozy in worn sweats, I joined the two men on the couch. I brooded over getting a "not found" error when I tried to track Gideon's smartphone with the instructions he'd given me.

I ended up sleeping in the living room, preferring the couch to a bed that might smell like my missing husband.

I woke up to the smell of him anyway, and the feel of his arms around me as he lifted me. Weary, I rested my head against Gideon's chest and listened to the sound of his heart beating strong and sure. He carried me to my bedroom.

"Where have you been?" I muttered.

"California."

I jolted. "What?"

He shook his head. "We'll talk in the morning."

"Gideon . . ."

"In the morning, Eva," he said sternly, putting me to bed and pressed a rough kiss to my forehead.

I caught his wrist as he straightened. "Don't you dare leave me."

"I haven't slept in damn near two days." There was an edge to his voice that set off alarms.

Pushing onto my elbows, I tried to see his face in the semidarkness, but it was too hard and I was still trying to shrug off sleep. I could tell he was wearing jeans and a long-sleeved shirt, and that was about it. "So? Got a bed right here."

He heaved out an exasperated, weary breath. "Lie down. I'll get my prescription."

It wasn't until he'd been gone too long that I remembered he kept a bottle of his pills in my bathroom. He'd left for no other reason than to leave. I shoved the blankets off me and stumbled out of the room, making my way through my darkened living room to find my keys. I went to Gideon's apartment and let myself in, nearly tripping over a suitcase left carelessly by the door.

He must have taken just enough time to drop it off before coming to me. And yet he hadn't intended to spend the night in my bed. Why had he come? Just to see me sleep? To check up on me?

Fuck. Would I ever understand him?

I searched for him and found him sprawled facedown on the master bed, his head on my pillow and his clothes still on. His boots lay a few feet apart from each other at the end of the bed, as if he'd kicked them off in a rush, and his smartphone and wallet were tossed on the nightstand.

The phone was irresistible.

I picked it up, typed in *angel* as the password, and scrolled through it without shame. If he caught me doing it, I wouldn't care. If he wasn't going to give me answers, I had every right to search for them myself.

The last thing I expected to find were so many pictures of me in his photo album. There were dozens: some of us together taken by paparazzi, others that he'd taken with his phone when I was unaware. Candid shots that afforded me the opportunity to see myself through his eyes.

I stopped worrying. He loved me. Adored me. No man could take the pictures he did of me otherwise, with messy hair and no makeup, doing nothing more interesting than reading something or standing in front of an open refrigerator contemplating what I wanted. Pictures of me sleeping and eating and frowning in concentration . . . Boring, commonplace things.

His phone log showed mostly calls placed between him and Angus, Raúl, or Scott. There were voice mails from Corinne I refused to torture myself by listening to, but I could see he hadn't answered her or called her in a while. There were calls between him and business associates—a couple with Arnoldo, and several with his attorneys.

And three calls exchanged between him and Deanna Johnson.

My gaze narrowed. Those ranged from several minutes long to a quarter of an hour.

I checked his text messages and found the one he'd sent to Angus when we were at the hospital.

I need her out of here.

Sinking into the armchair in the corner of the room, I stared at the message. *Need*, not *want*. For some reason, the word choice changed my perception of what happened. I still didn't get it completely, but I didn't feel quite so . . . pushed aside.

There were also texts between him and Ireland, which made me happy. I didn't read them but could see that the last one had come in on Monday.

Returning the phone to its former spot, I watched the man I loved sink into the deep sleep of exhaustion. Sprawled as he was, dressed as he was, he looked his age. He carried so much responsibility and he made it look so effortless . . . so innately artless, that it was easy to forget he was as vulnerable to being overworked and stressed out as anyone.

It was my job as his wife to help him deal with it. But that was impossible for me to do if he shut me out. In saving me worry, he took more onto himself.

We'd be talking about that as soon as he caught some sleep.

I woke with a crick in my neck and the lingering sense that something was wrong. Moving gingerly so as not to pull something, I unfolded from my curled-up position in the armchair and noted that the dawn was well on its way. Pinkish-orange light was visible through the windows, and a quick glance at the bedside clock told me it was creeping into morning.

Gideon groaned and I stilled, dread sliding through me at the sound.

It was a terrible noise, the sound of a creature wounded in both body and soul. A chill swept over me as he moaned again, everything in me reacting violently to his torment.

Rushing to the bed, I climbed on it, kneeling as I pushed at his shoulder. "Gideon. Wake up."

He flinched away from me, curling around my pillow and squeezing it. His body jerked as a sob escaped him.

I spooned behind him, wrapping one arm around his waist. "Shh, baby," I whispered. "I've got you. I'm here."

I rocked him as he cried in his sleep, my tears wetting his shirt.

"WAKE up, angel mine," Gideon murmured, his lips brushing over my jaw. "I need you."

I stretched, feeling lingering aches from the last two nights of hard training and the few hours I'd spent sleeping in the armchair before moving to the bed and joining him.

My T-shirt was pushed up, exposing my breasts to his avid, hungry mouth. A hand pushed beneath the waistband of my sweats and then my panties, finding my cleft and expertly coaxing me to a swift arousal.

"Gideon . . ." I could feel the need in his touch, the desire that was far more than skin deep.

He took my mouth, hushing me with a kiss. My hips arched as his fingers pushed into me, fucking me gently. Eager to answer his silent demand for more, I pushed at my sweats, kicking restlessly until I got them off.

I reached for the button fly of his jeans, yanking it open and shoving the denim and cotton boxer briefs out of the way.

"Put me inside you," he whispered against my lips.

I circled his thick erection with my fingers, positioning him and then lifting to take the first inch of him inside me.

Burying his face in my neck, he thrust, sinking into me, moaning with pleasure as I closed tight around him. "Christ, Eva. I need you so much."

My arms and legs caged him, holding him tight.

Time and everything else in the world ceased to matter. Gideon renewed all the promises he'd made to me on the sands of a Caribbean beach, and I tried to heal him, hoping to give him the strength he needed to face another day.

I was putting on my makeup when Gideon joined me in the bathroom, setting a steaming mug of creamy sweet coffee on the marble counter next to me. He wore nothing but pajama pants, so I guessed he wasn't going into the office or at least not right away.

Eyeing him in the mirror, I searched for signs that he remembered his dreams. I'd never seen him so deeply troubled, as if his heart were breaking.

"Eva," he said quietly, "we need to talk."

"I'm on board with that."

Leaning back against the counter, he held his mug in both hands. He stared down into his coffee for a long minute before asking, "Did you make a sex tape with Brett Kline?"

"What?" I faced him, my hand tightening on the handle of my makeup brush. "No. Fuck no. Why would you ask me that?"

He held my gaze. "When I came back from the hospital the other night, Deanna caught up with me in the lobby. After the situation with Corinne, I knew brushing her off was the wrong approach."

"I told you that."

"I know. You were right. So I took her to the bar up the street, bought her a glass of wine, and apologized."

"You took her out for wine," I repeated.

"No, I took her out to tell her I'm sorry for how I treated her. I bought her the wine so we had a reason to be sitting in the damn bar," he said irritably. "I figured you'd prefer a public place over bringing her up to the apartment, which would have been more convenient and private."

He was right, and I appreciated his thinking of how I'd react and making accommodations for it. But I was still annoyed that Deanna had snagged a pseudo date with him.

Gideon must have known what I was feeling because his lips tilted up on one side. "So possessive, angel. You're lucky I like it so much."

"Shut up. What does Deanna have to do with a sex tape? Did she tell you there was one? It's a lie. She's lying."

"She's not. My apology smoothed things over enough for her to throw me a bone. She told me about the tape and that an auction for it was imminent."

"I'm telling you, she's full of shit," I argued.

"You know a guy named Sam Yimara?"

Everything stopped. Anxiety pooled in the pit of my stomach. "Yes, he was the band's wannabe videographer."

"Right." He took a sip of his coffee, his eyes hard as they looked at me over the rim of his mug. "He apparently set up remote cameras at some of the band's shows to gather backstage material. He claims to have re-created the 'Golden' video with actual explicit footage."

"Oh my God." I covered my mouth, feeling sick.

It was bad enough thinking about strangers watching Brett and me fucking, but it was a million times worse imagining Gideon seeing it. I could still picture the look on his face when he'd watched the music video, and *that* had been terrible. He and I would never be the same if he viewed the real deal. I knew I'd never be able to scrub images of him and another woman out of my mind. And over time, they'd eat at me like acid.

"That's why you went to California," I whispered, horrified.

"Deanna gave me what information she had, and I secured a temporary injunction barring Yimara from licensing or selling the video."

I couldn't get a clue about what he was thinking or feeling from his body language. He was closed tight and restrained, rigidly in control. While I felt like I was coming apart at the seams. "You can't stop it from getting out," I whispered.

"We have a temporary seal on the court proceedings."

"That video hits one of those file-sharing sites and it'll spread like the plague."

He shook his head, the ends of his inky hair brushing over his shoulders. "I've got an IT team dedicated to nothing but looking twenty-four-seven for that file on the Internet, but Yimara won't make any money giving the footage away. It's only worth something as an exclusive. He's not going to fuck that up before he exhausts all other options—including selling it to me."

"Deanna will tell. It's her job to expose secrets, not keep them."

"I offered her a forty-eight-hour exclusive on our wedding photos, if she keeps a lid on this."

"And she was okay with that?" I asked skeptically. "That woman's hot for you. She can't have been happy about you being off the market. Permanently."

"There is a point at which it becomes clear there's no hope," he said dryly. "I think I managed to make that point. Trust me, she was happy enough with the money to be made on the wedding exclusive."

I moved to the toilet, dropped the lid down, and sat. The reality of what he'd told me sank in. "I'm sick over this, Gideon."

He set his coffee down next to mine and came to crouch in front of me. "Look at me."

I did as he ordered, but it was hard.

"I will *never* let anyone hurt you," he said. "Do you understand? I *will* take care of this."

"I'm sorry," I breathed. "I'm so sorry you have to deal with this. And with everything else you have going on—"

Gideon caught my hands. "Someone violated your privacy, Eva. Don't apologize for that. As for dealing with this . . . that's my right. My honor. You'll always come first."

"It didn't seem like I came first at the hospital," I argued, needing to get the resentment out before it festered. And needing him to explain why he was always pushing me away when he was trying to protect me. "Everything went to hell and you shoved me at Angus when I wanted to be there for you. You took off to *another state* and didn't call . . . didn't say anything."

His jaw tightened. "And I didn't sleep. It took every minute I had and too many favors to count to get that injunction done in the time I had to work with. You have to trust me, Eva. Even if you don't understand what I'm doing, trust that I'm always thinking of you and doing what's best for you. For us."

I looked away, hating that answer. "Corinne's pregnant."

He exhaled harshly. "She was, yes. Four months along."

One word chilled me. "Was?"

"She miscarried as the doctors were treating the overdose. I'm choosing to believe she didn't know about the baby."

I searched his face and tried to hide the pitiful relief on my own. "Four months? The baby was Giroux's, then."

"I would hope so," he said curtly. "He seems to think it was his, and that I'm responsible for her losing it."

"Jesus."

Gideon's head dropped to my lap, his cheek resting on my thigh. "She *had* to be clueless. She couldn't risk a baby over something so stupid."

"I won't let you blame yourself for this, Gideon," I told him sternly.

He wrapped his arms around my waist. "Christ. Am I cursed?"

I hated Corinne so much in that moment I felt violent. She'd known

Gideon's father had committed suicide. If she knew Gideon at all, she would know how much her attempt would devastate him.

"You are not responsible for this." I ran my fingers through his hair, offering comfort. "Do you hear me? Only Corinne is responsible for what happened. *She'll* have to live with what she's done, not you and me."

"Eva." He hugged me, his breath warm through the silk of my robe.

A quarter hour after Gideon left me in the bathroom to take a call from Raúl, I was still standing at the vanity, staring into the sink.

"You'll be late for work," he said gently, joining me and hugging me from behind.

"I'm thinking about just calling in." I never did that, but I was tired and feeling worn out. I couldn't imagine pulling it together enough to give my job the focus it deserved.

"You could, but it won't look good when you're photographed at the gala tonight."

I looked at him in the mirror. "We're not going!"

"Yes, we are."

"Gideon, if that footage of me and Brett gets out, you don't want your name linked to mine."

His body went stiff, and then he turned me around to face him. "Say that again."

"You heard me. The Cross name has been through enough, don't you think?"

"Angel, I'm as close as I've ever been to taking you across my knee. Luckily for you, I don't play rough when I'm mad."

His gruff teasing didn't distract me from the fact that he was determined to protect the girl I'd been, the girl I was ashamed of. He was willing to stand between me and scandal, shielding me as best he could and taking the hit alongside me, if it came to that.

I didn't think it was possible to love him more than I did, but he kept proving me wrong.

He cupped my face in his hands. "Whatever we face, we face together. And you'll do it with my name."

"Gideon—"

"I can't tell you how proud I am for you to have it." He brushed his mouth across my brow. "How much it means to me that you've taken it and made it yours."

"Oh, Gideon." I pushed onto my tiptoes and surged into him. "I love you so much."

I was a half hour late to work and found a temp at Megumi's desk. I smiled and said hi, but worry ate at me. I popped my head into Mark's office and apologized profusely for being late. Then I called Megumi's cell when I got to my cubicle, but she didn't answer. I headed over to Will's.

"Got a question for you," I said, when I reached him.

"Let's hope I have the answer," he shot back, swiveling in his chair to look up at me through his stylish glasses.

"Who does Megumi call to say she's sick?"

"She reports to Daphne for everything. Why?"

"I'm just worried. She hasn't called me back. I'm wondering if I pissed her off somehow." I shifted on my feet. "I hate not knowing or being able to help."

"Well, for what it's worth, Daphne said she sounds horrible."

"That sucks. But thanks."

I headed back to my cubicle. Mark gestured me into his office as I walked by.

"They're hanging the six-story banner for Tungsten scarves today."

"Yeah?"

He grinned. "Want to go check it out?"

"Really?" As scattered as I was feeling, getting out in the muggy August heat was preferable to sitting at my cool desk. "That'd be awesome!"

He grabbed his jacket off the back of his chair. "Let's go."

WHEN I got home shortly after five o'clock, I found my living room taken over by a team of white-coated beauty technicians. Cary and Trey were kicked back on the couch with green goop on their faces and towels under their heads to protect the white upholstery. My mother was chatting away while her hair was styled in a sexy cap of waves and curls.

I took a quick shower, then joined them. In an hour, they managed to take me from bedraggled to glamorous, affording me the time to think about everything I'd ruthlessly suppressed all day—the video, Corinne, Giroux, Deanna, and Brett.

Someone was going to have to tell Brett. That someone was me.

When the beautician came toward me with a lip brush, I held up my hand. "Red, please."

She paused a minute, her head canting as she examined me. "Yes, you're right."

I was holding my breath through a finishing blast of hair spray when my smartphone vibrated in the pocket of my robe. Seeing Gideon's name on the screen, I answered. "Hi, ace."

"What color are you wearing?" he asked, without a hello.

"Silver."

"Really?" His voice took on a warm purr that made my toes flex. "I can't wait to see you in it. And out of it."

"You won't be waiting," I admonished. "You'd better have your fine ass over here in about ten minutes."

"Yes, ma'am."

My eyes narrowed. "Hurry up or we won't have any limo time."

"Umm . . . I'll be there in five."

He hung up and I held my phone for a minute, smiling.

"Who was that?" my mom asked, coming up beside me.

"Gideon."

Her eyes lit up. "He's escorting you tonight?"

"Yes."

"Oh, Eva." She hugged me. "I'm so glad."

With my arms around her, I figured it was as good a time as any to start spreading the engagement news. I knew Gideon wasn't going to wait long before insisting on sharing our marriage with the world.

I said quietly, "He asked Dad for permission to marry me."

"Did he?" When she pulled back, she was smiling. "He talked to Richard, too, which I think is such a nice touch, don't you? I've already started planning. I was thinking June, at the Pierre, of course. We'll—"

"I suggest December, at the latest."

My mother gasped, her eyes widening. "Don't be ridiculous. There's no way to pull off a wedding in that amount of time. It's impossible."

I shrugged. "Tell Gideon you're thinking of June next year. See what he says."

"Well, I have to wait until he actually proposes first!"

"Right." I kissed her cheek. "I'm going to get dressed."

23

I WAS IN my room, sliding the strapless gown up over my matching bustier, when Gideon came in. I literally stopped breathing, my gaze drinking in his reflection in my cheval mirror. Standing behind me in a tuxedo tailored just for him, with a lovely gray tie that matched my dress so well, he was dazzling. I'd never seen him look so gorgeous.

"Wow," I breathed, entranced. "You are *so* getting laid tonight."

His mouth quirked. "Does that mean I can skip zipping you up?"

"Does that mean we can skip going to this thing?"

"Not a chance, angel. I'm showing off my wife tonight."

"No one knows I'm your wife."

"*I* know it." He came up behind me and secured my zipper. "And soon—really soon—the world will know it."

I leaned back into him, admiring our joint reflection. We took great pictures together.

Which made me think of other pictures . . .

"Promise me," I said, "that you'll never watch the video."

When he didn't answer me, I turned to look at him directly. When I saw the closed-off look on his face, I started freaking out. "Gideon. Did you watch it already?"

His jaw tightened. "A minute or two. Nothing explicit. Just enough to prove validity."

"Oh my God. Promise me you won't watch it." My voice rose and grew sharp as panic spread through me. "Promise me!"

His hands encircled my wrists and squeezed hard enough to make my breath catch. I stared at him, wide-eyed, confused by the sudden aggression.

"Calm down," he said quietly.

The oddest rush of warmth spread outward from where he touched me. My heart beat faster, but also steadier. I stared at our hands, my attention catching on his ruby ring. Red. Like the cuffs he'd bought for me. I felt similarly captured and bound now. And it soothed me in a way I didn't understand.

But Gideon obviously did.

That was why I'd been afraid to marry him so quickly, I realized. He was taking me on a journey that had an unknown destination and I had agreed to follow him blindfolded. It wasn't about where we'd end up as a couple, because that was never in question. We were obsessed, dependent on each other in the unrelenting way of addicts. Where *I* would end up, who I'd be at the end, was what I didn't know.

Gideon's transformation had been almost violent, happening in a moment of sharp clarity when he'd comprehended that he wouldn't—couldn't—live without me. My change was more gradual, so painstakingly measured that I'd believed I wouldn't have to change at all.

I was wrong.

Swallowing past the lump in my throat, I spoke more steadily. "Gideon, listen. Whatever's on that video, it's nothing compared to what you and I have. The only memories I want in your head are ones

346 · SYLVIA DAY

we make. What we've got together . . . that's the only thing that's real. The only thing that matters. So please . . . promise me."

He closed his eyes briefly, then nodded. "All right. I promise."

I breathed out a sigh of relief. "Thank you."

Lifting my hands to his mouth, he kissed them. "You're mine, Eva."

BY silent, mutual agreement, we refrained from mussing each other up in the limo before our first public appearance as a married couple. I was nervous, and while an orgasm or two would help alleviate that, looking less than perfect would only make it worse. And people would notice. Not only was my silver gown eye-catching, with its brilliant sheen and short train, but my arm-candy husband was an impossible-to-miss accessory.

Attention would be on us, and Gideon seemed determined to keep it that way. He helped me out of the limo when we arrived at Fifth Avenue and Central Park South, taking a moment to slide his lips across my temple. "That dress is going to look amazing on my bedroom floor."

I laughed at the cheesy line, which I knew he'd intended, and camera flashes went off in a storm of blinding light. Once he turned away from me, all warmth left his face, the beautiful planes settling into a closed expression that gave nothing away. He set his hand at the small of my back and led me across the red carpet and into Cipriani's.

Once inside, he found a spot he approved of and we stayed there for an hour as business associates and acquaintances circled around us. He wanted me at his side and he wanted to be at mine as well, something he proved a short while later when we were headed to the dance floor.

"Introduce me," he said simply and I followed his gaze to where Christine Field and Walter Leaman, of Waters Field & Leaman, were laughing along with the group of people they were standing with. Christine looked restrained and elegant in a black beaded dress that covered her from throat to wrists to ankles except for the plunging back, and Walter, who was a large man, looked successful and confident in a nicely cut tuxedo and bow tie.

"They know who you are," I pointed out.

"Do they know who I am *to you*?"

I wrinkled my nose a little, knowing my world was going to change drastically once my single-girl self was subsumed by my identity as Eva Cross. "Come on, ace."

We headed over there, weaving through round tables covered in white linens and decorated with candelabras wrapped in floral garlands that lent a wonderful fragrance to the room.

My bosses spotted Gideon first, of course. I don't think they even recognized me until Gideon quite obviously deferred to me by letting me speak first.

"Good evening," I said, shaking Christine's and Walter's hands. "I know you're both familiar with Gideon Cross, my . . ."

I paused, my brain grinding to a halt.

"Fiancé," Gideon finished, shaking hands.

Congratulations were exchanged; smiles got bigger, eyes brighter.

"This doesn't mean we're losing you, does it?" Christine asked, diamond drop earrings glinting in the soft light of the chandeliers.

"No. I'm not going anywhere."

That earned me a sharp pinch on my butt from Gideon.

We were going to have to deal with the work issue at some point, but I figured I could hold him off at least until our next wedding.

We talked a bit about the Kingsman Vodka campaign, which was mostly a way to emphasize what a good job Waters Field & Leaman had done so the agency could hook more Cross Industries business. Gideon knew the game, of course, and played it well. He was polite, charming, and clearly not a man who could be easily influenced.

After that, we ran out of things to talk about. Gideon made our excuses.

"Let's dance," he murmured in my ear. "I want to hold you."

We moved onto the dance floor, where Cary was drawing attention with a stunning redhead. Flashes of a pale, shapely leg could be seen through the risqué slit in her emerald green dress. He moved her into a spin, then a dip. Undeniably suave.

Trey hadn't been able to come because of an evening class, and I was sorry about that. I was sorry, too, that I was glad Cary hadn't brought Tatiana instead. Thinking that way made me feel bitchy, and I seriously disliked catty bitches.

"Look at me."

I tilted my head at Gideon's command and found his eyes on me. "Hi, ace."

With his hand at my back and my hand in his, we swept casually around the dance floor.

"Crossfire," he whispered, his gaze hot on my face.

I touched his cheek with my fingertips. "We're learning from our mistakes."

"You read my mind."

"It feels good."

He smiled, his eyes so blue and his hair so damn sexy I wanted to run my fingers through it right then and there. He pulled me closer. "Not as good as you feel."

We stayed on the dance floor through two songs. Then the music ended when the bandleader turned to the mic and made an announcement: Dinner was about to be served. Seated at our table were my mother and Richard, Cary, a plastic surgeon and his wife, and a guy who said he'd just wrapped up shooting the pilot episode to a new television show he hoped would be picked up for a full-season run.

The meal was some sort of Asian fusion and I ate everything, because it was good and the portions weren't that big. Gideon had his hand on my thigh beneath the table, his thumb rubbing lightly in small circles that made me squirm.

He leaned over. "Sit still."

"Stop it," I whispered back.

"Keep wiggling and I'll put my fingers inside you."

"You wouldn't dare."

He smirked. "Try me and see."

Because I wouldn't put it past him, I sat still, even though it killed me.

"Excuse me," Cary said abruptly, pushing back from the table.

I watched him walk away and caught his gaze lingering on a nearby table. When the redhead in green followed him out of the room a few moments later, I wasn't too surprised, but I was very disappointed. I knew the situation with Tatiana was stressing him out and I knew mindless sex was Cary's cure-all, but it also fucked with his self-esteem and led to more problems than it fixed.

It was good that we were only a couple days away from seeing Dr. Travis.

Leaning into Gideon, I whispered, "Cary and I are going to San Diego this weekend."

His head swiveled toward me. "You're telling me this *now*?"

"Well, between your exes and my ex, my parents, Cary, and everything else, it keeps slipping my mind! I figured I'd better tell you before I forgot again."

"Angel . . ." He shook his head.

"Hang on." I pushed to my feet. I needed to remind him that Brett had a tour stop in San Diego at the same time, but I had to catch Cary first.

He looked at me quizzically as he stood.

"Be right back," I told him, adding very quietly, "Got some cock-blocking to do."

"Eva—"

I heard the warning in his tone and ignored it, lifting my skirt and hurrying after Cary. I'd just made it past the ballroom entrance, when I ran into a familiar face.

"Magdalene," I said in surprise, stopping. "I didn't know you were here."

"Gage was wrapped up in a project, so we ran a little late. Missed dinner entirely, but at least I got my hands on one of those chocolate mousse things they served for dessert."

"Kick-ass," I agreed.

"Totally." Magdalene smiled.

I thought to myself that she looked really good. Softer, sweeter. Still stunning and sultry in a one-shouldered red lace dress, her dark hair framing a delicate face and crimson lips. Getting away from Christopher Vidal had done her a lot of good. And having a new man in her life surely helped. I remembered her mentioning a guy named Gage when she'd visited me at work a couple weeks before.

"I saw you with Gideon," she said. "And I noticed your ring."

"You should've come over and said hi."

"I was eating that dessert."

I laughed. "A girl's got to have her priorities."

Magdalene reached out and touched my arm briefly. "I'm happy for you, Eva. Happy for Gideon."

"Thank you. You should stop by our table and tell him that."

"I will. Catch you later."

She walked off and I stared after her for a minute, still wary but thinking she might not be so bad after all.

The one negative about running into Magdalene was losing Cary. By the time I resumed chasing after him, he'd already ducked out of sight somewhere.

I headed back to Gideon, mentally preparing the ass-chewing I was going to give Cary. Elizabeth Vidal halted me in my tracks.

"Excuse me," I said, when I nearly bumped into her.

She grabbed me by the elbow and pulled me over to a dark corner. Then she caught my hand and looked at my gorgeous Asscher diamond. "That's my ring."

I tugged free. "It *was* your ring. It's mine now. Your son gave it to me around the time he asked me to marry him."

She looked at me with those blue eyes that were so like her son's. So like Ireland's. She was a beautiful woman, glamorous and elegant. As much a head-turner as my mother, really, but she had Gideon's iciness.

"I won't let you take him away from me," she bit out between brilliantly white teeth.

"You've got it all wrong." I crossed my arms. "I want to get you two together, so we can put everything out in the open."

"You're filling his head with lies."

"Oh my God. Seriously? The next time he tells you what happened— and I'll make sure he does—you're going to believe him. And you're going to apologize, and find some fucking way to make it easier for him to bear. Because I want him healed and healthy and whole."

Elizabeth stared at me, clearly fuming. She obviously wasn't on board with that plan.

"Are we done?" I asked, disgusted with her deliberate blindness.

"Not even close," she hissed, leaning into me. "I know about you and that lead singer. I'm on to you."

I shook my head. Had Christopher talked to her? What would he have said? Knowing what he'd done to Magdalene, I believed him capable of pretty much anything. "Unbelievable. You believe the lies and ignore the truth."

I started walking away but stopped. "What I think is really interesting is that after I confronted you last time, you didn't ask Gideon about what happened. 'Hey, son, your crazy girlfriend told me this crazy story.' I can't figure out why you didn't ask him. I don't suppose you'd want to explain?"

"Fuck you."

"Yeah, I didn't think you would."

I left her behind before she opened her mouth again and ruined my night.

Unfortunately, when I started heading toward my table, I saw Deanna Johnson sitting in my seat, talking to Gideon.

"Are you kidding me?" I muttered, my gaze narrowing at the way the reporter kept putting her hand on his forearm as she talked. Cary was off doing what he shouldn't be doing; my mom and Stanton were on the dance floor. And Deanna had slid in like a snake.

Whatever Gideon thought, it was obvious to me that her interest in him was as hot as ever. And while he offered no encouragement aside from listening to whatever she was saying, just the fact that he was giving her attention was watering that weed.

"She must be great in bed. He fucks her a lot."

I stiffened and turned toward the woman talking to me. It was Cary's redhead, who had the flushed, bright-eyed look of a woman who'd just had a very nice orgasm. Still, she was older than I'd first thought from a distance.

"You should watch out for him," she said, looking at Gideon. "He uses women. I've seen it happen. More than it should."

"I can handle myself."

"They all say that." Her sympathetic smile rubbed me the wrong way. "I know of two women who've experienced severe depression over him. Certainly, they won't be the last."

"You shouldn't listen to gossip," I snapped.

She walked away with an irritatingly serene smile, reaching up to pat her hair as she skirted tables on the way to her own.

It wasn't until she was halfway across the room that I placed her face.

"Crap."

I hurried back to Gideon. He stood when I reached him.

"I need you real quick," I said briskly, before shooting a look at the brunette in my chair. "Deanna, always a pleasure."

She ignored the dig. "Hi, Eva. I was just leaving—"

But I'd already tuned her out. I caught Gideon's hand and tugged. "Come on."

"All right, hang on." He said something to Deanna, but I didn't catch it, pulling him along instead. "Christ, Eva. What the hell is the rush?"

I stopped by the wall and looked out over the room, searching for green and red. Seemed to me he would have noticed his former lover—unless she'd been deliberately avoiding him. Of course she looked so different without her former pixie haircut, and I hadn't seen her white-haired husband, which would have made it easier to identify her sooner. "Do you know if Anne Lucas is here?"

His hand tightened on mine. "I haven't seen her. Why?"

"Emerald green dress, long red hair. Seen that woman?"

"No."

"She was dancing with Cary earlier."

"I wasn't paying attention."

I looked at him, getting aggravated. "Jesus, Gideon. It was hard to miss her."

"Forgive me for having eyes only for my wife," he said dryly.

I squeezed his hand. "I'm sorry. I just need to know if it was her."

"Explain why. Did she come up to you?"

"Yeah, she did. Shoveled some shit my way, then wandered off. I think Cary sneaked off with her, too. You know, for a quickie."

Gideon's face turned hard. He turned his attention to the room, sweeping it from one side to the other, with a slow searching glance. "I don't see her. Or anyone like you described."

"Isn't Anne a therapist?"

"Psychiatrist."

A sense of foreboding made me restless. "Can we go now?"

He studied me. "Tell me what she said to you."

"Nothing I haven't heard before."

354 · SYLVIA DAY

"That's reassuring," he muttered. "Yes, let's go."

We went back to our table for my clutch and to say good-bye to everyone.

"Can I hitch a ride with you?" Cary asked, after I hugged my mom good-bye.

Gideon nodded. "Come on."

ANGUS shut the door of the limo.

Cary, Gideon, and I settled back into the bench seats, and just a couple of minutes later we pulled away from Cipriani's and into traffic.

My best friend shot me a look. "Don't start."

He hated when I laid into him about his behavior, and I didn't blame him. I wasn't his mother. But I was someone who loved him and wanted good things for him. I knew how self-destructive he could be when left unchecked.

But that wasn't my biggest concern at that moment.

"What was her name?" I asked, praying he knew so I could identify the redhead once and for all.

"Who cares?"

"Jesus." My hands flexed restlessly around my clutch. "Do you know it or not?"

"I didn't ask," he retorted. "Drop it."

"Watch the tone, Cary," Gideon admonished quietly. "You've got a problem, fine. Don't take it out on Eva for giving a shit about you."

Cary's jaw tightened and he looked out the window.

I sat back and Gideon drew me into the curve of his shoulder, his hand running up and down my bare arm.

No one said another word on the ride home.

⬿

WHEN we reached my apartment, Gideon headed into the kitchen to grab a bottle of water and ended up on the phone, his gaze meeting mine across the breakfast bar and the several feet separating us.

Cary stalked off to his bedroom, then turned abruptly at the hallway and came back to hug me. *Hard.*

With his face in the curve of my shoulder, he whispered, "Sorry, baby girl."

I hugged him back. "You deserve better than the way you treat yourself."

"I didn't do her," he said quietly, pulling back to look at me. "I was going to. I thought I wanted to. But when it came down to it, it hit me that I have a kid coming. A *kid*, Eva. And I don't want him—or her— growing up thinking of me the way I do my mom. I gotta get my shit straight."

I hugged him again. "I'm proud of you."

"Yeah, well." He pulled back, looking sheepish. "I still rubbed her off, since I'd taken it that far, but my dick stayed tucked in my pants."

"TMI, Cary," I said. "Totally TMI."

"We still heading out to San Diego tomorrow?" His hopeful look twisted my heart.

"Hell, yeah. I'm looking forward to it."

His grin was tinged with relief. "Good. I've got us flying out at eight thirty."

Gideon rejoined us just then, and the look he gave me told me we weren't done talking about my going away for the weekend. But when Cary headed down the hallway to his room, I grabbed Gideon and kissed him hard, delaying that conversation. As I'd hoped, he didn't hesitate to pull me in and take over, his mouth eating at mine with lush, deep licks.

Moaning, I let him sweep me away. The world could go crazy by itself for a night. Tomorrow was soon enough to face it and everything we had to deal with.

356 · SYLVIA DAY

I grabbed him by the tie. "Tonight, you're mine."

"I'm yours every night," he said in that warm, raspy voice that stirred the hottest fantasies.

"Start now." I walked backward, pulling him toward my room. "And don't stop."

He didn't. Not 'til morning.

AUTHOR'S NOTE

Yes, dear reader, you're right. This can't possibly be the end.

Gideon and Eva's journey isn't quite finished yet. I look forward to seeing where they'll take us next. Look for Captivated by You, *available now!*

All my best,
Sylvia

CAPTIVATED BY YOU

Available now from Berkley!

REFLECTED IN YOU

Sylvia Day

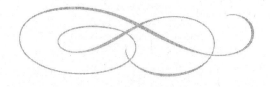

BERKLEY

New York

BERKLEY
An imprint of Penguin Random House LLC
penguinrandomhouse.com

Copyright © 2012 by Sylvia Day
Penguin Random House supports copyright. Copyright fuels creativity, encourages diverse voices,
promotes free speech, and creates a vibrant culture. Thank you for buying an authorized edition
of this book and for complying with copyright laws by not reproducing, scanning,
or distributing any part of it in any form without permission. You are supporting writers and
allowing Penguin Random House to continue to publish books for every reader.

BERKLEY and the BERKLEY & B colophon are registered trademarks of Penguin Random House LLC.

Library of Congress Cataloging-in-Publication Data

Day, Sylvia.
Reflected in you / Sylvia Day.—Berkley trade paperback ed.
p.   cm.
ISBN 978-0-425-26391-4
1. Erotic fiction.   2. Love stories.   I. Title.
PS3604.A9875R44 2012
813'.6—dc23
2012037035

First Edition: October 2012

Printed in the United States of America
16th Printing

This one is for Nora Roberts,
an inspiration and a true class act.

ACKNOWLEDGMENTS

I'm so grateful to Cindy Hwang and Leslie Gelbman for their support and encouragement, and most important, their love for Gideon and Eva's story. It takes passion to write a book and passion to sell it. I'm very thankful they have it.

I could write an entire book about everything I need to thank my agent Kimberly Whalen for. The Crossfire series is a massive multinational, multiformat endeavor, and she never misses a trick. Because she's always on the ball, I'm freed to focus on my part of our collaboration—the writing!—and I love her for it.

Behind Cindy, Leslie, Kim, Claire Pelly, and Tom Weldon are dynamic teams at Penguin and Trident Media Group. I wish I could mention everyone by name, but really, it takes a village. There are literally dozens of people to thank for their hard work and enthusiasm. The Crossfire series is being cared for and looked after by Trident and Penguin on a worldwide scale and I'm so grateful for the time you've all spent on my books.

My deepest gratitude to editor Hilary Sares, who is so instrumental in making the Crossfire series what it is. She keeps me straight.

Big thanks to my publicist, Gregg Sullivan, who makes my life easier in many ways.

I must also thank all of my international publishers (more than three dozen of you at the time I'm writing this) for welcoming Gideon and Eva into your countries and sharing them with your readers. You've all been so wonderful and I appreciate you.

And to all the readers around the world who've embraced Gideon and Eva's story—thank you! When I wrote *Bared to You* I was so sure I'd be the only person who loved it. I'm so thrilled that you do, too, and that we're following along on Eva and Gideon's journey together. Hot, bumpy roads are best traveled with friends!

I LOVED NEW York with the kind of mad passion I reserved for only one other thing in my life. The city was a microcosm of new world opportunities and old world traditions. Conservatives rubbed shoulders with bohemians. Oddities coexisted with priceless rarities. The pulsing energy of the city fueled international business bloodlines and drew people from all over the world.

And the embodiment of all that vibrancy, driving ambition, and world-renowned power had just screwed me to two toe-curlingly awesome orgasms.

As I padded over to his massive walk-in closet, I glanced at Gideon Cross's sex-rumpled bed and shivered with remembered pleasure. My hair was still damp from a shower, and the towel wrapped around me was my only article of clothing. I had an hour and a half before I had to be at work, which was cutting it a little too close for comfort. Obviously, I was going to have to allot time in my morning routine for sex, otherwise I'd always be scrambling. Gideon woke up ready to conquer the world, and he liked to start that domination with me.

How lucky was I?

Because it was sliding into July in New York and the temperature was heating up, I chose a slim pair of pressed natural-linen slacks and a sleeveless poplin shell in a soft gray that matched my eyes. Since I had no hairstyling talent, I pulled my long blond hair back in a simple ponytail, then made up my face. When I was presentable, I left the bedroom.

I heard Gideon's voice the moment I stepped into the hallway. A tiny shiver moved through me when I realized he was angry, his voice low and clipped. He didn't rile easily . . . unless he was ticked off with me. I could get him to raise his voice and curse, even shove his hands through his glorious shoulder-length mane of inky black hair.

For the most part, though, Gideon was a testament to leashed power. There was no need for him to shout when he could get people to quake in their shoes with just a look or a tersely spoken word.

I found him in his home office. He stood with his back to the door and a Bluetooth receiver in his ear. His arms were crossed and he was staring out the windows of his Fifth Avenue penthouse apartment, giving the impression of a very solitary man, an individual who was separate from the world around him, yet entirely capable of ruling it.

Leaning into the doorjamb, I drank him in. I was certain my view of the skyline was more awe-inspiring than his. My vantage point included him superimposed over those towering skyscrapers, an equally powerful and impressive presence. He'd finished his shower before I managed to crawl out of bed. His seriously addictive body was now dressed in two pieces of an expensively tailored three-piece suit—an admitted hot button of mine. The rear view of him showcased a perfect ass and a powerful back encased in a vest.

On the wall was a massive collage of photos of us as a couple and one very intimate one that he'd taken of me while I was sleeping. Most were pictures taken by the paparazzi who followed his every move. He was Gideon Cross, of Cross Industries, and at the ridiculous age of twenty-eight, he was one of the top twenty-five richest people in the world. I was pretty sure he owned a significant chunk of Manhattan; I was positive he was the hottest man on the planet. And he kept photos of me everywhere he worked, as if I could possibly be as fun to look at as he was.

He turned, pivoting gracefully to catch me with his icy blue gaze. Of course he'd known I was there, watching him. There was a crackling in the air when we were near each other, a sense of anticipation like the coiled silence before the boom of thunder. He'd probably deliberately waited a beat before facing me, giving me the opportunity to check him out because he knew I loved to look at him.

Dark and Dangerous. And all mine.

God . . . I never got used to the impact of that face. Those sculpted cheekbones and dark winged brows, the thickly lashed blue eyes, and those lips . . . perfectly etched to be both sensual and wicked. I loved when they smiled with sexual invitation, and I shivered when they thinned into a stern line. And when he pressed those lips to my body, I burned for him.

Jeez, listen to yourself. My mouth curved, remembering how annoyed I used to get at pals who waxed poetic about their boyfriends' good looks. But here I was, constantly awed by the gorgeousness of the complicated, frustrating, messed-up, sexy-as-sin man I was falling deeper in love with every day.

As we stared at each other, his scowl didn't lessen, nor did he cease speaking to the poor soul on the receiving end of his call, but his gaze warmed from its chilly irritation to scorching heat.

I should've become used to the change that came over him when he looked at me, but it still hit me with a force strong enough to rock me on my feet. That look conveyed how hard and deep he wanted to fuck me—which he did every chance he got—and it also afforded me a glimpse of his raw, unrelenting force of will. A core of strength and command marked everything Gideon did in life.

"See you at eight on Saturday," he finished, before yanking off the earpiece and tossing it on his desk. "Come here, Eva."

Another shiver slid through me at the way he said my name, with the same authoritative bite he used when he said *Come, Eva*, while I was beneath him . . . filled with him . . . desperate to climax for him . . .

"No time for that, ace." I backed into the hallway, because I was weak where he was concerned. The soft rasp in his smooth, cultured voice was nearly capable of making me orgasm just listening to it. And whenever he touched me, I caved.

I hurried to the kitchen to make us some coffee.

He muttered something under his breath and followed me out, his long stride easily gaining on mine. I found myself pinned to the hallway wall by six feet, two inches of hard, hot male.

"You know what happens when you run, angel." Gideon nipped my lower lip with his teeth and then soothed the sting with the caress of his tongue. "I catch you."

Inside me, something sighed with happy surrender and my body went lax with pleasure at being pressed so close to his. I craved him constantly, so deeply it was a physical ache. What I felt was lust, but it was also so much more. Something so precious and profound that Gideon's lust for me wasn't the trigger it would've been with another man. If anyone else had attempted to subdue me with the weight of his body, I would've freaked out. But it had never been an issue with Gideon. He knew what I needed and how much I could take.

The sudden flash of his grin stopped my heart.

Confronted with that breathtaking face framed by that lustrous dark hair, I felt my knees weaken just a little. He was so polished and urbane except for the decadent length of those silky strands.

He nuzzled his nose against mine. "You can't smile at me like that, then walk away. Tell me what you were thinking about when I was on the phone."

My lips twisted wryly. "How gorgeous you are. It's sickening how often I think about that. I need to get over it already."

He cupped the back of my thigh and urged me tighter against him, teasing me with an expert roll of his hips against mine. He was outrageously gifted in bed. And he knew it. "Damned if I'll let you."

"Oh?" Heat slid sinuously through my veins, my body too greedy for the feel of his. "You can't tell me you want another starry-eyed woman hanging on you, Mr. Hates-Exaggerated-Expectations."

"What I want," he purred, cupping my jaw and rubbing my bottom lip with the pad of his thumb, "is you being too busy thinking about me to think about anyone else."

I pulled in a slow and shaky breath. I was completely seduced by the smoldering look in his eyes, the provocative tone of his voice, the heat of his body, and the mouthwatering scent of his skin. He was my drug, and I had no desire to kick the habit.

"Gideon," I breathed, entranced.

With a soft groan, he sealed his chiseled mouth over mine, stealing away thoughts of what time it was with a lush, deep kiss . . . a kiss that almost succeeded in distracting me from seeing the insecurity he'd just revealed.

I pushed my fingers into his hair to hold him still and kissed him back, my tongue sliding along his, stroking. We'd been a couple for such a short period of time. Less than a month. Worse, neither of us knew how to have a relationship like the one we were attempting to build—a relationship in which we refused to pretend we weren't both seriously broken.

His arms banded around me and tightened possessively. "I wanted to spend the weekend with you down in the Florida Keys—naked."

"Umm, sounds nice." More than nice. As big of a kick as I got out of Gideon in a three-piece suit, I much preferred him stripped to the skin. I avoided pointing out that I wouldn't be available this weekend . . .

"Now I've got to spend the weekend taking care of business," he muttered, his lips moving against mine.

"Business you put off to be with me?" He'd been leaving work early to spend time with me, and I knew that had to be costing him. My mother was on her third marriage, and all of her spouses were successful, wealthy moguls of one kind or another. I knew the price for ambition was very late hours.

"I pay other people a generous salary so I can be with you."

Nice dodge, but noting the flash of irritation in his gaze, I distracted him. "Thank you. Let's get some coffee before we run out of time."

Gideon stroked his tongue along my bottom lip, then released me. "I'd like to get off the ground by eight tomorrow night. Pack cool and light. Arizona's got dry heat."

"What?" I blinked at his retreating back as it disappeared into his office. "Arizona is where your business is?"

"Unfortunately."

Uh . . . whoa. Instead of risking my shot at coffee, I postponed arguing and continued on to the kitchen. I passed through Gideon's spacious apartment with its stunning prewar architecture and slender arched windows, my heels alternately clicking over gleaming hardwood and muffled by Aubusson rugs. Decorated in dark woods and neutral fabrics, the luxurious space was brightened by jeweled accents. As much as his place screamed money, it managed to remain warm and welcoming, a comfortable place to relax and feel pampered.

When I reached the kitchen, I wasted no time in shoving a travel mug under the one-cup coffeemaker. Gideon joined me with his jacket draped over one arm and his cell phone in his hand. I put another portable mug under the spout for him before I went to the fridge for some half-and-half.

"It might be fortunate after all." I faced him and reminded him of my roommate issue. "I need to knock heads with Cary this weekend."

Gideon dropped his phone into the inner pocket of his jacket, then hung the garment off the back of one of the bar stools at the island. "You're coming with me, Eva."

Exhaling in a rush, I added half-and-half to my coffee. "To do what? Lie around naked, waiting for you to finish work and fuck me?"

His gaze held mine as he collected his mug and sipped his steaming coffee with too-calm deliberation. "Are we going to argue?"

"Are you going to be difficult? We talked about this. You know I can't leave Cary after what happened last night." The multibody tangle I'd found in my living room gave new meaning to the word *clusterfuck*.

I put the carton back in the fridge and absorbed the sensation of being drawn to him inexorably by the force of his will. It'd been that way from the beginning. When he chose to, Gideon could make me *feel* his demands. And it was very, very difficult to ignore the part of me that begged to give him whatever he wanted. "You're going to take care of business and I'm going to take care of my best friend, then we'll go back to taking care of each other."

"I won't be back until Sunday night, Eva."

Oh . . . I felt a sharp twinge in my belly at hearing we'd be apart that long. Most couples didn't spend every free moment together, but we weren't like most people. We both had hang-ups, insecurities, and an addiction to each other that required regular contact to keep us functioning properly. I hated being apart from him. I rarely went more than a couple of hours without thinking of him.

"You can't stand the thought, either," he said quietly, studying me in that way he had that saw everything. "By Sunday we'll both be worthless."

I blew on the surface of my coffee, then took a quick sip. I was unsettled at the thought of going the entire weekend without him. Worse, I hated the thought of him spending that amount of time away from me. He had a world of choices and possibilities out there, women who weren't so screwed up and difficult to be with.

Still, I managed to say, "We both know that's not exactly healthy, Gideon."

"Says who? No one else knows what it's like to be us."

Okay, I'd give him that.

"We need to get to work," I said, knowing this impasse was going to drive both of us crazy all day. We'd sort it out later, but for now we were stuck with it.

Resting his hip against the counter, he crossed his ankles and stubbornly settled in. "What we need is for you to come with me."

"Gideon." My foot began to tap against the travertine tile. "I can't just give up my life for you. If I turn into arm candy, you'll get bored real quick. Hell, I'd get sick of myself. It shouldn't kill us to spend a couple days straightening out other parts of our lives, even if we hate doing it."

His gaze captured mine. "You're too much trouble to be arm candy."

"Takes a troublemaker to know one."

Gideon straightened, shrugging off his brooding sensuality and instantly capturing me with his severe intensity. So mercurial—like me. "You've gotten a lot of press lately, Eva. It's no secret that you're in New York. I can't leave you here while I'm gone. Bring Cary with us if you have to. You can butt heads with him while you're waiting for me to finish work and fuck you."

"Ha." Even as I acknowledged his attempt to lighten the strain with humor, I realized what his real objection to being apart from me was—*Nathan*. My former stepbrother was a living nightmare from my past that Gideon seemed to fear might reappear in my present. It frightened me to concede that he wasn't totally wrong. The shield of anonymity that had protected me for years had been shattered by our highly public relationship.

God . . . we totally didn't have the time to get into *that* mess, but I knew it wasn't a point Gideon would concede on. He was a man who claimed his possessions utterly, fought off his competitors with ruthless precision, and would never allow any harm to come to me. I was his safe place, which made me rare and invaluable to him.

Gideon glanced at his watch. "Time to go, angel."

He fetched his jacket, then gestured for me to precede him through his luxurious living room, where I grabbed my purse and the bag holding my walking shoes and other necessities. A few moments later, we'd finished the descent to the ground floor in his private elevator and slid into the back of his black Bentley SUV.

"Hi, Angus," I greeted his driver, who touched the brim of his old-fashioned chauffeur's hat.

"Good morning, Miss Tramell," he replied, smiling. He was an older gentleman, with a liberal sprinkling of white in his red hair. I liked him for a lot of reasons, not the least of which was the fact that he'd been driving Gideon around since grade school and genuinely cared for him.

A quick glance at the Rolex my mother and stepfather had given me told me I'd make it to work on time . . . if we didn't get boxed in by traffic. Even as I thought this, Angus slid deftly into the sea of taxis and cars on the street. After the tense quiet of Gideon's apartment, the noise of Manhattan woke me as effectively as a jolt of caffeine. The blaring of horns and the thud of tires over a manhole cover invigorated me. Rapid-moving streams of pedestrians flanked both sides of the clogged street, while buildings stretched ambitiously toward the sky, keeping us in shadow even as the sun climbed.

God, I seriously loved New York. I took the time every day to absorb it, to try to draw it into me.

I settled into the leather seat back and reached for Gideon's hand, giving it a squeeze. "Would you feel better if Cary and I left town for the weekend? Maybe a quick trip to Vegas?"

Gideon's gaze narrowed. "Am I a threat to Cary? Is that why you won't consider Arizona?"

"What? No. I don't think so." Shifting in the seat, I faced him. "Sometimes it takes an all-nighter before I can get him to open up."

"You don't think so?" he repeated my answer, ignoring everything but the first words out of my mouth.

"He might feel like he can't reach out to me when he needs to talk because I'm always with you," I clarified, steadying my mug with two hands as we drove over a pothole. "Listen, you're going to have to get over any jealousy about Cary. When I say he's like a brother to me, Gideon, I'm not kidding. You don't have to like him, but you have to understand that he's a permanent part of my life."

"Do you tell him the same thing about me?"

"I don't have to. He knows. I'm trying to reach a compromise here—"

"I never compromise."

My brows rose. "In business, I'm sure you don't. But this is a relationship, Gideon. It requires give and—"

Gideon's growl cut me off. "My plane, my hotel, and if you leave the premises, you take a security team with you."

His sudden, reluctant capitulation surprised me silent for a long minute. Long enough for his brow to arch over those piercing blue eyes in a look that said *take it or leave it.*

"Don't you think that's a little extreme?" I prodded. "I'll have Cary with me."

"You'll forgive me if I don't trust him with your safety after last night." As he drank his coffee, his posture made it very clear that the conversation was done in his mind. He'd given me his acceptable options.

I might've gotten bitchy about that kind of high-handedness if I didn't understand that taking care of me was his motivation. My past had vicious skeletons, and dating Gideon had put me in a media spotlight that could bring Nathan Barker right to my door.

Plus, controlling everything around him was just part of who Gideon was. It came with the package and I had to make accommodations for that.

"Okay," I agreed. "Which hotel is yours?"

"I have a few. You can take your pick." He turned his head to look out the window. "Scott will e-mail you the list. When you've decided, let him know and he'll make the arrangements. We'll fly out together and return together."

Leaning my shoulder into the seat, I took a drink of my coffee and noted the way his hand was fisted on his thigh. In the tinted window's reflection, Gideon's face was impassive, but I could feel his moodiness.

"Thank you," I murmured.

"Don't. I'm not happy about this, Eva." A muscle in his jaw twitched. "Your roommate fucks up and I have to spend the weekend without you."

Hating that he was unhappy, I took his coffee from him and set our travel mugs in the backseat cup holders. Then I climbed into his lap, straddling him. I draped my arms around his shoulders. "I appreciate you bending on this, Gideon. It means a lot to me."

He caught me in his fierce blue gaze. "I knew you were going to drive me insane the moment I saw you."

I smiled, recalling how we'd met. "Sprawled on my ass on the lobby floor of the Crossfire Building?"

"Before. Outside."

Frowning, I asked, "Outside where?"

"On the sidewalk." Gideon gripped my hips, squeezing in that possessive, commanding way of his that made me ache for him. "I was leaving for a meeting. A minute later and I would've missed you. I'd just gotten into the car when you came around the corner."

I remembered the Bentley idling at the curb that day. I'd been too awed by the building to take note of the sleek vehicle when I arrived, but I had noticed it when I left.

"You hit me the instant I saw you," he said gruffly. "I couldn't look away. I wanted you immediately. Excessively. Almost violently."

How could I not have known that there'd been more to our first meeting than I'd realized? I thought we'd stumbled across each other by accident. But he'd been leaving for the day . . . which meant he had deliberately backtracked inside. For me.

"You stopped right next to the Bentley," he went on, "and your head tilted back. You were looking up at the building and I pictured you on your knees, looking up at me that same way."

The low growl in Gideon's voice had me squirming in his lap. "What way?" I whispered, mesmerized by the fire in his eyes.

"With excitement. A little awe . . . a little intimidation." Cupping my rear, he urged me tighter against him. "There was no way to stop myself from following you inside. And there you were, right where I'd wanted you, damn near kneeling in front of me. In that minute, I had a half dozen fantasies about what I was going to do to you when I got you naked."

I swallowed, remembering my similar reaction to him. "Looking at you for the first time made me think about sex. Screaming, sheet-clawing sex."

"I saw that." His hands slid up either side of my spine. "And I knew you saw *me*, too. Saw what I am . . . what I have inside me. You saw right through me."

And that was what had knocked me on my ass—literally. I'd looked into his eyes and realized how tightly reined he was, what a shadowed soul he had. I had seen power and hunger and control and demand. Somewhere inside me, I'd known he would take me over. It was a relief to know he'd felt the same upheaval over me.

Gideon's hands hugged my shoulder blades and pulled me closer, until our foreheads touched. "No one's ever seen before, Eva. You're the only one."

My throat tightened painfully. In so many ways, Gideon was a hard man, yet he could be so sweet to me. Almost childishly so, which I loved because it was pure and uncontrolled. If no one else bothered to look beyond his striking face and impressive bank account, they didn't deserve to know him. "I had no idea. You were so . . . cool. I didn't seem to affect you at all."

"Cool?" he scoffed. "I was on fire for you. I've been fucked up ever since."

"Gee. Thanks."

"You made me need you," he rasped. "Now I can't stand the thought of two days without you."

Holding his jaw in my hands, I kissed him tenderly, my lips coaxing and apologetic. "I love you, too," I whispered against his beautiful mouth. "I can't stand being away from you, either."

His returning kiss was greedy, devouring, and yet the way he held me close to him was gentle and reverent. As if I were precious. When he pulled back, we were both breathing hard.

"I'm not even your type," I teased, trying to lighten the mood before we went into work. Gideon's preference for brunettes was well known and well documented.

I felt the Bentley pull over and to a halt. Angus got out of the car to give us privacy, leaving the engine and air-conditioning running. I looked out the window and saw the Crossfire beside us.

"About the type thing—" Gideon's head fell back to rest against the seat. He took a deep breath. "Corinne was surprised by you. You weren't what she'd expected."

My jaw tightened at the mention of Gideon's former fiancée. Even knowing that their relationship had been about friendship and loneliness for him, not love, didn't stop the claws of envy from digging into me. Jealousy was one of my virulent flaws. "Because I'm blond?"

"Because . . . you don't look like her."

My breath caught. I hadn't considered that Corinne had set the standard for him. Even Magdalene Perez—one of Gideon's friends who wished she were more—had said she'd kept her dark hair long to emulate Corinne. But I hadn't grasped the complexity of that observation. My God . . . if it was true, Corinne had tremendous power over Gideon, way more than I could bear. My heart rate quickened and my stomach churned. I hated her irrationally. Hated that she'd had even a piece of him. Hated every woman who'd known his touch . . . his lust . . . his amazing body.

I started sliding off him.

"Eva." He stayed me by tightening his grip on my thighs. "I don't know if she's right."

I looked down at where he held me, and the sight of my promise ring on the finger of his right hand—my brand of ownership—calmed me. So did the look of confusion on his face when I met his gaze. "You don't?"

"If that's what it was, it wasn't conscious. I wasn't looking for her in other women. I didn't know I was looking for anything until I saw you."

My hands slid down his lapels as relief filled me. Maybe he hadn't been consciously looking for her, but even if he had, I couldn't be more different from Corinne in appearance and temperament. I was unique to him; a woman apart from his others in every way. I wished that could be enough to kill my jealousy.

"Maybe it wasn't a preference so much as a pattern." I smoothed his frown line with a fingertip. "You should ask Dr. Petersen when we see him tonight. I wish I had more answers after all my years of therapy, but I don't. There's a lot that's inexplicable between us, isn't there? I still have no idea what you see in me that's hooked you."

"It's what *you* see in *me*, angel," he said quietly, his features softening. "That you can know what I have in me and still want me as much as I want you. I go to sleep every night afraid I'll wake up and you'll be gone. Or that I scared you away . . . that I dreamed you—"

"No. Gideon." *Jesus.* He broke my heart every day. Shattered me.

"I know I don't tell you how I feel about you in the same way you tell me, but you have me. You know that."

"Yes, I know you love me, Gideon." Insanely. Outrageously. Obsessively. Just like my feelings for him.

"I'm caught up with you, Eva." With his head tilted back, Gideon pulled me down for the sweetest of kisses, his firm lips moving gently beneath mine. "I'd kill for you," he whispered, "give up everything I own for you . . . but I won't give *you* up. Two days is my limit. Don't ask for more than that; I can't give it to you."

I didn't take his words lightly. His wealth insulated him, gave him the power and control that had been stolen from him at some point in his life. He'd suffered brutality and violation, just as I had. That he would consider it worthwhile to lose his peace of mind just to keep me meant more than the words *I love you*.

"I just need the two days, ace, and I'll make them worth your while."

The starkness of his gaze bled away, replaced by sexual heat. "Oh? Planning on pacifying me with sex, angel?"

"Yes," I admitted shamelessly. "Lots of it. After all, the tactic seems to work well for you."

His mouth curved, but his gaze had a sharpness that quickened my breath. The dark look he gave me reminded me—as if I could forget—that Gideon wasn't a man who could be managed or tamed.

"Ah, Eva," he purred, sprawled against the seat with the predatory insouciance of a sleek panther who'd neatly trapped a mouse in his den.

A delicious shiver moved through me. When it came to Gideon, I was more than willing to be devoured.

2

JUST BEFORE I exited the elevator into the vestibule of Waters
Field & Leaman, the advertising firm I worked for on the twentieth floor, Gideon whispered in my ear, "Think about me all day."

I squeezed his hand surreptitiously in the crowded car. "Always do."

He continued the ride up to the top floor, which housed the
headquarters of Cross Industries. The Crossfire was his, one of many
properties he owned throughout the city, including the apartment
complex I lived in.

I tried not to pay attention to that. My mom was a career trophy
wife. She'd given up my father's love for an affluent lifestyle, which
I couldn't relate to at all. I'd prefer love over wealth any day, but I
suppose that was easy for me to say because I had money—a sizable
investment portfolio—of my own. Not that I ever touched it. I

wouldn't. I'd paid too high a price and couldn't imagine anything worth the cost.

Megumi, the receptionist, buzzed me through the glass security door and greeted me with a big smile. She was a pretty woman, young like me, with a stylish bob of glossy black hair framing stunning Asian features.

"Hey," I said, stopping by her desk. "Got any plans for lunch?"

"I do now."

"Awesome." My grin was wide and genuine. As much as I loved Cary and enjoyed spending time with him, I needed girlfriends, too. Cary had already started building a network of acquaintances and friends in our adopted city, but I'd been sucked into the Gideon vortex almost from the outset. As much as I'd prefer to spend every moment with him, I knew it wasn't healthy. Female friends would give it to me straight when I needed it, and I was going to have to cultivate those friendships if I wanted them.

Setting off, I headed down the long hallway to my cubicle. When I reached my desk, I put my bag and purse in the bottom drawer, keeping my smartphone out so I could silence it. I found a text from Cary: I'm sorry, baby girl.

"Cary Taylor," I sighed. "I love you . . . even when you're pissing me off."

And he'd pissed me off royally. No woman wanted to come home to a sexual clusterfuck in progress on her living room floor. Especially not while in the middle of a fight with her new boyfriend.

I texted back, Block off the wknd 4 me if u can.

There was a long pause and I imagined him absorbing my request. Damn, he texted back finally. Must be some ass kicking u have planned.

"Maybe a little," I muttered, shuddering as I remembered the . . . *orgy* I'd walked in on. But mostly I thought Cary and I needed to

REFLECTED IN YOU · 19

spend some quality downtime together. We hadn't been living in Manhattan long. It was a new town for us, new apartment, new jobs and experiences, new boyfriends for both of us. We were out of our element and struggling, and since we both had barge loads of baggage from our pasts, we didn't handle struggling well. Usually we leaned on each other for balance, but we hadn't had much time for that lately. We really needed to make the time. Up for a trip to Vegas? Just u and me?

Fuck yeah!

K . . . more later. As I silenced my phone and put it away, my gaze passed briefly over the two collage photo frames next to my monitor—one filled with photos of both of my parents and one of Cary, and the other filled with photos of me and Gideon. Gideon had put the latter collection together himself, wanting me to have a reminder of him just like the reminder he had of me on his desk. As if I needed it . . .

I loved having those images of the people I loved close by: my mom with her golden cap of curls and her bombshell smile, her curvy body scarcely covered by a tiny bikini as she enjoyed the French Riviera on my stepdad's yacht; my stepfather, Richard Stanton, looking regal and distinguished, his silver hair oddly complementing the looks of his much younger wife; and Cary, who was captured in all his photogenic glory, with his lustrous brown hair and sparkling green eyes, his smile wide and mischievous. That million-dollar face was starting to pop up in magazines everywhere and soon would grace billboards and bus stops advertising Grey Isles clothing.

I looked across the strip of hallway and through the glass wall that encased Mark Garrity's very small office and saw his jacket hung over the back of his Aeron chair, even though the man himself wasn't in sight. I wasn't surprised to find him in the break room scowling into his coffee mug; he and I shared a java dependency.

"I thought you had the hang of it," I said, referring to his trouble with the one-cup coffeemaker.

"I do, thanks to you." Mark lifted his head and offered a charmingly crooked smile. He had gleaming dark skin, a trim goatee, and soft brown eyes. In addition to being easy on the eyes, he was a great boss—very open to educating me about the ad business and quick to trust that he didn't have to show me how to do something twice. We worked well together, and I hoped that would be the case for a long time to come.

"Try this," he said, reaching for a second steaming cup waiting on the counter. He handed it to me and I accepted it gratefully, appreciating that he'd been thoughtful about adding cream and sweetener, which was how I liked it.

I took a cautious sip, since it was hot, then coughed over the unexpected—and unwelcome—flavor. "What *is* this?"

"Blueberry-flavored coffee."

Abruptly, I was the one scowling. "Who the hell wants to drink that?"

"Ah, see . . . it's our job to figure out who, then sell this to them." He lifted his mug in a toast. "Here's to our latest account!"

Wincing, I straightened my spine and took another sip.

I was pretty sure the sickly sweet taste of artificial blueberries was still coating my tongue two hours later. Since it was time for my break, I started an Internet search for Dr. Terrence Lucas, a man who'd clearly rubbed Gideon the wrong way when I'd seen the two men together at dinner the night before. I hadn't gotten any further than typing the doctor's name in the search box when my desk phone rang.

"Mark Garrity's office," I answered. "Eva Tramell speaking."

"Are you serious about Vegas?" Cary asked without preamble.

"Totally."

There was a pause. "Is this when you tell me you're moving in with your billionaire boyfriend and I've got to go?"

"What? *No.* Are you nuts?" I squeezed my eyes shut, understanding how insecure Cary was but thinking we were too far along in our friendship for those kinds of doubts. "You're stuck with me for life, you know that."

"And you just up and decided we should go to Vegas?"

"Pretty much. Figured we could sip mojitos by the pool and live off room service for a couple days."

"I'm not sure how much I can pitch in for that."

"Don't worry, it's on Gideon. His plane, his hotel. We'll just cover our food and drinks." A lie, since I planned on covering everything except the airfare, but Cary didn't need to know that.

"And he's not coming with us?"

I leaned back in my chair and stared at one of the photos of Gideon. I missed him already and it'd been only a couple of hours since we'd been together. "He's got business in Arizona, so he'll share the flights back and forth, but it'll be just you and me in Vegas. I think we need it."

"Yeah." He exhaled harshly. "I could do with a change of scenery and some quality time with my best girl."

"Okay, then. He wants to fly out by eight tomorrow night."

"I'll start packing. Want me to put a bag together for you, too?"

"Would you? That'd be great!" Cary could've been a stylist or personal shopper. He had serious talent when it came to clothes.

"Eva?"

"Yeah?"

He sighed. "Thank you for putting up with my shit."

"Shut up."

After we hung up, I stared at the phone for a long minute, hating that Cary was so unhappy when everything in his life was going so well. He was an expert at self-sabotage, never truly believing he was worthy of happiness.

As I returned my attention to work, the Google search on my monitor reminded me of my interest in Dr. Terry Lucas. A few articles about him had been posted on the Web, complete with pictures that cemented the verification.

Pediatrician. Forty-five years of age. Married for twenty years. Nervously, I searched for "Dr. Terrence Lucas and wife," inwardly cringing at the thought of seeing a golden-skinned, long-haired brunette. I exhaled my relief when I saw that Mrs. Lucas was a pale-skinned woman with short, bright red hair.

But that left me with more questions. I'd figured it would be a woman who'd caused the trouble between the two men.

The fact was, Gideon and I really didn't know that much about each other. We knew the ugly stuff—at least he knew mine; I'd mostly guessed his from some pretty obvious clues. We knew some of the basic cohabitation stuff about each other after spending so many nights sleeping over at our respective apartments. He'd met half of my family and I'd met all of his. But we hadn't been together long enough to touch on a whole lot of the periphery stuff. And frankly, I think we weren't as forthcoming or inquisitive as we could've been, as if we were afraid to pile any more crap onto an already struggling relationship.

We were together because we were addicted to each other. I was never as intoxicated as I was when we were happy together, and I knew it was the same for him. We were putting ourselves through the wringer for those moments of perfection between us, but they were so tenuous that only our stubbornness, determination, and love kept us fighting for them.

Enough with making yourself crazy.

I checked my e-mail, and found my daily Google alert on "Gideon Cross." The day's digest of links led mostly to photos of Gideon, in black tie sans tie, and me at the charity dinner at the Waldorf Astoria the night before.

"God." I couldn't help but be reminded of my mother when looking at the pictures of me in a champagne Vera Wang cocktail dress. Not just because of how closely my looks mirrored my mom's—aside from my hair being long and straight—but also because of the megamogul whose arm I graced.

Monica Tramell Barker Mitchell Stanton was very, very good at being a trophy wife. She knew precisely what was expected of her and delivered without fail. Although she'd been divorced twice, both times had been by her choice and both divorces had left her exes despondent over losing her. I didn't think less of my mother, because she gave as good as she got and didn't take anyone for granted, but I'd grown up striving for independence. My right to say no was my most valued possession.

Minimizing my e-mail window, I pushed my personal life aside and went back to searching for market comparisons on fruity coffee. I coordinated some initial meetings between the strategists and Mark and helped Mark with brainstorming a campaign for a gluten-free restaurant. Noon approached and I was starting to feel seriously hungry when my phone rang. I answered with my usual greeting.

"Eva?" an accented female voice greeted me. "It's Magdalene. Do you have a minute?"

I leaned back in my chair, alert. Magdalene and I had once shared a moment of sympathy over Corinne's unexpected and unwanted reappearance in Gideon's life, but I'd never forget how vicious Magdalene had been to me the first time we'd met. "Just. What's up?"

She sighed, then spoke quickly, her words flowing in a rush. "I was sitting at the table behind Corinne last night. I could hear a bit of what was being said between her and Gideon during dinner."

My stomach tensed, preparing for an emotional blow. Magdalene knew just how to exploit my insecurities about Gideon. "Stirring up crap while I'm at work is a new low," I said coldly. "I don't—"

"He wasn't ignoring you."

My mouth hung open a second, and she quickly filled the silence.

"He was managing her, Eva. She was making suggestions for where to take you around New York since you're new in town, but she was doing it by playing the old remember-when-you-and-I-went-there game."

"A walk down memory lane," I muttered, grateful now that I hadn't been able to hear much of Gideon's low-voiced conversation with his ex.

"Yes." Magdalene took a deep breath. "You left because you thought he was ignoring you for her. I just want you to know that he seemed to be thinking about you, trying to keep Corinne from upsetting you."

"Why do you care?"

"Who says I do? I owe you one, Eva, for the way I introduced myself."

I thought about that. Yeah, she owed me for when she ambushed me in the bathroom with her catty jealous bullshit. Not that I bought it as her sole motivation. Maybe I was just the lesser of two evils. Maybe she was keeping her enemies close. "All right. Thank you."

No denying I felt better. A weight I hadn't realized I was carrying around was suddenly relieved.

"Something else," Magdalene went on. "He went after you."

My grip tightened on the phone receiver. Gideon always came after me . . . because I was always running. My recovery was so fragile that I'd learned to protect it at all costs. When something threatened my stability, I ditched it.

"There have been other women in his life who've tried ultimatums like that, Eva. They got bored or they wanted his attention or some kind of grand gesture . . . So they walked away and expected him to come after them. You know what he did?"

"Nothing," I said softly, knowing my man. A man who never spent social time with women he slept with and never slept with women he associated with socially. Corinne and I were the sole exceptions to that rule, which was yet another reason why his ex sent me into fits of jealousy.

"Nothing more than making sure Angus dropped them off safely," she confirmed, making me think it'd been a tactic she'd tried at some point. "But when you left, he couldn't chase after you fast enough. And he wasn't himself when he said good-bye. He seemed . . . off."

Because he'd felt fear. My eyes closed as I mentally kicked myself. Hard.

Gideon had told me more than once that it terrified him when I ran, because he couldn't handle the thought that I might not come back. What good did it do to say that I couldn't imagine living without him when I so often showed him otherwise with my actions? Was it any wonder he hadn't opened up to me about his past?

I had to stop running. Gideon and I were both going to have to stand and fight for this, for *us*, if we were going to have any hope of making our relationship work.

"Do I owe you now?" I asked neutrally, returning Mark's wave as he left for lunch.

Magdalene exhaled in a rush. "Gideon and I have known each

other a long time. Our mothers are best friends. You and I will see each other around, Eva, and I'm hoping we can find a way to avoid any awkwardness."

The woman had come up to me and told me that the minute Gideon "shoved his dick" in me, I was "done." And she'd hit me with that at a moment when I was especially vulnerable.

"Listen, Magdalene, if you don't cause drama, we'll get by." And since she was being so forthright . . . "I can screw up my relationship with Gideon all by myself, trust me. I don't need any help."

She laughed softly. "That was my mistake, I think—I was too careful and too accommodating. He has to work at it with you. Anyway . . . I've taken up my minute. I'll let you go."

"Enjoy your weekend," I said, in lieu of thanks. I still couldn't trust her motivation.

"You, too."

As I returned the receiver to its cradle, my gaze went to the photos of me and Gideon. I was abruptly overwhelmed by feelings of greed and possession. He was mine, yet I couldn't be sure from one day to the next whether he'd stay mine. And the thought of any other woman having him made me insane.

I pulled open my bottom drawer and dug my smartphone out of my purse. Driven by the need to have him thinking as fiercely about me, I texted him about my sudden desperate hunger to devour him whole: I'd give anything to be sucking your cock right now.

Just thinking about how he looked when I took him in my mouth . . . the feral sounds he made when he was about to come . . .

Standing, I deleted the text the moment I saw it'd been delivered, then dropped my phone back in my purse. Since it was noon, I closed all the windows on my computer and headed out to reception to find Megumi.

"You hungry for anything in particular?" she asked, pushing to her feet and giving me a chance to admire her belted, sleeveless lavender dress.

I coughed because her question came so soon after my text. "No. Your choice. I'm not picky."

We pushed out through the glass doors to reach the elevators.

"I am *so* ready for the weekend," Megumi said with a groan as she stabbed the call button with an acrylic-tipped finger. "A day and a half left to go."

"Got something fun planned?"

"That remains to be seen." She sighed and tucked her hair behind her ear. "Blind date," she explained ruefully.

"Ah. Do you trust the person setting you up?"

"My roommate. I expect the guy will at least be physically attractive, because I know where she sleeps at night and paybacks are a bitch."

I was smiling as an elevator car reached our floor and we stepped inside. "Well, that ups your odds for a good time."

"Not really, since she found him by going on a blind date with him first. She swears he's great, just more my type than hers."

"Hmm."

"I know, right?" Megumi shook her head and looked up at the decorative, old-fashioned needle above the car doors that marked the passing floors.

"You'll have to let me know how it goes."

"Oh, yeah. Wish me luck."

"Absolutely." We'd just stepped out into the lobby when I felt my purse vibrate beneath my arm. As we passed through the turnstiles, I dug for my phone and felt my stomach tighten at the sight of Gideon's name. He was calling, not sexting me back.

"Excuse me," I said to Megumi before answering.

She waved it off nonchalantly. "Go for it."

"Hey," I greeted him playfully.

"Eva."

I missed a step hearing the way he growled my name. There was a wealth of promise in the roughness of his voice.

Slowing, I found I was speechless, just from hearing him say my name with that edginess I craved—the sharp bite that told me he wanted to be inside me more than he wanted anything else in the world.

While people flowed around me, entering and exiting the building, I was halted by the weighted silence on my phone. The unspoken and nearly irresistible demand. He made no sound at all—I couldn't even hear him breathing—but I felt his hunger. If I didn't have Megumi waiting patiently for me, I'd be riding an elevator to the top floor to satisfy his unvoiced command to make good on my offer.

The memory of the time I'd sucked him off in his office simmered through me, making my mouth water. I swallowed. "Gideon . . ."

"You wanted my attention—now you have it. I want to hear you say those words."

I felt my face flush. "I can't. Not here. Let me call you later."

"Step over by the column and out of the way."

Startled, I looked around for him. Then I remembered that the Caller ID put him in his office. My gaze lifted, searching for the security cameras. Immediately, I felt his eyes on me, hot and wanting. Arousal surged through me, spurred by his desire.

"Hurry along, angel. Your friend's waiting."

I moved to the column, my breathing fast and audible.

"Now tell me. Your text made me hard, Eva. What are you going to do about it?"

My hand went to my throat, my gaze sliding helplessly to Megumi, who watched me with raised brows. I lifted one finger up, asking for another minute, then turned my back to her and whispered, "I want you in my mouth."

"Why? To play with me? To tease me like you're doing now?" There was no heat in his voice, just calm severity.

I knew to pay careful attention when Gideon got serious about sex.

"No." I lifted my face to the tinted dome in the ceiling that concealed the nearest security camera. "To make you come. I love making you come, Gideon."

He exhaled harshly. "A gift, then."

Only I knew what it meant for Gideon to view a sexual act as a gift. For him, sex had previously been about pain and degradation or lust and necessity. Now, with me, it was about pleasure and love. "Always."

"Good. Because I treasure you, Eva, and what we have. Even our driving urge to fuck each other constantly is precious to me, because it matters."

I sagged into the column, admitting to myself that I'd fallen into an old destructive habit—I'd exploited sexual attraction to ease my insecurities. If Gideon was lusting after me, he couldn't be lusting after anyone else. How did he always know what was going on in my mind?

"Yes," I breathed, closing my eyes. "It matters."

There'd been a time when I'd turned to sex to feel affection, confusing momentary desire with genuine caring. Which was why I now insisted on having some sort of friendly framework in place before I went to bed with a man. I never again wanted to roll out of a lover's bed feeling worthless and dirty.

And I sure as hell didn't want to cheapen what I shared with Gideon just because I was irrationally scared of losing him.

It hit me then that I was off balance. I had this sick feeling in my gut, like something awful was going to happen.

"You can have what you want after work, angel." His voice deepened, grew raspier. "In the meantime, enjoy lunch with your coworker. I'll be thinking about you. And your mouth."

"I love you, Gideon."

It took a couple of deep breaths after I hung up to compose myself enough to join Megumi again. "I'm sorry about that."

"Everything all right?"

"Yes. Everything's fine."

"Things still hot and heavy with you and Gideon Cross?" She glanced at me with a slight smile.

"Umm . . ." *Oh yes.* "Yes, that's fine, too." And I wished desperately that I could talk about it. I wished I could just open the valve and gush about my overwhelming feelings for him. How thoughts of him consumed me, how the feel of him beneath my hands drove me wild, how the passion of his tortured soul cut into me like the sharpest blade.

But I couldn't. Not ever. He was too visible, too well known. Private tidbits about his life were worth a small fortune. I couldn't risk it.

"He sure is," Megumi agreed. "Damn fine. Did you know him before you started working here?"

"No. Although I suppose we would have met eventually." Because of our pasts. My mother gave generously to many abused children's charities, as did Gideon. It was inevitable that Gideon and I would've crossed paths at some point. I wondered what that meeting would have been like—him with a gorgeous brunette on his arm and me with Cary. Would we have had the same visceral reaction to each other from a distance as we'd had up close in the Crossfire lobby?

He'd wanted me the moment he saw me on the street.

"I wondered." Megumi pushed through the revolving lobby door.

"I read that it was serious between you two," she went on when I joined her outside on the sidewalk. "So I thought maybe you'd known him before."

"Don't believe everything you read on those gossip blogs."

"So it's not serious?"

"I didn't say that." It was *too* serious at times. Painfully, brutally so.

She shook her head. "God . . . listen to me pry. Sorry. Gossip is one of my vices. So are extremely hot men like Gideon Cross. I can't help but wonder what it'd be like to hook up with a guy whose body screams *sex* like that. Tell me he's awesome in bed."

I smiled. It was good to hang out with another girl. Not that Cary couldn't also be appreciative of a hot guy, but nothing beat girl talk. "You won't hear me complaining."

"Lucky bitch." Bumping shoulders with me to show she was teasing, she said, "How about that roommate of yours? From the photos I saw, he's gorgeous, too. Is he single? Wanna hook me up?"

Turning my head quickly, I hid a wince. I'd learned the hard way never to set up an acquaintance or friend with Cary. He was so easy to love, which led to a lot of broken hearts because he couldn't love back the same way. The moment things started going too well, Cary sabotaged them. "I don't know if he's single or not. Things are . . . complicated in his life at the moment."

"Well, if the opportunity presents itself, I'm certainly not opposed. Just sayin'. You like tacos?"

"Love 'em."

"I know a great place a couple blocks up. Come on."

THINGS were going well in my world as Megumi and I headed back from lunch. Forty minutes of gossip, guy-ogling, and three awesome carne asada tacos later, I was feeling pretty good. And we were returning to work a little over ten minutes early, which I was glad for since I hadn't been the most punctual employee lately, even though Mark never complained.

The city was thrumming around us, taxis and people surging through the growing heat and humidity as they crammed what they could into the insufficient hours of the day. I people-watched shamelessly, my eyes skimming over everyone and everything.

Men in business suits walked alongside women in flowing skirts and flip-flops. Ladies in haute couture and five-hundred-dollar shoes teetered past steaming hot dog vendor carts and shouting hawkers. The eclectic mix of New York was heaven to me, stirring an excitement that made me feel more vibrant here than anyplace else I'd ever lived.

We were stopped by a traffic light directly across from the Crossfire, and my gaze was immediately drawn to the black Bentley sitting in front of it. Gideon must've just gotten back from lunch. I couldn't help but think about him sitting in his car on the day we'd met, watching me as I took in the imposing beauty of his Crossfire Building. It made me tingly just thinking about it—

Suddenly, I went cold.

Because a striking brunette breezed out of the revolving doors just then and paused, giving me a good, long look at her—Gideon's ideal, whether he'd been aware of it or not. A woman I'd witnessed him fixate on the moment he'd seen her in the Waldorf Astoria ballroom. A woman whose poise and hold over Gideon brought out all my worst insecurities.

Corinne Giroux looked like a breath of fresh air in a cream-colored sheath dress and cherry red heels. She ran a hand over her waist-length dark hair, which wasn't quite as sleek as it'd appeared last night when I'd met her. In fact, it looked a little disheveled. And her fingers were rubbing at her mouth, wiping along the outline of her lips.

I pulled my smartphone out, activated the camera, and snapped a picture. With the proximity of the zoom, I could see why she was fussing with her lipstick—it was smeared. No, more like *mashed*. As if from a passionate kiss.

The light changed. Megumi and I moved with the flow, closing the distance between me and the woman who'd once had Gideon's promise to marry her. Angus stepped out of the Bentley and came around, speaking to her briefly before opening the back door for her. The feeling of betrayal—Angus's and Gideon's—was so fierce, I couldn't catch my breath. I swayed on my feet.

"Hey." Megumi caught my arm to steady me. "And we only had virgin margaritas, lightweight!"

I watched Corinne's willowy body slide into the back of Gideon's car with practiced grace. My fists clenched as fury surged through me. Through the haze of my angry tears, the Bentley pulled away from the curb and disappeared.

3

WHEN MEGUMI AND I stepped into an elevator, I hit the button for the top floor.

"I'll be back in five minutes, if anyone asks," I told her, as she stepped off at Waters Field & Leaman.

"Give him a kiss for me, will you?" she said, playfully fanning herself. "Makes me hot just thinking about living vicariously through you."

I managed a smile before the doors closed and the car continued its ascent. When it reached the end of the line, I exited into a tastefully ornate and undeniably masculine entrance foyer. Smoky glass security doors were sandblasted with CROSS INDUSTRIES and softened by hanging baskets of ferns and lilies.

Gideon's redheaded receptionist was unusually cooperative and buzzed me in before I reached the door. Then she grinned at me in a way that got my back up. I'd always gotten the impression she didn't like me, so I didn't trust that smile for a minute. It made me twitchy. Still, I waved and said hello, because I wasn't a catty bitch—unless I was given good reason to be.

I took the long hallway that led to Gideon, stopping at a large secondary reception area where his secretary, Scott, manned the desk.

Scott stood as I approached. "Hello, Eva," he greeted me, reaching for his phone. "I'll let him know you're here."

The glass wall that separated Gideon's office from the rest of the floor was usually crystal clear but could be made opaque with the push of a button. It was frosted now, which increased my uneasiness. "Is he alone?"

"Yes, but—"

Whatever else he said was lost as I pushed through the glass door and into Gideon's domain. It was a massive space, with three distinct seating areas, each larger than my boss Mark's entire office. In contrast to the elegant warmth of Gideon's apartment, his office was decorated in a cool palette of black, gray, and white broken only by the jewel-toned crystal decanters that decorated the wall behind a bar.

Floor-to-ceiling windows overlooked the city on two sides. The one solid wall opposite the immense desk was covered in flat screens streaming news channels from around the world.

My gaze swept the room and caught on the throw pillow that had been carelessly knocked to the floor. Beside it were indents in the area rug that betrayed where the couch feet were usually planted. The piece of furniture had, apparently, been bumped askew by a few inches.

My heart rate sped up and my palms grew damp. That awful anxiety I'd felt earlier intensified.

I had just noticed the open door to the washroom when Gideon stepped into view, stealing my breath with the beauty of his exposed torso. His hair was damp, as if from a recent shower, and his neck and upper chest were still flushed, as they became when he exerted himself physically.

He froze when he saw me, his gaze darkening for an instant before his perfect, implacable mask slid effortlessly into place.

"It's not a good time, Eva," he said, shrugging into a dress shirt he'd had draped over the back of a bar stool . . . a different shirt from the one he'd been wearing earlier that morning. "I'm running late to an appointment."

I gripped my purse tightly. Seeing him so intimately brought home how badly I wanted him. I loved him insanely, needed him like I needed to breathe . . . which only made it easier for me to understand how Magdalene and Corinne felt, and to relate to any lengths they might go to in trying to lure him away from me. "Why are you half dressed?"

There was no help for it. My body responded instinctively to the sight of his, which made it even harder for me to rein in my rioting emotions. His open, neatly pressed dress shirt revealed golden skin stretched tightly over washboard abs and perfectly defined pectorals. A dusting of dark hair over his chest arrowed down and darkened into a thin line, leading to a cock presently encased in boxer briefs and slacks. Just thinking about how he felt inside me made me ache with longing.

"I got something on my shirt." He began buttoning up, his abs flexing with his movements as he crossed over to the bar, where I saw his cuff links waiting. "I have to run. If you need something, let Scott know and he'll see to it. Or I'll take care of it when I get back. I shouldn't be more than two hours."

"Why are you running late?"

He didn't look at me when he answered, "I had to squeeze in a last-minute meeting."

Did you now? "You showered this morning." *After making love to me for an hour.* "Why did you have to shower again?"

"Why the inquisition?" he snapped.

Needing answers, I went to the washroom. The lingering humidity was oppressive. Ignoring the voice in my head telling me not to look for trouble I couldn't bear to find, I dug his shirt out of the laundry basket . . . and saw red lipstick smeared like a bloodstain on one of the cuffs. Pain twisted through my chest.

Dropping the garment on the floor, I pivoted and left, needing to get as far away from Gideon as possible. Before I threw up or started sobbing.

"Eva!" he snapped as I hurried past him. "What the hell is the matter with you?"

"Fuck you, asswipe."

"Excuse me?"

My hand was on the door handle when he caught me, yanking me back by the elbow. Spinning, I slapped him with enough force to turn his head and set my palm on fire.

"Goddamn it," he growled, grabbing me by the arms and shaking me. "Don't fucking hit me!"

"Don't touch me!" The feel of his bare hands on the bare skin of my arms was too much.

He shoved back and away from me. "What the fuck's gotten into you?"

"I *saw* her, Gideon."

"Saw who?"

"Corinne!"

He scowled. "What are you talking about?"

Pulling my smartphone out, I thrust the photo in his face. "Busted."

Gideon's gaze narrowed on the screen, and then his scowl cleared. "Busted doing what, exactly?" he asked, too softly.

"Oh, screw you." I turned toward the door, shoving my phone in my purse. "I'm not spelling it out for you."

His palm slapped against the glass, holding the door closed. Caging me with his body, he leaned down and hissed in my ear, "Yes. Yes, you goddamn will spell it out."

I squeezed my eyes shut as our position at the door brought back a flood of heated memories from the first time I'd been in Gideon's office. He'd stopped me just like this, seducing me deftly, drawing us into a passionate embrace on the very couch that had recently seen some kind of action forceful enough to shove it out of position.

"Doesn't a picture say a thousand words?" I bit out through clenched teeth.

"So Corinne was manhandled. What does that have to do with me?"

"Are you kidding me? Let me out."

"I don't find anything even remotely funny about this. In fact, I don't think I've ever been this pissed off at a woman. You come in here with your half-assed accusations and self-righteous bullshit—"

"I *am* righteous!" I twisted around and ducked beneath his arm, putting some much-needed distance between us. Being close to him hurt too much. "I would never cheat on you! If I wanted to fuck around, I'd break it off with you first."

Leaning into the door, Gideon crossed his arms. His shirt remained untucked and open at the collar, a look I found hot and tempting, which only made me angrier.

"You think I cheated on you?" His tone was clipped and icy.

I sucked in a deep breath to get through the pain of imagining him with Corinne on the sofa behind me. "Explain to me why she was here at the Crossfire, looking like she did. Why your office looks like this. Why you look like that."

His gaze went to the couch, then to the cushion on the floor, then back to me. "I don't know why Corinne was here or why she looked like that. I haven't seen her since last night, when you were with me."

Last night seemed like it'd happened forever ago. I wished that it had never happened at all.

"But I wasn't with you," I pointed out. "She batted her eyelashes and said she wanted to introduce you to someone, and you left me standing there."

"Christ." His eyes blazed. "Not this again."

I swiped angrily at a tear that slid down my cheek.

He growled. "You think I went with her because I was overcome with the need to be with her and get away from you?"

"I don't know, Gideon. *You* ditched *me*. You're the one with the answers."

"You ditched me first."

My mouth fell open. "I did not!"

"The hell you didn't. Almost the second we arrived, you took off. I had to hunt you down and when I did, you were dancing with that prick."

"Martin is Stanton's nephew!" And since Richard Stanton was my stepdad, I thought of Martin as family.

"I don't care if he's a damned priest. He wants to nail you."

"Oh my God. That's absurd! Stop deflecting. You were talking business with your associates. It was awkward standing there. For them as well as me."

"That's your place, awkward or not!"

My head jerked back as if he'd slapped me. "Come again?"

"How would you feel if I walked away from you at a Waters Field and Leaman party because you started talking about a campaign? Then, when you found me, I was slow dancing with Magdalene?"

"I—" *God.* I hadn't thought of it like that.

Gideon appeared smooth and unruffled with his powerful frame lounging against the door, but I could sense the anger vibrating beneath that calm surface. He was riveting always, but most especially when he was seething with passion. "It's my place to stand beside you, and support you, and yes, just fucking look pretty on your arm sometimes. It's my right, my duty, and my privilege, Eva, just as it's yours in reverse."

"I thought I was doing you a favor by getting out of the way."

His arched brow was a silent, sarcastic comeback.

My arms crossed in front of me. "Is that why you walked off with Corinne? Were you punishing me?"

"If I wanted to punish you, Eva, I'd take you over my knee."

My gaze narrowed. *That* was never going to happen.

"I know how you get," he said curtly. "I didn't want you jealous over Corinne before I had a chance to explain. I needed a few minutes to make sure she understood how serious you and I are, and how important it was to me that you enjoy the evening. That's the only reason I walked away with her."

"You told her not to say anything about you two, didn't you? You told her to keep quiet about what she is to you. Too bad Magdalene screwed that up."

And maybe Corinne and Magdalene had planned it that way. Corinne knew Gideon well enough to anticipate his moves; it might've been easy for her to plan around his reaction to her unexpected appearance in New York.

Which shed a whole new light on why Magdalene had called

me today. She and Corinne had been talking at the Waldorf when Gideon and I spotted them. Two women who wanted a man who was with another woman. Nothing was going to happen for them while I was in the picture, and because of that, I couldn't rule out the possibility that they might be working together.

"I wanted you to hear it from me," he said tightly.

I waved that off, more concerned about what was happening now. "I saw Corinne get into the Bentley, Gideon. Right before I came up here."

His other brow rose to match the first. "Did you?"

"Yes, I did. Can you explain that?"

"I can't, no."

Injured fury burned through me. I suddenly couldn't bear to even look at him. "Then get out of my way, I have to get back to work."

He didn't move. "I just want to be clear on something before you go: Do you believe I fucked her?"

Hearing him say it aloud made me flinch. "I don't know what to believe. The evidence sure—"

"I wouldn't care if the 'evidence' included you finding me and her naked in a bed together." He uncoiled so swiftly, I stumbled back in surprise. He stalked closer. "I want to know if you think I fucked her. If you think I would. Or could. Do you?"

My foot began to tap, but I didn't retreat. "Explain the lipstick on your shirt, Gideon."

His jaw tightened. "No."

"What?" The flat-out refusal sent me into a tailspin.

"Answer my question."

I studied his face and saw the mask he wore around other people but had never worn with me. He reached his hand toward me as if to brush my cheek with his fingertips, then pulled back at the last minute. In that brief instant in which he pulled away, I heard his teeth grind, as if *not* touching me was a struggle. Agonized, I was grateful he hadn't.

"I *need* you to explain," I whispered, wondering if I imagined the wince that crossed his face. Sometimes I wanted to believe something so badly, I deliberately manufactured excuses and ignored painful reality.

"I've given you no reason to doubt me."

"You're giving me one now, Gideon." I exhaled in a rush, deflating. Withdrawing. He was standing in front of me, but he seemed miles away. "I understand you need time before you share secrets that are painful for you. I've been where you're at, knowing I needed to talk about what happened to me but just not ready. That's why I've tried very hard not to push you or rush you. But this secret is one that's hurting *me*, and that's different. Don't you see that?"

Cursing under his breath, he cupped my face with cool hands. "I go out of my way to make sure you don't have any reason to feel jealous, but when you do get possessive, I like it. I want you to fight for me. I want you to care that much. I want you crazy about me. But possessiveness without trust is hell. If you don't trust me, we've got nothing."

"Trust goes both ways, Gideon."

He sucked in a deep breath. "Damn it. Don't look at me like that."

"I'm trying to figure out who you are. Where's the man who came right out and said he wanted to fuck me? The man who didn't hesitate to tell me I tie him up in knots, even as I was breaking up with him? I believed you'd always be brutally honest like that. I counted on it. Now—" I shook my head, my throat too tight to say anything else.

Grimness thinned his lips, but they stayed stubbornly closed.

Catching his wrists, I pulled his hands away. I was cracking open inside, breaking. "I won't run this time, but you can push me away. You might want to think about that."

I left. Gideon didn't stop me.

I spent the rest of the afternoon focused on work. Mark loved to brainstorm out loud, which was an awesome learning exercise for me, and his confident and amiable way of dealing with his accounts was inspiring. I watched him breeze through two client meetings in which he conveyed an air of command that was both reassuring and nonthreatening.

Then we tackled a baby-toy company's needs analysis, zeroing in on poor return expenditures as well as untapped avenues, such as mom-blog advertising. I was grateful that my job was a distraction from my personal life, and I was looking forward to going to my Krav Maga class later, so I could burn off some of my edgy restlessness.

It was just past four when my desk phone rang. I answered briskly and felt my heart leap at the sound of Gideon's voice.

"We should leave at five," he said, "to get to Dr. Petersen's on time."

"Oh." I'd forgotten that our couples therapy sessions were on Thursdays at six P.M. It would be our first.

Abruptly, I wondered if it would also be our last.

"I'll come get you," he went on gruffly, "when it's time."

I sighed, feeling far from up to it. I was already raw and irritable from our fight earlier. "I'm sorry I hit you. I shouldn't have done that. I hate that I did."

"Angel." Gideon exhaled harshly. "You didn't ask the one question that matters."

My eyes closed. It was irritating how he read my mind. "Either way, it doesn't change the fact that you're keeping secrets."

"Secrets are something we can work through; cheating isn't."

I rubbed at the ache behind my forehead. "You're right about that."

"There's only you, Eva." His voice was clipped and hard.

A tremor moved through me at the fury underlying his words. He was still angry that I'd doubted him. Oh well. I was still angry, too. "I'll be ready at five."

He was prompt, as usual. While I put my computer to sleep and grabbed my belongings, he spoke with Mark about the ongoing work on the Kingsman Vodka account. I watched Gideon furtively. He cut an imposing figure with his tall, leanly muscular frame in his dark suit and carried himself in a way that projected impenetrability, yet I'd seen him terribly vulnerable.

I was in love with that tender, deeply emotional man. And I resented the façade and his attempts to hide himself from me.

Turning his head, he caught me staring. I saw a glimpse of my beloved Gideon in his wild blue gaze, which briefly exposed a helpless yearning. Then he was gone, replaced by the cool mask. "Ready?"

It was so obvious that he was holding something back, and it killed me to have that gulf between us. To know there were things he wouldn't trust me with.

As we exited through reception, Megumi rested her chin on her fist and gave a dramatic sigh.

"She's crushing on you, Cross," I murmured, as we made our way out and he hit the call button for the elevator.

"Whatever." He snorted. "What does she know about me?"

"I've been asking myself that same question all day," I said quietly.

That time, I was certain he winced.

DR. Lyle Petersen was tall, with neatly groomed gray hair and sharp yet kind denim blue eyes. His office was tastefully decorated in neutral shades and his furniture was extremely comfortable, something I noted on every one of my visits to him. It was a little weird for me to see him as *my* therapist now. In the past, he'd met with me only as my mother's daughter. He'd been my mom's shrink for the last couple of years.

I watched as he settled into the gray wingback chair across from the sofa Gideon and I sat on. His keen gaze shifted between us, clearly noting how we'd each taken seats on opposite ends of the sofa, our stiff postures revealing our defensiveness. We'd made the drive over in the same way.

Flipping open the cover of his tablet, Dr. Petersen gripped his stylus and said, "Shall we start with the cause of the tension between you?"

I waited a beat, to give Gideon a chance to speak first. I wasn't terribly surprised when he just sat there, silent. "Well . . . in the last twenty-four hours I've met the fiancée I didn't know Gideon had—"

"Ex-fiancée," Gideon growled.

"—I found out the reason he's dated brunettes exclusively is because of her—"

"It wasn't dating."

"—and I caught her leaving his office after lunch looking like this—" I dug out my phone.

"She was leaving the building," Gideon bit out, "not my office."

I pulled up the picture and passed my phone over to Dr. Petersen. "And getting into *your* car, Gideon!"

"Angus just told you before we got here that he saw her standing there, recognized her, and was being polite."

"Like he'd say anything different!" I shot back. "He's been your driver since you were a kid. Of course he'd cover your ass."

"Oh, it's a conspiracy now?"

"What was he doing there, then?" I challenged.

"Driving me to lunch."

"Where? I'll just verify you were there and she wasn't, and we'll get that part out of the way."

Gideon's jaw clenched. "I told you. I had an unexpected appointment. I didn't make it to lunch."

"Who was the appointment?"

"It wasn't Corinne."

"That's not an answer!" I turned back to Dr. Petersen, who calmly returned my phone to me. "When I went up to his office to ask him what the hell was going on, I discovered him half dressed and freshly showered, with one of his sofas bumped out of place, pillows strewn all over the floor—"

"One goddamned pillow!"

"—and red lipstick on his shirt."

"There are two dozen businesses in the Crossfire," Gideon said coldly. "She could have been visiting any one of them."

"Right," I drawled, my voice dripping sarcasm. "Of course."

"Wouldn't I have taken her to the hotel?"

I sucked in a sharp breath, reeling. "You still have that room?"

His mask slipped, revealing a flare of panic. The realization that he still had his sex pad—a hotel room he used exclusively for fucking and somewhere *I'd* never go again—hit me like a physical blow, sending a sharp pain through my chest. A low sound left me, a pained whimper that had me squeezing my eyes shut.

"Let's slow down," Dr. Petersen interrupted, scribbling rapidly. "I want to backtrack a bit. Gideon, why didn't you tell Eva about Corinne?"

"I had every intention of doing so," Gideon said tightly.

"He doesn't tell me anything," I whispered, digging for a tissue in my purse so I wouldn't have mascara running down my face. *Why would he keep that room?* The only explanation was that he intended to use it with someone other than me.

"What do you talk about?" Dr. Petersen asked, directing the question at both of us.

"I'm usually apologizing," Gideon muttered.

Dr. Petersen looked up. "For what?"

"Everything." He raked a hand through his hair.

"Do you feel that Eva's too demanding or expects too much from you?"

I felt Gideon's gaze on my profile. "No. She doesn't ask for anything."

"Except the truth," I corrected, turning toward him.

His eyes blazed, searing me with heat. "I've never lied to you."

"Do you want her to ask you for things, Gideon?" Dr. Petersen queried.

Gideon frowned.

"Think about that. We'll come back to it." Dr. Petersen turned his attention to me. "I'm intrigued by the photo you took, Eva. You were confronted with a situation that many women would find deeply upsetting—"

"There was no situation," Gideon reiterated coldly.

"Her perception of a situation," Dr. Petersen qualified.

"A patently ridiculous perception, considering the physical aspect of our relationship."

"All right. Let's talk about that. How many times a week do you have sex? On average."

My face heated. I looked at Gideon, who returned my look with a smirk.

"Umm . . ." My lips twisted ruefully. "A lot."

"Daily?" Dr. Petersen's brows rose when I uncrossed and re-crossed my legs, nodding. "Multiple times daily?"

Gideon stepped in, "On average."

Laying his tablet flat on his lap, Dr. Petersen met Gideon's gaze. "Is this level of sexual activity customary for you?"

"Nothing about my relationship with Eva is customary, Doctor."

"What was the frequency of your sexual encounters prior to Eva?"

Gideon's jaw tensed, and he glanced at me.

"It's okay," I told him, even as I conceded that I wouldn't want to answer that question in front of him.

He reached his hand out, spanning the distance between us. I placed mine in his and appreciated the reassuring squeeze he gave me. "Twice a week," he said tightly. "On average."

The number of women quickly added up in my mind. My free hand fisted in my lap.

Dr. Petersen sat back. "Eva has brought up concerns of infidelity and lack of communication in your relationship. How often is sex used to resolve disagreements?"

Gideon's brow arched. "Before you assume Eva's suffering under the demands of my overactive libido, you should know that she initiates sex at least as often as I do. If one of us were going to have concerns about keeping up, it'd be me just by virtue of possessing male anatomy."

Dr. Petersen looked at me for confirmation.

"Most interactions between us lead to sex," I conceded, "includ-ing fights."

"Before or after the conflict is considered resolved by both of you?"

I sighed. "Before."

He dropped the stylus and started typing. I thought he might end up with a novel's worth by the time all was said and done.

"Your relationship has been highly sexualized from the beginning?" he asked.

I nodded, even though he wasn't looking. "We're very attracted to each other."

"Obviously." He glanced up and offered a kind smile. "However, I'd like to discuss the possibility of abstinence while we—"

"There is no possibility," Gideon interjected. "That's a nonstarter. I suggest we focus on what's *not* working without eliminating one of the few things that is."

"I'm not sure it *is* working, Gideon," Dr. Petersen said evenly. "Not the way it should be."

"Doctor." Gideon set one ankle on the opposite knee and settled back, creating a picture of unyielding decisiveness. "The only way I'm keeping my hands off her is if I'm dead. Find another way to fix us."

"I'm new to this therapy thing," Gideon said later, after we'd gotten back into the Bentley and were heading home. "So I'm not sure. Was that the train wreck it felt like it was?"

"It could've gone better," I said wearily, leaning my head back and closing my eyes. I was bone tired. Too tired to even think about catching the eight o'clock Krav Maga class. "I'd kill for a quick shower and my bed."

"I have some things to take care of before I can call it a day."

"That's fine." I yawned. "Why don't we take the night off and see each other tomorrow?"

Thick silence greeted my suggestion. After a moment, it became so fraught with tension that I was motivated to lift both my head and my heavy eyelids to look at him.

His gaze was on my face, his lips thinned into a frustrated line. "You're cutting me off."

"No, I'm—"

"The hell you're not! You've tried and convicted me, and now you're shutting me out."

"I'm exhausted, Gideon! There's only so much bullshit I can take before I'm buried in it. I need sleep and—"

"*I* need *you*," he snapped. "What is it going to take to make you believe me?"

"I don't think you cheated. Okay? As suspicious as it all looks, I can't convince myself you'd do that. It's the secrets that are getting to be too much. I'm giving all I've got to this and you're—"

"You think I'm not?" He twisted in the seat, sliding one bent leg in between us so that he faced me directly. "I've never worked so hard for anything in my life as I have for you."

"You can't make the effort for me. You have to do it for you."

"Don't give me that crap! I wouldn't need to work on my relationship skills for anyone else."

With a low moan, I rested my cheek against the seat and closed my eyes again. "I'm tired of fighting, Gideon. I just want some peace and quiet for a night. I've been feeling off all day."

"Are you sick?" He shifted, cupping the back of my neck gently and pressing his lips to my forehead. "You don't feel hot. Is your stomach upset?"

I breathed him in, absorbing the delicious scent of his skin. The urge to press my face into the crook of his neck was nearly overwhelming.

"No." And then it hit me. I groaned.

"What is it?" He pulled me into his lap, cradling me close. "What's wrong? Do you need a doctor?"

"It's my period," I whispered, not wanting Angus to overhear. "It should start any day now. I don't know why I didn't realize it before. No wonder I'm so tired and cranky; I'm hormonal."

He stilled. After a heartbeat or two, I tilted my head back to search his face.

With his lips twisted ruefully, he admitted, "That's a new one for me. Not something that comes up in the course of a casual sex life."

"Lucky you. You get to experience the inconvenience reserved for men with girlfriends and wives."

"I *am* lucky." Gideon brushed loose strands of my hair away from my temples, his own luxuriant hair falling around that chiseled face. "And maybe, if I'm really lucky, you'll feel better tomorrow and like me again."

Ah, God. My heart ached in my chest. "I like you now, Gideon. I just don't like you keeping secrets. It's going to break us up."

"Don't let it," he murmured, tracing my brows with his fingertip. "Trust me."

"You have to trust me back."

Folding over me, he pressed his lips softly to mine. "Don't you know, angel?" he breathed. "There's no one I trust more."

Sliding my arms beneath his jacket, I hugged him, soaking up the warmth of his lean, hard body. I couldn't help but worry that we were beginning to drift from one another.

Gideon pressed the advantage, his tongue dipping into my mouth, lightly touching and teasing mine with velvet licks. Deceptively unhurried. I sought a deeper contact, needing more. Always more. Hating that aside from this, he gave me so little of himself.

He groaned into my mouth, an erotic sound of pleasure and need that vibrated through me. Tilting his head, he sealed those beautifully sculpted lips over mine. The kiss deepened, our tongues stroking, our breaths quickening.

The arm he'd banded beneath my back tightened, pulling me closer. His other hand slid beneath my shirt, cradling my spine in his warm palm. His fingertips flexed, gentling me even as the kiss grew wild. I arched into the caress, needing the reassurance of his touch against my bare skin.

"Gideon . . ." For the first time, our physical closeness wasn't enough to calm the desperate wanting inside me.

"Shh," he soothed. "I'm here. Not going anywhere."

Closing my eyes, I buried my face in his neck, wondering if we'd both be too stubborn and stay, even if it turned out that it would be best to let go.

4

I WOKE WITH a cry that was muffled by the sweaty palm mashed over my mouth. A crushing weight cut off my air as another hand shoved up beneath my nightgown, groping and bruising. Panic gripped me and I thrashed, my legs kicking frantically.

No . . . Please, no . . . No more. Not again.

Panting like a dog, Nathan yanked my legs apart. The hard thing between his legs poked blindly, ramming into my inner thigh. I fought, my lungs burning, but he was so strong. I couldn't buck him off. I couldn't get away.

Stop it! Get off me. Don't touch me. Oh, God . . . please don't do that to me . . . don't hurt me . . .

Ma-ma!

Nathan's hand pressed down on me, squashing my head into the pillow. The more I struggled, the more excited he became. Gasping horrible, nasty words in my ear, he found the tender spot between my legs and shoved into me, groaning. I froze, locking in a vise of horrendous pain.

"Yeah," he grunted, *"... like it once it's in you ... hot little slut ... you like it ..."*

I couldn't breathe, my lungs shuddering with sobs, my nostrils plugged by the heel of his palm. Spots danced before my eyes; my chest burned. I fought again ... needing air ... desperate for air—

"Eva! Wake up!"

My eyes snapped open at the barked command. I heaved myself away from the hands gripping my biceps, gaining my freedom. I clawed away ... fighting the sheets that bound my legs ... tumbling down ...

The jolting impact of hitting the floor woke me fully, and an awful sound of pain and fear scraped up through my throat.

"Christ! Eva, damn it. Don't hurt yourself!"

I sucked in air with deep gulps and scrambled toward the bathroom on all fours.

Gideon scooped me up and gripped me to his chest. *"Eva."*

"Sick," I gasped, slapping a hand over my mouth as my stomach roiled.

"I've got you," he said grimly, carrying me with brisk, powerful strides. He took me to the toilet and tossed up the seat. Kneeling beside me, he held my hair back as I heaved, his warm hand stroking up and down my spine.

"Shh ... angel," he murmured, over and over. "It's okay. You're safe."

When my stomach was empty, I flushed the toilet and rested my sweat-drenched face on my forearm, trying to focus on anything but the remnants of my dream.

"Baby girl."

I turned my head to find Cary standing in the threshold of my bathroom, his handsome face marred by a frown. He was fully dressed in loose jeans and a henley, which made me aware that Gideon was fully dressed, too. He'd lost the suit earlier when we'd first come back to my apartment, but he wasn't wearing the sweats he had put on then. Instead he was in jeans and a black T-shirt.

Disoriented by their appearances, I glanced at my watch and saw it was just after midnight. "What are you guys doing?"

"I was just coming in," Cary said. "And caught up with Cross on his way up."

I looked at Gideon, whose concerned frown matched my roommate's. "You went out?"

Gideon helped me to my feet. "I told you I had some things to take care of."

Until midnight? "What things?"

"It's not important."

I shrugged out of his hold and went to the sink to brush my teeth. Another secret. How many did he have?

Cary appeared at my elbow, his gaze meeting mine in the reflection of my vanity mirror. "You haven't had a bad dream in a long time."

Looking into his worried green eyes, I let him see how worn down I was.

He gave my shoulder a reassuring squeeze. "We'll take it easy this weekend. Recharge. We both need it. You gonna be all right tonight?"

"I've got her." Gideon straightened from his perch on the lip of my bathtub, where he'd taken off his boots.

"That doesn't mean I'm not here." Cary pressed a quick kiss to my temple. "Holler if you need me."

The look he gave me before he left the room spoke volumes—he wasn't comfortable with Gideon sleeping over. Truth was, I had some reservations, too. I thought my lingering wariness over Gideon's sleep disorder was contributing a lot to my wild emotional state. As Cary had recently said, the man I loved was a ticking time bomb, and I shared a bed with him.

I rinsed out my mouth and dropped my toothbrush back into its holder. "I need a shower."

I'd taken one before I crashed, but now I felt dirty again. Cold sweat clung to my skin and when I closed my eyes, I could smell *him*—Nathan—on me.

Gideon turned on the water, then started stripping, blessedly distracting me with the sight of his gloriously tight body. His muscles were hard and well defined, his build lean yet powerful and elegant.

I left my clothes where they fell and stepped beneath the steamy spray with a groan. He entered the stall behind me, brushing my hair aside and pressing a kiss to my shoulder. "How are you?"

"Better." *Because you're near.*

His arms wrapped carefully around my waist and he released a shaky exhalation. "I . . . Jesus, Eva. Were you dreaming about Nathan?"

I took a deep breath. "Maybe one day we'll talk about our dreams, huh?"

He inhaled sharply, his fingertips flexing against my hip. "It's like that, is it?"

"Yeah," I muttered. "It's like that."

We stood there for a long moment, surrounded by steam and secrets, physically close yet emotionally distant. I hated it. The urge to cry was overwhelming and I didn't fight it. It felt good to get it out. All the pressure of the long day seemed to flow out of me as I sobbed.

REFLECTED IN YOU · 59

"Angel . . ." Gideon pressed into my back, his arms tight around my waist, soothing me with the protective shield of his big body. "Don't cry . . . God. I can't take it. Tell me what you need, angel. Tell me what I can do."

"Wash it away," I whispered, leaning into him, needing the comfort of his tender possessiveness. My fingers laced with his against my stomach. "Make me clean."

"You are."

I sucked in a shuddering breath, shaking my head.

"Listen to me, Eva. No one can touch you," he said fiercely. "No one can get to you. Never again."

My fingers tightened on his.

"They'd have to get through me, Eva. And that will never happen."

I couldn't speak past the ache in my throat. The thought of Gideon facing my nightmare . . . seeing the man who'd done those things to me . . . tightened the cold knot that had been sitting in my gut all day.

Gideon reached for my shampoo and I closed my eyes, shutting it all out, everything but the man whose sole focus at that moment was me.

I waited, breathless, for the feel of his magic fingers. When it came, I reached out to the wall in front of me for balance. With both palms pressed flat against the cool tile, I savored the feel of his fingertips kneading into my scalp and moaned.

"Feel good?" he asked, his voice low and rough.

"Always."

I drifted in bliss as he washed and conditioned my hair, shivering lightly as he ran a wide-toothed comb through the soaked strands. I was disappointed when he finished and must have made some sound of regret, because he leaned forward and promised, "I'm not nearly done."

I smelled my body wash, then—

"*Gideon.*"

I arched into his soap-slick hands. His thumbs dug gently into the knots in my shoulders, melting them with the perfect amount of pressure. Then he worked his way down my spine . . . my buttocks . . . my legs . . .

"I'm going to fall," I slurred, drunk with pleasure.

"I'll catch you, angel. I'll always catch you."

The pain and degradation of my memories washed away beneath the selfless reverence of Gideon's patient caretaking. More than the soap and water, it was his touch that freed me from the nightmare. I turned around at his urging and looked at him crouched before me, his hands gliding up my calves, his body an amazing display of taut flexing muscle. Cupping his jaw, I tilted his head up.

"You can be so good for me, Gideon," I told him softly. "I don't know how I could ever forget that. Even for a minute."

His chest expanded on a quick, deep breath. He straightened, his hands gliding up my thighs, until he towered over me again. His lips touched mine, softly. Lightly. "I know today was all kinds of fucked up. Shit . . . the whole week. It's been hard for me, too."

"I know." I hugged him, pressing my cheek to his heart. He was so solid and strong. I loved the way I felt when I was in his arms.

He was already thick and hard between us, but he grew more so as I cuddled into him. "Eva . . ." He cleared his throat. "Let me finish, angel."

I nipped his jaw with my teeth and reached down to grip his perfect ass, tugging him tighter against me. "Why don't you get started instead?"

"That isn't where this was headed."

As if it could've ended any other way when we were both naked and running our hands all over each other. Gideon could put his hand to the small of my back while we were walking and make me as needy as if he'd put his hand between my legs. "Well . . . revisit and revise, ace."

Gideon's hands came up and gripped the sides of my throat, his thumbs beneath my chin to push it up. His frown gave him away, and before he could tell me why it wasn't a good idea to make love now, I caught his cock in my hands.

He growled, his hips jerking. "Eva . . ."

"It would be a shame to waste this."

"I can't screw this up with you." His eyes were dark as sapphires. "If you ever freaked out while I was touching you, I'd lose my mind."

"Gideon, please—"

"I say when." The command in his voice was unmistakable.

My grip loosened automatically.

He stepped back and away, his hand dropping to fist his cock.

I shifted restlessly, my attention riveted to that dexterous hand and its long, elegant fingers. As the distance between us widened, I began to ache, my body responding to the loss of his. The heated languidness he'd instilled with his touch turned into a slow burn, as if he'd banked a fire that had suddenly been stoked.

"See something you like?" he purred, pleasuring himself.

Astonished that he'd taunt me after denying me, I looked up . . . and my breath caught.

Gideon was smoldering, too. I couldn't think of another word to describe him. He was watching me with a heavy-lidded gaze like he wanted to eat me alive. His tongue slid leisurely along the seam of his lips, as if he tasted me. When he caught the full lower curve between his teeth, I could've sworn I felt it between my legs. I knew that look so well . . . knew what came after it . . . knew how ferocious he could be when he wanted me that badly.

It was a look that screamed SEX. Hard, deep, endless, mind-blowing sex. He stood on the far side of my shower, his feet planted wide, his ripped body flexing rhythmically as he caressed his beautiful cock with long, slow strokes.

I'd never seen anything so blatantly sexual or boldly masculine.

"Oh my God," I breathed, riveted. "You are so fucking hot."

The gleam in his eyes told me he knew what he was doing to me. His free hand slid slowly up his ridged abdomen and squeezed his pectoral, making me jealous. "Could you come watching me?"

Realization struck me. He was afraid to touch me sexually so soon after my nightmare, afraid of what it might do to us if he triggered me. But he was willing to put on a show for me—*inspire* me—so I could touch myself. The surge of emotion I felt in that moment was devastating. Gratitude and affection, desire and tenderness.

"I love you, Gideon."

His eyes squeezed shut, as if the words were too much for him to take. When they opened again, the force of his will sent a shiver of need through me. "Show me."

The wide head of his cock was engulfed in his palm. He squeezed, bringing a flush to his face that had me pressing my thighs together. His thumb rubbed over the flat disk of his nipple. Once. Twice. He groaned a rough sound of delight that had me salivating.

The water pounding at my back and the billowing steam that plumed between us only added to the eroticism of the picture he presented. His hand quickened, sliding rhythmically up and down. He was so long and thick. Undeniably virile.

Unable to bear the ache of my tightened nipples, I cupped my breasts and squeezed.

"There you go, angel. Show me what I do to you."

There was a moment in which I wondered if I could. It hadn't been so long ago that I'd been embarrassed to talk about my vibrator with Gideon face-to-face.

"Look at me, Eva." He cupped his balls in one hand and his cock in the other. Shameless, which was such a turn-on. "I don't want to come without you. I need you with me."

I wanted to be as hot for him. I wanted him as aching and needy as I felt. I wanted my body—my *desire*—to be burned onto his brain the way this image of him would be burned onto mine.

With my eyes locked with his, my hands glided over my body. I watched his movements . . . listened for the catch of his breath . . . used his clues to know what drove him wild.

It was somehow as intimate as when he was inside me, maybe more so because we were wide open and on display. Totally bared. Our pleasure reflected in each other.

He started telling me what he wanted in that raspy sex god voice: *Tug your nipples, angel . . . Touch yourself—are you wet? Push your fingers inside you . . . Feel how tight you are? A hot, tight, plush little heaven for my dick . . . You're so fucking gorgeous . . . So sexy. I'm so damn stiff it hurts . . . See what you do to me? I'm going to come so hard for you . . .*

"Gideon." I gasped, my fingertips massaging my clit in rapid circles, my hips grinding into my touch.

"Right there with you," he said hoarsely, his hand jacking his cock with brutal speed and violence in his race to orgasm.

At the first jolting contraction of my core, I cried out, my legs quaking. My palm slapped against the glass enclosure for balance, the climax stealing the strength from my muscles. Gideon was on me in a second, gripping my hipbone in a way that conveyed greed and possession, his fingers flexing with restless agitation.

"Eva!" he growled, as the first thick, hot burst of semen hit my belly. "Fuck."

Hunching over me, his teeth sank into the tender spot between my shoulder and neck, a painless hold that conveyed the rawness of his pleasure. His groans vibrated against me and he came violently, spurting repeatedly against my stomach.

It was a little after six o'clock in the morning when I slipped out of my bedroom. I'd been up for a while, watching Gideon sleep. It was a rare treat, because I hardly ever managed to wake up before he did. I could stare at him without any worries that he'd be weirded out.

I padded down the hallway until it emptied into the expansive open floor plan of the main living area. It was ridiculous that Cary and I lived on the Upper West Side in an apartment large enough for a family, but I'd long ago learned to pick my battles when it came to arguing with my mother and stepfather over my safety. There was no way they were budging on location or security features like a doorman and front desk, but I could exploit my cooperation on my living arrangements to get them to ease up on other points.

I was in the kitchen waiting for the coffee to finish brewing when Cary joined me. He strolled in looking amazing in a pair of gray San Diego State University sweats, sleep-mussed chocolate brown hair, and a day's worth of stubble along his square jaw.

"Morning, baby girl," he murmured, pressing a kiss to my temple as he passed me.

"You're up early."

"Look who's talking." He grabbed two mugs out of the cupboard, then the half-and-half out of the fridge. He brought them over and studied me. "How are you doing?"

"I'm good. Really," I insisted, when he shot me a skeptical look. "Gideon took care of me."

"Okay, but is that really so great if he's the reason you were stressed enough to have the nightmare to begin with?"

I filled mugs for both of us, adding sugar to mine and cream to both. As I did, I told him about Corinne and the Waldorf dinner, then the argument I'd had with Gideon over her appearance at the Crossfire.

Cary stood with his hip cocked into the counter, his legs crossed at the ankle, and one arm banding his chest. He sipped his coffee. "No explanation, huh?"

I shook my head, feeling the weight of Gideon's silence. "How about you? How are you doing?"

"You just gonna change the subject?"

"What else is there to say? It's a one-sided story."

"You ever stop to think that he might always have secrets?"

Frowning, I lowered my mug. "What do you mean?"

"I mean he's the twenty-eight-year-old son of a suicidal Ponzi scheme swindler, and he just happens to own a large chunk of Manhattan." One brow arched upward in challenge. "Think about it. Can they really be mutually exclusive things?"

Lowering my gaze to my mug, I took a drink and didn't confess that I'd wondered the same thing once or twice. The extent of Gideon's fortune and empire was staggering, especially considering his age. "I can't see Gideon bilking people, not when it's more of a challenge to accomplish what he has legitimately."

"With all the secrets he's got, can you be sure you know him well enough to make that judgment call?"

I thought of the man who'd spent the night with me and felt relief at how sure I was about my answer—at least at that moment. "Yes."

"All right, then." Cary shrugged. "I talked to Dr. Travis yesterday."

My thoughts immediately veered in another direction at the mention of our therapist in San Diego. "You did?"

"Yeah. I really fucked up the other night."

From the agitated way he scooped his long bangs back from his face, I knew he was referring to the orgy I'd walked in on.

"Cross broke Ian's nose and split his lip," he said, reminding me of how violently Gideon had responded to Cary's . . . *friend* rudely propositioning me to join them. "I saw Ian yesterday and he looks like he was hit in the face with a brick. He was asking who clocked him, so he could press charges."

"Oh." My lungs seized for the length of two heartbeats. "Oh, crap."

"I know. Billionaire plus lawsuit equals beaucoup bucks. What the fuck was I thinking?" Cary closed his eyes and rubbed them. "I told him I didn't know who your date was, that it was some guy you picked up and dragged home. Cross blindsided him, so Ian didn't see shit."

"The two girls with you got a real good look at Gideon," I said grimly.

"They took off out that door"—Cary pointed across the living room as if our door were still reverberating with the slam—"like she-bats out of hell. They didn't go to the urgent care with us, and neither of us knows who they are. If Ian doesn't run into them again, we're okay."

I rubbed at the quiver in my tummy, feeling unsettled again.

"I'll keep an eye on the situation," he assured me. "The whole night was a major wake-up call, and talking it out in therapy gave me some perspective. Afterward, I went to see Trey. To apologize."

Hearing Trey's name made me sad. I'd hoped Cary's budding relationship with the veterinary student would work out, but Cary had sabotaged that. As usual. "How'd that go?"

He shrugged again, but the movement was awkward. "I hurt him the other night because I'm an asshole. Then I hurt him again yesterday trying to do the right thing."

"Did you break it off?" I held my hand out to him and squeezed his when he placed it in mine.

"It's seriously cooled off. Like on ice. He wants me to be gay, and I'm not."

It was painful to hear that someone wanted Cary to be anything other than who he was, because it'd always been that way for him. I couldn't understand why. To me, he was wonderful as is. "I'm so sorry, Cary."

"So am I, because he's a great guy. I'm just not ready for the stress and demands of a complicated relationship right now. I'm working a lot. I'm not stable enough yet to be fucked up in the head." His lips pursed. "You might want to think about that, too. We just moved out here. We've both still got some settling in to do."

I nodded, understanding where he was coming from and not disagreeing, but unwavering in my decision to see my relationship with Gideon through. "Did you talk to Tatiana, too?"

"No need." His thumb brushed over my knuckles before he released me. "She's easy."

Snorting, I took a large gulp of my cooling coffee.

"Not just *that* way," he chided, giving me a wicked grin. "I mean she doesn't expect anything or make any demands. As long as I suit up and she orgasms at least as many times as I do, she's good. I'm actually okay with her, and not just because she could suck chrome off a bumper. It's relaxing being with someone who just wants to have fun and causes no stress."

"Gideon knows me. He understands and tries to work around my issues. He's working for this, too, Cary. It's not easy for him, either."

"Do you think Cross had a nooner with his ex?" he asked bluntly.

"No."

"Are you sure?"

Sucking in a deep breath, I took a fortifying gulp and admitted, "Mostly. I think I'm the one doing it for him now. It's pretty hot with us, you know? But his ex has some kind of hold on him. He says it's guilt, but that doesn't explain his brunette fascination."

"It explains why you lost it and hit him—her being around again is eating at you. And he still won't tell you what's going on. Does that sound healthy to you?"

It wasn't. I knew that. I hated it. "We saw Dr. Petersen last night."

His brows rose. "How'd that go?"

"He didn't tell us to run far, far away from each other as fast as we can."

"And if he does? Will you listen?"

"I'm not bailing when things get rough this time. Seriously, Cary"—I held his gaze—"am I really all that far ahead if I can't take any waves?"

"Baby girl, Cross is a tsunami."

"Ha!" I smiled, unable to help it. Cary could get me to smile through tears. "To tell you the truth, if I don't work this out with Gideon, I have doubts I'll work it out with anyone."

"That's your shitty self-esteem talking."

"He knows what I'm carrying around in me."

"All right."

My brows shot up. "All right?" *That was too easy.*

"I'm not sold. But I'll deal." He grabbed my hand. "Come on. Let's get your hair done."

I smiled, grateful. "You're the best."

He bumped his hip into mine. "And I won't let you forget it."

5

"A s far as death traps go," Cary said, "this one's pretty swank."
I shook my head as I preceded him into the main cabin of
Gideon's private jet. "You are *not* going to die. Flying is safer than
driving."

"And you don't think the airline industry paid for the compila-
tion of those statistics?"

Pausing to smack him in the shoulder with a laugh, I glanced at
the amazingly opulent interior and felt more than a little awe. I'd
seen my share of private planes over the years, but as usual, Gideon
went to lengths to which few could afford to go.

The cabin was spacious, with a wide center aisle. The underlying
palette was neutral with accents of chocolate brown and ice blue.
Deep, swiveling bucket seats with tables were positioned on the left,
while a sectional sofa sat on the right. Each chair had a private

entertainment console beside it. I knew a bedroom would be found at the back of the plane and a luxurious bathroom or two.

A male flight attendant took my duffel bag and Cary's, then gestured for us to take a seat at one of the groupings of chairs that had a table. "Mr. Cross is expected within the next ten minutes," he said. "In the meantime, can I serve you something to drink?"

"Water for me, please." I glanced at my watch. It was just past seven thirty.

"Bloody Mary," Cary ordered, "if you've got it."

The steward smiled. "We've got everything."

Cary caught my look. "What? I haven't had dinner. The tomato juice will hold me over until we eat, and the alcohol will help the Dramamine kick in faster."

"I didn't say anything," I protested.

I turned to look out the window at the evening sky, and my thoughts settled on Gideon, as usual. He'd been quiet all day, starting with when he'd woken up. The ride to work had been made in silence, and when my day ended at five, he'd called just long enough to tell me that Angus would take me home alone, then drive me and Cary to the airport, where he'd meet us.

I opted to walk home instead, since I hadn't hit the gym the night before and didn't have time to work out prior to the flight. Angus had cautioned that Gideon wouldn't like me refusing the ride, even though I'd done it politely and with good reason. I think Angus thought I was still upset with him for giving Corinne a ride, which I kind of was. I was sorry to say that a tiny part of me hoped he'd feel bad about it. A bigger part of me hated that I could be that petty.

As I'd walked through Central Park, taking a meandering path through tall trees, I had determined that I wasn't going to be small over a guy. Not even Gideon. I wasn't going to let my frustration with him get in the way of having a good time in Vegas with my best friend.

Halfway home, I'd stopped and turned, picking out Gideon's penthouse high above Fifth Avenue. I wondered if he was there, packing and planning for a weekend without me. Or if he was still at work, wrapping up the week's pressing business.

"Uh-oh," Cary singsonged, as the flight attendant returned with a tray laden with our drinks. "You've got that look."

"What look?"

"The hell-on-wheels look." He clinked his tall, slender glass against the side of my squat tumbler. "Wanna talk about it?"

I was about to reply when Gideon stepped onto the plane. He looked grim and carried a briefcase in one hand and a duffel in the other. After passing his bag over to the attendant, he paused by me and Cary, giving my roommate a cursory nod before brushing the backs of his fingers across my cheek. The simple touch shot through me like a surge of electricity. Then he was gone, slipping into a cabin in the back and shutting the door.

I scowled. "He's so damn moody."

"And seriously hot. What he does for that suit . . ."

Most suits made the man. Gideon did things to a three-piece suit that should've been illegal.

"Don't distract me with his looks," I groused.

"Give him a blowjob. That's a guaranteed mood improver."

"Spoken like a man."

"You expected something different?" Cary grabbed the frosty glass bottle holding the excess water that wouldn't fit in my crystal tumbler. "Check this out."

He showed me the label, which was branded to the Cross Towers and Casino. "Now *that's* swank."

My lips twisted wryly. "For the whales."

"What?"

"Casino high rollers. Gamblers who don't blink an eye at dropping a hundred grand or more on the turn of a card. They get a lot of comps to lure them in—food, suites, and travel to and fro. My mom's second husband was a whale. It's one of the reasons why she left him."

He shook his head at me. "The shit you know. So this is a company jet?"

"One of five," the attendant said, returning with a tray of fruit and cheese.

"Jesus," Cary muttered. "That's a damned fleet."

I watched as he dug a travel packet of Dramamine out of his pocket and washed the pills down with his Bloody Mary.

"Want some?" he asked, tapping at the wrapper on the table.

"Nope. Thanks."

"You gonna deal with Mr. Hot and Moody?"

"Not sure. I may just pull out my e-reader."

He nodded. "Probably safer for your sanity."

Thirty minutes later, Cary was snoring lightly in his fully reclined seat, his ears covered with noise-canceling headphones. I watched him for a long minute, appreciating the sight of him looking restful and relaxed, the shallow grooves around his mouth softening in slumber.

Then I got up and went to the cabin I'd seen Gideon disappear into earlier. I debated knocking, then thought against it. He was shutting me out elsewhere; I wasn't going to give him the opportunity to do so now.

He glanced up when I walked in, his face showing no surprise at my abrupt appearance. He sat at a desk, listening to a woman who was speaking to him via satellite video. His coat was hung on the back of his chair and his tie was loosened. After that one brief glance at me, he resumed his conversation.

I started stripping.

My tank top came off first, followed by my sandals and jeans. The woman continued talking, mentioning "concerns" and "discrepancies," but Gideon's eyes were on me—hot and avid.

"We'll pick this up in the morning, Allison," he interjected, hitting a button on the keyboard that darkened the screen just before my bra landed on his head.

"I'm the one with PMS," I said, "but you're the one having mood swings."

He pulled my bra into his lap and leaned back in his chair, setting his elbows on the armrests and steepling his fingers together. "And you're putting on a striptease to improve my mood?"

"Ha! Men are so predictable. Cary suggested I blow you to make you happy. No . . . don't get excited. That's not going to happen." I hooked my thumbs in the waistband of my panties and rocked back on my heels. I had to give him points for keeping his eyes on mine and not on my breasts. "I think you owe me, ace. Big-time. I've been an exceptionally understanding girlfriend under the circumstances, don't you think?"

His brow arched.

"I mean, I'd like to see what you would do," I went on, "if you came over to my place and caught an ex-boyfriend stepping outside still tucking his shirt in his pants. Then, when you came upstairs, you found my couch messed up and me fresh from a shower."

Gideon's jaw tightened. "Neither of us wants to see what I'd do."

"So we're both agreed that I've been pretty damn awesome under extraordinary circumstances." I crossed my arms, knowing how that would showcase the assets he loved. "You've made it very clear how you'd choose to punish me. How would you choose to reward me?"

"Is it my choice?" he drawled, his eyes heavy-lidded.

I smiled. "No."

He set my bra on his keyboard and unfolded from the chair in a leisurely, graceful rise. "Then that's your reward, angel. What do you want?"

"I want you to stop being grumpy, for starters."

"Grumpy?" His lips twitched with a suppressed smile. "Well, I woke up without you, and now I face two more mornings of the same."

I dropped my arms to my sides and went to him, placing my palms flat to his broad chest. "Is that really all it is?"

"Eva." He was such a strong, physically powerful man, and yet he could touch me with such reverence.

I ducked my head, knowing something in my voice had given me away. He was too perceptive.

Cupping my jaw in his hands, Gideon tipped my head back and searched my face. "Talk to me."

"I feel like you're pulling away."

A low growl rumbled through the air between us. "I've got a lot on my mind. That doesn't mean I'm not thinking about you."

"I *feel* it, Gideon. There's distance between us that wasn't there before."

His hands slid down to my neck, wrapping around it. "There's no distance. You've got me by the throat, Eva." His grip tightened fractionally. "Can't you feel *that*?"

I sucked in a quick, tight breath. Agitation spurred my heartbeat, a physical response to fear that came entirely from within and not from Gideon, who I knew absolutely would never physically harm me or put me in danger.

"Sometimes," he said huskily, watching me with searing intensity, "I can hardly breathe."

I might've broken free if not for his eyes, which revealed such yearning and turmoil. He was making me feel the same loss of power, the same sense of being dependent on someone else for every breath I took.

So I did the opposite of running. Tilting my head back, I surrendered, and the tingles of fear left me in a rush. I was learning that Gideon was right about my desire to give up control to him. Doing so soothed something inside me, some need I hadn't realized I possessed.

There was a long pause, filled only by his breathing. I sensed him warring with his emotions and wondered what they were, wondered why he was so conflicted.

He released the tension with a deep exhalation. "What do you need, Eva?"

"You—a mile high."

His hands slid over my shoulders and squeezed, then caressed the length of my arms. His fingers linked with mine and he nuzzled our temples together. "What is it with you, sex, and modes of transportation?"

"I'll take you any way I can get you," I told him, repeating the sentiment he'd once said to me. "It'll probably be next weekend before I'm good to go again, thanks to my period."

"Fuck."

"That's the idea."

Reaching for his coat, he wrapped it around me and ushered me out of the cabin.

"Oh, God." My hands fisted the sheets beneath me, my back arching as Gideon pinned my hips to the bed and fluttered his tongue across

my clit. My skin was coated in a fine sheen of sweat, my vision blurring as my core tightened viciously in preparation for orgasm. My pulse was thrumming, racing in unison with the steady hum of the jet's engines.

I'd come twice already, as much from the sight of his dark head between my legs as from his wickedly gifted mouth. My panties were ruined, literally shredded by his grip, and he was still fully dressed.

"I'm ready." I pushed my fingers into his hair, feeling the dampness at the roots. His restraint was costing him. He was always so careful with me, taking the time to make sure I was soft and wet before filling me too full with his long, thick cock.

"I'll decide when you're ready."

"I want you inside—" The plane shook suddenly, then dropped, leaving me weightless but for the suction of Gideon's mouth. *"Gideon!"*

I trembled through another climax, my body arching with the need to feel him in me. Through the roaring of blood in my ears, I heard a voice making an announcement over the comm system, but I couldn't register the words.

"You're so sensitive now." Lifting his head, he licked his lips. "You're coming like crazy."

I gasped. "I'd come harder if you were inside me."

"I'll keep that in mind."

"It doesn't matter if I get a little sore now," I argued. "I'll have days to recover."

Something sparked in the depths of his gaze. He rose. "No, Eva."

My postorgasmic haze faded at the harshness of his voice. I levered up onto my elbows and watched him begin to strip, his moves quick and economically graceful.

"My choice," I reminded.

In short order he removed his vest, tie, and cuff links. His voice was too even when he asked, "You really want to play that card, angel?"

"If that's what it takes."

"It'll take more than that for me to hurt you deliberately." His shirt and slacks followed more slowly, a striptease that was far more seductive than mine had been. "For us, pain and pleasure are mutually exclusive."

"I didn't mean—"

"I know what you meant." He straightened from shoving his boxer briefs down, then knelt on the foot of the bed and crawled toward me like a sleek panther on the prowl. "You ache without my cock inside you. You'll say anything to have me there."

"Yes."

He hovered over me, his hair falling in a dark curtain around his face, his big body casting a shadow over mine. Tilting his head, he lowered his mouth and lightly traced the seam of my lips with the tip of his tongue. "You crave it. You feel empty without it."

"Yes, damn you." I gripped his lean hips, arching upward to try to feel his body against mine. I never felt closer to him than when we were making love, and I needed that closeness now, needed to feel like we were okay before we spent the weekend without each other.

He settled between my legs, his erection lying hard and hot between the lips of my sex. "It hurts you a little when I push all the way in, and there's no help for that—you have a tight little cunt and I cram you full. Sometimes I lose control and get rough, and there's no help for that, either. But don't *ever* ask me to hurt you deliberately. I can't."

"I want you," I breathed, rubbing my wet cleft shamelessly along the heated length of his cock.

"Not yet." He moved, rolling his hips to find me with the broad head of his penis. He pushed gently against me, parting me, spreading me open as he slipped just the tip inside. I writhed against the tight fit, my body resisting. "You're not ready yet."

"Fuck me. God . . . just fuck me!"

He reached down with one hand and grabbed my hip, stemming my frenzied attempts to push up and take more of him. "You're swollen."

I fought his hold. My nails dug into the tight curves of his ass and I tugged him against me. I didn't care that it might hurt. If I didn't get him in me I thought I'd lose my mind. "Give it to me."

Gideon slid his hand into my hair, fisting it to hold me where he wanted me. "Look at me."

"Gideon!"

"Look at me."

I stilled at the command in his voice. I stared up at him, my frustration melting as I watched a slow, gradual transformation sweep over his handsome face.

His features tightened first, as if he were pained. A wince knit his brow. His lips parted with a gasp, his chest beginning to heave with labored breaths. A tic began in his jaw, the muscle spasming violently. His skin grew hot, searing me. But what mesmerized me most was his piercing blue eyes and the unmistakable vulnerability that sifted through them like smoke.

My pulse quickened in response to the change in him. The mattress shifted as he dug his feet in, his body bracing—

"Eva." He jerked, then started coming, spurting hotly into me. His pleasured groan vibrated against me, his cock sinking through the sudden flood of semen to bottom out inside me. "Ah . . . Christ."

All the while he looked at me, showing me his face when he usually hid in the crook of my neck. I saw what he'd wanted me to see . . . the point he'd wanted to make—

There was nothing between us.

Rolling his hips, he rubbed out the rest of his orgasm, emptying himself inside me, lubricating me so there would be no pain or resistance. He released my hip and let me rock upward; let me seek the perfect pressure on my clit to set me off. With his eyes still on mine, he reached behind him to claim my wrists. One at a time, he lifted my arms over my head, restraining me.

Pinned to the mattress by his grip, his weight, and his unflagging erection, I was completely at his mercy. He began to thrust, stroking through the trembling walls of my sex with the thickly veined length of his big cock. Claiming me. Possessing me.

"Crossfire," he whispered, reminding me of my safe word.

I moaned as my sex rippled in climax, tightening and squeezing, milking him greedily.

"Feel that?" Gideon's tongue traced the shell of my ear, his breath gusting in humid pants. "You've got me by the throat and the balls. Where's the distance, angel?"

For the next three hours, there was none.

THE hotel manager threw open the double doors to our suite and Cary gave a long, low whistle.

"Hell yeah," he said, hustling me into the room with a hand on my elbow. "Look at the size of this place. You could do cartwheels in here."

He was right, but I'd have to wait until the morning to prove it. My legs were still shaky from my induction into the Mile-High Club.

Directly in front of us was a dazzling view of the Vegas Strip at night. The windows were floor to ceiling, wrapping around a corner that was filled with a piano.

"Why are there always pianos in high-roller suites?" Cary asked, flipping up the cover and tapping out a quick tune on the keys.

I shrugged and looked toward the manager, but she'd already moved off, her stilettos moving silently over the thick white carpet. The suite was decorated in what I'd call fifties Hollywood chic. The double-sided fireplace was faced with rough gray stone and decorated with a piece of art that resembled a hubcap with spacey spokes protruding from the center. The sofas were seafoam green with wooden legs as slender as the manager's heels. Everything had a retro vibe that was at once glamorous and inviting.

It was way too much. I'd expected a nice room, but not the presidential suite. I was about to refuse it when Cary gifted me with a big grin and two thumbs up. Having no willpower to refuse his joy, I gave in and hoped we weren't putting Gideon out of a more profitable reservation.

"Still want a cheeseburger?" I asked him, reaching for the room service menu on the console table behind the sofa.

"And a beer. Make that two."

Cary followed the manager into a bedroom on the left side of the living area, and I picked up the vintage rotary phone to place our order.

Thirty minutes later, I was fresh from a quick shower and dressed in my pajamas, eating chicken Alfredo cross-legged on the area rug. Cary was plowing through his burger and looking at me with happy eyes from his position on the opposite side of the coffee table.

"You never eat a massive pile of carbs this late," he noted between bites.

"My period's coming."

"I'm sure the workout you got on the way here helped, too."

I narrowed my eyes at him. "How would you know? You were passed out."

"Deductive reasoning, baby girl. When I went to sleep, you looked irritated. When I woke up, you looked like you'd just smoked a fat joint."

"How did Gideon look?"

"He looked the same—tight-assed and hot as hell."

I stabbed my fork into my noodles. "That's not fair."

"Who cares?" He gestured around us. "Look how he puts you up."

"I don't need a sugar daddy, Cary."

He munched on a French fry. "Have you thought any more about what you *do* need? You've got his time, his rockin' bod, and access to everything he owns. That's not bad."

"No," I agreed, twirling my fork. I knew from my mom's many marriages to powerful men that getting their time was the most important thing of all, because for them, it was truly the most valuable thing in their lives. "It's not bad. It's just not enough."

"THIS is the life," Cary pronounced, while lying like a god on a lounger by the pool. He wore pale green trunks and dark shades and caused an unusually large volume of women to walk on our side of the pool. "The only thing missing is a mojito. Gotta have alcohol to celebrate."

My mouth curved. I was sunbathing on the lounger beside him, enjoying the dry heat and occasional splashes of water. Celebrating was habitual for Cary, something I'd always considered quite charming. "What are we celebrating?"

"Summer."

"Okay, then." I sat up and slid my legs off the lounger, tying my sarong around my hips before I stood. My hair was still damp from an earlier dip in the pool and pinned atop my head with a lobster clip. The scorching sun felt good on my skin, a sensual kiss that was nearly enough to make me less self-conscious about the water I was retaining—thanks to my period starting.

I headed over to the pool bar, my gaze raking the other loungers and cabanas through the purple tint of my sunglasses. The area was packed with guests, many of whom were attractive enough to warrant second and third looks. One couple in particular caught my eye, because they reminded me of myself and Gideon. The blonde lay on her stomach, her torso propped up on her arms and her legs kicking playfully. Her very yummy dark-haired man stretched out on the chair beside her, his head propped on one hand while the fingers of the other hand stroked up and down her spine.

She caught me staring and her smile instantly faded. I couldn't see her eyes behind her Jackie O shades, but I knew she was glaring at me. With a smile, I looked away, knowing just how she felt about finding another woman checking out her man.

I found an empty space at the bar and gestured at the bartender to let him know I was ready to order when he was. Misters attached to the ceiling cooled my skin and lured me to slide onto a suddenly vacated bar stool while I waited.

"What are you drinking?"

Turning my head, I looked at the man who'd talked to me. "Nothing yet, but I'm considering a mojito."

"Let me buy you one." He smiled, revealing perfectly white but slightly crooked teeth. He extended his hand to me, a movement that brought my attention to his nicely defined arms. "Daniel."

I placed my hand in his. "Eva. Nice to meet you."

He crossed his arms on the bar and leaned over it. "What brings you to Vegas? Business or pleasure?"

"R and R. You?" Daniel had an interesting tattoo written in a foreign language on his right biceps, and I admired it. He wasn't traditionally good-looking, but he had confidence and poise, two things I found more attractive in a man than just his physical features.

"Work."

I shot a look at his swimming trunks. "I've got the wrong job."

"I sell—"

"Excuse me."

We both turned to face the woman who had intruded on our conversation. She was a compact brunette dressed in a dark polo shirt embroidered with both her name—*Sheila*—and *Cross Towers and Casino*. The earpiece in her ear and the utility belt around her waist gave her away as security.

"Miss Tramell." She greeted me with a nod.

My brows rose. "Yes?"

"There's a server who can take your order by your cabana."

"Cool, thanks. But I don't mind waiting here."

When I didn't move, Sheila turned her attention to Daniel. "If you'll move to the other end of the bar, sir, the bartender will see that your next drinks are on the house."

He gave a cursory nod, then smiled winningly at me. "I'm good here, too, thanks."

"I'm afraid I'll have to insist."

"What?" His smile turned into a scowl. "Why?"

I blinked at Sheila as realization sank in. *Gideon had me under watch.* And he thought he could control what I did from a distance.

Sheila returned my look, her face impassive. "I'll escort you back to your cabana, Miss Tramell."

For a minute, I considered making her day hell, maybe grabbing Daniel and kissing him senseless just to send a message to my overbearing boyfriend, but I managed to restrain my temper. She was only doing what she was paid to do. It was her boss who needed the kick in the ass.

"Sorry, Daniel," I said, flushing with embarrassment. I felt like a scolded kid and that *really* irked me. "It was nice meeting you."

He shrugged. "If you change your mind . . ."

I felt Sheila's gaze on my back as I preceded her to my lounger. Abruptly, I faced her. "So, is getting hit on the only time you're instructed to step in? Or do you have a list of situations?"

She hesitated a moment, then sighed. I could only imagine what she must think of me, the pretty blond piece of ass who couldn't be trusted to be out mingling in public. "There's a list."

"Of course there is." Gideon wouldn't leave anything to chance. I wondered when he'd worked on the list, if he'd compiled it just since I mentioned Vegas or if he'd had it on hand. Maybe it was a list he had formed while he was with other women. Maybe he'd written it for Corinne.

The more I thought about it, the angrier I got.

"Un-fucking-believable," I complained to Cary when she'd stepped a discreet distance away, as if that action alone would be enough to make me forget she was hovering. "I've got a babysitter."

"What?"

I told him what happened and watched his jaw tighten.

"That's crazy, Eva," he snapped.

"No shit. And I'm not putting up with it. He's got to learn that relationships don't work that way. And after all the crap he gave me about trust." I collapsed on my lounger. "How much does he trust me, if he's got to have someone shadowing me to chase strangers away?"

"I'm not down with this, Eva." He sat up and swung his legs over the side of his chair. "This isn't okay."

"You think I don't know that? And what's with her being a woman? Nothing against my gender and tough jobs. I'm just wondering if he expects her to follow me into ladies' rooms or just doesn't trust a guy to watch me."

"Are you serious? Why the hell are you sunbathing instead of chewing him a new one?"

The idea I'd been toying with fully formed in my mind. "I'm plotting."

"Oh?" His mouth curved in a wicked grin. "Do tell."

I picked my smartphone up from the little mosaic-topped table between us and scrolled through my contacts until I found *Benjamin Clancy*—my stepfather's personal bodyguard.

"Hey, Clancy. It's Eva," I greeted him when he answered after the first ring.

Cary's eyes widened behind his shades. "Ooh . . ."

Pushing to my feet, I mouthed, *I'm going upstairs*.

He nodded. "Everything's fine," I said, in answer to Clancy's query. I waited until I'd ducked indoors and knew Sheila was several paces behind me and still outside. "Listen, I have a favor to ask you."

I'D just ended my call with Clancy when another call came in. I grinned when I saw the Caller ID and answered with an exuberant, "Hi, Daddy!"

He laughed. "How's my girl?"

"Causing trouble and enjoying it." I spread my sarong out on a dining room chair and took a seat. "How are you?"

"Stopping trouble from happening and occasionally enjoying it."

Victor Reyes was an Oceanside, California, street cop, which was why I'd chosen to attend SDSU. My mom had been going through a rough patch with husband number two and I'd been in a rebellious phase, making my own life hell as I tried to forget what Nathan had done to me for so long.

Moving out of my mom's suffocating orbit had been one of the best decisions I'd ever made. My dad's quietly unshakeable love for me, his only child, had changed my life. He gave me much-needed freedom—within clearly defined limits—and arranged for me to see Dr. Travis, which led to the start of my long journey of recovery and my friendship with Cary.

"I miss you," I told him. I loved my mom dearly and knew she loved me back, but my relationship with her was a rocky one and it was just so easy with my dad.

"You might be happy about my news, then. I can come out and see you in about two weeks—the week after this upcoming one—if that works for you. I don't want to put you out."

"Oh my God, Dad. You could never put me out. I'd love to see you!"

"It'll be a short trip. I'd come in on the red-eye Thursday night and fly out again Sunday evening."

"I'm stoked! Yay! I'll make plans. We'll have a blast."

My dad's soft chuckle sent warmth flowing through me. "I'm coming to see *you*, not New York. Don't go crazy with any sightseeing or anything."

"Don't worry. I'll make sure we have lots of downtime. And you'll get to meet Gideon." Just the thought of the two of them together made my tummy flutter.

"Gideon Cross? You said nothing was going on there."

"Yeah." I wrinkled my nose. "We'd hit a rough spot at the time. I thought we were over."

There was a pause. "Is it serious?"

I paused, too, shifting restlessly. My dad was a trained observer;

he'd see right away that Gideon and I had tension between us—sexual and otherwise. "Yes. It's not always easy. It's a lot of work—*I'm* a lot of work—but we're both making the effort."

"Does he appreciate you, Eva?" My dad's voice was gruff and far too serious. "I don't care how much money he has; you don't have anything to prove to him."

"It's not like that!" I stared at my wriggling pedicured toes and realized the meeting would be more complicated than just a protective father being introduced to his daughter's new boyfriend. My dad had issues with rich men, thanks to my mom. "You'll see how it is when you meet him."

"All right." Skepticism colored his voice.

"Really, Dad." I couldn't begrudge him his concern, since it'd been my self-destructive run with not-so-good-for-me guys that had led him to finding Dr. Travis. He'd especially had trouble with a lead singer for whom I'd been little more than a groupie and a tattoo artist whom my dad had pulled over to find him getting a blowjob while driving—and not from me. "Gideon's good for me. He gets me."

"I'll keep an open mind, okay? And I'll e-mail you a copy of my itinerary when I book the flight. How's everything else going?"

"We just started working on a campaign for blueberry-flavored coffee."

Another pause. "You're kidding."

I laughed. "If only. Wish us luck trying to sell that! I'll be sure to stock some up for you to try."

"I thought you loved me."

"With all my heart. How's your love life going? Did your date go well?"

"Yeah . . . it wasn't bad."

Snorting, I asked, "Are you going to see her again?"

"That's the plan so far."

"You're a font of information, Dad."

He chuckled again and I heard his favorite chair creak as he shifted. "You don't really want to know about your old man's love life."

"True." Although I did sometimes wonder what his relationship had been like with my mom. He'd been the Latino boy from the wrong side of the tracks and she'd been the golden debutante with dollar signs in her blue eyes. I figured it must've been pretty hot between them.

We talked for a few more minutes, both of us excited to see each other again. I'd hoped we wouldn't drift apart after I moved away after college, which was why I'd made it a necessity to have a weekly catch-up call on Saturdays. Having him visit so soon helped to ease that worry.

I'd just hung up when Cary strolled in, looking every bit like the model he was.

"Still plotting?" he asked.

I stood. "All done. That was my dad. He's coming out to New York next week."

"Really? Rock on. Victor's cool."

We both moved into the kitchen, and he grabbed two beers out of the refrigerator. I'd noticed earlier that a number of items and products I used at home had been stocked in the suite. I wondered if Gideon was just that observant or if he'd found the information another way—like from looking at my receipts. I couldn't put it past him. Recognizing the boundaries between us was very difficult for him, as evidenced by his siccing his guards on me.

"When's the last time your parents were in the same state together?" Cary asked, prying the caps off the bottles with a bottle opener. "Let alone the same city."

Ah, God . . . "I'm not sure. Before I was born?" I took a long pull on the beer he handed me. "I'm not planning on putting them together."

"Here's to best-laid plans." He clinked the necks of our beers together. "Speaking of which, I was considering a quick bang with a chick I met at the pool, but I came up here instead. Figured you and I'd both go without today and just spend the time together."

"I'm honored," I said dryly. "I was going to come back down."

"Too hot out. That sun is brutal."

"Same sun we have in New York, isn't it?"

"Smart-ass." His green eyes sparkled. "How about we clean up and go out to lunch somewhere? My treat."

"Sure. But I can't say Sheila won't insist on tagging along."

"Fuck her and her boss. What is it with rich people and control issues?"

"They get rich because they take control."

"Whatever. I prefer our kind of crazy—we pretty much only screw with ourselves." He crossed one arm over his chest and leaned into the counter. "You gonna put up with his bullshit?"

"Depends."

"On what?"

I grinned and started backing out toward my bedroom. "Get ready. I'll tell you about it over lunch."

6

I'D JUST BARELY finished repacking my bag for the trip home when I heard the unmistakable sound of Gideon's voice in the living room. A rush of adrenaline pumped through my veins. Gideon had yet to say a word to me about what I'd done, even though we'd talked the night before after Cary and I had gotten back from clubbing and again this morning when I'd woken up.

Feigning ignorance was slightly nerve-racking. I'd wondered if Clancy had even managed to do what I had asked of him, but when I double-checked with my stepdad's bodyguard, he assured me that all was going as I'd planned.

On bare feet, I padded over to the open door of my bedroom just in time to see Cary walk out the door of our suite. Gideon stood alone in the small foyer, his inscrutable gaze on me as if he'd expected me to appear at any moment. He wore loose-fitting jeans and a black T-shirt, and I'd missed the sight of him so much my eyes stung.

"Hi, angel."

The fingers of my right hand toyed restlessly with the material of my black yoga pants. "Hi, ace."

His beautifully etched lips thinned for a moment. "Is there a particular meaning behind that endearment?"

"Well . . . you ace everything you do. And it's the nickname of a fictional character I have a crush on. You remind me of him sometimes."

"I'm not sure I like you having a crush on anyone but me, fictional or not."

"You'll get over it."

Shaking his head, he started toward me. "Like I'll get over the sumo wrestler you have shadowing me?"

I bit the inside of my cheek to keep from laughing. I hadn't been specific about appearance when I'd asked Clancy to arrange for someone he knew in the Phoenix area to guard Gideon the way Sheila was guarding me. I'd just asked for a man and provided a relatively small list of things to intercede with. "Where's Cary going?"

"Downstairs to play with the credit I arranged for him."

"We're not leaving right away?"

He slowly closed the distance between us. There was no mistaking the danger inherent in the way he stalked me. It was visible in the set of his shoulders and the gleam in his eyes. I might've been more worried if the sinuousness of his stride hadn't been so blatantly sexual. "You on your period?"

I nodded.

"Then I'll just have to come in your mouth."

My brows rose. "Is that right?"

"Oh, yeah." His mouth curved. "Don't worry, angel. I'll take care of you first."

He lunged and caught me up, surging into the bedroom and toppling us onto the bed. I gasped and his mouth was on mine, the kiss deep and ravenous. I was swept away by his passion and the beloved feel of his weight pressing me into the mattress. He smelled so good. His skin was so warm.

"I missed you," I moaned, wrapping my arms and legs around him. "Even though you're seriously irritating sometimes."

Gideon growled. "You're the most exasperating, infuriating woman I've ever met."

"Yeah, well, you pissed me off. I'm not a possession. You can't—"

"Yes, you are." He nipped my earlobe with his teeth, causing a sharp sting that made me cry out. "And yes, I can."

"Then you are, too. And I can, too."

"So you demonstrated. Have any idea how difficult it is to do business with someone when they can't get within three feet of you?"

I froze, because I'd made the three-feet rule applicable only to women. "Why would someone need to be that close to you?"

"To point out areas of interest on design schematics spread out in front of me and to fit alongside me within camera range for a teleconference—two things you made very difficult." Lifting his head, he looked down at me. "I was working. You were playing."

"I don't care. If it's good for me, it's good for you." But I was secretly pleased that Gideon had put up with the inconvenience, just as I had.

Reaching down, he caught me by the back of the thigh and yanked my legs wider apart. "You're not going to get a hundred percent equality in this relationship."

"The hell I'm not."

His hips settled into the opening he'd made. He rocked against me, rubbing the thick ridge of his erection against my sex. "You're not," he repeated, his hands pushing into my hair to grip my scalp and hold me in place.

Rolling his hips, he massaged my hypersensitive clit. The seam of his jeans was in the perfect place to stir my ever-simmering lust for him. Arousal spiked in my blood. "Stop it. I can't think when you do that."

"Don't think. Just listen, Eva. Who I am and what I've built makes me a target. You know the score, because you know what it's like to live with wealth and the attention it attracts."

"The guy at the bar wasn't a threat."

"That's debatable."

Irritation burned through me. It was the perceived lack of trust that bugged me, mostly because he didn't trust me with whatever secrets he was keeping, and I was dealing with that. "Get off me."

"I'm comfortable right here." He hitched his hips, rubbing against me.

"I'm pissed at you."

"I can tell." He didn't stop moving. "That won't stop you from coming."

I shoved at his hips, but he was too heavy to budge. "I can't when I'm mad!"

"Prove it."

He was way too smug, which made my anger swell. Since I couldn't turn my head, I closed my eyes, shutting him out. He didn't care. He kept on flexing against me. The clothes between us and the lack of penetration made me even more aware of the elegant fluidity of his body.

The man knew how to fuck.

Gideon didn't just shove his big dick in and out of a woman. He worked her with it, exploiting friction, changing angles and depth of penetration. The nuances of his skill were lost when I was writhing beneath him and focused only on the sensations he stoked in my body. But I felt them all now.

I fought against the pleasure, but I couldn't stifle a moan.

"That's it, angel," he coaxed. "Feel how hard I am for you? Feel what you do to me?"

"Don't use sex to punish me," I complained, my heels digging into the mattress.

He stilled for a moment, and then his mouth was suckling at my throat, his body undulating as if he were fucking me through our clothes. "I'm not mad, angel."

"Whatever. You're pushing me around."

"And you're driving me insane. You know what happened when I realized what you'd done?"

I glared at him through slitted eyes. "What?"

"I got hard."

My eyes opened wide.

"Inconveniently and publicly." He cupped my breast in his hand, his thumb stroking over the hardened point of my nipple. "I had to drag out a finished discussion while I waited for it to go down. It turns me on when you challenge me, Eva." His voice lowered and became raspier, dripping with sex and sin. "It makes me want to fuck you. For a very, very long time."

"God." My hips pumped upward, my core tightening with the need to come.

"And since I can't," he purred, "I'm going to get you off like this, then watch you return the favor with your mouth."

A whimper escaped me, my mouth watering at the promise of pleasing him that way. He was always so attuned to me when we made love. The only time he really let go and focused on his own pleasure was when I went down on him.

"That's it," he murmured, "keep rubbing your cunt against me like that. Christ, you're so damn hot."

"Gideon." My hands were gliding all over his flexing back and buttocks, my body arching and grinding into his. I came with a long and drawn-out moan, the tension breaking in a rush of relief.

His mouth covered mine, drinking in the sounds I made as I shivered beneath him. I clutched his hair, kissing him back.

He rolled us so that he was beneath me, his hands going to his button fly and ripping it open. "Now, Eva."

I scrambled down the bed, as eager to taste him as he was to have me do so. The moment he shoved his boxer briefs down, I had his penis in my hands, my lips flowing over the wide crest.

Groaning, Gideon grabbed a pillow and shoved it under his head. My gaze met his and I pulled him deeper.

"Yes," he hissed, the fingers of his right hand tangling in my hair. "Suck it hard and fast; I want to come."

I breathed in the scent of him, feeling the satiny softness of his heated flesh on my tongue. Then I took him at his word.

Hollowing my cheeks, I took him to the back of my throat, then pulled up to the crown. Over and over. Focusing on suction and speed, as greedy for his orgasm as he was, spurred by the abandoned sounds he made and the sight of his fingers clawing restlessly at the comforter. His hips churned, his hand in my hair guiding my pace.

"Ah, God." He watched me with dark, hot eyes. "I love the way you suck me off. Like you can't get enough."

I couldn't. I didn't think I ever could. His pleasure meant so much to me, because it was real and raw. For him, sex had always been staged and methodical. He couldn't hold back with me because he wanted me beyond reason. Two days without me and he was . . . undone.

I pumped him with my fist, feeling the thick veins throbbing beneath the smooth skin. A ragged sound tore from his throat and salty warmth spurted on my tongue. He was close, his face flushed and his lips parted with gasping breaths. Sweat misted my brow. My excitement mounted along with his. He was completely at my mercy, near mindless with the need to climax, muttering filthy sexy things about what he was going to do to me the next time he fucked me.

"That's it, angel. Milk it . . . make me come for you." His neck arched, his breath exploding from his lungs. *"Fuck."*

He came as I had—hard and brutal. Semen burst from the tip of his cock in a thick, hot rush that I struggled to swallow. He growled my name, his hips pumping upward into my working mouth, taking what he needed from me, giving me all he had until he was emptied.

Then he curled toward me, pulling me into a strangling embrace that pinned me to his heaving chest. For long moments, he just held me. I listened as his raging heartbeat slowed and his breathing returned to normal.

Finally, he spoke with his lips in my hair. "Needed that. Thank you."

I smiled and snuggled into him. "My pleasure, ace."

"I missed you," he said softly, his lips pressing to my brow. "So damn much. And not just for this."

"I know." We needed this—the physical closeness, the frenzied touching, the rush of orgasm—to release some of the wild, overwhelming emotions that affected us when we were together. "My dad's coming out to visit next week."

He stilled. Lifting his head, he looked at me wryly. "You have to tell me that while my dick's still hanging out?"

I laughed. "Caught you with your pants down?"

"Hell." He pressed his lips to my forehead, then rolled to his back and righted his clothes. "You have an idea of how you want the first meeting to go? Dinner out or in? Your place or mine?"

"I'll cook at my place." I stretched, then tugged the wrinkles out of my shirt.

He nodded, but his vibe changed. My sated, grateful lover of a moment before was replaced by the grim-faced man who'd been around more frequently lately.

"Would you prefer something different?" I asked.

"No. It's a good plan and what I would've suggested. He'll feel comfortable there."

"Will you?"

"Yes." He propped his head on one hand and looked down at me, brushing my hair back from my forehead. "I'd rather not hit him in the face with my money if we can help it."

I took a deep breath. "I hadn't considered that. I just thought I'd be less anxious about making a mess in my own kitchen than in yours. But you're right. It'll be okay, though, Gideon. Once he sees how you feel about me, he'll be good with us being together."

"I only care what he thinks if it affects how *you* feel. If he doesn't like me and that changes something between us—"

"You're the only one who can do that."

He gave a curt nod, which didn't help me feel better about what he was feeling. A lot of men got nervous meeting their girlfriend's parents, but Gideon wasn't like other men. He didn't rattle. Usually. I wanted him and my dad to be loose and easy around each other, not tense and defensive.

I changed the subject. "Did you get everything worked out in Phoenix?"

"Yes. One of the project managers noted some anomalies in accounting, and she was right to push me to look deeper into it. Embezzling isn't something I tolerate."

I winced, thinking of Gideon's father, who'd bilked investors out of millions before killing himself. "What's the project?"

"A golf resort."

"Nightclubs, resorts, luxury living, vodka, casinos . . . with a chain of gyms thrown in to keep fit for the high life?" I knew from checking out the Cross Industries website that Gideon also had software and games divisions, and a growing social media platform for young urban professionals. "You're a pleasure god in more ways than one."

"Pleasure god?" His eyes sparkled with humor. "I spend all my energy worshipping you."

"How did you get to be so rich?" I blurted out, pricked by the memory of Cary's insinuations about how Gideon could've amassed so much at such a young age.

"People like to have fun, and they'll pay for the privilege."

"That's not what I meant. How did you get Cross Industries started? Where did you get the capital to get things going?"

His eyes took on a speculative gleam. "Where do you think I got it?"

"I have no idea," I told him honestly.

"Blackjack."

I blinked. "Gambling? Are you kidding?"

"No." He laughed and tightened his arms around me.

But I couldn't see Gideon as a gambler. I'd learned, thanks to my mom's third husband, that gambling could become a very nasty and insidious disease that caused total lack of control. I just couldn't see someone as rigidly controlled as Gideon finding anything appealing about something so dependent on luck and chance.

Then it hit me. "You count cards."

"When I played," he agreed. "I don't anymore. And the contacts I made over card tables were as instrumental as the money I made."

I tried to absorb that information, struggled with it, then let it go for the moment. "Remind me not to play cards with you."

"Strip poker could be fun."

"For you."

He reached down and squeezed my ass. "And for you. You know how I get when you're naked."

I shot a pointed glance down at my fully dressed body. "And when I'm not naked."

Gideon's grin flashed, dazzling and entirely unapologetic.

"Do you still gamble?"

"Every day. But only in business and with you."

"With me? With our relationship?"

His gaze was soft on my face, filled with a sudden tenderness that made my throat tight. "You're the greatest risk I've ever taken." His pressed his lips gently to mine. "And the greatest reward."

WHEN I got to work Monday morning, I felt like things were finally settling back into their natural pre-Corinne rhythm. Gideon and I were dealing with adjusting to my period, which had never been an issue for either of us in any previous relationship we'd had, but was in ours because sex was how he showed me what he was feeling. He could say with his body what he couldn't with words, and my lust for him was how I proved my faith in us, something he needed to feel connected to me.

I could tell him I loved him over and over again, and I know it affected him when I did, but he needed the total surrender of my body—a display of trust he knew meant a great deal because of my past—to really believe it.

As he'd told me once, he had been the recipient of many *I love you*s over the years, but he'd never believed them because they hadn't been backed up with truth, trust, and honesty. The words meant little to him, which was why he refused to say them to me. I tried not to let him see how it hurt me that he wouldn't say them. I figured that was an adjustment I'd have to make to be with him.

"Good morning, Eva."

I glanced up from my desk and found Mark standing by my cubicle. His slightly crooked smile was always a winner. "Hey. I'm ready to roll when you are."

"Coffee first. You up for a refill?"

Grabbing my empty mug off my desk, I stood. "You bet."

We headed toward the break room.

"You look like you got a tan," Mark said, glancing over at me.

"Yeah, I did a little sun lounging over the weekend. It was good to be lazy and do nothing. Actually, that's probably one of my favorite things to do, period."

"I'm envious. Steven can't sit still for too long. He always wants to drag me somewhere for something."

"My roommate's the same way. It's exhausting how he runs around."

"Oh, before I forget." He gestured for me to enter the break room first. "Shawna wants you to get in touch. She's got concert tickets for some new rock band. I think she wants to see if you'd want them."

I thought of the attractive red-haired waitress I'd met the week before. She was Steven's sister, and Steven was Mark's longtime partner. The two men had met in college and had been together ever since. I really liked Steven. I was pretty sure I'd really like Shawna, too.

"Are you okay with me reaching out to her?" I had to ask, because she was—for all intents and purposes—Mark's sister-in-law and Mark was my boss.

"Of course. Don't worry. It won't be weird."

"All right." I smiled and hoped to add another girlfriend to my new life in New York. "Thanks."

"Thank me with a cup of coffee," he said, pulling out a mug from the cupboard and handing it to me. "You make it taste better than I do."

I shot him a look. "My dad uses that line."

"Must be true, then."

"Must be a standard guy finagle," I shot back. "How do you and Steven divvy up coffee making?"

"We don't." He grinned. "There's a Starbucks on the corner by our place."

"I'm sure there's a way to call that cheating, but I haven't had enough caffeine to think of it yet." I passed over his filled mug to him. "Which probably means I shouldn't share the idea that just came to me."

"Go for it. If it really sucks, I can hold it against you forever."

"Gee. Thanks." I held my mug between both hands. "Would it work to market the blueberry coffee like tea instead? You know, the coffee in a chintz teacup and saucer with maybe a scone and some clotted cream in the background? Give it a high-end, midafternoon snack sort of treatment? Throw in a fabulously handsome English-man to sip it with?"

Mark's lips pursed as he thought about it. "I think I like it. Let's go run it by the creatives."

"WHY didn't you tell me you were going to Las Vegas?"

I sighed inwardly at the high note of irritated anxiety in my mother's voice and adjusted my grip on the receiver of my desk phone. I'd barely returned my butt to my chair when the phone had rung. I suspected if I checked my voice mail, I'd find a message or two from her. When she got worked up about something, she couldn't let it go. "Hi, Mom. I'm sorry. I planned on calling you at lunch and catching up."

"I love Vegas."

"You do?" I thought she hated anything remotely related to gambling. "I didn't know that."

"You would've if you'd asked."

There was a hurt note in my mother's breathy voice that made me wince. "I'm sorry, Mom," I said again, having learned as a child that repeated apologies went a long way with her. "I needed to spend some downtime with Cary. We can talk about a future trip to Vegas, though, if you'd like to go sometime."

"Wouldn't that be fun? I'd like to do fun things with you, Eva."

"I'd like that, too." My eyes went to the picture of my mother and Stanton. She was a beautiful woman, one who radiated a vulnerable sensuality to which men responded helplessly. The vulnerability was real—my mom was fragile in many ways—but she was a man-eater, too. Men didn't take advantage of my mom; she walked all over them.

"Do you have plans for lunch? I could make a reservation and come get you."

"Can I bring a co-worker?" Megumi had hit me up with a lunch invitation when I'd come in, promising to regale me with the tale of her blind date.

"Oh, I'd love to meet the people you work with!"

My mouth curved with genuine affection. My mom drove me nuts a lot, but at the end of the day, her biggest fault was that she loved me too much. Combined with her neurosis, it was a maddening flaw, but one motivated by the best of intentions. "Okay. Pick us up at noon. And remember, we only get an hour, so it'll have to be close by and quick."

"I'll take care of it. I'm excited! See you soon."

MEGUMI and my mother took to each other right away. I recognized the familiar starry-eyed look on Megumi's face when they met, because I'd seen it so often over the years. Monica Stanton was a stunning woman, the kind of classic beauty you couldn't help but stare at because you couldn't believe anyone could be that perfect. Plus, the royal purple hue of the wingback she'd elected to sit in was an amazing backdrop for her golden hair and blue eyes.

For her part, my mom was delighted by Megumi's fashion sense. While my wardrobe choices leaned more toward traditional and ready-to-wear, Megumi favored unique combinations and color, much like the décor of the trendy café near Rockefeller Center my mom had taken us to.

The place reminded me of *Alice in Wonderland*, with its gilt and jewel-toned velvets used on uniquely shaped furniture. The chaise Megumi was perched on had an exaggerated curved back, while my mother's wingback had gargoyles for feet.

"I'm still trying to figure out what's wrong with him," Megumi went on. "I was looking, let me tell you. I mean a guy that great shouldn't be slumming it with blind dates."

"Hardly slumming it," my mom protested. "I'm sure he's wondering how he lucked out with you."

"Thanks!" Megumi grinned at me. "He was seriously hot. Not Gideon Cross hot, but hot all the same."

"How is Gideon, by the way?"

I didn't take my mom's question lightly. She was aware that

Gideon knew about the abuse I'd suffered as a child, and she'd taken the news hard. It was her greatest shame that she hadn't known what was going on under her own roof, and her guilt was enormous, as well as entirely undeserved. She hadn't known because I'd hidden it. Nathan had made me fear what he'd do if I ever told anyone. Still, my mother was anxious about Gideon's knowing. I hoped that she'd soon come to realize that Gideon didn't hold it against her any more than I did.

"He's working hard," I answered. "You know how it is. I've taken up a lot of his time since we hooked up, and I think he's paying for it now."

"You're worth it."

I took a large gulp of my water when I felt the nearly overwhelming urge to tell her that my dad was coming to visit. She'd be an ally in convincing him of Gideon's affection for me, but that was a selfish reason to say anything. I had no idea how she would react to Victor's being in New York, but it was highly possible she'd be distressed, and that would make everyone's life hell. Whatever her reasons, she preferred to have no contact with him whatsoever. I couldn't ignore how she'd managed to avoid seeing or talking to him since I'd become old enough to communicate with him directly.

"I saw a picture of Cary on the side of a bus yesterday," she said.

"Really?" I sat up straighter. "Where?"

"On Broadway. A jeans ad, I think it was."

"I saw one, too," Megumi said. "Not that I paid any attention to what he was wearing. That man is *fine*."

The conversation made me smile. My mother was adept at admiring men. It was one of the many reasons they adored her—she made them feel good. Megumi was more than her match in the guy-appreciation department.

"He's been getting recognized on the street," I said, glad that in this case we were talking about an ad and not a tabloid candid with me. The gossips thought it was so juicy that Gideon Cross's girlfriend lived with a sexy male model.

"Of course," my mom said, with a slight note of chastisement. "You didn't doubt he would eventually?"

"I'd hoped," I qualified. "For his sake. It's a sad fact that male models don't make as much or work as often as the women do." Although I'd expected Cary would break through somehow. Emotionally, he couldn't afford not to. He'd learned to put so much value on his looks that I didn't think he could allow himself to fail. It was one of my deepest fears that his career choice would come back to haunt him in ways neither of us could bear.

My mother took a delicate sip of her Pellegrino. The café specialized in cacao-laced menu items, but she was careful not to waste her daily calorie allotment on one meal. I was less cautious. I'd ordered a soup and sandwich combination plus a dessert that was going to cost me at least an extra hour on the treadmill later. I excused the indulgence with a mental reminder that I was on my period, which was a carte blanche chocolate zone in my opinion.

"So," Monica smiled at Megumi, "will you be seeing your blind date again?"

"I hope so."

"Darling, don't leave it to chance!"

As my mom started doling out her wisdom in regard to managing men, I sat back and enjoyed the show. She was of the firm belief that every woman deserved to have a wealthy man to dote on her, and for the first time in forever, she wasn't concentrating her matchmaking efforts on me. While I was worried about how my dad and Gideon would hit it off, I had no concerns about my mom's feelings on the matter. We both thought I was with the right guy for me, although for different reasons.

"Your mom rocks," Megumi said, when Monica ducked into the ladies' room to freshen up before we left. "And you look just like her, lucky you. How bad would it suck to have a mom who's hotter than you are?"

Laughing, I told her, "I'll have to drag you along with us again. This worked out great."

"I'd like that."

When it was time to go, I looked at Clancy and the town car waiting at the curb for us and realized I wanted to walk off some of my lunch before I got back to work. "I think I'm going to hoof it back," I told them. "I ate too much. You two go on without me."

"I'll go with you," Megumi said. "I could use the air, hot as it is. That canned air in the office makes my skin dry."

"I'll come, too," my mom offered.

I eyed her delicate heels skeptically, but then again, my mom wore nothing but heels. For her, walking in those was probably the same as walking in flats was to me.

We headed back to the Crossfire at the standard stride rate for Manhattan, which was something of a steady, purposeful clip. While weaving around human obstacles was usually part of the process, it was far less of an issue with my mom in the lead. Men moved reverently off to the side for her, then followed her with their eyes. In her simple, sexy wrap dress of ice blue, she looked cool and refreshing in the humid heat.

We'd just turned the corner to reach the Crossfire when she came to an abrupt halt that caused Megumi and me to crash into the back of her. She stumbled forward, wobbling, and I barely caught her by the elbow before she teetered over.

I looked at the ground to see what had held her up, but when I didn't see anything I looked at her. She was staring at the Crossfire in a daze.

"Jesus, Mom." I urged her out of the flow of pedestrians. "You're white as a sheet. Is the heat getting to you? Do you feel dizzy?"

"What?" Her hand went to her throat. Her dilated gaze remained fixed on the Crossfire.

Turning my head, I followed her line of sight, trying to see whatever it was that she did.

"What are you two looking at?" Megumi asked, frowning down the street.

"Mrs. Stanton." Clancy approached, having abandoned the town car he'd been driving at a safe but discreet distance behind us. "Is everything all right?"

"Did you see—?" she began, looking to him with her question.

"See what?" I demanded, as his head snapped up and his trained gaze raked the length of the street. The absoluteness of his focus sent a shiver down my spine.

"Let me drive you three the rest of the way," he said quietly.

The entrance to the Crossfire was literally across the street, but something in Clancy's tone brooked no argument. We all climbed in, with my mother taking the front seat.

"What was that about?" Megumi asked after we'd been dropped off and had moved into the cool interior of the building. "Your mom looked like she'd seen a ghost."

"I have no idea." But I felt ill.

Something had frightened my mother. It was going to drive me crazy until I found out what it was.

7

MY BACK HIT the mat with enough force to knock the air from my lungs. Stunned, I blinked up at the ceiling, trying to catch my breath.

Parker Smith's face came into view. "You're wasting my time. If you're going to be here, be *here*. One hundred percent. Not a million miles away in your head somewhere."

I grabbed the hand he extended to me, and he yanked me to my feet. Around us, a dozen more of Parker's Krav Maga students were hard at work. The Brooklyn-based studio was alive with noise and activity.

He was right. My thoughts were still stuck on my mom and the bizarre way she'd reacted when we returned to the Crossfire after lunch.

"Sorry," I muttered. "I've got something on my mind."

He moved like lightning, tagging me first on one knee, then my shoulder with rapid-fire slaps. "Do you think an attacker is going to wait until you're alert and ready before he comes after you?"

I crouched, forcing myself to focus. Parker crouched as well, his brown eyes hard and watchful. His shaved head and café au lait skin gleamed beneath the overhead fluorescent lighting. The studio was in a converted warehouse, which had been left rough for both economic reasons and atmosphere. My mother and stepfather were paranoid enough to have Clancy accompany me to my classes. The neighborhood was presently undergoing revitalization, which I thought was encouraging but they thought was troubling.

When Parker came at me again, I blocked him. The tagging came fast and furious then, and I pushed all other thoughts aside until later, when I was home.

When Gideon came over about an hour later, he found me in the bath surrounded by vanilla-scented candles. He undressed to join me, even though his damp hair told me he'd already showered after spending time with his own personal trainer. I watched him strip, riveted. The play of muscles beneath his skin and the inherent gracefulness in the way he moved sent a delicious sense of contentment sliding through me.

He climbed into the deep oval tub behind me, his long legs sliding in on either side of mine. His arms wrapped around me, and then he surprised me by lifting me up and back, so that I was sitting on his lap and my legs were draped over his.

"Lean into me, angel," he murmured. "I need to feel you."

I sighed with pleasure, sinking into the hardness of his powerful body as he cradled me. My aching muscles softened in surrender, eager as always to become completely pliable to his touch. I loved moments like this, when the world and our emotional triggers were far away. Moments when I *felt* the love he wouldn't profess for me.

"Soaking more bruises?" he asked with his cheek pressed to mine.

"My fault. My head wasn't in the game."

"Thinking about me?" he purred, nuzzling against my ear.

"I wish."

He paused, then switched gears. "Tell me what's bugging you."

I loved how easily he could read me, then revise and revisit his approach on the fly. I tried to be as adaptable for him. Really, flexibility was a requirement in a relationship between two high-maintenance people.

Linking my fingers with his, I told him about my mother's weird reaction after lunch.

"I almost expected to turn around and see my dad or something. I was wondering . . . You have security cameras that cover the front of the building, don't you?"

"Of course. I'll look into it."

"It's a ten-minute window of time, max. I just want to see if I can figure out what went on."

"Consider it done."

I tilted my head back and kissed his jaw. "Thank you."

His lips pressed to the top of my shoulder. "Angel, there's nothing I wouldn't do for you."

"Including talking about your past?" I felt him tense and mentally kicked myself. "Not right this second," I hastened to add, "but sometime. Just tell me we'll get there."

"Have lunch with me tomorrow. In my office."

"Are you going to talk about it then?"

Gideon exhaled harshly. "Eva."

I turned my face away and released him, disappointed with his evasion. Reaching for the edges of the tub, I prepared to get out and away from the man who somehow made me feel more connected to another human being than I'd ever been, yet was impossibly distant as well. Being with him fucked with my head, made me doubt the very things I'd been sure of just moments before. Rinse and repeat.

"I'm done," I muttered, blowing out the nearest candle. Smoke curled up and away, as intangible as my grasp on the man I loved. "I'm getting out."

"No." He cupped my breasts, restraining me. Water lapped around us, as agitated as I was.

"Let go, Gideon." I caught his wrists to pull his hands away.

He buried his face in my neck, obstinately holding on. "We'll get there. Okay? Just— We'll get there."

I deflated, feeling little of the triumph I had hoped to feel when I'd first asked and anticipated his answer.

"Can we give it a rest tonight?" he asked gruffly, still clinging tight. "Give it all a rest? I just want to be with you, all right? Order something in for dinner, watch TV, hold you when I sleep. Can we do that?"

Realizing something was seriously off, I twisted to face him. "What's wrong?"

"I just want some time with you."

My eyes stung with tears. There was more he wasn't telling me, so much more. Our relationship was swiftly becoming a minefield of words left unsaid and secrets not shared. "Okay."

"I need it, Eva. You and me with no drama." His wet fingertips brushed across my cheek. "Give me that. Please. Then give me a kiss."

Turning around, I straddled his hips and cupped his face in my hands. I angled my head to find the perfect approach and pressed my lips to his. I started out soft and slow, licking and suckling. I tugged on his bottom lip, then coaxed him to forget our problems with teasing strokes of my tongue along his.

"Kiss me, damn it," he growled, his hands bracketing my spine and kneading restlessly. "Kiss me like you love me."

"I do," I promised, breathing the words into him. "I can't help it."

"Angel." Pushing his hands into my damp hair, he held me how he wanted me and kissed me senseless.

AFTER dinner, Gideon worked in bed, propping his back against my headboard and his laptop on a lap desk. I sprawled on the bed on my belly, facing the TV and kicking my feet in the air.

"Do you know every line in this movie?" he asked, luring me to turn my attention away from *Ghostbusters* to look at him. He wore black boxer briefs and nothing else.

I loved that I got to see him that way—relaxed, comfortable, intimate. I wondered if Corinne had ever seen this view. If so, I could imagine her desperation to see it again, because I was desperate to never lose the privilege.

"Maybe," I conceded.

"And you have to say them all aloud?"

"Got a problem with that, ace?"

"No." Amusement lit his eyes and curved his mouth. "How many times have you seen it?"

"A gazillion times." I curled around and rose up on my hands and knees. "Want more?"

A dark winged brow rose.

"Are you the keymaster?" I purred, crawling forward.

"Angel, when you're looking at me like that, I'm whatever you want me to be."

I looked at him beneath lowered eyelids and breathed, "Do you want this body?"

Grinning, he set his lap desk aside. "All the damn time."

Straddling his legs, I climbed his torso. I wrapped my arms around his shoulders and growled, "Kiss me, subcreature."

"That's not how that line goes. And what happened to me being a pleasure god? Now I'm a subcreature?"

I pressed my cleft against the hard ridge of his cock and rolled my hips. "You're whatever I want you to be, remember?"

Gideon gripped my rib cage and tipped his head back. "And what's that?"

"Mine." I nipped his throat with my teeth. "All mine."

I couldn't breathe. I tried to scream, but something blocked my nose . . . covered my mouth. A high-pitched moan was the only sound to escape, my frantic calls for help trapped inside my mind.

Get off me. Stop it! Don't touch me. Oh, God . . . please don't do that to me.

Where was Mama? *Ma-ma!*

Nathan's hand covered my mouth, mashing my lips. The weight of his body pressed down on me, squashing my head into the pillow. The more I fought, the more excited he became. Panting like the animal he was, he lunged into me, over and over . . . trying to shove himself inside me. My panties were in the way, protecting me from the tearing pain I'd lived through too many times to count.

As if he'd read my mind, he growled in my ear, "You haven't felt pain yet. But you will."

I froze. Awareness hit me like a bucket of ice water. I *knew* that voice.

Gideon. No!

My blood roared in my ears. Sickness spread through my gut. Bile flooded my mouth.

It was worse, so much worse, when the person trying to rape you was someone you trusted with everything you had.

Fear and fury blended in a potent rush. In a moment of clarity, I heard Parker's barked commands. I remembered the basics.

I attacked the man I loved, the man whose nightmares blended with mine in the most horrific way. We were both sexual-abuse survivors, but in my dreams I was still a victim. In his, he'd become the aggressor, viciously determined to inflict the same agony and humiliation on his attacker as he himself had suffered.

My stiffened fingers rammed into Gideon's throat. He reared back with a curse and shifted, and I slammed my knee between his legs. Doubled over, he fell away from me. I rolled out of bed and hit the floor with a thud. Scrambling to my feet, I threw myself toward the door to the hallway.

"Eva!" he gasped, awake and aware of what he'd almost done to me in his sleep. "God. *Eva.* Wait!"

I bolted out the door and ran into the living room.

Finding a darkened corner, I curled into a ball and struggled to breathe, my sobs echoing through the apartment. I pressed my lips to my knee when the light came on in my bedroom and didn't move or make a sound when Gideon stepped into the living room an eternity later.

"Eva? Jesus. Are you okay? Did I . . . hurt you?"

Atypical sexual parasomnia was what Dr. Petersen called it, a manifestation of Gideon's deep psychological trauma. I called it hell. And we were both trapped in it.

His body language broke my heart. His normally proud bearing was weighted with defeat, his shoulders slumped and his head bowed. He was dressed and carrying his overnight bag. He stopped by the breakfast bar. I opened my mouth to speak; then I heard a metallic *clink* against the stone countertop.

I'd stopped him the last time; I'd made him stay. This time, I didn't have it in me.

This time, I wanted him to go.

The barely audible latching of the front door lock reverberated through me. Something inside me died. Panic welled. I missed him the moment he was gone. I didn't want him to stay. I didn't want him to go.

I don't know how long I sat there in the corner before I found the strength to stand and move to the couch. I vaguely registered that dawn was lighting the night sky when I heard the distant sound of Cary's cell phone ringing. Shortly after that, he came running into the living room.

"Eva!" He was on me in a minute, crouching in front of me with his hands on my knees. "How far did he go?"

I blinked down at him. "What?"

"Cross called. Said he'd had another nightmare."

"Nothing happened." I felt a hot tear roll down my cheek.

"You look like something happened. You look . . ."

I caught his wrists when he surged to his feet with a curse. "I'm okay."

"Shit, Eva. I've never seen you look like this. I can't stand it." He took a seat beside me and pulled me into his shoulder. "Enough is enough. Cut him off."

"I can't make that decision now."

"What are you waiting for?" He forced me back to glare at me. "You're going to wait too long and then this won't be just another bad relationship, it'll be one that permanently fucks you up."

"If I give up on him, he'll have no one. I can't—"

"That's not your problem. Eva . . . Goddamn it. It's not your responsibility to save him."

"It's— You don't understand." I wrapped my arms around him. Burying my face in his shoulder, I cried. "He's saving me."

I threw up when I found Gideon's key to my apartment lying on the breakfast bar. I barely made it to the sink.

When my stomach was empty, I was left with pain so agonizing it was crippling. I clung to the edge of the counter, gasping and sweating, crying so hard I wondered how I'd make it through another five minutes, let alone the rest of the day. The rest of my life.

The last time Gideon had returned my keys to me, we'd broken up for four days. It was impossible not to think that repeating the gesture signified a more permanent break. What had I done? Why hadn't I stopped him? Talked to him? Made him stay?

My smartphone signaled an incoming text. I stumbled to my purse and dug it out, praying it was Gideon. He'd talked to Cary three times already, but he'd yet to contact me.

When I saw his name on the screen, a sweet, sharp ache pierced my chest.

I'm working from home today, his message read. Angus will be waiting out front to give you a ride to work.

My stomach cramped again with dread. It had been a tremendously difficult week for both of us. I could understand why he'd just given up. But that understanding was wrapped in a gut-gnawing fear so cold and insidious that goose bumps swept up my arms.

My fingers shook as I texted him back: Will I see you tonight?

There was a long pause, long enough that I was about to demand a yes or no answer when he sent: Don't count on it. I have my appt with Dr. Petersen and a lot of work to do.

My grip tightened on my phone. It took me three attempts before I was able to type: I want to see you.

For the longest time, my phone sat silently. I was reaching for my landline in a near panic when he replied: I'll see what I can do.

Oh God . . . Tears made it hard for me to see the letters. He was done. I knew it deep down in my heart. Don't run. I'm not.

It seemed like forever before he replied: You should.

I debated calling in sick after that, but I didn't. I couldn't. I had been down that road too many times. I knew I could so easily fall back into old self-destructive habits to dull pain. It would kill me to lose Gideon, but I'd be dead anyway if I lost myself.

I had to hang on. Get through. Get by. One step at a time.

And so I climbed into the back of the Bentley when I was supposed to, and while Angus's grim face only made me worry more, I locked it down and slid into the autopilot mode of self-preservation that would get me through the hours ahead.

My day passed in a blur. I worked hard and focused on my job, using it to keep me from going crazy, but my heart wasn't in it. I spent my lunch hour running an errand, unable to tolerate the thought of eating or making small talk. After my shift was over, I almost blew off going to my Krav Maga class, but I stuck it out and gave a similar amount of focus to the drills as I'd given to my work. I had to keep moving forward, even if I was heading in a direction I couldn't bear to go.

"Better," Parker said, during a break. "You're still off, but you're better than last night."

I nodded and wiped the sweat from my face with a towel. I'd started Parker's classes solely as a more intense alternative to my usual gym visits, but last night had shown me that personal safety was more than just a convenient side benefit.

The tribal tattoos that banded his biceps flexed as he lifted a water bottle to his lips. Because he was left-handed, his simple gold wedding band caught the light and my eye. I was reminded of the promise ring on my right hand and I looked down at it. I remembered when Gideon had given it to me and how he'd said that the diamond-crusted Xs wrapping around the roped gold were representative of him "holding on" to me. I wondered if he still thought that way; if he still thought it was worth it to try. God knew I did.

"Ready?" Parker asked, tossing his empty bottle in the recycle bin.

"Bring it."

He grinned. "There she is."

Parker still worked me over, but it wasn't from lack of trying on my part. I was in it every step of the way, venting my frustration with good, healthy exercise. The few victories I managed to earn spurred my determination to fight for my rocky relationship, too. I was willing to put in the time and effort to be there for Gideon, to be a better and stronger person so we could get through our issues. And I was going to tell him that, whether he wanted to hear it or not.

When my hour was over, I cleaned up and waved good-bye to my classmates and then shoved at the push bar of the exit door and stepped out into the still-warm evening air. Clancy had already brought the car around to the door and was leaning against the fender in a pose that only a moron would think was casual. Despite the heat, he wore a jacket, which concealed his sidearm.

"Things moving along?" He straightened to open the door for me. As long as I'd known him, he'd kept his dark blond hair in a military crew cut. It added to the impression of his being a very somber man.

"Working on it." Sliding into the backseat, I told Clancy to drop me off at Gideon's. I had my own key and I was prepared to use it.

On the drive over, I wondered if Gideon had gone to see Dr. Petersen for his appointment or if he'd blown it off. He'd agreed to individual therapy only because of me. If I wasn't part of the equation anymore, he might not see any reason to make the effort.

I entered the understated and elegant lobby of Gideon's apartment building and checked in with the front desk. It wasn't until I was alone in his private elevator that the nerves really hit me. He'd placed me on his approved list weeks before, a gesture that meant so much more to him and me than it would to others because Gideon's home was his sanctuary, a place he allowed few visitors to see. I was the only lover he'd ever entertained there and the only person, aside from his household staff, who had a key. Yesterday I wouldn't have doubted my welcome, but now . . .

I exited into a small foyer decorated with checkerboard marble tiles and an antique console bearing a massive arrangement of white calla lilies. Before I unlocked his front door, I took a deep breath, steeling myself for however I might find him. The one previous time he'd attacked me in his sleep, it had shattered him. I couldn't help but fear what the second time had done to him. I was terrified that his parasomnia might be the wedge that drove us apart.

But the moment I entered his apartment, I knew he wasn't home. The energy that thrummed through a space when he occupied it was markedly absent.

Lights that were activated by my movements came on when I entered the expansive living room, and I forced myself to settle in as if I belonged there. My room was down the hall and I went to it, pausing on the threshold to absorb the weirdness of seeing my bedroom replicated in Gideon's place. The duplication was uncanny, from the color on the walls to the furniture and fabrics, but its existence was more than a little unnerving.

Gideon had created it as my safe room, a place for me to run to when I needed some space. I supposed I was running to it now, in a way, by using it instead of his.

Leaving my workout bag and purse on the bed, I showered and changed into one of the Cross Industries T-shirts Gideon had set aside for me. I tried not to think about why he still wasn't home. I'd just poured a glass of wine and turned on the living room television when my smartphone rang.

"Hello?" I answered, unfamiliar with the number on the nameless Caller ID.

"Eva? It's Shawna."

"Oh, hey, Shawna." I tried not to sound disappointed.

"I hope it's not too late to call."

I looked at the screen of my phone, noting that it was almost nine o'clock. Jealousy mingled with my concern. Where was he? "No worries. I'm just watching TV."

"Sorry I missed your call last night. I know it's short notice, but I wanted to see if you'd be up for going to a Six-Ninths concert on Friday."

"A what concert?"

"Six-Ninths. You haven't heard of 'em? They were indie until late last year. I've been following them for a while and they gave their e-mail list first dibs, so I scored tickets. Thing is, everyone I know likes hip-hop and dance pop. Not to say you're my last hope, but . . . well, you're my last hope. Tell me you like alt rock."

"I like alt rock." My phone beeped. Incoming call. When I saw it was Cary, I let it go to voice mail. I didn't think I'd be on the phone with Shawna too long and I could call him back.

"How did I know that?" She laughed. "I've got four tickets if you've got someone you'd like to bring along. Meet up at six? Grab something to eat first? The show starts at nine."

Gideon walked in just as I answered, "You've got a date."

He stood just inside the door with his jacket slung over one arm, the top button of his dress shirt undone, and a briefcase in his hand. His mask was in place, showing no emotion whatsoever at finding me sprawled on his couch in his T-shirt with a glass of his wine on his table and his television on. He raked me with a head-to-toe glance, but nothing flickered in those beautiful eyes. I suddenly felt awkward and unwanted.

"I'll get back to you about the other ticket," I told Shawna, sitting up slowly so I didn't flash him. "Thanks for thinking of me."

"I'm just glad you're coming! We're going to have a great time."

We agreed to talk the next day and hung up. In the interim, Gideon set his briefcase down and tossed his jacket over the arm of one of the gilded chairs flanking the ends of the glass coffee table.

"How long have you been here?" he asked, yanking the knot of his tie loose.

I stood. My palms grew damp at the thought that he might kick me out. "Not long."

"Have you eaten?"

I shook my head. I hadn't been able to eat much all day. I'd gotten through the session with Parker courtesy of a protein drink I'd picked up during my lunch hour.

"Order something." He walked past me toward the hallway. "Menus are in the kitchen drawer by the fridge. I'm going to grab a quick shower."

"Do you want something?" I asked his retreating back.

He didn't stop or look at me. "Yes. I haven't eaten, either."

I'd finally settled upon a local deli boasting organic tomato soup and fresh baguettes—figuring my stomach could maybe handle that—when my phone rang again.

"Hey, Cary," I answered, wishing I were home with him and not about to face a painful breakup.

"Hey, Cross was just here looking for you. I told him to go to hell and stay there."

"Cary." I sighed. I couldn't blame him; I'd do the same thing for him. "Thanks for letting me know."

"Where are you?"

"At his place, waiting for him. He just showed. I'll probably be home sooner rather than later."

"You kicking him to the curb?"

"I think that's on his agenda."

He exhaled audibly. "I know it's not what you're ready for, but it's for the best. You should call Dr. Travis ASAP. Talk it out with him. He'll help you put things in perspective."

I had to swallow past the lump in my throat. "I'm— Yeah. Maybe."

"You okay?"

"Ending it face-to-face has dignity, at least. That's something."

My phone was pulled from my hand.

Gideon held my gaze as he said, "Good-bye, Cary," then powered off my phone and set it on the counter. His hair was damp and he wore black pajama bottoms that hung low on his hips. The sight of him hit me hard, reminding me of all that I stood to lose when I lost him—the breathless anticipation and desire, the comfort and intimacy, the ephemeral sense of *rightness* that made everything worthwhile.

"Who's the date?" he asked.

"Huh? Oh. Shawna—Mark's sister-in-law—has concert tickets for Friday."

"Have you figured out what you want to eat?"

I nodded, tugging at the thigh-length hem of my shirt because I felt self-conscious.

"Get me a glass of whatever you're drinking." He reached around me and picked up the menu I'd set out on the counter. "I'll order. What do you want?"

It was a relief to move over to the cabinet that held the wine-glasses. "Soup. Crusty bread."

As I tugged the cork out of the bottle of merlot I had left on the counter, I heard him call the deli and speak in that firm, raspy voice of his that I loved from the moment I'd first heard it. He ordered tomato soup and chicken noodle, which caused a painful tightness in my chest. Without being told, he'd ordered what I wanted. It was another of the many serendipitous things that always made me feel like we were destined to end up in the same place, together, if only we could make it that far.

I passed him the glass I'd poured for him and watched as he took a drink. He looked tired, and I wondered if he'd stayed up all night like I had.

Lowering the glass, he licked the lingering trace of wine off his lips. "I went to your place looking for you. I expect Cary told you."

I rubbed at the painful ache in my chest. "I'm sorry . . . about this and—" I gestured at what I was wearing. "Damn it. I didn't plan this well."

He leaned back into the counter and crossed one ankle over the other. "Go on."

"I figured you'd be home. I should've called first. When you weren't here, I should have just waited for another time instead of making myself at home." I rubbed at my stinging eyes. "I'm . . . confused about what's going on. I'm not thinking straight."

His chest expanded on a deep breath. "If you're waiting for me to break up with you, you can stop waiting."

I grabbed on to the kitchen island to steady myself. *That's it? That's the end?*

"I can't do it," he said flatly. "I can't even say I'll let you walk, if that's why you're here."

What? I frowned in confusion. "You left your key at my place."

"I want it back."

"Gideon." My eyes closed and tears tracked down my cheeks. "You're an ass."

I walked away, moving toward my bedroom with a quick and slightly weaving stride that had nothing to do with the small amount of wine I'd sipped.

I had scarcely cleared the doorway of my room when he grabbed my elbow.

"I won't follow you inside," he said gruffly, his head bent to reach my ear. "I promised you that. But I'm asking you to stay and talk to me. At least listen. You came all this way—"

"I have something for you." It was hard for me to get the words past my tight throat.

He released me and I hurried to my purse. When I faced him, I asked, "Were you breaking up with me when you left the key on my counter?"

He filled the doorway. His hands were extended above his shoulders, his knuckles white from the force with which he gripped the frame, as if he were physically restraining himself from following me. The pose displayed his body beautifully, defining every muscle, allowing the drawstring waistband of his pants to cling to his hip bones. I wanted him with every breath I took.

"I wasn't thinking that far ahead," he admitted. "I just wanted you to feel safe."

My grip tightened around the object in my hand. "You ripped my heart out, Gideon. You have no idea what seeing that key lying there did to me. How bad it hurt me. No idea."

His eyes squeezed shut and his head bowed. "I wasn't thinking clearly. I thought I was doing the right thing—"

"Fuck that. Fuck your damn chivalry or whatever the hell you think that was. Don't do it again." My voice took on an edge. "I'm telling you right now and I mean it like I've never meant anything before—you ever give me my keys back again, we're done. There's no coming back from that. Do you understand?"

"I do, yes. I'm not sure you do."

My breath left me in a shaky exhalation. I approached him. "Give me your hand."

His left hand stayed on the doorjamb, but his right lowered and extended toward me.

"I never gave you the key to my place; you just took it." I cupped his hand between both of mine, placing my gift in his palm. "I'm giving it to you now."

Stepping back, I released him, watching as he looked down at the gleaming monogrammed fob with my apartment key on it. It was the best way I could think of to show him that it belonged to him and that it was given freely.

His hand fisted, closing tightly around my gift. After a long minute, he looked up at me and I saw the tears that wet his face.

"No," I whispered, my heart breaking further. I cupped his face in my hands, my thumbs brushing over his cheekbones. "Please . . . don't."

Gideon caught me up, his lips pressing to mine. "I don't know how to walk away."

"Shh."

"I'll hurt you. I already am. You deserve better—"

"Shut up, Gideon." I climbed him and wrapped my legs around his waist, holding on.

"Cary told me how you looked . . ." He began to shake violently. "You don't see what I'm doing to you. I'm breaking you, Eva—"

"That's not true."

He sank to his knees on the floor, clasping me tightly. "I've trapped you in this. You don't see it now, but you knew from the beginning— You knew what I would do to you, but I wouldn't let you run."

"I'm not running anymore. You've made me stronger. You gave me a reason to try harder."

"God." His eyes were haunted. He sat, stretching his legs out, pulling me closer. "We're so fucked up, and I've handled everything all wrong. We're going to kill each other with this. We'll tear each other apart until there's nothing left."

"Shut up. I don't want to hear any more of that shit. Did you go to Dr. Petersen?"

His head fell back against the wall and his eyes closed. "Yes, damn it."

"Did you tell him about last night?"

"Yes." His jaw clenched. "And he said the same thing he started on last week. That we're in too deep. We're drowning each other. He thinks we need to pull back, date platonically, sleep separately, spend more time together with others and less time alone."

It would be better, I thought. Better for our sanity, better for our chances. "I hope he's got a Plan B."

Gideon opened his eyes and looked at my scowling face. "That's what I said. Again."

"So we're fucked up. Every relationship has issues."

He snorted.

"Seriously," I insisted.

"We *are* going to sleep separately. That's something I let go too far."

"Separate beds or separate apartments?"

"Beds. That's all I can stand."

"All right." I sighed and rested my head on his shoulder, so grateful that he was in my arms again and that we were together. "I can deal. For now."

His throat worked on a hard swallow. "When I came home and found you here—" His arms tightened around me. "God, Eva. I thought Cary was lying about you not being home, that you just didn't want to see me. Then I thought you might be out . . . moving on."

"You're not that easy to get over, Gideon." I didn't think I'd ever get over him. He was in my blood. I straightened so he could see my face.

He placed his hand over his heart, the hand with the key. "Thank you for this."

"Don't let that go," I warned again.

"Don't regret giving it to me." He pressed his forehead to mine. I felt the warmth of his breath on my skin and thought he might have whispered something, but I didn't catch it if he did.

It didn't matter. We were together. After the long awful day, nothing else was important.

8

THE SOUND OF my bedroom door opening ended my forgettable dream, but it was the mouthwatering aroma of coffee that really woke me up. I stretched but kept my eyes closed, allowing the anticipation to build.

Gideon took a seat on the edge of the mattress, and a moment later his fingers drifted across my cheek. "How did you sleep?"

"I missed you. Is that coffee I smell for me?"

"If you're good."

My eyes popped open. "But you like me bad."

His smile did crazy things to me. He'd dressed already in one of his amazingly sexy suits and looked much better this morning than he had the night before. "I like you bad *with me*. Tell me about this concert on Friday."

"It's a band called Six-Ninths. That's all I know. Wanna go?"

"It's not a question of whether I want to go. If you're going, so am I."

My brows rose. "Is that right? And what if I hadn't asked you?"

He reached for my hand and gently twirled my promise ring around my finger. "Then you wouldn't be going, either."

"Excuse me?" I shoved my hair back. Noting the set look on his gorgeous face, I sat up. "Gimme that coffee. I want to be caffeinated when I kick your ass."

Gideon grinned and handed the mug over.

"Don't look at me like that," I warned. "I'm seriously not happy with you telling me I can't go somewhere."

"We're talking specifically about a rock concert, and I didn't say you couldn't go, just that you can't go without me. I'm sorry you don't like it, but it is what it is."

"Who says it's rock? Maybe it's classical. Or Celtic. Or pop."

"Six-Ninths signed with Vidal Records."

"Oh." Vidal Records was run by Gideon's stepfather, Christopher Vidal Sr., but Gideon had controlling interest. I wondered how a boy grew up to take over his stepfather's family business. I figured whatever the reason was, it was also why Gideon's half brother, Christopher Jr., hated him to the extreme.

"I've seen videos of their indie shows," he said dryly. "I'm not risking you to a crowd like that."

I sucked down a big gulp of coffee. "I get it, but you can't order me around."

"Can't I? Shh." He placed his fingers over my lips. "Don't argue. I'm not a tyrant. I may occasionally have concerns, and you'll be sensible about acknowledging them."

I shoved his hand away. "'Sensible' being whatever you've decided is best?"

"Of course."

"That's bullshit."

He stood. "We're not going to fight over a hypothetical situation. You asked me to go to the concert with you on Friday and I said yes. There's nothing to argue about."

Setting my coffee on the nightstand, I kicked off the covers and slid out of bed. "I have to be able to live my life, Gideon. I still have to be *me* or this won't work."

"And I have to be me. I'm not the only one who needs to compromise."

That hit me hard. He wasn't wrong—I had a right to expect him to give me my space, but he had a right to be understood as the man he was. I had to make accommodations for the fact that he had triggers, too. "What if I want a girls' night out clubbing with my friends?"

He caught my jaw in both hands and kissed my forehead. "You can take the limo and stick to clubs I own."

"So you can have your security people spy on me?"

"Keep an eye on you," he corrected, his lips sliding over my brow. "Is that so terrible, angel? Is it so unforgivable that I hate taking my eyes off you?"

"Don't twist this around."

He tilted my head back and looked down at me with hard, determined eyes. "You need to understand that even if you take the limo and stick to my clubs, I'm still going to go crazy until you get home. If that means you're driven a little crazy with my safety precautions, isn't that part of the give-and-take?"

I growled. "How do you make something unreasonable sound reasonable?"

"It's a gift."

Grabbing his very fine, very taut ass in my hands, I squeezed. "I need more coffee to deal with your gift, ace."

∽

IT had become somewhat of a Wednesday tradition for Mark, his partner Steven, and me to go out to lunch. When Mark and I arrived at the little Italian restaurant he'd chosen and found Shawna waiting with Steven, I was really touched. Mark and I had a very professional relationship, but somehow we'd managed to make that personal and it meant a lot to me.

"I'm so jealous of your tan," Shawna said, looking casual and cute in jeans, embellished tank top, and filmy scarf. "The sun just makes me red and gives me more freckles."

"But you've got that beautiful hair to show for it," I pointed out, admiring the deep red hue.

Steven ran a hand through his hair, which was the exact same color as his sister's, and grinned. "The things one sacrifices to be hot."

"How would you know?" Shawna shoved at his shoulder with a laugh, an effort that didn't budge her brother even an inch. Where she was slender as a reed, Steven was big and strapping. I knew from talking to Mark that his partner was very hands-on with his construction business, which explained both his size and the rugged condition of his hands.

We entered the restaurant and were seated right away, thanks to the reservation I'd made when Mark had invited me to lunch. It was a small establishment, but it had great charm. Sunlight poured in through the floor-to-ceiling windows and the aroma of the food was so tantalizing it made my mouth water.

"I am so excited about Friday." Shawna's soft blue eyes were lit with anticipation.

"Yeah, she'll take *you*," Steven told me dryly, "and not her big brother."

REFLECTED IN YOU · 133

"Sooo not your scene," she shot back. "You hate crowds."

"Just gotta establish some personal space, that's all."

Shawna rolled her eyes. "You can't be a bruiser everywhere."

The talk about crowds had me thinking of Gideon and his protective streak. "Mind if I bring the guy I'm seeing?" I asked. "Or is that a buzzkill?"

"Not at all. Does he have a friend who'd like to come?"

"Shawna." Mark was clearly shocked. And disapproving. "What about Doug?"

"What about him? You didn't let me finish." She looked at me and explained, "Doug's my boyfriend. He's in Sicily for the summer taking a culinary course. He's a chef."

"Nice," I said. "I dig guys who can cook."

"Oh, yeah." She grinned, then aimed a glare at Mark. "He's a keeper and I know it, so if your guy has a friend who's fine with filling the empty seat with no possibility of a hookup, bring him along."

I immediately thought of Cary and grinned.

But later that day, after Gideon and I had spent quality time with our personal trainers and had returned to his apartment for the night, I changed my mind. I got up from the couch where I'd been trying unsuccessfully to read a book and padded down the hall to his home office.

I found him frowning at whatever he was working on, his fingers flying over the keyboard. The glow of the monitor and the spotlight aimed at the photo collage on the wall were the only sources of illumination in the room, which left much of the large space in shadow. He sat in the semidark, bare-chested and beautiful, alone and powerfully self-contained. As he always did while working, he looked solitary and unreachable. I felt lonely just looking at him.

The combination of the physical distance caused by my period and Gideon's understandable decision to sleep separately stirred my deepest insecurities, made me want to cling tighter and try harder to keep his attention focused on me.

That he was working instead of spending time with me shouldn't have rankled—I knew how busy he was—but it did. I felt abandoned and needy, which told me I was regressing into familiar bad patterns. The simple fact was, Gideon and I were the best and worst things that had ever happened to each other.

He looked up and pinned me with his gaze. I watched his focus shift from work to me.

"Am I neglecting you, angel?" he asked, leaning back in his chair.

I flushed, wishing he couldn't read me so well. "I'm sorry to interrupt."

"You should always come to me when you need something." Pushing his keyboard drawer in, he patted the empty space on the desk in front of him and wheeled his chair back. "Come sit."

A thrill rushed through me. I hurried over, making no effort to hide my eagerness. I hopped onto the desk in front of him and smiled wide when he rolled his chair forward to fill the space between my legs.

Draping his arms over my thighs, he hugged me around the hips and said, "I should've explained that I'm trying to clear my schedule so we can take off this weekend."

"Really?" I pushed my fingers through his hair.

"I want you all to myself for a while. And I really, really need to fuck you for a very long time. Maybe the whole time." His eyes closed as I touched him. "I miss being inside you."

"You're always inside me," I whispered.

His mouth curved in a slow, wicked smile and his eyes opened. "You're making me hard."

"What's new?"

"Everything."

I frowned.

"We'll get to that," he said. "For now, tell me what you came in here for."

I hesitated, still stuck on his cryptic comment.

"Eva." His firm tone focused me. "What do you need?"

"A date for Shawna. Uh . . . not really a date. Shawna's got a man, but he's out of the country. It'd just be better if we made it an even party of four."

"You don't want to ask Cary?"

"I thought of him first, but Shawna's *my* friend. I thought you might want someone *you* know to come. You know, keep the dynamic even."

"All right. I'll see who's free."

I realized then that I hadn't really expected him to take me up on my offer.

Some of my thoughts must have shown on my face, because he asked, "Is there more?"

"I . . ." How did I say what I was thinking without making an ass of myself? I shook my head. "No. Nothing."

"Eva." His voice was stern. "Tell me."

"It's stupid."

"That wasn't a request."

An electric tingle coursed through me, as it always did when he took on that commanding tone. "I just thought you socialized for business and screwed random women occasionally."

Saying that last part was hard. As lame as it was to be jealous of women in his past, I couldn't help it.

"You didn't think I had friends?" he asked, clearly amused.

"You've never introduced me to any," I said sullenly, picking at the hem of my T-shirt.

"Ah . . ." His amusement deepened, his eyes sparkling with laughter. "You're my sexy little secret. Have to wonder what I was thinking when I made sure we were photographed kissing in public."

"Well." My gaze moved to the collage on the wall where that very picture could be found, a picture that had been plastered all over gossip blogs for days. "When you put it like that . . ."

Gideon laughed, and the sound spread through me in a heated rush of pleasure. "I've introduced you to a few of my friends when we've been out."

"Oh." I'd assumed everyone I had met at the events we'd attended were business associates.

"But keeping you all to myself isn't a bad idea."

I shot him a look and revisited the point I'd made when we argued about my going to Vegas instead of Phoenix. "Why can't *you* be the one lying around naked waiting to be fucked?"

"Where's the fun in that?"

I shoved at his shoulders and he hauled me into his lap, laughing.

I couldn't believe how good his mood was and wondered what had set it off. When I glanced at his monitor, all I saw was a spreadsheet that made my eyes cross and a half-written e-mail. But something was different about him. And I liked it.

"It'd be a pleasure," he murmured, with his lips to my throat, "to lie around with a hard-on that you rode whenever the mood struck you."

My sex clenched at the visual in my mind. "You're making me horny."

"Good. I like you that way."

"So," I mused, "if my fantasy is you providing around-the-clock stud servicing—"

"Sounds like reality to me."

I nipped him on the jaw with my teeth.

He growled. "Want to play rough, angel?"

"I want to know what your fantasy is."

Gideon adjusted me so that I was draped across his lap. "You."

"It better be."

He grinned. "In a swing."

"Huh?"

"A sex swing, Eva. Your gorgeous ass in a seat, feet in stirrups, legs spread wide, your perfect cunt wet and waiting." He rubbed seductive circles into the small of my back. "Totally at my mercy and unable to do anything but take all the cum I can give you. You'd love it."

I pictured him standing between my legs, naked and glistening with sweat, his biceps and pecs flexing as he rocked me back and forth, sliding me on and off his beautiful cock. "You want me helpless."

"I want you bound. And not on the outside. I'm working my way in."

"Gideon—"

"I won't ever take it further than you can handle," he promised, his eyes glittering hotly in the muted lighting. "But I'll take you to the edge."

I squirmed, both aroused and disturbed by the thought of giving up that much control. "Why?"

"Because you want to be mine and I want to possess you. We'll get there." His hand slid under my shirt and cupped my breast, his fingers rolling and tugging my nipple, igniting my body.

"Have you done that before?" I asked breathlessly. "The swing?"

His face shuttered. "Don't ask questions like that."

Oh God. "I just—"

His mouth sealed over mine. He nipped my lower lip, then thrust his tongue into my mouth, holding me where he wanted me with his fist in my hair. The dominance of the act was undeniable. Hunger surged through me, a need for him I couldn't control or fight. I whimpered, my chest aching at the thought of him putting that much time and effort into gaining pleasure from someone else.

Gideon's hand shoved between my legs and cupped my sex. I jerked, surprised at his aggression. He made a low sound of reassurance and massaged me, rubbing my tender flesh with the consummate skill I'd grown so addicted to.

He broke the kiss, moving his arm to arch my back and lift my breast to his mouth. He bit my nipple through the cotton, then wrapped his lips around the aching peak, sucking so strongly I felt the echo in my core.

I was under siege, my brain short-circuiting as desire pumped through me. His fingers slid beneath the edge of my panties to touch my clit, the feel of flesh on flesh just what I needed. *"Gideon."*

He lifted his head and watched with dark eyes as he made me come for him. I cried out when the tremors rippled through me, the release of tension after days of deprivation almost too much to bear. But he didn't let up. He stroked my sex until I came again, until violent shivers racked my body and I squeezed my legs shut to stop the onslaught.

When he pulled his hand away, I sagged, boneless and breathing heavily. I curled into him, my face pressed into his throat, my arms wrapping around his neck. My heart felt as if it had swelled in my chest. Everything I felt for him, all the torment and love, overwhelmed me. I clawed at him, trying to get closer.

"Shh." He held me tighter, squeezing me until it was hard to breathe. "You're questioning everything and driving yourself crazy."

"I hate this," I whispered. "I shouldn't need you this much. It's not healthy."

"That's where you're wrong." His heart beat strongly beneath my ear. "And I take responsibility for that. I've taken the lead with some things and given it to you with others. That's left you confused and worried. I'm sorry about that, angel. It'll be easier moving forward."

I leaned back so I could search his face. My breath caught when our eyes met and he stared back at me unflinchingly. I comprehended the difference then—there was a calm, solid serenity about him. Seeing that settled something inside me, too. My breathing slowed and evened; my anxiety lessened.

"That's better." He kissed my forehead. "I was going to wait until the weekend to talk about this, but now works. We're going to come to an agreement. Once it's met, there's no turning back. Understand?"

I swallowed hard. "I'm trying."

"You know the way I am. You've seen me at my worst. Last night, you said you want me anyway." He waited for my nod. "That's where I fucked up. I didn't trust you to make that decision for yourself and I should have. Because I didn't, I've been too cautious. Your past scares me, Eva."

The thought of Nathan indirectly taking Gideon away from me was so painful, my knees drew even closer into my chest. "Don't give him that power."

"I won't. And you have to realize there's more than one answer for everything. Who says you need me too much? Who says it's not healthy? Not you. You're unhappy because you're holding yourself back."

"Men don't—"

"Fuck that. Neither of us is typical. *And that's okay.* Turn off that voice in your head that's screwing you up. Trust me to know what you need, even when you think I'm wrong. And I'll trust your decision to be with me despite my faults. Got it?"

I bit my lower lip to hide its trembling and nodded.

"You don't look convinced," he said softly.

"I'm afraid I'll lose myself in you, Gideon. I'm scared I'll lose the part of me I worked so hard to get back."

"I'd never let that happen," he promised fiercely. "What I want is for us both to feel safe. What you and I have together shouldn't be draining us like this. It should be the one rock-solid thing we both count on."

My eyes stung with tears at the thought. "I want that," I whispered. "So much."

"I'm going to give it to you, angel." Gideon bent his dark head and brushed his lips over mine. "I'm going to give it to both of us. And you're going to let me."

"THINGS seem to be looking better this week," Dr. Petersen said when Gideon and I arrived for our Thursday night therapy appointment.

We sat near each other this time, with our hands clasped together. Gideon's thumb caressed my knuckles, and I looked at him and smiled, feeling settled by the contact.

Dr. Petersen flipped open the protective case of his tablet and settled more comfortably in his seat. "Is there anything in particular you'd like to discuss?"

"Tuesday was tough," I said quietly.

"I imagine so. Let's talk about Monday night. Can you tell me what happened, Eva?"

I told him about waking up from my own nightmare to find myself trapped in Gideon's. I walked him through that night and the following day.

"So you're sleeping separately now?" Dr. Petersen asked.

"Yes."

"Your nightmares"—he looked up at me—"how often do you have them?"

"Rarely. Prior to dating Gideon, it'd been almost two years since my last one." I watched him set the stylus down and start typing quickly. Something about his somberness made me anxious. "I love him," I blurted.

Gideon stiffened beside me.

Dr. Petersen's head came up, and he studied me. He glanced at Gideon, then back to me. "I don't doubt it. What made you say that, Eva?"

I shrugged awkwardly, hyperaware of Gideon's gaze on my profile.

"She wants your approval," Gideon said grimly.

His words rubbed over me like sandpaper.

"Is that true?" Dr. Petersen asked me.

"No."

"The hell it isn't." The rasp in Gideon's voice was pronounced.

"It's not," I argued, although I'd needed him to say it aloud for me to understand that. "I just . . . It's just the truth. That's the way I feel."

I looked at Dr. Petersen. "We have to make this work. We're *going* to make this work," I stressed. "I just want to know that you're on the same page. I need to know that you understand that failure isn't an option."

"Eva." He smiled kindly. "You and Gideon have a lot to work through, but it's certainly not insurmountable."

My breath left me in a rush of relief. "I love him," I said again, with a decisive nod.

Gideon surged to his feet, his grip crushingly tight on my hand. "If you'll excuse us a minute, Doctor."

Confused and a little worried, I stood and followed him out to the empty reception area. Dr. Petersen's receptionist had already gone home, and we were his last appointment of the day. I knew from my mother that these evening appointments came at a premium. I was grateful that Gideon was willing to pay for them not once but twice a week.

The door shut behind us, and I faced him. "Gideon, I swear it's not—"

"Hush." He cupped my face in both hands and kissed me, his mouth moving softly but urgently over mine.

Startled, it took me the length of two heartbeats to slide my hands beneath his jacket and grip his lean waist. When his tongue stroked deep into my mouth, a low moan escaped me.

He pulled back and I looked up at him, seeing the same gorgeous businessman in a dark suit that I'd first met, but the look in his eyes . . .

My throat burned.

The power and scorching intensity, the hunger and need. His fingertips brushed over my temples, across my cheeks, down to my throat. He tilted my jaw up and his lips pressed gently against mine. He didn't say anything, but he didn't have to. I got it.

He linked our fingers and led me back inside.

9

I HURRIED THROUGH the security turnstiles of the Crossfire and grinned when I saw Cary waiting for me in the lobby.

"Hey, you," I greeted him, admiring how he managed to make worn jeans and a V-neck T-shirt look expensive.

"Hey, stranger." He held out his hand to me and we stepped out of the building through the side door hand-in-hand. "You're looking happy."

The noonday heat hit me like a physical barrier. "Ugh. It's hot as hell. Let's pick somewhere close. You up for tacos?"

"Hell yeah."

I took him to the little Mexican place Megumi had introduced me to and tried not to let him see how guilty his greeting made me feel. I hadn't been home in a couple days and Gideon was planning a weekend trip away, which meant it would be another few days before I hung out with Cary again. It had been a relief when he'd agreed to meet me for lunch. I didn't want to go too long without checking in with him and making sure he was all right.

"Got any plans tonight?" I asked, after ordering for both of us.

"One of the photographers I've worked with is having a birthday bash tonight. I figured I'd pop in for a bit and see how it goes." He rocked back on his heels as we waited for our tacos and blended virgin margaritas. "You still planning on hanging with your boss's sister? You guys wanna come with?"

"Sister-in-law," I corrected. "And she's got concert tickets. I'm her last hope, she said, but even if I wasn't, I think it'll be fun. At least I hope so. I've never heard of the band, so I'm just hoping they don't suck."

"Who is it?"

"Six-Ninths. Know 'em?"

His eyes widened. "Six-Ninths? Really? They're good. You'll like them."

I grabbed our drinks off the counter and left the tray with our plates for him to carry. "You've heard of them and Shawna's a big fan. Where have I been?"

"Under Cross and his hard place. You taking him with you?"

"Yes." I hurried to grab a table as two businessmen stood to leave. I didn't tell Cary about Gideon's assertion that I couldn't go without him. I knew that wouldn't go over well with Cary, which made me wonder why I'd let it go as easily as I did. Usually Cary and I agreed about stuff like that.

"Can't see Cross liking alt rock." Cary sank fluidly into the chair across from me. "Does he know how much *you* like it? Especially the musicians who play it?"

I stuck my tongue out at him. "I can't believe you brought that up. Ancient history."

"So? Brett was hot. Ever think about him?"

"With shame." I picked up one of the carne asada tacos. "So I try not to."

"He was a decent guy," Cary said, before slurping up a hefty swallow of margarita-flavored slush.

"I'm not saying he wasn't. He just wasn't good for me." Just thinking about that time in my life made me want to squirm in embarrassment. Brett Kline was hot and he had a voice that made me wet just hearing it, but he was also one of the prime examples of an unfortunate choice in my previously sordid love life. "Moving on . . . You talk to Trey lately?"

Cary's smile faded. "This morning."

I waited patiently.

Finally, he sighed. "I miss him. Miss talking to him. He's so fucking smart, you know? Like you. He's going to that party with me tonight."

"As friends? Or as a date?"

"These are really good." He chewed a bite of one of his tacos before replying. "We're supposed to be going as friends, but you know I'll probably screw that up and fuck him. I asked him to meet me there and to head home from there so we're not alone, but I can always bang him in the bathroom or a goddamn maintenance closet. I have no willpower and he can't say no to me."

My heart hurt at his dejected tone.

"I know what that's like," I reminded him softly. That'd been me once. I'd been so desperate to feel connected with somebody. "Why don't you . . . you know . . . take care of it beforehand. Maybe that'll help."

A slow, mischievous smile spread across his handsome face. "Can I get you to record that for my voice mail message?"

I threw my wadded-up napkin at him.

He caught it with a laugh. "You can be such a prude sometimes. I love it."

"I love *you*. And I want you to be happy."

Lifting my hand to his lips, he kissed the back. "I'm working on it, baby girl."

"I'm here if you need me, even if I'm not home."

"I know." He squeezed my hand before releasing it.

"I'll be around a lot next week. Gotta get ready for my dad's visit." I bit into a taco and my feet did a little happy tap dance at how delicious it was. "I wanted to ask you about Friday. I've got to work, so if you're around, would you keep an eye on him? I'll stock up on the food he likes and leave him some city maps, but—"

"No problem." Cary winked at a pretty blonde as she walked by. "He'll be in good hands."

"Want to see a show with us while he's in town?"

"Eva honey, I'm always game to hang with you. Just let me know where and when, and I'll keep things clear as much as possible."

"Oh!" I quickly chewed and swallowed. "Mom told me she saw your pretty mug on the side of a bus the other day."

He grinned. "I know. She forwarded a pic she'd taken with her phone. Awesome, right?"

"Beyond. We'll need to celebrate," I said, stealing his signature line.

"Hell yeah."

"Whoa!" Shawna paused on the sidewalk outside her Brooklyn apartment complex and gaped at the limousine idling in the street. "You went all out."

"Not me," I said dryly, checking out her tight red shorts and strategically slashed Six-Ninths screened T-shirt. Her bright hair had been pulled up and teased, and her lips were painted to match her shorts. She looked hot and ready to party, and I felt vindicated in my clothing choice of ultra-short black leather pleated skirt, fitted white ribbed tank top, and cherry red sixteen-eye Doc Martens.

Gideon, who'd had his back to us while talking to Angus, turned to face us, and I found myself as dumbstruck now as I'd been when I first saw him after he had showered and changed. He wore loose-fitting black jeans and a plain black T-shirt with heavy black boots and somehow made the severely casual combination look so fucking sexy, I wanted to jump his bones. As Dark and Dangerous as he was in a suit, he was even more so when ready to rock. He looked younger and every bit as mouthwateringly gorgeous.

"Holy shit, tell me that's for me," Shawna whispered, gripping my wrist like a vise.

"Hey, you've got your own. That one's mine." And it gave me a huge thrill to say so. Mine to claim, to touch, to kiss. And later on, to fuck to exhaustion. *Oh yeah . . .*

She laughed when I rocked onto my tiptoes in anticipation. "All right. I'll settle for an introduction."

I did the honors, then waited for her to hop into the limo first. I was about to climb in after her when I felt Gideon's hand slide up beneath my skirt to squeeze my butt.

He pressed against my back and whispered in my ear, "Make sure I'm standing behind you when you bend over, angel, or I'll be spanking this pretty ass."

Turning my head, I leaned my cheek against his. "My period's over."

He growled, his fingertips biting into the flesh of my hip. "Why didn't you tell me that earlier?"

"Delayed gratification, ace," I told him, using a phrase he'd once tormented me with. I was laughing at his curse when I dropped onto the bench seat beside Shawna.

Angus slid behind the wheel and we headed out, breaking into a bottle of Armand de Brignac on the way. By the time we pulled up to Tableau One, a hot new fusion bistro that had a healthy line out front and energetic music pouring out onto the street, the combination of the champagne and Gideon's hot gaze on the nearly indecent hemline of my skirt had me feeling giddy.

Shawna slid forward on the seat and stared wide-eyed through the tinted windows. "Doug tried to get us in here before he left, but the waiting list is two months long. You can walk up, but the wait can be hours and there's no guarantee you'll be seated."

The limo door opened and Angus helped her out, then me. Gideon joined us, taking my arm as if we were dressed for a gala and not a rock concert. We were escorted inside so quickly, with the manager being so gushy and welcoming, that I looked at Gideon and mouthed, *One of yours?*

"Yes, in partnership."

I just sighed, reconciled to the inevitable. "Is your friend going to meet us for dinner?"

Gideon gestured with an easy nod of his chin. "He's already here."

I followed his gaze to an attractive man sporting blue jeans and a Six-Ninths T-shirt. The gentleman was acting as the focal point in a photo op with two pretty women on each side. He smiled wide for the person wielding a smartphone camera, then waved at Gideon and excused himself.

"Oh my God." Shawna bounced on her feet. "That's Arnoldo Ricci! He owns this place. And he's got a show on the Food Network!"

Gideon released me to clasp hands with Arnoldo and engage in the backslapping ritual of close male friends. "Arnoldo, my girlfriend, Eva Tramell."

I extended my hand and Arnoldo grabbed it, pulled me closer, and kissed me straight on the mouth.

"Back off," Gideon snapped, tugging me behind him.

Arnoldo grinned, his dark eyes flashing with humor. "And who's this vision?" he asked, turning to Shawna and lifting her hand to his lips.

"Shawna, this will be your escort, Arnoldo Ricci, *if* he manages to survive dinner." Gideon shot his friend a warning look. "Arnoldo, Shawna Ellison."

She practically glowed. "My boyfriend's a huge fan of yours. I am, too. He made your lasagna recipe once and it was. To. Die. For."

"Gideon told me your man is in Sicily now." Arnoldo's voice was flavored with a delicious accent. "I hope you can make the time to visit with him there."

My gaze darted to Gideon, knowing damn well I'd never given him that much information about Shawna's boyfriend. He glanced down at me with a look of mock innocence and an almost imperceptible smirk.

I shook my head, exasperated, but I couldn't deny that this would be a night Shawna would never forget.

The next hour passed in a blur of excellent food and fine wine. I was polishing off an extraordinary zabaione with raspberries when I caught Arnoldo watching me with a wide smile.

"*Bellissima*," he praised. "Always a joy to see a woman with a healthy appetite."

I flushed, slightly embarrassed. I couldn't help it; I loved food.

Gideon draped his arm along the back of my chair and toyed with the hair at my nape. His other hand lifted a glass of red wine to his mouth and when he licked his lips, I *knew* he was thinking about tasting me instead. His desire was charging the air between us. I had been falling under its spell all through dinner.

Reaching beneath the tablecloth, I cupped his cock through his jeans and squeezed. He went from semihard to stone instantly but gave no other outward indication of his arousal.

I couldn't help but see that as a challenge.

I began to stroke the rigid length of him with my fingers, careful to keep my movements slow and easy to prevent detection. To my delight, Gideon continued his conversation without a hitch in his voice or change of expression. His control excited me, made me bolder. I reached for his button fly, turned on by the thought of releasing him and stroking him skin on skin.

Gideon took another leisurely sip, then set his wineglass down.

"Only you, Arnoldo," he said dryly in response to something his friend had said.

My wrist was caught just as I tugged at the top button of his jeans. He lifted my hand to his lips, the gesture appearing to be an absentminded show of affection. The quick nip of his teeth into the pad of my finger caught me by surprise and made me gasp.

Arnoldo smiled; it was the knowing and slightly mocking smile one bachelor gave to another who'd been caught by a woman. He said something in Italian. Gideon replied, his pronunciation sounding fluid and sexy, his tone wry. Arnoldo threw his dark head back and laughed.

I squirmed in my seat. I loved seeing Gideon like this, relaxed and enjoying himself.

He looked at my empty dessert plate, then at me. "Ready to go?"

"Oh, yes." I was dying to see how the rest of the night would go, how many more sides of Gideon I'd get to discover. Because I loved this side of the man as much as I loved the powerful businessman in the suit and the dominant lover in my bed and the broken child who couldn't hide his tears and the tender partner who held me when I cried.

He was so complex and still a huge mystery to me. I'd barely scratched the surface of who he was. Which didn't stop me from being in too deep.

"THESE guys are good!" Shawna yelled as the opening act barreled headlong into their fifth song.

We'd left our seats after the third, working our way through a writhing crowd to the railing that divided the seating area from the mosh pit in front of the stage. Gideon surrounded me, his arms caging me on both sides, his hands gripping the rail. The audience pressed in around us, collectively pushing forward, but I was cushioned from it by his body, just as Shawna was by Arnoldo beside us.

I was sure Gideon could have gotten us way better seats, but I didn't have to tell him that the way Shawna had scored her fan-only tickets and the fact that *she'd* invited *us* meant her seats were our only option. I loved him for understanding that and for going with the flow.

Turning my head, I looked at him. "Is this band with Vidal, too?"

"No. But I like them."

I was stoked that he was enjoying the show. Lifting my arms in the air, I screamed, feeling pumped by the energy of the crowd and the driving beat. I danced within the circle of Gideon's arms, my body drenched in sweat, my blood raging.

When the act was done, the stagehands quickly set to work breaking down the equipment and setting up for Six-Ninths. Grateful for the evening, for the joy, for the awesomeness of going wild with the man I loved, I turned and threw my arms around Gideon's neck, mashing my lips to his.

He lifted me and urged my legs around his waist, kissing me violently. He was hard and pressing against me, luring me to grind into him. Around us people whistled and catcalled things that ranged from "Get a room" to "Fuck her, man!" but I didn't care and neither did Gideon, who seemed as swept away by the sensual craziness as I was. His hand on my buttocks rocked me into his erection while the other fisted in my hair, holding me where he wanted me as he kissed me as if he couldn't stop, as if he were starving for the taste of me.

Our open mouths slid desperately across each other. He tongued me deep and fast, fucking my mouth, making love to it. I drank him in, licking and tasting, moaning at his insatiable need. He sucked on my tongue, the circle of his lips sliding along it. It was too much. I was slick and aching for his cock, nearly frantic with the need to feel him filling me.

"You're going to make me come," he growled, before tugging on my bottom lip with his teeth.

I was so into him and the ferocity of his passion for me that I barely registered when Six-Ninths started. It wasn't until the vocals kicked in that I was jolted back to where I was.

I stiffened, my mind clawing its way up through the fog of desire to process what I was hearing. I knew the song. My eyes opened as Gideon pulled back. Over his shoulder I saw handwritten signs held up in the air.

BRETT KLINE IS MINE! And BANG ME, BRETT! And my personal favorite, BRETT, I'D HIT IT WITH YOU LIKE THE WRATH OF GOD!!!

Hell. What were the chances?

And Cary had known, of course. He'd known and hadn't warned

me. Probably thought it'd be hysterical for me to find out by accident instead.

My legs loosened from around Gideon's hips and he set me down, protecting me from the frenzied fans with the shield of his body. I turned to face the stage, feeling a mad fluttering in my belly. Sure enough, it was Brett Kline at the mic, his deep, powerful, sexy-as-hell voice pouring over the thousands who'd come to see him in action. His short hair was spiked and tipped with platinum, his lean body clothed in olive cargo pants and a black tank top. It was impossible to see from where I was, but I knew his eyes were a brilliant emerald green, his face was ruggedly handsome, and his killer smile revealed a dimple that drove women crazy.

Tearing my eyes away from him, I looked at the other band members, recognizing all of them. They hadn't been called Six-Ninths back in San Diego, though. They'd been called Captive Soul then, and I wondered what had led to the name change.

"Good, aren't they?" Gideon asked with his mouth to my ear so I could hear him. He had one hand on the railing and the other around my waist, keeping me pulled up tight against him as he moved to the music. The combination of his body and Brett's voice did insane things to my already raging sex drive.

I closed my eyes, focusing on the man behind me and the unique rush I'd always felt while listening to Brett sing. The music throbbed through my veins, bringing back memories—some good and some bad. I swayed in Gideon's arms, desire pounding through me. I was achingly aware of his hunger. It poured off him like heat waves, sinking into me, making me crave him until the physical distance between us was painful.

Grabbing the hand he had pressed flat against my stomach, I urged it downward.

"Eva." His voice was harsh with lust. I'd been pushing him all night, from the moment I told him my period was over, to the hand job beneath the restaurant table, to the scorching kiss during intermission.

He gripped my bare thigh and squeezed. "Open."

I set my left foot on the bottom of the railing. My head fell back against his shoulder and a heartbeat later, his hand was under my skirt. His tongue traced the shell of my ear, his breathing hard and fast. I felt him groan as much as heard it when he discovered how wet I was.

One song blended into another. Gideon rubbed me through the crotch of my boyshorts, moving in circles, then vertically through my cleft. My hips rolled into his touch, my core clenching, my ass grinding into the hard ridge of his erection. I was going to come right there, inches away from dozens of people, because that was what Gideon did to me. That was how insanely he turned me on. Nothing mattered when his hands were on me, his attention completely riveted to me.

"That's it, angel." His fingers pushed my underwear aside and two sank into me. "I'm going to fuck this gorgeous cunt for days."

With bodies pressing in all around us, music pounding over us, and privacy granted only by distraction, Gideon slid his fingers deep into my soaked sex and stayed there. The solid, unmoving penetration drove me wild. I ground my hips into his hand, working toward the orgasm I needed so desperately.

The song ended and the lights went out. Drenched in darkness, the crowd roared. Anticipation weighted the audience, building until the strum of guitar strings broke the heavy expectation. Shouts rang out, then lighters flickered to life, turning the sea of people into thousands of fireflies.

A spotlight hit the stage, revealing Brett sitting on a bar stool, shirtless and glistening with sweat. His chest was hard and defined,

REFLECTED IN YOU · 155

his abs ridged with muscle. He lowered the height of the microphone stand and the piercings in his nipples glittered with his movements. The women in the audience screamed, including Shawna, who jumped in place and gave an earsplitting whistle.

I totally got it. Sitting there as he was, with his feet propped on the rungs of the stool and his muscular arms covered in sleeves of black and gray tattoos, Brett looked insanely sexy and extremely fuckable. For six months nearly four years ago I'd debased myself to get him naked every chance I could, so infatuated with him and desperate to be loved that I took whatever scraps he threw me.

Gideon's fingers began to slide in and out of me. The bass kicked in. Brett began to sing a song I'd never heard before, his voice low and soulful, the words crystal clear. He had the voice of a fallen angel. Mesmerizing. Seductive. And the face and body to enhance the temptation.

Golden girl, there you are.
I'm singing for the crowd, the music's loud.
I'm living my dream, riding the high,
But I see you there, sunlight in your hair,
And I'm ready to go, desperate to fly.

Golden girl, there you are.
Dancing for the crowd, the music's loud.
I want you so bad. I can't look away.
Later, you'll drop to your knees. You'll beg me please.
And then you'll go, it's only your body I know.

Golden girl, where'd you go?
You're not there, with sunlight in your hair.
I could have you in the bar or the back of my car,

But never your heart. I'm falling apart.
I'll drop to my knees, I'll beg you. Please.

Please don't go. There's so much more I want to know.
Eva, please. I'm on my knees.

Golden girl, where'd you go?
I'm singing for the crowd, the music's loud.
And you're not there, with sunlight in your hair.
Eva, please. I'm on my knees.

The spotlight went dark. A long moment passed as the music faded. Then the lights came back on and the drums exploded with sound. The flames winked out and the crowd went crazy.

But I was lost to the roaring in my ears, the tightness in my chest, and a confusion that had me reeling.

"That song," Gideon growled in my ear, his fingers fucking me forcefully, "makes me think of you."

His palm pressed into my clit and massaged, and I climaxed in a rush that took me by storm. Tears came to my eyes. I cried out, shaking in his arms. Gripping the railing in front of me, I held on and let the unstoppable pleasure pulse through me.

When the show was over, all I could think about was getting to a phone and calling Cary. While we waited for the crowd to thin, I leaned heavily into Gideon, drawing support from the strength of his arms around me.

"You okay?" he asked, running his hands up and down my back.

"I'm fine," I lied. Honestly, I didn't know how I was feeling. It shouldn't matter that Brett wrote a song about me that painted a different light on our fuck-buddy history. I was in love with someone else.

"I want to go, too," he murmured. "I'm dying to get inside you, angel. I can barely think straight."

I pushed my hands into the back pockets of his jeans. "So let's get out of here."

"I've got backstage access." He kissed the tip of my nose when I leaned back to look up at him. "We don't have to tell them, if you'd rather get out of here."

I seriously debated it for a moment. After all, the night had been great as it was, thanks to Gideon. But I knew it'd bother me later if I denied Shawna and Arnoldo—who was also a Six-Ninths fan— something they'd remember for the rest of their lives. And I'd be lying if I didn't admit to myself that I wanted to catch a glimpse of Brett up close. I didn't want him to see me, but I wanted to see him. "No. Let's take them back there."

Gideon grabbed my hand and spoke to our friends, whose excitement over the news gave me the excuse to say I'd done it solely for them. We headed down toward the stage, then off to the side of it, where Gideon spoke to the massive man acting as security. When the guy spoke into the mic of his headset, Gideon pulled out his cell and told Angus to bring the limo around to the back. While he spoke, his eyes met mine. The heat in them and the promise of pleasure took my breath away.

"Your man is the ultimate," Shawna said, eyeing Gideon with a look of near reverence. It wasn't a predatory look, just an appreciative one. "I can't believe this night. I owe you big-time for this."

She pulled me in for a quick, hard hug. "Thank you."

I hugged her back. "Thank you for inviting me."

A tall, rangy man with blue streaks in his hair and stylish black-framed glasses approached us. "Mr. Cross," he greeted Gideon, extending his hand. "I didn't know you'd be coming tonight."

Gideon shook the man's hand. "I didn't tell you," he replied smoothly, reaching his other hand out to me.

I caught it and he pulled me forward, introducing me to Robert Phillips, Six-Ninths' manager. Shawna and Arnoldo were introduced next; then we were led back through the wings, where activity was high and groupies loitered.

I suddenly didn't want to catch even a glimpse of Brett. It was so easy to forget how it'd been between us while I was listening to him sing. It was so easy to *want* to forget after listening to the song he'd written. But that time in my past was something I was far from proud of.

"The band's right in here," Robert was saying, gesturing to an open door from which music and raucous laughter poured out. "They'll be excited to meet you."

My feet dug in suddenly and Gideon paused, glancing at me with a frown.

I pushed up onto my toes and whispered, "I'm not all that interested in meeting them. If you don't mind, I'm going to hit the backstage bathroom and head out to the limo."

"Can you wait a few minutes and I'll go with you?"

"I'll be okay. Don't worry about me."

He touched my forehead. "Are you feeling all right? You look flushed."

"I'm feeling great. I'll show you exactly how great as soon as we get home."

That did the trick. His frown faded and his mouth curved. "I'll hurry this along, then." He looked at Robert Phillips and gestured at Arnoldo and Shawna. "Can you take them in? I need a minute."

"Gideon, really . . ." I protested.

"I'm walking you over there."

I knew that tone. I let him walk me the twenty feet to the bathroom. "I can take it from here, ace."

"I'll wait."

"Then we'll never get out of here. Go do your thing. I'll be fine."

He gave me a very patient look. "Eva, I'm not leaving you alone."

"I can manage. Seriously. The exit is right there." I pointed down the hall to the open double doors beneath a lighted exit sign. Roadies were already transporting equipment out. "Angus is right out there, isn't he?"

Gideon leaned his shoulder into the wall and crossed his arms.

I threw up my hands. "Okay. Fine. Have it your way."

"You're learning, angel," he said with a smile.

Muttering under my breath, I went into the bathroom and took care of business. As I washed up at the sink, I looked into the mirror and winced. I had raccoon eyes from sweating so damn much and my pupils were dark and dilated.

"What does he see in you?" I asked myself derisively, thinking of how awesome he still looked. As hot and sweaty as he'd been, he looked none the worse for wear, while I looked damp and limp. But more so than my exterior, it was my personal failings I was thinking of. I couldn't get away from them. Not while Brett was in the same building with us.

I rubbed a dampened square of paper towel under my eyes to get rid of the black smudges, then headed back out to the hall. Gideon waited a few feet away, talking with Robert, or more accurately, listening to him. The band's manager was clearly excited about something.

Gideon spotted me and held up a hand to get me to wait a minute, but I didn't want to take the risk. I gestured down the hall at the exit, then turned and headed that way before he could stall me. I hurried past the greenroom door, chancing a quick glance inside to see Shawna laughing with a beer in her hand. The room was packed and boisterous, and she looked like she was having a great time.

I made my escape with a sigh of relief, feeling ten times lighter the moment I left. Spotting Angus standing next to Gideon's limo on the far side of the line of buses, I waved and set off toward him.

Looking back on the night, I was tantalized by how uninhibited Gideon had been. He sure as hell hadn't been the man who'd used mergers and acquisitions as parlance for getting me into bed.

I couldn't wait to get him naked.

A burst of flame in the darkness to my right startled me. I jolted to a halt and watched Brett Kline lift a match to the clove cigarette hanging from his lips. As he stood in the shadows to the side of the exit, the flickering light of the flame caressed his face and threw me back in time for a long minute.

He glanced up, caught me in his gaze, and froze. We stared at each other. My heart kicked into a mad beat, a combination of excitement and apprehension. He cursed suddenly, shaking out the match as it burned his fingers.

I took off, struggling to maintain a casual pace as I made a beeline for Angus and the limo.

"Hey! Hold up," Brett shouted. I heard his footsteps approaching at a jog, and adrenaline surged through me. A roadie was pushing a flat hand truck loaded with heavy gear and I darted around him, using him as cover to duck between two buses. I pressed my back flat against the side of one, standing between two open cargo compartments. I cringed into the shadows, feeling like a coward, but knowing I had nothing to say to Brett. I wasn't the girl he knew anymore.

I watched him rush by. I decided to wait, give him time to look and give up. I was hyperaware of the time passing, of the fact that Gideon would be looking for me soon.

"Eva."

I flinched at the sound of my name. Turning my head, I found Brett approaching from the other side. While I'd been looking to the right, he'd come up on the left.

"It *is* you," he said roughly. He dropped his clove smoke on the ground and crushed it beneath his boot.

I heard myself saying something familiar. "You should quit."

"So you keep telling me." He approached cautiously. "You saw the show?"

I nodded and stepped away from the bus, backing up. "It was awesome. You guys sound really great. I'm happy for you."

He took a step forward for every one of mine backward. "I was hoping I'd find you like this, at one of the shows. I had a hundred different ideas about how it might go if I saw you at one."

I didn't know what to say to that. The tension between us was so thick it was hard to breathe.

The attraction was still there.

It was nothing like what I felt with Gideon. Nothing more than a shadow of that, but it was there nonetheless.

I retreated back out into the open, where the activity was high and there were lots of people milling around.

"Why are you running?" he asked. In the pool of light from a parking lot lamp, I saw him clearly. He was even better looking than before.

"I can't . . ." I swallowed. "There's nothing to say."

"Bullshit." The intensity of his glare burned through me. "You stopped coming around. Didn't say a word, just stopped showing up. Why?"

I rubbed at the knot in my stomach. What was I going to say? *I finally grew a pair and decided I deserved better than to be one of the many chicks you fucked in a bathroom stall between sets?*

"Why, Eva? We had something going and you just fucking disappeared."

Turning my head, I looked for Gideon or Angus. Neither was anywhere in sight. The limo waited alone. "It was a long time ago."

Brett lunged forward and caught me by the arms, startling me, briefly frightening me with the sudden aggressive movement. If we hadn't been so near other people, it might have triggered panic.

"You owe me an explanation," he bit out.

"It's not—"

He kissed me. He had the softest lips, and he sealed them over mine and kissed me. By the time I registered what was happening, he'd tightened his grip on my arms and I couldn't move away. Couldn't push him away.

And for a brief span of time I didn't want to.

I even kissed him back, because the attraction was still there and it soothed something hurting inside me to think I might've been more than a convenient piece of ass. He tasted like cloves, smelled seductively like hardworking male, and he took my mouth with all the passion of a creative soul. He was familiar, in very intimate ways.

But in the end, it didn't matter that he got to me still. It didn't matter that we had a history, painful as it was for me. It didn't matter that I was flattered and affected by the lyrics he'd written, that after six months of watching him enjoy other women while nailing me anywhere with a door that locked, it was *me* he was thinking about when he seduced screaming-for-it women from the stage.

None of that mattered because I was madly in love with Gideon Cross, and he was what I needed.

I wrenched away with a gasp—

—and faced Gideon charging at a dead run, his speed unchecked as he rammed into Brett and took him down.

10

I STUMBLED BACK from the impact, nearly falling. The two men hit the asphalt with a sickening thud. Someone yelled. A woman screamed. I could do nothing. I stood frozen and silent, emotions twisting through me in a frenzied tangle.

Gideon pinned Brett by the throat and pummeled his ribs with a relentless series of blows. He was like a machine, silent and unstoppable. Brett grunted with each brutal impact and struggled to break free.

"Cross! *Dio mio.*"

I wept when Arnoldo appeared. He leaped forward, reaching for Gideon, only to scramble back as Brett wrenched to the side and the two men rolled.

Brett's bandmates pushed in through the growing crowd around the front of the buses, prepared to brawl . . . until they saw *who* Brett was fighting with—the man with the money behind their record label.

"Kline, you fuckhead!" Darrin, the drummer, gripped his own hair in both fists. "What the hell are you doing?"

Brett broke free, lurched to his feet, and tackled Gideon into the side of a bus. Gideon linked his hands and hammered Brett's back like a club, forcing Brett to lurch away. Pressing the advantage, Gideon lashed out with a roundhouse kick and followed with a lightning-quick jab to the gut. Brett swung, his powerful biceps bunching with his fist, but Gideon ducked fluidly and retaliated with an uppercut that snapped Brett's head back.

Jesus.

Gideon didn't make a sound, not when he struck out and not when Brett landed a direct hit to his jaw. The quiet intensity of his fury was chilling. I could feel the rage pumping off him, saw it in his eyes, but he remained controlled and eerily methodical. He'd disconnected in some way, retreated to a place where he could objectively observe his body doing serious damage to someone else.

I'd caused that. I had turned the warm, wickedly playful man who'd enchanted me all evening into the cold, murderous fighter in front of me.

"Miss Tramell." Angus grabbed my elbow.

I looked at him desperately. "You have to stop him."

"Please, return to the limousine."

"What?" I looked over and saw blood dripping from Brett's nose. No one was intervening. "Are you crazy?"

"We need to take Miss Ellison home. She's your guest; you need to see to her."

Brett swung and when Gideon feinted to the side, Brett rammed his other fist forward, nailing Gideon in the shoulder and sending him backward a few steps.

I grabbed Angus by the arms. "What's the matter with you?! Stop them!"

His pale blue eyes softened. "He knows when to stop, Eva."

"Are you *shitting* me?!"

He looked over my shoulder. "Mr. Ricci, if you would, please."

The next thing I knew, I was slung over Arnoldo's shoulder and en route to the limo. Lifting my head, I saw the circle of bystanders close in with my absence, blocking my view. I screamed my frustration and pounded at Arnoldo's back, but it didn't faze him. He climbed right into the back of the limo with me, and when Shawna hopped in a moment later, Angus shut the door as if everything was totally fucking normal.

"What the hell are you doing?" I snapped at Arnoldo, scrambling for the door handle as the limo rolled smoothly into motion. It wouldn't open and no matter what I did, I couldn't get it to unlock. "He's your friend! You're just going to leave him like that?"

"He's your boyfriend." The calm neutrality in Arnoldo's voice cut me deep. "And *you* are the one who left him like that."

I slumped back into the seat, my stomach churning and my palms damp. *Gideon . . .*

"You're the Eva in the song 'Golden,' aren't you?" Shawna asked quietly, from her position on the opposite bench seat.

Arnoldo started, obviously surprised by the connection. "I wonder if Gideon—" He sighed. "Of course he knows."

"That was a long time ago!" I said defensively.

"Not long enough, apparently," he pointed out.

Desperate to get to Gideon, I couldn't sit still. My feet tapped, my body battling against restlessness so intense I felt like crawling out of my skin.

I'd hurt the man I loved and through him, another man who'd done nothing more than be himself. And I had no good explanation for it. Looking back, I had no idea what had come over me. Why hadn't I pulled away sooner? Why had I kissed Brett back?

And what was Gideon going to do about it?

The thought that he might break up with me triggered overwhelming panic. I was sick with worry. Was he hurt? God . . . the thought of Gideon in pain ate at me like acid. Was he in trouble? He'd assaulted Brett. My palms went damp when I remembered Cary's news that his clusterfuck buddy also wanted to press assault charges.

Gideon's life was spiraling out of control—because of me. At some point he was going to realize I wasn't worth the trouble.

I glanced at Shawna. She was looking out the window pensively. I'd blown her awesome night. And Arnoldo's, too. "I'm sorry." I sighed miserably. "I screwed up everything."

She looked at me and shrugged, then offered a sympathetic smile that made my throat burn. "No big. I had a great time. I hope you work things out for the best."

The best thing for me was Gideon. Had I blown that? Had I thrown away the most important thing in my life over some weird, inexplicable head trip?

I still felt Brett's mouth on mine. I scrubbed at my lips, wishing I could erase the last half hour of my life as easily.

My anxiety made it feel like it took an eternity to drive Shawna home. I got out and gave her a hug on the sidewalk in front of her apartment building.

"I'm sorry," I said again, for both earlier and then, because I was dying to get to Gideon—wherever he was—and I was afraid my impatience showed. I wasn't sure I'd ever forgive Angus or Arnoldo for taking me away when and how they did.

Arnoldo hugged Shawna and told her that she and Doug had a

REFLECTED IN YOU · 167

standing reservation for Tableau One anytime. I softened a little toward him. He'd taken good care of her all night.

We climbed back into the limo and set off for the restaurant. I curled into a darkened corner of the seat and cried silently, unable to contain the flood of despair overwhelming me. When we arrived at the restaurant, I used my tank top to dry my face. Arnoldo stopped me from getting out.

"Be gentle with him," he scolded, staring hard at my face. "I have never seen him the way he is with you. I can't say you are worthy of him, but you can make him happy. I saw that myself. Do it or walk. Don't fuck with his head."

I couldn't speak past the lump in my throat, so I nodded, hoping he could see in my eyes how much Gideon meant to me. *Everything.*

Arnoldo disappeared into the restaurant. Before Angus shut the door, I slid forward on the seat. "Where is he? I need to see him. Please."

"He called." Angus's face was kind, which made me start crying again. "I'm taking you to him now."

"Is he okay?"

"I don't know."

I pushed back into the seat, feeling physically ill. I barely paid attention to where we were headed, my only thought being that I needed to explain. I needed to tell Gideon that I loved him, that I'd never leave him if he'd still have me, that he was the only man I wanted, the only man who set my blood on fire.

Eventually, the car slowed and I looked out, realizing we'd returned to the amphitheater. As I peered out the window, searching for him, the door behind me opened, startling me, and I shifted around to see Gideon duck inside and settle on the opposite bench from me.

I lurched toward him. "Gideon—"

"Don't." His voice whipped with anger, sending me recoiling and falling on my rear. The limo set into motion, jostling me.

Crying, I watched him pour a glass of amber liquor at the bar and toss it back. I waited on the floorboards, my stomach churning with fear and grief. He refilled his glass before shutting the bar and dropping back in his seat. I wanted to ask him if Brett was okay or badly hurt. I wanted to ask how Gideon was, if he was injured or fine. But I couldn't. I didn't know if he would take the questions the wrong way and assume my concern for Brett meant more than it did.

His face was impassive, his eyes hard as sapphires. "What is he to you?"

I swiped at the tears streaming down my face. "A mistake."

"Then? Or now?"

"Both."

His lip curled in a sneer. "You always kiss your mistakes like that?"

My chest heaved as I tried to stem the need to sob. I shook my head violently.

"You want him?" he asked tightly, before taking another drink.

"No," I whispered. "I only want you. I love *you*, Gideon. So much it hurts."

His eyes closed and his head fell back. I took the opportunity to crawl closer, needing to bridge the physical distance between us, at least.

"Did you come for me when I had my fingers inside you, Eva? Or because of his goddamn song?"

Oh my God . . . How he could doubt—?

I made him doubt. I did that. "You. You're the only one who can get to me like that. Make me forget where I am. Make it so I don't care who's around or what's happening as long as you're touching me."

"Isn't that what happened when he kissed you?" Gideon's eyes opened and focused on me. "He's had his dick in you. He's fucked you . . . blown his load inside you."

I cringed away from the horrible bitterness in his tone, the vicious nastiness. I knew just how he felt. How badly the mental images could sting and claw until you felt like you were going mad. In my mind, he and Corinne had fucked dozens of times while I watched in sick, jealous fury.

He straightened suddenly, leaning forward to rub his thumb roughly across my lips. "He's had your mouth."

I grabbed his glass and drank what was left in it, hating the harsh taste and searing burn. I swallowed by force of will alone. My stomach roiled, protesting. The heat of the alcohol spread outward from my gut.

Gideon sagged back into the seat, his arm thrown across his face. I knew he was still seeing me kissing Brett. Knew it was eating a hole in his mind.

Dropping the glass on the floor, I surged between his legs and fumbled with his button fly.

He caught my fingers in an iron grip but kept his eyes covered with his forearm. "What the fuck are you doing?"

"Come in my mouth," I begged. "Wash it away."

There was a long pause. He sat there, utterly still except for the heavy lift and fall of his chest.

"Please, Gideon."

With muttered curse, he released me, his hand falling limply to his side. "Do it."

I rushed to get to him, my pulse pounding at the thought that he might change his mind and deny me . . . that he might decide he was done with me. The only help he gave me was a momentary lift of his hips, so I could yank his jeans and boxer briefs out of the way.

Then his big, beautiful cock was in my hands. My mouth. I moaned at the taste of him, at the warmth and satiny softness of his skin, at the smell of him. I nuzzled my cheek against his groin and balls, wanting his scent all over me, marking me as his. My tongue followed the thick veins coursing the length of him, licking him up and down.

I heard his teeth grind when I sucked him with long drawing pulls, moans of apology and bliss vibrating in my throat. It broke my heart that he was so silent, my vocal lover who always talked dirty to me. Always told me what he wanted and needed . . . how good he felt when I made love to him. He was holding himself back, denying me the satisfaction of knowing I pleased him.

Pumping the thick root with my fist, I milked him, sucking on the plush crown, luring his pre-cum to the tip where I could lick it up with rapid flutters of my tongue. His thighs bunched, his breath came in fierce pants. I felt him coil tight and I went wild, double-fisting him, my mouth working so hard that my jaw ached. His spine straightened, his head lifting from the seat only to slam backward as the first thick spurt exploded in my mouth.

I whimpered, his flavor igniting my senses, making me crave more. I swallowed convulsively, my hands pulling and rubbing on his throbbing penis to lure more of his rich, creamy semen onto my tongue. His body quaked as he came for long minutes, filling my mouth until he spilled out of the sides of my lips. He made no sound, as unnaturally silent as he'd been during the fight.

I would've sucked him off for hours. I wanted to, but he put both hands on my shoulders and urged me away. I looked up into his heartrendingly gorgeous face, saw his eyes glittering in the semi-darkness. He touched my lips with his thumb, smearing his semen over and around the swollen curves.

"Slide your tight cunt around me," he ordered hoarsely. "I've got more to give you."

Shaky and frightened by his harsh remoteness, I wriggled out of my boy shorts.

"Take it all off. Everything except the boots."

I did as he said, my body quickening at his command. I'd do anything he wanted. I would prove to him that I was his and only his. I would atone however he needed me to so he'd know I loved him. I unzipped my skirt and pushed it off, then whipped my tank top over my head and threw it on the opposite bench. My bra followed.

When I straddled him, Gideon caught my hips and looked up at me. "Are you wet?"

"Yes."

"It turns you on to suck my cock."

My nipples hardened further. The blunt, crude way he talked about sex turned me on, too. "Always."

"Why did you kiss him?"

The abrupt change in topic knocked me askew. My lower lip trembled. "I don't know."

He released me, reaching up and over his shoulders with both hands to grip the sides of the headrest. His biceps bulged with the pose. I was aroused by the sight, as I was by everything about him. I wanted to see his bare chest glistening with sweat, his abs tightening and flexing as he pumped his cock into me.

I licked my lips, tasting him. "Take your shirt off."

His gaze narrowed. "This isn't for you."

I stilled, my heart racing in my chest. He was using sex against me. In the limo where we'd first made love, in the same position I'd first taken him . . . "You're punishing me."

"You've earned it."

It didn't matter that he was right. If I'd earned it, so had he.

I gripped the top of the seat back for balance and wrapped the fingers of my other hand around his cock. He was still hard, still throbbing. A muscle in his neck twitched as I stroked him in my fist, priming him. I placed the wide crest between the lips of my cleft, rubbing him back and forth, coating him with the slickness of my desire.

My gaze never left his. I watched him as I teased us both, looking for any sign of the passionate lover I adored. He wasn't there. A furious stranger glared back at me, daring me, taunting me with his detachment.

I let the first thick inch push inside me, spreading me open. Then I slammed my hips down, crying out as he pierced me deep and stretched me almost unbearably.

"Jesus. Fuck," he bit out, shuddering. "Goddamn it."

His uncontrolled outburst spurred me. Digging my knees into the seat, I set my hands on either side of his and lifted, pulling off him, my trembling sex clinging tightly. I pushed back down, the glide easier now that he was wet from me. When my buttocks hit his thighs I found his muscles hard as stone, his body giving away the lie—he wasn't indifferent.

I lifted again, slowly, making us both feel every nuance of the delicious friction. When I pushed back down, I tried to be as stoic as he was, but the sensation of fullness, the heated connection, was too exquisite to contain. I moaned, and he shifted restlessly, his hips moving in a delicious little circle before he could stop himself.

"You feel so good," I whispered, stroking his raging cock with my eager, aching sex. Sliding up and down. "You're all I need, Gideon. All I want. You were made for me."

"You forgot that," he bit out, his knuckles white from his grip on the seat back.

I wondered if he was just holding on or physically restraining himself from reaching for me. "Never. I could never forget. You're a part of me."

"Tell me why you kissed him."

"I don't know." I rested my damp forehead against his, feeling the tears burning behind my eyes. "God, Gideon. I swear I don't know."

"Then shut up and make me come."

If he'd slapped my face, it couldn't have shocked me more. I straightened and leaned away from him. "Fuck you."

"Now you're getting the idea."

Hot tears slid down my face. "Don't treat me like a whore."

"Eva." His voice was low and raspy, filled with warning, but his eyes were dark and desolate. Filled with pain that matched my own. "You want to stop, you know what to say."

Crossfire. With one word I could unmistakably, irrefutably put an end to this agony. But I couldn't use it now. Just the fact that he brought up my safe word told me he was testing me. Pushing me. He had an agenda, and if I gave up now, I'd never know what it was.

Reaching behind me, I set my hands on his knees. I arched my back and dragged my soaked sex along the rigid length of his cock, then slammed back down. I adjusted the angle, lifted and fell again, gasping at the feel of him. Mad as hell or not, my body worshipped his. Loved the feel of him, the sense of *rightness* that was there despite the anger and hurt.

His breath was powering out of his lungs with every plunge of my hips. His body was hot, so hot, radiating heat like a blast furnace. I pumped my hips. Up. Down. Taking the pleasure he refused to give me. My thighs, buttocks, stomach, and core tightened with every lift, fisting him from root to tip. They relaxed when I dropped, letting him sink deep.

I fucked him with everything I had, pounding myself onto his cock. His breath hissed out between his clenched teeth. Then he was coming hard, jetting inside me so fiercely I felt each scorching burst of semen like a separate thrust. I cried out, loving the feel of it, chasing an orgasm that would shatter me. I was wound so tightly, my body desperate for release after pleasing him twice.

But he moved, grabbing me by the waist and restraining my movements, holding himself deep as he pumped me full. I choked off a scream when I realized he was deliberately preventing me from coming.

"Tell me why, Eva," he growled. *"Why?"*

"I don't know!" I yelled, trying to grind my hips onto him, pounding his shoulders with my fists when his grip tightened.

Holding me pinned to his pelvis and filled with his cock, Gideon pushed to his feet and everything shifted. He pulled out of me, flipped me to face away from him, then bent me over the edge of the seat with my knees on the floorboard. With one hand at the small of my back, holding me down, he cupped my sex and rubbed, massaging his semen into my cleft. He spread it around, coating me with it. My hips circled, seeking that perfect bit of pressure to get me off . . .

He kept it from me. Deliberately.

The pounding in my clit and the needy clenching of my empty core was driving me mad, my body hungry for release. He pushed two fingers into me and my nails dug into the black leather seat. He finger-fucked me leisurely, sliding lazily in and out, keeping me on the edge.

"Gideon," I sobbed, the sensitive tissues inside me rippling greedily around him. I was coated in sweat, barely able to breathe. I began to pray for the car to stop, for us to reach our destination, holding my breath in desperate anticipation of escape. But the limo never pulled over. It kept driving and driving, and I was restrained so completely that I couldn't rise up enough to see where we were.

He folded over my back, his cock lying within the seam of my ass. "Tell me why, Eva," he crooned in my ear. "You knew I'd be coming after you . . . that I'd find you . . ."

My eyes squeezed shut, my hands clenching into fists. "I. Don't. Know. Damn you! I don't fucking know!"

His fingers pulled free and then his cock was pushing into me. My sex spasmed around the delicious hardness, sucking him deeper. I heard his breath catch on a muffled groan, and then he was taking me.

I cried with the pleasure of it, my entire body shivering with delight as he fucked me thoroughly, the wide head of his gorgeous penis rubbing and tugging at tender, hyperstimulated nerves. The pressure built and built, brewing like a storm . . .

"*Yes,*" I gasped, stretched tight with anticipation.

He pulled out at the first grasp of my sex and left me hanging on the precipice again. I screamed with frustration, fighting to get up and away from the lover who'd become the source of unbearable torment.

He whispered in my ear like the devil himself. "Tell me why, Eva. Are you thinking of him now? Are you wishing it were his cock inside you? Wishing it were his cock fucking your perfect little cunt?"

I screamed again. "I hate you! You're a sadistic, selfish son of a—"

He was in me again, filling me, stroking rhythmically into my quivering core.

Unable to stand it a minute longer, I struggled to reach my clit with my fingers, knowing a single stroke would have me coming violently.

"No." Gideon caught my wrists and held my hands down on the seat, his thighs between my own, keeping my legs spread wide so he could sink deep. Over and over. The tempo of his thrusts unfaltering and relentless.

I was thrashing, screaming, losing my mind. He could make me come with just his cock, giving me an intense vaginal orgasm just from riding me at the right angle, rubbing his thick crest over and over whatever spot I needed him to, a random place inside me he knew instinctively every time he had me.

"I hate you," I sobbed, tears of frustration wetting my face and the seat beneath my cheek.

Bending over me, he gasped in my ear, "Tell me why, Eva."

Fury boiled up inside me and spewed out. "Because you deserved it! Because you should know what it feels like! How bad it hurts, you self-centered asshole!"

He stilled. I felt his breath heave out of him. My blood was roaring in my ears, so loudly that at first I thought I was deliriously imagining his voice softening with tenderness.

"Angel." His lips brushed over my shoulder blade, his hands releasing my wrists to slide beneath me and cup my full, heavy breasts. "My stubborn, beautiful angel. Finally, we get to the truth."

Gideon lifted me up, straightening me. Exhausted, my head lolled against his shoulder, my tears dripping onto my chest. I had nothing left to fight with, barely able to whimper when he rolled an aching nipple between his fingertips and reached between my splayed legs. His hips began to lunge, his cock pumping upward into me as he pinched the lips of my sex around my throbbing clit and rubbed.

I came with a hoarse cry of his name, my entire body convulsing in fierce tremors as the relief exploded through me. The orgasm lasted forever and Gideon was tireless, extending my pleasure with the perfect thrusts I'd been so frantic for earlier.

When I finally collapsed in his arms, panting and soaked with sweat, he lifted me carefully off him and placed me lengthwise on the bench seat. Shattered, I covered my face with my hands, incapable of stopping him when he pushed my thighs apart and put his mouth on me. I was soaked with his semen and he didn't care, tonguing and suckling my clit until I came again. And again.

My back arched with each orgasm, my breath soughing from my lungs. I lost track of how many times I climaxed after they began rolling into each other, cresting and waning like the tide. I tried to curl away from him, but he just straightened and yanked his shirt off, climbing over me with one knee on the seat and the other leg extended to the floor. He placed his hands on the window above my head, putting his body on display as he'd refused to do before.

I shoved at him. "No more! I can't take any more."

"I know." His abs tightened as he slid into me, his eyes on my face as he pushed carefully through swollen tissues. "I just want to be inside you."

My neck arched as he slid deeper, a low sound escaping me because it felt *sooo* good. As worn out and overstimulated as I was, I still craved to possess him and to be possessed by him. I knew I always would.

Bending his head, he pressed his lips to my forehead. "You're all I want, Eva. There's no one else. There will never be anyone else."

"Gideon." He understood, as I hadn't, that the night had fallen apart because of *my* jealousy and the deep-seated need I had to make him feel it for himself.

He kissed me softly, reverently, erasing every memory of anyone else's lips on mine.

◯

"Angel." Gideon's voice was a warm rasp in my ear. "Wake up."

I moaned, squeezing my eyes shut tighter and burying my face deeper in his neck. "Leave me alone, you sex fiend."

His silent laughter shook me. He pressed a hard kiss to my forehead and wiggled out from under me. "We're here."

Cracking one eye open, I watched him put his shirt back on. He'd never gotten out of his jeans. I realized the sun was out. I sat up and looked out the windows, gasping when I saw the ocean. We'd stopped for gas once but I hadn't been able to get my bearings or figure out where we were. Gideon had declined to tell me when I asked, saying only that it was a surprise.

"Where are we?" I breathed, thrilled by the sight of the sun climbing over the water. It had to be solidly into morning. Maybe even midmorning.

"North Carolina. Lift your arms."

I obeyed automatically, and he slid my tank top over my head. "I need my bra," I muttered, when I could see him again.

"No one's here to see you but me and we're going straight into the bathtub."

I looked again at the weathered shingle-covered building we'd parked beside. It was at least three stories, with wraparound decks and balconies on the front and sides, and a quaint single-door entrance off the back. It stood on stilts at the shoreline, so close to the water that I knew the tide must come up right beneath it. "How long have we been driving?"

"Almost ten hours." Gideon slid my skirt up my legs and I stood, allowing him to twist it straight and pull up the zipper. "Let's go."

He got out first, then held his hand out for me. The bracing, salty breeze hit my face, waking me. The rhythmic surge of the ocean grounded me to the moment and where we were. Angus was nowhere to be seen, which was a relief, since I was very aware of my lack of underwear. "Angus drove all night?"

"We switched drivers when we stopped for gas."

I looked at Gideon and my pulse stuttered at the tender, haunted way he was looking at me. A shadow of a bruise marred his jaw and I reached up to touch it, my chest aching when he nuzzled into my palm.

"Are you hurt anywhere else?" I asked, feeling so emotionally raw after the long night we'd had.

He caught my wrist and pulled my hand down to press flat over his heart. "Here."

My love . . . It had been hard on him, too. "I'm so sorry."

"So am I." He kissed my fingertips, then linked our hands and led me up to the house.

The door was unlocked and he walked right in. A wire mesh basket sat on a console just inside the door, holding a bottle of wine and two glasses tied with ribbon. As Gideon turned the dead bolt with a firm click, I plucked the *Welcome* envelope out and opened it. A key fell into my palm.

"We won't be needing that." He took the key from me and set it on the console. "For the next two days, we're going to be hermits together."

A hum of pleasure warmed me from the inside, followed by more than a little awe that a man like Gideon Cross could enjoy my company so much he didn't need anyone else.

"Come on," he said, tugging me toward the stairs. "We'll break into that wine later."

"Yeah. Coffee first."

I took in the décor of the house. It was rustic on the outside and modern contemporary on the inside. The wainscoted walls were painted a bright white and decorated with massive black-and-white photos of seashells. The furniture was all white, and most of the accessory pieces were glass and metal. It would have been stark if not for the gorgeous view of the ocean and the color introduced in the area rugs covering the hardwood floors and the collection of hardcover books filling built-in bookcases.

When we reached the top floor, I felt a flutter of happiness. The master suite was a totally open space, with only two support columns to break it up. Bouquets of white roses, white tulips, and white calla lilies covered nearly every flat surface, and some even sat on the floor in strategic areas. The bed was massive and covered in white satin, which made me think of a bridal suite, an impression reinforced by the black-and-white photo of a filmy scarf or veil blowing in the breeze hanging over the headboard.

I looked at Gideon. "Have you been here before?"

He reached up and freed my now-lopsided ponytail. "No. What reason would I have to come here?"

Right. He didn't take women anywhere but his hotel fuck pad—that he apparently still had. My eyes closed wearily as he ran his fingers through the loosened tresses of my hair. I didn't have the energy to get riled up about that.

"Take your clothes off, angel. I'll start the bath."

He backed up. I opened my eyes and caught him by the shirt. I didn't know what to say; I just didn't want him to go.

He understood, because he got me.

"I'm not going anywhere, Eva." Gideon cupped my jaw in his hands and stared into my eyes, showing me the intensity and laser focus that had snared me from the first. "If you wanted him, it wouldn't be enough for me to let you go. I want you too much. I want you with me, in my life, in my bed. If I can have that, nothing else matters. I'm not too proud to take what I can get."

I swayed into him, drawn to his obsessive and insatiable raw need for me, which reflected the depth of my need for him. My hand fisted in the cotton of his T-shirt.

"Angel," he breathed, lowering his head to press his cheek to mine. "You can't let me go, either."

He swept me up in his arms and carried me into the bathroom with him.

I RECLINED WITH my eyes closed, my back cradled against Gideon's chest, listening to the sound of lapping water as his hands glided lazily over me in the claw-foot tub.

He'd washed my hair and then my body, pampering me, spoiling me. I knew he was making up for last night and the method he'd used to get me to face the truth—a truth he'd clearly known but needed me to see as well.

How did he know me so well . . . better than I knew myself?

"Tell me about him," he murmured, his arms wrapping around my waist.

I took a deep breath. I'd been waiting for him to ask about Brett. I knew Gideon well, too. "First, tell me if he's okay."

There was a pause before he answered. "There's no permanent damage. Would you care if there was?"

"Of course I'd care." I heard his teeth grind.

"I want to know about you two," he demanded tightly.

"No."

"Eva . . ."

"Don't take that tone with me, Gideon. I'm tired of being an open book for you while you hoard all your secrets." My head rolled to the side so that my cheek was pressed against his damp chest. "If all I get of you is your body, I'll take it. But I can't give you more in return."

"You mean you *won't*. Let's be—"

"I *can't*." I pulled away from him, twisting so that I faced him. "Look what it's doing to me! I *hurt* you last night. On purpose. Without even realizing it, because the resentment is eating at me even while I'm convincing myself that I can live with everything you're not telling me."

Sitting up, he spread his arms. "I'm wide open for you, Eva! You're making it sound like you don't know me . . . that all we have is sex . . . when you know me better than anyone else."

"Let's talk about what I *don't* know. Why do you own so much of Vidal Records? Why do you hate your family home? Why are you estranged from your parents? What's between you and Dr. Terrence Lucas? Where'd you go the other night when I had that nightmare? What's behind *your* nightmares? Why—"

"Enough!" he snapped, shoving his hands through his wet hair.

I settled back, watching and waiting as he clearly struggled with himself. "You should know you can tell me anything," I said softly.

"Can I?" He pierced me with his gaze. "Don't you have enough to look past as it is? How much shit can I pile on you before you run like hell?"

Laying my arms along the rim of the tub, I leaned my head back and closed my eyes. "Okay, then. We'll just be fuck buddies who bitch to a therapist once a week. Good to know."

"I screwed her," he spat. "There. Do you feel better?"

I shot up so fast, water surged over the edge of the tub. My stomach cramped. "You screwed Corinne?"

"No, damn it." His face was flushed. "Lucas's wife."

"Oh . . ." I remembered the photo I'd found of her through my Google search. "She's a redhead," I said lamely.

"My attraction to Anne was based entirely on her relationship to Lucas."

I frowned, confused. "So things were off between you and Dr. Lucas *before* you slept with his wife? Or because of it?"

Gideon set his elbow on the side of the tub and scrubbed at his face. "He alienated me from my family. I returned the favor."

"You broke them up?"

"I broke *her*." He exhaled harshly. "She came on to me at a fundraiser. I brushed her off until I learned who she was. I knew it'd kill Lucas to know I'd banged her, and the opening was there so I took it. It was just supposed to be that once, but Anne contacted me the next day. Because it would hurt him more to know she couldn't get enough, I let it go on. When she was ready to leave him for me, I sent her back to her husband."

I stared at him, noting his defiant embarrassment. He would do it again, but he was ashamed of what he'd done.

"Say something!" he snapped.

"Did she think you loved her?"

"No. Fuck. I'm an asshole for nailing another man's wife, but I didn't promise her anything. I was screwing Lucas through her—I didn't expect for her to become collateral damage. I wouldn't have let it get that far, if I had."

"Gideon." I sighed and shook my head.

"What?" He was practically bristling with restless, anxious energy. "Why did you say my name like that?"

"Because you're ridiculously dense for such a smart guy. You were sleeping with her regularly and didn't expect her to fall in love with you?"

"Jesus." His head fell back with a groan. "Not this again."

Then he straightened abruptly. "Actually, you know what? You keep on thinking I'm God's gift to women, angel. It's better for me if you believe I'm the best you can get."

I splashed him. The ease with which he dismissed his appeal was another way he mirrored me. We knew our strengths and played up our assets. But we couldn't see what made us unique enough for someone to really love us.

Gideon lunged forward and caught my hands. "Now, tell me what the fuck you had with Brett Kline."

"You didn't tell me what Dr. Lucas did to piss you off."

"Yes, I did."

"Not the details," I argued.

"It's your turn to spill. Out with it."

It took me a long time to get the words out. No guy wanted a recovering slut for his girlfriend. But Gideon waited patiently. Obstinately. I knew he wasn't going to let me get out of the tub until I told him about Brett.

"I was nothing but a convenient fuck for Brett," I confessed in a rush, wanting to get it over with, "and I put up with it—went out of my way for it—because in that period of my life, sex was the only way I knew how to feel loved."

"He wrote a love song about you, Eva."

I looked away. "The truth wouldn't make much of a ballad, would it?"

"Did you love him?"

"I— No." I looked at Gideon when he exhaled audibly, as if he'd been holding his breath. "I had a crush on him and the way he sings, but it was totally superficial. I never got to really know him."

His entire body visibly relaxed. "He was part of a . . . phase? That's it?"

I nodded and tried to pull my hands free of his, wishing I could get past my feelings of shame. I didn't blame Brett or any of the guys who'd drifted through my life then. I had no one to blame but myself.

"Come here." Gideon caught me by the waist and pulled me closer, tucking me against his chest again. His embrace was the most wonderful feeling in the world. His hands stroked the length of my spine, gentling me. "I won't lie. I want to beat the hell out of any man who's had you—you'd be smart to keep them the hell away from me—but nothing in your past can change how I feel about you. And God knows I'm no saint."

"I wish I could make it go away," I whispered. "I don't like remembering the girl I was then."

He rested his chin atop the crown of my head. "I get it. It didn't matter how long I showered after I'd been with Anne, it was never long enough to feel clean."

I tightened my arms around his waist, giving comfort and acceptance. And gratefully accepting both in return.

THE white silk robe I found hanging in the closet was gorgeous. It was lined with the softest terry cloth and embroidered with silver thread at the cuffs. I loved it, which was a good thing since it was, apparently, the only article of clothing for me in the entire house.

I watched Gideon pull on a pair of black silk pajama pants and tie the drawstring. "Why do you get clothes and I get a robe?"

He glanced up at me through a lock of inky hair that draped over his brow. "Because I'm the one who arranged everything?"

"Fiend."

"Just makes it easier for me to keep up with your insatiable sexual demands."

"*My* insatiable demands?" I headed into the bathroom to take the towel off my head. "I clearly remember begging to be left alone last night. Or was it this morning, after an all-nighter?"

He filled the doorway behind me. "You'll be begging again tonight, too. I'll go make some coffee."

In the mirror, I watched him turn away and saw the darkening bruise on his side. It was low on his back, where I hadn't had a chance to see it before. I spun around. "Gideon! You're hurt. Let me see."

"I'm fine." He was partway down the stairs before I could stop him. "Don't take too long."

Guilt swamped me, and a terrible urge to cry. My hand shook as I ran a wide-toothed comb through my damp hair. The bathroom had been stocked with my usual toiletries, demonstrating once again how thoughtful and attentive Gideon was, which only emphasized my deficits. I was making his life hell. After all he'd already suffered, my issues were the last thing he needed to deal with.

I took the stairs down to the first floor and found myself unable to join Gideon in the kitchen. I needed a minute to pull myself together and put on a happy face. I didn't want to ruin the weekend for him, too.

I stepped out through the French doors that led to the deck. The roar of the surf and the biting salt spray hit me at once. The hem of my robe whipped gently in the ocean breeze, cooling me in a way I found invigorating.

Taking a deep breath, I gripped the railing and closed my eyes, trying to find the peace I needed to keep Gideon from worrying. My problem was *me*, and I didn't want to concern him with something he couldn't change. Only *I* could make myself a stronger person, and I needed to, if I wanted to make him happy and offer him the security he so desperately wanted from me.

The door opened behind me, and I took a deep breath before turning to face him with a smile. Gideon came out with two steaming mugs gripped in one hand—one filled with black coffee and the other lightened with half-and-half. I knew it would be made perfectly to my tastes and delicious, because Gideon knew exactly what I liked. Not because I'd told him, but because he paid attention to everything about me.

"Stop beating yourself up," he ordered sternly, setting the mugs on the railing.

I sighed. Of course I couldn't hide my mood from him with just a smile. He saw right through me.

He caught my face in his hands and glared down at me. "It's over and done with. Forget it."

I reached out and ran my fingertips over the place where I'd seen the bruise.

"It needed to happen," he said curtly. "No. Shut up and listen to me. I thought I understood your feelings about Corinne, and, frankly, I thought you just weren't dealing with it well. But I had no clue. I was a self-centered idiot."

"I'm *not* dealing with it well. I hate her fucking guts. I can't think about her without feeling violent."

"I get it now. I didn't before." His mouth twisted ruefully. "Sometimes it takes something drastic to shake me up. Luckily, you've always been very good at getting my attention."

"Don't try to tease this away, Gideon. You could've been seriously hurt because of me."

He caught me by the waist when I would've turned away. "I *was* seriously hurt because of you. Seeing you in another guy's arms, kissing him . . ." His eyes grew hot and dark. "It shredded me, Eva. Cut me open and left me bleeding. I kicked his ass in self-defense."

"Oh, God," I breathed, devastated by his brutal honesty. "Gideon."

"I'm disgusted with myself for not being more understanding about Corinne. If a kiss could make me feel like that . . ." He wrapped his arms tight around me, one arm banding my hips while the other crossed my back so he could grip the back of my head. Capturing me.

"If you ever cheated on me," he said hoarsely, "it would kill me."

Turning my head, I pressed my lips to his throat. "That stupid kiss meant nothing. Less than nothing."

His hand gripped my hair and tilted my head back. "You don't understand what your kisses mean to me, Eva. For you to just give one away and call it stupid—"

Gideon dipped his head and sealed his mouth over mine. It started softly, sweet and teasing, his tongue stroking across my bottom lip. I opened my mouth, my tongue flicking out to touch his. He tilted his head and licked into my mouth. Fast, shallow licks that stirred a simmering desire.

I reached up and slid my fingers into his damp hair, pushing up onto my tiptoes to deepen the kiss. I moaned when he sucked on my tongue, leaning heavily against him. His lips moved against mine, growing wetter and hotter. We ate at each other, growing wilder by the second until we were fucking each other's mouths, passionately mating with lips and tongues and tiny bites. I was panting with my hunger for him, my lips slanting over his, needy sounds spilling from my throat.

His kisses were gifts. He kissed with everything he had, with power and passion and hunger and love. He held nothing back, giving everything, exposing everything.

Tension gripped his powerful frame, his rough satin skin growing feverishly hot. His tongue was plunging into my mouth, tangling with mine, his quickened breaths mingling with my own and filling my lungs. My senses were drenched in him, in his flavor and scent, my mind spinning as I angled my head, seeking a deeper taste. Wanting to lick deeper, suck harder. Devour.

I wanted him so much.

His hands ran up and down my spine, trembling and restless. He groaned and my sex tightened in answer. Tugging at the belt of my robe, he loosened it, spreading open the halves to grip my bare hips in his hands. He tugged on my lower lip, sinking his teeth into it, his tongue caressing it. I whimpered, wanting more, my mouth feeling swollen and sensitive.

No matter how close we were, it was never close enough.

Gideon gripped both cheeks of my ass and pulled me up hard against him, his erection like hot steel burning my belly through the thin silk of his pants. He released my lip and took my mouth again, filling me with the taste of his desire and need, his tongue a velvet lash of tormenting pleasure.

A hard shudder shook him and he growled, his hips circling. His fingers bit into my rear and his groan vibrated against my lips. I felt his cock jerk between us, then scorching warmth spread over my skin. He came with a tormented groan, soaking the silk between us.

I cried out, melting and aching, so insanely aroused by the knowledge that I could make him lose control with just a kiss.

His grip loosened, his lungs heaving. "Your kisses are *mine.*"

"Yes. *Gideon* . . ." I was shaken, left emotionally raw and open by the most erotic moment of my life.

He sank to his knees and tongued me to a shattering climax.

⌒

WE showered and napped the morning away. It felt so good to sleep beside him again, with my head pillowed on his chest, my arm draped over his rock-hard stomach, and my legs tangled with his.

When we woke shortly after one in the afternoon, I was starving. We headed down to the kitchen together and I found that I liked the ultra-stark modern look in that space. The watered-glass cabinet doors and granite paired beautifully with the dark hardwood. Better yet, the pantry was fully stocked. There was no need to leave the house for anything.

We went the easy route and made sandwiches, which we took into the living room and ate cross-legged on the couch facing each other.

I was halfway through when I caught Gideon watching me with a grin.

"What?" I asked, around a bite.

"Arnoldo's right. It's fun watching you eat."

"Shut up."

His grin widened. He looked so carefree and happy it made my heart hurt.

"How did you find this place?" I asked him. "Or how did Scott find it?"

"I found it." He shoved a potato chip in his mouth and licked the salt from his lips, which I found sexy as hell. "I wanted to take you away to an island, where no one could bother us. This is pretty close to that, without the travel time. I planned for us to fly down originally."

I ate thoughtfully, remembering the long drive. As insanity-inducing as the trip had been, there was something exciting about the idea of him rearranging our schedule just to fuck me senseless

REFLECTED IN YOU · 193

over hours, using my need for him to face a truth I'd blocked. Imagining all the frustration and fury that must have driven his plans . . . his thoughts focused on unleashing all of that seething passion on my helpless, willing body . . .

"You're getting that fuck-me look on your face," he observed. "And you call me a sex fiend."

"Sorry."

"Not complaining."

I rewound my thoughts to earlier in the evening. "Arnoldo doesn't like me anymore."

One dark brow arched. "You're getting the fuck-me look and thinking about Arnoldo? Do I have to kick *his* ass now, too?"

"No. Jeez. I threw that out there to distract us from sex and because it needs to be addressed."

He shrugged. "I'll talk to him."

"I think *I* should do it, for what it's worth."

Gideon studied me with those amazing blue eyes. "What would you say?"

"That he's right. I don't deserve you and I fucked up bad. But I'm crazy in love with you and I'd like a chance to prove to you both that I can be what you need."

"Angel, if I needed you more, I couldn't function." He lifted my hand to his lips to kiss my fingertips. "And I don't care what anyone else thinks. We've got our own rhythm and it works for us."

"*Does* it work for you?" I grabbed my bottle of iced tea off the coffee table and took a drink. "I know it drains you. Do you ever think it's just too hard or too painful?"

"You do realize how suggestive that sounds, right?"

"Oh my God." I laughed. "You're terrible."

His eyes sparkled with amusement. "That's not what you usually say."

Shaking my head, I went back to eating.

"I'd rather argue with you, angel, than laugh with anyone else."

Jesus. It took me a minute to be able to swallow the last bite in my mouth. "You know . . . I love you madly."

He smiled. "Yes, I know."

AFTER we'd cleaned up the mess from lunch, I tossed the sponge into the sink and said, "I need to make my Saturday phone call to my dad."

Gideon shook his head. "Not possible. You'll have to wait 'til Monday."

"Huh? Why?"

He caged me to the counter by gripping the edge on either side of me. "No phones."

"Are you serious? What about your cell phone?" I'd left mine at home before we went to the concert, knowing I had no place to carry it and having no intention of using it anyway.

"It's heading back to New York with the limo. No Internet, either. I had the modem and phones taken out before we got here."

I was speechless. With all the responsibilities and commitments he had, cutting himself off for the weekend was . . . unbelievable. "Wow. When's the last time you fell off the face of the earth like this?"

"Hmm . . . that would be never."

"There have to be at least a half dozen people freaking out because they can't run something by you."

He lifted one shoulder in a careless shrug. "They'll deal with it."

Pleasure surged through me. "I have you all to myself?"

"Completely." His mouth curved in a wicked smile. "What will you do with me, angel?"

I smiled back, ecstatically happy. "I'm sure I'll think of something."

WE went for a walk on the beach.

I rolled up a pair of Gideon's pajama bottoms and put on my white tank top, which was indecent since my bra was heading back to New York along with Gideon's cell phone.

"I have died and gone to heaven," he pronounced, checking out my chest as we strolled along the shore, "where the embodiment of every wet-dream, spank-bank fantasy of my adolescence is real and totally mine."

I bumped my shoulder into his. "How do you go from devastatingly romantic to crude in the space of an hour?"

"It's another one of my many talents." His gaze dropped again to the prominent points of my nipples, which were hard from exposure to the ocean breeze. He squeezed my hand and gave an exaggerated happy sigh. "Heaven with my angel. It doesn't get any better than this."

I had to agree. The beach was beautiful in a moody, untamed way that reminded me a lot of the man whose hand I held. The sounds of the surf and the crying of the gulls filled me with a unique sense of contentment. The water was cold on my bare feet, and the wind whipped my hair across my face. It had been a long time since I'd felt so good, and I was grateful to Gideon for giving us this time away to enjoy each other. We were perfect together when we were alone.

"You like it here," he noted.

"I've always loved being close to the water. My mother's second husband had a lake house. I remember walking along the shore like this with her and thinking I'd buy something on the water for myself one day."

He released my hand and draped his arm around my shoulders instead. "So let's do it. How about this place? You like it?"

I glanced up at him, loving the sight of the wind sifting through his hair. "Is it for sale?"

He looked down the stretch of beach in front of us. "Everything's for sale at the right price."

"Do *you* like it?"

"The interior's a little cold with all that white, although I like the master bedroom the way it is. We could change all the rest. Make it more us."

"Us," I repeated, wondering what that would be. I loved his apartment with its old world elegance. I think he felt comfortable at my place, which was more modern traditional. Combining the two . . . "Big step, buying a property together."

"Inevitable step," he corrected. "You told Dr. Petersen failure isn't an option."

"Yep, I did." We walked a little farther in silence. I tried to figure out how I felt about Gideon wanting to have a more tangible tie between us. I also wondered why he'd choose joint property ownership as the way to achieve it. "So I take it you like it here, too?"

"I like the beach." He brushed his hair back from his face. "There's a picture of me and my father building a sand castle on a beach."

It was a miracle my steps didn't falter. Gideon volunteered so little information about his past that when he did, it was nearly an earthshaking event. "I'd like to see it."

"My mother has it." We took a few more steps before he said, "I'll get it for you."

"I'll go with you." He hadn't told me why yet, but he'd told me once that the Vidal home was a nightmare for him. I suspected that whatever was at the root of his parasomnia had taken place there.

Gideon's chest expanded on a deep breath. "I can have it couriered."

"All right." I turned my head to kiss his bruised knuckles where they rested on my shoulder. "But my offer stands."

"What did you think of my mother?" he asked suddenly.

"She's very beautiful. Very elegant. She seemed gracious." I studied him, seeing Elizabeth Vidal's inky black hair and stunning blue eyes. "She also seems to love you a lot. It was in her eyes when she looked at you."

He kept looking straight ahead. "She didn't love me enough."

My breath left me in a rush. Because I didn't know what had given him such tormenting nightmares, I'd wondered if maybe she'd loved him too much. It was a relief to know that wasn't the case. It was awful enough that his father committed suicide. To be betrayed by his mother, too, might be more than he could ever recover from.

"How much is enough, Gideon?"

His jaw tightened. His chest expanded on a deep breath. "She didn't believe me."

I came to a dead stop and pivoted to face him. "You told her what happened to you? You told her and she didn't believe you?"

His gaze was trained over my head. "It doesn't matter now. It's long done."

"Bullshit. It matters. It matters a lot." I was furious for him. Furious that a mother hadn't done her job and stood by her child. Furious that the child had been Gideon. "I bet it hurts like fucking hell, too."

His gaze lowered to my face. "Look at you, so pissed off and upset. I shouldn't have said anything."

"You should've said something earlier."

The tension in his shoulders eased and his mouth curved ruefully. "I haven't told you anything."

"Gideon—"

"And of course you believe me, angel. You've had to sleep in a bed with me."

I grabbed his face in my hands and stared hard up into his eyes. "I. Believe. You."

His face contorted with pain for a split second before he picked me up in a bear hug. "Eva."

I slung my legs around his waist and wrapped my arms around his shoulders. "I believe you."

WHEN we got back to the house, Gideon went into the kitchen to open a bottle of wine and I perused the bookshelves in the living room, smiling when I came across the first book in the series I'd told him about, the one where'd I'd picked up his nickname, *ace*.

We sprawled on the couch and I read to him while he played absently with my hair. He was in a pensive mood after our walk, his mind seemingly far from me. I didn't resent that. We'd given each other a lot to think about over the last couple of days.

When the tide came in, it did indeed rush up under the house, which sounded amazing and looked even more so. We stepped out onto the deck and watched it ebb and flow, turning the house into an island in the surf.

"Let's make s'mores," I said, while leaning over the railing with Gideon wrapped around my back. "On that portable patio fireplace."

His teeth caught my earlobe and he whispered, "I want to lick melted chocolate off your body."

Yes, please . . . I teased him, "Wouldn't that burn?"

"Not if I do it right."

I turned to face him, and he picked me up and sat me on the wide handrail. Then he stepped between my legs and hugged me around the hips. There was a wonderful peace that accompanied the twilight and we both sank into it. I ran my hands through his hair, just as the night breeze did.

"Have you talked to Ireland at all?" I asked, thinking of his half sister, who was as beautiful as their mother. I'd met her at a Vidal Records party, and it became evident pretty quickly that she was hungry for any word or news about her eldest brother.

"No."

"What do you think about bringing her over for dinner when my dad's in town?"

Gideon's head tilted to the side as he observed me. "You want to invite a seventeen-year-old to dinner with me and your dad."

"No, I want your family to meet my family."

"She'll be bored."

"How would you know?" I challenged. "In any case, I think your sister hero-worships you. As long as you pay attention to her, I'm sure she'll be thrilled."

"Eva." He sighed, clearly exasperated. "Be real. I haven't the slightest idea how to entertain a teenage girl."

"Ireland's not some random kid, she's—"

"She might as well be!" He scowled at me.

It struck me then. "You're afraid of her."

"Come on," he scoffed.

"You are. She scares you." And I doubted it had anything to do with his sister's age or that she was a girl.

"What's gotten into you?" he complained. "You're stuck on Ireland. Leave her alone."

"She's the only family you've got, Gideon." And I was willing to support that choice. His half brother, Christopher, was an asshole, and his mother didn't deserve to have him in her life.

"I have *you!*"

"Baby." I sighed and wrapped my legs around him. "Yes, you've got me. But there's room for more people who love you in your life."

"She doesn't love me," he muttered. "She doesn't know me."

"I think you're wrong about that, but if not, she'd love you if she knew you. So let her know you."

"Enough. Let's go back to talking about s'mores."

I tried to stare him down, but it was impossible. When he considered a subject exhausted, there was no continuing it. So I'd have to go around it instead.

"You wanna talk about s'mores, ace?" I traced my lower lip with my tongue. "All that melty gooey chocolate on our fingers."

Gideon's gaze narrowed.

I ran my splayed fingers over his shoulders and down his chest. "I could be persuaded to let you smear that chocolate all over me. I could also be persuaded to smear some all over you."

His brow arched. "Are you trying to bribe me with sex again?"

"Did I say that?" I blinked innocently. "I don't think I said that."

"It was implied. So let's be clear." His voice was dangerously low, his eyes dark as his hand slid up under the hem of my tank top and cupped my bare breast. "I'll invite Ireland to dinner with your father because it'll make you happy and that makes me happy."

"Thank you," I said breathlessly, because he'd begun to tug rhythmically on my nipple, making me whimper in delight.

"I'm going to do whatever the hell I want with melted chocolate and your body because it'll please me and that will please you. I say when, I say how. Repeat that."

"You say—" I gasped as his mouth wrapped around my other nipple through the ribbed cotton. "Oh, God."

He nipped me with his teeth. "Finish."

My entire body tightened, so quick to respond to that authoritative tone. "You say when. You say how."

"There are things you can bargain with, angel, but your body and sex aren't negotiable."

My hands clutched his hair, an instinctive response to his relentless, delicious milking of my sensitive nipple. I gave up trying to understand why I wanted him in control. I just did. "What else can I bargain with? You have everything."

"Your time and attention are the two things you can leverage. I'll do anything for them."

A shiver moved through me. "I'm wet for you," I whispered.

Gideon stepped away from the railing, carrying me with him. "Because that's how I want you."

12

GIDEON AND I arrived back in Manhattan just before midnight on Sunday. We'd spent the previous night sleeping apart, but most of the day together in the master bed. Kissing and touching. Laughing and whispering.

By silent agreement we didn't talk about painful things during the rest of our time away. We didn't turn on the television or radio, because it seemed wrong to share our time with anyone. We walked on the beach again. We made long, slow, lazy love on the third-story deck. We played cards and he won every hand. We recharged and reminded ourselves that what we'd found with each other was worth fighting for.

It was the most perfect day of my life.

We returned to my apartment when we got back into the city. Gideon unlocked the door for us with the key I'd given him, and we entered the darkened space as quietly as possible so that we didn't wake Cary. Gideon gave me one of his soul-melting kisses good night and headed to the guest room, and I crawled into my lonely bed without him. Missing him. I wondered how long we'd be sleeping apart from each other. Months? Years?

Hating to think of it, I closed my eyes and started to drift.

The light flicked on.

"Eva. Get up." Gideon strode into the room and straight to my dresser, digging through my clothes.

I blinked at him, noting that he'd changed into slacks and a button-down dress shirt. "What's wrong?"

"It's Cary," he said grimly. "He's in the hospital."

A cab was waiting for us at the curb when we left my apartment building. Gideon ushered me in, then slid in beside me.

The cab seemed to pull away very slowly. Everything seemed to be moving slowly.

I clutched at Gideon's sleeve. "What happened?"

"He was attacked Friday night."

"How do you know?"

"Your mother and Stanton both left messages on my cell phone."

"My mother . . . ?" I looked at him blankly. "Why didn't she . . . ?"

No, she *couldn't* call me. I hadn't had my phone. Guilt and worry drowned me, making it hard to breathe.

"Eva." He put his arm around my shoulders, urging me to rest my head against him. "Don't worry until we know more."

"It's been *days*, Gideon. And I wasn't here."

Tears poured down my face and wouldn't stop, even after we arrived at the hospital. I barely registered the exterior of the building, my attention dulled by the hard-driving anxiety pounding through me. I thanked God for Gideon, who was so calm and in control. A staff member provided the number of Cary's room, but his helpfulness ended there. Gideon made a few middle-of-the-night phone calls that got me access to see Cary, even though it was well outside visiting hours. Gideon had been a very generous benefactor at times and that wasn't easily dismissed or forgotten.

When I stepped into Cary's private room and saw him, my heart shattered so completely, my knees went weak. Only Gideon kept me from falling. The man I thought of as my brother, the best friend I'd ever had or ever would have, lay silent and unmoving in the bed. His head was bandaged and his eyes blackened. One of his arms was stuck with intravenous lines, while the other was in a cast. I wouldn't have recognized him, if I hadn't known who he was.

Flowers covered every flat surface, cheerful and colorful bouquets. There were balloons, too, and a few cards. I knew some would be from my mother and Stanton, who were certainly paying for Cary's care as well.

We were his family. And everyone had been there for him but me.

Gideon led me closer, his arm tight around my waist to hold me up. I was sobbing, the tears flowing thick and hot. It was everything I could do to remain silent.

Still, Cary must have heard me or sensed me. His eyelids fluttered, then opened. His beautiful green eyes were bloodshot and unfocused. It took him a minute to find me. When he did, he blinked a few times, and then tears started rolling down his temples.

"Cary." I rushed to him and slipped my hand in his. "I'm here."

He gripped me so tightly, it was painful. "Eva."

"I'm sorry I took so long. I didn't have my phone. I had no idea. I would've been here if I'd known."

"S'okay. You're here now." His throat worked on a swallow. "God . . . everything hurts."

"I'll get a nurse," Gideon said, running his hand down my back before slipping silently out of the room.

I saw a small pitcher and cup with straw on the rolling tray table. "Are you thirsty?"

"Very."

"Can I sit you up? Or no?" I was afraid to do anything to cause him pain.

"Yeah."

Using the remote lying near his hand, I raised the top part of the bed so that he was reclined. Then I brought the straw to his lips and watched him drink greedily.

He relaxed with a sigh. "You're a sight for sore eyes, baby girl."

"What the hell happened?" I set the empty cup down and grabbed his hand again.

"Fuck if I know." His voice was weak, almost a whisper. "Got jumped. With a bat."

"With *a bat*?" Just the thought made me physically ill. The brutality of it. The violence . . . "Was he insane?"

"Of course," he snapped, a deep line of pain between his brows.

I backed up a half step. "I'm sorry."

"No, don't. Shit. I'm—" His eyes closed. "I'm exhausted."

Just then the nurse came in wearing scrubs decorated with cartoon tongue depressors and animated stethoscopes. She was young and pretty, with dark hair and sloe eyes. She checked Cary over, took his blood pressure, then pressed the button on a remote wrapped around the guardrail.

"You can self-administer every thirty minutes for pain," she told him. "Just press this button. It won't dispense a dose if it's not time, so you don't have to worry about pressing it too often."

"Once is too often," he muttered, looking at me.

I understood his reluctance; he had an addictive personality. He'd traveled a short ways down the junkie road before I kicked some sense into him.

But it was a relief to see the lines of pain on his forehead smooth out and his breathing settle into a deeper rhythm.

The nurse looked at me. "He needs his rest. You should come back during visiting hours."

Cary looked at me desperately. "Don't go."

"She's not going anywhere," Gideon said, reentering the room. "I've arranged to have a cot brought in tonight."

I didn't think it was possible to love Gideon more than I already did, but he somehow kept finding ways to prove me wrong.

The nurse smiled shyly at Gideon.

"Cary could use more water," I told her, watching her pull her gaze reluctantly away from my boyfriend to look at me.

She grabbed the pitcher and left the room.

Gideon stepped closer to the bed and spoke to Cary. "Tell me what happened."

Cary sighed. "Trey and I went out Friday, but he had to bail early. I walked him out to grab a cab, but it was nuts right in front of the club, so we went around the corner. He'd just taken off when I got nailed in the back of the head. Took me straight down and whaled on me a few times. Never got a chance to defend myself."

My hands began to shake, and Cary's thumb rubbed soothingly over the back.

"Hey," he murmured. "Teaches me. Don't stick my dick in the wrong chick."

"What?"

I watched Cary's eyes drift shut, and a moment later it was clear he was sleeping. I glanced helplessly across the bed at Gideon.

"I'll look into it," he said. "Step out with me for a minute."

I followed him, my gaze repeatedly turning back to Cary. When the door closed behind us, I said, "God, Gideon. He looks terrible."

"He got knocked around good," he said grimly. "He's got a skull fracture, a nasty concussion, three cracked ribs, and a broken arm."

The list of injuries was horribly painful to listen to. "I don't understand why someone would do this."

He pulled me close and pressed his lips to my forehead. "The doctor said it's possible Cary will be allowed to leave in a day or two, so I'll make arrangements for home care. I'll also let your work know you won't be coming in."

"Cary's agency needs to know."

"I'll see to it."

"Thank you." I hugged him hard. "What would I do without you?"

"You're never going to find out."

My mother woke me at nine the next morning, gliding fretfully into Cary's room as soon as visiting hours began. She pulled me out to the hallway, drawing the attention of everyone in the immediate area. It was early, but she looked amazing in eye-catching red-soled Louboutins and an ivory sleeveless sheath dress.

"Eva. I can't believe you went the entire weekend without your cell phone! What were you thinking? What if there had been an emergency?"

"There *was* an emergency."

"Exactly!" She threw up one hand, since the other arm had her clutch tucked beneath it. "No one could get hold of you or Gideon. He left a message saying that he was taking you away for the weekend, but no one knew where you were. I can't believe he was so irresponsible! What was he thinking?"

"Thank you," I interjected, because she was getting wound up and repeating herself, "for taking care of Cary. It means a lot to me."

"Well, of course." My mother took it down a notch. "We love him, too, you know. I'm devastated this happened."

Her lower lip trembled and she dug in her bag for her ever-ready handkerchief.

"Are the police investigating?" I asked.

"Yes, of course, but I don't know how much good it will do." She dabbed at the corners of her eyes. "I love Cary dearly, but he's a tramp. I doubt he can recall all the women and men he's been with. Remember the charity auction you attended with Gideon? When I bought you that stunning red dress?"

"Yes." I'd never forget it. It was the night Gideon and I first made love.

"I'm certain Cary slept with a blonde he danced with that night—while they were there! They disappeared and when they came back . . . Well, I know what a satisfied man looks like. I would be surprised if he knew her name."

I remembered what Cary had said before he fell asleep. "You think this attack has something to do with someone he slept with?"

My mother blinked at me, seeming to remember that I didn't know anything. "Cary was told to keep his hands off 'her'—whoever 'her' is. The detectives will be coming back later today to try to pull some names out of him."

"Jesus." I scrubbed at my eyes, needing my face wash badly and a cup of coffee even more. "They need to talk to Tatiana Cherlin."

"Who's that?"

"Someone Cary's been seeing. I think she'd get a kick out of something like this. Cary's boyfriend caught them together and she ate it up with a spoon. She loved being the cause of the drama."

I rubbed at the back of my neck, then realized the tingle I felt was for another reason entirely. I looked over my shoulder and saw Gideon approaching, his long legs closing the distance between us with that measured stride. Dressed for work in a suit, with a large cup of coffee in one hand and a small black bag in the other, he was exactly what I needed at just the moment I needed him.

"Excuse me." I walked toward Gideon and straight into his arms.

"Hey," he greeted me, with his lips in my hair. "How are you holding up?"

"It's awful. And senseless." My eyes burned. "He didn't need another disaster in his life. He's had more than his share."

"So have you, and you're suffering along with him."

"And you're doing the same with me." I pushed up onto my tiptoes and kissed his jaw, then stepped back. "Thank you."

He handed me the coffee. "I brought some things for you—a change of clothes, your cell and tablet, bathroom stuff."

I knew his thoughtfulness had to come at a price—literally. After a weekend away, he should be digging his way out of a small mountain of work worth millions, not running around taking care of me. "God. I love you."

"Eva!" My mother's startled exclamation made me wince. She advocated withholding the words *I love you* until the wedding night.

"Sorry, Mom. Can't help it."

Gideon brushed coffee-warmed fingertips down my cheek.

"Gideon," my mother began, coming up right beside us, "you should know better than to take Eva away without any means of calling for help. You do *know* better."

She was clearly referring to my past. I wasn't sure why she thought

I was so delicate that I couldn't function on my own. She was far more fragile.

I shot a sympathetic glance Gideon's way.

He held out the bag he'd brought for me, the calm and confident look on his face conveying his total comfort in dealing with my mother. So I left him to it. I didn't have it in me to deal with her until I'd caffeinated myself.

I slipped back into Cary's room and found him awake. Just the sight of him made the tears well and my throat close up tight. He was such a strong and vibrant man, so full of life and mischief. It was the worst pain to see him looking so broken.

"Hey," he muttered. "Quit the waterworks every time you see me. Makes me feel like I'm gonna die or something."

Hell. He was right. My tears didn't do him any good. Instead, what little relief they gave me just put more of the burden on him. I needed to be a better friend than that.

"I can't help it," I said, sniffling. "It sucks. Someone beat me to it and kicked your ass before I could."

"Is that right?" His scowl faded. "What'd I do now?"

"You didn't tell me about Brett and Six-Ninths."

"Oh yeah . . ." A bit of his old sparkle came back into his eyes. "How'd he look?"

"Good. Really good." Very hot, but I kept that thought to myself. "Although right now, he might not look much better than you."

I told him about the kiss and the resulting fight.

"Cross threw down, huh?" Cary shook his head, then winced and stopped. "Taking on Brett took guts—he's a barroom brawler who loves a good fight."

"And Gideon is a trained mixed martial artist." I began digging through the bag Gideon had brought. "Why didn't you tell me Captive Soul had signed with a major label?"

"Because you didn't need to fall into that hole again. There are girls who can date rock stars; you're not one of them. All that time on the road, all those groupies . . . You'd drive yourself and him insane."

I shot him a look. "I'm in total agreement with you. But I'm insulted that you'd think I'd run back to him just because he made it big."

"That's not why. I didn't want you to hear their first single if it could be helped."

"'Golden'?"

"Yeah . . ." He studied me as I headed toward the bathroom. "What'd you think of it?"

"It's better than a song titled 'Tapped That.'"

"Ha!" He waited until I came out again with my face washed and hair brushed. "So . . . you kissed him."

"That's the beginning and end of that story," I said dryly. "Have you talked to Trey since Friday?"

"No. They've got my phone somewhere. My wallet, too, I'm guessing. When I came to, I was here, wearing this"—he pinched at his hospital gown—"freakin' thing."

"I'll get your stuff for you." I dumped my toiletries back in the bag, then went to sit in the chair beside him with my coffee in hand. "Gideon's making arrangements to get you home with a private nurse."

"Ooh . . . that's a fantasy of mine. Can you make sure the nurse is hot? And single?"

My brows rose. Inside, though, I was so relieved to see him looking and sounding more like himself. "You're obviously feeling better, if you're feeling frisky. How did things go with Trey?"

"Good." He sighed. "I'd worried that the party wouldn't be his scene. I forgot that he knew a lot of the people already."

Cary and Trey had met at a photo shoot, with Cary modeling and Trey assisting the photographer behind the camera. "I'm glad you had a good time."

"Yeah. He was totally set on *not* getting laid."

"So you tried . . . after you said you wouldn't."

"This is *me* we're talking about." He rolled his eyes. "Hell yeah, I tried. He's hot and great in bed—"

"—and in love with you."

He released his pent-up breath in a rush, wincing as his chest expanded. "No one's perfect."

I had to bite back a laugh. "Cary Taylor. Loving you isn't a character defect."

"Well, it's not very smart. I was such an asshole to him," he muttered, looking disgruntled. "He could do so much better."

"That isn't your decision to make for him."

"Someone needs to make it."

"And you're volunteering because you love him, too." My mouth curved. "Don't you think that sounds ass-backwards?"

"I don't love him enough." All traces of levity were wiped from his face, leaving behind the wounded and lonely man I knew all too well. "I can't be faithful like he wants. Just him and me. I like women. Love them, actually. I'd be cutting off half of who I am. Just thinking about it makes me resent him."

"You fought too hard to accept yourself," I said softly, remembering that time with more than a little twinge of sadness. "I totally understand and don't disagree, but have you tried talking to Trey about it?"

"Yes, I talked to him about it. He listened." He rubbed his fingers over his brow. "I get it, I do. If he told me he wanted to bang some other guy while seeing me, it'd bother the fuck out of me."

"But not if it were a woman?"

"No. I don't know. Shit." His bloodshot green eyes pleaded with me. "Would it make a difference to you if Cross were banging another man? Or just another woman?"

The door opened and Gideon walked in. I held his gaze when I said, "If Gideon's dick touched anything but his hand or me, we'd be over."

His brows rose. "Well, then."

I smiled sweetly and winked. "Hi, ace."

"Angel." He looked at Cary. "How are you feeling this morning?"

Cary's lips twisted wryly. "Like I got hit by a bus . . . or a bat."

"We're working on getting you set up at home. It looks like we can make that happen by Wednesday."

"Big tits, please," Cary said. "Or bulging muscles. Either will do."

Gideon looked at me.

I grinned. "The private nurse."

"Ah."

"If it's a woman," Cary went on, "can you get her to wear one of those white nurse dresses with the zipper down the front."

"I can only imagine the media frenzy over that sexual-harassment lawsuit," Gideon said dryly. "How about a collection of naughty-nurse porn instead?"

"Dude." Cary smiled wide and looked, for a moment, like his old self. "You're the man."

Gideon looked at me. "Eva."

I stood and bent over to kiss Cary on the cheek. "I'll be right back."

We stepped out of the room and I saw my mother in conversation with the doctor, who looked dazzled by her.

"I talked to Garrity this morning," Gideon said, referring to Mark, my boss. "So don't worry about that."

I hadn't been, because he said he'd handle it. "Thank you. I'll need to go in tomorrow. I'm going to see if I can get hold of Trey, Cary's boyfriend. Maybe he can stop in while I'm at work."

"Let me know if you need any help with that." Gideon glanced at his watch. "You'll want to stay here again tonight?"

"Yes, if that's possible. Until Cary comes home."

He took my face in his hands and pressed his lips to mine. "All right. I have a lot of work to catch up on. Charge your cell so I can reach you."

I heard a faint buzzing. Gideon backed away and reached into an inner jacket pocket to withdraw his phone. He read the screen, then said, "I have to get this. I'll talk to you later."

Then he was gone, striding down the hallway as quickly as he'd arrived.

"He's going to marry you," my mother said, coming up to stand beside me. "You know that, don't you?"

I didn't, no. I still felt a little flare of gratitude every morning when I woke up and realized that we were still together. "What makes you say that?"

My mother looked at me with her baby blue eyes. It was one of the rare physical traits we didn't share. "He's completely taken you over and assumed control of everything."

"That's just his nature."

"That's the nature of all powerful men," she said, reaching up to fuss with my no-nonsense ponytail. "And he'll indulge you, because he's making an investment in you. You're an asset to him. You're beautiful, well bred and well connected, and independently wealthy. You're also in love with him and he can't take his eyes off you. I bet he can't keep his hands off you, either."

"Mother, please." I was so *not* in the mood for one of her lectures on the fine points of catching and marrying a rich man.

"Eva Lauren," she scolded, facing me directly. "I don't care if you listen to me because I'm your mother and you have to—or because you love him and don't want to lose him, but you *will* listen."

"Like I have a choice," I muttered.

"You're an asset now," she repeated. "See that your life choices don't make you a liability."

"Are you talking about Cary?" Anger sharpened my voice.

"I'm talking about the bruise on Gideon's jaw! Tell me that has nothing to do with you."

I flushed.

She *tsk*ed. "I knew it. Yes, he's your lover and you see an intimate side to him that few see, but don't ever forget that he's also Gideon Cross. You've got everything you need to be the perfect wife for a man of his stature, but you're still replaceable, Eva. What he's built is not. You jeopardize his empire and he'll leave you."

My jaw tightened. "Are you done?"

She ran her fingertips over my brows, her gaze shrewd and assessing. I knew she was giving me a mini-makeover in her mind, thinking of ways to improve what she'd given me from birth. "You think I'm a coldhearted gold digger, but my concern is maternal, believe it or not. I want very desperately for you to be with a man who has the money and wherewithal to guard you with everything he has, so I'll know you're safe. And I want you to be with a man you love."

"I've found him."

"And I can't tell you how thrilled I am. I'm thrilled he's young and still open to taking risks, so he's more forgiving and understanding of your . . . quirks. And he *knows*," she whispered, her gaze softening and growing liquid. "Just be careful. That's all I'm trying to say. Don't give him any reason to turn away from you."

"If he did, that wouldn't be love."

Her lips curved wryly and she pressed a kiss to my forehead. "Come now. You're my daughter. You can't be that naïve."

"Eva!"

I turned at the sound of my name and felt a rush of relief to see Trey hurrying toward me. He was of average height and nicely muscular, with unruly blond hair, hazel eyes, and a slight angle to his nose that told me it'd been broken at some point. He was dressed in faded, frayed jeans and a T-shirt, and I was struck by the fact that he wasn't Cary's usual flashy type. For once, it seemed, the attraction had been more than skin deep.

"I just found out," he said when he reached me. "Detectives came by my work this morning and questioned me. I can't believe this happened Friday night and I'm only just finding out about it."

I couldn't hold his slightly accusatory tone against him. "I just found out early this morning myself. I was out of town."

After a quick introduction between my mother and Trey, she excused herself to go sit with Cary, leaving me to elaborate on the information Trey had gleaned from the detectives.

Trey shoved his hands through his hair, making it look even messier. "This wouldn't have happened if I'd taken him with me when I left."

"You can't blame yourself for this."

"Who else do I blame for the fact that he's screwing around with another guy's girl?" He gripped the back of his neck. "I'm the one who's not enough for him. He's got the drive of a hormonal teenager and I'm working or in school all the damn time."

Ugh. Total TMI. It was a struggle not to wince. But I understood that Trey likely didn't have anyone else he felt comfortable discussing Cary with.

"He's bisexual, Trey," I said softly, reaching out to run a comforting hand down his biceps. "That doesn't mean you're lacking."

"I don't know how to live with this."

"Would you consider counseling? With both of you, I mean."

He looked at me with haunted eyes for a long minute; then his shoulders slumped. "I don't know. I think I have to decide if I can live with him cheating. Could you do it, Eva? Could you sit at home waiting for your man, knowing he was sticking it somewhere else?"

"No." An icy shiver coursed through me at the mere words. "No, I couldn't."

"And I don't even know if Cary would agree to counseling. He keeps pushing me away. He wants me, and then he doesn't. He's committed, and then he isn't. I want in, Eva, like he's let you in, but he keeps shutting me out."

"It took me a long time to break through to him. He tried pushing me away with sex, always coming on to me, taunting me. I think you made the right decision keeping it platonic on Friday. Cary puts his value on his looks and sex appeal. You need to show him that it's not just his body you want."

Trey sighed and crossed his arms. "Is that how you two got close? Because you wouldn't sleep with him?"

"Partly. Mostly it's because I'm a mess. It's not as obvious now as it was when we met, but he knows I'm not perfect."

"Neither am I! Who is?"

"He believes you're better than he is, that you deserve better." I grinned. "Me . . . well, I bet part of him thinks I deserve him. That we deserve each other."

"Crazy fucker," he muttered.

"He is that," I agreed. "That's why we love him, isn't it? Do you want to go in and see him? Or do you want to go home and think about it?"

"No, I want to see him." Trey's shoulders rolled back and his chin lifted. "I don't care what put him here. I want to be with him while he's going through this."

"I'm glad to hear that." I linked my arm with his and led him to Cary's room.

We entered to the sound of my mother's trilling, girlish laughter. She sat on the edge of the bed, with Cary smiling adoringly at her. She was as much a mother to him as she was to me, and he loved her so much for that. His own mother had hated him, abused him, and allowed others to abuse him.

He looked over and saw us, and the emotions that swept across his face in that moment caused a tightness in my chest. I heard Trey's breath catch as he got his first sight of Cary's condition. I kicked myself for not telling him in advance not to make the mistake of getting weepy like I had.

Trey cleared his throat. "Drama queen," he said with gruff affection. "If you wanted flowers, you should've just asked for them. This is extreme."

"And ineffective, apparently," Cary rejoined hoarsely, clearly trying to pull himself together. "I don't see any flowers."

"I see a ton." Trey's gaze did a brief slide across the room, then went back to Cary. "Just wanted to see what I was up against, so I could beat out my competition."

There was no way to miss the double meaning in that statement.

My mom rose from the bed. She leaned over and kissed Cary's cheek. "I'll take Eva out to breakfast. We'll see you in about an hour or so."

"Gimme a sec," I said, passing the bed quickly, "and I'll get out of your hair, guys."

I grabbed my phone and charger out of my bag and plugged it into an outlet by the window.

As soon as the screen flickered to life, I sent a quick group text message to Shawna and my dad, saying simply: I'll call later. Then I made sure my phone was silenced and left it on the window ledge.

"Ready?" my mom asked.

"As I'll ever be."

13

I HAD TO get up before dawn Tuesday morning. I left a note for Cary where he'd see it as soon as he woke up, then headed out to grab a cab back to our place. I showered, dressed, made coffee, and tried to talk myself out of feeling like something was off. I was stressed and suffering from lack of sleep, which always led to tiny bouts of depression.

I told myself that it had nothing to do with Gideon, but the knot in my stomach said differently.

Looking at the clock, I saw it was a little after eight. I'd have to leave soon, because Gideon hadn't called or texted to say that he'd be giving me a ride. It had been almost twenty-four hours since I'd last seen him or even really talked to him. The call I'd made to him at nine the night before had been less than brief. He'd been in the middle of something and barely said hello and good-bye.

I knew he had a lot of work to do. I knew I shouldn't resent him for having to pay for the time away with extra hours of work getting caught up. He'd done a lot to help me deal with Cary's situation, more than anyone could've expected. It was up to me to deal with how I was feeling about it.

Finishing my coffee, I rinsed out my mug, then grabbed my purse and bag on the way out. My tree-lined street was quiet, but the rest of New York was wide awake, its ceaseless energy thrumming with a tangible force. Women in chic office wear and men in suits tried to hail taxis that streaked by, before settling for packed buses or the subway instead. Flower stands exploded with brilliant color, the sight of them always capable of cheering me up in the morning, as did the sight and smell of the neighborhood bakery, which was doing a brisk business at that hour.

I was a little ways down Broadway before my phone rang.

The little thrill that shot through me at the sight of Gideon's name quickened my steps. "Hey, stranger."

"Where the hell are you?" he snapped.

A frisson of unease dampened my excitement. "I'm on my way to work."

"Why?" He spoke to someone offline, then, "Are you in a cab?"

"I'm walking. Jeez. Did you wake up on the wrong side of the bed or what?"

"You should have waited to be picked up."

"I didn't hear from you, and I didn't want to be late after missing work yesterday."

"You could've called me instead of just taking off." His voice was low and angry.

I became angry, too. "The last time I called, you were too busy to give me more than a minute of your time."

"I've got things to take care of, Eva. Give me a break."

"Sure thing. How about now?" I hung up and dropped my phone back into my bag.

It began ringing again immediately and I ignored it, my blood simmering. When the Bentley pulled up beside me a few minutes later, I kept walking. It followed, the front passenger window sliding down.

Angus leaned over. "Miss Tramell, please."

I paused, looking at him. "Are you alone?"

"Yes."

With a sigh, I got in the car. My phone was still ringing nonstop, so I reached in and shut the ringer off. One block later, I heard Gideon's voice coming through the car's speakers.

"Do you have her?"

"Yes, sir," Angus replied.

The line cut out.

"What the hell crawled up his ass and died?" I asked, looking at Angus in the rearview mirror.

"He's got a lot on his mind."

Whatever it was, it sure wasn't me. I couldn't believe what a jerk he was being. He'd been curt on the phone the night before, too, but not rude.

Within a few minutes after I arrived at work, Mark came up to my cubicle. "I'm sorry to hear about your roommate," he said, setting a fresh cup of coffee on my desk. "Is he going to be all right?"

"Eventually. Cary's tough; he'll pull through." I dropped my stuff in the bottom drawer of my desk and picked up the steaming mug with gratitude. "Thank you. And thanks for yesterday, too."

His dark eyes were warm with concern. "I'm surprised you're here today."

"I need to work." I managed a smile, despite feeling all twisted up and achy inside. Nothing was right in my world when things weren't right between me and Gideon. "Catch me up on what I missed."

THE morning passed swiftly. I had a checklist of follow-ups waiting from the week before, and Mark had an eleven thirty deadline to turn around a request for proposal for a promotional items manufacturer. By the time we sent the RFP off, I was back in the groove and willing to just forget Gideon's mood that morning. I wondered if he'd had another nightmare and hadn't slept well. I decided to call him when lunchtime rolled around, just in case.

And then I checked my inbox.

The Google alert I'd set up for Gideon's name was waiting for me. I opened the e-mail hoping to get an idea of what he might be working on. The words *former fiancée* in some of the headlines leaped out at me. The knot I'd had in my gut earlier returned, tighter than before.

I clicked on the first link, and it took me to a gossip blog sporting pictures of Gideon and Corinne having dinner at Tableau One. They sat close together in the front window, her hand resting intimately on his forearm. He was wearing the suit he'd worn to the hospital the day before, but I checked the date anyway, desperately hoping the photos were old. They weren't.

My palms began to sweat. I tortured myself by clicking through all the links and studying every photo I found. He was smiling in a few of them, looking remarkably content for a man whose girlfriend was at a hospital with her beaten-half-to-death best friend. I felt like throwing up. Or screaming. Or storming up to Gideon's office and asking him what the hell was going on.

He'd blown me off when I'd called him the night before—to go to dinner with his ex.

I jumped when my desk phone rang. I picked it up and woodenly recited, "Mark Garrity's office, Eva Tramell speaking."

"Eva." It was Megumi in reception, sounding as bubbly as usual. "There's someone asking for you downstairs—Brett Kline."

I sat there for a long minute, letting that sink into my fevered brain. I forwarded the alert digest to Gideon's e-mail so he'd know that I knew. Then I said, "I'll be right down."

I saw Brett in the lobby the minute I pushed through the security turnstiles. He wore black jeans and a Six-Ninths T-shirt. Sunglasses hid his eyes, but the spiky hair with its bleached tips was eye-catching, as was his body. Brett was tall and muscular, more muscular than Gideon, who was powerful without any bulk.

Brett's hands came out of his pockets when he saw me coming, his posture straightening. "Hey. Look at you."

I glanced down at my cap-sleeved dress with its flattering ruching and acknowledged that he'd never seen me dressed up. "I'm surprised you're still in town."

More surprised that he'd looked me up, but I didn't say that. I was glad he had, because I'd been worried about him.

"We sold out our Jones Beach show over the weekend, then played the Meadowlands last night. I skipped out on the guys because I wanted to see you before we head south. I searched for you online, found out where you worked, and came up."

Good old Google, I thought miserably. "I'm so stoked that everything's working out for you now. Do you have time to grab lunch?"

"Yes."

His answer came quickly and fervently, which set off a little warning. I was pissed, extremely hurt, and eager to retaliate against Gideon, but I didn't want to mislead Brett. Still, I couldn't resist taking him to the restaurant where Cary and I had once been pho-tographed together, in the hopes of getting caught by the paparazzi again. It would serve Gideon right to see what it felt like.

On the cab ride over, Brett asked about Cary and wasn't sur-prised to learn that my best friend had moved across the country with me.

"You two were always inseparable," he said. "Except when he was getting laid. Tell him I said hi."

"Sure." I didn't mention that Cary was in the hospital, because it felt too private to share.

It wasn't until we were seated in the restaurant that Brett took off his shades, so that was the first time I got a glimpse of the shiner that encompassed the area from his right eyebrow down to his cheekbone.

"Jesus," I breathed, wincing. "I'm sorry."

He shrugged. "Makeup made it disappear on stage. And you've seen me with worse. Besides, I got a couple good hits in, didn't I?"

Remembering the bruising on Gideon's jaw and back, I nodded. "You did."

"So . . ." He paused as the waiter came by and dropped off two glasses and a chilled bottle of water. "You're dating Gideon Cross."

I wondered why that question always seemed to pop up at a time when I wasn't sure the relationship would last another minute. "We've been seeing each other."

"Is it serious?"

"Sometimes it seems that way," I said honestly. "Are you seeing anyone?"

"Not now."

We took some time to read the menu and place our orders. The restaurant was busy and noisy, the background music barely heard over the hum of conversation and clatter of plates from the nearby kitchen. We looked across the table at each other, sizing each other up. I felt the thrum of attraction between us. When he wet his lips with the tip of his tongue, I knew he was aware of it, too.

"Why did you write 'Golden'?" I asked suddenly, unable to hold back my curiosity a moment longer. I'd been playing it off as nothing big with both Gideon and Cary, but it was driving me crazy.

Brett sat back in his chair. "Because I think about you a lot. I can't stop thinking about you actually."

"I don't understand why."

"We had it going on for six months, Eva. That's the longest I've ever been with someone."

"But we weren't *with* each other," I argued. My voice lowered. "Aside from sexually."

His mouth thinned. "I understand what I was to you, but that doesn't mean I didn't get hurt."

I stared at him for a long minute, my heart beating too quickly in my chest. "I feel like I'm stoned or something. The way I remember it, we'd hook up after shows, then you'd go about your business. And if I wasn't there to put out, you'd grab someone else."

He leaned forward. "Bullshit. I tried getting you to hang out. I was always asking you to stick around."

I took a couple of quick, deep breaths to calm myself down. I could hardly believe that now, almost four years too late, Brett Kline was talking to me like I'd once wanted him to. We were out in public together, having a meal, almost like a date. It was messing with my head, which was already confused and scattered because of Gideon.

"I had the biggest crush on you, Brett. I wrote your name with little hearts around it like a lovesick teenager. I wanted desperately to be your girlfriend."

"Are you kidding me?" He reached out and caught my hand. "What the fuck happened, then?"

I looked down at where he was absently twirling the ring Gideon had given me. "Remember when we went to the pool hall?"

"Yeah. How could I forget that?" He bit his lower lip, clearly recalling how I'd fucked his brains out in the back of his car, determined to be the best lay he'd ever had so he wouldn't bother with other girls. "I thought we were getting to the point where we'd start seeing each other outside the bar, but you ditched me the minute we got inside."

"I went to the bathroom," I said quietly, remembering the pain and embarrassment as if the incident had just happened, "and when I came out you and Darrin were at the change machine getting quarters for the tables. Your back was to me so you didn't see me. I heard you guys talking . . . and laughing."

I pulled in a deep breath and tugged my hand away from him.

To his credit, Brett shifted in obvious embarrassment. "I can't remember exactly what was said, but . . . Shit, Eva. I was twenty-one years old. The band was just starting to get popular. The chicks were everywhere."

"I know," I said dryly. "I was one of them."

"I'd been with you a few times by then. Bringing you along to the pool hall made a statement to the guys that things were picking up between us." He rubbed at his brow in a very familiar gesture. "I didn't have the balls to own up to how I was feeling about you. I made it about the sex, but that wasn't true."

I lifted my glass and drank, forcing down the lump in my throat.

His hand dropped onto the armrest. "So I screwed it up with my big mouth. That's why you bailed that night. That's why you never went anywhere with me again."

"I was desperate, Brett," I admitted, "but I didn't want to show it."

The waiter brought our food. I wondered why I'd ordered anything—I was too unsettled to eat.

Brett started cutting into his steak, attacking it really. Suddenly, he set his knife and fork down. "I blew it back then, but now everyone knows what was going on in my head at the time. 'Golden' is our biggest single. It's what got us signed with Vidal."

The idea of closure made me smile. "It's a beautiful song, and your voice sounds amazing when you sing it. I'm really glad you came up and saw me again before you head out. It means a lot to me that we talked through this."

"What if I don't want to just head out and move on?" He took a deep breath and released it in a rush. "You've been my muse the last few years, Eva. Because of you, I've written the best material the band's ever had."

"That's very flattering," I began.

"We sizzled together. Still do. I know you feel it. The way you kissed me the other night . . ."

"That was a mistake." My hands clenched beneath the table. I couldn't deal with more drama. I couldn't go through another night like Friday. "And you need to think about the fact that Gideon controls your label. You don't want any friction there."

"Fuck it. What's he going to do?" His fingertips drummed onto the table. "I want another shot with you."

I shook my head and reached for my purse. "That's impossible. Even if I didn't have a boyfriend, I'm not the right girl for your lifestyle, Brett. I'm too high-maintenance."

"I remember," he said roughly. "God, do I remember."

I flushed. "That's not what I meant."

"And that's not all I want. I can be here for you. Look at me now—the band's on the road, but you and I are together. I can make time. I want to."

"It's not that easy." I pulled cash out of my wallet and dropped it on the table. "You don't know me. You have no idea what it would mean to have a relationship with me, how much work it would take."

"Try me," he challenged.

"I'm needy and clingy and insanely jealous. I'd drive you crazy within a week."

"You've always driven me crazy. I like it." His smile faded. "Stop running, Eva. Give me a chance."

I met his gaze and held it. "I'm in love with Gideon."

His brows rose. Even battered, his face was breathtaking. "I don't believe you."

"I'm sorry. I have to go." I pushed to my feet and moved to pass him.

He caught my elbow. "Eva—"

"Please don't make a scene," I whispered, regretting my impetuous decision to eat at a popular place.

"You didn't eat."

"I can't. I need to leave."

"Fine. But I'm not giving up." He released me. "I make mistakes, but I learn from them."

I bent over and said firmly, "There's no chance. None."

Brett stabbed his fork into a slice of his steak. "Prove it."

THE Bentley was waiting at the curb when I stepped out of the restaurant. Angus climbed out and opened the rear door for me.

"How did you know where I was?" I asked, unsettled by his unexpected appearance.

His answer was to smile kindly and touch the brim of his chauffeur's hat.

"This is creepy, Angus," I complained as I slid into the backseat.

"I don't disagree, Miss Tramell. I'm just doing my job."

I texted Cary on the ride back to the Crossfire: Had lunch with Brett. He wants another chance w/me.

Cary replied, When it rains it pours . . .

Whole day = royally fucked, I typed. I want a do-over.

My phone rang. It was Cary.

"Baby girl," he drawled. "I want to sympathize, I do, but the love triangle thing is just too delicious. The determined rock star and the possessive billionaire. *Rawr.*"

"Oh God. Hanging up now."

"See you tonight?"

"Yes. Please don't make me regret it." I hung up to the sound of his laughter, secretly thrilled to hear him sounding so happy. Trey's visit must have worked wonders.

Angus dropped me off at the curb in front of the Crossfire, and I hurried out of the heat into the cool lobby. I managed to catch an open elevator just before the doors closed. There were a half dozen other people in the car with me, forming two groups that chatted among themselves. I stood in the front corner and tried to put my personal life out of my mind. I couldn't deal with it at work.

"Hey, we passed our floor," the girl next to me said.

I looked at the needle over the door.

The guy nearest the control panel stabbed repeatedly at all the numbers, but none of them lit up . . . except for the one for the top floor. "The buttons aren't working."

My pulse quickened.

"Use the emergency phone," one of the other girls said.

The car raced up and the butterflies in my stomach got worse with every floor we passed. The elevator finally came to a gliding stop at the top and the doors opened.

Gideon stood on the threshold, his face a gorgeous impassive mask. His eyes were brilliantly blue . . . and cold as ice. The sight of him took my breath away.

No one in the car said a word. I didn't move, praying the doors would hurry up and close. Gideon reached in, grabbed my elbow, and hauled me out. I struggled, too furious to want anything to do with him. The doors closed behind me and he let me go.

"Your behavior today has been appalling," he growled.

"*My* behavior? What about yours?"

I crossed over to the call buttons and hit the down button. It wouldn't stay lit.

"I'm talking to you, Eva."

I glanced at the security doors to Cross Industries and was relieved to see that the redheaded receptionist was away from her station.

"Really?" I faced him, hating that I could still find him so irresistibly attractive when he was being so ugly. "Funny how that doesn't lead to me actually learning anything—like about you going out with Corinne last night."

"You shouldn't be snooping online about me," he bit out. "You're deliberately trying to find something to get upset about."

"So your actions aren't the problem?" I shot back, feeling the pressure of tears at the back of my throat. "Just my finding out about them is?"

His arms crossed. "You need to trust me, Eva."

"You're making that impossible! Why didn't you tell me that you were going out to dinner with Corinne?"

"Because I knew you wouldn't like it."

"But you did it anyway." And that hurt. After all we'd talked about over the weekend . . . after he'd said that he understood how I felt . . .

"And you went out with Brett Kline knowing *I* wouldn't like it."

"What did I tell you? You're setting the precedent for how I handle my exes."

"Tit for tat? What a remarkable show of maturity."

I stumbled back from him. There was none of the Gideon I knew in the man facing me. It felt as if the man I loved had disappeared and the man standing in front of me was a total stranger in Gideon's body.

"You're making me hate you," I whispered. "Stop it."

Something passed briefly over Gideon's face, but it was gone before I could identify it. I let his body language do the talking for him. He stood far from me, with his shoulders stiff and his jaw tight.

My heart bled and my gaze dropped. "I can't be around you right now. Let me go."

Gideon moved to the other bank of elevators and pushed the call button. With his back to me and his attention on the indicator arrow, he said, "Angus will pick you up every morning. Wait for him. And I prefer that you eat lunch at your desk. It's best if you're not running around right now."

"Why not?"

"I have a lot of things on my plate at the moment—"

"Like dinner with Corinne?"

"—and I can't be worrying about you," he went on, ignoring my interruption. "I don't think I'm asking too much."

Something was wrong.

"Gideon, why won't you talk to me?" I reached out and touched his shoulder, only to have him jerk away as if I'd burned him. More than anything else, his rejection of my touch wounded me deeply. "Tell me what's going on. If there's a problem—"

"The problem is that I don't know where the hell you are half the

234 · SYLVIA DAY

time!" he snapped, turning to scowl at me as the elevator doors opened. "Your roommate is in the hospital. Your dad is coming to visit. Just . . . focus on that."

I stepped into the elevator with burning eyes. Aside from pulling me out of the elevator when it first arrived, Gideon hadn't touched me. He hadn't run his fingertips down my cheek or made any attempt to kiss me. And he made no mention of wanting to see me later, skipping right over the rest of the day to tell me about Angus waiting for me in the morning.

I'd never been so confused. I couldn't figure out what was happening, why there was suddenly this huge gulf between us, why Gideon was so tense and angry, why he didn't seem to care that I'd had lunch with Brett.

Why he didn't seem to care about anything at all.

The doors started to close. *Trust me, Eva.*

Had he breathed those words in the second before the doors shut? Or did I just wish that he had?

THE moment I walked into Cary's private room, he knew I was running on fumes. I'd endured a tough Krav Maga session with Parker, then stopped by the apartment only long enough to shower and eat a tasteless instant-ramen meal. The shock of the salt and carbs to my system after a day without food was more than enough to exhaust me past the point of no return.

"You look like shit," he said, muting the television.

"Look who's talking," I shot back, feeling too raw to take any criticism.

"I got hit with a baseball bat. What's your excuse?"

I arranged the pillow and scratchy blanket on my cot, then told him about my day from beginning to end.

"And I haven't heard from Gideon since," I finished wearily. "Even Brett got in touch with me after lunch. He left an envelope at the security desk with his phone number in it."

He'd also included the cash I left at the restaurant.

"Are you going to call him?" Cary asked.

"I don't want to think about Brett!" I sprawled on my back on the cot and shoved my hands through my hair. "I want to know what's wrong with Gideon. He's had a total personality transplant in the last thirty-six hours!"

"Maybe it's this."

I lifted my head off the pillow and saw him pointing at something on his bedside table. Rolling to my feet, I checked it out—a local gay periodical.

"Trey brought that over today," he said.

Cary's picture capped a front-page piece covering his attack—including speculation that the assault might have been a hate crime. His living situation with me and my romantic entanglement with Gideon Cross were mentioned, for no other reason, it seemed, than for a salacious punch.

"It's on their website, too," he added quietly. "I figure someone at the agency gossiped, and it spread and turned into someone's political crap. Honestly, I'm having a hard time imagining Cross giving a shit—"

"About your sexual orientation? He doesn't. He's not like that."

"But his PR people might feel differently. Could be why he wants to keep you under the radar. And if he's worried that someone might go after you to get to me, that explains why he wants to keep you tucked away and off the streets."

"Why wouldn't he tell me that?" I set the paper down. "Why is he being such a prick? Everything was so wonderful while we were gone. *He* was wonderful. I thought we'd turned a corner. I kept thinking he wasn't anything like the man I'd first met, and now he's worse. There's this . . . I don't know. He's a million miles away from me now. I don't understand it."

"I'm not the guy to ask, Eva." Cary grabbed my hand and squeezed. "He's the one with the answers."

"You're right." I went to my purse and pulled out my phone. "I'll be back in a bit."

I went to the little enclosed balcony off the visitors' waiting area and called Gideon. The phone rang and rang, eventually going to voice mail. I tried his home number instead. After the third ring, Gideon answered.

"Cross," he said curtly.

"Hi."

There was silence for the length of a heartbeat, then, "Hang on."

I heard a door open. The sound on the phone changed—he'd stepped away from wherever he'd been.

"Is everything all right?" he asked.

"No." I rubbed at my tired eyes. "I miss you."

He sighed. "I . . . I can't talk now, Eva."

"Why not? I don't understand why you're acting so cold to me. Did I do something wrong?" I heard murmuring and realized he'd muffled the receiver to talk to someone else. A horrible feeling of betrayal tightened my chest, making it hard to breathe. "Gideon. Who's at your place with you?"

"I have to go."

"Tell me who's there with you!"

"Angus will be at the hospital at seven. Get some sleep, angel."

The line went dead.

I lowered my hand and stared at my phone, as if it could somehow reveal to me what the fuck had just happened.

I made it back to Cary's room, felt weighted down and miserable as I pushed open the door.

Cary took one look at me and sighed. "You look like your puppy just died, baby girl."

The dam broke. I started sobbing.

14

I HARDLY SLEPT all night. I tossed and turned, drifting in and out of consciousness. The frequent nurse visits to check on Cary also woke me. His brain scans and lab reports were looking good and there was nothing absolutely definitive to worry about, but I hadn't been there for him when he'd first gotten hurt. I felt like I needed to be there for him now, sleep or no sleep.

Just before six, I gave up and got out of bed.

Grabbing my tablet and wireless keyboard, I headed down to the cafeteria for coffee. I pulled up a chair at one of the tables and prepared to write a letter to Gideon. In the short amounts of time I'd managed to pin him down the last couple of days, I hadn't been able to get my thoughts across to him. Writing it all out would have to be the way it got done. Maintaining steady, open communication was the only way we were going to survive as a couple.

I sipped my coffee and began typing, starting with my thanks for the beautiful weekend away and how much it meant to me. I told him how I thought our relationship had taken a massive leap forward during the trip, which only made the week's backslide harder to bear—

"Eva. What a pleasant surprise!"

Turning my head, I found Dr. Terrence Lucas standing behind me holding a disposable coffee cup like the one I'd filled for myself. He was dressed for work in slacks and tie with a white lab coat. "Hi," I greeted him, hoping I hid my wariness.

"Mind if I join you?" he asked, rounding me.

"Not at all."

I watched him take the seat beside me, and I refreshed my memory of his appearance. His hair was pure white, without a hint of gray, but his handsome face was unlined. His eyes were an unusual shade of green and they were keen with intelligence. His smile was both reassuring and charming. I suspected he was popular with his patients—and their mothers.

"There has to be some special reason," he began, "for you to be in the hospital long before visiting hours."

"My roommate's here." I didn't volunteer any more information, but he guessed.

"So Gideon Cross threw his money around and made arrangements for you." He shook his head and took a sip of his coffee. "And you're grateful. But what will it cost you?"

I sat back, offended on Gideon's behalf that his generosity was reduced to having an ulterior motive. "Why do you two dislike each other so much?"

His eyes lost their softness. "He hurt someone very close to me."

"Your wife. He told me." I could tell that startled him. "But that wasn't the beginning, was it? That was a result."

REFLECTED IN YOU · 241

"You know what he did, and you're still with him?" Lucas set his elbows on the table. "He's doing the same thing to you. You look exhausted and depressed. That's part of the game to him, you know. He's an expert at worshipping a woman as if he needs her to breathe. Then suddenly he can't bear the sight of her."

The statement was a painfully accurate description of my present reality with Gideon. My pulse quickened.

His gaze slid to my throat, then back to my face. His mouth curved in a mocking, knowing smile. "You've experienced what I'm talking about. He's going to continue to play with you until you rely on his mood to gauge your own. Then he'll get bored and dump you."

"What happened between you?" I asked again, knowing that was key.

"Gideon Cross is a narcissistic sociopath," he went on as if I hadn't spoken. "I believe he's a misogynist. He uses his money to seduce women, then despises them for being shallow enough to find his wealth attractive. He uses sex to control, and you never know what sort of mood you'll find him in. That's part of the rush—when you're always steeling yourself for the worst, you psych yourself up for a surge of relief when he's at his best."

"You don't know him," I said smoothly, refusing to take the bait. "And neither does your wife."

"Neither do you." He sat back and drank his coffee, appearing as unruffled as I tried to be. "No one does. He's a master manipulator and liar. Don't underestimate him. He's a twisted, dangerous man capable of just about anything."

"The fact that you won't explain his grudge against you makes me think you're at fault."

"You shouldn't make assumptions. There are some things I'm not at liberty to discuss."

242 · SYLVIA DAY

"That's convenient."

He sighed. "I'm not your adversary, Eva, and Cross doesn't need anyone to fight his battles. You don't have to believe me. Frankly, I'm so bitter *I* wouldn't believe me if I were in your place. But you're a beautiful, smart young lady."

I hadn't been lately, but it was my responsibility to fix that. Or walk.

"If you take a step back," he continued, "and look at what he's doing to you, how you're feeling about yourself since you've been with him, and whether you're truly fulfilled by your relationship, you'll come to your own conclusions."

Something beeped and he pulled his smartphone out of his coat pocket. "Ah, my latest patient has just entered the world."

He pushed to his feet and looked down at me, setting his hand on my shoulder. "You'll be the one who gets away. I'm glad."

I watched him walk briskly out of the cafeteria and collapsed into the seat back the moment he disappeared from view, deflating from exhaustion and confusion. My gaze moved to the sleeping screen of my tablet. I didn't have the energy to finish my letter.

I packed up and went to get ready for Angus's arrival.

"You up for Chinese?"

I looked up from the layout of the blueberry coffee ad on my desk into the warm brown eyes of my boss. I realized it was Wednesday, our usual day to go eat with Steven.

For a second, I considered bowing out and eating at my desk because I wanted to make Gideon happy. But just as quickly, I knew I'd resent him if I did. I was still trying to build a new life in New York, which included making friends and having plans that existed outside the life I shared with him.

"Always up for Chinese," I said. My very first meal with Mark and Steven had been Chinese takeout here in the office, on a night when we'd worked well past closing and Steven had stopped by to feed us.

Mark and I headed out at noon, and I refused to feel guilty about something I enjoyed so much. Steven was waiting for us at the restaurant, seated at a round table with a lacquered lazy Susan in the middle.

"Hey, you." He greeted me with a big bear hug, then pulled a chair out for me. He studied me as we both sat down. "You look tired."

I guessed I must really look like shit, since everyone kept telling me that. "It's been a rough week so far."

The waitress came by and Steven ordered a dim sum appetizer and the same dishes we'd shared for that first late-evening meal—kung pao chicken and broccoli beef. When we were alone again, Steven said, "I didn't know your roommate was gay. Did you tell us that?"

"He's bi, actually." I realized Steven, or someone he knew, must have seen the same newspaper Cary had showed me. "I don't think it came up."

"How's he feeling?" Mark asked, looking genuinely concerned.

"Better. He might be coming home today." Which was something that had been weighing on me all morning, since Gideon hadn't called to tell me definitively one way or the other.

"Let us know if you need any help," Steven said, all traces of levity gone. "We're here for you."

"Thank you. It wasn't a hate crime," I clarified. "I don't know where the reporter got that. I used to respect journalists. Now, so few of them do their homework, and fewer still can write objectively."

"I'm sure it's tough living in the media spotlight." Steven squeezed my hand on the table. He was a gregarious, playful fellow, but beneath that fun exterior was a solid man with a kind heart. "But then you have to kinda expect it when you're juggling rock stars and billionaires."

"Steven," Mark scolded, frowning.

"Ugh." My nose wrinkled. "Shawna told you."

"Of course she did," Steven said. "Least she can do after not inviting me along to the concert. But don't worry. She's not a gossip. She won't be telling anyone else."

I nodded, having no anxiety about that; Shawna was good people. But it was still embarrassing having my boss know I'd kissed one man while dating another.

"Not that it would be a bad thing for Cross to get a taste of his own medicine," Steven muttered.

I frowned, confused. Then I caught Mark's sympathetic gaze.

I realized the gay newspaper wasn't the only news they'd seen. They must have seen the photos of Gideon and Corinne, too. I felt my face flush with humiliation.

"He'll get a taste," I muttered. "If I have to cram it down his throat."

Steven's brows shot up, and then he laughed and patted my hand. "Get him, girl."

I'D barely returned to my desk when my work phone rang.

"Mark Garrity's office, Eva—"

"Why is it so damn difficult for you to follow orders?" Gideon asked harshly.

I just sat there, staring at the collage of photos he'd given me, pictures of us looking connected and in love.

"Eva?"

"What do you want from me, Gideon?" I asked quietly.

There was a moment of silence, then he exhaled. "Cary will be moved to your apartment this afternoon under the supervision of his doctor and a private nurse. He should be there when you get home."

"Thank you." Another stretch of quiet filled the line between us, but he didn't hang up. Finally, I queried, "Are we done?"

The question had a double meaning. I wondered if he caught that or even cared.

"Angus will give you a ride home."

My grip tightened on the phone. "Good-bye, Gideon."

I hung up and got back to work.

I checked on Cary the minute I got home. His bed had been moved aside and propped vertically against the wall to make room for a hospital bed that he could adjust at will. He was asleep when I came in, his nurse sitting in a new recliner and reading an e-book. It was the same nurse I'd seen the first night in the hospital, the pretty and exotic-looking one who had trouble taking her eyes off Gideon.

I wondered when he'd spoken to her—if he'd done it himself or sent someone else to do it—and whether she'd agreed for the money or for Gideon or both.

The fact that I was too tired to care one way or another said a lot about my own disconnection. Maybe there were people out there whose love could survive anything, but mine was fragile. It needed to be nurtured in order to thrive and grow.

I took a long, hot shower, then crawled into bed. I pulled my tablet onto my lap and tried to continue my letter to Gideon. I wanted to express my thoughts and reservations in a mature and cogent way. I wanted to make it easy for him to understand my reactions to some of the things he did and said, so he could see things from my point of view.

In the end, I didn't have the energy.

I'm not elaborating any more, I wrote instead, *because if I keep going, I'll beg. And if you don't know me well enough to know that you're hurting me, a letter isn't going to fix our problems.*

I'm desperate for you. I'm miserable without you. I think about the weekend, and the hours we spent together, and I can't think of anything I wouldn't do to have you like that again. Instead, you're spending time with HER, while I'm alone on my fourth night without you.

Even knowing you've been with her, I want to crawl on my knees for you and beg for scraps. A touch. A kiss. One tender word. You've made me that weak.

I hate myself like this. I hate that I need you this much. I hate that I'm so obsessed with you.

I hate that I love you.

Eva

I attached it to an e-mail with the subject line *My thoughts— uncensored* and hit send.

"Don't be afraid."

I woke to those three words and utter darkness. The mattress dipped as Gideon sat beside me, leaning over me with his arms bracketing my body and the blankets between us, a cocoon and barrier that allowed my mind to wake without fear. The delicious and unmistakable fragrance of his soap and shampoo mixed with the scent of his skin, soothing me along with his voice.

"Angel." He took my mouth, his lips slanting over mine.

I touched his chest with my fingers, feeling bare skin. He

groaned and stood, bending over me so his mouth stayed connected to mine while he yanked the blankets off and away.

Then he was settling over me, his body nude and hot to the touch. His ardent mouth moved down my throat, his hands pushing up my camisole so he could get to my breasts. His lips surrounded my nipple and he suckled, his weight supported by one forearm on the mattress, his other hand pushing between my legs.

He cupped my sex, his fingertip gliding over the satin along the seam of my cleft. His tongue flickered over my nipple, making it hard and tight, his teeth sinking lightly into the taut flesh.

"Gideon!" Tears slid in rivulets down my temples, the protective numbness I'd felt earlier falling away, leaving me exposed. I'd been withering without him, the world around me losing its vibrancy, my body hurting from its separation from his. Having him with me . . . touching me . . . was like rain in a drought. My soul unfurled for him, opening wide to soak him in.

I loved him so much.

His hair tickled my skin as his open mouth slid over my cleavage, his chest expanding as he breathed me in, nuzzling and wallowing in my scent. He captured the tip of my other breast with hard, deep suction. The pleasure shot through me, echoing in the clenching of my sex against his teasing fingertip.

He moved down my torso, licking and nibbling a path across my stomach, the breadth of his shoulders forcing my legs wider until his hot breath gusted over my slick cleft. His nose pressed against the wet satin, stroking me. He inhaled with a groan.

"*Eva*. I've been starved for you."

With impatient fingers, Gideon shoved the crotch of my panties aside and his mouth was on me. He held me open with his thumbs, his tongue lashing over my throbbing clit. My back arched with a cry, all my senses painfully acute without the benefit of sight. Tilting his head, he thrust into the quivering opening of my sex, fucking rhythmically, teasing me with shallow plunges.

"Oh God!" I writhed with the pleasure, my core clenching and releasing with the first tingles of orgasm.

I came in a violent rush, sweat misting my skin, my lungs burning as I fought for breath. His lips were around my trembling opening, sucking, his tongue delving. He was eating me with an intensity I was helpless against. The flesh between my legs was so swollen and sensitive, so vulnerable to his ravenous hunger. I was climaxing again within moments, my nails scouring the sheets.

My eyes were opened and blinded by darkness when he ripped my underwear off me and crawled over me. I felt the wide crest of his cock notch into my cleft, and then he lunged, driving deep into me with an animalistic growl. I cried out, shocked by his aggression, turned on by it.

Gideon reared up, resting back on his heels, my thighs splayed over his. He gripped my hips, elevating them, tilting me to the angle he wanted. He rolled his hips, stirring his cock inside me, pulling me onto him until I gasped in pain at how deep he was. The lips of my sex clung to the very base of his penis, spread wide to encompass the thick root. I had all of him, every inch, crammed too full and loving it. I'd been empty for days, so lonely I ached.

He groaned my name and came, spurting hot and thick, the creamy heat spreading upward along his length because there was no room inside me. He shuddered violently, dripping sweat onto my skin, flooding me. "For you, Eva," he gasped. "Every drop."

Pulling out abruptly, he flipped me over onto my belly and yanked my hips up. I gripped my headboard, my damp face pressed into my pillow. I waited for him to push into me and shivered when

I felt his breath against my buttocks. Then I jerked violently at the feel of him licking along the seam. He rimmed me with the tip of his tongue, stimulating the puckered opening to my rear.

A broken sound escaped me. *I don't do anal play, Eva.*

The tight ring of muscle flexed as I remembered his words, helplessly responding to the delicate flutters. There was nothing in our bed but us. Nothing could touch us when we were touching each other.

Gideon squeezed both of my cheeks in his hands, grounding me in the moment. I was open and parted for him in every way, completely exposed to his lush dark kiss.

"Oh!" I tensed all over. His tongue was inside me, thrusting. My entire body began to quake from the feeling, my toes curling, my lungs heaving as he possessed me without shame or reservation. *"Ah . . . God."*

I lifted into his mouth, giving myself to him. The affinity between us was brutal and raw, nearly unbearable. I felt seared by his desire, my skin feverish, my chest shaking with sobs I couldn't hold back.

He reached beneath me, pressed the flat of his fingers against my aching clit and rubbing, massaging. His tongue was driving me insane. The orgasm brewing inside me was spurred by the knowledge that there were no longer any boundaries for him with my body. He would do anything he desired—possess it, use it, pleasure it. Burying my face in my pillow, I screamed as I came, the ecstasy so vicious my legs gave out and I melted into the mattress.

Gideon slid over my back, his knee pushing my legs wide, his perspiration-slick body blanketing mine. He mounted me, pushing his cock inside me, his fingers linking with mine and pinning my hands to the bed. I was soaked with him and he rocked against me, sliding in and out.

"I'm desperate for you," he said hoarsely. "I'm miserable without you."

I tensed. "Don't mock me."

"I need you as much." He nuzzled into my hair, fucking me slow and easy. "I'm just as obsessed. Why can't you trust me?"

I squeezed my eyes shut, hot tears leaking out. "I don't understand you. You're tearing me apart."

He turned his head and his teeth sank into the top of my shoulder. A pained growl rumbled through his chest and I felt him coming, his cock jerking as it pumped me full of scorching semen.

His jaw relaxed, releasing me. He panted, his hips still churning. "Your letter gutted me."

"You won't talk to me . . . you won't listen . . ."

"I can't." He groaned, his arms tightening around mine so that I was completely at his mercy. "I just . . . It has to be this way."

"I can't live like this, Gideon."

"I'm hurting, too, Eva. It's killing me, too. Can't you see that?"

"No." I cried, my pillow growing wet beneath my cheek.

"Then stop overthinking and *feel it*! Feel *me*."

The night passed in a blur. I punished him with greedy hands and teeth, my nails raking over sweat-slick skin and muscle until he hissed in pleasured pain.

His lust was frantic and insatiable, his need tinged with a desperation that frightened me because it felt hopeless. It felt like good-bye.

"Need your love," he whispered against my skin. "Need you."

He touched me everywhere. He was constantly inside me, with his cock or his fingers or his tongue.

My nipples burned, made raw by his sucking. My sex throbbed and felt bruised from his wild, hard drives. My skin was chafed from the stubble that prickled over his jaw. My jaw ached from sucking his thick cock. My last memory was of him spooned behind me, his arm banded around my waist as he filled me from behind, both of us sore and exhausted and unable to stop.

"Don't let go," I begged, after I'd sworn I wouldn't.

When I woke to my alarm, he was gone.

15

I STOPPED BY Cary's room before I left for work Thursday morning.
I cracked the door open and peeked in. When I saw he was sleeping, I started to back out.

"Hey," he murmured, blinking at me.

"Hey." I entered. "How are you feeling?"

"I'm glad to be home." He rubbed at the corners of his eyes. "Everything all right?"

"Yeah . . . I just wanted to check on you before I head to work.
I'll be home around eight. I'll grab dinner on the way back, so expect a text around seven to see what you're hungry—" I interrupted
myself with a yawn.

"What kind of vitamins does Cross take?"

"Huh?"

"I'm never *not* horny, and even I can't pile-drive all night like

254 · SYLVIA DAY

that. I kept thinking, 'He's got to be done now.' Then he'd start up again."

I flushed and shifted on my feet.

He howled with laughter. "It's dark in here, but I know you're blushing."

"You should've put your headphones on," I mumbled.

"Don't stress about it. It was good to find out my equipment still works. I hadn't had a chubby since before the attack."

"Eww . . . Gross, Cary." I started backing out of the room. "My dad comes in tonight. Technically tomorrow. His flight lands at five."

"You picking him up?"

"Of course."

His smile faded. "You're going to kill yourself at this rate. You haven't gotten any sleep all week."

"I'll catch up. See ya."

"Hey," he called after me. "Does last night mean you and Cross are okay again?"

I leaned into the doorjamb with a sigh. "Something's wrong, and he won't talk to me about it. I wrote him a letter basically puking out all my insecurities and neuroses."

"*Never* put stuff like that in writing, baby girl."

"Yeah, well . . . all it got me was fucked half to death with no better idea of what the problem is. He said it has to be this way. I don't even know what that means."

He nodded.

"You act like you get it," I said.

"I think I get the sex."

That sent a chill down my spine. "Get-it-out-of-your-system sex?"

"It's possible," he agreed softly.

I closed my eyes and let the confirmation slide through me. Then I straightened. "I gotta run. Catch you later."

THE thing about nightmares was that you couldn't prepare for them. They sneaked up on you when you were most vulnerable, wrecking havoc and mayhem when you were totally defenseless.

And they didn't always happen while you were sleeping.

I sat in an agonized daze as Mark and Mr. Waters went over the fine points of the Kingsman Vodka ads, achingly aware of Gideon sitting at the head of the table in a black suit with white shirt and tie.

He was pointedly ignoring me, had been from the moment I walked into the Cross Industries conference room aside from a cursory handshake when Mr. Waters introduced us. That brief touch of his skin against mine had sent a charge of awareness through me, my body immediately recognizing his as the one that had pleasured it all night. Gideon hadn't seemed to register the contact at all, his gaze trained above my head as he'd said, "Miss Tramell."

The contrast to the last time we'd been in the room was profound. Then, he hadn't been able to keep his eyes off me. His focus had been searing and blatant, and when we'd left the room he'd told me that he wanted to fuck me and would dispense with anything that got in the way of his doing so.

This time, he stood abruptly when the meeting was concluded, shook the hands of Mark and Mr. Waters, and strode out the door with only a short, inscrutable glance at me. His two directors scurried after him, both attractive brunettes.

Mark shot me a questioning look across the table. I shook my head.

I made it back to my desk. I worked industriously for the rest of the day. During my lunch break, I stayed in and looked up things to do with my dad. I decided on three possibilities—the Empire State Building, the Statue of Liberty, and a Broadway play, with the trip to the Statue of Liberty reserved for if he *really* had a desire to go. Otherwise, I figured we could skip the ferry and just check her out from the shore. His time in the city was short, and I didn't want to overload it with a bunch of running around.

On my last break of the day, I called Gideon's office.

"Hi, Scott," I greeted his secretary. "Is it possible for me to talk to your boss real quick?"

"Hold on a minute and I'll see."

I half-expected to have my call rejected, but a couple of minutes later I was put through.

"Yes, Eva?"

I took the length of a heartbeat to savor the sound of his voice. "I'm sorry to bother you. This is probably a stupid question, considering, but . . . are you coming to dinner tomorrow to meet my father?"

"I'll be there," he said gruffly.

"Are you bringing Ireland?" I was surprised there wasn't a tremor in my voice, considering the overwhelming relief I felt.

There was a pause. Then, "Yes."

"Okay."

"I have a late meeting tonight, so I'll have to meet you at Dr. Petersen's. Angus will drive you over. I'll grab a cab."

"All right." I sagged into my seat, feeling a spark of hope. Continuing therapy and meeting my dad could only be seen as positive signs. Gideon and I were struggling. But he hadn't given up yet. "I'll see you then."

Angus dropped me off at Dr. Petersen's office at a quarter to six. I went inside and Dr. Petersen waved at me through his open office door, rising from his seat behind his desk to shake my hand.

"How are you, Eva?"

"I've been better."

His gaze swept over my face. "You look tired."

"So everyone keeps telling me," I said dryly.

He looked over my shoulder. "Where's Gideon?"

"He had a late meeting, so he's coming separately."

"All right." He gestured at the sofa. "This is a nice opportunity for us to talk alone. Is there anything in particular you'd like to discuss before he arrives?"

I settled on the seat and spilled my guts, telling Dr. Petersen about the amazing trip to the Outer Banks and then the bizarre, inexplicable week we'd had since. "I just don't get it. I feel like he's in trouble, but I can't get him to open up at all. He's completely cut me off emotionally. Honestly, I'm beginning to get whiplash. I'm also worried that his change in behavior is because of Corinne. Every time we've hit one of these walls, it's because of her."

I looked at my fingers, which were twisted around each other. They reminded me of my mother's habit of twisting handkerchiefs, and I forced my hands to relax. "It almost seems like she's got some kind of hold on him and he can't break free of it, no matter how he feels about me."

Dr. Petersen looked up from his typing, studying me. "Did he tell you that he wasn't going to make his appointment on Tuesday?"

"No." The news hit me hard. "He didn't say anything."

"He didn't tell me, either. I wouldn't say that's typical behavior for him, would you?"

I shook my head.

Dr. Petersen crossed his hands in his lap. "At times, one or both of you will backtrack a bit. That's to be expected considering the nature of your relationship—you're not just working on you as a couple, but also as individuals so you can be a couple."

"I can't deal with this, though." I took a deep breath. "I can't do this yo-yo thing. It's driving me insane. The letter I sent him . . . It was awful. All true, but awful. We've had some really beautiful moments together. He's said some—"

I had to stop a minute, and when I continued, my voice was hoarse. "He's said some w-wonderful things to me. I don't want to lose those memories in a bunch of ugly ones. I keep debating whether I should quit while I'm ahead, but I'm hanging in here because I promised him—and myself—that I wouldn't run anymore. That I was going to dig my feet in and fight for this."

"That's something you're working on?"

"Yes. Yes, it is. And it's not easy. Because some of the things he does . . . I react in ways I've learned to avoid. For my own sanity! At some point you have to say you gave it your best shot and it didn't work out. Right?"

Dr. Petersen's head tilted to the side. "And if you don't, what's the worst that could happen?"

"You're asking me?"

"Yes. Worst-case scenario."

"Well . . ." I splayed my fingers on my thighs. "He keeps drifting away from me, which makes me cling harder and lose all sense of self-worth. And we end up with him going back to life as he knew it and me going back to therapy trying to get my head on straight again."

He continued to look at me, and something about his patient watchfulness prodded me to keep talking.

"I'm afraid that he won't cut me loose when it's time and that I won't know better. That I'll keep hanging on to the sinking ship and go down with it. I just wish I could trust that he'd end it, if it comes to that."

"Do you think that needs to happen?"

"I don't know. Maybe." I pulled my gaze away from the clock on the wall. "But considering it's nearly seven and he stood us both up tonight, it seems likely."

IT was crazy to me that I *wasn't* surprised to find the Bentley waiting outside my apartment at quarter to five in the morning. The driver who climbed out from behind the wheel when I stepped outside wasn't familiar to me. He was much younger than Angus; early thirties was my guess. He looked Latino, with rich caramel-hued skin, and dark hair and eyes.

"Thanks," I told him, when he rounded the front of the vehicle, "but I'll just grab a cab."

Hearing that, the night doorman to my building stepped out to the street to flag one down for me.

"Mr. Cross said I'm to take you to La Guardia," the driver said.

"You can tell Mr. Cross that I won't be requiring his transportation services now or in the future." I moved toward the cab the doorman had hailed, but stopped and turned around. "And tell him to go fuck himself, too."

I slid into the cab and settled back as it pulled away.

I'LL admit to some bias when I say my father stands out in a crowd, but that didn't make it less true.

As he exited the security area, Victor Reyes commanded attention. He was six feet tall, fit and well built, and had the commanding presence of a man who wore a badge. His gaze raked the immediate area around him, always a cop even when he wasn't on duty. He had a duffel bag slung over his shoulder and wore blue jeans with a black button-down shirt. His hair was dark and wavy, his eyes stormy and gray like mine. He was seriously hot in a brooding, dangerous, bad-boy sort of way, and I tried to picture him alongside my mother's fragile, haughty beauty. I'd never seen them together, not even in pictures, and I really wanted to. If only just once.

"Daddy!" I yelled, waving.

His face lit up when he saw me, and a wide smile curved his mouth.

"There's my girl." He picked me up in a hug that had my feet dangling above the floor. "I've missed you like crazy."

I started crying. I couldn't help it. Being with him again was the last emotional straw.

"Hey." He rocked me. "What's with the tears?"

I wrapped my arms tighter around his neck, so grateful to have him with me, knowing all the other troubles in my life would fade into the background while he was around.

"I missed you like crazy, too," I said, sniffling.

We took a cab back to my place. On the ride over, my dad asked me the same sort of investigative questions about Cary's attack as the detectives had asked Cary in the hospital. I tried to keep him distracted with that discussion when we pulled up outside my building, but it didn't do any good.

My dad's eagle eyes took in the modern glass overhang attached to the brick façade of the building. He stared at the doorman, Paul, who touched the brim of his hat and opened the door for us. He studied the front desk and concierge, and rocked back on his heels as we waited for the elevator.

He didn't say anything and kept his poker face on, but I knew he was thinking about how much my digs must cost in a city like New York. When I showed him into my apartment, his sweeping gaze took in the size of the place. The massive windows had a stunning view of the city, and the flat-screen television mounted on the wall was just one of the many top-of-the-line electronics on display.

He knew I couldn't afford the place on my own. He knew my mother's husband was providing for me in ways he would never be able to. And I wondered if he thought about my mother, and how what she needed was also beyond his means.

"The security here is really tight," I told him by way of explanation. "It's impossible to get past the front desk if you're not on the list and a resident can't be reached to vouch for you."

My dad exhaled in a rush. "That's good."

"Yeah. I don't think Mom could sleep at night otherwise."

That made some of the tension leave his shoulders.

"Let me show you to your room." I led him down the hallway to the guest room suite. It had its own bathroom and mini-bar with fridge. I saw him noting those things before he dropped his duffel on the king-size bed. "Are you tired?"

He looked at me. "I know you are. And you have to work today, don't you? Why don't we nap for a bit before you have to get up?"

I stifled a yawn and nodded, knowing I could use the couple of hours of shut-eye. "Sounds good."

"Wake me when you're up," he said, rolling his shoulders back. "I'll make the coffee while you're getting ready."

"Awesome." My voice came husky with suppressed tears. Gideon almost always had coffee waiting for me on days when he'd spent the night, because he got up before me. I missed that little ritual of ours.

Somehow, I'd have to learn to live without it.

Pushing up onto my tiptoes, I kissed my dad's cheek. "I'm so glad you're here, Daddy."

I closed my eyes and clung tightly when he hugged me.

I stepped out of the small market with my bags of grocery ingredients for dinner and frowned at finding Angus idling at the curb. I'd refused a ride in the morning and again when I'd left the Crossfire, and he was still following and shadowing. It was ridiculous. I couldn't help but wonder if Gideon didn't want me as a girlfriend anymore, but his neurotic lust for my body meant that he didn't want anyone else to have me—namely Brett.

As I walked home, I entertained thoughts of having Brett over for dinner instead, imagining Angus having to make that call to Gideon when Brett came strolling up to my place. It was just a quick vengeful fantasy, since I wouldn't lead Brett on that way and he was in Florida anyway, but it did the trick. My step lightened and when I entered my apartment, I was in my first really good mood in days.

I dumped all the dinner stuff off in the kitchen, then went to find my dad. He was hanging out in Cary's room playing a video game. Cary worked a nunchuk one-handed, since his other hand was in a cast.

"Woo!" my dad shouted. "Spanked."

"You should be ashamed of yourself," Cary shot back, "taking advantage of an invalid."

"I'm crying a river here."

Cary looked at me in the doorway and winked. I loved him so much in that moment I couldn't stop myself from crossing over to him and pressing a kiss to his bruised forehead.

"Thank you," I whispered.

"Thank me with dinner. I'm starving."

I straightened. "I got the goods to make enchiladas."

My dad looked at me, smiling, knowing I'd need his help. "Yeah?"

"When you're ready," I told him. "I'm going to grab a shower."

Forty-five minutes later, my dad and I were in the kitchen rolling cheese and store-bought rotisserie chicken—my little cheat to save time—into lard-soaked white corn tortillas. In the living room, the CD changer slipped in the next disk and Van Morrison's soulful voice piped through the surround sound speakers.

"Oh yeah," my dad said, reaching for my hand and tugging me away from the counter. "Hum-de-rum, hum-de-rum, moondance," he sang in his deep baritone, twirling me.

I laughed, delighted.

Using the back of his hand against my spine to keep his greasy fingers off me, he swept me into a dance around the island, both of us singing the song and laughing. We were making our second revolution when I noticed the two people standing at the breakfast bar.

My smile fled and I stumbled, forcing my dad to catch me.

"You got two left feet?" he teased, his eyes only on me.

"Eva's a wonderful dancer," Gideon interjected, his face arrested in that implacable mask I detested.

My dad turned, his smile fading, too.

Gideon rounded the bar and entered the kitchen. He'd dressed for the occasion in jeans and a Yankees T-shirt. It was a suitably casual choice and a conversation starter, since my dad was a die-hard Padres fan.

"I hadn't realized she was such a good singer, as well. Gideon Cross," he introduced himself, holding out his hand.

"Victor Reyes." My dad waved his shiny fingers. "I'm a bit messy."

"I don't mind."

Shrugging, my dad took his hand and sized him up.

I tossed the dish towel to the guys and made my way over to Ireland, who was positively glowing. Her blue eyes were bright, her cheeks flushed with pleasure.

"I'm so glad you could make it," I said, hugging her carefully. "You look gorgeous!"

"So do you!"

It was a fib, but I appreciated it anyway. I hadn't done anything to my face or hair after my shower, because I knew my dad wouldn't care and I hadn't expected Gideon to show up. After all, the last time I'd heard from him had been when he'd said he would meet me at Dr. Petersen's office.

She looked over at the counter where I'd dumped everything. "Can I help?"

"Sure. Just don't count calories in your head—it'll explode." I introduced her to my dad, who was much warmer to her than he was to Gideon, and then I led her to the sink, where she washed up.

In short order, I had her helping to roll the last few enchiladas, while my dad put the already chilled Dos Equis Gideon had brought into the fridge. I didn't even bother to wonder how Gideon knew I was serving Mexican food for dinner. I only wondered why he'd invest the time to find out when it was very clear he had other things to do—like ditch his appointments.

My dad went to his room to wash up. Gideon came up behind me and put his hands on my waist, his lips brushing over my temple. "Eva."

I tensed against the nearly irresistible urge to lean into him. "Don't," I whispered. "I'd rather we didn't pretend."

His breath left him in a rush that ruffled my hair. His fingers tightened on my hips, kneading for a moment. Then I felt his phone vibrate and he released me, backing away to look at the screen.

"Excuse me," he said gruffly, leaving the kitchen before answering.

Ireland sidled over and whispered, "Thank you. I know you made him bring me along."

I managed a smile for her. "Nobody can make Gideon do anything he doesn't want to."

"You could." She tossed her head, throwing her sleek waist-length black hair over her shoulder. "You didn't see him watching you dance with your dad. His eyes got all shiny. I thought he was going to cry. And on the way up here, in the elevator, he tried to play it off, but I could totally tell he was nervous."

I stared down at the can of enchilada sauce in my hands, feeling my heart break a little more.

"You're mad at him, aren't you?" Ireland asked.

I cleared my throat. "Some people are just better off as friends."

"But you said you love him."

"That's not always enough." I turned around to reach the can opener and found Gideon standing at the other end of the island, staring at me. I froze.

A muscle in his jaw twitched before he unclenched it. "Would you like a beer?" he asked gruffly.

I nodded. I could've used a shot, too. Maybe a few.

"Want a glass?"

"No."

He looked at Ireland. "You thirsty? There's soda, water, milk."

"How about one of those beers?" she shot back, flashing a winsome smile.

"Try again," he said wryly.

I watched Ireland, noting how she sparkled when Gideon focused on her. I couldn't believe he didn't see how she loved him. Maybe right now it was based on superficial things, but it was there and it would grow with a little encouragement. I hoped he'd work on that.

When Gideon handed me the chilled beer, his fingers brushed mine. He held on for a minute, looking into my eyes. I knew he was thinking about the other night.

It seemed like a dream now, as if his visit never really happened. I could almost believe that I'd made it up in a desperate delusion, so hungry for his touch and his love that I couldn't go another minute without giving my mind relief from the madness of wanting and craving. If it weren't for the lingering soreness deep inside me, I wouldn't know what was real and what was nothing but false hope.

I pulled the beer out of his grasp and turned away. I didn't want to say we were done and over, but it was certain now that we needed a break from each other. Gideon needed to figure out what he was doing, what he was looking for, and whether I had any meaningful place in his life. Because this roller-coaster ride we were on was going to break me, and I couldn't let that happen. I wouldn't.

"Can I help with anything?" he asked.

I answered without looking at him, because doing so was too painful. "Can you see if we can get Cary out here? He's got a wheelchair."

"All right."

He left the room, and I could suddenly breathe deeply again.

Ireland hurried over. "What happened to Cary?"

"I'll tell you about it while we set the table."

I was surprised I could eat. I think I was too fascinated by the silent showdown between my dad and Gideon to notice that I was stuffing food into my mouth. At one end of the table, Cary was charming Ireland into peals of laughter that kept making me smile. At the other end, my dad sat at the head of the table, with Gideon on his left and me on his right.

They were talking. The conversation had opened with baseball, as I'd expected, then migrated into golf. On the surface, both men seemed relaxed, but the air around them was highly charged. I noticed that Gideon wasn't wearing his expensive watch. He'd planned carefully to appear as "normal" as possible.

But nothing Gideon did on the outside could change who he was on the inside. It was impossible to hide what he was—a dominant male, a captain of industry, a man of privilege. It was in every gesture he made, every word he spoke, every look he gave.

So he and my father were in the position of struggling to find who would be the alpha, and I suspected *I* hung in the balance. As if anyone were in control of my life but me.

Still, I understood that my father had only really been allowed to *be* a dad in the last four years, and he wasn't ready to give it up. Gideon, however, was jockeying for a position I was no longer prepared to give him.

But he was wearing the ring I'd given him. I tried not to read anything into it, but I wanted to hope. I wanted to believe.

We'd all finished the main course and I was pushing to my feet to clear the table for dessert when the intercom buzzed. I answered.

"Eva? NYPD detectives Graves and Michna are here," the gal at the front desk said.

I glanced at Cary, wondering if the detectives had found out who'd attacked him. I gave the go-ahead for them to come up and hurried back to the dining table.

Cary looked at me with raised brows, curious.

"It's the detectives," I explained. "Maybe they have news."

My dad's focus immediately shifted. Honed. "I'll let them in."

Ireland helped me clear up. We'd just dumped the cups into the sink when the doorbell rang. I wiped my hands with a dish towel and went out to the living room.

The two detectives who entered weren't the ones I expected, because they weren't the ones who'd questioned Cary at the hospital on Monday.

Gideon appeared out of the hallway, shoving his phone into his pocket.

I wondered who'd been calling him all night.

"Eva Tramell," the female detective said, stepping deeper into my apartment. She was a thin woman with a severe face and sharply intelligent blue eyes, which were her best feature. Her hair was brown and curly, her face clean of makeup. She wore slacks over dark flats, a poplin shirt, and a lightweight jacket that didn't hide the badge and gun clipped to her belt. "I'm Detective Shelley Graves of the NYPD. This is my partner, Detective Richard Michna. We're sorry to disturb you on a Friday night."

Michna was older, taller, and portly. His hair was graying at the temples and receding at the top, but he had a strong face and dark eyes that raked the room while Graves focused on me.

"Hello," I greeted them.

My father shut the door, and something about the way he moved or carried himself caught Michna's attention. "You on the job?"

"In California," my dad confirmed. "I'm visiting Eva, my daughter. What's this about?"

"We'd just like to ask you a few questions, Miss Tramell," Graves said. She looked at Gideon. "And you, too, Mr. Cross."

"Does this have something to do with the attack on Cary?" I asked.

She glanced at him. "Why don't we sit down."

We all moved into the living room, but only Ireland and I ended up taking a seat. Everyone else remained on their feet, with my dad pushing Cary's wheelchair.

"Nice place you've got here," Michna said.

"Thank you." I looked at Cary, wondering what the hell was going on.

"How long are you in town?" the detective asked my dad.

"Just for the weekend."

Graves smiled at me. "You go out to California a lot to see your dad?"

"I just moved from there a couple months ago."

"I went to Disneyland once when I was a kid," she said. "That was a while ago, obviously. I've been meaning to get back out there."

I frowned, not understanding why we were making small talk.

"We just need to ask you a couple of questions," Michna said, pulling a notepad out of the interior pocket of his jacket. "We don't want to hold you up any longer than we have to."

Graves nodded, her eyes still on me. "Can you tell us if you're familiar with a man named Nathan Barker, Miss Tramell?"

The room spun. Cary cursed and pushed unsteadily to his feet, taking the few steps to reach the seat beside me. He caught up my hand.

"Miss Tramell?" Graves took a seat on the other end of the sectional.

"He's her former stepbrother," Cary snapped. "What's this about?"

"When's the last time you saw Barker?" Michna asked.

In a courtroom . . . I tried to swallow, but my mouth was dry as sawdust. "Eight years ago," I said hoarsely.

"Did you know he was here in New York?"

Oh God. I shook my head violently.

"Where's this going?" my dad asked.

I looked helplessly at Cary, then at Gideon. My dad didn't know about Nathan. I didn't want him to know.

Cary squeezed my hand. Gideon wouldn't even look at me.

"Mr. Cross," Graves said. "What about you?"

"What about me?"

"Do you know Nathan Barker?"

My eyes pleaded with Gideon not to say anything in front of my dad, but he never once glanced my way.

"You wouldn't be asking that question," he answered, "if you didn't already know the answer."

My stomach dropped. A violent shiver moved through me. Still, Gideon wouldn't look at me. My brain was trying to process what was happening . . . what it meant . . . what was going on . . .

"Is there a point to these questions?" my father asked.

The blood was roaring in my ears. My heart was pounding with something like terror. The mere thought of Nathan being so close was enough to send me into a panic. I was panting. The room was swimming before my eyes. I thought I might pass out.

Graves was watching me like a hawk. "Can you just tell us where you were yesterday, Miss Tramell?"

"Where I was?" I repeated. "Yesterday?"

"Don't answer that," my dad ordered. "This interview isn't going any further until we know what this is about."

Michna nodded, as if he'd expected the interruption. "Nathan Barker was found dead this morning."

16

As soon as Detective Michna finished his sentence, my dad cut the questioning off. "We're done here," he said grimly. "If you have any further questions, you can make an appointment for my daughter to come in with counsel."

"How about you, Mr. Cross?" Michna's gaze moved to Gideon. "Would you mind telling us where you were yesterday?"

Gideon moved from his position behind the couch. "Why don't we talk while I show you out?"

I stared at him, but he still wouldn't look at me.

What else didn't he want me to know? How much was he hiding from me?

Ireland's fingers threaded with mine. Cary sat on one side of me and Ireland on the other, while the man I loved stood several feet away and hadn't glanced at me in almost half an hour. I felt like a cold rock had settled in my gut.

The detectives took down my phone numbers, then left with Gideon. I watched the three of them walk out, saw my dad eyeing Gideon with a hard speculative look.

"Maybe he was buying you an engagement ring," Ireland whispered. "And he doesn't want to blow the surprise."

I squeezed her hand for being sweet and thinking so highly of her brother. I hoped he never let her down or disillusioned her. The way *I* was now disillusioned. Gideon and I were nothing—we had nothing together—if he couldn't be honest with me.

Why hadn't he told me about Nathan?

Releasing Cary and Ireland, I stood and went into the kitchen. My dad followed me.

"Want to fill me in with what's going on?" he asked.

"I have no idea. This is all news to me."

He leaned his hip into the counter and studied me. "What's the history with you and Nathan Barker? You heard his name and looked like you were going to pass out."

I started rinsing off the dishes and loading the dishwasher. "He was a bully, Dad. That's all. He didn't like that his dad remarried, and he especially didn't like that his new stepmom already had a kid."

"Why would Gideon have anything to do with him?"

"That's a really good question." As I gripped the edge of the sink, I bowed my head and closed my eyes. That was what had driven the wedge between me and Gideon—*Nathan*. I knew it.

"Eva?" My dad's hands settled on my shoulders and kneaded into the hard, aching muscles. "Are you okay?"

"I-I'm tired. I haven't been sleeping well." I shut off the water and left the rest of the dishes where they were. I went to the cupboard where we kept our vitamins and over-the-counter medicines and took out two nighttime painkillers. I wanted a deep, dreamless sleep. I needed it, so I could wake up in a condition to figure out what I needed to do.

I looked at my dad. "Can you take care of Ireland until Gideon gets back?"

"Of course." He kissed my forehead. "We'll talk in the morning."

Ireland found me before I could find her. "Are you okay?" she asked, stepping into the kitchen.

"I'm going to lie down, if you don't mind. I know that's rude."

"No, it's okay."

"Really, I'm sorry." I pulled her close for a hug. "We'll do this again. Maybe a girls' day? Hit the spa or go shopping?"

"Sure. Call me?"

"I will." I let her go and passed through the living room to get to the hallway.

The front door opened and Gideon walked in. Our gazes met and held. I could read nothing in his. I looked away, went to my room, and locked the door.

I was up at nine the next morning, feeling groggy and grumpy but no longer overwhelmingly tired. I knew I needed to call Stanton and my mom, but I needed caffeine first.

I washed my face, brushed my teeth, and shuffled out to the living room. I was almost to the kitchen—the source of the luscious smell of coffee—when the doorbell rang. My heart skipped a beat. I couldn't help the instinctive reaction I had to thoughts of Gideon, who was one of the three people on the list to get past the front desk.

But when I opened the door, it was my mother. I hoped I didn't look too disappointed, but I don't think she noticed anyway. She swept right past me in a seafoam green dress that looked painted on, and she pulled it off as very few women could, somehow making the outfit sexy and elegant and age-appropriate. Of course, she looked young enough to be my sister.

She raked a glance over my comfortable SDSU sweatpants and camisole before saying, "Eva. My God. You have no idea—"

"Nathan's dead." I shut the door and glanced nervously down the hallway at the guest bedroom, praying that my dad was still func- tioning on West Coast time and sleeping.

"Oh." She turned around and faced me, and I got my first good look at her. Her mouth was thinned with worry, her blue eyes haunted. "Have the police come by already? They only just left us."

"They were here last night." I headed into the kitchen and straight to the coffeemaker.

"Why didn't you call us? We should have been with you. You should've had *a lawyer* with you, at the very least."

"It was a real quick visit, Mom. Want some?" I held up the carafe.

"No, thank you. You shouldn't drink so much of that stuff. It's not good for you."

I put the carafe back and opened the fridge.

"Dear God, Eva," my mother muttered, watching me. "Do you realize how many calories are in half-and-half?"

I set a bottle of water in front of her and moved back to lighten my coffee. "They were here for about thirty minutes and then left. They didn't get anything out of me beyond Nathan being my former stepbrother and that I haven't seen him in eight years."

"Thank God you didn't say more." She twisted open her water.

I grabbed my mug. "Let's move to my sitting room."

"What? Why? You never sit in there."

She was right, but using it would help prevent a surprise run-in between my parents.

"But *you* like it," I pointed out. We entered through my bedroom and I shut the door behind us, breathing a sigh of relief.

"I do like it," my mother said, turning to take it all in.

Of course she liked it; she'd decorated it. I liked it, too, but didn't really have a use for it. I'd thought about turning it into an adjoining bedroom for Gideon, but everything could be changing now. He'd pulled away from me, hidden Nathan and a dinner with Corinne from me. I wanted an explanation, and depending on what that was, we were going to either recommit to moving forward or take the painful steps to move away from each other.

My mom settled gracefully on the chaise, her gaze coming to rest on me. "You'll have to be very careful with the police, Eva. If they want to talk to you again, let Richard know so he can have his lawyers present."

"Why? I don't understand why I should worry about what I say or don't say. I haven't done anything wrong. I didn't even know he was in town." I watched her gaze skitter away from mine, and my tone firmed. "What's going on, Mom?"

She took a drink before speaking. "Nathan showed up in Richard's office last week. He wanted two and a half million dollars."

There was a sudden roaring in my ears. *"What?"*

"He wanted money," she said stiffly. "A lot of it."

"Why the hell would he think he'd get any?"

"He has—*had*—photos, Eva." Her lower lip began to quiver. "And video. Of you."

"Oh my God." I set my coffee aside with shaking hands and bent over, putting my head between my knees. "Oh God, I'm going to be sick."

And Gideon had seen Nathan—he'd confessed as much when he answered the detectives' questions. If he'd seen the pictures . . . been disgusted by them . . . it would explain why he cut me off. Why he'd been so tormented when he came to my bed. He might still want me, but he might not be able to live with the images now filling his head.

It has to be this way, he'd said.

A horrible sound escaped me. I couldn't even begin to imagine what Nathan might have captured. I didn't want to.

No wonder Gideon couldn't stand to look at me. When he'd made love to me the last time, it had been in utter darkness, where he could hear me and smell me and feel me—but not see me.

I stifled a scream of pain by biting my forearm.

"Baby, no!" My mother sank to her knees in front of me, urging me gently off the chair and onto the floor where she could rock me. "Shh. It's over. He's dead."

I curled into her lap, sobbing, realizing it truly was over—I'd lost Gideon. He would hate himself for turning away from me, but I understood why he might not be able to stop himself. If looking at me now reminded him of his own brutal past, how could he stand it? How could I?

My mother's hand stroked over my hair. I felt her crying, too. "Shh," she hushed me, her voice shaking. "Shh, baby. I've got you. I'll take care of you."

Eventually there were no more tears left to cry. I was empty, but with that emptiness came new clarity. I couldn't change what had happened, but I could do what was necessary to make sure that no one I loved suffered for it.

I sat up and wiped at my eyes.

"You shouldn't do that," my mother scolded. "Rubbing at your eyes like that will give you wrinkles."

For some reason, I found her concern for my future crow's-feet hysterical. I tried to hold it in, but a snorted laugh broke free.

"Eva Lauren!"

I thought her indignation was funny, too. I laughed some more, and once I started, I couldn't stop. I laughed until my sides hurt and I fell over.

"Oh, stop it!" She shoved at my shoulder. "It's not funny."

I laughed until I managed to squeeze out a few more tears.

"Eva, really!" But she was starting to smile.

I laughed until I wasn't laughing so much as sobbing again, dry and silent. I heard my mother giggling, and that somehow blended perfectly with my wracking pain. I couldn't explain it, but as horrible and hopeless as I felt, my mother's presence—complete with all her little quirks and admonitions that drove me insane—was just what I needed.

With my hands on my cramping stomach, I took a deep cleansing breath. "Did he arrange it?" I asked softly.

Her smiled faded. "Who? Richard? Arrange what? The money? *Oh...*"

I waited.

"No!" she protested. "He wouldn't. His mind doesn't work that way."

"Okay. I just had to know." I couldn't see Stanton ordering a hit, either. But Gideon . . .

I knew from his nightmares that his desire for vengeance was colored by violence. And I'd seen him fight Brett. The memory was seared in my mind. Gideon was capable, and with his history—

I took a deep breath, then blew it out. "How much do the police know?"

"Everything." Her eyes were soft and wet with guilt. "The seal on Nathan's records was broken when he died."

"And how did he die?"

"They didn't say."

"I suppose it's not important. We have a motive." I ran my hand through my hair. "It probably doesn't matter that we didn't personally have the opportunity. Your time is accounted for, isn't it? And Stanton's?"

"Yes. And yours, too?"

"Yes." But I didn't know about Gideon's. Not that it mattered. No one would expect men like Gideon and Stanton to get their hands dirty cleaning up a mess like Nathan.

We had more than one motive—the blackmail and revenge for what he'd done to me—and means, and means gave us the opportunity.

I brushed my hair again and splashed water on my face, all the while thinking of how I was going to get my mom out of my apartment undetected. When I found her digging through the closet in my bedroom—concerned as always about my style and appearance—I knew what to do.

"Remember that skirt I picked up at Macy's?" I asked her. "The green one?"

"Oh, yes. Very pretty."

"I haven't been able to wear it, because I can't think of anything I have to go with it. Can you help me find something?"

"Eva," she said, exasperated. "You should've established a personal style by now—and it shouldn't be sweats!"

"Help me out, Mom. I'll be right back." I took my coffee mug with me to have a purpose for leaving her. "Don't go anywhere."

"Where would I go?" she replied, her voice muffled because she'd stepped deeper into my walk-in closet.

I did a quick check of the living room and kitchen. My dad was nowhere to be seen and his bedroom door was closed, as was Cary's. I hurried back into my room.

"How's this?" she asked, holding up a champagne-hued silk blouse. The combination was gorgeous and classy.

"I love it! You rock! Thank you. But I'm sure you have to go now, right? I don't want to hold you up."

My mom frowned at me. "I'm not in a hurry."

"What about Stanton? This has got to be weighing on his mind. And it's a Saturday—he always reserves his weekends for you. He needs to have the time with you."

And God, did I feel awful for his stress. Stanton had spent a great deal of his time and money on issues pertaining to me and Nathan over the four years he'd been married to my mother. It was too much to ask of anyone, but he'd come through for us. For the rest of my life, I would owe him for loving my mother so much.

"This is weighing on your mind, too," she argued. "I want to be here for you, Eva. I want to support you."

My throat tightened, understanding that she was trying to make amends for what had happened to me because she was unable to forgive herself. "It's okay," I said hoarsely. "I'll be okay. And honestly, I'd feel terrible keeping you away from Stanton after all he's done for us. You're his reward, his little piece of heaven at the end of an endless workweek."

Her lips curved in an enchanting smile. "What a lovely thing to say."

Yes, I'd thought so, too, the times Gideon had said similar things to me.

It seemed impossible that only a week before, we'd been at the beach house, madly in love and taking firm, sure steps forward in our relationship.

But now that relationship was broken, and now I knew why. I was angry and hurt that Gideon had kept something as monumental as Nathan being in New York hidden from me. I was furious that he hadn't talked to me about what he was thinking and feeling. But I understood, too. He was a man who'd avoided talking about anything personal for years and years, and we hadn't been together long enough for that lifetime habit to change. I couldn't blame him for being who he was, just as I couldn't blame him for deciding that he couldn't live with what I was.

With a sigh, I went to my mom and hugged her. "Having you here . . . it's what I needed, Mama. Crying and laughing and just sitting with you. Nothing could be more perfect than that. Thank you."

"Really?" She hugged me tightly, feeling so small and delicate in my arms, even though we were the same size and her heels made her taller. "I thought you were going crazy."

I pulled back and smiled. "I think I did for a little bit, but you brought me back. And Stanton is a good man. I'm grateful for all he's done for us. Please tell him I said so."

Linking my arm with hers, I grabbed her clutch from my bed and led her to the front door. She hugged me again, her hands stroking up and down my back. "Call me tonight and tomorrow. I want to make sure you're doing okay."

"All right."

She studied me. "And let's plan on a spa day next week. If the doctor doesn't approve of Cary going, we'll have the technicians come here. I think we could all use a little pampering and polish right now."

"That's a really nice way of saying I look like shit." We were both rough around the edges, although she hid it much better than I did.

Nathan was still hanging over us like a dark cloud, still capable of ruining lives and destroying our peace. But we'd pretend that we were better off than we were. That was just the way we did things. "But you're right—it'll be good for us and it'll make Cary feel a whole lot better, even if he can only get a mani and pedi."

"I'll make the arrangements. I can't wait!" My mother flashed her signature megawatt smile—

—which is what my dad was hit with when I opened the front door. He stood on the threshold with Cary's keys in his hand, having been caught just about to slide one into the lock. He was dressed in running shorts and athletic shoes, his sweat-soaked shirt tossed carelessly over his shoulder. Still breathing a little quickly and glistening with sweat over tanned skin and rippling muscles, Victor Reyes was one hot hunk of a man.

And he was staring at my mom in a way that was totally indecent.

Tearing my gaze away from my seriously smokin' dad to look at my glamorous mother, I was shocked to see her looking at my father the same way he was looking at her.

Of all the times to realize my parents were in love with each other. Well, I'd suspected my dad was heartbroken over my mom, but I thought she'd been embarrassed about him, as if he were a big mistake and error in judgment in her past.

"Monica." My dad's voice was lower and deeper than I'd ever heard it, and more obviously flavored with an accent.

"Victor." My mom was breathless. "What are you doing here?"

One of his brows rose. "Visiting our daughter."

"And now Mom has to go," I prodded, torn between the novelty of seeing my parents together and a loyalty to Stanton, who was exactly what my mother needed. "I'll call you later, Mom."

282 · SYLVIA DAY

My dad didn't move for a moment, his gaze sliding down the length of my mom from head to toe, then gliding back up again. Then he took a deep breath and stepped aside.

My mom stepped out into the hallway and turned toward the elevator, and then at the last minute she turned back. She placed her palm over my dad's heart and lifted onto her tiptoes, kissing one of his cheeks and then the other.

"Good-bye," she breathed.

I watched her walk unsteadily to the elevator and push the button, her back to us. My dad didn't look away until the car doors closed behind her.

He exhaled in a rush and came into my apartment.

I shut the door. "How is it that I didn't know you two are crazy in love with each other?"

The look in his eyes was painful to witness. The raw agony was like an open wound. "Because it doesn't mean anything."

"I don't believe that. Love means everything."

"It doesn't conquer all like they say." He snorted. "Can you see your mother being a cop's wife?"

I winced.

"Right," he said dryly, wiping his forehead with his shirt. "Sometimes love isn't enough. And if it's not enough, what good is it?"

The bitterness I heard in his words was something I knew very well myself. I passed him and went into the kitchen.

My dad followed me. "Are you in love with Gideon Cross?"

"Isn't it obvious?"

"Is he in love with you?"

Because I just didn't have the energy, I dumped my mug in the sink and pulled out new ones for me and my dad. "I don't know. I know he wants me, and sometimes he needs me. I think he'd do

REFLECTED IN YOU · 283

anything he could for me if I asked, because I've gotten under his skin a bit."

But he couldn't tell me that he loved me. He wouldn't tell me about his past. And he couldn't, apparently, live with the evidence of *my* past.

"You've got a good head on your shoulders."

I pulled coffee beans out of the freezer to make a fresh pot. "That's seriously debatable, Dad."

"You're honest with yourself. That's a good trait to have." He gave me a tight smile when I looked over my shoulder at him. "I used your tablet earlier to check my e-mail. It was on the coffee table. I hope you don't mind."

I shook my head. "Help yourself."

"I surfed the Internet while I was on there. Wanted to see what popped up about Cross."

My heart sank a little. "You don't like him."

"I'm withholding judgment." My dad's voice faded as he moved into the living room, then strengthened again as he returned with my tablet in hand.

As I ground the beans, he flipped open the tablet's protective case and started tapping at the screen.

"I had a hard time getting a bead on him last night. I just wanted a little more information. I found some pictures of the two of you together that looked promising." His gaze was on the screen. "Then I found something else."

He turned the tablet around to face me. "Can you explain this to me? Is this another sister of his?"

Leaving the ground coffee to sit, I moved closer, my eyes on the article my dad had found on Page Six. The picture was of Gideon and Corinne at some sort of cocktail party. He had his arm around her waist, and their body language was familiar and intimate. He was very close to her, his lips nearly touching her temple. She had a drink in her hand and was laughing.

I picked up the tablet and read the caption: *Gideon Cross, CEO of Cross Industries, and Corinne Giroux at the Kingsman Vodka publicity mixer.*

My fingers shook as I scrolled to the top of the page and read the brief article, searching for more information. I went numb when I saw the mixer had been Thursday, from six to nine, at one of Gideon's properties—one I knew all too well. He'd fucked me there, just as he'd fucked dozens of women there.

Gideon had stood me up for our appointment with Dr. Petersen to take Corinne to his fuck-pad hotel.

That was what he'd wanted to tell the detectives that he didn't want me to hear: His alibi was an evening—maybe the whole night—spent with another woman.

Setting the tablet down with more care than necessary, I released the breath I'd been holding. "That's not his sister."

"I didn't think so."

I looked at him. "Could you do me a favor and finish making the coffee? I have a call to make."

"Sure. Then I'm going to grab a shower." He reached over and set his hand on top of mine. "Let's go out and erase this whole morning. Sound good?"

"Sounds perfect."

I grabbed the phone off its base and went back to my bedroom. I hit the speed dial for Gideon's cell and waited for him to pick up. Three rings later, he did.

"Cross," he said, although his screen would've told him it was me. "I really can't talk right now."

"Then just listen. I'll time myself. One minute. One goddamn minute of your time. Can you give me that?"

"I really—"

"Did Nathan come to you with photos of me?"

"This isn't—"

"Did he?" I snapped.

"Yes," he bit out.

"Did you look at them?"

There was a long pause, then, "Yes."

I exhaled. "Okay. I think you're a total asshole for letting me go to Dr. Petersen's office when you knew you weren't coming because you were going out with another woman instead. That's just serious douche bag territory, Gideon. And worse, it was a Kingsman event, too, which should've had *some* sentimental value to you, considering that's how—"

There was the abrupt scraping noise of a chair being shoved back. I rushed on, desperate to say what needed to be said before he hung up.

"I think you're a coward for not coming right out and saying we're over, especially before you started fucking around with someone else."

"Eva. Goddamn it."

"But I want you to know that even though the way you've handled this is fucking *wrong* and you've broken my heart into millions of tiny pieces and I've lost all respect for you, I don't blame you for how you feel after seeing those pictures of me. I get it."

"Stop." His voice was little more than a whisper, making me wonder if Corinne was with him even now.

"I don't want you to blame yourself, okay? After what you and I have been through—not that I know what you've been through because you never told me—but anyway . . ." I sighed and winced at how shaky it came out. Worse, when I opened my mouth again, my words were watery with tears. "Don't blame yourself. I don't. I just want you to know that."

"Christ," he breathed. "Please stop, Eva."

"I'm done. I hope you find—" My hand clenched in my lap. "Never mind. Good-bye."

I hung up and dropped the phone on my bed. I stripped off my clothes on the way to the shower and set the ring Gideon had given me on the counter. I turned the water on as hot as I could stand it and sank numbly to the floor of the stall.

I had nothing left.

17

FOR THE REST of Saturday and Sunday, my dad and I bounced all over the city. I made sure he did the food thing, taking him to Junior's for cheesecake, Gray's Papaya for hot dogs, and John's for pizza, which we took back to the apartment to share with Cary. We went up to the top of the Empire State Building, which also satisfied the Statue of Liberty requirement as far as my dad was concerned. We enjoyed a matinee show on Broadway. We walked to Times Square, which was hot and crowded and smelled awful but had some interesting—and a few half-naked—street performers. I snapped pictures with my phone and sent them to Cary for a laugh.

My dad was impressed with the emergency responder presence in the city and liked seeing the police officers on horseback as much as I did. We took a ride around Central Park in a horse-drawn carriage and braved the subway together. I took him to Rockefeller

Center and Macy's and the Crossfire, which he admitted was an impressive building more than capable of holding its own among other impressive buildings. But through it all, we were just hanging out. Mostly walking and talking and simply being together.

I finally learned how he'd met my mom. Her sleek little sports car had gotten a flat tire and she'd ended up at the auto shop where he was working. Their story reminded me of the old Billy Joel hit "Uptown Girl," and I told him so. My dad laughed and said it was one of his favorite songs. He said he could still see her sliding out from behind the wheel of her expensive little toy car and rocking his world. She was the most beautiful thing he'd seen before or since . . . until I came along.

"Do you resent her, Daddy?"

"I used to." He put his arm around my shoulders. "I'm never going to forgive her for not giving you my last name when you were born. But I'm not mad about the money thing anymore. I'd never be able to make her happy in the long run, and she knew herself enough to know that."

I nodded, feeling sorry for all of us.

"And really"—he sighed and rested his cheek against the top of my head for a moment—"as much as I wish I could give you all the things her husbands can, I'm just glad you're getting them. I'm not too proud to appreciate that your life is better because of her choices. And I'm not upset with my lot. I've got a good life that makes me happy and a daughter who makes me so damn proud. I consider myself a rich man because there's nothing in this world I want that I don't already have."

I stopped walking and hugged him. "I love you, Daddy. I'm so happy you're here."

His arms came around me, and I thought I just might be all right eventually. Both my mom and my dad were living fulfilling lives without the one they loved.

I could do it, too.

I fell into a depression after my dad left. The next few days crawled by. Every day I told myself I wasn't waiting on some sort of contact from Gideon, but when I crawled into bed at night, I cried myself to sleep because another day had ended without a word from him.

The people around me worried. Steven and Mark were overly solicitous at lunch on Wednesday. We went to the Mexican restaurant where Shawna worked, and the three of them tried so hard to make me laugh and enjoy myself. I did, because I loved spending time with all three of them and hated the concern I saw in their eyes, but there was a hole inside me that nothing could fill and a niggling worry about the investigation into Nathan's death.

My mom called me every day, asking if the police had contacted me again—they hadn't—and filling me in if the police had contacted her or Stanton that day.

I worried that they were circling around Stanton, but I had to believe that because my stepfather was obviously innocent, there was nothing for them to find. Still . . . I wondered if they would end up finding anything. It was obviously a homicide or they wouldn't be investigating. With Nathan being new to the city, who did he know who'd want to kill him?

In the back of my mind, I couldn't help but think that Gideon had arranged it. That made it harder for me to get over him, because there was a part of me—the little girl I'd once been—who'd wanted Nathan dead for a long time. Who'd wanted him to hurt like he'd hurt me for years. I'd lost my innocence to him, as well as my vir-

290 · SYLVIA DAY

ginity. I'd lost my self-esteem and self-respect. And in the end, I'd lost a child in an agonizing miscarriage when I was no more than a child myself.

I got through every day one minute at a time. I forced myself to go to Parker for Krav Maga, to watch TV, to smile and laugh when it was appropriate—most especially around Cary—and to get up every morning and face a new day. I tried to ignore how dead I felt inside. Nothing was vivid to me beyond the pain that throbbed through me like a constant dull ache. I lost weight and slept a lot without feeling rested.

On Thursday, Day Six After Gideon: Round Two, I left a message with Dr. Petersen's receptionist letting her know that Gideon and I wouldn't be coming to our sessions anymore. That evening, I had Clancy swing by Gideon's apartment building, and I left the ring he'd given me and the key to his apartment in a sealed envelope with the front desk. I didn't leave a note because I'd said everything I had to say.

On Friday, one of the other junior account managers got an assistant, and Mark asked if I'd help the new hire get settled. His name was Will and I liked him right away. He had dark hair that was curly but worn short. He had long sideburns and wore square-framed glasses that were very flattering on him. He drank soda instead of coffee and was still dating his high school sweetheart.

I spent much of the morning showing him around the offices.

"You like it here," he said.

"I love it here." I smiled.

Will smiled back. "I'm glad. I wasn't sure at first. You didn't seem all that enthusiastic, even when you were saying good stuff."

"My bad. I'm going through a tough breakup." I tried to shrug it off. "It's hard for me to get excited about anything right now, even things I'm crazy about. This job being one of them."

"I'm sorry about the breakup," he said, his dark eyes warm with sympathy.

"Yeah. Me, too."

Cary was looking and feeling better by Saturday. His ribs were still bandaged and his arm was going to be in a cast for a while, but he was walking around on his own and didn't need the nurse anymore.

My mom brought a beauty team over to our apartment—six women in white lab coats who appropriated my living room. Cary was in heaven. He had no qualms whatsoever about enjoying spa day. My mom looked tired, which wasn't like her at all. I knew she was worried about Stanton. And she was maybe spending time thinking about my dad, too. It seemed impossible to me that she wouldn't, after seeing him for the first time in nearly twenty-five years. His longing for her had been hot and alive to me; I couldn't imagine what it must have felt like to her.

As for me, it was just great to be around two people who loved me and knew me well enough not to bring up Gideon or give me a hard time for being a bummer to hang around with. My mom brought me a box of my favorite Knipschildt truffles, which I savored slowly. It was the one indulgence she never scolded me about. Even she agreed that a woman had a right to chocolate.

"What are you going to have done?" Cary asked me, looking at me with a bunch of black goop smeared all over his face. He was getting his hair trimmed in its usual sexily floppy style, and his toenails were being trimmed and filed into perfect rounded squares.

I licked the chocolate off my fingers and considered my answer. The last time we'd had a spa date, I'd just agreed to have an affair with Gideon. He and I were going on our first date, and I knew we'd be having sex. I'd chosen a package designed for seduction, making my skin soft and fragrant with scents purported to have aphrodisiac properties.

Everything was different now. In a way, I had a second chance to do things over. The investigation into Nathan's death was a concern for us all, but the fact that he was gone from my life forever liberated me in a way I hadn't realized I'd needed. Somewhere in the back of my mind, the fear must have been lurking there. It was always a possibility that I could see him again as long as he was alive. Now I was free.

I also had a new chance to embrace my New York life in a way I hadn't before. I was accountable to no one. I could go anywhere with anyone. *I* could *be* anyone. Who was the Eva Tramell who lived in Manhattan and had her dream job at an advertising agency? I didn't know yet. Up until now, I'd been the San Diego transplant who got swept into the orbit of an enigmatic and incredibly powerful man. *That* Eva was on Day Eight After Gideon: Round Two curled in a corner licking her wounds and would be for a long time. Maybe forever, because I couldn't imagine that I'd ever fall in love again like I had with Gideon. For better or worse, he was my soul mate. The other half of me. In many ways, he was my reflection.

"Eva?" Cary prodded, studying me.

"I want everything done," I said decisively. "I want a new haircut. Something short and flirty and chic. I want my nails painted fire engine red—fingers and toes. I want to be a new Eva."

Cary's brows rose. "Nails, yes. Hair, maybe. You shouldn't make sweeping decisions when you're fucked up over a guy. They come back to haunt you."

My chin lifted. "I'm doing it, Cary Taylor. You can either help or just shut up and watch."

"Eva!" My mother practically squealed. "You're going to look amazing! I know just the thing to do with your hair. You'll *love* it!"

Cary's lips twitched. "All righty, then, baby girl. Let's see what New Eva looks like."

NEW Eva turned out to be a modern, slightly edgy sexpot. My once long, straight blond hair was now shoulder length and cut in long layers, with platinum highlights sprinkled throughout and framing my face. I'd had my makeup done, too, to see what sort of look I should pair with my new hairdo, and I learned that smoky gray for my eyes was the way to go, along with soft pink lip gloss.

In the end, I hadn't gone with red for my nails and chose chocolate instead. I really liked it. For now, anyway. I was willing to admit I might be going through a phase.

"Okay, I take it back," Cary said, whistling. "Clearly you wear breakups well."

"See?" my mother crowed, grinning. "I told you! Now you look like an urban sophisticate."

"Is that what you call it?" I studied my reflection, amazed at the transformation. I appeared a bit older. Definitely more polished. Certainly sexier. It boosted my spirits to see someone else looking back at me besides the hollow-eyed young woman I'd been seeing for nearly two weeks now. Somehow, my thinner face and sad eyes paired well with the bolder style.

My mom insisted we go out for dinner since we all looked so good. She called Stanton and told him to get ready for a night out, and I could tell from her end of the conversation that she was delighting him with her girlish excitement. She left it to him to pick the place and make the arrangements, then continued with my makeover by picking a little black dress out of my closet. As I slipped it on, she held up one of my ivory cocktail dresses.

"Go for it," I told her, finding it amusing and pretty amazing that my mother could pull off wearing the clothes of someone nearly twenty years younger.

When we were set, she went to Cary's room and helped him get ready.

I watched from the doorway as my mother fussed over him, talking the whole time in that way she had that didn't require reciprocal conversation. Cary stood there with a sweet smile on his face, his eyes following her around the room with something like joy.

Her hands brushed over his broad shoulders, smoothing the pressed linen of his dress shirt, and then she expertly knotted his tie and stepped back to take in her handiwork. The sleeve on his casted arm was unbuttoned and rolled up, and his face still had yellow and purple bruising, but nothing could detract from the overall effect of Cary Taylor dressed for a casually elegant night out.

My mother's smile lit up the room. "Stunning, Cary. Simply stunning."

"Thank you."

Stepping forward, she kissed him on the cheek. "Almost as beautiful on the outside as you are on the inside."

I watched him blink and look at me, his green eyes filled with confusion. I leaned into the doorjamb and said, "Some of us can see right through you, Cary Taylor. Those gorgeous looks don't fool us. We know you've got that big beautiful heart inside you."

"Come on!" my mom said, grabbing both of our hands and pulling us out of the room.

When we made it down to the lobby level, we found Stanton's limousine waiting. My stepfather climbed out of the back and wrapped his arms around my mom, pressing a gentle kiss to her cheek because he knew she wouldn't want to mess up her lipstick. Stanton was an attractive man, with snow white hair and denim blue eyes. His face bore some traces of his years, but he was still a very attractive man, one who stayed fit and active.

"Eva!" He hugged me, too, and kissed my cheek. "You look ravishing."

I smiled, not quite sure whether being "ravishing" meant I looked like I was going to ravish someone or was waiting to be ravished.

Stanton shook Cary's hand and gave him a gentle slap to the shoulder. "It's good to see you back on your feet, young man. You gave us all a scare."

"Thank you. For everything."

"No thanks necessary," Stanton said, waving it off. "Ever."

My mom took a deep breath, then let it out. Her eyes were bright as she watched Stanton. She caught me looking at her and smiled, and it was a peaceful smile.

We ended up at a private club with a big band and two excellent singers—one male and one female. They switched frequently throughout the evening, providing the perfect accompaniment to a candlelit meal served in a high-backed velvet booth right out of a classic Manhattan society photo. I couldn't help but be charmed.

Between dinner and dessert, Cary asked me to dance. We'd taken formal dance classes together, at my mother's insistence, but we had to take it easy with Cary's injuries. We basically just swayed in place, enjoying the contentment that came from ending a happy day with a good meal shared with loved ones.

"Look at them," Cary said, watching Stanton expertly lead my mom around the dance floor. "He's crazy about her."

"Yes. And she's good for him. They give each other what they need."

He looked down at me. "You thinking about your dad?"

"A little." I reached up and ran my fingers through his hair, thinking of longer and darker strands that felt like thick silk. "I never really thought of myself as romantic. I mean, I like romance and grand gestures and that tipsy feeling you get when you're crushing hard on someone. But the whole Prince Charming fantasy and marrying the love of your life wasn't my thing."

"You and me, baby girl, we're too jaded. We just want mind-blowing sex with someone who knows we're fucked up and accepts it."

My mouth twisted wryly. "Somewhere along the way, I deluded myself into thinking Gideon and I could have it all. That being in love was all we needed. I guess because I never really thought I'd ever fall in love like that, and there's the whole myth that when you do, you're supposed to live happily ever after."

Cary pressed his lips to my brow. "I'm sorry, Eva. I know you're hurting. I wish I could fix it."

"I don't know why it never occurred to me to just find someone I can be happy with."

"Too bad we don't want to bang each other. We'd be perfect."

I laughed and leaned my cheek against his heart.

When the song ended, we pulled apart and started toward our table. I felt fingers circle my wrist and turned my head—

I found myself looking into the eyes of Christopher Vidal Jr., Gideon's half brother.

"I'd like to have the next dance," he said, his mouth curved in a boyish grin. There was no sign of the malicious man I'd witnessed on a secret video Cary had captured during a garden party at the Vidal residence.

Cary stepped forward, looking at me for cues.

My first instinct was to refuse Christopher, and then I looked around. "Are you here alone?"

"Does it matter?" He tugged me into his arms. "You're the one I want to dance with. I've got her," he said to Cary, sweeping me off.

We'd first met just like this, with him asking me to dance. I'd been on my first date with Gideon, and things had already begun falling apart at that point.

"You look fantastic, Eva. I love your hair."

I managed a tight smile. "Thank you."

"Relax," he said. "You're so stiff. I won't bite."

"Sorry. Just want to be sure I don't offend whoever you're here with."

"Just my parents and the manager of a singer who'd like to sign with Vidal Records."

"Ah." My smile widened into one more genuine. That was just what I was hoping to hear.

As we danced, I kept searching the room. I saw it as a sign when the song ended and Elizabeth Vidal stood, catching my eye. She excused herself from her table and I excused myself from Christopher, who protested.

"I have to freshen up," I told him.

"All right. But I insist on buying you a drink when you come back."

I took off after his mother, debating whether I should just come out and tell Christopher I thought he was a total asswipe of epic proportions. I didn't know if Magdalene had told him about the video, and if she hadn't, I figured there was probably a good reason why.

I waited for Elizabeth just outside the bathroom. When she reappeared, she spotted me hanging out in the hallway and smiled. Gideon's mother was a beautiful woman, with long straight black hair and the same amazing blue eyes as her son and Ireland. Just looking at her made my heart hurt. I missed Gideon so much. It was an hourly battle with myself not to contact him and take whatever I could get.

"Eva." She greeted me with air kisses for each of my cheeks.

298 · SYLVIA DAY

"Christopher said it was you. I didn't recognize you at first. You look so different with your hair like that. I think it's lovely."

"Thanks. I need to talk to you. Privately."

"Oh?" She frowned. "Is something wrong? Is it Gideon?"

"Come on." I gestured deeper down the hallway, toward the emergency exit.

"What's this about?"

Once we were away from the bathrooms, I told her. "Remember when Gideon was a child and he told you he'd been abused or violated?"

Her face paled. "He told you about that?"

"No. But I've witnessed his nightmares. His horrible, ugly, vicious nightmares where he begs for mercy." My voice was low but throbbed with anger. It was all I could do to keep my hands to myself as she stood there looking both embarrassed and militant. "It was your job to protect and support him!"

Her chin went up. "You don't know—"

"You're not to blame for what happened before you knew." I got in her face, felt satisfaction when she took a step back. "But anything that happened after he told you is entirely your fault."

"Fuck you," she spat at me. "You have no idea what you're talking about. How dare you come up to me like this and say these things to me when you're clueless!"

"Yeah, I dare. Your son is seriously damaged by what happened to him, and your refusal to believe him made it a million times worse."

"You think I would tolerate the abuse of my own child?" Her face was flushed with anger and her eyes too bright. "I had Gideon examined by two separate pediatricians to look for . . . trauma. I did everything I could be expected to do."

"Except believe him. Which is what you should've done as his mother."

"I'm Christopher's mother, too, and he was there. He swears nothing happened. Who was I supposed to believe when there was no proof? No one could find anything to support Gideon's claims."

"He shouldn't have had to provide proof. He was a child!" The anger I felt was vibrating through me. My fists were clenched against the urge to hit her. Not just for what Gideon had lost, but for what we'd lost together. "You were supposed to take his side no matter what."

"Gideon was a troubled boy, struggling through therapy over his father's death, and desperate for attention. You don't know what he was like then."

"I know what he's like now. He's broken and hurting and doesn't think he's worth loving. And you helped make him that way."

"Go to hell." She stormed off.

"I'm already there," I shouted after her. "And so is your son."

I spent all day Sunday being Old Eva.

Trey had the day off and took Cary out for brunch and a movie. I was pleased to see them together, thrilled that they were both trying. Cary hadn't invited over any of the people who called his cell, and I wondered if he was rethinking his friendships. I suspected many were of the fair-weather variety—great fun but no substance.

Having the entire apartment to myself, I slept too much, ate crappy food, and never bothered to change out of my pajamas. I cried over Gideon in the privacy of my room, staring at the collage of photos that used to be on my desk at work. I missed the weight of his ring on my finger and the sound of his voice. I missed the feel of his hands and lips on me and the tenderly possessive way he took care of me.

When Monday came around, I left the apartment as New Eva. With smoky eyes, pink lips, and my new bouncy layered cut, I felt like I could pretend to be someone else for the day. Someone who wasn't heartbroken and lost and angry.

I saw the Bentley when I stepped outside, but Angus didn't bother to exit the car, knowing I wouldn't accept a ride. It puzzled me that Gideon would have him wasting his time hanging around, just in case I might have him drive me somewhere. It didn't make any sense unless Gideon was feeling guilty. I hated guilt, hated that it afflicted so many of the people in my life. I wish they'd just drop it and move on. Like I was trying to do.

The morning at Waters Field & Leaman went by swiftly, because I had Will, the new assistant, to help out as well as my regular work to do. I was glad that he wasn't afraid to ask lots of questions, because he kept me too busy to count the seconds, minutes, and hours since the last time I'd seen Gideon.

"You look good, Eva," Mark said when I first joined him in his office. "Are you doing all right?"

"Not really. But I'll get there."

He leaned forward, setting his elbows on his desk. "Steven and I broke up once, about a year and a half into our relationship. We'd had a rough couple weeks and decided it'd be easier to let it go. It was fucking awful," he said vehemently. "I hated every minute of it. Getting up every morning was a monumental feat and he was in the same shape. So anyway . . . if you need anything . . . "

"Thank you. The best thing you can do for me right now is keep me busy. I just don't want any time to think about anything but work."

"I can do that."

When lunch came around, Will and I grabbed Megumi and we headed to a nearby pizza place. Megumi filled me in on her growing relationship with her blind date, and Will told us about his adventures at Ikea as he and his girlfriend worked on filling their loft apartment with do-it-yourself furniture. I was glad I had my spa day to talk about.

"We're heading to the Hamptons this weekend," Megumi said as we returned to the Crossfire. "My guy's grandparents have a place out there. How cool is that?"

"Very." I passed through the turnstiles beside her. "I'm jealous you'll be able to get away from the heat."

"I know, right?"

"Better than furniture assembly," Will muttered, following a group of people onto one of the elevators. "I can't wait 'til we're done."

The doors started to close, and then they slid open again. Gideon stepped into the car after us. The familiar, palpable energy that always coursed between us hit me hard. Awareness rippled down my spine and flared outward, sending goose bumps racing across my skin. The hair on my nape prickled.

Megumi glanced at me, and I shook my head. I knew better than to look directly at him. I couldn't be sure I wouldn't do something rash or desperate. I craved him so deeply, and it had been too long since he'd held me. I used to have the right to touch him, to reach for his hand, to lean into him, to sift my fingers through his hair. It was a horrible ache inside me that I wasn't allowed to do those things anymore. I had to bite my lip to stifle a moan of agony at being this close to him again.

I kept my head down, but I *felt* Gideon's eyes on me. I continued talking to my co-workers, forcing myself to focus on the discussion of furniture and the compromises necessary for cohabiting with someone of the opposite sex.

As the car continued its ascent and frequent stops, the number of people in the car dwindled. I was acutely attuned to where Gideon was, aware that he never took elevators this crowded, suspecting and hoping and praying that he'd just wanted to see me, be with me, even if it was only in this terribly impersonal way.

When we arrived on the twentieth floor, I took a deep breath and prepared to step out, hating the inevitable separation from the one thing in the world that made me feel truly alive.

The doors opened.

"Wait."

My eyes closed. I was stopped by the softly rasped command. I knew I should keep going as if I hadn't heard him. I knew it was just going to hurt so much worse if I gave him any more of myself, even a minute more of my life. But how could I possibly resist? I'd never been able to when it came to Gideon.

I stepped aside so that my co-workers could exit. Will frowned when I didn't follow, confused, but Megumi tugged him out. The doors closed.

I moved into the corner, my heart pounding. Gideon waited on the opposite side, radiating expectation and demand. As we climbed to the top floor, my body responded to his near-tangible need. My breasts swelled and became heavy; my sex grew slick and swollen. I was greedy for him. Needful. My breathing quickened.

He hadn't even touched me and I was nearly panting with desire.

The elevator glided to a stop. Gideon pulled the key out of his pocket and plugged it into the panel, suspending the car. Then he came to me.

There were only inches between us. I kept my head bowed and stared at his gleaming oxfords. I heard his breathing, deep and quick like mine. I smelled the subtly masculine scent of his skin, and my pulse leaped.

"Turn around, Eva."

A shiver moved through me at the familiar and beloved authoritative tone. Closing my eyes, I turned, then gasped as he immediately pressed against my back, flattening me to the wall of the car. His fingers linked with mine, holding my hands up by my shoulders.

"You're so beautiful," he breathed, nuzzling into my hair. "It hurts to look at you."

"Gideon. What are you doing?"

I felt his hunger pouring off him, enveloping me. His powerful frame was hard and hot, and vibrating with tension. He was aroused, his thick cock a firm pressure I couldn't stop myself from grinding into. I wanted him. I wanted him inside me. Filling me. Completing me. I'd been so empty without him.

He took a deep shuddering breath. His fingers flexed restlessly between mine, as if he wanted to touch me elsewhere but restrained himself.

I felt the ring I'd given him digging into my flesh. I turned my head to look at it and tensed when I saw it, confused and agonized.

"Why?" I whispered. "What do you want from me? An orgasm? You want to fuck me, Gideon? Is that it? Blow your load inside me?"

His breath hissed out at having those crude words thrown back in his face. "Don't."

"Don't call it what it is?" I closed my eyes. "Fine. Just do it. But don't put that ring on and act like this is something it's not."

"I never take it off. I won't. *Ever.*" His right hand released mine and he reached into his pocket. I watched as he slid the ring he'd given me back onto my finger, and then he lifted my hand to his mouth. He kissed it, then pressed his lips—quick, hard, angry—to my temple.

"Wait," he snapped.

Then he was gone. The car began its descent. My right hand curled into a fist and I backed away from the wall, breathing hard.

Wait. For what?

18

W HEN I EXITED the elevator on the twentieth floor, I was dry-eyed and determined. Megumi buzzed me through the security doors and pushed to her feet. "Is everything all right?"

I stopped by her desk. "I have no fucking clue. That man is a total head trip."

Her brows rose. "Keep me posted."

"I should just write a book," I muttered, resuming my walk back to my cubicle and wondering why in hell everyone was so interested in my dating life.

When I got to my desk, I dropped my purse in the drawer and sat down to call Cary.

"Hey," I said, when he answered. "If you get bored—"

"If?" He snorted.

306 · SYLVIA DAY

"Remember that folder of information you compiled on Gideon? Can you make me one of those on Dr. Terrence Lucas?"

"Okay. Do I know this guy?"

"No. He's a pediatrician."

There was a pause, then, "Are you pregnant?"

"No! Jeez. And if I were, I'd need an obstetrician."

"Whew. All right. Spell his name for me."

I gave Cary what he needed, then looked up Dr. Lucas's office and made an appointment to see him. "I won't need to fill out any new-patient paperwork," I told the receptionist. "I just want a quick consult."

After that, I called Vidal Records and left a message for Christopher to call me.

When Mark came back from lunch, I went over and knocked on his open door. "Hey. I need to ask for an hour in the morning for an appointment. Is it all right if I come in at ten and stay 'til six?"

"Ten to five is fine, Eva." He looked at me carefully. "Everything okay?"

"Getting better every day."

"Good." He smiled. "I'm really glad to hear that."

We dived back into work, but thoughts of Gideon weighed heavily on my mind. I kept staring at my ring, remembering what he had said when he'd first given it to me: *The Xs are me holding on to you.*

Wait. For him? For him to come back to me? Why? I couldn't understand why he'd cut me off the way he had, then expected me to take him back. Especially with Corinne in the picture.

I spent the rest of the afternoon going over the last few weeks in my mind, recalling conversations I'd had with Gideon, things he'd said or done, searching for answers. When I left the Crossfire at the end of the day, I saw the Bentley waiting out front and waved at Angus, who smiled back. I had issues with his boss, but Angus wasn't to blame for them.

It was hot and muggy outside. Miserable. I went to the Duane Reade around the corner for a bottle of cold water to drink on the walk home and a bag of mini chocolates to enjoy once I got through my Krav Maga class. When I left the drugstore, Angus was waiting just outside the door at the curb, shadowing me. As I turned the corner back toward the Crossfire to start the trip home, I saw Gideon step out to the street with Corinne. His hand was at the small of her back, leading her toward a sleek black Mercedes sedan I recognized as one of his. She was smiling. His expression was inscrutable.

Horrified, I couldn't move or look away. I stood there in the middle of the crowded sidewalk, my stomach twisting with grief and anger and a terrible, awful feeling of betrayal.

He looked up and saw me, freezing in place just as I had. The Latino driver I'd met the day my father arrived opened the back door and Corinne disappeared into the car. Gideon remained where he was, his gaze locked with mine.

There was no way he missed me lifting my hand and flipping him the bird.

Abruptly, I was struck by a thought.

I turned my back to Gideon and moved off to the side, digging into my purse for my phone. When I found it, I speed-dialed my mom, and when she answered, I said, "That day we went out to lunch with Megumi, you freaked out on the walk back to the Crossfire. You saw him, didn't you? Nathan. You saw Nathan at the Crossfire."

"Yes," she admitted. "That's why Richard decided it would be best to just pay him what he wanted. Nathan said he'd stay away from you as long as he had the money to leave the country. Why do you ask?"

"It didn't hit me until just now that Nathan was the reason why you reacted the way you did." I faced forward again and started walking quickly toward home. The Mercedes was gone, but my temper was rising. "I have to go, Mom. I'll call you later."

"Is everything all right?" she asked anxiously.

"Not yet, but I'm working on it."

"I'm here for you, if you need me."

I sighed. "I know. I'm okay. I love you."

When I got home, Cary was sitting on the couch with his laptop on his thighs and his bare feet on the coffee table.

"Hey," he called, his gaze still on his screen.

I dumped my stuff and kicked off my shoes. "You know what?"

He looked up at me from beneath a lock of hair that had fallen over his eyes. "What?"

"I thought Gideon took a hike because of Nathan. Everything was fine and then it wasn't, and shortly after that the police were telling us about Nathan. I figured one thing was linked to the other."

"Makes sense." He frowned. "I guess."

"But Nathan was at the Crossfire the Monday before you were attacked. I know he was there to see Gideon. I *know* it. Nathan wouldn't go there to see me. Not a place like that with all the security and people I know around."

He sat back. "Okay. So what does that mean?"

"It means Gideon was fine after Nathan." I threw up my hands. "He was fine that whole week. He was more than fine that weekend we took off together. He was fine Monday morning after we got back. Then—*bam*—he lost his fucking mind and went crazy on me Monday night."

"I'm following."

REFLECTED IN YOU · 309

"So what happened on Monday?"

Cary's brows rose. "You're asking me?"

"Grr." I grabbed my hair in my hands. "I'm asking the fucking universe. God. Anyone. What the hell happened to my boyfriend?"

"I thought we agreed you need to ask him."

"I get two answers from him: *Trust me* and *wait*. He gave my ring back today." I showed him my hand. "And he's still wearing the one I gave him. Do you have any idea how confusing that is? They're not just rings, they're promises. They're symbols of ownership and commitment. Why would he still wear his? Why is it so important to him that I wear mine? Does he seriously expect me to wait while he screws Corinne out of his system?"

"Is that what you think he's doing? Really?"

Closing my eyes, I let my head fall back. "No. And I can't decide if that makes me naïve or willfully delusional."

"Does this Dr. Lucas guy have anything to do with this?"

"No." I straightened and joined him on the couch. "Did you find anything?"

"Kind of hard, baby girl, when I don't know what I'm looking for."

"It's just a hunch." I looked at his screen. "What's that?"

"A transcript of an interview with Brett that was done yesterday on a Florida radio station."

"Oh? What are you reading that for?"

"I was listening to 'Golden' and decided to run a search on it, and this came up."

I tried reading, but my angle was bad. "What's it say?"

"He was asked if there's really an Eva out there and he said yes, there is, and he recently reconnected with her and hopes to make it work out a second time."

"What? No way!"

"Yes way." Cary grinned. "So you've got your rebound man lined up if Cross doesn't get his shit together."

I pushed to my feet. "Whatever. I'm hungry. Want something?"

"If your appetite's back, that's a good sign."

"Everything's coming back," I told him. "With a vengeance."

I was waiting at the curb for Angus the next morning. He pulled up and Paul, the doorman for my apartment building, opened the back door for me.

"Good morning, Angus," I greeted him.

"Good morning, Miss Tramell." His gaze met mine in the rear-view mirror, and he smiled.

As he started to pull away, I leaned forward between the two front seats. "Do you know where Corinne Giroux lives?"

He glanced at me. "Yes."

I sat back. "That's where I want to go."

CORINNE lived around the corner from Gideon. I was certain that wasn't a coincidence.

I checked in with the front desk and waited twenty minutes before I was given permission to go up to the tenth floor. I rang the bell to her apartment and the door swung open to reveal a flushed and disheveled Corinne in a floor-length black silk robe. She was seriously gorgeous, with her silky black hair and eyes like aquamarines, and she moved with a lithe grace I admired. I'd armored up in my favorite gray sleeveless dress and was very glad I had. She made me feel downright homely.

"Eva," she said breathlessly. "What a surprise."

"I'm sorry to barge in uninvited. I just need to ask you something real quick."

"Oh?" She kept the door partially closed and leaned into the jamb.

"Can I come in?" I asked tightly.

"Uh." She glanced over her shoulder. "It's best if you didn't."

"It doesn't bother me if you have company and I promise, this won't take but a minute."

"Eva." She licked her lips. "How do I say this . . . ?"

My hands were shaking and my stomach was a quivering mess, my brain taunting me with images of Gideon standing naked behind her, their early-morning fuck interrupted by the ex-girlfriend who wouldn't get a clue. I knew how well he liked sex in the morning.

But then I knew him well, period. Knew him enough to say, "Cut the shit, Corinne."

Her eyes widened.

My mouth curved derisively. "Gideon's in love with me. He's not fucking around with you."

She recovered quickly. "He's not fucking around with you, either. I would know, since he's spending all of his free time with me."

Fine. We'd talk about this in the hallway. "I know him. I don't always understand him, but that's a different story. I know he would've told you upfront that you and he weren't going anywhere, because he wouldn't want to lead you on. He hurt you before; he won't do it again."

"This is all very fascinating. Does he know you're here?"

"No, but you'll tell him. And that's fine. I just want to know what you were doing at the Crossfire that day you came out looking as freshly fucked as you do now."

Her smile was razor sharp. "What do you *think* I was doing?"

"Not Gideon," I said decisively, even though I was silently praying that I wasn't making a total idiot out of myself. "You saw me, didn't you? From the lobby, you had a direct view across the street and you saw me coming. Gideon told you at the Waldorf dinner that I was the jealous type. Did you have a nooner with someone from one of the other offices? Or did you muss yourself up before you stepped outside?"

I saw the answer on her face. It was lightning quick, there and gone, but I saw it.

"Both of those suggestions are absurd," she said.

I nodded, savoring a moment of profound relief and satisfaction. "Listen. You're never going to have him the way you want. And I know how that hurts. I've been living it the past two weeks. I'm sorry for you, I really am."

"Fuck you and your pity," she snapped. "Save it for yourself. I'm the one he's spending time with."

"And there's your saving grace, Corinne. If you're paying attention, you know he's hurting right now. Be his friend." I headed back to the elevators and called over my shoulder, "Have a nice day."

She slammed her door shut behind me.

When I got back to the Bentley, I told Angus to take me to Dr. Terrence Lucas's office. He paused in the act of closing the door and stared down at me. "Gideon will be very angry, Eva."

I nodded, understanding the warning. "I'll deal with it when the time comes."

The building that housed Dr. Lucas's private practice was unassuming, but his offices were warm and inviting. The waiting room was paneled in dark wood and the walls covered in a mixture of pictures of infants and children. Parenting magazines covered the tables and were neatly stored in racks, while the dedicated play area was tidy and supervised.

I signed in and took a seat, but I'd barely sat when I was called back by the nurse. I was taken to Dr. Lucas's office, not an exam room, and he rose from his chair when I entered, rounding the desk quickly.

"Eva." He held out his hand and I shook it. "You didn't have to make an appointment."

I managed a smile. "I didn't know how else to reach you."

"Have a seat."

I sat, but he remained standing, choosing to lean back against the desk and grip the edge with both hands. It was a power position, and I wondered why he felt the need to use it with me.

"What can I do for you?" he asked. He had a calm, confident air and a wide, open smile. With his good looks and affable manner, I was sure any mother would have confidence in his skill and integrity.

"Gideon Cross was a patient of yours, wasn't he?"

His face closed instantly and he straightened. "I'm not at liberty to discuss my patients."

"When you gave me that 'not at liberty to discuss' line at the hospital, I didn't put it together, and I should have." My fingertips drummed into the armrest. "You lied to his mother. Why?"

He returned to the other side of his desk, putting the furniture between us. "Did he tell you that?"

"No. I'm figuring this out as I go. Hypothetically speaking, why would you lie about the results of an exam?"

"I wouldn't. You need to leave."

"Oh, come on." I sat back and crossed my legs. "I expect more from you. Where are the assertions that Gideon is a soulless monster bent on corrupting the women of the world?"

"I've done my due diligence and warned you." His gaze was hard, his lip curled in a sneer. He wasn't quite so handsome anymore. "If you continue to throw your life away, there's nothing I can do about it."

314 · SYLVIA DAY

"I'm going to figure it out. I just needed to see your face. I had to know if I was right."

"You're not. Cross was never a patient of mine."

"Semantics—his mother consulted you. And while you go about your days seething over the fact that your wife fell in love with him, think about what you did to a small child who needed help." My voice took on an edge as anger surged. I couldn't think about what had happened to Gideon without wanting to do serious violence to anyone who contributed to his pain.

I uncrossed my legs and stood. "What happened between him and your wife happened between two consenting adults. What happened to him as a child was a crime and how you contributed to that is a travesty."

"Get out."

"My pleasure." I yanked the door open and nearly ran into Gideon, who'd been leaning against the wall just outside the office. His hand encircled my upper arm, but his gaze was on Dr. Lucas, icy with fury and hatred.

"Stay away from her," he said harshly.

Lucas's smile was filled with malice. "She came to me."

Gideon's returning smile made me shiver. "You see her coming, I suggest you run in the opposite direction."

"Funny. That's the advice I gave her in regard to you."

I flipped the good doctor the bird.

Snorting, Gideon caught my hand and pulled me back down the hall. "What is it with you and giving people the finger?"

"What? It's a classic."

"You can't just barge in here!" the receptionist snapped as we passed the counter.

He glanced at her. "You can cancel that call to security, we're leaving."

We exited out to the corridor. "Did Angus tattle on me?" I muttered, trying to pry my arm free.

"No. Stop wriggling. All the cars have GPS tracking."

"You're a nut job. You know that?"

He stabbed the elevator button and glared at me. "I am? What about you? You're all over the place. My mother. Corinne. Goddamned Lucas. What the fuck are you doing, Eva?"

"It's none of your business." I lifted my chin. "We broke up, remember?"

His jaw tightened. He stood there in his suit, looking so polished and urbane, while radiating a wild, feverish energy. The contrast between what I saw when I looked at him and what I felt goaded my hunger. I loved that I got to have the man inside the suit. Every delicious, untameable inch of him.

The car arrived and we stepped inside. Excitement sizzled through me. He'd come after me. That made me so hot. He shoved an elevator key into the control panel and I groaned.

"Is there anything you don't own in New York?"

He was on me in an instant, one hand in my hair and the other on my ass, his mouth on mine in a violent kiss. He wasted no time, his tongue thrusting between my lips, plunging deep and hard.

I moaned and gripped his waist, pushing onto my tiptoes to deepen the contact.

His teeth sank into my lower lip with enough force to hurt. "You think you can say a few words and end us? There is no end, Eva."

He flattened me into the side of the car. I was pinned by six feet, two inches of violently aroused male.

"I miss you," I whispered, grabbing his ass and urging him harder against me.

Gideon groaned. "Angel."

He was kissing me: deep, shamelessly desperate kisses that made my toes curl in my pumps.

"What are you doing?" he breathed. "You're going around, stirring up everything."

"I've got time on my hands," I shot back, just as breathless, "since I dumped my asshat boyfriend."

He growled, fiercely passionate, his hand in my hair pulling so tightly it pained me.

"You can't make this up with a kiss or a fuck, Gideon. Not this time." It was so hard to let him go; nearly impossible after the weeks I'd been denied the right and opportunity to touch him. I needed him.

His forehead pressed to mine. "You have to trust me."

I put my hands on his chest and shoved him back. He let me, his gaze searching my face.

"Not when you don't talk to me." I reached over, pulled the key from the control panel, and held it out to him. The car began its descent. "You put me through hell. On purpose. Made me suffer. And there's no end in sight. I don't know what the fuck you're doing, ace, but this Dr. Jekyll and Mr. Hyde shit ain't cutting it with me."

His hand went into his pocket, his movements leisurely and controlled, which was when he was at his most dangerous. "You're completely unmanageable."

"When I've got clothes on. Get used to it." The car doors opened and I stepped out. His hand went to the small of my back, and a shiver moved through me. That innocuous touch, through layers of material, had been inciting lust in me from the very first. "You put your hand on Corinne's back like this again, and I'm breaking your fingers."

"You know I don't want anyone else," he murmured. "I can't. I'm consumed with wanting you."

REFLECTED IN YOU · 317

Both the Bentley and the Mercedes were waiting at the curb. The sky had darkened while I'd been inside, as if it were brooding along with the man beside me. There was a weighted expectation in the air, an early sign of a gathering summer storm.

I stopped beneath the entrance overhang and looked at Gideon. "Make them ride together. You and I need to talk."

"That was the plan."

Angus touched the brim of his hat and slid behind the wheel. The other driver walked up to Gideon and handed him a set of keys.

"Miss Tramell," he said, by way of greeting.

"Eva, this is Raúl."

"We meet again," I said. "Did you pass on my message last time?"

Gideon's fingers flexed against my back. "He did."

I beamed. "Thank you, Raúl."

Raúl went around to the front passenger side of the Bentley, while Gideon escorted me to the Mercedes and opened the door for me. I felt a little thrill as he got behind the wheel and adjusted the seat to accommodate his long legs. He started the engine and merged into traffic, expertly and confidently navigating the powerful car through the craziness of New York city streets.

"Watching you drive makes me want you," I told him, noting how his easy grip on the wheel tightened.

"Christ." He glanced at me. "You have a transportation fetish."

"I have a Gideon fetish." My voice lowered. "It's been weeks."

"And I hate every second of it. This is torment for me, Eva. I can't focus. I can't sleep. I lose my temper at the slightest irritants. I'm in hell without you."

I never wanted him to suffer, but I'd be lying if I said it didn't make my own misery better knowing he was missing me as much as I was missing him.

I twisted in my seat to face him. "Why are you doing this to us?"

"I had an opportunity and I took it." His jaw firmed. "This separation is the price. It won't last forever. I need you to be patient."

I shook my head. "No, Gideon. I can't. Not anymore."

"You're *not* leaving me. I won't let you."

"I've already left. Don't you see that? I'm living my life and you're not in it."

"I'm in it every way I can be right now."

"By having Angus following me around? Come on. That's not a relationship." I leaned my cheek against the seat. "Not one I want anyway."

"Eva." He exhaled harshly. "My silence is the lesser of two evils. I feel like whether I explain or not, I'll drive you away, but explaining carries the greatest risk. You think you want to know, but if I tell you, you'll regret it. Trust me when I say there are some aspects of me you don't want to see."

"You have to give me something to work with." I set my hand on his thigh and felt the muscle bunch, then twitch in response to my touch. "I've got nothing right now. I'm empty."

He set his hand over mine. "You trust me. Despite what you see to the contrary, you've come to trust in what you know. That's huge, Eva. For both of us. For us, period."

"There is no us."

"Stop saying that."

"You wanted my blind trust and you have it, but that's all I can give you. You've shared so little of yourself and I've lived with it because I had you. And now I don't—"

"You have me," he protested.

"Not the way I need you." I lifted one shoulder in an awkward shrug. "You've given me your body and I've been greedy with it, because that's the only way you're really open to me. And now I don't have that, and when I look at what I do have, it's just promises. It's not enough for me. In the absence of you, all I have is a pile of things you won't tell me."

He stared straight ahead, his profile rigid. I pulled my hand out from under his and twisted the other way, giving him my back while I looked out the window at the teeming city.

"If I lose you, Eva," he said hoarsely, "I have nothing. Everything I've done is so I don't lose you."

"I need more." I rested my forehead against the glass. "If I can't have you on the outside, I need to have you on the inside, but you've never let me in."

We drove in silence, crawling along through the morning traffic. A fat drop of rain hit the windshield, followed by another.

"After my dad died," he said softly, "I had a hard time dealing with the changes. I remember that people liked him, liked being around him. He was making everyone rich, right? And then suddenly the world flipped on its head and everyone hated him. My mother, who'd been so happy all the time, was crying nonstop. And she and my dad were fighting every day. That's what I remember most—the constant yelling and screaming."

I looked at him, studying his stony profile, but I didn't say anything, afraid to lose the moment.

"She remarried right away. We moved out of the city. She got pregnant. I never knew when I'd run across someone my dad had fucked over, and I took a lot of shit for it from other kids. From their parents. Teachers. It was big news. To this day, people still talk about my dad and what he did. I was so angry. At everyone. I had tantrums all the time. I broke things."

He stopped at a light, breathing heavily. "After Christopher came along, I got worse, and when he was five, he imitated me, pitching a fit at dinner and shoving his plate across the table and onto the floor. My mom was pregnant with Ireland then, and she and Vidal decided it was time to put me into therapy."

Tears slid down my face at the picture he painted of the child he'd once been—scared and hurting and feeling like an outsider in his mom's new life.

"They came out to the house—the shrink and a doctoral candidate she was supervising. It started out all right. They both were nice, attractive, patient. But soon the shrink was spending most of the time counseling my mother, who was having a difficult pregnancy in addition to two young boys who were out of control. I was left alone with him more and more frequently."

Gideon pulled over and put the car into park. His hands gripped the wheel with white-knuckled force, his throat working. The steady patter of rain softened, leaving us alone with our painful truths.

"You don't have to tell me any more," I whispered, unbuckling my seat belt and reaching out to him. I touched his face with fingertips damp with my tears.

His nostrils flared on a sharply indrawn breath. "He made me come. Every goddamned time, he wouldn't stop until I came, so he could say I liked it."

I kicked off my shoes and pulled his hand away from the wheel so I could straddle his lap and hold him. His grip on me was excruciatingly tight, but I didn't complain. We were on an insanely busy street, with endless cars rumbling past on one side and a crush of pedestrians on the other, but neither of us cared. He was shaking violently, as if he were sobbing uncontrollably, but he made no sound and shed no tears.

The sky cried for him, the rain coming down hard and angry, steaming off the ground.

Holding his head in my hands, I pressed my wet face to his. "Hush, baby. I understand. I know how that feels, the way they gloat

REFLECTED IN YOU · 321

afterward. And the shame and confusion and guilt you felt. It's not your fault. You didn't want it. You didn't enjoy it."

"I let him touch me at first," he whispered. "He said it was my age . . . hormones . . . I needed to masturbate and I'd be calmer. Less angry all the time. He touched me, said he'd show me how to do it right. That I was doing it wrong—"

"Gideon, no." I pulled back to look at him, imagining in my mind how it would develop from that point on, all the things that would have been said to make it seem like Gideon was the instigator in his own rape. "You were a child in the hands of an adult who knew all the right buttons to push. They want to make it our fault so they have no culpability in their crime, but it's not true."

His eyes were huge and dark in his pale face. I pressed my lips gently to his, tasting my tears. "I love you. And I believe you. And none of this was your fault."

Gideon's hands were in my hair, holding me in place as he ravaged my mouth with desperate kisses. "Don't leave me."

"Leave you? I'm going to marry you."

He inhaled sharply. Then he pulled me closer, his hands careless and rough as they slid over me.

Impatient rapping against the window made me jerk in surprise. A cop in rain gear and safety vest looked at us through the untinted front window, scowling at us from beneath the brim of her hat. "You've got thirty seconds to move on or I'll cite you both for public indecency."

Embarrassed, my face flaming, I climbed back into my seat, sprawling in an ungraceful tumble. Gideon waited until I had my seat belt on, then put the car in drive. He tapped his brow in a salute to the officer, and pulled back out into traffic.

Reaching for my hand, he lifted it to his lips and kissed my fingertips. "I love you."

I froze, my heart pounding.

Linking our fingers together, he set them on his thigh. The windshield wipers slid from side to side, their rhythmic tempo mocking the racing of my pulse.

Swallowing hard, I whispered, "Say that again."

He slowed at a light. Turning his head, Gideon looked at me. He looked weary, as if all his usual pulsing energy had been expended and he was running on fumes. But his eyes were warm and bright, the curve of his mouth loving and hopeful. "I love you. Still not the right word, but I know you want to hear it."

"I need to hear it," I agreed softly.

"As long as you understand the difference." The light changed and he drove on. "People get over love. They can live without it, they can move on. Love can be lost and found again. But that won't happen for me. I won't survive you, Eva."

My breath caught at the look on his face when he glanced at me.

"I'm obsessed with you, angel. Addicted to you. You're everything I've ever wanted or needed, everything I've ever dreamed of. You're *everything*. I live and breathe you. For you."

I placed my other hand over our joined ones. "There's so much out there for you. You just don't know it yet."

"I don't need anything else. I get out of bed every morning and face the world because you're in it." He turned the corner and pulled up in front of the Crossfire behind the Bentley. He killed the engine, released his seat belt, and took a deep breath. "Because of you, the world makes sense to me in a way it didn't before. I have a place now, with you."

Suddenly I understood why he'd worked so hard, why he was so insanely successful at such a young age. He'd been driven to find his place in the world, to be more than an outsider.

His fingertips brushed across my cheek. I'd missed that touch so much, my heart bled at feeling it again.

"When are you coming back to me?" I asked softly.

"As soon as I can." Leaning forward, he pressed his lips to mine. "Wait."

19

WHEN I GOT to my desk, I found a voice mail from Christopher. I debated for a moment whether I should continue to pursue the truth. Christopher wasn't a man I wanted to invite any deeper into my life.

But I was haunted by the look that had been on Gideon's face when he told me about his past, and the sound of his voice, so hoarse with remembered shame and agony.

I felt his pain like my own.

In the end, there was no other choice. I returned Christopher's call and asked him out to lunch.

"Lunch with a beautiful woman?" There was a smile in his voice. "Absolutely."

"Any time you have free this week would be great."

"How about today?" he suggested. "I occasionally get a craving for that deli you took me to."

"Works for me. Noon?"

We set the time and I hung up just as Will stopped by my cubicle. He gave me puppy-dog eyes and said, "Help."

I managed a smile. "Sure."

The two hours flew by. When noon rolled around, I went downstairs and found Christopher waiting in the lobby. His auburn hair was a wild mess of short, loose waves and his grayish-green eyes sparkled. Wearing black slacks and a white dress shirt rolled up at the sleeves, he looked confident and attractive. He greeted me with his boyish grin, and it struck me then—I couldn't ask him about what he'd said to his mother long ago. He'd been a child himself, living in a dysfunctional home.

"I'm stoked you called me," he said. "But I have to admit, I'm curious about why. I'm wondering if it has anything to do with Gideon getting back together with Corinne."

That hurt. Terribly. I had to suck in a deep breath, then release my tension with it. I knew better. I had no doubts. But I was honest enough to admit that I wanted ownership of Gideon. I wanted to claim him, possess him, have everyone know that he was *mine*.

"Why do you hate him so much?" I asked, preceding him through the revolving doors. Thunder rumbled in the distance, but the hot, driving rain had ceased, leaving the streets awash in dirty water.

He joined me on the sidewalk and set his hand at the small of my back. It sent a shiver of revulsion through me. "Why? You want to exchange notes?"

"Sure. Why not?"

By the time lunch was over, I'd gotten a pretty good idea of what fueled Christopher's hatred. All he cared about was the man he saw in the mirror. Gideon was more handsome, richer, more powerful, more confident . . . just *more*. And Christopher was obviously being eaten alive by jealousy. His memories of Gideon were colored by the belief that Gideon had received all the attention as a child. Which might have been true, considering how troubled he was. Worse, the sibling rivalry had crossed over into their professional lives when Cross Industries acquired a majority share of Vidal Records. I made a mental note to ask Gideon why he'd done that.

We stopped outside the Crossfire to part ways. A taxi racing through a huge puddle sent a plume of foaming water right at me. Swearing under my breath, I dodged the spray and almost stumbled into Christopher.

"I'd like to take you out sometime, Eva. Dinner, perhaps?"

"I'll get in touch," I hedged. "My roommate's really sick right now and I need to be around for him as much as possible."

"You've got my number." He smiled and kissed the back of my hand, a gesture I'm sure he thought was charming. "And I'll keep in touch."

I made my way through the Crossfire's revolving doors and headed for the turnstiles.

One of the black-suited security guards at the desk stopped me. "Miss Tramell." He smiled. "Could you come with me, please?"

Curious, I followed him to the security office where I'd originally gotten my employee badge when I was hired. He opened the door for me, and Gideon was waiting inside.

Leaning back against the desk with his arms crossed, he looked beautiful and fuckable and wryly amused. The door shut behind me and he sighed, shaking his head.

"Are there other people in my life you plan on harassing on my behalf?" he asked.

"Are you spying on me again?"

328 · SYLVIA DAY

"Keeping a protective eye on you."

I arched a brow at him. "And how do you know if I harassed him or not?"

His faint smile widened. "Because I know you."

"Well, I didn't harass him. Really. I didn't," I argued when he shot me a look of disbelief. "I was going to, but then I didn't. And why are we in this room?"

"Are you on some kind of crusade, angel?"

We were talking around each other, and I wasn't sure why. And I didn't care, because something else struck me as more significant.

"Do you realize that your reaction to my lunch with Christopher is very calm? And so is my reaction to you spending time with Corinne? We're both reacting totally different from the way we would have just a month ago."

He was different. He smiled, and there was something unique about that warm curving of his lips. "We trust each other, Eva. It feels good, doesn't it?"

"Trusting you doesn't mean I'm any less baffled by what's going on between us. Why are we hiding in this office?"

"Plausible deniability." Gideon straightened and came to me. Cupping my face in his hands, he tilted my head back and kissed me sweetly. "I love you."

"You're getting good at saying that."

He ran his fingers through my new bangs. "Remember that night, when you had your nightmare and I was out late? You wondered where I was."

"I still wonder."

"I was at the hotel, clearing out that room. My fuck pad, as you called it. Explaining that while you were puking your guts out didn't seem to be the appropriate time."

My breath left me in a rush. It was a relief to know where he'd been. An even bigger relief to know that the fuck pad was no more.

His gaze was soft as he looked at me. "I'd completely forgotten about it until it came up with Dr. Petersen. We both know I'll never use it again. My girl prefers modes of transportation to beds."

He smiled and walked out. I stared after him.

The security guard filled the open doorway and I shoved aside my roiling thoughts to examine later, when I had the time to really grasp where they were leading me.

On the walk home, I picked up a bottle of sparkling apple juice in lieu of champagne. I saw the Bentley every now and then, following along, ever ready to pull over and pick me up. It used to irritate me, because the lingering connection it represented deepened my confusion over my breakup with Gideon. Now, the sight of it made me smile.

Dr. Petersen had been right. Abstinence and some space had cleared my head. Somehow, the distance between me and Gideon had made us stronger, made us appreciate each other more and take less for granted. I loved him more now than I ever had, and I felt that way while I was planning on a night just hanging out with my roommate, having no idea where Gideon was or who he might be with. It didn't matter. I knew I was in his thoughts, in his heart.

My phone rang and I pulled it out of my purse. Seeing my mother's name on the screen, I answered with, "Hi, Mom."

"I don't understand what they're looking for!" she complained, sounding angry and tearful. "They won't leave Richard alone. They went to his offices today and took copies of the security tapes."

"The detectives?"

"Yes. They're relentless. What do they want?"

I turned the corner to reach my street. "To catch a killer. They probably just want to see Nathan coming and going. Check the timing or something."

"That's ridiculous!"

"Yeah, it's also just a guess. Don't worry. There's nothing to find because Stanton's innocent. Everything will be okay."

"He's been so good about this, Eva," she said softly. "He's so good to me."

I sighed, hearing the pleading note in her voice. "I know, Mom. I get it. Dad gets it. You're where you should be. No one's judging you. We're all good."

It took me until I reached my front door to calm her down, during which time I wondered what the detectives would see if they pulled the Crossfire security tapes, too. The history of my relationship with Gideon could be chronicled through the times I'd been in the Cross Industries vestibule with him. He'd first propositioned me there, bluntly stating his desire. He'd pinned me to the wall there, right after I'd agreed to date him exclusively. And he'd rejected my touch that horrible day when he had first started pulling away from me. The detectives would see it all if they looked back far enough, those private and personal moments in time.

"Call me if you need me," I said as I dropped my bag and purse off at the breakfast bar. "I'll be home all night."

We hung up, and I noticed an unfamiliar trench coat slung over one of the bar stools. I shouted out to Cary, "Honey, I'm home!"

I put the bottle of apple juice in the fridge and headed down the hallway to my bedroom for a shower. I was on the threshold of my room when Cary's door opened and Tatiana came out. My eyes widened at the sight of her naughty nurse costume, complete with exposed garters and fishnets.

"Hey, honey," she said, looking smug. She was astonishingly tall in her heels, towering over me. A successful model, Tatiana Cherlin had the kind of face and body that could stop traffic. "Take care of him for me."

Blinking, I watched the leggy blonde disappear into the living room. I heard the front door shut a short time later.

Cary appeared in his doorway, looking mussed and flushed and wearing only his boxer briefs. He leaned into the doorway with a lazy, satisfied grin. "Hey."

"Hey, yourself. Looks like you had a good day."

"Hell yeah."

That made me smile. "No judgment here, but I assumed you and Tatiana were done."

"I never thought we got started." He ran a hand through his hair, ruffling it. "Then she showed up today all worried and apologetic. She's been in Prague and didn't hear about me until this morning. She rushed over wearing that, like she read my perverted mind."

I leaned into my doorway, too. "Guess she knows you."

"Guess she does." He shrugged. "We'll see how it goes. She knows Trey's in my life and I hope to keep him there. Trey, though . . . I know he won't like it."

I felt for both men. It was going to take a lot of compromising for their relationship to work out. "How about we forget about our significant others for a night and have an action movie marathon? I brought some nonalcoholic champagne home."

His brows rose. "Where's the fun in that?"

"Can't mix your meds with booze, you know," I said dryly.

"No Krav Maga for you tonight?"

"I'll make it up tomorrow. I feel like chilling with you. I want to sprawl on the couch, and eat pizza with chopsticks and Chinese food with my fingers."

332 · SYLVIA DAY

"You're a rebel, baby girl." He grinned. "And you've got yourself a date."

PARKER hit the mat with a grunt and I shouted, thrilled with my own success.

"Yes," I said with a fist pump. Learning to toss a guy as heavy as Parker was no small feat. Finding the right balance to gain the leverage I needed had taken me longer than it probably should have because I'd had such a hard time concentrating over the last couple of weeks.

There was no balance in my life when my relationship with Gideon was skewed.

Laughing, Parker reached out to me for a hand up. I gripped his forearm and tugged him to his feet.

"Good. Very good," he praised. "You're firing on all cylinders tonight."

"Thanks. Wanna try it again?"

"Take a ten-minute break and hydrate," he said. "I need to talk to Jeremy before he takes off."

Jeremy was one of Parker's co-instructors, a giant of a man that the students had to work their way up to. Right then, I couldn't imagine ever being able to fend off an assailant of his size, but I'd seen some really petite women in the class do it.

I grabbed my towel and my water and headed toward the aluminum bleachers lined up against the wall. My steps faltered when I saw one of the detectives who'd come to my apartment. Detective Shelley Graves wasn't dressed for work, though. She wore a sports top and matching pants with athletic shoes, and her dark, curly hair was pulled back in a ponytail.

Since she was just entering the building and the door happened to be next to the bleachers, I found myself walking toward her. I forced myself to look nonchalant when I felt anything but.

"Miss Tramell," she greeted me. "Fancy running into you here. Have you been working with Parker long?"

"About a month. It's good to see you, Detective."

"No, it's not." Her mouth twisted wryly. "At least you don't think so. Yet. Maybe you still won't when we're done chatting."

I frowned, confused by that tangle of words. Still, one thing was clear. "I can't speak to you without my attorney present."

She spread her arms wide. "I'm off-duty. But anyway, you don't have to say anything. I'll do all the talking."

Graves gestured toward the bleachers, and I reluctantly took a seat. I had damn good reason to be wary.

"How about we move a little higher?" She climbed to the top, and I stood and followed.

Once we were settled, she set her forearms on her knees and looked at the students below. "It's different here at night. I usually catch the day sessions. I told myself that on the off chance I happened to run into you off-duty someday, I'd talk to you. I figured the odds of that were nil. And lo and behold, here you are. It must be a sign."

I wasn't buying the additional explanation. "You don't strike me as the type to believe in signs."

"You've got me there, but I'll make an exception in this case." Her lips pursed for a moment, as if she were thinking hard about something. Then she looked at me. "I think your boyfriend killed Nathan Barker."

I stiffened, my breath catching audibly.

"I'll never be able to prove it," she said grimly. "He's too smart.

Too thorough. The whole thing was precisely premeditated. The moment Gideon Cross came to the decision to kill Nathan Barker, he had his ducks in a row."

I couldn't decide if I should stay or go—what the ramifications would be of either decision. And in that moment of indecisiveness, she kept talking.

"I believe it started the Monday after your roommate was attacked. When we searched the hotel room where Barker's body was discovered, we found photos. A lot of photos of you, but the ones I'm talking about were of your roommate."

"Cary?"

"If I were to present this to the ADA for an arrest warrant, I would say that Nathan Barker attacked Cary Taylor as a way to intimidate and threaten Gideon Cross. My guess is that Cross wasn't conceding to Barker's blackmail demands."

My hands twisted in my towel. I couldn't stand the thought of Cary suffering what he had because of me.

Graves looked at me, her gaze sharp and flat. Cop's eyes. My dad had them, too. "At that point, I think Cross perceived you to be in mortal danger. And you know what? He was right. I've seen the evidence we collected from Barker's room—photos, detailed notes of your daily schedule, news clippings . . . even some of your garbage. Usually when we find that sort of thing, it's too late."

"Nathan was watching me?" Just the thought sent a violent shiver through me.

"He was stalking you. The blackmail demands he made on your stepfather and Cross were just an escalation of that. I think Cross was getting too close to you, and Barker felt threatened by your relationship. I believe he hoped Cross would step away if he knew about your past."

I held the towel to my mouth, in case I became as sick as I felt.

REFLECTED IN YOU · 335

"So here's how I think it went down." Graves tapped her fingertips together, her attention seemingly on the strenuous drills below. "Cross cut you off, started seeing an old flame. That served two purposes—it made Barker relax, and it wiped out Cross's motive. Why would he kill a man over a woman he'd dumped? He set that up pretty well—he didn't tell you. You strengthened the lie with your honest reactions."

Her foot started tapping along with her fingers, her slim body radiating restless energy. "Cross doesn't hire out the job. That would be stupid. He doesn't want the money trail or a hit man who could rat him out. Besides, this is personal. *You're* personal. He wants the threat gone without a doubt. He sets up a last-minute party at one of his properties for some vodka company of his. Now he's got a rock-solid alibi. Even the press is there to snap pictures. And he knows precisely where you are and that your alibi is rock-solid, too."

My fingers clenched in the towel. *My God . . .*

The sounds of bodies hitting the mat, the hum of instructions being given, and the triumphant shouts of students all faded into a steady buzzing in my ears. There was a flurry of activity happening right in front of me and my brain couldn't process it. I had a sense of retreating down an endless tunnel, my reality shrinking to a tiny black point.

Opening her bottle of water, Graves drank deeply, then wiped her mouth with the back of her hand. "I'll admit, the party tripped me up a bit. How do you break an alibi like that? I had to go back to the hotel three times before I learned there was a fire in the kitchen that night. Nothing major, but the entire hotel was evacuated for close to an hour. All the guests were milling on the sidewalk. Cross was in and out of the hotel doing whatever an owner would do under those circumstances. I talked to a half dozen employees who saw him or talked to him around then, but none of them could pinpoint times for me. All agreed it was chaotic. Who could keep track of one guy in that mess?"

I felt myself shaking my head, as if she'd been directing the question at me.

She rolled her shoulders back. "I timed the walk from the service entrance—where Cross was seen talking to the FDNY—to Barker's hotel a couple blocks over. Fifteen minutes each way. Barker was taken out by a single stab wound to the chest. Right in the heart. Would've taken no more than a minute. No defensive wounds and he was found just inside the door. My guess? He opened the door to Cross and it was over before he could blink. And get this . . . *That* hotel is owned by a subsidiary of Cross Industries. And the security cameras in the building just happened to be down for an upgrade that's been in the works for several months."

"Coincidence," I said hoarsely. My heart was pounding. In a distant part of my brain, I registered that there were a dozen people just a few feet away, going about their lives without a clue that another human being in the room was dealing with a catastrophic event.

"Sure. Why not?" Graves shrugged, but her eyes gave her away. She *knew*. She couldn't prove it, but she knew. "So here's the thing: I could keep digging and spending time on this case while there are others on my desk. But what's the point? Cross isn't a danger to the public. My partner will tell you it's never okay to take the law into your own hands. And for the most part, I'm on the same page. But Nathan Barker was going to kill you. Maybe not next week. Maybe not next year. But someday."

She stood and brushed off her pants, picked up her water and towel, and ignored the fact that I was sobbing uncontrollably.

Gideon . . . I pressed the towel to my face, overwhelmed.

"I burned my notes," she went on. "My partner agrees we've hit a dead end. No one gives a shit that Nathan Barker isn't breathing our air anymore. Even his father told me he considered his son dead years ago."

I looked up at her, blinking to clear the haze of tears from my eyes. "I don't know what to say."

"You broke up with him on the Saturday after we interrupted your dinner, didn't you?" She nodded when I did. "He was in the station then, giving a statement. He stepped out of the room, but I could see him through the window in the door. The only time I've seen pain like that is when I'm notifying next of kin. To be honest, that's why I'm telling you this now—so you can go back to him."

"Thank you." I'd never put as much feeling into those two words as I did then.

Shaking her head, she started to walk back down the stairs, then stopped and turned, looking up at me. "I'm not the one you should be thanking."

SOMEHOW, I ended up at Gideon's apartment.

I don't remember leaving Parker's studio or telling Clancy where to take me. I don't remember checking in with the front desk or riding the elevator up. When I found myself in the private foyer facing Gideon's door, I had to stop a moment, unsure of how I'd gotten from the bleachers to that point.

I rang the bell and waited. When no one answered, I sank to the floor and leaned back against the door.

Gideon found me there. The elevator doors opened and he stepped out, stopping abruptly when he saw me. He was dressed in workout clothes and his hair was still damp with sweat. He'd never looked more wonderful.

He was staring at me, unmoving, so I explained, "I don't have a key anymore."

I didn't get up because I wasn't sure my legs would support me.

He crouched. "Eva? What's wrong?"

"I ran into Detective Graves tonight." I swallowed past the knot in my throat. "They're dropping the case."

His chest expanded on a deep breath.

With that sound, I *knew*.

Dark desolation shadowed Gideon's beautiful eyes. He knew that I knew. The truth hung heavy in the air between us, a near-tangible thing.

I'd kill for you, give up everything I own for you . . . but I won't give you *up*.

Gideon fell to his knees on the cold, hard marble. His head bowed. Waiting.

I shifted, mirroring his kneeling pose. I lifted his chin. Touched his face with my hands and my lips. My gratitude for his gift whispered over his skin: *Thank you . . . thank you . . . thank you.*

He caught me to him, his arms banded tight around me. His face pressed into my throat. "Where do we go from here?"

I held him. "Wherever this takes us. Together."

GIDEON AND EVA'S STORY CONTINUES

IN THE POWERFULLY SENSUAL

THIRD NOVEL IN THE CROSSFIRE SERIES

ENTWINED
WITH YOU

Now available from Berkley!

Ready to find
your next great read?

Let us help.

Visit prh.com/nextread

Penguin
Random
House

BARED TO YOU

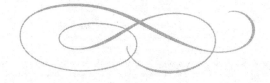

Sylvia Day

BERKLEY
New York

BERKLEY
An imprint of Penguin Random House LLC
penguinrandomhouse.com

Copyright © 2012 by Sylvia Day
Foreword copyright © 2023 by Sylvia Day
Readers Guide copyright © 2012 by Sylvia Day

ISBN: 9780425276761

The Library of Congress has cataloged the first Berkley trade edition of this book as follows:

Day, Sylvia.
Bared to you/Sylvia Day.—Berkley Trade pbk. ed.
p. cm.
ISBN 9780425260937
I. Title
PS3604.A9875B37 2012
813.'6—dc23 2012019475

First Berkley trade paperback edition / June 2012
Second Berkley trade paperback edition / February 2014

Printed in the United States of America
22nd Printing

This one is for Dr. David Allen Goodwin.
My love and gratitude are boundless.
Thank you, Dave. You saved my life.

FOREWORD

Every author has a theme to their stories, a connecting thread between who they are as an individual and the characters who give life to their work. I write about survivors. Surviving trauma is part of the human condition, and the resilience born from that universal experience is celebrated in each of my stories in varying degrees. My work covers the period of time after a traumatic event, at the point when the characters are still struggling with the aftermath, sometimes unaware that they are on the road to recovery.

In 2010, I began writing a historical romance that would later be titled *Seven Years to Sin*. As is my process, I began questioning the characters, which is how I learned that both Alistair and Jessica were survivors of childhood abuse. Alistair's torment was mental while Jessica's was physical.

As I worked with Jess and Alistair on their story (I often say that I'm more of a narrator than a creator), the beauty of their synergy was compelling. They understood each other in ways that others didn't and couldn't. Their shared experience of childhood trauma drew them together and facilitated their romance.

In reality, however, that's rarely how it works. Learning to love ourselves and reject guilt and doubt is a long process. Trying to heal while falling in love only complicates matters. Our partners' survival mechanisms can trigger our defenses. Instead of drawing survivors closer together, shared trauma often pushes them apart.

Seven Years to Sin is a stand-alone story written under a deadline, and it's a novel I'm very proud of. Still, I finished the story feeling like I'd barely skimmed the surface of deep and troubled waters. Jessica and Alistair's tale was complete, but their journey was one I wanted to revisit and explore more deeply. My research both broadened and narrowed. I started over and began writing *Bared to You*.

I changed the setting and time to the present day. Jessica and Eva look very much alike, as do Alistair and Gideon. There are even similar scenes in both novels. But Eva immediately established her more forceful personality, and when Gideon eventually walked onto the page, he turned my world upside down. Both of their childhood traumas were sexual, and their revelations exposed deep, painful vulnerabilities. They broke my heart, then put it back together again, and I am better for the experience.

I wrote *Bared to You* in a mad, feverish rush—literally. I had whooping cough and hardly left my bed for three months. I slept upright for mere minutes at a time. I can't say whether the incessant coughing or Eva's relentless talking kept me from sleeping properly; she narrated almost faster than I could type. As Gideon and Eva's story unfolded, they shed whatever vestiges of Jessica and Alistair remained and exerted themselves vehemently. They were in love, willing to fight for each other, and demanded absolute genuineness.

Before *Bared to You* was released, I made it available for early review. Within a week, the buzz was loud. It was enormous by the time the book launched on April 3, 2012.

Almost immediately, the emails began to pour into my inbox, bearing stories of survival and hope for unconditional love like Gideon and Eva's. Crossfire touched readers in different ways. Some simply fell in love with Gideon. Some felt seen for the first time. Some who'd been struggling with infertility found themselves expecting. Survivors who'd been silent for years found the courage to tell their stories; some opened up by asking loved ones to read particular scenes. Therapists had patients who brought the series to appointments to facilitate therapy. And some readers were inspired to train in self-defense, like Eva, which empowered them.

Every deeply personal story that's been shared with me will live in me always. Thank you for your trust. We all deserve and are worthy of love. I will always be grateful to Gideon and Eva for sharing that message with me and allowing me to share it with millions.

More than a decade later, not a single day has passed without someone mentioning Crossfire to me. Gideon and Eva have been a part of my daily life from the moment I typed the first word of their story. That's incredible, and I couldn't be more grateful. I think of all the Crossfire babies I met while touring the world, and it's amazing to consider how big of a leap ten years is for them. It's been the blink of an eye for me, yet my entire life has been irrevocably altered.

Whether I've met you at an event or we've never met, the fact that you're holding this book in your hands means we will always share the experience of being in the Crossfire together. If you're reading Eva and Gideon's story for the first time, I hope you love it and them. If you're reading their story for the hundredth time, welcome back. Eva and Gideon are dear friends who will never be far away, and I'm thrilled to celebrate their tenth anniversary with you!

With love always,
Sylvia

ACKNOWLEDGMENTS

I have great appreciation and respect for my editor, Cindy Hwang, for so many things involved in the process of turning over this series from my loving hands to hers. She wanted this story and fought hard to get it, and I'm grateful for her enthusiasm. Thank you, Cindy!

I can't say enough about my agent, Kimberly Whalen, who brings so much energy and drive to the table. She exceeded my expectations over and over again, leaving me in the lovely and much-longed-for position of saying, "Run with it." Thank you, Kim, for being just what I needed!

Behind Cindy and Kim are dynamic teams at Berkley and Trident Media Group. In every department, on every level, the support and excitement for the Crossfire series has been amazing. I'm so thankful, and I feel very blessed.

My deepest gratitude to editor Hilary Sares, who really dug into this story and made me work for it. Basically, she kicked my ass. By not pulling her punches or letting me shortchange the details, she made me work harder, and because of that, this story is a much, *much* better book. *Bared to You* wouldn't be what it is without you, Hilary. Thank you so much!

My thanks to Martha Trachtenberg, copy editor extraordinaire, and Victoria Colotta, interior text designer, for all their hard work on the self-published version of this book.

To Tera Kleinfelter, who read the first half of *Bared to You* and told me she loved it. Thank you, Tera!

To E. L. James, who wrote a story that captivated readers and created a hunger for more. You rocked it!

To Kati Brown, Jane Litte, Angela James, Maryse Black, Elizabeth Murach, Karla Parks, Gitte Doherty, Jenny Aspinall . . . oh, there are so many of you I need to thank for sharing *Bared to You* with others and saying such wonderful things about it! If I missed your name here, please believe I didn't miss you in my heart. I'm so grateful!

To all the girls who were at Cross Creek at some point in your adolescence: May all your dreams come true. You deserve it.

And to Alistair and Jessica, from *Seven Years to Sin*, who inspired me to write Gideon and Eva's story. I'm so glad the inspiration struck twice!

1

"WE SHOULD HEAD to a bar and celebrate."

I wasn't surprised by my roommate's emphatic pronouncement. Cary Taylor found excuses to celebrate, no matter how small and inconsequential. I'd always considered it part of his charm. "I'm sure drinking the night before starting a new job is a bad idea."

"Come on, Eva." Cary sat on our new living room floor amid half a dozen moving boxes and flashed his winning smile. We'd been unpacking for days, yet he still looked amazing. Leanly built, dark-haired, and green-eyed, Cary was a man who rarely looked anything less than absolutely gorgeous on any day of his life. I might have resented that if he hadn't been the dearest person on earth to me.

"I'm not talking about a bender," he insisted. "Just a glass of wine or two. We can hit a happy hour and be in by eight."

"I don't know if I'll make it back in time." I gestured at my yoga pants and fitted workout tank. "After I time the walk to work, I'm going to hit the gym."

"Walk fast, work out faster." Cary's perfectly executed arched brow made me laugh. I fully expected his million-dollar face to appear on billboards and fashion magazines all over the world one day. No matter his expression, he was a knockout.

"How about tomorrow after work?" I offered as a substitute. "If I make it through the day, that'll be worth celebrating."

"Deal. I'm breaking in the new kitchen for dinner."

"Uh . . ." Cooking was one of Cary's joys, but it wasn't one of his talents. "Great."

Blowing a wayward strand of hair off his face, he grinned at me. "We've got a kitchen most restaurants would kill for. There's no way to screw up a meal in there."

Dubious, I headed out with a wave, choosing to avoid a conversation about cooking. Taking the elevator down to the first floor, I smiled at the doorman when he let me out to the street with a flourish.

The moment I stepped outside, the smells and sounds of Manhattan embraced me and invited me to explore. I was not merely across the country from my former home in San Diego, but seemingly worlds away. Two major metropolises—one endlessly temperate and sensually lazy, the other teeming with life and frenetic energy. In my dreams, I'd imagined living in a walkup in Brooklyn, but being a dutiful daughter, I found myself on the Upper West Side instead. If not for Cary living with me, I would've been miserably lonely in the sprawling apartment that cost more per month than most people made in a year.

The doorman tipped his hat to me. "Good evening, Miss Tramell. Will you need a cab this evening?"

"No thanks, Paul." I rocked onto the rounded heels of my fitness shoes. "I'll be walking."

He smiled. "It's cooled down from this afternoon. Should be nice."

"I've been told I should enjoy the June weather before it gets wicked hot."

"Very good advice, Miss Tramell."

Stepping out from under the modern glass entrance overhang that somehow meshed with the age of the building and its neighbors, I enjoyed the relative quiet of my tree-lined street before I reached the bustle and flow of traffic on Broadway. One day soon, I hoped to blend right in, but for now I still felt like a fraudulent New Yorker. I had the address and the job, but I was still wary of the subway and had trouble hailing cabs. I tried not to walk around wide-eyed and distracted, but it was hard. There was just *so much* to see and experience.

The sensory input was astonishing—the smell of vehicle exhaust mixed with food from vendor carts, the shouts of hawkers blended with music from street entertainers, the awe-inspiring range of faces and styles and accents, the gorgeous architectural wonders . . . And the cars. *Jesus Christ.* The frenetic flow of tightly packed cars was unlike anything I'd ever seen anywhere.

There was always an ambulance, patrol car, or fire engine trying to part the flood of yellow taxis with the electronic wail of earsplitting sirens. I was in awe of the lumbering garbage trucks that navigated tiny one-way streets and the package delivery drivers who braved the bumper-to-bumper traffic while facing rigid deadlines.

Real New Yorkers cruised right through it all, their love for the city as comfortable and familiar as a favorite pair of shoes. They didn't view the steam billowing from potholes and vents in the sidewalks with romantic delight, and they didn't blink an eye when the ground vibrated beneath their feet as the subway roared by below, while I grinned like an idiot and flexed my toes. New York was a brand-new love affair for me. I was starry-eyed and it showed.

So I had to really work at playing it cool as I made my way over to the building where I would be working. As far as my job went, at least,

I'd gotten my way. I wanted to make a living based on my own merits, and that meant an entry-level position. Starting the next morning, I would be the assistant to Mark Garrity at Waters Field & Leaman, one of the preeminent advertising agencies in the United States. My stepfather, megafinancier Richard Stanton, had been annoyed when I took the job, pointing out that if I'd been less prideful I could've worked for a friend of his instead and reaped the benefits of that connection.

"You're as stubborn as your father," he'd said. "It'll take him forever to pay off your student loans on a cop's salary."

That had been a major fight, with my dad unwilling to back down. "Hell if another man's gonna pay for my daughter's education," Victor Reyes had said when Stanton made the offer. I respected that. I suspected Stanton did, too, although he would never admit it. I understood both men's sides, because I'd fought to pay off the loans myself . . . and lost. It was a point of pride for my father. My mother had refused to marry him, but he'd never wavered from his determination to be my dad in every way possible.

Knowing it was pointless to get riled up over old frustrations, I focused on getting to work as quickly as possible. I'd deliberately chosen to clock the short trip during a busy time on a Monday, so I was pleased when I reached the Crossfire Building, which housed Waters Field & Leaman, in less than thirty minutes.

I tipped my head back and followed the line of the building all the way up to the slender ribbon of sky. The Crossfire was seriously impressive, a sleek spire of gleaming sapphire that pierced the clouds. I knew from my previous interviews that the interior on the other side of the ornate copper-framed revolving doors was just as awe-inspiring, with golden-veined marble floors and walls and brushed-aluminum security desk and turnstiles.

I pulled my new ID card out of the inner pocket of my pants and held it up for the two guards in black business suits at the desk. They stopped me anyway, no doubt because I was majorly underdressed, but then they cleared me through. After I completed an elevator ride up to the twentieth floor, I'd have a general time frame for the whole route from door to door. Score.

I was walking toward the bank of elevators when a svelte, beautifully groomed brunette caught her purse on a turnstile and upended it, spilling a deluge of change. Coins rained onto the marble and rolled merrily away, and I watched people dodge the chaos and keep going as if they didn't see it. I winced in sympathy and crouched to help the woman collect her money, as did one of the guards.

"Thank you," she said, shooting me a quick, harried smile.

I smiled back. "No problem. I've been there."

I'd just squatted to reach a nickel lying near the entrance when I ran into a pair of luxurious black oxfords draped in tailored black slacks. I waited a beat for the man to move out of my way and when he didn't, I arched my neck back to allow my line of sight to rise. The custom three-piece suit hit more than a few of my hot buttons, but it was the tall, powerfully lean body inside it that made it sensational. Still, as impressive as all that magnificent maleness was, it wasn't until I reached the man's face that I went down for the count.

Wow. Just . . . *wow.*

He sank into an elegant crouch directly in front of me. Hit with all that exquisite masculinity at eye level, I could only stare. Stunned.

Then something shifted in the air between us.

As he stared back, he altered . . . as if a shield slid away from his eyes, revealing a scorching force of will that sucked the air from my lungs. The intense magnetism he exuded grew in strength, becoming a near-tangible impression of vibrant and unrelenting power.

Reacting purely on instinct, I shifted backward. And sprawled flat on my ass.

My elbows throbbed from the violent contact with the marble floor, but I scarcely registered the pain. I was too preoccupied with staring, riveted by the man in front of me. Inky black hair framed a breathtaking face. His bone structure would make a sculptor weep with joy, while a firmly etched mouth, a blade of a nose, and intensely blue eyes made him savagely gorgeous. Those eyes narrowed slightly, his features otherwise schooled into impassivity.

His dress shirt and suit were both black, but his tie perfectly matched those brilliant irises. His eyes were shrewd and assessing, and they bored into me. My heartbeat quickened; my lips parted to accommodate faster breaths. He smelled sinfully good. Not cologne. Body wash, maybe. Or shampoo. Whatever it was, it was mouth-watering, as was he.

He held out a hand to me, exposing gold and onyx cuff links and a very expensive-looking watch.

With a shaky inhalation, I placed my hand in his. My pulse leaped when his grip tightened. His touch was electric, sending a shock up my arm that raised the hairs on my nape. He didn't move for a moment, a frown line marring the space between arrogantly slashed brows.

"Are you all right?"

His voice was cultured and smooth, with a rasp that made my stomach flutter. It brought sex to mind. Extraordinary sex. I thought for a moment that he might be able to make me orgasm just by talking long enough.

My lips were dry, so I licked them before answering. "I'm fine."

He stood with economical grace, pulling me up with him. We maintained eye contact because I was unable to look away. He was younger than I'd assumed at first. Younger than thirty would be my guess, but his eyes were much worldlier. Hard and sharply intelligent.

I felt drawn to him, as if a rope bound my waist and he were slowly, inexorably pulling it.

Blinking out of my semidaze, I released him. He wasn't just beautiful; he was . . . enthralling. He was the kind of guy who made a woman want to rip his shirt open and watch the buttons scatter along

BARED TO YOU · 7

with her inhibitions. I looked at him in his civilized, urbane, outrageously expensive suit and thought of raw, primal, sheet-clawing fucking.

He bent down and retrieved the ID card I hadn't realized I'd dropped, freeing me from that provocative gaze. My brain stuttered back into gear.

I was irritated with myself for feeling so awkward while he was so completely self-possessed. And why? Because I was dazzled, damn it.

He glanced up at me, and the pose—him nearly kneeling before me—skewed my equilibrium again. He held my gaze as he rose. "Are you sure you're all right? You should sit down for a minute."

My face heated. How lovely to appear awkward and clumsy in front of the most self-assured and graceful man I'd ever met. "I just lost my balance. I'm okay."

Looking away, I caught sight of the woman who'd dumped the contents of her purse. She thanked the guard who'd helped her; then she turned to approach me, apologizing profusely. I faced her and held out the handful of coins I'd collected, but her gaze snagged on the god in the suit and she promptly forgot me altogether. After a beat, I just reached over and dumped the change into the woman's bag. Then I risked a glance at the man again, finding him watching me even as the brunette gushed thank-yous. *To him.* Not to me, of course, the one who'd actually helped.

I talked over her. "May I have my badge, please?"

He offered it back to me. Although I made an effort to retrieve it without touching him, his fingers brushed mine, sending that charge of awareness into me all over again.

"Thank you," I muttered before skirting him and pushing out to the street through the revolving door. I paused on the sidewalk, gulping in a breath of New York air redolent with a million different things, some good and some toxic.

There was a sleek black Bentley SUV in front of the building, and

I saw my reflection in the spotless tinted windows. I was flushed and my gray eyes were overly bright. I'd seen that look on my face before—in the bathroom mirror just before I went to bed with a man. It was my I'm-ready-to-fuck look and it had absolutely no business being on my face now.

Christ. Get a grip.

Five minutes with Mr. Dark and Dangerous, and I was filled with an edgy, restless energy. I could still feel the pull of him, the inexplicable urge to go back inside where he was. I could make the argument that I hadn't finished what I'd come to the Crossfire to do, but I knew I'd kick myself for it later. How many times was I going to make an ass of myself in one day?

"Enough," I scolded myself under my breath. "Moving on."

Horns blared as one cab darted in front of another with only inches to spare and then slammed on the brakes as daring pedestrians stepped into the intersection seconds before the light changed. Shouting ensued, a barrage of expletives and hand gestures that didn't carry real anger behind them. In seconds all the parties would forget the exchange, which was just one beat in the natural tempo of the city.

As I melded into the flow of foot traffic and set off toward the gym, a smile teased my mouth. *Ah, New York,* I thought, feeling settled again. *You rock.*

I'D planned on warming up on a treadmill, then capping off the hour with a few of the machines, but when I saw that a beginners' kickboxing class was about to start, I followed the mass of waiting students into that instead. By the time it was over, I felt more like myself. My muscles quivered with the perfect amount of fatigue, and I knew I'd sleep hard when I crashed later.

"You did really well."

I wiped the sweat off my face with a towel and looked at the young man who spoke to me. Lanky and sleekly muscular, he had keen brown eyes and flawless café au lait skin. His lashes were enviably thick and long, while his head was shaved bald.

"Thank you." My mouth twisted ruefully. "Pretty obvious it was my first time, huh?"

He grinned and held out his hand. "Parker Smith."

"Eva Tramell."

"You have a natural grace, Eva. With a little training you could be a literal knockout. In a city like New York, knowing self-defense is imperative." He gestured over to a corkboard hung on the wall. It was covered in thumbtacked business cards and flyers. Tearing off a flag from the bottom of a fluorescent sheet of paper, he held it out to me. "Ever heard of Krav Maga?"

"In a Jennifer Lopez movie."

"I teach it, and I'd love to teach you. That's my website and the number to the studio."

I admired his approach. It was direct, like his gaze, and his smile was genuine. I'd wondered if he was angling toward a pickup, but he was cool enough about it that I couldn't be sure.

Parker crossed his arms, which showed off cut biceps. He wore a black sleeveless shirt and long shorts. His Converse sneakers looked comfortably beat up, and tribal tattoos peeked out from his collar. "My website has the hours. You should come by and watch, see if it's for you."

"I'll definitely think about it."

"Do that." He extended his hand again, and his grip was solid and confident. "I hope to see you."

THE apartment smelled fabulous when I got back home, and Adele was crooning soulfully through the surround sound speakers about chasing pavements. I looked across the open floor plan into the kitchen and saw Cary swaying to the music while stirring something on the range. There was an open bottle of wine on the counter and two goblets, one of which was half-filled with red wine.

"Hey," I called out as I got closer. "Whatcha cooking? And do I have time for a shower first?"

He poured wine into the other goblet and slid it across the breakfast bar to me, his movements practiced and elegant. No one would know from looking at him that he'd spent his childhood bouncing between his drug-addicted mother and foster homes, followed by adolescence in juvenile detention facilities and state-run rehabs. "Pasta with meat sauce. And hold the shower, dinner's ready. Have fun?"

"Once I got to the gym, yeah." I pulled out one of the teakwood bar stools and sat. I told him about the kickboxing class and Parker Smith. "Wanna go with me?"

"Krav Maga?" Cary shook his head. "That's hard-core. I'd get all bruised up and that would cost me jobs. But I'll go with you to check it out, just in case this guy's a wack."

I watched him dump the pasta into a waiting colander. "A wack, huh?"

My dad had taught me to read guys pretty well, which was how I'd known the god in the suit was trouble. Regular people offered token smiles when they helped someone, just to make a momentary connection that smoothed the way.

Then again, I hadn't smiled at him either.

"Baby girl," Cary said, pulling bowls out of the cupboard, "you're a sexy, stunning woman. I question any man who doesn't have the balls to ask you outright for a date."

I wrinkled my nose at him.

He set a bowl in front of me. It contained tiny tubes of salad noodles covered in a skimpy tomato sauce with lumps of ground beef and peas. "You've got something on your mind. What is it?"

Hmm . . . I caught the handle of the spoon sticking out of the bowl and decided not to comment on the food. "I think I ran into the hottest man on the planet today. Maybe the hottest man in the history of the world."

"Oh? I thought that was me. Do tell me more." Cary stayed on the other side of the counter, preferring to stand and eat.

I watched him take a couple bites of his own concoction before I felt brave enough to try it myself. "Not much to tell, really. I ended up sprawled on my ass in the lobby of the Crossfire and he gave me a hand up."

"Tall or short? Blond or dark? Built or lean? Eye color?"

I washed down my second bite with some wine. "Tall. Dark. Lean *and* built. Blue eyes. Filthy rich, judging by his clothes and accessories. And he was insanely sexy. You know how it is—some good-looking guys don't make your hormones go crazy, while some unattractive guys have massive sex appeal. This guy had it all."

My belly fluttered as it had when Dark and Dangerous touched me. In my mind, I remembered his breathtaking face with crystal clarity. It should be illegal for a man to be that mind-blowing. I was *still* recovering from the frying of my brain cells.

Cary set his elbow on the counter and leaned in, his long bangs covering one vibrant green eye. "So what happened after he helped you up?"

I shrugged. "Nothing."

"Nothing?"

"I left."

"What? You didn't flirt with him?"

I took another bite. Really, the meal wasn't bad. Or else I was just starving. "He wasn't the kind of guy you flirt with, Cary."

"There is no such thing as a guy you can't flirt with. Even the happily married ones enjoy a little harmless flirtation now and then."

"There was nothing harmless about this guy," I said dryly.

"Ah, one of those." Cary nodded sagely. "Bad boys can be fun, if you don't get too close."

Of course he would know; men and women of all ages fell at his feet. Still, he somehow managed to pick the wrong partner every time. He'd dated stalkers, and cheaters, and lovers who threatened to kill themselves over him, and lovers with significant others they didn't tell him about . . . Name it, he'd been through it.

"I can't see this guy ever being fun," I said. "He was way too intense. Still, I bet he'd be awesome in the sack with all that intensity."

"Now you're talking. Forget the real guy. Just use his face in your fantasies and make him perfect there."

Preferring to get the guy out of my head altogether, I changed the subject. "You have any go-sees tomorrow?"

"Of course." Cary launched into the details of his schedule, mentioning a jeans advertisement, self-tanner, underwear, and cologne.

I shoved everything else out of my mind and focused on him and his growing success. The demand for Cary Taylor was increasing by the day, and he was building a reputation with photographers and accounts for being both professional and prompt. I was thrilled for him and so proud. He'd come a long way and been through so much.

It wasn't until after dinner that I noticed the two large gift boxes propped against the side of the sectional sofa.

"What are those?"

"Those," Cary said, joining me in the living room, "are the ultimate."

I knew immediately they were from Stanton and my mom. Money was something my mother needed to be happy, and I was glad Stanton, husband number three, was able to fill that need for her and all her many others as well. I often wished that could be the end of it, but my mom had a difficult time accepting that I didn't view money the same way she did. "What now?"

He threw his arm around my shoulders, easy enough for him to do because he was taller by five inches. "Don't be ungrateful. He loves your mom. He loves spoiling your mom, and your mom loves spoiling you. As much as you don't like it, he doesn't do it for you. He does it for her."

Sighing, I conceded his point. "What are they?"

"Glam threads for the advocacy center's fund-raiser dinner on Saturday. A bombshell dress for you and a Brioni tux for me, because buying gifts for me is what he does for you. You're more tolerant if you have me around to listen to you bitch."

"Damn straight. Thank God he knows that."

"Of course he knows. Stanton wouldn't be a bazillionaire if he didn't know everything." Cary caught my hand and tugged me over. "Come on. Take a look."

I pushed through the revolving door of the Crossfire into the lobby ten minutes before nine the next morning. Wanting to make the best impression on my first day, I'd gone with a simple sheath dress paired with black pumps that I slid on in replacement of my walking shoes during the elevator ride up. My blond hair was twisted up in an artful chignon that resembled a figure eight, courtesy of Cary. I was hair-inept, but he could create styles that were glamorous masterpieces. I wore the small pearl studs my dad had given me as a graduation gift and the Rolex from Stanton and my mother.

I had begun to think I'd put too much care into my appearance, but as I stepped into the lobby I remembered being sprawled across the floor in my workout clothes and I was grateful I didn't look anything like *that* graceless girl. The two security guards didn't seem to put two and two together when I flashed them my ID card on the way to the turnstiles.

Twenty floors later, I was exiting into the vestibule of Waters Field & Leaman. Before me was a wall of bulletproof glass that framed the double-door entrance to the reception area. The receptionist at the crescent-shaped desk saw the badge I held up to the glass. She hit the button that unlocked the doors as I put my ID away.

"Hi, Megumi," I greeted her when I stepped inside, admiring her cranberry-colored blouse. She was mixed race, a little bit Asian for sure, and very pretty. Her hair was dark and thick and cut into a sleek bob that was shorter in the back and razor sharp in the front. Her sloe eyes were brown and warm, and her lips were full and naturally pink.

"Eva, hi. Mark's not in yet, but you know where you're going, right?"

"Absolutely." With a wave, I took the hallway to the left of the reception desk all the way to the end, where I made another left turn and ended up in a formerly open space now partitioned into cubicles. One was mine and I went straight to it.

I dropped my purse and the bag holding my walking flats into the bottom drawer of my utilitarian metal desk, then booted up my computer. I'd brought a couple of things to personalize my space, and I pulled them out. One was a framed collage of three photos—me and Cary on Coronado Beach, my mom and Stanton on his yacht in the French Riviera, and my dad on duty in his City of Oceanside, California, police cruiser. The other item was a colorful arrangement of glass flowers that Cary had given me just that morning as a "first day" gift. I tucked it beside the small grouping of photos and sat back to take in the effect.

"Good morning, Eva."

I pushed to my feet to face my boss. "Good morning, Mr. Garrity."

"Call me Mark, please. Come on over to my office."

I followed him across the strip of hallway, once again thinking that my new boss was very easy to look at with his gleaming dark skin, trim goatee, and laughing brown eyes. Mark had a square jaw and a charmingly crooked smile. He was trim and fit, and he carried himself with a confident poise that inspired trust and respect.

He gestured at one of the two seats in front of his glass-and-chrome desk and waited until I sat to settle into his Aeron chair. Against the backdrop of sky and skyscrapers, Mark looked accomplished and powerful. He was, in fact, just a junior account manager, and his office was a closet compared to the ones occupied by the directors and executives, but no one could fault the view.

He leaned back and smiled. "Did you get settled into your new apartment?"

I was surprised he remembered, but I appreciated it, too. I'd met him during my second interview and liked him right away.

"For the most part," I answered. "Still a few stray boxes here and there."

"You moved from San Diego, right? Nice city, but very different from New York. Do you miss the palm trees?"

"I miss the dry air. The humidity here is taking some getting used to."

"Wait 'til summer hits." He smiled. "So . . . it's your first day and you're my first assistant, so we'll have to figure this out as we go. I'm not used to delegating, but I'm sure I'll pick it up quick."

I was instantly at ease. "I'm eager to be delegated to."

"Having you around is a big step up for me, Eva. I'd like you to be happy working here. Do you drink coffee?"

"Coffee is one of my major food groups."

"Ah, an assistant after my own heart." His smile widened. "I'm not going to ask you to fetch coffee for me, but I wouldn't mind if you helped me figure out how to use the new one-cup coffee brewers they just put in the break rooms."

I grinned. "No problem."

"How sad is it that I don't have anything else for you?" He rubbed the back of his neck sheepishly. "Why don't I show you the accounts I'm working on and we'll go from there?"

$\backsim$

THE rest of the day passed in a blur. Mark touched bases with two clients and had a long meeting with the creative team working on concept ideas for a trade school. It was a fascinating process seeing firsthand how the various departments picked up the baton from one another to carry a campaign from proposition to fruition. I might've stayed late just to get a better feel of the layout of the offices, but my phone rang at ten minutes to five.

"Mark Garrity's office. Eva Tramell speaking."

"Get your ass home so we can go out for the drink you rain-checked on yesterday."

Cary's mock sternness made me smile. "All right, all right. I'm coming."

Shutting down my computer, I cleared out. When I reached the bank of elevators, I pulled out my cell to text a quick On my way note to Cary. A ding alerted me to which car was stopping on my floor and I moved over to stand in front of it, briefly returning my attention to hitting the send button. When the doors opened, I took a step forward. I glanced up to watch where I was going and blue eyes met mine. My breath caught.

The sex god was the lone occupant.

2

His tie was silver and his shirt brilliantly white, the stark absence of color emphasizing those amazing blue irises. As he stood there with his jacket open and his hands shoved casually into his pants pockets, the sight of him was like running smack into a wall I hadn't known was there.

I jerked to a halt, my gaze riveted to the man who was even more striking than I'd remembered. I had never seen hair that purely black. It was glossy and slightly long, the ends drifting over his collar. That sexy length was the crowning touch of bad-boy allure over the successful businessman, like whipped cream topping on a hot-fudge brownie sundae. As my mother would say, only rogues and raiders had hair like that.

My hands clenched against the urge to touch it, to see if it felt like the rich silk it resembled.

The doors began to close. He took an easy step forward and pressed a button on the panel to hold them open. "There's plenty of room for both of us, Eva."

The sound of that smoky, implacable voice broke me out of my momentary daze. *How did he know my name?*

Then I remembered that he'd picked up my ID card when I'd dropped it in the lobby. For a second, I debated telling him I was waiting for someone so I could take another car down, but my brain lurched back into action.

What the hell was wrong with me? Clearly he worked in the Crossfire. I couldn't avoid him every time I saw him, and why should I? If I wanted to get to the point where I could look at him and take his hotness for granted, I needed to see him often enough that he became like furniture.

Ha! If only.

I stepped into the car. "Thank you."

He released the button and stepped back again. The doors closed and the elevator began its descent.

I immediately regretted my decision to share the car with him.

Awareness of him prickled across my skin. He was a potent force in such a small enclosure, radiating a palpable energy and sexual magnetism that had me shifting restlessly on my feet. My breathing became as ragged as my heartbeat. I felt that inexplicable pull to him again, as if he exuded a silent demand that I was instinctively attuned to answering.

"Enjoy your first day?" he asked, startling me.

His voice resonated, flowing over me in a seductive rhythm. *How the hell did he know it was my first day?*

"Yes, actually," I answered evenly. "How was yours?"

I felt his gaze slide over my profile, but I kept my attention trained on the brushed-aluminum elevator doors. My heart was racing in my chest, my stomach quivering madly. I felt jumbled and off my game.

"Well, it wasn't my first," he replied with a hint of amusement. "But it was successful. And getting better as it progresses."

I nodded and managed a smile, having no idea what that was supposed to mean. The car slowed on the twelfth floor and a friendly group of three got on, talking excitedly among themselves. I stepped back to make room for them, retreating into the opposite corner of the elevator from Dark and Dangerous. Except he sidestepped along with me. We were suddenly closer than we'd been before.

He adjusted his perfectly knotted tie, his arm brushing against mine as he did so. I sucked in a deep breath, trying to ignore my acute awareness of him by concentrating on the conversation taking place in front of us. It was impossible. He was just so *there*. Right there. All perfect and gorgeous and smelling divine. My thoughts ran away from me, fantasizing about how hard his body might be beneath the suit, how it might feel against me, how well endowed—or not—he might be . . .

When the car reached the lobby, I almost moaned in relief. I waited impatiently as the elevator emptied, and the first chance I got, I took a step forward. His hand settled firmly at the small of my back and he walked out beside me, steering me. The sensation of his touch on such a vulnerable place rippled through me.

We reached the turnstiles and his hand fell away, leaving me feeling oddly bereft. I glanced at him, trying to read him, but although he was looking at me, his face gave nothing away.

"Eva!"

The sight of Cary lounging casually against a marble column in the lobby shifted everything. He was wearing jeans that showcased his mile-long legs and an oversized sweater in soft green that emphasized his eyes. He easily drew the attention of everyone in the lobby. I slowed as I approached him and the sex god passed us, moving through the revolving door and sliding fluidly into the back of the chauffeured black Bentley SUV I'd seen at the curb the evening before.

Cary whistled as the car pulled away. "Well, well. From the way you were looking at him, that was the guy you told me about, right?"

"Oh, yeah. That was definitely him."

"You work together?" Linking arms with me, Cary tugged me out to the street through the stationary door.

"No." I stopped on the sidewalk to change into my walking flats, leaning into him as pedestrians flowed around us. "I don't know who he is, but he asked me if I'd had a good first day, so I better figure it out."

"Well . . ." He grinned and supported my elbow as I hopped awkwardly from one foot to the other. "No idea how anyone could get any work done around him. My brain sort of fried for a minute."

"I'm sure that's a universal effect." I straightened. "Let's go. I need a drink."

THE next morning arrived with a slight throbbing at the back of my skull that mocked me for having one too many glasses of wine. Still, as I rode the elevator up to the twentieth floor, I didn't regret the hangover as much as I should have. My choices were either too much alcohol or a whirl with my vibrator, and I was damned if I'd have a battery-provided orgasm starring Dark and Dangerous. Not that he'd know or even care that he made me so horny I couldn't see straight, but *I'd* know, and I didn't want to give the fantasy of him the satisfaction.

I dropped my stuff in the bottom drawer of my desk, and when I saw that Mark wasn't in yet, I grabbed a cup of coffee and returned to my cubicle to catch up on my favorite ad-biz blogs.

"Eva!"

I jumped when he appeared beside me, his grin a flash of white against his smooth dark skin. "Good morning, Mark."

"Is it ever. You're my lucky charm, I think. Come into my office. Bring your tablet. Can you work late tonight?"

I followed him over, catching on to his excitement. "Sure."

"I'd hoped you'd say that." He sank into his chair.

I took the one I'd sat in the day before and quickly opened a notepad program.

"So," he began, "we've received an RFP for Kingsman Vodka and they mentioned me by name. First time that's ever happened."

"Congratulations!"

"I appreciate that, but let's save them for when we've actually landed the account. We'll still have to bid, if we get past the request-for-proposal stage, and they want to meet with me tomorrow evening."

"Wow. Is that timeline usual?"

"No. Usually they'd wait until we had the RFP finished before meeting with us, but Cross Industries recently acquired Kingsman and C.I. has dozens of subsidiaries. That's good business if we can get it. They know it and they're making us jump through hoops, the first of which is meeting with me."

"Usually there would be a team, right?"

"Yes, we'd present as a group. But they're familiar with the drill—they know they'll get the pitch from a senior executive, then end up working with a junior like me—so they picked me out and now they want to vet me. But to be fair, the RFP provides a lot more information than it asks for in return. It's as good as a brief, so I really can't accuse them of being unreasonably demanding, just meticulous. Par for the course when dealing with Cross Industries."

He ran a hand over his tight curls, betraying the pressure he felt. "What do you think of Kingsman Vodka?"

"Uh . . . well . . . Honestly, I've never heard of it."

Mark fell back in his chair and laughed. "Thank God. I thought I was the only one. Well, the plus side is there's no bad press to get over. No news can be good news."

"What can I do to help? Besides research vodka and stay late."

His lips pursed a moment as he thought about it. "Jot this down . . ."

We worked straight through lunch and long after the office had emptied, going over some initial data from the strategists. It was a little after seven when Mark's smartphone rang, startling me with its abrupt intrusion into the quiet.

Mark activated the speaker and kept working. "Hey, baby."

"Have you fed that poor girl yet?" demanded a warm masculine voice over the line.

Glancing at me through his glass office wall, Mark said, "Ah . . . I forgot."

I looked away quickly, biting my lower lip to hide my smile.

A snort came clearly across the line. "Only two days on the job, and you're already overworking her and starving her to death. She's going to quit."

"Shit. You're right. Steve honey—"

"Don't 'Steve honey' me. Does she like Chinese?"

I gave Mark the thumbs-up.

He grinned. "Yes, she does."

"All right. I'll be there in twenty. Let security know I'm coming."

Almost exactly twenty minutes later, I buzzed Steven Ellison through the waiting area doors. He was a juggernaut of a fellow, dressed in dark jeans, scuffed work boots, and a neatly pressed button-down shirt. Red-haired with laughing blue eyes, he was as good looking as his partner was, just in a very different way. The three of us sat around Mark's desk and dumped kung pao chicken and broccoli beef onto paper plates, then added helpings of sticky white rice before digging in with chopsticks.

I discovered that Steven was a contractor, and that he and Mark

BARED TO YOU · 23

had been a couple since college. I watched them interact and felt awe and a dash of envy. Their relationship was so beautifully functional that it was a joy to spend time with them.

"Damn, girl," Steven said with a whistle, as I went for a third helping. "You can put it away. Where does it go?"

I shrugged. "To the gym with me. Maybe that helps . . . ?"

"Don't mind him," Mark said, grinning. "Steven's just jealous. He has to watch his girlish figure."

"Hell." Steven shot his partner a wry look. "I might have to take her out to lunch with the crew. I could win money betting on how much she can eat."

I smiled. "That could be fun."

"Ha. I knew you had a bit of a wild streak. It's in your smile."

Looking down at my food, I refused to let my mind wander into memories of just how wild I'd been in my rebellious, self-destructive phase.

Mark saved me. "Don't harass my assistant. And what do you know about wild women anyway?"

"I know some of them like hanging out with gay men. They like our perspective." His grin flashed. "I know a few other things, too. Hey . . . don't look so shocked, you two. I wanted to see if hetero sex lived up to the hype."

Clearly this was news to Mark, but from the twitching of his lips, he was secure enough in their relationship to find the whole exchange amusing. "Oh?"

"How'd that work out for you?" I asked bravely.

Steven shrugged. "I don't want to say it's overrated, 'cause clearly I'm the wrong demographic and I had a very limited sampling, but I can do without."

I thought it was very telling that Steven could relate his story in terms Mark worked with. They shared their careers with each other and listened, even though their chosen fields were miles apart.

"Considering your present living arrangement," Mark said to him, catching up a stem of broccoli with his chopsticks, "I'd say that's a very good thing."

By the time we finished eating, it was eight and the cleaning crew had arrived. Mark insisted on calling me a cab.

"Should I come in early tomorrow?" I asked.

Steven bumped shoulders with Mark. "You must've done something good in a past life to score this one."

"I think putting up with you in this life qualifies," Mark said dryly.

"Hey," Steven protested, "I'm housebroken. I put the toilet seat down."

Mark shot me an exasperated look that was warm with affection for his partner. "And that's helpful how?"

MARK and I scrambled all day Thursday to get ready for his four o'clock with the team from Kingsman. We grabbed an information-packed lunch with the two creatives who would be participating in the pitch when it got to that point in the process; then we went over the notes on Kingsman's Web presence and existing social media outreach.

I got a little nervous when three thirty rolled around because I knew traffic would be a bitch, but Mark kept working after I pointed out the time. It was quarter to four before he bounded out of his office with a broad smile, still shrugging into his jacket. "Join me, Eva."

I blinked up at him from my desk. "Really?"

"Hey, you worked hard on helping me prep. Don't you want to see how it goes?"

"Yes, absolutely." I pushed to my feet. Knowing my appearance would be a reflection on my boss, I smoothed my black pencil skirt and straightened the cuffs of my long-sleeved silk blouse. By a random twist of fate, my crimson shirt perfectly matched Mark's tie. "Thank you."

We headed out to the elevators and I was briefly startled when the car went up instead of down. When we reached the top floor, the waiting area we stepped into was considerably larger and more ornate than the one on the twentieth. Hanging baskets of ferns and lilies fragranced the air and a smoky glass security entrance was sandblasted with Cross Industries in a bold, masculine font.

We were buzzed in, and then asked to wait a moment. Both of us declined an offer of water or coffee, and less than five minutes after we arrived, we were directed to a closed conference room.

Mark looked at me with twinkling eyes as the receptionist reached for the door handle. "Ready?"

I smiled. "Ready."

The door opened and I was gestured in first. I made sure to smile brightly as I stepped inside . . . a smile that froze on my face at the sight of the man rising to his feet at my entrance.

My abrupt stop bottlenecked the threshold and Mark ran into my back, sending me stumbling forward. Dark and Dangerous caught me by the waist, hauling me off my feet and directly into his chest. The air left my lungs in a rush, followed immediately by every bit of common sense I possessed. Even through the layers of clothing between us, his biceps were like stone beneath my palms, his stomach a hard slab of muscle against my own. When he sucked in a sharp breath, my nipples tightened, stimulated by the expansion of his chest.

Oh no. I was cursed. A rapid-fire series of images flashed through my mind, showcasing a thousand ways I could stumble, fall, trip, skid, or crash in front of the sex god over the days, weeks, and months ahead.

"Hello again," he murmured, the vibration of his voice making me ache all over. "Always a pleasure running into you, Eva."

I flushed with embarrassment and desire, unable to find the will to push away despite the two other people in the room with him. It didn't help that his attention was solely on me, his hard body radiating that arresting impression of powerful demand.

"Mr. Cross," Mark said behind me. "Sorry about the entrance."

"Don't be. It was a memorable one."

I wobbled on my stilettos when Cross set me down, my knees weakened from the full-body contact. He was dressed in black again, with both his shirt and tie in a soft gray. As always, he looked too good.

What would it be like to be that amazing looking? There was no way he could go anywhere without causing a disturbance.

Reaching out, Mark steadied me and eased me back gently.

Cross's gaze stayed focused on Mark's hand at my elbow until I was released.

"Right. Okay then." Mark pulled himself together. "This is my assistant, Eva Tramell."

"We've met." Cross pulled out the chair next to his. "Eva."

I looked to Mark for guidance, still recovering from the moments I'd spent plastered against the sexual superconductor in Fioravanti.

Cross leaned closer and ordered quietly, "Sit, Eva."

Mark gave a brief nod, but I was already lowering into the chair at Cross's command, my body obeying instinctively before my mind caught up and objected.

I tried not to fidget for the next hour as Mark was grilled by Cross and the two Kingsman directors, both of whom were attractive brunettes in elegant pantsuits. The one in raspberry was especially enthusiastic about garnering Cross's attention, while the one in cream focused intently on my boss. All three seemed impressed by Mark's ability to articulate how the agency's work—and his facilitation of it with the client—created provable value for the client's brand.

I admired how cool Mark remained under pressure—pressure exerted by Cross, who easily dominated the meeting.

"Well done, Mr. Garrity," Cross praised lightly as they wrapped things up. "I look forward to going over the RFP when the time comes. What would entice you to try Kingsman, Eva?"

BARED TO YOU · 27

Startled, I blinked. "Excuse me?"

The intensity of his gaze was searing. It felt as if his entire focus were on me, which only reinforced my respect for Mark, who'd had to work under the weight of that stare for an hour.

Cross's chair was set parallel to the length of the table, facing me head on. His right arm rested on the smooth wooden surface, his long, elegant fingers stroking rhythmically along the top. I caught a glimpse of his wrist at the end of his cuff and for some crazy reason the sight of that small expanse of golden skin with its light dusting of dark hair arrested my attention. He was just so . . . *male*.

"Which of Mark's suggested concepts do you prefer?" he asked again.

"I think they're all brilliant."

His beautiful face was impassive when he said, "I'll clear the room to get your honest opinion, if that's what it takes."

My fingers curled around the ends of my chair's armrests. "I just gave you my honest opinion, Mr. Cross, but if you must know, I think sexy luxury on a budget will appeal to the largest demographic. But I lack—"

"I agree." Cross stood and buttoned his jacket. "You have a direction, Mr. Garrity. We'll revisit next week."

I sat for a moment, stunned by the breakneck pace of events. Then I looked at Mark, who seemed to be wavering between astonished joy and bewilderment.

Rising to my feet, I led the way to the door. I was hyperaware of Cross walking beside me. The way he moved, with animal grace and arrogant economy, was a major turn-on. I couldn't imagine him not fucking well and being aggressive about it, taking what he wanted in a way that made a woman wild to give it to him.

Cross stayed with me all the way to the bank of elevators. He said a few things to Mark about sports, I think, but I was too focused on the way I was reacting to him to care about the small talk. When the car arrived, I breathed a sigh of relief and hastily stepped forward with Mark.

"A moment, Eva," Cross said smoothly, holding me back with a hand at my elbow. "She'll be right down," he told Mark, as the elevator doors closed on my boss's astonished face.

Cross said nothing until the car was on its way down; then he pushed the call button again and asked, "Are you sleeping with anyone?"

The question was asked so casually, it took a second to process what he'd said.

I inhaled sharply. "Why is that any business of yours?"

He looked at me and I saw what I'd seen the first time we'd met—tremendous power and steely control. Both of which had me taking an involuntary step back. Again. At least I didn't fall this time; I was making progress.

"Because I want to fuck you, Eva. I need to know what's standing in my way, if anything."

The sudden ache between my thighs had me reaching for the wall to maintain my balance. He reached out to steady me, but I held him at bay with an uplifted hand. "Maybe I'm just not interested, Mr. Cross."

A ghost of a smile touched his lips and made him impossibly more handsome. *Dear God . . .*

The ding that signaled the approaching elevator made me jump, I was strung so tight. I'd never been so aroused. Never been so scorchingly attracted to another human being. Never been so offended by a person I lusted after.

I stepped into the elevator and faced him.

He smiled. "Until next time, Eva."

The doors closed and I sagged into the brass handrail, trying to regain my bearings. I'd barely pulled myself together when the doors opened and revealed Mark pacing in the waiting area on our floor.

"Jesus, Eva," Mark muttered, coming to an abrupt halt. "What the hell was that?"

"I have no freakin' clue." I exhaled in a rush, wishing I could share the confusing, irritating exchange I'd had with Cross, but well aware that my boss wasn't the appropriate outlet. "Who cares? You know he's going to give you the account."

A grin chased away his frown. "I'm thinking he might."

"As my roommate always says, you should celebrate. Should I make dinner reservations for you and Steven?"

"Why not? Pure Food and Wine at seven, if they can squeeze us in. If not, surprise us."

We'd barely returned to Mark's office when he was pounced on by the executives—Michael Waters, the CEO and president, and Christine Field and Walter Leaman, the executive chairman and vice chairman.

I skirted the four of them as quietly as possible and slid into my cubicle.

I called Pure Food and Wine and begged for a table for two. After some serious groveling and pleading, the hostess finally caved.

I left a message on Mark's voice mail: "It's definitely your lucky day. You're booked for dinner at seven. Have fun!"

Then I clocked out, eager to get home.

"He said *what*?" Cary sat on the opposite end of our white sectional sofa and shook his head.

"I know, right?" I enjoyed another sip of my wine. It was a crisp and nicely chilled sauvignon blanc I'd picked up on the walk home. "That was my reaction, too. I'm still not sure I didn't hallucinate the conversation while overdosing on his pheromones."

"So?"

I tucked my legs beneath me on the couch and leaned into the corner. "So what?"

"You know what, Eva." Grabbing his netbook off the coffee table, Cary propped it on his crossed legs. "Are you going to tap that or what?"

"I don't even *know* him. I don't even know his first name and he threw that curveball at me."

"He knew yours." He started typing on his keyboard. "And what about the thing with the vodka? Asking for your boss in particular?"

The hand I was running through my loose hair stilled. "Mark is very talented. If Cross has any sort of business sense at all, he'd pick up on that and exploit it."

"I'd say he knows business." Cary spun his netbook around and showed me the home page of Cross Industries, which boasted an awesome photo of the Crossfire. "That's his building, Eva. Gideon Cross owns it."

Damn it. My eyes closed. *Gideon Cross.* I thought the name suited him. It was as sexy and elegantly masculine as the man himself.

"He has people to handle marketing for his subsidiaries. Probably dozens of people to handle it."

"Stop talking, Cary."

"He's hot, rich, and wants to jump your bones. What's the problem?"

I looked at him. "It's going to be awkward running into him all the time. I'm hoping to hang on to my job for a long while. I really like it. I really like Mark. He's totally involved me in the process and I've learned so much from him already."

"Remember what Dr. Travis says about calculated risks? When your shrink tells you to take some, you should take some. You can deal with it. You and Cross are both adults." He turned his attention back to his Internet search. "Wow. Did you know he doesn't turn thirty for another two years? Think of the stamina."

"Think of the rudeness. I'm offended by how he just threw it out there. I hate feeling like a vagina with legs."

Cary paused and looked up at me, his eyes softening with sympathy. "I'm sorry, baby girl. You're so strong, so much stronger than I am. I just don't see you carrying around the baggage I do."

"I don't think I am, most of the time." I looked away because I didn't want to talk about what we'd been through in our pasts. "It's not like I wanted him to ask me out on a date. But there has to be a better way to tell a woman you want to take her to bed."

"You're right. He's an arrogant douche. Let him lust after you until he has blue balls. Serves him right."

That made me smile. Cary could always do that. "I doubt that man has ever had blue balls in his life, but it's a fun fantasy."

He shut his netbook with a decisive snap. "What should we do tonight?"

"I was thinking I'd like to go check out that Krav Maga studio in Brooklyn." I'd done a little research after meeting Parker Smith during my workout at Equinox, and as the week passed, the thought of having that kind of raw, physical outlet for stress seemed more and more ideal.

I knew it wouldn't be anything close to banging the hell out of Gideon Cross, but I suspected it would be a lot less dangerous to my health.

3

"THERE'S NO WAY your mom and Stanton are going to let you come out here at night multiple times a week," Cary said, hugging his stylish denim jacket around him even though it wasn't more than slightly chilly.

The converted warehouse Parker Smith used as his studio was a brick-faced building in a formerly industrial area of Brooklyn presently struggling to revitalize. The space was vast, and the massive metal delivery-bay doors offered no exterior clue as to what was taking place inside. Cary and I sat in aluminum bleachers, watching a half dozen combatants on the mats below.

"Ouch." I winced in sympathy as a guy took a kick to the groin. Even with padding, that had to sting. "How's Stanton going to find out, Cary?"

"Because you'll be in the hospital?" He glanced at me. "Seriously. Krav Maga is brutal. They're just sparring and it's full contact. And even if the bruises don't give you away, your stepdad will find out somehow. He always does."

"Because of my mom; she tells him everything. But I'm not telling her about this."

"Why not?"

"She won't understand. She'll think I want to protect myself because of what happened, and she'll feel guilty and give me grief about it. She won't believe my main interest is exercise and stress relief."

I propped my chin on my palm and watched Parker take the floor with a woman. He was a good instructor. Patient and thorough, and he explained things in an easy-to-understand way. His studio was in a rough neighborhood, but I thought it suited what he was teaching. It didn't get more reality based than a big, empty warehouse.

"That Parker guy is really hot," Cary murmured.

"He's also wearing a wedding band."

"I noticed. The good ones always get snatched up quick."

Parker joined us after the class was over, his dark eyes bright and his smile brighter. "What'd ya think, Eva?"

"Where do I sign up?"

His sexy smile made Cary reach over and squeeze the blood out of my hand.

"Step this way."

FRIDAY started out awesome. Mark walked me through the process of collecting information for an RFP, and he told me a little more about Cross Industries and Gideon Cross, pointing out that he and Cross were the same age.

"I have to remind myself of that," Mark said. "It's easy to forget he's so young when he's right in front of you."

"Yes," I agreed, secretly disappointed that I wouldn't see Cross for the next two days. As much as I told myself it didn't matter, I was bummed. I hadn't realized I'd been excited by the possibility that we might run into each other until that possibility was gone. It was just such a rush being near him. Plus he was a hell of a lot of fun to look at. I had nothing nearly as exciting planned for the weekend.

I was taking notes in Mark's office when I heard my desk phone ringing. Excusing myself, I rushed over to catch it. "Mark Garrity's office—"

"Eva, love. How are you?"

I sank into my chair at the sound of my stepfather's voice. Stanton always sounded like old money to me—cultured, entitled, and arrogant. "Richard. Is everything okay? Is Mom all right?"

"Yes. Everything's fine. Your mother is wonderful, as always."

His tone softened when he spoke of his wife, and I was grateful for that. I was grateful to him for a lot of things, actually, but it was sometimes hard to balance that against my feelings of disloyalty. I knew my dad was self-conscious about the massive differences in their income brackets.

"Good," I said, relieved. "I'm glad. Did you and Mom receive my thank-you note for the dress and Cary's tuxedo?"

"Yes, and it was thoughtful of you, but you know we don't expect you to thank us for such things. Excuse me a moment." He spoke to someone, most likely his secretary. "Eva, love, I'd like us to get together for lunch today. I'll send Clancy around to collect you."

"Today? But we'll be seeing each other tomorrow night. Can't it wait until then?"

"No, it should be today."

"But I only get an hour for lunch."

A tap on my shoulder turned me around to find Mark standing by my cubicle. "Take two," he whispered. "You earned it."

I sighed and mouthed a thank-you. "Will twelve o'clock work, Richard?"

"Perfectly. I look forward to seeing you."

I had no reason to look forward to private meetings with Stanton, but I dutifully left just before noon and found a town car waiting for me, idling at the curb. Clancy, Stanton's driver and bodyguard, opened the door for me as I greeted him. Then he slid behind the wheel and drove me downtown. By twenty after the hour, I was sitting at a conference table in Stanton's offices, eyeing a beautifully catered lunch for two.

Stanton came in shortly after my arrival, looking dapper and distinguished. His hair was pure white, his face lined but still very handsome. His eyes were the color of worn blue denim, and they were sharp with intelligence. He was trim and athletic, taking the time out of his busy days to stay fit even before he'd married his trophy wife—my mom.

I stood as he approached, and he bent to kiss my cheek. "You look lovely, Eva."

"Thank you." I looked like my mom, who was also a natural blonde. But my gray eyes came from my dad.

Taking a chair at the head of the table, Stanton was aware that the requisite backdrop of the New York skyline was behind him, and he took advantage of its impressiveness.

"Eat," he said, with the command so easily wielded by all men of power. Men like Gideon Cross.

Had Stanton been as driven at Cross's age?

I picked up my fork and started in on a chicken, cranberry, walnut, and feta salad. It was delicious, and I was hungry. I was glad Stanton didn't start talking right away so I could enjoy the meal, but the reprieve didn't last long.

"Eva love, I wanted to discuss your interest in Krav Maga."

I froze. "Excuse me?"

Stanton took a sip of iced water and leaned back, his jaw taking on the rigidity that warned me I wouldn't like what he was about to say. "Your mother was quite distraught last night when you went to that studio in Brooklyn. It took some time to calm her down and to assure her that I could make arrangements for you to pursue your interests in a safe manner. She doesn't want—"

"Wait." I set my fork down carefully, my appetite gone. "How did she know where I was?"

"She tracked your cell phone."

"No way," I breathed, deflating into my seat. The casualness of his reply, as if it were the most natural thing in the world, made me feel ill. My stomach churned, suddenly more interested in rejecting my lunch than digesting it. "That's why she insisted I use one of your company phones. It had nothing to do with saving me money."

"Of course that was part of it. But it also gives her peace of mind."

"Peace of mind? To spy on her grown daughter? It's not healthy, Richard. You've got to see that. Is she still seeing Dr. Petersen?"

He had the grace to look uncomfortable. "Yes, of course."

"Is she telling him what she's doing?"

"I don't know," he said stiffly. "That's Monica's private business. I don't interfere."

No, he didn't. He coddled her. Indulged her. Spoiled her. And allowed her obsession with my safety to run wild. "She has to let it go. *I've* let it go."

"You were an innocent, Eva. She feels guilty for not protecting you. We need to give her a little latitude."

"Latitude? She's a stalker!" My mind spun. How could my mom invade my privacy like that? *Why* would she? She was driving herself crazy, and me along with her. "This has to stop."

"It's an easy fix. I've already spoken with Clancy. He'll drive you when you need to venture into Brooklyn. Everything's been arranged. This will be much more convenient for you."

"Don't try to twist this around to being for my benefit." My eyes stung and my throat burned with unshed tears of frustration. I hated the way he talked about Brooklyn like it was a third-world country. "I'm a grown woman. I make my own decisions. It's the goddamn law!"

"Don't take that tone with me, Eva. I'm simply looking after your mother. And you."

I pushed back from the table. "You're enabling her. You're keeping her sick, and you're making me sick, too."

"Sit down. You need to eat. Monica worries that you're not eating healthy enough."

"She worries about *everything*, Richard. That's the problem." I dropped my napkin on the table. "I have to get back to work."

I turned away, striding toward the door to get out as quickly as possible. I retrieved my purse from Stanton's secretary and left my cell phone on her desk. Clancy, who had been waiting for me in the reception area, followed me, and I knew better than to try to blow him off. He didn't take orders from anyone but Stanton.

Clancy drove me back up to midtown, while I stewed in the backseat. I could bitch all I wanted, but in the end I wasn't any better than Stanton because I was going to give in. I was going to cave and let my mom have her way, because it hurt my heart to think of her suffering any more than she already did. She was so emotional and fragile, and she loved me to the point of being crazy about it.

My mood was still dark when I got back to the Crossfire. As Clancy pulled away from the curb, I stood on the crowded sidewalk and looked up and down the busy street for either a drugstore where I could get some chocolate or a wireless store where I could pick up a new phone.

I ended up walking around the block and buying a half dozen candy bars at a Duane Reade on the corner before heading back to the Crossfire. I'd been gone just about an hour, but I wasn't going to use the extra time Mark had given me. I needed work to distract me from my crazy-ass family.

As I caught an empty elevator car, I ripped open a bar and bit viciously into it. I was making strides toward filling my self-imposed chocolate quota before I hit the twentieth floor when the car stopped on the fourth. I appreciated the added time the stop gave me to enjoy the comfort of dark chocolate and caramel melting over my tongue.

The doors slid apart and revealed Gideon Cross talking with two other gentlemen.

As usual, I lost my breath at the sight of him, which reignited my fading irritation. Why did he have that effect on me? When was I going to become immune?

He glanced over and his lips curved into a slow, heart-stopping smile when he saw me.

Great. Just my crappy luck. I'd become some kind of challenge.

Cross's smile faded into a frown. "We'll finish this later," he murmured to his companions without looking away from me.

Stepping into the car, he lifted a hand to discourage them from following him. They blinked in surprise, glancing at me, then Cross, and then back again.

I stepped out, deciding it would be safer for my sanity to take a different car up.

"Not so fast, Eva." Cross caught me by the elbow and tugged me back. The doors shut and the elevator glided smoothly into motion.

"What are you doing?" I snapped. After dealing with Stanton, the last thing I needed was another domineering male trying to push me around.

Cross caught me by the upper arms and searched my face with that vivid blue gaze. "Something's wrong. What is it?"

The now-familiar electricity crackled to life between us, the pull made fiercer by my temper. "You."

"Me?" His thumbs stroked over my shoulders. Releasing me, he withdrew a lone key from his pocket and plugged it into the panel. All the lights cleared except for the one for the top floor.

He wore black again, with fine gray pinstripes. Seeing him from behind was a revelation. His shoulders were nicely broad without being bulky, emphasizing his lean waist and long legs. The silky strands of hair falling over his collar tempted me to clench them and pull. Hard. I wanted him to be as pissy as I was. I wanted a fight.

"I'm not in the mood for you now, Mr. Cross."

He watched the antique-style needle above the doors mark the passing floors. "I can get you in the mood."

"I'm not interested."

Cross glanced over his shoulder at me. His shirt and tie were both the same rich cerulean as his irises. The effect was striking. "No lies, Eva. Ever."

"That's not a lie. So what if I'm attracted to you? I expect most women are." Wrapping up what was left of my candy bar, I shoved it back into the shopping bag I'd tucked into my purse. I didn't need chocolate when I was sharing air with Gideon Cross. "But I'm not interested in doing anything about it."

He faced me then, turning in a leisurely pivot, that ghost of a smile softening his sinful mouth. His ease and unconcern aggravated me further. "*Attraction* is too tame a word for"—he gestured at the space between us—"this."

"Call me crazy, but I have to actually *like* someone before I get naked and sweaty with him."

"Not crazy," he said. "But I don't have the time or the inclination to date."

"That makes two of us. Glad we got that cleared up."

He stepped closer, his hand lifting to my face. I forced myself not to move away or give him the satisfaction of seeing me intimidated. His thumb brushed over the corner of my mouth, then lifted to his own. He sucked on the pad and purred, "Chocolate and you. Delicious."

A shiver moved through me, followed by a heated ache between my legs as I imagined licking chocolate off his lethally sexy body.

His gaze darkened and his voice lowered intimately. "Romance isn't in my repertoire, Eva. But a thousand ways to make you come are. Let me show you."

The car slowed to a halt. He withdrew the key from the panel and the doors opened.

I backed into the corner and shooed him out with a flick of my wrist. "I'm really not interested."

"We'll discuss." Cross caught me by the elbow and gently, but insistently, urged me out.

I went along because I liked the charge I got from being around him and because I was curious to see what he had to say when afforded more than five minutes of my time.

He was buzzed through the security door so quickly there was no need for him to break stride. The pretty redhead at the reception desk pushed hastily to her feet, about to impart some information until he shook his head impatiently. Her mouth snapped shut and she stared at me, her eyes wide, as we passed at a brisk pace.

The walk to Cross's office was mercifully short. His secretary stood when he saw his boss's approach but remained silent when he noted that Cross wasn't alone.

"Hold my calls, Scott," Cross said, steering me into his office through the open glass double doors.

Despite my irritation, I couldn't help but be impressed with Gideon Cross's spacious command center. Floor-to-ceiling windows overlooked the city on two sides, while a wall of glass faced the rest of the office space. The one opaque wall opposite the massive desk was covered in flatscreens streaming news channels from around the world. There were three distinct seating areas, each one larger than Mark's entire office, and a bar that showcased jeweled crystal decanters, which provided the only spots of color in a palette that was otherwise black, gray, and white.

Cross hit a button on his desk that closed the doors, then another that instantly frosted the clear glass wall, effectively shielding us from the view of his employees. With the beautiful sapphire-hued reflective film on the exterior windows, privacy was assured. He shrugged out of his jacket and hung it on a chrome coatrack. Then he returned to where I'd remained standing just inside the doors. "Something to drink, Eva?"

"No, thank you." Damn it. He was even yummier in just the vest. I could better see how fit he was. How strong his shoulders were. How beautifully his biceps and ass flexed as he moved.

He gestured toward a black leather sofa. "Have a seat."

"I have to go back to work."

"And I have a meeting at two. The sooner we work this out, the sooner we can both get back to business. Now, sit down."

"What do you think we're going to work out?"

Sighing, he scooped me up like a bride and carried me over to the sofa. He dropped me on my butt, then sat next to me. "Your objections. It's time to discuss what it's going to take to get you beneath me."

"A miracle." I pushed back from him, widening the space between us. I tugged at the hem of my emerald green skirt, wishing I'd worn pants instead. "I find your approach crude and offensive."

And a major turn-on, but I was never going to admit it.

He contemplated me with narrowed eyes. "It may be blunt, but it's honest. You don't strike me as the kind of woman who wants bullshit and flattery instead of the truth."

"What I want is to be seen as having more to offer than an inflatable sex doll."

Cross's brows shot up. "Well, then."

"Are we done?" I stood.

Wrapping my wrist with his fingers, he pulled me back down. "Hardly. We've established some talking points: We have an intense sexual attraction and neither of us wants to date. So what do you want—exactly? Seduction, Eva? Do you want to be seduced?"

I was equally fascinated and appalled by the conversation. And, yes, tempted. It was hard not to be while faced with such a gorgeous, virile male so determined to get hot and sweaty with me. Still, the dismay won out. "Sex that's planned like a business transaction is a turnoff for me."

"Establishing parameters in the beginning makes it less likely that there'll be exaggerated expectations and disappointment at the conclusion."

"Are you kidding?" I scowled. "Listen to yourself. Why even call it a fuck? Why not be clear and call it a seminal emission in a pre-approved orifice?"

He pissed me off by throwing his head back and laughing. The full, throaty sound flowed over me like a rush of warm water. My awareness of him heightened to a physically painful degree. His earthy amusement made him less sex god and more human. Flesh and blood. Real.

I pushed to my feet and backed out of reach. "Casual sex doesn't have to include wine and roses, but for God's sake, whatever else it is, sex should be personal. Friendly even. With mutual respect at the very least."

His humor fled as he stood, his eyes darkening. "There are no mixed signals in my private affairs. You want me to blur that line. I can't think of a good reason to."

"I don't want you to do jack shit, besides let me get back to work." I strode to the door and yanked on the handle, cursing softly when it didn't budge. "Let me out, Cross."

I felt him come up behind me. His palms pressed flat to the glass on either side of my shoulders, caging me in. I couldn't think of my own self-preservation when he was so close.

The strength and demand of his will exuded an almost tangible force field. When he stepped close enough, it surrounded me, closing me in with him. Everything outside that bubble ceased to exist, while inside it my entire body strained toward his. That he had such a profound, visceral effect on me while being so damn irritating had my mind spinning. How could I be so turned on by a man whose words should've turned me completely off?

"Turn around, Eva."

My eyes closed against the surge of arousal I felt at his authoritative tone. God, he smelled good. His powerful frame radiated heat and hunger, spurring my own wild desire for him. The uncontrollable response was intensified by my lingering frustration with Stanton and my more recent aggravation with Cross himself.

I wanted him. Bad. But he was no good for me. Honestly, I could screw up my life on my own. I didn't need any help.

My flushed forehead touched the air-conditioned glass. "Let it go, Cross."

"I am. You're too much trouble." His lips brushed behind my ear. One of his hands pressed flat to my stomach, the fingers splaying to urge me back against him. He was as aroused as I was, his cock hard and thick against my lower back. "Turn around and say good-bye."

Disappointed and regretful, I turned in his grip, sagging against the door to cool my heated back. He was curved over me, his luxurious hair framing his beautiful face, his forearm propped against the door to bring him closer. I had almost no room to breathe. The hand he'd had at my waist was now resting on the curve of my hip, tightening reflexively and driving me mad. He stared, his gaze searingly intense.

"Kiss me," he said hoarsely. "Give me that much."

Panting softly, I licked my dry lips. He groaned, tilted his head, and sealed his mouth over mine. I was shocked by how soft his firm

lips were and the gentleness of the pressure he exerted. I sighed and
his tongue dipped inside, tasting me in long, leisurely licks. His kiss
was confident, skilled, and just the right side of aggressive to turn me
on wildly.

I distantly registered my purse hitting the floor; then my hands
were in his hair. I pulled on the silky strands, using them to direct his
mouth over mine. He growled, deepening the kiss, stroking my tongue
with lush slides of his own. I felt the raging beat of his heart against
my chest, proof that he wasn't just a hopeless ideal conjured by my
fevered imagination.

He pushed away from the door. Cupping the back of my head
and the curve of my buttocks, he lifted me off my feet. "I want you,
Eva. Trouble or not, I can't stop."

I was pressed full-body against him, achingly aware of every hot,
hard inch of him. I kissed him back as if I could eat him alive. My skin
was damp and too sensitive, my breasts heavy and tender. My clit
throbbed for attention, pounding along with my raging heartbeat.

I was vaguely aware of movement, and then the couch was against
my back. Cross was levered over me with one knee on the cushion and
the other foot on the floor. His left arm supported his torso while his
right hand gripped the back of my knee, sliding upward along my
thigh in a firmly possessive glide.

His breath hissed out when he reached the point where my garter
clipped to the top of my silk stocking. He tore his gaze away from
mine and looked down, pushing my skirt higher to bare me from the
waist down.

"Jesus, Eva." A low rumble vibrated in his chest, the primitive
sound sending goose bumps racing across my skin. "Your boss is
damned lucky he's gay."

In a daze, I watched Cross's body lower to mine, my legs sliding
apart to accommodate the width of his hips. My muscles strained with
the urge to lift toward him, to hasten the contact between us that I'd

been craving since I first laid eyes on him. Lowering his head, he took my mouth again, bruising my lips with a fine edge of violence.

Abruptly, he yanked himself away, stumbling to his feet.

I lay there gasping and wet, so willing and ready. Then I realized why he'd reacted so fiercely.

Someone was behind him.

4

Mortified by the sudden intrusion into our privacy, I scrambled up and back into the armrest, yanking down my skirt.

". . . two o'clock appointment is here."

It took an endless moment to realize Cross and I were still alone in the room, that the voice I'd heard had come through a speaker. Cross stood at the far end of the sofa, flushed and scowling, his chest heaving. His tie was loosened and the fly of his slacks strained against a very impressive erection.

I had a nightmare vision in my head of what I must look like. And I was late getting back to work.

"Christ." He shoved both hands through his hair. "It's the middle of the fucking day. In my goddamn fucking office!"

I got to my feet and tried to straighten my appearance.

"Here." He came to me, yanking my skirt up again.

Furious at what I'd almost let happen when I should be at work, I smacked at his hands. "Stop it. Leave me alone."

"Shut up, Eva," he said grimly, catching the hem of my black silk blouse and tugging it into place, adjusting it so that the buttons once again formed a straight row between my breasts. Then he pulled down my skirt, smoothing it with calm, expert hands. "Fix your ponytail."

Cross retrieved his coat, shrugging into it before adjusting his tie. We reached the door at the same time, and when I crouched to fetch my purse, he lowered with me.

He caught my chin, forcing me to look at him. "Hey," he said softly. "You okay?"

My throat burned. I was aroused and mad and thoroughly embarrassed. I'd never in my life lost my mind like that. And I hated that I'd done so with *him*, a man whose approach to sexual intimacy was so clinical it depressed me just thinking about it.

I jerked my chin away. "Do I *look* okay?"

"You look beautiful and fuckable. I want you so badly it hurts. I'm dangerously close to taking you back to the couch and making you come 'til you beg me to stop."

"Can't accuse you of being silver-tongued," I muttered, aware that I wasn't offended. In fact, the rawness of his hunger for me was a serious aphrodisiac. Clutching the strap of my purse, I stood on shaky legs. I needed to get away from him. And, when my workday was done, I needed to be alone with a big glass of wine.

Cross stood with me. "I'll juggle what I have to and be done by five. I'll come get you then."

"No, you won't. This doesn't change anything."

"The hell it doesn't."

"Don't be arrogant, Cross. I lost my head for a second, but I still don't want what you want."

His fingers curled around the door handle. "Yes, you do. You just don't want it the way I want to give it to you. So, we'll revisit and revise."

More business. Cut-and-dried. My spine stiffened.

I set my hand over his and yanked on the handle, ducking under his arm to squeeze out the door. His secretary shoved quickly to his feet, gaping, as did the woman and two men who were waiting for Cross. I heard him speak behind me.

"Scott will show you into my office. I'll be just a moment."

He caught me by reception, his arm crossing my lower back to grip my hip. Not wanting to make a scene, I waited until we were by the elevators to pull away.

He stood calmly and hit the call button. "Five o'clock, Eva."

I stared at the lighted button. "I'm busy."

"Tomorrow, then."

"I'm busy all weekend."

Stepping in front of me, he asked tightly, "With whom?"

"That's none of your—"

His hand covered my mouth. "Don't. Tell me when, then. And before you say never, take a good look at me and tell me if you see a man who's easily deterred."

His face was hard, his gaze narrowed and determined. I shivered. I wasn't sure I'd win a battle of wills with Gideon Cross.

Swallowing, I waited until he lowered his hand and said, "I think we both need to cool off. Take a couple days to think."

He persisted. "Monday after work."

The elevator arrived and I stepped into it. Facing him, I countered, "Monday lunch."

We'd have only an hour, a guaranteed escape.

Just before the doors closed, he said, "We're going to happen, Eva."

It sounded as much like a threat as a promise.

"Don't sweat it, Eva," Mark said, when I arrived at my desk nearly a quarter after two. "You didn't miss anything. I had a late lunch with Mr. Leaman. I just barely got back myself."

"Thank you." No matter what he said, I still felt terrible. My kick-ass Friday morning seemed to have happened days ago.

We worked steadily until five, discussing a fast-food client and contemplating some possible tweaks to ad copy for a chain of organic grocery stores.

"Talk about strange bedfellows," Mark had teased, not knowing how apt that was in regard to my personal life.

I'd just shut down my computer and was pulling my purse out of the drawer when my phone rang. I glanced at the clock, saw it was exactly five, and considered ignoring the call because I was technically done for the day.

But since I was still feeling shitty about my overly long lunch, I considered it penance and answered. "Mark Garrity's—"

"Eva, honey. Richard says you forgot your cell phone at his office."

I exhaled in a rush and sagged back into my chair. I could picture the handkerchief wringing that usually accompanied that particular anxious tone of my mother's. It drove me nuts and it also broke my heart. "Hi, Mom. How are you?"

"Oh, I'm lovely. Thank you." My mom had a voice that was both girlish and breathy, like Marilyn Monroe crossed with Scarlett Johansson. "Clancy dropped your phone off with the concierge at your place. You really shouldn't go anywhere without it. You never know when you might need to call for someone—"

I'd been debating the logistics of just keeping the phone and forwarding calls to a new number I didn't share with my mom, but that wasn't my biggest concern. "What does Dr. Petersen say about you tracing my phone?"

The silence on the other end of the line was telling. "Dr. Petersen knows I worry about you."

Pinching the bridge of my nose, I said, "I think it's time for us to have another joint appointment, Mom."

"Oh . . . of course. He did mention that he'd like to see you again."

Probably because he suspects you're not being forthcoming. I changed the subject. "I really like my new job."

"That's wonderful, Eva! Is your boss treating you well?"

"Yes, he's great. I couldn't ask for anyone better."

"Is he handsome?"

I smiled. "Yes, very. And he's taken."

"Damn it. The good ones always are." She laughed and my smile widened.

I loved it when she was happy. I wished she were happy more often. "I can't wait to see you tomorrow at the advocacy dinner."

Monica Tramell Barker Mitchell Stanton was in her element at society functions, a gilded, shining beauty who'd never lacked male attention in her life.

"Let's make a day of it," my mom said breathlessly. "You, me, and Cary. We'll go to the spa, get pretty and polished. I'm sure you could use a massage after working so hard."

"I won't turn one down, that's for sure. And I know Cary will love it."

"Oh, I'm excited! I'll send a car by your place around eleven?"

"We'll be ready."

After I hung up, I leaned back in my chair and exhaled, needing a hot bath and an orgasm. If Gideon Cross somehow found out I masturbated while thinking about him, I didn't care. Being sexually frustrated was weakening my position, a weakness I knew he wouldn't be sharing. No doubt he'd have a preapproved orifice lined up before day's end.

As I swapped out my heels for my walking shoes, my phone rang again. My mother was rarely distracted for long. The five minutes since we'd ended our call was just about the right length of time for her to realize the cell phone issue hadn't been resolved. Once again, I debated ignoring the phone, but I didn't want to take any of the day's crap home with me.

I answered with my usual greeting, but it lacked its usual punch.

"I'm still thinking about you."

The velvet rasp of Cross's voice flooded me with such relief that I realized I'd been hoping to hear it again. Today.

God. The craving was so acute I knew he'd become a drug to my body, the prime source of some very intense highs.

"I can still feel you, Eva. Still taste you. I've been hard since you left, through two meetings and one teleconference. You've got the advantage; state your demands."

"Ah," I murmured. "Lemme think."

I let him wait, smiling as I remembered Cary's comment about blue balls. "Hmm . . . Nothing is coming to mind. But I do have some friendly advice. Go spend time with a woman who salivates at your feet and makes you feel like a god. Fuck her until neither of you can walk. When you see me on Monday you'll be totally over it and your life will return to its usual obsessive-compulsive order."

The creak of leather sounded over the phone and I imagined him leaning back in his desk chair. "That was your one free pass, Eva. The next time you insult my intelligence, I'll take you over my knee."

"I don't like that sort of thing." And yet the warning, given in that voice, aroused me. Dark and Dangerous for sure.

"We'll discuss. In the interim, tell me what you *do* like."

I stood. "You definitely have the voice for phone sex, but I've got to go. I have a date with my vibrator."

I should've hung up then, to gain the full effect of the brush-off, but I couldn't resist learning if he'd gloat like I had imagined he would. Plus, I was having fun with him.

"Oh, Eva." Cross spoke my name in a decadent purr. "You're determined to drive me to my knees, aren't you? What will it take to talk you into a threesome with B.O.B.?"

I ignored both questions as I slung my bag and purse over my shoulder, grateful he couldn't see how my hand shook. I was *not* discussing Battery-Operated Boyfriends with Gideon Cross. I'd never discussed masturbation openly with a man, let alone a man who was for all intents and purposes a stranger to me. "B.O.B. and I have a longtime understanding—when we're done with each other, we know exactly which one of us has been used, and it isn't me. Good night, Gideon."

I hung up and took the stairs, deciding the twenty-floor descent would serve double duty as both an avoidance technique and a replacement for a visit to the gym.

I was so grateful to be home after the day I'd had that I practically danced through my apartment's front door. My heartfelt "God, it's good to be home!" and accompanying spin was vehement enough to startle the couple on the couch.

"Oh," I said, wincing at my own silliness. Cary wasn't in a compromising position with his guest when I barged in, but they'd been sitting close enough to suggest intimacy.

Grudgingly, I thought of Gideon Cross, who preferred to strip all intimacy out of the most intimate act I could imagine. I'd had one-night stands and friends with benefits, and no one knew better than I that sex and making love were two very different things, but I didn't think I'd ever be able to view sex like a handshake. I thought it was sad that Cross did, even though he wasn't a man who inspired pity or sympathy.

"Hey, baby girl," Cary called out, pushing to his feet. "I was hoping you'd make it back before Trey had to leave."

BARED TO YOU · 53

"I have class in an hour," Trey explained, rounding the coffee table as I dropped my bag on the floor and put my purse on a bar stool at the breakfast bar. "But I'm glad I got to meet you before I left."

"Me, too." I shook the hand he extended to me, taking him in with a quick glance. He was about my age, I guessed. Average height and nicely muscular. He had unruly blond hair, soft hazel eyes, and a nose that had clearly been broken at some point.

"Mind if I grab a glass of wine?" I asked. "It's been a long day."

"Go for it," Trey replied.

"I'll take one, too." Cary joined us by the breakfast bar. He was wearing loose-fitting black jeans and an off-the-shoulder black sweater. The look was casual and elegant and did a phenomenal job of offsetting his dark brown hair and emerald eyes.

I went to the wine fridge and pulled out a random bottle.

Trey shoved his hands in the pockets of his jeans and rocked back on his heels, talking quietly with Cary as I uncorked and poured.

The phone rang and I grabbed the handset off the wall. "Hello?"

"Hey, Eva? It's Parker Smith."

"Parker, hi." I leaned my hip into the counter. "How are you?"

"I hope you don't mind my calling. Your stepdad gave me your home number when I couldn't reach you on your cell."

Gah. I'd had enough of Stanton for one day. "Not at all. What's up?"

"Honestly? Everything's looking up right now. Your stepdad is like my fairy godfather. He's funding a few safety improvements to the studio and some much-needed upgrades. That's why I'm calling. The studio's going to be out of commission next week. Classes will resume a week from Monday."

I closed my eyes, struggling to tamp down a flare of exasperation. It wasn't Parker's fault that Stanton and my mom were overprotective control freaks. Clearly they didn't see the irony of defending me while I was surrounded by people trained to do that very thing. "Sounds good. I can't wait. I'm really excited to be training with you."

"I'm excited, too. I'm going to work you hard, Eva. Your parents are going to get their money's worth."

I set a filled glass in front of Cary and took a big gulp out of my own. It never ceased to amaze me how much cooperation money could buy. But again, that wasn't Parker's fault. "No complaints here."

"We'll get started first thing the next week. Your driver has the schedule."

"Great. See you then." I hung up and caught the glance Trey shot Cary when he thought neither of us was looking. It was soft and filled with a sweet yearning, and it reminded me that my problems could wait. "I'm sorry I caught you on the way out, Trey. Do you have time for pizza Wednesday night? I'd love to do more than say hi and bye."

"I have class." He gave me a regretful smile and shot another side glance at Cary. "But I could come by on Tuesday."

"That'd be great." I smiled. "We could order in and have a movie night."

"I'd like that."

I was rewarded with the kiss Cary blew me as he headed to the door to show Trey out. When he returned to the kitchen he grabbed his wine and said, "All right. Spill it, Eva. You look stressed."

"I am," I agreed, grabbing the bottle and moving into the living room.

"It's Gideon Cross, isn't it?"

"Oh, yeah. But I don't want to talk about him." Although Gideon's pursuit was exhilarating, his goal sucked. "Let's talk about you and Trey instead. How did you two meet?"

"I ran across him on a job. He's working part time as a photographer's assistant. Sexy, isn't he?" His eyes were bright and happy. "And a real gentleman. In an old-school way."

"Who knew there were any of those left?" I muttered before polishing off my first glass.

"What's that supposed to mean?"

"Nothing. I'm sorry, Cary. He seemed great, and he obviously digs you. Is he studying photography?"

"Veterinary medicine."

"Wow. That's awesome."

"I think so, too. But forget about Trey for a minute. Talk about what's bugging you. Get it out."

I sighed. "My mom. She found out about my interest in Parker's studio and now she's freaking out."

"What? How'd she find out? I swear I haven't told anyone."

"I know you didn't. Never even crossed my mind." Grabbing the bottle off the table, I refilled my glass. "Get this. She's been tracking my cell phone."

Cary's brows rose. "Seriously? That's . . . creepy."

"I know, right? That's what I told Stanton, but he doesn't want to hear it."

"Well, hell." He ran a hand through his long bangs. "So what do you do?"

"Get a new phone. And meet with Dr. Petersen to see if he can't talk some sense into her."

"Good move. Turn it over to her shrink. So . . . is everything okay with your job? Do you still love it?"

"Totally." My head fell back into the sofa cushions and my eyes closed. "My work and you are my lifesavers right now."

"What about the young hottie bazillionaire who wants to nail you? Come on, Eva. You know I'm dying here. What happened?"

I told him, of course. I wanted his take on it all. But when I finished, he was quiet. I lifted my head to look at him, and found him bright-eyed and biting his lip.

"Cary? What are you thinking?"

"I'm feeling kind of hot from that story." He laughed, and the warm, richly masculine sound swept a lot of my irritation away. "He's got to be so confused right now. I would've paid money to see his face when you hit him with that bit he wanted to spank you over."

"I can't believe he said that." Just remembering Cross's voice when he made that threat had my palms damp enough to leave steam on my glass. "What the hell is he into?"

"Spanking's not deviant. Besides, he was going for missionary on the couch, so he's not averse to the basics." Cary fell into the sofa, a brilliant smile lighting up his handsome face. "You're a huge challenge to a guy who obviously thrives on them. And he's willing to make concessions to have you, which I'd bet he's not used to. Just tell him what you want."

I split the last of the wine between us, feeling marginally better with a bit of alcohol in my veins. What *did* I want? Aside from the obvious? "We're totally incompatible."

"Is that what you call what happened on his couch?"

"Cary, come on. Boil it down. He picked me up off the lobby floor and then asked me to fuck. That's really it. Even a guy I take home from a bar has more going for him than that. 'Hey, what's your name? Come here often? Who's your friend? What are you drinking? Like to dance? Do you work around here?'"

"All right, all right. I get it." He set his glass down on the table. "Let's go out. Hit a bar. Dance 'til we drop. Maybe meet some guys who'll talk you up some."

"Or at least buy me a drink."

"Hey, Cross offered you one of those in his office."

I shook my head and stood. "Whatever. Let me take a shower and we'll go."

I threw myself into clubbing like it was going out of style. Cary and I bounced all over downtown clubs from Tribeca to the East Village, wasting stupid money on cover charges and having a fabulous time. I danced until my feet felt like they were going to fall off, but I toughed it out until Cary complained about his heeled boots first.

We'd just stumbled out of a techno-pop club with a plan to buy me flip-flops at a nearby Walgreens when we ran across a hawker promoting a lounge a few blocks away.

"Great place to get off your feet for a while," he said, without the usual flashy smile or exaggerated hype most of the hawkers employed. His clothes—black jeans and turtleneck—were more upscale, which intrigued me. And he didn't have flyers or postcards. What he handed me was a business card made from papyrus paper and printed with a gilded font that caught the light of the electric signage around us. I made a mental note to hang on to it as a great piece of print advertising.

A stream of quickly moving pedestrians flowed around us. Cary squinted down at the lettering, having a few more drinks in him than I did. "Looks swank."

"Show them that card," the hawker urged. "You'll skip the cover."

"Sweet." Cary linked arms with me and dragged me along. "Let's go. You might find a quality guy in a swanky joint."

My feet were seriously killing me by the time we found the place, but I quit bitching when I saw the charming entrance. The line to get in was long, extending down the street and around the corner. Amy Winehouse's soulful voice drifted out of the open door, as did well-dressed customers who exited with big smiles.

True to the hawker's word, the business card was a magic key that granted us immediate and free entrance. A gorgeous hostess led us upstairs to a quieter VIP bar that overlooked the stage and dance floor below. We were shown to a small seating area by the balcony and settled at a table hugged by two half-moon velvet sofas. She propped a beverage menu in the center and said, "Your drinks are on the house. Enjoy your evening."

"Wow." Cary whistled. "We scored."

"I think that hawker recognized you from an ad."

"Wouldn't that rock?" He grinned. "God, it's a great night. Hanging out with my best girl and crushing on a new hunk in my life."

"Oh?"

"I think I've decided to see where things go with Trey."

That made me happy. It felt like I'd been waiting forever for him to find someone who'd treat him right. "Has he asked you out yet?"

"No, but I don't think it's because he doesn't want to." He shrugged and smoothed his artfully ripped T-shirt. Paired with black leather pants and spiked wristlets, it made him look sexy and wild. "I just think he's trying to figure out the situation with you first. He wigged when I told him I lived with a woman and that I'd moved across the country to be with you. He's worried I might be bi-curious and secretly hung up on you. That's why I wanted you two to meet today, so he could see how you and I are together."

"I'm sorry, Cary. I'll try to put him at ease about it."

"It's *not* your fault. Don't worry about it. It'll work out if it's supposed to."

His assurances didn't make me feel better. I tried to think of a way I could help.

Two guys stopped by our table. "Okay if we join you?" the taller one asked.

I glanced at Cary, and then back at the guys. They looked like brothers and they were very attractive. Both were smiling and confident, their stances loose and easy.

I was about to say, *Sure*, when a warm hand settled on my bare shoulder and squeezed firmly. "This one's taken."

Across from me, Cary gaped as Gideon Cross rounded the sofa and extended his hand to him. "Taylor. Gideon Cross."

"Cary Taylor." He shook Gideon's hand with a wide smile. "But you knew that. Nice to meet you. I've heard a lot about you."

I could've killed him. I seriously thought about it.

"Good to know." Gideon settled on the seat beside me, his arm draped behind me so that his fingertips could brush casually and possessively up and down my arm. "Maybe there's hope for me yet."

Twisting at the waist, I faced him and whispered fiercely, "What are you doing?"

He shot me a hard glance. "Whatever it takes."

"I'm going to dance." Cary stood with a mischievous grin. "Be back in a bit."

Ignoring my pleading glance, my best friend blew me a kiss and the guys followed him. I watched them all go, my heart racing. After another minute, ignoring Gideon became ridiculous, as well as impossible.

My gaze slid over him. He wore dress slacks in graphite gray and a black V-neck sweater, the overall effect being one of careless sophistication. I loved the look on him and was attracted to the softness it gave him, even though I knew it was only an illusion. He was a hard man in a lot of ways.

I took a deep breath, feeling like I needed to make an effort to socialize with him. After all, wasn't that my big complaint? That he wanted to skip past the getting-to-know-you stage and jump straight into bed?

"You look . . ." I paused. *Fantastic. Wonderful. Amazing. So damn sexy* . . . In the end, I went with the lame, "I like the way you look."

His brow arched. "Ah, something you like about me. Is that a general like of the overall package? Or just the clothes? Only the sweater? Or maybe it's the pants?"

The edge to his tone rubbed me the wrong way. "And if I say it's just the sweater?"

"I'll buy a dozen and wear them every damn day."

"That would be a shame."

"You don't like the sweater?" He was pissy, his words coming clipped and fast.

My hands flexed restlessly in my lap. "I love the sweater, but I also like the suits."

He stared at me a minute, and then nodded. "How was your date with B.O.B.?"

Oh hell. I looked away. It was a lot easier talking about masturbation over the phone. Doing it while squirming under that piercing blue stare was mortifying. "I don't kiss and tell."

He brushed the backs of his fingers over my cheek and murmured, "You're blushing."

I heard the amusement in his voice and swiftly changed topics. "Do you come here often?"

Shit. Where did that clichéd line come from?

His hand dropped to my lap and caught one of mine, his fingers curling into my palm. "When necessary."

A quick stab of jealousy made me stiffen. I glared at him, even though I was mad at myself for caring either way. "What does that mean? When you're on the prowl?"

Gideon's mouth curved into a genuine smile that hit me hard. "When expensive decisions need to be made. I own this club, Eva."

Of course he did. Jeez.

A pretty waitress set two pinkish-colored iced drinks in square tumblers on the table. She looked at Gideon and gave him a flirtatious smile. "Here you go, Mr. Cross. Two Stoli Elit and cranberries. Can I get you anything else?"

"That'll be all for now. Thanks."

I could totally see that she wanted to get on the preapproved list and I bristled at that; then I was distracted by what we'd been served. It was my beverage of choice when clubbing and what I'd been drinking all night. My nerves tingled. I watched him take a drink, swirl it around in his mouth like a fine wine, and then swallow it. The working of his throat made me hot, but that was nothing compared to what the intensity of his stare did to me.

"Not bad," he murmured. "Tell me if we made it right."

He kissed me. He moved in fast, but I saw it coming and didn't turn away. His mouth was cold and flavored with alcohol-laced cranberry. Delicious. All the chaotic emotion and energy that had been writhing around inside me abruptly became too much to contain. I shoved a hand in his glorious hair and clenched it tight, holding him still as I sucked on his tongue. His groan was the most erotic sound I'd ever heard, making the flesh between my legs tighten viciously.

Shocked by the fury of my reaction, I wrenched away, gasping.

Gideon followed, nuzzling the side of my face, his lips brushing over my ear. He was breathing hard, too, and the sound of the ice in his tumbler clinking against the glass skittered across my inflamed senses.

"I need to be inside you, Eva," he whispered roughly. "I'm aching for you."

My gaze fell to my drink on the table, my thoughts swirling around in my head, a clusterfuck of impressions and recollections and confusion. "How did you know?"

His tongue traced the shell of my ear and I shivered. It felt like every cell in my body was straining toward his. Resisting him took an impossible amount of energy, draining me and making me feel tired.

"Know what?" he asked.

"What I like to drink? What Cary's name is?"

He inhaled deeply and then pulled away. Setting his drink down, he shifted on the sofa and drew a knee up onto the cushion between us so that he faced me directly. His arm once again draped over the sofa back, his fingertips drawing circles on the curve of my shoulder. "You visited another of my clubs earlier. Your credit card popped and your drinks were recorded. And Cary Taylor is listed on the rental agreement for your apartment."

The room spun. *No way* . . . My cell phone. My credit card. My fucking apartment. I couldn't breathe. Between my mother and Gideon, I felt claustrophobic.

"Eva. Jesus. You're white as a ghost." He shoved a glass into my hand. "Drink."

It was the Stoli and cranberry. I pounded it, draining the tumbler. My stomach churned for a moment, then settled. "You own the building I live in?" I gasped.

"Oddly enough, yes." He moved to sit on the table, facing me, his legs on either side of mine. He took my glass and set it aside, then warmed my chilled hands with his.

"Are you crazy, Gideon?"

His mouth thinned. "Is that a serious question?"

"Yes. Yes, it is. My mom stalks me, too, and she sees a shrink. Do you have a shrink?"

"Not presently, but you're driving me crazy enough to make that a possibility."

"So this behavior isn't normal for you?" My heart was pounding. I could hear the blood rushing past my eardrums. "Or is it?"

He shoved a hand through his hair, restoring order to the strands I'd mussed when we'd kissed. "I accessed information you voluntarily made available to me."

"Not to you! Not for what you used it for! That has to violate some kind of privacy law." I stared at him, more confused than ever. "Why would you do that?"

He had the grace to look disgruntled, at least. "So I can figure you out, damn it."

"Why don't you just *ask* me, Gideon? Is that so fucking hard for people to do nowadays?"

"It is with you." He grabbed his drink off the table and tossed back most of it. "I can't get you alone for more than a few minutes at a time."

"Because the only thing you want to talk about is what you have to do to get laid!"

"Christ, Eva," he hissed, squeezing my hand. "Keep your voice down!"

I studied him, taking in every line and plane of his face. Unfortunately, cataloging the details didn't lessen my awe even a tiny bit. I was beginning to suspect I'd never get over being dazzled by his looks.

And I wasn't alone; I'd seen how other women reacted around him. And he was crazy rich, which made even old, bald, and paunchy guys attractive. It was no wonder he was used to snapping his fingers and scoring an orgasm.

His gaze darted over my face. "Why are you looking at me like that?"

"I'm thinking."

"About what?" His jaw tightened. "And I'm warning you, if you say anything about orifices, preapprovals, or seminal emissions, I won't be held accountable for my actions."

That almost made me smile. "I want to understand a few things, because I think it's possible I'm not giving you enough credit."

"I'd like to understand a few things myself," he muttered.

"I'm guessing the 'I want to fuck you' approach has a high success rate for you."

Gideon's face smoothed into unreadable impassivity. "I'm not touching that one, Eva."

"Okay. You want to figure out what it's going to take to get me into bed. Is that why you're here in this club right now? Because of me? And don't say what you think I want to hear."

His gaze was clear and steady. "I'm here for you, yes. I arranged it."

Suddenly the threads the street hawker had been wearing made sense. We'd been hustled by someone on Cross Industries' payroll. "Did you figure that getting me here would get you laid?"

His mouth twitched with suppressed amusement. "There's always the hope, but I expected it would take more work than a chance meeting over drinks."

"You're right. So why do it? Why not wait until Monday lunch?"

"Because you're out trolling. I can't do anything about B.O.B., but I can stop you from picking up some asshole in a bar. You want to score, Eva, I'm right here."

"I'm not trolling. I'm burning off tension after a stressful day."

"You're not the only one." He fingered one of my silver chandelier earrings. "So you drink and dance when you're tense. I work on the problem that's making me tense in the first place."

His voice had softened, and it stirred an alarming yearning. "Is that what I am? A problem?"

"Absolutely." But there was a hint of a smile around his lips.

I knew that was a lot of the appeal for him. Gideon Cross wouldn't be where he was, at such a young age, if he took "no" gracefully. "What's your definition of dating?"

A frown marred the space between his brows. "Lengthy social time spent with a woman during which we're not actively fucking."

"Don't you enjoy the company of women?"

The frown turned into a scowl. "Sure, as long as there aren't any exaggerated expectations or excessive demands on my time. I've found the best way to steer clear of those is to have mutually exclusive sexual relationships and friendships."

There were those pesky "exaggerated expectations" again. Clearly, those were a sticking point with him. "So, you do have female friends?"

BARED TO YOU · 65

"Of course." His legs tightened around mine, capturing me. "Where are you going with this?"

"You segregate sex from the rest of your life. You separate it from friendship, work . . . everything."

"I've got good reasons for doing that."

"I'm sure you do. Okay, here are my thoughts." It was difficult concentrating when I was so close to Gideon. "I told you I don't want to date and I don't. My job is priority number one and my personal life— as a single woman—is a close second. I don't want to sacrifice any of that time on a relationship, and there's really not enough left over to squeeze in anything steady."

"I'm right there with you."

"But I like sex."

"Good. Have it with me." His smile was an erotic invitation.

I shoved his shoulder. "I need a personal connection with the men I sleep with. It doesn't have to be intense or deep, but sex needs to be more than an emotionless transaction for me."

"Why?"

I could tell he wasn't being flippant. As bizarre as this conversation must be for him, Gideon was taking it seriously. "Call it one of my quirks, and I'm not saying that lightly. It pisses me off to feel used for sex. I feel devalued."

"Can't you look at it as *you* using *me* for sex?"

"Not with you." He was too forceful, too demanding.

A sizzling, predatory glimmer sparked in his eyes as I bared my weakness for him.

"Besides," I went on quickly, "that's semantics. I need an equal exchange in my sexual relationships. Or to have the upper hand."

"Okay."

"Okay? You said that really quickly, considering I'm telling you I need to combine two things you work so hard to avoid putting together."

"I'm not comfortable with it and I don't claim to understand, but I'm hearing you—it's an issue. Tell me how to get around it."

My breath left me in a rush. I hadn't expected that. He was a man who wanted no complications with his sex and I was a woman who found sex complicated, but he wasn't giving up. Yet.

"We need to be friendly, Gideon. Not best buds or confidants, but two people who know more about each other than their anatomy. To me, that means we have to spend time together when we're not actively fucking. And I'm afraid we'll have to spend time not actively fucking in places where we're forced to restrain ourselves."

"Isn't that what we're doing now?"

"Yes. And see, that's what I mean. I wasn't giving you credit for that. You should've done it in a less creepy manner"—I covered his lips with my fingers when he tried to cut me off—"but I admit you did try to set up a time to talk and I wasn't helpful."

He nipped my fingers with his teeth, making me yelp and yank my hand away.

"Hey. What was that for?"

He lifted my abused hand to his mouth and kissed the hurt, his tongue darting out to soothe. And incite.

In self-defense, I tugged my hand back to my lap. I still wasn't completely confident that we'd worked things out. "Just so you know there are no exaggerated expectations—when you and I spend time together not actively fucking, I won't think it's a date. All right?"

"That covers it." Gideon smiled, and my decision to be with him solidified for me. His smile was like lightning in the darkness, blinding and beautiful and mysterious, and I wanted him so badly it was physically painful.

His hands slid down to cup the backs of my thighs. Squeezing gently, he tugged me just a little bit closer. The hem of my short black halter dress slipped almost indecently high, and his gaze was riveted to the flesh he'd exposed. His tongue wet his lips in an action so carnal and suggestive I could almost feel the caress on my skin.

Duffy began begging for mercy, her voice drifting up from the dance floor below. An unwelcome ache developed in my chest and I rubbed at it.

I'd already had enough, but I heard myself saying, "I need another drink."

5

I HAD A VICIOUS hangover on Saturday morning and figured it was no less than I deserved. As much as I'd resented Gideon's insistence on negotiating sex with as much passion as he would a merger, in the end I'd negotiated in kind. Because I wanted him enough to take a calculated risk and break my own rules.

I took comfort in knowing he was breaking some of his own, too.

After a long, hot shower, I made my way into the living room and found Cary on the couch with his netbook, looking fresh and alert. Smelling coffee in the kitchen, I headed there and filled the biggest mug I could find.

"Morning, sunshine," Cary called out.

With my much-needed dose of caffeine wrapped between both palms, I joined him on the couch.

He pointed at a box on the end table. "That came for you while you were in the shower."

I set my mug on the coffee table and picked up the box. It was wrapped with brown paper and twine and had my name handwritten diagonally across the top with a decorative calligraphic flourish. Inside was an amber glass bottle with HANGOVER CURE painted on it in a white old-fashioned font and a note tied with raffia to the bottle's neck that said, *Drink me*. Gideon's business card was nestled in the cushioning tissue paper.

As I studied the gift, I found it very apt. Since meeting Gideon I'd felt like I'd fallen down the rabbit hole into a fascinating and seductive world where few of the known rules applied. I was in uncharted territory that was both exciting and scary.

I glanced at Cary, who eyed the bottle dubiously.

"Cheers." I pried the cork out and drank the contents without thinking twice about it. It tasted like sickly sweet cough syrup. My stomach quivered in distaste for a moment and then heated. I wiped my mouth with the back of my hand and shoved the cork back into the empty bottle.

"What was that?" Cary asked.

"From the burn, it's hair of the dog."

His nose wrinkled. "Effective but unpleasant."

And it was working. I already felt a little steadier.

Cary picked up the box and dug out Gideon's card. He flipped it over, then held it out to me. On the back Gideon had written *Call me* in bold slashing penmanship and jotted down a number.

I took the card, curling my hand around it. His gift was proof that he was thinking about me. His tenacity and focus were seductive. And flattering.

There was no denying I was in trouble where Gideon was concerned. I craved the way I felt when he touched me, and I loved the way he responded when I touched him back. When I tried to think of what I *wouldn't* agree to do to have his hands on me again, I couldn't come up with much.

When Cary tried to hand me the phone, I shook my head. "Not yet. I need a clear head when dealing with him, and I'm still fuzzy."

"You two seemed cozy last night. He's definitely into you."

"I'm definitely into him." Curling into the corner of the couch, I pressed my cheek into the cushion and hugged my legs to my chest. "We're going to hang out, get to know each other, have casual-but-physically-intense sex, and be otherwise completely independent. No strings, no expectations, no responsibilities."

Cary hit a button on his netbook and the printer on the other side of the room started spitting out pages. Then he snapped the computer closed, set it on the coffee table, and gave me all his attention. "Maybe it'll turn into something serious."

"Maybe not," I scoffed.

"Cynic."

"I'm not looking for happily-ever-after, Cary, especially not with a mega-mogul like Cross. I've seen what it's like for my mom being connected to powerful men. It's a full-time job with a part-time companion. Money keeps Mom happy, but it wouldn't be enough for me."

My dad had loved my mom. He'd asked her to marry him and share his life. She'd turned him down because he didn't have the hefty portfolio and sizable bank account she required in a husband. Love wasn't a requisite for marriage in Monica Stanton's opinion, and since her sultry-eyed, breathy-voiced beauty was irresistible to most men, she'd never had to settle for less than whatever she wanted. Unfortunately she hadn't wanted my dad for the long haul.

Glancing at the clock, I saw it was ten thirty. "I guess I should get ready."

"I love spa day with your mom." Cary smiled, and it chased the lingering shadows on my mood away. "I feel like a god when we're done."

"Me, too. Of the goddess persuasion."

We were so eager to be off that we went downstairs to meet the car rather than wait for the front desk to call up.

The doorman smiled as we stepped outside—me in heeled sandals and a maxi dress, and Cary in hip-hugging jeans and a long-sleeved T-shirt.

"Good morning, Miss Tramell. Mr. Taylor. Will you need a cab today?"

"No thanks, Paul. We're expecting a car." Cary grinned. "It's spa day at Perrini's!"

"Ah, Perrini's Day Spa." Paul gave a sage nod. "I bought my wife a gift certificate for our anniversary. She enjoyed it so much I plan to make it a tradition."

"You did good, Paul," I said. "Pampering a woman never goes out of style."

A black town car pulled up with Clancy at the wheel. Paul opened the rear door for us and we climbed in, squealing when we found a box of Knipschildt's Chocopologie on the seat. Waving at Paul, we settled back and dug in, taking tiny nibbles of the truffles that were worth savoring slowly.

Clancy drove us straight to Perrini's, where the relaxation began from the moment one walked in the door. Crossing the entrance threshold was like taking a vacation on the far side of the world. Every arched doorway was framed by lushly vibrant striped silks, while jeweled pillows decorated elegant chaises and oversized armchairs.

Birds chirped from suspended gilded cages, and potted plants filled every corner with lush fronds. Small decorative fountains added the sounds of running water, while stringed instrumental music was piped into the room via cleverly hidden speakers. The air was redolent with a mix of exotic spices and fragrances, making me feel like I'd stepped into *Arabian Nights*.

It was *this close* to being too much, but it didn't cross the line. Instead, Perrini's was exotic and luxurious, an indulgent treat for those who could afford it. Like my mother, who'd just finished a milk-and-honey bath when we arrived.

I studied the menu of treatments available, deciding to skip my usual "warrior woman" in favor of the "passionate pampering." I'd been waxed the week before, but the rest of the treatment—"designed to make you sexually irresistible"—sounded like exactly what I needed.

I'd finally managed to get my mind back into the safe zone of work when Cary spoke up from the pedicure chair beside mine.

"Mrs. Stanton, have you met Gideon Cross?"

I gaped at him. He knew damn well my mom went nuts over any news about my romantic—and not-so-romantic, as the case may be—relationships.

My mother, who sat in the chair on the other side of me, leaned forward with her usual girlish excitement over a rich, handsome man. "Of course. He's one of the wealthiest men in the world. Number twenty-five or so on *Forbes*'s list, if I'm remembering correctly. A very driven young man, obviously, and a generous benefactor to many of the children's charities I champion. Extremely eligible, of course, but I don't believe he's gay, Cary. He's got a reputation as a ladies' man."

"My loss." Cary grinned and ignored my violent headshaking. "But it'd be a hopeless crush anyway, since he's digging on Eva."

"Eva! I can't believe you didn't say anything. How could you not tell me something like that?"

I looked at my mom, whose scrubbed face appeared young, unlined, and very much like mine. I was very clearly my mother's daughter, right down to my surname. The one concession she'd made to my father had been to name me after his mother.

"There's nothing to tell," I insisted. "We're just . . . friends."

"We can do better than that," Monica said, with a look of calculation that struck fear in my heart. "I don't know how it escaped me that you work in the same building he does. I'm certain he was smitten the moment he saw you. Although he's known to prefer brunettes . . .

Hmm . . . Anyway. He's also known for his excellent taste. Clearly the latter won out with you."

"It's not like that. Please don't start meddling. You'll embarrass me."

"Nonsense. If anyone knows what to do with men, it's me."

I cringed, my shoulders creeping up to my ears. By the time my massage appointment came around, I was in desperate need of one. I stretched out on the table and closed my eyes, preparing to take a cat-nap to get through the long night ahead.

I loved dressing up and looking pretty as much as the next girl, but charity functions were a lot of work. Making small talk was exhausting, smiling nonstop was a pain, and conversations about businesses and people I didn't know were boring. If it weren't for Cary benefiting from the exposure, I'd put up a bigger fight about going.

I sighed. Who was I fooling? I'd end up going anyway. My mom and Stanton supported abused children's charities because they were significant to me. Going to the occasional stuffy event was a small price to pay for the return.

Taking a deep breath, I consciously relaxed. I made a mental note to call my dad when I got home and thought about how to send a thank-you note to Gideon for the hangover cure. I supposed I could e-mail him using the contact info on his business card, but that lacked class. Besides, I didn't know who read his inbox.

I'd just call him when I got home. Why not? He'd asked—no, *told*—me to; he'd written the demand on his business card. And I'd get to hear his luscious voice again.

The door opened and the masseuse came in. "Hello, Eva. You ready?"

Not quite. But I was getting there.

AFTER many lovely hours at the spa, my mom and Cary dropped me off at the apartment; then they headed out to hunt for new cuff links for Stanton. I used the time alone to call Gideon. Even with the much-needed privacy, I punched most of his phone number into the keypad a half dozen times before I finally put the call through.

He answered on the first ring. "Eva."

Startled that he'd known who was calling, my mind scrambled for a moment. *How did he have my name and number in his contact list?* "Uh . . . hi, Gideon."

"I'm a block away. Let the front desk know I'm coming."

"What?" I felt like I'd missed part of the conversation. "Coming where?"

"To your place. I'm rounding the corner now. Call the desk, Eva."

He hung up and I stared at the phone, trying to absorb the fact that Gideon was moments away from being with me again. Somewhat dazed, I went to the intercom and talked to the front desk, letting them know I was expecting him, and while I was talking, he walked into the lobby. A few moments after that, he was at my door.

It was then that I remembered I was dressed in only a thigh-length silk robe, and my face and hair were styled for the dinner. What kind of impression would he get from my appearance?

I tightened the belt of my robe before I let him in. It wasn't like I'd invited him over for a seduction or anything.

Gideon stood in the hallway for a long moment, his gaze raking me from my head down to my French-manicured toes. I was equally stunned by his appearance. The way he looked in worn jeans and a T-shirt made me want to undress him with my teeth.

"Worth the trip to find you like this, Eva." He stepped inside and locked the door behind him. "How are you feeling?"

"Good. Thanks to you. Thank you." My stomach quivered because he was here, with me, which made me feel almost . . . giddy. "That can't be why you came over."

"I'm here because it took you too long to call me."

"I didn't realize I had a deadline."

"I have to ask you something time-sensitive, but more than that, I wanted to know if you were feeling all right after last night." His eyes were dark as they swept over me, his breathtaking face framed by that luxurious curtain of inky hair. "God. You look beautiful, Eva. I can't remember ever wanting anything this much."

With just those few simple words I became hot and needy. Way too vulnerable. "What's so urgent?"

"Go with me to the advocacy center dinner tonight."

I pulled back, surprised and excited by the request. "You're going?"

"So are you. I checked, knowing your mother would be there. Let's go together."

My hand went to my throat, my mind torn between the weirdness of how much he knew about me and concern over what he was asking me to do. "That's not what I meant when I said we should spend time together."

"Why not?" The simple question was laced with challenge. "What's the problem with going together to an event we'd already planned on attending separately?"

"It's not very discreet. It's a high-profile event."

"So?" Gideon stepped closer and fingered a curl of my hair.

There was a dangerous purr to his voice that sent a shiver through me. I could feel the warmth of his big, hard body and smell the richly masculine scent of his skin. I was falling under his spell, deeper with every minute that passed.

"People will make assumptions, my mother in particular. She's already scenting your bachelor blood in the water."

Lowering his head, Gideon pressed his lips into the crook of my neck. "I don't care what people think. We know what we're doing. And I'll deal with your mother."

"If you think you can," I said breathlessly, "you don't know her very well."

"I'll pick you up at seven." His tongue traced the wildly throbbing vein in my throat and I melted into him, my body going lax as he pulled me close.

Still, I managed to say, "I haven't said yes."

"But you won't say no." He caught my earlobe between his teeth. "I won't let you."

I opened my mouth to protest and he sealed his lips over mine, shutting me up with a lush, wet kiss. His tongue did that slow, savoring licking that made me long to feel him doing the same between my legs. My hands went to his hair, sliding through it, tugging. When he wrapped his arms around me, I arched, curving into his hands.

Just as he had in his office, he had me on my back on the couch before I realized he was moving me, his mouth swallowing my surprised gasp. The robe gave way to his dexterous fingers; then he was cupping my breasts, kneading them with soft, rhythmic squeezes.

"Gideon—"

"Shh." He sucked on my lower lip, his fingers rolling and tugging my tender nipples. "It was driving me crazy knowing you were naked beneath your robe."

"You came over without— Oh! Oh, God . . ."

His mouth surrounded the tip of my breast, the wash of heat bringing a mist of perspiration to my skin.

My gaze darted frantically to the clock on the cable box. "Gideon, no."

His head lifted and he looked at me with stormy blue eyes. "It's insane, I know. I don't—I can't explain it, Eva, but I have to make you come. I've been thinking about it constantly for days now."

One of his hands pushed between my legs. They fell open shamelessly, my body so aroused I was flushed and almost feverish. His other hand continued to plump my breasts, making them heavy and unbearably sensitive.

"You're wet for me," he murmured, his gaze sliding down my body to where he was parting me with his fingers. "You're beautiful here, too. Plush and pink. So soft. You didn't wax today, did you?"

I shook my head.

"Thank God. I don't think I would've made it ten minutes without touching you, let alone ten hours." He slid one finger carefully into me.

My eyes closed against the unbearable vulnerability of being spread out naked and fingered by a man whose familiarity with the rules of Brazilian waxing betrayed an intimate knowledge of women. A man who was still fully clothed and kneeling on the floor beside me.

"You're so snug." Gideon pulled out and thrust gently back into me. My back bowed as I clenched eagerly around him. "And so greedy. How long has it been since the last time you were fucked?"

I swallowed hard. "I've been busy. I had my thesis, then job hunting and moving . . ."

"A while, then." He pulled out and pushed back into me with two fingers. I couldn't hold back a moan of delight. The man had talented hands, confident and skilled, and he took what he wanted with them.

"Are you on birth control, Eva?"

"Yes." My hands gripped the edges of the cushions. "Of course."

"I'll prove I'm clean and you'll do the same, and then you're going to let me come in you."

"Jesus, Gideon." I was panting for him, my hips circling shamelessly onto his thrusting fingers. I felt like I'd spontaneously combust if he didn't get me off.

I'd never been so turned on in my life. I was near mindless with the need for an orgasm. If Cary walked in right then and found me writhing in our living room while Gideon finger-fucked me, I didn't think I'd care.

Gideon was breathing hard, too. His face was flushed with lust. For me. When I'd done nothing more than respond helplessly to him.

His hand at my breast moved to my cheek and brushed over it. "You're blushing. I've scandalized you."

"Yes."

His smile was both wicked and delighted, and it made my chest tight. "I want to feel my cum in you when I fuck you with my fingers. I want *you* to feel my cum in you, so you think about how I looked and the sounds I made when I pumped it into you. And while you're thinking about that, you're going to look forward to me doing it again and again."

My sex rippled around his stroking fingers, the rawness of his words pushing me to the brink of orgasm.

"I'm going to tell you all the ways I want you to please me, Eva, and you're going to do it all . . . take it all, and we're going to have explosive, primal, no-holds-barred sex. You know that, don't you? You can feel how it'll be between us."

"Yes," I breathed, clutching my breasts to ease the deep ache of my hardened nipples. "Please, Gideon."

"Shh . . . I've got you." The pad of his thumb rubbed my clitoris in gentle circles. "Look into my eyes when you come for me."

Everything tightened in my core, the tension building as he massaged my clit and pushed his fingers in and out in a steady, unhurried rhythm.

"Give it up to me, Eva," he ordered. "Now."

I climaxed with a thready cry, my grip white-knuckled on the sides of the cushions as my hips pumped onto his hand, my mind far beyond shame or shyness. My gaze was locked to his, unable to look away, riveted by the fierce masculine triumph that flared in his eyes. In that moment he owned me. I'd do anything he wanted. And he knew it.

Searing pleasure pulsed through me. Through the roaring of blood in my ears, I thought I heard him speak hoarsely, but I lost the words when he hooked one of my legs over the back of the couch and covered my cleft with his mouth.

"No—" I pushed at his head with my hands. "I can't."

I was too swollen, too sensitive. But when his tongue touched my clit, fluttering over it, the hunger built again. More intense than the first time. He rimmed my trembling slit, teasing me, taunting me with the promise of another orgasm when I knew I couldn't have one again so quickly.

Then his tongue speared into me and I bit my lip to bite back a scream. I came a second time, my body quaking violently, tender muscles tightening desperately around his decadent licking. His growl vibrated through me. I didn't have the strength to push him away when he returned to my clit and sucked softly . . . tirelessly . . . until I climaxed again, gasping his name.

I was boneless as he straightened my leg and still breathless when he pressed kisses up my belly to my breasts. He licked each of my nipples, then hauled me up with his arms banded around my back. I hung lax and pliable in his grip while he took my mouth with suppressed violence, bruising my lips and betraying how close to the edge he was.

He closed my robe, then stood, staring down at me.

"Gideon . . . ?"

"Seven o'clock, Eva." He reached down and touched my ankle, his fingertips caressing the diamond anklet I'd put on in preparation for the evening. "And keep this on. I want to fuck you while you're wearing nothing else."

6

"Hey, Dad. I caught you." I adjusted my grip on the phone receiver and pulled up a stool at the breakfast bar. I missed my father. For the last four years we'd lived close enough to see each other at least once a week. Now his home in Oceanside was the entire country away. "How are you?"

He lowered the volume on the television. "Better, now that you've called. How was your first week at work?"

I went over my days from Monday through Friday, skipping over all the Gideon parts. "I really like my boss, Mark," I finished. "And the vibe of the agency is very energetic and kind of quirky. I'm happy going to work every day, and I'm bummed when it's time to go home."

"I hope it stays that way. But you need to make sure you have some downtime, too. Go out, be young, have fun. But not too much fun."

"Yeah, I had a little too much last night. Cary and I went clubbing, and I woke up with a mean hangover."

"Shit, don't tell me that." He groaned. "Some nights I wake up in a cold sweat thinking about you in New York. I get through it by telling myself you're too smart to take chances, thanks to two parents who've drilled safety rules into your DNA."

"Which is true," I said, laughing. "That reminds me . . . I'm going to start Krav Maga training."

"Really?" There was a thoughtful pause. "One of the guys on the force is big on it. Maybe I'll check it out and we can compare notes when I come out to visit you."

"You're coming to New York?" I couldn't hide my excitement. "Oh, Dad, I'd love it if you would. As much as I miss SoCal, Manhattan is really awesome. I think you'll like it."

"I'd like anyplace in the world as long as you're there." He waited a beat, then asked, "How's your mom?"

"Well . . . she's Mom. Beautiful, charming, and obsessive-compulsive."

My chest hurt and I rubbed at it. I thought my dad might still love my mom. He'd never married. That was one of the reasons I never told him about what happened to me. As a cop, he would've insisted on pressing charges and the scandal would have destroyed my mother. I also worried that he'd lose respect for her or even blame her, and it hadn't been her fault. As soon as she'd found out what her stepson was doing to me, she'd left a husband she was happy with and filed for divorce.

I kept talking, waving at Cary as he came rushing in with a little blue Tiffany & Co. bag. "We had a spa day today. It was a fun way to cap off the week."

I could hear the smile in his voice when he said, "I'm glad you two are managing to spend time together. What are your plans for the rest of the weekend?"

I hedged on the subject of the charity event, knowing the whole red-carpet business and astronomically priced dinner seats would just highlight the gap between my parents' lives. "Cary and I are going out to eat, and then I plan on staying in tomorrow. Sleeping in late, hanging out in my pajamas all day, maybe some movies and food delivery of some sort. A little vegetating before a new workweek kicks off."

"Sounds like heaven to me. I may copy you when my next day off rolls around."

Glancing at the clock, I saw it was creeping past six. "I have to get ready now. Be careful at work, okay? I worry about you, too."

"Will do. Bye, baby."

The familiar sign-off had me missing him so much my throat hurt. "Oh, wait! I'm getting a new cell phone. I'll text you the number as soon as I have it."

"Again? You just got a new one when you moved."

"Long, boring story."

"Hmm . . . Don't put it off. They're good for safety as well as for playing Angry Birds."

"I'm over that game!" I laughed, and warmth spread through me to hear him laughing, too. "I'll call you in a few days. Be good."

"That's *my* line."

We hung up. I sat for a few moments in the ensuing silence, feeling like everything was right in my world, which never lasted long. I brooded on that for minute; then Cary cranked up Hinder on his bedroom stereo and that kicked my butt into gear.

I hurried to my room to get ready for a night with Gideon.

"NECKLACE or no necklace?" I asked Cary, when he came into my bedroom looking seriously amazing. Dressed in his new Brioni tux, he was both debonair and dashing, and certain to attract attention.

"Hmm." His head tilted to the side as he studied me. "Hold it up again."

I lifted the choker of gold coins to my throat. The dress my mom had sent was fire engine red and styled for a Grecian goddess. It hung on one shoulder, cut diagonally across my cleavage, had ruching to the hip, and then split at my right upper thigh all the way down my leg. There was no back to speak of, aside from a slender strip of rhinestones that connected one side to the other to keep the front from falling off. Otherwise, the back was bared to just above the crack of my butt in a racy V-cut.

"Forget the necklace," he said. "I was leaning toward gold chandeliers, but now I'm thinking diamond hoops. The biggest ones you've got."

"What? Really?" I frowned at our reflections in my cheval mirror, watching as he moved to my jewelry box and dug through it.

"These." He brought them to me and I eyed the two-inch hoops my mother had given me for my eighteenth birthday. "Trust me, Eva. Try 'em on."

I did and found he was right. It was a very different look from the gold choker, less glam and more edgy sensuality. And the earrings went well with the diamond anklet on my right leg that I'd never think of the same way again after Gideon's comment. With my hair swept off my face into a cascade of thick, deliberately messy curls, I had a just-screwed look that was complemented by smoky eye shadow and glossy nude lips.

"What would I do without you, Cary Taylor?"

"Baby girl"—he set his hands on my shoulders and pressed his cheek to mine—"you'll never find out."

"You look awesome, by the way."

"Don't I?" He winked and stepped back, showing off.

In his own way, Cary could give Gideon a run for his money . . . er, looks. Cary was more finely featured, almost pretty compared to Gideon's savage beauty, but both were striking men who made you look twice, and then stare in greedy delight.

Cary hadn't been quite so perfect when I met him. He'd been

strung out and gaunt, his emerald eyes cloudy and lost. But I'd been drawn to him, going out of my way to sit next to him in group therapy. He'd finally propositioned me crudely, having come to believe the only reason people associated with him was because they wanted to fuck him. It was when I declined, firmly and irrevocably, that we finally connected and became best friends. He was the brother I'd never had.

The intercom buzzed and I jumped, making me realize how nervous I was. I looked at Cary. "I forgot to tell the front desk he was coming back."

"I'll get him."

"Are you going to be okay riding over with Stanton and my mom?"

"Are you kidding? They love me." His smile dimmed. "Having second thoughts about going with Cross?"

I took a deep breath, remembering where I'd been earlier—on my back in a multiorgasmic daze. "Not really, no. It's just that everything's happening so fast and going better than I expected or realized I wanted . . ."

"You're wondering what the catch is." Reaching out, he tapped my nose with his fingertip. "He's the catch, Eva. And you landed him. Enjoy yourself."

"I'm trying." I was grateful that Cary understood me and the way my mind worked. It was just so easy being with him, knowing he could fill in the blanks when I couldn't explain something.

"I researched the hell out of him this morning and printed out the interesting recent stuff. It's on your desk, if you decide you want to check it out."

I remembered him printing something before we got ready for the spa. Pushing onto my tiptoes, I kissed his cheek. "You're the best. I love you."

"Back atcha, baby girl." He headed out. "I'll head down to the front desk and bring him up. Take your time. He's ten minutes early."

Smiling, I watched him saunter into the hallway. The door had closed behind him when I moved into the small sitting room attached to my bedroom. On the very impractical escritoire my mother had picked out, I found a folder filled with articles and printed images. I settled into the chair and got lost in Gideon Cross's history.

It was like watching a train wreck to read that he was the son of Geoffrey Cross, former chairman of an investment securities firm later found to be a front for a massive Ponzi scheme. Gideon was just five years old when his dad committed suicide with a gunshot to the head rather than face prison time.

Oh, Gideon. I tried to picture him that young and imagined a handsome dark-haired boy with beautiful blue eyes filled with terrible confusion and sadness. The image broke my heart. How devastating his father's suicide—and the circumstances around it—must have been, for both him and his mother. The stress and strain at such a difficult time would've been enormous, especially for a child of that age.

His mother went on to marry Christopher Vidal, a music executive, and had two more children, Christopher Vidal Jr. and Ireland Vidal, but it seemed that a larger family and financial security had come too late to help Gideon stabilize after such a huge shakeup. He was too closed off not to bear some painful emotional scars.

With a critical and curious eye, I studied the women who'd been photographed with Gideon and thought about his approach to dating, socializing, and sex. I saw that my mom had been right—they were all brunettes. The woman who appeared with him most often bore the hallmarks of a Hispanic heritage. She was taller than me, willowy rather than curvy.

"Magdalene Perez," I murmured, grudgingly admitting that she was a stunner. Her posture had the kind of flamboyant confidence that I admired.

"Okay, it's been long enough," Cary interrupted with a soft note of amusement. He filled the doorway to my sitting room, leaning insolently into the doorjamb.

"Really?" I'd been so absorbed; I hadn't realized how much time had passed.

"I would guess you're about a minute away from him coming to find you. He's barely restraining himself."

I shut the folder and stood.

"Interesting reading, isn't it?"

"Very." How had Gideon's father—or more specifically, his father's suicide—influenced his life?

I knew that all the answers I wanted were waiting for me in the next room.

Leaving my bedroom, I took the hallway to the living room. I paused on the threshold, my gaze riveted to Gideon's back as he stood in front of the windows and looked out at the city. My heart rate kicked up. His reflection revealed a contemplative mood. His gaze was unfocused and his mouth grim. His crossed arms betrayed an inherent unease, as if he were out of his element. He looked remote and removed, a man who was inherently alone.

He sensed my presence, or maybe he felt my yearning. He pivoted, then went very still. I took the opportunity to drink him in, my gaze sliding all over him. He looked every inch the powerful magnate. So sensually handsome my eyes burned just from looking at him. The rakish fall of black hair around his face made my fingers flex with the urge to touch it. And the way he looked at me . . . my pulse leaped.

"Eva." He came toward me, his stride graceful and strong. He caught up my hand and lifted it to his mouth. His gaze was intense—intensely hot, intensely focused.

The feel of his lips against my skin sent goose bumps racing up my arm and stirred memories of that sinful mouth on other parts of my body. I was instantly aroused. "Hi."

Amusement warmed his eyes. "Hi, yourself. You look amazing. I can't wait to show you off."

I breathed through the delight I felt at the compliment. "Let's hope I can do you justice."

A slight frown knit the space between his brows. "Do you have everything you need?"

Cary appeared beside me, carrying my black velvet wrap and opera-length gloves. "Here you go. I tucked your gloss into your clutch."

"You're the best, Cary."

He winked at me—which told me he'd seen the condoms I had tucked into the small interior pocket. "I'll head down with you two."

Gideon took the wrap from Cary and draped it over my shoulders. He pulled my hair out from underneath it and the feel of his hands at my neck so distracted me, I barely paid attention when Cary pushed my gloves into my hands.

The elevator ride to the lobby was an exercise in surviving acute sexual tension. Not that Cary seemed to notice. He was on my left with both hands in his pockets, whistling. Gideon, on the other hand, was a tremendous force on the other side of me. Although he didn't move or make a sound, I could feel the edgy energy radiating from him. My skin tingled from the magnetic pull between us, and my breath came short and fast. I was relieved when the doors opened and freed us from the enclosed space.

Two women stood waiting to get on. Their jaws dropped when they saw Gideon and Cary, and that lightened my mood and made me smile.

"Ladies," Cary greeted them, with a smile that really wasn't fair. I could almost see their brain cells misfiring.

In contrast, Gideon gave a curt nod and led me out with a hand at the small of my back, skin to skin. The contact was electric, sending heat pouring through me.

I squeezed Cary's hand. "Save a dance for me."

"Always. See you in a bit."

A limousine was waiting at the curb, and the driver opened the door when Gideon and I stepped outside. I slid across the bench seat to the opposite side and adjusted my gown. When Gideon settled beside me and the door shut, I became highly conscious of how good he smelled. I breathed him in, telling myself to relax and enjoy his company. He took my hand and ran his fingertips over the palm, the simple touch sparking a fierce lust. I shrugged off my wrap, feeling too hot to wear it.

"Eva." He hit a button and the privacy glass behind the driver began to slide up. The next moment I was tugged across his lap and his mouth was on mine, kissing me fiercely.

I did what I'd wanted to do since I saw him in my living room: I shoved my hands in his hair and kissed him back. I loved the way he kissed me, as if he *had* to, as if he'd go crazy if he didn't and had nearly waited too long. I sucked on his tongue, having learned how much he liked it, having learned how much *I* liked it, how much it made me want to suck him elsewhere with the same eagerness.

His hands were sliding over my bare back and I moaned, feeling the prod of his erection against my hip. I shifted, moving to straddle him, shoving the skirt of my gown out of the way and making a mental note to thank my mom for the dress—which had such a convenient slit. With my knees on either side of his hips, I wrapped my arms around his shoulders and deepened the kiss. I licked into his mouth, nibbled on his lower lip, stroked my tongue along his . . .

Gideon gripped my waist and pushed me away. He leaned into the seat back, his neck arched to look up at my face, his chest heaving. "What are you doing to me?"

I ran my hands down his chest through his dress shirt, feeling the unforgiving hardness of his muscles. My fingers traced the ridges of his abdomen, my mind forming a picture of how he might look naked. "I'm touching you. Enjoying the hell out of you. I want you, Gideon."

BARED TO YOU · 89

He caught my wrists, stilling my movements. "Later. We're in the middle of Manhattan."

"No one can see us."

"That's not the point. It's not the time or place to start something we can't finish for hours. I'm losing my mind already from this afternoon."

"So let's make sure we finish it now."

His grip tightened painfully. "We can't do that here."

"Why not?" Then a surprising thought struck me. "Haven't you ever had sex in a limo?"

"No." His jaw hardened. "Have you?"

Looking away without answering, I saw the traffic and pedestrians surging around us. We were only inches away from hundreds of people, but the dark glass concealed us and made me feel reckless. I wanted to please him. I wanted to know I was capable of reaching into Gideon Cross, and there was nothing to stop me but him.

I rocked my hips against him, stroking myself with the hard length of his cock. His breath hissed out between clenched teeth.

"I need you, Gideon," I said breathlessly, inhaling his scent, which was richer now that he was aroused. I thought I might be slightly intoxicated, just from the enticing smell of his skin. "You drive me crazy."

He released my wrists and cupped my face, his lips pressing hard against mine. I reached for the fly of his slacks, freeing the two buttons to access the concealed zipper. He tensed.

"I need this," I whispered against his lips. "Give me this."

He didn't relax, but he made no further attempts to stop me either. When he fell heavily into my palms, he groaned, the sound both pained and erotic. I squeezed him gently, my touch deliberately tender as I sized him with my hands. He was so hard, like stone, and hot. I slid both of my fists up his length from root to tip, my breath catching when he quivered beneath me.

Gideon gripped my thighs, his hands sliding upward beneath the edges of my dress until his thumbs found the red lace of my thong. "Your cunt is so sweet," he murmured into my mouth. "I want to spread you out and lick you 'til you beg for my cock."

"I'll beg now, if you want." I stroked him with one hand and reached for my clutch with the other, snapping it open to grab a condom.

One of his thumbs slid beneath the edge of my panties, the pad sliding through the slickness of my desire. "I've barely touched you," he whispered, his eyes glittering up at me in the shadows of the backseat, "and you're ready for me."

"I can't help it."

"I don't want you to help it." He pushed his thumb inside me, biting his lower lip when I clenched helplessly around him. "It wouldn't be fair when I can't stop what you do to me."

I ripped the foil packet open with my teeth and held it out to him with the ring of the condom protruding from the tear. "I'm not good with these."

His hand curled around mine. "I'm breaking all my rules with you."

The seriousness of his low tone sent a burst of warmth and confidence through me. "Rules are made to be broken."

I saw his teeth flash white; then he hit a button on the panel beside him and said, "Drive until I say otherwise."

My cheeks heated. Another car's headlights pierced the dark tinted glass and slid over my face, betraying my embarrassment.

"Why, Eva," he purred, rolling the condom on deftly. "You've seduced me into having sex in my limousine, but blush when I tell my driver I don't want to be interrupted while you do it to me?"

His sudden playfulness made me desperate to have him. Setting my hands on his shoulders for balance, I lifted onto my knees, rising to gain the height I needed to hover over the crown of Gideon's thick cock. His hands fisted at my hips and I heard a snap as he tore my panties away. The abrupt sound and the violent action behind it spurred my desire to a fever pitch.

"Go slow," he ordered hoarsely, lifting his hips to push his pants down farther.

His erection brushed between my legs as he moved and I whimpered, so aching and empty, as if the orgasms he'd given me earlier had only deepened my craving rather than appeased it.

He tensed when I wrapped my fingers around him and positioned him, tucking the wide crest against the saturated folds of my cleft. The scent of our lust was heavy and humid in the air, a seductive mix of need and pheromones that awakened every cell in my body. My skin was flushed and tingling, my breasts heavy and tender.

This was what I'd wanted from the moment I first saw him—to possess him, to climb up his magnificent body and take him deep inside me.

"God. Eva," he gasped as I lowered onto him, his hands flexing restlessly on my thighs.

I closed my eyes, feeling too exposed. I'd wanted intimacy with him, and yet this seemed too intimate. We were eye-to-eye, only inches apart, cocooned in a small space with the rest of the world streaming by around us. I could sense his agitation, knew he was feeling as off-center as I was.

"You're so tight." His gasped words were threaded with a hint of delicious agony.

I took more of him, letting him slide deeper. I sucked in a deep breath, feeling exquisitely stretched.

Pressing his palm flat to my lower belly, he touched my throbbing clit with the pad of his thumb and began to massage it in slow, expertly soft circles. Everything in my core tightened and clenched, sucking him deeper. Opening my eyes, I looked at him from under heavy eyelids. He was so beautiful sprawled beneath me in his elegant tuxedo, his powerful body straining with the primal need to mate.

His neck arched, his head pressing hard into the seat back as if he were struggling against invisible bonds. "Ah, Christ," he bit out, his teeth grinding. "I'm going to come so hard."

The dark promise excited me. Sweat misted my skin. I became so wet and hot that I slid smoothly down the length of his cock until I'd nearly sheathed him. A breathless cry escaped me before I'd taken him to the root. He was so deep I could hardly stand it, forcing me to shift from side to side, trying to ease the unexpected bite of discomfort. But my body didn't seem to care that he was too big. It was rippling around him, squeezing, trembling on the verge of orgasm.

Gideon cursed and gripped my hip with his free hand, urging me to lean backward as his chest heaved with frantic breaths. The position altered my descent and I opened, accepting all of him. Immediately his body temperature rose, his torso radiating sultry heat through his clothes. Sweat dotted his upper lip.

Leaning forward, I slid my tongue along the sculpted curve, collecting the saltiness with a low murmur of delight. His hips churned impatiently. I lifted carefully, sliding up a few inches before he stopped me with that ferocious grasp on my hip.

"Slow," he warned again, with an authoritative bite that sent lust pulsing through me.

I lowered, taking him into me again, feeling an oddly luscious soreness as he pushed *just* past my limits. Our eyes locked on each other as the pleasure spread from the place where we connected. It struck me then that we were both fully clothed except for the most private and intimate parts of our bodies. I found that excruciatingly carnal, as were the sounds he made, as if the pleasure were as extreme for him as it was for me.

Wild for him, I pressed my mouth to his, my fingers gripping the sweat-damp roots of his hair. I kissed him as I rocked my hips, riding the maddening circling of his thumb, feeling the orgasm building with every slide of his long, thick penis into my melting core.

I lost my mind somewhere along the way, primitive instinct taking over until my body was completely in charge. I could focus on nothing but the driving urge to fuck, the ferocious need to ride his cock until the tension burst and set me free of this grinding hunger.

"It's so good," I sobbed, lost to him. "You feel . . . Ah, God, it's too good."

Using both hands, Gideon commanded my rhythm, tilting me into an angle that had the big crown of his cock rubbing a tender, aching spot inside me. As I tightened and shook, I realized I was going to come from that, just from the expert thrust of him inside me. *"Gideon."*

He captured me by the nape as the orgasm exploded through me, starting with the ecstatic spasms of my core and radiating outward until I was trembling all over. He watched me fall apart, holding my gaze when I would've closed my eyes. Possessed by his stare, I moaned and came harder than I ever had, my body jerking with every pulse of pleasure.

"Fuck, fuck, fuck," he growled, pounding his hips up at me, yanking my hips down to meet his punishing lunges. He hit the end of me with every deep thrust, battering into me. I could feel him growing harder and thicker.

I watched him avidly, needing to see it when he went over the edge for me. His eyes were wild with his need, losing their focus as his control frayed, his gorgeous face ravaged by the brutal race to climax.

"Eva!" He came with an animal sound of feral ecstasy, a snarling release that riveted me with its ferocity. He shook as the orgasm tore into him, his features softening for an instant with an unexpected vulnerability.

Cupping his face, I brushed my lips across his, comforting him as the forceful bursts of his gasping breaths struck my cheeks.

"Eva." He wrapped his arms around me and crushed me to him, pressing his damp face into the curve of my neck.

I knew just how he felt. Stripped. Laid bare.

We stayed like that for a long time, holding each other, absorbing the aftershocks. He turned his head and kissed me softly, the strokes of his tongue into my mouth soothing my ragged emotions.

"Wow," I breathed, shaken.

His mouth twitched. "Yeah."

I smiled, feeling dazed and high.

Gideon brushed the damp tendrils of hair off my temples, his fingertips gliding almost reverently across my face. The way he studied me made my chest hurt. He looked stunned and . . . grateful, his eyes warm and tender. "I don't want to break this moment."

Because I could hear it hanging in the air, I filled it in. "But . . . ?"

"But I can't blow off this dinner. I have a speech to give."

"Oh." The moment was effectively broken.

I lifted gingerly off him, biting my lip at the feel of him slipping wetly out of me. The friction was enough to make me want more. He'd barely softened.

"Damn it," he said roughly. "I want you again."

He caught me before I moved away, pulling a handkerchief out from somewhere and running it gently between my legs. It was a deeply intimate act, on par with the sex we'd just had.

When I was dry, I settled on the seat beside him and dug my lip gloss out of my clutch. I watched Gideon over the edge of my mirrored compact as he removed the condom and tied it off. He wrapped it in a cocktail napkin, then tossed it in a cleverly hidden trash receptacle. After restoring his appearance, he told the driver to head to our destination. Then he settled into the seat and stared out the window.

With every second that passed, I felt him withdrawing, the connection between us slipping further and further away. I found myself shrinking into the corner of the seat, away from him, mimicking the distance I felt building between us. All the warmth I'd felt receded into a marked chill, cooling me enough that I pulled my wrap around me again. He didn't move a muscle as I shifted beside him and put my compact away, as if he weren't even aware I was there.

Abruptly, Gideon opened the bar and pulled out a bottle. Without looking at me, he asked, "Brandy?"

"No, thank you." My voice was small, but he didn't seem to notice. Or maybe he didn't care. He poured a drink and tossed it back.

Confused and stung, I pulled on my gloves and tried to figure out what had gone wrong.

7

I DON'T REMEMBER MUCH of what happened after we arrived. Camera flashes burst around us like fireworks as we walked the length of the press gauntlet, but I scarcely paid them any mind, smiling by rote. I was drawn into myself and desperate to get away from the tension radiating in waves from Gideon.

The moment we crossed over into the building, someone called his name and he turned. I slipped away, darting around the rest of the guests clogging the carpeted entrance.

When I reached the reception hall, I snatched two glasses of champagne from a passing server and searched for Cary as I tossed one back. I spotted him on the far side of the room with my mom and Stanton, and I crossed to them, discarding my empty glass on a table as I passed it.

"Eva!" My mother's face lit up when she saw me. "That dress is stunning on you!"

She air-kissed each of my cheeks. She was gorgeous in a shimmering, fitted column of icy blue. Sapphires dripped from her ears, throat, and wrist, highlighting her eyes and her pale skin.

"Thank you." I took a gulp of champagne from my second glass, remembering that I'd planned on expressing gratitude for the dress. While I still appreciated the gift, I was no longer so happy about the convenient thigh slit.

Cary stepped forward, catching my elbow. One look at my face and he knew I was upset. I shook my head, not wanting to get into it now.

"More champagne, then?" he asked softly.

"Please."

I felt Gideon approaching before I saw my mother's face light up like the New Year's ball in Times Square. Stanton, too, seemed to straighten and gather himself.

"Eva." Gideon set his hand on the bare skin of my lower back and a shock of awareness moved through me. When his fingers flexed against me, I wondered if he felt it, too. "You ran off."

I stiffened against the reproof I heard in his tone. I shot him a look that said everything I couldn't while we were in public. "Richard, have you met Gideon Cross?"

"Yes, of course." The two men shook hands.

Gideon pulled me closer to his side. "We share the good fortune of escorting the two most beautiful women in New York."

Stanton agreed, smiling indulgently down at my mother.

I tossed back the rest of my champagne and gratefully exchanged the empty glass for the fresh one Cary handed me. There was a slight warmth growing in my belly from the alcohol, and it loosened the knot that had formed there.

Gideon leaned over and whispered harshly, "Don't forget you're here with me."

He was *mad*? What the hell? My gaze narrowed. "You're one to talk."

"Not here, Eva." He nodded at everyone and led me away. "Not now."

"Not ever," I muttered, going along with him just to spare my mother a scene.

Sipping my champagne, I slid into an autopilot mode of self-preservation I hadn't had to use in many years. Gideon introduced me to people, and I supposed I performed well enough—spoke at the appropriate moments and smiled when necessary—but I wasn't really paying attention. I was too conscious of the icy wall between us and my own hurt anger. If I'd needed any proof that Gideon was rigid about not socializing with women he slept with, I had it.

When dinner was announced, I went with him into the dining room and poked at my food. I drank a few glasses of the red wine they served with the meal and heard Gideon talking to our tablemates, although I didn't pay attention to the words, only to the cadence and the seductively deep, even tone. He made no attempt to draw me into the conversation, and I was glad. I didn't think I could say anything nice.

I didn't become engaged until he stood to a round of applause and took the stage. Then I turned in my seat and watched him cross to the lectern, unable to help admiring his animal grace and stunning good looks. Every step he took commanded attention and respect, which was a feat, considering his easy and unhurried stride.

He looked none the worse for wear after our abandoned fucking in his limo. In fact, he seemed like a totally different person. He was once again the man I'd met in the Crossfire lobby, supremely contained and quietly powerful.

"In North America," he began, "childhood sexual abuse is experienced by one in every four women and one in every six men. Take a good look around you. Someone at your table either is a survivor or knows someone who is. That's the unacceptable truth."

I was riveted. Gideon was a consummate orator, his vibrant baritone mesmerizing. But it was the topic, which hit so close to home, and his passionate and sometimes shocking way of discussing it, that moved me. I began to thaw, my bewildered fury and damaged self-confidence subverted by wonder. My view of him shifted, altering as I became simply another individual in a rapt audience. He wasn't the man who'd so recently hurt my feelings; he was just a skilled speaker discussing a subject that was deeply important to me.

When he finished, I stood and applauded, catching both him and myself by surprise. But others quickly joined me in the standing ovation and I heard the buzz of conversations around me, the quietly voiced compliments that were well deserved.

"You're a fortunate young lady."

I turned to look at the woman who spoke, a lovely redhead who appeared to be in her early forties. "We're just . . . friends."

Her serene smile somehow managed to argue with me.

People began stepping away from their tables. I was about to grab my clutch so I could leave for home when a young man came up to me. His wayward auburn hair inspired instant envy, and his eyes of grayish-green were soft and friendly. Handsome and sporting a boyish grin, he lured the first genuine smile out of me since the ride over in the limousine.

"Hello there," he said.

He seemed to know who I was, which put me in the awkward position of pretending I wasn't clueless as to who he was. "Hello."

He laughed, and the sound was light and charming. "I'm Christopher Vidal, Gideon's brother."

"Oh, of course." My face heated. I couldn't believe I'd been so lost in my own pity party that I hadn't made the connection at once.

"You're blushing."

"I'm sorry." I offered a sheepish smile. "Not sure how to say I read an article about you without sounding awkward."

He laughed. "I'm flattered you remembered it. Just don't tell me it was in Page Six."

The gossip column was notorious for getting the goods on New

York celebrities and socialites. "No," I said quickly. "*Rolling Stone*, maybe?"

"I can live with that." He extended his arm to me. "Would you like to dance?"

I glanced over to where Gideon was standing at the foot of the stairs that led to the stage. He was surrounded by people eager to talk to him, many of whom were women.

"You can see he'll be a while," Christopher said, with a note of amusement.

"Yes." I was about to look away when I recognized the woman standing next to Gideon—Magdalene Perez.

I picked up my clutch and managed a smile for Christopher. "I'd love to dance."

Arm in arm we headed into the ballroom and stepped onto the dance floor. The band began the first strains of a waltz and we moved easily, naturally into the music. He was a skilled dancer, agile and confident in his lead.

"So, how do you know Gideon?"

"I don't." I nodded at Cary when he glided by with a statuesque blonde. "I work in the Crossfire and we've run into each other once or twice."

"You work for him?"

"No. I'm an assistant at Waters Field and Leaman."

"Ah." He grinned. "Ad agency."

"Yes."

"Gideon must really be into you to go from meeting you once or twice to dragging you out on a date like this."

I cursed inwardly. I'd known assumptions would be made, but I wanted more than ever to avoid further humiliation. "Gideon's acquainted with my mother and she'd already arranged for me to come, so it's just a matter of two people going to the same event in one car rather than two."

"So you're available?"

I took a deep breath, feeling uncomfortable despite how fluidly we moved together. "Well, I'm not taken."

Christopher flashed his charismatic boyish grin. "My night just took a turn for the better."

He filled the rest of the dance with amusing anecdotes about the music industry that made me laugh and took my mind off Gideon.

When the dance ended, Cary was there to take the next one. We danced very well as a couple because we'd taken lessons together. I relaxed into his hold, grateful to have him as moral support.

"Are you enjoying yourself?" I asked him.

"I pinched myself during dinner when I realized I was sitting next to the top coordinator for Fashion Week. And she flirted with me!" He smiled, but his eyes were haunted. "Whenever I find myself in places like this . . . dressed like this . . . I can't believe it. You saved my life, Eva. Then you changed it completely."

"You save my sanity all the time. Trust me, we're even."

His hand tightened on mine, his gaze hardening. "You look miserable. How'd he fuck up?"

"I think I did that. We'll talk about it later."

"You're afraid I'll kick his ass here in front of everyone."

I sighed. "I'd rather you didn't, for my mom's sake."

Cary pressed his lips briefly to my forehead. "I warned him earlier. He knows it's coming."

"Oh, Cary." Love for him tightened my throat even as reluctant amusement curved my lips. I should've known Cary would give Gideon a big-brother threat of some sort. That was just so like him.

Gideon appeared beside us. "I'm cutting in."

It wasn't a request.

Cary stopped and looked at me. I nodded. He backed away with a bow, his gaze hot and fierce on Gideon's face.

Gideon pulled me close and took over the dance the way he took

over everything—with dominant confidence. It was an entirely different experience dancing with him than with my two previous partners.
Gideon had both the expertise of his brother and Cary's familiarity
with the way my body moved, but Gideon had a bold, aggressive style
that was inherently sexual.

It didn't help that being so close to a man I'd so recently been intimate with seduced my senses despite my unhappiness. He smelled
scrumptious, with undertones of sex, and the way he led me through
the bold, sweeping steps made me feel the soreness deep inside me,
reminding me that he'd been there not long ago.

"You keep taking off," he muttered, scowling down at me.

"Seemed like Magdalene picked up the slack quickly enough."

His brow arched and he drew me closer. "Jealous?"

"Seriously?" I looked away.

He made a frustrated noise. "Stay away from my brother, Eva."

"Why?"

"Because I said so."

My temper ignited, which felt good after all the self-recrimination
and doubts I'd been drowning in since we'd screwed like feral bunnies.
I decided to see if turnabout was fair play in Gideon Cross's world.
"Stay away from Magdalene, Gideon."

His jaw tightened. "She's just a friend."

"Meaning you haven't slept with her . . . ? Yet."

"No, damn it. And I don't want to. Listen—" The music wound
down and he slowed. "I have to go. I brought you here, and I would prefer to be the one who takes you home, but I don't want to pull you away
if you're enjoying yourself. Would you rather stick around and go home
with Stanton and your mother?"

Enjoying myself? Was he kidding or clueless? Or worse. Maybe
he'd written me off so completely that he wasn't paying attention to
me at all.

I pushed away from him, needing the distance. His scent was messing with my head. "I'll be fine. Forget about me."

"Eva." He reached for me and I stepped back quickly.

An arm came around my back and Cary spoke. "I've got her, Cross."

"Don't get in my way, Taylor," Gideon warned.

Cary snorted. "I get the impression you're doing a smokin' job of that all by yourself."

I swallowed past the lump in my throat. "You gave a wonderful speech, Gideon. It was the highlight of my evening."

He sucked in a sharp breath at the implied insult, then shoved a hand through his hair. Abruptly, he cursed and I realized why when he pulled his vibrating phone out of his pocket and glanced at the screen.

"I have to go." His gaze caught mine and held it. His fingertips drifted over my cheek. "I'll call you."

And then he was gone.

"Do you want to stay?" Cary asked quietly.

"No."

"I'll take you home, then."

"No, don't." I wanted to be alone for a bit. Soak in a hot bath with a bottle of cool wine and pull myself out of my funk. "You should be here. It could be good for your career. We can talk when you get home. Or tomorrow. I'm going the couch potato route all day."

His gaze darted over my face, searching. "You sure?"

I nodded.

"All right." But he looked unconvinced.

"If you could go out and ask a valet to have Stanton's limo brought around, I'll run to the ladies' room real quick."

"Okay." Cary ran his hand down my arm. "I'll get your wrap from the coatroom and see you out front."

It took longer to get to the restroom than it should have. For one, a surprising number of people stopped me for small talk, which had to be because I was Gideon Cross's date. And two, I avoided the nearest ladies' room, which had a steady flow of women pouring in and out of it, and I found one located farther away. I locked myself in a stall and took a few moments longer to finish my business than absolutely required. There was no one else in the room besides the attendant, so there was no one to rush me.

I was so hurt by Gideon it was hard to breathe, and I was so confused by his mood swings. Why had he touched my face like that? Why had he gotten mad when I didn't stay by his side? And why the hell had he threatened Cary? Gideon gave new meaning to the old adage about "running hot and cold."

Closing my eyes, I shored up my composure. *Jesus.* I didn't need this.

I'd bared my emotions in the limo and I still felt horribly vulnerable—a state I'd spent countless therapy hours learning to avoid. I wanted nothing more than to be home and hidden, freed from the pressure of acting like I was completely pulled together when I was anything but.

You set yourself up for this, I reminded myself. *Suck it up.*

Taking a deep breath, I stepped out and was resigned to finding Magdalene Perez leaning against the vanity with her arms crossed. She was clearly there for me, lying in wait at a time when my defenses were already weak. My step faltered; then I recovered and made my way to the sink to wash my hands.

She turned to face the mirror, studying my reflection. I studied her, too. She was even more gorgeous in person than she'd been in her photos. Tall and slender, with big dark eyes and a cascade of straight brown hair. Her lips were lush and red, her cheekbones high and sculpted. Her dress was modestly sexy, a flowing sheath of creamy satin that contrasted beautifully with her olive skin. She looked like a fucking supermodel and exuded an exotic sex appeal.

I accepted the hand towel the bathroom attendant handed me, and Magdalene spoke to the woman in Spanish, asking her to give us some privacy. I capped the request with, *"Por favor, gracias."* That earned me an arched brow from Magdalene and a closer examination, which I returned with equal coolness.

"Oh, dear," she murmured, the moment the attendant stepped out of earshot. She made a *tsk*ing noise that scraped over my nerves like nails on a chalkboard. "You've fucked him already."

"And you haven't."

That seemed to surprise her. "You're right, I haven't. You know why?"

I pulled a five-spot out of my clutch and dropped it in the silver tip tray. "Because he doesn't want to."

"And I don't want to either, because he can't commit. He's young, gorgeous, rich, and he's enjoying it."

"Yes." I nodded. "He certainly did."

Her gaze narrowed, her pleasant expression slipping slightly. "He doesn't respect the women he fucks. The minute he shoved his dick in you, you were done. Just like all the others. But I'm still here, because I'm the one he wants to keep around for the long haul."

I maintained my cool even though the blow had been a perfect hit right where the most damage could be done. "That's pathetic."

I walked out and didn't stop until I reached Stanton's limousine. Squeezing Cary's hand as I got in, I managed to wait until the car pulled away from the curb to start crying.

"Hey, baby girl," Cary called out when I shuffled into the living room the next morning. Dressed in nothing but a loose pair of old sweats, he was stretched out on the couch with his feet crossed and propped on the coffee table. He looked beautifully disheveled and comfortable in his own skin. "How'd you sleep?"

I gave him the thumbs-up and headed into the kitchen for coffee. I paused by the breakfast bar, my brows lifting at the massive arrangement of red roses on the counter. The fragrance was divine and I inhaled it with a deep breath. "What's this?"

"They came for you about an hour ago. A Sunday delivery. Pretty and super pricey."

I plucked the card off the clear plastic stake and opened it.

I'M STILL THINKING ABOUT YOU.
GIDEON

"From Cross?" Cary asked.

"Yes." My thumb brushed over what I assumed was his handwriting. It was bold and masculine and sexy. A romantic gesture for a guy who didn't have romance in his repertoire. I dropped the card on the counter as if it'd burned me and fetched a mug of coffee, praying caffeine would give me strength and restore my common sense.

"You don't seem impressed." He lowered the volume on the baseball game he was watching.

"He's bad news for me. He's like one giant trigger. I just need to stay away from him." Cary had been through therapy with me, and he knew the drill. He didn't look at me funny when I broke things down into therapeutic jargon, and he didn't have any trouble shooting it back to me the same way.

"The phone's been ringing all morning, too. I didn't want it to disturb you, so I shut the volume off."

Aware of the lingering ache between my legs, I curled up on the couch and fought the compulsion to listen to our voice mail to see if Gideon had called. I wanted to hear his voice, and an explanation that would make sense of what happened last night. "Sounds good to me. Let's leave it off all day."

"What happened?"

I blew steam off the top of my mug and took a tentative sip. "I fucked his brains out in his limo and he turned arctic afterward."

Cary watched me with those worldly emerald eyes, eyes that had seen more than anyone should be subjected to. "Rocked his world, did you?"

"Yeah, I did." And I got riled up just thinking about it. We'd connected. I *knew* it. I'd wanted him more than anything last night, and today I wanted nothing to do with him ever again. "It was intense. The best sexual experience of my life, and he was right there with me. I know he was. First time he'd ever made it in a car, and he was kind of resistant at first, but then I got him so hot for it he couldn't say no."

"Really? Never?" He ran a hand over his morning stubble. "Most guys scratch car banging off their fuck list in high school. In fact, I can't think of anyone who didn't, except for the nerds and fuglies, and he's neither."

I shrugged. "I guess car banging makes me a slut."

Cary grew very still. "Is that what he said?"

"No. He didn't say shit. I got that from his 'friend,' Magdalene. You know, that chick in most of the photos you printed off the Internet? She decided to sharpen her claws with a little catty girl chat in the bathroom."

"The bitch is jealous."

"Sexual frustration. She can't fuck him, because apparently girls who fuck him go into the discard pile."

"Did he say that?" Again, fury laced his quiet question.

"Not in so many words. He said he doesn't sleep with his female friends. He's got issues with women wanting more than a good time in the sack, so he keeps the women he bangs and the women he hangs out with in two separate camps." I took another sip of my coffee. "I warned him that sort of setup wasn't going to work for me and he said he'd make some adjustments, but I guess he's one of those guys who'll say whatever's necessary to get what he wants."

"Or else you have him running scared."

I glared. "Don't make excuses for him. Whose side are you on, anyway?"

"Yours, baby girl." He reached out and patted my knee. "Always yours."

I wrapped my hand around his muscular forearm and stroked my fingers gently along the underside in silent gratitude. I couldn't feel the multitude of fine white scars from cutting that marred his skin, but I never forgot they were there. I was thankful every day that he was alive, healthy, and a vital part of my life. "How'd your night go?"

"I can't complain." His eyes took on a mischievous glint. "I shagged that busty blonde in a maintenance closet. Her tits were real."

"Well, then." I smiled. "You made her night, I'm sure."

"I try." He picked up the phone receiver and winked at me. "What kind of delivery do you want? Subs? Chinese? Indian?"

"I'm not hungry."

"You're always hungry. If you don't pick something, I'll cook and you'll have to eat that."

I lifted my hand in surrender. "Okay, okay. You pick."

I got to work twenty minutes early on Monday, figuring I'd skip running into Gideon. When I reached my desk without incident, I felt such relief that I knew I was in serious trouble where he was concerned. My moods were shifting all over the place.

Mark arrived in high spirits, still floating from his major successes of the week before, and we dug right into work. I'd done some vodka market comparisons on Sunday and he was kind enough to go over those with me and listen to my impressions. Mark was also assigned the account for a new e-reader manufacturer, so we began the initial work on that.

With such a busy morning, time flew swiftly and I didn't have time to think about my personal life. I was really grateful for that. Then I answered the phone and heard Gideon on the line. I wasn't prepared.

"How's your Monday been so far?" he asked, his voice sending a shiver of awareness through me.

"Hectic." I glanced at the clock and was startled to see it was twenty minutes to noon.

"Good." There was a pause. "I tried calling you yesterday. I left a couple messages. I wanted to hear your voice."

My eyes closed on a deep breath. It had taken every bit of my willpower to make it through the day without listening to the voice mail. I'd even enlisted Cary in the cause, telling him to restrain me forcibly if it looked like I might succumb to the urge. "I did the hermit thing and worked a little."

"Did you get the flowers I sent?"

"Yes. They're lovely. Thank you."

"They reminded me of your dress."

What the hell was he doing? I was beginning to think he had multiple personality disorder. "Some women might say that's romantic."

"I only care what you say." His chair creaked as if he'd pushed to his feet. "I thought about stopping by. . . . I wanted to."

I sighed, surrendering to my confusion. "I'm glad you didn't."

There was another long pause. "I deserved that."

"I didn't say it to be a bitch. It's just the truth."

"I know. Listen . . . I arranged for lunch up here in my office so we don't waste any of the hour leaving and getting back."

After his parting *I'll call you*, I'd wondered if he would want to get together again after he settled down from whatever trip he'd been on. It was a possibility I'd been dreading since Saturday night, aware that

I needed to cut him off, but feeling strung out from the desire to be with him. I wanted to experience again that pure, perfect moment of intimacy we'd shared.

But I couldn't justify that one moment against all the other moments when he made me feel like crap.

"Gideon, we don't have any reason to have lunch together. We hashed things out Friday night, and we . . . took care of business Saturday. Let's just leave it at that."

"Eva." His voice turned gruff. "I know I fucked up. Let me explain."

"You don't have to. It's okay."

"It's not. I need to see you."

"I don't want—"

"We can do this the easy way, Eva. Or you can make it difficult." His tone took on a hard edge that made my pulse quicken. "Either way, you'll hear me out."

I closed my eyes, understanding that I wasn't lucky enough to get away with a quick good-bye phone chat. "Fine. I'll come up."

"Thank you." He exhaled audibly. "I can't wait to see you."

I returned the receiver to its cradle and stared at the photos on my desk, trying to formulate what I needed to say and steeling myself for the impact of seeing Gideon again. The ferocity of my physical response to him was impossible to control. Somehow I'd have to get past it and take care of business. Later, I'd think about having to see him in the building over the days, weeks, and months ahead. For the moment, I just had to focus on making it through lunch.

Yielding to the inevitable, I got back to work comparing the visual impact of some blow-in card samples.

"Eva."

I jumped and spun around in my chair, startled to find Gideon standing beside my cubicle. The sight of him blew me away, as usual, and my heart stuttered in my chest. A quick glance at the clock proved that a quarter hour had passed in no time at all.

"Gid—Mr. Cross. You didn't have to come down here."

His face was calm and impassive, but his eyes were stormy and hot. "Ready?"

I opened my drawer and pulled out my purse, taking the opportunity to suck in a deep, shaky breath. He smelled phenomenal.

"Mr. Cross." Mark's voice. "It's great to see you. Is there something—?"

"I'm here for Eva. We have a lunch date."

I straightened in time to see Mark's brows shoot up. He recovered quickly, his face smoothing into its usual good-natured handsomeness.

"I'll be back at one," I assured him.

"See you then. Enjoy your lunch."

Gideon put his hand at the small of my back and steered me out to the elevators, garnering raised brows from Megumi when we passed reception. I shifted restlessly as he hit the call button for the elevator, wishing I could've made it through the day without seeing the man whose touch I craved like a drug.

He faced me as we waited for the car, running his fingertips down the sleeve of my satin blouse. "Every time I close my eyes, I see you in that red dress. I hear the sounds you make when you're turned on. I feel you sliding over my cock, squeezing me like a fist, making me come so hard it hurts."

"Don't." I looked away, unable to bear the intimate way he was looking at me.

"I can't help it."

The arrival of the elevator was a relief. He caught my hand and pulled me inside. After he put his key in the panel, he tugged me closer. "I'm going to kiss you, Eva."

"I don't—"

He pulled me into him and sealed his mouth over mine. I resisted as long as I could; then I melted at the feel of his tongue stroking slow and sweet over mine. I'd wanted his kiss since we'd had sex. I wanted the reassurance that he valued what we'd shared, that it meant something to him as it had to me.

I was left bereft once again when he pulled away.

"Come on." He pulled the key out as the door opened.

Gideon's redheaded receptionist said nothing this time, although she eyed me strangely. In contrast, Gideon's secretary, Scott, stood when we approached and greeted me pleasantly by name.

"Good afternoon, Miss Tramell."

"Hi, Scott."

Gideon gave him a curt nod. "Hold my calls."

"Yes, of course."

I entered Gideon's expansive office, my gaze drifting to the sofa where he'd first touched me intimately.

Lunch was arranged on the bar—two plates covered in metal salvers.

"Can I take your purse?" he asked.

I looked at him, saw he'd taken off his jacket and slung it over his arm. He stood there in his tailored slacks and vest, his shirt and tie both a pristine white, his hair dark and thick around his breathtaking face, his eyes a wild and dazzling blue. In a word, he amazed me. I couldn't believe I'd made love to such a gorgeous man.

But then, it hadn't meant the same thing to him.

"Eva?"

"You're beautiful, Gideon." The words fell out of my mouth without conscious thought.

His brows lifted; then a softness came into his eyes. "I'm glad you like what you see."

I handed him my purse and moved away, needing the space. He hung his coat and my purse on the coatrack, then moved to the bar.

I crossed my arms. "Let's just get this over with. I don't want to see you anymore."

8

G IDEON SHOVED A hand through his hair and exhaled harshly. "You don't mean that."

I was suddenly very tired, exhausted from fighting with myself over him. "I really do. You and me . . . it was a mistake."

His jaw tightened. "It wasn't. The way I handled it afterward was the mistake."

I stared at him, startled by the fierceness of his denial. "I wasn't talking about the sex, Gideon. I'm talking about my agreeing to this crazy strangers-with-benefits deal between us. I knew it was all wrong from the beginning. I should've listened to my instincts."

"Do you want to be with me, Eva?"

"No. That's what—"

"Not like we discussed at the bar. More than that."

My heart started to pound. "What are you talking about?"

"Everything." He left the bar and came closer. "I want to be with you."

"You didn't seem like you did Saturday." My arms tightened around my middle.

"I was . . . reeling."

"So? I was, too."

His hands went to his hips. Then his arms crossed like mine. "Christ, Eva."

I watched him squirm and felt a flare of hope. "If that's all you've got, we're done."

"The hell we are."

"We've already hit a dead end if you're going to take a head trip every time we have sex."

He visibly struggled with what to say. "I'm used to having control. I *need* it. And you blew it all to hell in the limousine. I didn't handle that well."

"Ya think?"

"Eva." He approached. "I've never experienced anything like that. I didn't think it was possible for me to. Now that I have . . . I've got to have it. I've got to have *you*."

"It's just sex, Gideon. Super awesome sex, but that can seriously screw with your head when the two people doing it aren't good for each other."

"Bullshit. I've admitted I fucked up. I can't change what happened, but I can sure as shit get pissed that you want to cut me off because of it. You laid out your rules and I adjusted to accommodate them, but you won't make even a tiny adjustment for me. You have to meet me halfway." His face was hard with frustration. "At least give me a damn inch."

I stared at him, trying to figure out what he was doing and where this was going. "What do you want, Gideon?" I asked softly.

He caught me to him and cupped my cheek in one hand. "I want to keep feeling the way I feel when I'm with you. Just tell me what I have to do. And give me some room to screw up. I've never done this before. There's a learning curve."

I placed my palm over his heart and felt its pounding rhythm. He was anxious and passionate, and that had me on edge. How was I supposed to respond? Did I go with my gut or my common sense?

"Done what before?"

"Whatever it takes to spend as much time with you as possible. In and out of bed."

The rush of delight that swept through me was ridiculously powerful. "Do you understand how much work and time a relationship between us is going to take, Gideon? I'm wiped out already. Plus I'm still working on some personal stuff, and I have my new job . . . my crazy mother . . ." My fingers covered his mouth before he could open it. "But you're worth it, and I want you bad enough. So I guess I don't have a choice, do I?"

"Eva. Damn you." Gideon lifted me, hitching one arm beneath my rear to urge me to wrap my legs around his waist. He kissed me hard on the mouth and nuzzled his nose against mine. "We'll figure it out."

"You say that as if it'll be easy." I knew I was high-maintenance, and he was obviously going to be the same.

"Easy's boring." He carried me over to the bar and set me down on a bar stool. He pulled the dome off my place setting and revealed a massive cheeseburger and fries. The meal was still warm, thanks to a heated granite slab beneath the plate.

"Yum," I murmured, becoming aware of how hungry I was. Now that we'd talked, my appetite had returned full force.

He snapped open my napkin and laid it over my lap with a squeeze to my knee; then he took the seat beside me. "So, how do we do this?"

"Well, you pick it up with your hands and put it in your mouth."

He shot me a wry look that made me smile. It felt good to smile. It felt good to be with him. It usually did . . . for a little while. I took a bite of my burger, moaning when I got a full hit of its flavor. It was a traditional cheeseburger, but the taste was divine.

"Good, right?" he asked.

"Very good. In fact, a guy who knows about burgers this good might be worth keeping to myself." I wiped my mouth and hands. "How resistant are you to exclusivity?"

As he set his burger down, there was an eerie stillness to him. I couldn't begin to guess what he was thinking. "I assumed that was implied in our arrangement. But to avoid any doubts, I'll be clear and say there won't be any other men for you, Eva."

A shiver moved through me at the blunt finality in his tone and the iciness of his gaze. I knew he had a dark side; I'd learned long ago how to spot and avoid men who had dangerous shadows in their eyes. But the familiar alarm bells didn't ring around Gideon as they maybe should have. "But women are okay?" I asked, to lighten the mood.

His brows rose. "I know your roommate is bisexual. Are you?"

"Would that bother you?"

"Sharing you would bother me. It's not an option. Your body belongs to me, Eva."

"And yours belongs to me? Exclusively?"

His gaze turned hot. "Yes, and I expect you to take frequent and excessive advantage of it."

Well, then . . . "But you've seen me naked," I teased, my voice husky. "You know what you're getting. I don't. I love what I've seen of your body so far, but that hasn't been a whole lot."

"We can rectify that now."

The thought of him stripping for me made me squirm in my seat. He noticed and his mouth curved wickedly.

"You'd better not," I said regretfully. "I was late getting back on Friday."

"Tonight, then."

I swallowed hard. "Absolutely."

"I'll be sure to clear my schedule by five." He resumed eating, completely at ease with the fact that we'd both just penciled *mind-blowing sex* into our mental day calendars.

"You don't have to." I opened the mini ketchup bottle by my plate. "I need to hit the gym after work."

"We'll go together."

"Really?" I turned the bottle upside down and thumped the bottom with my palm.

He took it from me and used his knife to coax the ketchup onto my plate. "It's probably best for me to work off some energy before I get you naked. I'm sure you'd like to be able to walk tomorrow."

I stared at him, astonished by the casualness with which he'd made the statement and the rueful amusement on his face that told me he wasn't entirely kidding. My sex clenched in delicious anticipation. I could easily picture becoming seriously addicted to Gideon Cross.

I ate some fries, thinking of someone else who was addicted to Gideon. "Magdalene could be a problem for me."

He swallowed a bite of his burger and washed it down with a swig from his bottled water. "She told me she'd talked to you, and that it didn't go well."

I gave props to Magdalene's scheming and the clever attempt to cut me off at the pass. I'd have to be very careful with her, and Gideon was going to have to do something about her—like cut her off, period.

"No, it didn't go well," I agreed. "But then I don't appreciate being told that you don't respect the women you fuck and that the moment you shoved your dick into me you were done with me."

Gideon stilled. "She said that?"

"Word for word. She also said you're keeping her on ice until you're ready to settle down."

"Did she now?" His low voice had a chilling bite to it.

My stomach knotted, knowing things could go either really right or really wrong, depending on what Gideon said next. "Don't you believe me?"

"Of course I believe you."

"She could be a problem for me," I repeated, not letting it go.

"She won't be a problem. I'll talk to her."

I hated the thought of him talking to her, because it made me sick with jealousy. I figured that was an issue I should disclose up front. "Gideon . . ."

"Yes?" He'd finished his burger and was working on the fries.

"I'm a very jealous person. I can be irrational with it." I poked at my burger with a fry. "You might want to think about that, and whether you want to deal with someone who has self-esteem issues like I do. It was one of my sticking points when you first propositioned me, knowing it was going to drive me nuts having women salivating all over you and not having the right to say anything about it."

"You have the right now."

"You're not taking me seriously." I shook my head and took another bite of my cheeseburger.

"I've never been as serious about anything in my life." Reaching over, Gideon ran a fingertip over the corner of my mouth, then licked off the dab of sauce he'd collected. "You're not the only one who can get possessive. I'm very proprietary about what's mine."

I didn't doubt that for a minute.

I took another bite and thought of the night ahead. I was eager. Ridiculously so. I was dying to see Gideon naked. Dying to run my hands and lips all over him. Dying to have another go at driving him crazy. And I was damn near desperate to be under him, to feel him straining over me, pounding into me, coming hard and deep inside me . . .

"Keep thinking those thoughts," he said roughly, "and you'll be late again."

I looked at him with raised brows. "How did you know what I'm thinking?"

"You get this look on your face when you're turned on. I intend to put that look on your face as often as possible." Gideon covered his plate again and stood, withdrawing a business card from his pocket and setting it down beside me. I could see that he'd written his home and mobile numbers on the back. "I feel stupid asking this question considering our present conversation, but I need your cell phone number."

"Oh." I forcibly dragged my thoughts out of the bedroom. "I have to get one first. It's on my to-do list."

"What happened to the phone you were texting with last week?"

My nose wrinkled. "My mother was using it to track my movements around the city. She's a tad . . . overprotective."

"I see." He brushed the backs of his fingers down my cheek. "That's what you were talking about when you said your mom is stalking you."

"Yes, unfortunately."

"Okay, then. We'll take care of the phone after work before we head to the gym. It's safer for you to have one. And I want to be able to call you whenever I feel like it."

I set down the quarter of my burger that I couldn't eat and wiped my hands and mouth. "That was delicious. Thank you."

"It was my pleasure." He leaned over me and pressed his lips briefly to mine. "Do you need to use the washroom?"

"Yes. I need my toothbrush from my purse, too."

A few minutes later, I found myself standing in a washroom hidden behind a door that blended seamlessly with the mahogany paneling behind the flatscreens. We brushed our teeth side by side at the double-sink vanity, our gazes meeting in our mirrored reflections. It was such a domestic, *normal* thing to do and yet we both seemed to delight in it.

"I'll take you back down," he said, crossing his office to the coatrack.

I followed him but veered off when we reached his desk. I went to it and put my hand on the clear space in front of his chair. "Is this where you are most of the day?"

"Yes." He shrugged into his jacket and I wanted to bite him, he looked so delectable.

Instead, I hopped up to sit directly in front of his chair. According to my watch I had five minutes. Barely enough time to get back to work, but still. I couldn't resist exercising my new rights. I pointed at his chair. "Sit."

His brows rose, but he came over without argument and settled gracefully into the seat.

I spread my legs and crooked my finger. "Closer."

He rolled forward, filling the space between my thighs. He wrapped his arms around my hips and looked up at me. "One day soon, Eva, I'm going to fuck you right here."

"Just a kiss for now," I murmured, bending forward to take his mouth. With my hands on his shoulders for balance, I licked across his parted lips; then I slipped inside and teased him with gentleness.

Groaning, he deepened the kiss, eating at my mouth in a way that made me achy and wet.

"One day soon," I repeated against his lips, "I'm going to kneel beneath this desk and suck you off. Maybe while you're on the phone playing with your millions like Monopoly. You, Mr. Cross, will pass Go and collect your two hundred dollars."

His mouth curved against mine. "I can see how this is going to go. You're going to make me lose my mind coming everywhere I can in your tight, sexy body."

"Are you complaining?"

"Angel, I'm salivating."

I was bemused by the endearment, although I liked its sweetness. "Angel?"

He hummed a soft assent and kissed me.

I couldn't believe what a difference an hour made. I left Gideon's office in a completely different frame of mind than when I'd entered it. The feel of his hand at the small of my back made my body hum with anticipation rather than the misery I'd felt on the way in.

I waved bye to Scott and smiled brightly at the unsmiling receptionist.

"I don't think she likes me," I told Gideon, as we waited for the elevator.

"Who?"

"Your receptionist."

He glanced over that way, and the redhead beamed at him.

"Well," I murmured. "She likes you."

"I guarantee her paychecks."

My mouth curved. "Yes, I'm sure that's what it is. It couldn't possibly have anything to do with you being the sexiest man alive."

"Am I now?" He caged me to the wall and burned me with a searing gaze.

I set my hands against his abdomen, licking my lower lip when I felt the hard ridges of muscle tighten under my touch. "Just an observation."

"*I* like you." With his palms pressed flat to the wall on either side of my head, he lowered his mouth to mine and kissed me softly.

"I like you back. You do realize you're at work, don't you?"

"What good is being the boss if you can't do what you want?"

"Hmm."

When a car arrived, I ducked under Gideon's arm and slid into it. He prowled in after me, then circled me like a predator, sliding up behind me to pull me back against him. His hands pushed into my front pockets and splayed against my hip bones, keeping me tucked close.

The warmth of his touch so close to where I ached for him was a special brand of torture. In retaliation, I wriggled my butt against him and smiled when he hissed out a breath and hardened.

"Behave," he admonished gruffly. "I have a meeting in fifteen minutes."

"Will you think of me while you're sitting at your desk?"

"Undoubtedly. You'll definitely think about me while you're sitting at yours. That's an order, Miss Tramell."

My head fell back against his chest, loving the bite of command in his voice. "I don't see how I couldn't, Mr. Cross, considering how I think of you everywhere else I go."

He stepped out with me when we reached the twentieth floor. "Thank you for lunch."

"I think that's my line." I backed away. "See you later, Dark and Dangerous."

His brows rose at my nickname for him. "Five o'clock. Don't make me wait."

One of the cars in the left bank of elevators arrived. Megumi stepped out and Gideon stepped in, his gaze locked with mine until the doors closed.

"Whew," she said. "You scored. I'm pea green with envy."

I couldn't think of anything to say to that. It was all still too new and I was afraid to jinx it. In the back of my mind, I knew these feelings of happiness couldn't last. Everything was going *too* well.

I rushed to my desk and got to work.

"Eva." I looked up to see Mark standing in the threshold of his office. "Could I talk to you a minute?"

"Of course." I grabbed my tablet, even though his grim face and tone warned me it might not be needed. When Mark shut the door behind me, my apprehension increased. "Is everything all right?"

"Yes." He waited until I was seated, then took the chair beside me rather than the one behind his desk. "I don't know how to say this . . ."

"Just say it. I'll figure it out."

He looked at me with compassionate eyes and a cringe of embarrassment. "It's not my place to interfere. I'm just your boss and there's a line that comes with that, but I'm going to cross it because I like you, Eva, and I want you to work here for a long time."

My stomach tightened. "That's great. I really love my job."

"Good. Good, I'm glad." He shot me a quick smile. "Just . . . be careful with Cross, okay?"

I blinked, startled by the direction of the conversation. "Okay."

"He's brilliant, rich, and sexy, so I understand the appeal. As much as I love Steven, I get a little flustered around Cross myself. He's just got that kind of pull." Mark talked fast and shifted with obvious embarrassment. "And I can totally see why he's interested in you. You're beautiful, smart, honest, considerate . . . I could go on, because you're great."

"Thanks," I said quietly, hoping I didn't look as ill as I felt. This sort of warning from a friend, and knowing that others would think of me as just another babe-of-the-week, was exactly the type of thing that preyed on my insecurities.

"I just don't want to see you get hurt," he muttered, looking as miserable as I felt. "Part of that's selfish, I'll admit. I don't want to lose a great assistant because she doesn't want to work in a building owned by an ex."

"Mark, it means a lot to me that you care and that I'm valuable to you around here. But you don't have to worry about me. I'm a big girl. Besides, nothing is going to get me to quit this job."

He blew out his breath, clearly relieved. "All right. Let's put it away and get to work."

So we did, but I set myself up for future torture by subscribing to a daily Google alert for Gideon's name. And when five o'clock rolled around, my awareness of my many inadequacies was still spreading through my happiness like a stain.

Gideon was as prompt as he'd threatened to be, and he didn't seem to notice my introspective mood as we rode down in a crowded elevator. More than one woman in the car cast furtive glances in his direction, but that sort of thing I didn't mind. He was hot. I would've been surprised if they hadn't looked.

He caught my hand when we cleared the turnstiles, linking his fingers with mine. The simple, intimate gesture meant so much to me in that moment that my grip tightened on his. And I'd really have to watch out for that. The moment I became grateful he was spending time with me would be the beginning of the end. Neither of us would respect me if that happened.

The Bentley SUV sat at the curb and Gideon's driver stood at the ready by the rear door. Gideon looked at me. "I had some workout clothes packed and brought over, in case you were set on visiting your gym. Equinox, right? Or we can go to mine."

"Where's yours?"

"I prefer to go to the CrossTrainer on Thirty-fifth."

My curiosity over how he knew which gym I frequented vanished when I heard the "Cross" in the name of his gym. "You wouldn't happen to *own* the gym, would you?"

His grin flashed. "The chain. Usually, I practice mixed martial arts with a personal trainer, but I use the gym occasionally."

"The chain," I repeated. "Of course."

"Your choice," he said considerately. "I'll go wherever you want."

"By all means, let's go to your gym."

He opened the back door, and I slid in and over. I set my purse and my gym bag on my lap, and looked out the window as the car pulled away from the curb. The sedan driving next to us was so close I wouldn't have to lean far to touch it. Rush hour in Manhattan was something I was still getting used to. SoCal had bumper-to-bumper traffic, too, but it moved at a snail's pace. Here in New York, speed mixed with the crush in a way that often made me close my eyes and pray to survive the trip.

It was a whole new world. A new city, new apartment, new job, and new man. It was a lot to take on at once. I supposed it was understandable that I felt off-balance.

I glanced at Gideon and found him staring at me with an unreadable expression. Everything inside me twisted into a mess of wild lust and vibrating anxiety. I had no idea what I was doing with him, only that I couldn't stop even if I wanted to.

9

WE HIT THE wireless store first. The associate who helped us seemed highly susceptible to Gideon's magnetic pull. She practically fell all over herself the minute he showed the slightest interest in anything, quickly launching into detailed explanations and leaning into his personal space to demonstrate.

I tried separating from them and finding someone who'd actually help *me*, but Gideon's grip on my hand wouldn't let me move more than touching distance away. Then we argued over who was going to pay, which he seemed to think should be him even though the phone and account were mine.

"You got your way with picking the service provider," I pointed out, pushing his credit card aside and shoving mine at the girl.

"Because it's practical. We'll be on the same network, so calls to me are free." He swapped the cards deftly.

"I won't be calling you at all, if you don't put your damn credit card away!"

That did the trick, although I could tell he was unhappy about it. He'd just have to get over it.

Once we got back in the Bentley, his mood seemed restored.

"You can head to the gym now, Angus," he told his driver, settling back in the seat. Then he pulled his smartphone out of his pocket. He saved my new number into his contact list; then he took my new phone out of my hand and programmed my list with his home, office, and mobile numbers.

He'd barely finished when we arrived at CrossTrainer. Not surprisingly, the three-story fitness center was a health enthusiast's dream. I was impressed with every sleek, modern, top-of-the-line inch of it. Even the women's locker room was like something out of a science fiction movie.

But my awe was totally eclipsed by Gideon himself when I finished changing into my workout clothes and found him waiting for me out in the hallway. He'd changed into long shorts and a tank, which gave me my first look at his bare arms and legs.

I came to an abrupt halt and someone coming out behind me bumped into me. I could barely manage an apology; I was too busy visually devouring Gideon's body. His legs were toned and powerful, flawlessly proportional to his trim hips and waist. His arms made my mouth water. His biceps were precisely cut and his forearms were coursing with thick veins that were both brutal looking and sexy as hell. He'd tied his hair back, which showed off the definition of his neck and traps and the sculpted angles of his face.

Christ. I knew this man intimately. My brain couldn't wrap itself around that fact, not while faced with the irrefutable evidence of how uniquely beautiful he was.

And he was scowling at me.

Straightening away from the wall where he'd been leaning, he came toward me, then circled me. His fingertips ran along my bare midriff and back as he made the revolution, sending goose bumps racing over my skin. When he stopped in front of me, I threw my arms around his neck and pulled his mouth down for a quick, playfully smacking kiss.

"What the hell are you wearing?" he asked, looking marginally appeased by my enthusiastic greeting.

"Clothes."

"You look naked in that top."

"I thought you liked me naked." I was secretly pleased with my choice, which I'd made that morning before I'd known he'd be with me. The top was a triangle with long straps at the shoulders and ribs that secured with Velcro and could be worn in a variety of ways to allow the wearer to determine where her breasts needed the most support. It was specially designed for curvy women and was the first top I'd ever had that kept me from bouncing all over the place. What Gideon objected to was the nude color, which coordinated with the racing stripes on the matching black yoga pants.

"I like you naked *in private*," he muttered. "I'll need to be with you whenever you go to the gym."

"I won't complain, since I'm very much enjoying the view at the moment." Plus, I was perversely excited by his possessiveness after the hurt he'd inflicted with his withdrawal Saturday night. Two very different extremes—the first of many, I was sure.

"Let's get this over with." He grabbed my hand and led me away from the locker rooms, snatching two logo'd towels off a stack as we passed them. "I need to fuck you."

"I need to be fucked."

"Jesus, Eva." His grip on my hand tightened to the point that it hurt. "Where to? Free weights? Machines? Treadmills?"

"Treadmills. I want to run a bit."

He led me in that direction. I watched the way women followed him with their gazes, then their feet. They wanted to be in whatever section of the gym he was, and I couldn't blame them. I was dying to see him in action, too.

When we reached the seemingly endless rows of treadmills and bikes, we found that there weren't two treadmills free adjacent to each other.

Gideon walked up to a man who had one open on either side of him. "I'd be in your debt if you'd move over one."

The guy looked at me and grinned. "Yeah, sure."

"Thanks. I appreciate it."

Gideon took over the man's treadmill and motioned me to the one beside it. Before he programmed his workout, I leaned over to him. "Don't burn off too much energy," I whispered. "I want you missionary style the first time. I've been having this fantasy of you on top, banging the hell out of me."

His gaze burned into me. "Eva, you have no idea."

Nearly giddy with anticipation and a lovely surge of feminine power, I got on my treadmill and started at a brisk walk. While I warmed up, I set my iPod shuffle to random, and when "SexyBack" by Justin Timberlake came on, I hit my stride and went full-out. Running was both a mental and physical exercise for me. Sometimes I wished just running fast could get me away from whatever was troubling me.

After twenty minutes I slowed, then stopped, finally risking a glance at Gideon, who was running with the fluidity of a well-oiled machine. He was watching CNN on the overhead screens, but he flashed a grin at me as I wiped the sweat off my face. I swigged from my water bottle as I moved to the machines, picking one that gave me a clear view of him.

He went a full thirty on the treadmill; then he moved to free weights, always keeping me in his line of sight. As he worked out, quickly and efficiently, I couldn't help thinking how virile he was. It helped that I knew exactly what was in his shorts, but regardless, he was a man who worked behind a desk, yet kept his body in combat shape.

When I grabbed a fitness ball to do some crunches, one of the trainers came up to me. As one would expect in a top-of-the-line gym, he was handsome and very nicely built.

"Hi," he greeted me, with a movie star smile that showcased perfect white teeth. He had dark brown hair and eyes of nearly the same color. "First-timer, right? I haven't seen you in here before."

"Yes, first time."

"I'm Daniel." He extended his hand, and I gave him my name. "Are you finding everything you need, Eva?"

"So far so good, thanks."

"What flavor smoothie did you go for?"

I frowned. "Excuse me?"

"Your free orientation smoothie." He crossed his arms and his thick biceps strained the narrow cuffs of his uniform polo shirt. "You didn't get one from the bar downstairs when you signed up? You're supposed to."

"Ah, well." I shrugged sheepishly, thinking it was a nice touch all the same. "I didn't have the usual orientation."

"Did you get the tour? If not, let me take you around." He touched my elbow lightly and gestured toward the stairs. "You also get a free hour of personal training. We could do that tonight or make an appointment for later in the week. And I'd be happy to take you down to the health bar and scratch that off the list, too."

"Oh, I can't really." My nose wrinkled. "I'm not a member."

"Ah." He winked. "You're here on a temp pass? That's fine. You can't be expected to make up your mind if you don't get the full experience. I can assure you, though, that CrossTrainer is the best gym in Manhattan."

Gideon appeared at Daniel's shoulder. "The full experience is included," he said, coming around and behind me to slide his arms around my waist, "when you're the owner's girlfriend."

The word *girlfriend* reverberated through me, sending a crazy rush of adrenaline through my system. It was still sinking in that we had that level of commitment, but that didn't stop me from thinking the designation had a nice ring to it.

"Mr. Cross." Daniel straightened and took a step back, then extended his hand. "It's an honor to meet you."

"Daniel has me sold on the place," I said to Gideon, as they shook hands.

"I thought *I'd* done that." His hair was wet with sweat and he smelled divine. I'd never known a sweaty man could smell so damn good.

His hands stroked down my arms and I felt his lips on the crown of my head. "Let's go. See you later, Daniel."

I waved good-bye as we walked away. "Thanks, Daniel."

"Anytime."

"I bet," Gideon muttered. "He couldn't keep his eyes off your tits."

"They're very nice tits."

He made a low growling noise. I hid my amusement.

He smacked my butt hard enough to send me forward a step and leave behind a hot sting even through my pants. "That damned Band-Aid you call a shirt doesn't leave much to the imagination. Don't take long in the shower. You're just going to get sweaty again."

"Wait." I caught his arm before he passed the women's locker room on the way toward the men's. "Would it gross you out if I told you I didn't want you to shower? If I said I want to find someplace really close by where I could jump you while you're still dripping sweat?"

Gideon's jaw tightened and his gaze darkened dangerously. "I'm beginning to fear for your safety, Eva. Grab your stuff. There's a hotel around the corner."

Neither of us changed and we were outside in five minutes. Gideon walked briskly and I hurried to keep up. When he stopped abruptly, turned, and dipped me back in a lavish heated kiss on the crowded sidewalk, I was too stunned to do more than hold on. It was a soul-wrenching melding of our mouths, full of passion and sweet spontaneity that made my heart ache. Applause broke out around us.

When he straightened me again, I was breathless and dizzy. "What was that?" I gasped.

"A prelude." He resumed our dash to the nearest hotel, one I didn't catch the name of as he pulled me past the doorman and crossed straight to the elevator. It was clear to me that the property was one of Gideon's even before a manager greeted him by name just before the elevator doors closed.

Gideon dropped his duffel on the car floor and busied himself with figuring out how to extricate me from my sports top. I was slapping his hands away when the doors opened and he scooped up his bag. There was no one waiting on our floor and no one in the hallway. He pulled a master key out of somewhere, and a moment later we were in a room.

I pounced, pushing my hands up beneath his shirt to feel his damp skin and the hardness of the muscles beneath it. "Get naked. Like *now*."

He laughed as he toed off his sneakers and yanked his tank over his head.

Oh my God . . . seeing him in the flesh—all of him, as his shorts hit the floor—was synapse frying. There wasn't an ounce of excess flesh on him anywhere, just hard slabs of honed muscle. He had washboard abs and that super sexy V of muscle on his pelvis that Cary called the Loin of Apollo. Gideon didn't wax his chest like Cary did, but he groomed with the same care he showed to the rest of his body. He was pure primal male, the embodiment of everything I coveted, fantasized about, and wished for.

"I've died and gone to heaven," I said, staring unabashedly.

"You're still dressed." He attacked my clothes, whipping my loosened top off before I took a full breath. My pants were wrestled down and I kicked my shoes off in such a hurry that I lost my balance and fell on the bed. I barely caught my breath before he was on me.

We rolled across the mattress in a tangle. Everywhere he touched me left trails of fire behind. The clean, hardworking scent of his skin was an aphrodisiac and intoxicant at once, spurring my desire for him until I felt like I was about to lose my mind.

"You're so beautiful, Eva." He plumped one breast in his hand before taking my nipple into his mouth.

I cried out at the scorching heat and the lash of his tongue, my core tightening with every soft suck. My hands were greedy as they slid over his sweat-damp skin, stroking and kneading, searching for the spots that made him growl and moan. I scissored my legs with his and tried to roll him, but he was too heavy and too strong.

He lifted his head and smiled down at me. "It's my turn this time."

What I felt for him in that moment, seeing that smile and the heat in his eyes, was so intense it was painful. Too fast, I thought. I was falling too fast. "Gideon—"

He kissed me deeply, licking into my mouth in that way of his. I thought he could really make me come with just a kiss, if we stayed at it long enough. Everything about him turned me on, from the way he looked and felt beneath my hands to the way he watched me and touched me. His greed and the silent demands he made on my body, the forcefulness with which he pleasured me and took his pleasure in return, drove me wild.

I ran my hands through the wet silk of his hair. The crisp hairs on his chest teased my tightened nipples, and the feel of his rock-hard body against mine was enough to make me wet and needy.

"I love your body," he whispered, his lips moving across my cheek to my throat. His hand caressed the length of my torso from breast to hip. "I can't get enough of it."

"You haven't had very much of it yet," I teased.

"I don't think I'll ever have enough." Nibbling and licking across my shoulder, he slid down and caught my other nipple between his teeth. He tugged and the tiny dart of pain had my back arching on a soft cry. He soothed the sting with a soft suck, then kissed his way downward. "I've never wanted anything this badly."

"Then do me!"

"Not yet," he murmured, moving lower, rimming my navel with the tip of his tongue. "You're not ready yet."

"What? Ah, God . . . I can't get any readier." I tugged on his hair, trying to pull him up.

Gideon caught my wrists and pinned them to the mattress. "You have a tight little cunt, Eva. I'll bruise you if I don't get you soft and relaxed."

A violent shiver of arousal moved through me. It turned me on when he talked so bluntly about sex. Then he slid lower and I tensed. "No, Gideon. I need to shower for that."

He buried his face in my cleft and I struggled against his hold, flushed with sudden shame. He nipped at my inner thigh with his teeth. "Stop it."

"Don't. Please. You don't have to do that."

His glare stilled my frantic movements. "Do you think I feel differently about your body than you do mine?" he asked harshly. "I want you, Eva."

I licked my dry lips, so crazily turned on by his animal need that I couldn't form a single word. He growled softly and dove for the slick flesh between my legs. His tongue pushed into me, licking and parting the sensitive tissues. My hips churned restlessly, my body silently begging for more. It felt so good I could've wept.

"God, Eva. I've wanted my mouth on your cunt every day since I met you."

As the velvet softness of his tongue flickered over my swollen clit, my head pressed hard into the pillow. "Yes. Like that. Make me come."

He did, with the gentlest of suction and a hard lick. I writhed as the orgasm jolted through me, my core tensing violently, my limbs shaking. His tongue thrust into my sex as it convulsed, rippling along the shallow penetration, trying to pull him deeper. His groans vibrated against my swollen flesh, goading the climax to roll on and on. Tears stung my eyes and coursed down my temples, the physical pleasure destroying the wall that kept my emotions at bay.

And Gideon didn't stop. He circled the trembling entrance to my body with the tip of his tongue and lapped at my throbbing clit until I quickened again. Two fingers pushed inside me, curving and stroking. I was so sensitive I thrashed against the onslaught. When he drew on my clit with steady, rhythmic suction, I came again, crying out hoarsely. Then he had three fingers in me, twisting and opening me.

"No." My head tossed from side to side, every inch of my skin tingling and burning. "No more."

"Once more," he coaxed hoarsely. "Once more, then I'll fuck you."

"I can't . . ."

"You will." He blew a slow stream of air over my wet flesh, the coolness over fevered skin reawakening raw nerve endings. "I love watching you come, Eva. Love hearing the sounds you make, the way your body quivers . . ."

He massaged a tender spot inside me and an orgasm pulsed through me in a slow, heated roll of delight, no less devastating for being gentler than the two before it.

His weight and heat left me. In a distant corner of my dazed mind, I heard a drawer opening, followed swiftly by the sound of foil tearing. The mattress dipped as he returned, his hands rough now as he yanked me down to the center of the bed. He stretched himself on top of me, pinning me, tucking his forearms on the outside of my biceps and pressing them to my sides, capturing me.

My gaze was riveted to his austerely beautiful face. His features were harsh with lust, his skin stretched tight over his cheekbones and jaw. His eyes were so dark and dilated they were black, and I knew I was staring into the face of a man who'd passed the limits of his control. It was important to me that he'd made it that far for my benefit and that he'd done so to pleasure and prepare me for what I knew would be a hard ride.

My hands fisted in the bedspread, anticipation building. He'd made sure I got mine, over and over again. This would be for him.

"Fuck me," I ordered, daring him with my eyes.

"Eva." He snapped out my name as he rammed into me, sinking balls-deep in one fierce drive.

I gasped. He was big, hard as stone, and so damn deep. The connection was startlingly intense. Emotionally. Mentally. I'd never felt so completely . . . taken. Possessed.

I wouldn't have thought I could bear to be restrained during sex, not with my past being what it was, but Gideon's total domination of my body ratcheted my desire to an outrageous level. I'd never been so hot for it in my life, which seemed insane after what I'd experienced with him so far.

I clenched around him, relishing the feel of him inside me, filling me.

His hips ground against mine, prodding as if to say, *Feel me? I'm in you. I own you.*

His entire body hardened, the muscles of his chest and arms straining as he pulled out to the tip. The rigid tightening of his abs was the only warning I got before he slammed forward. Hard.

I cried out and his chest rumbled with a low, primitive sound. "Christ . . . You feel so good."

Tightening his hold, he starting fucking me, nailing my hips to the mattress with wildly fierce drives. Pleasure rippled through me again, pushing through me with every hot shove of his body into mine. *Like this,* I thought. *I want you just like this.*

He buried his face in my neck and held me tightly in place, plunging hard and fast, gasping raw, heated sex words that made me crazed with desire. "I've never been so hard and thick. I'm so deep in you . . . I can feel it against my stomach . . . feel my dick pounding into you."

I'd thought of this round as his, and yet he was still with me, still focused on me, swiveling his hips to stroke pleasure through my melting core. I made a small, helpless sound of need and his mouth slanted over mine. I was desperate for him, my nails digging into his pumping hips, struggling with the grinding urge to rock into the ferocious thrusts of his big cock.

We were dripping in sweat, our skin hot and slicked together, our chests heaving for air. As an orgasm brewed like a storm inside me, everything tightened and clenched, squeezing. He cursed and shoved one hand beneath my hip, cupping my rear and lifting me into his thrusts so that his cock head stroked over and over the spot that ached for him.

"Come, Eva," he ordered harshly. "Come now."

I climaxed in a rush that had me sobbing his name, the sensation enhanced and magnified by the way he'd confined my body. He threw his head back, shuddering.

"Ah, Eva!" He clasped me so tightly I couldn't breathe, his hips pumping as he came long and hard.

I've no idea how long we lay like that, leveled, mouths sliding over shoulders and throats to soothe and calm. My entire body tingled and pulsed.

"Wow," I managed finally.

"You'll kill me," he muttered with his lips at my jaw. "We're going to end up fucking each other to death."

"Me? I didn't do anything." He'd controlled me completely, and how freakin' sexy was *that*?

"You're breathing. That's enough."

I laughed, hugging him.

Lifting his head, he nuzzled my nose. "We're going to eat, and then we'll do that again."

My brows lifted. "You can do that again?"

"All night." He rolled his hips and I could feel that he was still semihard.

"You're a machine," I told him. "Or a god."

"It's you." With a soft, sweet kiss, he left me. He removed the condom, wrapped it in a tissue from the nightstand, and tossed the whole thing in the wastebasket by the bed. "We'll shower, then order from the restaurant downstairs. Unless you want to go down?"

"I don't think I can walk."

The flash of his grin stopped my heart for a minute. "Glad I'm not the only one."

"You look fine."

"I feel phenomenal." He sat back on the side of the bed and brushed my hair back from my forehead. His face was soft, his smile warmly affectionate.

I thought I saw something else in his eyes and the possibility closed my throat. It scared me.

"Shower with me," he said, running his hand down my arm.

"Gimme a minute to find my brain, then I'll join you."

"Okay." He went into the bathroom, giving me a prime view of his sculpted back and perfect ass. I sighed with pure female appreciation of a prime male specimen.

The water came on in the shower. I managed to sit up and slide my legs over the side of the bed, feeling exquisitely shaky. My gaze caught on the slightly open bedside drawer and I saw condoms through the gap.

My stomach twisted. The hotel was too upscale to be the kind that provided condoms along with the requisite Bible.

With a slightly trembling hand, I pulled the drawer out further and found a sizable quantity of prophylactics, including a bottle of feminine lubrication and spermicidal gel. My heart started pounding all over again. In my mind, I backtracked through our lust-fueled trip to the hotel. Gideon hadn't asked which rooms were available. Whether he had a master key or not, he'd need to know which rooms were occupied before he took one . . . unless he'd known beforehand that this particular suite would be empty.

Clearly it was *his* suite—a fuck pad outfitted with everything he'd need to have a good time with the women who served that purpose in his life.

As I pushed to my feet and walked over to the closet, I heard the glass shower door open in the bathroom, then close. I caught the two knobs of the louvered walnut closet doors and pushed them apart. There was a small selection of men's clothes hanging on the metal rod, some business shirts and slacks, as well as khakis and jeans. My temperature dropped and a sick misery spread through my orgasmic high.

The right-side dresser drawers held neatly folded T-shirts, boxer briefs, and socks. The top one on the left side held sex toys still in their packages. I didn't look at the drawers below that one. I'd seen enough.

I pulled on my pants and stole one of Gideon's shirts. As I dressed, my mind went through the steps I'd learned in therapy: *Talk it out. Explain what triggered the negative feelings to your partner. Face the trigger and work through it.*

Maybe if I'd been less shaken by the depth of my feelings for Gideon, I could have done all that. Maybe if we hadn't just had mind-blowing sex, I would have felt less raw and vulnerable. I'd never know. What I felt was slightly dirty, a little bit used, and a whole lot hurt. This particular revelation had hit me with excruciating force, and like a child, I wanted to hurt him back.

I scooped up the condoms, lube, and toys, and tossed them on the bed. Then, just as he called out my name in an amused and teasing voice, I picked up my bag and left him.

10

I KEPT MY HEAD down as I made the walk of shame past the registration desk and exited the hotel through a side door. I was red-faced with embarrassment remembering the manager who'd greeted Gideon as we got on the elevator. I could only imagine what he'd thought of me. He had to know what Gideon reserved that suite for. I couldn't stand the thought of being the next in a line of many, and yet that was exactly what I'd been from the moment we entered the hotel.

How hard would it have been to stop by the front desk and secure a room that was ours alone?

I started walking with no direction or destination in mind. It was dark out now, the city taking on a whole new life and energy from what it had during the business day. Steaming food carts dotted the sidewalks, along with a vendor selling framed artwork, another hawking novelty T-shirts, and yet another who had two folding tables covered in movie and television episode scripts.

With every step I took, the adrenaline from my flight burned away. The maliciously gleeful thoughts of Gideon coming out of the bathroom to find an empty room and a paraphernalia-strewn bed ran their course. I began to calm down . . . and seriously think about what had just happened.

Was it a coincidence that Gideon invited me to a gym that just so happened to be conveniently close to his fuck pad?

I remembered the conversation we'd had in his office over lunch and the way he'd struggled to express himself to keep me. He was as confused and torn about what was happening between us as I was, and I knew how easy it was to fall into established patterns. After all, hadn't I just fallen into one of my own by bailing? I'd spent enough years in therapy to know better than to wound and run when I was hurting.

Heartsick, I stepped into an Italian bistro and took a table. I ordered a glass of shiraz and a pizza margherita, hoping wine and food would calm the vibrating anxiety inside me so that I could think properly.

When the waiter returned with my wine, I gulped down half the glass without really tasting it. I missed Gideon already, missed the playful, happy mood he'd been in when I left. His scent was all over me—the smell of his skin and hot, grinding sex. My eyes stung and I let a few tears slide down my face, despite being in a very public, very busy restaurant. My food came and I picked at it. It tasted like cardboard, although I doubted that had anything to do with the chef or the venue.

Pulling over the chair where I'd set my bag, I dug out my new smartphone with the intention of leaving a message with Dr. Travis's answering service. He'd suggested we have video chat appointments until I found a new therapist in New York and I decided to take him up on that offer. That's when I noticed the twenty-one missed calls from Gideon and a text: I fucked up again. Don't break up with me. Talk to me. Pls.

The tears welled again. I held the phone to my heart, at a loss for what to do. I couldn't get the images of Gideon and other women out of my mind. I couldn't stop picturing him fucking the hell out of another woman on that same bed, using toys on her, driving her crazy, taking his pleasure from her body . . .

It was irrational and pointless to think of such things, and it made me feel petty and small and physically sick.

I startled when the phone vibrated against me, nearly dropping it. Nursing my misery, I debating letting it go to voice mail because I could see on the screen that it was Gideon—plus he was the only one who had the number—but I couldn't ignore it, because he was clearly frantic. As much as I'd wanted to wound him earlier, I couldn't stand to do it now.

"Hello." My voice didn't sound like mine, clogged as it was with tears and emotion.

"Eva! Thank God." Gideon sounded so anxious. "Where are you?"

Looking around, I didn't see anything that would tell me the name of the restaurant. "I don't know. I . . . I'm sorry, Gideon."

"No, Eva. Don't. It's my fault. I need to find you. Can you describe where you're at? Did you walk?"

"Yes. I walked."

"I know which exit you took. Which way did you head?" He was breathing quickly and I could hear the sounds of traffic and car horns in the background.

"To the left."

"Did you turn any corners after that?"

"I don't think so. I don't know." I looked around for a server I could ask. "I'm in a restaurant. Italian. There's seating on the sidewalk . . . and a wrought-iron fence. French doors . . . Jesus, Gideon, I—"

He appeared, silhouetted in the entrance with the phone held to his ear. I knew him immediately, watched as he froze when he saw me seated against the wall toward the back. Shoving the phone into the pocket of jeans he'd had stored at the hotel, he strode past the hostess who'd started speaking to him and headed straight for me. I barely managed to get to my feet before he hauled me against him and embraced me tightly.

"God." He shook slightly and buried his face in my neck. "Eva."

I hugged him back. He was fresh from a shower, making me achingly aware of my need for one.

"I can't be here," he said hoarsely, pulling back to cup my face in his hands. "I can't be in public right now. Will you come home with me?"

Something on my face must have betrayed my lingering wariness, because he pressed his lips to my forehead and murmured, "It won't be like the hotel, I promise. My mother's the only woman who's ever been to my place, aside from the housekeeper and staff."

"This is stupid," I muttered. "I'm being stupid."

"No." He brushed the hair back from my face and bent closer to whisper in my ear. "If you'd taken me to a place you reserved for fucking other men, I would've lost it."

The waiter returned and we pulled apart. "Should I get you a menu, sir?"

"That won't be necessary." Gideon dug his wallet out of his back pocket and handed over his credit card. "We're leaving."

WE took a cab to Gideon's place and he held on to my hand the entire time. I shouldn't have been so nervous riding a private elevator up to a penthouse apartment on Fifth Avenue. The sight of high ceilings and prewar architecture wasn't new to me, and really, it was all to be expected when dating a man who seemed to own damn near everything. And the coveted view of Central Park . . . well, of course he'd have one.

But Gideon's tension was palpable, and it made me realize that this was a big deal to *him*. When the elevator opened directly into his apartment's marbled entry foyer, his grip on my hand tightened before he released me. He unlocked the double-door entrance to usher me inside, and I could feel his anxiety as he watched for my reaction.

Gideon's home was as beautiful as the man himself. It was so very different from his office, which was sleek, modern, and cool. His private space was warm and sumptuous, filled with antiques and art anchored by gorgeous Aubusson rugs laid over gleaming hardwood floors.

"It's . . . amazing," I said softly, feeling privileged to see it. It was a glimpse into the private Gideon I was desperate to know, and it was stunning.

"Come in." He tugged me deeper into the apartment. "I want you to sleep here tonight."

"I don't have clothes and stuff . . ."

"All you need is the toothbrush in your purse. We can run by your place in the morning for the rest. I promise to get you to work on time." He pulled me into him and set his chin on the crown of my head. "I'd really like you to stay, Eva. I don't blame you for wanting to get out of the hotel, but finding you gone scared the hell out of me. I need to hang on to you for a while."

"I need to be held." I pushed my hands under the back of his T-shirt to caress the silken hardness of his bare back. "I could also use a shower."

With his nose in my hair, he inhaled deeply. "I like you smelling like me."

But he led me through the living room and down a hall to his bedroom.

"Wow," I breathed when he flicked on the light. A massive sleigh bed dominated the space, the wood dark—which he seemed to prefer—and the linens a soft cream. The rest of the furnishings matched the bed and the accents were brushed gold. It was a warm, masculine space with no art on the walls to detract from the serene night view of Central Park and the magnificent residential buildings on the other side. My side of Manhattan.

"The bathroom's in here."

As I took in the vanity, which appeared to have been made out of an antique claw-footed walnut cabinet, he pulled towels out of a companion armoire and set them out for me, moving with that confident, sensual grace I admired so much. Seeing him in his home, dressed so casually, touched me. Knowing I was the only woman to have this experience with him affected me even more. I felt like I was seeing him more naked now than I ever had. "Thank you."

He glanced at me and seemed to understand that I was talking about more than the towels. His stare burned through me. "It feels good to have you here."

"I have no idea how I ended up like this, with you." But I really, really liked it.

"Does it matter?" Gideon came to me, tilting my chin up to press a kiss to the tip of my nose. "I'll lay out a T-shirt for you on the bed. Caviar and vodka sound good to you?"

"Well . . . that's quite a step up from pizza."

He smiled. "Petrossian's Ossetra."

"I stand corrected." I smiled back. "Several hundred steps up."

I showered and dressed in the oversized Cross Industries shirt he laid out for me; then I called Cary to tell him I'd be out all night and give him a brief rundown about the hotel incident.

He whistled. "I'm not even sure what to say about that."

A speechless Cary Taylor spoke volumes.

I joined Gideon in the living room, and we sat on the floor at the coffee table to eat the prized caviar with mini toast and crème fraîche. We watched a rerun of a New York–set police procedural that just happened to include a scene filmed on the street in front of the Crossfire.

"I think it'd be cool to see a building I owned on TV like that," I said.

"It's not bad, if they don't close off the street for hours to film."

I bumped shoulders with him. "Pessimist."

We crawled into Gideon's bed at ten thirty and watched the last half of a show while curled up together. Sexual tension crackled in the air between us, but he didn't make any overtures so I didn't either. I suspected he was still trying to make amends for the hotel, trying to prove that he wanted to spend time with me not "actively fucking."

It worked. As much as I desired him, it felt good just hanging out together.

He slept in the nude, which was fabulous for me to cuddle up against. I tossed one leg over his, wrapped an arm around his waist, and rested my cheek over his heart. I don't remember the ending of the show, so I suppose I fell asleep before it was over.

When I woke it was still dark in the room and I'd rolled to the far side of my half of the bed. I sat up to see the digital clock face on Gideon's nightstand and found it was barely three in the morning. I usually slept straight through the night and thought maybe the strange surroundings were keeping me from sleeping deeply; then Gideon moaned and shifted restlessly, and I realized what had disturbed me. The sound he made was pained, his subsequent hiss of breath tormented.

"Don't touch me," he whispered harshly. "Get your fucking hands off me!"

I froze, my heart racing. His words sliced through the dark, filled with fury.

"You sick bastard." He writhed, his legs kicking at the covers. His back arched on a groan that sounded perversely erotic. "Don't. Ah, Christ . . . It *hurts*."

He strained, his body twisting. I couldn't bear it.

"Gideon." Because Cary had nightmares sometimes, I knew better than to touch a man in the throes of one. Instead, I knelt on my side of the bed and called his name. "Gideon, wake up."

Stilling abruptly, he fell to his back, tense and expectant. His chest heaved with panting breaths. His cock was hard and lay heavily along his belly.

I spoke firmly, although my heart was breaking. "Gideon. You're dreaming. Come back to me."

He deflated into the mattress. "Eva . . . ?"

"I'm here." Shifting, I moved out of the way of the moonlight but saw no luminous glitter that would tell me his eyes were open. "Are you awake?"

His breathing began to slow, but he didn't speak. His hands were fisted in the bottom sheet. I pulled the shirt I was wearing over my head and dropped it on the bed. I sidled closer, reaching out with a tentative hand to touch his arm. When he didn't move, I caressed him, my fingertips sliding gently over the hard muscle of his biceps.

"Gideon?"

He jerked awake. "What? What is it?"

I sat back on my heels with my hands on my thighs. I saw him blink at me, then shove both hands through his hair. I could feel the nightmare clinging to him, could sense it in the rigidness of his body.

"What's wrong?" he asked gruffly, pushing up onto one elbow. "You okay?"

"I want you." I stretched out against him, aligning my bare body to his. Pressing my face into his damp throat, I sucked gently on his salty skin. I knew from my own nightmares that being held and loved could push the specters back into the closet for a little while.

His arms came around me, his hands running up and down the curve of my spine. I felt him let go of the dream with a long, deep sigh.

Pushing him to his back, I climbed over him and sealed my mouth over his. His erection was notched between the lips of my sex and I rocked against him. The feel of his hands in my hair, holding me to take control of the kiss, quickly made me wet and ready. Fire licked just beneath my skin. I stroked my clit up and down his thick length, using him to masturbate until he made a rough sound of desire and rolled to put me beneath him.

"I don't have any condoms in the house," he murmured before wrapping his lips around my nipple and sucking gently.

I loved that he wasn't prepared. This wasn't his fuck pad; this was his home and I was the only lover he'd brought into it. "I know you mentioned swapping bills of health when we talked about birth control, and that's the responsible way to go, but—"

"I trust you." He lifted his head, looking at me in the faint light of the moon. Kneeing my legs open, he pushed the first bare inch inside me. He was scorching hot and silky soft.

"Eva," he breathed, clutching me tightly to him. "I've never . . . Christ, you feel so good. I'm so glad you're here."

I tugged his lips down to mine and kissed him. "Me, too."

I woke the way I'd fallen asleep, with Gideon on top of me and inside me. His gaze was heavy-lidded with desire as I rose from unconsciousness into heated pleasure. His hair hung around his shoulders and face, looking even sexier for being sleep-tousled. But best of all, there were no shadows in his gorgeous eyes, nothing lingering from the pain that haunted his dreams.

"I hope you don't mind," he murmured with a wicked grin, sliding in and out. "You're warm and soft. I can't help but want you."

I stretched my arms over my head and arched my back, pressing my breasts into his chest. Through the slender arch-topped windows, I saw the soft light of dawn filling the sky. "Umm . . . I could get used to waking up like this."

"That was my thought at three this morning." He rolled his hips and sank deep into me. "I thought I'd return the favor."

My body revved to life, my pulse quickening. "Yes, please."

CARY was gone when we got to my apartment; he'd left a note behind to tell me he was on a job but would be back in plenty of time for pizza with Trey. Since I'd been too upset to enjoy my pie the night before, I was ready to try again when I was having a good time.

"I have a business dinner tonight," Gideon said, leaning over my shoulder to read. "I was hoping you'd come with me and make it bearable."

"I can't bail out on Cary," I said apologetically, turning to face him. "Chicks before dicks and all that."

His mouth twitched and he caged me to the breakfast bar. He was dressed for work in a suit I'd picked out, a graphite gray Prada with a soft sheen. His tie was the blue one that matched his eyes, and as I'd lain on his bed and watched him dress, I'd had to fight the urge to take it all off him. "Cary isn't a chick. But I get the point. I want to see you tonight. Can I come over after the dinner and stay the night?"

Heated anticipation rushed through me. I smoothed my hands over his vest, feeling like I had a special secret because I knew exactly what he looked like without his clothes on. "I'd love it if you did."

"Good." He gave a satisfied nod. "I'll make us coffee, while you get dressed."

"The beans are in the freezer. The grinder's next to the coffeepot." I pointed. "And I like lots of milk and a little sweetener."

When I came out twenty minutes later, Gideon grabbed two travel mugs of coffee off the breakfast bar and we headed down to the lobby. Paul hustled us out the front door and into the backseat of Gideon's waiting Bentley SUV.

As Gideon's driver pulled into traffic, Gideon checked me out and said, "You're definitely trying to kill me. Are you wearing the garters again?"

Pulling the hem of my skirt up, I showed him where the top of my black silk stockings hooked to my black lace garter belt.

His muttered curse made me smile. I'd chosen a black short-sleeved silk turtleneck sweater paired with a decently short pleated skirt in lipstick red and heeled Mary Janes. Because Cary hadn't been around to manage something fancy with my hair, I'd pulled it back in a ponytail. "You like?"

"I'm hard." His voice was husky, and he adjusted himself in his trousers. "How the hell am I going to get through the day thinking about you dressed like that?"

"There's always lunch," I suggested, fantasizing about a nooner on Gideon's office couch.

"I have a business lunch today. I'd reschedule, if I hadn't moved it already yesterday."

"You rescheduled an appointment for me? I'm flattered."

He reached over and brushed his fingertips over my cheek, a now-habitual gesture of affection that was tender and fiercely intimate. I was coming to depend on receiving those touches.

I leaned my cheek into his palm. "Can you carve fifteen minutes out of your day for me?"

"I'll manage it."

"Call me when you know the time."

Taking a deep breath, I dug into my bag and wrapped my hand around a gift I wasn't sure he'd want, but I couldn't get the memory of his nightmare out of my head. I hoped that what I had for him would remind him of me and three A.M. sex, and help him cope. "I have something. I thought . . ."

It suddenly seemed conceited to give him what I'd brought.

He frowned. "What's wrong?"

"Nothing. It's just . . ." I exhaled in a rush. "Listen, I have something for you, but I just realized it's one of those gifts—well, it's not really a gift. I'm already thinking it's not appropriate and—"

He thrust out his hand. "Give it to me."

"You can totally decide not to take it—"

"Shut up, Eva." He crooked his fingers. "Give it to me."

I pulled it out of my bag and handed it over.

Gideon stared down at the framed photograph in complete silence. It was a novelty frame depicting die-cut images of things relating to graduation, including a digital clock face that read 3:00 A.M. The picture was of me posing on Coronado Beach in a coral bikini with a big floppy straw hat—I was tanned, happy, and blowing a kiss to Cary, who'd playacted the role of a high-fashion photographer by calling out ridiculous encouragements. *Beautiful, dahling. Show me sassy. Show me sexy. Brilliant. Show me catty . . . rawr . . .*

Embarrassed, I squirmed a little on the seat. "Like I said, you don't have to keep—"

"I—" He cleared his throat. "Thank you, Eva."

"Ah, well . . ." I was grateful to see the Crossfire outside my window. I jumped out quickly when the driver pulled over and ran my hands over my skirt, feeling self-conscious. "If you want, I can hang on to it until later."

Gideon shut the door of the Bentley and shook his head. "It's mine. You're not taking it back."

He linked our fingers together and gestured toward the revolving door with the hand holding the frame. I warmed when I realized he intended to take my picture into work with him.

ONE of the fun things about the ad business was that no day was ever the same as the one before it. I was hopping all morning and was just beginning to contemplate what to do about lunch when my phone rang. "Mark Garrity's office, Eva Tramell speaking."

"I've got news," Cary said by way of greeting.

"What?" I could tell by his voice that it was good news, whatever it was.

"I landed a Grey Isles campaign."

"Oh my God! Cary, that's awesome! I love their jeans."

"What are you doing for lunch?"

I grinned. "Celebrating with you. Can you be here at noon?"

"I'm already on my way."

I hung up and rocked back in my chair, so thrilled for Cary I felt like dancing. Needing something to do to kill the fifteen minutes remaining before my lunch break, I checked my inbox again and found a Google alert digest for Gideon's name. More than thirty mentions, in just one day.

I opened the e-mail and freaked out a little at the numerous "mystery woman" headlines. I clicked on the first link and found myself landing on a gossip blog.

There, in living color, was a photo of Gideon kissing me senseless on the sidewalk outside his gym. The accompanying article was short and to the point:

Gideon Cross, New York's most eligible bachelor since John F. Kennedy Jr., was spotted yesterday in a passionate public embrace. A source at Cross Industries identified the lucky mystery woman as socialite Eva Tramell, daughter of multimillionaire Richard Stanton and his wife, Monica. When queried about the nature of the relationship between Cross and Tramell, the source confirmed that Miss Tramell is "the significant woman" in the mogul's life at present. We imagine hearts are breaking across the country this morning.

"Oh, crap," I breathed.

11

I QUICKLY CLICKED THROUGH other links in the digest to find the same picture with similar captions and articles. Alarmed, I sat back and thought about what this meant. If one kiss was headline news, what chance would Gideon and I have to make a relationship work?

My hands weren't quite steady as I closed the browser tabs. I hadn't considered the press coverage, but I should have. "Damn it."

Anonymity was my friend. It protected me from my past. It protected my family from embarrassment, and Gideon, too. I didn't even have any social networking accounts, so people who weren't actively in my life couldn't find me.

A thin, invisible wall between me and exposure was gone.

"Hell," I breathed, finding myself in a painful situation I could have avoided if I'd dedicated any of my brain cells to something other than Gideon.

There was also *his* reaction to this mess to consider. . . . I cringed inwardly just thinking about it. And my mother. It wouldn't be long before she was calling and blowing everything out of—

"Shit." Remembering that she didn't have my new cell number, I picked up my desk phone and called my other voice mail to see if she'd already tried to reach me. I winced when I heard that my mailbox was full.

I hung up and grabbed my purse, then headed off to lunch, knowing Cary would help me put it all in perspective. I was so flustered when I reached the lobby level that I rushed out of the elevator with my only thought being to find my roommate. When I spotted him, I didn't take note of anyone else until Gideon sidestepped smoothly in front of me and blocked my path.

"Eva." He frowned down at me. Cupping my elbow, he turned me slightly around. That was when I saw the two women and a man who'd hidden him from my view.

I managed to find a smile for them. "Hello."

Gideon introduced me to his lunch dates. Then he excused us and tugged me off to the side. "What's wrong? You're upset."

"It's all over the place," I whispered. "A picture of us together."

He nodded. "I've seen it."

I blinked up at him, confused at his nonchalance. "You're okay with it?"

"Why wouldn't I be? For once, they're reporting the truth."

A sneaking suspicion niggled at me. "You planned it. You planted the story."

"Not entirely true," he said smoothly. "The photographer happened to be there. I just gave him a picture worth printing, and told PR to make it clear who you are and what you are to me."

"Why? Why would you do that?"

"You have your way of dealing with jealousy and I have mine. We're both off the market and now everyone knows it. Why is that a problem for you?"

"I was worried about your reaction, but there's more . . . There are things you don't know and I—" I took a deep, shaky breath. "It can't be that way between us, Gideon. We can't be public. I don't want— Damn it. I'll embarrass you."

"You couldn't. It's not possible." He brushed a loose lock of hair off my face. "Can we talk about this later? If you need me—"

"No, it's okay. Go."

Cary came over. Dressed in baggy black cargo pants and a V-neck white undershirt, he still managed to look expensive. "Everything all right?"

"Hi, Cary. Everything's fine." Gideon squeezed my hand. "Enjoy your lunch and don't worry."

He could say that because he didn't know better.

And I didn't know whether he'd still want me once he did.

Cary faced me as Gideon walked away. "Worry about what? What's wrong?"

"Everything." I sighed. "Let's get out of here, and I'll tell you over lunch."

"WELL," Cary murmured, looking at the link I'd forwarded from my smartphone to his. "That's some kiss. The dip was a great touch. He couldn't look more into you if he tried."

"That's the thing." I took another big gulp of water. "He did try."

He shoved his phone into his pocket. "Last week you kept shooting him down for only wanting your vagina. This week he's publicizing that he's in a committed, passionate relationship with you, and you're still unhappy. I'm starting to feel bad for the guy. He can't win for trying."

That stung. "Reporters are going to dig, Cary, and they're going to find dirt. And since it's juicy dirt, they're going to splash it all over hell and back, and it's going to embarrass Gideon."

"Baby girl." He set his hand over mine. "Stanton buried all that."

Stanton. I straightened. I hadn't thought of my stepfather. He'd see the disaster coming and keep a lid on it because he knew what the revelation would do to my mother. Still . . . "I'll have to talk to Gideon about it. He has a right to be warned."

Just the thought of that conversation made me miserable.

Cary knew how my brain worked. "If you think he's going to cut and run, I think you're wrong. He looks at you like you're the only person in the room."

I poked at my tuna Caesar salad. "He's got a few demons of his own. Nightmares. He's closed himself off, I think, because of whatever's eating at him."

"But he's let you in."

And he'd already shown hints of how possessive he could be about that connection. I accepted that because it was a flaw I shared, but still . . .

"You're analyzing this to death, Eva," Cary said. "You're thinking the way he feels about you has to be a fluke or a mistake. Someone like him couldn't really be into you for your big heart and sharp mind, right?"

"My self-esteem isn't *that* bad," I protested.

He took a sip of his champagne. "Isn't it? So tell me something *you* think he likes about you that doesn't have to do with sex or codependency."

I thought about it and came up empty, which made me scowl.

"Right," he went on with a nod. "And if Cross is anywhere near as messed up as we are, he's thinking the same thing in reverse, wondering what a hot babe like you sees in a guy like him. You've got money, so what has he got going for him besides being a stud who keeps screwing up?"

Sitting back in my chair, I absorbed everything he'd said. "Cary, I love you madly."

He grinned. "Back atcha, sweets. My advice, for what it's worth? Couples therapy. It's always been my plan to get into it when I find the one I want to settle down with. And try to have fun with him. You've got to have as many good times as bad, or it all becomes too painful and too much work."

I reached over and squeezed his hand. "Thank you."

"For what?" He shrugged off my gratitude with an elegant wave of his hand. "It's easy to pick apart someone else's life. You know I couldn't get through my rough spots without you."

"Which you don't have any of now," I pointed out, shifting the focus to him. "You're about to be splashed across a Times Square bill-board. You won't be my secret any longer. Should we upgrade dinner from pizza to something more worthy of the occasion? How about we haul out that case of Cristal Stanton gave us?"

"Now you're talking."

"Movies? Anything in particular you want to watch?"

"Whatever you want. I wouldn't want to screw with your big-dumb-blow-'em-up movie genius."

I grinned, feeling better as I'd known I would after an hour with Cary. "You'll let me know if I'm too dense to figure out when you and Trey want to be alone."

"Ha! Don't worry about that. Your tempestuous love life is making me feel dull and boring. I could use a hot, sweaty bang with my own stud."

"You just had a maintenance closet romp a couple days ago!"

He sighed. "I'd nearly forgotten. How sad is that?"

"It isn't when your eyes are laughing."

I'D just gotten back to my desk when I checked my smartphone and found a text from Gideon letting me know he had fifteen minutes to spare at quarter to three. I nursed a secret rush of anticipation for the next hour and a half, having decided to take Cary's advice and have a little fun. Gideon and I would have to wade through the ugliness of my past soon enough, but for now, I could give us both something to smile about.

I texted him just before I left, letting him know I was on my way. Considering the time constraints, we couldn't waste a minute. Gideon must have felt the same way, because I found Scott waiting for me at reception when I reached the Cross Industries waiting area. He walked me back after the receptionist buzzed me in.

"How's your day been?" I asked him.

He smiled. "Great so far. Yours?"

I smiled back. "I've had worse."

Gideon was on the phone when I entered his office. His tone was clipped and impatient as he told the person on the other end of the line that they should be able to manage the job without him having to oversee it personally.

He held up one finger to me to tell me he'd be another minute. I responded by blowing a big bubble with the gum I was chewing and popping it loudly.

His brows shot up, and he hit the buttons to close the doors and frost the glass wall.

Grinning, I sauntered over to his desk and hopped onto it, curling my fingers around the lip and swinging my legs. He popped the next bubble I blew with a quick jab of his finger. I pouted prettily.

"Deal with it," he said with quiet authority to whoever was on the phone. "It'll be next week before I can get out there, and waiting will set us back further. Stop talking. I have something time-sensitive on my desk and you're keeping me away from it. I guarantee that's not improving my disposition. Fix what needs fixing and report back to me tomorrow."

He returned the phone to its cradle with suppressed violence. "Eva—"

I held up one hand to cut him off and wrapped my gum in a Post-it I took from a dispenser on his desk. "Before you reprimand me, Mr. Cross, I want to say that when we reached an impasse in our merger discussions at the hotel yesterday, I shouldn't have walked out. It didn't help to resolve the situation. And I know I didn't react very well to the PR issue with the photo. But still . . . Even though I've been a naughty secretary, I think I should be given another chance to excel."

His gaze narrowed as he studied me, assessing and reevaluating the situation on the fly. "Did I ask for your opinion on the appropriate action to take, Miss Tramell?"

I shook my head and looked up at him from beneath my lashes. I could see the lingering frustration from his phone call falling away from him, replaced by his growing interest and arousal.

Hopping down from the desk, I sidled closer and smoothed his immaculate tie with both hands. "Can't we work something out? I do possess a wide variety of useful skills."

He caught me by the hips. "Which is one of the many reasons you're the only woman I've ever considered for the position."

Warmth flowed through me at his words. Boldly cupping his cock in my hand, I fondled him through his slacks. "Maybe I should reapply myself to my duties? I could demonstrate some of the ways I'm uniquely qualified to assist you."

Gideon hardened with delectable swiftness. "Such initiative, Miss Tramell. But my next meeting is less than ten minutes away. Also, I'm not accustomed to exploring job enrichment opportunities in my office."

I freed the button of his fly and lowered his zipper. With my lips to his jaw, I whispered, "If you think there's anywhere I won't make you come, you'll have to revisit and revise."

"Eva," he breathed, his eyes hot and tender. He cupped my throat, his thumbs brushing over my jaw. "You're unraveling me. Do you know that? Are you doing it on purpose?"

I reached inside his boxer briefs and wrapped my hands around him, offering up my lips for a kiss. He obliged me, taking my mouth with a fierceness that left me breathless.

"I want you," he growled.

I sank to my knees on the carpeted floor, pulling his pants down enough to give me the access I needed.

He exhaled harshly. "Eva, what are you—"

My lips flowed over the wide crown. He reached back for the edge of his desk, his hands curling around the lip with white-knuckled force. I held him with both hands and mouthed the plush head, sucking gently. The softness of his skin and his uniquely appealing scent made me moan. I felt the vibration ripple through his entire body and heard a rough sound rumble in his chest.

Gideon touched my cheek. "Lick it."

Aroused by the command, I fluttered my tongue across the underside and shivered with delight when he rewarded me with a hot burst of pre-cum. Fisting the root of him with one hand, I hollowed my cheeks and drew rhythmically, hoping for more.

I wished I had the time to make it last. Drive him crazy . . .

He made a sound filled with the sweetest agony. "God, Eva . . . your mouth. Keep sucking. Like that . . . hard and deep."

I was so turned on by his pleasure I squirmed. His hands pushed into my bound hair, pulling and tugging at the roots. I loved how he started out with tenderness, then grew rougher as the lust he felt for me overwhelmed his control.

The soft bite of pain made me hungrier, greedier. My head bobbed as I pleasured him, jacking him with one hand while I sucked and stroked the crest with my mouth. Heavy veins coursed the length of his cock, and I slid the flat of my tongue along them, tilting my head to find and caress each one.

He swelled, growing thicker and longer. My knees were uncomfortable, but I didn't care; my gaze was riveted to Gideon as his head fell back and he fought for breath.

"Eva, you suck me so good." He held my head still and took over. Thrusting his hips. Fucking my mouth. Stripped to a level of base need where only the race to orgasm mattered.

The thought made me crazed, the image in my mind of how we must look: Gideon in all his urbane sophistication, standing at the desk where he ruled an empire, stroking his big cock in and out of my greedy mouth.

I gripped his straining thighs in both hands, frantically working my lips and tongue, desperate for his climax. His balls were heavy and big, an audacious display of his powerful virility. I cupped them, rolling them gently, feeling them tighten and draw up.

"Ah, *Eva*." His voice was a guttural rasp. His grip tightened in my hair. "You're making me come."

The first spurt of semen was so thick, I struggled to swallow. Mindless in his pleasure, Gideon was thrusting against the back of my throat, his cock throbbing with every wrenching pulse into my mouth. My eyes watered and my lungs burned, but still I pumped my fists, milking him. His entire body shuddered as I took everything he had. The sounds he made and the muttered, breathless praise were the most gratifying I'd ever heard.

I licked him clean, marveling at how he didn't fully soften even after an explosive orgasm. He was still capable of fucking me senseless and more than willing to, I knew. But there was no time and I was happy about that. I wanted to do this for him. For us. For me, really, because I needed to know I could indulge in a selfless sexual act without feeling taken advantage of.

"I have to go," I murmured, standing and pressing my lips to his. "I hope the rest of your day is awesome, and your business dinner tonight, too."

I started to move away, but he caught my wrist, his gaze on the clock readout on his desk phone. I noticed my picture then, sitting in a place of prominence where he'd see it all day.

"Eva . . . Damn it. Wait."

I frowned at his tone, which sounded anxious. Frustrated.

He quickly restored his appearance, tucking himself back into his boxer briefs and straightening the tail of his shirt so he could fasten his pants. There was something sweet in watching him pull himself back together, restoring the façade he wore for the world while I knew at least a little of the man beneath it.

Tugging me close, Gideon pressed his lips to my brow. His hands moved through my hair to unclip my tortoise barrette. "I didn't get you off."

"No need." I loved the feel of his hands on my scalp. "That rocked just the way it was."

He was overly focused on fixing my hair, his cheeks flushed from his orgasm. "I know you need an even exchange," he argued gruffly. "I can't let you leave feeling like I used you."

A bittersweet tenderness pierced me. He'd listened. He cared.

I cupped his face in my hands. "You did use me, with my permission, and it was seriously hot. I wanted to give you this, Gideon. Remember? I warned you. I wanted you to have this memory of me."

His eyes widened with alarm. "Why the fuck do I need memories when I have you? Eva, if this is about the photo—"

"Shut up and enjoy the high." We didn't have the time to get into the photo issue now, and I didn't want to. It was going to ruin everything. "If we'd had an hour, I still wouldn't let you get me off. I'm not keeping score with you, ace. And honestly, you're the first guy I can say that to. Now, I have to go. You have to go."

I started away again, but he caught me back.

Scott's voice came through the speaker. "Excuse me, Mr. Cross. But your three o'clock is here."

"It's *okay*, Gideon," I assured him. "You're coming over tonight, right?"

"Nothing could keep me away."

I shoved up onto my tiptoes and kissed his cheek. "We'll talk then."

AFTER work, I took the stairs down to the ground floor to feel less guilty about skipping the gym and seriously regretted it by the time I reached the lobby. Lack of sleep from the night before had left me wiped out. I was contemplating taking the subway rather than walking when I saw Gideon's Bentley at the curb. When the driver got out and greeted me by name, I halted abruptly, surprised.

"Mr. Cross asked that I take you home," he said, looking smart in his black suit and chauffeur hat. He was an older gentleman with graying red hair, pale blue eyes, and the softest of cultured accents.

Considering how much my legs ached, I was grateful for the offer. "Thank you—I'm sorry, what was your name?"

"Angus, Miss Tramell."

How had I not remembered that? The name was so cool, it made me smile. "Thank you, Angus."

He tipped his hat. "My pleasure."

I slid through the back door he opened for me, and as I settled into the seat, I caught a glimpse of the handgun he wore in a shoulder holster beneath his jacket. It appeared that Angus, like Clancy, was both bodyguard and driver.

We pulled away from the curb and I asked, "How long have you been working for Mr. Cross, Angus?"

"Eight years now."

"Quite a while."

"I've known him longer than that," he volunteered, catching my gaze in the rearview mirror. "I drove him to school when he was a boy. He hired me away from Mr. Vidal when the time came."

Once again, I tried to picture Gideon as a child. No doubt he'd been beautiful and charismatic even then.

Had he enjoyed "normal" sexual relationships when he was a teenager? I couldn't imagine that women weren't throwing themselves at him even then. And as innately sexual as he was, I imagined he'd been a horny teen.

Digging in my purse, I pulled out my keys and leaned forward to set them on the front passenger seat. "Can you see that Gideon gets those? He's supposed to come over after whatever it is he's doing tonight, and depending on how late that is, I might not hear him knock."

"Of course."

Paul opened the door for me when we arrived at my apartment and he greeted Angus by name, reminding me that Gideon owned the building. I waved to both men, told the front desk Gideon would be coming over later, and then took myself upstairs. Cary's raised brows when he opened the door to me made me laugh.

"Gideon's coming over later," I explained, "but I'm feeling so hammered right now I may not stay up long. So I gave him my keys to let himself in. Did you order already?"

"I did. And I tossed a few bottles of Cristal in the wine fridge."

"You're the best." I shoved my bag at him.

I showered and called my mom from the phone in my room, wincing at her strident, "I have been trying to reach you *for days!*"

"Mom, if it's about Gideon Cross—"

"Well, of course, it's partly about him! For goodness' sake, Eva. You're being called the significant woman in his life. How could I not want to talk about that?"

"Mom—"

"But there's also the appointment you asked me to make with Dr. Petersen." The note of smug amusement in her voice made me smile. "We're scheduled to meet with him Thursday at six o'clock in the evening. I hope that works for you. He doesn't do many evening appointments."

I plopped backward onto my bed with a sigh. I'd been so distracted by work and Gideon that the appointment had slipped my mind. "Thursday at six will be fine. Thank you."

"Now, then. Tell me about Cross . . ."

When I emerged from my bedroom dressed in jersey pants and a San Diego State University sweatshirt, I found Trey seated with Cary in the living room. Both men stood when I came in, and Trey gifted me with an open, friendly smile.

"I'm sorry I look so ragged," I said sheepishly, running my fingers through my damp ponytail. "Taking the stairs at work almost killed me today."

"Elevator take the day off?" he asked.

"Nope. My brain did. What the hell was I thinking?" Spending the night with Gideon was enough of a workout.

The doorbell rang and Cary went to get it while I headed into the kitchen for the Cristal. I joined him at the breakfast bar as he signed the credit card receipt, and the look in his eyes when he glanced at Trey had me hiding a smile.

There were a lot of those looks going back and forth between the two men as the evening progressed. And I had to agree with Cary that Trey was a hottie. Dressed in distressed jeans, matching vest, and a long-sleeved shirt, the aspiring veterinarian looked casual but well put together. He was very different personality-wise from the type of guy Cary usually dated. Trey seemed more grounded; not quite somber, but definitely not flighty. I thought he'd be a good influence on Cary, if they stayed together long enough.

The three of us made it through two bottles of Cristal and two pizzas between us, plus all of *Demolition Man* before I called it a night. I urged Trey to stay for *Driven* to round out the Stallone mini-marathon; then

I went to my room and changed into a sexy black baby doll I'd been given as part of a bridesmaid gift bag—sans the matching panties.

Leaving a candle burning for Gideon, I crashed.

I woke to darkness and the scent of Gideon's skin, the lights and sounds of the city shut out by soundproofed windows and blackout drapes.

Gideon slid over me, a moving shadow, his bare skin cool to the touch. His mouth slanted over mine, kissing me slowly and deeply, tasting of mint and his own unique flavor. My hands slid down his sleekly muscular back, my legs parting so he could settle comfortably between them. The weight of him against me made my heart sigh and my blood warm with desire.

"Well, hello to you, too," I said breathlessly when he let me up for air.

"You'll come with me next time," he murmured in that sexy and decadent voice, nibbling at my throat.

"Will I?" I teased.

He reached down and cupped my butt in his hand, squeezing and lifting me into a deft roll of his hips. "Yes. I missed you, Eva."

I ran my fingers through his hair, wishing I could see him. "You haven't known me long enough to miss me."

"Shows how much you know," Gideon scoffed, sliding downward and nuzzling between my breasts.

I gasped as his mouth covered my nipple and sucked through the satin, deep pulls that echoed in the clenching of my core. He moved to my other breast, his hand pushing up the hem of my baby doll. I arched into him, lost to the magic of his mouth as it moved over my body, his tongue dipping into my navel, then sliding lower.

"And you missed me, too," he purred with masculine satisfaction, the tip of his middle finger rimming my cleft. "You're swollen and wet for me."

He pulled my legs over his shoulders and licked between my folds, soft and provocative laps of hot velvet against my sensitive flesh. My hands fisted in the sheet, my chest heaving as he circled my clit with the tip of his tongue, then nudged the hypersensitive knot of nerves. I keened, my hips moving restlessly into the devious torment, my muscles tightening with the clawing need to come.

The light, teasing flutters were driving me insane, giving me just enough to make me writhe but not enough to get me off. "Gideon, please."

"Not yet."

He tortured me, coaxing my body to the brink of orgasm, and then letting me slide back down. Over and over. Until sweat misted my skin and my heart felt like it would burst. His tongue was tireless and diabolical, cleverly focusing on my clit until a single stroke would set me off, then moving lower to thrust into me. The soft, shallow plunges were maddening, the flickering against the nerve-laden tissues making me desperate enough to beg shamelessly.

"Please, Gideon . . . let me come . . . I need to come, please."

"Shh, angel . . . I'll take care of you."

He finished me with a tenderness that made the orgasm roll through me like a crashing wave, building and swelling and spreading through me in a warm rush of pleasure.

He threaded his fingers with mine when he came over me again, restraining my arms. The head of his cock aligned with the slick entrance of my body and he pushed inexorably into me. I moaned, shifting to accommodate the heavy surge of his penis.

Gideon's breath gusted hard and humid against my throat, his big frame trembling as he slid carefully inside me. "You're so soft and warm. Mine, Eva. You're mine."

I wrapped my legs around his hips, welcoming him deeper, feeling his buttocks flex and release against my calves as he demonstrated to my body that it would indeed take his thick length all the way to the root.

With our hands linked, he took my mouth and began to move, gliding in and out with languid skill, the tempo precise and relentless yet smooth and easy. I felt every rock-hard inch of him, felt the unmistakable reiteration that every inch of me was his to possess. He drove the message home repeatedly until I was gasping against his mouth, thrashing restlessly beneath him, my hands bloodless from the strength of my grip on his.

He spoke heated praise and encouragement, telling me how beautiful I was . . . how perfect I felt to him . . . how he'd never stop . . . couldn't stop. I came with a sharp cry of relief, vibrating with the ecstasy of it, and he was right there with me. His pace quickened for several slamming thrusts; then he climaxed with a hiss of my name, spilling into me.

I sank lax into the mattress, sweaty and boneless and replete.

"I'm not done," he whispered darkly, adjusting his knees to increase the force of his thrusts. The pace remained expertly measured, each plunge staking a claim—*your body exists to serve me.*

Biting my lip, I fought back the sounds of helpless pleasure that might've broken the tranquillity of the night . . . and betrayed the frightening depths of emotion I was beginning to feel for Gideon Cross.

12

GIDEON FOUND ME in the shower the next morning. He strode into the master bath gloriously nude, walking with that sleek, confident grace I'd admired from the beginning. Watching the flexing of his muscles as he moved, I didn't even pretend not to stare at the magnificent package between his legs.

Despite the heat of the water, my nipples beaded tight and goose bumps raced across my skin.

His knowing smile as he joined me told me he knew exactly what kind of effect he had on me. I retaliated by running soapy hands all over his godlike body, then sitting on the bench and sucking him off with such enthusiasm he had to support himself with both palms pressed flat against the tile.

His raw, raspy instructions echoed in my mind the entire time I dressed for work, which I did quickly—before he had a chance to finish his shower and fuck the hell out of me as he'd threatened to just before spurting fiercely down my throat.

He'd had no nightmares during the night. Sex as a sedative seemed to be working, and I was extremely grateful for that.

"I hope you don't think you've gotten away," he said when he prowled after me into the kitchen. Immaculately dressed in a black pinstriped suit, he accepted the cup of coffee I handed him and gave me a look that promised all sorts of wicked things. I saw him in his supremely civilized attire and thought of the insatiable male who'd slipped into my bed during the night. My blood quickened. I was sore, my muscles thrumming with remembered pleasure, and I was still thinking about more.

"Keep looking at me like that," he warned, leaning casually into the counter and sipping his coffee. "See what happens."

"I'm going to lose my job over you."

"I'd give you another one."

I snorted. "As what? Your sex slave?"

"What a provocative suggestion. Let's discuss."

"Fiend," I muttered, rinsing out my mug in the sink and putting it in the dishwasher. "Ready? For *work*?"

He finished his coffee and I held out my hand for his mug, but he bypassed me and rinsed it out himself. Another mortal task that made him seem accessible, less of a fantasy I'd never have a chance of holding on to.

He faced me. "I want to take you out to dinner tonight, and then take you home to my bed."

"I don't want you to burn out on me, Gideon." He was a man used to being alone, a man who hadn't had a meaningful physical relationship in a long time, if ever. How long before his flight instincts kicked in? Besides, we really needed to stay out of the public eye as a couple. . . .

"Don't make excuses." His features hardened. "You don't get to decide I can't do this."

I kicked myself for offending him. He was trying and I needed to make sure he got credit for that, not discouragement. "That's not what I meant. I just don't want to crowd you. Plus we still need to—"

"Eva." He sighed, the hard tension leaving him with that frustrated exhalation. "You have to trust me. I'm trusting you. I've had to or we wouldn't be here now."

Okay. I nodded, swallowing hard. "Dinner and your place it is, then. I honestly can't wait."

GIDEON's words about trust lingered in my mind all morning, which was a good thing when the Google alert digest hit my inbox.

There was more than one photo this time around. Each article and blog post had several shots of me and Cary hugging good-bye outside the restaurant where we'd had lunch the day before. The captions speculated on the nature of our relationship, and some noted that we lived together. Others suggested I was reeling in "billionaire playboy Cross" while keeping my up-and-coming model boyfriend on the side.

The reason for the publicity became apparent when I saw the picture of Gideon mingled with the ones of me and Cary. It had been taken last night, while I was watching movies with Cary and Trey—and while Gideon was supposedly at a business dinner. In the photo, Gideon and Magdalene Perez smiled intimately at each other, her hand on his forearm as they stood outside a restaurant. The captions ranged between kudos for Gideon's "bevy of beautiful socialites" to speculation that he was hiding a broken heart over my infidelity by dating other women.

You have to trust me.

I closed my inbox, my breathing too quick and my heartbeat too fast. Jealous confusion twisted my gut. I knew he couldn't possibly have been physically intimate with another woman, and I knew he cared for me. But I hated Magdalene with a passion—certainly she'd given me good reason to during our bathroom chat—and I couldn't stand seeing her with Gideon. Couldn't stand seeing him smiling so fondly at her, especially after the way she'd treated me.

But I put it away. I shoved it into a box in my mind and I focused on my job. Mark was meeting with Gideon tomorrow to go over the RFP for the Kingsman campaign, and I was organizing the information flowing between Mark and the contributing departments.

"Hey, Eva." Mark poked his head out of his office. "Steve and I are meeting at Bryant Park Grill for lunch. He asked if you'd come. He'd like to see you again."

"I'd love to." My whole afternoon brightened at the thought of enjoying lunch at one of my favorite restaurants with two really charming guys. They'd distract me from thinking about the conversation I was hours away from having with Gideon about my past.

My privacy was clearly gone. I would have to grow a set of balls and talk to Gideon before we went out to dinner. Before he was seen in public with me any further. He needed to know the risk he was taking by being associated with me.

When I received an interoffice envelope a short while later, I assumed it was a small mock-up of one of the Kingsman ads, but found a note card from Gideon instead.

NOON. MY OFFICE.

"Really?" I muttered, irritated by the lack of salutation and closing. Not to mention the lack of a request. And who could forget the fact that Gideon hadn't even mentioned running into Magdalene at dinner?

Had he invited her as his date in my stead? That was what she was there for, after all. To be one of the women he socialized with outside his hotel room.

I flipped Gideon's card over and wrote the same number of words with no signature:

Sorry. Have plans.

A bratty reply, but he deserved it. When a quarter to noon rolled around, Mark and I headed down to the ground floor. When I was stopped by security and the guard called up to Gideon to tell him I was in the lobby, my irritation kicked into a temper.

"Let's go," I said to Mark, striding toward the revolving door and ignoring the pleas of the security guard to wait a moment. I felt bad putting him in the middle.

I saw Angus and the Bentley at the curb at the same moment I heard Gideon snap out my name like a whip crack behind me. I faced him as he joined us on the sidewalk with his face impassive and his gaze icy.

"I'm going to lunch with my boss," I told him, my chin lifting.

"Where are you headed, Garrity?" Gideon asked without taking his eyes off me.

"Bryant Park Grill."

"I'll see that she gets there." With that, he took my arm and steered me firmly toward the Bentley and the rear door that Angus held open for me. Gideon crowded in behind me, forcing me to scramble across the seat. The door shut and we were off.

I yanked the skirt of my sheath dress back into place. "What are you doing? Besides embarrassing me in front of my boss."

He draped one arm over the back of the seat and leaned toward me. "Is Cary in love with you?"

"What? No!"

"Have you fucked him?"

"Have you lost your mind?" Mortified, I shot a glance at Angus and found him acting like he was deaf. "Screw you, billionaire playboy with your bevy of beautiful socialites."

"So you did see the photos."

I was so mad I was panting. The nerve. I turned my head away, dismissing him and his idiotic accusations. "Cary's like a brother to me. You know that."

"Ah, but what are you to him? The photos were amazingly clear, Eva. I know love when I see it."

Angus slowed for a herd of pedestrians crossing the street. I shoved the door open and looked at Gideon over my shoulder, letting him take a good look at my face. "Obviously, you don't."

I slammed the door shut and set off briskly, righteous in my anger. I'd fought back my own questions and jealousy with herculean effort, and what did I get for it? An irrationally pissed-off Gideon.

"Eva. Stop right there."

I flipped him the bird over my shoulder and raced up the short steps into Bryant Park, a lushly green and tranquil oasis in the midst of the city. Just crossing up and over from the sidewalk was like being transported to a completely different realm. Dwarfed by the towering skyscrapers surrounding it, Bryant Park was a garden land behind a beautiful old library. A place where time slowed, children laughed over the innocent joy of a carousel ride, and books were treasured companions.

Unfortunately for me, the gorgeous ogre from one world chased me into the other. Gideon caught me by the waist.

"Don't run," he hissed in my ear.

"You're acting like a nut job."

"Maybe because you drive me fucking crazy." His arms tightened into steel bands. "You're mine. Tell me Cary knows that."

"Right. Like Magdalene knows you're mine." I wished he had something near my mouth that I could bite. "You're causing a scene."

"We could've done this in my office, if you weren't so damned stubborn."

"I had plans, asshat. And you're fucking them up for me." My voice broke, tears welling as I felt the number of eyes on us. I was going to get fired for being an embarrassing spectacle. "You're fucking up everything."

Gideon instantly released me, turning me to face him. His grip on my shoulders ensured I still couldn't get away.

"Christ." He crushed me against him, his lips in my hair. "Don't cry. I'm sorry."

I beat my fist against his chest, which was as effectual as hitting a rock wall. "What's *wrong* with you? You can go out with a catty bitch who calls me a whore and thinks she's going to marry you, but I can't have lunch with a dear friend who's been pulling for you from the beginning?"

"Eva." He cupped the back of my head with one hand and pressed his cheek to my temple. "Maggie just happened to be at the same restaurant where I had dinner with my business associates."

"I don't care. You want to talk about a look on someone's face. The look on yours . . . How could you look at her like that after what she said to me?"

"Angel . . ." His lips moved ardently over my face. "That look was for you. Maggie caught me outside and I told her I was heading home to you. I can't help how I look when I'm thinking about us being alone together."

"And you expect me to believe she smiled about that?"

"She told me to tell you hello, but I figured that wouldn't go over well, and there was no way I was ruining our night over her."

My arms slid around his waist beneath his jacket. "We need to talk. Tonight, Gideon. There are things I have to tell you. If a reporter looks in the right place and gets lucky . . . We have to keep our relationship private or end it. Either would be better for you."

Gideon cupped my face and pressed his forehead to mine. "Neither is an option. Whatever it is, we'll figure it out."

I pushed up onto my toes and pressed my mouth to his. Our tongues stroked and dipped, the kiss wildly passionate. I was vaguely aware of the multitude of people milling around us, the buzz of numerous conversations, and the steady rumble of the ceaseless midtown traffic, but none of it mattered while I was sheltered by Gideon. Cherished by him. He was both tormentor and pleasurer, a man whose mood swings and volatile passions rivaled my own.

"There," he whispered, running his fingertips down my cheek. "Let *that* go viral."

"You're not listening to me, you crazy stubborn man. I have to go."

"We'll ride home together after work." He backed away, holding my hand until distance pulled our fingers apart.

When I turned toward the ivy-draped restaurant, I saw Mark and Steven waiting for me by the entrance. They made such a pair with Mark in his suit and tie and Steven in his worn jeans and boots.

Steven stood with his hands in his pockets and a big grin on his attractive face. "I feel like I should applaud. That was better than watching a chick flick."

My face heated and I shifted on my feet.

Mark opened the door and waved me inside. "I think you can ignore my previous words of wisdom about Cross's womanizing."

"Thanks for not firing me," I replied wryly as we waited for the hostess to check our reservation. "Or at least for feeding me first."

Steven patted my shoulder. "Mark can't afford to lose you."

Pulling out a chair for me, Mark smiled. "How else will I give Steven regular updates on your love life? He's a soap opera addict, you know. He loves romantic dramas."

I snorted. "You're kidding."

Steven ran a hand over his chin and smiled. "I'll never admit it one way or the other. A man's got to have his secrets."

My mouth curved, but I was painfully aware of my own hidden truths. And how quickly time was passing before I'd have to reveal them.

FIVE o'clock found me steeling myself to divulge my secrets. I was tense and somber when Gideon and I slid into the Bentley, and my disquiet only worsened when I felt him studying the side of my averted face. When he took my hand and lifted it to his lips, I felt like crying. I was still trying to adjust after our argument in the park, and that was the least of what we had to deal with.

We didn't speak until we arrived at his apartment.

When we entered his home, he led me straight through his beautiful, expansive living room and down the hall to his bedroom. There, laid out on the bed, was a fabulous cocktail dress the color of Gideon's eyes and a floor-length black silk robe.

"I had a little time to shop before dinner yesterday," he explained.

My apprehension lifted slightly, softened by pleasure at his thoughtfulness. "Thank you."

He set my bag on a chair by the dresser. "I'd like you to get comfortable. You can wear the robe or something of mine. I'll open a bottle of wine and we'll just settle in. When you're ready, we'll talk."

"I'd like to take a quick shower." I wished we could separate what happened in the park from what I had to tell him so that each issue was dealt with on its own merits, but I didn't have a choice. Every day was another opportunity for someone else to tell Gideon what he needed to hear from me.

"Whatever you want, angel. Make yourself at home."

As I kicked off my heels and moved into the bathroom, I felt the weight of his concern, but my revelations would have to hold until I could compose myself better. In an effort to gain that control, I took my time in the shower. Unfortunately, it made me remember the one we'd taken together just that morning. Had that been both our first and last as a couple?

When I was ready, I found Gideon standing by the couch in the living room. He'd changed into black silk pajama bottoms that hung low around his hips. Nothing else. A small blaze flickered in the fireplace and a bottle of wine sat in an ice-filled bucket on the coffee table. A grouping of ivory candles had been clustered as a centerpiece, their golden glow the only illumination besides the fire.

"Excuse me," I said from the threshold of the room. "I'm looking for Gideon Cross, the man who doesn't have romance in his repertoire."

He grinned sheepishly, a boyish smile so at odds with the mature sexuality of his bared body. "I don't think about it that way. I just try to guess what might please you, and then I give it a shot and hope for the best."

"*You* please me." I crossed to him, the black robe swaying around my legs. I loved that he'd put on something that matched what he had given me.

"I want to," he said soberly. "I'm working on it."

Stopping in front of him, I drank in the beauty of his face and the sexy way the ends of his hair caressed the top of his shoulders. I ran my palms down his biceps, squeezing the hard muscle gently before stepping into him and pressing my face into his chest.

"Hey," he murmured, wrapping his arms around me. "Is this about me being an ass at lunch? Or whatever it is you need to say to me? Talk to me, Eva, so I can tell you it'll be okay."

I nuzzled my nose between his pecs, feeling the tickle of crisp chest hair against my cheek and breathing in the reassuring, familiar scent of his skin. "You should sit down. I have to tell you things about me. Ugly things."

Gideon reluctantly let me go when I pulled away from him. I curled up on his couch with my legs tucked underneath me, and he poured us both glasses of golden wine before taking a seat. Leaning toward me, he draped one arm over the back of the sofa and held his glass with the other hand, giving me every bit of his attention.

"Okay. Here goes." I took a deep breath before starting, feeling dizzy from the elevated rate of my pulse. I couldn't remember the last time I'd been so nervous or sick to my stomach.

"My mother and father never married. I really don't know too much about how they met, because neither of them talks about it. I know my mom came from money. Not as much as she married into, but more than most people have. She was a debutante. Had the whole white dress and presentation thing. Getting pregnant with me was a mistake that got her disowned, but she kept me."

I looked down into my glass. "I really admire her for that. There was a lot of pressure for her to make the baby—make *me*—go away, but she went through with the pregnancy anyway. Obviously."

His fingers sifted through my shower-damp hair. "Lucky me."

I caught his fingers and kissed his knuckles, then held his hand in my lap. "Even with a kid in tow, she was able to land herself a millionaire. He was a widower with a son just two years older than me, so I think they both thought they'd found the perfect arrangement. He traveled a lot and was rarely home, and my mom spent his money and took over raising his son."

"I understand the need for money, Eva," he murmured. "I have to have it, too. I need the power of it. The security."

Our eyes met. Something passed between us with that small admission. It made it easier for me to say what came next.

"I was ten the first time my stepbrother raped me—"

The stem of his glass snapped in his hand. He moved so swiftly he was a blur, catching the bowl of his goblet against his thigh before it spilled its contents.

I scrambled to my feet when he rose to his. "Did you cut yourself? Are you okay?"

"I'm fine," he bit out. He went into the kitchen and threw the broken glass away, shattering it further. I set my own glass down carefully, my hands shaking. I heard cupboards opening and closing. A few minutes later Gideon returned with a tumbler of something darker in his hand.

"Sit down, Eva."

I stared at him. His frame was rigid, his eyes icy cold. He scrubbed a hand over his face and said more gently, "Sit down . . . please."

My weakened knees gave out and I sat on the edge of the sofa, pulling the robe tighter around me.

Gideon remained standing, taking a large swallow of whatever was in his hand. "You said the first time. How many times were there?"

I took conscious breaths, trying to calm myself. "I don't know. I lost count."

"Did you tell anyone? Did you tell your mother?"

"No. My God, if she'd known, she would've gotten me out of there. But Nathan made sure I was too afraid to tell her." I tried to swallow past a tight, dry throat and winced at the painful sandpapery burn. When my voice came again, it was barely a whisper. "There was a time when it got so bad I almost told her anyway, but he knew. Nathan could tell I was close. So he broke my cat's neck and left her on my bed."

"Jesus Christ." His chest was heaving. "He wasn't just fucked up, he was insane. And he was touching you . . . *Eva.*"

"The servants had to know," I went on numbly, staring at my twisted hands. I just wanted to get it over with, to get it all out so I could put it back into the box in my mind where I forgot about it in my day-to-day life. "The fact that they didn't say anything either told me they were scared, too. They were grown-ups and they didn't say a word. I was a child. What could I do if they wouldn't do anything?"

"How did you get out?" he asked hoarsely. "When did it end?"

"When I was fourteen. I thought I was having my period, but there was too much blood. My mother panicked and took me to the emergency room. I'd had a miscarriage. In the course of the exam they found evidence of . . . other trauma. Vaginal and anal scarring—"

Gideon set his glass down on the end table with a harsh thud.

"I'm sorry," I whispered, feeling like I might be sick. "I'd spare you the details, but you need to know what someone might dig up. The hospital reported the abuse to child services. It's all a matter of public record, which has been sealed, but there are people who know the story. When my mom married Stanton, he went back and tightened those seals, paid out in return for nondisclosure agreements . . . stuff like that. But you have a right to know that this could come out and embarrass you."

"*Embarrass* me?" he snapped, vibrating with rage. "Embarrassment isn't on the list of what I'd feel."

"Gideon—"

"I would destroy the career of any reporter who wrote about this, and then I'd dismantle the publication that ran the piece." He was so cold with fury, he was icy. "I'm going to find the monster who hurt you, Eva, wherever he is, and I'm going to make him wish he were dead."

A shiver moved through me, because I believed him. It was in his face. His voice. In the energy he exuded and his sharply honed focus. He wasn't just dark and dangerous in his looks. Gideon was a man who got what he wanted, whatever it took.

I pushed to my feet. "He's not worth the effort. Not worth your time."

"*You* are. You're worth it. Damn it. Goddamn it to hell."

I moved closer to the fireplace, needing the warmth. "There's also a money trail. Cops and reporters always follow the money. Someone may wonder why my mother left her first marriage with two million dollars, but her daughter from a previous relationship left with five."

Without looking, I felt his sudden stillness. "Of course," I went on, "that blood money's probably grown to considerably more than that now. I won't touch it, but Stanton manages the brokerage account I dumped it in and everyone knows he has the Midas touch. If you ever had any concern that I wanted your money—"

"Stop talking."

I turned to face him. I saw his face, his eyes. Saw the pity and horror. But it was what I *didn't* see that hurt the most.

It was my greatest nightmare realized. I'd feared that my past might negatively impact his attraction to me. I'd told Cary that Gideon might stay with me for all the wrong reasons. That he might stay by my side, but that I'd still—for all intents and purposes—lose him anyway.

And it seemed I had.

13

I TIGHTENED THE BELT on my robe. "I'm going to get dressed and go."

"What?" Gideon glared. "Go where?"

"Home," I said, weary to the bone. "I think you need to digest all of this."

His arms crossed. "We can do that together."

"I don't think we can." My chin lifted, grief overwhelming my shame and heartrending disappointment. "Not while you're looking at me like you feel sorry for me."

"I'm not made of fucking stone, Eva. I wouldn't be human if I didn't care."

The emotions I'd run through since lunch coalesced into a searing pain in my chest and a cleansing burst of anger. "I don't want your goddamn pity."

He shoved both hands through his hair. "What the hell do you want, then?"

"You! I want you."

"You have me. How many times do I have to tell you that?"

"Your words don't mean shit when you can't back them up. From the moment we met, you've been hot for me. You haven't been able to look at me without making it damn clear you want to fuck my brains out. And that's gone, Gideon." My eyes burned. "That look . . . it's gone."

"You can't be serious." He stared at me as if I'd grown two heads.

"I don't think you know how your desire makes me feel." My arms wrapped around me, covering my breasts. I suddenly felt naked in the worst way. "It makes me feel beautiful. It makes me feel strong and alive. I—I can't bear to be with you if you don't feel that way about me anymore."

"Eva, I . . ." His voice faded into silence. He was hard-faced and distant, his fists clenched at his sides.

I loosened the sash of my robe and shrugged the whole garment off me. "Look at me, Gideon. Look at my body. It's the same one you couldn't get enough of last night. The same one you were so desperate to get into that you took me to that damn hotel room. If you don't want this anymore . . . if you don't get hard looking at it—"

"Is this hard enough for you?" He broke the drawstring of his pants, pushing them down to expose the heavy, thickly veined length of his erection.

We both lunged at the same time, colliding. Our mouths slid over each other as he lifted me to wrap my legs around his hips. He stumbled to the couch and fell, catching our combined weight with one outstretched hand.

I sprawled beneath him, breathless and sobbing, while he slid to his knees on the floor and tongued my cleft. He was rough and impatient, lacking the finesse I'd become used to, and I loved that he was. Loved it more when he levered over me and shoved his cock into me. I wasn't yet fully wet and the burn made me gasp, and then his thumb was on my clit, rubbing in circles that had my hips churning.

"Yes," I moaned, raking my nails down his back. He wasn't icy anymore. He was on fire. "Fuck me, Gideon. Fuck me hard."

"Eva." His mouth covered mine. He fisted my hair, holding me still as he lunged again and again, pounding hard and deep. He kicked off the armrest with one foot, powering into me, driving toward his orgasm with single-minded ferocity. "Mine . . . mine . . . mine . . ."

The rhythmic slap of his heavy balls against the curve of my buttocks and the harshness of his possessive litany drove me insane with lust. I felt myself quickening with every twinge of pain, felt my sex tightening with my growing arousal.

With a long, guttural groan he started coming, his flexing body quaking as he emptied himself inside me.

I held him as he climaxed, stroking his back, pressing kisses along his shoulder.

"Hold on," he said roughly, pushing his hands beneath me and flattening my breasts against him.

Gideon pulled me up, then sat down with me straddling his hips. I was slick from his orgasm, making it easy for him to push back inside me.

His hands brushed the hair away from my face, then wiped my tears of relief. "I'm always hard for you, always hot for you. I'm always half-crazy with wanting you. If anything could change that, I would've done it before we got this far. Understand?"

My hands wrapped around his wrists. "Yes."

"Now, show me that you still want *me* after that." His face was flushed and damp, his eyes dark and turbulent. "I need to know that losing control doesn't mean I've lost you."

I pulled his palms from my face and urged them down to my breasts. When he cupped them, I splayed my hands on his shoulders and rocked my hips. He was semihard, yet quickly thickened as I began to undulate. His fingers on my nipples, rolling and tugging, sent waves of pleasure through me, the gentle stimulation arrowing to my core. When he urged me closer and took a hardened tip in his mouth I cried out, my body igniting with need for more.

Clenching my thighs, I lifted. I closed my eyes to focus on the way he felt as he slid out; then I bit my lip at the way he stretched me sliding back in.

"That's it," he murmured, licking across my chest to my other nipple, fluttering his tongue over the tight, aching tip. "Come for me. I need you to come riding my cock."

Rolling my hips, I relished the exquisite feel of him filling me so perfectly. I had no shame, no regrets as I worked myself into a frenzy on his stiff penis, adjusting the angle so that the thick crown rubbed right where I needed it.

"Gideon," I breathed. "Oh, yes . . . oh, please . . ."

"You're so beautiful." He gripped the back of my neck in one hand and my waist in the other, arching his hips to push a little deeper. "So sexy. I'm going to come for you again. That's what you do to me, Eva. It's never enough."

I whimpered as everything tightened, as the sweet tension built from the deep rhythmic strokes. I was panting and frantic, pumping my hips. Reaching between my legs, I rubbed my clit with the pads of my fingers, hastening my climax.

He gasped, his head thrown back into the sofa cushion, his neck corded with strain. "I feel you getting ready to come. Your cunt gets so hot and tight, so greedy."

His words and his voice pushed me over. I cried out when the first hard tremor hit me, then again as the orgasm rippled through my body, my sex spasming around Gideon's steely erection.

Teeth grinding audibly, he held on until the clenches began to fade; then he clutched my hips aloft and pumped upward into me. Once, twice. On the third deep thrust, he growled my name and spurted hotly, laying the last of my fears and doubts to rest.

I don't know how long we sprawled on the couch like that, connected and close, my head on his shoulder and his hands caressing the curve of my spine.

Gideon pressed his lips to my temple and murmured, "Stay."

"Yes."

He hugged me. "You're so brave, Eva. So strong and honest. You're a miracle. My miracle."

"A miracle of modern therapy, maybe," I scoffed, my fingers playing in his luxuriant hair. "And even with that, I was really fucked up for a while and there are still some triggers I don't think I'll ever get past."

"God. The way I came on to you in the beginning . . . I could've ruined us before we even got started. And the advocacy dinner—" He shuddered and buried his face in my neck. "Eva, don't let me blow this. Don't let me chase you away."

Lifting my head, I searched his face. He was impossibly gorgeous. I had trouble taking it in at times. "You can't second-guess everything you do or say to me because of Nathan and what he did. It'll break us apart. It'll end us."

"Don't say that. Don't even think about it."

I smoothed his knit brow with strokes of my thumb. "I wish I could've never told you. I wish you didn't have to know."

He caught my hand and pressed my fingertips to his lips. "I have to know everything, every part of you, inside and out, every detail."

"A woman has to have some secrets," I teased.

"You won't have any with me." He captured me by my hair and an arm banded around my hips, urging me against him, reminding me—

as if I could forget—that he was still inside me. "I'm going to possess you, Eva. It's only fair since you've possessed me."

"And what about your secrets, Gideon?"

His face smoothed into an emotionless mask, an act so easily accomplished I knew it had become second nature to him. "I started from scratch when I met you. Everything I thought I was, everything I thought I needed . . ." He shook his head. "We're figuring out who I am together. You're the only one who knows me."

But I didn't. Not really. I was figuring him out, learning him bit by bit, but he was still a mystery to me in so many ways.

"Eva . . . If you just tell me what you want—" His throat worked on a swallow. "I can get better at this, if you give me the chance. Just don't . . . don't give up on me."

Jesus. He could shred me so easily. A few words, a desperate look, and I was cut wide open.

I touched his face, his hair, his shoulders. He was as broken as I was, in a way I didn't yet know about. "I need something from you, Gideon."

"Anything. Just tell me what it is."

"Every day, I need you to tell me something I don't know about you. Something insightful, no matter how small. I need you to promise me that you will."

Gideon eyed me warily. "Whatever I want?"

I nodded, unsure of myself and what I hoped to get out of him.

He exhaled harshly. "Okay."

I kissed him softly, a silent show of thanks.

Nuzzling his nose against mine, he asked, "Let's go out to dinner. Or do you want to order in?"

"Are you sure we should go out?"

"I want to go on a date with you."

There was no way I could say no to that, not when I knew what a big step it was for him. A big step for both of us, really, since the last time we'd gone on a date it'd ended in disaster. "Sounds romantic. And irresistible."

His joyful smile was my reward, as was the shower we took to clean up. I loved the intimacy of washing his body as much as I loved the feel of his palms gliding over me. When I took his hand and put it between my legs, urging two of his fingers inside me, I saw the familiar and very welcome heat in his eyes as he felt the slick essence he'd left behind.

He kissed me and murmured, "Mine."

Which prompted me to slide both hands over his cock and whisper the same claim back to him.

In the bedroom, I lifted my new blue dress off the bed and hugged it to me. "You picked this out, Gideon?"

"I did, yes. Do you like it?"

"It's beautiful." I smiled. "My mother said you had excellent taste . . . except for your preference for brunettes."

He glanced at me just before his very fine, very firm naked ass disappeared into his massive walk-in closet. "What brunettes?"

"Ooh, nicely done."

"Look in the top drawer on the right," he called out.

Was he trying to distract me from thinking about all the brunettes he'd been photographed with—including Magdalene?

I left the dress on the bed and opened the drawer. Inside were a dozen Carine Gilson lingerie sets, all in my size, in a wide range of colors. There were also garters and silk stockings still in their packages.

I looked up at Gideon as he reappeared with his clothes in hand. "I have a drawer?"

"You have three in the dresser and two in the bathroom."

"Gideon." I smiled. "Working up to a drawer usually takes a few months."

"How would you know?" He laid his clothes on the bed. "You've lived with a man other than Cary?"

I shot him a look. "Having a drawer isn't living with someone."

"That's not an answer." He walked over and brushed me gently aside to grab a pair of boxer briefs.

Sensing his withdrawal and darkening mood, I replied before he moved away. "I haven't lived with any other men, no."

Leaning over, Gideon pressed a brusque kiss to my forehead before returning to the bed. He paused at the footboard with his back to me. "I want this relationship to mean more to you than any others you've had."

"It does. By far." I tightened the knot of the towel between my breasts. "I'm struggling with that a little. It's become important so quickly. Maybe too quickly. I keep thinking it's too good to be true."

Turning, he faced me. "Maybe it is. If so, we deserve it."

I went to him and let him pull me into his arms. It was where I wanted to be more than anywhere else.

He pressed a kiss to the crown of my head. "I can't stand the thought that you're waiting for this to end. That's what you're doing, isn't it? That's what you sound like."

"I'm sorry."

"We just have to make you feel secure." He ran his fingers through my hair. "How do we do that?"

I hesitated a moment, then went for it. "Would you go to couples therapy with me?"

The stroking of his fingers paused. He stood silently for a moment, breathing deeply.

"Just think about it," I suggested. "Maybe look into it, see what it's about."

"Am I doing this wrong? You and me? Am I fucking it up that much?"

I pulled back to look at him. "No, Gideon. You're perfect. Perfect for me, anyway. I'm crazy about you. I think you're—"

He kissed me. "I'll do it. I'll go."

I loved him in that moment. Wildly. And the moment after that. And all through the ride to what turned out to be a dazzling, intimate dinner at Masa. We were one of only three parties in the restaurant and Gideon was greeted by name on sight. The food we were served was otherworldly good and the wine too expensive to think about or I wouldn't have been able to swallow it. Gideon was darkly charismatic; his charm was relaxed and seductive.

I felt beautiful in the dress he'd chosen and my mood was light. He knew the worst of what there was to know about me, but he was still with me.

His fingertips caressed my shoulder . . . drew circles on my nape . . . slid down my back. He kissed my temple and nuzzled beneath my ear, his tongue lightly touching the sensitive skin. Beneath the table, his hand squeezed my thigh and cupped the back of my knee. My entire body vibrated with awareness of him. I wanted him so badly I ached.

"How did you meet Cary?" he asked, eyeing me over the lip of his wineglass.

"Group therapy." I set my hand over his to still its upward slide on my leg, smiling at the mischievous glimmer in his eyes. "My dad's a cop and he'd heard of this therapist who supposedly had mad skills with wild kids, which I was. Cary was seeing Dr. Travis, too."

"Mad skills, huh?" Gideon smiled.

"Dr. Travis isn't like any other therapist I've ever met. His office is an old gymnasium he converted. He had an open-door policy with 'his kids,' and hanging out there was more real to me than lying on a couch. Plus he had a no-bullshit rule. It was straight-up honesty both ways or he'd get pissed. I've always liked that about him, that he cared enough to get emotional."

"Did you choose SDSU because your dad's in Southern California?"

My mouth twisted wryly as he revealed another bit of knowledge about me that I hadn't given him. "How much have you dug up on me?"

"Whatever I could find."

"Do I want to know how extensive that is?"

He lifted my hand to his lips and kissed the back. "Probably not."

I shook my head, exasperated. "Yes, that's why I attended SDSU. I didn't get to spend a lot of time with my dad while I was growing up. Plus my mother was smothering me to death."

"And you never told your dad about what happened to you?"

"No." I rolled the stem of my wineglass between my fingers. "He knows I was an angry troublemaker with self-esteem issues, but he doesn't know about Nathan."

"Why not?"

"Because he can't change what happened. Nathan was lawfully punished. His father paid a large sum for damages. Justice was served."

Gideon spoke coolly. "I disagree."

"What more can you expect?"

He drank deeply before replying. "It's not fit to describe over dinner."

"Oh." Because that sounded ominous, especially when paired with the ice of his gaze, I returned my attention to the food in front of me. There was no menu at Masa, only *omakase*, so every bite was a surprise delight, and the dearth of patrons made it seem almost as if we had the whole place to ourselves.

After a moment, he said, "I love watching you eat."

I shot him a look. "What's that supposed to mean?"

"You eat with gusto. And your little moans of pleasure make me hard."

I bumped my shoulder into his. "By your own admission, you're always hard."

"Your fault," he said, grinning, which made me grin, too.

Gideon ate with more deliberation than I did and didn't bat an eye at the astronomical check.

Before we stepped outside, he slid his jacket over my shoulders and said, "Let's go to your gym tomorrow."

I glanced at him. "Yours is nicer."

"Of course it is. But I'll go wherever you like."

"Someplace without helpful trainers named Daniel?" I asked sweetly.

He looked at me with an arched brow and a wry curving of his lips. "Watch yourself, angel. Before I think of a suitable consequence for mocking my possessiveness where you're concerned."

I noted he didn't threaten me with a spanking again. Did he understand that administered pain with sex was a major trigger for me? It took me back to a mental place I never wanted to return to.

On the ride back to Gideon's place, I curled into him in the back of the Bentley, my legs slung over one of his thighs and my head on his shoulder. I thought about the ways Nathan's abuse still affected my life—my sex life in particular.

How many of those ghosts could Gideon and I exorcise together? After that brief glimpse of toys I'd seen in the hotel room drawer, it was clear he was more experienced and sexually adventurous than I was. And the pleasure I'd derived from the ferocity of his lovemaking on the couch earlier proved to me that he could do things to me no one else could.

"I trust you," I whispered.

His arms tightened around me. With his lips in my hair, he murmured, "We're going to be good for each other, Eva."

When I fell asleep in his arms later that night, it was with those words in my head.

"DON'T . . . No. No, don't. . . . Please."

Gideon's cries had me jackknifing up in the bed, my heart thudding violently. I fought for breath, glancing wild-eyed at the man thrashing next to me.

He snarled like a feral beast, his hands fisted and his legs kicking restlessly. I moved back, afraid he'd strike out at me unknowingly in his dreams.

"Get off me," he panted.

"Gideon! Wake up."

"Get . . . off . . ." His hips arched upward with a hiss of pain. He hovered there, teeth gritted, his back bowed as if the bed were on fire beneath him. Then he collapsed, the mattress jolting as he bounced off it.

"Gideon." I reached for the bedside lamp, my throat burning. I couldn't reach it, had to throw the tangled blankets off to get closer. Gideon was writhing in agony, thrashing so violently he shook the bed.

The room lit up in a sudden flare of illumination. I turned toward him . . .

And found him masturbating with shocking viciousness.

His right hand gripped his cock with white-knuckled force, pumping brutally fast. His left hand clenched the fitted sheet. Torment and pain twisted his beautiful face.

Fearing for his safety, I shoved his shoulder with both hands. "Gideon, goddamn it. *Wake up!*"

My scream broke through the nightmare. His eyes flew open and he jerked upright, his eyes darting frantically.

"What?" he gasped, his chest heaving. His face was flushed, his lips and cheeks red with arousal. "What is it?"

"Jesus." I shoved my hands through my hair and slid out of bed, snatching up the black robe I'd hung over the footboard.

What was in his mind? What could make someone have such violently sexual dreams?

My voice shook. "You were having a nightmare. You scared the hell out of me."

"Eva." He looked down at his erection, and his color darkened with shame.

I stared at him from my safe place by the window, tying the sash of my robe with a yank. "What were you dreaming about?"

He shook his head, his gaze lowered with humiliation, a vulnerable posture I didn't know or recognize in him. It was as if someone else had taken over Gideon's body. "I don't know."

"Bullshit. Something's in you, something's eating at you. What is it?"

He rallied visibly as his brain struggled free of sleep. "It was just a dream, Eva. People have them."

I stared at him, hurt blooming that he would take that tone with me, as if I were being irrational. "Screw you."

His shoulders squared, and he tugged the sheet over his lap. "Why are you mad?"

"Because you're lying."

His chest expanded on a deep breath; then he released it in a rush. "I'm sorry I woke you."

I pinched the bridge of my nose, feeling a headache gathering strength. My eyes stung with the need to cry for him, to cry for whatever torment he'd once lived through. And to cry for us, because if he didn't let me in, our relationship had nowhere to go.

"One more time, Gideon: What were you dreaming about?"

"I don't remember." He ran a hand through his hair and slid his legs off the edge of the bed. "I have some business on my mind and it's probably keeping me up. I'm going to work in my home office for a while. Come back to bed, and try to get some sleep."

"There were a few right answers to that question, Gideon. 'Let's talk about it tomorrow' would've been one. 'Let's talk about it over the weekend' would've been another. And even 'I'm not ready to talk about it' would be okay. But you have some nerve acting like you don't know what I'm talking about while speaking to me like I'm unreasonable."

"Angel—"

"Don't." My arms wrapped around my waist. "Do you think it was easy telling you about my past? Do you think it was painless cutting myself open and letting the ugliness spill out? It would've been simpler to cut *you* off and date someone less prominent. I took the risk because I want to be with you. Maybe someday you'll feel the same way about me."

I left the room.

"Eva! Eva, damn it, come back here. What's wrong with you?"

I walked faster. I knew how he felt: the sickness in the gut that spread like cancer, the helpless anger, and the need to curl up in private and find the strength to shove the memories back into the deep, dark hole they still lived in.

It wasn't an excuse for lying or deflecting the blame onto me.

I snatched my purse off the chair where I'd dropped it on the way in from dinner and rushed out the front door into the foyer to the elevator. The car doors were closing with me inside when I saw him step into the living room through the open front door. His nakedness ensured he couldn't come after me, while the look in his eyes ensured I wouldn't stay. He'd donned his mask again, that striking implacable face that kept the world a safe distance away.

Shaking, I leaned heavily against the brass handrail for support. I was torn between my concern for him, which urged me to stay, and my hard-won knowledge, which assured me that his coping strategy wasn't one I could live with. The road to recovery for me was paved with hard truths, not denials and lies.

Swiping at my wet cheeks when I passed the third floor, I took deep breaths and collected myself before the doors opened on the lobby level.

The doorman whistled down a passing cab for me and was such a consummate professional that he acted like I was dressed for work rather than sporting bare feet and a black dressing gown. I thanked him sincerely.

And I was so grateful to the cabbie for getting me home quickly that I tipped him well and didn't care about the furtive looks I got from my own doorman and the front desk staffer. I didn't even care about the look I got from the stunning, statuesque blonde who stepped out of the elevator I was waiting for, until I smelled Cary's cologne on her and realized the T-shirt she was wearing was one of his.

She took in my half-dressed state with an amused glance. "Nice robe."

"Nice shirt."

The blonde took off with a smirk.

When I reached my floor, I found Cary lounging in the open doorway in a robe of his own.

He straightened and opened his arms to me. "Come here, baby girl."

I walked straight into him and hugged him tight, smelling a woman's perfume and hard sex all over him. "Who's the chick that just left?"

"Another model. Don't worry about her." He drew me into the apartment and shut and locked the door. "Cross called. He said you were heading back and he has your keys. He wanted to be sure I was here and awake to let you in. For what it's worth, he sounded torn up and anxious. You wanna talk about it?"

Setting my purse down on the breakfast bar, I went into the kitchen. "He had another nightmare. A really bad one. When I asked him about it he denied, he lied, then he acted like I was nuts."

"Ah, the classics."

The phone started ringing. I flicked the switch on the base that turned the ringer off and Cary did the same to the handset he'd left on the counter. Then I pulled out my smartphone, closed the alert that said I'd missed numerous calls from Gideon, and sent him a text message: Home safe. Hope you sleep well the rest of the night.

I powered the phone off and tossed it back in my purse; then I grabbed a bottle of water from the fridge. "The kicker is that I told him all my junk earlier tonight."

Cary's brows shot up. "So you did it. How'd he take it?"

"Better than I had any right to expect. Nathan ought to hope they never run into each other." I finished the bottle. "And Gideon agreed to the couples counseling you suggested. I thought we'd turned a corner. Maybe we did, but we hit a brick wall anyway."

"You seem okay, though." He leaned into the breakfast bar. "No tears. Really calm. Should I be worried?"

I rubbed my belly to ease the fear that had rooted there. "No, I'll be all right. I just . . . I want it to work out between us. I want to be with him, but lying about serious issues is a deal breaker for me."

God. I couldn't let myself even consider that we might not get past this. I was already feeling antsy. The need to be with Gideon was a frantic beat in my blood.

"You're a tough cookie, baby girl. I'm proud of you." He came to me, linked our arms, and turned off the kitchen lights. "Let's crash and start a new day when we wake up."

"I thought things were going well with you and Trey."

His grin was glorious. "Honey, I think I'm in love."

"With who?" I leaned my cheek against his shoulder. "Trey or the blonde?"

"Trey, silly. The blonde just provided a workout."

I had a lot to say about that, but it wasn't the time to get into Cary's history of sabotaging his own happiness. And maybe focusing on how good things were with Trey was the best way to handle this instance of it. "So you've finally fallen for a good guy. We should celebrate."

"Hey, that's my line."

14

THE NEXT MORNING dawned with an odd surreality. I made it to work, and then through most of my prelunch day in a kind of chilly fog. I couldn't get warm enough, despite wearing a cardigan over my blouse and a scarf that didn't match either one. It took me a few minutes longer to process requests than it should have, and I couldn't shake a feeling of dread.

Gideon made no contact with me whatsoever.

Nothing on my smartphone or e-mail after my text last night. Nothing in my e-mail inbox. No interoffice note.

The silence was excruciating. Especially when the day's Google alert hit my inbox and I saw the photos and phone videos of me and Gideon in Bryant Park. Seeing how we looked together—the passion and need, the painful longing on our faces, and the gratefulness of reconciliation—was bittersweet.

Pain twisted in my chest. *Gideon.*

If we couldn't work this out, would I ever stop thinking about him and wishing we had?

I struggled to pull myself together. Mark was meeting with Gideon today. Maybe that was why Gideon hadn't felt pressed to contact me. Or maybe he was just really busy. I knew he had to be, considering his business calendar. And as far as I knew, we still had plans to go to the gym after work. I exhaled in a rush and told myself that things would straighten out somehow. They just had to.

It was quarter to noon when my desk phone rang. Seeing from the readout that the call was coming from reception, I sighed with disappointment and answered.

"Hey, Eva," Megumi said cheerily. "You have a Magdalene Perez here to see you."

"Do I?" I stared at my monitor, confused and irritated. Had the Bryant Park photos lured Magdalene out from under whatever troll bridge she called home?

Regardless of the reason, I had no interest in talking to her. "Keep her up there for me, will you? I have to take care of something first."

"Sure. I'll tell her to have a seat."

I hung up, then pulled out my smartphone and scrolled through the contact list until I found the number to Gideon's office. I dialed and was relieved when Scott answered.

"Hey, Scott. It's Eva Tramell."

"Hi, Eva. Would you like to speak to Mr. Cross? He's in a meeting at the moment, but I can buzz him."

"No. No, don't bother him."

"It's a standing order. He won't mind."

It soothed me immensely to hear that. "I hate to throw this in your lap, but I have a request for you."

"Anything you need. That's also a standing order." The amusement in his voice relaxed me further.

"Magdalene Perez is down here on the twentieth floor. Frankly, the only thing she and I have in common is Gideon, and that's not a good thing. If she has something to say, it's your boss she should be talking to. Could you please have someone escort her up?"

"Absolutely. I'll take care of it now."

"Thanks, Scott. I appreciate you."

"It's my pleasure, Eva."

I hung up the phone and sagged back in my seat, feeling better already and proud of myself for not letting jealousy get the better of me. While I still really hated the idea of her having any of Gideon's time, I hadn't lied when I'd said I trusted him. I believed he had strong, deep feelings for me. I just didn't know if they were enough to override his survival instinct.

Megumi called me again.

"Oh my God," she said, laughing. "You should've seen her face when whoever that was came to get her."

"Good." I grinned. "I figured she was up to no good. Is she gone, then?"

"Yep."

"Thanks." I crossed the narrow strip of hallway to Mark's door and poked my head in to see if he wanted me to pick him up some lunch.

He frowned, thinking about it. "No, thanks. I'll be too nervous to eat until after the presentation with Cross. By then whatever you pick up will be hours old."

"How about a protein smoothie, then? It'll give you some easy fuel until you can eat."

"That'd be great." His smile lit up his dark eyes. "Something that goes good with vodka, just to get me in the mood."

"Anything you don't like? Any allergies?"

"Nada."

"Okay. See you in an hour." I knew just the place to go. The deli I had in mind was a couple blocks up and offered smoothies, salads, and a variety of made-to-order paninis with quick service.

I headed downstairs and tried not to think about Gideon's radio silence. I'd kind of expected to hear *something* after the Magdalene incident. Getting no reaction had me worrying all over again. I pushed out to the street through the revolving door and scarcely paid any attention to the man who climbed out of the back of a town car at the curb until he called my name.

Turning, I found myself facing Christopher Vidal.

"Oh . . . Hi," I greeted him. "How are you?"

"Better, now that I've seen you. You look fantastic."

"Thanks. I can say the same to you."

As different as he was from Gideon, he was gorgeous in his own way with his mahogany waves, grayish-green eyes, and charming smile. He was dressed in loose-fitting jeans and a cream V-neck sweater, a very sexy look for him.

"Are you here to see your brother?" I asked.

"Yes, and you."

"Me?"

"Heading to lunch? I'll join you and explain."

I was briefly reminded of Gideon's warning to stay away from Christopher, but by now I figured he trusted me. Especially with his brother.

"I'm going to a deli up the street," I said. "If you're game."

"Absolutely."

We started walking.

"What did you want to see me about?" I asked, too curious to wait.

He reached into one of two large cargo pockets of his jeans and pulled out a formal invitation in a vellum envelope. "I came to invite you to a garden party we're having at my parents' estate on Sunday. A mix of business and pleasure. Many of the artists signed to Vidal Records will be there. I was thinking it'd be great networking for your roommate—he's got the right look for music video."

I brightened. "That would be wonderful!"

Christopher grinned and passed the invite over. "And you'll both have fun. No one throws a party like my mother."

I glanced briefly at the envelope in my hand. Why hadn't Gideon said anything about the event?

"If you're wondering why Gideon didn't tell you about it," he said, seemingly reading my mind, "it's because he won't come. He never does. Even though he's the majority shareholder in the company, I think he finds the music industry and musicians too unpredictable for his tastes. By now, you know how he is."

Dark and intense. Powerfully magnetic and hotly sexual. Yes, I knew how he was. And he preferred to know what he was getting into at all costs.

I gestured at the deli when we reached it, and we stepped inside and got in line.

"This place smells awesome," Christopher said, his gaze on his phone as he typed out a quick text.

"The aroma delivers on its promise, trust me."

He smiled a delightful boyish smile that I was sure knocked most women on their asses. "My parents are really looking forward to meeting you, Eva."

"Oh?"

"Seeing the photos of you and Gideon over the last week has been a real surprise. A good surprise," he qualified quickly when I winced. "It's the first time we've seen him really into someone he's dating."

I sighed, thinking he wasn't so into me right now. Had I made a terrible mistake by leaving him alone last night?

When we reached the counter, I ordered a grilled vegetable-and-cheese panini with two pomegranate smoothies, asking them to hold the one with a protein shot for thirty minutes so I could eat in. Christopher ordered the same, and we managed to find a table in the crowded deli.

We talked about work, laughing over both a recent baby food commercial faux-blooper that had gone viral and some backstage anecdotes about acts Christopher had worked with. The time passed swiftly, and when we parted ways at the entrance of the Crossfire, I said good-bye with genuine affection.

I headed up to the twentieth floor and found Mark still at his desk. He offered me a quick smile despite his air of concentration.

"If you don't really need me," I said, "I think it'd be good for me to sit this presentation out."

Although he tried to hide it, I saw the lightning-quick flash of relief. It didn't offend me. Stress was stress, and my volatile relationship with Gideon was something Mark didn't need to think about while he was working on an important account.

"You're golden, Eva. You know that?"

I smiled and set the drink carrier down in front of him. "Drink your smoothie. It's really good, and the protein will keep you from feeling too hungry for a little bit longer. I'll be at my desk if you need me."

Before I put my purse in the drawer, I texted Cary to ask if he had plans on Sunday and if he'd like to go to a Vidal Records party. Then I got back to work. I'd started organizing Mark's files on the server, tagging them and placing them in directories to make it easier for us to assemble portfolios on the fly.

When Mark left for the meeting with Gideon, my heartbeat quickened and a clutch of anticipation tightened my stomach. I couldn't believe my excitement just from knowing what Gideon was doing at that particular moment, and that he'd have to think of me when he saw Mark. I hoped I'd hear from him after that. My mood picked up at the thought.

For the next hour, I was restless waiting to hear how things had gone. When Mark reappeared with a big grin and a spring in his step, I stood up in my cubicle and applauded him.

He took a gallant, exaggerated bow. "Thank you, Miss Tramell."

"I'm so stoked for you!"

"Cross asked me to give you this." He handed me a sealed manila envelope. "Come to my office and I'll give you all the deets."

The envelope had weight and rattled. I knew from touch what I'd find inside before I opened it, but still the sight of my keys sliding out and into my palm hit me hard. Gasping with a pain more intense than any I could remember, I read the accompanying note card.

> THANK YOU, EVA. FOR EVERYTHING.
> YOURS, G

A Dear Jane brush-off. It had to be. Otherwise, he would've given me the keys after work on the way to the gym.

There was a dull roaring in my ears. I felt dizzy. Disoriented. I was frightened and agonized. Furious.

I was also at work.

Closing my eyes and clenching my fists, I pulled myself together and fought off the driving urge to go upstairs and call Gideon a coward. He probably saw me as a threat, someone who'd come in, unwanted and uninvited, and shaken up his orderly world. Someone who'd demanded more from him than just his hot body and hefty bank account.

I shut my emotions behind a glass wall, where I was aware of them waiting in the background, but I was able to get through the rest of my workday. By the time I clocked out and headed downstairs, I still hadn't heard from Gideon. I was such an emotional disaster at that point I felt only a single, sharp twinge of despair as I exited the Crossfire.

I made it to the gym. I shut my brain off and ran full-bore on the treadmill, fleeing the anguish that would hit me soon enough. I ran until sweat coursed in rivulets down my face and body, and rubber legs forced me to stop.

Feeling battered and exhausted, I hit the showers. Then I called my mother and asked her to send Clancy to the gym to pick me up for our appointment with Dr. Petersen. As I put my work clothes back on, I mustered the energy to get through that last task before I could go home and collapse on my bed.

I waited for the town car at the curb, feeling separate and apart from the city teeming around me. When Clancy pulled up and hopped out to open the back door for me, I was startled to see my mom already inside. It was early yet. I'd expected to be driven solo to the apartment she shared with Stanton and wait on her for twenty minutes or so. That was our usual routine.

"Hey, Mom," I said wearily, settling on the seat beside her.

"How could you, Eva?" She was crying into a monogrammed handkerchief, her face beautiful even while reddened and wet with tears. *"Why?"*

Jolted out of my torment by her misery, I frowned and asked, "What did I do now?"

The new smartphone, if she'd somehow found out about it, wouldn't trigger this much drama. And it was too soon after the fact for her to know about my breakup with Gideon.

"You told Gideon Cross about . . . what happened to you." Her lower lip trembled with distress.

My head jerked back in shock. How could she know that? My God . . . Had she bugged my new place? My purse . . . ? *"What?"*

"Don't act clueless!"

"How do you know I told him?" My voice was a pained whisper.

"We just talked last night."

"He went to see Richard about it today."

I tried to picture Stanton's face during *that* conversation. I couldn't imagine my stepfather taking it well. "Why would he do that?"

"He wanted to know what's been done to prevent information

leaks. And he wanted to know where Nathan is—" She sobbed. "He wanted to know everything."

My breath hissed out between my teeth. I wasn't sure what Gideon's motivation was, but the possibility that he'd dumped me over Nathan and was now making sure that he was safe from scandal hurt worse than anything. I twisted in pain, my spine arching away from the seat back. I'd thought it was *his* past that drove a wedge between us, but it made more sense that it was *mine*.

For once I was grateful for my mother's self-absorption, which kept her from seeing how devastated I was.

"He had a right to know," I managed in a voice so raw it sounded nothing like my own. "And he has a right to try to protect himself from any blowback."

"You've never told any of your other boyfriends."

"I've never dated anyone who makes national headlines by sneezing either." I stared out the car window at the traffic that boxed us in. "Gideon Cross and Cross Industries are global news, Mother. He's light-years away from the guys I dated in college."

She spoke more, but I didn't hear her. I shut down for self-protection, cutting off the reality that was suddenly too painful to be endured.

DR. Petersen's office was exactly as I remembered. Decorated in soothing neutrals, it was both professional and comfortable. Dr. Petersen was the same—a handsome man with gray hair and gentle, intelligent blue eyes.

He welcomed us into his office with a wide smile, commenting on how lovely my mother looked and how like her I was. He said he was happy to see me again and that I looked well, but I could tell he spoke for my mother's benefit. He was too trained an observer to miss the raging emotions I suppressed.

"So," he began, settling into his chair across from the sofa my mother and I sat on. "What brings you both in today?"

I told him about the way my mom had been tracking my movements via my cell phone signal and how violated I felt. Mom told him about my interest in Krav Maga and how she took it as a sign that I wasn't feeling safe. I told him about how my mom and Stanton had pretty much taken over Parker's studio, which made me feel suffocated and claustrophobic. She told him I'd betrayed her trust by divulging deeply personal matters to strangers, which made her feel naked and painfully exposed.

Through it all, Dr. Petersen listened attentively, took notes, and spoke rarely, until we'd purged everything.

Once we'd quieted, he asked, "Monica, why didn't you tell me about tracking Eva's cell phone?"

The angle of her chin altered, a familiar defensive posture. "I didn't see anything wrong with it. Many parents track their children through their cell phones."

"Underage children," I shot back. "I'm an adult. My personal time is exactly that."

"If you were to envision yourself in her place, Monica," Dr. Petersen interjected, "would it be possible that you might feel as she does? What if you discovered someone was monitoring your movements without your knowledge or permission?"

"Not if the someone was my mother and I knew it gave her peace of mind," she argued.

"And have you considered how your actions affect Eva's peace of mind?" he queried gently. "Your need to protect her is understandable, but you should discuss the steps you wish to take openly with her. It's important to gain her input—and expect cooperation only when she chooses to give it. You have to honor her prerogative to set limits that may not be as broad as you'd like them to be."

My mother sputtered indignantly.

"Eva needs her boundaries, Monica," he continued, "and a sense of control over her own life. Those things were taken from her for a long time, and we have to respect her right to establish them now in the manner that best suits her."

"Oh." My mother twisted her handkerchief around her fingers. "I hadn't thought of it that way."

I reached out for my mother's hand when her lower lip trembled violently. "Nothing could've stopped me from talking to Gideon about my past. But I could have forewarned you. I'm sorry I didn't think of it."

"You're much stronger than I ever was," my mother said, "but I can't help worrying."

"My suggestion," Dr. Petersen said, "would be for you to take some time, Monica, and really think about what sorts of events and situations cause you anxiety. Then write them down."

My mother nodded.

"When you have what will surely not be an exhaustive list but a strong start," he went on, "you can sit down with Eva and discuss strategies for addressing those concerns—strategies you can both live with comfortably. For example, if not hearing from Eva for a few days troubles you, perhaps a text message or an e-mail will alleviate that."

"Okay."

"If you like, we can go over the list together."

The back-and-forth between the two made me want to scream. It was insult to injury. I hadn't expected Dr. Petersen to smack some sense into my mom, but I'd hoped he would at least take a harder line—God knew someone needed to, someone whose authority she respected.

When the hour ended and we were on our way out, I asked my mom to wait a moment so I could ask Dr. Petersen one last personal and private question.

"Yes, Eva?" He stood in front of me, looking infinitely patient and wise.

"I just wondered . . ." I paused, needing to swallow past a lump in my throat. "Is it possible for two abuse survivors to have a functional romantic relationship?"

"Absolutely." His immediate, unequivocal answer forced the trapped air from my lungs.

I shook his hand. "Thank you."

WHEN I got home, I unlocked my door with the keys Gideon had returned to me and went straight to my room, offering a lame wave to Cary, who was practicing yoga in the living room to a DVD.

I stripped off my clothes as I crossed the distance from my closed bedroom door to the bed, finally crawling between the cool sheets in just my underwear. I hugged a pillow and closed my eyes, so tired and drained I had nothing left.

The door opened at my back, and a moment later Cary sat beside me.

He brushed my hair away from my tear-streaked face. "What's the matter, baby girl?"

"I got kicked to the curb today. Courtesy of a fucking note card."

He sighed. "You know the drill, Eva. He's going to keep pushing you away, because he's expecting you to fail him like everyone else has."

"And I keep proving him right." I recognized myself in the description Cary had just given. I ran when the going got tough, because I was so sure it was all going to end badly. The only control I had was to be the one who left, instead of the one who was left behind.

"Because you're fighting to protect your own recovery." He lay down and spooned against my back, wrapping one leanly muscular arm around me and tucking me tight against him.

I snuggled into the physical affection I hadn't realized I needed. "He might've dumped me because of *my* past, not his."

"If that's true, it's good it's over. But I think you two will find each other eventually. At least I'm hoping you will." His sigh was soft on my neck. "I want there to be happily-ever-afters for the fucked-up crowd. Show me the way, Eva honey. Make me believe."

15

FRIDAY FOUND TREY sharing breakfast with Cary and me after an overnighter. As I drank the day's first cup of coffee, I watched him interact with Cary and was genuinely thrilled to see the intimate smiles and covert touches they gave each other.

I'd had easy relationships like that and hadn't appreciated them at the time. They had been comfortable and uncomplicated, but they'd been superficial in a fundamental way, too.

How deep could a love affair get if you didn't know the darkest recesses of your lover's soul? That was the dilemma I'd faced with Gideon.

Day Two After Gideon had begun. I found myself wanting to go to him and apologize for leaving him. I wanted to tell him I was there for him, ready to listen or simply offer silent comfort. But I was too emotionally invested. I got wounded too easily. I was too afraid of rejection. And knowing he wouldn't let me get too close only intensified that fear. Even if we did figure things out, I'd only tear myself apart trying to live with just the bits and pieces he decided to share with me.

At least my job was going well. The celebratory lunch the executives gave in honor of the agency landing the Kingsman account made me genuinely happy. I felt blessed to work in such a positive environment. But when I heard that Gideon had been invited—although no one expected him to show up—I returned quietly to my desk and focused on work the rest of the afternoon.

I hit the gym on the way home, then picked up some items to make fettuccini alfredo for dinner with crème brûlée for dessert—comfort food guaranteed to put me in a carbohydrate coma. I expected sleep to offer me a break from the endless what-ifs my brain was recycling, hopefully long into Saturday morning.

Cary and I ate in the living room with chopsticks, his idea to cheer me up. He said dinner was great, but I couldn't tell. I snapped out of it when he fell silent, too, and I realized I was being a less than stellar friend.

"When are the Grey Isles campaign ads going up?" I asked.

"I'm not sure, but get this . . ." He grinned. "You know how it is with male models—we're tossed around like condoms at an orgy. It's tough to stand out from the crowd, unless you're dating someone famous. Which I'm suddenly reported to be doing since those photos of you and me were plastered everywhere. I'm the side piece of action in your relationship with Gideon Cross. You've done wonders for making me a hot commodity."

I laughed. "You didn't need my help for that."

"Well, it certainly didn't hurt. Anyway, they called me back for a couple more shoots. I think they might just use me for more than five minutes."

"We'll have to celebrate," I teased.

"Absolutely. When you're up for it."

We ended up hanging out and watching the original *Tron*. His smartphone rang twenty minutes into the movie and I heard him speaking to his agency. "Sure. I'll be there in fifteen, tops. I'll call you when I get there."

"Got a job?" I asked after he'd hung up.

"Yeah. A model showed up for a night shoot so trashed he's worthless." He studied me. "You wanna come?"

I stretched my legs out on the couch. "Nope. I'm good right here."

"You sure you're okay?"

"All I need is mindless entertainment. Just the thought of getting dressed again exhausts me." I'd be happy wearing my flannel pajama bottoms and holey old tank top all weekend. As much as I hurt inside, total comfort outside seemed like a necessity. "Don't worry about me. I know I've been a mess lately, but I'll get it together. Go on and enjoy yourself."

After Cary rushed out, I paused the movie and went to the kitchen for some wine. I stopped by the breakfast bar, my fingertips gliding over the roses Gideon had sent me the previous weekend. Petals fell to the countertop like tears. I thought about cutting the stems and using the flower food packet that came with the bouquet, but it was pointless hanging on to them. I'd throw the arrangement away tomorrow, the last reminder of my equally doomed relationship.

I'd gotten further with Gideon in one week than I had with other relationships that lasted two years. I would always love him for that. Maybe I'd always love him, period.

And one day, that might not hurt so badly.

"RISE and shine, sleepyhead," Cary singsonged as he yanked the comforter off me.

"Ugh. Go away."

"You've got five minutes to get your ass up and in the shower, or the shower's coming to you."

Opening one eye, I peeked at him. He was shirtless and wearing baggy pants that barely clung to his hips. As far as wake-up calls went, he was prime. "Why do I have to get up?"

"Because when you're flat on your back you're not on your feet."

"Wow. That was deep, Cary Taylor."

He crossed his arms and shot me an arch look. "We need to go shopping."

I buried my face in the pillow. "No."

"Yes. I seem to remember you saying this was a 'Sunday garden party' and 'rock star gathering' in the same sentence. What the hell do I wear to something like that?"

"Ah, well. Good point."

"What are you wearing?"

"I . . . I don't know. I was leaning toward the 'English tea with hat' look, but now I'm not so sure."

He gave a brisk nod. "Right. Let's hit the shops and find something sexy, classy, and cool."

Growling a token protest, I rolled out of bed and padded over to the bathroom. It was impossible to shower without thinking of Gideon, without picturing his perfect body and remembering the desperate sounds he made when he came in my mouth. Everywhere I looked, Gideon was there. I'd even started hallucinating black Bentley SUVs all around town. I thought I spotted one damn near everywhere I went.

Cary and I had lunch; then we bounced all over the city, hitting the best of the Upper East Side thrift stores and Madison Avenue boutiques before taking a taxi downtown to SoHo. Along the way, Cary had two teenage girls ask for his autograph, which tickled me more than him, I think.

"Told you," he crowed.

"Told me what?"

"They recognized me from an entertainment news blog. One of the posts about you and Cross."

I snorted. "Glad my love life is working out for someone."

He was due at another job around three and I went with him, spending a few hours in the studio of a loud and brash photographer. Remembering it was Saturday, I slipped into a far corner and made my weekly call to my dad.

"You still happy in New York?" he asked me above the background noise of dispatch talking over the radio in his cruiser.

"So far so good." A lie, but the truth helped no one.

His partner said something I didn't catch. My dad snorted and said, "Hey, Chris insists he saw you on television the other day. Some cable channel, celebrity gossip thing. The guys won't leave me alone about it."

I sighed. "Tell them watching those shows is bad for their brain cells."

"So you're not dating one of the richest men in America?"

"No. What about your love life?" I asked, quickly diverting. "Are you seeing anyone?"

"Nothing serious. Hang on." He responded to a call on the radio, then said, "Sorry, sweetheart. I have to run. I love you. Miss you like crazy."

"I miss you, too, Daddy. Be careful."

"Always. Bye."

I killed the call and went back to my former spot to wait for Cary to wrap things up. In the lull, my mind tormented me. Where was Gideon now? What was he doing?

Would Monday bring me an inbox full of photos of him with another woman?

SUNDAY afternoon I borrowed Clancy and one of Stanton's town cars for the drive out to the Vidal estate in Dutchess County. Leaning back in the seat, I looked out the window, absently admiring the serene vista of rolling meadows and green woodlands that stretched to the distant horizon. I realized I was working on Day Four After Gideon. The pain I'd felt the first few days had turned into a dull throbbing that felt almost like the flu. Every part of my body ached, as if I were going through some sort of physical withdrawal, and my throat burned with unshed tears.

"Are you nervous?" Cary asked me.

I glanced at him. "Not really. Gideon won't be there."

"You're sure about that?"

"I wouldn't be going if I thought otherwise. I do have some pride, you know." I watched him drum his fingers on the armrest between our two seats. For all the shopping we'd done yesterday, he'd made only one purchase: a black leather tie. I'd teased him mercilessly about it, he of the perfect fashion sense going with something like that.

He caught me looking at it. "What? You still don't like my tie? I think it works well with the emo jeans and my lounge lizard jacket."

"Cary"—my lips quirked—"you can wear anything."

It was true. Cary could pull off any look, a benefit of having a sculpted, rangy body and a face that could make angels weep.

I set my hand over his restless fingers. "Are *you* nervous?"

"Trey didn't call last night," he muttered. "He said he would."

I gave his hand a reassuring squeeze. "It's just one missed call, Cary. I'm sure it doesn't mean anything serious."

"He could've called this morning," he argued. "Trey's not flaky like the others I've dated. He wouldn't have forgotten to call, which means he just doesn't want to."

"The rat bastard. I'll be sure to take lots of pictures of you having a great time looking sexy, classy, and cool to torment him with on Monday."

His mouth twitched. "Ah, the deviousness of the female mind. It's a shame Cross won't see you today. I think I got a semi when you came out of your room in that dress."

"Eww!" I smacked his shoulder and mock-glared when he laughed.

The dress had seemed perfect to both of us when we'd found it. It was cut in a classic garden party style—fitted bodice with a knee-length skirt that flared out from the waist. It was even white with flowers. But that was where the tea-and-crumpets style ended.

The edginess came from the strapless form, the alternating layers of black and crimson satin underskirts that gave it volume, and the black leather flowers that looked like wicked pinwheels. Cary had picked the red Jimmy Choo peep-toe pumps out of my closet and the ruby drop earrings to give it all the finishing touch. We'd decided to leave my hair loose around my shoulders, in case we arrived and learned that hats were required. All in all, I felt pretty and confident.

Clancy drove us through an imposing set of monogrammed gates and turned into a circular driveway, following the direction of a valet. Cary and I got out by the entrance, and he took my arm as my heels sank into blue-gray gravel on the walk to the house.

Upon entering the Vidals' sprawling Tudor-style mansion, we were warmly greeted by Gideon's family in a receiving line—his mother, his stepfather, Christopher, and their sister.

I took in the sight, thinking the Vidal family could only look more perfect if Gideon were lined up with them. His mother and sister had his coloring, both women boasting the same glossy obsidian hair and thickly lashed blue eyes. They were both beautiful in a finely wrought way.

"Eva!" Gideon's mother drew me toward her, then air-kissed both of my cheeks. "I'm so pleased to finally meet you. What a gorgeous girl you are! And your dress. I love it."

"Thank you."

Her hands brushed over my hair, cupped my face, and then slid down my arms. It was hard for me to bear it, because touching was sometimes an anxiety trigger for me when the person was a stranger. "Your hair, is it naturally blond?"

"Yes," I replied, startled and confused by the question. Who asked a question like that of a stranger?

"How fascinating. Well, welcome. I hope you have a wonderful time. We're so glad you could make it."

Feeling strangely unsettled, I was grateful when her attention moved to Cary and zeroed in.

"And you must be Cary," she crooned. "Here I'd been certain my two boys were the most attractive in the world. I see I was wrong about that. You are simply divine, young man."

Cary flashed his megawatt smile. "Ah, I think I'm in love, Mrs. Vidal."

She laughed with throaty delight. "Please. Call me Elizabeth. Or Lizzie, if you're brave enough."

Looking away, I found my hand clasped by Christopher Vidal Sr. In many ways, he reminded me of his son, with his slate green eyes and boyish smile. In others, he was a pleasant surprise. Dressed in khakis, loafers, and a cashmere cardigan, he looked more like a college professor than a music company executive.

"Eva. May I call you Eva?"

"Please do."

"Call me Chris. It makes it a little easier to distinguish between me and Christopher." His head tilted to the side as he contemplated me through quirky brass spectacles. "I can see why Gideon is so taken with you. Your eyes are a stormy gray, yet they're so clear and direct. Quite the most beautiful eyes I think I've ever seen, aside from my wife's."

I flushed. "Thank you."

"Is Gideon coming?"

"Not that I'm aware of." Why didn't his parents know the answer to that question?

"We always hope." He gestured at a waiting servant. "Please head back to the gardens and make yourself at home."

Christopher greeted me with a hug and a kiss on the cheek, while Gideon's sister, Ireland, sized me up in a sulky way that only a teenager could pull off. "You're a blonde," she said.

Jeez. Was Gideon's preference for dark-haired women a damn law or something? "And you're a very lovely brunette."

Cary offered me his arm and I accepted it gratefully.

As we walked away, he asked me quietly, "Were they what you expected?"

"His mom, maybe. His stepdad, no." I looked back over my shoulder, taking in the elegant floor-length cream sheath dress that clung to Elizabeth Vidal's svelte figure. I thought of what little I knew about Gideon's family. "How does a boy grow up to be a businessman who takes over his stepfather's family business?"

"Cross owns shares in Vidal Records?"

"Controlling interest."

"Hmm. Maybe it was a bailout?" he offered. "A helping hand during a trying time for the music industry?"

"Why not just give him the money?" I wondered.

"Because he's a shrewd businessman?"

With a sharp exhalation, I waved the question away and cleared my mind. I was attending the party for Cary, not Gideon, and I was going to keep that first and foremost in my thoughts.

Once we'd moved outside, we found a large, elaborately decorated marquee erected in the rear garden. Although the day was beautiful enough to stay out in the sun, I found a seat at a circular table covered in white damask instead.

Cary patted my shoulder. "You relax. I'll network."

"Go get 'em."

He moved away, intent on his agenda.

I sipped champagne and chatted with everyone who stopped by to strike up a conversation. There were a lot of recording artists at the party whose work I listened to, and I watched them covertly, a bit star-struck. For all the elegance of the surroundings and the endless number of servants, the overall vibe was casual and relaxed.

I was starting to enjoy myself when someone I'd hoped never to see again stepped out of the house onto the terrace: Magdalene Perez, looking phenomenal in a rose-hued chiffon gown that floated around her knees.

A hand settled on my shoulder and squeezed, setting my heart racing because it reminded me of the night Cary and I had gone to Gideon's club. But the figure that rounded me this time was Christopher.

"Hey, Eva." He took the chair next to mine and set his elbows on his knees, leaning toward me. "Are you having fun? You're not min-gling much."

"I'm having a great time." At least I had been. "Thank you for inviting me."

"Thank you for coming. My parents are stoked you're here. Me, too, of course." His grin made me smile, as did his tie, which had car-toon vinyl records all over it. "Are you hungry? The crab cakes are great. Grab one when the tray comes by."

"I'll do that."

"Let me know if you need anything. And save a dance for me." He winked, then hopped up and away.

Ireland took his seat, arranging herself with the practiced grace of a finishing-school graduate. Her hair fell in a single length to her waist, and her beautiful eyes were direct in a way I could appreciate. She looked worldlier than the seventeen years I'd calculated her to be, based on the newspaper clippings Cary had collected. "Hi."

"Hello."

"Where's Gideon?"

I shrugged at the blunt question. "I'm not sure."

She nodded sagely. "He's good at being a loner."

"Has he always been that way?"

"I guess. He moved out when I was little. Do you love him?"

My breath caught for a second. I released it in a rush and said simply, "Yes."

"I thought so when I saw that video of you two in Bryant Park." She bit her lush lower lip. "Is he fun? You know . . . to hang around with?"

"Oh. Well . . ." God. Did *anyone* know Gideon? "I wouldn't say he's fun, but he's never boring."

The live band began playing "Come Fly with Me," and Cary appeared beside me as if by magic. "Time to make me look good, Ginger."

"I'll try my best, Fred." I smiled at Ireland. "Excuse me a minute."

"Three minutes, nineteen seconds," she corrected, displaying some of her family's expertise in music.

Cary led me onto the empty dance floor and pulled me into a swift foxtrot. It took me a minute to get into it, because I'd been stiff and tight with misery for days. Then the synergy of longtime partners kicked in and we glided across the floor with sweeping steps.

When the singer's voice faded with the music, we stopped, breathless. We were pleasantly surprised by applause. Cary gave an elegant bow and I held on to his hand for stability as I dipped into a curtsy.

When I lifted my head and straightened, I found Gideon standing in front of me. Startled, I stumbled back a step. He was seriously underdressed in jeans and an untucked white dress shirt that was open at the collar and rolled up at the sleeves, but he was so damn fine he still put every other man in attendance to shame.

The tremendous yearning I felt at the sight of him overwhelmed me. Distantly I was aware of the band's singer pulling Cary away, but

I couldn't tear my gaze away from Gideon, whose wildly blue eyes burned into mine.

"What are you doing here?" he snapped, scowling.

I recoiled from his harshness. "Excuse me?"

"You shouldn't be here." He grabbed me by the elbow and started hauling me toward the house. "I don't want you here."

If he'd spit in my face, it couldn't have devastated me more. I yanked my arm free of him and walked briskly toward the house with my head held high, praying I could make it to the privacy of the town car and Clancy's protective watch before the tears started falling.

Behind me, I heard a come-hither female voice call out Gideon's name, and I sent up a prayer that the woman would stall him long enough for me to get out without further confrontation.

I thought I just might make it when I passed into the cool interior of the house.

"Eva, wait."

My shoulders hunched at the sound of Gideon's voice and I refused to look at him. "Get lost. I can show myself out."

"I'm not done—"

"I am!" I pivoted to face him. "You don't get to talk to me that way. Who do you think you are? You think I came here for *you*? That I was hoping I'd see you and you'd throw me a goddamn scrap or bone . . . some pathetic acknowledgment of my existence? Maybe I'd be able to harass you into a quick, dirty fuck in a corner somewhere in a pitiful effort to win you back?"

"Shut up, Eva." His gaze was scorching hot, his jaw tight and hard. "Listen to me—"

"I'm only here because I was told you *wouldn't* be. I'm here for Cary and his career. So you can go back to the party and forget about me all over again. I assure you, when I walk out the door, I'll be doing the same to you."

"Shut your damned mouth." He caught me by the elbows and

shook me so hard my teeth snapped together. "Just shut up and let me talk."

I slapped him hard enough to turn his head. "Don't touch me."

With a growl, Gideon hauled me into him and kissed me hard, bruising my lips. His hand was in my hair, fisting it roughly, holding me in place so I couldn't turn away. I bit the tongue he thrust aggressively into my mouth, then his lower lip, tasting blood, but he didn't stop. I shoved at his shoulders with everything I had, but I couldn't budge him.

Goddamn Stanton! If not for him and my crazy-assed mother, I'd have had a few Krav Maga classes under my belt by now. . . .

Gideon kissed me as if he were starved for the taste of me, and my resistance began to melt. He smelled so good, so familiar. His body felt so perfectly *right* against mine. My nipples betrayed me, hardening into tight points, and a slow, hot trickle of arousal gathered in my core. My heart thundered in my chest.

God, I wanted him. The craving hadn't gone away, not even for a minute.

He picked me up. Imprisoned by his tight grip, I had trouble breathing and my head began to spin. When he carried me through a door and kicked it shut behind him, I couldn't do more than make a feeble sound of protest.

I found myself pressed against a heavy glass door on the other side of a library, Gideon's hard and powerful body subduing my own. His arm at my waist slid lower, his hand delving beneath my skirts and finding the curves of my butt exposed by my lacy boy shorts underwear. He wrenched my hips hard to his, making me feel how hard he was, how aroused. My sex trembled with want, achingly empty.

All the fight left me. My arms fell to my sides, my palms pressing flat to the glass. I felt the brittle tension drain from his body as I softened in surrender, the pressure of his mouth easing and his kiss turning into a passionate coaxing.

"Eva," he breathed gruffly. "Don't fight me. I can't take it."

My eyes closed. "Let me go, Gideon."

He nuzzled his cheek against mine, his breath gusting hard and fast over my ear. "I can't. I know you're disgusted by what you saw the other night . . . what I was doing to myself—"

"Gideon, no!" *God.* Did he think I left him because of that? "That's not why—"

"I'm losing my mind without you." His lips were gliding down my neck, his tongue stroking over my racing pulse. He sucked on my skin, and pleasure radiated through me. "I can't think. I can't work or sleep. My body aches for you. I can make you want me again. Let me try."

Tears slipped free and ran down my face. They splashed on the upper swell of my breasts and he licked at them, lapping them away.

How would I ever recover if he made love to me again? How would I survive if he didn't?

"I never stopped wanting you," I whispered. "I can't stop. But you hurt me, Gideon. You have the power to hurt me like no one else can."

His gaze was stark and confused on my face. "I hurt you? How?"

"You lied to me. You shut me out." I cupped his face, needing him to understand this one thing without question. "Your past doesn't have the power to push me away. Only you can do that, and you did."

"I didn't know what to do," he rasped. "I never wanted you to see me like that . . ."

"That's the problem, Gideon. I want to know who you are, the good *and* the bad, and you want to keep parts of yourself hidden from me. If you don't open up, we're going to lose each other down the road and I won't be able to take it. I'm barely surviving it now. I've crawled through the last four days of my life. Another week, a month . . . It'll break me to give you up."

"I can let you in, Eva. I'm trying. But your first response when I screw up is to run away. You do it every time and I can't stand feeling like any moment I'm going to do or say something wrong and you're going to bolt."

His mouth was tender again as he brushed his lips back and forth over mine. I didn't argue with him. How could I, when he was right?

"I had hoped you'd come back on your own," he murmured, "but I can't stay away anymore. I'll carry you out of here if I have to. Whatever it takes to get you back in the same room with me, talking this out."

My heart stuttered. "You were hoping I'd come back? I thought . . . You gave me back my keys. I thought we were over."

He pulled back, his face set in fierce lines. "We'll *never* be over, Eva."

I looked at him, my heart aching like an open wound at how beautiful he was, how broken and in pain he was—pain I'd caused to some degree.

On tiptoes, I kissed the reddened handprint I'd left on his cheek, clutching his thick silky hair in my hands.

Gideon bent his knees to align our bodies, his breathing harsh and erratic. "I'll do whatever you want, whatever you need. Anything. Just take me back."

Maybe I should have been scared by the depth of his need, but I felt the same passionate insanity for him.

Running my hands down his chest in an effort to soothe his trembling, I gave him the hard truth. "We can't seem to stop making each other miserable. I can't keep doing this to you and I can't keep going through these crazy highs and lows. We need help, Gideon. We're seriously dysfunctional."

"I saw Dr. Petersen on Friday. He's going to take me on as a patient, and—if you agree—he'll take us both on as a couple. I figured if you can trust him, I can try."

"Dr. Petersen?" I remembered the brief jolt I'd felt at seeing a black Bentley SUV when Clancy pulled away from the doctor's office. At the time, I'd told myself it was wishful thinking. After all, there were countless black SUVs in New York. "You had me followed."

His chest expanded on a deep breath. He didn't deny it.

I bit back my anger. I could only imagine how terrible it must be for him to be so dependent on something—*someone*—he couldn't control. What mattered most at that moment were his willingness to try and the fact that it wasn't just talk. He'd actually taken steps. "It's going to be a lot of work, Gideon," I warned him.

"I'm not afraid of work." He was touching me restlessly, his hands sliding over my thighs and buttocks as if caressing my bare skin were as necessary to him as breathing. "I'm only afraid of losing you."

I pressed my cheek to his. We completed each other. Even now, as his hands roamed possessively over me, I felt a thawing in my soul, the desperate relief of being held—finally—by the man who understood and satisfied my deepest, most intimate desires.

"I need you." His mouth was sliding over my cheek and down my throat. "I need to be inside you . . ."

"*No.* My God. Not here." But my protest sounded weak even to my own ears. I wanted him anywhere, anytime, any way. . . .

"It has to be here," he muttered, dropping to his knees. "It has to be now."

He chafed my skin ripping the lace of my panties away; then he shoved my skirts to my waist and licked my cleft, his tongue parting my folds to stroke over my throbbing clit.

I gasped and tried to recoil, but there was nowhere to go. Not with the door at my back and a grimly determined Gideon in front, one hand keeping me pinned while the other lifted my left leg over his shoulder, opening me to his ardent mouth.

My head thudded against the glass, heat pulsing through my blood from the point where his tongue was driving me mad. My leg flexed against his back, urging him closer, my hands cupping his head to hold him still as I rocked into him. Feeling the rough satin strands of his hair against my sensitive inner thighs was its own provocation, heightening my awareness of everything around me. . . .

We were in Gideon's parents' house, in the midst of a party attended by dozens of famous people, and he was on his knees, growling his hunger as he licked and sucked my slick, aching cleft. He knew just how to get to me, knew what I liked and needed. He had an understanding of my nature that went above and beyond his incredible oral skills. The combination was devastating and addicting.

My body shook, my eyelids heavy from the illicit pleasure. "Gideon . . . You make me come so hard."

His tongue rubbed over and over the clenching entrance to my body, teasing me, making me grind shamelessly into his working mouth. His hands cupped my bare butt, kneading, urging me onto his tongue as he thrust it inside me. There was reverence in the greedy way he enjoyed me, the unmistakable sense that he worshipped my body, that pleasuring it and taking pleasure from it was as vital to him as the blood in his veins.

"Yes," I hissed, feeling the orgasm building. I was buzzed by champagne and the heated scent of Gideon's skin mixed with my own arousal. My breasts strained within the increasingly too-tight confines of my strapless bra, my body trembling on the edge of a desperately needed orgasm. "I'm so close."

A movement on the far side of the room caught my eye and I froze, my gaze locking with Magdalene's. She stood just inside the door, halted midstride, staring wide-eyed and openmouthed at the back of Gideon's moving head.

But he was either oblivious or too impassioned to care. His lips circled my clit and his cheeks hollowed. Sucking rhythmically, he massaged the hypersensitive knot with the tip of his tongue.

Everything tightened viciously, then released in a fiery burst of pleasure.

The orgasm poured through me in a scorching wave. I cried out, pumping my hips mindlessly into his mouth, lost to the primal connection between us. Gideon held me up as my knees weakened, tonguing my quivering flesh until the last tremor faded.

When I opened my eyes again, our audience of one had fled.

Standing in a rush, Gideon picked me up and carried me to the couch. He dropped me lengthwise on the cushion, then hauled my hips up to rest on the armrest, arching my spine.

I eyed him up the length of my torso. Why not just fold me over and fuck me from behind?

Then he ripped open his button fly and pulled his big, beautiful penis out, and I didn't care how he took me just so long as he did. I whimpered as he shoved into me, my body struggling to accommodate the wonderful fullness I craved. Yanking my hips to meet his powerful thrusts, Gideon battered my tender sex with that brutally thick column of rigid flesh, his gaze dark and possessive, his breath leaving him in primitive grunts every time he hit the end of me.

A trembling moan left me, the friction of his drives stirring my never-sated need to be fucked senseless by him. Only him.

A handful of strokes and his head fell back as he gasped my name, his hips rolling to stir me into a frenzy. "Squeeze me, Eva. Squeeze my dick."

When I complied, the ragged sound he made was so erotic my sex trembled in appreciation. "Yeah, angel . . . just like that."

I tightened around him and he cursed. His gaze found mine, the stunning blue hazed with sexual euphoria. A convulsive shudder racked his powerful frame, followed by an agonized sound of ecstasy. His cock jerked inside me, once, twice, and then he was coming long and hard, spurting hotly into the clutching depths of my body.

I didn't have time to climax again, but it didn't matter. I watched him with awe and pure female triumph. *I* could do this to *him*.

In the moments of orgasm, I owned him as completely as he owned me.

16

GIDEON FOLDED OVER me, his hair falling forward to tickle my chest, his lungs heaving. "God. I can't go days without this. Even the hours at work are too long."

I ran my fingers through the sweat-damp roots of his hair. "I missed you, too."

He nuzzled my breasts. "When you're not with me, I feel— Don't run anymore, Eva. I can't take it."

He pulled me up to stand in front of him, keeping his cock in me until the soles of my heels touched the hardwood floor. "Come home with me now."

"I can't leave Cary."

"Then we'll drag him out of here with us. Shh . . . Before you complain, whatever he hopes to get out of this party, I can make happen. Being here accomplishes nothing."

"Maybe he's having fun."

"I don't want you here." He suddenly seemed distant, his tone far too controlled.

"Do you know how badly it hurts me when you say that?" I cried softly, my chest tight with the pain of it. "What's wrong with me that you don't want me around your family?"

"Angel, no." He hugged me, his hands roaming my back in soothing caresses. "There's nothing wrong with you. It's this place. I don't—I *can't* be here. You want to know what's in my dreams? It's this house."

"Oh." My stomach knotted with worry and confusion. "I'm sorry. I didn't know."

Something in my voice lured him to press a kiss between my eyebrows. "I've been rough with you today. I'm sorry. I'm edgy and agitated being here, but that's no excuse."

I cupped his face and stared into his eyes, seeing the tumultuous emotions he was so used to hiding. "Don't ever apologize for being yourself with me. It's what I want. I want to be your safe place, Gideon."

"You are. You don't know how much, but I'll find a way to tell you." He rested his forehead against mine. "Let's go home. I bought some things for you."

"Oh? I love gifts." Especially when they came from my self-professed unromantic boyfriend.

Cautiously, he began to pull out of me. I was shocked to feel how wet I was, how copiously he'd come. The final few inches of his cock slid out in a rush and semen slicked my inner thighs. A moment later, two audacious droplets fell to the hardwood floor between my spread legs.

"Oh, shit." He groaned. "That's so damn hot. I'm getting hard again."

I stared at the brazen display of his virility and felt warm. "You can't go again after *that*."

"Hell if I can't." Cupping my sex in his hand, he rubbed the slickness all over me, coating the outer lips and massaging it into the folds. Euphoria spread through me like the warmth of fine liquor, a sense of contentment that came solely from the knowledge that Gideon found gratification in me and my body.

"I'm an animal with you," he murmured. "I want to mark you. I want to possess you so completely there's no separation between us."

My hips began to move in tiny circles as his words and touch reignited the desire he'd goaded with the thrusts of his cock. I wanted to come again, knew I'd be miserable if I had to wait until we reached his bed. I was a sexual creature with him, too, so physically attuned to him and so positive that he would never physically hurt me, that I was . . . free.

I encircled his wrist with my fingers and gently directed his hand around my hip to reach for me from behind. Nipping his jaw with my teeth, I gathered the courage he inspired in me and whispered, "Touch me here with your fingers. Mark me there."

He froze, his chest lifting and falling rapidly. "I don't"—his voice strengthened—"I don't do anal play, Eva."

Looking into his eyes, I saw something dark and volatile. Something very painful.

Of all the things for us to have in common. . . .

The raw passion of our lust gentled into the warm familiarity of love. With my heart breaking, I confessed, "I don't either. At least not voluntarily."

"Then . . . why?" The confusion in his voice moved me deeply.

I hugged him, pressing my cheek to his shoulder and listening to the slightly panicked beat of his heart. "Because I believe your touch can erase Nathan's."

"Oh, Eva." His cheek pressed to the crown of my head.

I snuggled closer. "You make me feel safe."

We held each other for long moments. I listened as his heartbeat slowed and his breathing smoothed out. I inhaled deeply, relishing the mix of his personal scent with the scent of hard lust and harder sex.

When the tip of his middle finger slid gossamer-soft over the pucker of my anus, I stilled and pulled back to look at him. "Gideon?"

"Why me?" he asked softly, his beautiful eyes dark and stormy. "You know I'm fucked up, Eva. You saw what I . . . That night you woke me . . . You *saw*, damn it. How can you trust me with your body this way?"

"I trust my heart and what it tells me." I smoothed the frown line between his brows. "You can give my body back to me, Gideon. I believe you're the only one who can."

His eyes closed and his damp forehead touched mine. "Do you have a safeword, Eva?"

Startled, I pulled back again to study his face. A few members of my therapy group had talked about Dom/sub relationships. Some required total control to feel safe during sex. Others fell on the opposite side of the line, finding that bondage and humiliation satisfied their deep-seated need to feel pain to experience pleasure. For those who practiced that lifestyle, a safeword was an unambiguous way to say *Stop*. But I couldn't see how that had any relevance to me and Gideon. "Do you?"

"I don't need one." Between my legs, the gentle stroke of his finger became less tentative. He repeated his question, "Do you have a safeword?"

"No. I've never needed one. Missionary, doggy style, B.O.B. . . . that's about the extent of my mad skills in the sack."

That brought a touch of amusement to his otherwise severe face. "Thank God. I wouldn't survive you otherwise."

And still that fingertip massaged me, spurring a dark yearning. Gideon could do that to me, make me forget everything that happened before. I had no negative sexual triggers with him, no hesitation or fears. He'd given that to me. In return, I wanted to give him the body he'd freed from my past.

The long case clock near the door began to chime the hour.

"Gideon, we've been gone a long time. Someone will come looking for us."

He put the slightest pressure against my sensitive rosette, barely pressing. "Do you really care if they do?"

My hips arched into the touch. Anticipation was making me hot all over again. "I don't care about anything but you when you're touching me."

His free hand lifted to my hair and held it at the roots, keeping my head still. "Did you ever enjoy anal play? Accidentally or by deliberation?"

"No."

"And yet you trust me enough to ask me for this." He kissed my forehead as he drew the slickness of his semen back to my rear.

I gripped his waistband. "You don't have to—"

"Yes, I do." His voice had that wickedly assertive bite to it. "If you crave something, I'll be the one to give it to you. All of your needs, Eva, are mine to fulfill. Whatever it costs me."

"Thank you, Gideon." My hips shifted restlessly as he continued to lubricate me gently. "I want to be what you need, too."

"I've told you what I need, Eva—control." He brushed his parted lips back and forth over mine. "You're asking me to lead you back into painful places, and I will, if that's what you need. But we have to be extremely careful."

"I know."

"Trust is hard for both of us. If we break it, we could lose everything. Think of a word you associate with power. *Your* safeword, angel. Choose it."

The pressure of that single fingertip became more insistent. I moaned, "Crossfire."

"Umm . . . I like it. Very fitting." His tongue dipped into my mouth, barely touching mine before retreating. His finger rimmed my anus over and over, pushing his semen into the puckered hole, a soft growl escaping him as it flexed in a silent plea for more.

The next time he pressed against the ring, I pushed out and he slipped his fingertip inside me. The feeling of penetration was shockingly intense.

Just as before, surrender weighted my body, leaving me languid.

"Are you okay?" Gideon asked harshly as I sagged against him. "Should I stop?"

"No . . . Don't stop."

He pushed fractionally deeper and I clenched around him, a helpless reaction to the feel of something gliding across tender tissues. "You're snug and scorching hot," he murmured. "And so soft. Does it hurt?"

"No. Please. More."

Gideon withdrew to his fingertip; then he slid in to the knuckle, slow and easy. I quivered in delight, astonished by how good it felt, that teasing bit of fullness in my rear.

"How's that?" he asked hoarsely.

"Good. Everything you do to me feels good."

He withdrew again, glided deep again. Leaning forward, I thrust my hips back to give him easier access and pressed my breasts against his chest. His fist in my hair tightened, pulling my head back so he could take my mouth in a lush, wet kiss. Our open mouths slid across each other, growing more frantic as my arousal built. The feel of Gideon's finger in that darkly sexual place, thrusting in that gentle rhythm, had me rocking backward to meet his inward drives.

"You're so beautiful," he murmured, his voice infinitely gentle. "I love making you feel good. Love watching an orgasm move through your body."

"Gideon." I was lost, drowning in the powerful joy of being held by him, loved by him. Four days alone had taught me how miserable I'd be if we couldn't work things out, how dull and colorless my world would be without him in it. "I need you."

"I know." He licked across my lips, making my head spin. "I'm here. Your cunt's trembling and tightening. You're going to come for me again."

With shaking hands, I reached between us for his cock, finding it hard. I lifted the layers of my underskirts so I could insert him into my drenched sex. He slid in a few inches, our standing positions preventing deeper penetration, but the connection alone was enough. I wrapped my arms around his shoulders, burying my face in his neck as my knees weakened. His hand left my hair, his arm clasping my back and holding me close.

"Eva." The tempo of his finger thrusts quickened. "Do you know what you do to me?"

His hips nudged against mine, the wide crest of his penis massaging a sweetly tender spot. "You're milking the head of my dick with those hungry little squeezes. You're going to make me come for you. When you go off, I'm going with you."

I was distantly aware of the helpless noises spilling from my throat. My senses were overloaded by Gideon's scent and the heat of his hard body, the feel of his cock rubbing inside me and his finger pumping into my rear. I was surrounded by him, filled with him, blissfully possessed in every way. A climax was building in force, pounding through me, pooling in my core. Not just from the physical pleasure but from the knowledge that he'd been willing to take a risk. Once again. For me.

His finger stilled and I made a sound of protest.

"Hush," he whispered. "Someone's coming."

"Oh God! Magdalene came in earlier and saw us. What if she told—"

"Don't move." Gideon didn't let me go. He stood just as he was, filling me front and back, his hand caressing the length of my spine and smoothing my dress down. "Your skirts hide everything."

With my back to the room's entrance, I pressed my flaming face into his shirt.

The door opened. There was a pause, then, "Is everything all right?"

Christopher. I felt awkward being unable to turn around.

"Of course," Gideon said smoothly, coolly in control. "What do you want?"

To my horror, he resumed the push and withdrawal of his finger. Not with the deep strokes of before, but slow, shallow thrusts that didn't disturb my skirts. Already aroused to a fever pitch and hovering on the verge of orgasm, I dug my nails into his neck. The tension in my body from having Christopher in the room only ramped up the erotic sensations.

"Eva?" Christopher asked.

I swallowed hard. "Yes?"

"Are you okay?"

Gideon adjusted his stance, which moved his cock inside me and bumped his pelvis against my pulsing clit.

"Y-yes. We're just . . . talking. About. Dinner." My eyes closed as Gideon's fingertip grazed the thin wall separating his penis from his touch. If he nudged my clit again, I'd come. I was too wound up to stop it.

Gideon's chest vibrated against my cheek as he spoke. "We'd be done sooner if you'd go, so tell me what you need."

"Mom's looking for you."

"Why?" Gideon shifted again, rocking into my clit at the same moment he gave a quick, deep thrust of his finger into my rear.

I climaxed. Afraid of the wail of pleasure that wanted out of me, I sank my teeth into Gideon's hard pectoral. He grunted softly and started coming, his cock jerking as it pumped thick spurts of scorching semen into me.

The rest of the conversation was lost beneath the roar of my blood. Christopher said something, Gideon replied, and then the door shut again. I was lifted to sit on the armrest and Gideon started thrusting between my spread thighs, using my body to rub out the rest of his orgasm, growling in my mouth as we finished off the rawest, most exhibitionistic sexual encounter of my life.

AFTERWARD, Gideon led me by the hand to a bathroom, where he lightly soaped a washcloth and cleansed between my legs before he paid the same attention to his cock. The way he took care of me was sweetly intimate, demonstrating yet again that as primal as his desire for me was, I was precious to him.

"I don't want us to fight anymore," I said quietly from my perch on the counter.

He tossed the washcloth down a concealed laundry chute and re-fastened his fly. Then he came to me, brushing his cool fingertips down my cheek. "We don't fight, angel. We just have to learn not to scare the hell out of each other."

"You make it sound so easy," I grumbled. To call either of us vir-gins would be ridiculous, yet emotionally that was just what we were. Fumbling in the dark and too eager, completely out of our depths and self-conscious, trying to impress and missing all the subtle nuances.

"Easy or hard, doesn't matter. We'll get through this because we have to." He pushed his fingers through my hair, restoring order to the disheveled strands. "We'll discuss when we get home. I think I've dis-covered the crux of our problem."

His conviction and determination soothed the restlessness I'd been feeling the last few days. Closing my eyes, I relaxed and enjoyed the tactile delight of having my hair played with. "Your mother seemed startled that I'm a blonde."

"Did she?"

"My mother was, too. Not about me being a blonde," I qualified. "That you'd be interested in one."

"Was she?"

"Gideon!"

"Hmm?" He kissed the end of my nose and ran his hands down my arms.

"I'm not the type you usually go for, am I?"

His brow arched. "I have one type: Eva Lauren Tramell. That's it."

I rolled my eyes. "Okay. Whatever."

"What does it matter? You're the woman I'm with."

"It doesn't matter. I'm just curious. People don't usually stray from their preferred type."

Stepping between my legs, he put his arms around my hips. "Lucky for me that I fit your type."

"Gideon, you don't fit any type," I drawled. "You're in a class by yourself."

His eyes sparkled. "Like what you see, do you?"

"You know I do, which is why we really should get out of here before we start screwing like minks again."

Pressing his cheek to mine, he murmured, "Only you could blow my mind in a place that's always made my skin crawl. Thank you for being exactly what I want and need."

"Oh, Gideon." I wrapped my arms and legs around him, holding him as close to me as possible. "You came here for me, didn't you? To take me away from this place you hate."

"I'd walk into hell for you, Eva, and this is pretty damn close." He exhaled harshly. "I was about to go to your apartment and drag you away with me when I learned you'd come here. You have to stay away from Christopher."

"Why do you keep saying that? He seems very nice."

Gideon pulled back, sifting my hair through his fingers. His eyes stayed fiercely locked to mine. "He takes sibling rivalry to the extreme, and he's unstable enough to make him dangerous. He's reaching out to you because he knows he can hurt me through you. You have to trust me on this."

Why was Gideon so suspicious of his half brother's motives? He had to have a good reason. It was yet another thing he didn't fully share with me. "I do trust you. Of course I do. I'll keep my distance."

"Thank you." Catching me by the waist, he lifted me off the counter and set me on my feet. "Let's grab Cary and get the hell out of here."

We made our way back outside with my hand in his. I was uncomfortably aware that we'd been gone a very long time. The sun was going down. And I was pantyless. My ruined boy shorts were presently stuffed into the front pocket of Gideon's jeans.

He glanced at me as we entered the marquee. "I should've told you before. You look gorgeous, Eva. That dress is amazing on you and so are those fuck-me red heels."

"Well, clearly they work." I bumped my shoulder into him. "Thank you."

"For the compliment? Or the fucking?"

"Hush," I admonished, flushing.

His dark velvet laugh turned every female head in hearing distance and some of the men's, too. Placing our linked hands at the small of my back, he pulled me close and smacked a kiss on my mouth.

"Gideon!" His mother glided toward us with sparkling eyes and a wide smile on her lovely face. "I'm so happy you're here."

She looked like she might hug him, but his posture altered subtly, charging the air around him with an invisible field of power that encompassed me as well.

Elizabeth drew to an abrupt halt.

"Mother," he greeted her with all the warmth of an arctic storm. "You can thank Eva for my being here. I've come to take her away."

"But she's having a good time, aren't you, Eva? You should stay for her sake." Elizabeth looked at me with a plea in her eyes.

My fingers flexed around Gideon's hand. He came first, that was never in question, but I couldn't help but wish I knew the story behind his coldness toward a mother who seemed to love him. Her adoring gaze slid over the face that had shades of her own, drinking in every feature hungrily. How long had it been since the last time she'd seen him in person?

Then I wondered if maybe she'd loved him *too much*. . . .

Revulsion made my spine stiffen.

"Don't put Eva on the spot," Gideon said, rubbing his knuckles against my tense back. "You've gotten what you wanted—you've met her."

"Perhaps you'll both come to dinner later this week?"

His only answer was an arched brow. Then his gaze lifted, luring my attention to follow it. I found Cary emerging from what appeared to be a hedgerow maze with a very recognizable pop princess on his arm. Gideon gestured him over.

"Oh, not Cary, too!" Elizabeth protested. "He's the life of the party."

"I thought you might like him." Gideon bared his teeth in something that was too sharp to be a smile. "Just remember that he's Eva's friend, Mother. That makes him mine as well."

I was hugely relieved when Cary joined us, breaking the tension in his easygoing way.

"I was looking for you," he said to me. "I was hoping you'd be ready to go. I got that call I was expecting."

Looking into his sparkling eyes, I knew Trey had reached him. "Yes, we're ready."

Cary and I walked around to say our good-byes and offer our thanks. Gideon remained at my side like a possessive shadow, his demeanor calm but markedly aloof.

We were all walking toward the house when I spotted Ireland off to the side staring at Gideon. I stopped and looked up at him. "Go get your sister so we can say good-bye."

"What?"

"She's standing to your left." I looked to our right to hide my prodding from the young girl whom I suspected might hero-worship her eldest brother.

He gestured Ireland over with a brusque wave of his hand. She took her time ambling over, her pretty face schooled into an expression of militant boredom. I looked at Cary with a shake of my head, remembering those days all too well.

"Listen." I squeezed Gideon's wrist. "Tell her you're sorry you two didn't get to catch up while you were here and she should call you sometime, if she wants."

Gideon shot me an arch look. "Catch up on what?"

Rubbing his biceps, I said, "She'll do all the talking if given a chance."

He scowled. "She's a teenage girl. Why would I give her a chance to talk my ear off?"

I pushed onto my tiptoes and whispered in his ear, "Because I'll owe you one."

"You're up to something." He eyed me warily for a moment; then he pressed a hard kiss to my lips with a growl. "So we'll leave it open and say you owe me more than one. Quantity to be determined."

I nodded. Cary rocked back on his heels and twirled one index finger around another in a sign meaning *wrapped around your finger.*

Only fair, I thought, since he was wrapped around my heart.

I was surprised when Gideon accepted the keys to the Bentley SUV from one of the valets. "*You* drove? Where's Angus?"

"Day off." He nuzzled against my temple. "I missed you, Eva."

I settled into the front passenger seat, and he shut the door behind me. As I secured my seat belt, I saw him pause by the hood, making eye contact with two men dressed in black who waited beside a sleek black Mercedes sedan at the end of the drive. They nodded and got in the Benz. When Gideon pulled out of the Vidal driveway, they followed directly behind us.

"Security detail?" I asked.

"Yes. I took off fast when I was told you were here, and they lost the tail for a while."

Cary went home with Clancy, so Gideon and I headed straight to the penthouse. I found myself getting turned on from watching Gideon drive. He handled the luxury vehicle the way he handled everything—confidently, aggressively, and with skillful control. He drove fast but not recklessly, weaving easily over the curves and straightaways of the scenic route back to the city. There was almost no traffic until we hit the gridlock of Manhattan.

When we arrived at his apartment, we both went straight into the master bathroom and undressed for a shower. As if he couldn't stop touching me, Gideon washed me from head to toe; then he dried me with a towel and wrapped me in a new robe of embroidered teal silk with kimono sleeves. He finished by pulling a pair of similarly hued drawstring silk pants out of a drawer for himself.

"Don't I get panties?" I asked, thinking about my drawer of sexy underwear.

"No. There's a phone hanging on the wall in the kitchen. Hit speed dial one and tell the man who answers that I want him to pick up double my usual dinner order from Peter Luger."

"All right." I headed out to the living room and made the call; then I had to search for Gideon. I found him in his home office, a room I hadn't been in before.

I didn't get a good look at the space at first because the only lighting came from an angled picture light on the wall and a barrister's lamp on his polished wood desk. Plus my eyes were more interested in focusing on him. He looked utterly sensual and compelling sprawled in his big black leather chair. He held a tulip glass of some liquor that he warmed between his hands, and the beauty of his flexing biceps sent tingles racing through me, as did the tight lacing of muscles on his abdomen.

His gaze was on the wall illuminated by the picture light, which snagged my attention, too. I was startled when I saw the art—a huge collage of blown-up photos of him and me: the picture of our kiss on the street outside the gym . . . a shot of us from the press gauntlet at the advocacy dinner . . . a candid of the tender aftermath of our fight in Bryant Park . . .

The focal point was the image in the center that had been taken while I slept in my own bed, lit only by the candle I'd left burning for him. It was an intimate voyeuristic shot, one that said more about the photographer than it did the subject.

I was deeply touched by the proof that he'd been falling along with me.

Gideon gestured at the drink he'd poured for me in advance and set on the edge of his desk. "Have a seat."

I complied, curious. There was an edge to him that was new, a sense of purpose and calm determination paired with laser-precise focus.

What had brought on his mood? And what did it mean for the rest of our evening?

Then I saw the small photo collage frame lying on the desktop next to my drink, and my worry faded. The frame was very similar to the one already on my desk, but this one held three photos of Gideon and me together.

"I want you to take that to work," he said quietly.

"Thank you." For the first time in days, I was happy. I hugged the frame to my chest with one hand and picked up my glass with the other.

His eyes glittered as he watched me take a seat. "You blow kisses at me all day from your picture on my desk. I think it's only fair that you be equally reminded of me. Of us."

246 · SYLVIA DAY

I exhaled in a rush, my heartbeat not quite steady. "I never forget about you or us."

"I wouldn't let you if you tried." Gideon took a deep drink, his throat working on a swallow. "I think I've figured out where we made our first misstep, the one that's led to all the stumbles we've had since."

"Oh?"

"Take a drink of your Armagnac, angel. I think you'll need it."

I took a cautious sip of the liquor, feeling the instantaneous burn, followed by recognition that I liked the flavor. I took a bigger drink.

Rolling his glass between his palms, Gideon took another drink and eyed me thoughtfully. "Tell me which was hotter, Eva: sex in the limo when you were in charge or sex in the hotel when I was?"

I shifted restlessly, unsure of where the conversation was leading. "I thought you enjoyed what happened in the limo. While it was happening, I mean. Obviously not later."

"I loved it," he said with quiet conviction. "The image of you in that red dress, moaning and telling me how good my cock feels inside you, will haunt me as long as I live. If you'd like to top me again in the future, I'm definitely game."

My stomach tensed. The muscles in my shoulders began to knot. "Gideon, I'm starting to freak out a little. All this talk of safewords and topping . . . it feels like this conversation is leading somewhere I can't go."

"You're thinking of bondage and pain. I'm talking about a consensual power exchange." Gideon studied me intently. "Would you like more brandy? You're very pale."

"You think?" I set the drained glass down. "It sounds like you're telling me you're a Dominant."

"Angel, you knew that already." His mouth curved in a soft, sexy smile. "What I'm telling you is that you're submissive."

17

I PUSHED TO MY feet in a rush.

"Don't," he warned in a dark purr. "You're not running yet. We're not done."

"You don't know what you're talking about." Being under someone else's thumb—*losing my right to say no!*—was never going to happen again. "You know what I went through. I need control as much as you do."

"Sit down, Eva."

I stayed on my feet, just to prove my point.

His smile widened and my insides melted. "Do you have any idea how crazy I am about you?" he murmured.

"You're crazy all right, if you think I'm going to put up with being ordered around, especially sexually."

"Come on, Eva. You know I don't want to beat you, punish you, hurt you, demean you, or order you around like a pet. Those aren't needs either of us has." Straightening, Gideon leaned forward and placed his elbows on the desktop. "You're the most important thing in my life. I treasure you. I want to protect you and make you feel safe. That's why we're talking about this."

God. How could he be so wonderful and so insane at the same time? "I don't need to be dominated!"

"What you need is someone to trust—No. Close your mouth, Eva. You'll wait until I'm finished."

My protest spluttered into silence.

"You've asked me to reacquaint your body with acts previously used to hurt and terrorize you. I can't tell you what your trust means to me or what it would do to me if I broke that trust. I can't risk it, Eva. We have to do this right."

I crossed my arms. "I guess I'm dumber than bricks. I thought our sex life was rockin'."

Setting his glass down, Gideon kept going as if I hadn't spoken. "You asked me to meet a need of yours today and I agreed. Now we need to—"

"If I'm not what you want, just spit it out!" I set the picture frame and my glass down before I did something with them I'd regret. "Don't try to pretty it up with—"

He was around the desk and on me before I could stumble back more than a couple steps. His mouth sealed over mine; his arms caged me. As he'd done earlier, he carried me to a wall and restrained me against it, his hands banding my wrists and lifting them high above my head.

Trapped, I could do nothing as he bent his knees and stroked my cleft with the rigid length of his erection. Once, twice. Silk rasped against my swollen clit. The bite of his teeth on my covered nipple sent a shiver through me, while the clean scent of his warm skin intoxicated me. With a gasp, I sagged into his embrace.

"See how easily you submit when I take over?" His lips followed the arch of my brow. "And it feels good, doesn't it? It feels right."

"That's not fair." I stared up at him. How could he expect me to respond any differently? As disturbed and confounded as I was, I was helplessly drawn to him.

"Of course it is. It's also true."

My gaze roamed over that glorious mane of inky hair and the chiseled lines of his incomparable face. The longing I felt was so acute it was painful. The hidden damage inside him only made me love him more. There were times when I felt like I'd found the other half of myself in him.

"I can't help it that you turn me on," I muttered. "My body is physiologically supposed to soften and relax, so you can shove that big cock inside me."

"Eva. Let's be honest. You *want* me to have total control. It's important to you that you can trust me to take care of you. There's nothing wrong with that. The reverse is true for me—I need you to trust me enough to give up that control."

I couldn't think when he was pressed up against me, my body achingly aware of every hard inch of him. "I am *not* submissive."

"You are with me. If you look back, you'll see you've been yielding to me all along."

"You're good in bed! And have more experience. Of course I let you do what you want to me." I bit my lower lip to stop it from quivering. "I'm sorry I haven't been as exciting for you."

"Bullshit, Eva. You know how much I enjoy making love to you. If I could get away with it, I'd do nothing else. We're not talking about games that get me off."

"Then we're talking about what gets *me* off? Is that what this is?"

"Yes. I thought so." He frowned. "You're upset. I didn't mean— Damn it. I thought discussing this would help us."

"Gideon." My eyes stung, then flooded with tears. He looked as wounded and confused as I felt. "You're breaking my heart."

Releasing my wrists, he stepped back and swept me up in his arms, carrying me out of his office and down the hallway to a closed door. "Turn the knob," he said quietly.

We entered a candlelit room that still smelled faintly of new paint. For a few seconds I was disoriented, unable to comprehend how we'd stepped out of Gideon's apartment and into my bedroom.

"I don't understand." A serious understatement, but my brain was still trying to get past the feeling of being teleported from one residence to another. "You . . . moved me in with you?"

"Not quite." He set me down, but kept an arm around me. "I recreated your room based on the photo I took of you sleeping."

"*Why?*"

What the hell? Who did something like that? Was this all to keep me from witnessing his nightmares?

The thought shattered my heart further. I felt like Gideon and I were drifting further away from each other by the moment.

His hands sifted through my damp hair, which only increased my agitation. I felt like batting his touch away and putting at least the length of the room between us. Maybe two rooms.

"If you feel the need to run," he said softly, "you can come in here and shut the door. I promise not to bother you until you're ready. This way, you have your safe place and I know that you haven't left me."

A million questions and speculations roared through my mind, but the one thing that stuck out was, "Are we still going to share a bed when we're sleeping?"

"Every night." Gideon's lips touched my forehead. "How could you think otherwise? Talk to me, Eva. What's going through that beautiful head of yours?"

"What's going through *my* head?" I snapped. "What the fuck is going on in yours? What happened to you in the four days we were broken up?"

His jaw tightened. "We never broke up, Eva."

The phone rang in the other room. I cursed under my breath. I wanted us to talk and I wanted him to go away, both at the same time. He squeezed my shoulders, and then let me go. "That's our dinner."

I didn't follow him when he left, feeling too unsettled to eat. Instead, I crawled onto the bed that was exactly like my own and curled around a pillow, closing my eyes. I didn't hear Gideon come back, but I felt him as he drew to a stop at the edge of the bed.

"Please don't make me eat alone," he said to my rigid back.

"Why don't you just order me to eat with you?"

He sighed, and then slid onto the bed to spoon behind me. His warmth was welcome, chasing away the chill that had brought goose bumps to my skin. He didn't say anything for a long while, just gave me the comfort of having him close. Or maybe he was taking comfort in me.

"Eva." His fingers caressed the length of my silk-clad arm. "I can't stand you being unhappy. Talk to me."

"I don't know what to say. I thought we were finally coming to a point where things would smooth out between us." I hugged the pillow tighter.

"Don't tense up, Eva. It hurts when you pull away from me."

I felt like he was *pushing* me away.

Rolling, I shoved him to his back; then I mounted him, my robe parting as I straddled his hips. I ran the palms of my hands over his powerful chest and raked the tanned flesh with my nails. My hips undulated over him, stroking my bare cleft over his cock. Through the thin silk of his pants, I could feel every ridge and thick vein. From the way his eyes darkened and his sculpted mouth parted on quickened breaths, I knew he could feel the outline and damp heat of me as well.

"Is this so awful for you?" I asked, rocking my hips. "Are you lying there thinking you're not giving me what I want because I'm in charge?"

Gideon set his hands on my thighs. Even that innocuous touch seemed dominating.

The edginess and sharpened focus I'd detected not long ago abruptly made sense to me—he wasn't restraining his force of will anymore.

The tremendous power coiled inside him was now directed at me like a blast of heat.

"I've told you before," he said huskily. "I'll take you however I can get you."

"Whatever. Don't think I don't know you're topping from the bottom."

His mouth curved with unapologetic amusement.

Sliding down, I teased the flat disk of his nipple with the tip of my tongue. I blanketed him as he'd done to me in the past, stretching my body over his hips and legs, my hands shoving beneath his gorgeous ass to squeeze the firm flesh and hold him tight against me. His cock was a thick column against my belly, renewing my fierce appetite for him.

"Are you going to punish me with pleasure?" he asked quietly. "Because you can. You can bring me to my knees, Eva."

My forehead dropped to his chest and the air left my lungs in an audible rush. "I wish."

"Please don't be so worried. We'll get through this along with everything else."

"You're so positive you're right." My gaze narrowed. "You're trying to prove a point."

"And you might prove yours." Gideon licked his lower lip and my sex clenched in silent demand.

There was a brilliant depth of emotion in his eyes. Whatever else was going on in our relationship, there was no doubt we were seriously twisted up over each other.

And I was about to demonstrate that in the flesh.

Gideon's neck arched as my mouth moved over his torso. "Oh, Eva."

"Your world's about to be rocked, Mr. Cross."

It was. I made sure of it.

FEELING goofy with feminine triumph, I sat at Gideon's dining table and remembered him as he'd been just a short time ago—damp with sweat and panting, cursing as I took my time savoring his luscious body.

He swallowed a bite of his steak, which had been kept hot courtesy of a warming drawer, and said calmly, "You're insatiable."

"Well, duh. You're gorgeous, sexy, and very well hung."

"I'm glad you approve. I'm also extremely wealthy."

I waved one hand carelessly, encompassing the whole of what had to be a fifty-million-dollar apartment. "Who cares about that?"

"Well, I do, actually." His mouth curved.

I stabbed my fork into a German fried potato, thinking that Peter Luger food was almost as good as sex. Almost. "I'm interested in your money only if it means you can afford to stop working in favor of lounging around naked as my sex slave."

"I could afford to financially, yes. But you'd get bored and dump me, and then where would I be?" His look was warmly amused. "Think you proved your point, do you?"

I chewed, then said, "Should I prove it again?"

"The fact that you're still horny enough to want to proves *my* point."

"Hmm." I drank my wine. "Are you projecting?"

He shot me a look and casually chewed another bite of the tenderest steak I'd ever had.

Restless and worried, I took a deep breath and asked, "Would you tell me if our sex life didn't satisfy you?"

"Don't be ridiculous, Eva."

What else could have prompted him to bring this up after our four-day breakup? "I'm sure it doesn't help that I'm not the type you usually go for. And we haven't used any of those toys you had in the hotel—"

"Stop talking."

"Excuse me?"

Gideon set his utensils down. "I'm not going to listen to you shred your self-esteem."

"What? You're the only one who gets to do all the talking?"

"You can pick a fight with me, Eva, but it's still not going to get you fucked."

"Who said—" I shut up when he glared. He was right. I still wanted him. I wanted him on top of me, explosively lustful, completely in control of both my pleasure and his.

Pushing away from the table, he said curtly, "Wait here."

When he returned a moment later, he set a black leather ring box beside my plate and resumed his seat. The sight of it hit me like a physical blow. Fear struck me first, icy cold. Followed swiftly by a longing that was white-hot.

My hands shook in my lap. I clasped my fingers together and realized my whole body was shaking. Lost, I lifted my gaze to Gideon's face.

The feel of his fingertips brushing down my cheek soothed much of the vibrating anxiety inside me, leaving behind the terrible yearning.

"It's not *that* ring," he murmured gently. "Not yet. You're not ready."

Something inside me wilted. Then relief flooded me. It *was* too soon. Neither of us was ready. But if I'd ever wondered how deeply I had fallen in love with Gideon, now I knew.

I nodded.

"Open it," he said.

With cautious fingers, I pulled the box closer and thumbed open the lid. "Oh."

Nestled inside the black leather and velvet was a ring like no other. Gold ropelike bands were intertwined and decorated with Xs covered in diamonds.

"Bonds," I murmured, "secured by crosses." Gideon *Cross*.

"Not quite. I see the ropes as representative of the many threads of you, not bondage. But yes, the *X*s are me holding on to you. By my fingernails, it feels like." He finished his glass of wine and refilled both our glasses.

I sat unmoving, stunned, trying to take it all in. Everything he'd done in the time we'd been apart—the photos, the ring, Dr. Petersen, the replicated bedroom, and whoever had been following me around— told me I'd never been far from his mind, if I'd even left it at all.

"You gave me my keys back," I whispered, still remembering the pain.

His hand reached out and covered mine. "There are a lot of reasons why I did that. You left me wearing nothing but a robe, Eva, and without your keys. I can't stand thinking about what could've happened if Cary hadn't been home to let you in right away."

Lifting his hand to my mouth, I kissed the back, then released him and closed the lid of the ring box. "It's beautiful, Gideon. Thank you. It means a lot to me."

"But you won't wear it." It wasn't a question.

"After the conversation we've had tonight, it feels like a collar."

After a moment, he nodded. "You're not altogether wrong."

My brain hurt and my heart ached. Four nights of restless sleeping didn't help. I couldn't understand why he felt I was so necessary, even though I felt that way about him. There were thousands of women in New York alone who could replace me in his life, but there was only one Gideon Cross.

"I feel like I'm disappointing you, Gideon. After everything we've talked about tonight . . . I feel like this is the beginning of the end."

Pushing his chair back, he angled toward me and touched my cheek. "It's not."

"When do we see Dr. Petersen?"

"I'll go alone on Tuesdays. After you talk to him and agree to couples counseling, we can go together on Thursdays."

"Two hours of your week, every week. Not including the travel back and forth. That's a big commitment." I reached up and brushed the hair back from his cheek. "Thank you."

Gideon caught my hand and kissed the palm. "It's no sacrifice, Eva."

He went into his office to work a bit before bed, and I carried the ring box into the master bathroom with me. I studied it further while I brushed my teeth and hair.

There was a soft hum of need beneath my skin, a persistent level of arousal that shouldn't have been possible considering the number of orgasms I'd already had over the course of the day. It was an emotionally driven need to connect to Gideon, to reassure myself that we were okay.

Clutching the ring box in my hand, I went to my side of Gideon's bed and set it on the nightstand. I wanted it where I'd see it first thing in the morning, after a good night's sleep.

With a sigh, I draped my beautiful new robe over the footboard and crawled into bed. After tossing and turning for a long while, I finally crashed.

I woke sometime in the middle of the night to a racing pulse and quick, shallow breathing. Disoriented, I lay still for a moment, gathering my bearings and remembering where I was. I tensed when it sank in, my ears straining to hear if Gideon was having another nightmare. When I discovered him lying quietly beside me, his breathing deep and even, I relaxed with a sigh.

What time had he finally come to bed? After the days we'd spent apart, it worried me that he might have felt a need to be alone.

Then it hit me. I was *aroused*. Painfully so.

My breasts were full and heavy, my nipples furled and tight. My core was aching and my cleft wet. As I lay there in the moonlit darkness, I realized that my own body had woken me with its demands. Had I dreamed something erotic? Or was it enough that Gideon was lying beside me?

Pushing up onto my elbows, I looked at him. The sheet and comforter clung to his waist, leaving his sculpted chest and biceps bared. His right arm was tossed over his head, framing the fall of dark hair around his face. His left arm lay between us on the blankets, the hand fisted and bringing to relief the network of thick veins that coursed up his forearms. Even in repose he looked fierce and powerful.

I became more aware of the tension inside me, the sense that I was drawn to him by the silent exertion of his formidable will. It wasn't possible that he could demand my surrender while he was sleeping, yet it felt that way, felt like that invisible rope between us was pulling me to him.

The throbbing between my legs grew unbearable and I pressed one hand against the violent pulsing, hoping to dull the ache. The pressure worsened it instead.

I couldn't stay still. Throwing the covers off, I slid my legs off the side of the mattress and thought about trying a glass of warm milk with the brandy Gideon had given me earlier. Abruptly, I paused, riveted by the moonlight gleaming off the leather of the ring box on the nightstand. I thought of the jewelry inside it and my desire surged. At that moment, the thought of being collared by Gideon filled me with heated yearning.

You're just horny, I scolded myself.

One of the girls in group had talked about how her "master" could use her body any time and in any way he wanted, for his pleasure alone. There was nothing about that I'd found sexy . . . until I put Gideon in the picture. I loved getting him off. I loved making him come. Just because.

My fingers brushed over the lid of the tiny box. Exhaling a shaky breath, I picked it up and opened it. A moment later I was sliding the cool band onto the ring finger of my right hand.

"Do you like it, Eva?"

A shiver moved through me at the sound of Gideon's voice, deeper and rougher than I'd ever heard it. He'd been awake, watching me.

How long had he been conscious? Was he as attuned to me while sleeping as I seemed to be to him?

"I love it." *I love you.*

Setting the box aside, I turned my head to find him sitting up. His eyes glittered in a way that made me impossibly aroused but also sent a bite of fear through me. It was an unguarded look, like the one that had literally knocked me on my ass when we met—scorching and possessive, filled with dark threats of ecstasy. His gorgeous face was harsh in the shadows, his jaw taut as he lifted my right hand to his mouth and kissed the ring he'd given me.

I moved to kneel on the bed and draped my arms around his neck. "Take me. Carte blanche."

He cupped my butt and squeezed. "How does it feel to say that?"

"Almost as good as the orgasms you're going to give me."

"Ah, a challenge." The tip of his tongue teased the seam of my lips, tempting me with the promise of a kiss he deliberately withheld.

"Gideon!"

"Lie back, angel, and grip your pillow with both hands." His mouth curved in a wicked smile. "Don't let go for any reason. Understand?"

Swallowing hard, I did as I was told, so turned on I thought I might come from just the relentless spasming of my needy sex.

He kicked the covers down to the footboard. "Spread your legs and pull up your knees."

My breath caught audibly as my nipples hardened further, causing a deep ache in my breasts. God, Gideon was hot as hell like this. I was panting with excitement, my mind spinning with the possibilities. The flesh between my legs trembled with want.

"Oh, Eva," he crooned, running his index finger through my slick cleft. "Look how greedy you are for me. It's a full-time job keeping this sweet little cunt satisfied."

That single rigid finger pushed into me, parting the swollen tissues. I tightened around him, so close to coming I could taste it. He withdrew and lifted his hand to his mouth, licking my flavor from his skin. My hips arched without volition, my body straining toward his.

"Your fault I'm so hot for you," I gasped. "You slacked on the job for days."

"Then I better make up for lost time." Sliding down into a prone position, he settled his shoulders beneath my thighs and rimmed the quivering entrance to my body with the tip of his tongue. Around and around. Ignoring my clit and refraining from fucking me even when I begged.

"Gideon, please."

"Shh. I have to get you ready first."

"I'm ready. I was ready before you woke up."

"Then you should've woken me earlier. I'll always take care of you, Eva. I live for it."

Whimpering in distress, I rocked my hips into that teasing tongue. Only when I was soaked with my own arousal, creaming desperately for the feel of any part of him I could get inside me, did he crawl over me and settle between my spread thighs, placing his forearms flat on the bed.

He held my gaze. His cock, feverishly hot and hard as stone, lay against the lips of my sex. I wanted it inside me more than I wanted to breathe. "Now," I gasped. "Now."

With a practiced shift of his hips, he rammed deep into me, shoving me up the bed.

"Ah, God," I gasped, convulsing ecstatically around the thick column of flesh that possessed me. This was what I'd needed since we'd talked in his home office, what I'd craved as I rode up and down his steely erection before dinner, what I'd needed even as I climaxed around his thick length.

"Don't come," he murmured in my ear, cupping my breasts in his hands and rolling my nipples between his thumb and forefingers.

"*What?*" I was pretty sure if he'd just take a deep breath I'd go off.

"And don't let go of the pillow."

Gideon began to move in a slow, lazy rhythm. "You're going to want to," he murmured, nuzzling the sensitive spot beneath my ear. "You love to grab my hair and rake your nails down my back. And when you're close to coming, you like to squeeze my ass and yank me deeper. Makes me so damn hard when you go wild like that, when you show me how much you love how I feel inside you."

"No fair," I moaned, knowing he was deliberately provoking me. The cadence of his raspy voice was perfectly timed with the relentless surging of his hips. "You're torturing me."

"Good things come to those who wait." His tongue traced the shell of my ear, and then dipped inside at the same moment he tugged on my nipples.

I bucked into his next thrust and nearly came. Gideon knew my body so well, knew all its secrets and erogenous zones. He was expertly stroking his cock inside me, rubbing over and over the tender bundle of nerves that quivered in delight.

Rolling his hips, he screwed into me, exploiting other spots. I made a plaintive sound, on fire for him, desperately infatuated. My fingers cramped with the grip I had on my pillow, my head thrashing against the driving need to orgasm. He could get me there just by rubbing inside me, the only man who'd ever been skilled enough to give me an intense vaginal orgasm.

"Don't come," he repeated, his voice hoarse. "Make it last."

"I c-can't. It feels too good. God, Gideon . . ." Tears leaked out of the corners of my eyes. "I . . . I'm lost in you."

I cried softly, afraid to say the other L-word too soon and risk upsetting the delicate balance between us.

"Oh, Eva." He rubbed his cheek against my damp face. "I must've wished for you so hard and so often you had no choice but to come true."

"Please," I begged softly. "Slow down."

Gideon lifted his head to look at me, choosing that moment to pinch my nipples with just enough force to inflict a hint of pain. The tender muscles inside me clenched down so hard that his next thrust caused him to groan.

"Please," I pleaded again, trembling with the effort to stave off my building climax. "I'm going to come if you don't slow down."

His gaze was hot on my face, his hips still lunging in a measured tempo that was slowly stealing my sanity. "Don't you want to come, Eva?" he purred in that voice that could lure me into hell with a dreamy smile. "Isn't that what you've been working toward all night?"

My neck arched as his lips drifted across my throat. "Only when you say I can," I gasped. "Only . . . when you say."

"Angel." One hand moved to my face, brushing back the strands of hair that clung to the perspiration on my skin. He kissed me deeply, reverently, licking deep into my mouth.

Yes . . .

"Come for me," he coaxed, quickening his pace. "Come, Eva."

On command, the orgasm struck me like a blow, shocking my system with an overload of sensation. Wave after wave of pulsing heat rolled through me, contracting my sex and tightening my core. I cried out, first with an inarticulate sound of agonized pleasure, then with his name. Chanting it over and over as he drove his beautiful cock into me, prolonging my climax, before pushing me into another one.

"Touch me," he rasped, as I fell apart beneath him. "Hold me."

Freed from his command to hold the pillow, I bound him to my sweat-slick body with arms and legs. He pounded deep and hard, driving strenuously toward his climax.

He came with a growl, his head thrown back as he spurted into me for long minutes. I held him until our bodies cooled and our breathing evened.

When Gideon finally rolled off me, he didn't go far. He wrapped himself around my back and whispered, "Sleep now."

I don't remember if I stayed awake long enough to reply.

18

MONDAY MORNINGS COULD be awesome, when they began with Gideon Cross. We rode to work with my back propped against his side and his arm slung over my shoulder so that his fingers could link with mine.

As he toyed with the ring he'd given me, I kicked out my legs and eyed the classic nude heels he'd bought me along with some outfits to wear on the occasions I slept over. To start out the new week, I'd decided on a black pinstriped sheath dress with a thin blue belt that reminded me of his eyes. He had excellent taste; I had to give him that.

Unless he was sending one of his brunette "acquaintances" out on buying sprees . . . ?

I pushed the unpleasant thought aside.

When I'd checked out the drawers he had set aside for me in his bathroom, I found all of my usual cosmetics and toiletries in all my usual shades. I didn't bother to ask how he knew, which might've led to me freaking out. Instead, I chose to look at it as more proof of his attentiveness. He thought of everything.

The highlight of my morning had been helping Gideon dress in one of his seriously sexy suits. I'd buttoned his shirt; he'd tucked it into his pants. I'd fastened his fly; he had knotted his tie. He'd shrugged into his vest; I'd smoothed the finely tailored material over his equally fine shirt, amazed to find that it could be just as sexy putting clothes *on* him as it was to take them *off*. It was like wrapping my own gift.

The world would see the beauty of the packaging, but only I knew the man inside it and how precious he was. His intimate smiles and his deep husky laugh, the gentleness of his touch and the ferocity of his passion were all reserved for me.

The Bentley bounced lightly over a pothole in the road and Gideon tightened his hold. "What's the plan after work?"

"I get to start my Krav Maga classes today." I couldn't keep the excitement out of my voice.

"Ah, that's right." His lips brushed over my temple. "You know I'm going to have to watch you go through drills. Just thinking about it makes me hard."

"Didn't we already establish that *everything* makes you hard?" I teased, nudging him with my elbow.

"Everything about *you*. Which is lucky for us, since you're insatiable. Text me when you're done and I'll meet you at your place."

Digging in my purse, I pulled out my smartphone to see if it still had a charge and saw a message from Cary. I opened it and found a video plus a text: Does X know his bro is a douche? Stay away from CV, baby girl *smooches*

I started the playback but it took me a minute to figure out what I was seeing. When comprehension set in, I froze.

"What is it?" Gideon asked with his lips in my hair. Then he stiffened behind me, which told me he was looking over my shoulder.

Cary had filmed the video at the Vidals' garden party. From the eight-foot-high hedges in the background, he was in the maze, and from the leaves framing the screen, he was in hiding. The star of the show was a couple locked in a passionate embrace. The woman was beautifully teary, while the man kissed over her frantic words and soothed her with gentle strokes of his hands.

They were talking about me and Gideon, talking about how I was using my body to get my hands on his millions.

"Don't worry," Christopher crooned to a distraught Magdalene. "You know Gideon gets bored fast."

"He's different with her. I—I think he loves her."

He kissed her forehead. "She's not his type."

The fingers I had linked with Gideon's tightened.

As we watched, Magdalene's demeanor slowly changed. She began to nuzzle into Christopher's touch, her voice softening, her mouth seeking. To an observer, it was clear he knew her body well—where to pet and where to rub. When she responded to his skilled seduction, he lifted her dress and fucked her. That he was taking advantage of her was obvious. It was there in the contemptuously triumphant look on his face as he screwed her until she was limp.

I didn't recognize the Christopher on the screen. His face, his posture, his voice . . . it was like he was a different man.

I was grateful when my smartphone battery died and the screen abruptly winked off. Gideon wrapped his arms around me.

"Yuck," I whispered, snuggling carefully into him so I didn't get makeup on his lapel. "Majorly creepy. I feel bad for her."

He exhaled harshly. "That's Christopher."

"Asshole. That smug look on his face—ugh." I shuddered.

Pressing his lips to my hair, he murmured, "I thought Maggie would be safe from him. Our mothers have known each other for years. I forget how much he hates me."

"Why?"

I wondered briefly if the nightmares Gideon had were related to Christopher, then put the thought aside. No way. Gideon was older by several years and tougher all the way around. He'd kick Christopher's ass.

"He thinks I got all the attention when we were younger," Gideon said wearily, "because everyone was worried about how I was handling my father's suicide. So he wants what's mine. Everything he can get his hands on."

I turned into him, pushing my arms underneath his jacket to get closer. There was something in his voice that made me hurt for him. His family home was a place he said haunted his nightmares and he was terribly distant from his family.

He'd never been loved. It was as simple—and as complicated—as that.

"Gideon?"

"Hmm?"

I pulled back to look at him. Reaching up, I traced the bold arch of his brow. "I love you."

A violent shudder moved through him, one hard enough to shake me, too.

"I don't mean to freak you out," I reassured him quickly, averting my face to give him some privacy. "You don't have to do anything about it. I just didn't want another minute to go by without you knowing how I feel. You can tuck it away now."

One of his hands gripped my nape; the other dug almost painfully into my waist. Gideon held me there, immobile, locked against him as if I might blow away. His breathing was ragged, his heartbeat pounding. He didn't say another word the rest of the ride to work, but he didn't let me go either.

I planned on telling him again one day in the future, but as far as first times went, I thought we'd both done okay.

AT ten o'clock sharp, I had two dozen long-stemmed red roses delivered to Gideon's office with the note:

In celebration of red dresses and limo rides.

Ten minutes later, I received an interoffice envelope with a note card that read:

LET'S DO THAT AGAIN. SOON.

At eleven o'clock, I had a black-and-white calla lily arrangement delivered to his office with the note:

*In honor of black & white garden party dresses
and being dragged into libraries . . .*

Ten minutes later, I received his reply:

I'LL BE DRAGGING YOU TO THE
FLOOR IN A MINUTE . . .

At noon, I went shopping. Ring shopping. I hit six different shops before I found a piece that struck me as being absolutely perfect. Made of platinum and studded with black diamonds, it was an industrial-looking ring that made me think of power and bondage. It was a dominant ring, very bold and masculine. I had to open a new charge account with the store to cover the hefty cost, but I considered the months of payments ahead of me worth it.

I called Gideon's office and talked with Scott, who helped me arrange a fifteen-minute window in Gideon's packed day for me to stop by.

"Thank you so much for your help, Scott."

"You're very welcome. I've enjoyed watching him receive your flowers today. I don't think I've ever seen him smile like that."

A warm rush of love flowed through me. I wanted to make Gideon happy. As he'd said, I lived for it.

I went back to work with a smile of my own. At two o'clock, I had a tiger lily arrangement delivered to Gideon's office followed by a private note sent via interoffice envelope:

In gratitude for all the jungle sex.

His reply:

SKIP THE KRAV MAGA. I'LL GIVE YOU A WORKOUT.

When three forty rolled around—five minutes before my appointment with Gideon—I got nervous. I stood up from my chair on shaky legs and paced in the elevator on the way up to his floor. Now that the time had come to give him my gift, I worried that maybe he didn't like rings . . . after all, he didn't wear any.

Was it too presumptuous and possessive of me to want him to wear one just because I did?

The redheaded receptionist didn't give me any trouble getting in and when Scott spotted me emerging from the hallway, he stood from his desk and greeted me with a wide grin. When I stepped into Gideon's office, Scott closed the door behind me.

I was immediately struck by the lovely fragrance of the flowers and the way they warmed the starkly modern office.

Gideon looked up from his monitor, his brows lifting when he saw me. He pushed fluidly to his feet. "Eva. Is something wrong?"

I watched him shift gears from professional to personal, his gaze softening as he looked at me.

"No. It's just . . ." I took a deep breath and went to him. "I have something for you."

"More? Did I forget a special occasion?"

I set the ring box down in the center of his desk. Then I turned away, feeling queasy. I seriously doubted the wisdom of my impetuous gift. It seemed like a stupid idea now.

What could I say to absolve him of guilt for not wanting it? As if it weren't bad enough I'd dropped the L-bomb on him today; then I had to follow it up with a damned ring. He was probably feeling the ball and chain already, dragging after him as he ran. And the noose tightening—

I heard the ring box snap open and Gideon's sharply drawn breath. "Eva."

His voice was dark and dangerous. I turned carefully, wincing at the austerity of his features and the starkness of his gaze. His hands were white-knuckled on the box.

"Too much?" I asked hoarsely.

"Yes." He set the box down and rounded the desk. "Too damn much. I can't sit still, I can't concentrate. I can't get you out of my head. I'm fucking restless, and I never am when I'm at work. I'm too busy. But you have me under siege."

I knew damn well how demanding his work had to be, yet I hadn't taken that into consideration when the mood to surprise him—again and again—hit me. "I'm sorry, Gideon. I wasn't thinking."

He approached with the sexy stride that hinted at how great he was in the sack. "Don't be sorry. Today has been the best day of my life."

"Really?" I watched him slide the ring onto his right ring finger. "I wanted to please you. Does it fit? I had to guess . . ."

"It's perfect. You're perfect." Gideon caught up my hands and kissed my ring, then watched as I repeated the gesture with his. "What you make me feel, Eva . . . it hurts."

My pulse leaped. "Is that bad?"

"It's wonderful." He cupped my face, his ring cool against my cheek. He kissed me passionately, his lips demanding against mine, his tongue thrusting with wicked skill into my mouth.

I wanted more, but restrained myself, thinking that I'd already gone overboard enough for one day. Plus, he'd been too distracted by my unexpected appearance to frost the glass wall to give us privacy.

"Tell me again what you said in the car," he whispered.

"Hmm . . . I don't know." I brushed my free hand over his vest. I was afraid to tell him again that I loved him. He'd taken it hard the first time, and I wasn't sure he'd fully taken in what it meant for us. For him. "You're ridiculously handsome, you know. It's a sucker punch every time I see you. Anyway . . . I don't want to risk scaring you away."

Leaning toward me, he touched his forehead to mine. "You regret what you said, don't you? All the flowers, the ring—"

"Do you really like it?" I asked anxiously, pulling back to study his face and see if he was hedging on the truth. "I don't want you to wear it for me if you hate it."

His fingers traced the shell of my ear. "It's perfect. It's how you see me. I'm proud to wear it."

I loved that he got it. Of course, that was because he got me.

"If you're trying to soften the blow of taking back what you said—" he began, his gaze betraying a surprising anxiety.

I couldn't resist the soft plea in his eyes. "I meant every word, Gideon."

"I'll make you say it again," he threatened in a seductive purr. "You'll scream it by the time I'm done with you."

I grinned and backed away. "Get back to work, fiend."

"I'll give you a lift home at five." He watched me move to the door. "I want your cunt naked and wet when you come down to the car. If you touch yourself to get there, don't make yourself come or there will be consequences."

Consequences. A little shiver moved through me, but it carried a level of fear I could deal with. I trusted Gideon to know just how far to push me. "Will you be hard and ready?"

A wry smile twisted his lips. "When am I not, with you? Thank you for today, Eva. Every minute of it."

I blew him a kiss and watched his eyes darken. The look on his face stayed with me the rest of the day.

It was six o'clock before I made it back to my apartment in a state of well-fucked dishevelment. I'd known what I was in for when I found Gideon's limousine at the curb after work instead of the Bentley. He'd damn near tackled me as I climbed into the back, then proceeded to demonstrate his phenomenal oral skills before nailing me into the seat with vigorous enthusiasm.

I was grateful that I kept in shape. Otherwise, Gideon's insatiable sexual appetite combined with his seemingly endless stamina might've exhausted me by now. Not that I was complaining. Just an observation.

Clancy was already waiting for me in the lobby of my apartment building when I came rushing in. If he noted my hideously wrinkled dress, flushed cheeks, and messy hair, he didn't point it out. I changed swiftly upstairs and we took off for Parker's studio. I hoped the orientation would start out easy because my legs were still a bit jellied from two toe-curling orgasms.

By the time we arrived at the converted warehouse in Brooklyn, I was excited and ready to learn. About a dozen students were engaged in various exercises, with Parker overseeing and offering encouragement from the edge of the mats. When he saw me, he came over and directed me to a far corner of the sparring area where we could work one-on-one.

"So . . . how's it going?" I asked, to break my own tension.

He smiled, showing off a very interesting and arresting face. "Nervous?"

"A little."

"We're going to work on your physical strength and stamina, as well as your awareness. I'm also going to start training you not to freeze or hesitate in unexpected confrontations."

Before we began, I thought I had pretty good physical strength and stamina, but I learned both could be better. We started out with a brief introduction to the equipment and layout of the space, and then moved on to an explanation of both fighting and neutral/passive stances. We warmed up with basic bodyweight calisthenics, then progressed to "tagging," where we tried to tag each other's shoulders and knees while standing face-to-face and blocking countermoves.

Parker was amazing at tagging, of course, but I started to get the hang of it. The majority of the time, however, was spent covering groundwork and I really sank my teeth into that. I knew very well what it was like to be down and at a disadvantage.

If Parker noted my underlying vehemence, he didn't comment on it.

WHEN Gideon showed up at my apartment later that evening, he found me soaking my aching body in my bathtub. Although I could tell he was fresh from a shower after his own workout with his personal trainer, he stripped and slid into the bath behind me, cradling me with his arms and legs. I whimpered as he rocked me.

"That good, huh?" he teased, catching my earlobe in his teeth.

"Who knew rolling around for an hour with a hot guy could be so exhausting?" Cary had been right about Krav Maga causing bruises; I could see a few shadows blooming beneath my skin already and we hadn't even gotten to the hard stuff yet.

"I might be jealous," Gideon murmured, squeezing my breasts, "if I didn't know Smith was married with children."

I snorted at yet another tidbit of knowledge he shouldn't know. "Do you also know his shoe and hat sizes?"

"Not yet." He laughed at my exasperated growl and I couldn't hold back a smile at hearing the rare sound.

One day soon we were going to have to talk about his obsession with information gathering, but today wasn't the day to get into it. We'd been at odds too much lately and Cary's warning about making sure we had as much fun as not was ever-present in my mind.

Playing with the ring on Gideon's finger, I told him about the conversation I'd had with my dad on Saturday and how his fellow cops had been ribbing him over the gossip about me dating *the* Gideon Cross.

He sighed. "I'm sorry."

Turning, I faced him. "It's not your fault you're news. You can't help being insanely attractive."

"One of these days," he said dryly, "I'll figure out whether my face is a curse or not."

"Well, if my opinion counts for anything, I'm rather fond of it."

Gideon's lips twitched and he touched my cheek. "Your opinion is the only one that means anything. And your dad's. I want him to like me, Eva, not think I'm exposing his daughter to invasions of her privacy."

"You'll win him over. He just wants me to be safe and happy."

He visibly relaxed and pulled me closer. "Do I make you happy?"

"Yes." I rested my cheek over his heart. "I love being with you. When we're not together, I wish we were."

"You said you didn't want to fight anymore," he murmured in my hair. "It's been bugging me. Are you getting tired of me fucking up all the time?"

"You do *not* fuck up all the time. And I've screwed up, too. Relationships are hard, Gideon. Most of them don't have kick-ass sex like we do. I put us in the lucky column."

He cupped water in his hand and poured it down my back, over and over, soothing me with its sinuous warmth. "I don't really remember my dad."

"Oh?" I tried to not tense up and reveal my surprise. Or my agitated excitement and desperate hunger to learn more about him. He'd never talked about his family before. It killed me not to prod with questions, but I didn't want to push if he wasn't ready. . . .

His chest lifted and fell on a deep exhale. There was something in the sound of his sigh that brought my head up and ruined my intention to be cautious.

I ran my hand over his hard pectorals. "Want to talk about what you *do* remember?"

"Just . . . impressions. He wasn't around much. He worked a lot. I guess I get my drive from him."

"Maybe workaholism—is that a word?—is something you have in common, but that's it."

"How would you know?" he shot back, defiant.

Reaching up, I brushed the hair back from his face. "I'm sorry, Gideon, but your father was a fraud who took the easy, selfish way out. You don't have it in you to be that way."

"Not that way, no." He paused. "But I don't think he ever learned how to connect to people, how to care about anything but his own immediate needs."

I studied him. "Do you think that describes you?"

"I don't know," he answered quietly.

"Well, I know, and it doesn't." I pressed a kiss to the tip of his nose. "You're a keeper."

"I better be." His arms tightened around me. "I can't think about you with someone else, Eva. Just the idea of another man seeing you the way I do, seeing you like this . . . putting his hands on you . . . It takes me to a dark place."

"It's not going to happen, Gideon." I knew how he felt. I wouldn't be able to bear it if he was intimate with another woman.

"You've changed everything for me. I couldn't stand losing you."

I hugged him. "The feeling's mutual."

Tilting my head back, Gideon took my mouth in a fierce kiss.

In moments it became clear we were soon going to be sloshing water all over the floor. I pulled away. "I need to eat if you want to go at it again, fiend."

"Says the girlfriend rubbing her wet naked body all over me." He sat back with a sinful smile.

"Let's order cheap Chinese and eat it out of the box with chopsticks."

"Let's order good Chinese and do that."

19

Cary joined us in the living room for excellent Chinese, a sweet plum wine, and Monday night television. As we flipped channels and laughed over the hilarious names of some reality television shows, I watched as two of the most important men in my life enjoyed some relaxation time and each other. They got along well, ribbing and playfully insulting each other in that way men had. I'd never seen that side of Gideon before and I loved it.

While I hogged one whole side of our sectional sofa, the two guys sat cross-legged on the floor and used the coffee table as a dining table. Both were wearing loose sweatpants and fitted T-shirts, and I appreciated the view. Was I a lucky girl or what?

Cracking his knuckles, Cary dramatically prepared to open his fortune cookie. "Let's see. Will I be rich? Famous? About to meet Mr. or Ms. Tall, Dark, and Tasty? Traveling to distant lands? What'd you guys get?"

"Mine's lame," I said. *"In the end all things will be known."* Duh. I didn't need a fortune to figure that out."

Gideon opened his and read, *"Prosperity will knock on your door soon."*

I snorted.

Cary shot me a look. "I know, right? You snatched someone else's cookie, Cross."

"He better not be anywhere near someone else's cookie," I said dryly.

Reaching over, Gideon plucked half of mine out of my fingers. "Don't worry, angel. Your cookie is the only one I want." He popped it in his mouth with a wink.

"Gag," Cary muttered. "Get a room." He cracked his fortune with a flourish, and then scowled. "What the fuck?"

I leaned forward. "What's it say?"

"Confucius say," Gideon ad-libbed, "man with hand in pocket feel cocky all day."

Cary threw half his cookie at Gideon, who caught it deftly and grinned.

"Give me that." I snatched the fortune out from between Cary's fingers and read it. Then laughed.

"Fuck you, Eva."

"Well?" Gideon prodded.

"Pick another cookie."

Gideon smiled. *"Pwned* by a fortune."

Cary threw the other half of his cookie.

I was reminded of similar evenings spent with Cary when I was attending SDSU, which made me try to picture what Gideon had been like in college. From the articles I'd read, I knew he'd attended Columbia for his undergraduate studies, then left to focus on his expanding business interests.

Had he associated with the other students? Did he go to frat parties, screw around, and/or drink too much? He was such a controlled man that I had a hard time picturing him that carefree, and yet here he was being exactly that with me and Cary.

He glanced at me then, still smiling, and my heart turned over in my chest. He looked his age for once, young and seriously fine and so very normal. At that moment, we were just a twenty-something couple relaxing at home with a roommate and a remote control. He was just my boyfriend, hanging out. It was all so sweet and uncomplicated, and I found the illusion a poignant one.

The intercom buzzed and Cary leaped to his feet to answer it. He glanced at me with a smile. "Maybe it's Trey."

I held up a hand with my fingers crossed.

But when Cary answered the door a few minutes later, it was the leggy blonde from the other night who came in.

"Hey," she said, taking in the remnants of dinner on the table. She eyed Gideon appraisingly as he politely unfolded and stood in that powerfully graceful way of his. She shot me a smirk, then unleashed a dazzling supermodel smile on Gideon and held out her hand. "Tatiana Cherlin."

He shook her hand. "Eva's boyfriend."

My brows lifted at his introduction. Was he protecting his identity? Or his personal space? Either way, I liked his response.

Cary came back into the room with a bottle of wine and two glasses. "Come on," he said, gesturing down the hallway to his bedroom.

Tatiana gave a little wave and preceded Cary out. I mouthed behind her back to Cary, *What are you doing?*

He winked and whispered, "Picking another cookie."

Gideon and I called it a night shortly after and headed to my room. As we got ready for bed, I asked him something I'd wondered about earlier. "Did you have a fuck pad in college, too?"

His T-shirt cleared his head. "Excuse me?"

"You know, like the hotel room. You're a randy guy. I just wondered if you'd had some kind of setup even then."

He was shaking his head as I ogled his divinely perfect torso and lean hips. "I've had as much sex since I met you as I've had in the last two years combined."

"No way."

"I work hard and I work out harder, both of which keep me pleasantly exhausted most of the time. Occasionally, I might've gotten an offer I didn't refuse, but otherwise I could take or leave sex until I met you."

"Bullshit." I found that impossible to believe.

He shot me a look before he headed toward the bathroom with a black leather toiletry bag. "Keep doubting me, Eva. See what happens."

"What?" I followed him, enjoying the sight of his delectable ass. "You're going to prove that you can take or leave sex by doing me again?"

"It takes two." He opened his bag and pulled out a new toothbrush that he extricated from its packaging and dropped into my toothbrush holder. "You've initiated sex between us as much as I have. You need the connection as much as I do."

"You're right. It's just . . ."

"Just what?" He pulled open a drawer, frowned at finding it full, and moved on to pull open another.

"Other sink," I said, smiling at his presumption that he would get drawers at my place, too, and his scowl when he couldn't find them. "They're all yours."

Gideon moved over to the second sink and began unpacking his bag into the drawers. "Just what?" he repeated, taking shampoo and body wash over to my shower.

Leaning my hip into the sink and crossing my arms, I watched him stake his claim all over my bathroom. There was no doubt that was what he was doing, just as there was no doubt that anyone walking into the room would know right away there was a man in my life.

It struck me then that I had a similar claim on his private space. His household staff had to know their boss was in a committed relationship now. The thought gave me a little thrill.

"I was thinking about you in college earlier," I went on, "when we were eating dinner, imagining what it would be like to see you around on campus. I would've been obsessed with you. I would have gone out of my way to see you around just to enjoy the view. I would've tried to get in the same classes as you, so I could daydream during lectures about getting into your pants."

"Sex maniac." He kissed the tip of my nose as he passed me and went to brush his teeth. "We both know what would've happened once I saw you."

I brushed my hair and teeth, then washed my face. "So . . . did you have a sex pad for the rare occasions some lucky bitch got you in bed?"

His gaze caught my soapy reflection in the mirror. "I've always used the hotel."

"That's the only place you've had sex? Before me?"

"The only place I've had consensual sex," he said quietly, "before you."

"Oh." My heart broke.

I walked over to him, hugging him from behind. I rubbed my cheek against his back.

We went to bed and wrapped ourselves around each other. I buried my face in his neck and breathed him in, snuggling. His body was hard, yet it was wonderfully comfortable against mine. He was so warm and strong, so powerfully male. I only had to think of him to want him.

I slid my leg over his hips and rose above him, my hands splayed atop the ridges of his abdomen. It was dark. I couldn't see him, but I didn't need to. As much as I loved that face of his—the one he resented at times—it was the way he touched me and murmured to me that really got to me. As if there were no one else in the world for him, nothing he wanted more.

"Gideon." I didn't need to say anything else.

Sitting up, he wrapped his arms around me and kissed me deeply. Then he rolled me beneath him and made love to me with a tender possessiveness that rocked me to my soul.

I woke with a jolt of surprise. A heavy weight crushed me and a harsh voice spit ugly, nasty words into my ear. Panic gripped me, cutting off my air.

Not again. No . . . Please, no . . .

My stepbrother's hand covered my mouth and he yanked my legs apart. I felt the hard thing between his legs poking blindly, trying to push into my body. My scream was muffled by his palm smashed over my lips and I cringed away, my heart pounding so hard I thought it would burst. Nathan was so heavy. So heavy and strong. I couldn't buck him off. I couldn't shove him away.

Stop it! Get off me. Don't touch me. Oh, God . . . please don't do that to me . . . not again . . .

Where was Mama? *Mama!*

I screamed, but Nathan's hand covered my mouth. It pressed down on me, squashing my head into the pillow. The more I fought, the more excited he became. Panting like a dog, he rammed against me over and over . . . trying to shove himself inside me . . .

"You're going to know what it feels like."

I froze. I knew that voice. I knew it wasn't Nathan's.

Not a dream. Still a nightmare.

God, no. Blinking madly in the darkness, I struggled to see. The blood was roaring through my ears. I couldn't hear.

But I knew the smell of his skin. Knew his touch, even when it was cruel. Knew the feel of his body on mine, even as it tried to invade me.

Gideon's erection battered into the crease of my thigh. Panicked, I heaved upward with all my strength. His hand on my face dislodged.

Sucking air into my lungs, I screamed.

His chest heaved as he growled, "Not so neat and tidy when you're the one getting fucked."

"Crossfire," I gasped.

A flash of light from the hallway blinded me, followed by the blessed removal of Gideon's smothering weight. Rolling to my side, I sobbed, my eyes streaming tears that blurred my view of Cary shoving Gideon across the room and into the wall, denting the drywall.

"Eva! Are you okay?" Cary turned on the bedside light, cursing when he saw me curled in a fetal position, rocking violently.

When Gideon straightened, Cary rounded on him. "Move one fucking muscle before the cops get here and I'll beat you to a bloody pulp!"

Swallowing past my burning throat, I pushed up to a seated position. My gaze locked with Gideon's and I watched the haze of sleep leave his eyes, replaced by a dawning horror.

"Dream," I choked out, catching Cary's arm as he reached for the phone. "He's d-dreaming."

Cary glanced at where Gideon crouched naked on the floor like a wild animal. Cary's arm dropped back to his side. "Jesus Christ," he breathed. "And I thought I was fucked up."

Sliding off the bed, I stood on shaky legs, sick with lingering fear. My knees gave out and Cary caught me, lowering to the floor with me and holding me as I cried.

"I'M gonna crash on the couch." Cary ran a hand through his sleep-mussed hair and leaned into the hallway wall. The door to my bedroom was open behind me and Gideon was inside, looking pale and haunted. "I'll set out some blankets and pillows for him, too. I don't think he should go home alone. He's shredded."

"Thanks, Cary." The arms I had wrapped around my middle tightened. "Is Tatiana still here?"

"Hell, no. It's not like that. We just fuck."

"What about Trey?" I asked quietly, my mind already drifting back to Gideon.

"I love Trey. I think he's the best person I've ever met aside from you." He bent forward and kissed my forehead. "And what he doesn't know won't hurt him. Stop worrying about me and take care of you."

I looked up at him, my eyes swimming in tears. "I don't know what to do."

Cary sighed, his green eyes dark and serious. "I think you need to decide if you're in over your head, baby girl. Some people can't be fixed. Look at me. I've got a great guy and I'm giving it to a girl I can't stand."

"Cary . . ." Reaching out, I touched his shoulder.

He caught my hand and squeezed it. "I'm here if you need me."

Gideon was zipping up his duffel bag when I returned to my room. He looked at me and fear slithered in my gut. Not for me, but for him. I'd never seen anyone look so desolate, so utterly broken. The bleakness in his beautiful eyes frightened me. There was no life in him. He was gray as death with deep shadows in all the angles and planes of his breathtaking face.

"What are you doing?" I whispered.

He backed up, as if he wanted to be as far away from me as he could get. "I can't stay."

It worried me that I felt a surge of relief at the thought of being alone. "We agreed—no running."

"That was before I attacked you!" he snapped, showing the first sign of spirit in more than an hour.

"You were unconscious."

"You're not going to be a victim ever again, Eva. My God . . . what I almost did to you . . ." He turned his back to me, his shoulders hunched in a way that scared me as much as the attack had.

"If you leave, we lose and our pasts win." I saw my words hit him like a blow. Every light in my room was on, as if electricity alone could banish all the shadows on our souls. "If you give up now, I'm afraid it'll be easier for you to stay away and for me to let you. We'll be over, Gideon."

"How can I stay? Why would you want me to?" Turning around, he looked at me with such longing it brought fresh tears to my eyes. "I'd kill myself before I hurt you."

Which was one of my fears. I had a difficult time picturing the Gideon I knew—the dominant, willful force of nature—taking his own life, but the Gideon standing before me was an entirely different person. And he was the child of a suicidal parent.

My fingers plucked at the hem of my T-shirt. "You'd never hurt me."

"You're afraid of me," he said hoarsely. "I can see it on your face. *I'm* afraid of me. Afraid of sleeping with you and doing something that will destroy us both."

He was right. I was afraid. Dread chilled my stomach.

Now I knew the explosive violence in him. The festering fury. And we were so impassioned with each other. I'd slapped his face at the garden party, lashing out physically when I *never* did that.

It was the nature of our relationship to be lusty and emotional, earthy and raw. The trust that held us together also opened us up to each other in ways that made us both vulnerable and dangerous. And it would get worse before it got better.

He shoved a hand through his hair. "Eva, I—"

"I love you, Gideon."

"God." He looked at me with something that resembled disgust.

Whether it was directed at me or himself, I didn't know. "How can you say that?"

"Because it's the truth."

"You just see this—" He gestured at himself with a wave of his hand. "You're not seeing the fucked-up, broken mess inside."

I inhaled sharply. "You can say that to me? When you know I'm fucked up and broken, too?"

"Maybe you're wired to go for someone who's terrible for you," he said bitterly.

"Stop it. I know you're hurting, but lashing out at me is only going to make you hurt worse." I glanced at the clock and saw it was four in the morning. I walked toward him, needing to get past my fear of touching him and being touched by him.

He held up a hand as if to hold me off. "I'm going home, Eva."

"Sleep on the couch here. Don't fight me about this, Gideon. Please. I'll worry myself sick if you go."

"You'll be more worried if I stay." He stared at me, looking lost and angry and filled with terrible yearning. His eyes pleaded with me for forgiveness, but he wouldn't accept it when I tried to give it to him.

I went to him and took his hand, fighting back the surge of apprehension that hit me when we touched. My nerves were still raw, my throat and mouth still sore, the memory of his attempts at penetration—so like Nathan's—still too fresh. "We'll g-get through this," I promised him, hating that my voice quavered. "You'll talk to Dr. Petersen and we'll go from there."

His hand lifted as if to touch my face. "If Cary hadn't been here—"

"He was, and I'll be fine. I love you. We'll get past this." I walked into him, hugging him, pushing my hands beneath his shirt to touch his bare skin. "We're not going to let the past get in the way of what we have."

I wasn't sure which of us I was trying to convince.

"Eva." His returning hug squeezed all of the air out of me. "I'm sorry. It's killing me. Please. Forgive me . . . I can't lose you."

"You won't." My eyes closed, focusing on the feel of him. The smell of him. Remembering that I once feared nothing when I was with him.

"I'm so sorry." His shaking hands stroked the curve of my spine. "I'll do anything . . ."

"Shh. I love you. We'll be okay."

Turning his head, he kissed me softly. "Forgive me, Eva. I need you. I'm afraid of what I'll become if I lose you . . ."

"I'm not going anywhere." My skin tingled beneath the restless glide of his hands on my back. "I'm right here. No more running."

He paused, his breath gusting harshly against my lips. Then he tilted his head and sealed his mouth over mine. My body responded to the gentle coaxing of his kiss. I arched into him without volition, pulling him closer.

He cupped my breasts in his hands, kneading them, circling the pads of his thumbs over my nipples until they peaked and ached. I moaned with a mixture of fear and hunger, and he quivered at the sound.

"Eva . . . ?"

"I—I can't." The memory of how I'd woken up was too fresh in my mind. It hurt me to deny him, knowing he needed the same thing from me as I'd needed from him when I told him about Nathan— proof that the desire was still there, that as ugly as the scars of our pasts were, they didn't affect what we were to each other now.

But I couldn't give him that. Not yet. I felt too raw and vulnerable. "Just hold me, Gideon. Please."

He nodded, wrapping his arms around me.

I urged him to sink to the floor with me, hoping I could get him to fall asleep. I curled into his side, my leg thrown over his, my arm draped over his hard stomach. He squeezed me gently, pressing his lips to my forehead, whispering over and over again how sorry he was.

"Don't leave me," I whispered. "Stay."

Gideon didn't answer, didn't make any promises, but he didn't let me go either.

I woke sometime later, hearing Gideon's heart beating steadily beneath my ear. All the lights were still on, and the carpeted floor was hard and uncomfortable.

Gideon lay on his back, his beautiful face youthful in sleep, his shirt lifted just enough to expose his navel and the ripped muscles of his abdomen.

This was the man I loved. This was the man whose body gave me such pleasure, whose thoughtfulness moved me over and over again. He was still here. And from the frown that marred the space between his brows, he was still hurting.

I slid my hand into his sweatpants. For the first time since we'd been together, he wasn't hot steel in my palms, but he quickly swelled and thickened as I tentatively stroked him from root to tip. Fear lingered just beneath my arousal, but I was more afraid of losing him than of living with the demons inside him.

He stirred, his arm tightening around my back. "Eva . . . ?"

This time I answered him the way I couldn't before. "Let's forget," I breathed into his mouth. "Make us forget."

"Eva."

He rolled into me, peeling my shirt off with cautious movements. I was similarly tentative in undressing him. We approached each other as if each of us were breakable. The bond between us was fragile just then, both of us apprehensive about the future and the wounds we could inflict with all of our jagged edges.

His lips wrapped around my nipple, his cheeks hollowing slowly, his seduction subdued. The tender suckling felt so good I gasped and arched into his hand. He caressed my side from breast to hip and back again, over and over, gentling me as my heart raced wildly.

He kissed across my chest to the other breast, murmuring words of apology and need in a voice broken by regret and misery. His tongue lapped at the hardened point, worrying it, before surrounding it with wet heat and suction.

"Gideon." The delicate pulls expertly coaxed desire through my skittish mind. My body was already lost in him, greedily seeking the pleasure and beauty of his.

"Don't be afraid of me," he whispered. "Don't pull away."

He kissed my navel and then moved lower, his hair caressing my stomach as he settled between my legs. He held me open with shaking hands and nuzzled my clit. His light, teasing licks through my cleft and the fluttering dips into my trembling sex took me to the edge of insanity.

My back bowed. Hoarse pleas left my lips. Tension spread through my body, tightening everything until I felt like I might snap under the pressure. And then he pushed me into orgasm with the softest nudge of the tip of his tongue.

I cried out, heated relief pulsing through my writhing body.

"I can't let you go, Eva." Gideon levered over me as I vibrated with pleasure. "I can't."

Brushing away the tear tracks from his face, I stared into his reddened eyes. His torment was painful for me to witness, hurting my heart. "I wouldn't let you if you tried."

He took himself in hand and fed his cock slowly, carefully into me. My head pressed hard into the floor as he sank deeper, possessing my body one thick inch at a time.

When I'd taken all of him, he began to move in measured, deliberate thrusts. I closed my eyes and focused on the connection between us. Then he settled onto me, his stomach pressed to mine, and my pulse leaped with panic. Abruptly frightened, I hesitated.

"Look at me, Eva." His voice was so hoarse it was unrecognizable.

I did, and saw his anguish.

"Make love to me," he begged in a breathless whisper. "Make love *with* me. Touch me, angel. Put your hands on me."

"Yes." My palms pressed flat to his back, then stroked over the quivering muscles to his ass. Squeezing the hard, flexing flesh, I urged him to move faster, plunge deeper.

The rhythmic strokes of his heavy cock through the clenching depths of my sex pushed ecstasy through me in heated waves. He felt so good. My legs wrapped around his plunging hips, my breath quickening as the cold knot inside me began to melt. Our gazes held.

Tears coursed down my temples. "I love you, Gideon."

"Please . . ." His eyes squeezed shut.

"I love you."

He lured me to orgasm with the skilled rolling of his hips, stirring his cock inside me. My sex clenched tightly, trying to hold him, trying to keep him deep in me.

"Come, Eva," he gasped against my throat.

I struggled for it, struggled to get past the lingering apprehension that came from having him on top of me. The anxiety mingled with the desire, keeping me on edge.

He made a hoarse sound filled with pain and regret. "Need you to come, Eva . . . need to feel you . . . Please . . ."

Cupping my buttocks, he angled my hips and stroked over and over that sensitive spot inside me. He was tireless, relentless, fucking me long and hard until my mind lost control of my body and I came violently. I bit his shoulder to stem my cries as I shook beneath him, the tiny muscles inside me trembling with ecstatic ripples. He groaned deep in his chest, a serrated sound of tormented pleasure.

"More," he ordered, deepening his drives to give me that delectable bite of soreness. That he once again trusted us both enough to introduce that little touch of pain chased away the last of my reservations. As much as we trusted each other, we were learning to trust our instincts, too.

I came again, ferociously, my toes curling until they cramped. I felt the familiar tension grip Gideon and tightened my grasp on his hips, spurring him on, desperate to feel him spurting inside me.

"No!" He wrenched away, falling to his back and throwing an arm over his eyes. Punishing himself by denying his body the comfort and pleasure of mine.

His chest heaved and glistened with sweat. His cock lay heavily on his belly, brutal-looking with its broad purpled head and thick roping of veins.

I dove for it with hands and mouth, ignoring his vicious curse. Pinning his torso with my forearm, I pumped him hard with my other fist and sucked voraciously on the sensitive crown. His thighs quivered, his legs kicking restlessly.

"Damn it, Eva. Fuck." He stiffened and gasped, his hands shoving into my hair, his hips bucking. "Oh, fuck. Suck it hard . . . Ah, Christ . . ."

He exploded in a powerful rush that almost choked me, coming hard, flooding my mouth. I took it all, my fist milking pulse after pulse up the throbbing length of his cock, swallowing repeatedly until he shuddered with the surfeit of sensation and begged me to stop.

I straightened and Gideon sat up and wrapped himself around me. He took me back down to the floor, where he buried his face in my throat and cried until dawn.

I wore a black, long-sleeved silk blouse and slacks to work on Tuesday, feeling the need to have a barrier between myself and the world. In the kitchen, Gideon cupped my face in his hands and brushed his mouth across mine with heartrending tenderness. His gaze remained haunted.

"Lunch?" I asked, feeling like we needed to cling to the connection between us.

"I have a business lunch." He ran his fingers through my loose hair.

"Would you come? I'll make sure Angus gets you back to work on time."

"I'd love to come along." I thought of the schedule of evening events, meetings, and appointments he'd sent to my smartphone. "And tomorrow night we have a benefit dinner at the Waldorf-Astoria?"

His gaze softened. Dressed for work, he looked somber yet collected. I knew he was anything but.

"You really won't give up on me, will you?" he asked quietly.

I held up my right hand and showed him my ring. "You're stuck with me, Cross. Get used to it."

On the drive to work, he cuddled me in his lap, and again on the ride to lunch at Jean Georges. I didn't speak more than a dozen words during the meal, which Gideon ordered for me and I enjoyed immensely.

I sat quietly at his side, my left hand resting on his hard thigh beneath the tablecloth, a wordless affirmation of my commitment to him. To us. One of his hands rested over mine, warm and strong, as he discussed a new property in development on St. Croix. We kept that connection throughout the entire meal, each of us choosing to eat one-handed rather than separate.

With each hour that passed, I felt the horror of the night before drain away from both of us. It would be another scar to add to his collection, another bitter memory he'd always have, a memory I would share and fear along with him, but it wouldn't rule us. We wouldn't let it.

ANGUS was waiting to take me home when my day ended. Gideon was working late and then going directly from the Crossfire to Dr. Petersen's office. I used the length of the drive to steel myself for the next round of training with Parker. I debated skipping it but ended up deciding it was important to keep to a routine. So much in my life was

292 · SYLVIA DAY

uncontrollable at the moment. Following a schedule was one of the few things totally within my power.

After an hour and a half of tagging and groundwork with Parker at the studio, I was relieved when Clancy dropped me off at home and proud of myself for working out when it was the last thing I'd wanted to do.

When I stepped into the lobby, I found Trey talking to the front desk.

"Hey," I greeted him. "Going up?"

He turned to face me, his hazel eyes warm and his smile open. Trey had a gentleness to him, a kind of straightforward naïveté that was different from the other relationships Cary'd had before. Or maybe I should just say Trey was "normal," which so few of the people in my and Cary's lives were.

"Cary's not in," he said. "They just tried calling."

"You're welcome to come up with me and wait. I won't be going out again."

"If you really don't mind." He fell into step beside me as I waved at the gal at the front desk and moved toward the elevators. "I brought something for him."

"I don't mind at all," I assured him, returning his sweet smile.

He eyed my yoga pants and tank top. "You just get back from the gym?"

"Yeah. Despite it being one of those days when I'd rather have done *anything* else."

He laughed as we stepped into the elevator. "I know that feeling."

As we rode up, silence descended. It was weighted.

"Everything all right?" I asked him.

"Well . . ." Trey adjusted the sling of his backpack. "Cary's just seemed a little off the last few days."

"Oh?" I bit my lower lip. "In what way?"

"I don't know. It's hard to explain. I just feel like maybe something's up with him and I'm missing what it is."

I thought of the blonde and winced inwardly. "Maybe he's stressed about the Grey Isles job and he doesn't want to bother you with it. He knows you've got your hands full with your job and school."

The tension in his shoulders softened. "Maybe that's it. It makes sense. Okay. Thank you."

I let us in to the apartment and told him to make himself at home. Trey headed to Cary's room to drop his stuff, while I went to the phone to check the voice mail.

A shout from down the hallway had me reaching for the phone for a different reason, my heart thudding with thoughts of intruders and imminent danger. More yelling followed, with one voice clearly belonging to Cary.

I exhaled in a rush, relieved. With the phone in my hand, I ventured to see what the hell was going on. I was nearly run over by Tatiana rounding the hallway corner, still buttoning her blouse.

"Oops," she said, with an unapologetic grin. "See ya."

I couldn't hear the door shut behind her over Trey's shouting.

"Fuck you, Cary. We talked about this! You promised!"

"You're blowing this out of proportion," Cary barked. "It's not what you think."

Trey came storming out of Cary's bedroom in such a rush that I plastered myself to the hallway wall to get out of his way. Cary followed, with a sheet slung around his waist. As he passed me, I shot him a narrow-eyed glance that earned me a fuck-off middle finger.

I left the two men alone and escaped into my shower, angry at Cary for once again ruining something good in his life. It was a pattern I kept hoping he'd break, but he couldn't seem to kick it.

When I came out to the kitchen a half hour later, the stillness in the apartment was absolute. I focused on cooking dinner, deciding to go with a pork roast and new potatoes with asparagus, one of Cary's favorite dinners, in case he was home for dinner and needed some cheering up.

The sight of Trey stepping into the hallway while I was putting the roast in the oven surprised me, and then it made me sad. I hated to see him leave looking flushed, disheveled, and crying. My pity turned to fierce disappointment when Cary joined me in the kitchen with the scent of male sweat and sex clinging to him. He shot me a scowl as he passed me on his way to the wine fridge.

I faced him with my arms crossed. "Screwing a heartbroken lover on the same sheets he's just caught you cheating on isn't going to make things better."

"Shut up, Eva."

"He's probably hating himself right now for giving in."

"I said shut the fuck up."

"Fine." I turned away from him and focused on seasoning the potatoes to put in the oven with the roast.

Cary grabbed wineglasses out of the cupboard. "I can feel you judging me. Stop it. He wouldn't be half as pissed if it'd been a man he caught me fucking."

"It's all his fault, huh?"

"Newsflash: Your love life isn't perfect either."

"Low blow, Cary. I'm not going to be your punching bag over this. You messed up, and then you made it worse. It's all on you."

"Don't get on your damn high horse. You're sleeping with a man who's going to rape you any day now."

"It's not like that!"

He snorted and leaned his hip against the counter, his green eyes filled with pain and anger. "If you're going to make excuses for him because he's sleeping when he attacks you, you'll have to make those same excuses for drunks and druggies. They don't know what they're doing either."

The truth of his words struck me hard, as did the fact that he was deliberately trying to wound me. "You can put down a bottle. You can't quit sleeping."

Straightening, Cary opened the bottle he'd selected and poured two glasses, sliding one across the counter toward me. "If anyone knows what it's like to be involved with people who hurt you, it's me. You love him. You want to save him. But who's going to save you, Eva? I'm not always going to be around when you're with him, and he's a ticking time bomb."

"You wanna talk about being in relationships that hurt, Cary?" I shot back, deflecting him away from my painful truths. "Did you screw Trey over to protect yourself? Did you figure you'd push him away before he had the chance to disappoint you?"

Cary's mouth curved bitterly. He tapped his glass to mine, which still sat on the counter. "Cheers to us, the seriously fucked up. At least we have each other."

He stalked out of the room and I deflated. I'd known this was coming—the unraveling of circumstances too good to be true. Contentment and happiness didn't exist in my life for more than a few moments at a time, and they were really only illusionary.

There was always something hidden. Lying in wait to spring up and ruin everything.

20

GIDEON ARRIVED JUST as dinner was coming out of the oven. He had a garment bag in one hand and a laptop case in the other. I'd worried that he would try to go home alone after his session with Dr. Petersen and was relieved when he'd called to say he was on his way. Still, when I first opened the door and saw him on the threshold, a shiver of unease slid through me.

"Hey," he said quietly, following me back into the kitchen. "Smells delicious in here."

"I hope you're hungry. There's a lot of food and I'll be surprised if Cary joins us to help eat it all."

Gideon dropped his stuff on the breakfast bar and approached me cautiously, his gaze searching my face as he neared. "I brought some things with me to stay the night, but I'll go if you want. At any time. Just tell me."

I blew out my breath in a harsh rush, determined not to let fear dictate my actions. "I want you here."

"I want to be here." He paused beside me. "Can I hold you?"

I turned into him and squeezed him hard. "Please."

He pressed his cheek against mine and hugged me close. The embrace wasn't as natural and easy as we'd grown used to. There was a new wariness between us that was different from anything we'd felt before.

"How are you doing?" he murmured.

"Better now that you're here."

"But still nervous." He pressed his lips to my forehead. "Me, too. I don't know how we're ever going to fall asleep next to each other again."

Pulling back slightly, I looked at him. That was my fear as well, and my earlier conversation with Cary didn't help matters. *He's a ticking time bomb. . . .*

"We'll figure it out," I said.

He was quiet for a long moment. "Has Nathan ever contacted you?"

"No." Although I had a deep-rooted fear that I might see him again one day, whether accidentally or deliberately. He was out there somewhere, breathing the same air . . . "Why?"

"It was on my mind today."

I pulled back to search his face, a knot forming in my throat at how tormented he looked. "Why?"

"Because we've got a lot of baggage between us."

"Are you thinking it's too much?"

Gideon shook his head. "I can't think that way."

I didn't know what to do or say. What assurances could I give him, when I wasn't sure my love and his need would be enough to make our relationship work?

"What's going through your mind?" he asked.

"Thoughts of food. I'm starving. Why don't you go see if Cary wants to eat? Then we can get started on dinner."

GIDEON found Cary sleeping, so he and I ate a candlelit dinner for two at the dining table, a somewhat formal meal while lounging in the worn T-shirts and pajama bottoms we'd put on after our respective showers. I was worried about Cary, but spending quiet downtime alone with Gideon felt like just what we needed.

"I had lunch with Magdalene in my office yesterday," he said after we'd enjoyed a few initial bites.

"Oh?" While I'd been ring shopping, Magdalene had been enjoying private time with my man?

"Don't take that tone," he admonished. "She ate a meal in an office covered in your flowers, with you blowing kisses from my desk. You were as much there as she was."

"Sorry. Knee-jerk reaction."

He lifted my hand to his mouth and pressed a quick, hard kiss to the back. "I'm relieved you can still get jealous over me."

I sighed. My emotions had been all over the map all day; I couldn't decide how I felt about anything. "Did you say anything to her about Christopher?"

"That was the point of the lunch. I showed her the video."

"What?" I frowned, remembering my phone had died in his car. "How'd you do that?"

"I took your phone up to my office and pulled the video off via USB. Didn't you notice I brought it back last night, fully charged?"

"No." I set my silverware down. Dominant or not, Gideon and I were going to have to work on which lines crossed over into my freak-out zone. "You can't just hack into my phone, Gideon."

"I didn't hack into it. You haven't set a password yet."

"That's not the point! It's a serious invasion of my fucking privacy.

Jesus . . ." Why in hell did no one in my life understand that I had boundaries? "Would you like me rummaging through your stuff?"

"I've got nothing to hide." He pulled his smartphone out of an inner pocket of his sweats and held it out to me. "And you won't either."

I didn't want to get into a fight now—things were too shaky as it was—but I'd let this go long enough. "It doesn't matter whether I have something I don't want you to see. I have a right to space and privacy, and you need to ask before you help yourself to my information and my belongings. You have to stop taking whatever you want without my permission."

"What was private about it?" he asked with a frown. "You showed it to me yourself."

"Don't be like my mother, Gideon!" I shouted. "There's only so much crazy I can handle."

He jerked back at my vehemence, clearly surprised by how upset I was. "Okay. I'm sorry."

I gulped down my wine, trying to rein in my temper and unease. "Sorry I'm mad? Or sorry you did it?"

After the length of several heartbeats, Gideon said, "I'm sorry you're mad."

He really didn't get it. "Why don't you see how weird this is?"

"Eva." He sighed and shoved a hand through his hair. "I spend a quarter of every day *inside* you. When you set limits outside that I can't help but see them as arbitrary."

"Well, they're not. They're important to me. If there's something you want to know, you need to ask me."

"All right."

"Don't do it anymore," I warned. "I'm not kidding, Gideon."

His jaw tightened. "Okay. I get it."

Then, because I really didn't want to fight, I moved on. "What did she say when she saw it?"

He visibly relaxed. "It was difficult, of course. Even more difficult to know I'd seen it."

"She saw us in the library."

"We didn't talk about that directly, but then, what was there to say? I won't apologize for making love to my girlfriend in a closed room." He leaned back in his chair and exhaled harshly. "Seeing Christopher's face on the video—seeing what he really thought of her—*that* hurt her. It's hard to see yourself being used that way. Especially by someone you think you know, someone who's supposed to care about you."

To hide my reaction, I busied myself with refilling both my glass and his. He spoke as if from experience. What exactly had been done to him?

After a quick gulp of wine, I asked, "How are *you* doing with it?"

"What can I do? Over the years, I've made every attempt to talk to Christopher. I've tried throwing money at him. I've tried threatening him. He's never shown any inclination to change. I realized long ago that I can only do damage control. And keep you as far away from him as possible."

"I'll be helping you with that, now that I know."

"Good." He took a drink, eyeing me over the lip of his glass. "You're not asking me about my appointment with Dr. Petersen."

"It's none of my business. Unless you want to share." I met his gaze, willing him to do just that. "I'm here to listen whenever you need an ear, but I'm not going to pry. When you're ready to let me in, you will. That said, I'd love to know if you like him."

"So far." He smiled. "He talks me around in circles. Not many people can do that."

"Yes. Talks you back around and makes you come at it from a different angle that has you thinking, 'Now why didn't I see it like that?'"

Gideon's fingers stroked up and down the stem of his glass. "He prescribed something for me to take at night before bed. I filled it before I came over."

"How do you feel about taking drugs?"

He looked at me with dark, haunted eyes. "I feel it's necessary. I have to be with you and I have to make that safe for you, whatever it takes. Dr. Petersen says the drug combined with therapy has been successful for other 'atypical sexual parasomniacs.' I have to believe that."

I reached over to squeeze his hand. Taking medication was a big step, especially for someone who'd avoided facing his problems for a long time. "Thank you."

Gideon's grip tightened. "Apparently there are enough people with this problem that there have been sleep studies on it. He told me about a documented case where a man sexually assaulted his wife in his sleep for twelve years before they sought help."

"Twelve years? Jesus."

"Apparently part of the reason they waited so long was because the man was a better lay when he was asleep," he said dryly. "And if that's not a killer blow to the ego, I don't know what is."

I stared at him. "Well, shit."

"I know, right?" His wry smile faded. "But I don't want you to feel pressured to share a bed with me, Eva. There is no magic pill. I can sleep on the couch or I can go home, although of the two choices I'd prefer the couch. My whole day is better after getting ready for work with you."

"For me, too."

Reaching over, Gideon caught my hand and lifted it to his lips. "I never imagined I could have this . . . Someone in my life who knows what you do about me. Someone who could talk about my fuck-ups over dinner because they accept me anyway . . . I'm grateful for you, Eva."

My heart twisted with a sweet pain in my chest. He could say such beautiful things, the perfect things.

"I feel the same way about you, ace." Deeper, maybe, because I loved him. But I didn't say that aloud. He'd get there someday. I wasn't going to give up until he was absolutely, irrevocably mine.

⌒

WITH his bare feet propped on the coffee table and his computer on his lap, Gideon looked so at home and relaxed that he kept distracting me from my television shows.

How did we get here? I asked myself. This extravagantly sexy man and me?

"You're staring," he murmured, his gaze on his laptop screen.

I stuck my tongue out at him.

"Is that a sexual suggestion, Miss Trammell?"

"How do you see me while staring at whatever you're working on?"

He looked up then and caught my gaze. His blue eyes blazed with power and heat. "I've always seen you, angel. From the moment you found me, I've seen nothing but you."

WEDNESDAY started with Gideon's cock pushing into me from behind, my new favorite way to wake up.

"Well, then," I said hoarsely, rubbing the sleep from my eyes as his arm hitched around my waist and hauled me closer to his warm, hard chest. "You're frisky this morning."

"You're gorgeous and sexy every morning," he murmured, nibbling on my shoulder. "I love waking up to you."

We celebrated a night of uninterrupted sleep with a handful of orgasms between us.

MUCH later in the day, I had lunch with Mark and Steven at a lovely Mexican restaurant tucked beneath the street. We descended a short set of cement stairs into a surprisingly spacious restaurant with black-vested waitstaff and plenty of light.

BARED TO YOU · 303

"You'll need to bring your man back here," Steven said, "and have him buy you one of the pomegranate margaritas."

"Good stuff?" I asked.

"Oh, yeah."

When the waitress came to take our orders, she flirted outrageously with Mark, fluttering enviously long lashes. Mark flirted back. As the meal progressed, the exuberant redhead—whose name tag introduced her as Shawna—became bolder, touching Mark's shoulders and the back of his neck every time she came by. In return, Mark's banter became more suggestive, until I eyed Steven nervously, watching his face redden and his scowl deepen by the moment. Shifting uncomfortably, I was counting down the minutes until the tension-fraught meal was over.

"Let's get together tonight," Shawna said to Mark when she brought the check. "One night with me and I'll cure you."

I gaped. Seriously?

"Seven o'clock work for you?" Mark purred. "I'll ruin you, Shawna. You know what happens once you go black. . . ."

I inhaled my water down the wrong pipe and choked.

Steven leaped to his feet and rounded the table, pounding me on the back. "Hell, Eva," he said, laughing. "We're just playing with you. Don't die on us."

"What?" I gasped, my eyes watering.

Grinning, he came around my shoulder and tossed his arm around the waitress. "Eva, meet my sister, Shawna. Shawna, Eva here is the one who makes Mark's life easier."

"That's good," Shawna said, "since he's got you to make things harder."

Steven winked at me. "That's why he keeps me around."

Seeing the brother and sister pair so close together, I finally caught the resemblance I'd missed before. I sagged into my seat and narrowed my eyes at Mark. "That was rotten. I thought Steven was going to blow a gasket."

Mark held up his hands in a show of surrender. "It was all his idea. He's the drama queen, remember?"

Rocking back on his heels, Steven grinned and said, "Now, Eva. You know Mark's the idea man in this relationship."

Shawna dug a business card out of her pocket and handed it to me. "My number's on the flipside. Gimme a call. I've got the inside dirt on these two. You can pay 'em back really good."

"Traitor!" Steven accused.

"Hey." Shawna shrugged. "Us girls have to stick together."

AFTER work, Gideon and I went to his gym. Angus dropped us off at the curb and we headed inside. The place was hopping and the locker room crowded. I changed and stowed my stuff, then met Gideon in the hallway.

I waved at Daniel, the trainer who'd talked to me on my first visit to CrossTrainer, and got a smack on the ass for it.

"Hey," I protested, swatting at Gideon's chastising hand. "Cut it out."

He tugged my ponytail and gently urged my head back, tilting my mouth up so he could mark his territory with a deep, lush kiss.

The way he pulled my hair sent electricity sweeping across my skin. "If this is your idea of a deterrent," I whispered against his lips, "I have to say it's much more of an incentive."

"I'm quite willing to take it up a notch." He nipped my lower lip with his teeth. "But I wouldn't suggest testing my limits that way, Eva."

"Don't worry. I have other ways to do it."

Gideon hit the treadmill first, affording me the pleasure of seeing his body glistening with sweat . . . in public. As often as I saw him that way in private, it never ceased to be a major turn-on.

And God, I loved the way he looked with his hair tied back. And the flex of his muscles beneath lightly tanned skin. And the graceful power of his movements. Seeing such an elegantly urbane man shed the suits and show off his animal side hit all my hot buttons.

I couldn't stop staring and was happy I didn't have to. He was mine, after all, a fact that sent warm pleasure sliding through me. Besides, every other woman in the gym was checking him out, too. As he moved from station to station, dozens of admiring eyes followed.

When he caught me ogling, I shot him a suggestive glance and ran my tongue along my lower lip. His arched brow and rueful half-smile made me tingly. I couldn't remember the last time I'd been so motivated while working out. An hour and a half just flew by.

By the time we got back in the Bentley and headed to the penthouse, I was squirming in my seat. My gaze slid repeatedly to Gideon in silent invitation.

He linked his fingers with mine. "You'll wait for it."

That pronouncement startled me. *"What?"*

"You heard me." He kissed my fingers and had the nerve to give me a wicked smile. "Delayed gratification, angel."

"Why would we do that?"

"Think of how crazed we'll be for each other after dinner."

I leaned closer so Angus didn't overhear me, although I knew he was professional enough to ignore us. "That's a given, waiting or not. I say we go with not."

But he wouldn't budge. Instead, he tortured us both. Having us undress each other for a steamy shower, our hands petting and caressing the curves and hollows of each other's bodies, then dressing for dinner. He went all out in black tie, but skipped the tie. His crisp white shirt was unbuttoned at the collar, revealing a flash of skin. The cocktail dress he selected for me was a champagne silk Vera Wang with a strapless bustier bodice, an open back, and a tiered skirt that ended a few inches above my knees.

I smiled when I saw it, knowing it was going to drive him nuts seeing me in that dress all night. It was gorgeous and I loved it, but it was a style meant for tall, slender models, not short curvy girls. In a pitiful bid for modesty, I left my hair down to hang over my breasts, but it didn't help much if Gideon's expression was any indication.

"My God, Eva." He adjusted himself in his slacks. "I've changed my mind about that dress. You shouldn't wear it in public."

"We don't have time for you to change your mind."

"I thought there was more material than that."

I shrugged with a grin. "What can I say? You bought it."

"I'm having second thoughts. How long could it possibly take to remove it?"

Sliding my tongue along my lower lip, I said, "I don't know. Why don't you find out?"

His eyes turned dark. "We'd never get out of here."

"I wouldn't complain." He looked so damn hot and I wanted him—as always—really damned bad.

"Isn't there a jacket or something you can put over that? A parka, maybe? Or a trench coat?"

Laughing, I grabbed my clutch off the dresser and wrapped my arm around his. "Don't worry. Everyone will be too busy checking you out to even bother noticing me."

He scowled as I tugged him out of the bedroom. "Seriously. Have your tits gotten bigger? They're spilling out over the top of that thing."

"I'm twenty-four years old, Gideon," I said dryly. "I stopped developing years ago. What you see is what you get."

"Yes, but I'm the only one who's supposed to be seeing, since I'm the only one who's allowed to be getting."

We moved into the living room. In the short time it took us to pass through to the foyer, I relished the quiet beauty of Gideon's home. I loved how warm and inviting it was. The Old World charm of the décor was so elegant, yet it was also remarkably comfortable. The stunning view out of the arched windows complemented the interior, but didn't distract from it.

The mixture of dark woods, distressed stone, warm colors, and vivid jeweled accents was clearly expensive, as was the art hung on the walls, but it was a tasteful display of wealth. I couldn't imagine anyone feeling awkward about what to touch or where to sit. It just wasn't that kind of space.

We caught the private elevator and Gideon faced me as the doors closed. He immediately tried tugging my bodice up.

"If you're not careful," I warned, "you'll expose my crotch instead."

"Damn it."

"We could have fun with this. I could play the role of a bubble-headed blond bimbo who's after your cock and your millions, and you can be yourself—the billionaire playboy with his latest toy. Just look bored and indulgent while I rub up against you and coo about how brilliant you are."

"That's not funny." Then he brightened. "What about a scarf?"

ONCE we checked in for the gala dinner benefiting a new crisis shelter for women and children, we were directed to a press gauntlet, triggering my fear of exposure. I focused on Gideon because nothing distracted me as thoroughly as he did. And because I was paying such close attention, I was able to watch the change from private man to public persona as it happened.

The mask slipped smoothly into place. His irises chilled to an icy blue and his sensual mouth lost any hint of curve. I could almost feel the force of his will enclosing us. There was a shield between us and the rest of the world simply because he wished it to be there. Standing beside him, I knew no one would approach or speak to me until he gave them some sign that they could.

Still, the don't-touch vibe didn't extend to looking. Gideon turned heads as we walked to the ballroom and eyes followed him. I got a nervous twitch from all the attention he garnered, but he seemed oblivious and completely unruffled.

If I'd had my heart set on cooing and rubbing all over Gideon, I would've had to wait in line. He was pretty much mobbed the moment we stopped walking. I stepped away to make room for those vying to catch his attention and wandered off to find some champagne. Waters Field & Leaman had done the pro bono advertising for the gala, and I spotted a few people I knew.

I'd managed to snag a glass off a passing waiter's tray when I heard someone call out my name. Turning, I saw Stanton's nephew approaching with a broad smile. Dark-haired and green-eyed, he was around my age. I knew him from the times I'd visited my mother on holiday breaks and was glad to see him.

"Martin!" I greeted him with open arms and we hugged briefly. "How are you? You look fabulous."

"I was about to say the same." He eyed my dress appreciatively. "I'd heard you'd moved to New York and meant to look you up. How long have you been in town?"

"Not long. A few weeks."

"Drink your champagne," he said. "And let's dance."

The wine was still bubbling nicely through my system when we moved onto the dance floor to the sound of Billie Holiday singing "Summertime."

"So," he began, "are you working?"

As we danced, I told him about my job and I asked what he was up to. I wasn't surprised to hear he was working for Stanton's investment firm and doing well.

"I'd love to come uptown and take you out to lunch sometime," he said.

"That would be great." I stepped back as the music ended and bumped into someone behind me. Hands went to my waist to steady me and I looked over my shoulder to find Gideon at my back.

"Hello," he purred, his icy gaze on Martin. "Introduce us."

"Gideon, this is Martin Stanton. We've known each other for a few years now. He's my stepfather's nephew." I took a deep breath and went for it. "Martin, this is the significant man in my life, Gideon Cross."

"Cross." Martin grinned and held out his hand. "I know who you are, of course. It's a pleasure to meet you. If things work out, maybe I'll be seeing you at some of the family gatherings."

Gideon's arm slid around my shoulders. "Count on it."

Martin was hailed by someone he knew, and he leaned forward to kiss my cheek. "I'll call you about lunch. Next week maybe?"

"Great." I was highly conscious of Gideon vibrating with energy beside me, although when I glanced at him, his face was calm and impassive.

He pulled me into a dance, with Louis Armstrong singing "What a Wonderful World." "Not sure I like him," he muttered.

"Martin's a very nice guy."

"Just so long as he knows you're mine." He pressed his cheek to my temple and placed his hand within the cutout back of my dress, skin to skin. There was no way to doubt that I belonged to him when he was holding me like that.

I relished the opportunity to be so close to his scrumptious body in public. Breathing him in, I relaxed into his expert hold. "I like this."

Nuzzling against me, he murmured, "That's the idea."

Bliss. It lasted as long as the dance did.

We were exiting the dance floor when I caught sight of Magdalene off to the side. It took me a moment to recognize her because she'd cut her hair into a sleek bob. She looked slender and classy in a simple black cocktail dress but was eclipsed by the striking brunette she was speaking to.

Gideon's stride faltered, slowing fractionally before resuming his usual pace. I was looking down, thinking he'd avoided something on the floor, when he said quietly, "I need to introduce you to someone."

My attention shifted to see where we were going. The woman with Magdalene had spotted Gideon and turned to face him. I felt his forearm tense beneath my fingers the moment their gazes met.

I could see why.

The woman, whoever she was, was deeply in love with Gideon. It was there on her face and in her pale, otherworldly blue eyes. Her beauty was stunning, so exquisite as to be surreal. Her hair was black as ink and hung thick and straight almost to her waist. Her dress was the same icy hue as her eyes, her skin golden from the sun, her body long and perfectly curved.

"Corinne," he greeted her, the natural rasp in his voice even more pronounced. He released me and caught her hands. "You didn't tell me you were back. I would've picked you up."

"I left a few messages on your voice mail at home," she said, in a voice that was cultured and smooth.

"Ah, I haven't been there much lately." As if that reminded him I was next to him, he released her and drew me up to his side. "Corinne, this is Eva Tramell. Eva, Corinne Giroux. An old friend."

I extended my hand to her and she shook it.

"Any friend of Gideon's is a friend of mine," she said with a warm smile.

"I hope that applies to girlfriends as well."

When her gaze met mine, it was knowing. "Especially girlfriends. If you could spare him a moment, I've been hoping to introduce him to an associate of mine."

"Of course." My voice was calm; I was anything but.

Gideon gave me a perfunctory kiss on the temple before he stepped closer to Corinne and offered his arm to her, leaving Magdalene standing awkwardly next to me.

I actually felt sorry for her, she looked so dejected. "Your new hairstyle is very flattering, Magdalene."

She glanced at me, her mouth tight, and then it softened with a sigh that sounded filled with resignation. "Thank you. It was time for a change. Time for many changes, I think. Also, there was no reason to imitate the one who got away now that she's back."

I frowned in confusion. "You lost me."

"I'm talking about Corinne." She studied my face. "You don't know. She and Gideon were engaged, for more than a year. She broke it off, married a wealthy Frenchman, and moved to Europe. But the marriage fell apart. They're now getting divorced and she's moved back to New York."

Engaged. I felt the blood drain from my face, my gaze shifting to where the man I loved stood with the woman he must've once loved, his hand moving to the small of her back to steady her as she leaned into him with a laugh.

As my stomach twisted with jealousy and sick fear, it struck me that I'd assumed he had never had a serious romantic relationship before me. Stupid. As hot as he was, I should've known better.

Magdalene touched my shoulder. "You should sit down, Eva. You're very pale."

I knew I was breathing too fast and my speeding pulse rate was dangerously high. "You're right."

Moving to the nearest available chair, I got off my feet. Magdalene sat beside me.

"You love him," she said. "I didn't see it. I'm sorry. And I'm sorry for what I said to you the first time we met."

"You love him, too," I replied woodenly, my gaze unfocused. "And at that time, I didn't. Not yet."

"Doesn't excuse me, does it?"

I gratefully accepted another glass of champagne when it was offered to me and took a second for Magdalene before the waiter straightened to move on. We clinked glasses in a pitiful display of scorned female solidarity. I wanted to leave. I wanted to get up and walk out. I wanted Gideon to realize I'd left, to be forced to leave after me. I wanted him to feel some of the pain I felt. Stupid, immature, hurtful imaginings that made me feel small.

I took comfort from Magdalene sitting silently beside me in commiseration. She knew how it felt to love Gideon and want him too much. That I sensed she was as miserable as I was confirmed what a threat Corinne might be.

Had he been pining for her this whole time? Was she the reason he'd closed himself off from other women?

"There you are."

I looked up as Gideon found me. Of course Corinne was still on his arm and I got the full effect of the two of them as a couple. They were, quite simply, impossibly gorgeous together.

Corinne took a seat beside me and Gideon brushed his fingertips over my cheek. "I have to speak with someone," he said. "Would you like me to bring you back anything?"

"Stoli and cranberry. Make it a double." I needed a buzz. Bad.

"All right." But he frowned at my request before he walked away.

"I'm so glad to meet you, Eva," Corinne said. "Gideon has told me so much about you."

"It can't have been too much. You two weren't gone that long."

"We talk nearly every day." She smiled, and there was nothing fake or malicious in her expression. "We've been friends a long time."

"More than friends," Magdalene said pointedly.

Corinne frowned at Magdalene, and I realized I wasn't supposed to know. Was it she or Gideon or both of them that had decided it was best not to tell me? Why cover up something if there was nothing to hide?

"Yes, that's true," she admitted with obvious reluctance. "Although that was some years ago now."

I twisted in my seat to face her. "You still love him."

"You can't blame me for that. Any woman who spends time with him falls in love with him. He's beautiful and untouchable. That's an irresistible combination." Her smile softened. "He tells me you've inspired him to start opening up. I'm grateful to you for that."

I was about to say, *I didn't do it for you.* Then an insidious doubt drifted through my mind, making a vulnerable spot inside me fold in on itself.

Was I doing it for her without knowing it?

I twisted the base of my empty champagne flute around and around on the table. "He was going to marry you."

"And it was the biggest mistake of my life walking away." Her hand went to her throat, her slender fingers restlessly stroking, as if toying with a necklace she'd normally find there. "I was young and in some ways he frightened me. He was so possessive. It wasn't until after I married that I realized possessiveness is much better than indifference. At least for me."

I looked away, fighting the nausea that rose in my throat.

"You're awfully quiet," she said.

"What is there to say?" Magdalene tossed out.

We all loved him. We were all available to him. In the end, he would make a choice between us.

"You should know, Eva," Corinne began, looking at me with those clear aquamarine eyes, "he's told me how special you are to him. It took me some time to gather the courage to come back here and face you two together. I even canceled a flight I had booked a couple weekends ago. I interrupted him at some charity event he was giving a speech at, poor guy, to tell him I was on my way and to ask for his help getting settled."

I froze, feeling as brittle as cracked glass. She had to be talking about the advocacy center dinner, the night Gideon and I had sex for the first time. The night we'd christened his limo and he'd immediately withdrew, then left me abruptly.

"When he called me back," she continued, "he told me he'd met someone. That he wanted you and me to meet when I got into town. I ended up chickening out. He's never asked me to meet a woman in his life before."

Oh my God. I glanced at Magdalene. Gideon had left me in a rush that night for *her.* For Corinne.

21

"E XCUSE ME." I pushed back from the table and searched for
Gideon. I saw him at the bar and went to him.

He was just turning away from the bartender with two glasses in
his hands when I intercepted him. I took my drink and gulped it
down, my teeth aching as the cubes of ice knocked against them.

"Eva—" There was a soft note of chastisement in his voice.

"I'm leaving," I said flatly, stepping around him to set my empty
glass on the bar top. "I don't consider that running, because I'm telling
you in advance and giving you the option of coming with me."

He exhaled harshly and I could see that he understood my mood.
He knew I knew. "I can't leave."

I turned away.

He caught my arm. "You know I can't stay if you go. You're upset
over nothing, Eva."

"Nothing?" I stared at where his hand gripped me. "I warned you I get upset and jealous. This time, you've given me good reason."

"Warning me is supposed to excuse you when you get ridiculous about it?" His face was relaxed, his voice low and calm. No one looking from a distance would pick up on the tension between us, but it was there in his eyes. Burning lust and icy fury. He was so good at putting those two together.

"Who's ridiculous? What about Daniel, the personal trainer? Or Martin, a member of my stepfamily?" I leaned closer and whispered, "I've never fucked either of them, let alone agreed to a marriage! I sure as hell don't talk to them every damn day!"

Abruptly, he caught me by the waist and hauled me up tight against him. "You need to be fucked now," he hissed in my ear, nipping the lobe with his teeth. "I shouldn't have made us wait."

"Maybe you were planning ahead," I shot back. "Saving it up in case an old flame popped back into your life, one you'd prefer to screw instead."

Gideon tossed back his drink, then secured me to his side with a steely arm around my waist and led me through the crowd to the door. He pulled his smartphone out of his pocket and ordered the limo brought around. By the time we reached the street, the long, sleek car was there. Gideon pushed me through the door Angus held open and told him, "Drive around the block until I say otherwise."

Then he slid in directly behind me, so closely I could feel his breath against my bare back. I scrambled toward the opposite seat, determined to get away from him. . . .

"Stop," he snapped.

I sank to my knees on the carpeted floor, breathing hard. I could run to the ends of the earth and I still wouldn't be able to escape the fact that Corinne Giroux had to be better for Gideon than I was. She was calm and cool, a soothing presence even to me—the person freaking out over the unwelcome fact of her existence. My worst nightmare.

His hand twisted into my loose hair, restraining me. His spread legs surrounded mine, his grip tightening so that my head was pulled back gently to touch his shoulder. "I'm going to give you what we both need, Eva. We're going to fuck as long as it takes to dull the edge enough to get through dinner. And you're not going to worry about Corinne, because while she's inside the ballroom, I'll be deep inside you."

"Yes," I whispered, licking dry lips.

"You forget who submits, Eva," he said gruffly. "I've given up control for you. I've bent and adjusted for you. I'll do anything to keep you and make you happy. But I won't be tamed or topped. Don't mistake indulgence for weakness."

I swallowed hard, my blood on fire for him. "Gideon . . ."

"Reach up with both hands and hold on to the grab handle above the window. Don't let go until I tell you, understand?"

I did as he ordered, pushing my hands through the leather loop. As my grip secured, my body sparked to life, making me aware of how right he was about what I needed. He knew me so well, this lover of mine.

Shoving his hands into my bodice, Gideon squeezed my full, aching breasts. When he rolled and tugged my nipples, my head lolled against him, the tension leaving my body in a rush.

"God." He nuzzled his mouth against my temple. "It's so perfect when you give yourself over to me like that . . . all at once, as if it's a huge relief."

"Fuck me," I begged, needing the connection. "Please."

Releasing my hair, he reached under my dress and pulled my panties down my thighs. His jacket flew past me to land on the seat; then his hand pushed between my legs from the front. He growled at finding me wet and swollen. "You were made for me, Eva. You can't go long without me inside you."

Still he primed me, running his skilled fingers through my cleft, spreading the moisture over my clit and the lips of my sex. He pushed two fingers into me, scissoring them, preparing me for the thrust of his long, thick cock.

"Do you want me, Gideon?" I asked hoarsely, needing to ride his thrusting fingers, but hampered by how far I had to reach to grab the strap.

"More than my next breath." His lips moved over my throat and the top of my shoulder, the warm velvet of his tongue sliding seductively across my skin. "I can't go long without you either, Eva. You're an addiction . . . my obsession . . ."

His teeth bit gently into my flesh, conveying his animal need with a rough sound of desire. All the while he fucked me with his fingers, his other hand massaging my clit, making me come again and again from the simultaneous stimulation.

"Gideon!" I gasped, when my damp fingers began to slip from the leather.

His hands left me and I heard the erotic rasp of his zipper lowering. "Let go and lie on your back with your legs spread."

I moved to the seat and stretched along it, offering my body to him in quivering anticipation. His gaze met mine, his face briefly lit by a passing swath of headlights.

"Don't be afraid." He came over me, setting his weight onto me with excruciating care.

"I'm too horny to be scared." I caught him and pulled my body up to press against the hardness of his. "I want you."

His cock head nudged against the lips of my sex. With a flex of his hips, he pushed into me, his breath hissing just as mine did at the searing connection. I went lax against the seat, my fingers barely clinging to his lean waist.

"I love you," I whispered, watching his face as he began to move. Every inch of my skin burned as if from the sun, and my chest was so tight with longing and emotion that it was hard to breathe. "And I need you, Gideon."

"You have me," he whispered, his cock sliding in and out. "I couldn't be more yours."

I quivered and tensed, my hips meeting his relentlessly measured drives. I climaxed with a breathless cry, shuddering as the ecstasy rippled through my sex, milking him until he grunted and started powering into me.

"*Eva.*"

I rocked into his ferocious lunges, urging him on. He clutched at me, riding me hard and fast. My head thrashed and I moaned shamelessly, loving the feel of him, that decadent sensation of being possessed and ruthlessly pleasured.

We were wild for each other, fucking like feral beasts, and I was so turned on by our primal lust I thought I'd die from the orgasm building inside me.

"You're so good at this, Gideon. So good . . ."

He gripped my buttock and yanked me up to meet his next thrust, hitting the end of me, forcing a gasp of pleasure/pain from my throat. I came again, clenching down hard on him.

"Ah, God. *Eva.*" With a serrated groan, he erupted violently, flooding me with his heat. Pinning my hips, he ground against me, emptying himself as deep in me as he could get.

When he finished, he sucked in a harsh breath and gathered my hair in his hands, kissing the side of my damp throat. "I wish you knew what you do to me. I wish I could tell you."

I held him tightly. "I can't help it that I'm stupid over you. It's just too much, Gideon. It's—"

"—uncontrollable." He started over again, thrusting rhythmically. Leisurely. As if we had all the time in the world. Thickening and lengthening with each push and pull.

"And you need control." I lost my breath on a particularly masterful stroke.

"I need *you*, Eva." His gaze was fierce on my face as he moved inside me. "I need you."

GIDEON didn't leave my side, or allow me to leave his, the rest of the evening. He kept his right hand linked with my left all the way through dinner, once again choosing to eat one-handed rather than release his hold on me.

Corinne—who'd taken a seat on the other side of him at our table—gave him a curious look. "I seem to remember you being right-handed."

"I still am," he said, lifting our joined hands from under the table and kissing my fingertips. I felt foolish and insecure when he did that—and conscious of Corinne's scrutiny.

Unfortunately, the romantic gesture didn't keep him from talking to Corinne throughout the meal, not me—which left me feeling fidgety and unhappy. I saw more of the back of Gideon's head than his face.

"At least it's not chicken."

I turned my head toward the man sitting beside me. I'd been so focused on trying to eavesdrop on Gideon's conversation that I hadn't paid any mind to our tablemates.

"I like chicken," I said. And I had liked the tilapia served for dinner—I'd cleaned my plate.

"Not rubberized, certainly." He grinned and suddenly looked much younger than his pure-white hair would suggest. "Ah, there's a smile," he murmured. "And it's a beautiful one."

"Thank you." I introduced myself.

"Dr. Terrence Lucas," he said. "But I prefer Terry."

"Dr. Terry. It's lovely to meet you."

He smiled again. "Just Terry, Eva."

Over the course of the few minutes we'd spoken, I'd come to believe Dr. Lucas wasn't a whole lot older than me, just prematurely gray. Aside from that, his face was handsome and unlined, his green eyes intelligent and kind. I revised my guesstimate of his age to be mid-to-late thirties.

"You look as bored as I feel," he said. "These events raise a considerable amount of money for the shelter, but they can be dull. Would you like to accompany me to the bar? I'll buy you a drink."

Beneath the table, I tested Gideon's grip by flexing my hand. His tightened.

"What are you doing?" he murmured.

Looking over my shoulder, I saw him watching me. Then I watched his gaze lift as Dr. Lucas stood behind me. Gideon's gaze noticeably cooled.

"She's going to alleviate the boredom of being ignored, Cross," Terry said, setting his hands on the back of my chair, "by spending time with someone who's more than happy to pay attention to such a beautiful woman."

I was immediately uncomfortable, aware of the crackling animosity between the two men. I tugged on his hand, but Gideon wouldn't release me.

"Walk away, Terry," Gideon warned.

"You've been so preoccupied with Mrs. Giroux, you didn't even notice when I sat at your table." Terry's smile took on an edge. "Eva. Shall we?"

"Don't move, Eva."

I shivered at the ice in Gideon's voice but felt stung enough to say, "It's not his fault he has a point."

Gideon's grip tightened painfully. "Not now."

Terry's gaze moved to my face. "You don't have to tolerate him talking to you that way. All the money in the world doesn't give anyone the right to order you around."

Infuriated and horribly embarrassed, I looked at Gideon. "Crossfire."

I wasn't sure I could use the safeword outside the bedroom, but he released me as if I'd burned him. I shoved my chair back and threw my napkin onto my plate. "Excuse me. Both of you."

With my clutch in hand, I walked away from the table, my stride easy and smooth. I made a beeline toward the restrooms, intending to freshen my makeup and collect myself, but then I saw the lighted exit sign and went with my urge to bail.

I pulled out my smartphone when I hit the sidewalk and texted Gideon: Not running. Just leaving.

I managed to hail a passing cab and headed home to nurse my anger.

I was jonesing for a hot bath and a bottle of wine when I reached my apartment. Shoving my key into the lock, I turned the knob and stepped into a porn video.

In the few shocked seconds it took for my brain to register what I was seeing, I stood riveted on the threshold, flooding the hallway behind me with blaring technopop. There were so many body parts involved, I had time to hastily slam the door behind me before I pieced them all together. One woman was spread-eagled on the floor. Another woman's face was in her crotch. Cary was banging the hell out of her while another man was drilling him in the ass.

I threw my head back and screamed bloody murder, completely fed up with everyone in my life. And because I was competing with the sound system, I ripped off one of my heels and threw it in that direction. The CD skipped, which jolted the *ménage à quatre* in progress on my living room floor into awareness of my presence. I limped over and shut off the volume, then faced the lot of them.

"Get the fuck out of my house," I snapped. "Right now."

"Who the hell is that?" the redhead at the bottom of the pile asked. "Your wife?"

There was a brief flash of embarrassment and guilt on Cary's face, and then he shot me a cocky smile. "My roommate. There's room for more, baby girl."

"Cary Taylor. Don't push me," I warned. "It's really, *really* not a good night."

The dark-haired male on top disengaged from Cary and stood, sauntering toward me. As he got closer, I saw that his brown eyes were unnaturally dilated and the pulse in his neck was throbbing viciously. "I can make it better," he offered with a leer.

"Back the fuck up." I adjusted my stance, preparing to ward him off physically if necessary.

"Leave her alone, Ian," Cary snapped, pushing to his feet.

"Come on, baby girl," Ian coaxed, making me sick by using Cary's pet name for me. "You need a good time. Let me show you one."

One minute he was inches in front of me, the next he was sailing into the couch with a scream. Gideon moved into place between me and the others, vibrating with fury. "Take it to your room, Cary," he bit out. "Or take it somewhere else."

Ian was squealing on my sofa, his nose spraying blood despite the two hands he tried to stanch it with.

Cary snatched his jeans off the floor. "You're not my fucking mother, Eva."

I sidestepped around Gideon. "Wasn't screwing up with Trey enough of a fucking lesson for you, you idiot?"

"This isn't about Trey!"

"Who's Trey?" the bottle blonde asked as she got to her feet. When she caught a good look at Gideon, she visibly preened, showing off an admittedly pretty body.

Her efforts earned her a glance so disdainfully dismissive and unimpressed that she finally had the grace to blush and cover herself with a slinky gold lamé dress she picked up off the floor. And because I was in a mood, I said, "Don't take it personally. He prefers brunettes."

The look Gideon shot me was lethal. I'd never seen him look so livid. He was literally vibrating with suppressed violence.

Frightened by that glare, I took an involuntary step back. He cursed viciously and shoved both of his hands through his hair.

Suddenly bone weary and desperately disappointed with the men in my life, I turned away. "Get this mess out of my house, Cary."

I headed down the hallway, kicking off my other heel en route. I was out of my dress before I reached my bathroom and in the shower less than a minute beyond that. I stayed out of the range of the spray until the water warmed, and then I stood directly beneath it. Too tired to stand for long, I sank to the floor and just sat beneath the stream with my eyes closed and my arms wrapped around my knees.

"Eva."

I cringed when I heard Gideon's voice, and tucked into an even tighter ball.

"Goddamn it," he snapped. "You piss me off worse than anyone else I know."

I looked at him through the veil of my wet hair. He was pacing the length of my bathroom, his jacket shed somewhere and his shirt untucked. "Go home, Gideon."

He halted and shot me an incredulous look. "I'm not fucking leaving you here. Cary's lost his damned mind! That amped-up asshole was seconds away from putting his hands on you when I got here."

"Cary wouldn't have let that happen. But either way, I can't deal with him and you at the same time." I didn't want to deal with either of them, actually. I just wanted to be alone.

"Then you'll just deal with me."

I scooped my hair back from my face with an impatient swipe of my hand. "Oh? I'm supposed to make *you* the priority?"

He recoiled as if I'd hit him. "I was under the impression we were both each other's priorities."

"Yeah, I thought that, too. Until tonight."

"Jesus. Will you drop it with Corinne already?" He spread his arms wide. "I'm here with you, aren't I? I barely said good-bye to her because I was chasing after you. *Again*."

"Fuck you. Don't do me any favors."

Gideon lunged into the shower fully dressed. He yanked me to my feet and kissed me. Hard. His mouth devoured mine, his hands gripping my upper arms to hold me in place.

But I didn't soften this time. I didn't give in. Even when he tried coaxing me with lush, suggestive licks.

"Why?" he muttered, his lips sliding down to my throat. "Why are you driving me insane?"

"I don't know what your problem is with Dr. Lucas, and I honestly don't give a shit. But he was right. Corinne got way too much of your attention tonight. You pretty much ignored me during dinner."

"It's impossible for me to ignore you, Eva." His face was hard and tight. "If you're in the same room with me, I don't see anyone else."

"Funny. Every time I looked at you, you were looking at her."

"This is stupid." He released me and shoved the wet hair out of his face. "You know how I feel about you."

"Do I? You want me. You need me. But do you love Corinne?"

"Oh, for fuck's sake. *No*." He shut the water off, caging me to the glass with both arms. "You want me to tell you I love you, Eva? Is that what this is about?"

My stomach cramped as if he'd struck me with the full force of his fist. I'd never felt that kind of pain before, hadn't known it existed. My eyes burned and I ducked under his arm before I embarrassed myself by crying. "Go home, Gideon. Please."

"I *am* home." He caught me from behind and buried his face in my soaked hair. "I'm with you."

I struggled to get free, but I was too wiped out. Physically. Emotionally. The tears came in a torrent and I couldn't stop them. And I hated crying in front of anyone. "Go away. *Please*."

"I love you, Eva. Of course I do."

"Oh my God." I kicked at him, flailing. Anything to get away from the person who'd become a massive source of pain and misery. "I don't want your fucking pity. I just want you to *go away*."

"I can't. You know I can't. Eva, stop fighting. Listen to me."

"Everything you're saying *hurts*, Gideon."

"It's not the right word, Eva," he pressed on stubbornly, his lips at my ear. "That's why I haven't said it. It's not the right word for you and what I feel for you."

"Shut up. If you care about me at all, you'll just shut up and go away."

"I've been loved before—by Corinne, by other women . . . But what the hell do they know about me? What the hell are they in love with when they don't know how fucked up I am? If that's love, it's nothing compared to what I feel for you."

I stilled, trembling, my gaze on the mirror's reflection of my mascara-smeared face and bedraggled wet hair next to Gideon's ravaged beauty. His features were overcome by volatile emotion as he wrapped himself tightly around me. We looked all wrong for each other.

And yet I understood the alienation of being around others who couldn't really see you or chose not to. I'd felt the self-loathing that came with being a fraud, portraying an image of what you wished you could be but weren't. I'd lived with the fear that the people you loved might turn away from you if they ever got to know the true person hidden inside.

"Gideon—"

His lips touched my temple. "I think I loved you the moment I saw you. Then we made love that first time in the limo and it became something else. Something more."

"Whatever. You cut me off that night and left me behind to take care of Corinne. How could you, Gideon?"

He released me only long enough to scoop me up and carry me over to where my bathrobe hung from a hook on the back of the door. He bundled me up, then had me sit on the edge of the tub while he went to the sink and pulled my makeup remover wipes out of the drawer. Crouching in front of me, he stroked the cloth over my cheek.

"When Corinne called during the advocacy dinner, it was the perfect time to make me do something stupid." His gaze was soft and warm on my tear-streaked face. "You and I had just made love, and I wasn't thinking clearly. I told her I was busy and that I was with someone, and when I heard the pain in her voice, I knew I had to deal with her so I could move forward with you."

"I don't understand. You left me behind for her. How does that move us forward?"

"I screwed up with Corinne, Eva." He tilted my chin back to rub at my raccoon eyes. "I met her my first year at Columbia. I noticed her, of course. She's beautiful and sweet, and never had an unkind word to say about anyone. When she pursued me, I let myself be caught and she became my first consensual sexual experience."

"I hate her."

That made his mouth curve slightly.

"I'm not kidding, Gideon. I'm sick with jealousy right now."

"It was just sex with her, angel. As raw as you and I fuck, it's still making love. Every time, from the very first time. You're the only one who's ever gotten to me that way."

I heaved out a breath. "Okay. I'm marginally better."

He kissed me. "I guess you could say we dated. We were exclusive sexually and we often ended up going to the same places as a couple.

Still, when she told me she loved me, I was surprised. And flattered. I cared about her. I enjoyed spending time with her."

"Still do, apparently," I muttered.

"Keep listening." He chastised me with a tap of his finger to the end of my nose. "I thought maybe I might love her, too, in my own way . . . the only way I knew how. I didn't want her to be with anyone else. So I said yes when she proposed."

I jerked back to look at him. "*She* proposed?"

"Don't look so shocked," he said wryly. "You're bruising my ego."

Relief flooded me in a rush that made me dizzy. I threw myself at him, hugging him as tight as I could.

"Hey." His returning embrace was just as fierce. "You okay?"

"Yes. Yes, I'm getting there." I pulled back and cupped his jaw in my hand. "Keep going."

"I said yes for all the wrong reasons. After two years of hanging out, we'd never spent a full night together. Never talked about any of the things I talk to you about. She didn't know me, not really, and yet I convinced myself that being loved at all was something to hang on to. Who else was going to do it right, if not her?"

He moved his attention to my other eye, cleaning away the black streaks. "I think she was hoping that being engaged would take us to a different level. Maybe I'd open up more. Maybe we'd stay the night at the hotel—which she thought was romantic, by the way—instead of calling it an early night because of classes in the morning. I don't know."

I thought it sounded terribly lonely. My poor Gideon. He'd been alone for so long. Maybe his whole life.

"And maybe when she broke it off after a year," he went on, "she was hoping that would kick-start things, too. That I'd make a bigger effort to keep her. Instead, I was relieved because I'd started to realize it was going to be impossible to share a home with her. What excuse was I going to come up with to sleep in separate rooms and have my own space?"

"You never considered telling her?"

"No." He shrugged. "Until you, I didn't consider my past an issue. Yes, it affected certain ways I did things, but everything had its place and I wasn't unhappy. In fact, I thought I had a comfortable and uncomplicated life."

"Oh, boy." My nose wrinkled. "Hello, Mr. Comfortable. I'm Miss Complicated."

His grin flashed. "Never a dull moment."

22

Gideon tossed the makeup remover wipe in the trash. Then he grabbed a towel to throw over the puddle he'd left on the floor and toed off his shoes. To my utter delight, he began stripping out of his wet clothes.

Watching him raptly, I said, "You feel guilty because she still loves you."

"I do, yes. I knew her husband. He was a good guy and he was crazy about her, until he figured out she didn't feel the same way and things fell apart."

He looked at me as he peeled his shirt off. "I couldn't figure out why he let it get to him. He was married to the girl he wanted, they lived in a different country away from me, so what was his problem? Now, I understand. If *you* loved someone else, Eva, it'd shred me to pieces, every single day. It'd kill me even if you were with me and not him. But unlike Giroux, I wouldn't let you go. Maybe I wouldn't have all of you, but you'd still be mine and I'd take what I could get."

My fingers laced in my lap. "That's what scares me, Gideon. You don't know what you're worth."

"Actually, I do. Twelve bill—"

"Shut up." My head spun and I pressed my fingertips to my eyes. "It shouldn't be such a mystery that women fall in love with you and stay in love. Did you know that Magdalene kept her hair long hoping it'd remind you of Corinne?"

He dropped his slacks and frowned at me. "Why?"

I sighed at his cluelessness. "Because she believes Corinne is who you want."

"Then she's not paying attention."

"Isn't she? Corinne told me she talks to you almost every day."

"Not quite. I'm often not available. You know how busy I am." His gaze took on the heated look I was so familiar with. I knew he was thinking about the times he got busy with me.

"That's nuts, Gideon. Her calling every day. That's stalking." Which reminded me of her assertion that he'd been as possessive over her as he was about me. That niggled at me in a terrible way.

"Where are you going with this?" he asked, in a voice laced with warm amusement.

"Don't you get it? You drive women off the deep end because you're the ultimate. You're the grand prize. If a woman can't have you, they know they're settling for less than the best. So they can't think about not having you. They just think of crazy ways to try to get you."

"Except for the one I want," he retorted dryly, "who spends a lot of time running in the opposite direction."

I stared unabashedly, drinking him in as he stood naked in front of me. "Answer one question for me, Gideon. Why do you want me, when you can have your pick of perfection instead? And I'm not fishing for compliments or reassurances. I'm asking an honest question."

He caught me up and moved us into the bedroom. "Eva, if you don't stop thinking of us as temporary, I'm going to take you over my knee and make damn sure you like it."

Setting me down in a chair, he went to rifle through my drawers.

I watched him pulling out underwear, yoga pants, and a top. "Have you forgotten I sleep in the nude with you?"

"We're not staying here." He faced me. "I don't trust Cary not to bring more intoxicated jerks home, and once we turn in for the night I'll be drugged on the medication Dr. Petersen prescribed and possibly unable to protect you. So we're going to my place."

I looked down at my twisted hands, thinking about how I might need protection from Gideon, too. "I've been down this road with Cary before, Gideon. I can't just hole up at your place and hope he comes out of it on his own. He needs me to be around more than I have been."

"Eva." Gideon brought me my clothes and crouched in front of me. "I know you need to support Cary. We'll figure out how tomorrow."

I cupped his face. "Thank you."

"I need you, too, though," he said quietly.

"We need each other."

He pushed to his feet. Moving back to the dresser, he pulled open his drawers and grabbed clothes for himself.

Standing, I began to dress. "Listen . . ."

He pulled on a pair of low-slung jeans. "Yes?"

"I feel tons better now that I know the score, but Corinne is still going to be a problem for me." I paused with my shirt in my hands. "You wanna nip her hopes in the bud real quick. Stow the guilt, Gideon, and start weaning her off."

He sat on the edge of the bed to pull on his socks. "She's a friend, Eva, and she's in a rough spot. It's a cruel time to cut her off."

"Think carefully, Gideon. I have exes in my past, too. You're setting the precedent now for how I'll handle them. I'm taking my cues from you."

He stood with a scowl. "You're threatening me."

"I prefer to see it as coercion. Relationships work both ways. You're not her only friend. She can find someone more appropriate to lean on in her time of crisis."

We grabbed what we needed and walked back into the living room. I saw the mess left behind—an aqua-hued bra beneath an end table and blood spray on my cream sectional—and I wished Cary were still around to smack some sense into.

"I'm digging into it with him tomorrow," I bit out, my jaw tight with anger and worry. "Goddamn it, I should've decked him when I had the chance. I should've knocked him out cold, and then locked him up in his room until he gets his brain working again."

Gideon's hand at the small of my back rubbed soothingly. "It'll be better to do that tomorrow, when he's alone and hungover. More effective that way."

ANGUS was waiting for us when we got downstairs. I was about to climb into the back of the limo when Gideon cursed under his breath, stopping me.

"What?" I asked him.

"I forgot something."

"Let me get my keys." I reached for the overnight bag Gideon was holding, which had my purse inside.

"No need. I have a set." He shot me an unapologetic grin when my brows rose. "I had copies made before I gave them back to you."

"Seriously?"

"If you'd paid attention"—he kissed the top of my head—"you might've noticed that you've had the key to my place on your key ring since I returned it."

I gaped after him as he darted past the doorman and back into the building. I remembered the torment of those four days when I'd thought we'd broken up and the excruciating pain I'd felt when those keys slid out of the envelope and into my palm.

I'd had the key to being with him all along.

Shaking my head, I looked around at my adopted city, loving everything about it and feeling grateful for the crazy well of happiness I'd found here.

Gideon and I still had so much work ahead of us. As much as we loved each other, it was no guarantee that we'd survive our personal wounds. But we communicated, we were honest with each other, and God knew we were both too stubborn to quit without a fight.

Gideon reappeared just as two large, beautifully groomed poodles walked by with their equally coiffed owner.

I climbed into the limo. As we pulled away from the curb, Gideon tugged me onto his lap and cuddled me close. "We had a rough night, but we got through it."

"Yeah, we did." Tipping my head back, I offered my mouth for a kiss. He obliged me with one that was slow and sweet—a simple reaffirmation of our precious, complicated, maddening, necessary connection.

Cupping his nape, I ran my fingers through his silky hair. "I can't wait to get you back in bed."

He gave a sexy little growl and attacked my neck with tickling nips and kisses, banishing our ghosts and their shadows.

At least for a little while . . .

Readers Guide for

BARED TO YOU

by Sylvia Day

DISCUSSION QUESTIONS

1. Eva's move from California to New York brings her closer to her mother. While the move was a good one for both her and Cary's careers, it could have been avoided. Why do you think she chose to start her new life in New York?

2. Cary is dependent on Eva materially and emotionally, even though she turns to him as a sounding board more often than he turns to her. What needs does Eva meet for Cary?

3. Initially, it's the physical attraction that draws Gideon to Eva, but by the time he lures her to his nightclub there's something deeper involved. What is it about Eva that causes Gideon to pursue her so relentlessly?

4. Gideon has a difficult time accepting any privacy barriers between him and Eva. Do you think Eva is too soft or too tough on the issue? How would you respond?

5. Eva values transparency in her relationships, but she allows Gideon to keep his secrets. Why do you think that is? Do you agree or disagree?

6. Gideon's life revolves around his work and his philanthropic commitments; Eva's social life is more personal. How do these differences affect them as a couple?

7. Gideon and Eva have a very sexual relationship. Considering their pasts, why do you think sex is such an important way for them to communicate?

GIDEON AND EVA'S STORY CONTINUES
IN THE POWERFULLY SENSUAL SECOND NOVEL IN THE
CROSSFIRE SERIES,

REFLECTED IN YOU

Now available from Berkley Books!

Ready to find
your next great read?

Let us help.

Visit prh.com/nextread

Penguin
Random
House